THE COLLECTED FICTION OF

H. P. LOVECRAFT

Volume I

*Howard P. Lovecraft collection, John Hay Library,
Brown University*

THE COLLECTED FICTION OF
H. P. LOVECRAFT

Volume I

weldonowen

CONTENTS

*The stories indicated are analyzed in detail in the companion *A Reader's Guide to Selected Works by H. P. Lovecraft.*

INTRODUCTION TO *THE COLLECTED FICTION OF H. P. LOVECRAFT*

No one would be more surprised by the H. P. Lovecraft Experience than Lovecraft himself. Lovecraft, often referred to by his initials HPL, lived a quiet life as a writer and editor in Providence, Rhode Island. His career gained him little fame and even less wealth during his lifetime. He died believing he had made no lasting literary mark on the world and would soon be forgotten.

Yet, fewer than ninety years after his death in 1937, H. P. Lovecraft has gained international fame as the "Father of Gothic Horror," and he stands as the most important American author of horror fiction since Edgar Allan Poe. His works have been translated into dozens of languages and remain in print in hundreds of editions, accompanied by mountains of scholarly commentary and critical analysis. His creations have both directly and indirectly inspired legions of other artists, and he continues to find new fans through films and television, role-playing games, audio dramas, graphic novels, musical compositions, fine arts, and more. His creations have infiltrated popular culture with freewheeling ease, and collectors pay thousands of dollars for his original manuscripts and other relics of his creativity. Even NASA scientists have joined in, naming a newly discovered region of the dwarf planet Pluto "Cthulhu Regio" after one of his most famous creatures, Cthulhu. Lovecraft is everywhere.

This posthumous reversal in fame and fortune is stunning, and there's little doubt that Lovecraft, who was plagued with self-doubt about his work, would have been amazed. In a March 7, 1920, letter to Rheinhart Kleiner, he noted:

> I should describe mine own nature as tripartite, my interests consisting of three parallel and dissociated groups—(a) Love of the strange & the fantastic. (b) Love of the abstract truth & of scientific logick. (c) Love of the ancient & the permanent. Sundry combinations of these three strains will probably account for all my odd tastes & eccentricities.

He was indeed a man of odd tastes and eccentricities, but he was also an author with a visionary imagination whose legacy matches that of the most influential American writers.

A Brief Biography

Howard Phillips Lovecraft was born on August 20, 1890, at his family's home in Providence, Rhode Island. His father, Winfield Scott Lovecraft, was the son of English immigrants and worked as a traveling salesman. Winfield was hospitalized with complications of syphilis when Howard was just three years old, and the elder Lovecraft died five years later without ever recovering or seeing his son again. (It is unclear whether Lovecraft understood the nature of his father's illness and death.) In the absence of his father, young Lovecraft was raised primarily by his mother, Sarah Susan Phillips Lovecraft, and his grandfather, Whipple Phillips. Grandfather Whipple was a prosperous industrialist and avid reader, and young HPL grew up in a mansion filled with books. He was the only child in a doting but conservative New England family.

Gifted with great intelligence and an eidetic memory, the precocious HPL learned to read fluently before other children his age, and he struggled to fit in comfortably in school. His mother was artistically gifted and was, seemingly, both overly protective and overly critical of her son. Young Howard suffered from intense headaches and other "nervous conditions," resulting in extended absences from school. For the most part, he educated himself by reading the books in his grandfather's tremendous private library and through the tutelage of his uncles—one a medical doctor and the other a newspaper editor. When Lovecraft did attend school, he had disciplinary problems with teachers he perceived to be less well informed than himself. His problems at school notwithstanding, he made lasting friendships with neighborhood boys, with whom he played elaborate world-building games revolving around railroads, detectives, Arabian conjurers, and other dime-novel figures. He acted out the plays of William Shakespeare using homemade pasteboard puppets. Young HPL's imagination fed on classical Greco-Roman mythology, *One Thousand and One Nights*, astronomy, and the works of Edgar Allan Poe.

In 1904, when Lovecraft was just fourteen, his grandfather's business ventures collapsed, and Whipple died of a stroke. With the family fortune gone, he and his mother were forced to abandon the Phillips mansion and move into a modest duplex not far away. The change was a massive shock to his system. Lovecraft had been raised as the proud heir to a long tradition of aristocratic English gentlemen. But, at the turn of the twentieth century, Providence was changing from an erstwhile English colony into a modern, industrial American city. The population doubled with an influx of immigrants seeking work in the new factories. With their long Anglophile pedigree and upperclass lifestyle now greatly diminished, the Lovecrafts surely felt their position undermined by foreign-born newcomers. Against this backdrop, Lovecraft suffered a health crisis, which in modern times would probably be considered a nervous breakdown. Between 1908 and 1913, he was plagued by nervous conditions, nightmares, depression, and thoughts of suicide. As a result, he was unable to complete his formal high school education, and failed to enroll in Brown University, which he had long anticipated attending. His condition left him unable to engage with people, and he withdrew from the world into near-total isolation. Sequestered at home with his mother, who increasingly struggled with mental health issues of her own, young Lovecraft suffered an untenable physical and emotional state during this five-year span, finding himself utterly debilitated.

Young HPL avidly read the popular boys' magazines of the day, including *Argosy* and *All-Story Weekly*, and was a big fan of Edgar Rice Burroughs and Zane Grey, among others. But as a youth more than usually familiar with fine English literature, he also found much to criticize there. Starting in 1913, he wrote a number of rather scathing letters to the editor, igniting a "flame war" with other readers. His witty rejoinders caught the attention of participants in the United Amateur Press Association, who urged him to join their organization. Lovecraft became involved with this group, and it proved to be one of the most impactful actions of his young life. In a 1921 essay titled "What Amateurdom and I Have Done for Each Other," he wrote:

> In 1914 when the kindly hand of amateurdom was handed to me, I was as close to the state of vegetation as any animal well can be... With the advent of the United I obtained a new will to live; a renewed sense of existence as other than a superfluous weight; and found a sphere in which I could feel that my efforts were not wholly futile.

The United Amateur Press Association, founded in 1895, was one of several highly structured groups formed originally by printers to practice their craft and share their work. They produced a wide range of journals, fanzines, booklets, and the like, ranging in quality from basic to lavish. Some members of the United did their own printing, but others, like Lovecraft, served primarily as editors or writers. The term "amateur press" ought not suggest that its participants were exclusively beginning or unskilled writers—quite the contrary. Instead, it was a community of eager participants whose goals were neither commercial nor professional. This was a movement of journalism pursued for the pure pleasure of it. Lovecraft derived two key benefits from his involvement in this community. First, he began to correspond with a growing network of like-minded friends; Lovecraft's voluminous letter writing distinguished him as one of the most prolific epistolarians in the history of the United States. Second, as his confidence grew, he returned to an endeavor he'd enjoyed in his youth—writing stories.

Lovecraft's celebrated fiction is the smallest part of his literary output. He wrote and published poetry and essays on a broad variety of topics, both in the publications of his colleagues and in his own journal, *The Conservative*, which made quite a splash in the amateur world:

> … many were immediately aware that a brilliant new talent had made itself known. The entire contents of the issue, both prose and verse, were the work of the editor, who obviously knew exactly what he wished to say and no less exactly how to say it.
>
> —Rheinhart Kleiner, "Howard Phillips Lovecraft,"
> *The Californian* 5, no. 1 (Summer 1937)

The Conservative was published in thirteen issues between 1915 and 1923, and it contained some unvarnished and offensive opinions and philosophical points of view, which more than lived up to the journal's title and stoked lingering controversy among its readers. Though not everyone agreed with him, Lovecraft had the respect of the amateur journalism community, and he served terms as president of both the United and its rival National Amateur Press Association.

Though he is known today chiefly for his stories, Lovecraft wrote many influential essays. His most famous essay is "Supernatural Horror in Literature," a 28,000-word survey written in 1927 and revised in 1934. It was commissioned by his friend W. Paul Cook, who wanted to publish it in his own amateur journal, *The Recluse*. It is a comprehensive study of the history of Western weird/horror fiction, from antiquity to the modern era, and an analysis of its principles. The longest essay Lovecraft ever wrote had nothing to do with horror: "A Description of the Town of Quebeck" was a 78,000-word history and travelogue of the Canadian city inspired by his visit there in 1930. He wrote it purely for his own enjoyment, and it remained unpublished until 1976.

As a correspondent, Lovecraft's letters are legendary. It is estimated that he wrote roughly 90,000 letters over the course of his lifetime, which works out to an astonishing average of fourteen letters every day of his adult life. While some letters are brief notes and postcards, others run sixty or more pages of dense, handwritten text. His circle of correspondents involved about seventy friends, colleagues, fans, and other aspiring writers, only a small number of whom he ever met in person. They included Robert E. Howard (creator of Conan the Barbarian) and Clark Ashton Smith (writer and visual artist who created the fantastical realms of Zothique and Hyperborea). His letters document his life in exhaustive detail, covering a vast array of fascinating topics and historical details. Of the approximately 10 percent of his letters that remain extant, many have been published, and a large number are preserved at Brown University's John Hay Library. Because of the intricate detail in these letters, Lovecraft's biographers have a vast amount of information from which to draw. It's from his letters that we know about his love of cats, his fondness for cheese, coffee and long walks, his hatred of cold weather and seafood, and his preference for working late at night, among many other things.

Lovecraft is best known, of course, for his tales of weird fiction, which are the focus of these volumes. In addition to creating his own stories, he worked with other writers, often vastly expanding on their ideas in collaborations. From childhood through his forty-seven years of life, he wrote just over one hundred stories. All of these stories are included in this collection, with the exception of his juvenilia and collaborations with other authors.

Strongly influenced by his love for the macabre work of Edgar Allan Poe, Lovecraft began his career writing in a similar vein. He produced brooding, eerie stories rich in atmosphere. Around 1919, he discovered and was enchanted by the fantasy works of Lord Dunsany and wrote several tales in a Dunsanian style, set in an imaginative dreamland. Over time, Lovecraft's stories became less imitative. When he finally found his own narrative voice, his stories became richer and more creative, and it was during this phase of his career that he created his "cosmic horror" and the Cthulhu Mythos (both discussed below).

In late May 1921, Lovecraft's mother died from complications following gallbladder surgery. Their relationship had been close and emotionally complicated, and her death was quite traumatic for him. Just six weeks later, he met Sonia Haft Greene, a fellow writer seven years his senior, at an amateur press convention in Boston. Whether it was because he felt liberated from his mother, or wished, perhaps, to replace her presence in his life, he began spending a lot of time with Sonia. In a move that shocked his aunts and his closest friends, in March 1924 Lovecraft announced they had married and planned to set up a household in New York City.

Having never had a day job, Lovecraft sought work in New York and found the process of trying to earn a living in the diverse cosmopolitan setting incredibly dispiriting. He considered himself a "gentleman," above the fray of the hustling, immigrant crowds he saw all around him. Sonia supported both of them with her work as a milliner for fashionable ladies, but she was unable to maintain a steady job, bouncing among various hat shops and department stores in Cincinnati and Cleveland. Lovecraft, unwilling to relocate to Ohio, took a bachelor flat in the Red Hook neighborhood of Brooklyn. Despite having many friends and an active social life in New York, he hated living in a community so different from, and more diverse than, his hometown. In May 1926, he returned alone to Providence, moving in with his Aunt Lillian. His marriage to Sonia had lasted little more than a year. Tensions between Lovecraft and his aunts over Sonia prevented the two from reuniting and, while never legally divorced, they went their separate ways.

Lovecraft did get odd jobs and seasonal work on occasion, but he made most of his sparse living as a ghostwriter and reviser for other authors. While many of them were unknown aspirants trying to break into magazine fiction markets, he had a few famous clients as well. He did ghostwriting for the magician Harry Houdini and the popular (and now forgotten) poet and pop psychologist David Van Bush. He formed revision-service partnerships with a number of his friends, and he advertised for clients in professional writers' journals. He revised and edited books of poetry, educational courses, and treacly romance fiction.

Years of experience taught Lovecraft how commercial writing worked but, in his own personal efforts, he continued to pursue what he considered to be artistic, rather than commercial, success. Between 1926 and 1931, back in Providence, Lovecraft flourished creatively, writing some of his finest and most enduring works. His successes were not remunerative, however; he struggled to sell his works to the poorly paying pulp magazines like *Weird Tales*. While he found an audience among the pulp readership, few books of his stories were published during his lifetime. Lovecraft tried to be philosophical about his disappointments, but he took them to heart, and he came to believe that he had failed as a writer and would make no lasting literary mark. His feelings of defeat notwithstanding, he greatly enjoyed the fellowship of other writers in the genre, and he traveled as far and as often as his meager resources permitted to visit some of them in person.

Through the course of the Great Depression, Lovecraft's conservative views softened, but his creative output, fortunes, and health all declined. In March 1937, Lovecraft died from cancer of the small intestine. A writer to the bitter end, he kept a daily journal of his disease's progression until he could no longer hold a pen. He was survived by his aunt Annie Phillips Gamwell. His estranged wife Sonia didn't learn of his death until 1946. Lovecraft was buried beside the family monument at Swan Point Cemetery in Providence but without his own headstone. In 1977, a group of fans purchased a headstone in his name with the apt epitaph, taken from one of his own letters, "I am Providence."

Lovecraft's Legacy

The Creation of Cosmic Horror

Lovecraft was a lifelong astronomy enthusiast, and his passion for all things astronomical guided his fiction in a new direction. He appreciated the unfathomably vast size of the universe and the infinite timescale involved in its history. When considering the vastness of space, Lovecraft refused to believe that anything that might happen on Earth, a tiny planet in an unremarkable solar system in a small galaxy, could be of any relevance to the cosmos at large. Thus, he paid little heed to the insignificant lives of human beings and instead began to focus on a "cosmic horror." This idea was revolutionary. And it caught on.

The Cthulhu Mythos

Over time, Lovecraft created a kind of mythology—or at least a recurrent set of godlike beings that he wove through many of his stories. This mythology has come to be known as the Cthulhu Mythos (see the companion *A Reader's Guide to Selected Works by H. P. Lovecraft* for more information). Great, powerful entities with alien names like Yog-Sothoth, Cthulhu, Azathoth, Nyarlathotep, and others haunt his tales, along with his other creations like the Necronomicon and Miskatonic University (also discussed in the Reader's Guide). Lovecraft was playful in deploying his pantheon, referring to it as "Yog-Sothothery." He made liberal, if not always internally consistent, use of these creations and encouraged his friends and colleagues to do likewise. His generosity in sharing his intellectual creations no doubt contributed to the longevity and popularization of his work.

Posthumous Fame

Lovecraft might well have faded into the obscurity he expected were it not for the devoted efforts of his young protégé and literary executor, Robert H. Barlow, and his friends August Derleth and Donald Wandrei. Barlow preserved and typed as many of Lovecraft's manuscripts as he could, and arranged for their donation to the John Hay Library at Brown University. Upon Lovecraft's death, Derleth and Wandrei endeavored to get a collection of his tales published in book form. After being rejected by several established publishers, they formed their own publishing company—Arkham House. In 1939, under the Arkham House imprint, they published a collection of thirty-six stories, entitled *The Outsider and Others*. This collection, and other titles that followed, made Lovecraft's widely scattered works accessible to his fans and was an essential step in preserving his literary legacy.

In the 1980s, two additional events proved essential to Lovecraft's elevation from well-regarded author of weird tales to pop-culture icon. First, in 1981, Chaosium Inc. published the tabletop role-playing game Call of Cthulhu™ by Sandy Petersen. Following the success of games like Dungeons & Dragons, Call of Cthulhu™ let players take on the roles of 1920s investigators probing Lovecraftian mysteries. Instead of seeking and amassing treasure and power, characters in Call of Cthulhu™ had the decidedly Lovecraftian experience of losing their sanity as they gained knowledge of dark secrets. The game was an immediate hit and introduced a new generation to the works of Lovecraft. More than forty years later, the award-winning game maintains strong sales all over the world, continuing to be a powerful point of entry to the works of H. P. Lovecraft.

The second key event was the 1985 release of the motion picture *Re-Animator* by director Stuart Gordon. The film took Lovecraft's Frankenstein-esque tale of "Herbert West—Reanimator" and gave it an over-the-top injection of sex and violence. Although there had been a few previous cinematic adaptations of Lovecraft's work, *Re-Animator* became an instant cult classic and introduced a new mass audience to his fiction, paving the way for many subsequent film adaptations of his stories.

Lovecraft got in at the ground floor of modern pop culture: movies, radio, pulp magazines, comic books, and popular music. Mass communication was invented during Lovecraft's lifetime, and the seeds he planted have taken root in all those mediums and grown ubiquitously. Lovecraftian influences are commonplace today, even if sometimes unacknowledged. Both his creations and style of horror have been embraced by filmmakers and creators of video games. The dreaded otherworldly monstrosity of Cthulhu can be found in plush slippers. One can buy a Cthulhu Monopoly board game. The character Cthulhu himself has made guest appearances on the television shows *South Park* and *The Simpsons*. Heavy metal bands bang their heads to songs like "Call of Ktulu" and "Behind the Wall of Sleep." Allusions to Lovecraft are woven throughout the works of Neil Gaiman, George R. R. Martin, and Stephen King.

In addition to these popular works, a vibrant community of academic scholars of Lovecraft keeps his work and name alive. Dirk Mosig, S. T. Joshi, David E. Schultz, Robert M. Price, Donovan Loucks, Bobby Derie, Michel Houellebecq, Marc Michaud, and many others have studied his life and works in minute detail, producing academic journals, podcasts, reprints, websites, conferences, and prodigious treatises. It is safe to say that no author whose work appeared primarily in pulp magazines has been the subject of so much serious scholarly attention, and for good reason. Simply put, Lovecraft study is rewarding. Lovecraft left behind so much to examine—and in such a fertile intersection of literature, history, science, philosophy, and art—that there will always be more to discover and contemplate.

The John Hay Library at Brown University maintains a massive collection of original Lovecraft manuscripts and related materials, and the library works actively to make it available to scholars and the public via the Brown Digital Repository. Since 1988, an annual Lovecraft Forum has taken place at the State University of New York at New Paltz, and since 1993, a biannual convention, NecronomiCon–Providence, has been held in Lovecraft's hometown of Providence, Rhode Island. There, thousands of scholars and fans of Lovecraft gather in a long-weekend celebration of his life and legacy.

The H. P. Lovecraft Historical Society

We founded the H. P. Lovecraft Society in Denver, Colorado, in the mid-1980s. We and our friends became interested in the works and worlds of Lovecraft through the Call of Cthulhu™ role-playing game. We thought it would be fun to put on costumes and play out our Lovecraftian adventures live in the real world. In that era before the Internet existed, we thought we had invented live-action roleplaying. We called our game Cthulhu Lives!, and we launched our own monthly 'zine, *Strange Eons*. Over the years we wrote and produced more than sixty live-action games that steadily grew in scale until we realized we were doing the same amount of work on these as would be required to produce small films. So, we started producing small films. Our society now has thousands of members all over the world and has produced award-winning movie adaptations of Lovecraft stories, along with 1930s-style audio dramas, audiobooks, a podcast, music and book projects, games and props, and a lot more. We strive to produce Lovecraftian entertainment of all kinds with a unique blend of respect for the source material, respect for humankind, authentic period details, high production value, and a sense of humor.

Enduring Controversy

H. P. Lovecraft is not without detractors. Some have criticized him as a "bad writer" because of his reckless use of polysyllabic adjectives or thinly drawn human characters. To us, this is like declaring that Pablo Picasso was a "bad painter" because he used too much blue or didn't work in a photorealistic style. Lovecraft is not for everyone, as he was the first to recognize, but to say that he was a bad writer because he himself was not interested in following popular stylistic trends is to miss the point entirely.

While we can dismiss such writerly criticisms without too much trouble, we cannot dismiss the fact that H. P. Lovecraft was a racist. It must be acknowledged that in some of his stories, and particularly in his essays and personal letters, he used offensive language and expressed antisemitic and white supremacist ideas. Some critics have suggested that, because of this, he should be dismissed and his works no longer read. We can understand that sentiment, but we believe that, like Picasso, Thomas Jefferson, Abraham Lincoln, Edgar Allan Poe, and Mark Twain, Lovecraft's positive contributions outweigh his negative ones. Lovecraft was a deeply flawed human being, and while we cannot retroactively change the beliefs of historical figures, we can choose to actively reject such ideologies while simultaneously appreciating their work. In the case of Lovecraft, we can choose to admire the enduring nature of his fantastical imagination and worlds of ancient mystery.

The Collected Fiction of H. P. Lovecraft

The text of the stories in these volumes has been meticulously compiled and edited by celebrated Lovecraft scholar S. T. Joshi. Mr. Joshi has, wherever possible, gone back to the original manuscripts and typescripts of the tales to provide the most accurate representation of Lovecraft's intent with each story. Many of these tales were first published in pulp magazines and amateur journals, where errors and omissions of all sorts were introduced—and some of these have persisted for years. These mistakes frustrated Lovecraft wildly, and he frequently lamented the damage done to his stories by careless editing. We have no doubt he would be pleased to know that every effort has been made to ensure that our readers can enjoy his stories exactly as he wrote them, with only the flaws of the author himself remaining.

Conclusion

Why does this ongoing fascination with Lovecraft continue? What is it in these tales that draws the modern world to this 1920s writer with his 1840s vocabulary and 1760s sensibility? Why does his popularity continue to grow a century after his death? Part of what makes Lovecraft's work so compelling is its setting in time. The number of years from the American Revolution to when young Lovecraft was coming of age is about the same as the number of years from his youth to today, so it's not hard for us to view his era the way he viewed Colonial America—as a kind of golden age. Lovecraft wrote between the wars, in an age before satellites, cell phones, or deep-sea submersibles, when our world had more mystery and innocence and romance. That context is part of what makes his horrors so disturbing.

We posit that Lovecraft gives us horror at its ultimate level. His horror doesn't arise from a bunch of zombies coming to get us, nor from the old mansion being haunted by unquiet spirits. No, Lovecraft's horror transcends the mundane entirely. Lovecraft shows us an existence where humankind is overshadowed by great and monstrous beings that eclipse everything humans have ever done. He strips away salvation: There is no useful vial of holy water or kindly god looking out for humanity. Lovecraft orphans us, forcing us to come face to face with the endless dark universe that surrounds us—our only hope being the good fortune not to fully understand the monstrous chaos that lurks at every turn. He exposes us to what he defined as humanity's oldest and strongest fear—fear of the unknown.

Lovecraft's works have been a source of thrills and inspiration to us for more than forty years. They have set our imaginations on fire and given us access to fantastical realms. We've transformed these stories into games, motion pictures, stage plays, audio dramas, rock operas, and much more. Lovecraft's imagination has been a catalyst for ours, and we hope it will prove to be one for yours as well. For almost a half-century, we've had cause to revisit these stories again and again, and those return trips have proven as enjoyable and rewarding as our first discovery. Lovecraft's works reward rereading. Whether this is your first excursion into his strange fiction or you're a devoted admirer of Lovecraft's unique narrative voice, we hope The H. P. Lovecraft Experience provides you with a delightful exploration of some of the most extraordinarily weird tales yet written.

Sean Branney, Andrew Leman
Founders, The H. P. Lovecraft Historical Society

THE BEAST IN THE CAVE

The horrible conclusion which had been gradually obtruding itself upon my confused and reluctant mind was now an awful certainty. I was lost, completely, hopelessly lost in the vast and labyrinthine recesses of the Mammoth Cave. Turn as I might, in no direction could my straining vision seize on any object capable of serving as a guidepost to set me on the outward path. That nevermore should I behold the blessed light of day, or scan the pleasant hills and dales of the beautiful world outside, my reason could no longer entertain the slightest unbelief. Hope had departed. Yet, indoctrinated as I was by a life of philosophical study, I derived no small measure of satisfaction from my unimpassioned demeanour; for although I had frequently read of the wild frenzies into which were thrown the victims of similar situations, I experienced none of these, but stood quiet as soon as I clearly realised the loss of my bearings.

Nor did the thought that I had probably wandered beyond the utmost limits of an ordinary search cause me to abandon my composure even for a moment. If I must die, I reflected, then was this terrible yet majestic cavern as welcome a sepulchre as that which any churchyard might afford; a conception which carried with it more of tranquillity than of despair.

Starving would prove my ultimate fate; of this I was certain. Some, I knew, had gone mad under circumstances such as these, but I felt that this end would not be mine. My disaster was the result of no fault save my own, since unbeknown to the guide I had separated myself from the regular party of sightseers; and, wandering for over an hour in forbidden avenues of the cave, had found myself unable to retrace the devious windings which I had pursued since forsaking my companions.

Already my torch had begun to expire; soon I would be enveloped by the total and almost palpable blackness of the bowels of the earth. As I stood in the waning, unsteady light, I idly wondered over the exact circumstances of my coming end. I remembered the accounts which I had heard of the colony of consumptives, who, taking their residence in the gigantic grotto to find health from the apparently salubrious air of the underground world, with its steady, uniform temperature, pure air, and peaceful quiet, had found, instead, death in strange and ghastly form. I had seen the sad remains of their ill made cottages as I passed them by with the party, and had wondered what unnatural influence a long sojourn in this immense and silent cavern would exert upon one as healthy and as vigorous as I. Now, I grimly told myself, my opportunity for settling this point had arrived, provided that want of food should not bring me too speedy a departure from this life.

As the last fitful rays of my torch faded into obscurity, I resolved to leave no stone unturned, no possible source of escape neglected, so summoning all the powers possessed by my lungs, I set up a series of loud shoutings, in the vain hope of attracting the attention of the guide by my clamour, yet, as I called, I believed in my heart that my cries were to no purpose, and that my voice, magnified and reflected by the numberless ramparts of the black maze about me, fell upon no ears save my own. All at once, however, my attention was fixed with a start as I fancied that I heard the sound of soft approaching steps on the rocky floor of the cavern. Was my deliverance about to be accomplished so soon? Had, then, all my horrible apprehensions been for naught, and was the guide, having marked my unwarranted absence from the party, following my course and seeking me out in this limestone labyrinth? Whilst these joyful queries arose in my brain, I was on the point of renewing my cries, in order that my discovery might come the sooner, when in an instant my delight was turned to horror as I listened; for my ever acute ear, now sharpened in even greater degree by the complete silence of the cave, bore to my benumbed understanding the unexpected and dreadful knowledge that these footfalls were *not like those of any mortal man.* In the unearthly stillness of this subterranean region, the tread of the booted guide would have sounded like a series of sharp and incisive blows. These impacts were soft, and stealthy, as of the padded paws of some feline. Besides, *at times,* when I listened carefully, I seemed to trace the falls of *four* instead of *two* feet.

I was now convinced that I had by my cries aroused and attracted some wild beast, perhaps a mountain lion which had accidentally strayed within the cave. Perhaps, I considered, the Almighty had chosen for me a swifter and more merciful death than that of hunger. Yet the instinct of self-preservation, never wholly dormant, was stirred in my breast, and though escape from the oncoming peril might but spare me for a sterner and more lingering end, I determined nevertheless to part with my life at as high a price as I could command. Strange as it may seem, my mind conceived of no intent on the part of the visitor save that of hostility. Accordingly, I became very quiet, in the hope that the unknown beast would, in the absence of a guiding sound, lose its direction as had I, and thus pass me by. But this hope was not destined for realisation, for the strange footfalls steadily advanced, the animal evidently having obtained my scent, which in an atmosphere so absolutely free from all distracting influences as is that of the cave, could doubtless be followed at a great distance.

Seeing therefore that I must be armed for defence against an uncanny and unseen attack in the dark, I grouped about me the largest of the fragments of rock which were strown upon all parts of the floor of the cavern in the vicinity, and, grasping one in each hand for immediate use, awaited with resignation the inevitable result. Meanwhile the hideous pattering of the paws drew near. Certainly, the conduct of the creature was exceedingly strange. Most of the time, the tread seemed to be that of a quadruped, walking with a singular *lack of unison* betwixt hind and fore feet, yet at brief and infrequent intervals I fancied that but two feet were engaged in the process of locomotion. I wondered what species of animal was to confront me; it must, I thought, be some unfortunate beast who had paid for its curiosity to investigate one of the entrances of the fearful grotto with a lifelong confinement in its interminable recesses. It doubtless obtained as food the eyeless fish, bats, and rats of the cave, as well as some of the ordinary fish that are wafted in at every freshet of Green River, which communicates in some occult manner with the waters of the cave. I occupied my terrible vigil with grotesque conjectures of what alterations cave life might have wrought in the physical structure of the beast, remembering the awful appearances ascribed by local tradition to the consumptives who had died after long residence in the cavern. Then I remembered with a start that, even should I succeed in killing my antagonist, I should *never behold its form,* as my torch had long since been extinct, and I was entirely unprovided with matches. The tension on my brain now became frightful. My disordered fancy conjured up hideous and fearsome shapes from the sinister darkness that surrounded me, and that actually seemed to *press* upon my body. Nearer, nearer, the dreadful footfalls approached. It seemed that I must give vent to a piercing scream, yet had I been sufficiently irresolute to attempt such a thing, my voice could scarce have responded. I was petrified, rooted to the spot. I doubted if my right arm would allow me to hurl its missile at the oncoming thing when the crucial moment should arrive. Now the steady *pat, pat,* of the steps was close at hand; now, *very* close. I could hear the laboured breathing of the animal, and terror-struck as I was, I realised that it must have come from a considerable distance, and was correspondingly fatigued. Suddenly the spell broke. My right hand, guided by my ever trustworthy sense of hearing, threw with full force the sharp-angled bit of limestone which it contained, toward that point in the darkness from which emanated the breathing and pattering, and, wonderful to relate, it nearly reached its goal, for I heard the thing jump, landing at a distance away, where it seemed to pause.

Having readjusted my aim, I discharged my second missile, this time most effectively, for with a flood of joy I listened as the creature fell in what sounded like a complete collapse, and evidently remained prone and unmoving. Almost overpowered by the great relief which rushed over me, I reeled back against the wall. The breathing continued, in heavy, gasping inhalations and expirations, whence I realised that I had no more than wounded the creature. And now all desire to examine the *thing* ceased. At last something allied to groundless, superstitious, fear had entered my brain, and I did not approach the body, nor did I continue to cast stones at it in order to complete the extinction of its life. Instead, I ran at full speed in what was, as nearly as I could estimate in my frenzied condition, the direction from which I had come. Suddenly I heard a sound, or rather, a regular succession of sounds. In another instant they had resolved themselves into a series of sharp, metallic clicks. This time there was no doubt. *It was the guide.* And then I shouted, yelled, screamed, even shrieked with joy as I beheld in the vaulted arches above the faint and glimmering effulgence which I knew to be the reflected light of an approaching torch. I ran to meet the flare, and before I could completely understand what had occurred, was lying upon the ground at the feet of the guide, embracing his boots, and gibbering, despite my boasted reserve, in a most meaningless and idiotic manner, pouring out my terrible story, and at the same time overwhelming my auditor with protestations of gratitude. At length I awoke to something like my normal consciousness. The guide had noted my absence upon the arrival of the party at the entrance of the cave, and had, from his own intuitive sense of direction, proceeded to make a thorough canvass of the by-passages just ahead of where he had last spoken to me, locating my whereabouts after a quest of about four hours.

By the time he had related this to me, I, emboldened by his torch and his company, began to reflect upon the strange beast which I had wounded but a short distance back in the darkness, and suggested that we ascertain, by the rushlight's aid, what manner of creature was my victim. Accordingly I retraced my steps, this time with a courage born of companionship, to the scene of my terrible experience. Soon we descried a white object upon the floor, an object whiter even than the gleaming limestone itself. Cautiously advancing, we gave vent to a simultaneous ejaculation of wonderment, for of all the unnatural monsters either of us had in our lifetimes beheld, this was in surpassing degree the strangest. It appeared to be an anthropoid ape of large proportions, escaped, perhaps, from some itinerant menagerie. Its hair was snow-white, a thing due no doubt to the bleaching action of a long existence within the inky confines of the cave, but it was also surprisingly thin, being indeed largely absent save on the head, where it was of such length and abundance that it fell over the shoulders in considerable profusion. The face was turned away from us, as the creature lay almost directly upon it. The inclination of the limbs was very singular, explaining, however, the alternation in their use which I had before noted, whereby the beast used sometimes all four, and on other occasions but two for its progress. From the tips of the fingers or toes long nail-like claws extended. The hands or feet were not prehensile, a fact that I ascribed to that long residence in the cave which, as I before mentioned, seemed evident from the all-pervading and almost unearthly *whiteness* so characteristic of the whole anatomy. No tail seemed to be present.

The respiration had now grown very feeble, and the guide had drawn his pistol with the evident intent of despatching the creature, when a sudden *sound* emitted by the latter caused the weapon to fall unused. The sound was of a nature difficult to describe. It was not like the normal note of any known species of simian, and I wondered if this unnatural quality were not the result of a long continued and complete silence, broken by the sensations produced by the advent of the light, a thing which the beast could not have seen since its first entrance into the cave. The sound, which I might feebly attempt to classify as a kind of deep toned chattering, was faintly continued. All at once a fleeting spasm of energy seemed to pass through the frame of the beast. The paws went through a convulsive motion, and the limbs contracted. With a jerk, the white body rolled over so that its face was turned in our direction. For a moment I was so struck with horror at the eyes thus revealed that I noted nothing else. They were black, those eyes, deep, jetty black, in hideous contrast to the snow-white hair and flesh. Like those of other cave denizens, they were deeply sunken in their orbits, and were entirely destitute of iris. As I looked more closely, I saw that they were set in a face less prognathous than that of the average ape, and infinitely more hairy. The nose was quite distinct.

As we gazed upon the uncanny sight presented to our vision, the thick lips opened, and several *sounds* issued from them, after which the *thing* relaxed in death.

The guide clutched my coat-sleeve and trembled so violently that the light shook fitfully, casting weird, moving shadows on the walls about us.

I made no motion, but stood rigidly still, my horrified eyes fixed upon the floor ahead.

Then fear left, and wonder, awe, compassion, and reverence succeeded in its place, for the *sounds* uttered by the stricken figure that lay stretched out on the limestone had told us the awesome truth. The creature I had killed, the strange beast of the unfathomed cave was, or had at one time been, a **MAN!!!**

THE ALCHEMIST

High up, crowning the grassy summit of a swelling mound whose sides are wooded near the base with the gnarled trees of the primeval forest, stands the old chateau of my ancestors. For centuries its lofty battlements have frowned down upon the wild and rugged countryside about, serving as a home and stronghold for the proud house whose honoured line is older even than the moss-grown castle walls. These ancient turrets, stained by the storms of generations and crumbling under the slow yet mighty pressure of time, formed in the ages of feudalism one of the most dreaded and formidable fortresses in all France. From its machicolated parapets and mounted battlements Barons, Counts, and even Kings had been defied, yet never had its spacious halls resounded to the footsteps of the invader.

But since those glorious years all is changed. A poverty but little above the level of dire want, together with a pride of name that forbids its alleviation by the pursuits of commercial life, have prevented the scions of our line from maintaining their estates in pristine splendour; and the falling stones of the walls, the overgrown vegetation in the parks, the dry and dusty moat, the ill-paved courtyards, and toppling towers without, as well as the sagging floors, the worm-eaten wainscots, and the faded tapestries within, all tell a gloomy tale of fallen grandeur. As the ages passed, first one, then another of the four great turrets were left to ruin, until at last but a single tower housed the sadly reduced descendants of the once mighty lords of the estate.

It was in one of the vast and gloomy chambers of this remaining tower that I, Antoine, last of the unhappy and accursed Comtes de C——, first saw the light of day, ninety long years ago. Within these walls, and amongst the dark and shadowy forests, the wild ravines and grottoes of the hillside below, were spent the first years of my troubled life. My parents I never knew. My father had been killed at the age of thirty-two, a month before I was born, by the fall of a stone somehow dislodged from one of the deserted parapets of the castle; and my mother having died at my birth, my care and education devolved solely upon one remaining servitor, an old and trusted man of considerable intelligence, whose name I remember as Pierre. I was an only child, and the lack of companionship which this fact entailed upon me was augmented by the strange care exercised by my aged guardian in excluding me from the society of the peasant children whose abodes were scattered here and there upon the plains that surround the base of the hill. At the time, Pierre said that this restriction was imposed upon me because my noble birth placed me above association with such plebeian company. Now I know that its real object was to keep from my ears the idle tales of the dread curse upon our line, that were nightly told and magnified by the simple tenantry as they conversed in hushed accents in the glow of their cottage hearths.

Thus isolated, and thrown upon my own resources, I spent the hours of my childhood in poring over the ancient tomes that filled the shadow-haunted library of the chateau, and in roaming without aim or purpose through the perpetual dusk of the spectral wood that clothes the sides of the hill near its foot. It was perhaps an effect of such surroundings that my mind early acquired a shade of melancholy. Those studies and pursuits which partake of the dark and occult in Nature most strongly claimed my attention.

Of my own race I was permitted to learn singularly little, yet what small knowledge of it I was able to gain, seemed to depress me much. Perhaps it was at first only the manifest reluctance of my old preceptor to discuss with me my paternal ancestry that gave rise to the terror which I ever felt at the mention of my great house; yet as I grew out of childhood, I was able to piece together disconnected fragments of discourse, let slip from the unwilling tongue which had begun to falter in approaching senility, that had a sort of relation to a certain circumstance which I had always deemed strange, but which now became dimly terrible. The circumstance to which I allude is the early age at which all the Comtes of my line had met their end. Whilst I had hitherto considered this but a natural attribute of a family of short-lived men, I afterward pondered long upon these premature deaths, and began to connect them with the wanderings of the old man, who often spoke of a curse which for centuries had prevented the lives of the holders of my title from much exceeding the span of thirty-two years. Upon my twenty-first birthday, the aged Pierre gave to me a family document which he said had for many generations been handed down from father to son, and continued by each possessor. Its contents were of the most startling nature, and its perusal confirmed the gravest of my apprehensions. At this time, my belief in the supernatural was firm and deep-seated, else I should have dismissed with scorn the incredible narrative unfolded before my eyes.

The paper carried me back to the days of the thirteenth century, when the old castle in which I sat had been a feared and impregnable fortress. It told of a certain ancient man who had once dwelt on our estates, a person of no small accomplishments, though little above the rank of peasant; by name, Michel, usually designated by the surname of Mauvais, the Evil, on account of his sinister reputation. He had studied beyond the custom of his kind, seeking such things as the Philosopher's Stone, or the Elixir of Eternal Life, and was reputed wise in the terrible secrets of Black Magic and Alchemy. Michel Mauvais had one son, named Charles, a youth as proficient as himself in the hidden arts, and who had therefore been called Le Sorcier, or the Wizard. This pair, shunned by all honest folk, were suspected of the most hideous practices. Old Michel was said to have burnt his wife alive as a sacrifice to the Devil, and the unaccountable disappearances of many small peasant children were laid at the dreaded door of these two. Yet through the dark natures of the father and the son ran one redeeming ray of humanity; the evil old man loved his offspring with fierce intensity, whilst the youth had for his parent a more than filial affection.

One night the castle on the hill was thrown into the wildest confusion by the vanishment of young Godfrey, son to Henri the Comte. A searching party, headed by the frantic father, invaded the cottage of the sorcerers and there came upon old Michel Mauvais, busy over a huge and violently boiling cauldron. Without certain cause, in the ungoverned madness of fury and despair, the Comte laid hands on the aged wizard, and ere he released his murderous hold his victim was no more. Meanwhile joyful servants were proclaiming aloud the finding of young Godfrey in a distant and unused chamber of the great edifice, telling too late that poor Michel had been killed in vain. As the Comte and his associates turned away from the lowly abode of the alchemists, the form of Charles Le Sorcier appeared through the trees. The excited chatter of the menials standing about told him what had occurred, yet he seemed at first unmoved at his father's fate. Then, slowly advancing to meet the Comte, he pronounced in dull yet terrible accents the curse that ever afterward haunted the house of C——.

> "May ne'er a noble of thy murd'rous line
> Survive to reach a greater age than thine!"

spake he, when, suddenly leaping backwards into the black wood, he drew from his tunic a phial of colourless liquid which he threw in the face of his father's slayer as he disappeared behind the inky curtain of the night. The Comte died without utterance, and was buried the next day, but little more than two and thirty years from the hour of his birth. No trace of the assassin could be found, though relentless bands of peasants scoured the neighbouring woods and the meadow-land around the hill.

Thus time and the want of a reminder dulled the memory of the curse in the minds of the late Comte's family, so that when Godfrey, innocent cause of the whole tragedy and now bearing the title, was killed by an arrow whilst hunting, at the age of thirty-two, there were no thoughts save those of grief at his demise. But when, years afterward, the next young Comte, Robert by name, was found dead in a nearby field from no apparent cause, the peasants told in whispers that their seigneur had but lately passed his thirty-second birthday when surprised by early death. Louis, son to Robert, was found drowned in the moat at the same fateful age, and thus down through the centuries ran the ominous chronicle; Henris, Roberts, Antoines, and Armands snatched from happy and virtuous lives when a little below the age of their unfortunate ancestor at his murder.

That I had left at most but eleven years of further existence was made certain to me by the words which I read. My life, previously held at small value, now became dearer to me each day, as I delved deeper and deeper into the mysteries of the hidden world of black magic. Isolated as I was, modern science had produced no impression upon me, and I laboured as in the Middle Ages, as wrapt as had been old Michel and young Charles themselves in the acquisition of daemonological and alchemical learning. Yet read as I might, in no manner could I account for the strange curse upon my line. In unusually rational moments, I would even go so far as to seek a natural explanation, attributing the early deaths of my ancestors to the sinister Charles Le Sorcier and his heirs; yet having found upon careful inquiry that there were no known descendants of the alchemist, I would fall back to my occult studies, and once more endeavour to find a spell that would release my house from its terrible burden. Upon one thing I was absolutely resolved. I should never wed, for since no other branches of my family were in existence, I might thus end the curse with myself.

As I drew near the age of thirty, old Pierre was called to the land beyond. Alone I buried him beneath the stones of the courtyard about which he had loved to wander in life. Thus was I left to ponder on myself as the only human creature within the great fortress, and in my utter solitude my mind began to cease its vain protest against the impending doom, to become almost reconciled to the fate which so many of my ancestors had met. Much of my time was now occupied in the exploration of the ruined and abandoned halls and towers of the old chateau, which in youth fear had caused me to shun, and some of which, old Pierre had once told me, had not been trodden by human foot for over four centuries. Strange and awesome were many of the objects I encountered. Furniture, covered by the dust of ages and crumbling with the rot of long dampness, met my eyes. Cobwebs in a profusion never before seen by me were spun everywhere, and huge bats flapped their bony and uncanny wings on all sides of the otherwise untenanted gloom.

Of my exact age, even down to days and hours, I kept a most careful record, for each movement of the pendulum of the massive clock in the library told off so much more of my doomed existence. At length I approached that time which I had so long viewed with apprehension. Since most of my ancestors had been seized some little while before they reached the exact age of the Comte Henri at his end, I was every moment on the watch for the coming of the unknown death. In what strange form the curse should overtake me, I knew not; but I was resolved, at least, that it should not find me a cowardly or a passive victim. With new vigour I applied myself to my examination of the old chateau and its contents.

It was upon one of the longest of all my excursions of discovery in the deserted portion of the castle, less than a week before that fatal hour which I felt must mark the utmost limit of my stay on earth, beyond which I could have not even the slightest hope of continuing to draw breath, that I came upon the culminating event of my whole life. I had spent the better part of the morning in climbing up and down half-ruined staircases in one of the most dilapidated of the ancient turrets. As the afternoon progressed, I sought the lower levels, descending into what appeared to be either a mediaeval place of confinement, or a more recently excavated storehouse for gunpowder. As I slowly traversed the nitre-encrusted passageway at the foot of the last staircase, the paving became very damp, and soon I saw by the light of my flickering torch that a blank, water-stained wall impeded my journey. Turning to retrace my steps, my eye fell upon a small trap-door with a ring, which lay directly beneath my feet. Pausing, I succeeded with difficulty in raising it, whereupon there was revealed a black aperture, exhaling noxious fumes which caused my torch to sputter, and disclosing in the unsteady glare the top of a flight of stone steps. As soon as the torch, which I lowered into the repellent depths, burned freely and steadily, I commenced my descent. The steps were many, and led to a narrow stone-flagged passage which I knew must be far underground. This passage proved of great length, and terminated in a massive oaken door, dripping with the moisture of the place, and stoutly resisting all my attempts to open it. Ceasing after a time my efforts in this direction, I had proceeded back some distance toward the steps, when there suddenly fell to my experience one of the most profound and maddening shocks capable of reception by the human mind. Without warning, *I heard the heavy door behind me creak slowly open upon its rusted hinges.* My immediate sensations are incapable of analysis. To be confronted in a place as thoroughly deserted as I had deemed the old castle with evidence of the presence of man or spirit, produced in my brain a horror of the most acute description. When at last I turned and faced the seat of the sound, my eyes must have started from their orbits at the sight that they beheld. There in the ancient Gothic doorway stood a human figure. It was that of a man clad in a skull-cap and long mediaeval tunic of dark colour. His long hair and flowing beard were of a terrible and intense black hue, and of incredible profusion. His forehead, high beyond the usual dimensions; his cheeks, deep sunken and heavily lined with wrinkles; and his hands, long, claw-like, and gnarled, were of such a deathly, marble-like whiteness as I have never elsewhere seen in man. His figure, lean to the proportions of a skeleton, was strangely bent and almost lost within the voluminous folds of his peculiar garment. But strangest of all were his eyes; twin caves of abysmal blackness, profound in expression of understanding, yet inhuman in degree of wickedness. These were now fixed upon me, piercing my soul with their hatred, and rooting me to the spot whereon I stood. At last the figure spoke in a rumbling voice that chilled me through with its dull hollowness and latent malevolence. The language in which the discourse was clothed was that debased form of Latin in use amongst the more learned men of the Middle Ages, and made familiar to me by my prolonged researches into the works of the old alchemists and daemonologists. The apparition spoke of the curse which had hovered over my house, told me of my coming end, dwelt on the wrong perpetrated by my ancestor against old Michel Mauvais, and gloated over the revenge of Charles Le Sorcier. He told how the young Charles had escaped into the night, returning in after years to kill Godfrey the heir with an arrow just as he approached the age which had been his father's at his assassination; how he had secretly returned to the estate and established himself, unknown, in the even then deserted subterranean chamber whose doorway now framed the hideous narrator; how he had seized Robert, son of Godfrey, in a field, forced poison down his throat, and left him to die at the age of thirty-two, thus maintaining the foul provisions of his vengeful curse. At this point I was left to imagine the solution of the greatest mystery of all, how the curse had been fulfilled since that time when Charles Le Sorcier must in the course of Nature have died, for the man digressed into an account of the deep alchemical studies of the two wizards, father and son, speaking most particularly of the researches of Charles Le Sorcier concerning the elixir which should grant to him who partook of it eternal life and youth.

His enthusiasm had seemed for the moment to remove from his terrible eyes the hatred that had at first so haunted them, but suddenly the fiendish glare returned, and with a shocking sound like the hissing of a serpent, the stranger raised a glass phial with the evident intent of ending my life as had Charles Le Sorcier, six hundred years before, ended that of my ancestor. Prompted by some preserving instinct of self-defence, I broke through the spell that had hitherto held me immovable, and flung my now dying torch at the creature who menaced my existence. I heard the phial break harmlessly against the stones of the passage as the tunic of the strange man caught fire and lit the horrid scene with a ghastly radiance. The shriek of fright and impotent malice emitted by the would-be assassin proved too much for my already shaken nerves, and I fell prone upon the slimy floor in a total faint.

When at last my senses returned, all was frightfully dark, and my mind remembering what had occurred, shrank from the idea of beholding more; yet curiosity overmastered all. Who, I asked myself, was this man of evil, and how came he within the castle walls? Why should he seek to avenge the death of poor Michel Mauvais, and how had the curse been carried on through all the long centuries since the time of Charles Le Sorcier? The dread of years was lifted off my shoulders, for I knew that he whom I had felled was the source of all my danger from the curse; and now that I was free, I burned with the desire to learn more of the sinister thing which had haunted my line for centuries, and made of my own youth one long-continued nightmare. Determined upon further exploration, I felt in my pockets for flint and steel, and lit the unused torch which I had with me. First of all, the new light revealed the distorted and blackened form of the mysterious stranger. The hideous eyes were now closed. Disliking the sight, I turned away and entered the chamber beyond the Gothic door. Here I found what seemed much like an alchemist's laboratory. In one corner was an immense pile of a shining yellow metal that sparkled gorgeously in the light of the torch. It may have been gold, but I did not pause to examine it, for I was strangely affected by that which I had undergone. At the farther end of the apartment was an opening leading out into one of the many wild ravines of the dark hillside forest. Filled with wonder, yet now realising how the man had obtained access to the chateau, I proceeded to return. I had intended to pass by the remains of the stranger with averted face, but as I approached the body, I seemed to hear emanating from it a faint sound, as though life were not yet wholly extinct. Aghast, I turned to examine the charred and shrivelled figure on the floor.

Then all at once the horrible eyes, blacker even than the seared face in which they were set, opened wide with an expression which I was unable to interpret. The cracked lips tried to frame words which I could not well understand. Once I caught the name of Charles Le Sorcier, and again I fancied that the words "years" and "curse" issued from the twisted mouth. Still I was at a loss to gather the purport of his disconnected speech. At my evident ignorance of his meaning, the pitchy eyes once more flashed malevolently at me, until, helpless as I saw my opponent to be, I trembled as I watched him.

Suddenly the wretch, animated with his last burst of strength, raised his hideous head from the damp and sunken pavement. Then, as I remained, paralysed with fear, he found his voice and in his dying breath screamed forth those words which have ever afterward haunted my days and my nights. "Fool," he shrieked, "can you not guess my secret? Have you no brain whereby you may recognise the will which has through six long centuries fulfilled the dreadful curse upon your house? Have I not told you of the great elixir of eternal life? Know you not how the secret of Alchemy was solved? I tell you, it is I! I! *I! that have lived for six hundred years to maintain my revenge,* FOR I AM CHARLES LE SORCIER!"

THE TOMB

"Sedibus ut saltem placidis in morte quiescam."
—*Virgil.*

In relating the circumstances which have led to my confinement within this refuge for the demented, I am aware that my present position will create a natural doubt of the authenticity of my narrative. It is an unfortunate fact that the bulk of humanity is too limited in its mental vision to weigh with patience and intelligence those isolated phenomena, seen and felt only by a psychologically sensitive few, which lie outside its common experience. Men of broader intellect know that there is no sharp distinction betwixt the real and the unreal; that all things appear as they do only by virtue of the delicate individual physical and mental media through which we are made conscious of them; but the prosaic materialism of the majority condemns as madness the flashes of super-sight which penetrate the common veil of obvious empiricism.

My name is Jervas Dudley, and from earliest childhood I have been a dreamer and a visionary. Wealthy beyond the necessity of a commercial life, and temperamentally unfitted for the formal studies and social recreations of my acquaintances, I have dwelt ever in realms apart from the visible world; spending my youth and adolescence in ancient and little-known books, and in roaming the fields and groves of the region near my ancestral home. I do not think that what I read in these books or saw in these fields and groves was exactly what other boys read and saw there; but of this I must say little, since detailed speech would but confirm those cruel slanders upon my intellect which I sometimes overhear from the whispers of the stealthy attendants around me. It is sufficient for me to relate events without analysing causes.

I have said that I dwelt apart from the visible world, but I have not said that I dwelt alone. This no human creature may do; for lacking the fellowship of the living, he inevitably draws upon the companionship of things that are not, or are no longer, living. Close by my home there lies a singular wooded hollow, in whose twilight deeps I spent most of my time; reading, thinking, and dreaming. Down its moss-covered slopes my first steps of infancy were taken, and around its grotesquely gnarled oak trees my first fancies of boyhood were woven. Well did I come to know the presiding dryads of those trees, and often have I watched their wild dances in the struggling beams of a waning moon—but of these things I must not now speak. I will tell only of the lone tomb in the darkest of the hillside thickets; the deserted tomb of the Hydes, an old and exalted family whose last direct descendant had been laid within its black recesses many decades before my birth.

The vault to which I refer is of ancient granite, weathered and discoloured by the mists and dampness of generations. Excavated back into the hillside, the structure is visible only at the entrance. The door, a ponderous and forbidding slab of stone, hangs upon rusted iron hinges, and is fastened *ajar* in a queerly sinister way by means of heavy iron chains and padlocks, according to a gruesome fashion of half a century ago. The abode of the race whose scions are here inurned had once crowned the declivity which holds the tomb, but had long since fallen victim to the flames which sprang up from a stroke of lightning. Of the midnight storm which destroyed this gloomy mansion, the older inhabitants of the region sometimes speak in hushed and uneasy voices; alluding to what they call "divine wrath" in a manner that in later years vaguely increased the always strong fascination which I had felt for the forest-darkened sepulchre. One man only had perished in the fire. When the last of the Hydes was buried in this place of shade and stillness, the sad urnful of ashes had come from a distant land; to which the family had repaired when the mansion burned down. No one remains to lay flowers before the granite portal, and few care to brave the depressing shadows which seem to linger strangely about the water-worn stones.

The Tomb

I shall never forget the afternoon when first I stumbled upon the half-hidden house of death. It was in mid-summer, when the alchemy of Nature transmutes the sylvan landscape to one vivid and almost homogeneous mass of green; when the senses are well-nigh intoxicated with the surging seas of moist verdure and the subtly indefinable odours of the soil and the vegetation. In such surroundings the mind loses its perspective; time and space become trivial and unreal, and echoes of a forgotten prehistoric past beat insistently upon the enthralled consciousness. All day I had been wandering through the mystic groves of the hollow; thinking thoughts I need not discuss, and conversing with things I need not name. In years a child of ten, I had seen and heard many wonders unknown to the throng; and was oddly aged in certain respects. When, upon forcing my way between two savage clumps of briers, I suddenly encountered the entrance of the vault, I had no knowledge of what I had discovered. The dark blocks of granite, the door so curiously ajar, and the funereal carvings above the arch, aroused in me no associations of mournful or terrible character. Of graves and tombs I knew and imagined much, but had on account of my peculiar temperament been kept from all personal contact with churchyards and cemeteries. The strange stone house on the woodland slope was to me only a source of interest and speculation; and its cold, damp interior, into which I vainly peered through the aperture so tantalisingly left, contained for me no hint of death or decay. But in that instant of curiosity was born the madly unreasoning desire which has brought me to this hell of confinement. Spurred on by a voice which must have come from the hideous soul of the forest, I resolved to enter the beckoning gloom in spite of the ponderous chains which barred my passage. In the waning light of day I alternately rattled the rusty impediments with a view to throwing wide the stone door, and essayed to squeeze my slight form through the space already provided; but neither plan met with success. At first curious, I was now frantic; and when in the thickening twilight I returned to my home, I had sworn to the hundred gods of the grove that *at any cost* I would some day force an entrance to the black, chilly depths that seemed calling out to me. The physician with the iron-grey beard who comes each day to my room once told a visitor that this decision marked the beginning of a pitiful monomania; but I will leave final judgment to my readers when they shall have learnt all.

The months following my discovery were spent in futile attempts to force the complicated padlock of the slightly open vault, and in carefully guarded inquiries regarding the nature and history of the structure. With the traditionally receptive ears of the small boy, I learned much; though an habitual secretiveness caused me to tell no one of my information or my resolve. It is perhaps worth mentioning that I was not at all surprised or terrified on learning of the nature of the vault. My rather original ideas regarding life and death had caused me to associate the cold clay with the breathing body in a vague fashion; and I felt that the great and sinister family of the burned-down mansion was in some way represented within the stone space I sought to explore. Mumbled tales of the weird rites and godless revels of bygone years in the ancient hall gave to me a new and potent interest in the tomb, before whose door I would sit for hours at a time each day. Once I thrust a candle within the nearly closed entrance, but could see nothing save a flight of damp stone steps leading downward. The odour of the place repelled yet bewitched me. I felt I had known it before, in a past remote beyond all recollection; beyond even my tenancy of the body I now possess.

The year after I first beheld the tomb, I stumbled upon a worm-eaten translation of Plutarch's "Lives" in the book-filled attic of my home. Reading the life of Theseus, I was much impressed by the passage telling of the great stone beneath which the boyish hero was to find his tokens of destiny whenever he should become old enough to lift its enormous weight. This legend had the effect of dispelling my keenest impatience to enter the vault, for it made me feel that the time was not yet ripe. Later, I told myself, I should grow to a strength and ingenuity which might enable me to unfasten the heavily chained door with ease; but until then I would do better by conforming to what seemed the will of Fate.

Accordingly my watches by the dank portal became less persistent, and much of my time was spent in other though equally strange pursuits. I would sometimes rise very quietly in the night, stealing out to walk in those churchyards and places of burial from which I had been kept by my parents. What I did there I may not say, for I am not now sure of the reality of certain things; but I know that on the day after such a nocturnal ramble I would often astonish those about me with my knowledge of topics almost forgotten for many generations. It was after a night like this that I shocked the community with a queer conceit about the burial of the rich and celebrated Squire Brewster, a maker of local history who was interred in 1711, and whose slate headstone, bearing a graven skull and crossbones, was slowly crumbling to powder. In a moment of childish imagination I vowed not only that the undertaker, Goodman Simpson, had stolen the silver-buckled shoes, silken hose, and satin small-clothes of the deceased before burial; but that the Squire himself, not fully inanimate, had turned twice in his mound-covered coffin on the day after interment.

But the idea of entering the tomb never left my thoughts; being indeed stimulated by the unexpected genealogical discovery that my own maternal ancestry possessed at least a slight link with the supposedly extinct family of the Hydes. Last of my paternal race, I was likewise the last of this older and more mysterious line. I began to feel that the tomb was *mine,* and to look forward with hot eagerness to the time when I might pass within that stone door and down those slimy stone steps in the dark. I now formed the habit of *listening* very intently at the slightly open portal, choosing my favourite hours of midnight stillness for the odd vigil. By the time I came of age, I had made a small clearing in the thicket before the mould-stained facade on the hillside, allowing the surrounding vegetation to encircle and overhang the space like the walls and roof of a sylvan bower. This bower was my temple, the fastened door my shrine, and here I would lie outstretched on the mossy ground, thinking strange thoughts and dreaming strange dreams.

The night of the first revelation was a sultry one. I must have fallen asleep from fatigue, for it was with a distinct sense of awakening that I heard the *voices.* Of those tones and accents I hesitate to speak; of their *quality* I will not speak; but I may say that they presented certain uncanny differences in vocabulary, pronunciation, and mode of utterance. Every shade of New England dialect, from the uncouth syllables of the Puritan colonists to the precise rhetoric of fifty years ago, seemed represented in that shadowy colloquy, though it was only later that I noticed the fact. At the time, indeed, my attention was distracted from this matter by another phenomenon; a phenomenon so fleeting that I could not take oath upon its reality. I barely fancied that as I awoke, a *light* had been hurriedly extinguished within the sunken sepulchre. I do not think I was either astounded or panic-stricken, but I know that I was greatly and permanently *changed* that night. Upon returning home I went with much directness to a rotting chest in the attic, wherein I found the key which next day unlocked with ease the barrier I had so long stormed in vain.

It was in the soft glow of late afternoon that I first entered the vault on the abandoned slope. A spell was upon me, and my heart leaped with an exultation I can but ill describe. As I closed the door behind me and descended the dripping steps by the light of my lone candle, I seemed to know the way; and though the candle sputtered with the stifling reek of the place, I felt singularly at home in the musty, charnel-house air. Looking about me, I beheld many marble slabs bearing coffins, or the remains of coffins. Some of these were sealed and intact, but others had nearly vanished, leaving the silver handles and plates isolated amidst certain curious heaps of whitish dust. Upon one plate I read the name of Sir Geoffrey Hyde, who had come from Sussex in 1640 and died here a few years later. In a conspicuous alcove was one fairly well-preserved and untenanted casket, adorned with a single name which brought to me both a smile and a shudder. An odd impulse caused me to climb upon the broad slab, extinguish my candle, and lie down within the vacant box.

In the grey light of dawn I staggered from the vault and locked the chain of the door behind me. I was no longer a young man, though but twenty-one winters had chilled my bodily frame. Early-rising villagers who observed my homeward progress looked at me strangely, and marvelled at the signs of ribald revelry which they saw in one whose life was known to be sober and solitary. I did not appear before my parents till after a long and refreshing sleep.

Henceforward I haunted the tomb each night; seeing, hearing, and doing things I must never recall. My speech, always susceptible to environmental influences, was the first thing to succumb to the change; and my suddenly acquired archaism of diction was soon remarked upon. Later a queer boldness and recklessness came into my demeanour, till I unconsciously grew to possess the bearing of a man of the world despite my lifelong seclusion. My formerly silent tongue waxed voluble with the easy grace of a Chesterfield or the godless cynicism of a Rochester. I displayed a peculiar erudition utterly unlike the fantastic, monkish lore over which I had pored in youth; and covered the fly-leaves of my books with facile impromptu epigrams which brought up suggestions of Gay, Prior, and the sprightliest of the Augustan wits and rhymesters. One morning at breakfast I came close to disaster by declaiming in palpably liquorish accents an effusion of eighteenth-century Bacchanalian mirth; a bit of Georgian playfulness never recorded in a book, which ran something like this:

> Come hither, my lads, with your tankards of ale,
> And drink to the present before it shall fail;
> Pile each on your platter a mountain of beef,
> For 'tis eating and drinking that bring us relief:
> So fill up your glass,
> For life will soon pass;
> When you're dead ye'll ne'er drink to your king or your lass!

Anacreon had a red nose, so they say;
But what's a red nose if ye're happy and gay?
Gad split me! I'd rather be red whilst I'm here
Than white as a lily—and dead half a year!
So Betty, my miss,
Come give me a kiss;
In hell there's no innkeeper's daughter like this!

Young Harry, propp'd up just as straight as he's able,
Will soon lose his wig and slip under the table;
But fill up your goblets and pass 'em around—
Better under the table than under the ground!
So revel and chaff
As ye thirstily quaff:
Under six feet of dirt 'tis less easy to laugh!

The fiend strike me blue! I'm scarce able to walk,
And damn me if I can stand upright or talk!
Here, landlord, bid Betty to summon a chair;
I'll try home for a while, for my wife is not there!
So lend me a hand;
I'm not able to stand,
But I'm gay whilst I linger on top of the land!

About this time I conceived my present fear of fire and thunderstorms. Previously indifferent to such things, I had now an unspeakable horror of them; and would retire to the innermost recesses of the house whenever the heavens threatened an electrical display. A favourite haunt of mine during the day was the ruined cellar of the mansion that had burned down, and in fancy I would picture the structure as it had been in its prime. On one occasion I startled a villager by leading him confidently to a shallow sub-cellar, of whose existence I seemed to know in spite of the fact that it had been unseen and forgotten for many generations.

At last came that which I had long feared. My parents, alarmed at the altered manner and appearance of their only son, commenced to exert over my movements a kindly espionage which threatened to result in disaster. I had told no one of my visits to the tomb, having guarded my secret purpose with religious zeal since childhood; but now I was forced to exercise care in threading the mazes of the wooded hollow, that I might throw off a possible pursuer. My key to the vault I kept suspended from a cord about my neck, its presence known only to me. I never carried out of the sepulchre any of the things I came upon whilst within its walls.

One morning as I emerged from the damp tomb and fastened the chain of the portal with none too steady hand, I beheld in an adjacent thicket the dreaded face of a watcher. Surely the end was near; for my bower was discovered, and the objective of my nocturnal journeys revealed. The man did not accost me, so I hastened home in an effort to overhear what he might report to my careworn father. Were my sojourns beyond the chained door about to be proclaimed to the world? Imagine my delighted astonishment on hearing the spy inform my parent in a cautious whisper *that I had spent the night in the bower outside the tomb*; my sleep-filmed eyes fixed upon the crevice where the padlocked portal stood ajar! By what miracle had the watcher been thus deluded? I was now convinced that a supernatural agency protected me. Made bold by this heaven-sent circumstance, I began to resume perfect openness in going to the vault; confident that no one could witness my entrance. For a week I tasted to the full the joys of that charnel conviviality which I must not describe, when the *thing* happened, and I was borne away to this accursed abode of sorrow and monotony.

I should not have ventured out that night; for the taint of thunder was in the clouds, and a hellish phosphorescence rose from the rank swamp at the bottom of the hollow. The call of the dead, too, was different. Instead of the hillside tomb, it was the charred cellar on the crest of the slope whose presiding daemon beckoned to me with unseen fingers. As I emerged from an intervening grove upon the plain before the ruin, I beheld in the misty moonlight a thing I had always vaguely expected. The mansion, gone for a century, once more reared its stately height to the raptured vision; every window ablaze with the splendour of many candles. Up the long drive rolled the coaches of the Boston gentry, whilst on foot came a numerous assemblage of powdered exquisites from the neighbouring mansions. With this throng I mingled, though I knew I belonged with the hosts rather than with the guests. Inside the hall were music, laughter, and wine on every hand. Several faces I recognised; though I should have known them better had they been shrivelled or eaten away by death and decomposition. Amidst a wild and reckless throng I was the wildest and most abandoned. Gay blasphemy poured in torrents from my lips, and in my shocking sallies I heeded no law of God, Man, or Nature. Suddenly a peal of thunder, resonant even above the din of the swinish revelry, clave the very roof and laid a hush of fear upon the boisterous company. Red tongues of flame and searing gusts of heat engulfed the house; and the roysterers, struck with terror at the descent of a calamity which seemed to transcend the bounds of unguided Nature, fled shrieking into the night. I alone remained, riveted to my seat by a grovelling fear which I had never felt before. And then a second horror took possession of my soul. Burnt alive to ashes, my body dispersed by the four winds, *I might never lie in the tomb of the Hydes!* Was not my coffin prepared for me? Had I not a right to rest till eternity amongst the descendants of Sir Geoffrey Hyde? Aye! I would claim my heritage of death, even though my soul go seeking through the ages for another corporeal tenement to represent it on that vacant slab in the alcove of the vault. *Jervas Hyde* should never share the sad fate of Palinurus!

As the phantom of the burning house faded, I found myself screaming and struggling madly in the arms of two men, one of whom was the spy who had followed me to the tomb. Rain was pouring down in torrents, and upon the southern horizon were flashes of the lightning that had so lately passed over our heads. My father, his face lined with sorrow, stood by as I shouted my demands to be laid within the tomb; frequently admonishing my captors to treat me as gently as they could. A blackened circle on the floor of the ruined cellar told of a violent stroke from the heavens; and from this spot a group of curious villagers with lanterns were prying a small box of antique workmanship which the thunderbolt had brought to light. Ceasing my futile and now objectless writhing, I watched the spectators as they viewed the treasure-trove, and was permitted to share in their discoveries. The box, whose fastenings were broken by the stroke which had unearthed it, contained many papers and objects of value; but I had eyes for one thing alone. It was the porcelain miniature of a young man in a smartly curled bag-wig, and bore the initials "J. H." The face was such that as I gazed, I might well have been studying my mirror.

On the following day I was brought to this room with the barred windows, but I have been kept informed of certain things through an aged and simple-minded servitor, for whom I bore a fondness in infancy, and who like me loves the churchyard. What I have dared relate of my experiences within the vault has brought me only pitying smiles. My father, who visits me frequently, declares that at no time did I pass the chained portal, and swears that the rusted padlock had not been touched for fifty years when he examined it. He even says that all the village knew of my journeys to the tomb, and that I was often watched as I slept in the bower outside the grim facade, my half-open eyes fixed on the crevice that leads to the interior. Against these assertions I have no tangible proof to offer, since my key to the padlock was lost in the struggle on that night of horrors. The strange things of the past which I learnt during those nocturnal meetings with the dead he dismisses as the fruits of my lifelong and omnivorous browsing amongst the ancient volumes of the family library. Had it not been for my old servant Hiram, I should have by this time become quite convinced of my madness.

But Hiram, loyal to the last, has held faith in me, and has done that which impels me to make public at least a part of my story. A week ago he burst open the lock which chains the door of the tomb perpetually ajar, and descended with a lantern into the murky depths. On a slab in an alcove he found an old but empty coffin whose tarnished plate bears the single word "*Jervas*". In that coffin and in that vault they have promised me I shall be buried.

DAGON

I am writing this under an appreciable mental strain, since by tonight I shall be no more. Penniless, and at the end of my supply of the drug which alone makes life endurable, I can bear the torture no longer; and shall cast myself from this garret window into the squalid street below. Do not think from my slavery to morphine that I am a weakling or a degenerate. When you have read these hastily scrawled pages you may guess, though never fully realise, why it is that I must have forgetfulness or death.

It was in one of the most open and least frequented parts of the broad Pacific that the packet of which I was supercargo fell a victim to the German sea-raider. The great war was then at its very beginning, and the enemy's navy had not reached its later degree of ruthlessness; so that our vessel was made a legitimate prize, whilst we of her crew were treated with all the fairness and consideration due us as naval prisoners. So liberal, indeed, was the discipline of our captors, that five days after we were taken I managed to escape alone in a small boat with water and provisions for a good length of time.

When I finally found myself adrift and free, I had but little idea of my surroundings. Never a competent navigator, I could only guess vaguely by the sun and stars that I was somewhat south of the equator. Of the longitude I knew nothing, and no island or coast-line was in sight. The weather kept fair, and for uncounted days I drifted aimlessly beneath the scorching sun; waiting either for some passing ship, or to be cast on the shores of some habitable land. But neither ship nor land appeared, and I began to despair in my solitude upon the heaving vastnesses of unbroken blue.

The change happened whilst I slept. Its details I shall never know; for my slumber, though troubled and dream-infested, was continuous. When at last I awaked, it was to discover myself half sucked into a slimy expanse of hellish black mire which extended about me in monotonous undulations as far as I could see, and in which my boat lay grounded some distance away.

Though one might well imagine that my first sensation would be of wonder at so prodigious and unexpected a transformation of scenery, I was in reality more horrified than astonished; for there was in the air and in the rotting soil a sinister quality which chilled me to the very core. The region was putrid with the carcasses of decaying fish, and of other less describable things which I saw protruding from the nasty mud of the unending plain. Perhaps I should not hope to convey in mere words the unutterable hideousness that can dwell in absolute silence and barren immensity. There was nothing within hearing, and nothing in sight save a vast reach of black slime; yet the very completeness of the stillness and the homogeneity of the landscape oppressed me with a nauseating fear.

The sun was blazing down from a sky which seemed to me almost black in its cloudless cruelty; as though reflecting the inky marsh beneath my feet. As I crawled into the stranded boat I realised that only one theory could explain my position. Through some unprecedented volcanic upheaval, a portion of the ocean floor must have been thrown to the surface, exposing regions which for innumerable millions of years had lain hidden under unfathomable watery depths. So great was the extent of the new land which had risen beneath me, that I could not detect the faintest noise of the surging ocean, strain my ears as I might. Nor were there any sea-fowl to prey upon the dead things.

For several hours I sat thinking or brooding in the boat, which lay upon its side and afforded a slight shade as the sun moved across the heavens. As the day progressed, the ground lost some of its stickiness, and seemed likely to dry sufficiently for travelling purposes in a short time. That night I slept but little, and the next day I made for myself a pack containing food and water, preparatory to an overland journey in search of the vanished sea and possible rescue.

On the third morning I found the soil dry enough to walk upon with ease. The odour of the fish was maddening; but I was too much concerned with graver things to mind so slight an evil, and set out boldly for an unknown goal. All day I forged steadily westward, guided by a far-away hummock which rose higher than any other elevation on the rolling desert. That night I encamped, and on the following day still travelled toward the hummock, though that object seemed scarcely nearer than when I had first espied it. By the fourth evening I attained the base of the mound, which turned out to be much higher than it had appeared from a distance; an intervening valley setting it out in sharper relief from the general surface. Too weary to ascend, I slept in the shadow of the hill.

I know not why my dreams were so wild that night; but ere the waning and fantastically gibbous moon had risen far above the eastern plain, I was awake in a cold perspiration, determined to sleep no more. Such visions as I had experienced were too much for me to endure again. And in the glow of the moon I saw how unwise I had been to travel by day. Without the glare of the parching sun, my journey would have cost me less energy; indeed, I now felt quite able to perform the ascent which had deterred me at sunset. Picking up my pack, I started for the crest of the eminence.

I have said that the unbroken monotony of the rolling plain was a source of vague horror to me; but I think my horror was greater when I gained the summit of the mound and looked down the other side into an immeasurable pit or canyon, whose black recesses the moon had not yet soared high enough to illumine. I felt myself on the edge of the world; peering over the rim into a fathomless chaos of eternal night. Through my terror ran curious reminiscences of "Paradise Lost", and of Satan's hideous climb through the unfashioned realms of darkness.

As the moon climbed higher in the sky, I began to see that the slopes of the valley were not quite so perpendicular as I had imagined. Ledges and outcroppings of rock afforded fairly easy footholds for a descent, whilst after a drop of a few hundred feet, the declivity became very gradual. Urged on by an impulse which I cannot definitely analyse, I scrambled with difficulty down the rocks and stood on the gentler slope beneath, gazing into the Stygian deeps where no light had yet penetrated.

All at once my attention was captured by a vast and singular object on the opposite slope, which rose steeply about a hundred yards ahead of me; an object that gleamed whitely in the newly bestowed rays of the ascending moon. That it was merely a gigantic piece of stone, I soon assured myself; but I was conscious of a distinct impression that its contour and location were not altogether the work of Nature. A closer scrutiny filled me with sensations I cannot express; for despite its enormous magnitude, and its position in an abyss which had yawned at the bottom of the sea since the world was young, I perceived beyond a doubt that the strange object was a well-shaped monolith whose massive bulk had known the workmanship and perhaps the worship of living and thinking creatures.

Dazed and frightened, yet not without a certain thrill of the scientist's or archaeologist's delight, I examined my surroundings more closely. The moon, now near the zenith, shone weirdly and vividly above the towering steeps that hemmed in the chasm, and revealed the fact that a far-flung body of water flowed at the bottom, winding out of sight in both directions, and almost lapping my feet as I stood on the slope. Across the chasm, the wavelets washed the base of the Cyclopean monolith; on whose surface I could now trace both inscriptions and crude sculptures. The writing was in a system of hieroglyphics unknown to me, and unlike anything I had ever seen in books; consisting for the most part of conventionalised aquatic symbols such as fishes, eels, octopi, crustaceans, molluscs, whales, and the like. Several characters obviously represented marine things which are unknown to the modern world, but whose decomposing forms I had observed on the ocean-risen plain.

It was the pictorial carving, however, that did most to hold me spellbound. Plainly visible across the intervening water on account of their enormous size, were an array of bas-reliefs whose subjects would have excited the envy of a Doré. I think that these things were supposed to depict men—at least, a certain sort of men; though the creatures were shewn disporting like fishes in the waters of some marine grotto, or paying homage at some monolithic shrine which appeared to be under the waves as well. Of their faces and forms I dare not speak in detail; for the mere remembrance makes me grow faint. Grotesque beyond the imagination of a Poe or a Bulwer, they were damnably human in general outline despite webbed hands and feet, shockingly wide and flabby lips, glassy, bulging eyes, and other features less pleasant to recall. Curiously enough, they seemed to have been chiselled badly out of proportion with their scenic background; for one of the creatures was shewn in the act of killing a whale represented as but little larger than himself. I remarked, as I say, their grotesqueness and strange size; but in a moment decided that they were merely the imaginary gods of some primitive fishing or seafaring tribe; some tribe whose last descendant had perished eras before the first ancestor of the Piltdown or Neanderthal Man was born. Awestruck at this unexpected glimpse into a past beyond the conception of the most daring anthropologist, I stood musing whilst the moon cast queer reflections on the silent channel before me.

Then suddenly I saw it. With only a slight churning to mark its rise to the surface, the thing slid into view above the dark waters. Vast, Polyphemus-like, and loathsome, it darted like a stupendous monster of nightmares to the monolith, about which it flung its gigantic scaly arms, the while it bowed its hideous head and gave vent to certain measured sounds. I think I went mad then.

Of my frantic ascent of the slope and cliff, and of my delirious journey back to the stranded boat, I remember little. I believe I sang a great deal, and laughed oddly when I was unable to sing. I have indistinct recollections of a great storm some time after I reached the boat; at any rate, I know that I heard peals of thunder and other tones which Nature utters only in wild and terrible moods.

When I came out of the shadows I was in a San Francisco hospital; brought thither by the captain of the American ship which had picked up my boat in mid-ocean. In my delirium I had said much, but found that my words had been given scant attention. Of any land upheaval in the Pacific, my rescuers knew nothing; nor did I deem it necessary to insist upon a thing which I knew they could not believe. Once I sought out a celebrated ethnologist, and amused him with peculiar questions regarding the ancient Philistine legend of Dagon, the Fish-God; but soon perceiving that he was hopelessly conventional, I did not press my inquiries.

It is at night, especially when the moon is gibbous and waning, that I see the thing. I tried morphine; but the drug has given only transient surcease, and has drawn me into its clutches as a hopeless slave. So now I am to end matters, having written a full account for the information or the contemptuous amusement of my fellow-men. Often I ask myself if it could not all have been a pure phantasm—a mere freak of fever as I lay sun-stricken and raving in the open boat after my escape from the German man-of-war. This I ask myself, but ever does there come before me a hideously vivid vision in reply. I cannot think of the deep sea without shuddering at the nameless things that may at this very moment be crawling and floundering on its slimy bed, worshipping their ancient stone idols and carving their own detestable likenesses on submarine obelisks of water-soaked granite. I dream of a day when they may rise above the billows to drag down in their reeking talons the remnants of puny, war-exhausted mankind—of a day when the land shall sink, and the dark ocean floor shall ascend amidst universal pandemonium.

The end is near. I hear a noise at the door, as of some immense slippery body lumbering against it. It shall not find me. God, *that hand!* The window! The window!

A REMINISCENCE OF DR. SAMUEL JOHNSON

The Privilege of Reminiscence, however rambling or tiresome, is one generally allow'd to the very aged; indeed, 'tis frequently by means of such Recollections that the obscure occurrences of History, and the lesser Anecdotes of the Great, are transmitted to Posterity.

Tho' many of my readers have at times observ'd and remark'd a Sort of antique Flow in my Stile of Writing, it hath pleased me to pass amongst the Members of this Generation as a young Man, giving out the Fiction that I was born in 1890, in *America.* I am now, however, resolv'd to unburthen myself of a secret which I have hitherto kept thro' Dread of Incredulity; and to impart to the Publick a true knowledge of my long years, in order to gratifie their taste for authentick Information of an Age with whose famous Personages I was on familiar Terms. Be it then known that I was born on the family Estate in *Devonshire,* of the 10th day of August, 1690, (or in the new *Gregorian* Stile of Reckoning, the 20th of August) being therefore now in my 228th year. Coming early to *London,* I saw as a Child many of the celebrated Men of King *William's* Reign, including the lamented Mr. *Dryden,* who sat much at the Tables of *Will's* Coffee-House. With Mr. *Addison* and Dr. *Swift* I later became very well acquainted, and was an even more familiar Friend to Mr. *Pope,* whom I knew and respected till the Day of his Death. But since it is of my more recent Associate, the late Dr. *Johnson*, that I am at this time desir'd to write; I will pass over my Youth for the present.

I had first Knowledge of the Doctor in May of the year 1738, tho' I did not at that Time meet him. Mr. *Pope* had just compleated his Epilogue to his *Satires*, (the Piece beginning: "Not twice a Twelvemonth you appear in Print.") and had arrang'd for its Publication. On the very Day it appear'd, there was also publish'd a Satire in Imitation of *Juvenal*, intitul'd "*London*", by the then unknown *Johnson*; and this so struck the Town, that many Gentlemen of Taste declared, it was the Work of a greater Poet than Mr. *Pope*. Notwithstanding what some Detractors have said of Mr. *Pope's* petty Jealousy, he gave the Verses of his new Rival no small Praise; and having learnt thro' Mr. *Richardson* who the Poet was, told me 'that Mr. *Johnson* wou'd soon be *deterré*.'

I had no personal Acquaintance with the Doctor till 1763, when I was presented to him at the *Mitre* Tavern by Mr. *James Boswell*, a young *Scotchman* of excellent Family and great Learning, but small Wit, whose metrical Effusions I had sometimes revis'd.

Dr. *Johnson*, as I beheld him, was a full, pursy Man, very ill drest, and of slovenly Aspect. I recall him to have worn a bushy Bob-Wig, untyed and without Powder, and much too small for his Head. His cloaths were of rusty brown, much wrinkled, and with more than one Button missing. His Face, too full to be handsom, was likewise marred by the Effects of some scrofulous Disorder; and his Head was continually rolling about in a sort of convulsive way. Of this Infirmity, indeed, I had known before; having heard of it from Mr. *Pope*, who took the Trouble to make particular Inquiries.

Being nearly seventy-three, full nineteen Years older than Dr. *Johnson*, (I say Doctor, tho' his Degree came not till two Years afterward) I naturally expected him to have some Regard for my Age; and was therefore not in that Fear of him, which others confess'd. On my asking him what he thought of my favourable Notice of his Dictionary in *The Londoner*, my periodical Paper, he said: "Sir, I possess no Recollection of having perus'd your Paper, and have not a great Interest in the Opinions of the less thoughtful Part of Mankind." Being more than a little piqued at the Incivility of one whose Celebrity made me solicitous of his Approbation, I ventur'd to retaliate in kind, and told him, I was surpris'd that a Man of Sense shou'd judge the Thoughtfulness of one whose Productions he admitted never having read. "Why, Sir," reply'd *Johnson*, "I do not require to become familiar with a Man's Writings in order to estimate the Superficiality of his Attainments, when he plainly shews it by his Eagerness to mention his own Productions in the first Question he puts to me." Having thus become Friends, we convers'd on many Matters. When, to agree with him, I said I was distrustful of the Authenticity of *Ossian's* Poems, Mr. *Johnson* said: "That, Sir, does not do your Understanding particular Credit; for what all the Town is sensible of, is no great Discovery for a *Grub-Street* Critick to make. You might as well say, you have a strong Suspicion that *Milton* wrote 'Paradise Lost'!"

I thereafter saw *Johnson* very frequently, most often at Meetings of THE LITERARY CLUB, which was founded the next Year by the Doctor, together with Mr. *Burke*, the parliamentary Orator, Mr. *Beauclerk*, a Gentleman of Fashion, Mr. *Langton*, a pious Man and Captain of Militia, Sir J. *Reynolds*, the widely known Painter, Dr. *Goldsmith*, the prose and poetick Writer, Dr. *Nugent*, father-in-law to Mr. *Burke*, Sir *John Hawkins*, Mr. *Anthony Chamier*, and my self. We assembled generally at seven o'clock of an Evening, once a Week, at the *Turk's-Head*, in *Gerrard-Street, Soho*, till that Tavern was sold and made into a private Dwelling; after which Event we mov'd our Gatherings successively to *Prince's* in *Sackville-Street*, *Le Tellier's* in *Dover-Street*, and *Parsloe's* and *The Thatched House* in *St. James's-Street*. In these Meetings we preserv'd a remarkable Degree of Amity and Tranquillity, which contrasts very favourably with some of the Dissensions and Disruptions I observe in the literary and amateur Press Associations of today. This Tranquillity was the more remarkable, because we had amongst us Gentlemen of very opposed Opinions. Dr. *Johnson* and I, as well as many others, were high Tories; whilst Mr. *Burke* was a *Whig*, and against the *American* War, many of his Speeches on that Subject having been widely publish'd. The least congenial Member was one of the Founders, Sir *John Hawkins*, who hath since written many misrepresentations of our Society. Sir *John*, an eccentrick Fellow, once declin'd to pay his part of the Reckoning for Supper, because 'twas his Custom at Home to eat no Supper. Later he insulted Mr. *Burke* in so intolerable a Manner, that we all took Pains to shew our Disapproval; after which Incident he came no more to our Meetings. However, he never openly fell out with the Doctor, and was the Executor of his Will; tho' Mr. *Boswell* and others have Reason to question the genuineness of his Attachment. Other and later Members of the CLUB were Mr. *David Garrick*, the Actor and early Friend of Dr. *Johnson*, Messieurs *Tho.* and *Jos. Warton*, Dr. *Adam Smith*, Dr. *Percy*, Author of the "Reliques", Mr. *Edw. Gibbon*, the Historian, Dr. *Burney*, the Musician, Mr. *Malone*, the Critick, and Mr. *Boswell*. Mr. *Garrick* obtain'd Admittance only with Difficulty; for the Doctor, notwithstanding his great Friendship, was for ever affecting to decry the Stage and all Things connected with it. *Johnson*, indeed, had a most singular Habit of speaking for *Davy* when others were against him, and of arguing against him, when others were for him. I have no Doubt but that he sincerely lov'd Mr. *Garrick*, for he never alluded to him as he did to *Foote*, who was a very coarse Fellow despite his comick Genius. Mr. *Gibbon* was none too well lik'd, for he had an odious sneering Way which offended even those of us who most admir'd his historical Productions. Mr. *Goldsmith*, a little Man very vain of his Dress and very deficient in Brilliancy of Conversation, was my particular Favourite; since I was equally unable to shine in the Discourse. He was vastly jealous of Dr. *Johnson*, tho' none the less liking and respecting him. I remember that once a Foreigner, a *German*, I think, was in our Company; and that whilst *Goldsmith* was speaking, he observ'd the Doctor preparing to utter something. Unconsciously looking upon *Goldsmith* as a meer Encumbrance when compar'd to the greater Man, the Foreigner bluntly interrupted him and incurr'd his lasting Hostility by crying, "Hush, Toctor *Shonson* iss going to speak!"

In this luminous Company I was tolerated more because of my Years than for my Wit or Learning; being no Match at all for the rest. My Friendship for the celebrated Monsieur *Voltaire* was ever a Cause of Annoyance to the Doctor; who was deeply orthodox, and who us'd to say of the *French* Philosopher: "Vir est acerrimi Ingenii et paucarum Literarum."

Mr. *Boswell*, a little teazing Fellow whom I had known for some Time previously, us'd to make Sport of my aukward Manners and old-fashion'd Wig and Cloaths. Once coming in a little the worse for Wine (to which he was addicted) he endeavour'd to lampoon me by means of an Impromptu in verse, writ on the Surface of the Table; but lacking the Aid he usually had in his Composition, he made a bad grammatical Blunder. I told him, he shou'd not try to pasquinade the Source of his Poesy. At another time *Bozzy* (as we us'd to call him) complain'd of my Harshness toward new Writers in the Articles I prepar'd for *The Monthly Review*. He said, I push'd every Aspirant off the Slopes of Parnassus. "Sir," I reply'd, "you are mistaken. They who lose their Hold do so from their own Want of Strength; but desiring to conceal their Weakness, they attribute the Absence of Success to the first Critick that mentions them." I am glad to recall that Dr. *Johnson* upheld me in this Matter.

Dr. *Johnson* was second to no Man in the Pains he took to revise the bad Verses of others; indeed, 'tis said that in the book of poor blind old Mrs. Williams, there are scarce two lines which are not the Doctor's. At one Time *Johnson* recited to me some lines by a Servant to the Duke of *Leeds*, which had so amus'd him, that he had got them by Heart. They are on the Duke's Wedding, and so much resemble in Quality the Work of other and more recent poetick Dunces, that I cannot forbear copying them:

"When the Duke of *Leeds* shall marry'd be
To a fine young Lady of high Quality
How happy will that Gentlewoman be
In his Grace of *Leeds'* good Company."

I ask'd the Doctor, if he had ever try'd making Sense of this Piece; and upon his saying he had not, I amus'd myself with the following Amendment of it:

When Gallant LEEDS auspiciously shall wed
The virtuous Fair, of antient Lineage bred,
How must the Maid rejoice with conscious Pride
To win so great an Husband to her Side!

On shewing this to Dr. *Johnson*, he said, "Sir, you have straightened out the Feet, but you have put neither Wit nor Poetry into the Lines."

It wou'd afford me Gratification to tell more of my Experiences with Dr. *Johnson* and his circle of Wits; but I am an old Man, and easily fatigued. I seem to ramble along without much Logick or Continuity when I endeavour to recall the Past; and fear I light upon but few Incidents which others have not before discuss'd. Shou'd my present Recollections meet with Favour, I might later set down some further Anecdotes of old Times of which I am the only Survivor. I recall many Things of *Sam Johnson* and his Club, having kept up my Membership in the Latter long after the Doctor's Death, at which I sincerely mourn'd. I remember how *John Burgoyne,* Esq., the General, whose Dramatick and Poetical Works were printed after his Death, was blackballed by three Votes; probably because of his unfortunate Defeat in the *American* War, at *Saratoga*. Poor *John!* His Son fared better, I think, and was made a Baronet. But I am very tired. I am old, very old, and it is Time for my Afternoon Nap.

POLARIS

Into the north window of my chamber glows the Pole Star with uncanny light. All through the long hellish hours of blackness it shines there. And in the autumn of the year, when the winds from the north curse and whine, and the red-leaved trees of the swamp mutter things to one another in the small hours of the morning under the horned waning moon, I sit by the casement and watch that star. Down from the heights reels the glittering Cassiopeia as the hours wear on, while Charles' Wain lumbers up from behind the vapour-soaked swamp trees that sway in the night-wind. Just before dawn Arcturus winks ruddily from above the cemetery on the low hillock, and Coma Berenices shimmers weirdly afar off in the mysterious east; but still the Pole Star leers down from the same place in the black vault, winking hideously like an insane watching eye which strives to convey some strange message, yet recalls nothing save that it once had a message to convey. Sometimes, when it is cloudy, I can sleep.

Well do I remember the night of the great Aurora, when over the swamp played the shocking coruscations of the daemon-light. After the beams came clouds, and then I slept.

And it was under a horned waning moon that I saw the city for the first time. Still and somnolent did it lie, on a strange plateau in a hollow betwixt strange peaks. Of ghastly marble were its walls and its towers, its columns, domes, and pavements. In the marble streets were marble pillars, the upper parts of which were carven into the images of grave bearded men. The air was warm and stirred not. And overhead, scarce ten degrees from the zenith, glowed that watching Pole Star. Long did I gaze on the city, but the day came not. When the red Aldebaran, which blinked low in the sky but never set, had crawled a quarter of the way around the horizon, I saw light and motion in the houses and the streets. Forms strangely robed, but at once noble and familiar, walked abroad, and under the horned waning moon men talked wisdom in a tongue which I understood, though it was unlike any language I had ever known. And when the red Aldebaran had crawled more than half way around the horizon, there were again darkness and silence.

When I awaked, I was not as I had been. Upon my memory was graven the vision of the city, and within my soul had arisen another and vaguer recollection, of whose nature I was not then certain. Thereafter, on the cloudy nights when I could sleep, I saw the city often; sometimes under that horned waning moon, and sometimes under the hot yellow rays of a sun which did not set, but which wheeled low around the horizon. And on the clear nights the Pole Star leered as never before.

Gradually I came to wonder what might be my place in that city on the strange plateau betwixt strange peaks. At first content to view the scene as an all-observant uncorporeal presence, I now desired to define my relation to it, and to speak my mind amongst the grave men who conversed each day in the public squares. I said to myself, "This is no dream, for by what means can I prove the greater reality of that other life in the house of stone and brick south of the sinister swamp and the cemetery on the low hillock, where the Pole Star peers into my north window each night?"

One night as I listened to the discourse in the large square containing many statues, I felt a change; and perceived that I had at last a bodily form. Nor was I a stranger in the streets of Olathoë, which lies on the plateau of Sarkis, betwixt the peaks Noton and Kadiphonek. It was my friend Alos who spoke, and his speech was one that pleased my soul, for it was the speech of a true man and patriot. That night had the news come of Daikos' fall, and of the advance of the Inutos; squat, hellish, yellow fiends who five years ago had appeared out of the unknown west to ravage the confines of our kingdom and finally to besiege our towns. Having taken the fortified places at the foot of the mountains, their way now lay open to the plateau, unless every citizen could resist with the strength of ten men. For the squat creatures were mighty in the arts of war, and knew not the scruples of honour which held back our tall, grey-eyed men of Lomar from ruthless conquest.

Alos, my friend, was commander of all the forces on the plateau, and in him lay the last hope of our country. On this occasion he spoke of the perils to be faced, and exhorted the men of Olathoë, bravest of the Lomarians, to sustain the traditions of their ancestors, who when forced to move southward from Zobna before the advance of the great ice-sheet (even as our descendants must some day flee from the land of Lomar), valiantly and victoriously swept aside the hairy, long-armed, cannibal Gnophkehs that stood in their way. To me Alos denied a warrior's part, for I was feeble and given to strange faintings when subjected to stress and hardships. But my eyes were the keenest in the city, despite the long hours I gave each day to the study of the Pnakotic manuscripts and the wisdom of the Zobnarian Fathers; so my friend, desiring not to doom me to inaction, rewarded me with that duty which was second to nothing in importance. To the watch-tower of Thapnen he sent me, there to serve as the eyes of our army. Should the Inutos attempt to gain the citadel by the narrow pass behind the peak Noton, and thereby surprise the garrison, I was to give the signal of fire which would warn the waiting soldiers and save the town from immediate disaster.

Alone I mounted the tower, for every man of stout body was needed in the passes below. My brain was sore dazed with excitement and fatigue, for I had not slept in many days; yet was my purpose firm, for I loved my native land of Lomar, and the marble city of Olathoë that lies betwixt the peaks of Noton and Kadiphonek.

But as I stood in the tower's topmost chamber, I beheld the horned waning moon, red and sinister, quivering through the vapours that hovered over the distant valley of Banof. And through an opening in the roof glittered the pale Pole Star, fluttering as if alive, and leering like a fiend and tempter. Methought its spirit whispered evil counsel, soothing me to traitorous somnolence with a damnable rhythmical promise which it repeated over and over:

"Slumber, watcher, till the spheres
Six and twenty thousand years
Have revolv'd, and I return
To the spot where now I burn.
Other stars anon shall rise
To the axis of the skies;
Stars that soothe and stars that bless
With a sweet forgetfulness:
Only when my round is o'er
Shall the past disturb thy door."

Vainly did I struggle with my drowsiness, seeking to connect these strange words with some lore of the skies which I had learnt from the Pnakotic manuscripts. My head, heavy and reeling, drooped to my breast, and when next I looked up it was in a dream; with the Pole Star grinning at me through a window from over the horrible swaying trees of a dream-swamp. And I am still dreaming.

In my shame and despair I sometimes scream frantically, begging the dream-creatures around me to waken me ere the Inutos steal up the pass behind the peak Noton and take the citadel by surprise; but these creatures are daemons, for they laugh at me and tell me I am not dreaming. They mock me whilst I sleep, and whilst the squat yellow foe may be creeping silently upon us. I have failed in my duty and betrayed the marble city of Olathoë; I have proven false to Alos, my friend and commander. But still these shadows of my dream deride me. They say there is no land of Lomar, save in my nocturnal imaginings; that in those realms where the Pole Star shines high and red Aldebaran crawls low around the horizon, there has been naught save ice and snow for thousands of years, and never a man save squat yellow creatures, blighted by the cold, whom they call "Esquimaux".

And as I writhe in my guilty agony, frantic to save the city whose peril every moment grows, and vainly striving to shake off this unnatural dream of a house of stone and brick south of a sinister swamp and a cemetery on a low hillock; the Pole Star, evil and monstrous, leers down from the black vault, winking hideously like an insane watching eye which strives to convey some strange message, yet recalls nothing save that it once had a message to convey.

BEYOND THE WALL OF SLEEP

"I have an exposition of sleep come upon me."
—*Shakespeare.*

I have frequently wondered if the majority of mankind ever pause to reflect upon the occasionally titanic significance of dreams, and of the obscure world to which they belong. Whilst the greater number of our nocturnal visions are perhaps no more than faint and fantastic reflections of our waking experiences—Freud to the contrary with his puerile symbolism—there are still a certain remainder whose immundane and ethereal character permits of no ordinary interpretation, and whose vaguely exciting and disquieting effect suggests possible minute glimpses into a sphere of mental existence no less important than physical life, yet separated from that life by an all but impassable barrier. From my experience I cannot doubt but that man, when lost to terrestrial consciousness, is indeed sojourning in another and uncorporeal life of far different nature from the life we know; and of which only the slightest and most indistinct memories linger after waking. From those blurred and fragmentary memories we may infer much, yet prove little. We may guess that in dreams life, matter, and vitality, as the earth knows such things, are not necessarily constant; and that time and space do not exist as our waking selves comprehend them. Sometimes I believe that this less material life is our truer life, and that our vain presence on the terraqueous globe is itself the secondary or merely virtual phenomenon.

It was from a youthful reverie filled with speculations of this sort that I arose one afternoon in the winter of 1900–1901, when to the state psychopathic institution in which I served as an interne was brought the man whose case has ever since haunted me so unceasingly. His name, as given on the records, was Joe Slater, or Slaader, and his appearance was that of the typical denizen of the Catskill Mountain region; one of those strange, repellent scions of a primitive colonial peasant stock whose isolation for nearly three centuries in the hilly fastnesses of a little-travelled countryside has caused them to sink to a kind of barbaric degeneracy, rather than advance with their more fortunately placed brethren of the thickly settled districts. Among these odd folk, who correspond exactly to the decadent element of "white trash" in the South, law and morals are non-existent; and their general mental status is probably below that of any other section of the native American people.

Joe Slater, who came to the institution in the vigilant custody of four state policemen, and who was described as a highly dangerous character, certainly presented no evidence of his perilous disposition when first I beheld him. Though well above the middle stature, and of somewhat brawny frame, he was given an absurd appearance of harmless stupidity by the pale, sleepy blueness of his small watery eyes, the scantiness of his neglected and never-shaven growth of yellow beard, and the listless drooping of his heavy nether lip. His age was unknown, since among his kind neither family records nor permanent family ties exist; but from the baldness of his head in front, and from the decayed condition of his teeth, the head surgeon wrote him down as a man of about forty.

From the medical and court documents we learned all that could be gathered of his case. This man, a vagabond, hunter, and trapper, had always been strange in the eyes of his primitive associates. He had habitually slept at night beyond the ordinary time, and upon waking would often talk of unknown things in a manner so bizarre as to inspire fear even in the hearts of an unimaginative populace. Not that his form of language was at all unusual, for he never spoke save in the debased patois of his environment; but the tone and tenor of his utterances were of such mysterious wildness, that none might listen without apprehension. He himself was generally as terrified and baffled as his auditors, and within an hour after awakening would forget all that he had said, or at least all that had caused him to say what he did; relapsing into a bovine, half-amiable normality like that of the other hill-dwellers.

As Slater grew older, it appeared, his matutinal aberrations had gradually increased in frequency and violence; till about a month before his arrival at the institution had occurred the shocking tragedy which caused his arrest by the authorities. One day near noon, after a profound sleep begun in a whiskey debauch at about five of the previous afternoon, the man had roused himself most suddenly; with ululations so horrible and unearthly that they brought several neighbours to his cabin—a filthy sty where he dwelt with a family as indescribable as himself. Rushing out into the snow, he had flung his arms aloft and commenced a series of leaps directly upward in the air; the while shouting his determination to reach some 'big, big cabin with brightness in the roof and walls and floor, and the loud queer music far away'. As two men of moderate size sought to restrain him, he had struggled with maniacal force and fury, screaming of his desire and need to find and kill a certain 'thing that shines and shakes and laughs'. At length, after temporarily felling one of his detainers with a sudden blow, he had flung himself upon the other in a daemoniac ecstasy of bloodthirstiness, shrieking fiendishly that he would 'jump high in the air and burn his way through anything that stopped him'. Family and neighbours had now fled in a panic, and when the more courageous of them returned, Slater was gone, leaving behind an unrecognisable pulp-like thing that had been a living man but an hour before. None of the mountaineers had dared to pursue him, and it is likely that they would have welcomed his death from the cold; but when several mornings later they heard his screams from a distant ravine, they realised that he had somehow managed to survive, and that his removal in one way or another would be necessary. Then had followed an armed searching party, whose purpose (whatever it may have been originally) became that of a sheriff's posse after one of the seldom popular state troopers had by accident observed, then questioned, and finally joined the seekers.

On the third day Slater was found unconscious in the hollow of a tree, and taken to the nearest gaol; where alienists from Albany examined him as soon as his senses returned. To them he told a simple story. He had, he said, gone to sleep one afternoon about sundown after drinking much liquor. He had awaked to find himself standing bloody-handed in the snow before his cabin, the mangled corpse of his neighbour Peter Slader at his feet. Horrified, he had taken to the woods in a vague effort to escape from the scene of what must have been his crime. Beyond these things he seemed to know nothing, nor could the expert questioning of his interrogators bring out a single additional fact. That night Slater slept quietly, and the next morning he wakened with no singular feature save a certain alteration of expression. Dr. Barnard, who had been watching the patient, thought he noticed in the pale blue eyes a certain gleam of peculiar quality; and in the flaccid lips an all but imperceptible tightening, as if of intelligent determination. But when questioned, Slater relapsed into the habitual vacancy of the mountaineer, and only reiterated what he had said on the preceding day.

On the third morning occurred the first of the man's mental attacks. After some show of uneasiness in sleep, he burst forth into a frenzy so powerful that the combined efforts of four men were needed to bind him in a strait-jacket. The alienists listened with keen attention to his words, since their curiosity had been aroused to a high pitch by the suggestive yet mostly conflicting and incoherent stories of his family and neighbours. Slater raved for upward of fifteen minutes, babbling in his backwoods dialect of great edifices of light, oceans of space, strange music, and shadowy mountains and valleys. But most of all did he dwell upon some mysterious blazing entity that shook and laughed and mocked at him. This vast, vague personality seemed to have done him a terrible wrong, and to kill it in triumphant revenge was his paramount desire. In order to reach it, he said, he would soar through abysses of emptiness, *burning* every obstacle that stood in his way. Thus ran his discourse, until with the greatest suddenness he ceased. The fire of madness died from his eyes, and in dull wonder he looked at his questioners and asked why he was bound. Dr. Barnard unbuckled the leathern harness and did not restore it till night, when he succeeded in persuading Slater to don it of his own volition, for his own good. The man had now admitted that he sometimes talked queerly, though he knew not why.

Within a week two more attacks appeared, but from them the doctors learned little. On the *source* of Slater's visions they speculated at length, for since he could neither read nor write, and had apparently never heard a legend or fairy tale, his gorgeous imagery was quite inexplicable. That it could not come from any known myth or romance was made especially clear by the fact that the unfortunate lunatic expressed himself only in his own simple manner. He raved of things he did not understand and could not interpret; things which he claimed to have experienced, but which he could not have learned through any normal or connected narration. The alienists soon agreed that abnormal dreams were the foundation of the trouble; dreams whose vividness could for a time completely dominate the waking mind of this basically inferior man. With due formality Slater was tried for murder, acquitted on the ground of insanity, and committed to the institution wherein I held so humble a post.

I have said that I am a constant speculator concerning dream life, and from this you may judge of the eagerness with which I applied myself to the study of the new patient as soon as

I had fully ascertained the facts of his case. He seemed to sense a certain friendliness in me; born no doubt of the interest I could not conceal, and the gentle manner in which I questioned him. Not that he ever recognised me during his attacks, when I hung breathlessly upon his chaotic but cosmic word-pictures; but he knew me in his quiet hours, when he would sit by his barred window weaving baskets of straw and willow, and perhaps pining for the mountain freedom he could never enjoy again. His family never called to see him; probably it had found another temporary head, after the manner of decadent mountain folk.

By degrees I commenced to feel an overwhelming wonder at the mad and fantastic conceptions of Joe Slater. The man himself was pitiably inferior in mentality and language alike; but his glowing, titanic visions, though described in a barbarous and disjointed jargon, were assuredly things which only a superior or even exceptional brain could conceive. How, I often asked myself, could the stolid imagination of a Catskill degenerate conjure up sights whose very possession argued a lurking spark of genius? How could any backwoods dullard have gained so much as an idea of those glittering realms of supernal radiance and space about which Slater ranted in his furious delirium? More and more I inclined to the belief that in the pitiful personality who cringed before me lay the disordered nucleus of something beyond my comprehension; something infinitely beyond the comprehension of my more experienced but less imaginative medical and scientific colleagues.

And yet I could extract nothing definite from the man. The sum of all my investigation was, that in a kind of semi-uncorporeal dream life Slater wandered or floated through resplendent and prodigious valleys, meadows, gardens, cities, and palaces of light; in a region unbounded and unknown to man. That there he was no peasant or degenerate, but a creature of importance and vivid life; moving proudly and dominantly, and checked only by a certain deadly enemy, who seemed to be a being of visible yet ethereal structure, and who did not appear to be of human shape, since Slater never referred to it as a *man*, or as aught save a *thing*. This *thing* had done Slater some hideous but unnamed wrong, which the maniac (if maniac he were) yearned to avenge. From the manner in which Slater alluded to their dealings, I judged that he and the luminous *thing* had met on equal terms; that in his dream existence the man was himself a luminous *thing* of the same race as his enemy. This impression was sustained by his frequent references to *flying through space* and *burning* all that impeded his progress. Yet these conceptions were formulated in rustic words wholly inadequate to convey them, a circumstance which drove me to the conclusion that if a true dream-world indeed existed, oral language was not its medium for the transmission of thought. Could it be that the dream-soul inhabiting this inferior body was desperately struggling to speak things which the simple and halting tongue of dulness could not utter? Could it be that I was face to face with intellectual emanations which would explain the mystery if I could but learn to discover and read them? I did not tell the older physicians of these things, for middle age is sceptical, cynical, and disinclined to accept new ideas. Besides, the head of the institution had but lately warned me in his paternal way that I was overworking; that my mind needed a rest.

It had long been my belief that human thought consists basically of atomic or molecular motion, convertible into ether waves of radiant energy like heat, light, and electricity. This belief had early led me to contemplate the possibility of telepathy or mental communication by means of suitable apparatus, and I had in my college days prepared a set of transmitting and receiving instruments somewhat similar to the cumbrous devices employed in wireless telegraphy at that crude, pre-radio period. These I had tested with a fellow-student; but achieving no result, had soon packed them away with other scientific odds and ends for possible future use. Now, in my intense desire to probe into the dream life of Joe Slater, I sought these instruments again; and spent several days in repairing them for action. When they were complete once more I missed no opportunity for their trial. At each outburst of Slater's violence, I would fit the transmitter to his forehead and the receiver to my own; constantly making delicate adjustments for various hypothetical wave-lengths of intellectual energy. I had but little notion of how the thought-impressions would, if successfully conveyed, arouse an intelligent response in my brain; but I felt certain that I could detect and interpret them. Accordingly I continued my experiments, though informing no one of their nature.

It was on the twenty-first of February, 1901, that the thing finally occurred. As I look back across the years I realise how unreal it seems; and sometimes half wonder if old Dr. Fenton was not right when he charged it all to my excited imagination. I recall that he listened with great kindness and patience when I told him, but afterward gave me a nerve-powder and arranged for the half-year's vacation on which I departed the next week. That fateful night I was wildly agitated and perturbed, for despite the excellent care he had received, Joe Slater was unmistakably dying. Perhaps it was his mountain freedom that he missed, or perhaps the turmoil in his brain had grown too acute for his rather sluggish physique; but at all events the flame of vitality flickered low in the decadent body. He was drowsy near the end, and as darkness fell he dropped off into a troubled sleep. I did not strap on the strait-jacket as was customary when he slept, since I saw that he was too feeble to be dangerous, even if he woke in mental disorder once more before passing away. But I did place upon his head and mine the two ends of my cosmic "radio"; hoping against hope for a first and last message from the dream-world in the brief time remaining. In the cell with us was one nurse, a mediocre fellow who did not understand the purpose of the apparatus, or think to inquire into my course. As the hours wore on I saw his head droop awkwardly in sleep, but I did not disturb him. I myself, lulled by the rhythmical breathing of the healthy and the dying man, must have nodded a little later.

The sound of weird lyric melody was what aroused me. Chords, vibrations, and harmonic ecstasies echoed passionately on every hand; while on my ravished sight burst the stupendous spectacle of ultimate beauty. Walls, columns, and architraves of living fire blazed effulgently around the spot where I seemed to float in air; extending upward to an infinitely high vaulted dome of indescribable splendour. Blending with this display of palatial magnificence, or rather, supplanting it at times in kaleidoscopic rotation, were glimpses of wide plains and graceful valleys, high mountains and inviting grottoes; covered with every lovely attribute of scenery which my delighted eye could conceive of, yet formed wholly of some glowing, ethereal, plastic entity, which in consistency partook as much of spirit as of matter. As I gazed, I perceived that my own brain held the key to these enchanting metamorphoses; for each vista which appeared to me, was the one my changing mind most wished to behold. Amidst this elysian realm I dwelt not as a stranger, for each sight and sound was familiar to me; just as it had been for uncounted aeons of eternity before, and would be for like eternities to come.

Then the resplendent aura of my brother of light drew near and held colloquy with me, soul to soul, with silent and perfect interchange of thought. The hour was one of approaching triumph, for was not my fellow-being escaping at last from a degrading periodic bondage; escaping for ever, and preparing to follow the accursed oppressor even unto the uttermost fields of ether, that upon it might be wrought a flaming cosmic vengeance which would shake the spheres? We floated thus for a little time, when I perceived a slight blurring and fading of the objects around us, as though some force were recalling me to earth—where I least wished to go. The form near me seemed to feel a change also, for it gradually brought its discourse toward a conclusion, and itself prepared to quit the scene; fading from my sight at a rate somewhat less rapid than that of the other objects. A few more thoughts were exchanged, and I knew that the luminous one and I were being recalled to bondage, though for my brother of light it would be the last time. The sorry planet-shell being well-nigh spent, in less than an hour my fellow would be free to pursue the oppressor along the Milky Way and past the hither stars to the very confines of infinity.

A well-defined shock separates my final impression of the fading scene of light from my sudden and somewhat shamefaced awakening and straightening up in my chair as I saw the dying figure on the couch move hesitantly. Joe Slater was indeed awaking, though probably for the last time. As I looked more closely, I saw that in the sallow cheeks shone spots of colour which had never before been present. The lips, too, seemed unusual; being tightly compressed, as if by the force of a stronger character than had been Slater's. The whole face finally began to grow tense, and the head turned restlessly with closed eyes. I did not arouse the sleeping nurse, but readjusted the slightly disarranged head-bands of my telepathic "radio", intent to catch any parting message the dreamer might have to deliver. All at once the head turned sharply in my direction and the eyes fell open, causing me to stare in blank amazement at what I beheld. The man who had been Joe Slater, the Catskill decadent, was now gazing at me with a pair of luminous, expanded eyes whose blue seemed subtly to have deepened. Neither mania nor degeneracy was visible in that gaze, and I felt beyond a doubt that I was viewing a face behind which lay an active mind of high order.

At this juncture my brain became aware of a steady external influence operating upon it. I closed my eyes to concentrate my thoughts more profoundly, and was rewarded by the positive knowledge that *my long-sought mental message had come at last.* Each transmitted idea formed rapidly in my mind, and though no actual language was employed, my habitual association of conception and expression was so great that I seemed to be receiving the message in ordinary English.

"*Joe Slater is dead,*" came the soul-petrifying voice or agency from beyond the wall of sleep. My opened eyes sought the couch of pain in curious horror, but the blue eyes were still calmly gazing, and the countenance was still intelligently animated. "He is better dead, for he was unfit to bear the active intellect of cosmic entity. His gross body could not undergo the needed adjustments between ethereal life and planet life. He was too much of an animal, too little a man; yet it is through his deficiency that you have come to discover me, for the cosmic and planet souls rightly should never meet. He has been my torment and diurnal prison for forty-two of your terrestrial years. I am an entity like that which you yourself become in the freedom of dreamless sleep. I am your brother of light, and have floated with you in the effulgent valleys. It is not permitted me to tell your waking earth-self of your real self, but we are all roamers of vast spaces and travellers in many ages. Next year I may be dwelling in the dark Egypt which you call ancient, or in the cruel empire of Tsan-Chan which is to come three thousand years hence. You and I have drifted to the worlds that reel about the red Arcturus, and dwelt in the bodies of the insect-philosophers that crawl proudly over the fourth moon of Jupiter. How little does the earth-self know of life and its extent! How little, indeed, ought it to know for its own tranquillity! Of the oppressor I cannot speak. You on earth have unwittingly felt its distant presence—you who without knowing idly gave to its blinking beacon the name of *Algol, the Daemon-Star.* It is to meet and conquer that oppressor that I have vainly striven for aeons, held back by bodily encumbrances. Tonight I go as a Nemesis bearing just and blazingly cataclysmic vengeance. *Watch me in the sky close by the Daemon-Star.* I cannot speak longer, for the body of Joe Slater grows cold and rigid, and the coarse brains are ceasing to vibrate as I wish. You have been my friend in the cosmos; you have been my only friend on this planet—the only soul to sense and seek for me within the repellent form which lies on this couch. We shall meet again—perhaps in the shining mists of Orion's Sword, perhaps on a bleak plateau in prehistoric Asia. Perhaps in unremembered dreams tonight; perhaps in some other form an aeon hence, when the solar system shall have been swept away."

At this point the thought-waves abruptly ceased, and the pale eyes of the dreamer—or can I say dead man?—commenced to glaze fishily. In a half-stupor I crossed over to the couch and felt of his wrist, but found it cold, stiff, and pulseless. The sallow cheeks paled again, and the thick lips fell open, disclosing the repulsively rotten fangs of the degenerate Joe Slater. I shivered, pulled a blanket over the hideous face, and awakened the nurse. Then I left the cell and went silently to my room. I had an insistent and unaccountable craving for a sleep whose dreams I should not remember.

The climax? What plain tale of science can boast of such a rhetorical effect? I have merely set down certain things appealing to me as facts, allowing you to construe them as you will. As I have already admitted, my superior, old Dr. Fenton, denies the reality of everything I have related. He vows that I was broken down with nervous strain, and badly in need of the long vacation on full pay which he so generously gave me. He assures me on his professional honour that Joe Slater was but a low-grade paranoiac, whose fantastic notions must have come from the crude hereditary folk-tales which circulate in even the most decadent of communities. All this he tells me—yet I cannot forget what I saw in the sky on the night after Slater died. Lest you think me a biased witness, another's pen must add this final testimony, which may perhaps supply the climax you expect. I will quote the following account of the star *Nova Persei* verbatim from the pages of that eminent astronomical authority, Prof. Garrett P. Serviss:

> "On February 22, 1901, a marvellous new star was discovered by Dr. Anderson of Edinburgh, *not very far from Algol.* No star had been visible at that point before. Within twenty-four hours the stranger had become so bright that it outshone Capella. In a week or two it had visibly faded, and in the course of a few months it was hardly discernible with the naked eye."

MEMORY

In the valley of Nis the accursed waning moon shines thinly, tearing a path for its light with feeble horns through the lethal foliage of a great upas-tree. And within the depths of the valley, where the light reaches not, move forms not meet to be beheld. Rank is the herbage on each slope, where evil vines and creeping plants crawl amidst the stones of ruined palaces, twining tightly about broken columns and strange monoliths, and heaving up marble pavements laid by forgotten hands. And in trees that grow gigantic in crumbling courtyards leap little apes, while in and out of deep treasure-vaults writhe poison serpents and scaly things without a name.

Vast are the stones which sleep beneath coverlets of dank moss, and mighty were the walls from which they fell. For all time did their builders erect them, and in sooth they yet serve nobly, for beneath them the grey toad makes his habitation.

At the very bottom of the valley lies the river Than, whose waters are slimy and filled with weeds. From hidden springs it rises, and to subterranean grottoes it flows, so that the Daemon of the Valley knows not why its waters are red, nor whither they are bound.

The Genie that haunts the moonbeams spake to the Daemon of the Valley, saying, "I am old, and forget much. Tell me the deeds and aspect and name of them who built these things of stone." And the Daemon replied, "I am Memory, and am wise in lore of the past, but I too am old. These beings were like the waters of the river Than, not to be understood. Their deeds I recall not, for they were but of the moment. Their aspect I recall dimly, for it was like to that of the little apes in the trees. Their name I recall clearly, for it rhymed with that of the river. These beings of yesterday were called Man."

So the Genie flew back to the thin horned moon, and the Daemon looked intently at a little ape in a tree that grew in a crumbling courtyard.

OLD BUGS

An Extemporaneous Sob Story
by Marcus Lollius, Proconsul of Gaul

Sheehan's Pool Room, which adorns one of the lesser alleys in the heart of Chicago's stockyard district, is not a nice place. Its air, freighted with a thousand odours such as Coleridge may have found at Cologne, too seldom knows the purifying rays of the sun; but fights for space with the acrid fumes of unnumbered cheap cigars and cigarettes which dangle from the coarse lips of unnumbered human animals that haunt the place day and night. But the popularity of Sheehan's remains unimpaired; and for this there is a reason—a reason obvious to anyone who will take the trouble to analyse the mixed stenches prevailing there. Over and above the fumes and sickening closeness rises an aroma once familiar throughout the land, but now happily banished to the back streets of life by the edict of a benevolent government—the aroma of strong, wicked whiskey—a precious kind of forbidden fruit indeed in this year of grace 1950.

Sheehan's is the acknowledged centre to Chicago's subterranean traffic in liquor and narcotics, and as such has a certain dignity which extends even to the unkempt attachés of the place; but there was until lately one who lay outside the pale of that dignity—one who shared the squalor and filth, but not the importance, of Sheehan's. He was called "Old Bugs", and was the most disreputable object in a disreputable environment. What he had once been, many tried to guess; for his language and mode of utterance when intoxicated to a certain degree were such as to excite wonderment; but what he *was,* presented less difficulty—for "Old Bugs", in superlative degree, epitomised the pathetic species known as the "bum" or the "down-and-outer". Whence he had come, no one could tell. One night he had burst wildly into Sheehan's, foaming at the mouth and screaming for whiskey and hasheesh; and having been supplied in exchange for a promise to perform odd jobs, had hung about ever since, mopping floors, cleaning cuspidors and glasses, and attending to a hundred similar menial duties in exchange for the drink and drugs which were necessary to keep him alive and sane.

He talked but little, and usually in the common jargon of the underworld; but occasionally, when inflamed by an unusually generous dose of crude whiskey, would burst forth into strings of incomprehensible polysyllables and snatches of sonorous prose and verse which led certain habitués to conjecture that he had seen better days. One steady patron—a bank defaulter under cover—came to converse with him quite regularly, and from the tone of his discourse ventured the opinion that he had been a writer or professor in his day. But the only tangible clue to Old Bugs' past was a faded photograph which he constantly carried about with him—the photograph of a young woman of noble and beautiful features. This he would sometimes draw from his tattered pocket, carefully unwrap from its covering of tissue paper, and gaze upon for hours with an expression of ineffable sadness and tenderness. It was not the portrait of one whom an underworld denizen would be likely to know, but of a lady of breeding and quality, garbed in the quaint attire of thirty years before. Old Bugs himself seemed also to belong to the past, for his nondescript clothing bore every hallmark of antiquity. He was a man of immense height, probably more than six feet, though his stooping shoulders sometimes belied this fact. His hair, a dirty white and falling out in patches, was never combed; and over his lean face grew a mangy stubble of coarse beard which seemed always to remain at the bristling stage—never shaven—yet never long enough to form a respectable set of whiskers. His features had perhaps been noble once, but were now seamed with the ghastly effects of terrible dissipation. At one time—probably in middle life—he had evidently been grossly fat; but now he was horribly lean, the purple flesh hanging in loose pouches under his bleary eyes and upon his cheeks. Altogether, Old Bugs was not pleasing to look upon.

The disposition of Old Bugs was as odd as his aspect. Ordinarily he was true to the derelict type—ready to do anything for a nickel or a dose of whiskey or hasheesh—but at rare intervals he shewed the traits which earned him his name. Then he would try to straighten up, and a certain fire would creep into the sunken eyes. His demeanour would assume an unwonted grace and even dignity; and the sodden creatures around him would sense something of superiority—something which made them less ready to give the usual kicks and cuffs to the poor butt and drudge. At these times he would shew a sardonic humour and make remarks which the folk of Sheehan's deemed foolish and irrational. But the spells would soon pass, and once more Old Bugs would resume his eternal floor-scrubbing and cuspidor-cleaning. But for one thing Old Bugs would have been an ideal slave to the establishment—and that one thing was his conduct when young men were introduced for their first drink. The old man would then rise from the floor in anger and excitement, muttering threats and warnings, and seeking to dissuade the novices from embarking upon their course of "seeing life as it is". He would sputter and fume, exploding into sesquipedalian admonitions and strange oaths, and animated by a frightful earnestness which brought a shudder to more than one drug-racked mind in the crowded room. But after a time his alcohol-enfeebled brain would wander from the subject, and with a foolish grin he would turn once more to his mop or cleaning-rag.

I do not think that many of Sheehan's regular patrons will ever forget the day that young Alfred Trever came. He was rather a "find"—a rich and high-spirited youth who would "go the limit" in anything he undertook—at least, that was the verdict of Pete Schultz, Sheehan's "runner", who had come across the boy at Lawrence College, in the small town of Appleton, Wisconsin. Trever was the son of prominent parents in Appleton. His father, Karl Trever, was an attorney and citizen of distinction, whilst his mother had made an enviable reputation as a poetess under her maiden name of Eleanor Wing. Alfred was himself a scholar and poet of distinction, though cursed with a certain childish irresponsibility which made him an ideal prey for Sheehan's runner. He was blond, handsome, and spoiled; vivacious and eager to taste the several forms of dissipation about which he had read and heard. At Lawrence he had been prominent in the mock-fraternity of "Tappa Tappa Keg", where he was the wildest and merriest of the wild and merry young roysterers; but this immature, collegiate frivolity did not satisfy him. He knew deeper vices through books, and he now longed to know them at first hand. Perhaps this tendency toward wildness had been stimulated somewhat by the repression to which he had been subjected at home; for Mrs. Trever had particular reason for training her only child with rigid severity. She had, in her own youth, been deeply and permanently impressed with the horror of dissipation by the case of one to whom she had for a time been engaged.

Young Galpin, the fiancé in question, had been one of Appleton's most remarkable sons. Attaining distinction as a boy through his wonderful mentality, he won vast fame at the

University of Wisconsin, and at the age of twenty-three returned to Appleton to take up a professorship at Lawrence and to slip a diamond upon the finger of Appleton's fairest and most brilliant daughter. For a season all went happily, till without warning the storm burst. Evil habits, dating from a first drink taken years before in woodland seclusion, made themselves manifest in the young professor; and only by a hurried resignation did he escape a nasty prosecution for injury to the habits and morals of the pupils under his charge. His engagement broken, Galpin moved east to begin life anew; but before long, Appletonians heard of his dismissal in disgrace from New York University, where he had obtained an instructorship in English. Galpin now devoted his time to the library and lecture platform, preparing volumes and speeches on various subjects connected with *belles lettres,* and always shewing a genius so remarkable that it seemed as if the public must some time pardon him for his past mistakes. His impassioned lectures in defence of Villon, Poe, Verlaine, and Oscar Wilde were applied to himself as well, and in the short Indian summer of his glory there was talk of a renewed engagement at a certain cultured home on Park Avenue. But then the blow fell. A final disgrace, compared to which the others had been as nothing, shattered the illusions of those who had come to believe in Galpin's reform; and the young man abandoned his name and disappeared from public view. Rumour now and then associated him with a certain "Consul Hasting" whose work for the stage and for motion-picture companies attracted a certain degree of attention because of its scholarly breadth and depth; but Hasting soon disappeared from the public eye, and Galpin became only a name for parents to quote in warning accents. Eleanor Wing soon celebrated her marriage to Karl Trever, a rising young lawyer, and of her former admirer retained only enough memory to dictate the naming of her only son, and the moral guidance of that handsome and headstrong youth. Now, in spite of all that guidance, Alfred Trever was at Sheehan's and about to take his first drink.

"Boss," cried Schultz, as he entered the vile-smelling room with his young victim, "meet my friend Al Trever, bes' li'l' sport up at Lawrence—thas' 'n Appleton, Wis., y' know. Some swell guy, too—'s father's a big corp'ration lawyer up in his burg, 'n' 's mother's some lit'ry genius. He wants to see life as she is—wants to know what the real lightnin' juice tastes like—so jus' remember he's me friend an' treat 'im right."

As the names Trever, Lawrence, and Appleton fell on the air, the loafers seemed to sense something unusual. Perhaps it was only some sound connected with the clicking balls of the pool tables or the rattling glasses that were brought from the cryptic regions in the rear—perhaps only that, plus some strange rustling of the dirty draperies at the one dingy window—but many thought that someone in the room had gritted his teeth and drawn a very sharp breath.

"Glad to know you, Sheehan," said Trever in a quiet, well-bred tone. "This is my first experience in a place like this, but I am a student of life, and don't want to miss any experience. There's poetry in this sort of thing, you know—or perhaps you don't know, but it's all the same."

"Young feller," responded the proprietor, "ya come tuh th' right place tuh see life. We got all kinds here—reel life an' a good time. The damn' government can try tuh make folks good ef it wants tuh, but it can't stop a feller from hittin' 'er up when he feels like it. Whaddya want, feller—booze, coke, or some other sorta dope? Yuh can't ask for nothin' we ain't got."

Habitués say that it was at this point they noticed a cessation in the regular, monotonous strokes of the mop.

"I want whiskey—good old-fashioned rye!" exclaimed Trever enthusiastically. "I'll tell you, I'm good and tired of water after reading of the merry bouts fellows used to have in the old days. I can't read an Anacreontic without watering at the mouth—and it's something a lot stronger than water that my mouth waters for!"

"Anacreontic—what 'n hell's that?" several hangers-on looked up as the young man went slightly beyond their depth. But the bank defaulter under cover explained to them that Anacreon was a gay old dog who lived many years ago and wrote about the fun he had when all the world was just like Sheehan's.

"Let me see, Trever," continued the defaulter, "didn't Schultz say your mother is a literary person, too?"

"Yes, damn it," replied Trever, "but nothing like the old Teian! She's one of those dull, eternal moralisers that try to take all the joy out of life. Namby-pamby sort—ever heard of her? She writes under her maiden name of Eleanor Wing."

Here it was that Old Bugs dropped his mop.

"Well, here's yer stuff," announced Sheehan jovially as a tray of bottles and glasses was wheeled into the room. "Good old rye, an' as fiery as ya kin find anyw'eres in Chi'."

The youth's eyes glistened and his nostrils curled at the fumes of the brownish fluid which an attendant was pouring out for him. It repelled him horribly, and revolted all his inherited delicacy; but his determination to taste life to the full remained with him, and he maintained a bold front. But before his resolution was put to the test, the unexpected intervened. Old Bugs, springing up from the crouching position in which he had hitherto been, leaped at the youth and dashed from his hands the uplifted glass, almost simultaneously attacking the tray of bottles and glasses with his mop, and scattering the contents upon the floor in a confusion of odoriferous fluid and broken bottles and tumblers. Numbers of men, or things which had been men, dropped to the floor and began lapping at the puddles of spilled liquor, but most remained immovable, watching the unprecedented actions of the barroom drudge and derelict. Old Bugs straightened up before the astonished Trever, and in a mild and cultivated voice said, "Do not do this thing. I was like you once, and I did it. Now I am like—this."

"What do you mean, you damned old fool?" shouted Trever. "What do you mean by interfering with a gentleman in his pleasures?"

Sheehan, now recovering from his astonishment, advanced and laid a heavy hand on the old waif's shoulder.

"This is the last time for you, old bird!" he exclaimed furiously. "When a gen'l'man wants tuh take a drink here, by God, he shall, without you interferin'. Now get th' hell outa here afore I kick hell outa ya."

But Sheehan had reckoned without scientific knowledge of abnormal psychology and the effects of nervous stimulus. Old Bugs, obtaining a firmer hold on his mop, began to wield it like the javelin of a Macedonian hoplite, and soon cleared a considerable space around himself, meanwhile shouting various disconnected bits of quotation, among which was prominently repeated, " … the sons of Belial, blown with insolence and wine."

The room became pandemonium, and men screamed and howled in fright at the sinister being they had aroused. Trever seemed dazed in the confusion, and shrank to the wall as the strife thickened. "He shall not drink! He shall not drink!" Thus roared Old Bugs as he seemed to run out of—or rise above—quotations. Policemen appeared at the door, attracted by the noise, but for a time they made no move to intervene. Trever, now thoroughly terrified and cured for ever of his desire to see life via the vice route, edged closer to the blue-coated newcomers. Could he but escape and catch a train for Appleton, he reflected, he would consider his education in dissipation quite complete.

Then suddenly Old Bugs ceased to wield his javelin and stopped still—drawing himself up more erectly than any denizen of the place had ever seen him before. "*Ave, Caesar, Moriturus te saluto!*" he shouted, and dropped to the whiskey-reeking floor, never to rise again.

Subsequent impressions will never leave the mind of young Trever. The picture is blurred, but ineradicable. Policemen ploughed a way through the crowd, questioning everyone closely both about the incident and about the dead figure on the floor. Sheehan especially did they ply with inquiries, yet without eliciting any information of value concerning Old Bugs. Then the bank defaulter remembered the picture, and suggested that it be viewed and filed for identification at police headquarters. An officer bent reluctantly over the loathsome glassy-eyed form and found the tissue-wrapped cardboard, which he passed around among the others.

"Some chicken!" leered a drunken man as he viewed the beautiful face, but those who were sober did not leer, looking with respect and abashment at the delicate and spiritual features. No one seemed able to place the subject, and all wondered that the drug-degraded derelict should have such a portrait in his possession—that is, all but the bank defaulter, who was meanwhile eyeing the intruding bluecoats rather uneasily. *He* had seen a little deeper beneath Old Bugs' mask of utter degradation.

Then the picture was passed to Trever, and a change came over the youth. After the first start, he replaced the tissue wrapping around the portrait, as if to shield it from the sordidness of the place. Then he gazed long and searchingly at the figure on the floor, noting its great height, and the aristocratic cast of features which seemed to appear now that the wretched flame of life had flickered out. No, he said hastily, as the question was put to him, he did not know the subject of the picture. It was so old, he added, that no one now could be expected to recognise it.

But Alfred Trever did not speak the truth, as many guessed when he offered to take charge of the body and secure its interment in Appleton. Over the library mantel in his home hung the exact replica of that picture, and all his life he had known and loved its original.

For the gentle and noble features were those of his own mother.

THE TRANSITION OF JUAN ROMERO

Of the events which took place at the Norton Mine on October 18th and 19th, 1894, I have no desire to speak. A sense of duty to science is all that impels me to recall, in these last years of my life, scenes and happenings fraught with a terror doubly acute because I cannot wholly define it. But I believe that before I die I should tell what I know of the—shall I say transition—of Juan Romero.

My name and origin need not be related to posterity; in fact, I fancy it is better that they should not be, for when a man suddenly migrates to the States or the Colonies, he leaves his past behind him. Besides, what I once was is not in the least relevant to my narrative; save perhaps the fact that during my service in India I was more at home amongst white-bearded native teachers than amongst my brother-officers. I had delved not a little into odd Eastern lore when overtaken by the calamities which brought about my new life in America's vast West—a life wherein I found it well to accept a name—my present one—which is very common and carries no meaning.

In the summer and autumn of 1894 I dwelt in the drear expanses of the Cactus Mountains, employed as a common labourer at the celebrated Norton Mine; whose discovery by an aged prospector some years before had turned the surrounding region from a nearly unpeopled waste to a seething cauldron of sordid life. A cavern of gold, lying deep below a mountain lake, had enriched its venerable finder beyond his wildest dreams, and now formed the seat of extensive tunnelling operations on the part of the corporation to which it had finally been sold. Additional grottoes had been found, and the yield of yellow metal was exceedingly great; so that a mighty and heterogeneous army of miners toiled day and night in the numerous passages and rock hollows. The Superintendent, a Mr. Arthur, often discussed the singularity of the local geological formations; speculating on the probable extent of the chain of caves, and estimating the future of the titanic mining enterprise. He considered the auriferous cavities the result of the action of water, and believed that the last of them would soon be opened up.

It was not long after my arrival and employment that Juan Romero came to the Norton Mine. One of a large herd of unkempt Mexicans attracted thither from the neighbouring country, he at first commanded attention only because of his features; which though plainly of the Red Indian type, were yet remarkable for their light colour and refined conformation, being vastly unlike those of the average "Greaser" or Piute of the locality. It is curious that although he differed so widely from the mass of Hispanicised and tribal Indians, Romero gave not the least impression of Caucasian blood. It was not the Castilian conquistador or the American pioneer, but the ancient and noble Aztec, whom imagination called to view when the silent peon would rise in the early morning and gaze in fascination at the sun as it crept above the eastern hills, meanwhile stretching out his arms to the orb as if in the performance of some rite whose nature he did not himself comprehend. But save for his face, Romero was not in any way suggestive of nobility. Ignorant and dirty, he was at home amongst the other brown-skinned Mexicans; having come (so I was afterward told) from the very lowest sort of surroundings. He had been found as a child in a crude mountain hut, the only survivor of an epidemic which had stalked lethally by. Near the hut, close to a rather unusual rock fissure, had lain two skeletons, newly picked by vultures, and presumably forming the sole remains of his parents. No one recalled their identity, and they were soon forgotten by the many. Indeed, the crumbling of the adobe hut and the closing of the rock fissure by a subsequent avalanche had helped to efface even the scene from recollection. Reared by a Mexican cattle-thief who had given him his name, Juan differed little from his fellows.

The attachment which Romero manifested toward me was undoubtedly commenced through the quaint and ancient Hindoo ring which I wore when not engaged in active labour. Of its nature, and manner of coming into my possession, I cannot speak. It was my last link with a chapter of life for ever closed, and I valued it highly. Soon I observed that the odd-looking Mexican was likewise interested; eyeing it with an expression that banished all suspicion of mere covetousness. Its hoary hieroglyphs seemed to stir some faint recollection in his untutored but active mind, though he could not possibly have beheld their like before. Within a few weeks after his advent, Romero was like a faithful servant to me; this notwithstanding the fact that I was myself but an ordinary miner. Our conversation was necessarily limited. He knew but a few words of English, whilst I found my Oxonian Spanish was something quite different from the patois of the peon of New Spain.

The event which I am about to relate was unheralded by long premonitions. Though the man Romero had interested me, and though my ring had affected him peculiarly, I think that neither of us had any expectation of what was to follow when the great blast was set off. Geological considerations had dictated an extension of the mine directly downward from the deepest part of the subterranean area; and the belief of the Superintendent that only solid rock would be encountered, had led to the placing of a prodigious charge of dynamite. With this work Romero and I were not connected, wherefore our first knowledge of extraordinary conditions came from others. The charge, heavier perhaps than had been estimated, had seemed to shake the entire mountain. Windows in shanties on the slope outside were shattered by the shock, whilst miners throughout the nearer passages were knocked from their feet. Jewel Lake, which lay above the scene of action, heaved as in a tempest. Upon investigation it was seen that a new abyss yawned indefinitely below the seat of the blast; an abyss so monstrous that no handy line might fathom it, nor any lamp illuminate it. Baffled, the excavators sought a conference with the Superintendent, who ordered great lengths of rope to be taken to the pit, and spliced and lowered without cessation till a bottom might be discovered.

Shortly afterward the pale-faced workmen apprised the Superintendent of their failure. Firmly though respectfully they signified their refusal to revisit the chasm, or indeed to work further in the mine until it might be sealed. Something beyond their experience was evidently confronting them, for so far as they could ascertain, the void below was infinite. The Superintendent did not reproach them. Instead, he pondered deeply, and made many plans for the following day. The night shift did not go on that evening.

At two in the morning a lone coyote on the mountain began to howl dismally. From somewhere within the works a dog barked in answer; either to the coyote—or to something else. A storm was gathering about the peaks of the range, and weirdly shaped clouds scudded horribly across the blurred patch of celestial light which marked a gibbous moon's[1] attempts to shine through many layers of cirro-stratus vapours. It was Romero's voice, coming from the bunk above, that awaked me; a voice excited and tense with some vague expectation I could not understand:

"*¡Madre de Dios!—el sonido—ese sonido—¡oiga Vd!—¿lo oye Vd?—Señor,* THAT SOUND!"

I listened, wondering what sound he meant. The coyote, the dog, the storm, all were audible; the last named now gaining ascendancy as the wind shrieked more and more frantically. Flashes of lightning were visible through the bunk-house window. I questioned the nervous Mexican, repeating the sounds I had heard:

"*¿El coyote?—¿el perro?—¿el viento?*"

But Romero did not reply. Then he commenced whispering as in awe:

"*El ritmo, Señor—el ritmo de la tierra*—THAT THROB DOWN IN THE GROUND!"

And now I also heard; heard and shivered without knowing why. Deep, deep, below me was a sound—a rhythm, just as the peon had said—which, though exceedingly faint, yet dominated even the dog, the coyote, and the increasing tempest. To seek to describe it were useless—for it was such that no description is possible. Perhaps it was like the pulsing of the engines far down in a great liner, as sensed from the deck, yet it was not so mechanical; not so devoid of the element of life and consciousness. Of all its qualities, *remoteness* in the earth most impressed me. To my mind rushed fragments of a passage in Joseph Glanvill which Poe has quoted with tremendous effect[2]—

> "—the vastness, profundity, and unsearchableness of His works, *which have a depth in them greater than the well of Democritus.*"

Suddenly Romero leaped from his bunk; pausing before me to gaze at the strange ring on my hand, which glistened queerly in every flash of lightning, and then staring intently in the direction of the mine shaft. I also rose, and both stood motionless for a time, straining our ears as the uncanny rhythm seemed more and more to

---

[1] AUTHOR'S NOTE: Here is a lesson in scientific accuracy for fiction writers. I have just looked up the moon's phases for October, 1894, to find when a gibbous moon was visible at 2 a.m., and have changed the dates to fit!!

[2] Motto of "A Descent into the Maelstrom"

take on a vital quality. Then without apparent volition we began to move toward the door, whose rattling in the gale held a comforting suggestion of earthly reality. The chanting in the depths—for such the sound now seemed to be—grew in volume and distinctness; and we felt irresistibly urged out into the storm and thence to the gaping blackness of the shaft.

We encountered no living creature, for the men of the night shift had been released from duty, and were doubtless at the Dry Gulch settlement pouring sinister rumours into the ear of some drowsy bartender. From the watchman's cabin, however, gleamed a small square of yellow light like a guardian eye. I dimly wondered how the rhythmic sound had affected the watchman; but Romero was moving more swiftly now, and I followed without pausing.

As we descended the shaft, the sound beneath grew definitely composite. It struck me as horribly like a sort of Oriental ceremony, with beating of drums and chanting of many voices. I have, as you are aware, been much in India. Romero and I moved without material hesitancy through drifts and down ladders; ever toward the thing that allured us, yet ever with a pitifully helpless fear and reluctance. At one time I fancied I had gone mad—this was when, on wondering how our way was lighted in the absence of lamp or candle, I realised that the ancient ring on my finger was glowing with eery radiance, diffusing a pallid lustre through the damp, heavy air around.

It was without warning that Romero, after clambering down one of the many rude ladders, broke into a run and left me alone. Some new and wild note in the drumming and chanting, perceptible but slightly to me, had acted on him in startling fashion; and with a wild outcry he forged ahead unguided in the cavern's gloom. I heard his repeated shrieks before me, as he stumbled awkwardly along the level places and scrambled madly down the rickety ladders. And frightened as I was, I yet retained enough of perception to note that his speech, when articulate, was not of any sort known to me. Harsh but impressive polysyllables had replaced the customary mixture of bad Spanish and worse English, and of these only the oft repeated cry "*Huitzilopotchli*" seemed in the least familiar. Later I definitely placed that word in the works of a great historian[3]—and shuddered when the association came to me.

The climax of that awful night was composite but fairly brief, beginning just as I reached the final cavern of the journey. Out of the darkness immediately ahead burst a final shriek from

---

[3] Prescott, *Conquest of Mexico*

the Mexican, which was joined by such a chorus of uncouth sound as I could never hear again and survive. In that moment it seemed as if all the hidden terrors and monstrosities of earth had become articulate in an effort to overwhelm the human race. Simultaneously the light from my ring was extinguished, and I saw a new light glimmering from lower space but a few yards ahead of me. I had arrived at the abyss, which was now redly aglow, and which had evidently swallowed up the unfortunate Romero. Advancing, I peered over the edge of that chasm which no line could fathom, and which was now a pandemonium of flickering flame and hideous uproar. At first I beheld nothing but a seething blur of luminosity; but then shapes, all infinitely distant, began to detach themselves from the confusion, and I saw—was it Juan Romero?—*but God! I dare not tell you what I saw!* ... Some power from heaven, coming to my aid, obliterated both sights and sounds in such a crash as may be heard when two universes collide in space. Chaos supervened, and I knew the peace of oblivion.

I hardly know how to continue, since conditions so singular are involved; but I will do my best, not even trying to differentiate betwixt the real and the apparent. When I awaked, I was safe in my bunk and the red glow of dawn was visible at the window. Some distance away the lifeless body of Juan Romero lay upon a table, surrounded by a group of men including the camp doctor. The men were discussing the strange death of the Mexican as he lay asleep; a death seemingly connected in some way with the terrible bolt of lightning which had struck and shaken the mountain. No direct cause was evident, and an autopsy failed to shew any reason why Romero should not be living. Snatches of conversation indicated beyond a doubt that neither Romero nor I had left the bunk-house during the night; that neither had been awake during the frightful storm which had passed over the Cactus range. That storm, said men who had ventured down the mine shaft, had caused extensive caving in, and had completely closed the deep abyss which had created so much apprehension the day before. When I asked the watchman what sounds he had heard prior to the mighty thunderbolt, he mentioned a coyote, a dog, and the snarling mountain wind—nothing more. Nor do I doubt his word.

Upon the resumption of work Superintendent Arthur called on some especially dependable men to make a few investigations around the spot where the gulf had appeared. Though hardly eager, they obeyed; and a deep boring was made. Results were very curious. The roof of the void, as seen whilst it was open, was not by any means thick; yet now the drills of the investigators met with what appeared to be a limitless extent of solid rock. Finding nothing else, not even gold, the Superintendent abandoned his attempts; but a perplexed look occasionally steals over his countenance as he sits thinking at his desk.

One other thing is curious. Shortly after waking on that morning after the storm, I noticed the unaccountable absence of my Hindoo ring from my finger. I had prized it greatly, yet nevertheless felt a sensation of relief at its disappearance. If one of my fellow-miners appropriated it, he must have been quite clever in disposing of his booty, for despite advertisements and a police search the ring was never seen again. Somehow I doubt if it was stolen by mortal hands, for many strange things were taught me in India.

My opinion of my whole experience varies from time to time. In broad daylight, and at most seasons I am apt to think the greater part of it a mere dream; but sometimes in the autumn, about two in the morning when the winds and animals howl dismally, there comes from inconceivable depths below a damnable suggestion of rhythmical throbbing … and I feel that the transition of Juan Romero was a terrible one indeed.

THE WHITE SHIP

I am Basil Elton, keeper of the North Point light that my father and grandfather kept before me. Far from the shore stands the grey lighthouse, above sunken slimy rocks that are seen when the tide is low, but unseen when the tide is high. Past that beacon for a century have swept the majestic barques of the seven seas. In the days of my grandfather there were many; in the days of my father not so many; and now there are so few that I sometimes feel strangely alone, as though I were the last man on our planet.

From far shores came those white-sailed argosies of old; from far Eastern shores where warm suns shine and sweet odours linger about strange gardens and gay temples. The old captains of the sea came often to my grandfather and told him of these things, which in turn he told to my father, and my father told to me in the long autumn evenings when the wind howled eerily from the East. And I have read more of these things, and of many things besides, in the books men gave me when I was young and filled with wonder.

But more wonderful than the lore of old men and the lore of books is the secret lore of ocean. Blue, green, grey, white, or black; smooth, ruffled, or mountainous; that ocean is not silent. All my days have I watched it and listened to it, and I know it well. At first it told to me only the plain little tales of calm beaches and near ports, but with the years it grew more friendly and spoke of other things; of things more strange and more distant in space and in time. Sometimes at twilight the grey vapours of the horizon have parted to grant me glimpses of the ways beyond; and sometimes at night the deep waters of the sea have grown clear and phosphorescent, to grant me glimpses of the ways beneath. And these glimpses have been as often of the ways that were and the ways that might be, as of the ways that are; for ocean is more ancient than the mountains, and freighted with the memories and the dreams of Time.

Out of the South it was that the White Ship used to come when the moon was full and high in the heavens. Out of the South it would glide very smoothly and silently over the sea. And whether the sea was rough or calm, and whether the wind was friendly or adverse, it would always glide smoothly and silently, its sails distent and its long strange tiers of oars moving rhythmically. One night I espied upon the deck a man, bearded and robed, and he seemed to beckon me to embark for fair unknown shores. Many times afterward I saw him under the full moon, and ever did he beckon me.

Very brightly did the moon shine on the night I answered the call, and I walked out over the waters to the White Ship on a bridge of moonbeams. The man who had beckoned now spoke a welcome to me in a soft language I seemed to know well, and the hours were filled with soft songs of the oarsmen as we glided away into a mysterious South, golden with the glow of that full, mellow moon.

And when the day dawned, rosy and effulgent, I beheld the green shore of far lands, bright and beautiful, and to me unknown. Up from the sea rose lordly terraces of verdure, tree-studded, and shewing here and there the gleaming white roofs and colonnades of strange temples. As we drew nearer the green shore the bearded man told me of that land, the Land of Zar, where dwell all the dreams and thoughts of beauty that come to men once and then are forgotten. And when I looked upon the terraces again I saw that what he said was true, for among the sights before me were many things I had once seen through the mists beyond the horizon and in the phosphorescent depths of ocean. There too were forms and fantasies more splendid than any I had ever known; the visions of young poets who died in want before the world could learn of what they had seen and dreamed. But we did not set foot upon the sloping meadows of Zar, for it is told that he who treads them may nevermore return to his native place.

As the White Ship sailed silently away from the templed terraces of Zar, we beheld on the distant horizon ahead the spires of a mighty city; and the bearded man said to me, "This is Thalarion, the City of a Thousand Wonders, wherein reside all those mysteries that man has striven in vain to fathom." And I looked again, at closer range, and saw that the city was greater than any city I had known or dreamed of before. Into the sky the spires of its temples reached, so that no man might behold their peaks; and far back beyond the horizon stretched the grim, grey walls, over which one might spy only a few roofs, weird and ominous, yet adorned with rich friezes and alluring sculptures. I yearned mightily to enter this fascinating yet repellent city, and besought the bearded man to land me at the stone pier by the huge carven gate Akariel; but he gently denied my wish, saying: "Into Thalarion, the City of a Thousand Wonders, many have passed but none returned. Therein walk only daemons and mad things that are no longer men, and the streets are white with the unburied bones of those who have looked upon the eidolon Lathi, that reigns over the city." So the White Ship sailed on past the walls of Thalarion, and followed for many days a southward-flying bird, whose glossy plumage matched the sky out of which it had appeared.

Then came we to a pleasant coast gay with blossoms of every hue, where as far inland as we could see basked lovely groves and radiant arbours beneath a meridian sun. From bowers beyond our view came bursts of song and snatches of lyric harmony, interspersed with faint laughter so delicious that I urged the rowers onward in my eagerness to reach the scene. And the bearded man spoke no word, but watched me as we approached the lily-lined shore. Suddenly a wind blowing from over the flowery meadows and leafy woods brought a scent at which I trembled. The wind grew stronger, and the air was filled with the lethal, charnel odour of plague-stricken towns and uncovered cemeteries. And as we sailed madly away from that damnable coast the bearded man spoke at last, saying: "This is Xura, the Land of Pleasures Unattained."

So once more the White Ship followed the bird of heaven, over warm blessed seas fanned by caressing, aromatic breezes. Day after day and night after night did we sail, and when the moon was full we would listen to soft songs of the oarsmen, sweet as on that distant night when we sailed away from my native land. And it was by moonlight that we anchored at last in the harbour of Sona-Nyl, which is guarded by twin headlands of crystal that rise from the sea and meet in a resplendent arch. This is the Land of Fancy, and we walked to the verdant shore upon a golden bridge of moonbeams.

In the Land of Sona-Nyl there is neither time nor space, neither suffering nor death; and there I dwelt for many aeons. Green are the groves and pastures, bright and fragrant the flowers, blue and musical the streams, clear and cool the fountains, and stately and gorgeous the temples, castles, and cities of Sona-Nyl. Of that land there is no bound, for beyond each vista of beauty rises another more beautiful. Over the countryside and amidst the splendour of cities rove at will the happy folk, of whom all are gifted with unmarred grace and unalloyed happiness. For the aeons that I dwelt there I wandered blissfully through gardens where quaint pagodas peep from pleasing clumps of bushes, and where the white walks are bordered with delicate blossoms. I climbed gentle hills from whose summits I could see entrancing panoramas of loveliness, with steepled towns nestling in verdant valleys, and with the golden domes of gigantic cities glittering on the infinitely distant horizon. And I viewed by moonlight the sparkling sea, the crystal headlands, and the placid harbour wherein lay anchored the White Ship.

It was against the full moon one night in the immemorial year of Tharp that I saw outlined the beckoning form of the celestial bird, and felt the first stirrings of unrest. Then I spoke with the bearded man, and told him of my new yearning to depart for remote Cathuria, which no man hath seen, but which all believe to lie beyond the basalt pillars of the West. It is the Land of Hope, and in it shine the perfect ideals of all that we know elsewhere; or at least so men relate. But the bearded man said to me: "Beware of those perilous seas wherein men say Cathuria lies. In Sona-Nyl there is no pain nor death, but who can tell what lies beyond the basalt pillars of the West?" Natheless at the next full moon I boarded the White Ship, and with the reluctant bearded man left the happy harbour for untravelled seas.

And the bird of heaven flew before, and led us toward the basalt pillars of the West, but this time the oarsmen sang no soft songs under the full moon. In my mind I would often picture the unknown Land of Cathuria with its splendid groves and palaces, and would wonder what new delights there awaited me. "Cathuria," I would say to myself, "is the abode of gods and the land of unnumbered cities of gold. Its forests are of aloe and sandalwood, even as the fragrant groves of Camorin, and among the trees flutter gay birds sweet with song. On the green and flowery mountains of Cathuria stand temples of pink marble rich with carven and painted glories, and having in their courtyards cool fountains of silver, where purl with ravishing music the scented waters that come from the grotto-born river Narg. And the cities of Cathuria are cinctured with golden walls, and their pavements are also of gold. In the gardens of these cities are strange orchids, and perfumed lakes whose beds are of coral and amber. At night the streets and the gardens are lit with gay lanthorns fashioned from the three-coloured shell of the tortoise, and here resound the soft notes of the singer and the lutanist. And the houses of the cities of Cathuria are all palaces, each built over a fragrant canal bearing the waters of the sacred Narg. Of marble and porphyry are the houses, and roofed with glittering gold that reflects the rays of the sun and enhances the splendour of the cities as blissful gods view them from the distant peaks. Fairest of all is the palace of the great monarch Dorieb, whom some say to be a demigod and others a god. High is the palace of Dorieb, and many are the turrets of marble upon its walls. In its wide halls may multitudes assemble, and here hang the trophies of the ages. And the roof is of pure gold, set upon tall pillars of ruby and azure, and having such carven figures of gods and heroes that he who looks up to those heights seems to gaze upon the living Olympus. And the floor is of glass, under which flow the cunningly lighted waters of the Narg, gay with gaudy fish not known beyond the bounds of lovely Cathuria."

Thus would I speak to myself of Cathuria, but ever would the bearded man warn me to turn back to the happy shores of Sona-Nyl; for Sona-Nyl is known of men, while none hath ever beheld Cathuria.

And on the thirty-first day that we followed the bird, we beheld the basalt pillars of the West. Shrouded in mist they were, so that no man might peer beyond them or see their summits—which indeed some say reach even to the heavens. And the bearded man again implored me to turn back, but I heeded him not; for from the mists beyond the basalt pillars I fancied there came the notes of singer and lutanist; sweeter than the sweetest songs of Sona-Nyl, and sounding mine own praises; the praises of me, who had voyaged far under the full moon and dwelt in the Land of Fancy.

So to the sound of melody the White Ship sailed into the mist betwixt the basalt pillars of the West. And when the music ceased and the mist lifted, we beheld not the Land of Cathuria, but a swift-rushing resistless sea, over which our helpless barque was borne toward some unknown goal. Soon to our ears came the distant thunder of falling waters, and to our eyes appeared on the far horizon ahead the titanic spray of a monstrous cataract, wherein the oceans of the world drop down to abysmal nothingness. Then did the bearded man say to me with tears on his cheek, "We have rejected the beautiful Land of Sona-Nyl, which we may never behold again. The gods are greater than men, and they have conquered." And I closed my eyes before the crash that I knew would come, shutting out the sight of the celestial bird which flapped its mocking blue wings over the brink of the torrent.

Out of that crash came darkness, and I heard the shrieking of men and of things which were not men. From the East tempestuous winds arose, and chilled me as I crouched on the slab of damp stone which had risen beneath my feet. Then as I heard another crash I opened my eyes and beheld myself upon the platform of that lighthouse from whence I had sailed so many aeons ago. In the darkness below there loomed the vast blurred outlines of a vessel breaking up on the cruel rocks, and as I glanced out over the waste I saw that the light had failed for the first time since my grandfather had assumed its care.

And in the later watches of the night, when I went within the tower, I saw on the wall a calendar which still remained as when I had left it at the hour I sailed away. With the dawn I descended the tower and looked for wreckage upon the rocks, but what I found was only this: a strange dead bird whose hue was as of the azure sky, and a single shattered spar, of a whiteness greater than that of the wave-tips or of the mountain snow.

And thereafter the ocean told me its secrets no more; and though many times since has the moon shone full and high in the heavens, the White Ship from the South came never again.

THE STREET

There be those who say that things and places have souls, and there be those who say they have not; I dare not say, myself, but I will tell of The Street.

Men of strength and honour fashioned that Street; good, valiant men of our blood who had come from the Blessed Isles across the seas. At first it was but a path trodden by bearers of water from the woodland spring to the cluster of houses by the beach. Then, as more men came to the growing cluster of houses and looked about for places to dwell, they built cabins along the north side; cabins of stout oaken logs with masonry on the side toward the forest, for many Indians lurked there with fire-arrows. And in a few years more, men built cabins on the south side of The Street.

Up and down The Street walked grave men in conical hats, who most of the time carried muskets or fowling pieces. And there were also their bonneted wives and sober children. In the evening these men with their wives and children would sit about gigantic hearths and read and speak. Very simple were the things of which they read and spoke, yet things which gave them courage and goodness and helped them by day to subdue the forest and till the fields. And the children would listen, and learn of the laws and deeds of old, and of that dear England which they had never seen, or could not remember.

There was war, and thereafter no more Indians troubled The Street. The men, busy with labour, waxed prosperous and as happy as they knew how to be. And the children grew up comfortably, and more families came from the Mother Land to dwell on The Street. And the children's children, and the newcomers' children, grew up. The town was now a city, and one by one the cabins gave place to houses; simple, beautiful houses of brick and wood, with stone steps and iron railings and fanlights over the doors. No flimsy creations were these houses, for they were made to serve many a generation. Within there were carven mantels and graceful stairs, and sensible, pleasing furniture, china, and silver, brought from the Mother Land.

So The Street drank in the dreams of a young people, and rejoiced as its dwellers became more graceful and happy. Where once had been only strength and honour, taste and learning now abode as well. Books and paintings and music came to the houses, and the young men went to the university which rose above the plain to the north. In the place of conical hats and muskets there were three-cornered hats and small-swords, and lace and snowy periwigs. And there were cobblestones over which clattered many a blooded horse and rumbled many a gilded coach; and brick sidewalks with horse blocks and hitching-posts.

There were in that Street many trees; elms and oaks and maples of dignity; so that in the summer the scene was all soft verdure and twittering bird-song. And behind the houses were walled rose-gardens with hedged paths and sundials, where at evening the moon and stars would shine down bewitchingly while fragrant blossoms glistened with dew.

So The Street dreamed on, past wars, calamities, and changes. Once most of the young men went away, and some never came back. That was when they furled the Old Flag and put up a new Banner of Stripes and Stars. But though men talked of great changes, The Street felt them not; for its folk were still the same, speaking of the old familiar things in the old familiar accents. And the trees still sheltered singing birds, and at evening the moon and stars still looked down upon dewy blossoms in the walled rose-gardens.

In time there were no more swords, three-cornered hats, or periwigs in The Street. How strange seemed the denizens with their walking-sticks, tall beavers, and cropped heads! New sounds came from the distance—first strange puffings and shrieks from the river a mile away, and many years later strange puffings and shrieks and rumblings from other directions. The air was not quite so pure as before, but the spirit of the place had not changed. The blood and soul of the people were as the blood and soul of their ancestors who had fashioned The Street. Nor did the spirit change when they tore open the earth to lay down strange pipes, or when they set up tall posts bearing weird wires. There was so much ancient lore in that Street, that the past could not easily be forgotten.

Then came days of evil, when many who had known The Street of old knew it no more; and many knew it, who had not known it before. And those who came were never as those who went away; for their accents were coarse and strident, and their mien and faces unpleasing. Their thoughts, too, fought with the wise, just spirit of The Street. So The Street pined silently as its houses fell into decay, and its trees died one by one, and its rose-gardens grew rank with weeds and waste. But it felt a stir of pride one day when again marched forth young men, some of whom never came back. These young men were clad in blue.

With the years worse fortune came to The Street. Its trees were all gone now, and its rose-gardens were displaced by the backs of cheap, ugly new buildings on parallel streets. Yet the houses remained, despite the ravages of the years and the storms and worms, for they had been made to serve many a generation. New kinds of faces appeared in The Street; swarthy, sinister faces with furtive eyes and odd features, whose owners spoke unfamiliar words and placed signs in known and unknown characters upon most of the musty houses. Push-carts crowded the gutters. A sordid, undefinable stench settled over the place, and the ancient spirit slept.

Great excitement once came to The Street. War and revolution were raging across the seas; a dynasty had collapsed, and its degenerate subjects were flocking with dubious intent to the Western Land. Many of these took lodgings in the battered houses that had once known the song of birds and the scent of roses. Then the Western Land itself awoke, and joined the Mother Land in her titanic struggle for civilisation. Over the cities once more floated the Old Flag, companioned by the New Flag and by a plainer yet glorious Tri-colour. But not many flags floated over The Street, for therein brooded only fear and hatred and ignorance. Again young men went forth, but not quite as did the young men of those other days. Something was lacking. And the sons of those young men of other days, who did indeed go forth in olive-drab with the true spirit of their ancestors, went from distant places and knew not The Street and its ancient spirit.

Over the seas there was a great victory, and in triumph most of the young men returned. Those who had lacked something lacked it no longer, yet did fear and hatred and ignorance still brood over The Street; for many had stayed behind, and many strangers had come from distant places to the ancient houses. And the young men who had returned dwelt there no longer. Swarthy and sinister were most of the strangers, yet among them one might find a few faces like those who fashioned The Street and moulded its spirit. Like and yet unlike, for there was in the eyes of all a weird, unhealthy glitter as of greed, ambition, vindictiveness, or misguided zeal. Unrest and treason were abroad amongst an evil few who plotted to strike the Western Land its death-blow, that they might mount to power over its ruins; even as assassins had mounted in that unhappy frozen land from whence most of them had come. And the heart of that plotting was in The Street, whose crumbling houses teemed with alien makers of discord and echoed with the plans and speeches of those who yearned for the appointed day of blood, flame, and crime.

Of the various odd assemblages in The Street, the law said much but could prove little. With great diligence did men of hidden badges linger and listen about such places as Petrovitch's Bakery, the squalid Rifkin School of Modern Economics, the Circle Social Club, and the Liberty Cafe. There congregated sinister men in great numbers, yet always was their speech guarded or in a foreign tongue. And still the old houses stood, with their forgotten lore of nobler, departed centuries; of sturdy colonial tenants and dewy rose-gardens in the moonlight. Sometimes a lone poet or traveller would come to view them, and would try to picture them in their vanished glory; yet of such travellers and poets there were not many.

The rumour now spread widely that these houses contained the leaders of a vast band of terrorists, who on a designated day were to launch an orgy of slaughter for the extermination of America and of all the fine old traditions which The Street had loved. Handbills and papers fluttered about filthy gutters; handbills and papers printed in many tongues and in many characters, yet all bearing messages of crime and rebellion. In these writings the people were urged to tear down the laws and virtues that our fathers had exalted; to stamp out the soul of the old America—the soul that was bequeathed through a thousand and a half years of Anglo-Saxon freedom, justice, and moderation. It was said that the swart men who dwelt in The Street and congregated in its rotting edifices were the brains of a hideous revolution; that at their word of command many millions of brainless, besotted beasts would stretch forth their noisome talons from the slums of a thousand cities, burning, slaying, and destroying till the land of our fathers should be no more. All this was said and repeated, and many looked forward in dread to the fourth day of July, about which the strange writings hinted much; yet could nothing be found to place the guilt. None could tell just whose arrest might cut off the damnable plotting at its source. Many times came bands of blue-coated police to search the shaky houses, though at last they ceased to come; for they too had grown tired of law and order, and had abandoned all the city to its fate. Then men in olive-drab came, bearing muskets; till it seemed as if in its sad sleep The Street must have some haunting dreams of those other days, when musket-bearing men in conical hats walked along it from the woodland spring to the cluster of houses by the beach. Yet could no act be performed to check the impending cataclysm, for the swart, sinister men were old in cunning.

So The Street slept uneasily on, till one night there gathered in Petrovitch's Bakery and the Rifkin School of Modern Economics, and the Circle Social Club, and the Liberty Cafe, and in other places as well, vast hordes of men whose eyes were big with horrible triumph and expectation. Over hidden wires strange messages travelled, and much was said of still stranger messages yet to travel; but most of this was not guessed till afterward, when the Western Land was safe from the peril. The men in olive-drab could not tell what was happening, or what they ought to do; for the swart, sinister men were skilled in subtlety and concealment.

And yet the men in olive-drab will always remember that night, and will speak of The Street as they tell of it to their grandchildren; for many of them were sent there toward morning on a mission unlike that which they had expected. It was known that this nest of anarchy was old, and that the houses were tottering from the ravages of the years and the storms and the worms; yet was the happening of that summer night a surprise because of its very queer uniformity. It was, indeed, an exceedingly singular happening; though after all a simple one. For without warning, in one of the small hours beyond midnight, all the ravages of the years and the storms and the worms came to a tremendous climax; and after the crash there was nothing left standing in The Street save two ancient chimneys and part of a stout brick wall. Nor did anything that had been alive come alive from the ruins.

A poet and a traveller, who came with the mighty crowd that sought the scene, tell odd stories. The poet says that all through the hours before dawn he beheld sordid ruins but indistinctly in the glare of the arc-lights; that there loomed above the wreckage another picture wherein he could descry moonlight and fair houses and elms and oaks and maples of dignity. And the traveller declares that instead of the place's wonted stench there lingered a delicate fragrance as of roses in full bloom. But are not the dreams of poets and the tales of travellers notoriously false?

There be those who say that things and places have souls, and there be those who say they have not; I dare not say, myself, but I have told you of The Street.

THE DOOM THAT CAME TO SARNATH

There is in the land of Mnar a vast still lake that is fed by no stream and out of which no stream flows. Ten thousand years ago there stood by its shore the mighty city of Sarnath, but Sarnath stands there no more.

It is told that in the immemorial years when the world was young, before ever the men of Sarnath came to the land of Mnar, another city stood beside the lake; the grey stone city of Ib, which was old as the lake itself, and peopled with beings not pleasing to behold. Very odd and ugly were these beings, as indeed are most beings of a world yet inchoate and rudely fashioned. It is written on the brick cylinders of Kadatheron that the beings of Ib were in hue as green as the lake and the mists that rise above it; that they had bulging eyes, pouting, flabby lips, and curious ears, and were without voice. It is also written that they descended one night from the moon in a mist; they and the vast still lake and the grey stone city of Ib. However this may be, it is certain that they worshipped a sea-green stone idol chiselled in the likeness of Bokrug, the great water-lizard; before which they danced horribly when the moon was gibbous. And it is written in a papyrus of Ilarnek, that they one day discovered fire, and thereafter kindled flames on many ceremonial occasions. But not much is written of these beings, because they lived in very ancient times, and man is young, and knows but little of the very ancient living things.

After many aeons men came to the land of Mnar; dark shepherd folk with their fleecy flocks, who built Thraa, Ilarnek, and Kadatheron on the winding river Ai. And certain tribes, more hardy then the rest, pushed on to the border of the lake and built Sarnath at a spot where precious metals were found in the earth.

Not far from the grey city of Ib did the wandering tribes lay the first stones of Sarnath, and at the beings of Ib they marvelled greatly. But with their marvelling was mixed hate, for they thought it not meet that beings of such aspect should walk about the world of men at dusk. Nor did they like the strange sculptures upon the grey monoliths of Ib, for those sculptures were terrible with great antiquity. Why the beings and the sculptures lingered so late in the world, even until the coming of men, none can tell; unless it was because the land of Mnar is very still, and remote from most other lands both of waking and of dream.

As the men of Sarnath beheld more of the beings of Ib their hate grew, and it was not less because they found the beings weak, and soft as jelly to the touch of stones and spears and arrows. So one day the young warriors, the slingers and the spearmen and the bowmen, marched against Ib and slew all the inhabitants thereof, pushing the queer bodies into the lake with long spears, because they did not wish to touch them. And because they did not like the grey sculptured monoliths of Ib they cast these also into the lake; wondering from the greatness of the labour how ever the stones were brought from afar, as they must have been, since there is naught like them in all the land of Mnar or in the lands adjacent.

Thus of the very ancient city of Ib was nothing spared save the sea-green stone idol chiselled in the likeness of Bokrug, the water-lizard. This the young warriors took back with them to Sarnath as a symbol of conquest over the old gods and beings of Ib, and a sign of leadership in Mnar. But on the night after it was set up in the temple a terrible thing must have happened, for weird lights were seen over the lake, and in the morning the people found the idol gone, and the high-priest Taran-Ish lying dead, as from some fear unspeakable. And before he had died, Taran-Ish had scrawled upon the altar of chrysolite with coarse shaky strokes the sign of DOOM.

After Taran-Ish there were many high-priests in Sarnath, but never was the sea-green stone idol found. And many centuries came and went, wherein Sarnath prospered exceedingly, so that only priests and old women remembered what Taran-Ish had scrawled upon the altar of chrysolite. Betwixt Sarnath and the city of Ilarnek arose a caravan route, and the precious metals from the earth were exchanged for other metals and rare cloths and jewels and books and tools for artificers and all things of luxury that are known to the people who dwell along the winding river Ai and beyond. So Sarnath waxed mighty and learned and beautiful, and sent forth conquering armies to subdue the neighbouring cities; and in time there sate upon a throne in Sarnath the kings of all the land of Mnar and of many lands adjacent.

The wonder of the world and the pride of all mankind was Sarnath the magnificent. Of polished desert-quarried marble were its walls, in height three hundred cubits and in breadth seventy-five, so that chariots might pass each other as men drave them along the top. For full five hundred stadia did they run, being open only on the side toward the lake; where a green stone sea-wall kept back the waves that rose oddly once a year at the festival of the destroying of Ib. In Sarnath were fifty streets from the lake to the gates of the caravans, and fifty more intersecting them. With onyx were they paved, save those whereon the horses and camels and elephants trod, which were paved with granite. And the gates of Sarnath were as many as the landward ends of the streets, each of bronze, and flanked by the figures of lions and elephants carven from some stone no longer known among men. The houses of Sarnath were of glazed brick and chalcedony, each having its walled garden and crystal lakelet. With strange art were they builded, for no other city had houses like them; and travellers from Thraa and Ilarnek and Kadatheron marvelled at the shining domes wherewith they were surmounted.

But more marvellous still were the palaces and the temples, and the gardens made by Zokkar the olden king. There were many palaces, the least of which was mightier than any in Thraa or Ilarnek or Kadatheron. So high were they that one within might sometimes fancy himself beneath only the sky; yet when lighted with torches dipt in the oil of Dothur their walls shewed vast paintings of kings and armies, of a splendour at once inspiring and stupefying to the beholder. Many were the pillars of the palaces, all of tinted marble, and carven into designs of surpassing beauty. And in most of the palaces the floors were mosaics of beryl and lapis-lazuli and sardonyx and carbuncle and other choice materials, so disposed that the beholder might fancy himself walking over beds of the rarest flowers. And there were likewise fountains, which cast scented waters about in pleasing jets arranged with cunning art. Outshining all others was the palace of the kings of Mnar and of the lands adjacent. On a pair of golden crouching lions rested the throne, many steps above the gleaming floor. And it was wrought of one piece of ivory, though no man lives who knows whence so vast a piece could have come. In that palace were also many galleries, and many amphitheatres where lions and men and elephants battled at the pleasure of the kings.

Sometimes the amphitheatres were flooded with water conveyed from the lake in mighty aqueducts, and then were enacted stirring sea-fights, or combats betwixt swimmers and deadly marine things.

Lofty and amazing were the seventeen tower-like temples of Sarnath, fashioned of a bright multi-coloured stone not known elsewhere. A full thousand cubits high stood the greatest among them, wherein the high-priests dwelt with a magnificence scarce less than that of the kings. On the ground were halls as vast and splendid as those of the palaces; where gathered throngs in worship of Zo-Kalar and Tamash and Lobon, the chief gods of Sarnath, whose incense-enveloped shrines were as the thrones of monarchs. Not like the eikons of other gods were those of Zo-Kalar and Tamash and Lobon, for so close to life were they that one might swear the graceful bearded gods themselves sate on the ivory thrones. And up unending steps of shining zircon was the tower-chamber, wherefrom the high-priests looked out over the city and the plains and the lake by day; and at the cryptic moon and the significant stars and planets, and their reflections in the lake, by night. Here was done the very secret and ancient rite in detestation of Bokrug, the water-lizard, and here rested the altar of chrysolite which bore the DOOM-scrawl of Taran-Ish.

Wonderful likewise were the gardens made by Zokkar the olden king. In the centre of Sarnath they lay, covering a great space and encircled by a high wall. And they were surmounted by a mighty dome of glass, through which shone the sun and moon and stars and planets when it was clear, and from which were hung fulgent images of the sun and moon and stars and planets when it was not clear. In summer the gardens were cooled with fresh odorous breezes skilfully wafted by fans, and in winter they were heated with concealed fires, so that in those gardens it was always spring. There ran little streams over bright pebbles, dividing meads of green and gardens of many hues, and spanned by a multitude of bridges. Many were the waterfalls in their courses, and many were the lilied lakelets into which they expanded. Over the streams and lakelets rode white swans, whilst the music of rare birds chimed with the melody of the waters. In ordered terraces rose the green banks, adorned here and there with bowers of vines and sweet blossoms, and seats and benches of marble and porphyry. And there were many small shrines and temples where one might rest or pray to small gods.

Each year there was celebrated in Sarnath the feast of the destroying of Ib, at which time wine, song, dancing, and merriment of every kind abounded. Great honours were then paid to the shades of those who had annihilated the odd ancient beings, and the memory of those beings and of their elder gods was derided by dancers and lutanists crowned with roses from the gardens of Zokkar. And the kings would look out over the lake and curse the bones of the dead that lay beneath it. At first the high-priests liked not these festivals, for there had descended amongst them queer tales of how the sea-green eikon of Bokrug had vanished, and how Taran-Ish had died from fear and left a warning. And they said that from their high tower they sometimes saw lights beneath the waters of the lake. But as many years passed without calamity even the priests laughed and cursed and joined in the orgies of the feasters. Indeed, had they not themselves, in their high tower, often performed the very secret and ancient rite in detestation of Bokrug, the water-lizard? And a thousand years of riches and delight passed over Sarnath, wonder of the world and pride of all mankind.

Gorgeous beyond thought was the feast of the thousandth year of the destroying of Ib. For a decade had it been talked of in the land of Mnar, and as it drew nigh there came to Sarnath on horses and camels and elephants men from Thraa, Ilarnek, and Kadatheron, and all the cities of Mnar and the lands beyond. Before the marble walls on the appointed night were pitched the pavilions of princes and the tents of travellers, and all the shore resounded with the song of happy revellers. Within his banquet-hall reclined Nargis-Hei, the king, drunken with ancient wine from the vaults of conquered Pnoth, and surrounded by feasting nobles and hurrying slaves. There were eaten many strange delicacies at that feast; peacocks from the isles of Nariel in the Middle Ocean, young goats from the distant hills of Implan, heels of camels from the Bnazic desert, nuts and spices from Cydathrian groves, and pearls from wave-washed Mtal dissolved in the vinegar of Thraa. Of sauces there were an untold number, prepared by the subtlest cooks in all Mnar, and suited to the palate of every feaster. But most prized of all the viands were the great fishes from the lake, each of vast size, and served up on golden platters set with rubies and diamonds.

Whilst the king and his nobles feasted within the palace, and viewed the crowning dish as it awaited them on golden platters, others feasted elsewhere. In the tower of the great temple the priests held revels, and in pavilions without the walls the princes of neighbouring lands made merry. And it was the high-priest Gnai-Kah who first saw the shadows that descended from the gibbous moon into the lake, and the damnable green mists that arose from the lake to meet the moon and to shroud in a sinister haze the towers and the domes of fated Sarnath. Thereafter those in the towers and without the walls beheld strange lights on the water, and saw that the grey rock Akurion, which was wont to rear high above it near the shore, was almost submerged. And fear grew vaguely yet swiftly, so that the princes of Ilarnek and of far Rokol took down and folded their tents and pavilions and departed for the river Ai, though they scarce knew the reason for their departing.

Then, close to the hour of midnight, all the bronze gates of Sarnath burst open and emptied forth a frenzied throng that blackened the plain, so that all the visiting princes and travellers fled away in fright. For on the faces of this throng was writ a madness born of horror unendurable, and on their tongues were words so terrible that no hearer paused for proof. Men whose eyes were wild with fear shrieked aloud of the sight within the king's banquet-hall, where through the windows were seen no longer the forms of Nargis-Hei and his nobles and slaves, but a horde of indescribable green voiceless things with bulging eyes, pouting, flabby lips, and curious ears; things which danced horribly, bearing in their paws golden platters set with rubies and diamonds and containing uncouth flames. And the princes and travellers, as they fled from the doomed city of Sarnath on horses and camels and elephants, looked again upon the mist-begetting lake and saw that the grey rock Akurion was quite submerged.

Through all the land of Mnar and the lands adjacent spread the tales of those who had fled from Sarnath, and caravans sought that accursed city and its precious metals no more. It was long ere any traveller went thither, and even then only the brave and adventurous young men of distant Falona dared make the journey; adventurous young men of yellow hair and blue eyes, who are no kin to the men of Mnar. These men indeed went to the lake to view Sarnath; but though they found the vast still lake itself, and the grey rock Akurion which rears high above it near the shore, they beheld not the wonder of the world and pride of all mankind. Where once had risen walls of three hundred cubits and towers yet higher, now stretched only the marshy shore, and where once had dwelt fifty millions of men now crawled only the detestable green water-lizard. Not even the mines of precious metal remained, for DOOM had come to Sarnath.

But half buried in the rushes was spied a curious green idol of stone; an exceedingly ancient idol coated with seaweed and chiselled in the likeness of Bokrug, the great water-lizard. That idol, enshrined in the high temple at Ilarnek, was subsequently worshipped beneath the gibbous moon throughout the land of Mnar.

THE STATEMENT OF RANDOLPH CARTER

I repeat to you, gentlemen, that your inquisition is fruitless. Detain me here for ever if you will; confine or execute me if you must have a victim to propitiate the illusion you call justice; but I can say no more than I have said already. Everything that I can remember, I have told with perfect candour. Nothing has been distorted or concealed, and if anything remains vague, it is only because of the dark cloud which has come over my mind—that cloud and the nebulous nature of the horrors which brought it upon me.

Again I say, I do not know what has become of Harley Warren; though I think—almost hope—that he is in peaceful oblivion, if there be anywhere so blessed a thing. It is true that I have for five years been his closest friend, and a partial sharer of his terrible researches into the unknown. I will not deny, though my memory is uncertain and indistinct, that this witness of yours may have seen us together as he says, on the Gainesville pike, walking toward Big Cypress Swamp, at half past eleven on that awful night. That we bore electric lanterns, spades, and a curious coil of wire with attached instruments, I will even affirm; for these things all played a part in the single hideous scene which remains burned into my shaken recollection. But of what followed, and of the reason I was found alone and dazed on the edge of the swamp next morning, I must insist that I know nothing save what

I have told you over and over again. You say to me that there is nothing in the swamp or near it which could form the setting of that frightful episode. I reply that I know nothing beyond what I saw. Vision or nightmare it may have been—vision or nightmare I fervently hope it was—yet it is all that my mind retains of what took place in those shocking hours after we left the sight of men. And why Harley Warren did not return, he or his shade—or some nameless *thing* I cannot describe—alone can tell.

As I have said before, the weird studies of Harley Warren were well known to me, and to some extent shared by me. Of his vast collection of strange, rare books on forbidden subjects I have read all that are written in the languages of which I am master; but these are few as compared with those in languages I cannot understand. Most, I believe, are in Arabic; and the fiend-inspired book which brought on the end—the book which he carried in his pocket out of the world—was written in characters whose like I never saw elsewhere. Warren would never tell me just what was in that book. As to the nature of our studies—must I say again that I no longer retain full comprehension? It seems to me rather merciful that I do not, for they were terrible studies, which I pursued more through reluctant fascination than through actual inclination. Warren always dominated me, and sometimes I feared him. I remember how I shuddered at his facial expression on the night before the awful happening, when he talked so incessantly of his theory, *why certain corpses never decay, but rest firm and fat in their tombs for a thousand years.* But I do not fear him now, for I suspect that he has known horrors beyond my ken. Now I fear *for* him.

Once more I say that I have no clear idea of our object on that night. Certainly, it had much to do with something in the book which Warren carried with him—that ancient book in undecipherable characters which had come to him from India a month before—but I swear I do not know what it was that we expected to find. Your witness says he saw us at half past eleven on the Gainesville pike, headed for Big Cypress Swamp. This is probably true, but I have no distinct memory of it. The picture seared into my soul is of one scene only, and the hour must have been long after midnight; for a waning crescent moon was high in the vaporous heavens.

The place was an ancient cemetery; so ancient that I trembled at the manifold signs of immemorial years. It was in a deep, damp hollow, overgrown with rank grass, moss, and curious creeping weeds, and filled with a vague stench which my idle fancy associated absurdly with rotting stone. On every hand were the signs of neglect and decrepitude, and I seemed haunted by the notion that Warren and I were the first living creatures to invade a lethal silence of centuries. Over the valley's rim a wan, waning crescent moon peered through the noisome vapours that seemed to emanate from unheard-of catacombs, and by its feeble, wavering beams I could distinguish a repellent array of antique slabs, urns, cenotaphs, and mausolean facades; all crumbling, moss-grown, and moisture-stained, and partly concealed by the gross luxuriance of the unhealthy vegetation. My first vivid impression of my own presence in this terrible necropolis concerns the act of pausing with Warren before a certain half-obliterated sepulchre, and of throwing down some burdens which we seemed to have been carrying. I now observed that I had with me an electric lantern and two spades, whilst my companion was supplied with a similar lantern and a portable telephone outfit. No word was uttered, for the spot and the task seemed known to us; and without delay we seized our spades and commenced to clear away the grass, weeds, and drifted earth from the flat, archaic mortuary. After uncovering the entire surface, which consisted of three immense granite slabs, we stepped back some distance to survey the charnel scene; and Warren appeared to make some mental calculations. Then he returned to the sepulchre, and using his spade as a lever, sought to pry up the slab lying nearest to a stony ruin which may have been a monument in its day. He did not succeed, and motioned to me to come to his assistance. Finally our combined strength loosened the stone, which we raised and tipped to one side.

The removal of the slab revealed a black aperture, from which rushed an effluence of miasmal gases so nauseous that we started back in horror. After an interval, however, we approached the pit again, and found the exhalations less unbearable. Our lanterns disclosed the top of a flight of stone steps, dripping with some detestable ichor of the inner earth, and bordered by moist walls encrusted with nitre. And now for the first time my memory records verbal discourse, Warren addressing me at length in his mellow tenor voice; a voice singularly unperturbed by our awesome surroundings.

"I'm sorry to have to ask you to stay on the surface," he said, "but it would be a crime to let anyone with your frail nerves go down there. You can't imagine, even from what you have read and from what I've told you, the things I shall have to see and do. It's fiendish work, Carter, and I doubt if any man without ironclad sensibilities could ever see it through and come up alive and sane. I don't wish to offend you, and heaven knows I'd be glad enough to have you with me; but the responsibility is in a certain sense mine, and I couldn't drag a bundle of nerves like you down to probable death or madness. I tell you, you can't imagine what the thing is really like! But I promise to keep you informed over the telephone of every move—you see I've enough wire here to reach to the centre of the earth and back!"

I can still hear, in memory, those coolly spoken words; and I can still remember my remonstrances. I seemed desperately anxious to accompany my friend into those sepulchral depths, yet he proved inflexibly obdurate. At one time he threatened to abandon the expedition if I remained insistent; a threat which proved effective, since he alone held the key to the *thing*. All this I can still remember, though I no longer know what manner of *thing* we sought. After he had secured my reluctant acquiescence in his design, Warren picked up the reel of wire and adjusted the instruments. At his nod I took one of the latter and seated myself upon an aged, discoloured gravestone close by the newly uncovered aperture. Then he shook my hand, shouldered the coil of wire, and disappeared within that indescribable ossuary. For a moment I kept sight of the glow of his lantern, and heard the rustle of the wire as he laid it down after him; but the glow soon disappeared abruptly, as if a turn in the stone staircase had been encountered, and the sound died away almost as quickly. I was alone, yet bound to the unknown depths by those magic strands whose insulated surface lay green beneath the struggling beams of that waning crescent moon.

In the lone silence of that hoary and deserted city of the dead, my mind conceived the most ghastly phantasies and illusions; and the grotesque shrines and monoliths seemed to assume a hideous personality—a half-sentience. Amorphous shadows seemed to lurk in the darker recesses of the weed-choked hollow and to flit as in some blasphemous ceremonial procession past the portals of the mouldering tombs in the hillside; shadows which could not have been cast by that pallid, peering crescent moon. I constantly consulted my watch by the light of my electric lantern, and listened with feverish anxiety at the receiver of the telephone; but for more than a quarter of an hour heard nothing. Then a faint clicking came from the instrument, and I called down to my friend in a tense voice. Apprehensive as I was, I was nevertheless unprepared for the words which came up from that uncanny vault in accents more alarmed and quivering than any I had heard before from Harley Warren. He who had so calmly left me a little while previously, now called from below in a shaky whisper more portentous than the loudest shriek:

"*God! If you could see what I am seeing!*"

I could not answer. Speechless, I could only wait. Then came the frenzied tones again:

"*Carter, it's terrible—monstrous—unbelievable!*"

This time my voice did not fail me, and I poured into the transmitter a flood of excited questions. Terrified, I continued to repeat, "Warren, what is it? What is it?"

Once more came the voice of my friend, still hoarse with fear, and now apparently tinged with despair:

"*I can't tell you, Carter! It's too utterly beyond thought—I dare not tell you—no man could know it and live—Great God! I never dreamed of THIS!*" Stillness again, save for my now incoherent torrent of shuddering inquiry. Then the voice of Warren in a pitch of wilder consternation:

"*Carter! for the love of God, put back the slab and get out of this if you can! Quick!—leave everything else and make for the outside—it's your only chance! Do as I say, and don't ask me to explain!*"

I heard, yet was able only to repeat my frantic questions. Around me were the tombs and the darkness and the shadows; below me, some peril beyond the radius of the human imagination. But my friend was in greater danger than I, and through my fear I felt a vague resentment that he should deem me capable of deserting him under such circumstances. More clicking, and after a pause a piteous cry from Warren:

"*Beat it! For God's sake, put back the slab and beat it, Carter!*"

Something in the boyish slang of my evidently stricken companion unleashed my faculties. I formed and shouted a resolution, "Warren, brace up! I'm coming down!" But at this offer the tone of my auditor changed to a scream of utter despair:

"*Don't! You can't understand! It's too late—and my own fault. Put back the slab and run—there's nothing else you or anyone can do now!*" The tone changed again, this time acquiring a softer quality, as of hopeless resignation. Yet it remained tense through anxiety for me.

"*Quick—before it's too late!*" I tried not to heed him; tried to break through the paralysis which held me, and to fulfil my vow to rush down to his aid. But his next whisper found me still held inert in the chains of stark horror.

"*Carter—hurry! It's no use—you must go—better one than two—the slab—*" A pause, more clicking, then the faint voice of Warren:

"*Nearly over now—don't make it harder—cover up those damned steps and run for your life—you're losing time— So long, Carter—won't see you again.*" Here Warren's whisper swelled into a cry; a cry that gradually rose to a shriek fraught with all the horror of the ages—

"*Curse these hellish things—legions—* My God! *Beat it! Beat it! Beat it!*"

After that was silence. I know not how many interminable aeons I sat stupefied; whispering, muttering, calling, screaming into that telephone. Over and over again through those aeons I whispered and muttered, called, shouted, and screamed, "Warren! Warren! Answer me—are you there?"

And then there came to me the crowning horror of all—the unbelievable, unthinkable, almost unmentionable thing. I have said that aeons seemed to elapse after Warren shrieked forth his last despairing warning, and that only my own cries now broke the hideous silence. But after a while there was a further clicking in the receiver, and I strained my ears to listen. Again I called down, "Warren, are you there?", and in answer heard the *thing* which has brought this cloud over my mind. I do not try, gentlemen, to account for that *thing*—that voice—nor can I venture to describe it in detail, since the first words took away my consciousness and created a mental blank which reaches to the time of my awakening in the hospital. Shall I say that the voice was deep; hollow; gelatinous; remote; unearthly; inhuman; disembodied? What shall I say? It was the end of my experience, and is the end of my story. I heard it, and knew no more. Heard it as I sat petrified in that unknown cemetery in the hollow, amidst the crumbling stones and the falling tombs, the rank vegetation and the miasmal vapours. Heard it well up from the innermost depths of that damnable open sepulchre as I watched amorphous, necrophagous shadows dance beneath an accursed waning moon. And this is what it said:

"*YOU FOOL, WARREN IS DEAD!*"

THE TERRIBLE OLD MAN

It was the design of Angelo Ricci and Joe Czanek and Manuel Silva to call on the Terrible Old Man. This old man dwells all alone in a very ancient house in Water Street near the sea, and is reputed to be both exceedingly rich and exceedingly feeble; which forms a situation very attractive to men of the profession of Messrs. Ricci, Czanek, and Silva, for that profession was nothing less dignified than robbery.

The inhabitants of Kingsport say and think many things about the Terrible Old Man which generally keep him safe from the attentions of gentlemen like Mr. Ricci and his colleagues, despite the almost certain fact that he hides a fortune of indefinite magnitude somewhere about his musty and venerable abode. He is, in truth, a very strange person, believed to have been a captain of East India clipper ships in his day; so old that no one can remember when he was young, and so taciturn that few know his real name. Among the gnarled trees in the front yard of his aged and neglected place he maintains a strange collection of large stones, oddly grouped and painted so that they resemble the idols in some obscure Eastern temple. This collection frightens away most of the small boys who love to taunt the Terrible Old Man about his long white hair and beard, or to break the small-paned windows of his dwelling with wicked missiles; but there are other things which frighten the older and more curious folk who sometimes steal up to the house to peer in through the dusty panes. These folk say that on a table in a bare room on the ground floor are many peculiar bottles, in each a small piece of lead suspended pendulum-wise from a string. And they say that the Terrible Old Man talks to these bottles, addressing them by such names as Jack, Scar-Face, Long Tom, Spanish Joe, Peters, and Mate Ellis, and that whenever he speaks to a bottle the little lead pendulum within makes certain definite vibrations as if in answer. Those who have watched the tall, lean, Terrible Old Man in these peculiar conversations do not watch him again. But Angelo Ricci and Joe Czanek and Manuel Silva were not of Kingsport blood; they were of that new and heterogeneous alien stock which lies outside the charmed circle of New-England life and traditions, and they saw in the Terrible Old Man merely a tottering, almost helpless greybeard, who could not walk without the aid of his knotted cane, and whose thin, weak hands shook pitifully. They were really quite sorry in their way for the lonely, unpopular old fellow, whom everybody shunned, and at whom all the dogs barked singularly. But business is business, and to a robber whose soul is in his profession, there is a lure and a challenge about a very old and very feeble man who has no account at the bank, and who pays for his few necessities at the village store with Spanish gold and silver minted two centuries ago.

Messrs. Ricci, Czanek, and Silva selected the night of April 11th for their call. Mr. Ricci and Mr. Silva were to interview the poor old gentleman, whilst Mr. Czanek waited for them and their presumable metallic burden with a covered motor-car in Ship Street, by the gate in the tall rear wall of their host's grounds. Desire to avoid needless explanations in case of unexpected police intrusions prompted these plans for a quiet and unostentatious departure.

As prearranged, the three adventurers started out separately in order to prevent any evil-minded suspicions afterwards. Messrs. Ricci and Silva met in Water Street by the old man's front gate, and although they did not like the way the moon shone down upon the painted stones through the budding branches of the gnarled trees, they had more important things to think about than mere idle superstition. They feared it might be unpleasant work making the Terrible Old Man loquacious concerning his hoarded gold and silver, for aged sea-captains are notably stubborn and perverse. Still, he was very old and very feeble, and there were two visitors. Messrs. Ricci and Silva were experienced in the art of making unwilling persons voluble, and the screams of a weak and exceptionally venerable man can be easily muffled. So they moved up to the one lighted window and heard the Terrible Old Man talking childishly to his bottles with pendulums. Then they donned masks and knocked politely at the weather-stained oaken door.

Waiting seemed very long to Mr. Czanek as he fidgeted restlessly in the covered motor-car by the Terrible Old Man's back gate in Ship Street. He was more than ordinarily tender-hearted, and he did not like the hideous screams he had heard in the ancient house just after the hour appointed for the deed. Had he not told his colleagues to be as gentle as possible with the pathetic old sea-captain? Very nervously he watched that narrow oaken gate in the high and ivy-clad stone wall. Frequently he consulted his watch, and wondered at the delay. Had the old man died before revealing where his treasure was hidden, and had a thorough search become necessary? Mr. Czanek did not like to wait so long in the dark in such a place. Then he sensed a soft tread or tapping on the walk inside the gate, heard a gentle fumbling at the rusty latch, and saw the narrow, heavy door swing inward. And in the pallid glow of the single dim street-lamp he strained his eyes to see what his colleagues had brought out of that sinister house which loomed so close behind. But when he looked, he did not see what he had expected; for his colleagues were not there at all, but only the Terrible Old Man leaning quietly on his knotted cane and smiling hideously. Mr. Czanek had never before noticed the colour of that man's eyes; now he saw that they were yellow.

Little things make considerable excitement in little towns, which is the reason that Kingsport people talked all that spring and summer about the three unidentifiable bodies, horribly slashed as with many cutlasses, and horribly mangled as by the tread of many cruel boot-heels, which the tide washed in. And some people even spoke of things as trivial as the deserted motor-car found in Ship Street, or certain especially inhuman cries, probably of a stray animal or migratory bird, heard in the night by wakeful citizens. But in this idle village gossip the Terrible Old Man took no interest at all. He was by nature reserved, and when one is aged and feeble one's reserve is doubly strong. Besides, so ancient a sea-captain must have witnessed scores of things much more stirring in the far-off days of his unremembered youth.

THE TREE

"Fata viam invenient."

On a verdant slope of Mount Maenalus, in Arcadia, there stands an olive grove about the ruins of a villa. Close by is a tomb, once beautiful with the sublimest sculptures, but now fallen into as great decay as the house. At one end of that tomb, its curious roots displacing the time-stained blocks of Pentelic marble, grows an unnaturally large olive tree of oddly repellent shape; so like to some grotesque man, or death-distorted body of a man, that the country folk fear to pass it at night when the moon shines faintly through the crooked boughs. Mount Maenalus is a chosen haunt of dreaded Pan, whose queer companions are many, and simple swains believe that the tree must have some hideous kinship to these weird Panisci; but an old bee-keeper who lives in a neighbouring cottage told me a different story.

Many years ago, when the hillside villa was new and resplendent, there dwelt within it the two sculptors Kalos and Musides. From Lydia to Neapolis the beauty of their work was praised, and none dared say that the one excelled the other in skill. The Hermes of Kalos stood in a marble shrine in Corinth, and the Pallas of Musides surmounted a pillar in Athens, near the Parthenon. All men paid homage to Kalos and Musides, and marvelled that no shadow of artistic jealousy cooled the warmth of their brotherly friendship.

But though Kalos and Musides dwelt in unbroken harmony, their natures were not alike. Whilst Musides revelled by night amidst the urban gaieties of Tegea, Kalos would remain at home; stealing away from the sight of his slaves into the cool recesses of the olive grove. There he would meditate upon the visions that filled his mind, and there devise the forms of beauty which later became immortal in breathing marble. Idle folk, indeed, said that Kalos conversed with spirits of the grove, and that his statues were but images of the fauns and dryads he met there—for he patterned his work after no living model.

So famous were Kalos and Musides, that none wondered when the Tyrant of Syracuse sent to them deputies to speak of the costly statue of Tyché which he had planned for his city. Of great size and cunning workmanship must the statue be, for it was to form a wonder of nations and a goal of travellers. Exalted beyond thought would be he whose work should gain acceptance, and for this honour Kalos and Musides were invited to compete. Their brotherly love was well known, and the crafty Tyrant surmised that each, instead of concealing his work from the other, would offer aid and advice; this charity producing two images of unheard-of beauty, the lovelier of which would eclipse even the dreams of poets.

With joy the sculptors hailed the Tyrant's offer, so that in the days that followed their slaves heard the ceaseless blows of chisels. Not from each other did Kalos and Musides conceal their work, but the sight was for them alone. Saving theirs, no eyes beheld the two divine figures released by skilful blows from the rough blocks that had imprisoned them since the world began.

At night, as of yore, Musides sought the banquet halls of Tegea whilst Kalos wandered alone in the olive grove. But as time passed, men observed a want of gaiety in the once sparkling Musides. It was strange, they said amongst themselves, that depression should thus seize one with so great a chance to win art's loftiest reward. Many months passed, yet in the sour face of Musides came nothing of the sharp expectancy which the situation should arouse.

Then one day Musides spoke of the illness of Kalos, after which none marvelled again at his sadness, since the sculptors' attachment was known to be deep and sacred. Subsequently many went to visit Kalos, and indeed noticed the pallor of his face; but there was about him a happy serenity which made his glance more magical than the glance of Musides—who was clearly distracted with anxiety, and who pushed aside all the slaves in his eagerness to feed and wait upon his friend with his own hands. Hidden behind heavy curtains stood the two unfinished figures of Tyché, little touched of late by the sick man and his faithful attendant.

As Kalos grew inexplicably weaker and weaker despite the ministrations of puzzled physicians and of his assiduous friend, he desired to be carried often to the grove which he so loved. There he would ask to be left alone, as if wishing to speak with unseen things. Musides ever granted his requests, though his eyes filled with visible tears at the thought that Kalos should care more for the fauns and the dryads than for him. At last the end drew near, and Kalos discoursed of things beyond this life. Musides, weeping, promised him a sepulchre more lovely than the tomb of Mausolus; but Kalos bade him speak no more of marble glories. Only one wish now haunted the mind of the dying man; that twigs from certain olive trees in the grove be buried by his resting-place—close to his head. And one night, sitting alone in the darkness of his olive grove, Kalos died.

Beautiful beyond words was the marble sepulchre which stricken Musides carved for his beloved friend. None but Kalos himself could have fashioned such bas-reliefs, wherein were displayed all the splendours of Elysium. Nor did Musides fail to bury close to Kalos' head the olive twigs from the grove.

As the first violence of Musides' grief gave place to resignation, he laboured with diligence upon his figure of Tyché. All honour was now his, since the Tyrant of Syracuse would have the work of none save him or Kalos. His task proved a vent for his emotion, and he toiled more steadily each day, shunning the gaieties he once had relished. Meanwhile his evenings were spent beside the tomb of his friend, where a young olive tree had sprung up near the sleeper's head. So swift was the growth of this tree, and so strange was its form, that all who beheld it exclaimed in surprise; and Musides seemed at once fascinated and repelled.

Three years after the death of Kalos, Musides despatched a messenger to the Tyrant, and it was whispered in the agora at Tegea that the mighty statue was finished. By this time the tree by the tomb had attained amazing proportions, exceeding all other trees of its kind, and sending out a singularly heavy branch above the great apartment in which Musides laboured. As many visitors came to view the prodigious tree, as to admire the art of the sculptor, so that Musides was seldom alone. But he did not mind his multitude of guests; indeed, he seemed to dread being alone now that his absorbing work was done. The bleak mountain wind, sighing through the olive grove and the tomb-tree, had an uncanny way of forming vaguely articulate sounds.

The sky was dark on the evening that the Tyrant's emissaries came to Tegea. It was definitely known that they had come to bear away the great image of Tyché and bring eternal honour to

Musides, so their reception by the proxenoi was of great warmth. As the night wore on, a violent storm of wind broke over the crest of Maenalus, and the men from far Syracuse were glad that they rested snugly in the town. They talked of their illustrious Tyrant, and of the splendour of his capital; and exulted in the glory of the statue which Musides had wrought for him. And then the men of Tegea spoke of the goodness of Musides, and of his heavy grief for his friend; and how not even the coming laurels of art could console him in the absence of Kalos, who might have worn those laurels instead. Of the tree which grew by the tomb, near the head of Kalos, they also spoke. The wind shrieked more horribly, and both the Syracusans and the Arcadians prayed to Aiolos.

In the sunshine of the morning the proxenoi led the Tyrant's messengers up the slope to the abode of the sculptor, but the night-wind had done strange things. Slaves' cries ascended from a scene of desolation, and no more amidst the olive grove rose the gleaming colonnades of that vast hall wherein Musides had dreamed and toiled. Lone and shaken mourned the humbler courts and the lower walls, for upon the sumptuous greater peristyle had fallen squarely the heavy overhanging bough of the strange new tree, reducing the stately poem in marble with odd completeness to a mound of unsightly ruins.

Strangers and Tegeans stood aghast, looking from the wreckage to the great, sinister tree whose aspect was so weirdly human and whose roots reached so queerly into the sculptured sepulchre of Kalos. And their fear and dismay increased when they searched the fallen apartment; for of the gentle Musides, and of the marvellously wrought image of Tyché, no trace could be discovered. Amidst such stupendous ruin only chaos dwelt, and the representatives of two cities left disappointed; Syracusans that they had no statue to bear home, Tegeans that they had no artist to crown. However, the Syracusans obtained after a while a very splendid statue in Athens, and the Tegeans consoled themselves by erecting in the agora a marble temple commemorating the gifts, virtues, and brotherly piety of Musides.

But the olive grove still stands, as does the tree growing out of the tomb of Kalos, and the old bee-keeper told me that sometimes the boughs whisper to one another in the night-wind, saying over and over again, "Οἶδα! Οἶδα!—*I know! I know!*"

THE CATS OF ULTHAR

It is said that in Ulthar, which lies beyond the river Skai, no man may kill a cat; and this I can verily believe as I gaze upon him who sitteth purring before the fire. For the cat is cryptic, and close to strange things which men cannot see. He is the soul of antique Ægyptus, and bearer of tales from forgotten cities in Meroë and Ophir. He is the kin of the jungle's lords, and heir to the secrets of hoary and sinister Africa. The Sphinx is his cousin, and he speaks her language; but he is more ancient than the Sphinx, and remembers that which she hath forgotten.

In Ulthar, before ever the burgesses forbade the killing of cats, there dwelt an old cotter and his wife who delighted to trap and slay the cats of their neighbours. Why they did this I know not; save that many hate the voice of the cat in the night, and take it ill that cats should run stealthily about yards and gardens at twilight. But whatever the reason, this old man and woman took pleasure in trapping and slaying every cat which came near to their hovel; and from some of the sounds heard after dark, many villagers fancied that the manner of slaying was exceedingly peculiar. But the villagers did not discuss such things with the old man and his wife; because of the habitual expression on the withered faces of the two, and because their cottage was so small and so darkly hidden under spreading oaks at the back of a neglected yard. In truth, much as the owners of cats hated these odd folk, they feared them more; and instead of berating them as brutal assassins, merely took care that no cherished pet or mouser should stray toward the remote hovel under the dark trees. When through some unavoidable oversight a cat was missed, and sounds heard after dark, the loser would lament impotently; or console himself by thanking Fate that it was not one of his children who had thus vanished. For the people of Ulthar were simple, and knew not whence it is that all cats first came.

One day a caravan of strange wanderers from the South entered the narrow cobbled streets of Ulthar. Dark wanderers they were, and unlike the other roving folk who passed through the village twice every year. In the market-place they told fortunes for silver, and bought gay beads from the merchants. What was the land of these wanderers none could tell; but it was seen that they were given to strange prayers, and that they had painted on the sides of their wagons strange figures with human bodies and the heads of cats, hawks, rams, and lions. And the leader of the caravan wore a head-dress with two horns and a curious disc betwixt the horns.

There was in this singular caravan a little boy with no father or mother, but only a tiny black kitten to cherish. The plague had not been kind to him, yet had left him this small furry thing to mitigate his sorrow; and when one is very young, one can find great relief in the lively antics of a black kitten. So the boy whom the dark people called Menes smiled more often than he wept as he sate playing with his graceful kitten on the steps of an oddly painted wagon.

On the third morning of the wanderers' stay in Ulthar, Menes could not find his kitten; and as he sobbed aloud in the market-place certain villagers told him of the old man and his wife, and of sounds heard in the night. And when he heard these things his sobbing gave place to meditation, and finally to prayer. He stretched out his arms toward the sun and prayed in a tongue no villager could understand; though indeed the villagers did not try very hard to understand, since their attention was mostly taken up by the sky and the odd shapes the clouds were assuming. It was very peculiar, but as the little boy uttered his petition there seemed to form overhead the shadowy, nebulous figures of exotic things; of hybrid creatures crowned with horn-flanked discs. Nature is full of such illusions to impress the imaginative.

That night the wanderers left Ulthar, and were never seen again. And the householders were troubled when they noticed that in all the village there was not a cat to be found. From each hearth the familiar cat had vanished; cats large and small, black, grey, striped, yellow, and white. Old Kranon, the burgomaster, swore that the dark folk had taken the cats away in revenge for the killing of Menes' kitten; and cursed the caravan and the little boy. But Nith, the lean notary, declared that the old cotter and his wife were more likely persons to suspect; for their hatred of cats was notorious and increasingly bold. Still, no one durst complain to the sinister couple; even when little Atal, the innkeeper's son, vowed that he had at twilight seen all the cats of Ulthar in that accursed yard under the trees, pacing very slowly and solemnly in a circle around the cottage, two abreast, as if in performance of some unheard-of rite of beasts. The villagers did not know how much to believe from so small a boy; and though they feared that the evil pair had charmed the cats to their death, they preferred not to chide the old cotter till they met him outside his dark and repellent yard.

So Ulthar went to sleep in vain anger; and when the people awaked at dawn—behold! every cat was back at his accustomed hearth! Large and small, black, grey, striped, yellow, and white, none was missing. Very sleek and fat did the cats appear, and sonorous with purring content. The citizens talked with one another of the affair, and marvelled not a little. Old Kranon again insisted that it was the dark folk who had taken them, since cats did not return alive from the cottage of the ancient man and his wife. But all agreed on one thing; that the refusal of all the cats to eat their portions of meat or drink their saucers of milk was exceedingly curious. And for two whole days the sleek, lazy cats of Ulthar would touch no food, but only doze by the fire or in the sun.

It was fully a week before the villagers noticed that no lights were appearing at dusk in the windows of the cottage under the trees. Then the lean Nith remarked that no one had seen the old man or his wife since the night the cats were away. In another week the burgomaster decided to overcome his fears and call at the strangely silent dwelling as a matter of duty, though in doing so he was careful to take with him Shang the blacksmith and Thul the cutter of stone as witnesses. And when they had broken down the frail door they found only this: two cleanly picked human skeletons on the earthen floor, and a number of singular beetles crawling in the shadowy corners.

There was subsequently much talk amongst the burgesses of Ulthar. Zath, the coroner, disputed at length with Nith, the lean notary; and Kranon and Shang and Thul were overwhelmed with questions. Even little Atal, the innkeeper's son, was closely questioned and given a sweetmeat as reward. They talked of the old cotter and his wife, of the caravan of dark wanderers, of small

Menes and his black kitten, of the prayer of Menes and of the sky during that prayer, of the doings of the cats on the night the caravan left, and of what was later found in the cottage under the dark trees in the repellent yard.

And in the end the burgesses passed that remarkable law which is told of by traders in Hatheg and discussed by travellers in Nir; namely, that in Ulthar no man may kill a cat.

THE TEMPLE

(Manuscript found on the coast of Yucatan.)

On August 20, 1917, I, Karl Heinrich, Graf von Altberg-Ehrenstein, Lieutenant-Commander in the Imperial German Navy and in charge of the submarine U-29, deposit this bottle and record in the Atlantic Ocean at a point to me unknown but probably about N. Latitude 20°, W. Longitude 35°, where my ship lies disabled on the ocean floor. I do so because of my desire to set certain unusual facts before the public; a thing I shall not in all probability survive to accomplish in person, since the circumstances surrounding me are as menacing as they are extraordinary, and involve not only the hopeless crippling of the U-29, but the impairment of my iron German will in a manner most disastrous.

On the afternoon of June 18, as reported by wireless to the U-61, bound for Kiel, we torpedoed the British freighter *Victory*, New York to Liverpool, in N. Latitude 45° 16′, W. Longitude 28° 34′; permitting the crew to leave in boats in order to obtain a good cinema view for the admiralty records. The ship sank quite picturesquely, bow first, the stern rising high out of the water whilst the hull shot down perpendicularly to the bottom of the sea. Our camera missed nothing, and I regret that so fine a reel of film should never reach Berlin. After that we sank the lifeboats with our guns and submerged.

When we rose to the surface about sunset a seaman's body was found on the deck, hands gripping the railing in curious fashion. The poor fellow was young, rather dark, and very handsome; probably an Italian or Greek, and undoubtedly of the *Victory's* crew. He had evidently sought refuge on the very ship which had been forced to destroy his own—one more victim of the unjust war of aggression which the English pig-dogs are waging upon the Fatherland. Our men searched him for souvenirs, and found in his coat pocket a very odd bit of ivory carved to represent a youth's head crowned with laurel. My fellow-officer, Lieut. Klenze, believed that the thing was of great age and artistic value, so took it from the men for himself. How it had ever come into the possession of a common sailor, neither he nor I could imagine.

As the dead man was thrown overboard there occurred two incidents which created much disturbance amongst the crew. The fellow's eyes had been closed; but in the dragging of his body to the rail they were jarred open, and many seemed to entertain a queer delusion that they gazed steadily and mockingly at Schmidt and Zimmer, who were bent over the corpse. The Boatswain Müller, an elderly man who would have known better had he not been a superstitious Alsatian swine, became so excited by this impression that he watched the body in the water; and swore that after it sank a little it drew its limbs into a swimming position and sped away to the south under the waves. Klenze and I did not like these displays of peasant ignorance, and severely reprimanded the men, particularly Müller.

The next day a very troublesome situation was created by the indisposition of some of the crew. They were evidently suffering from the nervous strain of our long voyage, and had had bad dreams. Several seemed quite dazed and stupid; and after satisfying myself that they were not feigning their weakness, I excused them from their duties. The sea was rather rough, so we descended to a depth where the waves were less troublesome. Here we were comparatively calm, despite a somewhat puzzling southward current which we could not identify from our oceanographic charts. The moans of the sick men were decidedly annoying; but since they did not appear to demoralise the rest of the crew, we did not resort to extreme measures. It was our plan to remain where we were and intercept the liner *Dacia*, mentioned in information from agents in New York.

In the early evening we rose to the surface, and found the sea less heavy. The smoke of a battleship was on the northern horizon, but our distance and ability to submerge made us safe. What worried us more was the talk of Boatswain Müller, which grew wilder as night came on. He was in a detestably childish state, and babbled of some illusion of dead bodies drifting past the undersea portholes; bodies which looked at him intensely, and which he recognised in spite of bloating as having seen dying during some of our victorious German exploits. And he said that the young man we had found and tossed overboard was their leader. This was very gruesome and abnormal, so we confined Müller in irons and had him soundly whipped. The men were not pleased at his punishment, but discipline was necessary. We also denied the request of a delegation headed by Seaman Zimmer, that the curious carved ivory head be cast into the sea.

On June 20, Seamen Bohm and Schmidt, who had been ill the day before, became violently insane. I regretted that no physician was included in our complement of officers, since German lives are precious; but the constant ravings of the two concerning a terrible curse were most subversive of discipline, so drastic steps were taken. The crew accepted the event in a sullen fashion, but it seemed to quiet Müller; who thereafter gave us no trouble. In the evening we released him, and he went about his duties silently.

In the week that followed we were all very nervous, watching for the *Dacia.* The tension was aggravated by the disappearance of Müller and Zimmer, who undoubtedly committed suicide as a result of the fears which had seemed to harass them, though they were not observed in the act of jumping overboard. I was rather glad to be rid of Müller, for even his silence had unfavourably affected the crew. Everyone seemed inclined to be silent now, as though holding a secret fear. Many were ill, but none made a disturbance. Lieut. Klenze chafed under the strain, and was annoyed by the merest trifles—such as the school of dolphins which gathered about the U-29 in increasing numbers, and the growing intensity of that southward current which was not on our chart.

It at length became apparent that we had missed the *Dacia* altogether. Such failures are not uncommon, and we were more pleased than disappointed; since our return to Wilhelmshaven was now in order. At noon June 28 we turned northeastward, and despite some rather comical entanglements with the unusual masses of dolphins were soon under way.

The explosion in the engine room at 2 p.m. was wholly a surprise. No defect in the machinery or carelessness in the men had been noticed, yet without warning the ship was racked from end to end with a colossal shock. Lieut. Klenze hurried to the engine room, finding the fuel-tank and most of the mechanism shattered, and Engineers Raabe and Schneider instantly killed. Our situation had suddenly become grave indeed; for though the chemical air regenerators were intact, and though we could use the devices for raising and submerging the ship and opening the hatches as long as compressed air and storage batteries might hold out, we were powerless to propel or guide the submarine. To seek rescue in the lifeboats would be to deliver ourselves into the hands of enemies unreasonably embittered against our great German nation, and our wireless had failed ever since the *Victory* affair to put us in touch with a fellow U-boat of the Imperial Navy.

From the hour of the accident till July 2 we drifted constantly to the south, almost without plans and encountering no vessel. Dolphins still encircled the U-29, a somewhat remarkable circumstance considering the distance we had covered. On the morning of July 2 we sighted a warship flying American colours, and the men became very restless in their desire to surrender. Finally Lieut. Klenze had to shoot a seaman named Traube, who urged this un-German act with especial violence. This quieted the crew for the time, and we submerged unseen.

The next afternoon a dense flock of sea-birds appeared from the south, and the ocean began to heave ominously. Closing our hatches, we awaited developments until we realised that we must either submerge or be swamped in the mounting waves. Our air pressure and electricity were diminishing, and we wished to avoid all unnecessary use of our slender mechanical resources; but in this case there was no choice. We did not descend far, and when after several hours the sea was calmer, we decided to return to the surface. Here, however, a new trouble developed; for the ship failed to respond to our direction in spite of all that the mechanics could do. As the men grew more frightened at this undersea imprisonment, some of them began to mutter again about Lieut. Klenze's ivory image, but the sight of an automatic pistol calmed them. We kept the poor devils as busy as we could, tinkering at the machinery even when we knew it was useless.

Klenze and I usually slept at different times; and it was during my sleep, about 5 a.m., July 4, that the general mutiny broke loose. The six remaining pigs of seamen, suspecting that we were lost, had suddenly burst into a mad fury at our refusal to surrender to the Yankee battleship two days before; and were in a delirium of cursing and destruction. They roared like the animals they were, and broke instruments and furniture indiscriminately; screaming about such nonsense as the curse of the ivory image and the dark dead youth who looked at them and swam away. Lieut. Klenze seemed paralysed and inefficient, as one might expect of a soft, womanish Rhinelander. I shot all six men, for it was necessary, and made sure that none remained alive.

We expelled the bodies through the double hatches and were alone in the U-29. Klenze seemed very nervous, and drank heavily. It was decided that we remain alive as long as possible, using the large stock of provisions and chemical supply of oxygen, none of which had suffered from the crazy antics of those swine-hound seamen. Our compasses, depth gauges, and other delicate instruments were ruined; so that henceforth our only reckoning would be guesswork, based on our watches, the calendar, and our apparent drift as judged by any objects we might spy through the portholes or from the conning tower. Fortunately we had storage batteries still capable of long use, both for interior lighting and for the searchlight. We often cast a beam around the ship, but saw only dolphins, swimming parallel to our own drifting course. I was scientifically interested in those dolphins; for though the ordinary *Delphinus delphis* is a cetacean mammal, unable to subsist without air, I watched one of the swimmers closely for two hours, and did not see him alter his submerged condition.

With the passage of time Klenze and I decided that we were still drifting south, meanwhile sinking deeper and deeper. We noted the marine fauna and flora, and read much on the subject in the books I had carried with me for spare moments. I could not help observing, however, the inferior scientific knowledge of my companion. His mind was not Prussian, but given to imaginings and speculations which have no value. The fact of our coming death affected him curiously, and he would frequently pray in remorse over the men, women, and children we had sent to the bottom; forgetting that all things are noble which serve the German state. After a time he became noticeably unbalanced, gazing for hours at his ivory image and weaving fanciful stories of the lost and forgotten things under the sea. Sometimes, as a psychological experiment, I would lead him on in these wanderings, and listen to his endless poetical quotations and tales of sunken ships. I was very sorry for him, for I dislike to see a German suffer; but he was not a good man to die with. For myself I was proud, knowing how the Fatherland would revere my memory and how my sons would be taught to be men like me.

On August 9, we espied the ocean floor, and sent a powerful beam from the searchlight over it. It was a vast undulating plain, mostly covered with seaweed, and strown with the shells of small molluscs. Here and there were slimy objects of puzzling contour, draped with weeds and encrusted with barnacles, which Klenze declared must be ancient ships lying in their graves. He was puzzled by one thing, a peak of solid matter, protruding above the ocean bed nearly four feet at its apex; about two feet thick, with flat sides and smooth upper surfaces which met at a very obtuse angle. I called the peak a bit of outcropping rock, but Klenze thought he saw carvings on it. After a while he began to shudder, and turned away from the scene as if frightened; yet could give no explanation save that he was overcome with the vastness, darkness, remoteness, antiquity, and mystery of the oceanic abysses. His mind was tired, but I am always a German, and was quick to notice two things: that the U-29 was standing the deep-sea pressure splendidly, and that the peculiar dolphins were still about us, even at a depth where the existence of high organisms is considered impossible by most naturalists. That I had previously overestimated our depth, I was sure; but none the less we must still be deep enough to make these phenomena remarkable. Our southward speed, as gauged by the ocean floor, was about as I had estimated from the organisms passed at higher levels.

It was at 3:15 p.m., August 12, that poor Klenze went wholly mad. He had been in the conning tower using the searchlight when I saw him bound into the library compartment where I sat reading, and his face at once betrayed him. I will repeat here what he said, underlining the words he emphasised: "He is calling! He is calling! I hear him! We must go!" As he spoke he took his ivory image from the table, pocketed it, and seized my arm in an effort to drag me up the companionway to the deck. In a moment I understood that he meant to open the hatch and plunge with me into the water outside, a vagary of suicidal and homicidal mania for which I was scarcely prepared. As I hung back and attempted to soothe him he grew more violent, saying: "Come now—do not wait until later; it is better to repent and be forgiven than to defy and be condemned." Then I tried the opposite of the soothing plan, and told him he was mad—pitifully demented. But he was unmoved, and cried: "If I am mad, it is mercy! May the gods pity the man who in his callousness can remain sane to the hideous end! Come and be mad whilst *he* still calls with mercy!"

This outburst seemed to relieve a pressure in his brain; for as he finished he grew much milder, asking me to let him depart alone if I would not accompany him. My course at once became clear. He was a German, but only a Rhinelander and a commoner; and he was now a potentially dangerous madman. By complying with his suicidal request I could immediately free myself from one who was no longer a companion but a menace. I asked him to give me the ivory image before he went, but this request brought from him such uncanny laughter that I did not repeat it. Then I asked him if he wished to leave any keepsake or lock of hair for his family in Germany in case I should be rescued, but again he gave me that strange laugh. So as he climbed the ladder I went to the levers, and allowing proper time-intervals operated the machinery which sent him to his death. After I saw that he was no longer in the boat I threw the searchlight around the water in an effort to obtain a last glimpse of him; since I wished to ascertain whether the water-pressure would flatten him as it theoretically should, or whether the body would be unaffected, like those extraordinary dolphins. I did not, however, succeed in finding my late companion, for the dolphins were massed thickly and obscuringly about the conning tower.

That evening I regretted that I had not taken the ivory image surreptitiously from poor Klenze's pocket as he left, for the memory of it fascinated me. I could not forget the youthful, beautiful head with its leafy crown, though I am not by nature an artist. I was also sorry that I had no one with whom to converse. Klenze, though not my mental equal, was much better than no one. I did not sleep well that night, and wondered exactly when the end would come. Surely, I had little enough chance of rescue.

The next day I ascended to the conning tower and commenced the customary searchlight explorations. Northward the view was much the same as it had been all the four days since we had sighted the bottom, but I perceived that the drifting of the U-29 was less rapid. As I swung the beam around to the south, I noticed that the ocean floor ahead fell away in a marked declivity, and bore curiously regular blocks of stone in certain places, disposed as if in accordance with definite patterns. The boat did not at once descend to match the greater ocean depth, so I was soon forced to adjust the searchlight to cast a sharply downward beam. Owing to the abruptness of the change a wire was disconnected, which necessitated a delay of many minutes for repairs; but at length the light streamed on again, flooding the marine valley below me.

I am not given to emotion of any kind, but my amazement was very great when I saw what lay revealed in that electrical glow. And yet as one reared in the best *Kultur* of Prussia I should not have been amazed, for geology and tradition alike tell us of great transpositions in oceanic and continental areas. What I saw was an extended and elaborate array of ruined edifices; all of magnificent though unclassified architecture, and in various stages of preservation. Most appeared to be of marble, gleaming whitely in the rays of the searchlight, and the general plan was of a large city at the bottom of a narrow valley, with numerous isolated temples and villas on the steep slopes above. Roofs were fallen and columns were broken, but there still remained an air of immemorially ancient splendour which nothing could efface.

Confronted at last with the Atlantis I had formerly deemed largely a myth, I was the most eager of explorers. At the bottom of that valley a river once had flowed; for as I examined the scene more closely I beheld the remains of stone and marble bridges and sea-walls, and terraces and embankments once verdant and beautiful. In my enthusiasm I became nearly as idiotic and sentimental as poor Klenze, and was very tardy in noticing that the southward current had ceased at last, allowing the U-29 to settle slowly down upon the sunken city as an aëroplane settles upon a town of the upper earth. I was slow, too, in realising that the school of unusual dolphins had vanished.

In about two hours the boat rested in a paved plaza close to the rocky wall of the valley. On one side I could view the entire city as it sloped from the plaza down to the old river-bank; on the other side, in startling proximity, I was confronted by the richly ornate and perfectly preserved facade of a great building, evidently a temple, hollowed from the solid rock. Of the original workmanship of this titanic thing I can only make conjectures. The facade, of immense magnitude, apparently covers a continuous hollow recess; for its windows are many and widely distributed. In the centre yawns a great open door, reached by an impressive flight of steps, and surrounded by exquisite carvings like the figures of Bacchanals in relief. Foremost of all are the great columns and frieze, both decorated with sculptures of inexpressible beauty; obviously portraying idealised pastoral scenes and processions of priests and priestesses bearing strange ceremonial devices in adoration of a radiant god. The art is of the most phenomenal perfection, largely Hellenic in idea, yet strangely individual. It imparts an impression of terrible antiquity, as though it were the remotest rather than the immediate ancestor of Greek art. Nor can I doubt that every detail of this massive product was fashioned from the virgin hillside rock of our planet. It is palpably a part of the valley wall, though how the vast interior was ever excavated I cannot imagine. Perhaps a cavern or series of caverns furnished the nucleus. Neither age nor submersion has corroded the pristine grandeur of this awful fane—for fane indeed it must be—and today after thousands of years it rests untarnished and inviolate in the endless night and silence of an ocean chasm.

I cannot reckon the number of hours I spent in gazing at the sunken city with its buildings, arches, statues, and bridges, and the colossal temple with its beauty and mystery. Though I knew that death was near, my curiosity was consuming; and I threw the searchlight's beam about in eager quest. The shaft of light permitted me to learn many details, but refused to shew anything within the gaping door of the rock-hewn temple; and after a time I turned off the current, conscious of the need of conserving power. The rays were now perceptibly dimmer than they had been during the weeks of drifting. And as if sharpened by the coming deprivation of light, my desire to explore the watery secrets grew. I, a German, should be the first to tread those aeon-forgotten ways!

I produced and examined a deep-sea diving suit of jointed metal, and experimented with the portable light and air regenerator. Though I should have trouble in managing the double hatches alone, I believed I could overcome all obstacles with my scientific skill and actually walk about the dead city in person.

On August 16 I effected an exit from the U-29, and laboriously made my way through the ruined and mud-choked streets to the ancient river. I found no skeletons or other human remains, but gleaned a wealth of archaeological lore from sculptures and coins. Of this I cannot now speak save to utter my awe at a culture in the full noon of glory when cave-dwellers roamed Europe and the Nile flowed unwatched to the sea. Others, guided by this manuscript if it shall ever be found, must unfold the mysteries at which I can only hint. I returned to the boat as my electric batteries grew feeble, resolved to explore the rock temple on the following day.

On the 17th, as my impulse to search out the mystery of the temple waxed still more insistent, a great disappointment befell me; for I found that the materials needed to replenish the portable light had perished in the mutiny of those pigs in July. My rage was unbounded, yet my German sense forbade me to venture unprepared into an utterly black interior which might prove the lair of some indescribable marine monster or a labyrinth of passages from whose windings I could never extricate myself. All I could do was to turn on the waning searchlight of the U-29, and with its aid walk up the temple steps and study the exterior carvings. The shaft of light entered the door at an upward angle, and I peered in to see if I could glimpse anything, but all in vain. Not even the roof was visible; and though I took a step or two inside after testing the floor with a staff, I dared not go farther. Moreover, for the first time in my life I experienced the emotion of dread. I began to realise how some of poor Klenze's moods had arisen, for as the temple drew me more and more, I feared its aqueous abysses with a blind and mounting terror. Returning to the submarine, I turned off the lights and sat thinking in the dark. Electricity must now be saved for emergencies.

Saturday the 18th I spent in total darkness, tormented by thoughts and memories that threatened to overcome my German will. Klenze had gone mad and perished before reaching this sinister remnant of a past unwholesomely remote, and had advised me to go with him. Was, indeed, Fate preserving my reason only to draw me irresistibly to an end more horrible and unthinkable than any man has dreamed of? Clearly, my nerves were sorely taxed, and I must cast off these impressions of weaker men.

I could not sleep Saturday night, and turned on the lights regardless of the future. It was annoying that the electricity should not last out the air and provisions. I revived my thoughts of euthanasia, and examined my automatic pistol. Toward morning I must have dropped asleep with the lights on, for I awoke in darkness yesterday afternoon to find the batteries dead. I struck several matches in succession, and desperately regretted the improvidence which had caused us long ago to use up the few candles we carried.

After the fading of the last match I dared to waste, I sat very quietly without a light. As I considered the inevitable end my mind ran over preceding events, and developed a hitherto dormant impression which would have caused a weaker and more superstitious man to shudder. *The head of the radiant god in the sculptures on the rock temple is the same as that carven bit of ivory which the dead sailor brought from the sea and which poor Klenze carried back into the sea.*

I was a little dazed by this coincidence, but did not become terrified. It is only the inferior thinker who hastens to explain the singular and the complex by the primitive short cut of supernaturalism. The coincidence was strange, but I was too sound a reasoner to connect circumstances which admit of no logical connexion, or to associate in any uncanny fashion the disastrous events which had led from the *Victory* affair to my present plight. Feeling the need of more rest, I took a sedative and secured some more sleep. My nervous condition was reflected in my dreams, for I seemed to hear the cries of drowning persons, and to see dead faces pressing against the portholes of the boat. And among the dead faces was the living, mocking face of the youth with the ivory image.

I must be careful how I record my awaking today, for I am unstrung, and much hallucination is necessarily mixed with fact. Psychologically my case is most interesting, and I regret that it cannot be observed scientifically by a competent German authority. Upon opening my eyes my first sensation was an overmastering desire to visit the rock temple; a desire which grew every instant, yet which I automatically sought to resist through some emotion of fear which operated in the reverse direction.

Next there came to me the impression of *light* amidst the darkness of dead batteries, and I seemed to see a sort of phosphorescent glow in the water through the porthole which opened toward the temple. This aroused my curiosity, for I knew of no deep-sea organism capable of emitting such luminosity. But before I could investigate there came a third impression which because of its irrationality caused me to doubt the objectivity of anything my senses might record. It was an aural delusion; a sensation of rhythmic, melodic sound as of some wild yet beautiful chant or choral hymn, coming from the outside through the absolutely sound-proof hull of the U-29. Convinced of my psychological and nervous abnormality, I lighted some matches and poured a stiff dose of sodium bromide solution, which seemed to calm me to the extent of dispelling the illusion of sound. But the phosphorescence remained, and I had difficulty in repressing a childish impulse to go to the porthole and seek its source. It was horribly realistic, and I could soon distinguish by its aid the familiar objects around me, as well as the empty sodium bromide glass of which I had had no former visual impression in its present location. The last circumstance made me ponder, and I crossed the room and touched the glass. It was indeed in the place where I had seemed to see it. Now I knew that the light was either real or part of an hallucination so fixed and consistent that I could not hope to dispel it, so abandoning all resistance I ascended to the conning tower to look for the luminous agency. Might it not actually be another U-boat, offering possibilities of rescue?

It is well that the reader accept nothing which follows as objective truth, for since the events transcend natural law, they are necessarily the subjective and unreal creations of my overtaxed mind. When I attained the conning tower I found the sea in general far less luminous than I had expected. There was no animal or vegetable phosphorescence about, and the city that sloped down to the river was invisible in blackness. What I did see was not spectacular, not grotesque or terrifying, yet it removed my last vestige of trust in my consciousness. *For the door and windows of the undersea temple hewn from the rocky hill were vividly aglow with a flickering radiance, as from a mighty altar-flame far within.*

Later incidents are chaotic. As I stared at the uncannily lighted door and windows, I became subject to the most extravagant visions—visions so extravagant that I cannot even relate them. I fancied that I discerned objects in the temple; objects both stationary and moving; and seemed to hear again the unreal chant that had floated to me when first I awaked. And over all rose thoughts and fears which centred in the youth from the sea and the ivory image whose carving was duplicated on the frieze and columns of the temple before me. I thought of poor Klenze, and wondered where his body rested with the image he had carried back into the sea. He had warned me of something, and I had not heeded—but he was a soft-headed Rhinelander who went mad at troubles a Prussian could bear with ease.

The rest is very simple. My impulse to visit and enter the temple has now become an inexplicable and imperious command which ultimately cannot be denied. My own German will no longer controls my acts, and volition is henceforward possible only in minor matters. Such madness it was which drove Klenze to his death, bareheaded and unprotected in the ocean; but I am a Prussian and man of sense, and will use to the last what little will I have. When first I saw that I must go, I prepared my diving suit, helmet, and air regenerator for instant donning; and immediately commenced to write this hurried chronicle in the hope that it may some day reach the world. I shall seal the manuscript in a bottle and entrust it to the sea as I leave the U-29 for ever.

I have no fear, not even from the prophecies of the madman Klenze. What I have seen cannot be true, and I know that this madness of my own will at most lead only to suffocation when my air is gone. The light in the temple is a sheer delusion, and I shall die calmly, like a German, in the black and forgotten depths. This daemoniac laughter which I hear as I write comes only from my own weakening brain. So I will carefully don my diving suit and walk boldly up the steps into that primal shrine; that silent secret of unfathomed waters and uncounted years.

FACTS CONCERNING THE LATE ARTHUR JERMYN AND HIS FAMILY

Life is a hideous thing, and from the background behind what we know of it peer daemoniacal hints of truth which make it sometimes a thousandfold more hideous. Science, already oppressive with its shocking revelations, will perhaps be the ultimate exterminator of our human species—if separate species we be—for its reserve of unguessed horrors could never be borne by mortal brains if loosed upon the world. If we knew what we are, we should do as Sir Arthur Jermyn did; and Arthur Jermyn soaked himself in oil and set fire to his clothing one night. No one placed the charred fragments in an urn or set a memorial to him who had been; for certain papers and a certain boxed *object* were found, which made men wish to forget. Some who knew him do not admit that he ever existed.

Arthur Jermyn went out on the moor and burned himself after seeing the boxed *object* which had come from Africa. It was this *object*, and not his peculiar personal appearance, which made him end his life. Many would have disliked to live if possessed of the peculiar features of Arthur Jermyn, but he had been a poet and scholar and had not minded. Learning was in his blood, for his great-grandfather, Sir Robert Jermyn, Bt., had been an anthropologist of note, whilst his great-great-great-grandfather, Sir Wade Jermyn, was one of the earliest explorers of the Congo region, and had written eruditely of its tribes, animals, and supposed antiquities. Indeed, old Sir Wade had possessed an intellectual zeal amounting almost to a mania; his bizarre conjectures on a prehistoric white Congolese civilisation earning him much ridicule when his book, "Observations on the Several Parts of Africa", was published. In 1765 this fearless explorer had been placed in a madhouse at Huntingdon.

Madness was in all the Jermyns, and people were glad there were not many of them. The line put forth no branches, and Arthur was the last of it. If he had not been, one cannot say what he would have done when the *object* came. The Jermyns never seemed to look quite right—something was amiss, though Arthur was the worst, and the old family portraits in Jermyn House shewed fine faces enough before Sir Wade's time. Certainly, the madness began with Sir Wade, whose wild stories of Africa were at once the delight and terror of his few friends. It shewed in his collection of trophies and specimens, which were not such as a normal man would accumulate and preserve, and appeared strikingly in the Oriental seclusion in which he kept his wife. The latter, he had said, was the daughter of a Portuguese trader whom he had met in Africa; and did not like English ways. She, with an infant son born in Africa, had accompanied him back from the second and longest of his trips, and had gone with him on the third and last, never returning. No one had ever seen her closely, not even the servants; for her disposition had been violent and singular. During her brief stay at Jermyn House she occupied a remote wing, and was waited on by her husband alone. Sir Wade was, indeed, most peculiar in his solicitude for his family; for when he returned to Africa he would permit no one to care for his young son save a loathsome black woman from Guinea. Upon coming back, after the death of Lady Jermyn, he himself assumed complete care of the boy.

But it was the talk of Sir Wade, especially when in his cups, which chiefly led his friends to deem him mad. In a rational age like the eighteenth century it was unwise for a man of learning to talk about wild sights and strange scenes under a Congo moon; of the gigantic walls and pillars of a forgotten city, crumbling and vine-grown, and of damp, silent, stone steps leading interminably down into the darkness of abysmal treasure-vaults and inconceivable catacombs. Especially was it unwise to rave of the living things that might haunt such a place; of creatures half of the jungle and half of the impiously aged city—fabulous creatures which even a Pliny might describe with scepticism; things that might have sprung up after the great apes had overrun the dying city with the walls and the pillars, the vaults and the weird carvings. Yet after he came home for the last time Sir Wade would speak of such matters with a shudderingly uncanny zest, mostly after his third glass at the Knight's Head; boasting of what he had found in the jungle and of how he had dwelt among terrible ruins known only to him. And finally he had spoken of the living things in such a manner that he was taken to the madhouse. He had shewn little regret when shut into the barred room at Huntingdon, for his mind moved curiously. Ever since his son had commenced to grow out of infancy he had liked his home less and less, till at last he had seemed to dread it. The Knight's Head had been his headquarters, and when he was confined he expressed some vague gratitude as if for protection. Three years later he died.

Wade Jermyn's son Philip was a highly peculiar person. Despite a strong physical resemblance to his father, his appearance and conduct were in many particulars so coarse that he was universally shunned. Though he did not inherit the madness which was feared by some, he was densely stupid and given to brief periods of uncontrollable violence. In frame he was small, but intensely powerful, and was of incredible agility. Twelve years after succeeding to his title he married the daughter of his gamekeeper, a person said to be of gypsy extraction, but before his son was born joined the navy as a common sailor, completing the general disgust which his habits and mesalliance had begun. After the close of the American war he was heard of as a sailor on a merchantman in the African trade, having a kind of reputation for feats of strength and climbing, but finally disappearing one night as his ship lay off the Congo coast.

In the son of Sir Philip Jermyn the now accepted family peculiarity took a strange and fatal turn. Tall and fairly handsome, with a sort of weird Eastern grace despite certain slight oddities of proportion, Robert Jermyn began life as a scholar and investigator. It was he who first studied scientifically the vast collection of relics which his mad grandfather had brought from Africa, and who made the family name as celebrated in ethnology as in exploration. In 1815 Sir Robert married a daughter of the seventh Viscount Brightholme and was subsequently blessed with three children, the eldest and youngest of whom were never publicly seen on account of deformities in mind and body. Saddened by these family misfortunes, the scientist sought relief in work, and made two long expeditions in the interior of Africa. In 1849 his second son, Nevil, a singularly repellent person who seemed to combine the surliness of Philip Jermyn with the hauteur of the Brightholmes, ran away with a vulgar dancer, but was pardoned upon his return in the following year. He came back to Jermyn

House a widower with an infant son, Alfred, who was one day to be the father of Arthur Jermyn.

Friends said that it was this series of griefs which unhinged the mind of Sir Robert Jermyn, yet it was probably merely a bit of African folklore which caused the disaster. The elderly scholar had been collecting legends of the Onga tribes near the field of his grandfather's and his own explorations, hoping in some way to account for Sir Wade's wild tales of a lost city peopled by strange hybrid creatures. A certain consistency in the strange papers of his ancestor suggested that the madman's imagination might have been stimulated by native myths. On October 19, 1852, the explorer Samuel Seaton called at Jermyn House with a manuscript of notes collected among the Ongas, believing that certain legends of a grey city of white apes ruled by a white god might prove valuable to the ethnologist. In his conversation he probably supplied many additional details; the nature of which will never be known, since a hideous series of tragedies suddenly burst into being. When Sir Robert Jermyn emerged from his library he left behind the strangled corpse of the explorer, and before he could be restrained, had put an end to all three of his children; the two who were never seen, and the son who had run away. Nevil Jermyn died in the successful defence of his own two-year-old son, who had apparently been included in the old man's madly murderous scheme. Sir Robert himself, after repeated attempts at suicide and a stubborn refusal to utter any articulate sound, died of apoplexy in the second year of his confinement.

Sir Alfred Jermyn was a baronet before his fourth birthday, but his tastes never matched his title. At twenty he had joined a band of music-hall performers, and at thirty-six had deserted his wife and child to travel with an itinerant American circus. His end was very revolting. Among the animals in the exhibition with which he travelled was a huge bull gorilla of lighter colour than the average; a surprisingly tractable beast of much popularity with the performers. With this gorilla Alfred Jermyn was singularly fascinated, and on many occasions the two would eye each other for long periods through the intervening bars. Eventually Jermyn asked and obtained permission to train the animal, astonishing audiences and fellow-performers alike with his success. One morning in Chicago, as the gorilla and Alfred Jermyn were rehearsing an exceedingly clever boxing match, the former delivered a blow of more than usual force, hurting both the body and dignity of the amateur trainer. Of what followed, members of "The Greatest Show on Earth" do not like to speak. They did not expect to hear Sir Alfred Jermyn emit a shrill, inhuman scream, or to see him seize his clumsy antagonist with both hands, dash it to the floor of the cage, and bite fiendishly at its hairy throat. The gorilla was off its guard, but not for long, and before anything could be done by the regular trainer the body which had belonged to a baronet was past recognition.

II.

Arthur Jermyn was the son of Sir Alfred Jermyn and a music-hall singer of unknown origin. When the husband and father deserted his family, the mother took the child to Jermyn House; where there was none left to object to her presence. She was not without notions of what a nobleman's dignity should be, and saw to it that her son received the best education which limited money could provide. The family resources were now sadly slender, and Jermyn House had fallen into woeful disrepair, but young Arthur loved the old edifice and all its contents. He was not like any other Jermyn who had ever lived, for he was a poet and a dreamer. Some of the neighbouring families who had heard tales of old Sir Wade Jermyn's unseen Portuguese wife declared that her Latin blood must be shewing itself; but most persons merely sneered at his sensitiveness to beauty, attributing it to his music-hall mother, who was socially unrecognised. The poetic delicacy of Arthur Jermyn was the more remarkable because of his uncouth personal appearance. Most of the Jermyns had possessed a subtly odd and repellent cast, but Arthur's case was very striking. It is hard to say just what he resembled, but his expression, his facial angle, and the length of his arms gave a thrill of repulsion to those who met him for the first time.

It was the mind and character of Arthur Jermyn which atoned for his aspect. Gifted and learned, he took highest honours at Oxford and seemed likely to redeem the intellectual fame of his family. Though of poetic rather than scientific temperament, he planned to continue the work of his forefathers in African ethnology and antiquities, utilising the truly wonderful though strange collection of Sir Wade. With his fanciful mind he thought often of the prehistoric civilisation in which the mad explorer had so implicitly believed, and would weave tale after tale about the silent jungle city mentioned in the latter's wilder notes and paragraphs. For the nebulous utterances concerning a nameless, unsuspected race of jungle hybrids he had a peculiar feeling of mingled terror and attraction; speculating on the possible basis of such a fancy, and seeking to obtain light among the more recent data gleaned by his great-grandfather and Samuel Seaton amongst the Ongas.

In 1911, after the death of his mother, Sir Arthur Jermyn determined to pursue his investigations to the utmost extent. Selling a portion of his estate to obtain the requisite money, he outfitted an expedition and sailed for the Congo. Arranging with the Belgian authorities for a party of guides, he spent a year in the Onga and Kaliri country, finding data beyond the highest of his expectations. Among the Kaliris was an aged chief called Mwanu, who possessed not only a highly retentive memory, but a singular degree of intelligence and interest in old legends. This ancient confirmed every tale which Jermyn had heard, adding his own account of the stone city and the white apes as it had been told to him.

According to Mwanu, the grey city and the hybrid creatures were no more, having been annihilated by the warlike N'bangus many years ago. This tribe, after destroying most of the edifices and killing the live beings, had carried off the stuffed goddess which had been the object of their quest; the white ape-goddess which the strange beings worshipped, and which was held by Congo tradition to be the form of one who had reigned as a princess among those beings. Just what the white ape-like creatures could have been, Mwanu had no idea, but he thought they were the builders of the ruined city. Jermyn could form no conjecture, but by close questioning obtained a very picturesque legend of the stuffed goddess.

The ape-princess, it was said, became the consort of a great white god who had come out of the West. For a long time they had reigned over the city together, but when they had a son all three went away. Later the god and the princess had returned, and upon the death of the princess her divine husband had mummified the body and enshrined it in a vast house of stone, where it was worshipped. Then he had departed alone. The legend here seemed to present three variants. According to one story nothing further happened save that the stuffed goddess became a symbol of supremacy for whatever tribe might possess it. It was for this reason that the N'bangus carried it off. A second story told of the god's return and death at the feet of his enshrined wife. A third told of the return of the son, grown to manhood—or apehood or godhood, as the case might be—yet unconscious of his identity. Surely the imaginative blacks had made the most of whatever events might lie behind the extravagant legendry.

Of the reality of the jungle city described by old Sir Wade, Arthur Jermyn had no further doubt; and was hardly astonished when early in 1912 he came upon what was left of it. Its size must have been exaggerated, yet the stones lying about proved that it was no mere negro village. Unfortunately no carvings could be found, and the small size of the expedition prevented operations toward clearing the one visible passageway that seemed to lead down into the system of vaults which Sir Wade had mentioned. The white apes and the stuffed goddess were discussed with all the native chiefs of the region, but it remained for a European to improve on the data offered by old Mwanu. M. Verhaeren, Belgian agent at a trading-post on the Congo, believed that he could not only locate but obtain the stuffed goddess, of which he had vaguely heard; since the once mighty N'bangus were now the submissive servants of King Albert's government, and with but little persuasion could be induced to part with the gruesome deity they had carried off. When Jermyn sailed for England, therefore, it was with the exultant probability that he would within a few months receive a priceless ethnological relic confirming the wildest of his great-great-great-grandfather's narratives—that is, the wildest which he had ever heard. Countrymen near Jermyn House had perhaps heard wilder tales handed down from ancestors who had listened to Sir Wade around the tables of the Knight's Head.

Arthur Jermyn waited very patiently for the expected box from M. Verhaeren, meanwhile studying with increased diligence the manuscripts left by his mad ancestor. He began to feel closely akin to Sir Wade, and to seek relics of the latter's personal life in England as well as of his African exploits. Oral accounts of the mysterious and secluded wife had been numerous, but no tangible relic of her stay at Jermyn House remained. Jermyn wondered what circumstance had prompted or permitted such an effacement, and decided that the husband's insanity was the prime cause. His great-great-great-grandmother, he recalled, was said to have been the daughter of a Portuguese trader in Africa. No doubt her practical heritage and superficial knowledge of the Dark Continent had caused her to flout Sir Wade's tales of the interior, a thing which such a man would not be likely to forgive. She had died in Africa, perhaps dragged thither by a husband determined to prove what he had told. But as Jermyn indulged in these reflections he could not but smile at their futility, a century and a half after the death of both of his strange progenitors.

In June, 1913, a letter arrived from M. Verhaeren, telling of the finding of the stuffed goddess. It was, the Belgian averred, a most extraordinary object; an object quite beyond the power of a layman to classify. Whether it was human or simian only a scientist could determine, and the process of determination would be greatly hampered by its imperfect condition. Time and the Congo climate are not kind to mummies; especially when their preparation is as amateurish as seemed to be the case here. Around the creature's neck had been found a golden chain bearing an empty locket on which were armorial designs; no doubt some hapless traveller's keepsake, taken by the N'bangus and hung upon the goddess as a charm. In commenting on the contour of the mummy's face, M. Verhaeren suggested a whimsical comparison; or rather, expressed a humorous wonder just how it would strike his correspondent, but was too much interested scientifically to waste many words in levity. The stuffed goddess, he wrote, would arrive duly packed about a month after receipt of the letter.

The boxed object was delivered at Jermyn House on the afternoon of August 3, 1913, being conveyed immediately to the large chamber which housed the collection of African specimens as arranged by Sir Robert and Arthur. What ensued can best be gathered from the tales of servants and from things and papers later examined. Of the various tales that of aged Soames, the family butler, is most ample and coherent. According to this trustworthy man, Sir Arthur Jermyn dismissed everyone from the room before opening the box, though the instant sound of hammer and chisel shewed that he did not delay the operation. Nothing was heard for some time; just how long Soames cannot exactly estimate; but it was certainly less than a quarter of an hour later that the horrible scream, undoubtedly in Jermyn's voice, was heard. Immediately afterward Jermyn emerged from the room, rushing frantically toward the front of the house as if pursued by some hideous enemy. The expression on his face, a face ghastly enough in repose, was beyond description. When near the front door he seemed to think of something, and turned back in his flight, finally disappearing down the stairs to the cellar. The servants were utterly dumbfounded, and watched at the head of the stairs, but their master did not return. A smell of oil was all that came up from the regions below. After dark a rattling was heard at the door leading from the cellar into the courtyard; and a stable-boy saw Arthur Jermyn, glistening from head to foot with oil and redolent of that fluid, steal furtively out and vanish on the black moor surrounding the house. Then, in an exaltation of supreme horror, everyone saw the end. A spark appeared on the moor, a flame arose, and a pillar of human fire reached to the heavens. The house of Jermyn no longer existed.

The reason why Arthur Jermyn's charred fragments were not collected and buried lies in what was found afterward, principally the thing in the box. The stuffed goddess was a nauseous sight, withered and eaten away, but it was clearly a mummified white ape of some unknown species, less hairy than any recorded variety, and infinitely nearer mankind—quite shockingly so. Detailed description would be rather unpleasant, but two salient particulars must be told, for they fit in revoltingly with certain notes of Sir Wade Jermyn's African expeditions and with the Congolese legends of the white god and the ape-princess. The two particulars in question are these: the arms on the golden locket about the creature's neck were the Jermyn arms, and the jocose suggestion of M. Verhaeren about a certain resemblance as connected with the shrivelled face applied with vivid, ghastly, and unnatural horror to none other than the sensitive Arthur Jermyn, great-great-great-grandson of Sir Wade Jermyn and an unknown wife. Members of the Royal Anthropological Institute burned the thing and threw the locket into a well, and some of them do not admit that Arthur Jermyn ever existed.

CELEPHAÏS

In a dream Kuranes saw the city in the valley, and the seacoast beyond, and the snowy peak overlooking the sea, and the gaily painted galleys that sail out of the harbour toward distant regions where the sea meets the sky. In a dream it was also that he came by his name of Kuranes, for when awake he was called by another name. Perhaps it was natural for him to dream a new name; for he was the last of his family, and alone among the indifferent millions of London, so there were not many to speak to him and remind him who he had been. His money and lands were gone, and he did not care for the ways of people about him, but preferred to dream and write of his dreams. What he wrote was laughed at by those to whom he shewed it, so that after a time he kept his writings to himself, and finally ceased to write. The more he withdrew from the world about him, the more wonderful became his dreams; and it would have been quite futile to try to describe them on paper. Kuranes was not modern, and did not think like others who wrote. Whilst they strove to strip from life its embroidered robes of myth, and to shew in naked ugliness the foul thing that is reality, Kuranes sought for beauty alone. When truth and experience failed to reveal it, he sought it in fancy and illusion, and found it on his very doorstep, amid the nebulous memories of childhood tales and dreams.

There are not many persons who know what wonders are opened to them in the stories and visions of their youth; for when as children we listen and dream, we think but half-formed thoughts, and when as men we try to remember, we are dulled and prosaic with the poison of life. But some of us awake in the night with strange phantasms of enchanted hills and gardens, of fountains that sing in the sun, of golden cliffs overhanging murmuring seas, of plains that stretch down to sleeping cities of bronze and stone, and of shadowy companies of heroes that ride caparisoned white horses along the edges of thick forests; and then we know that we have looked back through the ivory gates into that world of wonder which was ours before we were wise and unhappy.

Kuranes came very suddenly upon his old world of childhood. He had been dreaming of the house where he was born; the great stone house covered with ivy, where thirteen generations of his ancestors had lived, and where he had hoped to die. It was moonlight, and he had stolen out into the fragrant summer night, through the gardens, down the terraces, past the great oaks of the park, and along the long white road to the village. The village seemed very old, eaten away at the edge like the moon which had commenced to wane, and Kuranes wondered whether the peaked roofs of the small houses hid sleep or death. In the streets were spears of long grass, and the window-panes on either side were either broken or filmily staring. Kuranes had not lingered, but had plodded on as though summoned toward some goal. He dared not disobey the summons for fear it might prove an illusion like the urges and aspirations of waking life, which do not lead to any goal. Then he had been drawn down a lane that led off from the village street toward the channel cliffs, and had come to the end of things—to the precipice and the abyss where all the village and all the world fell abruptly away into the unechoing emptiness of infinity, and where even the sky ahead was empty and unlit by the crumbling moon and the peering stars. Faith had urged him on, over the precipice and into the gulf, where he had floated down, down, down; past dark, shapeless, undreamed dreams, faintly glowing spheres that may have been partly dreamed dreams, and laughing winged things that seemed to mock the dreamers of all the worlds. Then a rift seemed to open in the darkness before him, and he saw the city of the valley, glistening radiantly far, far below, with a background of sea and sky, and a snow-capped mountain near the shore.

Kuranes had awaked the very moment he beheld the city, yet he knew from his brief glance that it was none other than Celephaïs, in the Valley of Ooth-Nargai beyond the Tanarian Hills, where his spirit had dwelt all the eternity of an hour one summer afternoon very long ago, when he had slipt away from his nurse and let the warm sea-breeze lull him to sleep as he watched the clouds from the cliff near the village. He had protested then, when they had found him, waked him, and carried him home, for just as he was aroused he had been about to sail in a golden galley for those alluring regions where the sea meets the sky. And now he was equally resentful of awaking, for he had found his fabulous city after forty weary years.

But three nights afterward Kuranes came again to Celephaïs. As before, he dreamed first of the village that was asleep or dead, and of the abyss down which one must float silently; then the rift appeared again, and he beheld the glittering minarets of the city, and saw the graceful galleys riding at anchor in the blue harbour, and watched the gingko trees of Mount Aran swaying in the sea-breeze. But this time he was not snatched away, and like a winged being settled gradually over a grassy hillside till finally his feet rested gently on the turf. He had indeed come back to the Valley of Ooth-Nargai and the splendid city of Celephaïs.

Down the hill amid scented grasses and brilliant flowers walked Kuranes, over the bubbling Naraxa on the small wooden bridge where he had carved his name so many years ago, and through the whispering grove to the great stone bridge by the city gate. All was as of old, nor were the marble walls discoloured, nor the polished bronze statues upon them tarnished. And Kuranes saw that he need not tremble lest the things he knew be vanished; for even the sentries on the ramparts were the same, and still as young as he remembered them. When he entered the city, past the bronze gates and over the onyx pavements, the merchants and camel-drivers greeted him as if he had never been away; and it was the same at the turquoise temple of Nath-Horthath, where the orchid-wreathed priests told him that there is no time in Ooth-Nargai, but only perpetual youth. Then Kuranes walked through the Street of Pillars to the seaward wall, where gathered the traders and sailors, and strange men from the regions where the sea meets the sky. There he stayed long, gazing out over the bright harbour where the ripples sparkled beneath an unknown sun, and where rode lightly the galleys from far places over the water. And he gazed also upon Mount Aran rising regally from the shore, its lower slopes green with swaying trees and its white summit touching the sky.

More than ever Kuranes wished to sail in a galley to the far places of which he had heard so many strange tales, and he sought again the captain who had agreed to carry him so long ago. He found the man, Athib, sitting on the same chest of spices he had sat upon before, and Athib seemed not to realise that any time had passed. Then the two rowed to a galley in the harbour, and giving orders to the oarsmen, commenced to sail out into the billowy Cerenarian Sea that leads to the sky. For several days they glided undulatingly over the water, till finally they came to the horizon, where the sea meets the sky. Here the galley paused not at all, but floated easily in the blue of the sky among fleecy clouds tinted with rose. And far beneath the keel Kuranes could see strange lands and rivers and cities of surpassing beauty, spread indolently in the sunshine which seemed never to lessen or disappear. At length Athib told him that their journey was near its end, and that they would soon enter the harbour of Serannian, the pink marble city of the clouds, which is built on that ethereal coast where the west wind flows into the sky; but as the highest of the city's carven towers came into sight there was a sound somewhere in space, and Kuranes awaked in his London garret.

For many months after that Kuranes sought the marvellous city of Celephaïs and its sky-bound galleys in vain; and though his dreams carried him to many gorgeous and unheard-of places, no one whom he met could tell him how to find Ooth-Nargai, beyond the Tanarian Hills. One night he went flying over dark mountains where there were faint, lone campfires at great distances apart, and strange, shaggy herds with tinkling bells on the leaders; and in the wildest part of this hilly country, so remote that few men could ever have seen it, he found a hideously ancient wall or causeway of stone zigzagging along the ridges and valleys; too gigantic ever to have risen by human hands, and of such a length that neither end of it could be seen. Beyond that wall in the grey dawn he came to a land of quaint gardens and cherry trees, and when the sun rose he beheld such beauty of red and white flowers, green foliage and lawns, white paths, diamond brooks, blue lakelets, carven bridges, and red-roofed pagodas, that he for a moment forgot Celephaïs in sheer delight. But he remembered it again when he walked down a white path toward a red-roofed pagoda, and would have questioned the people of that land about it, had he not found that there were no people there, but only birds and bees and butterflies. On another night Kuranes walked up a damp stone spiral stairway endlessly, and came to a tower window overlooking a mighty plain and river lit by the full moon; and in the silent city that spread away from the river-bank he thought he beheld some feature or arrangement which he had known before. He would have descended and asked the way to Ooth-Nargai had not a fearsome aurora sputtered up from some remote place beyond the horizon, shewing the ruin and antiquity of the city, and the stagnation of the reedy river, and the death lying upon that land, as it had lain since King Kynaratholis came home from his conquests to find the vengeance of the gods.

So Kuranes sought fruitlessly for the marvellous city of Celephaïs and its galleys that sail to Serannian in the sky, meanwhile seeing many wonders and once barely escaping from the high-priest not to be described, which wears a yellow silken mask over its face and dwells all alone in a prehistoric stone monastery on the cold desert plateau of Leng. In time he grew so impatient of the bleak intervals of day that he began buying drugs in order to increase his periods of sleep. Hasheesh helped a great deal, and once sent him to a part of space where form does not exist, but where glowing gases study the secrets of existence. And a violet-coloured gas told him that this part of space was outside what he had called infinity. The gas had not heard of planets and organisms before, but identified Kuranes merely as one from the infinity where matter, energy, and gravitation exist. Kuranes was now very anxious to return to minaret-studded Celephaïs, and increased his doses of drugs; but eventually he had no more money left, and could buy no drugs. Then one summer day he was turned out of his garret, and wandered aimlessly through the streets, drifting over a bridge to a place where the houses grew thinner and thinner. And it was there that fulfilment came, and he met the cortege of knights come from Celephaïs to bear him thither for ever.

Handsome knights they were, astride roan horses and clad in shining armour with tabards of cloth-of-gold curiously emblazoned. So numerous were they, that Kuranes almost mistook them for an army, but their leader told him they were sent in his honour; since it was he who had created Ooth-Nargai in his dreams, on which account he was now to be appointed its chief god for evermore. Then they gave Kuranes a horse and placed him at the head of the cavalcade, and all rode majestically through the downs of Surrey and onward toward the region where Kuranes and his ancestors were born. It was very strange, but as the riders went on they seemed to gallop back through Time; for whenever they passed through a village in the twilight they saw only such houses and villagers as Chaucer or men before him might have seen, and sometimes they saw knights on horseback with small companies of retainers. When it grew dark they travelled more swiftly, till soon they were flying uncannily as if in the air. In the dim dawn they came upon the village which Kuranes had seen alive in his childhood, and asleep or dead in his dreams. It was alive now, and early villagers courtesied as the horsemen clattered down the street and turned off into the lane that ends in the abyss of dream. Kuranes had previously entered that abyss only at night, and wondered what it would look like by day; so he watched anxiously as the column approached its brink. Just as they galloped up the rising ground to the precipice a golden glare came somewhere out of the east and hid all the landscape in its effulgent draperies. The abyss was now a seething chaos of roseate and cerulean splendour, and invisible voices sang exultantly as the knightly entourage plunged over the edge and floated gracefully down past glittering clouds and silvery coruscations. Endlessly down the horsemen floated, their chargers pawing the aether as if galloping over golden sands; and then the luminous vapours spread apart to reveal a greater brightness, the brightness of the city Celephaïs, and the seacoast beyond, and the snowy peak overlooking the sea, and the gaily painted galleys that sail out of the harbour toward distant regions where the sea meets the sky.

And Kuranes reigned thereafter over Ooth-Nargai and all the neighbouring regions of dream, and held his court alternately in Celephaïs and in the cloud-fashioned Serannian. He reigns there still, and will reign happily for ever, though below the cliffs at Innsmouth the channel tides played mockingly with the body of a tramp who had stumbled through the half-deserted village at dawn; played mockingly, and cast it upon the rocks by ivy-covered Trevor Towers, where a notably fat and especially offensive millionaire brewer enjoys the purchased atmosphere of extinct nobility.

FROM BEYOND

Horrible beyond conception was the change which had taken place in my best friend, Crawford Tillinghast. I had not seen him since that day, two months and a half before, when he had told me toward what goal his physical and metaphysical researches were leading; when he had answered my awed and almost frightened remonstrances by driving me from his laboratory and his house in a burst of fanatical rage. I had known that he now remained mostly shut in the attic laboratory with that accursed electrical machine, eating little and excluding even the servants, but I had not thought that a brief period of ten weeks could so alter and disfigure any human creature. It is not pleasant to see a stout man suddenly grown thin, and it is even worse when the baggy skin becomes yellowed or greyed, the eyes sunken, circled, and uncannily glowing, the forehead veined and corrugated, and the hands tremulous and twitching. And if added to this there be a repellent unkemptness; a wild disorder of dress, a bushiness of dark hair white at the roots, and an unchecked growth of pure white beard on a face once clean-shaven, the cumulative effect is quite shocking. But such was the aspect of Crawford Tillinghast on the night his half-coherent message brought me to his door after my weeks of exile; such the spectre that trembled as it admitted me, candle in hand, and glanced furtively over its shoulder as if fearful of unseen things in the ancient, lonely house set back from Benevolent Street.

That Crawford Tillinghast should ever have studied science and philosophy was a mistake. These things should be left to the frigid and impersonal investigator, for they offer two equally tragic alternatives to the man of feeling and action; despair if he fail in his quest, and terrors unutterable and unimaginable if he succeed. Tillinghast had once been the prey of failure, solitary and melancholy; but now I knew, with nauseating fears of my own, that he was the prey of success. I had indeed warned him ten weeks before, when he burst forth with his tale of what he felt himself about to discover. He had been flushed and excited then, talking in a high and unnatural, though always pedantic, voice.

"What do we know," he had said, "of the world and the universe about us? Our means of receiving impressions are absurdly few, and our notions of surrounding objects infinitely narrow. We see things only as we are constructed to see them, and can gain no idea of their absolute nature. With five feeble senses we pretend to comprehend the boundlessly complex cosmos, yet other beings with a wider, stronger, or different range of senses might not only see very differently the things we see, but might see and study whole worlds of matter, energy, and life which lie close at hand yet can never be detected with the senses we have. I have always believed that such strange, inaccessible worlds exist at our very elbows, *and now I believe I have found a way to break down the barriers.* I am not joking. Within twenty-four hours that machine near the table will generate waves acting on unrecognised sense-organs that exist in us as atrophied or rudimentary vestiges. Those waves will open up to us many vistas unknown to man, and several unknown to anything we consider organic life. We shall see that at which dogs howl in the dark, and that at which cats prick up their ears after midnight. We shall see these things, and other things which no breathing creature has yet seen. We shall overleap time, space, and dimensions, and without bodily motion peer to the bottom of creation."

When Tillinghast said these things I remonstrated, for I knew him well enough to be frightened rather than amused; but he was a fanatic, and drove me from the house. Now he was no less a fanatic, but his desire to speak had conquered his resentment, and he had written me imperatively in a hand I could scarcely recognise. As I entered the abode of the friend so suddenly metamorphosed to a shivering gargoyle, I became infected with the terror which seemed stalking in all the shadows. The words and beliefs expressed ten weeks before seemed bodied forth in the darkness beyond the small circle of candle light, and I sickened at the hollow, altered voice of my host. I wished the servants were about, and did not like it when he said they had all left three days previously. It seemed strange that old Gregory, at least, should desert his master without telling as tried a friend as I. It was he who had given me all the information I had of Tillinghast after I was repulsed in rage.

Yet I soon subordinated all my fears to my growing curiosity and fascination. Just what Crawford Tillinghast now wished of me I could only guess, but that he had some stupendous secret or discovery to impart, I could not doubt. Before I had protested at his unnatural pryings into the unthinkable; now that he had evidently succeeded to some degree I almost shared his spirit, terrible though the cost of victory appeared. Up through the dark emptiness of the house I followed the bobbing candle in the hand of this shaking parody on man. The electricity seemed to be turned off, and when I asked my guide he said it was for a definite reason.

"It would be too much … I would not dare," he continued to mutter. I especially noted his new habit of muttering, for it was not like him to talk to himself. We entered the laboratory in the attic, and I observed that detestable electrical machine, glowing with a sickly, sinister, violet luminosity. It was connected with a powerful chemical battery, but seemed to be receiving no current; for I recalled that in its experimental stage it had sputtered and purred when in action. In reply to my question Tillinghast mumbled that this permanent glow was not electrical in any sense that I could understand.

He now seated me near the machine, so that it was on my right, and turned a switch somewhere below the crowning cluster of glass bulbs. The usual sputtering began, turned to a whine, and terminated in a drone so soft as to suggest a return to silence. Meanwhile the luminosity increased, waned again, then assumed a pale, outré colour or blend of colours which I could neither place nor describe. Tillinghast had been watching me, and noted my puzzled expression.

"Do you know what that is?" he whispered. "*That is ultra-violet.*" He chuckled oddly at my surprise. "You thought ultra-violet was invisible, and so it is—but you can see that and many other invisible things *now*.

"Listen to me! The waves from that thing are waking a thousand sleeping senses in us; senses which we inherit from aeons of evolution from the state of detached electrons to the state of organic humanity. I have seen *truth*, and I intend to shew it to you. Do you wonder how it will seem? I will tell you." Here Tillinghast seated himself directly opposite me, blowing out his candle and staring hideously into my eyes. "Your existing sense-organs—ears first, I think—will pick up many of the impressions, for they are closely connected with the dormant organs. Then there will be others. You have heard of the pineal gland? I laugh at the shallow endocrinologist, fellow-dupe and fellow-parvenu of the Freudian. That gland is the great sense-organ of organs—*I have found out*. It is like sight in the end, and transmits visual pictures to the brain. If you are normal, that is the way you ought to get most of it … I mean get most of the evidence from *beyond*."

I looked about the immense attic room with the sloping south wall, dimly lit by rays which the every-day eye cannot see. The far corners were all shadows, and the whole place took on a hazy unreality which obscured its nature and invited the imagination to symbolism and phantasm. During the interval that Tillinghast was silent I fancied myself in some vast and incredible temple of long-dead gods; some vague edifice of innumerable black stone columns reaching up from a floor of damp slabs to a cloudy height beyond the range of my vision. The picture was very vivid for a while, but gradually gave way to a more horrible conception; that of utter, absolute solitude in infinite, sightless, soundless space. There seemed to be a void, and nothing more, and I felt a childish fear which prompted me to draw from my hip pocket the revolver I always carried after dark since the night I was held up in East Providence. Then, from the farthermost regions of remoteness, the *sound* softly glided into existence. It was infinitely faint, subtly vibrant, and unmistakably musical, but held a quality of surpassing wildness which made its impact feel like a delicate torture of my whole body. I felt sensations like those one feels when accidentally scratching ground glass. Simultaneously there developed something like a cold draught, which apparently swept past me from the direction of the distant sound. As I waited breathlessly I perceived that both sound and wind were increasing; the effect being to give me an odd notion of myself as tied to a pair of rails in the path of a gigantic approaching locomotive. I began to speak to Tillinghast, and as I did so all the unusual impressions abruptly vanished. I saw only the man, the glowing machine, and the dim apartment. Tillinghast was grinning repulsively at the revolver which I had almost unconsciously drawn, but from his expression I was sure he had seen and heard as much as I, if not a great deal more. I whispered what I had experienced, and he bade me remain as quiet and receptive as possible.

"Don't move," he cautioned, "for in these rays *we are able to be seen as well as to see.* I told you the servants left, but I didn't tell you *how.* It was that thick-witted housekeeper—she turned on the lights downstairs after I had warned her not to, and the wires picked up sympathetic vibrations. It must have been frightful—I could hear the screams up here in spite of all I was seeing and hearing from another direction, and later it was rather awful to find those empty heaps of clothes around the house. Mrs. Updike's clothes were close to the front hall switch—that's how I know she did it. It got them all. But so long as we don't move we're fairly safe. Remember we're dealing with a hideous world in which we are practically helpless.... *Keep still!*"

The combined shock of the revelation and of the abrupt command gave me a kind of paralysis, and in my terror my mind again opened to the impressions coming from what Tillinghast called "*beyond*". I was now in a vortex of sound and motion, with confused pictures before my eyes. I saw the blurred outlines of the room, but from some point in space there seemed to be pouring a seething column of unrecognisable shapes or clouds, penetrating the solid roof at a point ahead and to the right of me. Then I glimpsed the temple-like effect again, but this time the pillars reached up into an aërial ocean of light, which sent down one blinding beam along the path of the cloudy column I had seen before. After that the scene was almost wholly kaleidoscopic, and in the jumble of sights, sounds, and unidentified sense-impressions I felt that I was about to dissolve or in some way lose the solid form. One definite flash I shall always remember. I seemed for an instant to behold a patch of strange night sky filled with shining, revolving spheres, and as it receded I saw that the glowing suns formed a constellation or galaxy of settled shape; this shape being the distorted face of Crawford Tillinghast. At another time I felt huge animate things brushing past me and occasionally *walking or drifting through my supposedly solid body*, and thought I saw Tillinghast look at them as though his better trained senses could catch them visually. I recalled what he had said of the pineal gland, and wondered what he saw with this preternatural eye.

Suddenly I myself became possessed of a kind of augmented sight. Over and above the luminous and shadowy chaos arose a picture which, though vague, held the elements of consistency and permanence. It was indeed somewhat familiar, for the unusual part was superimposed upon the usual terrestrial scene much as a cinema view may be thrown upon the painted curtain of a theatre. I saw the attic laboratory, the electrical machine, and the unsightly form of Tillinghast opposite me; but of all the space unoccupied by familiar material objects not one particle was vacant. Indescribable shapes both alive and otherwise were mixed in disgusting disarray, and close to every known thing were whole worlds of alien, unknown entities. It likewise seemed that all the known things entered into the composition of other unknown things, and vice versa. Foremost among the living objects were great inky, jellyish monstrosities which flabbily quivered in harmony with the vibrations from the machine. They were present in loathsome profusion, and I saw to my horror that they *overlapped*; that they were semi-fluid and capable of passing through one another and through what we know as solids. These things were never still, but seemed ever floating about with some malignant purpose. Sometimes they appeared to devour one another, the attacker launching itself at its victim and instantaneously obliterating the latter from sight. Shudderingly I felt that I knew what had obliterated the unfortunate servants, and could not exclude the things from my mind as I strove to observe other properties of the newly visible world that lies unseen around us. But Tillinghast had been watching me, and was speaking.

"You see them? You see them? You see the things that float and flop about you and through you every moment of your life? You see the creatures that form what men call the pure air and the blue sky? Have I not succeeded in breaking down the barrier; have I not shewn you worlds that no other living men have seen?" I heard him scream through the horrible chaos, and looked at the wild face thrust so offensively close to mine. His eyes were pits of flame, and they glared at me with what I now saw was overwhelming hatred. The machine droned detestably.

"You think those floundering things wiped out the servants? Fool, they are harmless! But the servants *are* gone, aren't they? You tried to stop me; you discouraged me when I needed every drop of encouragement I could get; you were afraid of the cosmic truth, you damned coward, but now I've got you! What swept up the servants? What made them scream so loud? ... Don't know, eh? You'll know soon enough! Look at me—listen to what I say—do you suppose there are really any such things as time and magnitude? Do you fancy there are such things as form or matter? I tell you, I have struck depths that your little brain can't picture! I have seen beyond the bounds of infinity and drawn down daemons from the stars.... I have harnessed the shadows that stride from world to world to sow death and madness.... Space belongs to me, do you hear? Things are hunting me now—the things that devour and dissolve—but I know how to elude them. It is you they will get, as they got the servants. Stirring, dear sir? I told you it was dangerous to move. I have saved you so far by telling you to keep still—saved you to see more sights and to listen to me. If you had moved, they would have been at you long ago. Don't worry, they won't *hurt* you. They didn't hurt the servants—it was *seeing* that made the poor devils scream so. My pets are not pretty, for they come out of places where aesthetic standards are—*very different*. Disintegration is quite painless, I assure you—but *I want you to see them*. I almost saw them, but I knew how to stop. You are not curious? I always knew you were no scientist! Trembling, eh? Trembling with anxiety to see the ultimate things I have discovered? Why don't you move, then? Tired? Well, don't worry, my friend, *for they are coming....* Look! Look, curse you, look! ... It's just over your left shoulder...."

What remains to be told is very brief, and may be familiar to you from the newspaper accounts. The police heard a shot in the old Tillinghast house and found us there—Tillinghast dead and me unconscious. They arrested me because the revolver was in my hand, but released me in three hours, after they found it was apoplexy which had finished Tillinghast and saw that my shot had been directed at the noxious machine which now lay hopelessly shattered on the laboratory floor. I did not tell very much of what I had seen, for I feared the coroner would be sceptical; but from the evasive outline I did give, the doctor told me that I had undoubtedly been hypnotised by the vindictive and homicidal madman.

I wish I could believe that doctor. It would help my shaky nerves if I could dismiss what I now have to think of the air and the sky about and above me. I never feel alone or comfortable, and a hideous sense of pursuit sometimes comes chillingly on me when I am weary. What prevents me from believing the doctor is this one simple fact—that the police never found the bodies of those servants whom they say Crawford Tillinghast murdered.

NYARLATHOTEP

Nyarlathotep ... the crawling chaos ... I am the last ... I will tell the audient void....

I do not recall distinctly when it began, but it was months ago. The general tension was horrible. To a season of political and social upheaval was added a strange and brooding apprehension of hideous physical danger; a danger widespread and all-embracing, such a danger as may be imagined only in the most terrible phantasms of the night. I recall that the people went about with pale and worried faces, and whispered warnings and prophecies which no one dared consciously repeat or acknowledge to himself that he had heard. A sense of monstrous guilt was upon the land, and out of the abysses between the stars swept chill currents that made men shiver in dark and lonely places. There was a daemoniac alteration in the sequence of the seasons—the autumn heat lingered fearsomely, and everyone felt that the world and perhaps the universe had passed from the control of known gods or forces to that of gods or forces which were unknown.

And it was then that Nyarlathotep came out of Egypt. Who he was, none could tell, but he was of the old native blood and looked like a Pharaoh. The fellahin knelt when they saw him, yet could not say why. He said he had risen up out of the blackness of twenty-seven centuries, and that he had heard messages from places not on this planet. Into the lands of civilisation came Nyarlathotep, swarthy, slender, and sinister, always buying strange instruments of glass and metal and combining them into instruments yet stranger. He spoke much of the sciences—of electricity and psychology—and gave exhibitions of power which sent his spectators away speechless, yet which swelled his fame to exceeding magnitude. Men advised one another to see Nyarlathotep, and shuddered. And where Nyarlathotep went, rest vanished; for the small hours were rent with the screams of nightmare. Never before had the screams of nightmare been such a public problem; now the wise men almost wished they could forbid sleep in the small hours, that the shrieks of cities might less horribly disturb the pale, pitying moon as it glimmered on green waters gliding under bridges, and old steeples crumbling against a sickly sky.

I remember when Nyarlathotep came to my city—the great, the old, the terrible city of unnumbered crimes. My friend had told me of him, and of the impelling fascination and allurement of his revelations, and I burned with eagerness to explore his uttermost mysteries. My friend said they were horrible and impressive beyond my most fevered imaginings; that what was thrown on a screen in the darkened room prophesied things none but Nyarlathotep dared prophesy, and that in the sputter of his sparks there was taken from men that which had never been taken before yet which shewed only in the eyes. And I heard it hinted abroad that those who knew Nyarlathotep looked on sights which others saw not.

It was in the hot autumn that I went through the night with the restless crowds to see Nyarlathotep; through the stifling night and up the endless stairs into the choking room. And shadowed on a screen, I saw hooded forms amidst ruins, and yellow evil faces peering from behind fallen monuments. And I saw the world battling against blackness; against the waves of destruction from ultimate space; whirling, churning; struggling around the dimming, cooling sun. Then the sparks played amazingly around the heads of the spectators, and hair stood up on end whilst shadows more grotesque than I can tell came out and squatted on the heads. And when I, who was colder and more scientific than the rest, mumbled a trembling protest about "imposture" and "static electricity", Nyarlathotep drave us all out, down the dizzy stairs into the damp, hot, deserted midnight streets. I screamed aloud that I was *not* afraid; that I never could be afraid; and others screamed with me for solace. We sware to one another that the city *was* exactly the same, and still alive; and when the electric lights began to fade we cursed the company over and over again, and laughed at the queer faces we made.

I believe we felt something coming down from the greenish moon, for when we began to depend on its light we drifted into curious involuntary marching formations and seemed to know our destinations though we dared not think of them. Once we looked at the pavement and found the blocks loose and displaced by grass, with scarce a line of rusted metal to shew where the tramways had run. And again we saw a tram-car, lone, windowless, dilapidated, and almost on its side. When we gazed around the horizon, we could not find the third tower by the river, and noticed that the silhouette of the second tower was ragged at the top. Then we split up into narrow columns, each of which seemed drawn in a different direction. One disappeared in a narrow alley to the left, leaving only the echo of a shocking moan. Another filed down a weed-choked subway entrance, howling with a laughter that was mad. My own column was sucked toward the open country, and presently felt a chill which was not of the hot autumn; for as we stalked out on the dark moor, we beheld around us the hellish moon-glitter of evil snows. Trackless, inexplicable snows, swept asunder in one direction only, where lay a gulf all the blacker for its glittering walls. The column seemed very thin indeed as it plodded dreamily into the gulf. I lingered behind, for the black rift in the green-litten snow was frightful, and I thought I had heard the reverberations of a disquieting wail as my companions vanished; but my power to linger was slight. As if beckoned by those who had gone before, I half floated between the titanic snowdrifts, quivering and afraid, into the sightless vortex of the unimaginable.

Screamingly sentient, dumbly delirious, only the gods that were can tell. A sickened, sensitive shadow writhing in hands that are not hands, and whirled blindly past ghastly midnights of rotting creation, corpses of dead worlds with sores that were cities, charnel winds that brush the pallid stars and make them flicker low. Beyond the worlds vague ghosts of monstrous things; half-seen columns of unsanctified temples that rest on nameless rocks beneath space and reach up to dizzy vacua above the spheres of light and darkness. And through this revolting graveyard of the universe the muffled, maddening beating of drums, and thin, monotonous whine of blasphemous flutes from inconceivable, unlighted chambers beyond Time; the detestable pounding and piping whereunto dance slowly, awkwardly, and absurdly the gigantic, tenebrous ultimate gods—the blind, voiceless, mindless gargoyles whose soul is Nyarlathotep.

THE PICTURE IN THE HOUSE

Searchers after horror haunt strange, far places. For them are the catacombs of Ptolemais, and the carven mausolea of the nightmare countries. They climb to the moonlit towers of ruined Rhine castles, and falter down black cobwebbed steps beneath the scattered stones of forgotten cities in Asia. The haunted wood and the desolate mountain are their shrines, and they linger around the sinister monoliths on uninhabited islands. But the true epicure in the terrible, to whom a new thrill of unutterable ghastliness is the chief end and justification of existence, esteems most of all the ancient, lonely farmhouses of backwoods New England; for there the dark elements of strength, solitude, grotesqueness, and ignorance combine to form the perfection of the hideous.

Most horrible of all sights are the little unpainted wooden houses remote from travelled ways, usually squatted upon some damp, grassy slope or leaning against some gigantic outcropping of rock. Two hundred years and more they have leaned or squatted there, while the vines have crawled and the trees have swelled and spread. They are almost hidden now in lawless luxuriances of green and guardian shrouds of shadow; but the small-paned windows still stare shockingly, as if blinking through a lethal stupor which wards off madness by dulling the memory of unutterable things.

In such houses have dwelt generations of strange people, whose like the world has never seen. Seized with a gloomy and fanatical belief which exiled them from their kind, their ancestors sought the wilderness for freedom. There the scions of a conquering race indeed flourished free from the restrictions of their fellows, but cowered in an appalling slavery to the dismal phantasms of their own minds. Divorced from the enlightenment of civilisation, the strength of these Puritans turned into singular channels; and in their isolation, morbid self-repression, and struggle for life with relentless Nature, there came to them dark furtive traits from the prehistoric depths of their cold Northern heritage. By necessity practical and by philosophy stern, these folk were not beautiful in their sins. Erring as all mortals must, they were forced by their rigid code to seek concealment above all else; so that they came to use less and less taste in what they concealed. Only the silent, sleepy, staring houses in the backwoods can tell all that has lain hidden since the early days; and they are not communicative, being loath to shake off the drowsiness which helps them forget. Sometimes one feels that it would be merciful to tear down these houses, for they must often dream.

It was to a time-battered edifice of this description that I was driven one afternoon in November, 1896, by a rain of such chilling copiousness that any shelter was preferable to exposure. I had been travelling for some time amongst the people of the Miskatonic Valley in quest of certain genealogical data; and from the remote, devious, and problematical nature of my course, had deemed it convenient to employ a bicycle despite the lateness of the season. Now I found myself upon an apparently abandoned road which I had chosen as the shortest cut to Arkham; overtaken by the storm at a point far from any town, and confronted with no refuge save the antique and repellent wooden building which blinked with bleared windows from between two huge leafless elms near the foot of a rocky hill. Distant though it was from the remnant of a road, this house none the less impressed me unfavourably the very moment I espied it. Honest, wholesome structures do not stare at travellers so slyly and hauntingly, and in my genealogical researches I had encountered legends of a century before which biased me against places of this kind. Yet the force of the elements was such as to overcome my scruples, and I did not hesitate to wheel my machine up the weedy rise to the closed door which seemed at once so suggestive and secretive.

I had somehow taken it for granted that the house was abandoned, yet as I approached it I was not so sure; for though the walks were indeed overgrown with weeds, they seemed to retain their nature a little too well to argue complete desertion. Therefore instead of trying the door I knocked, feeling as I did so a trepidation I could scarcely explain. As I waited on the rough, mossy rock which served as a doorstep, I glanced at the neighbouring windows and the panes of the transom above me, and noticed that although old, rattling, and almost opaque with dirt, they were not broken. The building, then, must still be inhabited, despite its isolation and general neglect. However, my rapping evoked no response, so after repeating the summons I tried the rusty latch and found the door unfastened. Inside was a little vestibule with walls from which the plaster was falling, and through the doorway came a faint but peculiarly hateful odour. I entered, carrying my bicycle, and closed the door behind me. Ahead rose a narrow staircase, flanked by a small door probably leading to the cellar, while to the left and right were closed doors leading to rooms on the ground floor.

Leaning my cycle against the wall I opened the door at the left, and crossed into a small low-ceiled chamber but dimly lighted by its two dusty windows and furnished in the barest and most primitive possible way. It appeared to be a kind of sitting-room, for it had a table and several chairs, and an immense fireplace above which ticked an antique clock on a mantel. Books and papers were very few, and in the prevailing gloom I could not readily discern the titles. What interested me was the uniform air of archaism as displayed in every visible detail. Most of the houses in this region I had found rich in relics of the past, but here the antiquity was curiously complete; for in all the room I could not discover a single article of definitely post-revolutionary date. Had the furnishings been less humble, the place would have been a collector's paradise.

As I surveyed this quaint apartment, I felt an increase in that aversion first excited by the bleak exterior of the house. Just what it was that I feared or loathed, I could by no means define; but something in the whole atmosphere seemed redolent of unhallowed age, of unpleasant crudeness, and of secrets which should be forgotten. I felt disinclined to sit down, and wandered about examining the various articles which I had noticed. The first object of my curiosity was a book of medium size lying upon the table and presenting such an antediluvian aspect that I marvelled at beholding it outside a museum or library. It was bound in leather with metal fittings, and was in an excellent state of preservation; being altogether an unusual sort of volume to encounter in an abode so lowly. When I opened it to the title page my wonder grew even greater, for it proved to be nothing less rare than Pigafetta's account of the Congo region, written in Latin from the notes of the sailor Lopez and printed at Frankfort in 1598. I had often heard of this work, with its curious illustrations by the brothers De Bry, hence for a moment forgot my uneasiness in my desire to turn the pages before me. The engravings were indeed interesting, drawn wholly from imagination and careless descriptions, and represented negroes with white skins and Caucasian features; nor would I soon have closed the book had not an exceedingly trivial circumstance upset my tired nerves and revived my sensation of disquiet. What annoyed me was merely the persistent way in which the volume tended to fall open of itself at Plate XII, which represented in gruesome detail a butcher's shop of the cannibal Anziques. I experienced some shame at my susceptibility to so slight a thing, but the drawing nevertheless disturbed me, especially in connexion with some adjacent passages descriptive of Anzique gastronomy.

I had turned to a neighbouring shelf and was examining its meagre literary contents—an eighteenth-century Bible, a "Pilgrim's Progress" of like period, illustrated with grotesque woodcuts and printed by the almanack-maker Isaiah Thomas, the rotting bulk of Cotton Mather's "Magnalia Christi Americana", and a few other books of evidently equal age—when my attention was aroused by the unmistakable sound of walking in the room overhead. At first astonished and startled, considering the lack of response to my recent knocking at the door, I immediately afterward concluded that the walker had just awaked from a sound sleep; and listened with less surprise as the footsteps sounded on the creaking stairs. The tread was heavy, yet seemed to contain a curious quality of cautiousness; a quality which I disliked the more because the tread was heavy. When I had entered the room I had shut the door behind me. Now, after a moment of silence during which the walker may have been inspecting my bicycle in the hall, I heard a fumbling at the latch and saw the panelled portal swing open again.

In the doorway stood a person of such singular appearance that I should have exclaimed aloud but for the restraints of good breeding. Old, white-bearded, and ragged, my host possessed a countenance and physique which inspired equal wonder and respect. His height could not have been less than six feet, and despite a general air of age and poverty he was stout and powerful in proportion. His face, almost hidden by a long beard which grew high on the cheeks, seemed abnormally ruddy and less wrinkled than one might expect; while over a high forehead fell a shock of white hair little thinned by the years. His blue eyes, though a trifle bloodshot, seemed inexplicably keen and burning. But for his horrible unkemptness the man would have been as distinguished-looking as he was impressive. This unkemptness, however, made him offensive despite his face and figure. Of what his clothing consisted I could hardly tell, for it seemed to me no more than a mass of tatters surmounting a pair of high, heavy boots; and his lack of cleanliness surpassed description.

The appearance of this man, and the instinctive fear he inspired, prepared me for something like enmity; so that I almost shuddered through surprise and a sense of uncanny incongruity when he motioned me to a chair and addressed me in a thin, weak voice full of fawning respect and ingratiating hospitality. His speech was very curious, an extreme form of Yankee dialect I had thought long extinct; and I studied it closely as he sat down opposite me for conversation.

"Ketched in the rain, be ye?" he greeted. "Glad ye was nigh the haouse en' hed the sense ta come right in. I calc'late I was asleep, else I'd a heerd ye—I ain't as young as I uster be, an' I need a paowerful sight o' naps naowadays. Trav'lin' fur? I hain't seed many folks 'long this rud sence they tuk off the Arkham stage."

I replied that I was going to Arkham, and apologised for my rude entry into his domicile, whereupon he continued.

"Glad ta see ye, young Sir—new faces is scurce arount here, an' I hain't got much ta cheer me up these days. Guess yew hail from Bosting, don't ye? I never ben thar, but I kin tell a taown man when I see 'im—we hed one fer deestrick schoolmaster in 'eighty-four, but he quit suddent an' no one never heerd on 'im sence—" Here the old man lapsed into a kind of chuckle, and made no explanation when I questioned him. He seemed to be in an aboundingly good humour, yet to possess those eccentricities which one might guess from his grooming. For some time he rambled on with an almost feverish geniality, when it struck me to ask him how he came by so rare a book as Pigafetta's "Regnum Congo". The effect of this volume had not left me, and I felt a certain hesitancy in speaking of it; but curiosity overmastered all the vague fears which had steadily accumulated since my first glimpse of the house. To my relief, the question did not seem an awkward one; for the old man answered freely and volubly.

"Oh, thet Afriky book? Cap'n Ebenezer Holt traded me thet in 'sixty-eight—him as was kilt in the war." Something about the name of Ebenezer Holt caused me to look up sharply. I had encountered it in my genealogical work, but not in any record since the Revolution. I wondered if my host could help me in the task at which I was labouring, and resolved to ask him about it later on. He continued.

"Ebenezer was on a Salem merchantman for years, an' picked up a sight o' queer stuff in every port. He got this in London, I guess—he uster like ter buy things at the shops. I was up ta his haouse onct, on the hill, tradin' hosses, when I see this book. I relished the picters, so he give it in on a swap. 'Tis a queer book—here, leave me git on my spetacles—" The old man fumbled among his rags, producing a pair of dirty and amazingly antique glasses with small octagonal lenses and steel bows. Donning these, he reached for the volume on the table and turned the pages lovingly.

"Ebenezer cud read a leetle o' this—'tis Latin—but I can't. I hed two er three schoolmasters read me a bit, and Passon Clark, him they say got draownded in the pond—kin yew make anything outen it?" I told him that I could, and translated for his benefit a paragraph near the beginning. If I erred, he was not scholar enough to correct me; for he seemed childishly pleased at my English version. His proximity was becoming rather obnoxious, yet I saw no way to escape without offending him. I was amused at the childish fondness of this ignorant old man for the pictures in a book he could not read, and wondered how much better he could read the few books in English which adorned the room. This revelation of simplicity removed much of the ill-defined apprehension I had felt, and I smiled as my host rambled on:

"Queer haow picters kin set a body thinkin'. Take this un here near the front. Hev yew ever seed trees like thet, with big leaves a-floppin' over an' daown? And them men—them can't be niggers—they dew beat all! Kinder like Injuns, I guess, even ef they be in Afriky. Some o' these here critters looks like monkeys, or half monkeys an' half men, but I never heerd o' nothing like this un." Here he pointed to a fabulous creature of the artist, which one might describe as a sort of dragon with the head of an alligator.

"But naow I'll shew ye the best un—over here nigh the middle—" The old man's speech grew a trifle thicker and his eyes assumed a brighter glow; but his fumbling hands, though seemingly clumsier than before, were entirely adequate to their mission. The book fell open, almost of its own accord and as if from frequent consultation at this place, to the repellent twelfth plate shewing a butcher's shop amongst the Anzique cannibals. My sense of restlessness returned, though I did not exhibit it. The especially bizarre thing was that the artist had made his Africans look like white men—the limbs and quarters hanging about the walls of the shop were ghastly, while the butcher with his axe was hideously incongruous. But my host seemed to relish the view as much as I disliked it.

"What d'ye think o' this—ain't never see the like hereabouts, eh? When I see this I telled Eb Holt, 'Thar's suthin' ta stir ye up an' make yer blood tickle!' When I read in Scripter about slayin'—like them Midianites was slew—I kinder think things, but I ain't got no picter of it. Here a body kin see all they is to it—I s'pose 'tis sinful, but ain't we all born an' livin' in sin?—Thet feller bein' chopped up gives me a tickle every time I look at 'im—I hev ta keep lookin' at 'im—see whar the butcher cut off his feet? Thar's his head on thet bench, with one arm side of it, an' t'other arm's on the graound side o' the meat block."

As the man mumbled on in his shocking ecstasy the expression on his hairy, spectacled face became indescribable, but his voice sank rather than mounted. My own sensations can scarcely be recorded. All the terror I had dimly felt before rushed upon me actively and vividly, and I knew that I loathed the ancient and abhorrent creature so near me with an infinite intensity. His madness, or at least his partial perversion, seemed beyond dispute. He was almost whispering now, with a huskiness more terrible than a scream, and I trembled as I listened.

"As I says, 'tis queer haow picters sets ye thinkin'. D'ye know, young Sir, I'm right sot on this un here. Arter I got the book off Eb I uster look at it a lot, especial when I'd heerd Passon Clark rant o' Sundays in his big wig. Onct I tried suthin' funny—here, young Sir, don't git skeert—all I done was ter look at the picter afore I kilt the sheep for market—killin' sheep was kinder more fun arter lookin' at it—" The tone of the old man now sank very low, sometimes becoming so faint that his words were hardly audible. I listened to the rain, and to the rattling of the bleared, small-paned windows, and marked a rumbling of approaching thunder quite unusual for the season. Once a terrific flash and peal shook the frail house to its foundations, but the whisperer seemed not to notice it.

"Killin' sheep was kinder more fun—but d'ye know, 'twan't quite *satisfyin'*. Queer haow a *cravin'* gits a holt on ye— As ye love the Almighty, young man, don't tell nobody, but I swar ter Gawd thet picter begun ta make me *hungry fer victuals I couldn't raise nor buy*—here, set still, what's ailin' ye?—I didn't do nothin', only I wondered haow 'twud be ef I *did*— They say meat makes blood an' flesh, an' gives ye new life, so I wondered ef 'twudn't make a man live longer an' longer ef 'twas *more the same*—" But the whisperer never continued. The interruption was not produced by my fright, nor by the rapidly increasing storm amidst whose fury I was presently to open my eyes on a smoky solitude of blackened ruins. It was produced by a very simple though somewhat unusual happening.

The open book lay flat between us, with the picture staring repulsively upward. As the old man whispered the words "*more the same*" a tiny spattering impact was heard, and something shewed on the yellowed paper of the upturned volume. I thought of the rain and of a leaky roof, but rain is not red. On the butcher's shop of the Anzique cannibals a small red spattering glistened picturesquely, lending vividness to the horror of the engraving. The old man saw it, and stopped whispering even before my expression of horror made it necessary; saw it and glanced quickly toward the floor of the room he had left an hour before. I followed his glance, and beheld just above us on the loose plaster of the ancient ceiling a large irregular spot of wet crimson which seemed to spread even as I viewed it. I did not shriek or move, but merely shut my eyes. A moment later came the titanic thunderbolt of thunderbolts; blasting that accursed house of unutterable secrets and bringing the oblivion which alone saved my mind.

EX OBLIVIONE

When the last days were upon me, and the ugly trifles of existence began to drive me to madness like the small drops of water that torturers let fall ceaselessly upon one spot of their victim's body, I loved the irradiate refuge of sleep. In my dreams I found a little of the beauty I had vainly sought in life, and wandered through old gardens and enchanted woods.

Once when the wind was soft and scented I heard the south calling, and sailed endlessly and languorously under strange stars.

Once when the gentle rain fell I glided in a barge down a sunless stream under the earth till I reached another world of purple twilight, iridescent arbours, and undying roses.

And once I walked through a golden valley that led to shadowy groves and ruins, and ended in a mighty wall green with antique vines, and pierced by a little gate of bronze.

Many times I walked through that valley, and longer and longer would I pause in the spectral half-light where the giant trees squirmed and twisted grotesquely, and the grey ground stretched damply from trunk to trunk, sometimes disclosing the mould-stained stones of buried temples. And always the goal of my fancies was the mighty vine-grown wall with the little gate of bronze therein.

After a while, as the days of waking became less and less bearable from their greyness and sameness, I would often drift in opiate peace through the valley and the shadowy groves, and wonder how I might seize them for my eternal dwelling-place, so that I need no more crawl back to a dull world stript of interest and new colours. And as I looked upon the little gate in the mighty wall, I felt that beyond it lay a dream-country from which, once it was entered, there would be no return.

So each night in sleep I strove to find the hidden latch of the gate in the ivied antique wall, though it was exceedingly well hidden. And I would tell myself that the realm beyond the wall was not more lasting merely, but more lovely and radiant as well.

Then one night in the dream city of Zakarion I found a yellowed papyrus filled with the thoughts of dream-sages who dwelt of old in that city, and who were too wise ever to be born in the waking world. Therein were written many things concerning the world of dream, and among them was lore of a golden valley and a sacred grove with temples, and a high wall pierced by a little bronze gate. When I saw this lore, I knew that it touched on the scenes I had haunted, and I therefore read long in the yellowed papyrus.

Some of the dream-sages wrote gorgeously of the wonders beyond the irrepassable gate, but others told of horror and disappointment. I knew not which to believe, yet longed more and more to cross for ever into the unknown land; for doubt and secrecy are the lure of lures, and no new horror can be more terrible than the daily torture of the commonplace. So when I learned of the drug which would unlock the gate and drive me through, I resolved to take it when next I awaked.

Last night I swallowed the drug and floated dreamily into the golden valley and the shadowy groves; and when I came this time to the antique wall, I saw that the small gate of bronze was ajar. From beyond came a glow that weirdly lit the giant twisted trees and tops of the buried temples, and I drifted on songfully, expectant of the glories of the land from whence I should never return.

But as the gate swung wider and the sorcery of drug and dream pushed me through, I knew that all sights and glories were at an end; for in that new realm was neither land nor sea, but only the white void of unpeopled and illimitable space. So, happier than I had ever dared hope to be, I dissolved again into that native infinity of crystal oblivion from which the daemon Life had called me for one brief and desolate hour.

SWEET ERMENGARDE; OR, THE HEART OF A COUNTRY GIRL

By Percy Simple

Chapter I.
A Simple Rustic Maid

Ermengarde Stubbs was the beauteous blonde daughter of Hiram Stubbs, a poor but honest farmer-bootlegger of Hogton, Vt. Her name was originally Ethyl Ermengarde, but her father persuaded her to drop the praenomen after the passage of the 18th Amendment, averring that it made him thirsty by reminding him of ethyl alcohol, C_2H_5OH. His own products contained mostly methyl or wood alcohol, CH_3OH. Ermengarde confessed to sixteen summers, and branded as mendacious all reports to the effect that she was thirty. She had large black eyes, a prominent Roman nose, light hair which was never dark at the roots except when the local drug store was short on supplies, and a beautiful but inexpensive complexion. She was about 5^{ft} $5.33...^{in}$ tall, weighed 115.47 lbs. on her father's corn scales—also off them—and was adjudged most lovely by all the village swains who admired her father's farm and liked his liquid crops.

Ermengarde's hand was sought in matrimony by two ardent lovers. 'Squire Hardman, who had a mortgage on the old home, was very rich and elderly. He was dark and cruelly handsome, and always rode horseback and carried a riding-crop. Long had he sought the radiant Ermengarde, and now his ardour was fanned to fever heat by a secret known to him alone—for upon the humble acres of

Farmer Stubbs he had discovered a vein of rich GOLD!! "Aha!" said he, "I will win the maiden ere her parent knows of his unsuspected wealth, and join to my fortune a greater fortune still!" And so he began to call twice a week instead of once as before.

But alas for the sinister designs of a villain—'Squire Hardman was not the only suitor for the fair one. Close by the village dwelt another—the handsome Jack Manly, whose curly yellow hair had won the sweet Ermengarde's affection when both were toddling youngsters at the village school. Jack had long been too bashful to declare his passion, but one day while strolling along a shady lane by the old mill with Ermengarde, he had found courage to utter that which was within his heart.

"O light of my life," said he, "my soul is so overburdened that I must speak! Ermengarde, my ideal [he pronounced it i-deel!], life has become an empty thing without you. Beloved of my spirit, behold a suppliant kneeling in the dust before thee. Ermengarde—oh, Ermengarde, raise me to an heaven of joy and say that you will some day be mine! It is true that I am poor, but have I not youth and strength to fight my way to fame? This I can do only for you, dear Ethyl—pardon me, Ermengarde—my only, my most precious—" but here he paused to wipe his eyes and mop his brow, and the fair responded:

"Jack—my angel—at last—I mean, this is so unexpected and quite unprecedented! I had never dreamed that you entertained sentiments of affection in connexion with one so lowly as Farmer Stubbs' child—for I am still but a child! Such is your natural nobility that I had feared—I mean thought—you would be blind to such slight charms as I possess, and that you would seek your fortune in the great city; there meeting and wedding one of those more comely damsels whose splendour we observe in fashion books.

"But, Jack, since it is really I whom you adore, let us waive all needless circumlocution. Jack—my darling—my heart has long been susceptible to your manly graces. I cherish an affection for thee—consider me thine own and be sure to buy the ring at Perkins' hardware store where they have such nice imitation diamonds in the window."

"Ermengarde, me love!"

"Jack—my precious!"

"My darling!"

"My own!"

"My Gawd!"

[Curtain]

Chapter II.
And the Villain Still Pursued Her

But these tender passages, sacred though their fervour, did not pass unobserved by profane eyes; for crouched in the bushes and gritting his teeth was the dastardly 'Squire Hardman! When the lovers had finally strolled away he leapt out into the lane, viciously twirling his moustache and riding-crop, and kicking an unquestionably innocent cat who was also out strolling.

"Curses!" he cried—Hardman, not the cat—"I am foiled in my plot to get the farm and the girl! But Jack Manly shall never succeed! I am a man of power—and we shall see!"

Thereupon he repaired to the humble Stubbs cottage, where he found the fond father in the still-cellar washing bottles under the supervision of the gentle wife and mother, Hannah Stubbs. Coming directly to the point, the villain spoke:

"Farmer Stubbs, I cherish a tender affection of long standing for your lovely offspring, Ethyl Ermengarde. I am consumed with love, and wish her hand in matrimony. Always a man of few words, I will not descend to euphemism. Give me the girl or I will foreclose the mortgage and take the old home!"

"But, Sir," pleaded the distracted Stubbs while his stricken spouse merely glowered, "I am sure the child's affections are elsewhere placed."

"She must be mine!" sternly snapped the sinister 'Squire. "I will make her love me—none shall resist my will! Either she becomes muh wife or the old homestead goes!"

And with a sneer and flick of his riding-crop 'Squire Hardman strode out into the night.

Scarce had he departed, when there entered by the back door the radiant lovers, eager to tell the senior Stubbses of their new-found happiness. Imagine the universal consternation which reigned when all was known! Tears flowed like white mule, till suddenly Jack remembered he was the hero and raised his head, declaiming in appropriately virile accents:

"Never shall the fair Ermengarde be offered up to this beast as a sacrifice while I live! I shall protect her—she is mine, mine, mine—and then some! Fear not, dear father and mother to be—I will defend you all! You shall have the old home still [adverb, not noun—although Jack was by no means out of sympathy with Stubbs' kind of farm produce] and I shall lead to the altar the beauteous Ermengarde, loveliest of her sex! To perdition with the crool 'Squire and his ill-gotten gold—the right shall always win, and a hero is always in the right! I will go to the great city and there make a fortune to save you all ere the mortgage fall due! Farewell, my love—I leave you now in tears, but I shall return to pay off the mortgage and claim you as my bride!"

"Jack, my protector!"

"Ermie, my tootsie roll!"

"Dearest!"

"Darling!—and don't forget that ring at Perkins'."

"Oh!"

"Ah!"

[Curtain]

Chapter III.
A Dastardly Act

But the resourceful 'Squire Hardman was not so easily to be foiled. Close by the village lay a disreputable settlement of unkempt shacks, populated by a shiftless scum who lived by thieving and other odd jobs. Here the devilish villain secured two accomplices—ill-favoured fellows who were very clearly no gentlemen. And in the night the evil three broke into the Stubbs cottage and abducted the fair Ermengarde, taking her to a wretched hovel in the settlement and placing her under the charge of Mother Maria, a hideous old hag. Farmer Stubbs was quite distracted, and would have advertised in the papers if the cost had been less than a cent a word for each insertion. Ermengarde was firm, and never wavered in her refusal to wed the villain.

"Aha, my proud beauty," quoth he, "I have ye in me power, and sooner or later I will break that will of thine! Meanwhile think of your poor old father and mother as turned out of hearth and home and wandering helpless through the meadows!"

"Oh, spare them, spare them!" said the maiden.

"Neverr … ha ha ha ha!" leered the brute.

And so the cruel days sped on, while all in ignorance young Jack Manly was seeking fame and fortune in the great city.

Chapter IV.
Subtle Villainy

One day as 'Squire Hardman sat in the front parlour of his expensive and palatial home, indulging in his favourite pastime of gnashing his teeth and swishing his riding-crop, a great thought came to him; and he cursed aloud at the statue of Satan on the onyx mantelpiece.

"Fool that I am!" he cried. "Why did I ever waste all this trouble on the girl when I can get the farm by simply foreclosing? I never thought of that! I will let the girl go, take the farm, and be free to wed some fair city maid like the leading lady of that burlesque troupe which played last week at the Town Hall!"

And so he went down to the settlement, apologised to Ermengarde, let her go home, and went home himself to plot new crimes and invent new modes of villainy.

The days wore on, and the Stubbses grew very sad over the coming loss of their home and still but nobody seemed able to do anything about it. One day a party of hunters from the city chanced to stray over the old farm, and one of them found the gold!! Hiding his discovery from his companions, he feigned rattlesnake-bite and went to the Stubbs cottage for aid of the usual kind. Ermengarde opened the door and saw him. He also saw her, and in that moment resolved to win her and the gold. "For my old mother's sake I must"—he cried loudly to himself. "No sacrifice is too great!"

Chapter V.
The City Chap

Algernon Reginald Jones was a polished man of the world from the great city, and in his sophisticated hands our poor little Ermengarde was as a mere child. One could almost believe that sixteen-year-old stuff. Algy was a fast worker, but never crude. He could have taught Hardman a thing or two about finesse in sheiking. Thus only a week after his advent to the Stubbs family circle, where he lurked like the vile serpent that he was, he had persuaded the heroine to elope! It was in the night that she went, leaving a note for her parents, sniffing the familiar mash for he last time, and kissing the cat goodbye—touching stuff! On the train Algernon became sleepy and slumped down in his seat, allowing a paper to fall out of his pocket by accident. Ermengarde, taking advantage of her supposed position as a bride-elect, picked up the folded sheet and began to read its perfumed expanse—when lo! she almost fainted! It was a love letter from another woman!!

"Perfidious deceiver!" she whispered at the sleeping Algernon, "so this is all that your boasted fidelity amounts to! I am done with you for all eternity!"

So saying, she pushed him out the window and settled down for a much needed rest.

Chapter VI.
Alone in the Great City

When the noisy train pulled into the dark station at the city, poor helpless Ermengarde was all alone without the money to get back to Hogton. "Oh why," she sighed in innocent regret, "didn't I take his pocketbook before I pushed him out? Oh well, I should worry! He told me all about the city so I can easily earn enough to get home if not to pay off the mortgage!"

But alas for our little heroine—work is not easy for a greenhorn to secure, so for a week she was forced to sleep on park benches and obtain food from the bread-line. Once a wily and wicked person, perceiving her helplessness, offered her a position as dish-washer in a fashionable and depraved cabaret; but our heroine was true to her rustic ideals and refused to work in such a gilded and glittering palace of frivolity—especially since she was offered only $3.00 per week with meals but no board. She tried to look up Jack Manly, her one-time lover, but he was nowhere to be found. Perchance, too, he would not have known her; for in her poverty she had perforce become a brunette again, and Jack had not beheld her in that state since school days. One day she found a neat but costly purse in the park; and after seeing that there was not much in it, took it to the rich lady whose card proclaimed her ownership. Delighted beyond words at the honesty of this forlorn waif, the aristocratic Mrs. Van Itty adopted Ermengarde to replace the little one who had been stolen from her so many years ago. "How like my precious Maude," she sighed, as she watched the fair brunette return to blondeness. And so several weeks passed, with the old folks at home tearing their hair and the wicked 'Squire Hardman chuckling devilishly.

Chapter VII.
Happy Ever Afterward

One day the wealthy heiress Ermengarde S. Van Itty hired a new second assistant chauffeur. Struck by something familiar in his face, she looked again and gasped. Lo! it was none other than the perfidious Algernon Reginald Jones, whom she had pushed from a car window on that fateful day! He had survived—this much was almost immediately evident. Also, he had wed the other woman, who had run away with the milkman and all the money in the house. Now wholly humbled, he asked forgiveness of our heroine, and confided to her the whole tale of the gold on her father's farm. Moved beyond words, she raised his salary a dollar a month and resolved to gratify at last that always unquenchable anxiety to relieve the worry of the old folks. So one bright day Ermengarde motored back to Hogton and arrived at the farm just as 'Squire Hardman was foreclosing the mortgage and ordering the old folks out.

"Stay, villain!" she cried, flashing a colossal roll of bills. "You are foiled at last! Here is your money—now go, and never darken our humble door again!"

Then followed a joyous reunion, whilst the 'Squire twisted his moustache and riding-crop in bafflement and dismay. But hark! What is this? Footsteps sound on the old gravel walk, and who should appear but our hero, Jack Manly—worn and seedy, but radiant of face. Seeking at once the downcast villain, he said:

"'Squire—lend me a ten-spot, will you? I have just come back from the city with my beauteous bride, the fair Bridget Goldstein, and need something to start things on the old farm." Then turning to the Stubbses, he apologised for his inability to pay off the mortgage as agreed.

"Don't mention it," said Ermengarde, "prosperity has come to us, and I will consider it sufficient repayment if you will forget for ever the foolish fancies of our childhood."

All this time Mrs. Van Itty had been sitting in the motor waiting for Ermengarde; but as she lazily eyed the sharp-faced Hannah Stubbs a vague memory started from the back of her brain. Then it all came to her, and she shrieked accusingly at the agrestic matron.

"You—you—Hannah Smith—I know you now! Twenty-eight years ago you were my baby Maude's nurse and stole her from the cradle!! Where, oh, where is my child?" Then a thought came as the lightning in a murky sky. "*Ermengarde*—you say she is *your* daughter.... She is mine! Fate has restored to me my own chee-ild—my tiny Maudie!—Ermengarde—Maude—come to your mother's loving arms!!!"

But Ermengarde was doing some tall thinking. How could she get away with the sixteen-year-old stuff if she had been stolen twenty-eight years ago? And if she was not Stubbs' daughter the gold would never be hers. Mrs. Van Itty was rich, but 'Squire Hardman was richer. So, approaching the dejected villain, she inflicted upon him the last terrible punishment.

"'Squire, dear," she murmured, "I have reconsidered all. I love you and your naive strength. Marry me at once or I will have you prosecuted for that kidnapping last year. Foreclose your mortgage and enjoy with me the gold your cleverness discovered. Come, dear!" And the poor dub did.

THE END.

THE NAMELESS CITY

When I drew nigh the nameless city I knew it was accursed. I was travelling in a parched and terrible valley under the moon, and afar I saw it protruding uncannily above the sands as parts of a corpse may protrude from an ill-made grave. Fear spoke from the age-worn stones of this hoary survivor of the deluge, this great-grandmother of the eldest pyramid; and a viewless aura repelled me and bade me retreat from antique and sinister secrets that no man should see, and no man else had ever dared to see.

Remote in the desert of Araby lies the nameless city, crumbling and inarticulate, its low walls nearly hidden by the sands of uncounted ages. It must have been thus before the first stones of Memphis were laid, and while the bricks of Babylon were yet unbaked. There is no legend so old as to give it a name, or to recall that it was ever alive; but it is told of in whispers around campfires and muttered about by grandams in the tents of sheiks, so that all the tribes shun it without wholly knowing why. It was of this place that Abdul Alhazred the mad poet dreamed on the night before he sang his unexplainable couplet:

> "That is not dead which can eternal lie,
> And with strange aeons even death may die."

I should have known that the Arabs had good reason for shunning the nameless city, the city told of in strange tales but seen by no living man, yet I defied them and went into the untrodden waste with my camel. I alone have seen it, and that is why no other face bears such hideous lines of fear as mine; why no other man shivers so horribly when the night-wind rattles the windows. When I came upon it in the ghastly stillness of unending sleep it looked at me, chilly from the rays of a cold moon amidst the desert's heat. And as I returned its look I forgot my triumph at finding it, and stopped still with my camel to wait for the dawn.

For hours I waited, till the east grew grey and the stars faded, and the grey turned to roseal light edged with gold. I heard a moaning and saw a storm of sand stirring among the antique stones though the sky was clear and the vast reaches of the desert still. Then suddenly above the desert's far rim came the blazing edge of the sun, seen through the tiny sandstorm which was passing away, and in my fevered state I fancied that from some remote depth there came a crash of musical metal to hail the fiery disc as Memnon hails it from the banks of the Nile. My ears rang and my imagination seethed as I led my camel slowly across the sand to that unvocal stone place; that place too old for Egypt and Meroë to remember; that place which I alone of living men had seen.

In and out amongst the shapeless foundations of houses and palaces I wandered, finding never a carving or inscription to tell of those men, if men they were, who built the city and dwelt therein so long ago. The antiquity of the spot was unwholesome, and I longed to encounter some sign or device to prove that the city was indeed fashioned by mankind. There were certain *proportions* and *dimensions* in the ruins which I did not like. I had with me many tools, and dug much within the walls of the obliterated edifices; but progress was slow, and nothing significant was revealed. When night and the moon returned I felt a chill wind which brought new fear, so that I did not dare to remain in the city. And as I went outside the antique walls to sleep, a small sighing sandstorm gathered behind me, blowing over the grey stones though the moon was bright and most of the desert still.

I awaked just at dawn from a pageant of horrible dreams, my ears ringing as from some metallic peal. I saw the sun peering redly through the last gusts of a little sandstorm that hovered over the nameless city, and marked the quietness of the rest of the landscape. Once more I ventured within those brooding ruins that swelled beneath the sand like an ogre under a coverlet, and again dug vainly for relics of the forgotten race. At noon I rested, and in the afternoon I spent much time tracing the walls, and the bygone streets, and the outlines of the nearly vanished buildings. I saw that the city had been mighty indeed, and wondered at the sources of its greatness. To myself I pictured all the splendours of an age so distant that Chaldaea could not recall it, and thought of Sarnath the Doomed, that stood in the land of Mnar when mankind was young, and of Ib, that was carven of grey stone before mankind existed.

All at once I came upon a place where the bed-rock rose stark through the sand and formed a low cliff; and here I saw with joy what seemed to promise further traces of the antediluvian people. Hewn rudely on the face of the cliff were the unmistakable facades of several small, squat rock houses or temples; whose interiors might preserve many secrets of ages too remote for calculation, though sandstorms had long since effaced any carvings which may have been outside.

Very low and sand-choked were all of the dark apertures near me, but I cleared one with my spade and crawled through it, carrying a torch to reveal whatever mysteries it might hold. When I was inside I saw that the cavern was indeed a temple, and beheld plain signs of the race that had lived and worshipped before the desert was a desert. Primitive altars, pillars, and niches, all curiously low, were not absent; and though I saw no sculptures nor frescoes, there were many singular stones clearly shaped into symbols by artificial means. The lowness of the chiselled chamber was very strange, for I could hardly more than kneel upright; but the area was so great that my torch shewed only part at a time. I shuddered oddly in some of the far corners; for certain altars and stones suggested forgotten rites of terrible, revolting, and inexplicable nature, and made me wonder what manner of men could have made and frequented such a temple. When I had seen all that the place contained, I crawled out again, avid to find what the other temples might yield.

Night had now approached, yet the tangible things I had seen made curiosity stronger than fear, so that I did not flee from the long moon-cast shadows that had daunted me when first I saw the nameless city. In the twilight I cleared another aperture and with a new torch crawled into it, finding more vague stones and symbols, though nothing more definite than the other temple had contained. The room was just as low, but much less broad, ending in a very narrow passage crowded with obscure and cryptical shrines. About these shrines I was prying when the noise of a wind and of my camel outside broke through the stillness and drew me forth to see what could have frightened the beast.

The moon was gleaming vividly over the primeval ruins, lighting a dense cloud of sand that seemed blown by a strong but decreasing wind from some point along the cliff ahead of me. I knew it was this chilly, sandy wind which had disturbed the camel, and was about to lead him to a place of better shelter when I chanced to glance up and saw that there was no wind atop the cliff. This astonished me and made me fearful again, but I immediately recalled the sudden local winds I had seen and heard before at sunrise and sunset, and judged it was a normal thing. I decided that it came from some rock fissure leading to a cave, and watched the troubled sand to trace it to its source; soon perceiving that it came from the black orifice of a temple a long distance south of me, almost out of sight. Against the choking sand-cloud I plodded toward this temple, which as I neared it loomed larger than the rest, and shewed a doorway far less clogged with caked sand. I would have entered had not the terrific force of the icy wind almost quenched my torch. It poured madly out of the dark door, sighing uncannily as it ruffled the sand and spread about the weird ruins. Soon it grew fainter and the sand grew more and more still, till finally all was at rest again; but a presence seemed stalking among the spectral stones of the city, and when I glanced at the moon it seemed to quiver as though mirrored in unquiet waters. I was more afraid than I could explain, but not enough to dull my thirst for wonder; so as soon as the wind was quite gone I crossed into the dark chamber from which it had come.

This temple, as I had fancied from the outside, was larger than either of those I had visited before; and was presumably a natural cavern, since it bore winds from some region beyond. Here I could stand quite upright, but saw that the stones and altars were as low as those in the other temples. On the walls and roof I beheld for the first time some traces of the pictorial art of the ancient race, curious curling streaks of paint that had almost faded or crumbled away; and on two of the altars I saw with rising excitement a maze of well-fashioned curvilinear carvings. As I held my torch aloft it seemed to me that the shape of the roof was too regular to be natural, and I wondered what the prehistoric cutters of stone had first worked upon. Their engineering skill must have been vast.

Then a brighter flare of the fantastic flame shewed me that for which I had been seeking, the opening to those remoter abysses whence the sudden wind had blown; and I grew faint when I saw that it was a small and plainly *artificial* door chiselled in the solid rock. I thrust my torch within, beholding a black tunnel with roof arching low over a rough flight of very small, numerous, and steeply descending steps. I shall always see those steps in my dreams, for I came to learn what they meant. At the time I hardly knew whether to call them steps or mere footholds in a precipitous descent. My mind was whirling with mad thoughts, and the words and warnings of Arab prophets seemed to float across the desert from the lands that men know to the nameless city that men dare not know. Yet I hesitated only a moment before advancing through the portal and commencing to climb cautiously down the steep passage, feet first, as though on a ladder.

It is only in the terrible phantasms of drugs or delirium that any other man can have had such a descent as mine. The narrow passage led infinitely down like some hideous haunted well, and the torch I held above my head could not light the unknown depths toward which I was crawling. I lost track of the hours and forgot to consult my watch, though I was frightened when I thought of the distance I must be traversing. There were changes of direction and of steepness, and once I came to a long, low, level passage where I had to wriggle feet first along the rocky floor, holding my torch at arm's length beyond my head. The place was not high enough for kneeling. After that were more of the steep steps, and I was still scrambling down interminably when my failing torch died out. I do not think I noticed it at the time, for when I did notice it I was still holding it high above me as if it were ablaze. I was quite unbalanced with that instinct for the strange and the unknown which has made me a wanderer upon earth and a haunter of far, ancient, and forbidden places.

In the darkness there flashed before my mind fragments of my cherished treasury of daemoniac lore; sentences from Alhazred the mad Arab, paragraphs from the apocryphal nightmares of Damascius, and infamous lines from the delirious "Image du Monde" of Gauthier de Metz. I repeated queer extracts, and muttered of Afrasiab and the daemons that floated with him down the Oxus; later chanting over and over again a phrase from one of Lord Dunsany's tales—"the unreverberate blackness of the abyss". Once when the descent grew amazingly steep I recited something in sing-song from Thomas Moore until I feared to recite more:

"A reservoir of darkness, black
As witches' cauldrons are, when fill'd
With moon-drugs in th' eclipse distill'd.
Leaning to look if foot might pass
Down thro' that chasm, I saw, beneath,
As far as vision could explore,
The jetty sides as smooth as glass,
Looking as if just varnish'd o'er
With that dark pitch the Sea of Death
Throws out upon its slimy shore."

Time had quite ceased to exist when my feet again felt a level floor, and I found myself in a place slightly higher than the rooms in the two smaller temples now so incalculably far above my head. I could not quite stand, but could kneel upright, and in the dark I shuffled and crept hither and thither at random. I soon knew that I was in a narrow passage whose walls were lined with cases of wood having glass fronts. As in that palaeozoic and abysmal place I felt of such things as polished wood and glass I shuddered at the possible implications. The cases were apparently ranged along each side of the passage at regular intervals, and were oblong and horizontal, hideously like coffins in shape and size. When I tried to move two or three for further examination, I found they were firmly fastened.

I saw that the passage was a long one, so floundered ahead rapidly in a creeping run that would have seemed horrible had any eye watched me in the blackness; crossing from side to side occasionally to feel of my surroundings and be sure the walls and rows of cases still stretched on. Man is so used to thinking visually that I almost forgot the darkness and pictured the endless corridor of wood and glass in its low-studded monotony as though I saw it. And then in a moment of indescribable emotion I did see it.

Just when my fancy merged into real sight I cannot tell; but there came a gradual glow ahead, and all at once I knew that I saw the dim outlines of the corridor and the cases, revealed by some unknown subterranean phosphorescence. For a little while all was exactly as I had imagined it, since the glow was very faint; but as I mechanically kept on stumbling ahead into the stronger light I realised that my fancy had been but feeble. This hall was no relic of crudity like the temples in the city above, but a monument of the most magnificent and exotic art. Rich, vivid, and daringly fantastic designs and pictures formed a continuous scheme of mural painting whose lines and colours were beyond description. The cases were of a strange golden wood, with fronts of exquisite glass, and contained the mummified forms of creatures outreaching in grotesqueness the most chaotic dreams of man.

To convey any idea of these monstrosities is impossible. They were of the reptile kind, with body lines suggesting sometimes the crocodile, sometimes the seal, but more often nothing of which either the naturalist or the paleaeontologist ever heard. In size they approximated a small man, and their fore legs bore delicate and evidently flexible feet curiously like human hands and fingers. But strangest of all were their heads, which presented a contour violating all known biological principles. To nothing can such things be well compared—in one flash I thought of comparisons as varied as the cat, the bulldog, the mythic Satyr, and the human being. Not Jove himself had so colossal and protuberant a forehead, yet the horns and the noselessness and the alligator-like jaw placed the things outside all established categories. I debated for a time on the reality of the mummies, half suspecting they were artificial idols; but soon decided they were indeed some palaeogean species which had lived when the nameless city was alive. To crown their grotesqueness, most of them were gorgeously enrobed in the costliest of fabrics, and lavishly laden with ornaments of gold, jewels, and unknown shining metals.

The importance of these crawling creatures must have been vast, for they held first place among the wild designs on the frescoed walls and ceiling. With matchless skill had the artist drawn them in a world of their own, wherein they had cities and gardens fashioned to suit their dimensions; and I could not but think that their pictured history was allegorical, perhaps shewing the progress of the race that worshipped them. These creatures, I said to myself, were to the men of the nameless city what the she-wolf was to Rome, or what some totem-beast is to a tribe of Indians.

Holding this view, I thought I could trace roughly a wonderful epic of the nameless city; the tale of a mighty seacoast metropolis that ruled the world before Africa rose out of the waves, and of its struggles as the sea shrank away, and the desert crept into the fertile valley that held it. I saw its wars and triumphs, its troubles and defeats, and afterward its terrible fight against the desert when thousands of its people—here represented in allegory by the grotesque reptiles—were driven to chisel their way down through the rocks in some marvellous manner to another world whereof their prophets had told them. It was all vividly weird and realistic, and its connexion with the awesome descent I had made was unmistakable. I even recognised the passages.

As I crept along the corridor toward the brighter light I saw later stages of the painted epic—the leave-taking of the race that had dwelt in the nameless city and the valley around for ten million years; the race whose souls shrank from quitting scenes their bodies had known so long, where they had settled as nomads in the earth's youth, hewing in the virgin rock those primal shrines at which they never ceased to worship. Now that the light was better I studied the pictures more closely, and, remembering that the strange reptiles must represent the unknown men, pondered upon the customs of the nameless city. Many things were peculiar and inexplicable. The civilisation, which included a written alphabet, had seemingly risen to a higher order than those immeasurably later civilisations of Egypt and Chaldaea, yet there were curious omissions. I could, for example, find no pictures to represent deaths or funeral customs, save such as were related to wars, violence, and plagues; and I wondered at the reticence shewn concerning natural death. It was as though an ideal of earthly immortality had been fostered as a cheering illusion.

Still nearer the end of the passage were painted scenes of the utmost picturesqueness and extravagance; contrasted views of the nameless city in its desertion and growing ruin, and of the strange new realm or paradise to which the race had hewed its way through the stone. In these views the city and the desert valley were shewn always by moonlight, a golden nimbus hovering over the fallen walls and half revealing the splendid perfection of former times, shewn spectrally and elusively by the artist. The paradisal scenes were almost too extravagant to be believed; portraying a hidden world of eternal day filled with glorious cities and ethereal hills and valleys. At the very last I thought I saw signs of an artistic anticlimax. The paintings were less skilful, and much more bizarre than even the wildest of the earlier scenes. They seemed to record a slow decadence of the ancient stock, coupled with a growing ferocity toward the outside world from which it was driven by the desert. The forms of the people—always represented by the sacred reptiles—appeared to be gradually wasting away, though their spirit as shewn hovering about the ruins by moonlight gained in proportion. Emaciated priests, displayed as reptiles in ornate robes, cursed the upper air and all who breathed it; and one terrible final scene shewed a primitive-looking man, perhaps a pioneer of ancient Irem, the City of Pillars, torn to pieces by members of the elder race. I remembered how the Arabs fear the nameless city, and was glad that beyond this place the grey walls and ceiling were bare.

As I viewed the pageant of mural history I had approached very closely the end of the low-ceiled hall, and was aware of a great gate through which came all of the illuminating phosphorescence. Creeping up to it, I cried aloud in transcendent amazement at what lay beyond; for instead of other and brighter chambers there was only an illimitable void of uniform radiance, such as one might fancy when gazing down from the peak of Mount Everest upon a sea of sunlit mist. Behind me was a passage so cramped that I could not stand upright in it; before me was an infinity of subterranean effulgence.

Reaching down from the passage into the abyss was the head of a steep flight of steps—small numerous steps like those of the black passages I had traversed—but after a few feet the glowing vapours concealed everything. Swung back open against the left-hand wall of the passage was a massive door of brass, incredibly thick and decorated with fantastic bas-reliefs, which could if closed shut the whole inner world of light away from the vaults and passages of rock. I looked at the steps, and for the nonce dared not try them. I touched the open brass door, and could not move it. Then I sank prone to the stone floor, my mind aflame with prodigious reflections which not even a death-like exhaustion could banish.

As I lay still with closed eyes, free to ponder, many things I had lightly noted in the frescoes came back to me with new and terrible significance—scenes representing the nameless city in its heyday, the vegetation of the valley around it, and the distant lands with which its merchants traded. The allegory of the crawling creatures puzzled me by its universal prominence, and I wondered that it should be so closely followed in a pictured history of such importance. In the frescoes the nameless city had been shewn in proportions fitted to the reptiles. I wondered what its real proportions and magnificence had been, and reflected a moment on certain oddities I had noticed in the ruins. I thought curiously of the lowness of the primal temples and of the underground corridor, which were doubtless hewn thus out of deference to the reptile deities there honoured; though it perforce reduced the worshippers to crawling. Perhaps the very rites had involved a crawling in imitation of the creatures. No religious theory, however, could easily explain why the level passage in that awesome descent should be as low as the temples—or lower, since one could not even kneel in it. As I thought of the crawling creatures, whose hideous mummified forms were so close to me, I felt a new throb of fear. Mental associations are curious, and I shrank from the idea that except for the poor primitive man torn to pieces in the last painting, mine was the only human form amidst the many relics and symbols of primordial life.

But as always in my strange and roving existence, wonder soon drove out fear; for the luminous abyss and what it might contain presented a problem worthy of the greatest explorer. That a weird world of mystery lay far down that flight of peculiarly small steps I could not doubt, and I hoped to find there those human memorials which the painted corridor had failed to give. The frescoes had pictured unbelievable cities, hills, and valleys in this lower realm, and my fancy dwelt on the rich and colossal ruins that awaited me.

My fears, indeed, concerned the past rather than the future. Not even the physical horror of my position in that cramped corridor of dead reptiles and antediluvian frescoes, miles below the world I knew and faced by another world of eery light and mist, could match the lethal dread I felt at the abysmal antiquity of the scene and its soul. An ancientness so vast that measurement is feeble seemed to leer down from the primal stones and rock-hewn temples in the nameless city, while the very latest of the astounding maps in the frescoes shewed oceans and continents that man has forgotten, with only here and there some vaguely familiar outline. Of what could have happened in the geological aeons since the paintings ceased and the death-hating race resentfully succumbed to decay, no man might say. Life had once teemed in these caverns and in the luminous realm beyond; now I was alone with vivid relics, and I trembled to think of the countless ages through which these relics had kept a silent and deserted vigil.

Suddenly there came another burst of that acute fear which had intermittently seized me ever since I first saw the terrible valley and the nameless city under a cold moon, and despite my exhaustion I found myself starting frantically to a sitting posture and gazing back along the black corridor toward the tunnels that rose to the outer world. My sensations were much like those which had made me shun the nameless city at night, and were as inexplicable as they were poignant. In another moment, however, I received a still greater shock in the form of a definite sound—the first which had broken the utter silence of these tomb-like depths. It was a deep, low moaning, as of a distant throng of condemned spirits, and came from the direction in which I was staring. Its volume rapidly grew, till soon it reverberated frightfully through the low passage, and at the same time I became conscious of an increasing draught of cold air, likewise flowing from the tunnels and the city above. The touch of this air seemed to restore my balance, for I instantly recalled the sudden gusts which had risen around the mouth of the abyss each sunset and sunrise, one of which had indeed served to reveal the hidden tunnels to me. I looked at my watch and saw that sunrise was near, so braced myself to resist the gale which was sweeping down to its cavern home as it had swept forth at evening. My fear again waned low, since a natural phenomenon tends to dispel broodings over the unknown.

More and more madly poured the shrieking, moaning night-wind into that gulf of the inner earth. I dropped prone again and clutched vainly at the floor for fear of being swept bodily through the open gate into the phosphorescent abyss. Such fury I had not expected, and as I grew aware of an actual slipping of my form toward the abyss I was beset by a thousand new terrors of apprehension and imagination. The malignancy of the blast awakened incredible fancies; once more I compared myself shudderingly to the only other human image in that frightful corridor, the man who was torn to pieces by the nameless race, for in the fiendish clawing of the swirling currents there seemed to abide a vindictive rage all the stronger because it was largely impotent. I think I screamed frantically near the last—I was almost mad—but if I did so my cries were lost in the hell-born babel of howling wind-wraiths. I tried to crawl against the murderous invisible torrent, but could not even hold my own as I was pushed slowly and inexorably toward the unknown world. Finally reason must have wholly snapped, for I fell to babbling over and over that unexplainable couplet of the mad Arab Alhazred, who dreamed of the nameless city:

> "That is not dead which can eternal lie,
> And with strange aeons even death may die."

Only the grim brooding desert gods know what really took place—what indescribable struggles and scrambles in the dark I endured or what Abaddon guided me back to life, where I must always remember and shiver in the night-wind till oblivion—or worse—claims me. Monstrous, unnatural, colossal, was the thing—too far beyond all the ideas of man to be believed except in the silent damnable small hours when one cannot sleep.

I have said that the fury of the rushing blast was infernal—cacodaemoniacal—and that its voices were hideous with the pent-up viciousness of desolate eternities. Presently those voices, while still chaotic before me, seemed to my beating brain to take articulate form behind me; and down there in the grave of unnumbered aeon-dead antiquities, leagues below the dawn-lit world of men, I heard the ghastly cursing and snarling of strange-tongued fiends. Turning, I saw outlined against the luminous aether of the abyss what could not be seen against the dusk of the corridor—a nightmare horde of rushing devils; hate-distorted, grotesquely panoplied, half-transparent; devils of a race no man might mistake—the crawling reptiles of the nameless city.

And as the wind died away I was plunged into the ghoul-peopled blackness of earth's bowels; for behind the last of the creatures the great brazen door clanged shut with a deafening peal of metallic music whose reverberations swelled out to the distant world to hail the rising sun as Memnon hails it from the banks of the Nile.

THE QUEST OF IRANON

Into the granite city of Teloth wandered the youth, vine-crowned, his yellow hair glistening with myrrh and his purple robe torn with briers of the mountain Sidrak that lies across the antique bridge of stone. The men of Teloth are dark and stern, and dwell in square houses, and with frowns they asked the stranger whence he had come and what were his name and fortune. So the youth answered:

"I am Iranon, and come from Aira, a far city that I recall only dimly but seek to find again. I am a singer of songs that I learned in the far city, and my calling is to make beauty with the things remembered of childhood. My wealth is in little memories and dreams, and in hopes that I sing in gardens when the moon is tender and the west wind stirs the lotos-buds."

When the men of Teloth heard these things they whispered to one another; for though in the granite city there is no laughter or song, the stern men sometimes look to the Karthian hills in the spring and think of the lutes of distant Oonai whereof travellers have told. And thinking thus, they bade the stranger stay and sing in the square before the Tower of Mlin, though they liked not the colour of his tattered robe, nor the myrrh in his hair, nor his chaplet of vine-leaves, nor the youth in his golden voice. At evening Iranon sang, and while he sang an old man prayed and a blind man said he saw a nimbus over the singer's head. But most of the men of Teloth yawned, and some laughed and some went away to sleep; for Iranon told nothing useful, singing only his memories, his dreams, and his hopes.

"I remember the twilight, the moon, and soft songs, and the window where I was rocked to sleep. And through the window was the street where the golden lights came, and where the shadows danced on houses of marble. I remember the square of moonlight on the floor, that was not like any other light, and the visions that danced in the moonbeams when my mother sang to me. And too, I remember the sun of morning bright above the many-coloured hills in summer, and the sweetness of flowers borne on the south wind that made the trees sing.

"O Aira, city of marble and beryl, how many are thy beauties! How loved I the warm and fragrant groves across the hyaline Nithra, and the falls of the tiny Kra that flowed through the verdant valley! In those groves and in that vale the children wove wreaths for one another, and at dusk I dreamed strange dreams under the yath-trees on the mountain as I saw below me the lights of the city, and the curving Nithra reflecting a ribbon of stars.

"And in the city were palaces of veined and tinted marble, with golden domes and painted walls, and green gardens with cerulean pools and crystal fountains. Often I played in the gardens and waded in the pools, and lay and dreamed among the pale flowers under the trees. And sometimes at sunset I would climb the long hilly street to the citadel and the open place, and look down upon Aira, the magic city of marble and beryl, splendid in a robe of golden flame.

"Long have I missed thee, Aira, for I was but young when we went into exile; but my father was thy King and I shall come again to thee, for it is so decreed of Fate. All through seven lands have I sought thee, and some day shall I reign over thy groves and gardens, thy streets and palaces, and sing to men who shall know whereof I sing, and laugh not nor turn away. For I am Iranon, who was a Prince in Aira."

That night the men of Teloth lodged the stranger in a stable, and in the morning an archon came to him and told him to go to the shop of Athok the cobbler, and be apprenticed to him.

"But I am Iranon, a singer of songs," he said, "and have no heart for the cobbler's trade."

"All in Teloth must toil," replied the archon, "for that is the law." Then said Iranon,

"Wherefore do ye toil; is it not that ye may live and be happy? And if ye toil only that ye may toil more, when shall happiness find you? Ye toil to live, but is not life made of beauty and song? And if ye suffer no singers among you, where shall be the fruits of your toil? Toil without song is like a weary journey without an end. Were not death more pleasing?" But the archon was sullen and did not understand, and rebuked the stranger.

"Thou art a strange youth, and I like not thy face nor thy voice. The words thou speakest are blasphemy, for the gods of Teloth have said that toil is good. Our gods have promised us a haven of light beyond death, where there shall be rest without end, and crystal coldness amidst which none shall vex his mind with thought or his eyes with beauty. Go thou then to Athok the cobbler or be gone out of the city by sunset. All here must serve, and song is folly."

So Iranon went out of the stable and walked over the narrow stone streets between the gloomy square houses of granite, seeking something green in the air of spring. But in Teloth was nothing green, for all was of stone. On the faces of men were frowns, but by the stone embankment along the sluggish river Zuro sate a young boy with sad eyes gazing into the waters to spy green budding branches washed down from the hills by the freshets. And the boy said to him:

"Art thou not indeed he of whom the archons tell, who seekest a far city in a fair land? I am Romnod, and born of the blood of Teloth, but am not old in the ways of the granite city, and yearn daily for the warm groves and the distant lands of beauty and song. Beyond the Karthian hills lieth Oonai, the city of lutes and dancing, which men whisper of and say is both lovely and terrible. Thither would I go were I old enough to find the way, and thither shouldst thou go an thou wouldst sing and have men listen to thee. Let us leave the city Teloth and fare together among the hills of spring. Thou shalt shew me the ways of travel and I will attend thy songs at evening when the stars one by one bring dreams to the minds of dreamers. And peradventure it may be that Oonai the city of lutes and dancing is even the fair Aira thou seekest, for it is told that thou hast not known Aira since old days, and a name often changeth. Let us go to Oonai, O Iranon of the golden head, where men shall know our longings and welcome us as brothers, nor ever laugh or frown at what we say." And Iranon answered:

"Be it so, small one; if any in this stone place yearn for beauty he must seek the mountains and beyond, and I would not leave thee to pine by the sluggish Zuro. But think not that delight and understanding dwell just across the Karthian hills, or in any spot thou canst find in a day's, or a year's, or a lustrum's journey.

Behold, when I was small like thee I dwelt in the valley of Narthos by the frigid Xari, where none would listen to my dreams; and I told myself that when older I would go to Sinara on the southern slope, and sing to smiling dromedary-men in the market-place. But when I went to Sinara I found the dromedary-men all drunken and ribald, and saw that their songs were not as mine, so I travelled in a barge down the Xari to onyx-walled Jaren. And the soldiers at Jaren laughed at me and drave me out, so that I wandered to many other cities. I have seen Stethelos that is below the great cataract, and have gazed on the marsh where Sarnath once stood. I have been to Thraa, Ilarnek, and Kadatheron on the winding river Ai, and have dwelt long in Olathoë in the land of Lomar. But though I have had listeners sometimes, they have ever been few, and I know that welcome shall wait me only in Aira, the city of marble and beryl where my father once ruled as King. So for Aira shall we seek, though it were well to visit distant and lute-blessed Oonai across the Karthian hills, which may indeed be Aira, though I think not. Aira's beauty is past imagining, and none can tell of it without rapture, whilst of Oonai the camel-drivers whisper leeringly."

At the sunset Iranon and small Romnod went forth from Teloth, and for long wandered amidst the green hills and cool forests. The way was rough and obscure, and never did they seem nearer to Oonai the city of lutes and dancing; but in the dusk as the stars came out Iranon would sing of Aira and its beauties and Romnod would listen, so that they were both happy after a fashion. They ate plentifully of fruit and red berries, and marked not the passing of time, but many years must have slipped away. Small Romnod was now not so small, and spoke deeply instead of shrilly, though Iranon was always the same, and decked his golden hair with vines and fragrant resins found in the woods. So it came to pass one day that Romnod seemed older than Iranon, though he had been very small when Iranon had found him watching for green budding branches in Teloth beside the sluggish stone-banked Zuro.

Then one night when the moon was full the travellers came to a mountain crest and looked down upon the myriad lights of Oonai. Peasants had told them they were near, and Iranon knew that this was not his native city of Aira. The lights of Oonai were not like those of Aira; for they were harsh and glaring, while the lights of Aira shine as softly and magically as shone the moonlight on the floor by the window where Iranon's mother once rocked him to sleep with song. But Oonai was a city of lutes and dancing, so Iranon and Romnod went down the steep slope that they might find men to whom songs and dreams would bring pleasure. And when they were come into the town they found rose-wreathed revellers bound from house to house and leaning from windows and balconies, who listened to the songs of Iranon and tossed him flowers and applauded when he was done. Then for a moment did Iranon believe he had found those who thought and felt even as he, though the town was not a hundredth as fair as Aira.

When dawn came Iranon looked about with dismay, for the domes of Oonai were not golden in the sun, but grey and dismal. And the men of Oonai were pale with revelling and dull with wine, and unlike the radiant men of Aira. But because the people had thrown him blossoms and acclaimed his songs Iranon stayed on, and with him Romnod, who liked the revelry of the town and wore in his dark hair roses and myrtle. Often at night Iranon sang to the revellers, but he was always as before, crowned only with the vine of the mountains and remembering the marble streets of Aira and the hyaline Nithra. In the frescoed halls of the Monarch did he sing, upon a crystal dais raised over a floor that was a mirror, and as he sang he brought pictures to his hearers till the floor seemed to reflect old, beautiful, and half-remembered things instead of the wine-reddened feasters who pelted him with roses. And the King bade him put away his tattered purple, and clothed him in satin and cloth-of-gold, with rings of green jade and bracelets of tinted ivory, and lodged him in a gilded and tapestried chamber on a bed of sweet carven wood with canopies and coverlets of flower-embroidered silk. Thus dwelt Iranon in Oonai, the city of lutes and dancing.

It is not known how long Iranon tarried in Oonai, but one day the King brought to the palace some wild whirling dancers from the Liranian desert, and dusky flute-players from Drinen in the East, and after that the revellers threw their roses not so much at Iranon as at the dancers and the flute-players. And day by day that Romnod who had been a small boy in granite Teloth grew coarser and redder with wine, till he dreamed less and less, and listened with less delight to the songs of Iranon. But though Iranon was sad he ceased not to sing, and at evening told again his dreams of Aira, the city of marble and beryl. Then one night the red and fattened Romnod snorted heavily amidst the poppied silks of his banquet-couch and died writhing, whilst Iranon, pale and slender, sang to himself in a far corner. And when Iranon had wept over the grave of Romnod and strown it with green budding branches, such as Romnod used to love, he put aside his silks and gauds and went forgotten out of Oonai the city of lutes and dancing clad only in the ragged purple in which he had come, and garlanded with fresh vines from the mountains.

Into the sunset wandered Iranon, seeking still for his native land and for men who would understand and cherish his songs and dreams. In all the cities of Cydathria and in the lands beyond the Bnazic desert gay-faced children laughed at his olden songs and tattered robe of purple; but Iranon stayed ever young, and wore wreaths upon his golden head whilst he sang of Aira, delight of the past and hope of the future.

So came he one night to the squalid cot of an antique shepherd, bent and dirty, who kept lean flocks on a stony slope above a quicksand marsh. To this man Iranon spoke, as to so many others:

"Canst thou tell me where I may find Aira, the city of marble and beryl, where flows the hyaline Nithra and where the falls of the tiny Kra sing to verdant valleys and hills forested with yath trees?" And the shepherd, hearing, looked long and strangely at Iranon, as if recalling something very far away in time, and noted each line of the stranger's face, and his golden hair, and his crown of vine-leaves. But he was old, and shook his head as he replied:

"O stranger, I have indeed heard the name of Aira, and the other names thou hast spoken, but they come to me from afar down the waste of long years. I heard them in my youth from the lips of a playmate, a beggar's boy given to strange dreams, who would weave long tales about the moon and the flowers and the west wind. We used to laugh at him, for we knew him from his birth though he thought himself a King's son. He was comely, even as thou, but full of folly and strangeness; and he ran away when small to find those who would listen gladly to his songs and dreams. How often hath he sung to me of lands that never were, and things that never can be! Of Aira did he speak much; of Aira and the river Nithra, and the falls of the tiny Kra. There would he ever say he once dwelt as a Prince, though here we knew him from his birth. Nor was there ever a marble city of Aira, nor those who could delight in strange songs, save in the dreams of mine old playmate Iranon who is gone."

And in the twilight, as the stars came out one by one and the moon cast on the marsh a radiance like that which a child sees quivering on the floor as he is rocked to sleep at evening, there walked into the lethal quicksands a very old man in tattered purple, crowned with withered vine-leaves and gazing ahead as if upon the golden domes of a fair city where dreams are understood. That night something of youth and beauty died in the elder world.

THE MOON-BOG

Somewhere, to what remote and fearsome region I know not, Denys Barry has gone. I was with him the last night he lived among men, and heard his screams when the thing came to him; but all the peasants and police in County Meath could never find him, or the others, though they searched long and far. And now I shudder when I hear the frogs piping in swamps, or see the moon in lonely places.

I had known Denys Barry well in America, where he had grown rich, and had congratulated him when he bought back the old castle by the bog at sleepy Kilderry. It was from Kilderry that his father had come, and it was there that he wished to enjoy his wealth among ancestral scenes. Men of his blood had once ruled over Kilderry and built and dwelt in the castle, but those days were very remote, so that for generations the castle had been empty and decaying. After he went to Ireland Barry wrote me often, and told me how under his care the grey castle was rising tower by tower to its ancient splendour; how the ivy was climbing slowly over the restored walls as it had climbed so many centuries ago, and how the peasants blessed him for bringing back the old days with his gold from over the sea. But in time there came troubles, and the peasants ceased to bless him, and fled away instead as from a doom. And then he sent a letter and asked me to visit him, for he was lonely in the castle with no one to speak to save the new servants and labourers he had brought from the North.

The bog was the cause of all these troubles, as Barry told me the night I came to the castle. I had reached Kilderry in the summer sunset, as the gold of the sky lighted the green of the hills and groves and the blue of the bog, where on a far islet a strange olden ruin glistened spectrally. That sunset was very beautiful, but the peasants at Ballylough had warned me against it and said that Kilderry had become accursed, so that I almost shuddered to see the high turrets of the castle gilded with fire. Barry's motor had met me at the Ballylough station, for Kilderry is off the railway. The villagers had shunned the car and the driver from the North, but had whispered to me with pale faces when they saw I was going to Kilderry. And that night, after our reunion, Barry told me why.

The peasants had gone from Kilderry because Denys Barry was to drain the great bog. For all his love of Ireland, America had not left him untouched, and he hated the beautiful wasted space where peat might be cut and land opened up. The legends and superstitions of Kilderry did not move him, and he laughed when the peasants first refused to help, and then cursed him and went away to Ballylough with their few belongings as they saw his determination. In their place he sent for labourers from the North, and when the servants left he replaced them likewise. But it was lonely among strangers, so Barry had asked me to come.

When I heard the fears which had driven the people from Kilderry I laughed as loudly as my friend had laughed, for these fears were of the vaguest, wildest, and most absurd character. They had to do with some preposterous legend of the bog, and of a grim guardian spirit that dwelt in the strange olden ruin on the far islet I had seen in the sunset. There were tales of dancing lights in the dark of the moon, and of chill winds when the night was warm; of wraiths in white hovering over the waters, and of an imagined city of stone deep down below the swampy surface. But foremost among the weird fancies, and alone in its absolute unanimity, was that of the curse awaiting him who should dare to touch or drain the vast reddish morass. There were secrets, said the peasants, which must not be uncovered; secrets that had lain hidden since the plague came to the children of Partholan in the fabulous years beyond history. In the "Book of Invaders" it is told that these sons of the Greeks were all buried at Tallaght, but old men in Kilderry said that one city was overlooked save by its patron moon-goddess; so that only the wooded hills buried it when the men of Nemed swept down from Scythia in their thirty ships.

Such were the idle tales which had made the villagers leave Kilderry, and when I heard them I did not wonder that Denys Barry had refused to listen. He had, however, a great interest in antiquities; and proposed to explore the bog thoroughly when it was drained. The white ruins on the islet he had often visited, but though their age was plainly great, and their contour very little like that of most ruins in Ireland, they were too dilapidated to tell the days of their glory. Now the work of drainage was ready to begin, and the labourers from the North were soon to strip the forbidden bog of its green moss and red heather, and kill the tiny shell-paved streamlets and the quiet blue pools fringed with rushes.

After Barry had told me these things I was very drowsy, for the travels of the day had been wearying and my host had talked late into the night. A manservant shewed me to my room, which was in a remote tower overlooking the village, and the plain at the edge of the bog, and the bog itself; so that I could see from my windows in the moonlight the silent roofs from which the peasants had fled and which now sheltered the labourers from the North, and too, the parish church with its antique spire, and far out across the brooding bog the remote olden ruin on the islet gleaming white and spectral. Just as I dropped to sleep I fancied I heard faint sounds from the distance; sounds that were wild and half musical, and stirred me with a weird excitement which coloured my dreams. But when I awaked next morning I felt it had all been a dream, for the visions I had seen were more wonderful than any sound of wild pipes in the night. Influenced by the legends that Barry had related, my mind had in slumber hovered around a stately city in a green valley, where marble streets and statues, villas and temples, carvings and inscriptions, all spoke in certain tones the glory that was Greece. When I told this dream to Barry we both laughed; but I laughed the louder, because he was perplexed about his labourers from the North. For the sixth time they had all overslept, waking very slowly and dazedly, and acting as if they had not rested, although they were known to have gone early to bed the night before.

That morning and afternoon I wandered alone through the sun-gilded village and talked now and then with idle labourers, for Barry was busy with the final plans for beginning his work of drainage. The labourers were not as happy as they might have been; for most of them seemed uneasy over some dream which they had had, yet which they tried in vain to remember. I told them of my dream, but they were not interested till I spoke of the weird sounds I thought I had heard. Then they looked oddly at me, and said that they seemed to remember weird sounds, too.

In the evening Barry dined with me and announced that he would begin the drainage in two days. I was glad, for although I disliked to see the moss and the heather and the little streams and lakes depart, I had a growing wish to discern the ancient secrets the deep-matted peat might hide. And that night my dreams of piping flutes and marble peristyles came to a sudden and disquieting end; for upon the city in the valley I saw a pestilence descend, and then a frightful avalanche of wooded slopes that covered the dead bodies in the streets and left unburied only the temple of Artemis on the high peak, where the aged moon-priestess Cleis lay cold and silent with a crown of ivory on her silver head.

I have said that I awaked suddenly and in alarm. For some time I could not tell whether I was waking or sleeping, for the sound of flutes still rang shrilly in my ears; but when I saw on the floor the icy moonbeams and the outlines of a latticed Gothic window I decided I must be awake and in the castle at Kilderry. Then I heard a clock from some remote landing below strike the hour of two, and knew I was awake. Yet still there came that monotonous piping from afar; wild, weird airs that made me think of some dance of fauns on distant Maenalus. It would not let me sleep, and in impatience I sprang up and paced the floor. Only by chance did I go to the north window and look out upon the silent village and the plain at the edge of the bog. I had no wish to gaze abroad, for I wanted to sleep; but the flutes tormented me, and I had to do or see something. How could I have suspected the thing I was to behold?

There in the moonlight that flooded the spacious plain was a spectacle which no mortal, having seen it, could ever forget. To the sound of reedy pipes that echoed over the bog there glided silently and eerily a mixed throng of swaying figures, reeling through such a revel as the Sicilians may have danced to Demeter in the old days under the harvest moon beside the Cyane. The wide plain, the golden moonlight, the shadowy moving forms, and above all the shrill monotonous piping, produced an effect which almost paralysed me; yet I noted amidst my fear that half of these tireless, mechanical dancers were the labourers whom I had thought asleep, whilst the other half were strange airy beings in white, half-indeterminate in nature, but suggesting pale wistful naiads from the haunted fountains of the bog. I do not know how long I gazed at this sight from the lonely turret window before I dropped suddenly in a dreamless swoon, out of which the high sun of morning aroused me.

My first impulse on awaking was to communicate all my fears and observations to Denys Barry, but as I saw the sunlight glowing through the latticed east window I became sure that there was no reality in what I thought I had seen. I am given to strange phantasms, yet am never weak enough to believe in them; so on this occasion contented myself with questioning the labourers, who slept very late and recalled nothing of the previous night save misty dreams of shrill sounds. This matter of the spectral piping harassed me greatly, and I wondered if the crickets of autumn had come before their time to vex the night and haunt the visions of men. Later in the day I watched Barry in the library poring over his plans for the great work which was to begin on the morrow, and for the first time felt a touch of the same kind of fear that had driven the peasants away. For some unknown reason I dreaded the thought of disturbing the ancient bog and its sunless secrets, and pictured terrible sights lying black under the unmeasured depth of age-old peat. That these secrets should be brought to light seemed injudicious, and I began to wish for an excuse to leave the castle and the village. I went so far as to talk casually to Barry on the subject, but did not dare continue after he gave his resounding laugh. So I was silent when the sun set fulgently over the far hills, and Kilderry blazed all red and gold in a flame that seemed a portent.

Whether the events of that night were of reality or illusion I shall never ascertain. Certainly they transcend anything we dream of in Nature and the universe; yet in no normal fashion can I explain those disappearances which were known to all men after it was over. I retired early and full of dread, and for a long time could not sleep in the uncanny silence of the tower. It was very dark, for although the sky was clear the moon was now well in the wane, and would not rise till the small hours. I thought as I lay there of Denys Barry, and of what would befall that bog when the day came, and found myself almost frantic with an impulse to rush out into the night, take Barry's car, and drive madly to Ballylough out of the menaced lands. But before my fears could crystallise into action I had fallen asleep, and gazed in dreams upon the city in the valley, cold and dead under a shroud of hideous shadow.

Probably it was the shrill piping that awaked me, yet that piping was not what I noticed first when I opened my eyes. I was lying with my back to the east window overlooking the bog, where the waning moon would rise, and therefore expected to see light cast on the opposite wall before me; but I had not looked for such a sight as now appeared. Light indeed glowed on the panels ahead, but it was not any light that the moon gives. Terrible and piercing was the shaft of ruddy refulgence that streamed through the Gothic window, and the whole chamber was brilliant with a splendour intense and unearthly. My immediate actions were peculiar for such a situation, but it is only in tales that a man does the dramatic and foreseen thing. Instead of looking out across the bog toward the source of the new light, I kept my eyes from the window in panic fear, and clumsily drew on my clothing with some dazed idea of escape. I remember seizing my revolver and hat, but before it was over I had lost them both without firing the one or donning the other. After a time the fascination of the red radiance overcame my fright, and I crept to the east window and looked out whilst the maddening, incessant piping whined and reverberated through the castle and over all the village.

Over the bog was a deluge of flaring light, scarlet and sinister, and pouring from the strange olden ruin on the far islet. The aspect of that ruin I cannot describe—I must have been mad, for it seemed to rise majestic and undecayed, splendid and column-cinctured, the flame-reflecting marble of its entablature piercing the sky like the apex of a temple on a mountaintop. Flutes shrieked and drums began to beat, and as I watched in awe and terror I thought I saw dark saltant forms silhouetted grotesquely against the vision of marble and effulgence. The effect was titanic—altogether unthinkable—and I might have stared indefinitely had not the sound of the piping seemed to grow stronger at my left. Trembling with a terror oddly mixed with ecstasy I crossed the circular room to the north window from which I could see the village and the plain at the edge of the bog. There my eyes dilated again with a wild wonder as great as if I had not just turned from a scene beyond the pale of Nature, for on the ghastly red-litten plain was moving a procession of beings in such a manner as none ever saw before save in nightmares.

Half gliding, half floating in the air, the white-clad bog-wraiths were slowly retreating toward the still waters and the island ruin in fantastic formations suggesting some ancient and solemn ceremonial dance. Their waving translucent arms, guided by the detestable piping of those unseen flutes, beckoned in uncanny rhythm to a throng of lurching labourers who followed dog-like with blind, brainless, floundering steps as if dragged by a clumsy but resistless daemon-will. As the naiads neared the bog, without altering their course, a new line of stumbling stragglers zigzagged drunkenly out of the castle from some door far below my window, groped sightlessly across the courtyard and through the intervening bit of village, and joined the floundering column of labourers on the plain. Despite their distance below me I at once knew they were the servants brought from the North, for I recognised the ugly and unwieldy form of the cook, whose very absurdness had now become unutterably tragic. The flutes piped horribly, and again I heard the beating of the drums from the direction of the island ruin. Then silently and gracefully the naiads reached the water and melted one by one into the ancient bog; while the line of followers, never checking their speed, splashed awkwardly after them and vanished amidst a tiny vortex of unwholesome bubbles which I could barely see in the scarlet light. And as the last pathetic straggler, the fat cook, sank heavily out of sight in that sullen pool, the flutes and the drums grew silent, and the blinding red rays from the ruins snapped instantaneously out, leaving the village of doom lone and desolate in the wan beams of a new-risen moon.

My condition was now one of indescribable chaos. Not knowing whether I was mad or sane, sleeping or waking, I was saved only by a merciful numbness. I believe I did ridiculous things such as offering prayers to Artemis, Latona, Demeter, Persephone, and Plouton. All that I recalled of a classic youth came to my lips as the horrors of the situation roused my deepest superstitions. I felt that I had witnessed the death of a whole village, and knew I was alone in the castle with Denys Barry, whose boldness had brought down a doom. As I thought of him new terrors convulsed me, and I fell to the floor; not fainting, but physically helpless. Then I felt the icy blast from the east window where the moon had risen, and began to hear the shrieks in the castle far below me. Soon those shrieks had attained a magnitude and quality which cannot be written of, and which make me faint as I think of them. All I can say is that they came from something I had known as a friend.

At some time during this shocking period the cold wind and the screaming must have roused me, for my next impression is of racing madly through inky rooms and corridors and out across the courtyard into the hideous night. They found me at dawn wandering mindless near Ballylough, but what unhinged me utterly was not any of the horrors I had seen or heard before. What I muttered about as I came slowly out of the shadows was a pair of fantastic incidents which occurred in my flight; incidents of no significance, yet which haunt me unceasingly when I am alone in certain marshy places or in the moonlight.

As I fled from that accursed castle along the bog's edge I heard a new sound; common, yet unlike any I had heard before at Kilderry. The stagnant waters, lately quite devoid of animal life, now teemed with a horde of slimy enormous frogs which piped shrilly and incessantly in tones strangely out of keeping with their size. They glistened bloated and green in the moonbeams, and seemed to gaze up at the fount of light. I followed the gaze of one very fat and ugly frog, and saw the second of the things which drove my senses away.

Stretching directly from the strange olden ruin on the far islet to the waning moon, my eyes seemed to trace a beam of faint quivering radiance having no reflection in the waters of the bog. And upward along that pallid path my fevered fancy pictured a thin shadow slowly writhing; a vague contorted shadow struggling as if drawn by unseen daemons. Crazed as I was, I saw in that awful shadow a monstrous resemblance—a nauseous, unbelievable caricature—a blasphemous effigy of him who had been Denys Barry.

THE OUTSIDER

That night the Baron dreamt of many a woe;
And all his warrior-guests, with shade and form
Of witch, and demon, and large coffin-worm,
Were long be-nightmared.

—*Keats.*

Unhappy is he to whom the memories of childhood bring only fear and sadness. Wretched is he who looks back upon lone hours in vast and dismal chambers with brown hangings and maddening rows of antique books, or upon awed watches in twilight groves of grotesque, gigantic, and vine-encumbered trees that silently wave twisted branches far aloft. Such a lot the gods gave to me—to me, the dazed, the disappointed; the barren, the broken. And yet I am strangely content, and cling desperately to those sere memories, when my mind momentarily threatens to reach beyond to the other.

I know not where I was born, save that the castle was infinitely old and infinitely horrible; full of dark passages and having high ceilings where the eye could find only cobwebs and shadows. The stones in the crumbling corridors seemed always hideously damp, and there was an accursed smell everywhere, as of the piled-up corpses of dead generations. It was never light, so that I used sometimes to light candles and gaze steadily at them for relief; nor was there any sun outdoors, since the terrible trees grew high above the topmost accessible tower. There was one black tower which reached above the trees into the unknown outer sky, but that was partly ruined and could not be ascended save by a well-nigh impossible climb up the sheer wall, stone by stone.

I must have lived years in this place, but I cannot measure the time. Beings must have cared for my needs, yet I cannot recall any person except myself; or anything alive but the noiseless rats and bats and spiders. I think that whoever nursed me must have been shockingly aged, since my first conception of a living person was that of something mockingly like myself, yet distorted, shrivelled, and decaying like the castle. To me there was nothing grotesque in the bones and skeletons that strowed some of the stone crypts deep down among the foundations. I fantastically associated these things with every-day events, and thought them more natural than the coloured pictures of living beings which I found in many of the mouldy books. From such books I learned all that I know. No teacher urged or guided me, and I do not recall hearing any human voice in all those years—not even my own; for although I had read of speech, I had never thought to try to speak aloud. My aspect was a matter equally unthought of, for there were no mirrors in the castle, and I merely regarded myself by instinct as akin to the youthful figures I saw drawn and painted in the books. I felt conscious of youth because I remembered so little.

Outside, across the putrid moat and under the dark mute trees, I would often lie and dream for hours about what I read in the books; and would longingly picture myself amidst gay crowds in the sunny world beyond the endless forest. Once I tried to escape from the forest, but as I went farther from the castle the shade grew denser and the air more filled with brooding fear; so that I ran frantically back lest I lose my way in a labyrinth of nighted silence.

So through endless twilights I dreamed and waited, though I knew not what I waited for. Then in the shadowy solitude my longing for light grew so frantic that I could rest no more, and I lifted entreating hands to the single black ruined tower that reached above the forest into the unknown outer sky. And at last I resolved to scale that tower, fall though I might; since it were better to glimpse the sky and perish, than to live without ever beholding day.

In the dank twilight I climbed the worn and aged stone stairs till I reached the level where they ceased, and thereafter clung perilously to small footholds leading upward. Ghastly and terrible was that dead, stairless cylinder of rock; black, ruined, and deserted, and sinister with startled bats whose wings made no noise. But more ghastly and terrible still was the slowness of my progress; for climb as I might, the darkness overhead grew no thinner, and a new chill as of haunted and venerable mould assailed me. I shivered as I wondered why I did not reach the light, and would have looked down had I dared. I fancied that night had come suddenly upon me, and vainly groped with one free hand for a window embrasure, that I might peer out and above, and try to judge the height I had attained.

All at once, after an infinity of awesome, sightless crawling up that concave and desperate precipice, I felt my head touch a solid thing, and I knew I must have gained the roof, or at least some kind of floor. In the darkness I raised my free hand and tested the barrier, finding it stone and immovable. Then came a deadly circuit of the tower, clinging to whatever holds the slimy wall could give; till finally my testing hand found the barrier yielding, and I turned upward again, pushing the slab or door with my head as I used both hands in my fearful ascent. There was no light revealed above, and as my hands went higher I knew that my climb was for the nonce ended; since the slab was the trap-door of an aperture leading to a level stone surface of greater circumference than the lower tower, no doubt the floor of some lofty and capacious observation chamber. I crawled through carefully, and tried to prevent the heavy slab from falling back into place; but failed in the latter attempt. As I lay exhausted on the stone floor I heard the eery echoes of its fall, but hoped when necessary to pry it up again.

Believing I was now at a prodigious height, far above the accursed branches of the wood, I dragged myself up from the floor and fumbled about for windows, that I might look for the first time upon the sky, and the moon and stars of which I had read. But on every hand I was disappointed; since all that I found were vast shelves of marble, bearing odious oblong boxes of disturbing size. More and more I reflected, and wondered what hoary secrets might abide in this high apartment so many aeons cut off from the castle below. Then unexpectedly my hands came upon a doorway, where hung a portal of stone, rough with strange chiselling. Trying it, I found it locked; but with a supreme burst of strength I overcame all obstacles and dragged it open inward. As I did so there came to me the purest ecstasy I have ever known; for shining tranquilly through an ornate grating of iron, and down a short stone passageway of steps that ascended from the newly found doorway, was the radiant full moon, which I had never before seen save in dreams and in vague visions I dared not call memories.

Fancying now that I had attained the very pinnacle of the castle, I commenced to rush up the few steps beyond the door; but the sudden veiling of the moon by a cloud caused me to stumble, and I felt my way more slowly in the dark. It was still very dark when I reached the grating—which I tried carefully and found unlocked, but which I did not open for fear of falling from the amazing height to which I had climbed. Then the moon came out.

Most daemoniacal of all shocks is that of the abysmally unexpected and grotesquely unbelievable. Nothing I had before undergone could compare in terror with what I now saw; with the bizarre marvels that sight implied. The sight itself was as simple as it was stupefying, for it was merely this: instead of a dizzying prospect of treetops seen from a lofty eminence, there stretched around me on a level through the grating nothing less than *the solid ground,* decked and diversified by marble slabs and columns, and overshadowed by an ancient stone church, whose ruined spire gleamed spectrally in the moonlight.

Half unconscious, I opened the grating and staggered out upon the white gravel path that stretched away in two directions. My mind, stunned and chaotic as it was, still held the frantic craving for light; and not even the fantastic wonder which had happened could stay my course. I neither knew nor cared whether my experience was insanity, dreaming, or magic; but was determined to gaze on brilliance and gaiety at any cost. I knew not who I was or what I was, or what my surroundings might be; though as I continued to stumble along I became conscious of a kind of fearsome latent memory that made my progress not wholly fortuitous. I passed under an arch out of that region of slabs and columns, and wandered through the open country; sometimes following the visible road, but sometimes leaving it curiously to tread across meadows where only occasional ruins bespoke the ancient presence of a forgotten road. Once I swam across a swift river where crumbling, mossy masonry told of a bridge long vanished.

Over two hours must have passed before I reached what seemed to be my goal, a venerable ivied castle in a thickly wooded park; maddeningly familiar, yet full of perplexing strangeness to me. I saw that the moat was filled in, and that some of the well-known towers were demolished; whilst new wings existed to confuse the beholder. But what I observed with chief interest and delight were the open windows—gorgeously ablaze with light and sending forth sound of the gayest revelry. Advancing to one of these I looked in and saw an oddly dressed company, indeed; making merry, and speaking brightly to one another. I had never, seemingly, heard human speech before; and could guess only vaguely what was said. Some of the faces seemed to hold expressions that brought up incredibly remote recollections; others were utterly alien.

I now stepped through the low window into the brilliantly lighted room, stepping as I did so from my single bright moment of hope to my blackest convulsion of despair and realisation. The nightmare was quick to come; for as I entered, there occurred immediately one of the most terrifying demonstrations I had ever conceived. Scarcely had I crossed the sill when there descended upon the whole company a sudden and unheralded fear of hideous intensity, distorting every face and evoking the most horrible screams from nearly every throat. Flight was universal, and in the clamour and panic several fell in a swoon and were dragged away by their madly fleeing companions. Many covered their eyes with their hands, and plunged blindly and awkwardly in their race to escape; overturning furniture and stumbling against the walls before they managed to reach one of the many doors.

The cries were shocking; and as I stood in the brilliant apartment alone and dazed, listening to their vanishing echoes, I trembled at the thought of what might be lurking near me unseen. At a casual inspection the room seemed deserted, but when I moved toward one of the alcoves I thought I detected a presence there—a hint of motion beyond the golden-arched doorway leading to another and somewhat similar room. As I approached the arch I began to perceive the presence more clearly; and then, with the first and last sound I ever uttered—a ghastly ululation that revolted me almost as poignantly as its noxious cause—I beheld in full, frightful vividness the inconceivable, indescribable, and unmentionable monstrosity which had by its simple appearance changed a merry company to a herd of delirious fugitives.

I cannot even hint what it was like, for it was a compound of all that is unclean, uncanny, unwelcome, abnormal, and detestable. It was the ghoulish shade of decay, antiquity, and desolation; the putrid, dripping eidolon of unwholesome revelation; the awful baring of that which the merciful earth should always hide. God knows it was not of this world—or no longer of this world—yet to my horror I saw in its eaten-away and bone-revealing outlines a leering, abhorrent travesty on the human shape; and in its mouldy, disintegrating apparel an unspeakable quality that chilled me even more.

I was almost paralysed, but not too much so to make a feeble effort toward flight; a backward stumble which failed to break the spell in which the nameless, voiceless monster held me. My eyes, bewitched by the glassy orbs which stared loathsomely into them, refused to close; though they were mercifully blurred, and shewed the terrible object but indistinctly after the first shock. I tried to raise my hand to shut out the sight, yet so stunned were my nerves that my arm could not fully obey my will. The attempt, however, was enough to disturb my balance; so that I had to stagger forward several steps to avoid falling. As I did so I became suddenly and agonisingly aware of the *nearness* of the carrion thing, whose hideous hollow breathing I half fancied I could hear. Nearly mad, I found myself yet able to throw out a hand to ward off the foetid apparition which pressed so close; when in one cataclysmic second of cosmic nightmarishness and hellish accident *my fingers touched the rotting outstretched paw of the monster beneath the golden arch.*

I did not shriek, but all the fiendish ghouls that ride the night-wind shrieked for me as in that same second there crashed down upon my mind a single and fleeting avalanche of soul-annihilating memory. I knew in that second all that had been; I remembered beyond the frightful castle and the trees, and recognised the altered edifice in which I now stood; I recognised, most terrible of all, the unholy abomination that stood leering before me as I withdrew my sullied fingers from its own.

But in the cosmos there is balm as well as bitterness, and that balm is nepenthe. In the supreme horror of that second I forgot what had horrified me, and the burst of black memory vanished in a chaos of echoing images. In a dream I fled from that haunted and accursed pile, and ran swiftly and silently in the moonlight. When I returned to the churchyard place of marble and went down the steps I found the stone trap-door immovable; but I was not sorry, for I had hated the antique castle and the trees. Now I ride with the mocking and friendly ghouls on the night-wind, and play by day amongst the catacombs of Nephren-Ka in the sealed and unknown valley of Hadoth by the Nile. I know that light is not for me, save that of the moon over the rock tombs of Neb, nor any gaiety save the unnamed feasts of Nitokris beneath the Great Pyramid; yet in my new wildness and freedom I almost welcome the bitterness of alienage.

For although nepenthe has calmed me, I know always that I am an outsider; a stranger in this century and among those who are still men. This I have known ever since I stretched out my fingers to the abomination within that great gilded frame; stretched out my fingers and touched *a cold and unyielding surface of polished glass.*

THE OTHER GODS

Atop the tallest of earth's peaks dwell the gods of earth, and suffer no man to tell that he hath looked upon them. Lesser peaks they once inhabited; but ever the men from the plains would scale the slopes of rock and snow, driving the gods to higher and higher mountains till now only the last remains. When they left their older peaks they took with them all signs of themselves; save once, it is said, when they left a carven image on the face of the mountain which they called Ngranek.

But now they have betaken themselves to unknown Kadath in the cold waste where no man treads, and are grown stern, having no higher peak whereto to flee at the coming of men. They are grown stern, and where once they suffered men to displace them, they now forbid men to come, or coming, to depart. It is well for men that they know not of Kadath in the cold waste, else they would seek injudiciously to scale it.

Sometimes when earth's gods are homesick they visit in the still night the peaks where once they dwelt, and weep softly as they try to play in the olden way on remembered slopes. Men have felt the tears of the gods on white-capped Thurai, though they have thought it rain; and have heard the sighs of the gods in the plaintive dawn-winds of Lerion. In cloud-ships the gods are wont to travel, and wise cotters have legends that keep them from certain high peaks at night when it is cloudy, for the gods are not lenient as of old.

The Other Gods

In Ulthar, which lies beyond the river Skai, once dwelt an old man avid to behold the gods of earth; a man deeply learned in the seven cryptical books of Hsan, and familiar with the Pnakotic Manuscripts of distant and frozen Lomar. His name was Barzai the Wise, and the villagers tell of how he went up a mountain on the night of the strange eclipse.

Barzai knew so much of the gods that he could tell of their comings and goings, and guessed so many of their secrets that he was deemed half a god himself. It was he who wisely advised the burgesses of Ulthar when they passed their remarkable law against the slaying of cats, and who first told the young priest Atal where it is that black cats go at midnight on St. John's Eve. Barzai was learned in the lore of earth's gods, and had gained a desire to look upon their faces. He believed that his great secret knowledge of gods could shield him from their wrath, so resolved to go up to the summit of high and rocky Hatheg-Kla on a night when he knew the gods would be there.

Hatheg-Kla is far in the stony desert beyond Hatheg, for which it is named, and rises like a rock statue in a silent temple. Around its peak the mists play always mournfully, for mists are the memories of the gods, and the gods loved Hatheg-Kla when they dwelt upon it in the old days. Often the gods of earth visit Hatheg-Kla in their ships of cloud, casting pale vapours over the slopes as they dance reminiscently on the summit under a clear moon. The villagers of Hatheg say it is ill to climb Hatheg-Kla at any time, and deadly to climb it by night when pale vapours hide the summit and the moon; but Barzai heeded them not when he came from neighbouring Ulthar with the young priest Atal, who was his disciple. Atal was only the son of an innkeeper, and was sometimes afraid; but Barzai's father had been a landgrave who dwelt in an ancient castle, so he had no common superstition in his blood, and only laughed at the fearful cotters.

Barzai and Atal went out of Hatheg into the stony desert despite the prayers of peasants, and talked of earth's gods by their campfires at night. Many days they travelled, and from afar saw lofty Hatheg-Kla with his aureole of mournful mist. On the thirteenth day they reached the mountain's lonely base, and Atal spoke of his fears. But Barzai was old and learned and had no fears, so led the way boldly up the slope that no man had scaled since the time of Sansu, who is written of with fright in the mouldy Pnakotic Manuscripts.

The way was rocky, and made perilous by chasms, cliffs, and falling stones. Later it grew cold and snowy; and Barzai and Atal often slipped and fell as they hewed and plodded upward with staves and axes. Finally the air grew thin, and the sky changed colour, and the climbers found it hard to breathe; but still they toiled up and up, marvelling at the strangeness of the scene and thrilling at the thought of what would happen on the summit when the moon was out and the pale vapours spread around. For three days they climbed higher, higher, and higher toward the roof of the world; then they camped to wait for the clouding of the moon.

For four nights no clouds came, and the moon shone down cold through the thin mournful mists around the silent pinnacle. Then on the fifth night, which was the night of the full moon, Barzai saw some dense clouds far to the north, and stayed up with Atal to watch them draw near. Thick and majestic they sailed, slowly and deliberately onward; ranging themselves round the peak high above the watchers, and hiding the moon and the summit from view. For a long hour the watchers gazed, whilst the vapours swirled and the screen of clouds grew thicker and more restless. Barzai was wise in the lore of earth's gods, and listened hard for certain sounds, but Atal felt the chill of the vapours and the awe of the night, and feared much. And when Barzai began to climb higher and beckon eagerly, it was long before Atal would follow.

So thick were the vapours that the way was hard, and though Atal followed on at last, he could scarce see the grey shape of Barzai on the dim slope above in the clouded moonlight. Barzai forged very far ahead, and seemed despite his age to climb more easily than Atal; fearing not the steepness that began to grow too great for any save a strong and dauntless man, nor pausing at wide black chasms that Atal scarce could leap. And so they went up wildly over rocks and gulfs, slipping and stumbling, and sometimes awed at the vastness and horrible silence of bleak ice pinnacles and mute granite steeps.

Very suddenly Barzai went out of Atal's sight, scaling a hideous cliff that seemed to bulge outward and block the path for any climber not inspired of earth's gods. Atal was far below, and planning what he should do when he reached the place, when curiously he noticed that the light had grown strong, as if the cloudless peak and moonlit meeting-place of the gods were very near. And as he scrambled on toward the bulging cliff and litten sky he felt fears more shocking than any he had known before. Then through the high mists he heard the voice of unseen Barzai shouting wildly in delight:

"I have heard the gods! I have heard earth's gods singing in revelry on Hatheg-Kla! The voices of earth's gods are known to

Barzai the Prophet! The mists are thin and the moon is bright, and I shall see the gods dancing wildly on Hatheg-Kla that they loved in youth! The wisdom of Barzai hath made him greater than earth's gods, and against his will their spells and barriers are as naught; Barzai will behold the gods, the proud gods, the secret gods, the gods of earth who spurn the sight of men!"

Atal could not hear the voices Barzai heard, but he was now close to the bulging cliff and scanning it for footholds. Then he heard Barzai's voice grow shriller and louder:

"The mists are very thin, and the moon casts shadows on the slope; the voices of earth's gods are high and wild, and they fear the coming of Barzai the Wise, who is greater than they.... The moon's light flickers, as earth's gods dance against it; I shall see the dancing forms of the gods that leap and howl in the moonlight.... The light is dimmer and the gods are afraid...."

Whilst Barzai was shouting these things Atal felt a spectral change in all the air, as if the laws of earth were bowing to greater laws; for though the way was steeper than ever, the upward path was now grown fearsomely easy, and the bulging cliff proved scarce an obstacle when he reached it and slid perilously up its convex face. The light of the moon had strangely failed, and as Atal plunged upward through the mists he heard Barzai the Wise shrieking in the shadows:

"The moon is dark, and the gods dance in the night; there is terror in the sky, for upon the moon hath sunk an eclipse foretold in no books of men or of earth's gods.... There is unknown magic on Hatheg-Kla, for the screams of the frightened gods have turned to laughter, and the slopes of ice shoot up endlessly into the black heavens whither I am plunging.... Hei! Hei! At last! *In the dim light I behold the gods of earth!*"

And now Atal, slipping dizzily up over inconceivable steeps, heard in the dark a loathsome laughing, mixed with such a cry as no man else ever heard save in the Phlegethon of unrelatable nightmares; a cry wherein reverberated the horror and anguish of a haunted lifetime packed into one atrocious moment:

"The *other* gods! The *other* gods! The gods of the outer hells that guard the feeble gods of earth! ... Look away! ... Go back! ... Do not see! ... Do not see! ... The vengeance of the infinite abysses ... That cursed, that damnable pit ... Merciful gods of earth, *I am falling into the sky!*"

And as Atal shut his eyes and stopped his ears and tried to jump downward against the frightful pull from unknown heights, there resounded on Hatheg-Kla that terrible peal of thunder which awaked the good cotters of the plains and the honest burgesses of Hatheg, and Nir, and Ulthar, and caused them to behold through the clouds that strange eclipse of the moon that no book ever predicted. And when the moon came out at last Atal was safe on the lower snows of the mountain without sight of earth's gods, or of the *other* gods.

Now it is told in the mouldy Pnakotic Manuscripts that Sansu found naught but wordless ice and rock when he climbed Hatheg-Kla in the youth of the world. Yet when the men of Ulthar and Nir and Hatheg crushed their fears and scaled that haunted steep by day in search of Barzai the Wise, they found graven in the naked stone of the summit a curious and Cyclopean symbol fifty cubits wide, as if the rock had been riven by some titanic chisel. And the symbol was like to one that learned men have discerned in those frightful parts of the Pnakotic Manuscripts which are too ancient to be read. This they found.

Barzai the Wise they never found, nor could the holy priest Atal ever be persuaded to pray for his soul's repose. Moreover, to this day the people of Ulthar and Nir and Hatheg fear eclipses, and pray by night when pale vapours hide the mountaintop and the moon. And above the mists on Hatheg-Kla earth's gods sometimes dance reminiscently; for they know they are safe, and love to come from unknown Kadath in ships of cloud and play in the olden way, as they did when earth was new and men not given to the climbing of inaccessible places.

THE MUSIC OF ERICH ZANN

I have examined maps of the city with the greatest care, yet have never again found the Rue d'Auseil. These maps have not been modern maps alone, for I know that names change. I have, on the contrary, delved deeply into all the antiquities of the place; and have personally explored every region, of whatever name, which could possibly answer to the street I knew as the Rue d'Auseil. But despite all I have done it remains an humiliating fact that I cannot find the house, the street, or even the locality, where, during the last months of my impoverished life as a student of metaphysics at the University, I heard the music of Erich Zann.

That my memory is broken, I do not wonder; for my health, physical and mental, was gravely disturbed throughout the period of my residence in the Rue d'Auseil, and I recall that I took none of my few acquaintances there. But that I cannot find the place again is both singular and perplexing; for it was within a half-hour's walk of the University and was distinguished by peculiarities which could hardly be forgotten by anyone who had been there. I have never met a person who has seen the Rue d'Auseil.

The Rue d'Auseil lay across a dark river bordered by precipitous brick blear-windowed warehouses and spanned by a ponderous bridge of dark stone. It was always shadowy along that river, as if the smoke of neighbouring factories shut out the sun perpetually. The river was also odorous with evil stenches which I have never smelled elsewhere, and which may some day help me to find it, since I should recognise them at once. Beyond the bridge were narrow cobbled streets with rails; and then came the ascent, at first gradual, but incredibly steep as the Rue d'Auseil was reached.

I have never seen another street as narrow and steep as the Rue d'Auseil. It was almost a cliff, closed to all vehicles, consisting in several places of flights of steps, and ending at the top in a lofty ivied wall. Its paving was irregular, sometimes stone slabs, sometimes cobblestones, and sometimes bare earth with struggling greenish-grey vegetation. The houses were tall, peaked-roofed, incredibly old, and crazily leaning backward, forward, and sidewise. Occasionally an opposite pair, both leaning forward, almost met across the street like an arch; and certainly they kept most of the light from the ground below. There were a few overhead bridges from house to house across the street.

The inhabitants of that street impressed me peculiarly. At first I thought it was because they were all silent and reticent; but later decided it was because they were all very old. I do not know how I came to live on such a street, but I was not myself when I moved there. I had been living in many poor places, always evicted for want of money; until at last I came upon that tottering house in the Rue d'Auseil, kept by the paralytic Blandot. It was the third house from the top of the street, and by far the tallest of them all.

My room was on the fifth story; the only inhabited room there, since the house was almost empty. On the night I arrived I heard strange music from the peaked garret overhead, and the next day asked old Blandot about it. He told me it was an old German viol-player, a strange dumb man who signed his name as Erich Zann, and who played evenings in a cheap theatre orchestra; adding that Zann's desire to play in the night after his return from the theatre was the reason he had chosen this lofty and isolated garret room, whose single gable window was the only point on the street from which one could look over the terminating wall at the declivity and panorama beyond.

Thereafter I heard Zann every night, and although he kept me awake, I was haunted by the weirdness of his music. Knowing little of the art myself, I was yet certain that none of his harmonies had any relation to music I had heard before; and concluded that he was a composer of highly original genius. The longer I listened, the more I was fascinated, until after a week I resolved to make the old man's acquaintance.

One night, as he was returning from his work, I intercepted Zann in the hallway and told him that I would like to know him and be with him when he played. He was a small, lean, bent person, with shabby clothes, blue eyes, grotesque, satyr-like face, and nearly bald head; and at my first words seemed both angered and frightened. My obvious friendliness, however, finally melted him; and he grudgingly motioned to me to follow him up the dark, creaking, and rickety attic stairs. His room, one of only two in the steeply pitched garret, was on the west side, toward the high wall that formed the upper end of the street. Its size was very great, and seemed the greater because of its extraordinary bareness and neglect. Of furniture there was only a narrow iron bedstead, a dingy washstand, a small table, a large bookcase, an iron music-rack, and three old-fashioned chairs. Sheets of music were piled in disorder about the floor. The walls were of bare boards, and had probably never known plaster; whilst the abundance of dust and cobwebs made the place seem more deserted than inhabited. Evidently Erich Zann's world of beauty lay in some far cosmos of the imagination.

Motioning me to sit down, the dumb man closed the door, turned the large wooden bolt, and lighted a candle to augment the one he had brought with him. He now removed his viol from its moth-eaten covering, and taking it, seated himself in the least uncomfortable of the chairs. He did not employ the music-rack, but offering no choice and playing from memory, enchanted me for over an hour with strains I had never heard before; strains which must have been of his own devising. To describe their exact nature is impossible for one unversed in music. They were a kind of fugue, with recurrent passages of the most captivating quality, but to me were notable for the absence of any of the weird notes I had overheard from my room below on other occasions.

Those haunting notes I had remembered, and had often hummed and whistled inaccurately to myself; so when the player at length laid down his bow I asked him if he would render some of them. As I began my request the wrinkled satyr-like face lost the bored placidity it had possessed during the playing, and seemed to shew the same curious mixture of anger and fright which I had noticed when first I accosted the old man. For a moment I was inclined to use persuasion, regarding rather lightly the whims of senility; and even tried to awaken my host's weirder mood by whistling a few of the strains to which I had listened the night before. But I did not pursue this course for more than a moment; for when the dumb musician recognised the whistled air his face grew suddenly distorted with an expression wholly beyond analysis, and his long, cold, bony right hand reached out to stop my mouth and silence the crude imitation. As he did this he further demonstrated his eccentricity by casting a startled glance toward the lone curtained window, as if fearful of some intruder; a glance doubly absurd, since the garret stood high and inaccessible above all the adjacent roofs—this window being the only point on the steep street, as the concierge had told me, from which one could see over the wall at the summit.

The old man's glance brought Blandot's remark to my mind, and with a certain capriciousness I felt a wish to look out over the wide and dizzying panorama of moonlit roofs and city lights beyond the hilltop, which of all the dwellers in the Rue d'Auseil only this crabbed musician could see. I moved toward the window and would have drawn aside the nondescript curtains, when with a frightened rage even greater than before the dumb lodger was upon me again; this time motioning with his head toward the door as he nervously strove to drag me thither with both hands. Now thoroughly disgusted with my host, I ordered him to release me, and told him I would go at once. His clutch relaxed, and as he saw my disgust and offence his own anger seemed to subside. He tightened his relaxing grip, but this time in a friendly manner; forcing me into a chair, then with an appearance of wistfulness crossing to the littered table where he wrote many words with a pencil in the laboured French of a foreigner.

The note which he finally handed me was an appeal for tolerance and forgiveness. Zann said that he was old, lonely, and afflicted with strange fears and nervous disorders connected with his music and with other things. He had enjoyed my listening to his music, and wished I would come again and not mind his eccentricities. But he could not play to another his weird harmonies, and could not bear hearing them from another; nor could he bear having anything in his room touched by another. He had not known until our hallway conversation that I could overhear his playing in my room, and now asked me if I would arrange with Blandot to take a lower room where I could not hear him in the night. He would, he wrote, defray the difference in rent.

As I sat deciphering the execrable French I felt more lenient toward the old man. He was a victim of physical and nervous suffering, as was I; and my metaphysical studies had taught me kindness. In the silence there came a slight sound from the window—the shutter must have rattled in the night-wind—and for some reason I started almost as violently as did Erich Zann. So when I had finished reading I shook my host by the hand, and departed as a friend. The next day Blandot gave me a more expensive room on the third floor, between the apartments of an aged money-lender and the room of a respectable upholsterer. There was no one on the fourth floor.

It was not long before I found that Zann's eagerness for my company was not as great as it had seemed while he was persuading me to move down from the fifth story. He did not ask me to call on him, and when I did call he appeared uneasy and played listlessly. This was always at night—in the day he slept and would admit no one. My liking for him did not grow, though the attic room and the weird music seemed to hold an odd fascination for me. I had a curious desire to look out of that window, over the wall and down the unseen slope at the glittering roofs and spires which must lie outspread there. Once I went up to the garret during theatre hours, when Zann was away, but the door was locked.

What I did succeed in doing was to overhear the nocturnal playing of the dumb old man. At first I would tiptoe up to my old fifth floor, then I grew bold enough to climb the last creaking staircase to the peaked garret. There in the narrow hall, outside the bolted door with the covered keyhole, I often heard sounds which filled me with an indefinable dread—the dread of vague wonder and brooding mystery. It was not that the sounds were hideous, for they were not; but that they held vibrations suggesting nothing on this globe of earth, and that at certain intervals they assumed a symphonic quality which I could hardly conceive as produced by one player. Certainly, Erich Zann was a genius of wild power. As the weeks passed, the playing grew wilder, whilst the old musician acquired an increasing haggardness and furtiveness pitiful to behold. He now refused to admit me at any time, and shunned me whenever we met on the stairs.

Then one night as I listened at the door I heard the shrieking viol swell into a chaotic babel of sound; a pandemonium which would have led me to doubt my own shaking sanity had there not come from behind that barred portal a piteous proof that the horror was real—the awful, inarticulate cry which only a mute can utter, and which rises only in moments of the most terrible fear or anguish. I knocked repeatedly at the door, but received no response. Afterward I waited in the black hallway, shivering with cold and fear, till I heard the poor musician's feeble effort to rise from the floor by the aid of a chair. Believing him just conscious after a fainting fit, I renewed my rapping, at the same time calling out my name reassuringly. I heard Zann stumble to the window and close both shutter and sash, then stumble to the door, which he falteringly unfastened to admit me. This time his delight at having me present was real; for his distorted face gleamed with relief, while he clutched at my coat as a child clutches at its mother's skirts.

Shaking pathetically, the old man forced me into a chair whilst he sank into another, beside which his viol and bow lay carelessly on the floor. He sat for some time inactive, nodding oddly, but having a paradoxical suggestion of intense and frightened listening. Subsequently he seemed to be satisfied, and crossing to a chair by the table wrote a brief note, handed it to me, and returned to the table, where he began to write rapidly and incessantly. The note implored me in the name of mercy, and for the sake of my own curiosity, to wait where I was while he prepared a full account in German of all the marvels and terrors which beset him. I waited, and the dumb man's pencil flew.

It was perhaps an hour later, while I still waited and while the old musician's feverishly written sheets still continued to pile up, that I saw Zann start as from the hint of a horrible shock. Unmistakably he was looking at the curtained window and listening shudderingly. Then I half fancied I heard a sound myself; though it was not a horrible sound, but rather an exquisitely low and infinitely distant musical note, suggesting a player in one of the neighbouring houses, or in some abode beyond the lofty wall over which I had never been able to look. Upon Zann the effect was terrible, for dropping his pencil suddenly he rose, seized his viol, and commenced to rend the night with the wildest playing I had ever heard from his bow save when listening at the barred door.

It would be useless to describe the playing of Erich Zann on that dreadful night. It was more horrible than anything I had ever overheard, because I could now see the expression of his face, and could realise that this time the motive was stark fear. He was trying to make a noise; to ward something off or drown something out—what, I could not imagine, awesome though I felt it must be. The playing grew fantastic, delirious, and hysterical, yet kept to the last the qualities of supreme genius which I know this strange old man possessed. I recognised the air—it was a wild Hungarian dance popular in the theatres, and I reflected for a moment that this was the first time I had ever heard Zann play the work of another composer.

Louder and louder, wilder and wilder, mounted the shrieking and whining of that desperate viol. The player was dripping with an uncanny perspiration and twisted like a monkey; always looking frantically at the curtained window. In his frenzied strains I could almost see shadowy satyrs and Bacchanals dancing and whirling insanely through seething abysses of clouds and smoke and lightning. And then I thought I heard a shriller, steadier note that was not from the viol; a calm, deliberate, purposeful, mocking note from far away in the west.

At this juncture the shutter began to rattle in a howling night-wind which had sprung up outside as if in answer to the mad playing within. Zann's screaming viol now outdid itself, emitting sounds I had never thought a viol could emit. The shutter rattled more loudly, unfastened, and commenced slamming against the window. Then the glass broke shiveringly under the persistent impacts, and the chill wind rushed in, making the candles sputter and rustling the sheets of paper on the table where Zann had begun to write out his horrible secret. I looked at Zann and saw that he was past conscious observation. His blue eyes were bulging, glassy, and sightless, and the frantic playing had become a blind, mechanical, unrecognisable orgy that no pen could even suggest.

A sudden gust, stronger than the others, caught up the manuscript and bore it toward the window. I followed the flying sheets in desperation, but they were gone before I reached the demolished panes. Then I remembered my old wish to gaze from this window, the only window in the Rue d'Auseil from which one might see the slope beyond the wall, and the city outspread beneath. It was very dark, but the city's lights always burned, and I expected to see them there amidst the rain and wind. Yet when I looked from that highest of all gable windows, looked while the candles sputtered and the insane viol howled with the night-wind, I saw no city spread below, and no friendly lights gleaming from remembered streets, but only the blackness of space illimitable; unimagined space alive with motion and music, and having no semblance of anything on earth. And as I stood there looking in terror, the wind blew out both the candles in that ancient peaked garret, leaving me in savage and impenetrable darkness with chaos and pandemonium before me, and the daemon madness of that night-baying viol behind me.

I staggered back in the dark, without the means of striking a light, crashing against the table, overturning a chair, and finally groping my way to the place where the blackness screamed with shocking music. To save myself and Erich Zann I could at least try, whatever the powers opposed to me. Once I thought some chill thing brushed me, and I screamed, but my scream could not be heard above that hideous viol. Suddenly out of the blackness the madly sawing bow struck me, and I knew I was close to the player. I felt ahead, touched the back of Zann's chair, and then found and shook his shoulder in an effort to bring him to his senses.

He did not respond, and still the viol shrieked on without slackening. I moved my hand to his head, whose mechanical nodding I was able to stop, and shouted in his ear that we must both flee the unknown things of the night. But he neither answered me nor abated the frenzy of his unutterable music, while all through the garret strange currents of wind seemed to dance in the darkness and babel. When my hand touched his ear I shuddered, though I knew not why—knew not why till I felt of the still face; the ice-cold, stiffened, unbreathing face whose glassy eyes bulged uselessly into the void. And then, by some miracle finding the door and the large wooden bolt, I plunged wildly away from that glassy-eyed thing in the dark, and from the ghoulish howling of that accursed viol whose fury increased even as I plunged.

Leaping, floating, flying down those endless stairs through the dark house; racing mindlessly out into the narrow, steep, and ancient street of steps and tottering houses; clattering down steps and over cobbles to the lower streets and the putrid canyon-walled river; panting across the great dark bridge to the broader, healthier streets and boulevards we know; all these are terrible impressions that linger with me. And I recall that there was no wind, and that the moon was out, and that all the lights of the city twinkled.

Despite my most careful searches and investigations, I have never since been able to find the Rue d'Auseil. But I am not wholly sorry; either for this or for the loss in undreamable abysses of the closely written sheets which alone could have explained the music of Erich Zann.

HERBERT WEST—REANIMATOR

I. From the Dark

Of Herbert West, who was my friend in college and in after life, I can speak only with extreme terror. This terror is not due altogether to the sinister manner of his recent disappearance, but was engendered by the whole nature of his life-work, and first gained its acute form more than seventeen years ago, when we were in the third year of our course at the Miskatonic University Medical School in Arkham. While he was with me, the wonder and diabolism of his experiments fascinated me utterly, and I was his closest companion. Now that he is gone and the spell is broken, the actual fear is greater. Memories and possibilities are ever more hideous than realities.

The first horrible incident of our acquaintance was the greatest shock I ever experienced, and it is only with reluctance that I repeat it. As I have said, it happened when we were in the medical school, where West had already made himself notorious through his wild theories on the nature of death and the possibility of overcoming it artificially. His views, which were widely ridiculed by the faculty and by his fellow-students, hinged on the essentially mechanistic nature of life; and concerned means for operating the organic machinery of mankind by calculated chemical action after the failure of natural processes. In his experiments with various animating solutions he had killed and treated immense numbers of rabbits, guinea-pigs, cats, dogs, and monkeys, till he had become the prime nuisance of the college. Several times he had actually obtained signs of life in animals supposedly dead; in many cases violent signs; but he soon saw that the perfection of his process, if indeed possible, would necessarily involve a lifetime of research. It likewise became clear that, since the same solution never worked alike on different organic species, he would require human subjects for further and more specialised progress. It was here that he first came into conflict with the college authorities, and was debarred from future experiments by no less a dignitary than the dean of the medical school himself—the learned and benevolent Dr. Allan Halsey, whose work in behalf of the stricken is recalled by every old resident of Arkham.

I had always been exceptionally tolerant of West's pursuits, and we frequently discussed his theories, whose ramifications and corollaries were almost infinite. Holding with Haeckel that all life is a chemical and physical process, and that the so-called "soul" is a myth, my friend believed that artificial reanimation of the dead can depend only on the condition of the tissues; and that unless actual decomposition has set in, a corpse fully equipped with organs may with suitable measures be set going again in the peculiar fashion known as life. That the psychic or intellectual life might be impaired by the slight deterioration of sensitive brain-cells which even a short period of death would be apt to cause, West fully realised. It had at first been his hope to find a reagent which would restore vitality before the actual advent of death, and only repeated failures on animals had shewn him that the natural and artificial life-motions were incompatible. He then sought extreme freshness in his specimens, injecting his solutions into the blood immediately after the extinction of life. It was this circumstance which made the professors so carelessly sceptical, for they felt that true death had not occurred in any case. They did not stop to view the matter closely and reasoningly.

It was not long after the faculty had interdicted his work that West confided to me his resolution to get fresh human bodies in some manner, and continue in secret the experiments he could no longer perform openly. To hear him discussing ways and means was rather ghastly, for at the college we had never procured anatomical specimens ourselves. Whenever the morgue proved inadequate, two local negroes attended to this matter, and they were seldom questioned. West was then a small, slender, spectacled youth with delicate features, yellow hair, pale blue eyes, and a soft voice, and it was uncanny to hear him dwelling on the relative merits of Christchurch Cemetery and the potter's field. We finally decided on the potter's field, because practically every body in Christchurch was embalmed; a thing of course ruinous to West's researches.

I was by this time his active and enthralled assistant, and helped him make all his decisions, not only concerning the source of bodies but concerning a suitable place for our loathsome work. It was I who thought of the deserted Chapman farmhouse beyond Meadow Hill, where we fitted up on the ground floor an operating room and a laboratory, each with dark curtains to conceal our midnight doings. The place was far from any road, and in sight of no other house, yet precautions were none the less necessary; since rumours of strange lights, started by chance nocturnal roamers, would soon bring disaster on our enterprise. It was agreed to call the whole thing a chemical laboratory if discovery should occur. Gradually we equipped our sinister haunt of science with materials either purchased in Boston or quietly borrowed from the college—materials carefully made unrecognisable save to expert eyes—and provided spades and picks for the many burials we should have to make in the cellar. At the college we used an incinerator, but the apparatus was too costly for our unauthorised laboratory. Bodies were always a nuisance—even the small guinea-pig bodies from the slight clandestine experiments in West's room at the boarding-house.

We followed the local death-notices like ghouls, for our specimens demanded particular qualities. What we wanted were corpses interred soon after death and without artificial preservation; preferably free from malforming disease, and certainly with all organs present. Accident victims were our best hope. Not for many weeks did we hear of anything suitable; though we talked with morgue and hospital authorities, ostensibly in the college's interest, as often as we could without exciting suspicion. We found that the college had first choice in every case, so that it might be necessary to remain in Arkham during the summer, when only the limited summer-school classes were held. In the end, though, luck favoured us; for one day we heard of an almost ideal case in the potter's field; a brawny young workman drowned only the morning before in Sumner's Pond, and buried at the town's expense without delay or embalming. That afternoon we found the new grave, and determined to begin work soon after midnight.

It was a repulsive task that we undertook in the black small hours, even though we lacked at that time the special horror of graveyards which later experiences brought to us. We carried spades and oil dark lanterns, for although electric torches were then manufactured, they were not as satisfactory as the tungsten contrivances of today. The process of unearthing was slow and sordid—it might have been gruesomely poetical if we had been artists instead of scientists—and we were glad when our spades struck wood. When the pine box was fully uncovered West scrambled down and removed the lid, dragging out and propping up the contents. I reached down and hauled the contents out of the grave, and then both toiled hard to restore the spot to its former appearance. The affair made us rather nervous, especially the stiff form and vacant face of our first trophy, but we managed to remove all traces of our visit. When we had patted down the last shovelful of earth we put the specimen in a canvas sack and set out for the old Chapman place beyond Meadow Hill.

On an improvised dissecting-table in the old farmhouse, by the light of a powerful acetylene lamp, the specimen was not very spectral looking. It had been a sturdy and apparently unimaginative youth of wholesome plebeian type—large-framed, grey-eyed, and brown-haired—a sound animal without psychological subtleties, and probably having vital processes of the simplest and healthiest sort. Now, with the eyes closed, it looked more asleep than dead; though the expert test of my friend soon left no doubt on that score. We had at last what West had always longed for—a real dead man of the ideal kind, ready for the solution as prepared according to the most careful calculations and theories for human use. The tension on our part became very great. We knew that there was scarcely a chance for anything like complete success, and could not avoid hideous fears at possible grotesque results of partial animation. Especially were we apprehensive concerning the mind and impulses of the creature, since in the space following death some of the more delicate cerebral cells might well have suffered deterioration. I, myself, still held some curious notions about the traditional "soul" of man, and felt an awe at the secrets that might be told by one returning from the dead. I wondered what sights this placid youth might have seen in inaccessible spheres, and what he could relate if fully restored to life. But my wonder was not overwhelming, since for the most part I shared the materialism of my friend. He was calmer than I as he forced a large quantity of his fluid into a vein of the body's arm, immediately binding the incision securely.

The waiting was gruesome, but West never faltered. Every now and then he applied his stethoscope to the specimen, and bore the negative results philosophically. After about three-quarters of an hour without the least sign of life he disappointedly pronounced the solution inadequate, but determined to make the most of his opportunity and try one change in the formula before disposing of his ghastly prize. We had that afternoon dug a grave in the cellar, and would have to fill it by dawn—for although we had fixed a lock on the house we wished to shun even the remotest risk of a ghoulish discovery. Besides, the body would not be even approximately fresh the next night. So taking the solitary acetylene lamp into the adjacent laboratory, we left our silent guest on the slab in the dark, and bent every energy to the mixing of a new solution; the weighing and measuring supervised by West with an almost fanatical care.

The awful event was very sudden, and wholly unexpected. I was pouring something from one test-tube to another, and West was busy over the alcohol blast-lamp which had to answer for a Bunsen burner in this gasless edifice, when from the pitch-black room we had left there burst the most appalling and daemoniac succession of cries that either of us had ever heard. Not more unutterable could have been the chaos of hellish sound if the pit itself had opened to release the agony of the damned, for in one inconceivable cacophony was centred all the supernal terror and unnatural despair of animate nature. Human it could not have been—it is not in man to make such sounds—and without a thought of our late employment or its possible discovery both West and I leaped to the nearest window like stricken animals; overturning tubes, lamp, and retorts, and vaulting madly into the starred abyss of the rural night. I think we screamed ourselves as we stumbled frantically toward the town, though as we reached the outskirts we put on a semblance of restraint—just enough to seem like belated revellers staggering home from a debauch.

We did not separate, but managed to get to West's room, where we whispered with the gas up until dawn. By then we had calmed ourselves a little with rational theories and plans for investigation, so that we could sleep through the day—classes being disregarded. But that evening two items in the paper, wholly unrelated, made it again impossible for us to sleep. The old deserted Chapman house had inexplicably burned to an amorphous heap of ashes; that we could understand because of the upset lamp. Also, an attempt had been made to disturb a new grave in the potter's field, as if by futile and spadeless clawing at the earth. That we could not understand, for we had patted down the mould very carefully.

And for seventeen years after that West would look frequently over his shoulder, and complain of fancied footsteps behind him. Now he has disappeared.

II. The Plague-Daemon

I shall never forget that hideous summer sixteen years ago, when like a noxious afrite from the halls of Eblis typhoid stalked leeringly through Arkham. It is by that satanic scourge that most recall the year, for truly terror brooded with bat-wings over the piles of coffins in the tombs of Christchurch Cemetery; yet for me there is a greater horror in that time—a horror known to me alone now that Herbert West has disappeared.

West and I were doing post-graduate work in summer classes at the medical school of Miskatonic University, and my friend had attained a wide notoriety because of his experiments leading toward the revivification of the dead. After the scientific slaughter of uncounted small animals the freakish work had ostensibly stopped by order of our sceptical dean, Dr. Allan Halsey; though West had continued to perform certain secret tests in his dingy boarding-house room, and had on one terrible and unforgettable occasion taken a human body from its grave in the potter's field to a deserted farmhouse beyond Meadow Hill.

I was with him on that odious occasion, and saw him inject into the still veins the elixir which he thought would to some extent restore life's chemical and physical processes. It had ended horribly—in a delirium of fear which we gradually came to attribute to our own overwrought nerves—and West had never afterward been able to shake off a maddening sensation of being haunted and hunted. The body had not been quite fresh enough; it is obvious that to restore normal mental attributes a body must be very fresh indeed; and the burning of the old house had prevented us from burying the thing. It would have been better if we could have known it was underground.

After that experience West had dropped his researches for some time; but as the zeal of the born scientist slowly returned, he again became importunate with the college faculty, pleading for the use of the dissecting-room and of fresh human specimens for the work he regarded as so overwhelmingly important. His pleas, however, were wholly in vain; for the decision of Dr. Halsey was inflexible, and the other professors all endorsed the verdict of their leader. In the radical theory of reanimation they saw nothing but the immature vagaries of a youthful enthusiast whose slight form, yellow hair, spectacled blue eyes, and soft voice gave no hint of the supernormal—almost diabolical—power of the cold brain within. I can see him now as he was then—and I shiver. He grew sterner of face, but never elderly. And now Sefton Asylum has had the mishap and West has vanished.

West clashed disagreeably with Dr. Halsey near the end of our last undergraduate term in a wordy dispute that did less credit to him than to the kindly dean in point of courtesy. He felt that he was needlessly and irrationally retarded in a supremely great work; a work which he could of course conduct to suit himself in later years, but which he wished to begin while still possessed of the exceptional facilities of the university. That the tradition-bound elders should ignore his singular results on animals, and persist in their denial of the possibility of reanimation, was inexpressibly disgusting and almost incomprehensible to a youth of West's logical temperament. Only greater maturity could help him understand the chronic mental limitations of the "professor-doctor" type—the product of generations of pathetic Puritanism; kindly, conscientious, and sometimes gentle and amiable, yet always narrow, intolerant, custom-ridden, and lacking in perspective. Age has more charity for these incomplete yet high-souled characters, whose worst real vice is timidity, and who are ultimately punished by general ridicule for their intellectual sins—sins like Ptolemaism, Calvinism, anti-Darwinism, anti-Nietzscheism, and every sort of Sabbatarianism and sumptuary legislation. West, young despite his marvellous scientific acquirements, had scant patience with good Dr. Halsey and his erudite colleagues; and nursed an increasing resentment, coupled with a desire to prove his theories to these obtuse worthies in some striking and dramatic fashion. Like most youths, he indulged in elaborate day-dreams of revenge, triumph, and final magnanimous forgiveness.

And then had come the scourge, grinning and lethal, from the nightmare caverns of Tartarus. West and I had graduated about the time of its beginning, but had remained for additional work at the summer school, so that we were in Arkham when it broke with full daemoniac fury upon the town. Though not as yet licenced physicians, we now had our degrees, and were pressed frantically into public service as the numbers of the stricken grew. The situation was almost past management, and deaths ensued too frequently for the local undertakers fully to handle. Burials without embalming were made in rapid succession, and even the Christchurch Cemetery receiving tomb was crammed with coffins of the unembalmed dead. This circumstance was not without effect on West, who thought often of the irony of the situation—so many fresh specimens, yet none for his persecuted researches! We were frightfully overworked, and the terrific mental and nervous strain made my friend brood morbidly.

But West's gentle enemies were no less harassed with prostrating duties. College had all but closed, and every doctor of the medical faculty was helping to fight the typhoid plague. Dr. Halsey in particular had distinguished himself in sacrificing service, applying his extreme skill with whole-hearted energy to cases which many others shunned because of danger or apparent hopelessness. Before a month was over the fearless dean had become a popular hero, though he seemed unconscious of his fame as he struggled to keep from collapsing with physical fatigue and nervous exhaustion. West could not withhold admiration for the fortitude of his foe, but because of this was even more determined to prove to him the truth of his amazing doctrines. Taking advantage of the disorganisation of both college work and municipal health regulations, he managed to get a recently deceased body smuggled into the university dissecting-room one night, and in my presence injected a new modification of his solution. The thing actually opened its eyes, but only stared at the ceiling with a look of soul-petrifying horror before collapsing into an inertness from which nothing could rouse it. West said it was not fresh enough—the hot summer air does not favour corpses. That time we were almost caught before we incinerated the thing, and West doubted the advisability of repeating his daring misuse of the college laboratory.

The peak of the epidemic was reached in August. West and I were almost dead, and Dr. Halsey did die on the 14th. The students all attended the hasty funeral on the 15th, and bought an impressive wreath, though the latter was quite overshadowed by the tributes sent by wealthy Arkham citizens and by the municipality itself. It was almost a public affair, for the dean had surely been a public benefactor. After the entombment we were all somewhat depressed, and spent the afternoon at the bar of the Commercial House; where West, though shaken by the death of his chief opponent, chilled the rest of us with references to his notorious theories. Most of the students went home, or to various duties, as the evening advanced; but West persuaded me to aid him in "making a night of it". West's landlady saw us arrive at his room about two in the morning, with a third man between us; and told her husband that we had all evidently dined and wined rather well.

Apparently this acidulous matron was right; for about 3 a.m. the whole house was aroused by cries coming from West's room, where when they broke down the door they found the two of us unconscious on the blood-stained carpet, beaten, scratched, and mauled, and with the broken remnants of West's bottles and instruments around us. Only an open window told what had become of our assailant, and many wondered how he himself had fared after the terrific leap from the second story to the lawn which he must have made. There were some strange garments in the room, but West upon regaining consciousness said they did not belong to the stranger, but were specimens collected for bacteriological analysis in the course of investigations on the transmission of germ diseases. He ordered them burnt as soon as possible in the capacious fireplace. To the police we both declared ignorance of our late companion's identity. He was, West nervously said, a congenial stranger whom we had met at some downtown bar of uncertain location. We had all been rather jovial, and West and I did not wish to have our pugnacious companion hunted down.

That same night saw the beginning of the second Arkham horror—the horror that to me eclipsed the plague itself. Christchurch Cemetery was the scene of a terrible killing; a watchman having been clawed to death in a manner not only too hideous for description, but raising a doubt as to the human agency of the deed. The victim had been seen alive considerably after midnight—the dawn revealed the unutterable thing. The manager of a circus at the neighbouring town of Bolton was questioned, but he swore that no beast had at any time escaped from its cage. Those who found the body noted a trail of blood leading to the receiving tomb, where a small pool of red lay on the concrete just outside the gate. A fainter trail led away toward the woods, but it soon gave out.

The next night devils danced on the roofs of Arkham, and unnatural madness howled in the wind. Through the fevered town had crept a curse which some said was greater than the plague, and which others whispered was the embodied daemon-soul of the plague itself. Eight houses were entered by a nameless thing which strowed red death in its wake—in all, seventeen maimed and shapeless remnants of bodies were left behind by the voiceless, sadistic monster that crept abroad. A few persons had half seen it in the dark, and said it was white and like a malformed ape or anthropomorphic fiend. It had not left behind quite all that it had attacked, for sometimes it had been hungry. The number it had killed was fourteen; three of the bodies had been in stricken homes and had not been alive.

On the third night frantic bands of searchers, led by the police, captured it in a house on Crane Street near the Miskatonic campus. They had organised the quest with care, keeping in touch by means of volunteer telephone stations, and when someone in the college district had reported hearing a scratching at a shuttered window, the net was quickly spread. On account of the general alarm and precautions, there were only two more victims, and the capture was effected without major casualties. The thing was finally stopped by a bullet, though not a fatal one, and was rushed to the local hospital amidst universal excitement and loathing.

For it had been a man. This much was clear despite the nauseous eyes, the voiceless simianism, and the daemoniac savagery. They dressed its wound and carted it to the asylum at Sefton, where it beat its head against the walls of a padded cell for sixteen years—until the recent mishap, when it escaped under circumstances that few like to mention. What had most disgusted the searchers of Arkham was the thing they noticed with the monster's face was cleaned—the mocking, unbelievable resemblance to a learned and self-sacrificing martyr who had been entombed but three days before—the late Dr. Allan Halsey, public benefactor and dean of the medical school of Miskatonic University.

To the vanished Herbert West and to me the disgust and horror were supreme. I shudder tonight as I think of it; shudder even more than I did that morning when West muttered through his bandages,

"Damn it, it wasn't *quite* fresh enough!"

III. Six Shots by Moonlight

It is uncommon to fire all six shots of a revolver with great suddenness when one would probably be sufficient, but many things in the life of Herbert West were uncommon. It is, for instance, not often that a young physician leaving college is obliged to conceal the principles which guide his selection of a home and office, yet that was the case with Herbert West. When he and I obtained our degrees at the medical school of Miskatonic University, and sought to relieve our poverty by setting up as general practitioners, we took great care not to say that we chose our house because it was fairly well isolated, and as near as possible to the potter's field.

Reticence such as this is seldom without a cause, nor indeed was ours; for our requirements were those resulting from a life-work distinctly unpopular. Outwardly we were doctors only, but beneath the surface were aims of far greater and more terrible moment—for the essence of Herbert West's existence was a quest amid black and forbidden realms of the unknown, in which he hoped to uncover the secret of life and restore to perpetual animation the graveyard's cold clay. Such a quest demands strange materials, among them fresh human bodies; and in order to keep supplied with these indispensable things one must live quietly and not far from a place of informal interment.

West and I had met in college, and I had been the only one to sympathise with his hideous experiments. Gradually I had come to be his inseparable assistant, and now that we were out of college we had to keep together. It was not easy to find a good opening for two doctors in company, but finally the influence of the university secured us a practice in Bolton—a factory town near Arkham, the seat of the college. The Bolton Worsted Mills are the largest in the Miskatonic Valley, and their polyglot employees are never popular as patients with the local physicians. We chose our house with the greatest care, seizing at last on a rather run-down cottage near the end of Pond Street; five numbers from the closest neighbour, and separated from the local potter's field by only a stretch of meadow land, bisected by a narrow neck of the rather dense forest which lies to the north. The distance was greater than we wished, but we could get no nearer house without going on the other side of the field, wholly out of the factory district. We were not much displeased, however, since there were no people between us and our sinister source of supplies. The walk was a trifle long, but we could haul our silent specimens undisturbed.

Our practice was surprisingly large from the very first—large enough to please most young doctors, and large enough to prove a bore and a burden to students whose real interest lay elsewhere. The mill-hands were of somewhat turbulent inclinations; and besides their many natural needs, their frequent clashes and stabbing affrays gave us plenty to do. But what actually absorbed our minds was the secret laboratory we had fitted up in the cellar—the laboratory with the long table under the electric lights, where in the small hours of the morning we often injected West's various solutions into the veins of the things we dragged from the potter's field. West was experimenting madly to find something which would start man's vital motions anew after they had been stopped by the thing we call death, but had encountered the most ghastly obstacles. The solution had to be differently compounded for different types—what would serve for guinea-pigs would not serve for human beings, and different human specimens required large modifications.

The bodies had to be exceedingly fresh, or the slight decomposition of brain tissue would render perfect reanimation impossible. Indeed, the greatest problem was to get them fresh enough—West had had horrible experiences during his secret college researches with corpses of doubtful vintage. The results of partial or imperfect animation were much more hideous than were the total failures, and we both held fearsome recollections of such things. Ever since our first daemoniac session in the deserted farmhouse on Meadow Hill in Arkham, we had felt a brooding menace; and West, though a calm, blond, blue-eyed scientific automaton in most respects, often confessed to a shuddering sensation of stealthy pursuit. He half felt that he was followed—a psychological delusion of shaken nerves, enhanced by the undeniably disturbing fact that at least one of our reanimated specimens was still alive—a frightful carnivorous thing in a padded cell at Sefton. Then there was another—our first—whose exact fate we had never learned.

We had fair luck with specimens in Bolton—much better than in Arkham. We had not been settled a week before we got an accident victim on the very night of burial, and made it open its eyes with an amazingly rational expression before the solution failed. It had lost an arm—if it had been a perfect body we might have succeeded better. Between then and the next January we secured three more; one total failure, one case of marked muscular motion, and one rather shivery thing—it rose of itself and uttered a sound. Then came a period when luck was poor; interments fell off, and those that did occur were of specimens either too diseased or too maimed for use. We kept track of all the deaths and their circumstances with systematic care.

One March night, however, we unexpectedly obtained a specimen which did not come from the potter's field. In Bolton the prevailing spirit of Puritanism had outlawed the sport of boxing—with the usual result. Surreptitious and ill-conducted bouts among the mill-workers were common, and occasionally professional talent of low grade was imported. This late winter night there had been such a match; evidently with disastrous results, since two timorous Poles had come to us with incoherently whispered entreaties to attend to a very secret and desperate case. We followed them to an abandoned barn, where the remnants of a crowd of frightened foreigners were watching a silent black form on the floor.

The match had been between Kid O'Brien—a lubberly and now quaking youth with a most un-Hibernian hooked nose—and Buck Robinson, "The Harlem Smoke". The negro had been knocked out, and a moment's examination shewed us that he would permanently remain so. He was a loathsome, gorilla-like thing, with abnormally long arms which I could not help calling fore legs, and a face that conjured up thoughts of unspeakable Congo secrets and tom-tom poundings under an eery moon. The body must have looked even worse in life—but the world holds many ugly things. Fear was upon the whole pitiful crowd, for they did not know what the law would exact of them if the affair were not hushed up; and they were very grateful when West, in spite of my involuntary shudders, offered to get rid of the thing quietly—for a purpose I knew too well.

There was bright moonlight over the snowless landscape, but we dressed the thing and carried it home between us through the deserted streets and meadows, as we had carried a similar thing one horrible night in Arkham. We approached the house from the field in the rear, took the specimen in the back door and down the cellar stairs, and prepared it for the usual experiment. Our fear of the police was absurdly great, though we had timed our trip to avoid the solitary patrolman of that section.

The result was wearily anticlimactic. Ghastly as our prize appeared, it was wholly unresponsive to every solution we injected in its black arm; solutions prepared from experience with white specimens only. So as the hour grew dangerously near to dawn, we did as we had done with the others—dragged the thing across the meadows to the neck of woods near the potter's field, and buried it there in the best sort of grave the frozen ground would furnish. The grave was not very deep, but fully as good as that of the previous specimen—the thing which had risen of itself and uttered a sound. In the light of our dark lanterns we carefully covered it with leaves and dead vines, fairly certain that the police would never find it in a forest so dim and dense.

The next day I was increasingly apprehensive about the police, for a patient brought rumours of a suspected fight and death. West had still another source of worry, for he had been called in the afternoon to a case which ended very threateningly. An Italian woman had become hysterical over her missing child—a lad of five who had strayed off early in the morning and failed to appear for dinner—and had developed symptoms highly alarming in view of an always weak heart. It was a very foolish hysteria, for the boy had often run away before; but Italian peasants are exceedingly superstitious, and this woman seemed as much harassed by omens as by facts. About seven o'clock in the evening she had died, and her frantic husband had made a frightful scene in his efforts to kill West, whom he wildly blamed for not saving her life. Friends had held him when he drew a stiletto, but West departed amidst his inhuman shrieks, curses, and oaths of vengeance. In his latest affliction the fellow seemed to have forgotten his child, who was still missing as the night advanced. There was some talk of searching the woods, but most of the family's friends were busy with the dead woman and the screaming man. Altogether, the nervous strain upon West must have been tremendous. Thoughts of the police and of the mad Italian both weighed heavily.

We retired about eleven, but I did not sleep well. Bolton had a surprisingly good police force for so small a town, and I could not help fearing the mess which would ensue if the affair of the night before were ever tracked down. It might mean the end of all our local work—and perhaps prison for both West and me. I did not like those rumours of a fight which were floating about. After the clock had struck three the moon shone in my eyes, but I turned over without rising to pull down the shade. Then came the steady rattling at the back door.

I lay still and somewhat dazed, but before long heard West's rap on my door. He was clad in dressing-gown and slippers, and had in his hands a revolver and an electric flashlight. From the revolver I knew that he was thinking more of the crazed Italian than of the police.

"We'd better both go," he whispered. "It wouldn't do not to answer it anyway, and it may be a patient—it would be like one of those fools to try the back door."

So we both went down the stairs on tiptoe, with a fear partly justified and partly that which comes only from the soul of the weird small hours. The rattling continued, growing somewhat louder. When we reached the door I cautiously unbolted it and threw it open, and as the moon streamed revealingly down on the form silhouetted there, West did a peculiar thing. Despite the obvious danger of attracting notice and bringing down on our heads the dreaded police investigation—a thing which after all was mercifully averted by the relative isolation of our cottage—my friend suddenly, excitedly, and unnecessarily emptied all six chambers of his revolver into the nocturnal visitor.

For that visitor was neither Italian nor policeman. Looming hideously against the spectral moon was a gigantic misshapen thing not to be imagined save in nightmares—a glassy-eyed, ink-black apparition nearly on all fours, covered with bits of mould, leaves, and vines, foul with caked blood, and having between its glistening teeth a snow-white, terrible, cylindrical object terminating in a tiny hand.

IV. The Scream of the Dead

The scream of a dead man gave to me that acute and added horror of Dr. Herbert West which harassed the latter years of our companionship. It is natural that such a thing as a dead man's scream should give horror, for it is obviously not a pleasing or ordinary occurrence; but I was used to similar experiences, hence suffered on this occasion only because of a particular circumstance. And, as I have implied, it was not of the dead man himself that I became afraid.

Herbert West, whose associate and assistant I was, possessed scientific interests far beyond the usual routine of a village physician. That was why, when establishing his practice in Bolton, he had chosen an isolated house near the potter's field. Briefly and brutally stated, West's sole absorbing interest was a secret study of the phenomena of life and its cessation, leading toward the reanimation of the dead through injections of an excitant solution. For this ghastly experimenting it was necessary to have a constant supply of very fresh human bodies; very fresh because even the least decay hopelessly damaged the brain structure, and human because we found that the solution had to be compounded differently for different types of organisms. Scores of rabbits and guinea-pigs had been killed and treated, but their trail was a blind one. West had never fully succeeded because he had never been able to secure a corpse sufficiently fresh. What he wanted were bodies from which vitality had only just departed; bodies with every cell intact and capable of receiving again the impulse toward that mode of motion called life. There was hope that this second and artificial life might be made perpetual by repetitions of the injection, but we had learned that an ordinary natural life would not respond to the action. To establish the artificial motion, natural life must be extinct—the specimens must be very fresh, but genuinely dead.

The awesome quest had begun when West and I were students at the Miskatonic University Medical School in Arkham, vividly conscious for the first time of the thoroughly mechanical nature of life. That was seven years before, but West looked scarcely a day older now—he was small, blond, clean-shaven, soft-voiced, and spectacled, with only an occasional flash of a cold blue eye to tell of the hardening and growing fanaticism of his character under the pressure of his terrible investigations. Our experiences had often been hideous in the extreme; the results of defective reanimation, when lumps of graveyard clay had been galvanised into morbid, unnatural, and brainless motion by various modifications of the vital solution.

One thing had uttered a nerve-shattering scream; another had risen violently, beaten us both to unconsciousness, and run amuck in a shocking way before it could be placed behind asylum bars; still another, a loathsome African monstrosity, had clawed out of its shallow grave and done a deed—West had had to shoot that object. We could not get bodies fresh enough to shew any trace of reason when reanimated, so had perforce created nameless horrors. It was disturbing to think that one, perhaps two, of our monsters still lived—that thought haunted us shadowingly, till finally West disappeared under frightful circumstances. But at the time of the scream in the cellar laboratory of the isolated Bolton cottage, our fears were subordinate to our anxiety for extremely fresh specimens. West was more avid than I, so that it almost seemed to me that he looked half-covetously at any very healthy living physique.

It was in July, 1910, that the bad luck regarding specimens began to turn. I had been on a long visit to my parents in Illinois, and upon my return found West in a state of singular elation. He had, he told me excitedly, in all likelihood solved the problem of freshness through an approach from an entirely new angle—that of artificial preservation. I had known that he was working on a new and highly unusual embalming compound, and was not surprised that it had turned out well; but until he explained the details I was rather puzzled as to how such a compound could help in our work, since the objectionable staleness of the specimens was largely due to delay occurring before we secured them. This, I now saw, West had clearly recognised; creating his embalming compound for future rather than immediate use, and trusting to fate to supply again some very recent and unburied corpse, as it had years before when we obtained the negro killed in the Bolton prize-fight. At last fate had been kind, so that on this occasion there lay in the secret cellar laboratory a corpse whose decay could not by any possibility have begun. What would happen on reanimation, and whether we could hope for a revival of mind and reason, West did not venture to predict. The experiment would be a landmark in our studies, and he had saved the new body for my return, so that both might share the spectacle in accustomed fashion.

West told me how he had obtained the specimen. It had been a vigorous man; a well-dressed stranger just off the train and on his way to transact some business with the Bolton Worsted Mills. The walk through the town had been long, and by the time the traveller paused at our cottage to ask the way to the factories his heart had become greatly overtaxed. He had refused a stimulant, and had suddenly dropped dead only a moment later. The body, as might be expected, seemed to West a heaven-sent gift. In his brief conversation the stranger had made it clear that he was unknown in Bolton, and a search of his pockets subsequently revealed him to be one Robert Leavitt of St. Louis, apparently without a family to make instant inquiries about his disappearance. If this man could not be restored to life, no one would know of our experiment. We buried our materials in a dense strip of woods between the house and the potter's field. If, on the other hand, he could be restored, our fame would be brilliantly and perpetually established. So without delay West had injected into the body's wrist the compound which would hold it fresh for use after my arrival. The matter of the presumably weak heart, which to my mind imperilled the success of our experiment, did not appear to trouble West extensively. He hoped at last to obtain what he had never obtained before—a rekindled spark of reason and perhaps a normal, living creature.

So on the night of July 18, 1910, Herbert West and I stood in the cellar laboratory and gazed at a white, silent figure beneath the dazzling arc-light. The embalming compound had worked uncannily well, for as I stared fascinatedly at the sturdy frame which had lain two weeks without stiffening I was moved to seek West's assurance that the thing was really dead. This assurance he gave readily enough; reminding me that the reanimating solution was never used without careful tests as to life; since it could have no effect if any of the original vitality were present. As West proceeded to take preliminary steps, I was impressed by the vast intricacy of the new experiment; an intricacy so vast that he could trust no hand less delicate than his own. Forbidding me to touch the body, he first injected a drug in the wrist just beside the place his needle had punctured when injecting the embalming compound. This, he said, was to neutralise the compound and release the system to a normal relaxation so that the reanimating solution might freely work when injected. Slightly later, when a change and a gentle tremor seemed to affect the dead limbs, West stuffed a pillow-like object violently over the twitching face, not withdrawing it until the corpse appeared quiet and ready for our attempt at reanimation. The pale enthusiast now applied some last perfunctory tests for absolute lifelessness, withdrew satisfied, and finally injected into the left arm an accurately measured amount of the vital elixir, prepared during the afternoon with a greater care than we had used since college days, when our feats were new and groping. I cannot express the wild, breathless suspense with which we waited for results on this first really fresh specimen—the first we could reasonably expect to open its lips in rational speech, perhaps to tell of what it had seen beyond the unfathomable abyss.

West was a materialist, believing in no soul and attributing all the workings of consciousness to bodily phenomena; consequently he looked for no revelation of hideous secrets from gulfs and caverns beyond death's barrier. I did not wholly disagree with him theoretically, yet held vague instinctive remnants of the primitive faith of my forefathers; so that I could not help eyeing the corpse with a certain amount of awe and terrible expectation. Besides—I could not extract from my memory that hideous, inhuman shriek we heard on the night we tried our first experiment in the deserted farmhouse at Arkham.

Very little time had elapsed before I saw that the attempt was not to be a total failure. A touch of colour came to cheeks hitherto chalk-white, and spread out under the curiously ample stubble of sandy beard. West, who had his hand on the pulse of the left wrist, suddenly nodded significantly; and almost simultaneously a mist appeared on the mirror inclined above the body's mouth. There followed a few spasmodic muscular motions, and then an audible breathing and visible motion of the chest. I looked at the closed eyelids, and thought I detected a quivering. Then the lids opened, shewing eyes which were grey, calm, and alive, but still unintelligent and not even curious.

In a moment of fantastic whim I whispered questions to the reddening ears; questions of other worlds of which the memory might still be present. Subsequent terror drove them from my mind, but I think the last one, which I repeated, was: "Where have you been?" I do not yet know whether I was answered or not, for no sound came from the well-shaped mouth; but I do know that at that moment I firmly thought the thin lips moved silently, forming syllables which I would have vocalised as "only now" if that phrase had possessed any sense or relevancy. At that moment, as I say, I was elated with the conviction that the one great goal had been attained; and that for the first time a reanimated corpse had uttered distinct words impelled by actual reason. In the next moment there was no doubt about the triumph; no doubt that the solution had truly accomplished, at least temporarily, its full mission of restoring rational and articulate life to the dead. But in that triumph there came to me the greatest of all horrors—not horror of the thing that spoke, but of the deed that I had witnessed and of the man with whom my professional fortunes were joined.

For that very fresh body, at last writhing into full and terrifying consciousness with eyes dilated at the memory of its last scene on earth, threw out its frantic hands in a life and death struggle with the air; and suddenly collapsing into a second and final dissolution from which there could be no return, screamed out the cry that will ring eternally in my aching brain:

"Help! Keep off, you cursed little tow-head fiend—keep that damned needle away from me!"

V. The Horror from the Shadows

Many men have related hideous things, not mentioned in print, which happened on the battlefields of the Great War. Some of these things have made me faint, others have convulsed me with devastating nausea, while still others have made me tremble and look behind me in the dark; yet despite the worst of them I believe I can myself relate the most hideous thing of all—the shocking, the unnatural, the unbelievable horror from the shadows.

In 1915 I was a physician with the rank of First Lieutenant in a Canadian regiment in Flanders, one of many Americans to precede the government itself into the gigantic struggle. I had not entered the army on my own initiative, but rather as a natural result of the enlistment of the man whose indispensable assistant I was—the celebrated Boston surgical specialist, Dr. Herbert West. Dr. West had been avid for a chance to serve as surgeon in a great war, and when the chance had come he carried me with him almost against my will. There were reasons why I would have been glad to let the war separate us; reasons why I found the practice of medicine and the companionship of West more and more irritating; but when he had gone to Ottawa and through a colleague's influence secured a medical commission as Major, I could not resist the imperious persuasion of one determined that I should accompany him in my usual capacity.

When I say that Dr. West was avid to serve in battle, I do not mean to imply that he was either naturally warlike or anxious for the safety of civilisation. Always an ice-cold intellectual machine; slight, blond, blue-eyed, and spectacled; I think he secretly sneered at my occasional martial enthusiasms and censures of supine neutrality. There was, however, something he wanted in embattled Flanders; and in order to secure it he had to assume a military exterior. What he wanted was not a thing which many persons want, but something connected with the peculiar branch of medical science which he had chosen quite clandestinely to follow, and in which he had achieved amazing and occasionally hideous results. It was, in fact, nothing more or less than an abundant supply of freshly killed men in every stage of dismemberment.

Herbert West needed fresh bodies because his life-work was the reanimation of the dead. This work was not known to the fashionable clientele who had so swiftly built up his fame after his arrival in Boston; but was only too well known to me, who had been his closest friend and sole assistant since the old days in Miskatonic University Medical School at Arkham. It was in those college days that he had begun his terrible experiments, first on small animals and then on human bodies shockingly obtained. There was a solution which he injected into the veins of dead things, and if they were fresh enough they responded in strange ways. He had had much trouble in discovering the proper formula, for each type of organism was found to need a stimulus especially adapted to it. Terror stalked him when he reflected on his partial failures; nameless things resulting from imperfect solutions or from bodies insufficiently fresh. A certain number of these failures had remained alive—one was in an asylum while others had vanished—and as he thought of conceivable yet virtually impossible eventualities he often shivered beneath his usual stolidity.

West had soon learned that absolute freshness was the prime requisite for useful specimens, and had accordingly resorted to frightful and unnatural expedients in body-snatching. In college, and during our early practice together in the factory town of Bolton, my attitude toward him had been largely one of fascinated admiration; but as his boldness in methods grew, I began to develop a gnawing fear. I did not like the way he looked at healthy living bodies; and then there came a nightmarish session in the cellar laboratory when I learned that a certain specimen had been a living body when he secured it. That was the first time he had ever been able to revive the quality of rational thought in a corpse; and his success, obtained at such a loathsome cost, had completely hardened him.

Of his methods in the intervening five years I dare not speak. I was held to him by sheer force of fear, and witnessed sights that no human tongue could repeat. Gradually I came to find Herbert West himself more horrible than anything he did—that was when it dawned on me that his once normal scientific zeal for prolonging life had subtly degenerated into a mere morbid and ghoulish curiosity and secret sense of charnel picturesqueness. His interest became a hellish and perverse addiction to the repellently and fiendishly abnormal; he gloated calmly over artificial monstrosities which would make most healthy men drop dead from fright and disgust; he became, behind his pallid intellectuality, a fastidious Baudelaire of physical experiment—a languid Elagabalus of the tombs.

Dangers he met unflinchingly; crimes he committed unmoved. I think the climax came when he had proved his point that rational life can be restored, and had sought new worlds to conquer by experimenting on the reanimation of detached parts of bodies. He had wild and original ideas on the independent vital properties of organic cells and nerve-tissue separated from natural physiological systems; and achieved some hideous preliminary results in the form of never-dying, artificially nourished tissue obtained from the nearly hatched eggs of an indescribable tropical reptile. Two biological points he was exceedingly anxious to settle—first, whether any amount of consciousness and rational action be possible without the brain, proceeding from the spinal cord and various nerve-centres; and second, whether any kind of ethereal, intangible relation distinct from the material cells may exist to link the surgically separated parts of what has previously been a single living organism. All this research work required a prodigious supply of freshly slaughtered human flesh—and that was why Herbert West had entered the Great War.

The phantasmal, unmentionable thing occurred one midnight late in March, 1915, in a field hospital behind the lines at St. Eloi. I wonder even now if it could have been other than a daemoniac dream of delirium. West had a private laboratory in an east room of the barn-like temporary edifice, assigned him on his plea that he was devising new and radical methods for the treatment of hitherto hopeless cases of maiming. There he worked like a butcher in the midst of his gory wares—I could never get used to the levity with which he handled and classified certain things. At times he actually did perform marvels of surgery for the soldiers; but his chief delights were of a less public and philanthropic kind, requiring many explanations of sounds which seemed peculiar even amidst that babel of the damned. Among these sounds were frequent revolver-shots—surely not uncommon on a battlefield, but distinctly uncommon in an hospital. Dr. West's reanimated specimens were not meant for long existence or a large audience. Besides human tissue, West employed much of the reptile embryo tissue which he had cultivated with such singular results. It was better than human material for maintaining life in organless fragments, and that was now my friend's chief activity. In a dark corner of the laboratory, over a queer incubating burner, he kept a large covered vat full of this reptilian cell-matter; which multiplied and grew puffily and hideously.

On the night of which I speak we had a splendid new specimen—a man at once physically powerful and of such high mentality that a sensitive nervous system was assured. It was rather ironic, for he was the officer who had helped West to his commission, and who was now to have been our associate. Moreover, he had in the past secretly studied the theory of reanimation to some extent under West. Major Sir Eric Moreland

Clapham-Lee, D.S.O., was the greatest surgeon in our division, and had been hastily assigned to the St. Eloi sector when news of the heavy fighting reached headquarters. He had come in an aëroplane piloted by the intrepid Lieut. Ronald Hill, only to be shot down when directly over his destination. The fall had been spectacular and awful; Hill was unrecognisable afterward, but the wreck yielded up the great surgeon in a nearly decapitated but otherwise intact condition. West had greedily seized the lifeless thing which had once been his friend and fellow-scholar; and I shuddered when he finished severing the head, placed it in his hellish vat of pulpy reptile-tissue to preserve it for future experiments, and proceeded to treat the decapitated body on the operating table. He injected new blood, joined certain veins, arteries, and nerves at the headless neck, and closed the ghastly aperture with engrafted skin from an unidentified specimen which had borne an officer's uniform. I knew what he wanted—to see if this highly organised body could exhibit, without its head, any of the signs of mental life which had distinguished Sir Eric Moreland Clapham-Lee. Once a student of reanimation, this silent trunk was now gruesomely called upon to exemplify it.

I can still see Herbert West under the sinister electric light as he injected his reanimating solution into the arm of the headless body. The scene I cannot describe—I should faint if I tried it, for there is madness in a room full of classified charnel things, with blood and lesser human debris almost ankle-deep on the slimy floor, and with hideous reptilian abnormalities sprouting, bubbling, and baking over a winking bluish-green spectre of dim flame in a far corner of black shadows.

The specimen, as West repeatedly observed, had a splendid nervous system. Much was expected of it; and as a few twitching motions began to appear, I could see the feverish interest on West's face. He was ready, I think, to see proof of his increasingly strong opinion that consciousness, reason, and personality can exist independently of the brain—that man has no central connective spirit, but is merely a machine of nervous matter, each section more or less complete in itself. In one triumphant demonstration West was about to relegate the mystery of life to the category of myth. The body now twitched more vigorously, and beneath our avid eyes commenced to heave in a frightful way. The arms stirred disquietingly, the legs drew up, and various muscles contracted in a repulsive kind of writhing. Then the headless thing threw out its arms in a gesture which was unmistakably one of desperation—an intelligent desperation apparently sufficient to prove every theory of Herbert West. Certainly, the nerves were recalling the man's last act in life; the struggle to get free of the falling aëroplane.

What followed, I shall never positively know. It may have been wholly an hallucination from the shock caused at that instant by the sudden and complete destruction of the building in a cataclysm of German shell-fire—who can gainsay it, since West and I were the only proved survivors? West liked to think that before his recent disappearance, but there were times when he could not; for it was queer that we both had the same hallucination. The hideous occurrence itself was very simple, notable only for what it implied.

The body on the table had risen with a blind and terrible groping, and we had heard a sound. I should not call that sound a voice, for it was too awful. And yet its timbre was not the most awful thing about it. Neither was its message—it had merely screamed, "Jump, Ronald, for God's sake, jump!" The awful thing was its source.

For it had come from the large covered vat in that ghoulish corner of crawling black shadows.

VI. The Tomb-Legions

When Dr. Herbert West disappeared a year ago, the Boston police questioned me closely. They suspected that I was holding something back, and perhaps suspected even graver things; but I could not tell them the truth because they would not have believed it. They knew, indeed, that West had been connected with activities beyond the credence of ordinary men; for his hideous experiments in the reanimation of dead bodies had long been too extensive to admit of perfect secrecy; but the final soul-shattering catastrophe held elements of daemoniac phantasy which make even me doubt the reality of what I saw.

I was West's closest friend and only confidential assistant. We had met years before, in medical school, and from the first I had shared his terrible researches. He had slowly tried to perfect a solution which, injected into the veins of the newly deceased, would restore life; a labour demanding an abundance of fresh corpses and therefore involving the most unnatural actions. Still more shocking were the products of some of the experiments—grisly masses of flesh that had been dead, but that West waked to a blind, brainless, nauseous animation. These were the usual results, for in order to reawaken the mind it was necessary to have specimens so absolutely fresh that no decay could possibly affect the delicate brain-cells.

This need for very fresh corpses had been West's moral undoing. They were hard to get, and one awful day he had secured his specimen while it was still alive and vigorous. A struggle, a needle, and a powerful alkaloid had transformed it to a very fresh corpse, and the experiment had succeeded for a brief and memorable moment; but West had emerged with a soul calloused and seared, and a hardened eye which sometimes glanced with a kind of hideous and calculating appraisal at men of especially sensitive brain and especially vigorous physique. Toward the last I became acutely afraid of West, for he began to look at me that way. People did not seem to notice his glances, but they noticed my fear; and after his disappearance used that as a basis for some absurd suspicions.

West, in reality, was more afraid than I; for his abominable pursuits entailed a life of furtiveness and dread of every shadow. Partly it was the police he feared; but sometimes his nervousness was deeper and more nebulous, touching on certain indescribable things into which he had injected a morbid life, and from which he had not seen that life depart. He usually finished his experiments with a revolver, but a few times he had not been quick enough. There was that first specimen on whose rifled grave marks of clawing were later seen. There was also that Arkham professor's body which had done cannibal things before it had been captured and thrust unidentified into a madhouse cell at Sefton, where it beat the walls for sixteen years. Most of the other possibly surviving results were things less easy to speak of—for in later years West's scientific zeal had degenerated to an unhealthy and fantastic mania, and he had spent his chief skill in vitalising not entire human bodies but isolated parts of bodies, or parts joined to organic matter other than human. It had become fiendishly disgusting by the time he disappeared; many of the experiments could not even be hinted at in print. The Great War, through which both of us served as surgeons, had intensified this side of West.

In saying that West's fear of his specimens was nebulous, I have in mind particularly its complex nature. Part of it came merely from knowing of the existence of such nameless monsters, while another part arose from apprehension of the bodily harm they might under certain circumstances do him. Their disappearance added horror to the situation—of them all West knew the whereabouts of only one, the pitiful asylum thing. Then there was a more subtle fear—a very fantastic sensation resulting from a curious experiment in the Canadian army in 1915. West, in the midst of a severe battle, had reanimated Major Sir Eric Moreland Clapham-Lee, D.S.O., a fellow-physician who knew about his experiments and could have duplicated them. The head had been removed, so that the possibilities of quasi-intelligent life in the trunk might be investigated. Just as the building was wiped out by a German shell, there had been a success. The trunk had moved intelligently; and, unbelievable to relate, we were both sickeningly sure that articulate sounds had come from the detached head as it lay in a shadowy corner of the laboratory. The shell had been merciful, in a way—but West could never feel as certain as he wished, that we two were the only survivors. He used to make shuddering conjectures about the possible actions of a headless physician with the power of reanimating the dead.

West's last quarters were in a venerable house of much elegance, overlooking one of the oldest burying-grounds in Boston. He had chosen the place for purely symbolic and fantastically aesthetic reasons, since most of the interments were of the colonial period and therefore of little use to a scientist seeking very fresh bodies. The laboratory was in a sub-cellar secretly constructed by imported workmen, and contained a huge incinerator for the quiet and complete disposal of such bodies, or fragments and synthetic mockeries of bodies, as might remain from the morbid experiments and unhallowed amusements of the owner. During the excavation of this cellar the workmen had struck some exceedingly ancient masonry; undoubtedly connected with the old burying-ground, yet far too deep to correspond with any known sepulchre therein. After a number of calculations West decided that it represented some secret chamber beneath the tomb of the Averills, where the last interment had been made in 1768. I was with him when he studied the nitrous, dripping walls laid bare by the spades and mattocks of the men, and was prepared for the gruesome thrill which would attend the uncovering of centuried grave-secrets; but for the first time West's new timidity conquered his natural curiosity, and he betrayed his degenerating fibre by ordering the masonry left intact and plastered over. Thus it remained till that final hellish night; part of the walls of the secret laboratory. I speak of West's decadence, but must add that it was a purely mental and intangible thing. Outwardly he was the same to the last—calm, cold, slight, and yellow-haired, with spectacled blue eyes and a general aspect of youth which years and fears seemed never to change. He seemed calm even when he thought of that clawed grave and looked over his shoulder; even when he thought of the carnivorous thing that gnawed and pawed at Sefton bars.

The end of Herbert West began one evening in our joint study when he was dividing his curious glance between the newspaper and me. A strange headline item had struck at him from the crumpled pages, and a nameless titan claw had seemed to reach down through sixteen years. Something fearsome and incredible had happened at Sefton Asylum fifty miles away, stunning the neighbourhood and baffling the police. In the small hours of the morning a body of silent men had entered the grounds and their leader had aroused the attendants. He was a menacing military figure who talked without moving his lips and whose voice seemed almost ventriloquially connected with an immense black case he carried. His expressionless face was handsome to the point of radiant beauty, but had shocked the superintendent when the hall light fell on it—for it was a wax face with eyes of painted glass. Some nameless accident had befallen this man. A larger man guided his steps; a repellent hulk whose bluish face seemed half eaten away by some unknown malady. The speaker had asked for the custody of the cannibal monster committed from Arkham sixteen years before; and upon being refused, gave a signal which precipitated a shocking riot. The fiends had beaten, trampled, and bitten every attendant who did not flee; killing four and finally succeeding in the liberation of the monster. Those victims who could recall the event without hysteria swore that the creatures had acted less like men than like unthinkable automata guided by the wax-faced leader. By the time help could be summoned, every trace of the men and of their mad charge had vanished.

From the hour of reading this item until midnight, West sat almost paralysed. At midnight the doorbell rang, startling him fearfully. All the servants were asleep in the attic, so I answered the bell. As I have told the police, there was no wagon in the street; but only a group of strange-looking figures bearing a large square box which they deposited in the hallway after one of them had grunted in a highly unnatural voice, "Express—prepaid." They filed out of the house with a jerky tread, and as I watched them go I had an odd idea that they were turning toward the ancient cemetery on which the back of the house abutted. When I slammed the door after them West came downstairs and looked at the box. It was about two feet square, and bore West's correct name and present address. It also bore the inscription, "From Eric Moreland Clapham-Lee, St. Eloi, Flanders." Six years before, in Flanders, a shelled hospital had fallen upon the headless reanimated trunk of Dr. Clapham-Lee, and upon the detached head which—perhaps—had uttered articulate sounds.

West was not even excited now. His condition was more ghastly. Quickly he said, "It's the finish—but let's incinerate—this." We carried the thing down to the laboratory—listening. I do not remember many particulars—you can imagine my state of mind—but it is a vicious lie to say it was Herbert West's body which I put into the incinerator. We both inserted the whole unopened wooden box, closed the door, and started the electricity. Nor did any sound come from the box, after all.

It was West who first noticed the falling plaster on that part of the wall where the ancient tomb masonry had been covered up. I was going to run, but he stopped me. Then I saw a small black aperture, felt a ghoulish wind of ice, and smelled the charnel bowels of a putrescent earth. There was no sound, but just then the electric lights went out and I saw outlined against some phosphorescence of the nether world a horde of silent toiling things which only insanity—or worse—could create. Their outlines were human, semi-human, fractionally human, and not human at all—the horde was grotesquely heterogeneous. They were removing the stones quietly, one by one, from the centuried wall. And then, as the breach became large enough, they came out into the laboratory in single file; led by a stalking thing with a beautiful head made of wax. A sort of mad-eyed monstrosity behind the leader seized on Herbert West. West did not resist or utter a sound. Then they all sprang at him and tore him to pieces before my eyes, bearing the fragments away into that subterranean vault of fabulous abominations. West's head was carried off by the wax-headed leader, who wore a Canadian officer's uniform. As it disappeared I saw that the blue eyes behind the spectacles were hideously blazing with their first touch of frantic, visible emotion.

Servants found me unconscious in the morning. West was gone. The incinerator contained only unidentifiable ashes. Detectives have questioned me, but what can I say? The Sefton tragedy they will not connect with West; not that, nor the men with the box, whose existence they deny. I told them of the vault, and they pointed to the unbroken plaster wall and laughed. So I told them no more. They imply that I am either a madman or a murderer—probably I am mad. But I might not be mad if those accursed tomb-legions had not been so silent.

HYPNOS

To S. L.

"Apropos of sleep, that sinister adventure of all our nights, we may say that men go to bed daily with an audacity that would be incomprehensible if we did not know that it is the result of ignorance of the danger."

—*Baudelaire.*

May the merciful gods, if indeed there be such, guard those hours when no power of the will, or drug that the cunning of man devises, can keep me from the chasm of sleep. Death is merciful, for there is no return therefrom, but with him who has come back out of the nethermost chambers of night, haggard and knowing, peace rests nevermore. Fool that I was to plunge with such unsanctioned phrensy into mysteries no man was meant to penetrate; fool or god that *he* was—my only friend, who led me and went before me, and who in the end passed into terrors which may yet be mine.

We met, I recall, in a railway station, where he was the centre of a crowd of the vulgarly curious. He was unconscious, having fallen in a kind of convulsion which imparted to his slight black-clad body a strange rigidity. I think he was then approaching forty years of age, for there were deep lines in the face, wan and hollow-cheeked, but oval and actually *beautiful*; and touches of grey in the thick, waving hair and small full beard which had once been of the deepest raven black. His brow was white as the marble of Pentelicus, and of a height and breadth almost godlike. I said to myself, with all the ardour of a sculptor, that this man was a faun's statue out of antique Hellas, dug from a temple's ruins and brought somehow to life in our stifling age only to feel the chill and pressure of devastating years. And when he opened his immense, sunken, and wildly luminous black eyes I knew he would be thenceforth my only friend—the only friend of one who had never possessed a friend before—for I saw that such eyes must have looked fully upon the grandeur and the terror of realms beyond normal consciousness and reality; realms which I had cherished in fancy, but vainly sought. So as I drove the crowd away I told him he must come home with me and be my teacher and leader in unfathomed mysteries, and he assented without speaking a word. Afterward I found that his voice was music—the music of deep viols and of crystalline spheres. We talked often in the night, and in the day, when I chiselled busts of him, and carved miniature heads in ivory to immortalise his different expressions.

Of our studies it is impossible to speak, since they held so slight a connexion with anything of the world as living men conceive it. They were of that vaster and more appalling universe of dim entity and consciousness which lies deeper than matter, time, and space, and whose existence we suspect only in certain forms of sleep—those rare dreams beyond dreams which come never to common men, and but once or twice in the lifetime of imaginative men. The cosmos of our waking knowledge, born from such an universe as a bubble is born from the pipe of a jester, touches it only as such a bubble may touch its sardonic source when sucked back by the jester's whim. Men of learning suspect it little, and ignore it mostly. Wise men have interpreted dreams, and the gods have laughed. One man with Oriental eyes has said that all time and space are relative, and men have laughed. But even that man with Oriental eyes has done no more than suspect. I had wished and tried to do more than suspect, and my friend had tried and partly succeeded. Then we both tried together, and with exotic drugs courted terrible and forbidden dreams in the tower studio chamber of the old manor-house in hoary Kent.

Among the agonies of these after days is that chief of torments—inarticulateness. What I learned and saw in those hours of impious exploration can never be told—for want of symbols or suggestions in any language. I say this because from first to last our discoveries partook only of the nature of *sensations*; sensations correlated with no impression which the nervous system of normal humanity is capable of receiving. They were sensations, yet within them lay unbelievable elements of time and space—things which at bottom possess no distinct and definite existence. Human utterance can best convey the general character of our experiences by calling them *plungings* or *soarings*; for in every period of revelation some part of our minds broke boldly away from all that is real and present, rushing aërially along shocking, unlighted, and fear-haunted abysses, and occasionally *tearing* through certain well-marked and typical obstacles describable only as viscous, uncouth clouds or vapours. In these black and bodiless flights we were sometimes alone and sometimes together. When we were together, my friend was always far ahead; I could comprehend his presence despite the absence of form by a species of pictorial memory whereby his face appeared to me, golden from a strange light and frightful with its weird beauty, its anomalously youthful cheeks, its burning eyes, its Olympian brow, and its shadowing hair and growth of beard.

Of the progress of time we kept no record, for time had become to us the merest illusion. I know only that there must have been something very singular involved, since we came at length to marvel why we did not grow old. Our discourse was unholy, and always hideously ambitious—no god or daemon could have aspired to discoveries and conquests like those which we planned in whispers. I shiver as I speak of them, and dare not be explicit; though I will say that my friend once wrote on paper a wish which he dared not utter with his tongue, and which made me burn the paper and look affrightedly out of the window at the spangled night sky. I will hint—only hint—that he had designs which involved the rulership of the visible universe and more; designs whereby the earth and the stars would move at his command, and the destinies of all living things be his. I affirm—I swear—that I had no share in these extreme aspirations. Anything my friend may have said or written to the contrary must be erroneous, for I am no man of strength to risk the unmentionable warfare in unmentionable spheres by which alone one might achieve success.

There was a night when winds from unknown spaces whirled us irresistibly into limitless vacua beyond all thought and entity. Perceptions of the most maddeningly untransmissible sort thronged upon us; perceptions of infinity which at the time convulsed us with joy, yet which are now partly lost to my memory and partly incapable of presentation to others. Viscous obstacles were clawed through in rapid succession, and at length I felt that we had been borne to realms of greater remoteness than any we had previously known. My friend was vastly in advance as we plunged in this awesome ocean of virgin aether, and I could see the sinister exultation on his floating, luminous, too youthful memory-face. Suddenly that face became dim and quickly disappeared, and in a brief space I found myself projected against an obstacle which I could not penetrate. It was like the others, yet incalculably denser; a sticky, clammy mass, if such terms can be applied to analogous qualities in a non-material sphere.

I had, I felt, been halted by a barrier which my friend and leader had successfully passed. Struggling anew, I came to the end of the drug-dream and opened my physical eyes to the tower studio in whose opposite corner reclined the pallid and still unconscious form of my fellow-dreamer, weirdly haggard and wildly beautiful as the moon shed gold-green light on his marble features. Then, after a short interval, the form in the corner stirred; and may pitying heaven keep from my sight and sound another thing like that which took place before me. I cannot tell you how he shrieked, or what vistas of unvisitable hells gleamed for a second in black eyes crazed with fright. I can only say that I fainted, and did not stir till he himself recovered and shook me in his phrensy for someone to keep away the horror and desolation.

That was the end of our voluntary searchings in the caverns of dream. Awed, shaken, and portentous, my friend who had been beyond the barrier warned me that we must never venture within those realms again. What he had seen, he dared not tell me; but he said from his wisdom that we must sleep as little as possible, even if drugs were necessary to keep us awake. That he was right, I soon learned from the unutterable fear which engulfed me whenever consciousness lapsed. After each short and inevitable sleep I seemed older, whilst my friend aged with a rapidity almost shocking. It is hideous to see wrinkles form and hair whiten almost before one's eyes. Our mode of life was now totally altered. Heretofore a recluse so far as I know—his true name and origin never having passed his lips—my friend now became frantic in his fear of solitude. At night he would not be alone, nor would the company of a few persons calm him. His sole relief was obtained in revelry of the most general and boisterous sort; so that few assemblies of the young and the gay were unknown to us. Our appearance and age seemed to excite in most cases a ridicule which I keenly resented, but which my friend considered a lesser evil than solitude. Especially was he afraid to be out of doors alone when the stars were shining, and if forced to this condition he would often glance furtively at the sky as if hunted by some monstrous thing therein. He did not always glance at the same place in the sky—it seemed to be a different place at different times. On spring evenings it would be low in the northeast. In the summer it would be nearly overhead. In the autumn it would be in the northwest. In winter it would be in the east, but mostly if in the small hours of morning. Midwinter evenings seemed least dreadful to him. Only after two years did I connect this fear with anything in particular; but then I began to see that he must be looking at a special spot on the celestial vault whose position at different times corresponded to the direction of his glance—a spot roughly marked by the constellation Corona Borealis.

We now had a studio in London, never separating, but never discussing the days when we had sought to plumb the mysteries of the unreal world. We were aged and weak from our drugs, dissipations, and nervous overstrain, and the thinning hair and beard of my friend had become snow-white. Our freedom from long sleep was surprising, for seldom did we succumb more than an hour or two at a time to the shadow which had now grown so frightful a menace. Then came one January of fog and rain, when money ran low and drugs were hard to buy. My statues and ivory heads were all sold, and I had no means to purchase new materials, or energy to fashion them even had I possessed them. We suffered terribly, and on a certain night my friend sank into a deep-breathing sleep from which I could not awaken him. I can recall the scene now—the desolate, pitch-black garret studio under the eaves with the rain beating down; the ticking of our lone clock; the fancied ticking of our watches as they rested on the dressing-table; the creaking of some swaying shutter in a remote part of the house; certain distant city noises muffled by fog and space; and worst of all the deep, steady, sinister breathing of my friend on the couch—a rhythmical breathing which seemed to measure moments of supernal fear and agony for his spirit as it wandered in spheres forbidden, unimagined, and hideously remote.

The tension of my vigil became oppressive, and a wild train of trivial impressions and associations thronged through my almost unhinged mind. I heard a clock strike somewhere—not ours, for that was not a striking clock—and my morbid fancy found in this a new starting-point for idle wanderings. Clocks—time—space—infinity—and then my fancy reverted to the local as I reflected that even now, beyond the roof and the fog and the rain and the atmosphere, Corona Borealis was rising in the northeast. Corona Borealis, which my friend had appeared to dread, and whose scintillant semicircle of stars must even now be glowing unseen through the measureless abysses of aether. All at once my feverishly sensitive ears seemed to detect a new and wholly distinct component in the soft medley of drug-magnified sounds—a low and damnably insistent whine from very far away; droning, clamouring, mocking, calling, *from the northeast.*

But it was not that distant whine which robbed me of my faculties and set upon my soul such a seal of fright as may never in life be removed; not that which drew the shrieks and excited the convulsions which caused lodgers and police to break down the door. It was not what I *heard,* but what I *saw;* for in that dark, locked, shuttered, and curtained room there appeared from the black northeast corner a shaft of horrible red-gold light—a shaft which bore with it no glow to disperse the darkness, but which streamed only upon the recumbent head of the troubled sleeper, bringing out in hideous duplication the luminous and strangely youthful memory-face as I had known it in dreams of abysmal space and unshackled time, when my friend had pushed beyond the barrier to those secret, innermost, and forbidden caverns of nightmare.

And as I looked, I beheld the head rise, the black, liquid, and deep-sunken eyes open in terror, and the thin, shadowed lips part as if for a scream too frightful to be uttered. There dwelt in that ghastly and inflexible face, as it shone bodiless, luminous, and rejuvenated in the blackness, more of stark, teeming, brain-shattering fear than all the rest of heaven and earth has ever revealed to me. No word was spoken amidst the distant sound that grew nearer and nearer, but as I followed the memory-face's mad stare along that cursed shaft of light to its source, the source whence also the whining came, I too saw for an instant what it saw, and fell with ringing ears in that fit of shrieking and epilepsy which brought the lodgers and the police. Never could I tell, try as I might, what it actually was that I saw; nor could the still face tell, for although it must have seen more than I did, it will never speak again. But always I shall guard against the mocking and insatiate Hypnos, lord of sleep, against the night sky, and against the mad ambitions of knowledge and philosophy.

Just what happened is unknown, for not only was my own mind unseated by the strange and hideous thing, but others were tainted with a forgetfulness which can mean nothing if not madness. They have said, I know not for what reason, that I never had a friend; but that art, philosophy, and insanity had filled all my tragic life. The lodgers and police on that night soothed me, and the doctor administered something to quiet me, nor did anyone see what a nightmare event had taken place. My stricken friend moved them to no pity, but what they found on the couch in the studio made them give me a praise which sickened me, and now a fame which I spurn in despair as I sit for hours, bald, grey-bearded, shrivelled, palsied, drug-crazed, and broken, adoring and praying to the object they found.

For they deny that I sold the last of my statuary, and point with ecstasy at the thing which the whining shaft of light left cold, petrified, and unvocal. It is all that remains of my friend; the friend who led me on to madness and wreckage; a godlike head of such marble as only old Hellas could yield, young with the youth that is outside time, and with beauteous bearded face, curved, smiling lips, Olympian brow, and dense locks waving and poppy-crowned. They say that that haunting memory-face is modelled from my own, as it was at twenty-five; but upon the marble base is carven a single name in the letters of Attica—ʽΥΠΝΟΣ.

WHAT THE MOON BRINGS

I hate the moon—I am afraid of it—for when it shines on certain scenes familiar and loved it sometimes makes them unfamiliar and hideous.

It was in the spectral summer when the moon shone down on the old garden where I wandered; the spectral summer of narcotic flowers and humid seas of foliage that bring wild and many-coloured dreams. And as I walked by the shallow crystal stream I saw unwonted ripples tipped with yellow light, as if those placid waters were drawn on in resistless currents to strange oceans that are not in the world. Silent and sparkling, bright and baleful, those moon-cursed waters hurried I knew not whither; whilst from the embowered banks white lotos blossoms fluttered one by one in the opiate night-wind and dropped despairingly into the stream, swirling away horribly under the arched, carven bridge, and staring back with the sinister resignation of calm, dead faces.

And as I ran along the shore, crushing sleeping flowers with heedless feet and maddened ever by the fear of unknown things and the lure of the dead faces, I saw that the garden had no end under that moon; for where by day the walls were, there stretched now only new vistas of trees and paths, flowers and shrubs, stone idols and pagodas, and bendings of the yellow-litten stream past grassy banks and under grotesque bridges of marble. And the lips of the dead lotos-faces whispered sadly, and bade me follow, nor did I cease my steps till the stream became a river, and joined amidst marshes of swaying reeds and beaches of gleaming sand the shore of a vast and nameless sea.

Upon that sea the hateful moon shone, and over its unvocal waves weird perfumes brooded. And as I saw therein the lotos-faces vanish, I longed for nets that I might capture them and learn from them the secrets which the moon had brought upon the night. But when that moon went over to the west and the still tide ebbed from the sullen shore, I saw in that light old spires that the waves almost uncovered, and white columns gay with festoons of green seaweed. And knowing that to this sunken place all the dead had come, I trembled and did not wish again to speak with the lotos-faces.

Yet when I saw afar out in the sea a black condor descend from the sky to seek rest on a vast reef, I would fain have questioned him, and asked him of those whom I had known when they were alive. This I would have asked him had he not been so far away, but he was very far, and could not be seen at all when he drew nigh that gigantic reef.

So I watched the tide go out under that sinking moon, and saw gleaming the spires, the towers, and the roofs of that dead, dripping city. And as I watched, my nostrils tried to close against the perfume-conquering stench of the world's dead; for truly, in this unplaced and forgotten spot had all the flesh of the churchyards gathered for puffy sea-worms to gnaw and glut upon.

Over those horrors the evil moon now hung very low, but the puffy worms of the sea need no moon to feed by. And as I watched the ripples that told of the writhing of worms beneath, I felt a new chill from afar out whither the condor had flown, as if my flesh had caught a horror before my eyes had seen it.

Nor had my flesh trembled without cause, for when I raised my eyes I saw that the waters had ebbed very low, shewing much of the vast reef whose rim I had seen before. And when I saw that this reef was but the black basalt crown of a shocking eikon whose monstrous forehead now shone in the dim moonlight and whose vile hooves must paw the hellish ooze miles below, I shrieked and shrieked lest the hidden face rise above the waters, and lest the hidden eyes look at me after the slinking away of that leering and treacherous yellow moon.

And to escape this relentless thing I plunged gladly and unhesitantly into the stinking shallows where amidst weedy walls and sunken streets fat sea-worms feast upon the world's dead.

AZATHOTH

When age fell upon the world, and wonder went out of the minds of men; when grey cities reared to smoky skies tall towers grim and ugly, in whose shadow none might dream of the sun or of spring's flowering meads; when learning stripped earth of her mantle of beauty, and poets sang no more save of twisted phantoms seen with bleared and inward-looking eyes; when these things had come to pass, and childish hopes had gone away for ever, there was a man who travelled out of life on a quest into the spaces whither the world's dreams had fled.

Of the name and abode of this man but little is written, for they were of the waking world only; yet it is said that both were obscure. It is enough to know that he dwelt in a city of high walls where sterile twilight reigned, and that he toiled all day among shadow and turmoil, coming home at evening to a room whose one window opened not on the fields and groves but on a dim court where other windows stared in dull despair. From that casement one might see only walls and windows, except sometimes when one leaned far out and peered aloft at the small stars that passed. And because mere walls and windows must soon drive to madness a man who reads and dreams much, the dweller in that room used night after night to lean out and peer aloft to glimpse some fragment of things beyond the waking world and the greyness of tall cities. After years he began to call the slow-sailing stars by name, and to follow them in fancy when they glided regretfully out of sight; till at length his vision opened to many secret vistas whose existence no common eye suspects. And one night a mighty gulf was bridged, and the dream-haunted skies swelled down to the lonely watcher's window to merge with the close air of his room and make him a part of their fabulous wonder.

There came to that room wild streams of violet midnight glittering with dust of gold; vortices of dusk and fire, swirling out of the ultimate spaces and heavy with perfumes from beyond the worlds. Opiate oceans poured there, litten by suns that the eye may never behold and having in their whirlpools strange dolphins and sea-nymphs of unrememberable deeps. Noiseless infinity eddied around the dreamer and wafted him away without even touching the body that leaned stiffly from the lonely window; and for days not counted in men's calendars the tides of far spheres bare him gently to join the dreams for which he longed; the dreams that men have lost. And in the course of many cycles they tenderly left him sleeping on a green sunrise shore; a green shore fragrant with lotus-blossoms and starred by red camalotes.

THE HOUND

In my tortured ears there sounds unceasingly a nightmare whirring and flapping, and a faint, distant baying as of some gigantic hound. It is not dream—it is not, I fear, even madness—for too much has already happened to give me these merciful doubts. St. John is a mangled corpse; I alone know why, and such is my knowledge that I am about to blow out my brains for fear I shall be mangled in the same way. Down unlit and illimitable corridors of eldritch phantasy sweeps the black, shapeless Nemesis that drives me to self-annihilation.

May heaven forgive the folly and morbidity which led us both to so monstrous a fate! Wearied with the commonplaces of a prosaic world, where even the joys of romance and adventure soon grow stale, St. John and I had followed enthusiastically every aesthetic and intellectual movement which promised respite from our devastating ennui. The enigmas of the symbolists and the ecstasies of the pre-Raphaelites all were ours in their time, but each new mood was drained too soon of its diverting novelty and appeal. Only the sombre philosophy of the decadents could hold us, and this we found potent only by increasing gradually the depth and diabolism of our penetrations. Baudelaire and Huysmans were soon exhausted of thrills, till finally there remained for us only the more direct stimuli of unnatural personal experiences and adventures. It was this frightful emotional need which led us eventually to that detestable course which even in my present fear I mention with shame and timidity—that hideous extremity of human outrage, the abhorred practice of grave-robing.

I cannot reveal the details of our shocking expeditions, or catalogue even partly the worst of the trophies adorning the nameless museum we prepared in the great stone house where we jointly dwelt, alone and servantless. Our museum was a blasphemous, unthinkable place, where with the satanic taste of neurotic virtuosi we had assembled an universe of terror and decay to excite our jaded sensibilities. It was a secret room, far, far underground; where huge winged daemons carven of basalt and onyx vomited from wide grinning mouths weird green and orange light, and hidden pneumatic pipes ruffled into kaleidoscopic dances of death the lines of red charnel things hand in hand woven in voluminous black hangings. Through these pipes came at will the odours our moods most craved; sometimes the scent of pale funereal lilies, sometimes the narcotic incense of imagined Eastern shrines of the kingly dead, and sometimes—how I shudder to recall it!—the frightful, soul-upheaving stenches of the uncovered grave.

Around the walls of this repellent chamber were cases of antique mummies alternating with comely, lifelike bodies perfectly stuffed and cured by the taxidermist's art, and with headstones snatched from the oldest churchyards of the world. Niches here and there contained skulls of all shapes, and heads preserved in various stages of dissolution. There one might find the rotting, bald pates of famous noblemen, and the fresh and radiantly golden heads of new-buried children. Statues and paintings there were, all of fiendish subjects and some executed by St. John and myself. A locked portfolio, bound in tanned human skin, held certain unknown and unnamable drawings which it was rumoured Goya had perpetrated but dared not acknowledge. There were nauseous musical instruments, stringed, brass, and wood-wind, on which St. John and I sometimes produced dissonances of exquisite morbidity and cacodaemoniacal ghastliness; whilst in a multitude of inlaid ebony cabinets reposed the most incredible and unimaginable variety of tomb-loot ever assembled by human madness and perversity. It is of this loot in particular that I must not speak—thank God I had the courage to destroy it long before I thought of destroying myself!

The predatory excursions on which we collected our unmentionable treasures were always artistically memorable events. We were no vulgar ghouls, but worked only under certain conditions of mood, landscape, environment, weather, season, and moonlight. These pastimes were to us the most exquisite form of aesthetic expression, and we gave their details a fastidious technical care. An inappropriate hour, a jarring lighting effect, or a clumsy manipulation of the damp sod, would almost totally destroy for us that ecstatic titillation which followed the exhumation of some ominous, grinning secret of the earth. Our quest for novel scenes and piquant conditions was feverish and insatiate—St. John was always the leader, and he it was who led the way at last to that mocking, that accursed spot which brought us our hideous and inevitable doom.

By what malign fatality were we lured to that terrible Holland churchyard? I think it was the dark rumour and legendry, the tales of one buried for five centuries, who had himself been a ghoul in his time and had stolen a potent thing from a mighty sepulchre. I can recall the scene in these final moments—the pale autumnal moon over the graves, casting long horrible shadows; the grotesque trees, drooping sullenly to meet the neglected grass and the crumbling slabs; the vast legions of strangely colossal bats that flew against the moon; the antique ivied church pointing a huge spectral finger at the livid sky; the phosphorescent insects that danced like death-fires under the yews in a distant corner; the odours of mould, vegetation, and less explicable things that mingled feebly with the night-wind from over far swamps and seas; and worst of all, the faint deep-toned baying of some gigantic hound which we could neither see nor definitely place. As we heard this suggestion of baying we shuddered, remembering the tales of the peasantry; for he whom we sought had centuries before been found in this selfsame spot, torn and mangled by the claws and teeth of some unspeakable beast.

I remembered how we delved in this ghoul's grave with our spades, and how we thrilled at the picture of ourselves, the grave, the pale watching moon, the horrible shadows, the grotesque trees, the titanic bats, the antique church, the dancing death-fires, the sickening odours, the gently moaning night-wind, and the strange, half-heard, directionless baying, of whose objective existence we could scarcely be sure. Then we struck a substance harder than the damp mould, and beheld a rotting oblong box crusted with mineral deposits from the long-undisturbed ground. It was incredibly tough and thick, but so old that we finally pried it open and feasted our eyes on what it held.

Much—amazingly much—was left of the object despite the lapse of five hundred years. The skeleton, though crushed in places by the jaws of the thing that had killed it, held together with surprising firmness, and we gloated over the clean white skull and its long, firm teeth and its eyeless sockets that once had glowed with a charnel fever like our own. In the coffin lay an amulet of curious and exotic design, which had apparently been worn around the sleeper's neck. It was the oddly conventionalised figure of a crouching winged hound, or sphinx with a semi-canine face, and was exquisitely carved in antique Oriental fashion from a small piece of green jade. The expression on its features was repellent in the extreme, savouring at once of death, bestiality, and malevolence. Around the base was an inscription in characters which neither St. John nor I could identify; and on the bottom, like a maker's seal, was graven a grotesque and formidable skull.

Immediately upon beholding this amulet we knew that we must possess it; that this treasure alone was our logical pelf from the centuried grave. Even had its outlines been unfamiliar we would have desired it, but as we looked more closely we saw that it was not wholly unfamiliar. Alien it indeed was to all art and literature which sane and balanced readers know, but we recognised it as the thing hinted of in the forbidden "Necronomicon" of the mad Arab Abdul Alhazred; the ghastly soul-symbol of the corpse-eating cult of inaccessible Leng, in Central Asia. All too well did we trace the sinister lineaments described by the old Arab daemonologist; lineaments, he wrote, drawn from some obscure supernatural manifestation of the souls of those who vexed and gnawed at the dead.

Seizing the green jade object, we gave a last glance at the bleached and cavern-eyed face of its owner and closed up the grave as we found it. As we hastened from that abhorrent spot, the stolen amulet in St. John's pocket, we thought we saw the bats descend in a body to the earth we had so lately rifled, as if seeking for some cursed and unholy nourishment. But the autumn moon shone weak and pale, and we could not be sure. So, too, as we sailed the next day away from Holland to our home, we thought we heard the faint distant baying of some gigantic hound in the background. But the autumn wind moaned sad and wan, and we could not be sure.

II.

Less than a week after our return to England, strange things began to happen. We lived as recluses; devoid of friends, alone, and without servants in a few rooms of an ancient manor-house on a bleak and unfrequented moor; so that our doors were seldom disturbed by the knock of the visitor. Now, however, we were troubled by what seemed to be frequent fumblings in the night, not only around the doors but around the windows also, upper as well as lower. Once we fancied that a large, opaque body darkened the library window when the moon was shining against it, and another time we thought we heard a whirring or flapping sound not far off. On each occasion investigation revealed nothing, and we began to ascribe the occurrences to imagination alone—that same curiously disturbed imagination which still prolonged in our ears the faint far baying we thought we had heard in the Holland churchyard. The jade amulet now reposed in a niche in our museum, and sometimes we burned strangely scented candles before it. We read much in Alhazred's "Necronomicon" about its properties, and about the relation of ghouls' souls to the objects it symbolised; and were disturbed by what we read. Then terror came.

On the night of September 24, 19—, I heard a knock at my chamber door. Fancying it St. John's, I bade the knocker enter, but was answered only by a shrill laugh. There was no one in the corridor. When I aroused St. John from his sleep, he professed entire ignorance of the event, and became as worried as I. It was that night that the faint, distant baying over the moor became to us a certain and dreaded reality. Four days later, whilst we were both in the hidden museum, there came a low, cautious scratching at the single door which led to the secret library staircase. Our alarm was now divided, for besides our fear of the unknown, we had always entertained a dread that our grisly collection might be discovered. Extinguishing all lights, we proceeded to the door and threw it suddenly open; whereupon we felt an unaccountable rush of air, and heard as if receding far away a queer combination of rustling, tittering, and articulate chatter. Whether we were mad, dreaming, or in our senses, we did not try to determine. We only realised, with the blackest of apprehensions, that the apparently disembodied chatter was beyond a doubt *in the Dutch language.*

After that we lived in growing horror and fascination. Mostly we held to the theory that we were jointly going mad from our life of unnatural excitements, but sometimes it pleased us more to dramatise ourselves as the victims of some creeping and appalling doom. Bizarre manifestations were now too frequent to count. Our lonely house was seemingly alive with the presence of some malign being whose nature we could not guess, and every night that daemoniac baying rolled over the windswept moor, always louder and louder. On October 29 we found in the soft earth underneath the library window a series of footprints utterly impossible to describe. They were as baffling as the hordes of great bats which haunted the old manor-house in unprecedented and increasing numbers.

The horror reached a culmination on November 18, when St. John, walking home after dark from the distant railway station, was seized by some frightful carnivorous thing and torn to ribbons. His screams had reached the house, and I had hastened to the terrible scene in time to hear a whir of wings and see a vague black cloudy thing silhouetted against the rising moon. My friend was dying when I spoke to him, and he could not answer coherently. All he could do was to whisper, "The amulet—that damned thing—." Then he collapsed, an inert mass of mangled flesh.

I buried him the next midnight in one of our neglected gardens, and mumbled over his body one of the devilish rituals he had loved in life. And as I pronounced the last daemoniac sentence I heard afar on the moor the faint baying of some gigantic hound. The moon was up, but I dared not look at it. And when I saw on the dim-litten moor a wide nebulous shadow sweeping from mound to mound, I shut my eyes and threw myself face down upon the ground. When I arose trembling, I know not how much later, I staggered into the house and made shocking obeisances before the enshrined amulet of green jade.

Being now afraid to live alone in the ancient house on the moor, I departed on the following day for London, taking with me the amulet after destroying by fire and burial the rest of the impious collection in the museum. But after three nights I heard the baying again, and before a week was over felt strange eyes upon me whenever it was dark. One evening as I strolled on Victoria Embankment for some needed air, I saw a black shape obscure one of the reflections of the lamps in the water. A wind stronger than the night-wind rushed by, and I knew that what had befallen St. John must soon befall me.

The next day I carefully wrapped the green jade amulet and sailed for Holland. What mercy I might gain by returning the thing to its silent, sleeping owner I knew not; but I felt that I must at least try any step conceivably logical. What the hound was, and why it pursued me, were questions still vague; but I had first heard the baying in that ancient churchyard, and every subsequent event including St. John's dying whisper had served to connect the curse with the stealing of the amulet. Accordingly I sank into the nethermost abysses of despair when, at an inn in Rotterdam, I discovered that thieves had despoiled me of this sole means of salvation.

The baying was loud that evening, and in the morning I read of a nameless deed in the vilest quarter of the city. The rabble were in terror, for upon an evil tenement had fallen a red death beyond the foulest previous crime of the neighbourhood. In a squalid thieves' den an entire family had been torn to shreds by an unknown thing which left no trace, and those around had heard all night above the usual clamour of drunken voices a faint, deep, insistent note as of a gigantic hound.

So at last I stood again in that unwholesome churchyard where a pale winter moon cast hideous shadows, and leafless trees drooped sullenly to meet the withered, frosty grass and cracking slabs, and the ivied church pointed a jeering finger at the unfriendly sky, and the night-wind howled maniacally from over frozen swamps and frigid seas. The baying was very faint now, and it ceased altogether as I approached the ancient grave I had once violated, and frightened away an abnormally large horde of bats which had been hovering curiously around it.

I know not why I went thither unless to pray, or gibber out insane pleas and apologies to the calm white thing that lay within; but, whatever my reason, I attacked the half-frozen sod with a desperation partly mine and partly that of a dominating will outside myself. Excavation was much easier than I expected, though at one point I encountered a queer interruption; when a lean vulture darted down out of the cold sky and pecked frantically at the grave-earth until I killed him with a blow of my spade. Finally I reached the rotting oblong box and removed the damp nitrous cover. This is the last rational act I ever performed.

For crouched within that centuried coffin, embraced by a close-packed nightmare retinue of huge, sinewy, sleeping bats, was the bony thing my friend and I had robbed; not clean and placid as we had seen it then, but covered with caked blood and shreds of alien flesh and hair, and leering sentiently at me with phosphorescent sockets and sharp ensanguined fangs yawning twistedly in mockery of my inevitable doom. And when it gave from those grinning jaws a deep, sardonic bay as of some gigantic hound, and I saw that it held in its gory, filthy claw the lost and fateful amulet of green jade, I merely screamed and ran away idiotically, my screams soon dissolving into peals of hysterical laughter.

Madness rides the star-wind ... claws and teeth sharpened on centuries of corpses ... dripping death astride a Bacchanale of bats from night-black ruins of buried temples of Belial.... Now, as the baying of that dead, fleshless monstrosity grows louder and louder, and the stealthy whirring and flapping of those accursed web-wings circles closer and closer, I shall seek with my revolver the oblivion which is my only refuge from the unnamed and unnamable.

THE LURKING FEAR

I. The Shadow on the Chimney

There was thunder in the air on the night I went to the deserted mansion atop Tempest Mountain to find the lurking fear. I was not alone, for foolhardiness was not then mixed with that love of the grotesque and the terrible which has made my career a series of quests for strange horrors in literature and in life. With me were two faithful and muscular men for whom I had sent when the time came; men long associated with me in my ghastly explorations because of their peculiar fitness.

We had started quietly from the village because of the reporters who still lingered about after the eldritch panic of a month before—the nightmare creeping death. Later, I thought, they might aid me; but I did not want them then. Would to God I had let them share the search, that I might not have had to bear the secret alone so long; to bear it alone for fear the world would call me mad or go mad itself at the daemon implications of the thing. Now that I am telling it anyway, lest the brooding make me a maniac, I wish I had never concealed it. For I, and I only, know what manner of fear lurked on that spectral and desolate mountain.

In a small motor-car we covered the miles of primeval forest and hill until the wooded ascent checked it. The country bore an aspect more than usually sinister as we viewed it by night and without the accustomed crowds of investigators, so that we were often tempted to use the acetylene headlight despite the attention it might attract. It was not a wholesome landscape after dark, and I believe I would have noticed its morbidity even had I been ignorant of the terror that stalked there. Of wild creatures there were none—they are wise when death leers close. The ancient lightning-scarred trees seemed unnaturally large and twisted, and the other vegetation unnaturally thick and feverish, while curious mounds and hummocks in the weedy, fulgurite-pitted earth reminded me of snakes and dead men's skulls swelled to gigantic proportions.

Fear had lurked on Tempest Mountain for more than a century. This I learned at once from newspaper accounts of the catastrophe which first brought the region to the world's notice. The place is a remote, lonely elevation in that part of the Catskills where Dutch civilisation once feebly and transiently penetrated, leaving behind as it receded only a few ruined mansions and a degenerate squatter population inhabiting pitiful hamlets on isolated slopes. Normal beings seldom visited the locality till the state police were formed, and even now only infrequent troopers patrol it. The fear, however, is an old tradition throughout the neighbouring villages; since it is a prime topic in the simple discourse of the poor mongrels who sometimes leave their valleys to trade hand-woven baskets for such primitive necessities as they cannot shoot, raise, or make.

The lurking fear dwelt in the shunned and deserted Martense mansion, which crowned the high but gradual eminence whose liability to frequent thunderstorms gave it the name of Tempest Mountain. For over a hundred years the antique, grove-circled stone house had been the subject of stories incredibly wild and monstrously hideous; stories of a silent colossal creeping death which stalked abroad in summer. With whimpering insistence the squatters told tales of a daemon which seized lone wayfarers after dark, either carrying them off or leaving them in a frightful state of gnawed dismemberment; while sometimes they whispered of blood-trails toward the distant mansion. Some said the thunder called the lurking fear out of its habitation, while others said the thunder was its voice.

No one outside the backwoods had believed these varying and conflicting stories, with their incoherent, extravagant descriptions of the half-glimpsed fiend; yet not a farmer or villager doubted that the Martense mansion was ghoulishly haunted. Local history forbade such a doubt, although no ghostly evidence was ever found by such investigators as had visited the building after some especially vivid tale of the squatters. Grandmothers told strange myths of the Martense spectre; myths concerning the Martense family itself, its queer hereditary dissimilarity of eyes, its long, unnatural annals, and the murder which had cursed it.

The terror which brought me to the scene was a sudden and portentous confirmation of the mountaineers' wildest legends. One summer night, after a thunderstorm of unprecedented violence, the countryside was aroused by a squatter stampede which no mere delusion could create. The pitiful throngs of natives shrieked and whined of the unnamable horror which had descended upon them, and they were not doubted. They had not seen it, but had heard such cries from one of their hamlets that they knew a creeping death had come.

In the morning citizens and state troopers followed the shuddering mountaineers to the place where they said the death had come. Death was indeed there. The ground under one of the squatters' villages had caved in after a lightning stroke, destroying several of the malodorous shanties; but upon this property damage was superimposed an organic devastation which paled it to insignificance. Of a possible seventy-five natives who had inhabited this spot, not one living specimen was visible. The disordered earth was covered with blood and human debris bespeaking too vividly the ravages of daemon teeth and talons; yet no visible trail led away from the carnage. That some hideous animal must be the cause, everyone quickly agreed; nor did any tongue now revive the charge that such cryptic deaths formed merely the sordid murders common in decadent communities. That charge was revived only when about twenty-five of the estimated population were found missing from the dead; and even then it was hard to explain the murder of fifty by half that number. But the fact remained that on a summer night a bolt had come out of the heavens and left a dead village whose corpses were horribly mangled, chewed, and clawed.

The excited countryside immediately connected the horror with the haunted Martense mansion, though the localities were over three miles apart. The troopers were more sceptical; including the mansion only casually in their investigations, and dropping it altogether when they found it thoroughly deserted. Country and village people, however, canvassed the place with infinite care; overturning everything in the house, sounding ponds and brooks, beating down bushes, and ransacking the nearby forests. All was in vain; the death that had come had left no trace save destruction itself.

By the second day of the search the affair was fully treated by the newspapers, whose reporters overran Tempest Mountain. They described it in much detail, and with many interviews to elucidate the horror's history as told by local grandams. I followed the accounts languidly at first, for I am a connoisseur in horrors; but after a week I detected an atmosphere which stirred me oddly, so that on August 5th, 1921, I registered among the reporters who crowded the hotel at Lefferts Corners, nearest village to Tempest Mountain and acknowledged headquarters of the searchers. Three weeks more, and the dispersal of the reporters left me free to begin a terrible exploration based on the minute inquiries and surveying with which I had meanwhile busied myself.

So on this summer night, while distant thunder rumbled, I left a silent motor-car and tramped with two armed companions up the last mound-covered reaches of Tempest Mountain, casting the beams of an electric torch on the spectral grey walls that began to appear through the giant oaks ahead. In this morbid night solitude and feeble shifting illumination, the vast box-like pile displayed obscure hints of terror which day could not uncover; yet I did not hesitate, since I had come with fierce resolution to test an idea. I believed that the thunder called the death-daemon out of some fearsome secret place; and be that daemon solid entity or vaporous pestilence, I meant to see it.

I had thoroughly searched the ruin before, hence knew my plan well; choosing as the seat of my vigil the old room of Jan Martense, whose murder looms so great in the rural legends. I felt subtly that the apartment of this ancient victim was best for my purposes. The chamber, measuring about twenty feet square, contained like the other rooms some rubbish which had once been furniture. It lay on the second story, on the southeast corner of the house, and had an immense east window and narrow south window, both devoid of panes or shutters. Opposite the large window was an enormous Dutch fireplace with scriptural tiles representing the prodigal son, and opposite the narrow window was a spacious bed built into the wall.

As the tree-muffled thunder grew louder, I arranged my plan's details. First I fastened side by side to the ledge of the large window three rope ladders which I had brought with me. I knew they reached a suitable spot on the grass outside, for I had tested them. Then the three of us dragged from another room a wide four-poster bedstead, crowding it laterally against the window. Having strown it with fir boughs, all now rested on it with drawn automatics, two relaxing while the third watched. From whatever direction the daemon might come, our potential escape was provided. If it came from within the house, we had the window ladders; if from outside, the door and the stairs. We did not think, judging from precedent, that it would pursue us far even at worst.

I watched from midnight to one o'clock, when in spite of the sinister house, the unprotected window, and the approaching thunder and lightning, I felt singularly drowsy. I was between my two companions, George Bennett being toward the window and William Tobey toward the fireplace. Bennett was asleep, having apparently felt the same anomalous drowsiness which affected me, so I designated Tobey for the next watch although even he was nodding. It is curious how intently I had been watching that fireplace.

The increasing thunder must have affected my dreams, for in the brief time I slept there came to me apocalyptic visions. Once I partly awaked, probably because the sleeper toward the window had restlessly flung an arm across my chest. I was not sufficiently awake to see whether Tobey was attending to his duties as sentinel, but felt a distinct anxiety on that score. Never before had the presence of evil so poignantly oppressed me. Later I must have dropped asleep again, for it was out of a phantasmal chaos that my mind leaped when the night grew hideous with shrieks beyond anything in my former experience or imagination.

In that shrieking the inmost soul of human fear and agony clawed hopelessly and insanely at the ebony gates of oblivion. I awoke to red madness and the mockery of diabolism, as farther and farther down inconceivable vistas that phobic and crystalline anguish retreated and reverberated. There was no light, but I knew from the empty space at my right that Tobey was gone, God alone knew whither. Across my chest still lay the heavy arm of the sleeper at my left.

Then came the devastating stroke of lightning which shook the whole mountain, lit the darkest crypts of the hoary grove, and splintered the patriarch of the twisted trees. In the daemon flash of a monstrous fireball the sleeper started up suddenly while the glare from beyond the window threw his shadow vividly upon the chimney above the fireplace from which my eyes had never strayed. That I am still alive and sane, is a marvel I cannot fathom. I cannot fathom it, for the shadow on that chimney was not that of George Bennett or of any other human creature, but a blasphemous abnormality from hell's nethermost craters; a nameless, shapeless abomination which no mind could fully grasp and no pen even partly describe. In another second I was alone in the accursed mansion, shivering and gibbering. George Bennett and William Tobey had left no trace, not even of a struggle. They were never heard of again.

II. A Passer in the Storm

For days after that hideous experience in the forest-swathed mansion I lay nervously exhausted in my hotel room at Lefferts Corners. I do not remember exactly how I managed to reach the motor-car, start it, and slip unobserved back to the village; for I retain no distinct impression save of wild-armed titan trees, daemoniac mutterings of thunder, and Charonian shadows athwart the low mounds that dotted and streaked the region.

As I shivered and brooded on the casting of that brain-blasting shadow, I knew that I had at last pried out one of earth's supreme horrors—one of those nameless blights of outer voids whose faint daemon scratchings we sometimes hear on the farthest rim of space, yet from which our own finite vision has given us a merciful immunity. The shadow I had seen, I hardly dared to analyse or identify. Something had lain between me and the window that night, but I shuddered whenever I could not cast off the instinct to classify it. If it had only snarled, or bayed, or laughed titteringly—even that would have relieved the abysmal hideousness. But it was so silent. It had rested a heavy arm or fore leg on my chest.... Obviously it was organic, or had once been organic.... Jan Martense, whose room I had invaded, was buried in the graveyard near the mansion.... I must find Bennett and Tobey, if they lived ... why had it picked them, and left me for the last? ... Drowsiness is so stifling, and dreams are so horrible....

In a short time I realised that I must tell my story to someone or break down completely. I had already decided not to abandon the quest for the lurking fear, for in my rash ignorance it seemed to me that uncertainty was worse than enlightenment, however terrible the latter might prove to be. Accordingly I resolved in my mind the best course to pursue; whom to select for my confidences, and how to track down the thing which had obliterated two men and cast a nightmare shadow.

My chief acquaintances at Lefferts Corners had been the affable reporters, of whom several still remained to collect final echoes of the tragedy. It was from these that I determined to choose a colleague, and the more I reflected the more my preference inclined toward one Arthur Munroe, a dark, lean man of about thirty-five, whose education, taste, intelligence, and temperament all seemed to mark him as one not bound to conventional ideas and experiences.

On an afternoon in early September Arthur Munroe listened to my story. I saw from the beginning that he was both interested and sympathetic, and when I had finished he analysed and discussed the thing with the greatest shrewdness and judgment. His advice, moreover, was eminently practical; for he recommended a postponement of operations at the Martense mansion until we might become fortified with more detailed historical and geographical data. On his initiative we combed the countryside for information regarding the terrible Martense family, and discovered a man who possessed a marvellously illuminating ancestral diary. We also talked at length with such of the mountain mongrels as had not fled from the terror and confusion to remoter slopes, and arranged to precede our culminating task—the exhaustive and definitive examination of the mansion in the light of its detailed history—with an equally exhaustive and definitive examination of spots associated with the various tragedies of squatter legend.

The results of this examination were not at first very enlightening, though our tabulation of them seemed to reveal a fairly significant trend; namely, that the number of reported horrors was by far the greatest in areas either comparatively near the avoided house or connected with it by stretches of the morbidly overnourished forest. There were, it is true, exceptions; indeed, the horror which had caught the world's ear had happened in a treeless space remote alike from the mansion and from any connecting woods.

As to the nature and appearance of the lurking fear, nothing could be gained from the scared and witless shanty-dwellers. In the same breath they called it a snake and a giant, a thunder-devil and a bat, a vulture and a walking tree. We did, however, deem ourselves justified in assuming that it was a living organism highly susceptible to electrical storms; and although certain of the stories suggested wings, we believed that its aversion for open spaces made land locomotion a more probable theory. The only thing really incompatible with the latter view was the rapidity with which the creature must have travelled in order to perform all the deeds attributed to it.

When we came to know the squatters better, we found them curiously likeable in many ways. Simple animals they were, gently descending the evolutionary scale because of their unfortunate ancestry and stultifying isolation. They feared outsiders, but slowly grew accustomed to us; finally helping vastly when we beat down all the thickets and tore out all the partitions of the mansion in our search for the lurking fear. When we asked them to help us find Bennett and Tobey they were truly distressed; for they wanted to help us, yet knew that these victims had gone as wholly out of the world as their own missing people. That great numbers of them had actually been killed and removed, just as the wild animals had long been exterminated, we were of course thoroughly convinced; and we waited apprehensively for further tragedies to occur.

By the middle of October we were puzzled by our lack of progress. Owing to the clear nights no daemoniac aggressions had taken place, and the completeness of our vain searches of house and country almost drove us to regard the lurking fear as a non-material agency. We feared that the cold weather would come on and halt our explorations, for all agreed that the daemon was generally quiet in winter. Thus there was a kind of haste and desperation in our last daylight canvass of the horror-visited hamlet; a hamlet now deserted because of the squatters' fears.

The ill-fated squatter hamlet had borne no name, but had long stood in a sheltered though treeless cleft between two elevations called respectively Cone Mountain and Maple Hill. It was closer to Maple Hill than to Cone Mountain, some of the crude abodes indeed being dugouts on the side of the former eminence. Geographically it lay about two miles northwest of the base of Tempest Mountain, and three miles from the oak-girt mansion. Of the distance between the hamlet and the mansion, fully two miles and a quarter on the hamlet's side was entirely open country; the plain being of fairly level character save for some of the low snake-like mounds, and having as vegetation only grass and scattered weeds. Considering this topography, we had finally concluded that the daemon must have come by way of Cone Mountain, a wooded southern prolongation of which ran to within a short distance of the westernmost spur of Tempest Mountain. The upheaval of ground we traced conclusively to a landslide from Maple Hill, a tall lone splintered tree on whose side had been the striking point of the thunderbolt which summoned the fiend.

As for the twentieth time or more Arthur Munroe and I went minutely over every inch of the violated village, we were filled with a certain discouragement coupled with vague and novel fears. It was acutely uncanny, even when frightful and uncanny things were common, to encounter so blankly clueless a scene after such overwhelming occurrences; and we moved about beneath the leaden, darkening sky with that tragic directionless zeal which results from a combined sense of futility and necessity of action. Our care was gravely minute; every cottage was again entered, every hillside dugout again searched for bodies, every thorny foot of adjacent slope again scanned for dens and caves, but all without result. And yet, as I have said, vague new fears hovered menacingly over us; as if giant bat-winged gryphons squatted invisibly on the mountaintops and leered with Abaddon-eyes that had looked on trans-cosmic gulfs.

As the afternoon advanced, it became increasingly difficult to see; and we heard the rumble of a thunderstorm gathering over Tempest Mountain. This sound in such a locality naturally stirred us, though less than it would have done at night. As it was, we hoped desperately that the storm would last until well after dark; and with that hope turned from our aimless hillside searching toward the nearest inhabited hamlet to gather a body of squatters as helpers in the investigation. Timid as they were, a few of the younger men were sufficiently inspired by our protective leadership to promise such help.

We had hardly more than turned, however, when there descended such a blinding sheet of torrential rain that shelter became imperative. The extreme, almost nocturnal darkness of the sky caused us to stumble sadly, but guided by the frequent flashes of lightning and by our minute knowledge of the hamlet we soon reached the least porous cabin of the lot; an heterogeneous combination of logs and boards whose still existing door and single tiny window both faced Maple Hill. Barring the door after us against the fury of the wind and rain, we put in place the crude window shutter which our frequent searches had taught us where to find. It was dismal sitting there on rickety boxes in the pitchy darkness, but we smoked pipes and occasionally flashed our pocket lamps about. Now and then we could see the lightning through cracks in the wall; the afternoon was so incredibly dark that each flash was extremely vivid.

The stormy vigil reminded me shudderingly of my ghastly night on Tempest Mountain. My mind turned to that odd question which had kept recurring ever since the nightmare thing had happened; and again I wondered why the daemon, approaching the three watchers either from the window or the interior, had begun with the men on each side and left the middle man till the last, when the titan fireball had scared it away. Why had it not taken its victims in natural order, with myself second, from whichever direction it had approached? With what manner of far-reaching tentacles did it prey? Or did it know that I was the leader, and save me for a fate worse than that of my companions?

In the midst of these reflections, as if dramatically arranged to intensify them, there fell nearby a terrific bolt of lightning followed by the sound of sliding earth. At the same time the wolfish wind rose to daemoniac crescendoes of ululation. We were sure that the lone tree on Maple Hill had been struck again, and Munroe rose from his box and went to the tiny window to ascertain the damage. When he took down the shutter the wind and rain howled deafeningly in, so that I could not hear what he said; but I waited while he leaned out and tried to fathom Nature's pandemonium.

Gradually a calming of the wind and dispersal of the unusual darkness told of the storm's passing. I had hoped it would last into the night to help our quest, but a furtive sunbeam from a knothole behind me removed the likelihood of such a thing. Suggesting to Munroe that we had better get some light even if more showers came, I unbarred and opened the crude door. The ground outside was a singular mass of mud and pools, with fresh heaps of earth from the slight landslide; but I saw nothing to justify the interest which kept my companion silently leaning out the window. Crossing to where he leaned, I touched his shoulder; but he did not move. Then, as I playfully shook him and turned him around, I felt the strangling tendrils of a cancerous horror whose roots reached into illimitable pasts and fathomless abysms of the night that broods beyond time.

For Arthur Munroe was dead. And on what remained of his chewed and gouged head there was no longer a face.

III. What the Red Glare Meant

On the tempest-racked night of November 8, 1921, with a lantern which cast charnel shadows, I stood digging alone and idiotically in the grave of Jan Martense. I had begun to dig in the afternoon, because a thunderstorm was brewing, and now that it was dark and the storm had burst above the maniacally thick foliage I was glad.

I believe that my mind was partly unhinged by events since August 5th; the daemon shadow in the mansion, the general strain and disappointment, and the thing that occurred at the hamlet in an October storm. After that thing I had dug a grave for one whose death I could not understand. I knew that others could not understand either, so let them think Arthur Munroe had wandered away. They searched, but found nothing. The squatters might have understood, but I dared not frighten them more. I myself seemed strangely callous. That shock at the mansion had done something to my brain, and I could think only of the quest for a horror now grown to cataclysmic stature in my imagination; a quest which the fate of Arthur Munroe made me vow to keep silent and solitary.

The scene of my excavations would alone have been enough to unnerve any ordinary man. Baleful primal trees of unholy size, age, and grotesqueness leered above me like the pillars of some hellish Druidic temple; muffling the thunder, hushing the clawing wind, and admitting but little rain. Beyond the scarred trunks in the background, illumined by faint flashes of filtered lightning, rose the damp ivied stones of the deserted mansion, while somewhat nearer was the abandoned Dutch garden whose walks and beds were polluted by a white, fungous, foetid, overnourished vegetation that never saw full daylight. And nearest of all was the graveyard, where deformed trees tossed insane branches as their roots displaced unhallowed slabs and sucked venom from what lay below. Now and then, beneath the brown pall of leaves that rotted and festered in the antediluvian forest darkness, I could trace the sinister outlines of some of those low mounds which characterised the lightning-pierced region.

History had led me to this archaic grave. History, indeed, was all I had after everything else ended in mocking Satanism. I now believed that the lurking fear was no material thing, but a wolf-fanged ghost that rode the midnight lightning. And I believed, because of the masses of local tradition I had unearthed in my search with Arthur Munroe, that the ghost was that of Jan Martense, who died in 1762. That is why I was digging idiotically in his grave.

The Martense mansion was built in 1670 by Gerrit Martense, a wealthy New-Amsterdam merchant who disliked the changing order under British rule, and had constructed this magnificent domicile on a remote woodland summit whose untrodden solitude and unusual scenery pleased him. The only substantial disappointment encountered in this site was that which concerned the prevalence of violent thunderstorms in summer. When selecting the hill and building his mansion, Mynheer Martense had laid these frequent natural outbursts to some peculiarity of the year; but in time he perceived that the locality was especially liable to such phenomena. At length, having found these storms injurious to his health, he fitted up a cellar into which he could retreat from their wildest pandemonium.

Of Gerrit Martense's descendants less is known than of himself; since they were all reared in hatred of the English civilisation, and trained to shun such of the colonists as accepted it. Their life was exceedingly secluded, and people declared that their isolation had made them heavy of speech and comprehension. In appearance all were marked by a peculiar inherited dissimilarity of eyes; one generally being blue and the other brown. Their social contacts grew fewer and fewer, till at last they took to intermarrying with the numerous menial class about the estate. Many of the crowded family degenerated, moved across the valley, and merged with the mongrel population which was later to produce the pitiful squatters. The rest had stuck sullenly to their ancestral mansion, becoming more and more clannish and taciturn, yet developing a nervous responsiveness to the frequent thunderstorms.

Most of this information reached the outside world through young Jan Martense, who from some kind of restlessness joined the colonial army when news of the Albany Convention reached Tempest Mountain. He was the first of Gerrit's descendants to see much of the world; and when he returned in 1760 after six years of campaigning, he was hated as an outsider by his father, uncles, and brothers, in spite of his dissimilar Martense eyes. No longer could he share the peculiarities and prejudices of the Martenses, while the very mountain thunderstorms failed to intoxicate him as they had before. Instead, his surroundings depressed him; and he frequently wrote to a friend in Albany of plans to leave the paternal roof.

In the spring of 1763 Jonathan Gifford, the Albany friend of Jan Martense, became worried by his correspondent's silence; especially in view of the conditions and quarrels at the Martense mansion. Determined to visit Jan in person, he went into the mountains on horseback. His diary states that he reached Tempest Mountain on September 20, finding the mansion in great decrepitude. The sullen, odd-eyed Martenses, whose unclean animal aspect shocked him, told him in broken gutturals that Jan was dead. He had, they insisted, been struck by lightning the autumn before; and now lay buried behind the neglected sunken gardens. They shewed the visitor the grave, barren and devoid of markers. Something in the Martenses' manner gave Gifford a feeling of repulsion and suspicion, and a week later he returned with spade and mattock to explore the sepulchral spot. He found what he expected—a skull crushed cruelly as if by savage blows—so returning to Albany he openly charged the Martenses with the murder of their kinsman.

Legal evidence was lacking, but the story spread rapidly round the countryside; and from that time the Martenses were ostracised by the world. No one would deal with them, and their distant manor was shunned as an accursed place. Somehow they managed to live on independently by the products of their estate, for occasional lights glimpsed from far-away hills attested their continued presence. These lights were seen as late as 1810, but toward the last they became very infrequent.

Meanwhile there grew up about the mansion and the mountain a body of diabolic legendry. The place was avoided with doubled assiduousness, and invested with every whispered myth tradition could supply. It remained unvisited till 1816, when the continued absence of lights was noticed by the squatters. At that time a party made investigations, finding the house deserted and partly in ruins.

There were no skeletons about, so that departure rather than death was inferred. The clan seemed to have left several years before, and improvised penthouses shewed how numerous it had grown prior to its migration. Its cultural level had fallen very low, as proved by decaying furniture and scattered silverware which must have been long abandoned when its owners left. But though the dreaded Martenses were gone, the fear of the haunted house continued; and grew very acute when new and strange stories arose among the mountain decadents. There it stood; deserted, feared, and linked with the vengeful ghost of Jan Martense. There it still stood on the night I dug in Jan Martense's grave.

I have described my protracted digging as idiotic, and such it indeed was in object and method. The coffin of Jan Martense had soon been unearthed—it now held only dust and nitre—but in my fury to exhume his ghost I delved irrationally and clumsily down beneath where he had lain. God knows what I expected to find—I only felt that I was digging in the grave of a man whose ghost stalked by night.

It is impossible to say what monstrous depth I had attained when my spade, and soon my feet, broke through the ground beneath. The event, under the circumstances, was tremendous; for in the existence of a subterranean space here, my mad theories had terrible confirmation. My slight fall had extinguished the lantern, but I produced an electric pocket lamp and viewed the small horizontal tunnel which led away indefinitely in both directions. It was amply large enough for a man to wriggle through; and though no sane person would have tried it at that time, I forgot danger, reason, and cleanliness in my single-minded fever to unearth the lurking fear. Choosing the direction toward the house, I scrambled recklessly into the narrow burrow; squirming ahead blindly and rapidly, and flashing but seldom the lamp I kept before me.

What language can describe the spectacle of a man lost in infinitely abysmal earth; pawing, twisting, wheezing; scrambling madly through sunken convolutions of immemorial blackness without an idea of time, safety, direction, or definite object? There is something hideous in it, but that is what I did. I did it for so long that life faded to a far memory, and I became one with the moles and grubs of nighted depths. Indeed, it was only by accident that after interminable writhings I jarred my forgotten electric lamp alight, so that it shone eerily along the burrow of caked loam that stretched and curved ahead.

I had been scrambling in this way for some time, so that my battery had burned very low, when the passage suddenly inclined sharply upward, altering my mode of progress. And as I raised my glance it was without preparation that I saw glistening in the distance two daemoniac reflections of my expiring lamp; two reflections glowing with a baneful and unmistakable effulgence, and provoking maddeningly nebulous memories. I stopped automatically, though lacking the brain to retreat. The eyes approached, yet of the thing that bore them I could distinguish only a claw. But what a claw! Then far overhead I heard a faint crashing which I recognised. It was the wild thunder of the mountain, raised to hysteric fury—I must have been crawling upward for some time, so that the surface was now quite near. And as the muffled thunder clattered, those eyes still stared with vacuous viciousness.

Thank God I did not then know what it was, else I should have died. But I was saved by the very thunder that had summoned it, for after a hideous wait there burst from the unseen outside sky one of those frequent mountainward bolts whose aftermath I had noticed here and there as gashes of disturbed earth and fulgurites of various sizes. With Cyclopean rage it tore through the soil above that damnable pit, blinding and deafening me, yet not wholly reducing me to a coma.

In the chaos of sliding, shifting earth I clawed and floundered helplessly till the rain on my head steadied me and I saw that I had come to the surface in a familiar spot; a steep unforested place on the southwest slope of the mountain. Recurrent sheet lightnings illumed the tumbled ground and the remains of the curious low hummock which had stretched down from the wooded higher slope, but there was nothing in the chaos to shew my place of egress from the lethal catacomb. My brain was as great a chaos as the earth, and as a distant red glare burst on the landscape from the south I hardly realised the horror I had been through.

But when two days later the squatters told me what the red glare meant, I felt more horror than that which the mound-burrow and the claw and eyes had given; more horror because of the overwhelming implications. In a hamlet twenty miles away an orgy of fear had followed the bolt which brought me above ground, and a nameless thing had dropped from an overhanging tree into a weak-roofed cabin. It had done a deed, but the squatters had fired the cabin in frenzy before it could escape. It had been doing that deed at the very moment the earth caved in on the thing with the claw and eyes.

IV. The Horror in the Eyes

There can be nothing normal in the mind of one who, knowing what I knew of the horrors of Tempest Mountain, would seek alone for the fear that lurked there. That at least two of the fear's embodiments were destroyed, formed but a slight guarantee of mental and physical safety in this Acheron of multiform diabolism; yet I continued my quest with even greater zeal as events and revelations became more monstrous.

When, two days after my frightful crawl through that crypt of the eyes and claw, I learned that a thing had malignly hovered twenty miles away at the same instant the eyes were glaring at me, I experienced virtual convulsions of fright. But that fright was so mixed with wonder and alluring grotesqueness, that it was almost a pleasant sensation. Sometimes, in the throes of a nightmare when unseen powers whirl one over the roofs of strange dead cities toward the grinning chasm of Nis, it is a relief and even a delight to shriek wildly and throw oneself voluntarily along with the hideous vortex of dream-doom into whatever bottomless gulf may yawn. And so it was with the waking nightmare of Tempest Mountain; the discovery that two monsters had haunted the spot gave me ultimately a mad craving to plunge into the very earth of the accursed region, and with bare hands dig out the death that leered from every inch of the poisonous soil.

As soon as possible I visited the grave of Jan Martense and dug vainly where I had dug before. Some extensive cave-in had obliterated all trace of the underground passage, while the rain had washed so much earth back into the excavation that I could not tell how deeply I had dug that other day. I likewise made a difficult trip to the distant hamlet where the death-creature had been burnt, and was little repaid for my trouble. In the ashes of the fateful cabin I found several bones, but apparently none of the monster's. The squatters said the thing had had only one victim; but in this I judged them inaccurate, since besides the complete skull of a human being, there was another bony fragment which seemed certainly to have belonged to a human skull at some time. Though the rapid drop of the monster had been seen, no one could say just what the creature was like; those who had glimpsed it called it simply a devil. Examining the great tree where it had lurked, I could discern no distinctive marks. I tried to find some trail into the black forest, but on this occasion could not stand the sight of those morbidly large boles, or of those vast serpent-like roots that twisted so malevolently before they sank into the earth.

My next step was to re-examine with microscopic care the deserted hamlet where death had come most abundantly, and where Arthur Munroe had seen something he never lived to describe. Though my vain previous searches had been exceedingly minute, I now had new data to test; for my horrible grave-crawl convinced me that at least one of the phases of the monstrosity had been an underground creature. This time, on the 14th of November, my quest concerned itself mostly with the slopes of Cone Mountain and Maple Hill where they overlook the unfortunate hamlet, and I gave particular attention to the loose earth of the landslide region on the latter eminence.

The afternoon of my search brought nothing to light, and dusk came as I stood on Maple Hill looking down at the hamlet and across the valley to Tempest Mountain. There had been a gorgeous sunset, and now the moon came up, nearly full and shedding a silver flood over the plain, the distant mountainside, and the curious low mounds that rose here and there. It was a peaceful Arcadian scene, but knowing what it hid I hated it. I hated the mocking moon, the hypocritical plain, the festering mountain, and those sinister mounds. Everything seemed to me tainted with a loathsome contagion, and inspired by a noxious alliance with distorted hidden powers.

Presently, as I gazed abstractedly at the moonlit panorama, my eye became attracted by something singular in the nature and arrangement of a certain topographical element. Without having any exact knowledge of geology, I had from the first been interested in the odd mounds and hummocks of the region. I had noticed that they were pretty widely distributed around Tempest Mountain, though less numerous on the plain than near the hilltop itself, where prehistoric glaciation had doubtless found feebler opposition to its striking and fantastic caprices. Now, in the light of that low moon which cast long weird shadows, it struck me forcibly that the various points and lines of the mound system had a peculiar relation to the summit of Tempest Mountain. That summit was undeniably a centre from which the lines or rows of points radiated indefinitely and irregularly, as if the unwholesome Martense mansion had thrown visible tentacles of terror. The idea of such tentacles gave me an unexplained thrill, and I stopped to analyse my reason for believing these mounds glacial phenomena.

The more I analysed the less I believed, and against my newly opened mind there began to beat grotesque and horrible analogies based on superficial aspects and upon my experience beneath the earth. Before I knew it I was uttering frenzied and disjointed words to myself: "My God! ... Molehills ... the damned place must be honeycombed ... how many ... that night at the mansion ... they took Bennett and Tobey first ... on each side of us...." Then I was digging frantically into the mound which had stretched nearest me; digging desperately, shiveringly, but almost jubilantly; digging and at last shrieking aloud with some unplaced emotion as I came upon a tunnel or burrow just like the one through which I had crawled on that other daemoniac night.

After that I recall running, spade in hand; a hideous run across moon-litten, mound-marked meadows and through diseased, precipitous abysses of haunted hillside forest; leaping, screaming, panting, bounding toward the terrible Martense mansion. I recall digging unreasoningly in all parts of the brier-choked cellar; digging to find the core and centre of that malignant universe of mounds. And then I recall how I laughed when I stumbled on the passageway; the hole at the base of the old chimney, where the thick weeds grew and cast queer shadows in the light of the lone candle I had happened to have with me. What still remained down in that hell-hive, lurking and waiting for the thunder to arouse it, I did not know. Two had been killed; perhaps that had finished it. But still there remained that burning determination to reach the innermost secret of the fear, which I had once more come to deem definite, material, and organic.

My indecisive speculation whether to explore the passage alone and immediately with my pocket-light or to try to assemble a band of squatters for the quest, was interrupted after a time by a sudden rush of wind from outside which blew out the candle and left me in stark blackness. The moon no longer shone through the chinks and apertures above me, and with a sense of fateful alarm I heard the sinister and significant rumble of approaching thunder. A confusion of associated ideas possessed my brain, leading me to grope back toward the farthest corner of the cellar. My eyes, however, never turned away from the horrible opening at the base of the chimney; and I began to get glimpses of the crumbling bricks and unhealthy weeds as faint glows of lightning penetrated the woods outside and illumined the chinks in the upper wall. Every second I was consumed with a mixture of fear and curiosity. What would the storm call forth—or was there anything left for it to call? Guided by a lightning flash I settled myself down behind a dense clump of vegetation, through which I could see the opening without being seen.

If heaven is merciful, it will some day efface from my consciousness the sight that I saw, and let me live my last years in peace. I cannot sleep at night now, and have to take opiates when it thunders. The thing came abruptly and unannounced; a daemon, rat-like scurrying from pits remote and unimaginable, a hellish panting and stifled grunting, and then from that opening beneath the chimney a burst of multitudinous and leprous life—a loathsome night-spawned flood of organic corruption more devastatingly hideous than the blackest conjurations of mortal madness and morbidity. Seething, stewing, surging, bubbling like serpents' slime it rolled up and out of that yawning hole, spreading like a septic contagion and streaming from the cellar at every point of egress—streaming out to scatter through the accursed midnight forests and strow fear, madness, and death.

God knows how many there were—there must have been thousands. To see the stream of them in that faint, intermittent lightning was shocking. When they had thinned out enough to be glimpsed as separate organisms, I saw that they were dwarfed, deformed hairy devils or apes—monstrous and diabolic caricatures of the monkey tribe. They were so hideously silent; there was hardly a squeal when one of the last stragglers turned with the skill of long practice to make a meal in accustomed fashion on a weaker companion. Others snapped up what it left and ate with slavering relish. Then, in spite of my daze of fright and disgust, my morbid curiosity triumphed; and as the last of the monstrosities oozed up alone from that nether world of unknown nightmare, I drew my automatic pistol and shot it under cover of the thunder.

Shrieking, slithering, torrential shadows of red viscous madness chasing one another through endless, ensanguined corridors of purple fulgurous sky … formless phantasms and kaleidoscopic mutations of a ghoulish, remembered scene; forests of monstrous overnourished oaks with serpent roots twisting and sucking unnamable juices from an earth verminous with millions of cannibal devils; mound-like tentacles groping from underground nuclei of polypous perversion … insane lightning over malignant ivied walls and daemon arcades choked with fungous vegetation…. Heaven be thanked for the instinct which led me unconscious to places where men dwell; to the peaceful village that slept under the calm stars of clearing skies.

I had recovered enough in a week to send to Albany for a gang of men to blow up the Martense mansion and the entire top of Tempest Mountain with dynamite, stop up all the discoverable mound-burrows, and destroy certain overnourished trees whose very existence seemed an insult to sanity. I could sleep a little after they had done this, but true rest will never come as long as I remember that nameless secret of the lurking fear. The thing will haunt me, for who can say the extermination is complete, and that analogous phenomena do not exist all over the world? Who can, with my knowledge, think of the earth's unknown caverns without a nightmare dread of future possibilities? I cannot see a well or a subway entrance without shuddering ... why cannot the doctors give me something to make me sleep, or truly calm my brain when it thunders?

What I saw in the glow of my flashlight after I shot the unspeakable straggling object was so simple that almost a minute elapsed before I understood and went delirious. The object was nauseous; a filthy whitish gorilla thing with sharp yellow fangs and matted fur. It was the ultimate product of mammalian degeneration; the frightful outcome of isolated spawning, multiplication, and cannibal nutrition above and below the ground; the embodiment of all the snarling chaos and grinning fear that lurk behind life. It had looked at me as it died, and its eyes had the same odd quality that marked those other eyes which had stared at me underground and excited cloudy recollections. One eye was blue, the other brown. They were the dissimilar Martense eyes of the old legends, and I knew in one inundating cataclysm of voiceless horror what had become of that vanished family; the terrible and thunder-crazed house of Martense.

THE RATS IN THE WALLS

On July 16, 1923, I moved into Exham Priory after the last workman had finished his labours. The restoration had been a stupendous task, for little had remained of the deserted pile but a shell-like ruin; yet because it had been the seat of my ancestors I let no expense deter me. The place had not been inhabited since the reign of James the First, when a tragedy of intensely hideous, though largely unexplained, nature had struck down the master, five of his children, and several servants; and driven forth under a cloud of suspicion and terror the third son, my lineal progenitor and the only survivor of the abhorred line. With this sole heir denounced as a murderer, the estate had reverted to the crown, nor had the accused man made any attempt to exculpate himself or regain his property. Shaken by some horror greater than that of conscience or the law, and expressing only a frantic wish to exclude the ancient edifice from his sight and memory, Walter de la Poer, eleventh Baron Exham, fled to Virginia and there founded the family which by the next century had become known as Delapore.

Exham Priory had remained untenanted, though later allotted to the estates of the Norrys family and much studied because of its peculiarly composite architecture; an architecture involving Gothic towers resting on a Saxon or Romanesque substructure, whose foundation in turn was of a still earlier order or blend of orders—Roman, and even Druidic or native Cymric, if legends speak truly. This foundation was a very singular thing, being merged on one side with the solid limestone of the precipice from whose brink the priory overlooked a desolate valley three miles west of the village of Anchester. Architects and antiquarians loved to examine this strange relic of forgotten centuries, but the country folk hated it. They had hated it hundreds of years before, when my ancestors lived there, and they hated it now, with the moss and mould of abandonment on it. I had not been a day in Anchester before I knew I came of an accursed house. And this week workmen have blown up Exham Priory, and are busy obliterating the traces of its foundations.

The bare statistics of my ancestry I had always known, together with the fact that my first American forbear had come to the colonies under a strange cloud. Of details, however, I had been kept wholly ignorant through the policy of reticence always maintained by the Delapores. Unlike our planter neighbours, we seldom boasted of crusading ancestors or other mediaeval and Renaissance heroes; nor was any kind of tradition handed down except what may have been recorded in the sealed envelope left before the Civil War by every squire to his eldest son for posthumous opening. The glories we cherished were those achieved since the migration; the glories of a proud and honourable, if somewhat reserved and unsocial Virginia line.

During the war our fortunes were extinguished and our whole existence changed by the burning of Carfax, our home on the banks of the James. My grandfather, advanced in years, had perished in that incendiary outrage, and with him the envelope that bound us all to the past. I can recall that fire today as I saw it then at the age of seven, with the Federal soldiers shouting, the women screaming, and the negroes howling and praying. My father was in the army, defending Richmond, and after many formalities my mother and I were passed through the lines to join him.

When the war ended we all moved north, whence my mother had come; and I grew to manhood, middle age, and ultimate wealth as a stolid Yankee. Neither my father nor I ever knew what our hereditary envelope had contained, and as I merged into the greyness of Massachusetts business life I lost all interest in the mysteries which evidently lurked far back in my family tree. Had I suspected their nature, how gladly I would have left Exham Priory to its moss, bats, and cobwebs!

My father died in 1904, but without any message to leave me, or to my only child, Alfred, a motherless boy of ten. It was this boy who reversed the order of family information; for although I could give him only jesting conjectures about the past, he wrote me of some very interesting ancestral legends when the late war took him to England in 1917 as an aviation officer. Apparently the Delapores had a colourful and perhaps sinister history, for a friend of my son's, Capt. Edward Norrys of the Royal Flying

Corps, dwelt near the family seat at Anchester and related some peasant superstitions which few novelists could equal for wildness and incredibility. Norrys himself, of course, did not take them seriously; but they amused my son and made good material for his letters to me. It was this legendry which definitely turned my attention to my transatlantic heritage, and made me resolve to purchase and restore the family seat which Norrys shewed to Alfred in its picturesque desertion, and offered to get for him at a surprisingly reasonable figure, since his own uncle was the present owner.

I bought Exham Priory in 1918, but was almost immediately distracted from my plans of restoration by the return of my son as a maimed invalid. During the two years that he lived I thought of nothing but his care, having even placed my business under the direction of partners. In 1921, as I found myself bereaved and aimless, a retired manufacturer no longer young, I resolved to divert my remaining years with my new possession. Visiting Anchester in December, I was entertained by Capt. Norrys, a plump, amiable young man who had thought much of my son, and secured his assistance in gathering plans and anecdotes to guide in the coming restoration. Exham Priory itself I saw without emotion, a jumble of tottering mediaeval ruins covered with lichens and honeycombed with rooks' nests, perched perilously upon a precipice, and denuded of floors or other interior features save the stone walls of the separate towers.

As I gradually recovered the image of the edifice as it had been when my ancestor left it over three centuries before, I began to hire workmen for the reconstruction. In every case I was forced to go outside the immediate locality, for the Anchester villagers had an almost unbelievable fear and hatred of the place. This sentiment was so great that it was sometimes communicated to the outside labourers, causing numerous desertions; whilst its scope appeared to include both the priory and its ancient family.

My son had told me that he was somewhat avoided during his visits because he was a de la Poer, and I now found myself subtly ostracised for a like reason until I convinced the peasants how little I knew of my heritage. Even then they sullenly disliked me, so that I had to collect most of the village traditions through the mediation of Norrys. What the people could not forgive, perhaps, was that I had come to restore a symbol so abhorrent to them; for, rationally or not, they viewed Exham Priory as nothing less than a haunt of fiends and werewolves.

Piecing together the tales which Norrys collected for me, and supplementing them with the accounts of several savants who had studied the ruins, I deduced that Exham Priory stood on the site of a prehistoric temple; a Druidical or ante-Druidical thing which must have been contemporary with Stonehenge. That indescribable rites had been celebrated there, few doubted; and there were unpleasant tales of the transference of these rites into the Cybele-worship which the Romans had introduced. Inscriptions still visible in the sub-cellar bore such unmistakable letters as "DIV ... OPS ... MAGNA. MAT ..." sign of the Magna Mater whose dark worship was once vainly forbidden to Roman citizens. Anchester had been the camp of the third Augustan legion, as many remains attest, and it was said that the temple of Cybele was splendid and thronged with worshippers who performed nameless ceremonies at the bidding of a Phrygian priest. Tales added that the fall of the old religion did not end the orgies at the temple, but that the priests lived on in the new faith without real change. Likewise was it said that the rites did not vanish with the Roman power, and that certain among the Saxons added to what remained of the temple, and gave it the essential outline it subsequently preserved, making it the centre of a cult feared through half the heptarchy. About 1000 A.D. the place is mentioned in a chronicle as being a substantial stone priory housing a strange and powerful monastic order and surrounded by extensive gardens which needed no walls to exclude a frightened populace. It was never destroyed by the Danes, though after the Norman Conquest it must have declined tremendously; since there was no impediment when Henry the Third granted the site to my ancestor, Gilbert de la Poer, First Baron Exham, in 1261.

Of my family before this date there is no evil report, but something strange must have happened then. In one chronicle there is a reference to a de la Poer as "cursed of God" in 1307, whilst village legendry had nothing but evil and frantic fear to tell of the castle that went up on the foundations of the old temple and priory. The fireside tales were of the most grisly description, all the ghastlier because of their frightened reticence and cloudy evasiveness. They represented my ancestors as a race of hereditary daemons beside whom Gilles de Retz and the Marquis de Sade would seem the veriest tyros, and hinted whisperingly at their responsibility for the occasional disappearances of villagers through several generations.

The worst characters, apparently, were the barons and their direct heirs; at least, most was whispered about these. If of healthier inclinations, it was said, an heir would early and mysteriously die to make way for another more typical scion.

There seemed to be an inner cult in the family, presided over by the head of the house, and sometimes closed except to a few members. Temperament rather than ancestry was evidently the basis of this cult, for it was entered by several who married into the family. Lady Margaret Trevor from Cornwall, wife of Godfrey, the second son of the fifth baron, became a favourite bane of children all over the countryside, and the daemon heroine of a particularly horrible old ballad not yet extinct near the Welsh border. Preserved in balladry, too, though not illustrating the same point, is the hideous tale of Lady Mary de la Poer, who shortly after her marriage to the Earl of Shrewsfield was killed by him and his mother, both of the slayers being absolved and blessed by the priest to whom they confessed what they dared not repeat to the world.

These myths and ballads, typical as they were of crude superstition, repelled me greatly. Their persistence, and their application to so long a line of my ancestors, were especially annoying; whilst the imputations of monstrous habits proved unpleasantly reminiscent of the one known scandal of my immediate forbears—the case of my cousin, young Randolph Delapore of Carfax, who went among the negroes and became a voodoo priest after he returned from the Mexican War.

I was much less disturbed by the vaguer tales of wails and howlings in the barren, windswept valley beneath the limestone cliff; of the graveyard stenches after the spring rains; of the floundering, squealing white thing on which Sir John Clave's horse had trod one night in a lonely field; and of the servant who had gone mad at what he saw in the priory in the full light of day. These things were hackneyed spectral lore, and I was at that time a pronounced sceptic. The accounts of vanished peasants were less to be dismissed, though not especially significant in view of mediaeval custom. Prying curiosity meant death, and more than one severed head had been publicly shewn on the bastions—now effaced—around Exham Priory.

A few of the tales were exceedingly picturesque, and made me wish I had learnt more of comparative mythology in my youth. There was, for instance, the belief that a legion of bat-winged devils kept Witches' Sabbath each night at the priory—a legion whose sustenance might explain the disproportionate abundance of coarse vegetables harvested in the vast gardens. And, most vivid of all, there was the dramatic epic of the rats—the scampering army of obscene vermin which had burst forth from the castle three months after the tragedy that doomed it to desertion—the lean, filthy, ravenous army which had swept all before it and devoured fowl, cats, dogs, hogs, sheep, and even two hapless human beings before its fury was spent. Around that unforgettable rodent army a whole separate cycle of myths revolves, for it scattered among the village homes and brought curses and horrors in its train.

Such was the lore that assailed me as I pushed to completion, with an elderly obstinacy, the work of restoring my ancestral home. It must not be imagined for a moment that these tales formed my principal psychological environment. On the other hand, I was constantly praised and encouraged by Capt. Norrys and the antiquarians who surrounded and aided me. When the task was done, over two years after its commencement, I viewed the great rooms, wainscotted walls, vaulted ceilings, mullioned windows, and broad staircases with a pride which fully compensated for the prodigious expense of the restoration. Every attribute of the Middle Ages was cunningly reproduced, and the new parts blended perfectly with the original walls and foundations. The seat of my fathers was complete, and I looked forward to redeeming at last the local fame of the line which ended in me. I would reside here permanently, and prove that a de la Poer (for I had adopted again the original spelling of the name) need not be a fiend. My comfort was perhaps augmented by the fact that, although Exham Priory was mediaevally fitted, its interior was in truth wholly new and free from old vermin and old ghosts alike.

As I have said, I moved in on July 16, 1923. My household consisted of seven servants and nine cats, of which latter species I am particularly fond. My eldest cat, "Nigger-Man", was seven years old and had come with me from my home in Bolton, Massachusetts; the others I had accumulated whilst living with Capt. Norrys' family during the restoration of the priory. For five days our routine proceeded with the utmost placidity, my time being spent mostly in the codification of old family data. I had now obtained some very circumstantial accounts of the final tragedy and flight of Walter de la Poer, which I conceived to be the probable contents of the hereditary paper lost in the fire at Carfax. It appeared that my ancestor was accused with much reason of having killed all the other members of his household, except four servant confederates, in their sleep, about two weeks after a shocking discovery which changed his whole demeanour, but which, except by implication, he disclosed to no one save perhaps the servants who assisted him and afterward fled beyond reach.

This deliberate slaughter, which included a father, three brothers, and two sisters, was largely condoned by the villagers, and so slackly treated by the law that its perpetrator escaped honoured, unharmed, and undisguised to Virginia; the general whispered sentiment being that he had purged the land of an immemorial curse. What discovery had prompted an act so terrible, I could scarcely even conjecture. Walter de la Poer must have known for years the sinister tales about his family, so that this material could have given him no fresh impulse. Had he, then, witnessed some appalling ancient rite, or stumbled upon some frightful and revealing symbol in the priory or its vicinity? He was reputed to have been a shy, gentle youth in England. In Viriginia he seemed not so much hard or bitter as harassed and apprehensive. He was spoken of in the diary of another gentleman-adventurer, Francis Harley of Bellview, as a man of unexampled justice, honour, and delicacy.

On July 22 occurred the first incident which, though lightly dismissed at the time, takes on a preternatural significance in relation to later events. It was so simple as to be almost negligible, and could not possibly have been noticed under the circumstances; for it must be recalled that since I was in a building practically fresh and new except for the walls, and surrounded by a well-balanced staff of servitors, apprehension would have been absurd despite the locality. What I afterward remembered is merely this—that my old black cat, whose moods I know so well, was undoubtedly alert and anxious to an extent wholly out of keeping with his natural character. He roved from room to room, restless and disturbed, and sniffed constantly about the walls which formed part of the old Gothic structure. I realise how trite this sounds—like the inevitable dog in the ghost story, which always growls before his master sees the sheeted figure—yet I cannot consistently suppress it.

The following day a servant complained of restlessness among all the cats in the house. He came to me in my study, a lofty west room on the second story, with groined arches, black oak panelling, and a triple Gothic window overlooking the limestone cliff and desolate valley; and even as he spoke I saw the jetty form of Nigger-Man creeping along the west wall and scratching at the new panels which overlaid the ancient stone. I told the man that there must be some singular odour or emanation from the old stonework, imperceptible to human senses, but affecting the delicate organs of cats even through the new woodwork. This I truly believed, and when the fellow suggested the presence of mice or rats, I mentioned that there had been no rats there for three hundred years, and that even the field mice of the surrounding country could hardly be found in these high walls, where they had never been known to stray. That afternoon I called on Capt. Norrys, and he assured me that it would be quite incredible for field mice to infest the priory in such a sudden and unprecedented fashion.

That night, dispensing as usual with a valet, I retired in the west tower chamber which I had chosen as my own, reached from the study by a stone staircase and short gallery—the former partly ancient, the latter entirely restored. This room was circular, very high, and without wainscotting, being hung with arras which I had myself chosen in London. Seeing that Nigger-Man was with me, I shut the heavy Gothic door and retired by the light of the electric bulbs which so cleverly counterfeited candles, finally switching off the light and sinking on the carved and canopied four-poster, with the venerable cat in his accustomed place across my feet. I did not draw the curtains, but gazed out at the narrow north window which I faced. There was a suspicion of aurora in the sky, and the delicate traceries of the window were pleasantly silhouetted.

At some time I must have fallen quietly asleep, for I recall a distinct sense of leaving strange dreams, when the cat started violently from his placid position. I saw him in the faint auroral glow, head strained forward, fore feet on my ankles, and hind feet stretched behind. He was looking intensely at a point on the wall somewhat west of the window, a point which to my eye had nothing to mark it, but toward which all my attention was now directed. And as I watched, I knew that Nigger-Man was not vainly excited. Whether the arras actually moved I cannot say. I think it did, very slightly. But what I can swear to is that behind it I heard a low, distinct scurrying as of rats or mice. In a moment the cat had jumped bodily on the screening tapestry, bringing the affected section to the floor with his weight, and exposing a damp, ancient wall of stone; patched here and there by the restorers, and devoid of any trace of rodent prowlers. Nigger-Man raced up and down the floor by this part of the wall, clawing the fallen arras and seemingly trying at times to insert a paw between the wall and the oaken floor. He found nothing, and after a time returned wearily to his place across my feet. I had not moved, but I did not sleep again that night.

In the morning I questioned all the servants, and found that none of them had noticed anything unusual, save that the cook remembered the actions of a cat which had rested on her windowsill. This cat had howled at some unknown hour of the night, awaking the cook in time for her to see him dart purposefully out of the open door down the stairs. I drowsed away the noontime, and in the afternoon called again on Capt. Norrys, who became exceedingly interested in what I told him. The odd incidents—so slight yet so curious—appealed to his sense of the picturesque, and elicited from him a number of reminiscences of local ghostly lore. We were genuinely perplexed at the presence of rats, and Norrys lent me some traps and paris-green, which I had the servants place in strategic localities when I returned.

I retired early, being very sleepy, but was harassed by dreams of the most horrible sort. I seemed to be looking down from an immense height upon a twilit grotto, knee-deep with filth, where a white-bearded daemon swineherd drove about with his staff a flock of fungous, flabby beasts whose appearance filled me with unutterable loathing. Then, as the swineherd paused and nodded over his task, a mighty swarm of rats rained down on the stinking abyss and fell to devouring beasts and man alike.

From this terrific vision I was abruptly awaked by the motions of Nigger-Man, who had been sleeping as usual across my feet. This time I did not have to question the source of his snarls and hisses, and of the fear which made him sink his claws into my ankle, unconscious of their effect; for on every side of the chamber the walls were alive with nauseous sound—the verminous slithering of ravenous, gigantic rats. There was now no aurora to shew the state of the arras—the fallen section of which had been replaced—but I was not too frightened to switch on the light.

As the bulbs leapt into radiance I saw a hideous shaking all over the tapestry, causing the somewhat peculiar designs to execute a singular dance of death. This motion disappeared almost at once, and the sound with it. Springing out of bed, I poked at the arras with the long handle of a warming-pan that rested near, and lifted one section to see what lay beneath. There was nothing but the patched stone wall, and even the cat had lost his tense realisation of abnormal presences. When I examined the circular trap that had been placed in the room, I found all of the openings sprung, though no trace remained of what had been caught and had escaped.

Further sleep was out of the question, so, lighting a candle, I opened the door and went out in the gallery toward the stairs to my study, Nigger-Man following at my heels. Before we had reached the stone steps, however, the cat darted ahead of me and vanished down the ancient flight. As I descended the stairs myself, I became suddenly aware of sounds in the great room below; sounds of a nature which could not be mistaken. The oak-panelled walls were alive with rats, scampering and milling, whilst Nigger-Man was racing about with the fury of a baffled hunter. Reaching the bottom, I switched on the light, which did not this time cause the noise to subside. The rats continued their riot, stampeding with such force and distinctness that I could finally assign to their motions a definite direction. These creatures, in numbers apparently inexhaustible, were engaged in one stupendous migration from inconceivable heights to some depth conceivably, or inconceivably, below.

I now heard steps in the corridor, and in another moment two servants pushed open the massive door. They were searching the house for some unknown source of disturbance which had thrown all the cats into a snarling panic and caused them to plunge precipitately down several flights of stairs and squat, yowling, before the closed door to the sub-cellar. I asked them if they had heard the rats, but they replied in the negative. And when I turned to call their attention to the sounds in the panels, I realised that the noise had ceased. With the two men I went down to the door of the sub-cellar, but found the cats already dispersed. Later I resolved to explore the crypt below; but for the present I merely made a round of the traps. All were sprung, yet all were tenantless. Satisfying myself that no one had heard the rats save the felines and me, I sat in my study till morning; thinking profoundly, and recalling every scrap of legend I had unearthed concerning the building I inhabited.

I slept some in the forenoon, leaning back in the one comfortable library chair which my mediaeval plan of furnishing could not banish. Later I telephoned to Capt. Norrys, who came over and helped me explore the sub-cellar. Absolutely nothing untoward was found, although we could not repress a thrill at the knowledge that this vault was built by Roman hands. Every low arch and massive pillar was Roman—not the debased Romanesque of the bungling Saxons, but the severe and harmonious classicism of the age of the Caesars; indeed, the walls abounded with inscriptions familiar to the antiquarians who had repeatedly explored the place—things like "P. GETAE. PROP … TEMP … DONA …" and "L. PRAEC … VS … PONTIFI … ATYS …"

The reference to Atys made me shiver, for I had read Catullus and knew something of the hideous rites of the Eastern god, whose worship was so mixed with that of Cybele. Norrys and I, by the light of lanterns, tried to interpret the odd and nearly effaced designs on certain irregularly rectangular blocks of stone generally held to be altars, but could make nothing of them. We remembered that one pattern, a sort of rayed sun, was held by students to imply a non-Roman origin, suggesting that these altars had merely been adopted by the Roman priests from some older and perhaps aboriginal temple on the same site. On one of these blocks were some brown stains which made me wonder. The largest, in the centre of the room, had certain features on the upper surface which indicated its connexion with fire—probably burnt offerings.

Such were the sights in that crypt before whose door the cats had howled, and where Norrys and I now determined to pass the night. Couches were brought down by the servants, who were told not to mind any nocturnal actions of the cats, and Nigger-Man was admitted as much for help as for companionship. We decided to keep the great oak door—a modern reproduction with slits for ventilation—tightly closed; and, with this attended to, we retired with lanterns still burning to await whatever might occur.

The vault was very deep in the foundations of the priory, and undoubtedly far down on the face of the beetling limestone cliff overlooking the waste valley. That it had been the goal of the scuffling and unexplainable rats I could not doubt, though why, I could not tell. As we lay there expectantly, I found my vigil occasionally mixed with half-formed dreams from which the uneasy motions of the cat across my feet would rouse me. These dreams were not wholesome, but horribly like the one I had had the night before. I saw again the twilit grotto, and the swineherd with his unmentionable fungous beasts wallowing in filth, and as I looked at these things they seemed nearer and more distinct—so distinct that I could almost observe their features. Then I did observe the flabby features of one of them—and awaked with such a scream that Nigger-Man started up, whilst Capt. Norrys, who had not slept, laughed considerably. Norrys might have laughed more—or perhaps less—had he known what it was that made me scream. But I did not remember myself till later. Ultimate horror often paralyses memory in a merciful way.

Norrys waked me when the phenomena began. Out of the same frightful dream I was called by his gentle shaking and his urging to listen to the cats. Indeed, there was much to listen to, for beyond the closed door at the head of the stone steps was a veritable nightmare of feline yelling and clawing, whilst Nigger-Man, unmindful of his kindred outside, was running excitedly around the bare stone walls, in which I heard the same babel of scurrying rats that had troubled me the night before.

An acute terror now rose within me, for here were anomalies which nothing normal could well explain. These rats, if not the creatures of a madness which I shared with the cats alone, must be burrowing and sliding in Roman walls I had thought to be of solid limestone blocks … unless perhaps the action of water through more than seventeen centuries had eaten winding tunnels which rodent bodies had worn clear and ample.… But even so, the spectral horror was no less; for if these were living vermin why did not Norrys hear their disgusting commotion? Why did he urge me to watch Nigger-Man and listen to the cats outside, and why did he guess wildly and vaguely at what could have aroused them?

By the time I had managed to tell him, as rationally as I could, what I thought I was hearing, my ears gave me the last fading impression of the scurrying; which had retreated *still downward,* far underneath this deepest of sub-cellars, till it seemed as if the whole cliff below were riddled with questing rats. Norrys was not as sceptical as I had anticipated, but instead seemed profoundly moved. He motioned to me to notice that the cats at the door had ceased their clamour, as if giving up the rats for lost; whilst Nigger-Man had a burst of renewed restlessness, and was clawing frantically around the bottom of the large stone altar in the centre of the room, which was nearer Norrys' couch than mine.

My fear of the unknown was at this point very great. Something astounding had occurred, and I saw that Capt. Norrys, a younger, stouter, and presumably more naturally materialistic man, was affected fully as much as myself—perhaps because of his lifelong and intimate familiarity with local legend. We could for the moment do nothing but watch the old black cat as he pawed with decreasing fervour at the base of the altar, occasionally looking up and mewing to me in that persuasive manner which he used when he wished me to perform some favour for him.

Norrys now took a lantern close to the altar and examined the place where Nigger-Man was pawing; silently kneeling and scraping away the lichens of centuries which joined the massive pre-Roman block to the tessellated floor. He did not find anything, and was about to abandon his efforts when I noticed a trivial circumstance which made me shudder, even though it implied nothing more than I had already imagined. I told him of it, and we both looked at its almost imperceptible manifestation with the fixedness of fascinated discovery and acknowledgment. It was only this—that the flame of the lantern set down near the altar was slightly but certainly flickering from a draught of air which it had not before received, and which came indubitably from the crevices between floor and altar where Norrys was scraping away the lichens.

We spent the rest of the night in the brilliantly lighted study, nervously discussing what we should do next. The discovery that some vault deeper than the deepest known masonry of the Romans underlay this accursed pile—some vault unsuspected by the curious antiquarians of three centuries—would have been sufficient to excite us without any background of the sinister. As it was, the fascination became twofold; and we paused in doubt whether to abandon our search and quit the priory for ever in superstitious caution, or to gratify our sense of adventure and brave whatever horrors might await us in the unknown depths. By morning we had compromised, and decided to go to London to gather a group of archaeologists and scientific men fit to cope with the mystery. It should be mentioned that before leaving the sub-cellar we had vainly tried to move the central altar which we now recognised as the gate to a new pit of nameless fear. What secret would open the gate, wiser men than we would have to find.

During many days in London Capt. Norrys and I presented our facts, conjectures, and legendary anecdotes to five eminent authorities, all men who could be trusted to respect any family disclosures which future explorations might develop. We found most of them little disposed to scoff, but instead intensely interested and sincerely sympathetic. It is hardly necessary to name them all, but I may say that they included Sir William Brinton, whose excavations in the Troad excited most of the world in their day. As we all took the train for Anchester I felt myself poised on the brink of frightful revelations, a sensation symbolised by the air of mourning among the many Americans at the unexpected death of the President on the other side of the world.

On the evening of August 7th we reached Exham Priory, where the servants assured me that nothing unusual had occurred. The cats, even old Nigger-Man, had been perfectly placid; and not a trap in the house had been sprung. We were to begin exploring on the following day, awaiting which I assigned well-appointed rooms to all my guests. I myself retired in my own tower chamber, with Nigger-Man across my feet. Sleep came quickly, but hideous dreams assailed me. There was a vision of a Roman feast like that of Trimalchio, with a horror in a covered platter. Then came that damnable, recurrent thing about the swineherd and his filthy drove in the twilit grotto. Yet when I awoke it was full daylight, with normal sounds in the house below. The rats, living or spectral, had not troubled me; and Nigger-Man was still quietly asleep. On going down, I found that the same tranquillity had prevailed elsewhere; a condition which one of the assembled savants—a fellow named Thornton, devoted to the psychic—rather absurdly laid to the fact that I had now been shewn the thing which certain forces had wished to shew me.

All was now ready, and at eleven a.m. our entire group of seven men, bearing powerful electric searchlights and implements of excavation, went down to the sub-cellar and bolted the door behind us. Nigger-Man was with us, for the investigators found no occasion to despise his excitability, and were indeed anxious that he be present in case of obscure rodent manifestations. We noted the Roman inscriptions and unknown altar designs only briefly, for three of the savants had already seen them, and all knew their characteristics. Prime attention was paid to the momentous central altar, and within an hour Sir William Brinton had caused it to tilt backward, balanced by some unknown species of counterweight.

There now lay revealed such a horror as would have overwhelmed us had we not been prepared. Through a nearly square opening in the tiled floor, sprawling on a flight of stone steps so prodigiously worn that it was little more than an inclined plane at the centre, was a ghastly array of human or semi-human bones. Those which retained their collocation as skeletons shewed attitudes of panic fear, and over all were the marks of rodent gnawing. The skulls denoted nothing short of utter idiocy, cretinism, or primitive semi-apedom. Above the hellishly littered steps arched a descending passage seemingly chiselled from the solid rock, and conducting a current of air. This current was not a sudden and noxious rush as from a closed vault, but a cool breeze with something of freshness in it. We did not pause long, but shiveringly began to clear a passage down the steps. It was then that Sir William, examining the hewn walls, made the odd observation that the passage, according to the direction of the strokes, must have been chiselled *from beneath.*

I must be very deliberate now, and choose my words.

After ploughing down a few steps amidst the gnawed bones we saw that there was light ahead; not any mystic phosphorescence, but a filtered daylight which could not come except from unknown fissures in the cliff that overlooked the waste valley. That such fissures had escaped notice from outside was hardly remarkable, for not only is the valley wholly uninhabited, but the cliff is so high and beetling that only an aëronaut could study its face in detail. A few steps more, and our breaths were literally snatched from us by what we saw; so literally that Thornton, the psychic investigator, actually fainted in the arms of the dazed man who stood behind him. Norrys, his plump face utterly white and flabby, simply cried out inarticulately; whilst I think that what I did was to gasp or hiss, and cover my eyes. The man behind me—the only one of the party older than I—croaked the hackneyed "My God!" in the most cracked voice I ever heard. Of seven cultivated men, only Sir William Brinton retained his composure; a thing more to his credit because he led the party and must have seen the sight first.

It was a twilit grotto of enormous height, stretching away farther than any eye could see; a subterraneous world of limitless mystery and horrible suggestion. There were buildings and other architectural remains—in one terrified glance I saw a weird pattern of tumuli, a savage circle of monoliths, a low-domed Roman ruin, a sprawling Saxon pile, and an early English edifice of wood—but all these were dwarfed by the ghoulish spectacle presented by the general surface of the ground. For yards about the steps extended an insane tangle of human bones, or bones at least as human as those on the steps. Like a foamy sea they stretched, some fallen apart, but others wholly or partly articulated as skeletons; these latter invariably in postures of daemoniac frenzy, either fighting off some menace or clutching other forms with cannibal intent.

When Dr. Trask, the anthropologist, stooped to classify the skulls, he found a degraded mixture which utterly baffled him. They were mostly lower than the Piltdown man in the scale of evolution, but in every case definitely human. Many were of higher grade, and a very few were the skulls of supremely and sensitively developed types. All the bones were gnawed, mostly by rats, but somewhat by others of the half-human drove. Mixed with them were many tiny bones of rats—fallen members of the lethal army which closed the ancient epic.

I wonder that any man among us lived and kept his sanity through that hideous day of discovery. Not Hoffmann or Huysmans could conceive a scene more wildly incredible, more frenetically repellent, or more Gothically grotesque than the twilit grotto through which we seven staggered; each stumbling on revelation after revelation, and trying to keep for the nonce from thinking of the events which must have taken place there three hundred, or a thousand, or two thousand, or ten thousand years ago. It was the antechamber of hell, and poor Thornton fainted again when Trask told him that some of the skeleton things must have descended as quadrupeds through the last twenty or more generations.

Horror piled on horror as we began to interpret the architectural remains. The quadruped things—with their occasional recruits from the biped class—had been kept in stone pens, out of which they must have broken in their last delirium of hunger or rat-fear. There had been great herds of them, evidently fattened on the coarse vegetables whose remains could be found as a sort of poisonous ensilage at the bottom of huge stone bins older than Rome. I knew now why my ancestors had had such excessive gardens—would to heaven I could forget! The purpose of the herds I did not have to ask.

Sir William, standing with his searchlight in the Roman ruin, translated aloud the most shocking ritual I have ever known; and told of the diet of the antediluvian cult which the priests of Cybele found and mingled with their own. Norrys, used as he was to the trenches, could not walk straight when he came out of the English building. It was a butcher shop and kitchen—he had expected that—but it was too much to see familiar English implements in such a place, and to read familiar English *graffiti* there, some as recent as 1610. I could not go in that building—that building whose daemon activities were stopped only by the dagger of my ancestor Walter de la Poer.

What I did venture to enter was the low Saxon building, whose oaken door had fallen, and there I found a terrible row of ten stone cells with rusty bars. Three had tenants, all skeletons of high grade, and on the bony forefinger of one I found a seal ring with my own coat-of-arms. Sir William found a vault with far older cells below the Roman chapel, but these cells were empty. Below them was a low crypt with cases of formally arranged bones, some of them bearing terrible parallel inscriptions carved in Latin, Greek, and the tongue of Phrygia. Meanwhile, Dr. Trask had opened one of the prehistoric tumuli, and brought to light skulls which were slighty more human than a gorilla's, and which bore indescribable ideographic carvings. Through all this horror my cat stalked unperturbed. Once I saw him monstrously perched atop a mountain of bones, and wondered at the secrets that might lie behind his yellow eyes.

Having grasped to some slight degree the frightful revelations of this twilit area—an area so hideously foreshadowed by my recurrent dream—we turned to that apparently boundless depth of midnight cavern where no ray of light from the cliff could penetrate. We shall never know what sightless Stygian worlds yawn beyond the little distance we went, for it was decided that such secrets are not good for mankind. But there was plenty to engross us close at hand, for we had not gone far before the searchlights shewed that accursed infinity of pits in which the rats had feasted, and whose sudden lack of replenishment had driven the ravenous rodent army first to turn on the living herds of starving things, and then to burst forth from the priory in that historic orgy of devastation which the peasants will never forget.

God! those carrion black pits of sawed, picked bones and opened skulls! Those nightmare chasms choked with the pithecanthropoid, Celtic, Roman, and English bones of countless unhallowed centuries! Some of them were full, and none can say how deep they had once been. Others were still bottomless to our searchlights, and peopled by unnamable fancies. What, I thought, of the hapless rats that stumbled into such traps amidst the blackness of their quests in this grisly Tartarus?

Once my foot slipped near a horribly yawning brink, and I had a moment of ecstatic fear. I must have been musing a long time, for I could not see any of the party but the plump Capt. Norrys. Then there came a sound from that inky, boundless, farther distance that I thought I knew; and I saw my old black cat dart past me like a winged Egyptian god, straight into the illimitable gulf of the unknown. But I was not far behind, for there was no doubt after another second. It was the eldritch scurrying of those fiend-born rats, always questing for new horrors, and determined to lead me on even unto those grinning caverns of earth's centre where Nyarlathotep, the mad faceless god, howls blindly in the darkness to the piping of two amorphous idiot flute-players.

My searchlight expired, but still I ran. I heard voices, and yowls, and echoes, but above all there gently rose that impious, insidious scurrying; gently rising, rising, as a stiff bloated corpse gently rises above an oily river that flows under endless onyx bridges to a black, putrid sea. Something bumped into me—something soft and plump. It must have been the rats; the viscous, gelatinous, ravenous army that feast on the dead and the living.... Why shouldn't rats eat a de la Poer as a de la Poer eats forbidden things? ... The war ate my boy, damn them all ... and the Yanks ate Carfax with flames and burnt Grandsire Delapore and the secret ... No, no, I tell you, I am *not* that daemon swineherd in the twilit grotto! It was *not* Edward Norrys' fat face on that flabby, fungous thing! Who says I am a de la Poer? He lived, but my boy died! ... Shall a Norrys hold the lands of a de la Poer? ... It's voodoo, I tell you ... that spotted snake ... Curse you, Thornton, I'll teach you to faint at what my family do! ... 'Sblood, thou stinkard, I'll learn ye how to gust ... wolde ye swynke me thilke wys? ... *Magna Mater! Magna Mater! ... Atys ... Dia ad aghaidh 's ad aodann ... agus bas dunach ort! Dhonas 's dholas ort, agus leat-sa! ... Ungl ... ungl ... rrrlh ... chchch ...*

That is what they say I said when they found me in the blackness after three hours; found me crouching in the blackness over the plump, half-eaten body of Capt. Norrys, with my own cat leaping and tearing at my throat. Now they have blown up

Exham Priory, taken my Nigger-Man away from me, and shut me into this barred room at Hanwell with fearful whispers about my heredity and experiences. Thornton is in the next room, but they prevent me from talking to him. They are trying, too, to suppress most of the facts concerning the priory. When I speak of poor Norrys they accuse me of a hideous thing, but they must know that I did not do it. They must know it was the rats; the slithering, scurrying rats whose scampering will never let me sleep; the daemon rats that race behind the padding in this room and beckon me down to greater horrors than I have ever known; the rats they can never hear; the rats, the rats in the walls.

THE UNNAMABLE

We were sitting on a dilapidated seventeenth-century tomb in the late afternoon of an autumn day at the old burying-ground in Arkham, and speculating about the unnamable. Looking toward the giant willow in the centre of the cemetery, whose trunk has nearly engulfed an ancient, illegible slab, I had made a fantastic remark about the spectral and unmentionable nourishment which the colossal roots must be sucking in from that hoary, charnel earth; when my friend chided me for such nonsense and told me that since no interments had occurred there for over a century, nothing could possibly exist to nourish the tree in other than an ordinary manner. Besides, he added, my constant talk about "unnamable" and "unmentionable" things was a very puerile device, quite in keeping with my lowly standing as an author. I was too fond of ending my stories with sights or sounds which paralysed my heroes' faculties and left them without courage, words, or associations to tell what they had experienced. We know things, he said, only through our five senses or our religious intuitions; wherefore it is quite impossible to refer to any object or spectacle which cannot be clearly depicted by the solid definitions of fact or the correct doctrines of theology—preferably those of the Congregationalists, with whatever modifications tradition and Sir Arthur Conan Doyle may supply.

With this friend, Joel Manton, I had often languidly disputed. He was principal of the East High School, born and bred in Boston and sharing New England's self-satisfied deafness to the delicate overtones of life. It was his view that only our normal, objective experiences possess any aesthetic significance, and that it is the province of the artist not so much to rouse strong emotion by action, ecstasy, and astonishment, as to maintain a placid interest and appreciation by accurate, detailed transcripts of every-day affairs. Especially did he object to my preoccupation with the mystical and the unexplained; for although believing in the supernatural much more fully than I, he would not admit that it is sufficiently commonplace for literary treatment. That a mind can find its greatest pleasure in escapes from the daily treadmill, and in original and dramatic re-combinations of images usually thrown by habit and fatigue into the hackneyed patterns of actual existence, was something virtually incredible to his clear, practical, and logical intellect. With him all things and feelings had fixed dimensions, properties, causes, and effects; and although he vaguely knew that the mind sometimes holds visions and sensations of far less geometrical, classifiable, and workable nature, he believed himself justified in drawing an arbitrary line and ruling out of court all that cannot be experienced and understood by the average citizen. Besides, he was almost sure that nothing can be really "unnamable". It didn't sound sensible to him.

Though I well realised the futility of imaginative and metaphysical arguments against the complacency of an orthodox sun-dweller, something in the scene of this afternoon colloquy moved me to more than usual contentiousness. The crumbling slate slabs, the patriarchal trees, and the centuried gambrel roofs of the witch-haunted old town that stretched around, all combined to rouse my spirit in defence of my work; and I was soon carrying my thrusts into the enemy's own country. It was not, indeed, difficult to begin a counter-attack, for I knew that Joel Manton actually half clung to many old-wives' superstitions which sophisticated people had long outgrown; beliefs in the appearance of dying persons at distant places, and in the impressions left by old faces on the windows through which they have gazed all their lives. To credit these whisperings of rural grandmothers, I now insisted, argued a faith in the existence of spectral substances on the earth apart from and subsequent to their material counterparts. It argued a capability of believing in phenomena beyond all normal notions; for if a dead man can transmit his visible or tangible image half across the world, or down the stretch of the centuries, how can it be absurd to suppose that deserted houses are full of queer sentient things, or that old graveyards teem with the terrible, unbodied intelligences of generations? And since spirit, in order to cause all the manifestations attributed to it, cannot be limited by any of the laws of matter; why is it extravagant to imagine psychically living dead things in shapes—or absences of shapes—which must for human spectators be utterly and appallingly "unnamable"? "Common sense" in reflecting on these subjects, I assured my friend with some warmth, is merely a stupid absence of imagination and mental flexibility.

Twilight had now approached, but neither of us felt any wish to cease speaking. Manton seemed unimpressed by my arguments, and eager to refute them, having that confidence in his own opinions which had doubtless caused his success as a teacher; whilst I was too sure of my ground to fear defeat. The dusk fell, and lights faintly gleamed in some of the distant windows, but we did not move. Our seat on the tomb was very comfortable, and I knew that my prosaic friend would not mind the cavernous rift in the ancient, root-disturbed brickwork close behind us, or the utter blackness of the spot brought by the intervention of a tottering, deserted seventeenth-century house between us and the nearest lighted road. There in the dark, upon that riven tomb by the deserted house, we talked on about the "unnamable", and after my friend had finished his scoffing I told him of the awful evidence behind the story at which he had scoffed the most.

My tale had been called "The Attic Window", and appeared in the January 1922 issue of *Whispers*. In a good many places, especially the South and the Pacific coast, they took the magazines off the stands at the complaints of silly milksops; but New England didn't get the thrill and merely shrugged its shoulders at my extravagance. The thing, it was averred, was biologically impossible to start with; merely another of those crazy country mutterings which Cotton Mather had been gullible enough to dump into his chaotic "Magnalia Christi Americana", and so poorly authenticated that even he had not ventured to name the locality where the horror occurred. And as to the way I amplified the bare jotting of the old mystic—that was quite impossible, and characteristic of a flighty and notional scribbler! Mather had indeed told of the thing as being born, but nobody but a cheap sensationalist would think of having it grow up, look into people's windows at night, and be hidden in the attic of a house, in flesh and in spirit, till someone saw it at the window centuries later and couldn't describe what it was that turned his hair grey. All this was flagrant trashiness, and my friend Manton was not slow to insist on that fact. Then I told him what I had found in an old diary kept between 1706 and 1723, unearthed among family papers not a mile from where we were sitting; that, and the certain reality of the scars on my ancestor's chest and back which the diary described. I told him, too, of the fears of others in that region, and how they were whispered down for generations; and how no mythical madness came to the boy who in 1793 entered an abandoned house to examine certain traces suspected to be there.

It had been an eldritch thing—no wonder sensitive students shudder at the Puritan age in Massachusetts. So little is known of what went on beneath the surface—so little, yet such a ghastly festering as it bubbles up putrescently in occasional ghoulish glimpses. The witchcraft terror is a horrible ray of light on what was stewing in men's crushed brains, but even that is a trifle. There was no beauty; no freedom—we can see that from the architectural and household remains, and the poisonous sermons of the cramped divines. And inside that rusted iron strait-jacket lurked gibbering hideousness, perversion, and diabolism. Here, truly, was the apotheosis of the unnamable.

Cotton Mather, in that daemoniac sixth book which no one should read after dark, minced no words as he flung forth his anathema. Stern as a Jewish prophet, and laconically unamazed as none since his day could be, he told of the beast that had brought forth what was more than beast but less than man—the thing with the blemished eye—and of the screaming drunken wretch that they hanged for having such an eye. This much he baldly told, yet without a hint of what came after. Perhaps he did not know, or perhaps he knew and did not dare to tell. Others knew, but did not dare to tell—there is no public hint of why they whispered about the lock on the door to the attic stairs in the house of a childless, broken, embittered old man who had put up a blank slate slab by an avoided grave, although one may trace enough evasive legends to curdle the thinnest blood.

It is all in that ancestral diary I found; all the hushed innuendoes and furtive tales of things with a blemished eye seen at windows in the night or in deserted meadows near the woods. Something had caught my ancestor on a dark valley road, leaving him with marks of horns on his chest and of ape-like claws on his back; and when they looked for prints in the trampled dust they found the mixed marks of split hooves and vaguely anthropoid paws. Once a post-rider said he saw an old man chasing and calling to a frightful, loping, nameless thing on Meadow Hill in the thinly moonlit hours before dawn, and many believed him. Certainly, there was strange talk one night in 1710 when the childless, broken old man was buried in the crypt behind his own house in sight of the blank slate slab. They never unlocked that attic door, but left the whole house as it was, dreaded and deserted. When noises came from it, they whispered and shivered; and hoped that the lock on that attic door was strong. Then they stopped hoping when the horror occurred at the parsonage, leaving not a soul alive or in one piece. With the years the legends take on a spectral character—I suppose the thing, if it was a living thing, must have died. The memory had lingered hideously—all the more hideous because it was so secret.

During this narration my friend Manton had become very silent, and I saw that my words had impressed him. He did not laugh as I paused, but asked quite seriously about the boy who went mad in 1793, and who had presumably been the hero of my fiction. I told him why the boy had gone to that shunned, deserted house, and remarked that he ought to be interested, since he believed that windows retained latent images of those who had sat at them. The boy had gone to look at the windows of that horrible attic, because of tales of things seen behind them, and had come back screaming maniacally.

Manton remained thoughtful as I said this, but gradually reverted to his analytical mood. He granted for the sake of argument that some unnatural monster had really existed, but reminded me that even the most morbid perversion of Nature need not be *unnamable* or scientifically indescribable. I admired his clearness and persistence, and added some further revelations I had collected among the old people. Those later spectral legends, I made plain, related to monstrous apparitions more frightful than anything organic could be; apparitions of gigantic bestial forms sometimes visible and sometimes only tangible, which floated about on moonless nights and haunted the old house, the crypt behind it, and the grave where a sapling had sprouted beside an illegible slab. Whether or not such apparitions had ever gored or smothered people to death, as told in uncorroborated traditions, they had produced a strong and consistent impression; and were yet darkly feared by very aged natives, though largely forgotten by the last two generations—perhaps dying for lack of being thought about. Moreover, so far as aesthetic theory was involved, if the psychic emanations of human creatures be grotesque distortions, what coherent representation could express or portray so gibbous and infamous a nebulosity as the spectre of a malign, chaotic perversion, itself a morbid blasphemy against Nature? Moulded by the dead brain of a hybrid nightmare, would not such a vaporous terror constitute in all loathsome truth the exquisitely, the shriekingly *unnamable?*

The hour must now have grown very late. A singularly noiseless bat brushed by me, and I believe it touched Manton also, for although I could not see him I felt him raise his arm. Presently he spoke.

"But is that house with the attic window still standing and deserted?"

"Yes," I answered. "I have seen it."

"And did you find anything there—in the attic or anywhere else?"

"There were some bones up under the eaves. They may have been what that boy saw—if he was sensitive he wouldn't have needed anything in the window-glass to unhinge him. If they all came from the same object it must have been an hysterical, delirious monstrosity. It would have been blasphemous to leave such bones in the world, so I went back with a sack and took them to the tomb behind the house. There was an opening where I could dump them in. Don't think I was a fool—you ought to have seen that skull. It had four-inch horns, but a face and jaw something like yours and mine."

At last I could feel a real shiver run through Manton, who had moved very near. But his curiosity was undeterred.

"And what about the window-panes?"

"They were all gone. One window had lost its entire frame, and in the other there was not a trace of glass in the little diamond apertures. They were that kind—the old lattice windows that went out of use before 1700. I don't believe they've had any glass for a hundred years or more—maybe the boy broke 'em if he got that far; the legend doesn't say."

Manton was reflecting again.

"I'd like to see that house, Carter. Where is it? Glass or no glass, I must explore it a little. And the tomb where you put those bones, and the other grave without an inscription—the whole thing must be a bit terrible."

"You did see it—until it got dark."

My friend was more wrought upon than I had suspected, for at this touch of harmless theatricalism he started neurotically away from me and actually cried out with a sort of gulping gasp which released a strain of previous repression. It was an odd cry, and all the more terrible because it was answered. For as it was still echoing I heard a creaking sound through the pitchy blackness, and knew that a lattice window was opening in that accursed old house beside us. And because all the other frames were long since fallen, I knew that it was the grisly glassless frame of that daemoniac attic window.

Then came a noxious rush of noisome, frigid air from that same dreaded direction, followed by a piercing shriek just beside me on that shocking rifted tomb of man and monster. In another instant I was knocked from my gruesome bench by the devilish threshing of some unseen entity of titanic size but undetermined nature; knocked sprawling on the root-clutched mould of that abhorrent graveyard, while from the tomb came such a stifled uproar of gasping and whirring that my fancy peopled the rayless gloom with Miltonic legions of the misshapen damned. There was a vortex of withering, ice-cold wind, and then the rattle of loose bricks and plaster; but I had mercifully fainted before I could learn what it meant.

Manton, though smaller than I, is more resilient; for we opened our eyes at almost the same instant, despite his greater injuries. Our couches were side by side, and we knew in a few seconds that we were in St. Mary's Hospital. Attendants were grouped about in tense curiosity, eager to aid our memory by telling us how we came there, and we soon heard of the farmer who had found us at noon in a lonely field beyond Meadow Hill, a mile from the old burying-ground, on a spot where an ancient slaughter-house is reputed to have stood. Manton had two malignant wounds in the chest, and some less severe cuts or gougings in the back. I was not so seriously hurt, but was covered with welts and contusions of the most bewildering character, including the print of a split hoof. It was plain that Manton knew more than I, but he told nothing to the puzzled and interested physicians till he had learned what our injuries were. Then he said we were the victims of a vicious bull—though the animal was a difficult thing to place and account for. After the doctors and nurses had left, I whispered an awestruck question:

"Good God, Manton, but *what was it?* Those scars—*was it like that?*"

And I was too dazed to exult when he whispered back a thing I had half expected—

"*No—it wasn't that way at all.* It was everywhere—a gelatine—a slime—yet it had shapes, a thousand shapes of horror beyond all memory. There were eyes—and a blemish. It was the pit—the maelstrom—the ultimate abomination. Carter, *it was the unnamable!*"

THE FESTIVAL

"Efficiunt Daemones, ut quae non sunt, sic tamen quasi sint, conspicienda hominibus exhibeant."

—*Lactantius.*

I was far from home, and the spell of the eastern sea was upon me. In the twilight I heard it pounding on the rocks, and I knew it lay just over the hill where the twisting willows writhed against the clearing sky and the first stars of evening. And because my fathers had called me to the old town beyond, I pushed on through the shallow, new-fallen snow along the road that soared lonely up to where Aldebaran twinkled among the trees; on toward the very ancient town I had never seen but often dreamed of.

It was the Yuletide, that men call Christmas though they know in their hearts it is older than Bethlehem and Babylon, older than Memphis and mankind. It was the Yuletide, and I had come at last to the ancient sea town where my people had dwelt and kept festival in the elder time when festival was forbidden; where also they had commanded their sons to keep festival once every century, that the memory of primal secrets might not be forgotten. Mine were an old people, and were old even when this land was settled three hundred years before. And they were strange, because they had come as dark furtive folk from opiate southern gardens of orchids, and spoken another tongue before they learnt the tongue of the blue-eyed fishers. And now they were scattered, and shared only the rituals of mysteries that none living could understand. I was the only one who came back that night to the old fishing town as legend bade, for only the poor and the lonely remember.

Then beyond the hill's crest I saw Kingsport outspread frostily in the gloaming; snowy Kingsport with its ancient vanes and steeples, ridgepoles and chimney-pots, wharves and small bridges, willow-trees and graveyards; endless labyrinths of steep, narrow, crooked streets, and dizzy church-crowned central peak that time durst not touch; ceaseless mazes of colonial houses piled and scattered at all angles and levels like a child's disordered blocks; antiquity hovering on grey wings over winter-whitened gables and gambrel roofs; fanlights and small-paned windows one by one gleaming out in the cold dusk to join Orion and the archaic stars. And against the rotting wharves the sea pounded; the secretive, immemorial sea out of which the people had come in the elder time.

Beside the road at its crest a still higher summit rose, bleak and windswept, and I saw that it was a burying-ground where black gravestones stuck ghoulishly through the snow like the decayed fingernails of a gigantic corpse. The printless road was very lonely, and sometimes I thought I heard a distant horrible creaking as of a gibbet in the wind. They had hanged four kinsmen of mine for witchcraft in 1692, but I did not know just where.

As the road wound down the seaward slope I listened for the merry sounds of a village at evening, but did not hear them. Then I thought of the season, and felt that these old Puritan folk might well have Christmas customs strange to me, and full of silent hearthside prayer. So after that I did not listen for merriment or look for wayfarers, but kept on down past the hushed lighted farmhouses and shadowy stone walls to where the signs of ancient shops and sea-taverns creaked in the salt breeze, and the grotesque knockers of pillared doorways glistened along deserted, unpaved lanes in the light of little, curtained windows.

I had seen maps of the town, and knew where to find the home of my people. It was told that I should be known and welcomed, for village legend lives long; so I hastened through Back Street to Circle Court, and across the fresh snow on the one full flagstone pavement in the town, to where Green Lane leads off behind the Market House. The old maps still held good, and I had no trouble; though at Arkham they must have lied when they said the trolleys ran to this place, since I saw not a wire overhead. Snow would have hid the rails in any case. I was glad I had chosen to walk, for the white village had seemed very beautiful from the hill; and now I was eager to knock at the door of my people, the seventh house on the left in Green Lane, with an ancient peaked roof and jutting second story, all built before 1650.

There were lights inside the house when I came upon it, and I saw from the diamond window-panes that it must have been kept very close to its antique state. The upper part overhung the narrow grass-grown street and nearly met the overhanging part of the house opposite, so that I was almost in a tunnel, with the low stone doorstep wholly free from snow. There was no sidewalk, but many houses had high doors reached by double flights of steps with iron railings. It was an odd scene, and because I was strange to New England I had never known its like before. Though it pleased me, I would have relished it better if there had been footprints in the snow, and people in the streets, and a few windows without drawn curtains.

When I sounded the archaic iron knocker I was half afraid. Some fear had been gathering in me, perhaps because of the strangeness of my heritage, and the bleakness of the evening, and the queerness of the silence in that aged town of curious customs. And when my knock was answered I was fully afraid, because I had not heard any footsteps before the door creaked open. But I was not afraid long, for the gowned, slippered old man in the doorway had a bland face that reassured me; and though he made signs that he was dumb, he wrote a quaint and ancient welcome with the stylus and wax tablet he carried.

He beckoned me into a low, candle-lit room with massive exposed rafters and dark, stiff, sparse furniture of the seventeenth century. The past was vivid there, for not an attribute was missing. There was a cavernous fireplace and a spinning-wheel at which a bent old woman in loose wrapper and deep poke-bonnet sat back toward me, silently spinning despite the festive season. An indefinite dampness seemed upon the place, and I marvelled that no fire should be blazing. The high-backed settle faced the row of curtained windows at the left, and seemed to be occupied, though I was not sure. I did not like everything about what I saw, and felt again the fear I had had. This fear grew stronger from what had before lessened it, for the more I looked at the old man's bland face the more its very blandness terrified me. The eyes never moved, and the skin was too like wax. Finally I was sure it was not a face at all, but a fiendishly cunning mask. But the flabby hands, curiously gloved, wrote genially on the tablet and told me I must wait a while before I could be led to the place of the festival.

Pointing to a chair, table, and pile of books, the old man now left the room; and when I sat down to read I saw that the books were hoary and mouldy, and that they included old Morryster's wild "Marvells of Science", the terrible "Saducismus Triumphatus" of Joseph Glanvill, published in 1681, the shocking "Daemonolatreia" of Remigius, printed in 1595 at Lyons, and worst of all, the unmentionable "Necronomicon" of the mad Arab Abdul Alhazred, in Olaus Wormius' forbidden Latin translation; a book which I had never seen, but of which I had heard monstrous things whispered. No one spoke to me, but I could hear the creaking of signs in the wind outside, and the whir of the wheel as the bonneted old woman continued her silent spinning, spinning. I thought the room and the books and the people very morbid and disquieting, but because an old tradition of my fathers had summoned me to strange feastings, I resolved to expect queer things. So I tried to read, and soon became tremblingly absorbed by something I found in that accursed "Necronomicon"; a thought and a legend too hideous for sanity or consciousness. But I disliked it when I fancied I heard the closing of one of the windows that the settle faced, as if it had been stealthily opened. It had seemed to follow a whirring that was not of the old woman's spinning-wheel. This was not much, though, for the old woman was spinning very hard, and the aged clock had been striking. After that I lost the feeling that there were persons on the settle, and was reading intently and shudderingly when the old man came back booted and dressed in a loose antique costume, and sat down on that very bench, so that I could not see him. It was certainly nervous waiting, and the blasphemous book in my hands made it doubly so. When eleven struck, however, the old man stood up, glided to a massive carved chest in a corner, and got two hooded cloaks; one of which he donned, and the other of which he draped round the old woman, who was ceasing her monotonous spinning. Then they both started for the outer door; the woman lamely creeping, and the old man, after picking up the very book I had been reading, beckoning me as he drew his hood over that unmoving face or mask.

We went out into the moonless and tortuous network of that incredibly ancient town; went out as the lights in the curtained windows disappeared one by one, and the Dog Star leered at the throng of cowled, cloaked figures that poured silently from every doorway and formed monstrous processions up this street and that, past the creaking signs and antediluvian gables, the thatched roofs and diamond-paned windows; threading precipitous lanes where decaying houses overlapped and crumbled together, gliding across open courts and churchyards where the bobbing lanthorns made eldritch drunken constellations.

Amid these hushed throngs I followed my voiceless guides; jostled by elbows that seemed preternaturally soft, and pressed by chests and stomachs that seemed abnormally pulpy; but seeing never a face and hearing never a word. Up, up, up the eery columns slithered, and I saw that all the travellers were converging as they flowed near a sort of focus of crazy alleys at the top of a high hill in the centre of the town, where perched a great white church. I had seen it from the road's crest when I looked at Kingsport in the new dusk, and it had made me shiver because Aldebaran had seemed to balance itself a moment on the ghostly spire.

There was an open space around the church; partly a churchyard with spectral shafts, and partly a half-paved square swept nearly bare of snow by the wind, and lined with unwholesomely archaic houses having peaked roofs and overhanging gables. Death-fires danced over the tombs, revealing gruesome vistas, though queerly failing to cast any shadows. Past the churchyard, where there were no houses, I could see over the hill's summit and watch the glimmer of stars on the harbour, though the town was invisible in the dark. Only once in a while a lanthorn bobbed horribly through serpentine alleys on its way to overtake the throng that was now slipping speechlessly into the church. I waited till the crowd had oozed into the black doorway, and till all the stragglers had followed. The old man was pulling at my sleeve, but I was determined to be the last. Then finally I went, the sinister man and the old spinning woman before me. Crossing the threshold into that swarming temple of unknown darkness, I turned once to look at the outside world as the churchyard phosphorescence cast a sickly glow on the hilltop pavement. And as I did so I shuddered. For though the wind had not left much snow, a few patches did remain on the path near the door; and in that fleeting backward look it seemed to my troubled eyes that they bore no mark of passing feet, not even mine.

The church was scarce lighted by all the lanthorns that had entered it, for most of the throng had already vanished. They had streamed up the aisle between the high white pews to the trap-door of the vaults which yawned loathsomely open just before the pulpit, and were now squirming noiselessly in. I followed dumbly down the footworn steps and into the dank, suffocating crypt. The tail of that sinuous line of night-marchers seemed very horrible, and as I saw them wriggling into a venerable tomb they seemed more horrible still. Then I noticed that the tomb's floor had an aperture down which the throng was sliding, and in a moment we were all descending an ominous staircase of rough-hewn stone; a narrow spiral staircase damp and peculiarly odorous, that wound endlessly down into the bowels of the hill past monotonous walls of dripping stone blocks and crumbling mortar. It was a silent, shocking descent, and I observed after a horrible interval that the walls and steps were changing in nature, as if chiselled out of the solid rock. What mainly troubled me was that the myriad footfalls made no sound and set up no echoes.

After more aeons of descent I saw some side passages or burrows leading from unknown recesses of blackness to this shaft of nighted mystery. Soon they became excessively numerous, like impious catacombs of nameless menace; and their pungent odour of decay grew quite unbearable. I knew we must have passed down through the mountain and beneath the earth of Kingsport itself, and I shivered that a town should be so aged and maggoty with subterraneous evil.

Then I saw the lurid shimmering of pale light, and heard the insidious lapping of sunless waters. Again I shivered, for I did not like the things that the night had brought, and wished bitterly that no forefather had summoned me to this primal rite. As the steps and the passage grew broader, I heard another sound, the thin, whining mockery of a feeble flute; and suddenly there spread out before me the boundless vista of an inner world—a vast fungous shore litten by a belching column of sick greenish flame and washed by a wide oily river that flowed from abysses frightful and unsuspected to join the blackest gulfs of immemorial ocean.

Fainting and gasping, I looked at that unhallowed Erebus of titan toadstools, leprous fire, and slimy water, and saw the cloaked throngs forming a semicircle around the blazing pillar. It was the Yule-rite, older than man and fated to survive him; the primal rite of the solstice and of spring's promise beyond the snows; the rite of fire and evergreen, light and music. And in that Stygian grotto I saw them do the rite, and adore the sick pillar of flame, and throw into the water handfuls gouged out of the viscous vegetation which glittered green in the chlorotic glare. I saw this, and I saw something amorphously squatted far away from the light, piping noisomely on a flute; and as the thing piped I thought I heard noxious muffled flutterings in the foetid darkness where I could not see. But what frightened me most was that flaming column; spouting volcanically from depths profound and inconceivable, casting no shadows as healthy flame should, and coating the nitrous stone above with a nasty, venomous verdigris. For in all that seething combustion no warmth lay, but only the clamminess of death and corruption.

The man who had brought me now squirmed to a point directly beside the hideous flame, and made stiff ceremonial motions to the semicircle he faced. At certain stages of the ritual they did grovelling obeisance, especially when he held above his head that abhorrent "Necronomicon" he had taken with him; and I shared all the obeisances because I had been summoned to this festival by the writings of my forefathers. Then the old man made a signal to the half-seen flute-player in the darkness, which player thereupon changed its feeble drone to a scarce louder drone in another key; precipitating as it did so a horror unthinkable and unexpected. At this horror I sank nearly to the lichened earth, transfixed with a dread not of this nor any world, but only of the mad spaces between the stars.

Out of the unimaginable blackness beyond the gangrenous glare of that cold flame, out of the tartarean leagues through which that oily river rolled uncanny, unheard, and unsuspected, there flopped rhythmically a horde of tame, trained, hybrid winged things that no sound eye could ever wholly grasp, or sound brain ever wholly remember. They were not altogether crows, nor moles, nor buzzards, nor ants, nor vampire bats, nor decomposed human beings; but something I cannot and must not recall. They flopped limply along, half with their webbed feet and half with their membraneous wings; and as they reached the throng of celebrants the cowled figures seized and mounted them, and rode off one by one along the reaches of that unlighted river, into pits and galleries of panic where poison springs feed frightful and undiscoverable cataracts.

The old spinning woman had gone with the throng, and the old man remained only because I had refused when he motioned me to seize an animal and ride like the rest. I saw when I staggered to my feet that the amorphous flute-player had rolled out of sight, but that two of the beasts were patiently standing by. As I hung back, the old man produced his stylus and tablet and wrote that he was the true deputy of my fathers who had founded the Yule worship in this ancient place; that it had been decreed I should come back, and that the most secret mysteries were yet to be performed. He wrote this in a very ancient hand, and when I still hesitated he pulled from his loose robe a seal ring and a watch, both with my family arms, to prove that he was what he said. But it was a hideous proof, because I knew from old papers that that watch had been buried with my great-great-great-great-grandfather in 1698.

Presently the old man drew back his hood and pointed to the family resemblance in his face, but I only shuddered, because I was sure that the face was merely a devilish waxen mask. The flopping animals were now scratching restlessly at the lichens, and I saw that the old man was nearly as restless himself. When one of the things began to waddle and edge away, he turned quickly to stop it; so that the suddenness of his motion dislodged the waxen mask from what should have been his head. And then, because that nightmare's position barred me from the stone staircase down which we had come, I flung myself into the oily underground river that bubbled somewhere to the caves of the sea; flung myself into that putrescent juice of earth's inner horrors before the madness of my screams could bring down upon me all the charnel legions these pest-gulfs might conceal.

At the hospital they told me I had been found half-frozen in Kingsport Harbour at dawn, clinging to the drifting spar that accident sent to save me. They told me I had taken the wrong fork of the hill road the night before, and fallen over the cliffs at Orange Point; a thing they deduced from prints found in the snow. There was nothing I could say, because everything was wrong. Everything was wrong, with the broad window shewing a sea of roofs in which only about one in five was ancient, and the sound of trolleys and motors in the streets below. They insisted that this was Kingsport, and I could not deny it. When I went delirious at hearing that the hospital stood near the old churchyard on Central Hill, they sent me to St. Mary's Hospital in Arkham, where I could have better care. I liked it there, for the doctors were broad-minded, and even lent me their influence in obtaining the carefully sheltered copy of Alhazred's objectionable "Necronomicon" from the library of Miskatonic University. They said something about a "psychosis", and agreed I had better get any harassing obsessions off my mind.

So I read again that hideous chapter, and shuddered doubly because it was indeed not new to me. I had seen it before, let footprints tell what they might; and where it was I had seen it were best forgotten. There was no one—in waking hours—who could remind me of it; but my dreams are filled with terror, because of phrases I dare not quote. I dare quote only one paragraph, put into such English as I can make from the awkward Low Latin.

> "The nethermost caverns," wrote the mad Arab, "are not for the fathoming of eyes that see; for their marvels are strange and terrific. Cursed the ground where dead thoughts live new and oddly bodied, and evil the mind that is held by no head. Wisely did Ibn Schacabao say, that happy is the tomb where no wizard hath lain, and happy the town at night whose wizards are all ashes. For it is of old rumour that the soul of the devil-bought hastes not from his charnel clay, but fats and instructs *the very worm that gnaws*; till out of corruption horrid life springs, and the dull scavengers of earth wax crafty to vex it and swell monstrous to plague it. Great holes secretly are digged where earth's pores ought to suffice, and things have learnt to walk that ought to crawl."

UNDER THE PYRAMIDS

(with Harry Houdini)

I.

Mystery attracts mystery. Ever since the wide appearance of my name as a performer of unexplained feats, I have encountered strange narratives and events which my calling has led people to link with my interests and activities. Some of these have been trivial and irrelevant, some deeply dramatic and absorbing, some productive of weird and perilous experiences, and some involving me in extensive scientific and historical research. Many of these matters I have told and shall continue to tell very freely; but there is one of which I speak with great reluctance, and which I am now relating only after a session of grilling persuasion from the publishers of this magazine, who had heard vague rumours of it from other members of my family.

The hitherto guarded subject pertains to my non-professional visit to Egypt fourteen years ago, and has been avoided by me for several reasons. For one thing, I am averse to exploiting certain unmistakably actual facts and conditions obviously unknown to the myriad tourists who throng about the pyramids and apparently secreted with much diligence by the authorities at Cairo, who cannot be wholly ignorant of them. For another thing, I dislike to recount an incident in which my own fantastic imagination must have played so great a part. What I saw—or thought I saw—certainly did not take place; but is rather to be viewed as a result of my then recent readings in Egyptology, and of the speculations anent this theme which my environment naturally prompted. These imaginative stimuli, magnified by the excitement of an actual event terrible enough in itself, undoubtedly gave rise to the culminating horror of that grotesque night so long past.

In January, 1910, I had finished a professional engagement in England and signed a contract for a tour of Australian theatres. A liberal time being allowed for the trip, I determined to make the most of it in the sort of travel which chiefly interests me; so accompanied by my wife I drifted pleasantly down the Continent and embarked at Marseilles on the P. & O. Steamer *Malwa,* bound for Port Said. From that point I proposed to visit the principal historical localities of lower Egypt before leaving finally for Australia.

The voyage was an agreeable one, and enlivened by many of the amusing incidents which befall a magical performer apart from his work. I had intended, for the sake of quiet travel, to keep my name a secret; but was goaded into betraying myself by a fellow-magician whose anxiety to astound the passengers with ordinary tricks tempted me to duplicate and exceed his feats in a manner quite destructive of my incognito. I mention this because of its ultimate effect—an effect I should have forseen before unmasking to a shipload of tourists about to scatter throughout the Nile Valley. What it did was to herald my identity wherever I subsequently went, and deprive my wife and me of all the placid inconspicuousness we had sought. Travelling to seek curiosities, I was often forced to stand inspection as a sort of curiosity myself!

We had come to Egypt in search of the picturesque and the mystically impressive, but found little enough when the ship edged up to Port Said and discharged its passengers in small boats. Low dunes of sand, bobbing buoys in shallow water, and a drearily European small town with nothing of interest save the great De Lesseps statue, made us anxious to get on to something more worth our while. After some discussion we decided to proceed at once to Cairo and the Pyramids, later going to Alexandria for the Australian boat and for whatever Graeco-Roman sights that ancient metropolis might present.

The railway journey was tolerable enough, and consumed only four hours and a half. We saw much of the Suez Canal, whose route we followed as far as Ismailiya, and later had a taste of Old Egypt in our glimpse of the restored fresh-water canal of the Middle Empire. Then at last we saw Cairo glimmering through the growing dusk; a twinkling constellation which became a blaze as we halted at the great Gare Centrale.

But once more disappointment seemed to await us, for all that we beheld was European save the costumes and the crowds. A prosaic subway led to a square teeming with carriages, taxicabs, and trolley-cars, and gorgeous with electric lights shining on tall buildings; whilst the very theatre where I was vainly requested to play, and which I later attended as a spectator, had recently been renamed the "American Cosmograph". We stopped at Shepherd's Hotel, reached in a taxi that sped along broad, smartly built-up streets; and amidst the perfect service of its restaurant, elevators, and generally Anglo-American luxuries the mysterious East and immemorial past seemed very far away.

The next day, however, precipitated us delightfully into the heart of the Arabian Nights atmosphere; and in the winding ways and exotic skyline of Cairo, the Bagdad of Haroun-al-Raschid seemed to live again. Guided by our Baedeker, we had struck east past the Ezbekiyeh Gardens along the Mouski in quest of the native quarter, and were soon in the hands of a clamorous cicerone who—notwithstanding later developments—was assuredly a master at his trade. Not until afterward did I see that I should have applied at the hotel for a licenced guide. This man, a shaven, peculiarly hollow-voiced, and relatively cleanly fellow who looked like a Pharaoh and called himself "Abdul Reis el Drogman", appeared to have much power over others of his kind; though subsequently the police professed not to know him, and to suggest that *reis* is merely a name for any person in authority, whilst "Drogman" is obviously no more than a clumsy modification of the word for a leader of tourist parties—*dragoman.*

Abdul led us among such wonders as we had before only read and dreamed of. Old Cairo is itself a story-book and a dream—labyrinths of narrow alleys redolent of aromatic secrets; Arabesque balconies and oriels nearly meeting above the cobbled streets; maelstroms of Oriental traffic with strange cries, cracking whips, rattling carts, jingling money, and braying donkeys; kaleidoscopes of polychrome robes, veils, turbans, and tarbushes; water-carriers and dervishes, dogs and cats, soothsayers and barbers; and over all the whining of blind beggars crouched in alcoves, and the sonorous chanting of muezzins from minarets limned delicately against a sky of deep, unchanging blue.

The roofed, quieter bazaars were hardly less alluring. Spice, perfume, incense, beads, rugs, silks, and brass—old Mahmoud Suleiman squats cross-legged amidst his gummy bottles while chattering youths pulverise mustard in the hollowed-out capital of an ancient classic column—a Roman Corinthian, perhaps from neighbouring Heliopolis, where Augustus stationed one of his three Egyptian legions. Antiquity begins to mingle with exoticism. And then the mosques and the museum—we saw them all, and tried not to let our Arabian revel succumb to the darker charm of Pharaonic Egypt which the museum's priceless treasures offered. That was to be our climax, and for the present we concentrated on the mediaeval Saracenic glories of the Caliphs whose magnificent tomb-mosques form a glittering faery necropolis on the edge of the Arabian Desert.

At length Abdul took us along the Sharia Mohammed Ali to the ancient mosque of Sultan Hassan, and the tower-flanked Bab-el-Azab, beyond which climbs the steep-walled pass to the mighty citadel that Saladin himself built with the stones of forgotten pyramids. It was sunset when we scaled that cliff, circled the modern mosque of Mohammed Ali, and looked down from the dizzy parapet over mystic Cairo—mystic Cairo all golden with its carven domes, its ethereal minarets, and its flaming gardens. Far over the city towered the great Roman dome of the new museum; and beyond it—across the cryptic yellow Nile that is the mother of aeons and dynasties—lurked the menacing sands of the Libyan Desert, undulant and iridescent and evil with older arcana. The red sun sank low, bringing the relentless chill of Egyptian dusk; and as it stood poised on the world's rim like that ancient god of Heliopolis—Re-Harakhte, the Horizon-Sun—we saw silhouetted against its vermeil holocaust the black outlines of the Pyramids of Gizeh—the palaeogean tombs that were hoary with a thousand years when Tut-Ankh-Amen mounted his golden throne in distant Thebes. Then we knew that we were done with Saracen Cairo, and that we must taste the deeper mysteries of primal Egypt—the black Khem of Re and Amen, Isis and Osiris.

The next morning we visited the Pyramids, riding out in a Victoria across the great Nile bridge with its bronze lions, the island of Ghizereh with its massive lebbakh trees, and the smaller English bridge to the western shore. Down the shore road we drove, between great rows of lebbakhs and past the vast Zoölogical Gardens to the suburb of Gizeh, where a new bridge to Cairo proper has since been built. Then, turning inland along the Sharia-el-Haram, we crossed a region of glassy canals and shabby native villages till before us loomed the objects of our quest, cleaving the mists of dawn and forming inverted replicas in the roadside pools. Forty centuries, as Napoleon had told his campaigners there, indeed looked down upon us.

The road now rose abruptly, till we finally reached our place of transfer between the trolley station and the Mena House Hotel. Abdul Reis, who capably purchased our Pyramid tickets, seemed to have an understanding with the crowding, yelling, and offensive Bedouins who inhabited a squalid mud village some distance away and pestiferously assailed every traveller; for he kept them very decently at bay and secured an excellent pair of camels for us, himself mounting a donkey and assigning the leadership of our animals to a group of men and boys more expensive than useful. The area to be traversed was so small that camels were hardly needed, but we did not regret adding to our experience this troublesome form of desert navigation.

The Pyramids stand on a high rock plateau, this group forming next to the northernmost of the series of regal and aristocratic cemeteries built in the neighbourhood of the extinct capital Memphis, which lay on the same side of the Nile, somewhat south of Gizeh, and which flourished between 3400 and 2000 B.C. The greatest pyramid, which lies nearest the modern road, was built by King Cheops or Khufu about 2800 B.C., and stands more than 450 feet in perpendicular height. In a line southwest from this are successively the Second Pyramid, built a generation later by King Khephren, and though slightly smaller, looking even larger because set on higher ground, and the radically smaller Third Pyramid of King Mycerinus, built about 2700 B.C. Near the edge of the plateau and due east of the Second Pyramid, with a face probably altered to form a colossal portrait of Khephren, its royal restorer, stands the monstrous Sphinx—mute, sardonic, and wise beyond mankind and memory.

Minor pyramids and the traces of ruined minor pyramids are found in several places, and the whole plateau is pitted with the tombs of dignitaries of less than royal rank. These latter were originally marked by *mastabas,* or stone bench-like structures above the deep burial shafts, as found in other Memphian cemeteries and exemplified by Perneb's Tomb in the Metropolitan Museum of New York. At Gizeh, however, all such visible things have been swept away by time and pillage; and only the rock-hewn shafts, either sand-filled or cleared out by archaeologists, remain to attest their former existence. Connected with each tomb was a chapel in which priests and relatives offered food and prayer to the hovering *ka* or vital principle of the deceased. The small tombs have their chapels contained in their stone *mastabas* or superstructures, but the mortuary chapels of the pyramids, where regal Pharaohs lay, were separate temples, each to the east of its corresponding pyramid, and connected by a causeway to a massive gate-chapel or propylon at the edge of the rock plateau.

The gate-chapel leading to the Second Pyramid, nearly buried in the drifting sands, yawns subterraneously southeast of the Sphinx. Persistent tradition dubs it the "Temple of the Sphinx"; and it may perhaps be rightly called such if the Sphinx indeed represents the Second Pyramid's builder Khephren. There are unpleasant tales of the Sphinx before Khephren—but whatever its elder features were, the monarch replaced them with his own that men might look at the colossus without fear. It was in the great gateway-temple that the life-size diorite statue of Khephren now in the Cairo Museum was found; a statue before which I stood in awe when I beheld it. Whether the whole edifice is now excavated I am not certain, but in 1910 most of it was below ground, with the entrance heavily barred at night. Germans were in charge of the work, and the war or other things may have stopped them. I would give much, in view of my experience and of certain Bedouin whisperings discredited or unknown in Cairo, to know what has developed in connexion with a certain well in a transverse gallery where statues of the Pharaoh were found in curious juxtaposition to the statues of baboons.

The road, as we traversed it on our camels that morning, curved sharply past the wooden police quarters, post-office, drug store, and shops on the left, and plunged south and east in a complete bend that scaled the rock plateau and brought us face to face with the desert under the lee of the Great Pyramid. Past Cyclopean masonry we rode, rounding the eastern face and looking down ahead into a valley of minor pyramids beyond which the eternal Nile glistened to the east, and the eternal desert shimmered to the west. Very close loomed the three major pyramids, the greatest devoid of outer casing and shewing its bulk of great stones, but the others retaining here and there the neatly fitted covering which had made them smooth and finished in their day.

Presently we descended toward the Sphinx, and sat silent beneath the spell of those terrible unseeing eyes. On the vast stone breast we faintly discerned the emblem of Re-Harakhte, for whose image the Sphinx was mistaken in a late dynasty; and though sand covered the tablet between the great paws, we recalled what Thutmosis IV inscribed thereon, and the dream he had when a prince. It was then that the smile of the Sphinx vaguely displeased us, and made us wonder about the legends of subterranean passages beneath the monstrous creature, leading down, down, to depths none might dare hint at—depths connected with mysteries older than the dynastic Egypt we excavate, and having a sinister relation to the persistence of abnormal, animal-headed gods in the ancient Nilotic pantheon. Then, too, it was I asked myself an idle question whose hideous significance was not to appear for many an hour.

Other tourists now began to overtake us, and we moved on to the sand-choked Temple of the Sphinx, fifty yards to the southeast, which I have previously mentioned as the great gate of the causeway to the Second Pyramid's mortuary chapel on the plateau. Most of it was still underground, and although we dismounted and descended through a modern passageway to its alabaster corridor and pillared hall, I felt that Abdul and the local German attendant had not shewn us all there was to see. After this we made the conventional circuit of the pyramid plateau, examining the Second Pyramid and the peculiar ruins of its mortuary chapel to the east, the Third Pyramid and its miniature southern satellites and ruined eastern chapel, the rock tombs and honeycombings of the fourth and fifth dynasties, and the famous Campell's Tomb whose shadowy shaft sinks precipitously for fifty-three feet to a sinister sarcophagus which one of our camel-drivers divested of the cumbering sand after a vertiginous descent by rope.

Cries now assailed us from the Great Pyramid, where Bedouins were besieging a party of tourists with offers of guidance to the top, or of displays of speed in the performance of solitary trips up and down. Seven minutes is said to be the record for such an ascent and descent, but many lusty sheiks and sons of sheiks assured us they could cut it to five if given the requisite impetus of liberal *baksheesh.* They did not get this impetus, though we did let Abdul take us up, thus obtaining a view of unprecedented magnificence which included not only remote and glittering Cairo with its crowned Citadel and background of gold-violet hills, but all the pyramids of the Memphian district as well, from Abu Roash on the north to the Dashur on the south. The Sakkara step-pyramid, which marks the evolution of the low *mastaba* into the true pyramid, shewed clearly and alluringly in the sandy distance. It is close to this transition-monument that the famed Tomb of Perneb was found—more than 400 miles north of the Theban rock valley where Tut-Ankh-Amen sleeps. Again I was forced to silence through sheer awe. The prospect of such antiquity, and the secrets each hoary monument seemed to hold and brood over, filled me with a reverence and sense of immensity nothing else ever gave me.

Fatigued by our climb, and disgusted with the importunate Bedouins whose actions seemed to defy every rule of taste, we omitted the arduous detail of entering the cramped interior passages of any of the pyramids, though we saw several of the hardiest tourists preparing for the suffocating crawl through Cheops' mightiest memorial. As we dismissed and overpaid our local bodyguard and drove back to Cairo with Abdul Reis under the afternoon sun, we half regretted the omission we had made. Such fascinating things were whispered about lower pyramid passages not in the guide-books; passages whose entrances had been hastily blocked up and concealed by certain uncommunicative archaeologists who had found and begun to explore them. Of course, this whispering was largely baseless on the face of it; but it was curious to reflect how persistently visitors were forbidden to enter the Pyramids at night, or to visit the lowest burrows and crypt of the Great Pyramid. Perhaps in the latter case it was the psychological effect which was feared—the effect on the visitor of feeling himself huddled down beneath a gigantic world of solid masonry; joined to the life he has known by the merest tube, in which he may only crawl, and which any accident or evil design might block. The whole subject seemed so weird and alluring that we resolved to pay the pyramid plateau another visit at the earliest possible opportunity. For me this opportunity came much earlier than I expected.

That evening, the members of our party feeling somewhat tired after the strenuous programme of the day, I went alone with Abdul Reis for a walk through the picturesque Arab quarter. Though I had seen it by day, I wished to study the alleys and bazaars in the dusk, when rich shadows and mellow gleams of light would add to their glamour and fantastic illusion. The native crowds were thinning, but were still very noisy and numerous when we came upon a knot of revelling Bedouins in the Suk-en-Nahhasin, or bazaar of the coppersmiths. Their apparent leader, an insolent youth with heavy features and saucily cocked tarbush, took some notice of us; and evidently recognised with no great friendliness my competent but admittedly supercilious and sneeringly disposed guide. Perhaps, I thought, he resented that odd reproduction of the Sphinx's half-smile which I had often remarked with amused irritation; or perhaps he did not like the hollow and sepulchral resonance of Abdul's voice. At any rate, the exchange of ancestrally opprobrious language became very brisk; and before long Ali Ziz, as I heard the stranger called when called by no worse name, began to pull violently at Abdul's robe, an action quickly reciprocated, and leading to a spirited scuffle in which both combatants lost their sacredly cherished headgear and would have reached an even direr condition had I not intervened and separated them by main force.

My interference, at first seemingly unwelcome on both sides, succeeded at last in effecting a truce. Sullenly each belligerent composed his wrath and his attire; and with an assumption of dignity as profound as it was sudden, the two formed a curious pact of honour which I soon learned is a custom of great antiquity in Cairo—a pact for the settlement of their difference by means of a nocturnal fist fight atop the Great Pyramid, long after the departure of the last moonlight sightseer. Each duellist was to assemble a party of seconds, and the affair was to begin at midnight, proceeding by rounds in the most civilised possible fashion. In all this planning there was much which excited my interest. The fight itself promised to be unique and spectacular, while the thought of the scene on that hoary pile overlooking the antediluvian plateau of Gizeh under the wan moon of the pallid small hours appealed to every fibre of imagination in me. A request found Abdul exceedingly willing to admit me to his party of seconds; so that all the rest of the early evening I accompanied him to various dens in the most lawless regions of the town—mostly northeast of the Ezbekiyeh—where he gathered one by one a select and formidable band of congenial cutthroats as his pugilistic background.

Shortly after nine our party, mounted on donkeys bearing such royal or tourist-reminiscent names as "Rameses", "Mark Twain", "J. P. Morgan", and "Minnehaha", edged through street labyrinths both Oriental and Occidental, crossed the muddy and mast-forested Nile by the bridge of the bronze lions, and cantered philosophically between the lebbakhs on the road to Gizeh. Slightly over two hours were consumed by the trip, toward the end of which we passed the last of the returning tourists, saluted the last in-bound trolley-car, and were alone with the night and the past and the spectral moon.

Then we saw the vast pyramids at the end of the avenue, ghoulish with a dim atavistical menace which I had not seemed to notice in the daytime. Even the smallest of them held a hint of the ghastly—for was it not in this that they had buried Queen Nitokris alive in the Sixth Dynasty; subtle Queen Nitokris, who once invited all her enemies to a feast in a temple below the Nile, and drowned them by opening the water-gates? I recalled that the Arabs whisper things about Nitokris, and shun the Third Pyramid at certain phases of the moon. It must have been over her that Thomas Moore was brooding when he wrote a thing muttered about by Memphian boatmen—

"The subterranean nymph that dwells
'Mid sunless gems and glories hid—
The lady of the Pyramid!"

Early as we were, Ali Ziz and his party were ahead of us; for we saw their donkeys outlined against the desert plateau at Kafr-el-Haram; toward which squalid Arab settlement, close to the Sphinx, we had diverged instead of following the regular road to the Mena House, where some of the sleepy, inefficient police might have observed and halted us. Here, where filthy Bedouins stabled camels and donkeys in the rock tombs of Khephren's courtiers, we were led up the rocks and over the sand to the Great Pyramid, up whose time-worn sides the Arabs swarmed eagerly, Abdul Reis offering me the assistance I did not need.

As most travellers know, the actual apex of this structure has long been worn away, leaving a reasonably flat platform twelve yards square. On this eery pinnacle a squared circle was formed, and in a few moments the sardonic desert moon leered down upon a battle which, but for the quality of the ringside cries, might well have occurred at some minor athletic club in America. As I watched it, I felt that some of our less desirable institutions were not lacking; for every blow, feint, and defence bespoke "stalling" to my not inexperienced eye. It was quickly over, and despite my misgivings as to methods I felt a sort of proprietary pride when Abdul Reis was adjudged the winner.

Reconciliation was phenomenally rapid, and amidst the singing, fraternising, and drinking which followed, I found it difficult to realise that a quarrel had ever occurred. Oddly enough, I myself seemed to be more of a centre of notice than the antagonists; and from my smattering of Arabic I judged that they were discussing my professional performances and escapes from every sort of manacle and confinement, in a manner which indicated not only a surprising knowledge of me, but a distinct hostility and scepticism concerning my feats of escape. It gradually dawned on me that the elder magic of Egypt did not depart without leaving traces, and that fragments of a strange secret lore and priestly cult-practices have survived surreptitiously amongst the fellaheen to such an extent that the prowess of a strange "hahwi" or magician is resented and disputed. I thought of how much my hollow-voiced guide Abdul Reis looked like an old Egyptian priest or Pharaoh or smiling Sphinx … and wondered.

Suddenly something happened which in a flash proved the correctness of my reflections and made me curse the denseness whereby I had accepted this night's events as other than the empty and malicious "frameup" they now shewed themselves to be. Without warning, and doubtless in answer to some subtle sign from Abdul, the entire band of Bedouins precipitated itself upon me; and having produced heavy ropes, soon had me bound as securely as I was ever bound in the course of my life, either on the stage or off. I struggled at first, but soon saw that one man could make no headway against a band of over twenty sinewy barbarians. My hands were tied behind my back, my knees bent to their fullest extent, and my wrists and ankles stoutly linked together with unyielding cords. A stifling gag was forced into my mouth, and a blindfold fastened tightly over my eyes. Then, as the Arabs bore me aloft on their shoulders and began a jouncing descent of the pyramid, I heard the taunts of my late guide Abdul, who mocked and jeered delightedly in his hollow voice, and assured me that I was soon to have my "magic powers" put to a supreme test which would quickly remove any egotism I might have gained through triumphing over all the tests offered by America and Europe. Egypt, he reminded me, is very old; and full of inner mysteries and antique powers not even conceivable to the experts of today, whose devices had so uniformly failed to entrap me.

How far or in what direction I was carried, I cannot tell; for the circumstances were all against the formation of any accurate judgment. I know, however, that it could not have been a great distance; since my bearers at no point hastened beyond a walk, yet kept me aloft a surprisingly short time. It is this perplexing brevity which makes me feel almost like shuddering whenever I think of Gizeh and its plateau—for one is oppressed by hints of the closeness to every- day tourist routes of what existed then and must exist still.

The evil abnormality I speak of did not become manifest at first. Setting me down on a surface which I recognised as sand rather than rock, my captors passed a rope around my chest and dragged me a few feet to a ragged opening in the ground, into which they presently lowered me with much rough handling. For apparent aeons I bumped against the stony irregular sides of a narrow hewn well which I took to be one of the numerous burial shafts of the plateau until the prodigious, almost incredible depth of it robbed me of all bases of conjecture.

The horror of the experience deepened with every dragging second. That any descent through the sheer solid rock could be so vast without reaching the core of the planet itself, or that any rope made by man could be so long as to dangle me in these unholy and seemingly fathomless profundities of nether earth, were beliefs of such grotesqueness that it was easier to doubt my agitated senses than to accept them. Even now I am uncertain, for I know how deceitful the sense of time becomes when one or more of the usual perceptions or conditions of life is removed or distorted. But I am quite sure that I preserved a logical consciousness that far; that at least I did not add any full-grown phantoms of imagination to a picture hideous enough in its reality, and explicable by a type of cerebral illusion vastly short of actual hallucination.

All this was not the cause of my first bit of fainting. The shocking ordeal was cumulative, and the beginning of the later terrors was a very perceptible increase in my rate of descent. They were paying out that infinitely long rope very swiftly now, and I scraped cruelly against the rough and constricted sides of the shaft as I shot madly downward. My clothing was in tatters, and I felt the trickle of blood all over, even above the mounting and excruciating pain. My nostrils, too, were assailed by a scarcely definable menace; a creeping odour of damp and staleness curiously unlike anything I had ever smelt before, and having faint overtones of spice and incense that lent an element of mockery.

Then the mental cataclysm came. It was horrible—hideous beyond all articulate description because it was all of the soul, with nothing of detail to describe. It was the ecstasy of nightmare and the summation of the fiendish. The suddenness of it was apocalyptic and daemoniac—one moment I was plunging agonisedly down that narrow well of million-toothed torture, yet the next moment I was soaring on bat-wings in the gulfs of hell; swinging free and swoopingly through illimitable miles of boundless, musty space; rising dizzily to measureless pinnacles of chilling ether, then diving gaspingly to sucking nadirs of ravenous, nauseous lower vacua.... Thank God for the mercy that shut out in oblivion those clawing Furies of consciousness which half unhinged my faculties, and tore Harpy-like at my spirit! That one respite, short as it was, gave me the strength and sanity to endure those still greater sublimations of cosmic panic that lurked and gibbered on the road ahead.

II.

It was very gradually that I regained my senses after that eldritch flight through Stygian space. The process was infinitely painful, and coloured by fantastic dreams in which my bound and gagged condition found singular embodiment. The precise nature of these dreams was very clear while I was experiencing them, but became blurred in my recollection almost immediately afterward, and was soon reduced to the merest outline by the terrible events—real or imaginary—which followed. I dreamed that I was in the grasp of a great and horrible paw; a yellow, hairy, five-clawed paw which had reached out of the earth to crush and engulf me. And when I stopped to reflect what the paw was, it seemed to me that it was Egypt. In the dream I looked back at the events of the preceding weeks, and saw myself lured and enmeshed little by little, subtly and insidiously, by some hellish ghoul-spirit of the elder Nile sorcery; some spirit that was in Egypt before ever man was, and that will be when man is no more.

I saw the horror and unwholesome antiquity of Egypt, and the grisly alliance it has always had with the tombs and temples of the dead. I saw phantom processions of priests with the heads of bulls, falcons, cats, and ibises; phantom processions marching interminably through subterraneous labyrinths and avenues of titanic propylaea beside which a man is as a fly, and offering unnamable sacrifices to indescribable gods. Stone colossi marched in endless night and drove herds of grinning androsphinxes down to the shores of illimitable stagnant rivers of pitch. And behind it all I saw the ineffable malignity of primordial necromancy, black and amorphous, and fumbling greedily after me in the darkness to choke out the spirit that had dared to mock it by emulation. In my sleeping brain there took shape a melodrama of sinister hatred and pursuit, and I saw the black soul of Egypt singling me out and calling me in inaudible whispers; calling and luring me, leading me on with the glitter and glamour of a Saracenic surface, but ever pulling me down to the age-mad catacombs and horrors of its dead and abysmal pharaonic heart.

Then the dream-faces took on human resemblances, and I saw my guide Abdul Reis in the robes of a king, with the sneer of the Sphinx on his features. And I knew that those features were the features of Khephren the Great, who raised the Second Pyramid, carved over the Sphinx's face in the likeness of his own, and built that titanic gateway temple whose myriad corridors the archaeologists think they have dug out of the cryptical sand and the uninformative rock. And I looked at the long, lean, rigid hand of Khephren; the long, lean, rigid hand as I had seen it on the diorite statue in the Cairo Museum—the statue they had found in the terrible gateway temple—and wondered that I had not shrieked when I saw it on Abdul Reis.... That hand! It was hideously cold, and it was crushing me; it was the cold and cramping of the sarcophagus ... the chill and constriction of unrememberable Egypt.... It was nighted, necropolitan Egypt itself ... that yellow paw ... and they whisper such things of Khephren....

But at this juncture I began to awake—or at least, to assume a condition less completely that of sleep than the one just preceding. I recalled the fight atop the pyramid, the treacherous Bedouins and their attack, my frightful descent by rope through endless rock depths, and my mad swinging and plunging in a chill void redolent of aromatic putrescence. I perceived that I now lay on a damp rock floor, and that my bonds were still biting into me with unloosened force. It was very cold, and I seemed to detect a faint current of noisome air sweeping across me. The cuts and bruises I had received from the jagged sides of the rock shaft were paining me woefully, their soreness enhanced to a stinging or burning acuteness by some pungent quality in the faint draught, and the mere act of rolling over was enough to set my whole frame throbbing with untold agony. As I turned I felt a tug from above, and concluded that the rope whereby I was lowered still reached to the surface. Whether or not the Arabs still held it, I had no idea; nor had I any idea how far within the earth I was. I knew that the darkness around me was wholly or nearly total, since no ray of moonlight penetrated my blindfold; but I did not trust my senses enough to accept as evidence of extreme depth the sensation of vast duration which had characterised my descent.

Knowing at least that I was in a space of considerable extent reached from the surface directly above by an opening in the rock, I doubtfully conjectured that my prison was perhaps the buried gateway chapel of old Khephren—the Temple of the Sphinx—perhaps some inner corridor which the guides had not shewn me during my morning visit, and from which I might easily escape if I could find my way to the barred entrance. It would be a labyrinthine wandering, but no worse than others out of which I had in the past found my way. The first step was to get free of my bonds, gag, and blindfold; and this I knew would be no great task, since subtler experts than these Arabs had tried every known species of fetter upon me during my long and varied career as an exponent of escape, yet had never succeeded in defeating my methods.

Then it occurred to me that the Arabs might be ready to meet and attack me at the entrance upon any evidence of my probable escape from the binding cords, as would be furnished by any decided agitation of the rope which they probably held. This, of course, was taking for granted that my place of confinement was indeed Khephren's Temple of the Sphinx. The direct opening in the roof, wherever it might lurk, could not be beyond easy reach of the ordinary modern entrance near the Sphinx; if in truth it were any great distance at all on the surface, since the total area known to visitors is not at all enormous. I had not noticed any such opening during my daytime pilgrimage, but knew that these things are easily overlooked amidst the drifting sands. Thinking these matters over as I lay bent and bound on the rock floor, I nearly forgot the horrors of the abysmal descent and cavernous swinging which had so lately reduced me to a coma. My present thought was only to outwit the Arabs, and I accordingly determined to work myself free as quickly as possible, avoiding any tug on the descending line which might betray an effective or even problematical attempt at freedom.

This, however, was more easily determined than effected. A few preliminary trials made it clear that little could be accomplished without considerable motion; and it did not surprise me when, after one especially energetic struggle, I began to feel the coils of falling rope as they piled up about me and upon me. Obviously, I thought, the Bedouins had felt my movements and released their end of the rope; hastening no doubt to the temple's true entrance to lie murderously in wait for me. The prospect was not pleasing—but I had faced worse in my time without flinching, and would not flinch now. At present I must first of all free myself of bonds, then trust to ingenuity to escape from the temple unharmed. It is curious how implicitly I had come to believe myself in the old temple of Khephren beside the Sphinx, only a short distance below the ground.

That belief was shattered, and every pristine apprehension of preternatural depth and daemoniac mystery revived, by a circumstance which grew in horror and significance even as I formulated my philosophical plan. I have said that the falling rope was piling up about and upon me. Now I saw that it was *continuing to pile,* as no rope of normal length could possibly do. It gained in momentum and became an avalanche of hemp, accumulating mountainously on the floor, and half burying me beneath its swiftly multiplying coils. Soon I was completely engulfed and gasping for breath as the increasing convolutions submerged and stifled me. My senses tottered again, and I vainly tried to fight off a menace desperate and ineluctable. It was not merely that I was tortured beyond human endurance—not merely that life and breath seemed to be crushed slowly out of me—it was the knowledge of *what those unnatural lengths of rope implied,* and the consciousness of what unknown and incalculable gulfs of inner earth must at this moment be surrounding me. My endless descent and swinging flight through goblin space, then, must have been real; and even now I must be lying helpless in some nameless cavern world toward the core of the planet. Such a sudden confirmation of ultimate horror was insupportable, and a second time I lapsed into merciful oblivion.

When I say oblivion, I do not imply that I was free from dreams. On the contrary, my absence from the conscious world was marked by visions of the most unutterable hideousness. God! . . . If only I had not read so much Egyptology before coming to this land which is the fount of all darkness and terror! This second spell of fainting filled my sleeping mind anew with shivering realisation of the country and its archaic secrets, and through some damnable chance my dreams turned to the ancient notions of the dead and their sojournings in soul *and body* beyond those mysterious tombs which were more houses than graves. I recalled, in dream-shapes which it is well that I do not remember, the peculiar and elaborate construction of Egyptian sepulchres; and the exceedingly singular and terrific doctrines which determined this construction.

All these people thought of was death and the dead. They conceived of a literal resurrection of the body which made them mummify it with desperate care, and preserve all the vital organs in canopic jars near the corpse; whilst besides the body they believed in two other elements, the soul, which after its weighing and approval by Osiris dwelt in the land of the blest, and the obscure and portentous *ka* or life-principle which wandered about the upper and lower worlds in a horrible way, demanding occasional access to the preserved body, consuming the food offerings brought by priests and pious relatives to the mortuary chapel, and sometimes—as men whispered—taking its body or the wooden double always buried beside it and stalking noxiously abroad on errands peculiarly repellent.

For thousands of years those bodies rested gorgeously encased and staring glassily upward when not visited by the *ka*, awaiting the day when Osiris should restore both *ka* and soul, and lead forth the stiff legions of the dead from their sunken houses of sleep. It was to have been a glorious rebirth—but not all souls were approved, nor were all tombs inviolate, so that certain grotesque *mistakes* and fiendish *abnormalities* were to be looked for. Even today the Arabs murmur of unsanctified convocations and unwholesome worship in forgotten nether abysses, which only winged invisible *kas* and soulless mummies may visit and return unscathed.

Perhaps the most leeringly blood-congealing legends are those which relate to certain perverse products of decadent priestcraft—*composite mummies* made by the artificial union of human trunks and limbs with the heads of animals in imitation of the elder gods. At all stages of history the sacred animals were mummified, so that consecrated bulls, cats, ibises, crocodiles, and the like might return some day to greater glory. But only in the decadence did they mix the human and animal in the same mummy—only in the decadence, when they did not understand the rights and prerogatives of the *ka* and the soul. What happened to those composite mummies is not told of—at least publicly—and it is certain that no Egyptologist ever found one. The whispers of Arabs are very wild, and cannot be relied upon. They even hint that old Khephren—he of the Sphinx, the Second Pyramid, and the yawning gateway temple—lives far underground wedded to the ghoul-queen Nitokris and ruling over the mummies that are neither of man nor of beast.

It was of these—of Khephren and his consort and his strange armies of the hybrid dead—that I dreamed, and that is why I am glad the exact dream-shapes have faded from my memory. My most horrible vision was connected with an idle question I had asked myself the day before when looking at the great carven riddle of the desert and wondering with what unknown depths the temple so close to it might be secretly connected. That question, so innocent and whimsical then, assumed in my dream a meaning of frenetic and hysterical madness … *what huge and loathsome abnormality was the Sphinx originally carven to represent?*

My second awakening—if awakening it was—is a memory of stark hideousness which nothing else in my life—save one thing which came after—can parallel; and that life has been full and adventurous beyond most men's. Remember that I had lost consciousness whilst buried beneath a cascade of falling rope whose immensity revealed the cataclysmic depth of my present position. Now, as perception returned, I felt the entire weight gone; and realised upon rolling over that although I was still tied, gagged, and blindfolded, *some agency had removed completely the suffocating hempen landslide which had overwhelmed me.* The significance of this condition, of course, came to me only gradually; but even so I think it would have brought unconsciousness again had I not by this time reached such a state of emotional exhaustion that no new horror could make much difference. I was alone … with *what?*

Before I could torture myself with any new reflection, or make any fresh effort to escape from my bonds, an additional circumstance became manifest. Pains not formerly felt were racking my arms and legs, and I seemed coated with a profusion of dried blood beyond anything my former cuts and abrasions could furnish. My chest, too, seemed pierced by a hundred wounds, as though some malign, titanic ibis had been pecking at it. Assuredly the agency which had removed the rope was a hostile one, and had begun to wreak terrible injuries upon me when somehow impelled to desist. Yet at the time my sensations were distinctly the reverse of what one might expect. Instead of sinking into a bottomless pit of despair, I was stirred to new courage and action; for now I felt that the evil forces were physical things which a fearless man might encounter on an even basis.

On the strength of this thought I tugged again at my bonds, and used all the art of a lifetime to free myself as I had so often done amidst the glare of lights and the applause of vast crowds. The familiar details of my escaping process commenced to engross me, and now that the long rope was gone I half regained my belief that the supreme horrors were hallucinations after all, and that there had never been any terrible shaft, measureless abyss, or interminable rope. Was I after all in the gateway temple of Khephren beside the Sphinx, and had the sneaking Arabs stolen in to torture me as I lay helpless there? At any rate, I must be free. Let me stand up unbound, ungagged, and with eyes open to catch any glimmer of light which might come trickling from any source, and I could actually delight in the combat against evil and treacherous foes!

How long I took in shaking off my encumbrances I cannot tell. It must have been longer than in my exhibition performances, because I was wounded, exhausted, and enervated by the experiences I had passed through. When I was finally free, and taking deep breaths of a chill, damp, evilly spiced air all the more horrible when encountered without the screen of gag and blindfold edges, I found that I was too cramped and fatigued to move at once. There I lay, trying to stretch a frame bent and mangled, for an indefinite period, and straining my eyes to catch a glimpse of some ray of light which would give a hint as to my position.

By degrees my strength and flexibility returned, but my eyes beheld nothing. As I staggered to my feet I peered diligently in every direction, yet met only an ebony blackness as great as that I had known when blindfolded. I tried my legs, blood-encrusted beneath my shredded trousers, and found that I could walk; yet could not decide in what direction to go. Obviously I ought not to walk at random, and perhaps retreat directly from the entrance I sought; so I paused to note the direction of the cold, foetid, natron-scented air-current which I had never ceased to feel. Accepting the point of its source as the possible entrance to the abyss, I strove to keep track of this landmark and to walk consistently toward it.

I had had a match-box with me, and even a small electric flashlight; but of course the pockets of my tossed and tattered clothing were long since emptied of all heavy articles. As I walked cautiously in the blackness, the draught grew stronger and more offensive, till at length I could regard it as nothing less than a tangible stream of detestable vapour pouring out of some aperture like the smoke of the genie from the fisherman's jar in the Eastern tale. The East … Egypt … truly, this dark cradle of civilisation was ever the well-spring of horrors and marvels unspeakable! The more I reflected on the nature of this cavern wind, the greater my sense of disquiet became; for although despite its odour I had sought its source as at least an indirect clue to the outer world, I now saw plainly that this foul emanation could have no admixture or connexion whatsoever with the clean air of the Libyan Desert, but must be essentially a thing vomited from sinister gulfs still lower down. I had, then, been walking in the wrong direction!

After a moment's reflection I decided not to retrace my steps. Away from the draught I would have no landmarks, for the roughly level rock floor was devoid of distinctive configurations. If, however, I followed up the strange current, I would undoubtedly arrive at an aperture of some sort, from whose gate I could perhaps work round the walls to the opposite side of this Cyclopean and otherwise unnavigable hall. That I might fail, I well realised. I saw that this was no part of Khephren's gateway temple which tourists know, and it struck me that this particular hall might be unknown even to archaeologists, and merely stumbled upon by the inquisitive and malignant Arabs who had imprisoned me. If so, was there any present gate of escape to the known parts or to the outer air?

What evidence, indeed, did I now possess that this was the gateway temple at all? For a moment all my wildest speculations rushed back upon me, and I thought of that vivid mélange of impressions—descent, suspension in space, the rope, my wounds, and the dreams that were frankly dreams. Was this the end of life for me? Or indeed, would it be merciful if this moment *were* the end? I could answer none of my own questions, but merely kept on till Fate for a third time reduced me to oblivion. This time there were no dreams, for the suddenness of the incident shocked me out of all thought either conscious or subconscious. Tripping on an unexpected descending step at a point where the offensive draught became strong enough to offer an actual physical resistance, I was precipitated headlong down a black flight of huge stone stairs into a gulf of hideousness unrelieved.

That I ever breathed again is a tribute to the inherent vitality of the healthy human organism. Often I look back to that night and feel a touch of actual *humour* in those repeated lapses of consciousness; lapses whose succession reminded me at the time of nothing more than the crude cinema melodramas of that period. Of course, it is possible that the repeated lapses never occurred; and that all the features of that underground nightmare were merely the dreams of one long coma which began with the shock of my descent into that abyss and ended with the healing balm of the outer air and of the rising sun which found me stretched on the sands of Gizeh before the sardonic and dawn-flushed face of the Great Sphinx.

I prefer to believe this latter explanation as much as I can, hence was glad when the police told me that the barrier to Khephren's gateway temple had been found unfastened, and that a sizeable rift to the surface did actually exist in one corner of the still buried part. I was glad, too, when the doctors pronounced my wounds only those to be expected from my seizure, blindfolding, lowering, struggling with bonds, falling some distance—perhaps into a depression in the temple's inner gallery—dragging myself to the outer barrier and escaping from it, and experiences like that … a very soothing diagnosis. And yet I know that there must be more than appears on the surface. That extreme descent is too vivid a memory to be dismissed—and it is odd that no one has ever been able to find a man answering the description of my guide Abdul Reis el Drogman—the tomb-throated guide who looked and smiled like King Khephren.

I have digressed from my connected narrative—perhaps in the vain hope of evading the telling of that final incident; that incident which of all is most certainly an hallucination. But I promised to relate it, and do not break promises. When I recovered—or seemed to recover—my senses after that fall down the black stone stairs, I was quite as alone and in darkness as before. The windy stench, bad enough before, was now fiendish; yet I had acquired enough familiarity by this time to bear it stoically. Dazedly I began to crawl away from the place whence the putrid wind came, and with my bleeding hands felt the colossal blocks of a mighty pavement. Once my head struck against a hard object, and when I felt of it I learned that it was the base of a column—a column of unbelievable immensity—whose surface was covered with gigantic chiselled hieroglyphics very perceptible to my touch. Crawling on, I encountered other titan columns at incomprehensible distances apart; when suddenly my attention was captured by the realisation of something which must have been impinging on my subconscious hearing long before the conscious sense was aware of it.

From some still lower chasm in earth's bowels were proceeding certain *sounds,* measured and definite, and like nothing I had ever heard before. That they were very ancient and distinctly ceremonial, I felt almost intuitively; and much reading in Egyptology led me to associate them with the flute, the sambuke, the sistrum, and the tympanum. In their rhythmic piping, droning, rattling, and beating I felt an element of terror beyond all the known terrors of earth—a terror peculiarly dissociated from personal fear, and taking the form of a sort of objective pity for our planet, that it should hold within its depths such horrors as must lie behind these aegipanic cacophonies. The sounds increased in volume, and I felt that they were approaching. Then—and may all the gods of all pantheons unite to keep the like from my ears again—I began to hear, faintly and afar off, *the morbid and millennial tramping of the marching things.*

It was hideous that footfalls *so dissimilar* should move in such perfect rhythm. The training of unhallowed thousands of years must lie behind that march of earth's inmost monstrosities … padding, clicking, walking, stalking, rumbling, lumbering, crawling … and all to the abhorrent discords of those mocking instruments. And then … God keep the memory of those Arab legends out of my head! The mummies without souls … the meeting-place of the wandering *kas* … the hordes of the devil-cursed pharaonic dead of forty centuries … the *composite mummies* led through the uttermost onyx voids by King Khephren and his ghoul-queen Nitokris.…

The tramping drew nearer—heaven save me from the sound of those feet and paws and hooves and pads and talons as it commenced to acquire detail! Down limitless reaches of sunless pavement a spark of light flickered in the malodorous wind, and I drew behind the enormous circumference of a Cyclopic column that I might escape for a while the horror that was stalking million-footed toward me through gigantic hypostyles of inhuman dread and phobic antiquity. The flickers increased, and the tramping and dissonant rhythm grew sickeningly loud. In the quivering orange light there stood faintly forth a scene of such stony awe that I gasped from a sheer wonder that conquered even fear and repulsion. Bases of columns whose middles were higher than human sight … mere bases of things that must each dwarf the Eiffel Tower to insignificance … hieroglyphics carved by unthinkable hands in caverns where daylight can be only a remote legend.…

I *would not* look at the marching things. That I desperately resolved as I heard their creaking joints and nitrous wheezing above the dead music and the dead tramping. It was merciful that they did not speak … but God! *their crazy torches began to cast shadows on the surface of those stupendous columns.* Heaven take it away! *Hippopotami should not have human hands and carry torches … men should not have the heads of crocodiles.…*

I tried to turn away, but the shadows and the sounds and the stench were everywhere. Then I remembered something I used to do in half-conscious nightmares as a boy, and began to repeat to myself, "This is a dream! This is a dream!" But it was of no use, and I could only shut my eyes and pray … at least, that is what I think I did, for one is never sure in visions—and I know this can have been nothing more. I wondered whether I should ever reach the world again, and at times would furtively open my eyes to see if I could discern any feature of the place other than the wind of spiced putrefaction, the topless columns, and the thaumatropically grotesque shadows of abnormal horror. The sputtering glare of multiplying torches now shone, and unless this hellish place were wholly without walls, I could not fail to see some boundary or fixed landmark soon. But I had to shut my eyes again when I realised *how many* of the things were assembling—and when I glimpsed a certain object walking solemnly and steadily *without any body above the waist.*

A fiendish and ululant corpse-gurgle or death-rattle now split the very atmosphere—the charnel atmosphere poisonous with naphtha and bitumen blasts—in one concerted chorus from the ghoulish legion of hybrid blasphemies. My eyes, perversely shaken open, gazed for an instant upon a sight which no human creature could even imagine without panic fear and physical exhaustion. The things had filed ceremonially in one direction, the direction of the noisome wind, where the light of their torches shewed their bended heads … or the bended heads of such as had heads.... They were worshipping before a great black foetor-belching aperture which reached up almost out of sight, and which I could see was flanked at right angles by two giant staircases whose ends were far away in shadow. One of these was indubitably the staircase I had fallen down.

The dimensions of the hole were fully in proportion with those of the columns—an ordinary house would have been lost in it, and any average public building could easily have been moved in and out. It was so vast a surface that only by moving the eye could one trace its boundaries … so vast, so hideously black, and so aromatically stinking.... Directly in front of this yawning Polyphemus-door the things were throwing objects—evidently sacrifices or religious offerings, to judge by their gestures. Khephren was their leader; sneering King Khephren *or the guide Abdul Reis,* crowned with a golden pshent and intoning endless formulae with the hollow voice of the dead. By his side knelt beautiful Queen Nitokris, whom I saw in profile for a moment, noting that the right half of her face was eaten away by rats or other ghouls. And I shut my eyes again when I saw *what* objects were being thrown as offerings to the foetid aperture or its possible local deity.

It occurred to me that judging from the elaborateness of this worship, the concealed deity must be one of considerable importance. Was it Osiris or Isis, Horus or Anubis, or some vast unknown God of the Dead still more central and supreme? There is a legend that terrible altars and colossi were reared to an Unknown One before ever the known gods were worshipped....

And now, as I steeled myself to watch the rapt and sepulchral adorations of those nameless things, a thought of escape flashed upon me. The hall was dim, and the columns heavy with shadow.

With every creature of that nightmare throng absorbed in shocking raptures, it might be barely possible for me to creep past to the far-away end of one of the staircases and ascend unseen; trusting to Fate and skill to deliver me from the upper reaches. Where I was, I neither knew nor seriously reflected upon—and for a moment it struck me as amusing to plan a serious escape from that which I knew to be a dream. Was I in some hidden and unsuspected lower realm of Khephren's gateway temple—that temple which generations have persistently called the Temple of the Sphinx? I could not conjecture, but I resolved to ascend to life and consciousness if wit and muscle could carry me.

Wriggling flat on my stomach, I began the anxious journey toward the foot of the left-hand staircase, which seemed the more accessible of the two. I cannot describe the incidents and sensations of that crawl, but they may be guessed when one reflects on *what I had to watch steadily in that malign, wind-blown torchlight* in order to avoid detection. The bottom of the staircase was, as I have said, far away in shadow; as it had to be to rise without a bend to the dizzy parapeted landing above the titanic aperture. This placed the last stages of my crawl at some distance from the noisome herd, though the spectacle chilled me even when quite remote at my right.

At length I succeeded in reaching the steps and began to climb; keeping close to the wall, on which I observed decorations of the most hideous sort, and relying for safety on the absorbed, ecstatic interest with which the monstrosities watched the foul-breezed aperture and the impious objects of nourishment they had flung on the pavement before it. Though the staircase was huge and steep, fashioned of vast porphyry blocks as if for the feet of a giant, the ascent seemed virtually interminable. Dread of discovery and the pain which renewed exercise had brought to my wounds combined to make that upward crawl a thing of agonising memory. I had intended, on reaching the landing, to climb immediately onward along whatever upper staircase might mount from there; stopping for no last look at the carrion abominations that pawed and genuflected some seventy or eighty feet below—yet a sudden repetition of that thunderous corpse-gurgle and death-rattle chorus, coming as I had nearly gained the top of the flight and shewing by its ceremonial rhythm that it was not an alarm of my discovery, caused me to pause and peer cautiously over the parapet.

The monstrosities were hailing something which had poked itself out of the nauseous aperture to seize the hellish fare proffered it. It was something quite ponderous, even as seen from my height; something yellowish and hairy, and endowed with a sort of nervous motion. It was as large, perhaps, as a good-sized hippopotamus; but very curiously shaped. It seemed to have no neck, but five separate shaggy heads springing in a row from a roughly cylindrical trunk; the first very small, the second good-sized, the third and fourth equal and largest of all, and the fifth rather small, though not so small as the first. Out of these heads darted curious rigid tentacles which seized ravenously on the *excessively great* quantities of unmentionable food placed before the aperture. Once in a while the thing would leap up, and occasionally it would retreat into its den in a very odd manner. Its locomotion was so inexplicable that I stared in fascination, wishing it would emerge farther from the cavernous lair beneath me.

Then it *did* emerge ... it *did* emerge, and at the sight I turned and fled into the darkness up the higher staircase that rose behind me; fled unknowingly up incredible steps and ladders and inclined planes to which no human sight or logic guided me, and which I must ever relegate to the world of dreams for want of any confirmation. It must have been dream, or the dawn would never have found me breathing on the sands of Gizeh before the sardonic dawn-flushed face of the Great Sphinx.

The Great Sphinx! God!—that *idle question* I asked myself on that sun-blest morning before ... *what huge and loathsome abnormality was the Sphinx originally carven to represent?* Accursed is the sight, be it in dream or not, that revealed to me the supreme horror—the Unknown God of the Dead, which licks its colossal chops in the unsuspected abyss, fed hideous morsels by soulless absurdities that should not exist. The five-headed monster that emerged ... that five-headed monster as large as a hippopotamus ... the five-headed monster—*and that of which it is the merest fore-paw....*

But I survived, and I know it was only a dream.

THE SHUNNED HOUSE

I.

From even the greatest of horrors irony is seldom absent. Sometimes it enters directly into the composition of the events, while sometimes it relates only to their fortuitous position among persons and places. The latter sort is splendidly exemplified by a case in the ancient city of Providence, where in the late forties Edgar Allan Poe used to sojourn often during his unsuccessful wooing of the gifted poetess, Mrs. Whitman. Poe generally stopped at the Mansion House in Benefit Street—the renamed Golden Ball Inn whose roof has sheltered Washington, Jefferson, and Lafayette—and his favourite walk led northward along the same street to Mrs. Whitman's home and the neighbouring hillside churchyard of St. John's, whose hidden expanse of eighteenth-century gravestones had for him a peculiar fascination.

Now the irony is this. In this walk, so many times repeated, the world's greatest master of the terrible and the bizarre was obliged to pass a particular house on the eastern side of the street; a dingy, antiquated structure perched on the abruptly rising side-hill, with a great unkempt yard dating from a time when the region was partly open country. It does not appear that he ever wrote or spoke of it, nor is there any evidence that he even noticed it. And yet that house, to the two persons in possession of certain information, equals or outranks in horror the wildest phantasy of the genius who so often passed it unknowingly, and stands starkly leering as a symbol of all that is unutterably hideous.

The house was—and for that matter still is—of a kind to attract the attention of the curious. Originally a farm or semi-farm building, it followed the average New England colonial lines of the middle eighteenth century—the prosperous peaked-roof sort, with two stories and dormerless attic, and with the Georgian doorway and interior panelling dictated by the progress of taste at that time. It faced south, with one gable end buried to the lower windows in the eastward rising hill, and the other exposed to the foundations toward the street. Its construction, over a century and a half ago, had followed the grading and straightening of the road in that especial vicinity; for Benefit Street—at first called Back Street—was laid out as a lane winding amongst the graveyards of the first settlers, and straightened only when the removal of the bodies to the North Burial Ground made it decently possible to cut through the old family plots.

At the start, the western wall had lain some twenty feet up a precipitous lawn from the roadway; but a widening of the street at about the time of the Revolution sheared off most of the intervening space, exposing the foundations so that a brick basement wall had to be made, giving the deep cellar a street frontage with door and two windows above ground, close to the new line of public travel. When the sidewalk was laid out a century ago the last of the intervening space was removed; and Poe in his walks must have seen only a sheer ascent of dull grey brick flush with the sidewalk and surmounted at a height of ten feet by the antique shingled bulk of the house proper.

The farm-like grounds extended back very deeply up the hill, almost to Wheaton Street. The space south of the house, abutting on Benefit Street, was of course greatly above the existing sidewalk level, forming a terrace bounded by a high bank wall of damp, mossy stone pierced by a steep flight of narrow steps which led inward between canyon-like surfaces to the upper region of mangy lawn, rheumy brick walks, and neglected gardens whose dismantled cement urns, rusted kettles fallen from tripods of knotty sticks, and similar paraphernalia set off the weather-beaten front door with its broken fanlight, rotting Ionic pilasters, and wormy triangular pediment.

What I heard in my youth about the shunned house was merely that people died there in alarmingly great numbers. That,

I was told, was why the original owners had moved out some twenty years after building the place. It was plainly unhealthy, perhaps because of the dampness and fungous growths in the cellar, the general sickish smell, the draughts of the hallways, or the quality of the well and pump water. These things were bad enough, and these were all that gained belief among the persons whom I knew. Only the notebooks of my antiquarian uncle, Dr. Elihu Whipple, revealed to me at length the darker, vaguer surmises which formed an undercurrent of folklore among old-time servants and humble folk; surmises which never travelled far, and which were largely forgotten when Providence grew to be a metropolis with a shifting modern population.

The general fact is, that the house was never regarded by the solid part of the community as in any real sense "haunted". There were no widespread tales of rattling chains, cold currents of air, extinguished lights, or faces at the window. Extremists sometimes said the house was "unlucky", but that is as far as even they went. What was really beyond dispute is that a frightful proportion of persons died there; or more accurately, *had* died there, since after some peculiar happenings over sixty years ago the building had become deserted through the sheer impossibility of renting it. These persons were not all cut off suddenly by any one cause; rather did it seem that their vitality was insidiously sapped, so that each one died the sooner from whatever tendency to weakness he may have naturally had. And those who did not die displayed in varying degree a type of anaemia or consumption, and sometimes a decline of the mental faculties, which spoke ill for the salubriousness of the building. Neighbouring houses, it must be added, seemed entirely free from the noxious quality.

This much I knew before my insistent questioning led my uncle to shew me the notes which finally embarked us both on our hideous investigation. In my childhood the shunned house was vacant, with barren, gnarled, and terrible old trees, long, queerly pale grass, and nightmarishly misshapen weeds in the high terraced yard where birds never lingered. We boys used to overrun the place, and I can still recall my youthful terror not only at the morbid strangeness of this sinister vegetation, but at the eldritch atmosphere and odour of the dilapidated house, whose unlocked front door was often entered in quest of shudders. The small-paned windows were largely broken, and a nameless air of desolation hung round the precarious panelling, shaky interior shutters, peeling wall-paper, falling plaster, rickety staircases, and such fragments of battered furniture as still remained. The dust and cobwebs added their touch of the fearful; and brave indeed was the boy who would voluntarily ascend the ladder to the attic, a vast raftered length lighted only by small blinking windows in the gable ends, and filled with a massed wreckage of chests, chairs, and spinning-wheels which infinite years of deposit had shrouded and festooned into monstrous and hellish shapes.

But after all, the attic was not the most terrible part of the house. It was the dank, humid cellar which somehow exerted the strongest repulsion on us, even though it was wholly above ground on the street side, with only a thin door and window-pierced brick wall to separate it from the busy sidewalk. We scarcely knew whether to haunt it in spectral fascination, or to shun it for the sake of our souls and our sanity. For one thing, the bad odour of the house was strongest there; and for another thing, we did not like the white fungous growths which occasionally sprang up in rainy summer weather from the hard earth floor. Those fungi, grotesquely like the vegetation in the yard outside, were truly horrible in their outlines; detestable parodies of toadstools and Indian-pipes, whose like we had never seen in any other situation. They rotted quickly, and at one stage became slightly phosphorescent; so that nocturnal passers-by sometimes spoke of witch-fires glowing behind the broken panes of the foetor-spreading windows.

We never—even in our wildest Hallowe'en moods—visited this cellar by night, but in some of our daytime visits could detect the phosphorescence, especially when the day was dark and wet. There was also a subtler thing we often thought we detected—a very strange thing which was, however, merely suggestive at most. I refer to a sort of cloudy whitish pattern on the dirt floor—a vague, shifting deposit of mould or nitre which we sometimes thought we could trace amidst the sparse fungous growths near the huge fireplace of the basement kitchen. Once in a while it struck us that this patch bore an uncanny resemblance to a doubled-up human figure, though generally no such kinship existed, and often there was no whitish deposit whatever. On a certain rainy afternoon when this illusion seemed phenomenally strong, and when, in addition, I had fancied I glimpsed a kind of thin, yellowish, shimmering exhalation rising from the nitrous pattern toward the yawning fireplace, I spoke to my uncle about the matter. He smiled at this odd conceit, but it seemed that his smile was tinged with reminiscence. Later I heard that a similar notion entered into some of the wild ancient tales of the common folk—a notion likewise alluding to ghoulish, wolfish shapes taken by smoke from the great chimney, and queer contours assumed by certain of the sinuous tree-roots that thrust their way into the cellar through the loose foundation-stones.

II.

Not till my adult years did my uncle set before me the notes and data which he had collected concerning the shunned house. Dr. Whipple was a sane, conservative physician of the old school, and for all his interest in the place was not eager to encourage young thoughts toward the abnormal. His own view, postulating simply a building and location of markedly unsanitary qualities, had nothing to do with abnormality; but he realised that the very picturesqueness which aroused his own interest would in a boy's fanciful mind take on all manner of gruesome imaginative associations.

The doctor was a bachelor; a white-haired, clean-shaven, old-fashioned gentleman, and a local historian of note, who had often broken a lance with such controversial guardians of tradition as Sidney S. Rider and Thomas W. Bicknell. He lived with one manservant in a Georgian homestead with knocker and iron-railed steps, balanced eerily on the steep ascent of North Court Street beside the ancient brick court and colony house where his grandfather—a cousin of that celebrated privateersman, Capt. Whipple, who burnt His Majesty's armed schooner *Gaspee* in 1772—had voted in the legislature on May 4, 1776, for the independence of the Rhode-Island Colony. Around him in the damp, low-ceiled library with the musty white panelling, heavy carved overmantel, and small-paned, vine-shaded windows, were the relics and records of his ancient family, among which were many dubious allusions to the shunned house in Benefit Street. That pest spot lies not far distant—for Benefit runs ledgewise just above the court-house along the precipitous hill up which the first settlement climbed.

When, in the end, my insistent pestering and maturing years evoked from my uncle the hoarded lore I sought, there lay before me a strange enough chronicle. Long-winded, statistical, and drearily genealogical as some of the matter was, there ran through it a continuous thread of brooding, tenacious horror and preternatural malevolence which impressed me even more than it had impressed the good doctor. Separate events fitted together uncannily, and seemingly irrelevant details held mines of hideous possibilities. A new and burning curiosity grew in me, compared to which my boyish curiosity was feeble and inchoate. The first revelation led to an exhaustive research, and finally to that shuddering quest which proved so disastrous to myself and mine. For at the last my uncle insisted on joining the search I had commenced, and after a certain night in that house he did not come away with me. I am lonely without that gentle soul whose long years were filled only with honour, virtue, good taste, benevolence, and learning. I have reared a marble urn to his memory in St. John's churchyard—the place that Poe loved—the hidden grove of giant willows on the hill, where tombs and headstones huddle quietly between the hoary bulk of the church and the houses and bank walls of Benefit Street.

The history of the house, opening amidst a maze of dates, revealed no trace of the sinister either about its construction or about the prosperous and honourable family who built it. Yet from the first a taint of calamity, soon increased to boding significance, was apparent. My uncle's carefully compiled record began with the building of the structure in 1763, and followed the theme with an unusual amount of detail. The shunned house, it seems, was first inhabited by William Harris and his wife Rhoby Dexter, with their children, Elkanah, born in 1755, Abigail, born in 1757, William, Jr., born in 1759, and Ruth, born in 1761. Harris was a substantial merchant and seaman in the West India trade, connected with the firm of Obadiah Brown and his nephews. After Brown's death in 1761, the new firm of Nicholas Brown & Co. made him master of the brig *Prudence*, Providence-built, of 120 tons, thus enabling him to erect the new homestead he had desired ever since his marriage.

The site he had chosen—a recently straightened part of the new and fashionable Back Street, which ran along the side of the hill above crowded Cheapside—was all that could be wished, and the building did justice to the location. It was the best that moderate means could afford, and Harris hastened to move in before the birth of a fifth child which the family expected. That child, a boy, came in December; but was still-born. Nor was any child to be born alive in that house for a century and a half.

The next April sickness occurred among the children, and Abigail and Ruth died before the month was over. Dr. Job Ives diagnosed the trouble as some infantile fever, though others declared it was more of a mere wasting-away or decline. It seemed, in any event, to be contagious; for Hannah Bowen, one of the two servants, died of it in the following June. Eli Liddeason, the other servant, constantly complained of weakness; and would have returned to his father's farm in Rehoboth but for a sudden attachment for Mehitabel Pierce, who was hired to succeed Hannah. He died the next year—a sad year indeed, since it marked the death of William Harris himself, enfeebled as he was by the climate of Martinique, where his occupation had kept him for considerable periods during the preceding decade.

The widowed Rhoby Harris never recovered from the shock of her husband's death, and the passing of her first-born Elkanah two years later was the final blow to her reason. In 1768 she fell victim to a mild form of insanity, and was thereafter confined to the upper part of the house; her elder maiden sister, Mercy Dexter, having moved in to take charge of the family. Mercy was a plain, raw-boned woman of great strength; but her health visibly declined from the time of her advent. She was greatly devoted to her unfortunate sister, and had an especial affection for her only surviving nephew William, who from a sturdy infant had become a sickly, spindling lad. In this year the servant Mehitabel died, and the other servant, Preserved Smith, left without coherent explanation—or at least, with only some wild tales and a complaint that he disliked the smell of the place. For a time Mercy could secure no more help, since the seven deaths and case of madness, all occurring within five years' space, had begun to set in motion the body of fireside rumour which later became so bizarre. Ultimately, however, she obtained new servants from out of town; Ann White, a morose woman from that part of North Kingstown now set off as the township of Exeter, and a capable Boston man named Zenas Low.

It was Ann White who first gave definite shape to the sinister idle talk. Mercy should have known better than to hire anyone from the Nooseneck Hill country, for that remote bit of backwoods was then, as now, a seat of the most uncomfortable superstitions. As lately as 1892 an Exeter community exhumed a dead body and ceremoniously burnt its heart in order to prevent certain alleged visitations injurious to the public health and peace, and one may imagine the point of view of the same section in 1768. Ann's tongue was perniciously active, and within a few months Mercy discharged her, filling her place with a faithful and amiable Amazon from Newport, Maria Robbins.

Meanwhile poor Rhoby Harris, in her madness, gave voice to dreams and imaginings of the most hideous sort. At times her screams became insupportable, and for long periods she would utter shrieking horrors which necessitated her son's temporary residence with his cousin, Peleg Harris, in Presbyterian-Lane near the new college building. The boy would seem to improve after these visits, and had Mercy been as wise as she was well-meaning, she would have let him live permanently with Peleg. Just what Mrs. Harris cried out in her fits of violence, tradition hesitates to say; or rather, presents such extravagant accounts that they nullify themselves through sheer absurdity. Certainly it sounds absurd to hear that a woman educated only in the rudiments of French often shouted for hours in a coarse and idiomatic form of that language, or that the same person, alone and guarded, complained wildly of a staring thing which bit and chewed at her.

In 1772 the servant Zenas died, and when Mrs. Harris heard of it she laughed with a shocking delight utterly foreign to her. The next year she herself died, and was laid to rest in the North Burial Ground beside her husband.

Upon the outbreak of trouble with Great Britain in 1775, William Harris, despite his scant sixteen years and feeble constitution, managed to enlist in the Army of Observation under General Greene; and from that time on enjoyed a steady rise in health and prestige. In 1780, as a Captain in the Rhode Island forces in New Jersey under Colonel Angell, he met and married Phebe Hetfield of Elizabethtown, whom he brought to Providence upon his honourable discharge in the following year.

The young soldier's return was not a thing of unmitigated happiness. The house, it is true, was still in good condition; and the street had been widened and changed in name from Back Street to Benefit Street. But Mercy Dexter's once robust frame had undergone a sad and curious decay, so that she was now a stooped and pathetic figure with hollow voice and disconcerting pallor—qualities shared to a singular degree by the one remaining servant Maria. In the autumn of 1782 Phebe Harris gave birth to a still-born daughter, and on the fifteenth of the next May Mercy Dexter took leave of a useful, austere, and virtuous life.

William Harris, at last thoroughly convinced of the radically unhealthful nature of his abode, now took steps toward quitting it and closing it for ever. Securing temporary quarters for himself and wife at the newly opened Golden Ball Inn, he arranged for the building of a new and finer house in Westminster Street, in the growing part of the town across the Great Bridge. There, in 1785, his son Dutee was born; and there the family dwelt till the encroachments of commerce drove them back across the river and over the hill to Angell Street, in the newer East Side residence district, where the late Archer Harris built his sumptuous but hideous French-roofed mansion in 1876. William and Phebe both succumbed to the yellow fever epidemic of 1797, but Dutee was brought up by his cousin Rathbone Harris, Peleg's son.

Rathbone was a practical man, and rented the Benefit Street house despite William's wish to keep it vacant. He considered it an obligation to his ward to make the most of all the boy's property, nor did he concern himself with the deaths and illnesses which caused so many changes of tenants, or the steadily growing aversion with which the house was generally regarded. It is likely that he felt only vexation when, in 1804, the town council ordered him to fumigate the place with sulphur, tar, and gum camphor on account of the much-discussed deaths of four persons, presumably caused by the then diminishing fever epidemic. They said the place had a febrile smell.

Dutee himself thought little of the house, for he grew up to be a privateersman, and served with distinction on the *Vigilant* under Capt. Cahoone in the War of 1812. He returned unharmed, married in 1814, and became a father on that memorable night of September 23, 1815, when a great gale drove the waters of the bay over half the town, and floated a tall sloop well up Westminster Street so that its masts almost tapped the Harris windows in symbolic affirmation that the new boy, Welcome, was a seaman's son.

Welcome did not survive his father, but lived to perish gloriously at Fredericksburg in 1862. Neither he nor his son Archer knew of the shunned house as other than a nuisance almost impossible to rent—perhaps on account of the mustiness and sickly odour of unkempt old age. Indeed, it never was rented after a series of deaths culminating in 1861, which the excitement of the war tended to throw into obscurity. Carrington Harris, last of the male line, knew it only as a deserted and somewhat picturesque centre of legend until I told him my experience. He had meant to tear it down and build an apartment house on the site, but after my account decided to let it stand, install plumbing, and rent it. Nor has he yet had any difficulty in obtaining tenants. The horror has gone.

III.

It may well be imagined how powerfully I was affected by the annals of the Harrises. In this continuous record there seemed to me to brood a persistent evil beyond anything in Nature as I had known it; an evil clearly connected with the house and not with the family. This impression was confirmed by my uncle's less systematic array of miscellaneous data—legends transcribed from servant gossip, cuttings from the papers, copies of death-certificates by fellow-physicians, and the like. All of this material I cannot hope to give, for my uncle was a tireless antiquarian and very deeply interested in the shunned house; but I may refer to several dominant points which earn notice by their recurrence through many reports from diverse sources. For example, the servant gossip was practically unanimous in attributing to the fungous and malodorous *cellar* of the house a vast supremacy in evil influence. There had been servants—Ann White especially—who would not use the cellar kitchen, and at least three well-defined legends bore upon the queer quasi-human or diabolic outlines assumed by tree-roots and patches of mould in that region. These latter narratives interested me profoundly, on account of what I had seen in my boyhood, but I felt that most of the significance had in each case been largely obscured by additions from the common stock of local ghost lore.

Ann White, with her Exeter superstition, had promulgated the most extravagant and at the same time most consistent tale; alleging that there must lie buried beneath the house one of those vampires—the dead who retain their bodily form and live on the blood or breath of the living—whose hideous legions send their preying shapes or spirits abroad by night. To destroy a vampire one must, the grandmothers say, exhume it and burn its heart, or at least drive a stake through that organ; and Ann's dogged insistence on a search under the cellar had been prominent in bringing about her discharge.

Her tales, however, commanded a wide audience, and were the more readily accepted because the house indeed stood on land once used for burial purposes. To me their interest depended less on this circumstance than on the peculiarly appropriate way in which they dovetailed with certain other things—the complaint of the departing servant Preserved Smith, who had preceded Ann and never heard of her, that something "sucked his breath" at night; the death-certificates of the fever victims of 1804, issued by Dr. Chad Hopkins, and shewing the four deceased persons all unaccountably lacking in blood; and the obscure passages of poor Rhoby Harris's ravings, where she complained of the sharp teeth of a glassy-eyed, half-visible presence.

Free from unwarranted superstition though I am, these things produced in me an odd sensation, which was intensified by a pair of widely separated newspaper cuttings relating to deaths in the shunned house—one from the *Providence Gazette and Country-Journal* of April 12, 1815, and the other from the *Daily Transcript and Chronicle* of October 27, 1845—each of which detailed an appallingly grisly circumstance whose duplication was remarkable. It seems that in both instances the dying person, in 1815 a gentle old lady named Stafford and in 1845 a school-teacher of middle age named Eleazar Durfee, became transfigured in a horrible way; glaring glassily and attempting to bite the throat of the attending physician. Even more puzzling, though, was the final case which put an end to the renting of the house—a series of anaemia deaths preceded by progressive madnesses wherein the patient would craftily attempt the lives of his relatives by incisions in the neck or wrist.

This was in 1860 and 1861, when my uncle had just begun his medical practice; and before leaving for the front he heard much of it from his elder professional colleagues. The really inexplicable thing was the way in which the victims—ignorant people, for the ill-smelling and widely shunned house could now be rented to no others—would babble maledictions in French, a language they could not possibly have studied to any extent. It made one think of poor Rhoby Harris nearly a century before, and so moved my uncle that he commenced collecting historical data on the house after listening, some time subsequent to his return from the war, to the first-hand account of Drs. Chase and Whitmarsh. Indeed, I could see that my uncle had thought deeply on the subject, and that he was glad of my own interest—an open-minded and sympathetic interest which enabled him to discuss with me matters at which others would merely have laughed. His fancy had not gone so far as mine, but he felt that the place was rare in its imaginative potentialities, and worthy of note as an inspiration in the field of the grotesque and macabre.

For my part, I was disposed to take the whole subject with profound seriousness, and began at once not only to review the evidence, but to accumulate as much more as I could. I talked with the elderly Archer Harris, then owner of the house, many times before his death in 1916; and obtained from him and his still surviving maiden sister Alice an authentic corroboration of all the family data my uncle had collected. When, however, I asked them what connexion with France or its language the house could have, they confessed themselves as frankly baffled and ignorant as I. Archer knew nothing, and all that Miss Harris could say was that an old allusion her grandfather, Dutee Harris, had heard of might have shed a little light. The old seaman, who had survived his son Welcome's death in battle by two years, had not himself known the legend; but recalled that his earliest nurse, the ancient Maria Robbins, seemed darkly aware of something that might have lent a weird significance to the French ravings of Rhoby Harris, which she had so often heard during the last days of that hapless woman. Maria had been at the shunned house from 1769 till the removal of the family in 1783, and had seen Mercy Dexter die. Once she hinted to the child Dutee of a somewhat peculiar circumstance in Mercy's last moments, but he had soon forgotten all about it save that it was something peculiar. The granddaughter, moreover, recalled even this much with difficulty. She and her brother were not so much interested in the house as was Archer's son Carrington, the present owner, with whom I talked after my experience.

Having exhausted the Harris family of all the information it could furnish, I turned my attention to early town records and deeds with a zeal more penetrating than that which my uncle had occasionally shewn in the same work. What I wished was a comprehensive history of the site from its very settlement in 1636—or even before, if any Narragansett Indian legend could be unearthed to supply the data. I found, at the start, that the land had been part of the long strip of home lot granted originally to John Throckmorton; one of many similar strips beginning at the Town Street beside the river and extending up over the hill to a line roughly corresponding with the modern Hope Street. The Throckmorton lot had later, of course, been much subdivided; and I became very assiduous in tracing that section through which Back or Benefit Street was later run. It had, as rumour indeed said, been the Throckmorton graveyard; but as I examined the records more carefully, I found that the graves had all been transferred at an early date to the North Burial Ground on the Pawtucket West Road.

Then suddenly I came—by a rare piece of chance, since it was not in the main body of records and might easily have been missed—upon something which aroused my keenest eagerness, fitting in as it did with several of the queerest phases of the affair. It was the record of a lease, in 1697, of a small tract of ground to an Etienne Roulet and wife. At last the French element had appeared—that, and another deeper element of horror which the name conjured up from the darkest recesses of my weird and heterogeneous reading—and I feverishly studied the platting of the locality as it had been before the cutting through and partial straightening of Back Street between 1747 and 1758. I found what I had half expected, that where the shunned house now stood the Roulets had laid out their graveyard behind a one-story and attic cottage, and that no record of any transfer of graves existed. The document, indeed, ended in much confusion; and I was forced to ransack both the Rhode Island Historical Society and Shepley Library before I could find a local door which the name of Etienne Roulet would unlock. In the end I did find something; something of such vague but monstrous import that I set about at once to examine the cellar of the shunned house itself with a new and excited minuteness.

The Roulets, it seemed, had come in 1696 from East Greenwich, down the west shore of Narragansett Bay. They were Huguenots from Caude, and had encountered much opposition before the Providence selectmen allowed them to settle in the town. Unpopularity had dogged them in East Greenwich, whither they had come in 1686, after the revocation of the Edict of Nantes, and rumour said that the cause of dislike extended beyond mere racial and national prejudice, or the land disputes which involved other French settlers with the English in rivalries which not even Governor Andros could quell. But their ardent Protestantism—too ardent, some whispered—and their evident distress when virtually driven from the village down the bay, had moved the sympathy of the town fathers. Here the strangers had been granted a haven; and the swarthy Etienne Roulet, less apt at agriculture than at reading queer books and drawing queer diagrams, was given a clerical post in the warehouse at Pardon Tillinghast's wharf, far south in Town Street. There had, however, been a riot of some sort later on—perhaps forty years later, after old Roulet's death—and no one seemed to hear of the family after that.

For a century and more, it appeared, the Roulets had been well remembered and frequently discussed as vivid incidents in the quiet life of a New England seaport. Etienne's son Paul, a surly fellow whose erratic conduct had probably provoked the riot which wiped out the family, was particularly a source of speculation; and though Providence never shared the witchcraft panics of her Puritan neighbours, it was freely intimated by old wives that his prayers were neither uttered at the proper time nor directed toward the proper object. All this had undoubtedly formed the basis of the legend known by old Maria Robbins. What relation it had to the French ravings of Rhoby Harris and other inhabitants of the shunned house, imagination or future discovery alone could determine. I wondered how many of those who had known the legends realised that additional link with the terrible which my wider reading had given me; that ominous item in the annals of morbid horror which tells of the creature *Jacques Roulet, of Caude,* who in 1598 was condemned to death as a daemoniac but afterward saved from the stake by the Paris parliament and shut in a madhouse. He had been found covered with blood and shreds of flesh in a wood, shortly after the killing and rending of a boy by a pair of wolves. One wolf was seen to lope away unhurt. Surely a pretty hearthside tale, with a queer significance as to name and place; but I decided that the Providence gossips could not have generally known of it. Had they known, the coincidence of names would have brought some drastic and frightened action—indeed, might not its limited whispering have precipitated the final riot which erased the Roulets from the town?

I now visited the accursed place with increased frequency; studying the unwholesome vegetation of the garden, examining all the walls of the building, and poring over every inch of the earthen cellar floor. Finally, with Carrington Harris's permission, I fitted a key to the disused door opening from the cellar directly upon Benefit Street, preferring to have a more immediate access to the outside world than the dark stairs, ground-floor hall, and front door could give. There, where morbidity lurked most thickly, I searched and poked during long afternoons when the sunlight filtered in through the cobwebbed above-ground windows, and a sense of security glowed from the unlocked door which placed me only a few feet from the placid sidewalk outside. Nothing new rewarded my efforts—only the same depressing mustiness and faint suggestions of noxious odours and nitrous outlines on the floor—and I fancy that many pedestrians must have watched me curiously through the broken panes.

At length, upon a suggestion of my uncle's, I decided to try the spot nocturnally; and one stormy midnight ran the beams of an electric torch over the mouldy floor with its uncanny shapes and distorted, half-phosphorescent fungi. The place had dispirited me curiously that evening, and I was almost prepared when I saw—or thought I saw—amidst the whitish deposits a particularly sharp definition of the "huddled form" I had suspected from boyhood. Its clearness was astonishing and unprecedented—and as I watched I seemed to see again the thin, yellowish, shimmering exhalation which had startled me on that rainy afternoon so many years before.

Above the anthropomorphic patch of mould by the fireplace it rose; a subtle, sickish, almost luminous vapour which as it hung trembling in the dampness seemed to develop vague and shocking suggestions of form, gradually trailing off into nebulous decay and passing up into the blackness of the great chimney with a foetor in its wake. It was truly horrible, and the more so to me because of what I knew of the spot. Refusing to flee, I watched it fade—and as I watched I felt that it was in turn watching me greedily with eyes more imaginable than visible. When I told my uncle about it he was greatly aroused; and after a tense hour of reflection, arrived at a definite and drastic decision. Weighing in his mind the importance of the matter, and the significance of our relation to it, he insisted that we both test—and if possible destroy—the horror of the house by a joint night or nights of aggressive vigil in that musty and fungus-cursed cellar.

IV.

On Wednesday, June 25, 1919, after a proper notification of Carrington Harris which did not include surmises as to what we expected to find, my uncle and I conveyed to the shunned house two camp chairs and a folding camp cot, together with some scientific mechanism of greater weight and intricacy. These we placed in the cellar during the day, screening the windows with paper and planning to return in the evening for our first vigil. We had locked the door from the cellar to the ground floor; and having a key to the outside cellar door, were prepared to leave our expensive and delicate apparatus—which we had obtained secretly and at great cost—as many days as our vigils might have to be protracted. It was our design to sit up together till very late, and then watch singly till dawn in two-hour stretches, myself first and then my companion; the inactive member resting on the cot.

The natural leadership with which my uncle procured the instruments from the laboratories of Brown University and the Cranston Street Armoury, and instinctively assumed direction of our venture, was a marvellous commentary on the potential vitality and resilience of a man of eighty-one. Elihu Whipple had lived according to the hygienic laws he had preached as a physician, and but for what happened later would be here in full vigour today. Only two persons suspect what did happen—Carrington Harris and myself. I had to tell Harris because he owned the house and deserved to know what had gone out of it. Then too, we had spoken to him in advance of our quest; and I felt after my uncle's going that he would understand and assist me in some vitally necessary public explanations. He turned very pale, but agreed to help me, and decided that it would now be safe to rent the house.

To declare that we were not nervous on that rainy night of watching would be an exaggeration both gross and ridiculous. We were not, as I have said, in any sense childishly superstitious, but scientific study and reflection had taught us that the known universe of three dimensions embraces the merest fraction of the whole cosmos of substance and energy. In this case an overwhelming preponderance of evidence from numerous authentic sources pointed to the tenacious existence of certain forces of great power and, so far as the human point of view is concerned, exceptional malignancy. To say that we actually believed in vampires or werewolves would be a carelessly inclusive statement. Rather must it be said that we were not prepared to deny the possibility of certain unfamiliar and unclassified modifications of vital force and attenuated matter; existing very infrequently in three-dimensional space because of its more intimate connexion with other spatial units, yet close enough to the boundary of our own to furnish us occasional manifestations which we, for lack of a proper vantage-point, may never hope to understand.

In short, it seemed to my uncle and me that an incontrovertible array of facts pointed to some lingering influence in the shunned house; traceable to one or another of the ill-favoured French settlers of two centuries before, and still operative through rare and unknown laws of atomic and electronic motion. That the family of Roulet had possessed an abnormal affinity for outer circles of entity—dark spheres which for normal folk hold only repulsion and terror—their recorded history seemed to prove. Had not, then, the riots of those bygone seventeen-thirties set moving certain kinetic patterns in the morbid brain of one or more of them—notably the sinister Paul Roulet—which obscurely survived the bodies murdered and buried by the mob, and continued to function in some multiple-dimensioned space along the original lines of force determined by a frantic hatred of the encroaching community?

Such a thing was surely not a physical or biochemical impossibility in the light of a newer science which includes the theories of relativity and intra-atomic action. One might easily imagine an alien nucleus of substance or energy, formless or otherwise, kept alive by imperceptible or immaterial subtractions from the life-force or bodily tissue and fluids of other and more palpably living things into which it penetrates and with whose fabric it sometimes completely merges itself. It might be actively hostile, or it might be dictated merely by blind motives of self-preservation. In any case such a monster must of necessity be in our scheme of things an anomaly and an intruder, whose extirpation forms a primary duty with every man not an enemy to the world's life, health, and sanity.

What baffled us was our utter ignorance of the aspect in which we might encounter the thing. No sane person had even seen it, and few had ever felt it definitely. It might be pure energy—a form ethereal and outside the realm of substance—or it might be partly material; some unknown and equivocal mass of plasticity, capable of changing at will to nebulous approximations of the solid, liquid, gaseous, or tenuously unparticled states. The anthropomorphic patch of mould on the floor, the form of the yellowish vapour, and the curvature of the tree-roots in some of the old tales, all argued at least a remote and reminiscent connexion with the human shape; but how representative or permanent that similarity might be, none could say with any kind of certainty.

We had devised two weapons to fight it; a large and specially fitted Crookes tube operated by powerful storage batteries and provided with peculiar screens and reflectors, in case it proved intangible and opposable only by vigorously destructive ether radiations, and a pair of military flame-throwers of the sort used in the world-war, in case it proved partly material and susceptible of mechanical destruction—for like the superstitious Exeter rustics, we were prepared to burn the thing's heart out if heart existed to burn. All this aggressive mechanism we set in the cellar in positions carefully arranged with reference to the cot and chairs, and to the spot before the fireplace where the mould had taken strange shapes. That suggestive patch, by the way, was only faintly visible when we placed our furniture and instruments, and when we returned that evening for the actual vigil. For a moment I half doubted that I had ever seen it in the more definitely limned form—but then I thought of the legends.

Our cellar vigil began at 10 p.m., daylight saving time, and as it continued we found no promise of pertinent developments. A weak, filtered glow from the rain-harassed street-lamps outside, and a feeble phosphorescence from the detestable fungi within, shewed the dripping stone of the walls, from which all traces of whitewash had vanished; the dank, foetid, and mildew-tainted hard earth floor with its obscene fungi; the rotting remains of what had been stools, chairs, and tables, and other more shapeless furniture; the heavy planks and massive beams of the ground floor overhead; the decrepit plank door leading to bins and chambers beneath other parts of the house; the crumbling stone staircase with ruined wooden hand-rail; and the crude and cavernous fireplace of blackened brick where rusted iron fragments revealed the past presence of hooks, andirons, spit, crane, and a door to the Dutch oven—these things, and our austere cot and camp chairs, and the heavy and intricate destructive machinery we had brought.

We had, as in my own former explorations, left the door to the street unlocked; so that a direct and practical path of escape might lie open in case of manifestations beyond our power to deal with. It was our idea that our continued nocturnal presence would call forth whatever malign entity lurked there; and that being prepared, we could dispose of the thing with one or the other of our provided means as soon as we had recognised and observed it sufficiently. How long it might require to evoke and extinguish the thing, we had no notion. It occurred to us, too, that our venture was far from safe; for in what strength the thing might appear no one could tell. But we deemed the game worth the hazard, and embarked on it alone and unhesitatingly; conscious that the seeking of outside aid would only expose us to ridicule and perhaps defeat our entire purpose. Such was our frame of mind as we talked—far into the night, till my uncle's growing drowsiness made me remind him to lie down for his two-hour sleep.

Something like fear chilled me as I sat there in the small hours alone—I say alone, for one who sits by a sleeper is indeed alone; perhaps more alone than he can realise. My uncle breathed heavily, his deep inhalations and exhalations accompanied by the rain outside, and punctuated by another nerve-racking sound of distant dripping water within—for the house was repulsively damp even in dry weather, and in this storm positively swamp-like. I studied the loose, antique masonry of the walls in the fungus-light and the feeble rays which stole in from the street through the screened windows; and once, when the noisome atmosphere of the place seemed about to sicken me, I opened the door and looked up and down the street, feasting my eyes on familiar sights and my nostrils on wholesome air. Still nothing occurred to reward my watching; and I yawned repeatedly, fatigue getting the better of apprehension.

Then the stirring of my uncle in his sleep attracted my notice. He had turned restlessly on the cot several times during the latter half of the first hour, but now he was breathing with unusual irregularity, occasionally heaving a sigh which held more than a few of the qualities of a choking moan. I turned my electric flashlight on him and found his face averted, so rising and crossing to the other side of the cot, I again flashed the light to see if he seemed in any pain. What I saw unnerved me most surprisingly, considering its relative triviality. It must have been merely the association of any odd circumstance with the sinister nature of our location and mission, for surely the circumstance was not in itself frightful or unnatural. It was merely that my uncle's facial expression, disturbed no doubt by the strange dreams which our situation prompted, betrayed considerable agitation, and seemed not at all characteristic of him. His habitual expression was one of kindly and well-bred calm, whereas now a variety of emotions seemed struggling within him. I think, on the whole, that it was this *variety* which chiefly disturbed me. My uncle, as he gasped and tossed in increasing perturbation and with eyes that had now started open, seemed not one but many men, and suggested a curious quality of alienage from himself.

All at once he commenced to mutter, and I did not like the look of his mouth and teeth as he spoke. The words were at first indistinguishable, and then—with a tremendous start—I recognised something about them which filled me with icy fear till I recalled the breadth of my uncle's education and the interminable translations he had made from anthropological and antiquarian articles in the *Revue des Deux Mondes*. For the venerable Elihu

Whipple was muttering *in French,* and the few phrases I could distinguish seemed connected with the darkest myths he had ever adapted from the famous Paris magazine.

Suddenly a perspiration broke out on the sleeper's forehead, and he leaped abruptly up, half awake. The jumble of French changed to a cry in English, and the hoarse voice shouted excitedly, "My breath, my breath!" Then the awakening became complete, and with a subsidence of facial expression to the normal state my uncle seized my hand and began to relate a dream whose nucleus of significance I could only surmise with a kind of awe.

He had, he said, floated off from a very ordinary series of dream-pictures into a scene whose strangeness was related to nothing he had ever read. It was of this world, and yet not of it—a shadowy geometrical confusion in which could be seen elements of familiar things in most unfamiliar and perturbing combinations. There was a suggestion of queerly disordered pictures superimposed one upon another; an arrangement in which the essentials of time as well as of space seemed dissolved and mixed in the most illogical fashion. In this kaleidoscopic vortex of phantasmal images were occasional snapshots, if one might use the term, of singular clearness but unaccountable heterogeneity.

Once my uncle thought he lay in a carelessly dug open pit, with a crowd of angry faces framed by straggling locks and three-cornered hats frowning down on him. Again he seemed to be in the interior of a house—an old house, apparently—but the details and inhabitants were constantly changing, and he could never be certain of the faces or the furniture, or even of the room itself, since doors and windows seemed in just as great a state of flux as the more presumably mobile objects. It was queer—damnably queer—and my uncle spoke almost sheepishly, as if half expecting not to be believed, when he declared that of the strange faces many had unmistakably borne the features of the Harris family. And all the while there was a personal sensation of choking, as if some pervasive presence had spread itself through his body and sought to possess itself of his vital processes. I shuddered at the thought of those vital processes, worn as they were by eighty-one years of continuous functioning, in conflict with unknown forces of which the youngest and strongest system might well be afraid; but in another moment reflected that dreams are only dreams, and that these uncomfortable visions could be, at most, no more than my uncle's reaction to the investigations and expectations which had lately filled our minds to the exclusion of all else.

Conversation, also, soon tended to dispel my sense of strangeness; and in time I yielded to my yawns and took my turn at slumber. My uncle seemed now very wakeful, and welcomed his period of watching even though the nightmare had aroused him far ahead of his allotted two hours. Sleep seized me quickly, and I was at once haunted with dreams of the most disturbing kind. I felt, in my visions, a cosmic and abysmal loneness; with hostility surging from all sides upon some prison where I lay confined. I seemed bound and gagged, and taunted by the echoing yells of distant multitudes who thirsted for my blood. My uncle's face came to me with less pleasant associations than in waking hours, and I recall many futile struggles and attempts to scream. It was not a pleasant sleep, and for a second I was not sorry for the echoing shriek which clove through the barriers of dream and flung me to a sharp and startled awakeness in which every actual object before my eyes stood out with more than natural clearness and reality.

V.

I had been lying with my face away from my uncle's chair, so that in this sudden flash of awakening I saw only the door to the street, the more northerly window, and the wall and floor and ceiling toward the north of the room, all photographed with morbid vividness on my brain in a light brighter than the glow of the fungi or the rays from the street outside. It was not a strong or even a fairly strong light; certainly not nearly strong enough to read an average book by. But it cast a shadow of myself and the cot on the floor, and had a yellowish, penetrating force that hinted at things more potent than luminosity. This I perceived with unhealthy sharpness despite the fact that two of my other senses were violently assailed. For on my ears rang the reverberations of that shocking scream, while my nostrils revolted at the stench which filled the place. My mind, as alert as my senses, recognised the gravely unusual; and almost automatically I leaped up and turned about to grasp the destructive instruments which we had left trained on the mouldy spot before the fireplace. As I turned, I dreaded what I was to see; for the scream had been in my uncle's voice, and I knew not against what menace I should have to defend him and myself.

Yet after all, the sight was worse than I had dreaded. There are horrors beyond horrors, and this was one of those nuclei of all dreamable hideousness which the cosmos saves to blast an accursed and unhappy few. Out of the fungus-ridden earth steamed up a vaporous corpse-light, yellow and diseased, which bubbled and lapped to a gigantic height in vague outlines half human and half monstrous, through which I could see the chimney and fireplace beyond. It was all eyes—wolfish and mocking—and the rugose insect-like head dissolved at the top to a thin stream of mist which curled putridly about and finally vanished up the chimney. I say that I saw this thing, but it is only in conscious retrospection that I ever definitely traced its damnable approach to form. At the time it was to me only a seething, dimly phosphorescent cloud of fungous loathsomeness, enveloping and dissolving to an abhorrent plasticity the one object on which all my attention was focussed. That object was my uncle—the venerable Elihu Whipple—who with blackening and decaying features leered and gibbered at me, and reached out dripping claws to rend me in the fury which this horror had brought.

It was a sense of routine which kept me from going mad. I had drilled myself in preparation for the crucial moment, and blind training saved me. Recognising the bubbling evil as no substance reachable by matter or material chemistry, and therefore ignoring the flame-thrower which loomed on my left, I threw on the current of the Crookes tube apparatus, and focussed toward that scene of immortal blasphemousness the strongest ether radiations which man's art can arouse from the spaces and fluids of Nature. There was a bluish haze and a frenzied sputtering, and the yellowish phosphorescence grew dimmer to my eyes. But I saw the dimness was only that of contrast, and that the waves from the machine had no effect whatever.

Then, in the midst of that daemoniac spectacle, I saw a fresh horror which brought cries to my lips and sent me fumbling and staggering toward that unlocked door to the quiet street, careless of what abnormal terrors I loosed upon the world, or what thoughts or judgments of men I brought down upon my head. In that dim blend of blue and yellow the form of my uncle had commenced a nauseous liquefaction whose essence eludes all description, and in which there played across his vanishing face such changes of identity as only madness can conceive. He was at once a devil and a multitude, a charnel-house and a pageant. Lit by the mixed and uncertain beams, that gelatinous face assumed a dozen—a score—a hundred—aspects; grinning, as it sank to the ground on a body that melted like tallow, in the caricatured likeness of legions strange and yet not strange.

I saw the features of the Harris line, masculine and feminine, adult and infantile, and other features old and young, coarse and refined, familiar and unfamiliar. For a second there flashed a degraded counterfeit of a miniature of poor mad Rhoby Harris that I had seen in the School of Design Museum, and another time I thought I caught the raw-boned image of Mercy Dexter as I recalled her from a painting in Carrington Harris's house.

It was frightful beyond conception; toward the last, when a curious blend of servant and baby visages flickered close to the fungous floor where a pool of greenish grease was spreading, it seemed as though the shifting features fought against themselves, and strove to form contours like those of my uncle's kindly face. I like to think that he existed at that moment, and that he tried to bid me farewell. It seems to me I hiccoughed a farewell from my own parched throat as I lurched out into the street; a thin stream of grease following me through the door to the rain-drenched sidewalk.

The rest is shadowy and monstrous. There was no one in the soaking street, and in all the world there was no one I dared tell. I walked aimlessly south past College Hill and the Athenaeum, down Hopkins Street, and over the bridge to the business section where tall buildings seemed to guard me as modern material things guard the world from ancient and unwholesome wonder. Then grey dawn unfolded wetly from the east, silhouetting the archaic hill and its venerable steeples, and beckoning me to the place where my terrible work was still unfinished. And in the end I went, wet, hatless, and dazed in the morning light, and entered that awful door in Benefit Street which I had left ajar, and which still swung cryptically in full sight of the early householders to whom I dared not speak.

The grease was gone, for the mouldy floor was porous. And in front of the fireplace was no vestige of the giant doubled-up form traced in nitre. I looked at the cot, the chairs, the instruments, my neglected hat, and the yellowed straw hat of my uncle. Dazedness was uppermost, and I could scarcely recall what was dream and what was reality. Then thought trickled back, and I knew that I had witnessed things more horrible than I had dreamed. Sitting down, I tried to conjecture as nearly as sanity would let me just what had happened, and how I might end the horror, if indeed it had been real. Matter it seemed not to be, nor ether, nor anything else conceivable by mortal mind. What, then, but some exotic *emanation*; some vampirish vapour such as Exeter rustics tell of as lurking over certain churchyards? This I felt was the clue, and again I looked at the floor before the fireplace where the mould and nitre had taken strange forms. In ten minutes my mind was made up, and taking my hat I set out for home, where I bathed, ate, and gave by telephone an order for a pickaxe, a spade, a military gas-mask, and six carboys of sulphuric acid, all to be delivered the next morning at the cellar door of the shunned house in Benefit Street. After that I tried to sleep; and failing, passed the hours in reading and in the composition of inane verses to counteract my mood.

At 11 a.m. the next day I commenced digging. It was sunny weather, and I was glad of that. I was still alone, for as much as I feared the unknown horror I sought, there was more fear in the thought of telling anybody. Later I told Harris only through sheer necessity, and because he had heard odd tales from old people which disposed him ever so little toward belief. As I turned up the stinking black earth in front of the fireplace, my spade causing a viscous yellow ichor to ooze from the white fungi which it severed, I trembled at the dubious thoughts of what I might uncover. Some secrets of inner earth are not good for mankind, and this seemed to me one of them.

My hand shook perceptibly, but still I delved; after a while standing in the large hole I had made. With the deepening of the hole, which was about six feet square, the evil smell increased; and I lost all doubt of my imminent contact with the hellish thing whose emanations had cursed the house for over a century and a half. I wondered what it would look like—what its form and substance would be, and how big it might have waxed through long ages of life-sucking. At length I climbed out of the hole and dispersed the heaped-up dirt, then arranging the great carboys of acid around and near two sides, so that when necessary I might empty them all down the aperture in quick succession. After that I dumped earth only along the other two sides; working more slowly and donning my gas-mask as the smell grew. I was nearly unnerved at my proximity to a nameless thing at the bottom of a pit.

Suddenly my spade struck something softer than earth. I shuddered, and made a motion as if to climb out of the hole, which was now as deep as my neck. Then courage returned, and I scraped away more dirt in the light of the electric torch I had provided. The surface I uncovered was fishy and glassy—a kind of semi-putrid congealed jelly with suggestions of translucency. I scraped further, and saw that it had form. There was a rift where a part of the substance was folded over. The exposed area was huge and roughly cylindrical; like a mammoth soft blue-white stovepipe doubled in two, its largest part some two feet in diameter. Still more I scraped, and then abruptly I leaped out of the hole and away from the filthy thing; frantically unstopping and tilting the heavy carboys, and precipitating their corrosive contents one after another down that charnel gulf and upon the unthinkable abnormality whose titan *elbow* I had seen.

The blinding maelstrom of greenish-yellow vapour which surged tempestuously up from that hole as the floods of acid descended, will never leave my memory. All along the hill people tell of the yellow day, when virulent and horrible fumes arose from the factory waste dumped in the Providence River, but I know how mistaken they are as to the source. They tell, too, of the hideous roar which at the same time came from some disordered water-pipe or gas main underground—but again I could correct them if I dared. It was unspeakably shocking, and I do not see how I lived through it. I did faint after emptying the fourth carboy, which I had to handle after the fumes had begun to penetrate my mask; but when I recovered I saw that the hole was emitting no fresh vapours.

The two remaining carboys I emptied down without particular result, and after a time I felt it safe to shovel the earth back into the pit. It was twilight before I was done, but fear had gone out of the place. The dampness was less foetid, and all the strange fungi had withered to a kind of harmless greyish powder which blew ash-like along the floor. One of earth's nethermost terrors had perished for ever; and if there be a hell, it had received at last the daemon soul of an unhallowed thing. And as I patted down the last spadeful of mould, I shed the first of the many tears with which I have paid unaffected tribute to my beloved uncle's memory.

The next spring no more pale grass and strange weeds came up in the shunned house's terraced garden, and shortly afterward Carrington Harris rented the place. It is still spectral, but its strangeness fascinates me, and I shall find mixed with my relief a queer regret when it is torn down to make way for a tawdry shop or vulgar apartment building. The barren old trees in the yard have begun to bear small, sweet apples, and last year the birds nested in their gnarled boughs.

THE HORROR AT RED HOOK

"There are sacraments of evil as well as of good about us, and we live and move to my belief in an unknown world, a place where there are caves and shadows and dwellers in twilight. It is possible that man may sometimes return on the track of evolution, and it is my belief that an awful lore is not yet dead."

—*Arthur Machen.*

I.

Not many weeks ago, on a street corner in the village of Pascoag, Rhode Island, a tall, heavily built, and wholesome-looking pedestrian furnished much speculation by a singular lapse of behaviour. He had, it appears, been descending the hill by the road from Chepachet; and encountering the compact section, had turned to his left into the main thoroughfare where several modest business blocks convey a touch of the urban. At this point, without visible provocation, he committed his astonishing lapse; staring queerly for a second at the tallest of the buildings before him, and then, with a series of terrified, hysterical shrieks, breaking into a frantic run which ended in a stumble and fall at the next crossing. Picked up and dusted off by ready hands, he was found to be conscious, organically unhurt, and evidently cured of his sudden nervous attack. He muttered some shamefaced explanations involving a strain he had undergone, and with downcast glance turned back up the Chepachet road, trudging out of sight without once looking behind him. It was a strange incident to befall so large, robust, normal-featured, and capable-looking a man, and the strangeness was not lessened by the remarks of a bystander who had recognised him as the boarder of a well-known dairyman on the outskirts of Chepachet.

He was, it developed, a New York police detective named Thomas F. Malone, now on a long leave of absence under medical treatment after some disproportionately arduous work on a gruesome local case which accident had made dramatic. There had been a collapse of several old brick buildings during a raid in which he had shared, and something about the wholesale loss of life, both of prisoners and of his companions, had peculiarly appalled him. As a result, he had acquired an acute and anomalous horror of any buildings even remotely suggesting the ones which had fallen in, so that in the end mental specialists forbade him the sight of such things for an indefinite period. A police surgeon with relatives in Chepachet had put forward that quaint hamlet of wooden colonial houses as an ideal spot for the psychological convalescence; and thither the sufferer had gone, promising never to venture among the brick-lined streets of larger villages till duly advised by the Woonsocket specialist with whom he was put in touch. This walk to Pascoag for magazines had been a mistake, and the patient had paid in fright, bruises, and humiliation for his disobedience.

So much the gossips of Chepachet and Pascoag knew; and so much, also, the most learned specialists believed. But Malone had at first told the specialists much more, ceasing only when he saw that utter incredulity was his portion. Thereafter he held his peace, protesting not at all when it was generally agreed that the collapse of certain squalid brick houses in the Red Hook section of Brooklyn, and the consequent death of many brave officers, had unseated his nervous equilibrium. He had worked too hard, all said, in trying to clean up those nests of disorder and violence; certain features were shocking enough, in all conscience, and the unexpected tragedy was the last straw. This was a simple explanation which everyone could understand, and because Malone was not a simple person he perceived that he had better let it suffice. To hint to unimaginative people of a horror beyond all human conception—a horror of houses and blocks and cities leprous and cancerous with evil dragged from elder worlds—would be merely to invite a padded cell instead of a restful rustication, and Malone was a man of sense despite his mysticism. He had the Celt's far vision of weird and hidden things, but the logician's quick eye for the outwardly unconvincing; an amalgam which had led him far afield in the forty-two years of his life, and set him in strange places for a Dublin University man born in a Georgian villa near Phoenix Park.

And now, as he reviewed the things he had seen and felt and apprehended, Malone was content to keep unshared the secret of what could reduce a dauntless fighter to a quivering neurotic; what could make old brick slums and seas of dark, subtle faces a thing of nightmare and eldritch portent. It would not be the first time his sensations had been forced to bide uninterpreted—for was not his very act of plunging into the polyglot abyss of New York's underworld a freak beyond sensible explanation? What could he tell the prosaic of the antique witcheries and grotesque marvels discernible to sensitive eyes amidst the poison cauldron where all the varied dregs of unwholesome ages mix their venom and perpetuate their obscene terrors? He had seen the hellish green flame of secret wonder in this blatant, evasive welter of outward greed and inward blasphemy, and had smiled gently when all the New-Yorkers he knew scoffed at his experiment in police work. They had been very witty and cynical, deriding his fantastic pursuit of unknowable mysteries and assuring him that in these days New York held nothing but cheapness and vulgarity. One of them had wagered him a heavy sum that he could not—despite many poignant things to his credit in the *Dublin Review*—even write a truly interesting story of New York low life; and now, looking back, he perceived that cosmic irony had justified the prophet's words while secretly confuting their flippant meaning. The horror, as glimpsed at last, could not make a story—for like the book cited by Poe's German authority, "*er lasst sich nicht lesen*—it does not permit itself to be read."

II.

To Malone the sense of latent mystery in existence was always present. In youth he had felt the hidden beauty and ecstasy of things, and had been a poet; but poverty and sorrow and exile had turned his gaze in darker directions, and he had thrilled at the imputations of evil in the world around. Daily life had for him come to be a phantasmagoria of macabre shadow-studies; now glittering and leering with concealed rottenness as in Beardsley's best manner, now hinting terrors behind the commonest shapes and objects as in the subtler and less obvious work of Gustave Doré. He would often regard it as merciful that most persons of high intelligence jeer at the inmost mysteries; for, he argued, if superior minds were ever placed in fullest contact with the secrets preserved by ancient and lowly cults, the resultant abnormalities would soon not only wreck the world, but threaten the very integrity of the universe. All this reflection was no doubt morbid, but keen logic and a deep sense of humour ably offset it. Malone was satisfied to let his notions remain as half-spied and forbidden visions to be lightly played with; and hysteria came only when duty flung him into a hell of revelation too sudden and insidious to escape.

He had for some time been detailed to the Butler Street station in Brooklyn when the Red Hook matter came to his notice. Red Hook is a maze of hybrid squalor near the ancient waterfront opposite Governor's Island, with dirty highways climbing the hill from the wharves to that higher ground where the decayed lengths of Clinton and Court Streets lead off toward the Borough Hall. Its houses are mostly of brick, dating from the first quarter to the middle of the nineteenth century, and some of the obscurer alleys and byways have that alluring antique flavour which conventional reading leads us to call "Dickensian". The population is a hopeless tangle and enigma; Syrian, Spanish, Italian, and negro elements impinging upon one another, and fragments of Scandinavian and American belts lying not far distant. It is a babel of sound and filth, and sends out strange cries to answer the lapping of oily waves at its grimy piers and the monstrous organ litanies of the harbour whistles. Here long ago a brighter picture dwelt, with clear-eyed mariners on the lower streets and homes of taste and substance where the larger houses line the hill. One can trace the relics of this former happiness in the trim shapes of the buildings, the occasional graceful churches, and the evidences of original art and background in bits of detail here and there—a worn flight of steps, a battered doorway, a wormy pair of decorative columns or pilasters, or a fragment of once green space with bent and rusted iron railing. The houses are generally in solid blocks, and now and then a many-windowed cupola arises to tell of days when the households of captains and ship-owners watched the sea.

From this tangle of material and spiritual putrescence the blasphemies of a hundred dialects assail the sky. Hordes of prowlers reel shouting and singing along the lanes and thoroughfares, occasional furtive hands suddenly extinguish lights and pull down curtains, and swarthy, sin-pitted faces disappear from windows when visitors pick their way through. Policemen despair of order or reform, and seek rather to erect barriers protecting the outside world from the contagion. The clang of the patrol is answered by a kind of spectral silence, and such prisoners as are taken are never communicative. Visible offences are as varied as the local dialects, and run the gamut from the smuggling of rum and prohibited aliens through diverse stages of lawlessness and obscure vice to murder and mutilation in their most abhorrent guises. That these visible affairs are not more frequent is not to the neighbourhood's credit, unless the power of concealment be an art demanding credit. More people enter Red Hook than leave it—or at least, than leave it by the landward side—and those who are not loquacious are the likeliest to leave.

Malone found in this state of things a faint stench of secrets more terrible than any of the sins denounced by citizens and bemoaned by priests and philanthropists. He was conscious, as one who united imagination with scientific knowledge, that modern people under lawless conditions tend uncannily to repeat the darkest instinctive patterns of primitive half-ape savagery in their daily life and ritual observances; and he had often viewed with an anthropologist's shudder the chanting, cursing processions of blear-eyed and pockmarked young men which wound their way along in the dark small hours of morning. One saw groups of these youths incessantly; sometimes in leering vigils on street corners, sometimes in doorways playing eerily on cheap instruments of music, sometimes in stupefied dozes or indecent dialogues around cafeteria tables near Borough Hall, and sometimes in whispering converse around dingy taxicabs drawn up at the high stoops of crumbling and closely shuttered old houses. They chilled and fascinated him more than he dared confess to his associates on the force, for he seemed to see in them some monstrous thread of secret continuity; some fiendish, cryptical, and ancient pattern utterly beyond and below the sordid mass of facts and habits and haunts listed with such conscientious technical care by the police. They must be, he felt inwardly, the heirs of some shocking and primordial tradition; the sharers of debased and broken scraps from cults and ceremonies older than mankind. Their coherence and definiteness suggested it, and it shewed in the singular suspicion of order which lurked beneath their squalid disorder. He had not read in vain such treatises as Miss Murray's "Witch-Cult in Western Europe"; and knew that up to recent years there had certainly survived among peasants and furtive folk a frightful and clandestine system of assemblies and orgies descended from dark religions antedating the Aryan world, and appearing in popular legends as Black Masses and Witches' Sabbaths. That these hellish vestiges of old Turanian-Asiatic magic and fertility-cults were even now wholly dead he could not for a moment suppose, and he frequently wondered how much older and how much blacker than the very worst of the muttered tales some of them might really be.

III.

It was the case of Robert Suydam which took Malone to the heart of things in Red Hook. Suydam was a lettered recluse of ancient Dutch family, possessed originally of barely independent means, and inhabiting the spacious but ill-preserved mansion which his grandfather had built in Flatbush when that village was little more than a pleasant group of colonial cottages surrounding the steepled and ivy-clad Reformed Church with its iron-railed yard of Netherlandish gravestones. In his lonely house, set back from Martense Street amidst a yard of venerable trees, Suydam had read and brooded for some six decades except for a period a generation before, when he had sailed for the Old World and remained there out of sight for eight years. He could afford no servants, and would admit but few visitors to his absolute solitude; eschewing close friendships and receiving his rare acquaintances in one of the three ground-floor rooms which he kept in order—a vast, high-ceiled library whose walls were solidly packed with tattered books of ponderous, archaic, and vaguely repellent aspect. The growth of the town and its final absorption in the Brooklyn district had meant nothing to Suydam, and he had come to mean less and less to the town. Elderly people still pointed him out on the streets, but to most of the recent population he was merely a queer, corpulent old fellow whose unkempt white hair, stubbly beard, shiny black clothes, and gold-headed cane earned him an amused glance and nothing more. Malone did not know him by sight till duty called him to the case, but had heard of him indirectly as a really profound authority on mediaeval superstition, and had once idly meant to look up an out-of-print pamphlet of his on the Kabbalah and the Faustus legend, which a friend had quoted from memory.

Suydam became a "case" when his distant and only relatives sought court pronouncements on his sanity. Their action seemed sudden to the outside world, but was really undertaken only after prolonged observation and sorrowful debate. It was based on certain odd changes in his speech and habits; wild references to impending wonders, and unaccountable hauntings of disreputable Brooklyn neighbourhoods. He had been growing shabbier and shabbier with the years, and now prowled about like a veritable mendicant; seen occasionally by humiliated friends in subway stations, or loitering on the benches around Borough Hall in conversation with groups of swarthy, evil-looking strangers. When he spoke it was to babble of unlimited powers almost within his grasp, and to repeat with knowing leers such mystical words or names as "Sephiroth", "Ashmodai", and "Samaël". The court action revealed that he was using up his income and wasting his principal in the purchase of curious tomes imported from London and Paris, and in the maintenance of a squalid basement flat in the Red Hook district where he spent nearly every night, receiving odd delegations of mixed rowdies and foreigners, and apparently conducting some kind of ceremonial service behind the green blinds of secretive windows. Detectives assigned to follow him reported strange cries and chants and prancing of feet filtering out from these nocturnal rites, and shuddered at their peculiar ecstasy and abandon despite the commonness of weird orgies in that sodden section. When, however, the matter came to a hearing, Suydam managed to preserve his liberty. Before the judge his manner grew urbane and reasonable, and he freely admitted the queerness of demeanour and extravagant cast of language into which he had fallen through excessive devotion to study and research. He was, he said, engaged in the investigation of certain details of European tradition which required the closest contact with foreign groups and their songs and folk dances. The notion that any low secret society was preying upon him, as hinted by his relatives, was obviously absurd; and shewed how sadly limited was their understanding of him and his work. Triumphing with his calm explanations, he was suffered to depart unhindered; and the paid detectives of the Suydams, Corlears, and Van Brunts were withdrawn in resigned disgust.

It was here that an alliance of Federal inspectors and police, Malone with them, entered the case. The law had watched the Suydam action with interest, and had in many instances been called upon to aid the private detectives. In this work it developed that Suydam's new associates were among the blackest and most vicious criminals of Red Hook's devious lanes, and that at least a third of them were known and repeated offenders in the matter of thievery, disorder, and the importation of illegal immigrants. Indeed, it would not have been too much to say that the old scholar's particular circle coincided almost perfectly with the worst of the organised cliques which smuggled ashore certain nameless and unclassified Asian dregs wisely turned back by Ellis Island. In the teeming rookeries of Parker Place—since renamed—where Suydam had his basement flat, there had grown up a very unusual colony of unclassified slant-eyed folk who used the Arabic alphabet but were eloquently repudiated by the great mass of Syrians in and around Atlantic Avenue. They could all have been deported for lack of credentials, but legalism is slow-moving, and one does not disturb Red Hook unless publicity forces one to.

These creatures attended a tumbledown stone church, used Wednesdays as a dance-hall, which reared its Gothic buttresses near the vilest part of the waterfront. It was nominally Catholic; but priests throughout Brooklyn denied the place all standing and authenticity, and policemen agreed with them when they listened to the noises it emitted at night. Malone used to fancy he heard terrible cracked bass notes from a hidden organ far underground when the church stood empty and unlighted, whilst all observers dreaded the shrieking and drumming which accompanied the visible services. Suydam, when questioned, said he thought the ritual was some remnant of Nestorian Christianity tinctured with the Shamanism of Thibet. Most of the people, he conjectured, were of Mongoloid stock, originating somewhere in or near Kurdistan—and Malone could not help recalling that Kurdistan is the land of the Yezidis, last survivors of the Persian devil-worshippers. However this may have been, the stir of the Suydam investigation made it certain that these unauthorised newcomers were flooding Red Hook in increasing numbers; entering through some marine conspiracy unreached by revenue officers and harbour police, overrunning Parker Place and rapidly spreading up the hill, and welcomed with curious fraternalism by the other assorted denizens of the region. Their squat figures and characteristic squinting physiognomies, grotesquely combined with flashy American clothing, appeared more and more numerously among the loafers and nomad gangsters of the Borough Hall section; till at length it was deemed necessary to compute their numbers, ascertain their sources and occupations, and find if possible a way to round them up and deliver them to the proper immigration authorities. To this task Malone was assigned by agreement of Federal and city forces, and as he commenced his canvass of Red Hook he felt poised upon the brink of nameless terrors, with the shabby, unkempt figure of Robert Suydam as arch-fiend and adversary.

IV.

Police methods are varied and ingenious. Malone, through unostentatious rambles, carefully casual conversations, well-timed offers of hip-pocket liquor, and judicious dialogues with frightened prisoners, learned many isolated facts about the movement whose aspect had become so menacing. The newcomers were indeed Kurds, but of a dialect obscure and puzzling to exact philology. Such of them as worked lived mostly as dock-hands and unlicenced pedlars, though frequently serving in Greek restaurants and tending corner news stands. Most of them, however, had no visible means of support; and were obviously connected with underworld pursuits, of which smuggling and "bootlegging" were the least indescribable. They had come in steamships, apparently tramp freighters, and had been unloaded by stealth on moonless nights in rowboats which stole under a certain wharf and followed a hidden canal to a secret subterranean pool beneath a house. This wharf, canal, and house Malone could not locate, for the memories of his informants were exceedingly confused, while their speech was to a great extent beyond even the ablest interpreters; nor could he gain any real data on the reasons for their systematic importation. They were reticent about the exact spot from which they had come, and were never sufficiently off guard to reveal the agencies which had sought them out and directed their course. Indeed, they developed something like acute fright when asked the reasons for their presence. Gangsters of other breeds were equally taciturn, and the most that could be gathered was that some god or great priesthood had promised them unheard-of powers and supernatural glories and rulerships in a strange land.

The attendance of both newcomers and old gangsters at Suydam's closely guarded nocturnal meetings was very regular, and the police soon learned that the erstwhile recluse had leased additional flats to accommodate such guests as knew his password; at last occupying three entire houses and permanently harbouring many of his queer companions. He spent but little time now at his Flatbush home, apparently going and coming only to obtain and return books; and his face and manner had attained an appalling pitch of wildness. Malone twice interviewed him, but was each time brusquely repulsed. He knew nothing, he said, of any mysterious plots or movements; and had no idea how the Kurds could have entered or what they wanted. His business was to study undisturbed the folklore of all the immigrants of the district; a business with which policemen had no legitimate concern. Malone mentioned his admiration for Suydam's old brochure on the Kabbalah and other myths, but the old man's softening was only momentary. He sensed an intrusion, and rebuffed his visitor in no uncertain way; till Malone withdrew disgusted, and turned to other channels of information.

What Malone would have unearthed could he have worked continuously on the case, we shall never know. As it was, a stupid conflict between city and Federal authority suspended the investigations for several months, during which the detective was busy with other assignments. But at no time did he lose interest, or fail to stand amazed at what began to happen to Robert Suydam. Just at the time when a wave of kidnappings and disappearances spread its excitement over New York, the unkempt scholar embarked upon a metamorphosis as startling as it was absurd. One day he was seen near Borough Hall with clean-shaved face, well-trimmed hair, and tastefully immaculate attire, and on every day thereafter some obscure improvement was noticed in him. He maintained his new fastidiousness without interruption, added to it an unwonted sparkle of eye and crispness of speech, and began little by little to shed the corpulence which had so long deformed him. Now frequently taken for less than his age, he acquired an elasticity of step and buoyancy of demeanour to match the new tradition, and shewed a curious darkening of the hair which somehow did not suggest dye. As the months passed, he commenced to dress less and less conservatively, and finally astonished his few friends by renovating and redecorating his Flatbush mansion, which he threw open in a series of receptions, summoning all the acquaintances he could remember, and extending a special welcome to the fully forgiven relatives who had so lately sought his restraint. Some attended through curiosity, others through duty; but all were suddenly charmed by the dawning grace and urbanity of the former hermit. He had, he asserted, accomplished most of his allotted work; and having just inherited some property from a half-forgotten European friend, was about to spend his remaining years in a brighter second youth which ease, care, and diet had made possible to him. Less and less was he seen at Red Hook, and more and more did he move in the society to which he was born. Policemen noted a tendency of the gangsters to congregate at the old stone church and dance-hall instead of at the basement flat in Parker Place, though the latter and its recent annexes still overflowed with noxious life.

Then two incidents occurred—wide enough apart, but both of intense interest in the case as Malone envisaged it. One was a quiet announcement in the *Eagle* of Robert Suydam's engagement to Miss Cornelia Gerritsen of Bayside, a young woman of excellent position, and distantly related to the elderly bridegroom-elect; whilst the other was a raid on the dance-hall church by city police, after a report that the face of a kidnapped child had been seen for a second at one of the basement windows. Malone had participated in this raid, and studied the place with much care when inside. Nothing was found—in fact, the building was entirely deserted when visited—but the sensitive Celt was vaguely disturbed by many things about the interior. There were crudely painted panels he did not like—panels which depicted sacred faces with peculiarly worldly and sardonic expressions, and which occasionally took liberties that even a layman's sense of decorum could scarcely countenance. Then, too, he did not relish the Greek inscription on the wall above the pulpit; an ancient incantation which he had once stumbled upon in Dublin college days, and which read, literally translated,

> "O friend and companion of night, thou who rejoicest in the baying of dogs and spilt blood, who wanderest in the midst of shades among the tombs, who longest for blood and bringest terror to mortals, Gorgo, Mormo, thousand-faced moon, look favourably on our sacrifices!"

When he read this he shuddered, and thought vaguely of the cracked bass organ notes he fancied he had heard beneath the church on certain nights. He shuddered again at the rust around the rim of a metal basin which stood on the altar, and paused nervously when his nostrils seemed to detect a curious and ghastly stench from somewhere in the neighbourhood. That organ memory haunted him, and he explored the basement with particular assiduity before he left. The place was very hateful to him; yet after all, were the blasphemous panels and inscriptions more than mere crudities perpetrated by the ignorant?

By the time of Suydam's wedding the kidnapping epidemic had become a popular newspaper scandal. Most of the victims were young children of the lowest classes, but the increasing number of disappearances had worked up a sentiment of the strongest fury. Journals clamoured for action from the police, and once more the Butler Street station sent its men over Red Hook for clues, discoveries, and criminals. Malone was glad to be on the trail again, and took pride in a raid on one of Suydam's Parker Place houses. There, indeed, no stolen child was found, despite the tales of screams and the red sash picked up in the areaway; but the paintings and rough inscriptions on the peeling walls of most of the rooms, and the primitive chemical laboratory in the attic, all helped to convince the detective that he was on the track of something tremendous. The paintings were appalling—hideous monsters of every shape and size, and parodies on human outlines which cannot be described. The writing was in red, and varied from Arabic to Greek, Roman, and Hebrew letters. Malone could not read much of it, but what he did decipher was portentous and cabbalistic enough. One frequently repeated motto was in a sort of Hebraised Hellenistic Greek, and suggested the most terrible daemon-evocations of the Alexandrian decadence:

> "HEL . HELOYM . SOTHER . EMMANVEL . SABAOTH . AGLA . TETRAGRAMMATON . AGYROS . OTHEOS . ISCHYROS . ATHANATOS . IEHOVA . VA . ADONAI . SADAY . HOMOVSION . MESSIAS . ESCHEREHEYE."

Circles and pentagrams loomed on every hand, and told indubitably of the strange beliefs and aspirations of those who dwelt so squalidly here. In the cellar, however, the strangest thing was found—a pile of genuine gold ingots covered carelessly with a piece of burlap, and bearing upon their shining surfaces the same weird hieroglyphics which also adorned the walls. During this raid the police encountered only a passive resistance from the squinting Orientals that swarmed from every door. Finding nothing relevant, they had to leave all as it was; but the precinct captain wrote Suydam a note advising him to look closely to the character of his tenants and protégés in view of the growing public clamour.

V.

Then came the June wedding and the great sensation. Flatbush was gay for the hour about high noon, and pennanted motors thronged the streets near the old Dutch church where an awning stretched from door to highway. No local event ever surpassed the Suydam-Gerritsen nuptials in tone and scale, and the party which escorted bride and groom to the Cunard Pier was, if not exactly the smartest, at least a solid page from the Social Register. At five o'clock adieux were waved, and the ponderous liner edged away from the long pier, slowly turned its nose seaward, discarded its tug, and headed for the widening water spaces that led to Old World wonders. By night the outer harbour was cleared, and late passengers watched the stars twinkling above an unpolluted ocean.

Whether the tramp steamer or the scream was first to gain attention, no one can say. Probably they were simultaneous, but it is of no use to calculate. The scream came from the Suydam stateroom, and the sailor who broke down the door could perhaps have told frightful things if he had not forthwith gone completely mad—as it is, he shrieked more loudly than the first victims, and thereafter ran simpering about the vessel till caught and put in irons. The ship's doctor who entered the stateroom and turned on the lights a moment later did not go mad, but told nobody what he saw till afterward, when he corresponded with Malone in Chepachet. It was murder—strangulation—but one need not say that the claw-mark on Mrs. Suydam's throat could not have come from her husband's or any other human hand, or that upon the white wall there flickered for an instant in hateful red a legend which, later copied from memory, seems to have been nothing less than the fearsome Chaldee letters of the word "LILITH". One need not mention these things because they vanished so quickly—as for Suydam, one could at least bar others from the room until one knew what to think oneself. The doctor has distinctly assured Malone that he did not see *IT*. The open porthole, just before he turned on the lights, was clouded for a second with a certain phosphorescence, and for a moment there seemed to echo in the night outside the suggestion of a faint and hellish tittering; but no real outline met the eye. As proof, the doctor points to his continued sanity.

Then the tramp steamer claimed all attention. A boat put off, and a horde of swart, insolent ruffians in officers' dress swarmed aboard the temporarily halted Cunarder. They wanted Suydam or his body—they had known of his trip, and for certain reasons were sure he would die. The captain's deck was almost a pandemonium; for at the instant, between the doctor's report from the stateroom and the demands of the men from the tramp, not even the wisest and gravest seaman could think what to do. Suddenly the leader of the visiting mariners, an Arab with a hatefully negroid mouth, pulled forth a dirty, crumpled paper and handed it to the captain. It was signed by Robert Suydam, and bore the following odd message:

> "In case of sudden or unexplained accident or death on my part, please deliver me or my body unquestioningly into the hands of the bearer and his associates. Everything, for me, and perhaps for you, depends on absolute compliance. Explanations can come later—do not fail me now.
>
> ROBERT SUYDAM."

Captain and doctor looked at each other, and the latter whispered something to the former. Finally they nodded rather helplessly and led the way to the Suydam stateroom. The doctor directed the captain's glance away as he unlocked the door and admitted the strange seamen, nor did he breathe easily till they filed out with their burden after an unaccountably long period of preparation. It was wrapped in bedding from the berths, and the doctor was glad that the outlines were not very revealing. Somehow the men got the thing over the side and away to their tramp steamer without uncovering it. The Cunarder started again, and the doctor and a ship's undertaker sought out the Suydam stateroom to perform what last services they could. Once more the physician was forced to reticence and even to mendacity, for a hellish thing had happened. When the undertaker asked him why he had drained off all of Mrs. Suydam's blood, he neglected to affirm that he had not done so; nor did he point to the vacant bottle-spaces on the rack, or to the odour in the sink which shewed the hasty disposition of the bottles' original contents. The pockets of those men—if men they were—had bulged damnably when they left the ship. Two hours later, and the world knew by radio all that it ought to know of the horrible affair.

VI.

That same June evening, without having heard a word from the sea, Malone was desperately busy among the alleys of Red Hook. A sudden stir seemed to permeate the place, and as if apprised by "grapevine telegraph" of something singular, the denizens clustered expectantly around the dance-hall church and the houses in Parker Place. Three children had just disappeared—blue-eyed Norwegians from the streets toward Gowanus—and there were rumours of a mob forming among the sturdy Vikings of that section. Malone had for weeks been urging his colleagues to attempt a general cleanup; and at last, moved by conditions more obvious to their common sense than the conjectures of a Dublin dreamer, they had agreed upon a final stroke. The unrest and menace of this evening had been the deciding factor, and just about midnight a raiding party recruited from three stations descended upon Parker Place and its environs. Doors were battered in, stragglers arrested, and candle-lighted rooms forced to disgorge unbelievable throngs of mixed foreigners in figured robes, mitres, and other inexplicable devices. Much was lost in the melee, for objects were thrown hastily down unexpected shafts, and betraying odours deadened by the sudden kindling of pungent incense. But spattered blood was everywhere, and Malone shuddered whenever he saw a brazier or altar from which the smoke was still rising.

He wanted to be in several places at once, and decided on Suydam's basement flat only after a messenger had reported the complete emptiness of the dilapidated dance-hall church. The flat, he thought, must hold some clue to a cult of which the occult scholar had so obviously become the centre and leader; and it was with real expectancy that he ransacked the musty rooms, noted their vaguely charnel odour, and examined the curious books, instruments, gold ingots, and glass-stoppered bottles scattered carelessly here and there. Once a lean, black-and-white cat edged between his feet and tripped him, overturning at the same time a beaker half full of a red liquid. The shock was severe, and to this day Malone is not certain of what he saw; but in dreams he still pictures that cat as it scuttled away with certain monstrous alterations and peculiarities. Then came the locked cellar door, and the search for something to break it down. A heavy stool stood near, and its tough seat was more than enough for the antique panels. A crack formed and enlarged, and the whole door gave way—but from the *other* side; whence poured a howling tumult of ice-cold wind with all the stenches of the bottomless pit, and whence reached a sucking force not of earth or heaven, which, coiling sentiently about the paralysed detective, dragged him through the aperture and down unmeasured spaces filled with whispers and wails, and gusts of mocking laughter.

Of course it was a dream. All the specialists have told him so, and he has nothing tangible to prove the contrary. Indeed, he would rather have it thus; for then the sight of old brick slums and dark foreign faces would not eat so deeply into his soul. But at the time it was all horribly real, and nothing can ever efface the memory of those nighted crypts, those titan arcades, and those half-formed shapes of hell that strode gigantically in silence holding half-eaten things whose still surviving portions screamed for mercy or laughed with madness. Odours of incense and corruption joined in sickening concert, and the black air was alive with the cloudy, semi-visible bulk of shapeless elemental things with eyes. Somewhere dark sticky water was lapping at onyx piers, and once the shivery tinkle of raucous little bells pealed out to greet the insane titter of a naked phosphorescent thing which swam into sight, scrambled ashore, and climbed up to squat leeringly on a carved golden pedestal in the background.

Avenues of limitless night seemed to radiate in every direction, till one might fancy that here lay the root of a contagion destined to sicken and swallow cities, and engulf nations in the foetor of hybrid pestilence. Here cosmic sin had entered, and festered by unhallowed rites had commenced the grinning march of death that was to rot us all to fungous abnormalities too hideous for the grave's holding. Satan here held his Babylonish court, and in the blood of stainless childhood the leprous limbs of phosphorescent Lilith were laved. Incubi and succubae howled praise to Hecate, and headless moon-calves bleated to the Magna Mater. Goats leaped to the sound of thin accursed flutes, and Ægipans chased endlessly after misshapen fauns over rocks twisted like swollen toads. Moloch and Ashtaroth were not absent; for in this quintessence of all damnation the bounds of consciousness were let down, and man's fancy lay open to vistas of every realm of horror and every forbidden dimension that evil had power to mould. The world and Nature were helpless against such assaults from unsealed wells of night, nor could any sign or prayer check the Walpurgis-riot of horror which had come when a sage with the hateful key had stumbled on a horde with the locked and brimming coffer of transmitted daemon-lore.

Suddenly a ray of physical light shot through these phantasms, and Malone heard the sound of oars amidst the blasphemies of things that should be dead. A boat with a lantern in its prow darted into sight, made fast to an iron ring in the slimy stone pier, and vomited forth several dark men bearing a long burden swathed in bedding. They took it to the naked phosphorescent thing on the carved golden pedestal, and the thing tittered and pawed at the bedding. Then they unswathed it, and propped upright before the pedestal the gangrenous corpse of a corpulent old man with stubbly beard and unkempt white hair. The phosphorescent thing tittered again, and the men produced bottles from their pockets and anointed its feet with red, whilst they afterward gave the bottles to the thing to drink from.

All at once, from an arcaded avenue leading endlessly away, there came the daemoniac rattle and wheeze of a blasphemous organ, choking and rumbling out the mockeries of hell in a cracked, sardonic bass. In an instant every moving entity was electrified; and forming at once into a ceremonial procession, the nightmare horde slithered away in quest of the sound—goat, satyr, and Ægipan, incubus, succuba, and lemur, twisted toad and shapeless elemental, dog-faced howler and silent strutter in darkness—all led by the abominable naked phosphorescent thing that had squatted on the carved golden throne, and that now strode insolently bearing in its arms the glassy-eyed corpse of the corpulent old man. The strange dark men danced in the rear, and the whole column skipped and leaped with Dionysiac fury. Malone staggered after them a few steps, delirious and hazy, and doubtful of his place in this or any world. Then he turned, faltered, and sank down on the cold damp stone, gasping and shivering as the daemon organ croaked on, and the howling and drumming and tinkling of the mad procession grew fainter and fainter.

Vaguely he was conscious of chanted horrors and shocking croakings afar off. Now and then a wail or whine of ceremonial devotion would float to him through the black arcade, whilst eventually there rose the dreadful Greek incantation whose text he had read above the pulpit of that dance-hall church.

"O friend and companion of night, thou who rejoicest in the baying of dogs (*here a hideous howl burst forth*) and spilt blood (*here nameless sounds vied with morbid shriekings*), who wanderest in the midst of shades among the tombs (*here a whistling sigh occurred*), who longest for blood and bringest terror to mortals (*short, sharp cries from myriad throats*), Gorgo (*repeated as response*), Mormo (*repeated with ecstasy*), thousand-faced moon (*sighs and flute notes*), look favourably on our sacrifices!"

As the chant closed, a general shout went up, and hissing sounds nearly drowned the croaking of the cracked bass organ. Then a gasp as from many throats, and a babel of barked and bleated words—"Lilith, Great Lilith, behold the Bridegroom!" More cries, a clamour of rioting, and the sharp, clicking footfalls of a running figure. The footfalls approached, and Malone raised himself to his elbow to look.

The luminosity of the crypt, lately diminished, had now slightly increased; and in that devil-light there appeared the fleeing form of that which should not flee or feel or breathe—the glassy-eyed, gangrenous corpse of the corpulent old man, now needing no support, but animated by some infernal sorcery of the rite just closed. After it raced the naked, tittering, phosphorescent thing that belonged on the carven pedestal, and still farther behind panted the dark men, and all the dread crew of sentient loathsomenesses. The corpse was gaining on its pursuers, and seemed bent on a definite object, straining with every rotting muscle toward the carved golden pedestal, whose necromantic importance was evidently so great. Another moment and it had reached its goal, whilst the trailing throng laboured on with more frantic speed. But they were too late, for in one final spurt of strength which ripped tendon from tendon and sent its noisome bulk floundering to the floor in a state of jellyish dissolution, the staring corpse which had been Robert Suydam achieved its object and its triumph. The push had been tremendous, but the force had held out; and as the pusher collapsed to a muddy blotch of corruption the pedestal he had pushed tottered, tipped, and finally careened from its onyx base into the thick waters below, sending up a parting gleam of carven gold as it sank heavily to undreamable gulfs of lower Tartarus. In that instant, too, the whole scene of horror faded to nothingness before Malone's eyes; and he fainted amidst a thunderous crash which seemed to blot out all the evil universe.

VII.

Malone's dream, experienced in full before he knew of Suydam's death and transfer at sea, was curiously supplemented by some odd realities of the case; though that is no reason why anyone should believe it. The three old houses in Parker Place, doubtless long rotten with decay in its most insidious form, collapsed without visible cause while half the raiders and most of the prisoners were inside; and of both the greater number were instantly killed. Only in the basements and cellars was there much saving of life, and Malone was lucky to have been deep below the house of Robert Suydam. For he really was there, as no one is disposed to deny. They found him unconscious by the edge of a night-black pool, with a grotesquely horrible jumble of decay and bone, identifiable through dental work as the body of Suydam, a few feet away. The case was plain, for it was hither that the smugglers' underground canal led; and the men who took Suydam from the ship had brought him home. They themselves were never found, or at least never identified; and the ship's doctor is not yet satisfied with the simple certitudes of the police.

Suydam was evidently a leader in extensive man-smuggling operations, for the canal to his house was but one of several subterranean channels and tunnels in the neighbourhood. There was a tunnel from this house to a crypt beneath the dance-hall church; a crypt accessible from the church only through a narrow secret passage in the north wall, and in whose chambers some singular and terrible things were discovered. The croaking organ was there, as well as a vast arched chapel with wooden benches and a strangely figured altar. The walls were lined with small cells, in seventeen of which—hideous to relate—solitary prisoners in a state of complete idiocy were found chained, including four mothers with infants of disturbingly strange appearance. These infants died soon after exposure to the light; a circumstance which the doctors thought rather merciful. Nobody but Malone, among those who inspected them, remembered the sombre question of old Delrio: "*An sint unquam daemones incubi et succubae, et an ex tali congressu proles nasci queat?*"

Before the canals were filled up they were thoroughly dredged, and yielded forth a sensational array of sawed and split bones of all sizes. The kidnapping epidemic, very clearly, had been traced home; though only two of the surviving prisoners could by any legal thread be connected with it. These men are now in prison, since they failed of conviction as accessories in the actual murders. The carved golden pedestal or throne so often mentioned by Malone as of primary occult importance was never brought to light, though at one place under the Suydam house the canal was observed to sink into a well too deep for dredging. It was choked up at the mouth and cemented over when the cellars of the new houses were made, but Malone often speculates on what lies beneath. The police, satisfied that they had shattered a dangerous gang of maniacs and man-smugglers, turned over to the Federal authorities the unconvicted Kurds, who before their deportation were conclusively found to belong to the Yezidi clan of devil-worshippers. The tramp ship and its crew remain an elusive mystery, though cynical detectives are once more ready to combat its smuggling and rum-running ventures. Malone thinks these detectives shew a sadly limited perspective in their lack of wonder at the myriad unexplainable details, and the suggestive obscurity of the whole case; though he is just as critical of the newspapers, which saw only a morbid sensation and gloated over a minor sadist cult when they might have proclaimed a horror from the universe's very heart. But he is content to rest silent in Chepachet, calming his nervous system and praying that time may gradually transfer his terrible experience from the realm of present reality to that of picturesque and semi-mythical remoteness.

Robert Suydam sleeps beside his bride in Greenwood Cemetery. No funeral was held over the strangely released bones, and relatives are grateful for the swift oblivion which overtook the case as a whole. The scholar's connexion with the Red Hook horrors, indeed, was never emblazoned by legal proof; since his death forestalled the inquiry he would otherwise have faced. His own end is not much mentioned, and the Suydams hope that posterity may recall him only as a gentle recluse who dabbled in harmless magic and folklore.

As for Red Hook—it is always the same. Suydam came and went; a terror gathered and faded; but the evil spirit of darkness and squalor broods on amongst the mongrels in the old brick houses, and prowling bands still parade on unknown errands past windows where lights and twisted faces unaccountably appear and disappear. Age-old horror is a hydra with a thousand heads, and the cults of darkness are rooted in blasphemies deeper than the well of Democritus. The soul of the beast is omnipresent and triumphant, and Red Hook's legions of blear-eyed, pockmarked youths still chant and curse and howl as they file from abyss to abyss, none knows whence or whither, pushed on by blind laws of biology which they may never understand. As of old, more people enter Red Hook than leave it on the landward side, and there are already rumours of new canals running underground to certain centres of traffic in liquor and less mentionable things.

The dance-hall church is now mostly a dance hall, and queer faces have appeared at night at the windows. Lately a policeman expressed the belief that the filled-up crypt has been dug out again, and for no simply explainable purpose. Who are we to combat poisons older than history and mankind? Apes danced in Asia to those horrors, and the cancer lurks secure and spreading where furtiveness hides in rows of decaying brick.

Malone does not shudder without cause—for only the other day an officer overheard a swarthy squinting hag teaching a small child some whispered patois in the shadow of an areaway. He listened, and thought it very strange when he heard her repeat over and over again,

> "O friend and companion of night, thou who rejoicest in the baying of dogs and spilt blood, who wanderest in the midst of shades among the tombs, who longest for blood and bringest terror to mortals, Gorgo, Mormo, thousand-faced moon, look favourably on our sacrifices!"

HE

I saw him on a sleepless night when I was walking desperately to save my soul and my vision. My coming to New York had been a mistake; for whereas I had looked for poignant wonder and inspiration in the teeming labyrinths of ancient streets that twist endlessly from forgotten courts and squares and waterfronts to courts and squares and waterfronts equally forgotten, and in the Cyclopean modern towers and pinnacles that rise blackly Babylonian under waning moons, I had found instead only a sense of horror and oppression which threatened to master, paralyse, and annihilate me.

The disillusion had been gradual. Coming for the first time upon the town, I had seen it in the sunset from a bridge, majestic above its waters, its incredible peaks and pyramids rising flower-like and delicate from pools of violet mist to play with the flaming golden clouds and the first stars of evening. Then it had lighted up window by window above the shimmering tides where lanterns nodded and glided and deep horns bayed weird harmonies, and itself become a starry firmament of dream, redolent of faery music, and one with the marvels of Carcassonne and Samarcand and El Dorado and all glorious and half-fabulous cities. Shortly afterward I was taken through those antique ways so dear to my fancy—narrow, curving alleys and passages where rows of red Georgian brick blinked with small-paned dormers above pillared doorways that had looked on gilded sedans and panelled coaches—and in the first flush of realisation of these long-wished things I thought I had indeed achieved such treasures as would make me in time a poet.

But success and happiness were not to be. Garish daylight shewed only squalor and alienage and the noxious elephantiasis of climbing, spreading stone where the moon had hinted of loveliness and elder magic; and the throngs of people that seethed through the flume-like streets were squat, swarthy strangers with hardened faces and narrow eyes, shrewd strangers without dreams and without kinship to the scenes about them, who could never mean aught to a blue-eyed man of the old folk, with the love of fair green lanes and white New England village steeples in his heart.

So instead of the poems I had hoped for, there came only a shuddering blankness and ineffable loneliness; and I saw at last a fearful truth which no one had ever dared to breathe before—the unwhisperable secret of secrets—the fact that this city of stone and stridor is not a sentient perpetuation of Old New York as London is of Old London and Paris of Old Paris, but that it is in fact quite dead, its sprawling body imperfectly embalmed and infested with queer animate things which have nothing to do with it as it was in life. Upon making this discovery I ceased to sleep comfortably; though something of resigned tranquillity came back as I gradually formed the habit of keeping off the streets by day and venturing abroad only at night, when darkness calls forth what little of the past still hovers wraith-like about, and old white doorways remember the stalwart forms that once passed through them. With this mode of relief I even wrote a few poems, and still refrained from going home to my people lest I seem to crawl back ignobly in defeat.

Then, on a sleepless night's walk, I met the man. It was in a grotesque hidden courtyard of the Greenwich section, for there in my ignorance I had settled, having heard of the place as the natural home of poets and artists. The archaic lanes and houses and unexpected bits of square and court had indeed delighted me, and when I found the poets and artists to be loud-voiced pretenders whose quaintness is tinsel and whose lives are a denial of all that pure beauty which is poetry and art, I stayed on for love of these venerable things. I fancied them as they were in their prime, when Greenwich was a placid village not yet engulfed by the town; and in the hours before dawn, when all the revellers had slunk away, I used to wander alone among their cryptical windings and brood upon the curious arcana which generations must have deposited there. This kept my soul alive, and gave me a few of those dreams and visions for which the poet far within me cried out.

The man came upon me at about two one cloudy August morning, as I was threading a series of detached courtyards; now accessible only through the unlighted hallways of intervening buildings, but once forming parts of a continuous network of picturesque alleys. I had heard of them by vague rumour, and realised that they could not be upon any map of today; but the fact that they were forgotten only endeared them to me, so that I had sought them with twice my usual eagerness. Now that I had found them, my eagerness was again redoubled; for something in their arrangement dimly hinted that they might be only a few of many such, with dark, dumb counterparts wedged obscurely betwixt high blank walls and deserted rear tenements, or lurking lamplessly behind archways, unbetrayed by hordes of the foreign-speaking or guarded by furtive and uncommunicative artists whose practices do not invite publicity or the light of day.

He spoke to me without invitation, noting my mood and glances as I studied certain knockered doorways above iron-railed steps, the pallid glow of traceried transoms feebly lighting my face. His own face was in shadow, and he wore a wide-brimmed hat which somehow blended perfectly with the out-of-date cloak he affected; but I was subtly disquieted even before he addressed me. His form was very slight, thin almost to cadaverousness; and his voice proved phenomenally soft and hollow, though not particularly deep. He had, he said, noticed me several times at my wanderings; and inferred that I resembled him in loving the vestiges of former years. Would I not like the guidance of one long practiced in these explorations, and possessed of local information profoundly deeper than any which an obvious newcomer could possibly have gained?

As he spoke, I caught a glimpse of his face in the yellow beam from a solitary attic window. It was a noble, even a handsome, elderly countenance; and bore the marks of a lineage and refinement unusual for the age and place. Yet some quality about it disturbed me almost as much as its features pleased me—perhaps it was too white, or too expressionless, or too much out of keeping with the locality, to make me feel easy or comfortable. Nevertheless I followed him; for in those dreary days my quest for antique beauty and mystery was all that I had to keep my soul alive, and I reckoned it a rare favour of Fate to fall in with one whose kindred seekings seemed to have penetrated so much farther than mine.

Something in the night constrained the cloaked man to silence, and for a long hour he led me forward without needless words; making only the briefest of comments concerning ancient names and dates and changes, and directing my progress very largely by gestures as we squeezed through interstices, tiptoed through corridors, clambered over brick walls, and once crawled on hands and knees through a low, arched passage of stone whose immense length and tortuous twistings effaced at last every hint of geographical location I had managed to preserve. The things we saw were very old and marvellous, or at least they seemed so in the few straggling rays of light by which I viewed them, and I shall never forget the tottering Ionic columns and fluted pilasters and urn-headed iron fence-posts and flaring-lintelled windows and decorative fanlights that appeared to grow quainter and stranger the deeper we advanced into this inexhaustible maze of unknown antiquity.

We met no person, and as time passed the lighted windows became fewer and fewer. The street-lights we first encountered had been of oil, and of the ancient lozenge pattern. Later I noticed some with candles; and at last, after traversing a horrible unlighted court where my guide had to lead with his gloved hand through total blackness to a narrow wooden gate in a high wall, we came upon a fragment of alley lit only by lanterns in front of every seventh house—unbelievably colonial tin lanterns with conical tops and holes punched in the sides. This alley led steeply uphill—more steeply than I thought possible in this part of New York—and the upper end was blocked squarely by the ivy-clad wall of a private estate, beyond which I could see a pale cupola, and the tops of trees waving against a vague lightness in the sky. In this wall was a small, low-arched gate of nail-studded black oak, which the man proceeded to unlock with a ponderous key. Leading me within, he steered a course in utter blackness over what seemed to be a gravel path, and finally up a flight of stone steps to the door of the house, which he unlocked and opened for me.

We entered, and as we did so I grew faint from a reek of infinite mustiness which welled out to meet us, and which must have been the fruit of unwholesome centuries of decay. My host appeared not to notice this, and in courtesy I kept silent as he piloted me up a curving stairway, across a hall, and into a room whose door I heard him lock behind us. Then I saw him pull the curtains of the three small-paned windows that barely shewed themselves against the lightening sky; after which he crossed to the mantel, struck flint and steel, lighted two candles of a candelabrum of twelve sconces, and made a gesture enjoining soft-toned speech.

In this feeble radiance I saw that we were in a spacious, well-furnished, and panelled library dating from the first quarter of the eighteenth century, with splendid doorway pediments, a delightful Doric cornice, and a magnificently carved overmantel with scroll-and-urn top. Above the crowded bookshelves at intervals along the walls were well-wrought family portraits; all tarnished to an enigmatical dimness, and bearing an unmistakable likeness to the man who now motioned me to a chair beside the graceful Chippendale table. Before seating himself across the table from me, my host paused for a moment as if in embarrassment; then, tardily removing his gloves, wide-brimmed hat, and cloak, stood theatrically revealed in full mid-Georgian costume from queued hair and neck ruffles to knee-breeches, silk hose, and the buckled shoes I had not previously noticed. Now slowly sinking into a lyre-back chair, he commenced to eye me intently.

Without his hat he took on an aspect of extreme age which was scarcely visible before, and I wondered if this unperceived mark of singular longevity were not one of the sources of my original disquiet. When he spoke at length, his soft, hollow, and carefully muffled voice not infrequently quavered; and now and then I had great difficulty in following him as I listened with a thrill of amazement and half-disavowed alarm which grew each instant.

"You behold, Sir," my host began, "a man of very eccentrical habits, for whose costume no apology need be offered to one with your wit and inclinations. Reflecting upon better times, I have not scrupled to ascertain their ways and adopt their dress and manners; an indulgence which offends none if practiced without ostentation. It hath been my good-fortune to retain the rural seat of my ancestors, swallowed though it was by two towns, first Greenwich, which built up hither after 1800, then New-York, which joined on near 1830. There were many reasons for the close keeping of this place in my family, and I have not been remiss in discharging such obligations. The squire who succeeded to it in 1768 studied sartain arts and made sartain discoveries, all connected with influences residing in this particular plot of ground, and eminently desarving of the strongest guarding. Some curious effects of these arts and discoveries I now purpose to shew you, under the strictest secrecy; and I believe I may rely on my judgment of men enough to have no distrust of either your interest or your fidelity."

He paused, but I could only nod my head. I have said that I was alarmed, yet to my soul nothing was more deadly than the material daylight world of New York, and whether this man were a harmless eccentric or a wielder of dangerous arts I had no choice save to follow him and slake my sense of wonder on whatever he might have to offer. So I listened.

"To—my ancestor—" he softly continued, "there appeared to reside some very remarkable qualities in the will of mankind; qualities having a little-suspected dominance not only over the acts of one's self and of others, but over every variety of force and substance in Nature, and over many elements and dimensions deemed more univarsal than Nature herself. May I say that he flouted the sanctity of things as great as space and time, and that he put to strange uses the rites of sartain half-breed red Indians once encamped upon this hill? These Indians shewed choler when the place was built, and were plaguy pestilent in asking to visit the grounds at the full of the moon. For years they stole over the wall each month when they could, and by stealth performed sartain acts. Then, in '68, the new squire catched them at their doings, and stood still at what he saw. Thereafter he bargained with them and exchanged the free access of his grounds for the exact inwardness of what they did; larning that their grandfathers got part of their custom from red ancestors and part from an old Dutchman in the time of the States-General. And pox on him, I'm afeared the squire must have sarved them monstrous bad rum—whether or not by intent—for a week after he larnt the secret he was the only man living that knew it. You, Sir, are the first outsider to be told there is a secret, and split me if I'd have risked tampering that much with—the powers—had ye not been so hot after bygone things."

I shuddered as the man grew colloquial—and with the familiar speech of another day. He went on.

"But you must know, Sir, that what—the squire—got from those mongrel salvages was but a small part of the larning he came to have. He had not been at Oxford for nothing, nor talked to no account with an ancient chymist and astrologer in Paris. He was, in fine, made sensible that all the world is but the smoke of our intellects; past the bidding of the vulgar, but by the wise to be puffed out and drawn in like any cloud of prime Virginia tobacco. What we want, we may make about us; and what we don't want, we may sweep away. I won't say that all this is wholly true in body, but 'tis sufficient true to furnish a very pretty spectacle now and then. You, I conceive, would be tickled by a better sight of sartain other years than your fancy affords you; so be pleased to hold back any fright at what I design to shew. Come to the window and be quiet."

My host now took my hand to draw me to one of the two windows on the long side of the malodorous room, and at the first touch of his ungloved fingers I turned cold. His flesh, though dry and firm, was of the quality of ice; and I almost shrank away from his pulling. But again I thought of the emptiness and horror of reality, and boldly prepared to follow whithersoever I might be led. Once at the window, the man drew apart the yellow silk curtains and directed my stare into the blackness outside. For a moment I saw nothing save a myriad of tiny dancing lights, far, far before me. Then, as if in response to an insidious motion of my host's hand, a flash of heat-lightning played over the scene, and I looked out upon a sea of luxuriant foliage—foliage unpolluted, and not the sea of roofs to be expected by any normal mind. On my right the Hudson glittered wickedly, and in the distance ahead I saw the unhealthy shimmer of a vast salt marsh constellated with nervous fireflies. The flash died, and an evil smile illumined the waxy face of the aged necromancer.

"That was before my time—before the new squire's time. Pray let us try again."

I was faint, even fainter than the hateful modernity of that accursed city had made me.

"Good God!" I whispered, "can you do that for *any time?*" And as he nodded, and bared the black stumps of what had once been yellow fangs, I clutched at the curtains to prevent myself from falling. But he steadied me with that terrible, ice-cold claw, and once more made his insidious gesture.

Again the lightning flashed—but this time upon a scene not wholly strange. It was Greenwich, the Greenwich that used to be, with here and there a roof or row of houses as we see it now, yet with lovely green lanes and fields and bits of grassy common. The marsh still glittered beyond, but in the farther distance I saw the steeples of what was then all of New York; Trinity and St. Paul's and the Brick Church dominating their sisters, and a faint haze of wood smoke hovering over the whole. I breathed hard, but not so much from the sight itself as from the possibilities my imagination terrifiedly conjured up.

"Can you—dare you—go *far?*" I spoke with awe, and I think he shared it for a second, but the evil grin returned.

"*Far?* What I have seen would blast ye to a mad statue of stone! Back, back—forward, *forward*—look, ye puling lack-wit!"

And as he snarled the phrase under his breath he gestured anew; bringing to the sky a flash more blinding than either which had come before. For full three seconds I could glimpse that pandaemoniac sight, and in those seconds I saw a vista which will ever afterward torment me in dreams. I saw the heavens verminous with strange flying things, and beneath them a hellish black city of giant stone terraces with impious pyramids flung savagely to the moon, and devil-lights burning from unnumbered windows. And swarming loathsomely on aërial galleries I saw the yellow, squint-eyed people of that city, robed horribly in orange and red, and dancing insanely to the pounding of fevered kettle-drums, the clatter of obscene crotala, and the maniacal moaning of muted horns whose ceaseless dirges rose and fell undulantly like the waves of an unhallowed ocean of bitumen.

I saw this vista, I say, and heard as with the mind's ear the blasphemous domdaniel of cacophony which companioned it. It was the shrieking fulfilment of all the horror which that corpse-city had ever stirred in my soul, and forgetting every injunction to silence I screamed and screamed and screamed as my nerves gave way and the walls quivered about me.

Then, as the flash subsided, I saw that my host was trembling too; a look of shocking fear half blotting from his face the serpent distortion of rage which my screams had excited. He tottered, clutched at the curtains as I had done before, and wriggled his head wildly, like a hunted animal. God knows he had cause, for as the echoes of my screaming died away there came another sound so hellishly suggestive that only numbed emotion kept me sane and conscious. It was the steady, stealthy creaking of the stairs beyond the locked door, as with the ascent of a barefoot or skin-shod horde; and at last the cautious, purposeful rattling of the brass latch that glowed in the feeble candlelight. The old man clawed and spat at me through the mouldy air, and barked things in his throat as he swayed with the yellow curtain he clutched.

"The full moon—damn ye—ye … ye yelping dog—ye called 'em, and they've come for me! Moccasined feet—dead men—Gad sink ye, ye red devils, but I poisoned no rum o' yours—han't I kept your pox-rotted magic safe?—ye swilled yourselves sick, curse ye, and ye must needs blame the squire—let go, you! Unhand that latch—I've naught for ye here—"

At this point three slow and very deliberate raps shook the panels of the door, and a white foam gathered at the mouth of the frantic magician. His fright, turning to steely despair, left room for a resurgence of his rage against me; and he staggered a step toward the table on whose edge I was steadying myself. The curtains, still clutched in his right hand as his left clawed out at me, grew taut and finally crashed down from their lofty fastenings; admitting to the room a flood of that full moonlight which the brightening of the sky had presaged. In those greenish beams the candles paled, and a new semblance of decay spread over the musk-reeking room with its wormy panelling, sagging floor, battered mantel, rickety furniture, and ragged draperies. It spread over the old man, too, whether from the same source or because of his fear and vehemence, and I saw him shrivel and blacken as he lurched near and strove to rend me with vulturine talons. Only his eyes stayed whole, and they glared with a propulsive, dilated incandescence which grew as the face around them charred and dwindled.

The rapping was now repeated with greater insistence, and this time bore a hint of metal. The black thing facing me had become only a head with eyes, impotently trying to wriggle across the sinking floor in my direction, and occasionally emitting feeble little spits of immortal malice. Now swift and splintering blows assailed the sickly panels, and I saw the gleam of a tomahawk as it cleft the rending wood. I did not move, for I could not; but watched dazedly as the door fell in pieces to admit a colossal, shapeless influx of inky substance starred with shining, malevolent eyes. It poured thickly, like a flood of oil bursting a rotten bulkhead, overturned a chair as it spread, and finally flowed under the table and across the room to where the blackened head with the eyes still glared at me. Around that head it closed, totally swallowing it up, and in another moment it had begun to recede; bearing away its invisible burden without touching me, and flowing again out of that black doorway and down the unseen stairs, which creaked as before, though in reverse order.

Then the floor gave way at last, and I slid gaspingly down into the nighted chamber below, choking with cobwebs and half swooning with terror. The green moon, shining through broken windows, shewed me the hall door half open; and as I rose from the plaster-strown floor and twisted myself free from the sagged ceiling, I saw sweep past it an awful torrent of blackness, with scores of baleful eyes glowing in it. It was seeking the door to the cellar, and when it found it, it vanished therein. I now felt the floor of this lower room giving as that of the upper chamber had done, and once a crashing above had been followed by the fall past the west window of something which must have been the cupola. Now liberated for the instant from the wreckage, I rushed through the hall to the front door; and finding myself unable to open it, seized a chair and broke a window, climbing frenziedly out upon the unkempt lawn where moonlight danced over yard-high grass and weeds. The wall was high, and all the gates were locked; but moving a pile of boxes in a corner I managed to gain the top and cling to the great stone urn set there.

About me in my exhaustion I could see only strange walls and windows and old gambrel roofs. The steep street of my approach was nowhere visible, and the little I did see succumbed rapidly to a mist that rolled in from the river despite the glaring moonlight. Suddenly the urn to which I clung began to tremble, as if sharing my own lethal dizziness; and in another instant my body was plunging downward to I knew not what fate.

The man who found me said that I must have crawled a long way despite my broken bones, for a trail of blood stretched off as far as he dared look. The gathering rain soon effaced this link with the scene of my ordeal, and reports could state no more than that I had appeared from a place unknown, at the entrance of a little black court off Perry Street.

I never sought to return to those tenebrous labyrinths, nor would I direct any sane man thither if I could. Of who or what that ancient creature was, I have no idea; but I repeat that the city is dead and full of unsuspected horrors. Whither *he* has gone, I do not know; but I have gone home to the pure New England lanes up which fragrant sea-winds sweep at evening.

IN THE VAULT

There is nothing more absurd, as I view it, than that conventional association of the homely and the wholesome which seems to pervade the psychology of the multitude. Mention a bucolic Yankee setting, a bungling and thick-fibred village undertaker, and a careless mishap in a tomb, and no average reader can be brought to expect more than a hearty albeit grotesque phase of comedy. God knows, though, that the prosy tale which George Birch's death permits me to tell has in it aspects beside which some of our darkest tragedies are light.

Birch acquired a limitation and changed his business in 1881, yet never discussed the case when he could avoid it. Neither did his old physician Dr. Davis, who died years ago. It was generally stated that the affliction and shock were results of an unlucky slip whereby Birch had locked himself for nine hours in the receiving tomb of Peck Valley Cemetery, escaping only by crude and disastrous mechanical means; but while this much was undoubtedly true, there were other and blacker things which the man used to whisper to me in his drunken delirium toward the last. He confided in me because I was his doctor, and because he probably felt the need of confiding in someone else after Davis died. He was a bachelor, wholly without relatives.

Birch, before 1881, had been the village undertaker of Peck Valley; and was a very calloused and primitive specimen even as such specimens go. The practices I heard attributed to him would be unbelievable today, at least in a city; and even Peck Valley would have shuddered a bit had it known the easy ethics of its mortuary artist in such debatable matters as the ownership of costly "laying-out" apparel invisible beneath the casket's lid, and the degree of dignity to be maintained in posing and adapting the unseen members of lifeless tenants to containers not always calculated with sublimest accuracy. Most distinctly Birch was lax, insensitive, and professionally undesirable; yet I still think he was not an evil man. He was merely crass of fibre and function—thoughtless, careless, and liquorish, as his easily avoidable accident proves, and without that modicum of imagination which holds the average citizen within certain limits fixed by taste.

Just where to begin Birch's story I can hardly decide, since I am no practiced teller of tales. I suppose one should start in the cold December of 1880, when the ground froze and the cemetery delvers found they could dig no more graves till spring. Fortunately the village was small and the death rate low, so that it was possible to give all of Birch's inanimate charges a temporary haven in the single antiquated receiving tomb. The undertaker grew doubly lethargic in the bitter weather, and seemed to outdo even himself in carelessness. Never did he knock together flimsier and ungainlier caskets, or disregard more flagrantly the needs of the rusty lock on the tomb door which he slammed open and shut with such nonchalant abandon.

At last the spring thaw came, and graves were laboriously prepared for the nine silent harvests of the grim reaper which waited in the tomb. Birch, though dreading the bother of removal and interment, began his task of transference one disagreeable April morning, but ceased before noon because of a heavy rain that seemed to irritate his horse, after having laid but one mortal tenement to its permanent rest. That was Darius Peck, the nonagenarian, whose grave was not far from the tomb. Birch decided that he would begin the next day with little old Matthew Fenner, whose grave was also near by; but actually postponed the matter for three days, not getting to work till Good Friday, the 15th. Being without superstition, he did not heed the day at all; though ever afterward he refused to do anything of importance on that fateful sixth day of the week. Certainly, the events of that evening greatly changed George Birch.

On the afternoon of Friday, April 15th, then, Birch set out for the tomb with horse and wagon to transfer the body of Matthew Fenner. That he was not perfectly sober, he subsequently admitted; though he had not then taken to the wholesale drinking by which he later tried to forget certain things. He was just dizzy and careless enough to annoy his sensitive horse, which as he drew it viciously up at the tomb neighed and pawed and tossed its head, much as on that former occasion when the rain had vexed it. The day was clear, but a high wind had sprung up; and Birch was glad to get to shelter as he unlocked the iron door and entered the side-hill vault. Another might not have relished the damp, odorous chamber with the eight carelessly placed coffins; but Birch in those days was insensitive, and was concerned only in getting the right coffin for the right grave. He had not forgotten the criticism aroused when Hannah Bixby's relatives, wishing to transport her body to the cemetery in the city whither they had moved, found the casket of Judge Capwell beneath her headstone.

The light was dim, but Birch's sight was good, and he did not get Asaph Saywer's coffin by mistake, although it was very similar. He had, indeed, made that coffin for Matthew Fenner; but had cast it aside at last as too awkward and flimsy, in a fit of curious sentimentality aroused by recalling how kindly and generous the little old man had been to him during his bankruptcy five years before. He gave old Matt the very best his skill could produce, but was thrifty enough to save the rejected specimen, and to use it when Asaph Sawyer died of a malignant fever. Sawyer was not a lovable man, and many stories were told of his almost inhuman vindictiveness and tenacious memory for wrongs real or fancied. To him Birch had felt no compunction in assigning the carelessly made coffin which he now pushed out of the way in his quest for the Fenner casket.

It was just as he had recognised old Matt's coffin that the door slammed to in the wind, leaving him in a dusk even deeper than before. The narrow transom admitted only the feeblest of rays, and the overhead ventilation funnel virtually none at all; so that he was reduced to a profane fumbling as he made his halting way among the long boxes toward the latch. In this funereal twilight he rattled the rusty handles, pushed at the iron panels, and wondered why the massive portal had grown so suddenly recalcitrant. In this twilight, too, he began to realise the truth and to shout loudly as if his horse outside could do more than neigh an unsympathetic reply. For the long-neglected latch was obviously broken, leaving the careless undertaker trapped in the vault, a victim of his own oversight.

The thing must have happened at about three-thirty in the afternoon. Birch, being by temperament phlegmatic and practical, did not shout long; but proceeded to grope about for some tools which he recalled seeing in a corner of the tomb. It is doubtful whether he was touched at all by the horror and exquisite weirdness of his position, but the bald fact of imprisonment so far from the daily paths of men was enough to exasperate him thoroughly. His day's work was sadly interrupted, and unless chance presently brought some rambler hither, he might have to remain all night or longer. The pile of tools soon reached, and a hammer and chisel selected, Birch returned over the coffins to the door. The air had begun to be exceedingly unwholesome; but to this detail he paid no attention as he toiled, half by feeling, at the heavy and corroded metal of the latch. He would have given much for a lantern or bit of candle; but lacking these, bungled semi-sightlessly as best he might.

When he perceived that the latch was hopelessly unyielding, at least to such meagre tools and under such tenebrous conditions as these, Birch glanced about for other possible points of escape. The vault had been dug from a hillside, so that the narrow ventilation funnel in the top ran through several feet of earth, making this direction utterly useless to consider. Over the door, however, the high, slit-like transom in the brick facade gave promise of possible enlargement to a diligent worker; hence upon this his eyes long rested as he racked his brains for means to reach it. There was nothing like a ladder in the tomb, and the coffin niches on the sides and rear—which Birch seldom took the trouble to use—afforded no ascent to the space above the door. Only the coffins themselves remained as potential stepping-stones, and as he considered these he speculated on the best mode of arranging them. Three coffin-heights, he reckoned, would permit him to reach the transom; but he could do better with four. The boxes were fairly even, and could be piled up like blocks; so he began to compute how he might most stably use the eight to rear a scalable platform four deep. As he planned, he could not but wish that the units of his contemplated staircase had been more securely made. Whether he had imagination enough to wish they were empty, is strongly to be doubted.

Finally he decided to lay a base of three parallel with the wall, to place upon this two layers of two each, and upon these a single box to serve as the platform. This arrangement could be ascended with a minimum of awkwardness, and would furnish the desired height. Better still, though, he would utilise only two boxes of the base to support the superstructure, leaving one free to be piled on top in case the actual feat of escape required an even greater altitude. And so the prisoner toiled in the twilight, heaving the unresponsive remnants of mortality with little ceremony as his miniature Tower of Babel rose course by course. Several of the coffins began to split under the stress of handling, and he planned to save the stoutly built casket of little Matthew Fenner for the top, in order that his feet might have as certain a surface as possible. In the semi-gloom he trusted mostly to touch to select the right one, and indeed came upon it almost by accident, since it tumbled into his hands as if through some odd volition after he had unwittingly placed it beside another on the third layer.

The tower at length finished, and his aching arms rested by a pause during which he sat on the bottom step of his grim device, Birch cautiously ascended with his tools and stood abreast of the narrow transom. The borders of the space were entirely of brick, and there seemed little doubt but that he could shortly chisel away enough to allow his body to pass. As his hammer blows began to fall, the horse outside whinnied in a tone which may have been encouraging and may have been mocking. In either case it would have been appropriate; for the unexpected tenacity of the easy-looking brickwork was surely a sardonic commentary on the vanity of mortal hopes, and the source of a task whose performance deserved every possible stimulus.

Dusk fell and found Birch still toiling. He worked largely by feeling now, since newly gathered clouds hid the moon; and though progress was still slow, he felt heartened at the extent of his encroachments on the top and bottom of the aperture. He could, he was sure, get out by midnight—though it is characteristic of him that this thought was untinged with eery implications. Undisturbed by oppressive reflections on the time, the place, and the company beneath his feet, he philosophically chipped away the stony brickwork; cursing when a fragment hit him in the face, and laughing when one struck the increasingly excited horse that pawed near the cypress tree. In time the hole grew so large that he ventured to try his body in it now and then, shifting about so that the coffins beneath him rocked and creaked. He would not, he found, have to pile another on his platform to make the proper height; for the hole was on exactly the right level to use as soon as its size might permit.

It must have been midnight at least when Birch decided he could get through the transom. Tired and perspiring despite many rests, he descended to the floor and sat a while on the bottom box to gather strength for the final wriggle and leap to the ground outside. The hungry horse was neighing repeatedly and almost uncannily, and he vaguely wished it would stop. He was curiously unelated over his impending escape, and almost dreaded the exertion, for his form had the indolent stoutness of early middle age. As he remounted the splitting coffins he felt his weight very poignantly; especially when, upon reaching the topmost one, he heard that aggravated crackle which bespeaks the wholesale rending of wood. He had, it seems, planned in vain when choosing the stoutest coffin for the platform; for no sooner was his full bulk again upon it than the rotting lid gave way, jouncing him two feet down on a surface which even he did not care to imagine. Maddened by the sound, or by the stench which billowed forth even to the open air, the waiting horse gave a scream that was too frantic for a neigh, and plunged madly off through the night, the wagon rattling crazily behind it.

Birch, in his ghastly situation, was now too low for an easy scramble out of the enlarged transom; but gathered his energies for a determined try. Clutching the edges of the aperture, he sought to pull himself up, when he noticed a queer retardation in the form of an apparent drag on both his ankles. In another moment he knew fear for the first time that night; for struggle as he would, he could not shake clear of the unknown grasp which held his feet in relentless captivity. Horrible pains, as of savage wounds, shot through his calves; and in his mind was a vortex of fright mixed with an unquenchable materialism that suggested splinters, loose nails, or some other attribute of a breaking wooden box. Perhaps he screamed. At any rate he kicked and squirmed frantically and automatically whilst his consciousness was almost eclipsed in a half-swoon.

Instinct guided him in his wriggle through the transom, and in the crawl which followed his jarring thud on the damp ground. He could not walk, it appeared, and the emerging moon must have witnessed a horrible sight as he dragged his bleeding ankles toward the cemetery lodge; his fingers clawing the black mould in brainless haste, and his body responding with that maddening slowness from which one suffers when chased by the phantoms of nightmare. There was evidently, however, no pursuer; for he was alone and alive when Armington, the lodge-keeper, answered his feeble clawing at the door.

Armington helped Birch to the outside of a spare bed and sent his little son Edwin for Dr. Davis. The afflicted man was fully conscious, but would say nothing of any consequence; merely muttering such things as "oh, my ankles!", "let go!", or "shut in the tomb". Then the doctor came with his medicine-case and asked crisp questions, and removed the patient's outer clothing, shoes, and socks. The wounds—for both ankles were frightfully lacerated about the Achilles' tendons—seemed to puzzle the old physician greatly, and finally almost to frighten him. His questioning grew more than medically tense, and his hands shook as he dressed the mangled members; binding them as if he wished to get the wounds out of sight as quickly as possible.

For an impersonal doctor, Davis' ominous and awestruck cross-examination became very strange indeed as he sought to drain from the weakened undertaker every least detail of his horrible experience. He was oddly anxious to know if Birch were sure—absolutely sure—of the identity of that top coffin of the pile; how he had chosen it, how he had been certain of it as the Fenner coffin in the dusk, and how he had distinguished it from the inferior duplicate coffin of vicious Asaph Sawyer. Would the firm Fenner casket have caved in so readily? Davis, an old-time village practitioner, had of course seen both at the respective funerals, as indeed he had attended both Fenner and Sawyer in their last illnesses. He had even wondered, at Sawyer's funeral, how the vindictive farmer had managed to lie straight in a box so closely akin to that of the diminutive Fenner.

After a full two hours Dr. Davis left, urging Birch to insist at all times that his wounds were caused entirely by loose nails and splintering wood. What else, he added, could ever in any case be proved or believed? But it would be well to say as little as could be said, and to let no other doctor treat the wounds. Birch heeded this advice all the rest of his life till he told me his story; and when I saw the scars—ancient and whitened as they then were—I agreed that he was wise in so doing. He always remained lame, for the great tendons had been severed; but I think the greatest lameness was in his soul. His thinking processes, once so phlegmatic and logical, had become ineffaceably scarred; and it was pitiful to note his response to certain chance allusions such as "Friday", "tomb", "coffin", and words of less obvious concatenation. His frightened horse had gone home, but his frightened wits never quite did that. He changed his business, but something always preyed upon him. It may have been just fear, and it may have been fear mixed with a queer belated sort of remorse for bygone crudities. His drinking, of course, only aggravated what it was meant to alleviate.

When Dr. Davis left Birch that night he had taken a lantern and gone to the old receiving tomb. The moon was shining on the scattered brick fragments and marred facade, and the latch of the great door yielded readily to a touch from the outside. Steeled by old ordeals in dissecting rooms, the doctor entered and looked about, stifling the nausea of mind and body that everything in sight and smell induced. He cried aloud once, and a little later gave a gasp that was more terrible than a cry. Then he fled back to the lodge and broke all the rules of his calling by rousing and shaking his patient, and hurling at him a succession of shuddering whispers that seared into the bewildered ears like the hissing of vitriol.

"It was Asaph's coffin, Birch, just as I thought! I knew his teeth, with the front ones missing on the upper jaw—never, for God's sake, shew those wounds! The body was pretty badly gone, but if ever I saw vindictiveness on any face—or former face.... You know what a fiend he was for revenge—how he ruined old Raymond thirty years after their boundary suit, and how he stepped on the puppy that snapped at him a year ago last August.... He was the devil incarnate, Birch, and I believe his eye-for-an-eye fury could beat old Father Death himself. God, what a rage! I'd hate to have it aimed at me!

"Why did you do it, Birch? He was a scoundrel, and I don't blame you for giving him a cast-aside coffin, but you always did go too damned far! Well enough to skimp on the thing some way, but you knew what a little man old Fenner was.

"I'll never get the picture out of my head as long as I live. You kicked hard, for Asaph's coffin was on the floor. His head was broken in, and everything was tumbled about. I've seen sights before, but there was one thing too much here. An eye for an eye! Great heavens, Birch, but you got what you deserved. The skull turned my stomach, but the other was worse—*those ankles cut neatly off to fit Matt Fenner's cast-aside coffin!*"

COOL AIR

You ask me to explain why I am afraid of a draught of cool air; why I shiver more than others upon entering a cold room, and seem nauseated and repelled when the chill of evening creeps through the heat of a mild autumn day. There are those who say I respond to cold as others do to a bad odour, and I am the last to deny the impression. What I will do is to relate the most horrible circumstance I ever encountered, and leave it to you to judge whether or not this forms a suitable explanation of my peculiarity.

It is a mistake to fancy that horror is associated inextricably with darkness, silence, and solitude. I found it in the glare of mid-afternoon, in the clangour of a metropolis, and in the teeming midst of a shabby and commonplace rooming-house with a prosaic landlady and two stalwart men by my side. In the spring of 1923 I had secured some dreary and unprofitable magazine work in the city of New York; and being unable to pay any substantial rent, began drifting from one cheap boarding establishment to another in search of a room which might combine the qualities of decent cleanliness, endurable furnishings, and very reasonable price. It soon developed that I had only a choice between different evils, but after a time I came upon a house in West Fourteenth Street which disgusted me much less than the others I had sampled.

The place was a four-story mansion of brownstone, dating apparently from the late forties, and fitted with woodwork and marble whose stained and sullied splendour argued a descent from high levels of tasteful opulence. In the rooms, large and lofty, and decorated with impossible paper and ridiculously ornate stucco cornices, there lingered a depressing mustiness and hint of obscure cookery; but the floors were clean, the linen tolerably regular, and the hot water not too often cold or turned off, so that I came to regard it as at least a bearable place to hibernate till one might really live again. The landlady, a slatternly, almost bearded Spanish woman named Herrero, did not annoy me with gossip or with criticisms of the late-burning electric light in my third-floor front hall room; and my fellow-lodgers were as quiet and uncommunicative as one might desire, being mostly Spaniards a little above the coarsest and crudest grade. Only the din of street cars in the thoroughfare below proved a serious annoyance.

I had been there about three weeks when the first odd incident occurred. One evening at about eight I heard a spattering on the floor and became suddenly aware that I had been smelling the pungent odour of ammonia for some time. Looking about, I saw that the ceiling was wet and dripping; the soaking apparently proceeding from a corner on the side toward the street. Anxious to stop the matter at its source, I hastened to the basement to tell the landlady; and was assured by her that the trouble would quickly be set right.

"Doctair Muñoz," she cried as she rushed upstairs ahead of me, "he have speel hees chemicals. He ees too seeck for doctair heemself—seecker and seecker all the time—but he weel not have no othair for help. He ees vairy queer in hees seeckness—all day he take funnee-smelling baths, and he cannot get excite or warm. All hees own housework he do—hees leetle room are full of bottles and machines, and he do not work as doctair. But he was great once—my fathair in Barcelona have hear of heem—and only joost now he feex a arm of the plumber that get hurt of sudden. He nevair go out, only on roof, and my boy Esteban he breeng heem hees food and laundry and mediceens and chemicals. My Gawd, the sal-ammoniac that man use for keep heem cool!"

Mrs. Herrero disappeared up the staircase to the fourth floor, and I returned to my room. The ammonia ceased to drip, and as I cleaned up what had spilled and opened the window for air, I heard the landlady's heavy footsteps above me. Dr. Muñoz I had never heard, save for certain sounds as of some gasoline-driven mechanism; since his step was soft and gentle. I wondered for a moment what the strange affliction of this man might be, and whether his obstinate refusal of outside aid were not the result of a rather baseless eccentricity. There is, I reflected tritely, an infinite deal of pathos in the state of an eminent person who has come down in the world.

I might never have known Dr. Muñoz had it not been for the heart attack that suddenly seized me one forenoon as I sat writing in my room. Physicians had told me of the danger of those spells, and I knew there was no time to be lost; so remembering what the landlady had said about the invalid's help of the injured workman, I dragged myself upstairs and knocked feebly at the door above mine. My knock was answered in good English by a curious voice some distance to the right, asking my name and business; and these things being stated, there came an opening of the door next to the one I had sought.

A rush of cool air greeted me; and though the day was one of the hottest of late June, I shivered as I crossed the threshold into a large apartment whose rich and tasteful decoration surprised me in this nest of squalor and seediness. A folding couch now filled its diurnal role of sofa, and the mahogany furniture, sumptuous hangings, old paintings, and mellow bookshelves all bespoke a gentleman's study rather than a boarding-house bedroom. I now saw that the hall room above mine—the "leetle room" of bottles and machines which Mrs. Herrero had mentioned—was merely the laboratory of the doctor; and that his main living quarters lay in the spacious adjoining room whose convenient alcoves and large contiguous bathroom permitted him to hide all dressers and obtrusive utilitarian devices. Dr. Muñoz, most certainly, was a man of birth, cultivation, and discrimination.

The figure before me was short but exquisitely proportioned, and clad in somewhat formal dress of perfect cut and fit. A high-bred face of masterful though not arrogant expression was adorned by a short iron-grey full beard, and an old-fashioned pince-nez shielded the full, dark eyes and surmounted an aquiline nose which gave a Moorish touch to a physiognomy otherwise dominantly Celtiberian. Thick, well-trimmed hair that argued the punctual calls of a barber was parted gracefully above a high forehead; and the whole picture was one of striking intelligence and superior blood and breeding.

Nevertheless, as I saw Dr. Muñoz in that blast of cool air, I felt a repugnance which nothing in his aspect could justify.

Only his lividly inclined complexion and coldness of touch could have afforded a physical basis for this feeling, and even these things should have been excusable considering the man's known invalidism. It might, too, have been the singular cold that alienated me; for such chilliness was abnormal on so hot a day, and the abnormal always excites aversion, distrust, and fear.

But repugnance was soon forgotten in admiration, for the strange physician's extreme skill at once became manifest despite the ice-coldness and shakiness of his bloodless-looking hands. He clearly understood my needs at a glance, and ministered to them with a master's deftness; the while reassuring me in a finely modulated though oddly hollow and timbreless voice that he was the bitterest of sworn enemies to death, and had sunk his fortune and lost all his friends in a lifetime of bizarre experiment devoted to its bafflement and extirpation. Something of the benevolent fanatic seemed to reside in him, and he rambled on almost garrulously as he sounded my chest and mixed a suitable draught of drugs fetched from the smaller laboratory room. Evidently he found the society of a well-born man a rare novelty in this dingy environment, and was moved to unaccustomed speech as memories of better days surged over him.

His voice, if queer, was at least soothing; and I could not even perceive that he breathed as the fluent sentences rolled urbanely out. He sought to distract my mind from my own seizure by speaking of his theories and experiments; and I remember his tactfully consoling me about my weak heart by insisting that will and consciousness are stronger than organic life itself, so that if a bodily frame be but originally healthy and carefully preserved, it may through a scientific enhancement of these qualities retain a kind of nervous animation despite the most serious impairments, defects, or even absences in the battery of specific organs. He might, he half-jestingly said, some day teach me to live—or at least to possess some kind of conscious existence—without any heart at all! For his part, he was afflicted with a complication of maladies requiring a very exact regimen which included constant cold. Any marked rise in temperature might, if prolonged, affect him fatally; and the frigidity of his habitation—some 55 or 56 degrees Fahrenheit—was maintained by an absorption system of ammonia cooling, the gasoline engine of whose pumps I had often heard in my own room below.

Relieved of my seizure in a marvellously short while, I left the shivery place a disciple and devotee of the gifted recluse. After that I paid him frequent overcoated calls; listening while he told of secret researches and almost ghastly results, and trembling a bit when I examined the unconventional and astonishingly ancient volumes on his shelves. I was eventually, I may add, almost cured of my disease for all time by his skilful ministrations. It seems that he did not scorn the incantations of the mediaevalists, since he believed these cryptic formulae to contain rare psychological stimuli which might conceivably have singular effects on the substance of a nervous system from which organic pulsations had fled. I was touched by his account of the aged Dr. Torres of Valencia, who had shared his earlier experiments and nursed him through the great illness of eighteen years before, whence his present disorders proceeded. No sooner had the venerable practitioner saved his colleague than he himself succumbed to the grim enemy he had fought. Perhaps the strain had been too great; for Dr. Muñoz made it whisperingly clear—though not in detail—that the methods of healing had been most extraordinary, involving scenes and processes not welcomed by elderly and conservative Galens.

As the weeks passed, I observed with regret that my new friend was indeed slowly but unmistakably losing ground physically, as Mrs. Herrero had suggested. The livid aspect of his countenance was intensified, his voice became more hollow and indistinct, his muscular motions were less perfectly coördinated, and his mind and will displayed less resilience and initiative. Of this sad change he seemed by no means unaware, and little by little his expression and conversation both took on a gruesome irony which restored in me something of the subtle repulsion I had originally felt.

He developed strange caprices, acquiring a fondness for exotic spices and Egyptian incense till his room smelled like the vault of a sepulchred Pharaoh in the Valley of Kings. At the same time his demands for cold air increased, and with my aid he amplified the ammonia piping of his room and modified the pumps and feed of his refrigerating machine till he could keep the temperature as low as 34° or 40°, and finally even 28°; the bathroom and laboratory, of course, being less chilled, in order that water might not freeze, and that chemical processes might not be impeded. The tenant adjoining him complained of the icy air from around the connecting door, so I helped him fit heavy hangings to obviate the difficulty. A kind of growing horror, of outré and morbid cast, seemed to possess him. He talked of death incessantly, but laughed hollowly when such things as burial or funeral arrangements were gently suggested.

All in all, he became a disconcerting and even gruesome companion; yet in my gratitude for his healing I could not well abandon him to the strangers around him, and was careful to dust his room and attend to his needs each day, muffled in a heavy ulster which I bought especially for the purpose. I likewise did much of his shopping, and gasped in bafflement at some of the chemicals he ordered from druggists and laboratory supply houses.

An increasing and unexplained atmosphere of panic seemed to rise around his apartment. The whole house, as I have said, had a musty odour; but the smell in his room was worse—and in spite of all the spices and incense, and the pungent chemicals of the now incessant baths which he insisted on taking unaided. I perceived that it must be connected with his ailment, and shuddered when I reflected on what that ailment might be. Mrs. Herrero crossed herself when she looked at him, and gave him up unreservedly to me; not even letting her son Esteban continue to run errands for him. When I suggested other physicians, the sufferer would fly into as much of a rage as he seemed to dare to entertain. He evidently feared the physical effect of violent emotion, yet his will and driving force waxed rather than waned, and he refused to be confined to his bed. The lassitude of his earlier ill days gave place to a return of his fiery purpose, so that he seemed about to hurl defiance at the death-daemon even as that ancient enemy seized him. The pretence of eating, always curiously like a formality with him, he virtually abandoned; and mental power alone appeared to keep him from total collapse.

He acquired a habit of writing long documents of some sort, which he carefully sealed and filed with injunctions that I transmit them after his death to certain persons whom he named—for the most part lettered East Indians, but including a once celebrated French physician now generally thought dead, and about whom the most inconceivable things had been whispered. As it happened, I burned all these papers undelivered and unopened. His aspect and voice became utterly frightful, and his presence almost unbearable. One September day an unexpected glimpse of him induced an epileptic fit in a man who had come to repair his electric desk lamp; a fit for which he prescribed effectively whilst keeping himself well out of sight. That man, oddly enough, had been through the terrors of the Great War without having incurred any fright so thorough.

Then, in the middle of October, the horror of horrors came with stupefying suddenness. One night about eleven the pump of the refrigerating machine broke down, so that within three hours the process of ammonia cooling became impossible. Dr. Muñoz summoned me by thumping on the floor, and I worked desperately to repair the injury while my host cursed in a tone whose lifeless, rattling hollowness surpassed description. My amateur efforts, however, proved of no use; and when I had brought in a mechanic from a neighbouring all-night garage we learned that nothing could be done till morning, when a new piston would have to be obtained. The moribund hermit's rage and fear, swelling to grotesque proportions, seemed likely to shatter what remained of his failing physique; and once a spasm caused him to clap his hands to his eyes and rush into the bathroom. He groped his way out with face tightly bandaged, and I never saw his eyes again.

The frigidity of the apartment was now sensibly diminishing, and at about 5 a.m. the doctor retired to the bathroom, commanding me to keep him supplied with all the ice I could obtain at all-night drug stores and cafeterias. As I would return from my sometimes discouraging trips and lay my spoils before the closed bathroom door, I could hear a restless splashing within, and a thick voice croaking out the order for "More—more!" At length a warm day broke, and the shops opened one by one. I asked Esteban either to help with the ice-fetching whilst I obtained the pump piston, or to order the piston whilst I continued with the ice; but instructed by his mother, he absolutely refused.

Finally I hired a seedy-looking loafer whom I encountered on the corner of Eighth Avenue to keep the patient supplied with ice from a little shop where I introduced him, and applied myself diligently to the task of finding a pump piston and engaging workmen competent to install it. The task seemed interminable, and I raged almost as violently as the hermit when I saw the hours slipping by in a breathless, foodless round of vain telephoning, and a hectic quest from place to place, hither and thither by subway and surface car. About noon I encountered a suitable supply house far downtown, and at approximately 1:30 p.m. arrived at my boarding-place with the necessary paraphernalia and two sturdy and intelligent mechanics. I had done all I could, and hoped I was in time.

Black terror, however, had preceded me. The house was in utter turmoil, and above the chatter of awed voices I heard a man praying in a deep basso. Fiendish things were in the air, and lodgers told over the beads of their rosaries as they caught the odour from beneath the doctor's closed door. The lounger I had hired, it seems, had fled screaming and mad-eyed not long after his second delivery of ice; perhaps as a result of excessive curiosity. He could not, of course, have locked the door behind him; yet it was now fastened, presumably from the inside. There was no sound within save a nameless sort of slow, thick dripping.

Briefly consulting with Mrs. Herrero and the workmen despite a fear that gnawed my inmost soul, I advised the breaking down of the door; but the landlady found a way to turn the key from the outside with some wire device. We had previously opened the doors of all the other rooms on that hall, and flung all the windows to the very top. Now, noses protected by handkerchiefs, we tremblingly invaded the accursed south room which blazed with the warm sun of early afternoon.

A kind of dark, slimy trail led from the open bathroom door to the hall door, and thence to the desk, where a terrible little pool had accumulated. Something was scrawled there in pencil in an awful, blind hand on a piece of paper hideously smeared as though by the very claws that traced the hurried last words. Then the trail led to the couch and ended unutterably.

What was, or had been, on the couch I cannot and dare not say here. But this is what I shiveringly puzzled out on the stickily smeared paper before I drew a match and burned it to a crisp; what I puzzled out in terror as the landlady and two mechanics rushed frantically from that hellish place to babble their incoherent stories at the nearest police station. The nauseous words seemed well-nigh incredible in that yellow sunlight, with the clatter of cars and motor trucks ascending clamorously from crowded Fourteenth Street, yet I confess that I believed them then. Whether I believe them now I honestly do not know. There are things about which it is better not to speculate, and all that I can say is that I hate the smell of ammonia, and grow faint at a draught of unusually cool air.

"The end," ran that noisome scrawl, "is here. No more ice—the man looked and ran away. Warmer every minute, and the tissues can't last. I fancy you know—what I said about the will and the nerves and the preserved body after the organs ceased to work. It was good theory, but couldn't keep up indefinitely. There was a gradual deterioration I had not foreseen. Dr. Torres knew, but the shock killed him. He couldn't stand what he had to do—he had to get me in a strange, dark place when he minded my letter and nursed me back. And the organs never would work again. It had to be done my way—artificial preservation—*for you see I died that time eighteen years ago.*"

THE CALL OF CTHULHU

(Found Among the Papers of the Late
Francis Wayland Thurston, of Boston)

"Of such great powers or beings there may be conceivably a survival ... a survivial of a hugely remote period when ... consciousness was manifested, perhaps, in shapes and forms long since withdrawn before the tide of advancing humanity ... forms of which poetry and legend alone have caught a flying memory and called them gods, monsters, mythical beings of all sorts and kinds...."

—*Algernon Blackwood.*

I.
The Horror in Clay.

The most merciful thing in the world, I think, is the inability of the human mind to correlate all its contents. We live on a placid island of ignorance in the midst of black seas of infinity, and it was not meant that we should voyage far. The sciences, each straining in its own direction, have hitherto harmed us little; but some day the piecing together of dissociated knowledge will open up such terrifying vistas of reality, and of our frightful position therein, that we shall either go mad from the revelation or flee from the deadly light into the peace and safety of a new dark age.

Theosophists have guessed at the awesome grandeur of the cosmic cycle wherein our world and human race form transient incidents. They have hinted at strange survivals in terms which would freeze the blood if not masked by a bland optimism. But it is not from them that there came the single glimpse of forbidden aeons which chills me when I think of it and maddens me when I dream of it. That glimpse, like all dread glimpses of truth, flashed out from an accidental piecing together of separated things—in this case an old newspaper item and the notes of a dead professor. I hope that no one else will accomplish this piecing out; certainly, if I live, I shall never knowingly supply a link in so hideous a chain. I think that the professor, too, intended to keep silent regarding the part he knew, and that he would have destroyed his notes had not sudden death seized him.

My knowledge of the thing began in the winter of 1926–27 with the death of my grand-uncle George Gammell Angell, Professor Emeritus of Semitic Languages in Brown University, Providence, Rhode Island. Professor Angell was widely known as an authority on ancient inscriptions, and had frequently been resorted to by the heads of prominent museums; so that his passing at the age of ninety-two may be recalled by many. Locally, interest was intensified by the obscurity of the cause of death. The professor had been stricken whilst returning from the Newport boat; falling suddenly, as witnesses said, after having been jostled by a nautical-looking negro who had come from one of the queer dark courts on the precipitous hillside which formed a short cut from the waterfront to the deceased's home in Williams Street. Physicians were unable to find any visible disorder, but concluded after perplexed debate that some obscure lesion of the heart, induced by the brisk ascent of so steep a hill by so elderly a man, was responsible for the end. At the time I saw no reason to dissent from this dictum, but latterly I am inclined to wonder—and more than wonder.

As my grand-uncle's heir and executor, for he died a childless widower, I was expected to go over his papers with some thoroughness; and for that purpose moved his entire set of files and boxes to my quarters in Boston. Much of the material which I correlated will be later published by the American Archaeological Society, but there was one box which I found exceedingly puzzling, and which I felt much averse from shewing to other eyes. It had been locked, and I did not find the key till it occurred to me to examine the personal ring which the professor carried always in his pocket. Then indeed I succeeded in opening it, but when I did so seemed only to be confronted by a greater and more closely locked barrier. For what could be the meaning of the queer clay bas-relief and the disjointed jottings, ramblings, and cuttings which I found? Had my uncle, in his latter years, become credulous of the most superficial impostures? I resolved to search out the eccentric sculptor responsible for this apparent disturbance of an old man's peace of mind.

The bas-relief was a rough rectangle less than an inch thick and about five by six inches in area; obviously of modern origin. Its designs, however, were far from modern in atmosphere and suggestion; for although the vagaries of cubism and futurism are many and wild, they do not often reproduce that cryptic regularity which lurks in prehistoric writing. And writing of some kind the bulk of these designs seemed certainly to be; though my memory, despite much familiarity with the papers and collections of my uncle, failed in any way to identify this particular species, or even to hint at its remotest affiliations.

Above these apparent hieroglyphics was a figure of evidently pictorial intent, though its impressionistic execution forbade a very clear idea of its nature. It seemed to be a sort of monster, or symbol representing a monster, of a form which only a diseased fancy could conceive. If I say that my somewhat extravagant imagination yielded simultaneous pictures of an octopus, a dragon, and a human caricature, I shall not be unfaithful to the spirit of the thing. A pulpy, tentacled head surmounted a grotesque and scaly body with rudimentary wings; but it was the *general outline* of the whole which made it most shockingly frightful. Behind the figure was a vague suggestion of a Cyclopean architectural background.

The writing accompanying this oddity was, aside from a stack of press cuttings, in Professor Angell's most recent hand; and made no pretence to literary style. What seemed to be the main document was headed "CTHULHU CULT" in characters painstakingly printed to avoid the erroneous reading of a word so unheard-of. The manuscript was divided into two sections, the first of which was headed "1925—Dream and Dream Work of H. A. Wilcox, 7 Thomas St., Providence, R.I.", and the second, "Narrative of Inspector John R. Legrasse, 121 Bienville St., New Orleans, La., at 1908 A. A. S. Mtg.—Notes on Same, & Prof. Webb's Acct." The other manuscript papers were all brief notes, some of them accounts of the queer dreams of different persons, some of them citations from theosophical books and magazines (notably W. Scott-Elliot's "Atlantis and the Lost Lemuria"), and the rest comments on long-surviving secret societies and hidden cults, with references to passages in such mythological and anthropological source-books as Frazer's "Golden Bough" and Miss Murray's "Witch-Cult in Western Europe". The cuttings largely alluded to outré mental illnesses and outbreaks of group folly or mania in the spring of 1925.

The first half of the principal manuscript told a very peculiar tale. It appears that on March 1st, 1925, a thin, dark young man of neurotic and excited aspect had called upon Professor Angell bearing the singular clay bas-relief, which was then exceedingly damp and fresh. His card bore the name of Henry Anthony Wilcox, and my uncle had recognised him as the youngest son of an excellent family slightly known to him, who had latterly been studying sculpture at the Rhode Island School of Design and living alone at the Fleur-de-Lys Building near that institution. Wilcox was a precocious youth of known genius but great eccentricity, and had from childhood excited attention through the strange stories and odd dreams he was in the habit of relating. He called himself "psychically hypersensitive", but the staid folk of the ancient commercial city dismissed him as merely "queer". Never mingling much with his kind, he had dropped gradually from social visibility, and was now known only to a small group of aesthetes from other towns. Even the Providence Art Club, anxious to preserve its conservatism, had found him quite hopeless.

On the occasion of the visit, ran the professor's manuscript, the sculptor abruptly asked for the benefit of his host's archaeological knowledge in identifying the hieroglyphics on the bas-relief. He spoke in a dreamy, stilted manner which suggested pose and alienated sympathy; and my uncle shewed some sharpness in replying, for the conspicuous freshness of the tablet implied kinship with anything but archaeology. Young Wilcox's rejoinder, which impressed my uncle enough to make him recall and record it verbatim, was of a fantastically poetic cast which must have typified his whole conversation, and which I have since found highly characteristic of him. He said, "It is new, indeed, for I made it last night in a dream of strange cities; and dreams are older than brooding Tyre, or the contemplative Sphinx, or garden-girdled Babylon."

It was then that he began that rambling tale which suddenly played upon a sleeping memory and won the fevered interest of my uncle. There had been a slight earthquake tremor the night before, the most considerable felt in New England for some years; and Wilcox's imagination had been keenly affected. Upon retiring, he had had an unprecedented dream of great Cyclopean cities of titan blocks and sky-flung monoliths, all dripping with green ooze and sinister with latent horror. Hieroglyphics had covered the walls and pillars, and from some undetermined point below had come a voice that was not a voice; a chaotic sensation which only fancy could transmute into sound, but which he attempted to render by the almost unpronounceable jumble of letters, "*Cthulhu fhtagn*".

This verbal jumble was the key to the recollection which excited and disturbed Professor Angell. He questioned the sculptor with scientific minuteness; and studied with almost frantic intensity the bas-relief on which the youth had found himself working, chilled and clad only in his night-clothes, when waking had stolen bewilderingly over him. My uncle blamed his old age, Wilcox afterward said, for his slowness in recognising both hieroglyphics and pictorial design. Many of his questions seemed highly out-of-place to his visitor, especially those which tried to connect the latter with strange cults or societies; and Wilcox could not understand the repeated promises of silence which he was offered in exchange for an admission of membership in some widespread mystical or paganly religious body. When Professor Angell became convinced that the sculptor was indeed ignorant of any cult or system of cryptic lore, he besieged his visitor with demands for future reports of dreams. This bore regular fruit, for after the first interview the manuscript records daily calls of the young man, during which he related startling fragments of nocturnal imagery whose burden was always some terrible Cyclopean vista of dark and dripping stone, with a subterrene voice or intelligence shouting monotonously in enigmatical sense-impacts uninscribable save as gibberish. The two sounds most frequently repeated are those rendered by the letters "*Cthulhu*" and "*R'lyeh*".

On March 23d, the manuscript continued, Wilcox failed to appear; and inquiries at his quarters revealed that he had been stricken with an obscure sort of fever and taken to the home of his family in Waterman Street. He had cried out in the night, arousing several other artists in the building, and had manifested since then only alternations of unconsciousness and delirium. My uncle at once telephoned the family, and from that time forward kept close watch of the case; calling often at the Thayer Street office of Dr. Tobey, whom he learned to be in charge. The youth's febrile mind, apparently, was dwelling on strange things; and the doctor shuddered now and then as he spoke of them. They included not only a repetition of what he had formerly dreamed, but touched wildly on a gigantic thing "miles high" which walked or lumbered about. He at no time fully described this object, but occasional frantic words, as repeated by Dr. Tobey, convinced the professor that it must be identical with the nameless monstrosity he had sought to depict in his dream-sculpture. Reference to this object, the doctor added, was invariably a prelude to the young man's subsidence into lethargy. His temperature, oddly enough, was not greatly above normal; but his whole condition was otherwise such as to suggest true fever rather than mental disorder.

On April 2nd at about 3 p.m. every trace of Wilcox's malady suddenly ceased. He sat upright in bed, astonished to find himself at home and completely ignorant of what had happened in dream or reality since the night of March 22nd. Pronounced well by his physician, he returned to his quarters in three days; but to Professor Angell he was of no further assistance. All traces of strange dreaming had vanished with his recovery, and my uncle kept no record of his night-thoughts after a week of pointless and irrelevant accounts of thoroughly usual visions.

Here the first part of the manuscript ended, but references to certain of the scattered notes gave me much material for thought—so much, in fact, that only the ingrained scepticism then forming my philosophy can account for my continued distrust of the artist. The notes in question were those descriptive of the dreams of various persons covering the same period as that in which young Wilcox had had his strange visitations. My uncle, it seems, had quickly instituted a prodigiously far-flung body of inquiries amongst nearly all the friends whom he could question without impertinence, asking for nightly reports of their dreams, and the dates of any notable visions for some time past. The reception of his request seems to have been varied; but he must, at the very least, have received more responses than any ordinary man could have handled without a secretary. This original correspondence was not preserved, but his notes formed a thorough and really significant digest. Average people in society and business—New England's traditional "salt of the earth"—gave an almost completely negative result, though scattered cases of uneasy but formless nocturnal impressions appear here and there, always between March 23d and April 2nd—the period of young Wilcox's delirium. Scientific men were little more affected, though four cases of vague description suggest fugitive glimpses of strange landscapes, and in one case there is mentioned a dread of something abnormal.

It was from the artists and poets that the pertinent answers came, and I know that panic would have broken loose had they been able to compare notes. As it was, lacking their original letters, I half suspected the compiler of having asked leading questions, or of having edited the correspondence in corroboration of what he had latently resolved to see. That is why I continued to feel that Wilcox, somehow cognisant of the old data which my uncle had possessed, had been imposing on the veteran scientist. These responses from aesthetes told a disturbing tale. From February 28th to April 2nd a large proportion of them had dreamed very bizarre things, the intensity of the dreams being immeasurably the stronger during the period of the sculptor's delirium. Over a fourth of those who reported anything, reported scenes and half-sounds not unlike those which Wilcox had described; and some of the dreamers confessed acute fear of the gigantic nameless thing visible toward the last. One case, which the note describes with emphasis, was very sad. The subject, a widely known architect with leanings toward theosophy and occultism, went violently insane on the date of young Wilcox's seizure, and expired several months later after incessant screamings to be saved from some escaped denizen of hell. Had my uncle referred to these cases by name instead of merely by number, I should have attempted some corroboration and personal investigation; but as it was, I succeeded in tracing down only a few. All of these, however, bore out the notes in full. I have often wondered if all the objects of the professor's questioning felt as puzzled as did this fraction. It is well that no explanation shall ever reach them.

The press cuttings, as I have intimated, touched on cases of panic, mania, and eccentricity during the given period. Professor Angell must have employed a cutting bureau, for the number of extracts was tremendous and the sources scattered throughout the globe. Here was a nocturnal suicide in London, where a lone sleeper had leaped from a window after a shocking cry. Here likewise a rambling letter to the editor of a paper in South America, where a fanatic deduces a dire future from visions he has seen. A despatch from California describes a theosophist colony as donning white robes en masse for some "glorious fulfilment" which never arrives, whilst items from India speak guardedly of serious native unrest toward the end of March. Voodoo orgies multiply in Hayti, and African outposts report ominous mutterings. American officers in the Philippines find certain tribes bothersome about this time, and New York policemen are mobbed by hysterical Levantines on the night of March 22–23. The west of Ireland, too, is full of wild rumour and legendry, and a fantastic painter named Ardois-Bonnot hangs a blasphemous "Dream Landscape" in the Paris spring salon of 1926. And so numerous are the recorded troubles in insane asylums, that only a miracle can have stopped the medical fraternity from noting strange parallelisms and drawing mystified conclusions. A weird bunch of cuttings, all told; and I can at this date scarcely envisage the callous rationalism with which I set them aside. But I was then convinced that young Wilcox had known of the older matters mentioned by the professor.

II.
The Tale of Inspector Legrasse.

The older matters which had made the sculptor's dream and bas-relief so significant to my uncle formed the subject of the second half of his long manuscript. Once before, it appears, Professor Angell had seen the hellish outlines of the nameless monstrosity, puzzled over the unknown hieroglyphics, and heard the ominous syllables which can be rendered only as "*Cthulhu*"; and all this in so stirring and horrible a connexion that it is small wonder he pursued young Wilcox with queries and demands for data.

The earlier experience had come in 1908, seventeen years before, when the American Archaeological Society held its annual meeting in St. Louis. Professor Angell, as befitted one of his authority and attainments, had had a prominent part in all the deliberations; and was one of the first to be approached by the several outsiders who took advantage of the convocation to offer questions for correct answering and problems for expert solution.

The chief of these outsiders, and in a short time the focus of interest for the entire meeting, was a commonplace-looking middle-aged man who had travelled all the way from New Orleans for certain special information unobtainable from any local source. His name was John Raymond Legrasse, and he was by profession an Inspector of Police. With him he bore the subject of his visit, a grotesque, repulsive, and apparently very ancient stone statuette whose origin he was at a loss to determine. It must not be fancied that Inspector Legrasse had the least interest in archaeology. On the contrary, his wish for enlightenment was prompted by purely professional considerations. The statuette, idol, fetish, or whatever it was, had been captured some months before in the wooded swamps south of New Orleans during a raid on a supposed voodoo meeting; and so singular and hideous were the rites connected with it, that the police could not but realise that they had stumbled on a dark cult totally unknown to them, and infinitely more diabolic than even the blackest of the African voodoo circles. Of its origin, apart from the erratic and unbelievable tales extorted from the captured members, absolutely nothing was to be discovered; hence the anxiety of the police for any antiquarian lore which might help them to place the frightful symbol, and through it track down the cult to its fountain-head.

Inspector Legrasse was scarcely prepared for the sensation which his offering created. One sight of the thing had been enough to throw the assembled men of science into a state of tense excitement, and they lost no time in crowding around him to gaze at the diminutive figure whose utter strangeness and air of genuinely abysmal antiquity hinted so potently at unopened and archaic vistas. No recognised school of sculpture had animated this terrible object, yet centuries and even thousands of years seemed recorded in its dim and greenish surface of unplaceable stone.

The figure, which was finally passed slowly from man to man for close and careful study, was between seven and eight inches in height, and of exquisitely artistic workmanship. It represented a monster of vaguely anthropoid outline, but with an octopus-like head whose face was a mass of feelers, a scaly, rubbery-looking body, prodigious claws on hind and fore feet, and long, narrow wings behind. This thing, which seemed instinct with a fearsome and unnatural malignancy, was of a somewhat bloated corpulence, and squatted evilly on a rectangular block or pedestal covered with undecipherable characters. The tips of the wings touched the back edge of the block, the seat occupied the centre, whilst the long, curved claws of the doubled-up, crouching hind legs gripped the front edge and extended a quarter of the way down toward the bottom of the pedestal. The cephalopod head was bent forward, so that the ends of the facial feelers brushed the backs of huge fore-paws which clasped the croucher's elevated knees. The aspect of the whole was abnormally lifelike, and the more subtly fearful because its source was so totally unknown. Its vast, awesome, and incalculable age was unmistakable; yet not one link did it shew with any known type of art belonging to civilisation's youth—or indeed to any other time. Totally separate and apart, its very material was a mystery; for the soapy, greenish-black stone with its golden or iridescent flecks and striations resembled nothing familiar to geology or mineralogy. The characters along the base were equally baffling; and no member present, despite a representation of half the world's expert learning in this field, could form the least notion of even their remotest linguistic kinship. They, like the subject and material, belonged to something horribly remote and distinct from mankind as we know it; something frightfully suggestive of old and unhallowed cycles of life in which our world and our conceptions have no part.

And yet, as the members severally shook their heads and confessed defeat at the Inspector's problem, there was one man in that gathering who suspected a touch of bizarre familiarity in the monstrous shape and writing, and who presently told with some diffidence of the odd trifle he knew. This person was the late William Channing Webb, Professor of Anthropology in Princeton University, and an explorer of no slight note. Professor Webb had been engaged, forty-eight years before, in a tour of Greenland and Iceland in search of some Runic inscriptions which he failed to unearth; and whilst high up on the West Greenland coast had encountered a singular tribe or cult of degenerate Esquimaux whose religion, a curious form of devil-worship, chilled him with its deliberate bloodthirstiness and repulsiveness. It was a faith of which other Esquimaux knew little, and which they mentioned only with shudders, saying that it had come down from horribly ancient aeons before ever the world was made. Besides nameless rites and human sacrifices there were certain queer hereditary rituals addressed to a supreme elder devil or *tornasuk*; and of this Professor Webb had taken a careful phonetic copy from an aged *angekok* or wizard-priest, expressing the sounds in Roman letters as best he knew how. But just now of prime significance was the fetish which this cult had cherished, and around which they danced when the aurora leaped high over the ice cliffs. It was, the professor stated, a very crude bas-relief of stone, comprising a hideous picture and some cryptic writing. And so far as he could tell, it was a rough parallel in all essential features of the bestial thing now lying before the meeting.

This data, received with suspense and astonishment by the assembled members, proved doubly exciting to Inspector Legrasse; and he began at once to ply his informant with questions. Having noted and copied an oral ritual among the swamp cult-worshippers his men had arrested, he besought the professor to remember as best he might the syllables taken down amongst the diabolist Esquimaux. There then followed an exhaustive comparison of details, and a moment of really awed silence when both detective and scientist agreed on the virtual identity of the phrase common to two hellish rituals so many worlds of distance apart. What, in substance, both the Esquimau wizards and the Louisiana swamp-priests had chanted to their kindred idols was something very like this—the word-divisions being guessed at from traditional breaks in the phrase as chanted aloud:

"*Ph'nglui mglw'nafh Cthulhu R'lyeh wgah'nagl fhtagn.*"

Legrasse had one point in advance of Professor Webb, for several among his mongrel prisoners had repeated to him what older celebrants had told them the words meant. This text, as given, ran something like this:

"*In his house at R'lyeh dead Cthulhu waits dreaming.*"

And now, in response to a general and urgent demand, Inspector Legrasse related as fully as possible his experience with the swamp worshippers; telling a story to which I could see my uncle attached profound significance. It savoured of the wildest dreams of myth-maker and theosophist, and disclosed an astonishing degree of cosmic imagination among such half-castes and pariahs as might be least expected to possess it.

On November 1st, 1907, there had come to the New Orleans police a frantic summons from the swamp and lagoon country to the south. The squatters there, mostly primitive but good-natured descendants of Lafitte's men, were in the grip of stark terror from an unknown thing which had stolen upon them in the night. It was voodoo, apparently, but voodoo of a more terrible sort than they had ever known; and some of their women and children had disappeared since the malevolent tom-tom had begun its incessant beating far within the black haunted woods where no dweller ventured. There were insane shouts and harrowing screams, soul-chilling chants and dancing devil-flames; and, the frightened messenger added, the people could stand it no more.

So a body of twenty police, filling two carriages and an automobile, had set out in the late afternoon with the shivering squatter as a guide. At the end of the passable road they alighted, and for miles splashed on in silence through the terrible cypress woods where day never came. Ugly roots and malignant hanging nooses of Spanish moss beset them, and now and then a pile of dank stones or fragment of a rotting wall intensified by its hint of morbid habitation a depression which every malformed tree and every fungous islet combined to create. At length the squatter settlement, a miserable huddle of huts, hove in sight; and hysterical dwellers ran out to cluster around the group of bobbing lanterns. The muffled beat of tom-toms was now faintly audible far, far ahead; and a curdling shriek came at infrequent intervals when the wind shifted. A reddish glare, too, seemed to filter through the pale undergrowth beyond endless avenues of forest night. Reluctant even to be left alone again, each one of the cowed squatters refused point-blank to advance another inch toward the scene of unholy worship, so Inspector Legrasse and his nineteen colleagues plunged on unguided into black arcades of horror that none of them had ever trod before.

The region now entered by the police was one of traditionally evil repute, substantially unknown and untraversed by white men. There were legends of a hidden lake unglimpsed by mortal sight, in which dwelt a huge, formless white polypous thing with luminous eyes; and squatters whispered that bat-winged devils flew up out of caverns in inner earth to worship it at midnight. They said it had been there before D'Iberville, before La Salle, before the Indians, and before even the wholesome beasts and birds of the woods. It was nightmare itself, and to see it was to die. But it made men dream, and so they knew enough to keep away. The present voodoo orgy was, indeed, on the merest fringe of this abhorred area, but that location was bad enough; hence perhaps the very place of the worship had terrified the squatters more than the shocking sounds and incidents.

Only poetry or madness could do justice to the noises heard by Legrasse's men as they ploughed on through the black morass toward the red glare and the muffled tom-toms. There are vocal qualities peculiar to men, and vocal qualities peculiar to beasts; and it is terrible to hear the one when the source should yield the other. Animal fury and orgiastic licence here whipped themselves to daemoniac heights by howls and squawking ecstasies that tore and reverberated through those nighted woods like pestilential tempests from the gulfs of hell. Now and then the less organised ululation would cease, and from what seemed a well-drilled chorus of hoarse voices would rise in sing-song chant that hideous phrase or ritual:

"*Ph'nglui mglw'nafh Cthulhu R'lyeh wgah'nagl fhtagn.*"

Then the men, having reached a spot where the trees were thinner, came suddenly in sight of the spectacle itself. Four of them reeled, one fainted, and two were shaken into a frantic cry which the mad cacophony of the orgy fortunately deadened. Legrasse dashed swamp water on the face of the fainting man, and all stood trembling and nearly hypnotised with horror.

In a natural glade of the swamp stood a grassy island of perhaps an acre's extent, clear of trees and tolerably dry. On this now leaped and twisted a more indescribable horde of human abnormality than any but a Sime or an Angarola could paint. Void of clothing, this hybrid spawn were braying, bellowing, and writhing about a monstrous ring-shaped bonfire; in the centre of which, revealed by occasional rifts in the curtain of flame, stood a great granite monolith some eight feet in height; on top of which, incongruous with its diminutiveness, rested the noxious carven statuette. From a wide circle of ten scaffolds set up at regular intervals with the flame-girt monolith as a centre hung, head downward, the oddly marred bodies of the helpless squatters who had disappeared. It was inside this circle that the ring of worshippers jumped and roared, the general direction of the mass motion being from left to right in endless Bacchanale between the ring of bodies and the ring of fire.

It may have been only imagination and it may have been only echoes which induced one of the men, an excitable Spaniard, to fancy he heard antiphonal responses to the ritual from some far and unillumined spot deeper within the wood of ancient legendry and horror. This man, Joseph D. Galvez, I later met and questioned; and he proved distractingly imaginative. He indeed went so far as to hint of the faint beating of great wings, and of a glimpse of shining eyes and a mountainous white bulk beyond the remotest trees—but I suppose he had been hearing too much native superstition.

Actually, the horrified pause of the men was of comparatively brief duration. Duty came first; and although there must have been nearly a hundred mongrel celebrants in the throng, the police relied on their firearms and plunged determinedly into the nauseous rout. For five minutes the resultant din and chaos were beyond description. Wild blows were struck, shots were fired, and escapes were made; but in the end Legrasse was able to count some forty-seven sullen prisoners, whom he forced to dress in haste and fall into line between two rows of policemen. Five of the worshippers lay dead, and two severely wounded ones were carried away on improvised stretchers by their fellow-prisoners. The image on the monolith, of course, was carefully removed and carried back by Legrasse.

Examined at headquarters after a trip of intense strain and weariness, the prisoners all proved to be men of a very low, mixed-blooded, and mentally aberrant type. Most were seamen, and a sprinkling of negroes and mulattoes, largely West Indians or Brava Portuguese from the Cape Verde Islands, gave a colouring of voodooism to the heterogeneous cult. But before many questions were asked, it became manifest that something far deeper and older than negro fetichism was involved. Degraded and ignorant as they were, the creatures held with surprising consistency to the central idea of their loathsome faith.

They worshipped, so they said, the Great Old Ones who lived ages before there were any men, and who came to the young world out of the sky. Those Old Ones were gone now, inside the earth and under the sea; but their dead bodies had told their secrets in dreams to the first men, who formed a cult which had never died. This was that cult, and the prisoners said it had always existed and always would exist, hidden in distant wastes and dark places all over the world until the time when the great priest Cthulhu, from his dark house in the mighty city of R'lyeh under the waters, should rise and bring the earth again beneath his sway. Some day he would call, when the stars were ready, and the secret cult would always be waiting to liberate him.

Meanwhile no more must be told. There was a secret which even torture could not extract. Mankind was not absolutely alone among the conscious things of earth, for shapes came out of the dark to visit the faithful few. But these were not the Great Old Ones. No man had ever seen the Old Ones. The carven idol was great Cthulhu, but none might say whether or not the others were precisely like him. No one could read the old writing now, but things were told by word of mouth. The chanted ritual was not the secret—that was never spoken aloud, only whispered. The chant meant only this: "In his house at R'lyeh dead Cthulhu waits dreaming."

Only two of the prisoners were found sane enough to be hanged, and the rest were committed to various institutions. All denied a part in the ritual murders, and averred that the killing had been done by Black Winged Ones which had come to them from their immemorial meeting-place in the haunted wood. But of those mysterious allies no coherent account could ever be gained. What the police did extract, came mainly from an immensely aged mestizo named Castro, who claimed to have sailed to strange ports and talked with undying leaders of the cult in the mountains of China.

Old Castro remembered bits of hideous legend that paled the speculations of theosophists and made man and the world seem recent and transient indeed. There had been aeons when other Things ruled on the earth, and They had had great cities. Remains of Them, he said the deathless Chinamen had told him, were still to be found as Cyclopean stones on islands in the Pacific. They all died vast epochs of time before men came, but there were arts which could revive Them when the stars had come round again to the right positions in the cycle of eternity. They had, indeed, come themselves from the stars, and brought Their images with Them.

These Great Old Ones, Castro continued, were not composed altogether of flesh and blood. They had shape—for did not this star-fashioned image prove it?—but that shape was not made of matter. When the stars were right, They could plunge from world to world through the sky; but when the stars were wrong, They could not live. But although They no longer lived, They would never really die. They all lay in stone houses in Their great city of

R'lyeh, preserved by the spells of mighty Cthulhu for a glorious resurrection when the stars and the earth might once more be ready for Them. But at that time some force from outside must serve to liberate Their bodies. The spells that preserved Them intact likewise prevented Them from making an initial move, and They could only lie awake in the dark and think whilst uncounted millions of years rolled by. They knew all that was occurring in the universe, but Their mode of speech was transmitted thought. Even now They talked in Their tombs. When, after infinities of chaos, the first men came, the Great Old Ones spoke to the sensitive among them by moulding their dreams; for only thus could Their language reach the fleshly minds of mammals.

Then, whispered Castro, those first men formed the cult around small idols which the Great Ones shewed them; idols brought in dim aeras from dark stars. That cult would never die till the stars came right again, and the secret priests would take great Cthulhu from His tomb to revive His subjects and resume His rule of earth. The time would be easy to know, for then mankind would have become as the Great Old Ones; free and wild and beyond good and evil, with laws and morals thrown aside and all men shouting and killing and revelling in joy. Then the liberated Old Ones would teach them new ways to shout and kill and revel and enjoy themselves, and all the earth would flame with a holocaust of ecstasy and freedom. Meanwhile the cult, by appropriate rites, must keep alive the memory of those ancient ways and shadow forth the prophecy of their return.

In the elder time chosen men had talked with the entombed Old Ones in dreams, but then something had happened. The great stone city R'lyeh, with its monoliths and sepulchres, had sunk beneath the waves; and the deep waters, full of the one primal mystery through which not even thought can pass, had cut off the spectral intercourse. But memory never died, and high-priests said that the city would rise again when the stars were right. Then came out of the earth the black spirits of earth, mouldy and shadowy, and full of dim rumours picked up in caverns beneath forgotten sea-bottoms. But of them old Castro dared not speak much. He cut himself off hurriedly, and no amount of persuasion or subtlety could elicit more in this direction. The *size* of the Old Ones, too, he curiously declined to mention. Of the cult, he said that he thought the centre lay amid the pathless deserts of Arabia, where Irem, the City of Pillars, dreams hidden and untouched. It was not allied to the European witch-cult, and was virtually unknown beyond its members. No book had ever really hinted of it, though the deathless Chinamen said that there were double meanings in the "Necronomicon" of the mad Arab Abdul Alhazred which the initiated might read as they chose, especially the much-discussed couplet:

> "That is not dead which can eternal lie,
> And with strange aeons even death may die."

Legrasse, deeply impressed and not a little bewildered, had inquired in vain concerning the historic affiliations of the cult. Castro, apparently, had told the truth when he said that it was wholly secret. The authorities at Tulane University could shed no light upon either cult or image, and now the detective had come to the highest authorities in the country and met with no more than the Greenland tale of Professor Webb.

The feverish interest aroused at the meeting by Legrasse's tale, corroborated as it was by the statuette, is echoed in the subsequent correspondence of those who attended; although scant mention occurs in the formal publications of the society. Caution is the first care of those accustomed to face occasional charlatanry and imposture. Legrasse for some time lent the image to Professor Webb, but at the latter's death it was returned to him and remains in his possession, where I viewed it not long ago. It is truly a terrible thing, and unmistakably akin to the dream-sculpture of young Wilcox.

That my uncle was excited by the tale of the sculptor I did not wonder, for what thoughts must arise upon hearing, after a knowledge of what Legrasse had learned of the cult, of a sensitive young man who had *dreamed* not only the figure and exact hieroglyphics of the swamp-found image and the Greenland devil tablet, but had come *in his dreams* upon at least three of the precise words of the formula uttered alike by Esquimau diabolists and mongrel Louisianans? Professor Angell's instant start on an investigation of the utmost thoroughness was eminently natural; though privately I suspected young Wilcox of having heard of the cult in some indirect way, and of having invented a series of dreams to heighten and continue the mystery at my uncle's expense. The dream-narratives and cuttings collected by the professor were, of course, strong corroboration; but the rationalism of my mind and the extravagance of the whole subject led me to adopt what I thought the most sensible conclusions. So, after thoroughly studying the manuscript again and correlating the theosophical and anthropological notes with the cult narrative of Legrasse, I made a trip to Providence to see the sculptor and give him the rebuke I thought proper for so boldly imposing upon a learned and aged man.

Wilcox still lived alone in the Fleur-de-Lys Building in Thomas Street, a hideous Victorian imitation of seventeenth-century Breton architecture which flaunts its stuccoed front amidst the lovely colonial houses on the ancient hill, and under the very shadow of the finest Georgian steeple in America. I found him at work in his rooms, and at once conceded from the specimens scattered about that his genius is indeed profound and authentic. He will, I believe, some time be heard from as one of the great decadents; for he has crystallised in clay and will one day mirror in marble those nightmares and phantasies which Arthur Machen evokes in prose, and Clark Ashton Smith makes visible in verse and in painting.

Dark, frail, and somewhat unkempt in aspect, he turned languidly at my knock and asked me my business without rising. When I told him who I was, he displayed some interest; for my uncle had excited his curiosity in probing his strange dreams, yet had never explained the reason for the study. I did not enlarge his knowledge in this regard, but sought with some subtlety to draw him out. In a short time I became convinced of his absolute sincerity, for he spoke of the dreams in a manner none could mistake. They and their subconscious residuum had influenced his art profoundly, and he shewed me a morbid statue whose contours almost made me shake with the potency of its black suggestion. He could not recall having seen the original of this thing except in his own dream bas-relief, but the outlines had formed themselves insensibly under his hands. It was, no doubt, the giant shape he had raved of in delirium. That he really knew nothing of the hidden cult, save from what my uncle's relentless catechism had let fall, he soon made clear; and again I strove to think of some way in which he could possibly have received the weird impressions.

He talked of his dreams in a strangely poetic fashion; making me see with terrible vividness the damp Cyclopean city of slimy green stone—whose *geometry*, he oddly said, was *all wrong*—and hear with frightened expectancy the ceaseless, half-mental calling from underground: "*Cthulhu fhtagn*", "*Cthulhu fhtagn*". These words had formed part of that dread ritual which told of dead Cthulhu's dream-vigil in his stone vault at R'lyeh, and I felt deeply moved despite my rational beliefs. Wilcox, I was sure, had heard of the cult in some casual way, and had soon forgotten it amidst the mass of his equally weird reading and imagining. Later, by virtue of its sheer impressiveness, it had found subconscious expression in dreams, in the bas-relief, and in the terrible statue I now beheld; so that his imposture upon my uncle had been a very innocent one. The youth was of a type, at once slightly affected and slightly ill-mannered, which I could never like; but I was willing enough now to admit both his genius and his honesty. I took leave of him amicably, and wish him all the success his talent promises.

The matter of the cult still remained to fascinate me, and at times I had visions of personal fame from researches into its origin and connexions. I visited New Orleans, talked with Legrasse and others of that old-time raiding-party, saw the frightful image, and even questioned such of the mongrel prisoners as still survived. Old Castro, unfortunately, had been dead for some years. What I now heard so graphically at first-hand, though it was really no more than a detailed confirmation of what my uncle had written, excited me afresh; for I felt sure that I was on the track of a very real, very secret, and very ancient religion whose discovery would make me an anthropologist of note. My attitude was still one of absolute materialism, *as I wish it still were,* and I discounted with almost inexplicable perversity the coincidence of the dream notes and odd cuttings collected by Professor Angell.

One thing I began to suspect, and which I now fear I *know,* is that my uncle's death was far from natural. He fell on a narrow hill street leading up from an ancient waterfront swarming with foreign mongrels, after a careless push from a negro sailor. I did not forget the mixed blood and marine pursuits of the cult-members in Louisiana, and would not be surprised to learn of secret methods and poison needles as ruthless and as anciently known as the cryptic rites and beliefs. Legrasse and his men, it is true, have been let alone; but in Norway a certain seaman who saw things is dead. Might not the deeper inquiries of my uncle after encountering the sculptor's data have come to sinister ears? I think Professor Angell died because he knew too much, or because he was likely to learn too much. Whether I shall go as he did remains to be seen, for I have learned much now.

III.
The Madness from the Sea.

If heaven ever wishes to grant me a boon, it will be a total effacing of the results of a mere chance which fixed my eye on a certain stray piece of shelf-paper. It was nothing on which I would naturally have stumbled in the course of my daily round, for it was an old number of an Australian journal, the *Sydney Bulletin* for April 18, 1925. It had escaped even the cutting bureau which had at the time of its issuance been avidly collecting material for my uncle's research.

I had largely given over my inquiries into what Professor Angell called the "Cthulhu Cult", and was visiting a learned friend in Paterson, New Jersey; the curator of a local museum and a mineralogist of note. Examining one day the reserve specimens roughly set on the storage shelves in a rear room of the museum, my eye was caught by an odd picture in one of the old papers spread beneath the stones. It was the *Sydney Bulletin* I have mentioned, for my friend has wide affiliations in all conceivable foreign parts; and the picture was a half-tone cut of a hideous stone image almost identical with that which Legrasse had found in the swamp.

Eagerly clearing the sheet of its precious contents, I scanned the item in detail; and was disappointed to find it of only moderate length. What it suggested, however, was of portentous significance to my flagging quest; and I carefully tore it out for immediate action. It read as follows:

MYSTERY DERELICT FOUND AT SEA

Vigilant Arrives With Helpless Armed New Zealand Yacht in Tow.
One Survivor and Dead Man Found Aboard. Tale of Desperate Battle and Deaths at Sea.
Rescued Seaman Refuses Particulars of Strange Experience.
Odd Idol Found in His Possession. Inquiry to Follow.

The Morrison Co.'s freighter *Vigilant*, bound from Valparaiso, arrived this morning at its wharf in Darling Harbour, having in tow the battled and disabled but heavily armed steam yacht *Alert* of Dunedin, N. Z., which was sighted April 12th in S. Latitude 34° 21′, W. Longitude 152° 17′ with one living and one dead man aboard.

The *Vigilant* left Valparaiso March 25th, and on April 2nd was driven considerably south of her course by exceptionally heavy storms and monster waves. On April 12th the derelict was sighted; and though apparently deserted, was found upon boarding to contain one survivor in a half-delirious condition and one man who had evidently been dead for more than a week. The living man was clutching a horrible stone idol of unknown origin, about a foot in height, regarding whose nature authorities at Sydney University, the Royal Society, and the Museum in College Street all profess complete bafflement, and which the survivor says he found in the cabin of the yacht, in a small carved shrine of common pattern.

This man, after recovering his senses, told an exceedingly strange story of piracy and slaughter. He is Gustaf Johansen, a

Norwegian of some intelligence, and had been second mate of the two-masted schooner *Emma* of Auckland, which sailed for Callao February 20th with a complement of eleven men. The *Emma*, he says, was delayed and thrown widely south of her course by the great storm of March 1st, and on March 22nd, in S. Latitude 49° 51´, W. Longitude 128° 34´, encountered the *Alert*, manned by a queer and evil-looking crew of Kanakas and half-castes. Being ordered peremptorily to turn back, Capt. Collins refused; whereupon the strange crew began to fire savagely and without warning upon the schooner with a peculiarly heavy battery of brass cannon forming part of the yacht's equipment. The *Emma's* men shewed fight, says the survivor, and though the schooner began to sink from shots beneath the waterline they managed to heave alongside their enemy and board her, grappling with the savage crew on the yacht's deck, and being forced to kill them all, the number being slightly superior, because of their particularly abhorrent and desperate though rather clumsy mode of fighting.

Three of the *Emma*'s men, including Capt. Collins and First Mate Green, were killed; and the remaining eight under Second Mate Johansen proceeded to navigate the captured yacht, going ahead in their original direction to see if any reason for their ordering back had existed. The next day, it appears, they raised and landed on a small island, although none is known to exist in that part of the ocean; and six of the men somehow died ashore, though Johansen is queerly reticent about this part of his story, and speaks only of their falling into a rock chasm. Later, it seems, he and one companion boarded the yacht and tried to manage her, but were beaten about by the storm of April 2nd. From that time till his rescue on the 12th the man remembers little, and he does not even recall when William Briden, his companion, died. Briden's death reveals no apparent cause, and was probably due to excitement or exposure. Cable advices from Dunedin report that the *Alert* was well known there as an island trader, and bore an evil reputation along the waterfront. It was owned by a curious group of half-castes whose frequent meetings and night trips to the woods attracted no little curiosity; and it had set sail in great haste just after the storm and earth tremors of March 1st. Our Auckland correspondent gives the *Emma* and her crew an excellent reputation, and Johansen is described as a sober and worthy man. The admiralty will institute an inquiry on the whole matter beginning tomorrow, at which every effort will be made to induce Johansen to speak more freely than he has done hitherto.

This was all, together with the picture of the hellish image; but what a train of ideas it started in my mind! Here were new treasuries of data on the Cthulhu Cult, and evidence that it had strange interests at sea as well as on land. What motive prompted the hybrid crew to order back the *Emma* as they sailed about with their hideous idol? What was the unknown island on which six of the *Emma's* crew had died, and about which the mate Johansen was so secretive? What had the vice-admiralty's investigation brought out, and what was known of the noxious cult in Dunedin? And most marvellous of all, what deep and more than natural linkage of dates was this which gave a malign and now undeniable significance to the various turns of events so carefully noted by my uncle?

March 1st—our February 28th according to the International Date Line—the earthquake and storm had come. From Dunedin the *Alert* and her noisome crew had darted eagerly forth as if imperiously summoned, and on the other side of the earth poets and artists had begun to dream of a strange, dank Cyclopean city whilst a young sculptor had moulded in his sleep the form of the dreaded Cthulhu. March 23d the crew of the *Emma* landed on an unknown island and left six men dead; and on that date the dreams of sensitive men assumed a heightened vividness and darkened with dread of a giant monster's malign pursuit, whilst an architect had gone mad and a sculptor had lapsed suddenly into delirium! And what of this storm of April 2nd—the date on which all dreams of the dank city ceased, and Wilcox emerged unharmed from the bondage of strange fever? What of all this—and of those hints of old Castro about the sunken, star-born Old Ones and their coming reign; their faithful cult *and their mastery of dreams?* Was I tottering on the brink of cosmic horrors beyond man's power to bear? If so, they must be horrors of the mind alone, for in some way the second of April had put a stop to whatever monstrous menace had begun its siege of mankind's soul.

That evening, after a day of hurried cabling and arranging, I bade my host adieu and took a train for San Francisco. In less than a month I was in Dunedin; where, however, I found that little was known of the strange cult-members who had lingered in the old sea-taverns. Waterfront scum was far too common for special mention; though there was vague talk about one inland trip these mongrels had made, during which faint drumming and red flame were noted on the distant hills. In Auckland I learned that Johansen had returned *with yellow hair turned white* after a perfunctory and inconclusive questioning at Sydney, and had thereafter sold his cottage in West Street and sailed with his wife to his old home in Oslo. Of his stirring experience he would tell his friends no more than he had told the admiralty officials, and all they could do was to give me his Oslo address.

After that I went to Sydney and talked profitlessly with seamen and members of the vice-admiralty court. I saw the *Alert*, now sold and in commercial use, at Circular Quay in Sydney Cove, but gained nothing from its non-committal bulk. The crouching image with its cuttlefish head, dragon body, scaly wings, and hieroglyphed pedestal, was preserved in the Museum at Hyde Park; and I studied it long and well, finding it a thing of balefully exquisite workmanship, and with the same utter mystery, terrible antiquity, and unearthly strangeness of material which I had noted in Legrasse's smaller specimen. Geologists, the curator told me, had found it a monstrous puzzle; for they vowed that the world held no rock like it. Then I thought with a shudder of what old Castro had told Legrasse about the primal Great Ones: "They had come from the stars, and had brought Their images with Them."

Shaken with such a mental revolution as I had never before known, I now resolved to visit Mate Johansen in Oslo. Sailing for London, I reëmbarked at once for the Norwegian capital; and one autumn day landed at the trim wharves in the shadow of the Egeberg. Johansen's address, I discovered, lay in the Old Town of King Harold Haardrada, which kept alive the name of Oslo during all the centuries that the greater city masqueraded as "Christiania". I made the brief trip by taxicab, and knocked with palpitant heart at the door of a neat and ancient building with plastered front. A sad-faced woman in black answered my summons, and I was stung with disappointment when she told me in halting English that Gustaf Johansen was no more.

He had not survived his return, said his wife, for the doings at sea in 1925 had broken him. He had told her no more than he had told the public, but had left a long manuscript—of "technical matters" as he said—written in English, evidently in order to safeguard her from the peril of casual perusal. During a walk through a narrow lane near the Gothenburg dock, a bundle of papers falling from an attic window had knocked him down. Two Lascar sailors at once helped him to his feet, but before the ambulance could reach him he was dead. Physicians found no adequate cause for the end, and laid it to heart trouble and a weakened constitution.

I now felt gnawing at my vitals that dark terror which will never leave me till I, too, am at rest; "accidentally" or otherwise. Persuading the widow that my connexion with her husband's "technical matters" was sufficient to entitle me to his manuscript, I bore the document away and began to read it on the London boat. It was a simple, rambling thing—a naive sailor's effort at a post-facto diary—and strove to recall day by day that last awful voyage. I cannot attempt to transcribe it verbatim in all its cloudiness and redundance, but I will tell its gist enough to shew why the sound of the water against the vessel's sides became so unendurable to me that I stopped my ears with cotton.

Johansen, thank God, did not know quite all, even though he saw the city and the Thing, but I shall never sleep calmly again when I think of the horrors that lurk ceaselessly behind life in time and in space, and of those unhallowed blasphemies from elder stars which dream beneath the sea, known and favoured by a nightmare cult ready and eager to loose them on the world whenever another earthquake shall heave their monstrous stone city again to the sun and air.

Johansen's voyage had begun just as he told it to the vice-admiralty. The *Emma,* in ballast, had cleared Auckland on February 20th, and had felt the full force of that earthquake-born tempest which must have heaved up from the sea-bottom the horrors that filled men's dreams. Once more under control, the ship was making good progress when held up by the *Alert* on March 22nd, and I could feel the mate's regret as he wrote of her bombardment and sinking. Of the swarthy cult-fiends on the *Alert* he speaks with significant horror. There was some peculiarly abominable quality about them which made their destruction seem almost a duty, and Johansen shews ingenuous wonder at the charge of ruthlessness brought against his party during the proceedings of the court of inquiry. Then, driven ahead by curiosity in their captured yacht under Johansen's command, the men sight a great stone pillar sticking out of the sea, and in S. Latitude 47° 9′, W. Longitude 126° 43′ come upon a coast-line of mingled mud, ooze, and weedy Cyclopean masonry which can be nothing less than the tangible substance of earth's supreme terror—the nightmare corpse-city of R'lyeh, that was built in measureless aeons behind history by the vast, loathsome shapes that seeped down from the dark stars. There lay great Cthulhu and his hordes, hidden in green slimy vaults and sending out at last, after cycles incalculable, the thoughts that spread fear to the dreams of the sensitive and called imperiously to the faithful to come on a pilgrimage of liberation and restoration. All this Johansen did not suspect, but God knows he soon saw enough!

I suppose that only a single mountaintop, the hideous monolith-crowned citadel whereon great Cthulhu was buried, actually emerged from the waters. When I think of the *extent* of all that may be brooding down there I almost wish to kill myself forthwith. Johansen and his men were awed by the cosmic majesty of this dripping Babylon of elder daemons, and must have guessed without guidance that it was nothing of this or of any sane planet. Awe at the unbelievable size of the greenish stone blocks, at the dizzying height of the great carven monolith, and at the stupefying identity of the colossal statues and bas-reliefs with the queer image found in the shrine on the *Alert,* is poignantly visible in every line of the mate's frightened description.

Without knowing what futurism is like, Johansen achieved something very close to it when he spoke of the city; for instead of describing any definite structure or building, he dwells only on broad impressions of vast angles and stone surfaces—surfaces too great to belong to any thing right or proper for this earth, and impious with horrible images and hieroglyphs. I mention his talk about *angles* because it suggests something Wilcox had told me of his awful dreams. He had said that the *geometry* of the dream-place he saw was abnormal, non-Euclidean, and loathsomely redolent of spheres and dimensions apart from ours. Now an unlettered seaman felt the same thing whilst gazing at the terrible reality.

Johansen and his men landed at a sloping mud-bank on this monstrous Acropolis, and clambered slipperily up over titan oozy blocks which could have been no mortal staircase. The very sun of heaven seemed distorted when viewed through the polarising miasma welling out from this sea-soaked perversion, and twisted menace and suspense lurked leeringly in those crazily elusive angles of carven rock where a second glance shewed concavity after the first shewed convexity.

Something very like fright had come over all the explorers before anything more definite than rock and ooze and weed was seen. Each would have fled had he not feared the scorn of the others, and it was only half-heartedly that they searched—vainly, as it proved—for some portable souvenir to bear away.

It was Rodriguez the Portuguese who climbed up the foot of the monolith and shouted of what he had found. The rest followed him, and looked curiously at the immense carved door with the now familiar squid-dragon bas-relief. It was, Johansen said, like a great barn-door; and they all felt that it was a door because of the ornate lintel, threshold, and jambs around it, though they could not decide whether it lay flat like a trap-door or slantwise like an outside cellar-door. As Wilcox would have said, the geometry of the place was all wrong. One could not be sure that the sea and the ground were horizontal, hence the relative position of everything else seemed phantasmally variable.

Briden pushed at the stone in several places without result. Then Donovan felt over it delicately around the edge, pressing each point separately as he went. He climbed interminably along the grotesque stone moulding—that is, one would call it climbing if the thing was not after all horizontal—and the men wondered how any door in the universe could be so vast. Then, very softly and slowly, the acre-great panel began to give inward at the top; and they saw that it was balanced. Donovan slid or somehow propelled himself down or along the jamb and rejoined his fellows, and everyone watched the queer recession of the monstrously carven portal. In this phantasy of prismatic distortion it moved anomalously in a diagonal way, so that all the rules of matter and perspective seemed upset.

The aperture was black with a darkness almost material. That tenebrousness was indeed a *positive quality*; for it obscured such parts of the inner walls as ought to have been revealed, and actually burst forth like smoke from its aeon-long imprisonment, visibly darkening the sun as it slunk away into the shrunken and gibbous sky on flapping membraneous wings. The odour arising from the newly opened depths was intolerable, and at length the quick-eared Hawkins thought he heard a nasty, slopping sound down there. Everyone listened, and everyone was listening still when It lumbered slobberingly into sight and gropingly squeezed Its gelatinous green immensity through the black doorway into the tainted outside air of that poison city of madness.

Poor Johansen's handwriting almost gave out when he wrote of this. Of the six men who never reached the ship, he thinks two perished of pure fright in that accursed instant. The Thing cannot be described—there is no language for such abysms of shrieking and immemorial lunacy, such eldritch contradictions of all matter, force, and cosmic order. A mountain walked or stumbled. God! What wonder that across the earth a great architect went mad, and poor Wilcox raved with fever in that telepathic instant? The Thing of the idols, the green, sticky spawn of the stars, had awaked to claim his own. The stars were right again, and what an age-old cult had failed to do by design, a band of innocent sailors had done by accident. After vigintillions of years great Cthulhu was loose again, and ravening for delight.

Three men were swept up by the flabby claws before anybody turned. God rest them, if there be any rest in the universe. They were Donovan, Guerrera, and Ångstrom. Parker slipped as the other three were plunging frenziedly over endless vistas of green-crusted rock to the boat, and Johansen swears he was swallowed up by an angle of masonry which shouldn't have been there; an angle which was acute, but behaved as if it were obtuse. So only Briden and Johansen reached the boat, and pulled desperately for the *Alert* as the mountainous monstrosity flopped down the slimy stones and hesitated floundering at the edge of the water.

Steam had not been suffered to go down entirely, despite the departure of all hands for the shore; and it was the work of only a few moments of feverish rushing up and down between wheel and engines to get the *Alert* under way. Slowly, amidst the distorted horrors of that indescribable scene, she began to churn the lethal waters; whilst on the masonry of that charnel shore that was not of earth the titan Thing from the stars slavered and gibbered like Polypheme cursing the fleeing ship of Odysseus. Then, bolder than the storied Cyclops, great Cthulhu slid greasily into the water and began to pursue with vast wave-raising strokes of cosmic potency. Briden looked back and went mad, laughing shrilly as he kept on laughing at intervals till death found him one night in the cabin whilst Johansen was wandering deliriously.

But Johansen had not given out yet. Knowing that the Thing could surely overtake the *Alert* until steam was fully up, he resolved on a desperate chance; and, setting the engine for full speed, ran lightning-like on deck and reversed the wheel. There was a mighty eddying and foaming in the noisome brine, and as the steam mounted higher and higher the brave Norwegian drove his vessel head on against the pursuing jelly which rose above the unclean froth like the stern of a daemon galleon. The awful squid-head with writhing feelers came nearly up to the bowsprit of the sturdy yacht, but Johansen drove on relentlessly. There was a bursting as of an exploding bladder, a slushy nastiness as of a cloven sunfish, a stench as of a thousand opened graves, and a sound that the chronicler would not put on paper. For an instant the ship was befouled by an acrid and blinding green cloud, and then there was only a venomous seething astern; where—God in heaven!—the scattered plasticity of that nameless sky-spawn was nebulously *recombining* in its hateful original form, whilst its distance widened every second as the *Alert* gained impetus from its mounting steam.

That was all. After that Johansen only brooded over the idol in the cabin and attended to a few matters of food for himself and the laughing maniac by his side. He did not try to navigate after the first bold flight, for the reaction had taken something out of his soul. Then came the storm of April 2nd, and a gathering of the clouds about his consciousness. There is a sense of spectral whirling through liquid gulfs of infinity, of dizzying rides through reeling universes on a comet's tail, and of hysterical plunges from the pit to the moon and from the moon back again to the pit, all livened by a cachinnating chorus of the distorted, hilarious elder gods and the green, bat-winged mocking imps of Tartarus.

Out of that dream came rescue—the *Vigilant,* the vice-admiralty court, the streets of Dunedin, and the long voyage back home to the old house by the Egeberg. He could not tell—they would think him mad. He would write of what he knew before death came, but his wife must not guess. Death would be a boon if only it could blot out the memories.

That was the document I read, and now I have placed it in the tin box beside the bas-relief and the papers of Professor Angell. With it shall go this record of mine—this test of my own sanity, wherein is pieced together that which I hope may never be pieced together again. I have looked upon all that the universe has to hold of horror, and even the skies of spring and the flowers of summer must ever afterward be poison to me. But I do not think my life will be long. As my uncle went, as poor Johansen went, so I shall go. I know too much, and the cult still lives.

Cthulhu still lives, too, I suppose, again in that chasm of stone which has shielded him since the sun was young. His accursed city is sunken once more, for the *Vigilant* sailed over the spot after the April storm; but his ministers on earth still bellow and prance and slay around idol-capped monoliths in lonely places. He must have been trapped by the sinking whilst within his black abyss, or else the world would by now be screaming with fright and frenzy. Who knows the end? What has risen may sink, and what has sunk may rise. Loathsomeness waits and dreams in the deep, and decay spreads over the tottering cities of men. A time will come—but I must not and cannot think! Let me pray that, if I do not survive this manuscript, my executors may put caution before audacity and see that it meets no other eye.

PICKMAN'S MODEL

You needn't think I'm crazy, Eliot—plenty of others have queerer prejudices than this. Why don't you laugh at Oliver's grandfather, who won't ride in a motor? If I don't like that damned subway, it's my own business; and we got here more quickly anyhow in the taxi. We'd have had to walk up the hill from Park Street if we'd taken the car.

I know I'm more nervous than I was when you saw me last year, but you don't need to hold a clinic over it. There's plenty of reason, God knows, and I fancy I'm lucky to be sane at all. Why the third degree? You didn't use to be so inquisitive.

Well, if you must hear it, I don't know why you shouldn't. Maybe you ought to, anyhow, for you kept writing me like a grieved parent when you heard I'd begun to cut the Art Club and keep away from Pickman. Now that he's disappeared I go around to the club once in a while, but my nerves aren't what they were.

No, I don't know what's become of Pickman, and I don't like to guess. You might have surmised I had some inside information when I dropped him—and that's why I don't want to think where he's gone. Let the police find what they can—it won't be much, judging from the fact that they don't know yet of the old North End place he hired under the name of Peters. I'm not sure that I could find it again myself—not that I'd ever try, even in broad daylight! Yes, I do know, or am afraid I know, why he maintained it. I'm coming to that. And I think you'll understand before I'm through why I don't tell the police. They would ask me to guide them, but I couldn't go back there even if I knew the way. There was something there—and now I can't use the subway or (and you may as well have your laugh at this, too) go down into cellars any more.

I should think you'd have known I didn't drop Pickman for the same silly reasons that fussy old women like Dr. Reid or Joe Minot or Bosworth did. Morbid art doesn't shock me, and when a man has the genius Pickman had I feel it an honour to know him, no matter what direction his work takes. Boston never had a greater painter than Richard Upton Pickman. I said it at first and I say it still, and I never swerved an inch, either, when he shewed that "Ghoul Feeding". That, you remember, was when Minot cut him.

You know, it takes profound art and profound insight into Nature to turn out stuff like Pickman's. Any magazine-cover hack can splash paint around wildly and call it a nightmare or a Witches' Sabbath or a portrait of the devil, but only a great painter can make such a thing really scare or ring true. That's because only a real artist knows the actual anatomy of the terrible or the physiology of fear—the exact sort of lines and proportions that connect up with latent instincts or hereditary memories of fright, and the proper colour contrasts and lighting effects to stir the dormant sense of strangeness. I don't have to tell you why a Fuseli really brings a shiver while a cheap ghost-story frontispiece merely makes us laugh. There's something those fellows catch—beyond life—that they're able to make us catch for a second. Doré had it. Sime has it. Angarola of Chicago has it. And Pickman had it as no man ever had it before or—I hope to heaven—ever will again.

Don't ask me what it is they see. You know, in ordinary art, there's all the difference in the world between the vital, breathing things drawn from Nature or models and the artificial truck that commercial small fry reel off in a bare studio by rule. Well, I should say that the really weird artist has a kind of vision which makes models, or summons up what amounts to actual scenes from the spectral world he lives in. Anyhow, he manages to turn out results that differ from the pretender's mince-pie dreams in just about the same way that the life painter's results differ from the concoctions of a correspondence-school cartoonist. If I had ever seen what Pickman saw—but no! Here, let's have a drink before we get any deeper. Gad, I wouldn't be alive if I'd ever seen what that man—if he was a man—saw!

You recall that Pickman's forte was faces. I don't believe anybody since Goya could put so much of sheer hell into a set of features or a twist of expression. And before Goya you have to go back to the mediaeval chaps who did the gargoyles and chimaeras on Notre Dame and Mont Saint-Michel. They believed all sorts of things—and maybe they saw all sorts of things, too, for the Middle Ages had some curious phases. I remember your asking Pickman yourself once, the year before you went away, wherever in thunder he got such ideas and visions. Wasn't that a nasty laugh he gave you? It was partly because of that laugh that Reid dropped him. Reid, you know, had just taken up comparative pathology, and was full of pompous "inside stuff" about the biological or evolutionary significance of this or that mental or physical symptom. He said Pickman repelled him more and more every day, and almost frightened him toward the last—that the fellow's features and expression were slowly developing in a way he didn't like; in a way that wasn't human. He had a lot of talk about diet, and said Pickman must be abnormal and eccentric to the last degree. I suppose you told Reid, if you and he had any correspondence over it, that he'd let Pickman's paintings get on his nerves or harrow up his imagination. I know I told him that myself—then.

But keep in mind that I didn't drop Pickman for anything like this. On the contrary, my admiration for him kept growing; for that "Ghoul Feeding" was a tremendous achievement. As you know, the club wouldn't exhibit it, and the Museum of Fine Arts wouldn't accept it as a gift; and I can add that nobody would buy it, so Pickman had it right in his house till he went. Now his father has it in Salem—you know Pickman comes of old Salem stock, and had a witch ancestor hanged in 1692.

I got into the habit of calling on Pickman quite often, especially after I began making notes for a monograph on weird art. Probably it was his work which put the idea into my head, and anyhow, I found him a mine of data and suggestions when I came to develop it. He shewed me all the paintings and drawings he had about; including some pen-and-ink sketches that would, I verily believe, have got him kicked out of the club if many of the members had seen them. Before long I was pretty nearly a devotee, and would listen for hours like a schoolboy to art theories and philosophic speculations wild enough to qualify him for the Danvers asylum. My hero-worship, coupled with the fact that people generally were commencing to have less and less to do with him, made him get very confidential with me; and one evening he hinted that if I were fairly close-mouthed and none too squeamish, he might shew me something rather unusual—something a bit stronger than anything he had in the house.

"You know," he said, "there are things that won't do for Newbury Street—things that are out of place here, and that can't be conceived here, anyhow. It's my business to catch the overtones of the soul, and you won't find those in a parvenu set of artificial streets on made land. Back Bay isn't Boston—it isn't anything yet, because it's had no time to pick up memories and attract local spirits. If there are any ghosts here, they're the tame ghosts of a salt marsh and a shallow cove; and I want human ghosts—the ghosts of beings highly organised enough to have looked on hell and known the meaning of what they saw.

"The place for an artist to live is the North End. If any aesthete were sincere, he'd put up with the slums for the sake of the massed traditions. God, man! Don't you realise that places like that weren't merely *made,* but actually *grew?* Generation after generation lived and felt and died there, and in days when people weren't afraid to live and feel and die. Don't you know there was a mill on Copp's Hill in 1632, and that half the present streets were laid out by 1650? I can shew you houses that have stood two centuries and a half and more; houses that have witnessed what would make a modern house crumble into powder. What do moderns know of life and the forces behind it? You call the Salem witchcraft a delusion, but I'll wager my four-times-great-grandmother could have told you things. They hanged her on Gallows Hill, with Cotton Mather looking sanctimoniously on. Mather, damn him, was afraid somebody might succeed in kicking free of this accursed cage of monotony—I wish someone had laid a spell on him or sucked his blood in the night!

"I can shew you a house he lived in, and I can shew you another one he was afraid to enter in spite of all his fine bold talk. He knew things he didn't dare put into that stupid 'Magnalia' or that puerile 'Wonders of the Invisible World'. Look here, do you know the whole North End once had a set of tunnels that kept certain people in touch with each other's houses, and the burying-ground, and the sea? Let them prosecute and persecute above ground—things went on every day that they couldn't reach, and voices laughed at night that they couldn't place!

"Why, man, out of ten surviving houses built before 1700 and not moved since, I'll wager that in eight I can shew you something queer in the cellar. There's hardly a month that you don't read of workmen finding bricked-up arches and wells leading nowhere in this or that old place as it comes down—you could see one near Henchman Street from the elevated last year. There were witches and what their spells summoned; pirates and what they brought in from the sea; smugglers; privateers—and I tell you, people knew how to live, and how to enlarge the bounds of life, in the old times! This wasn't the only world a bold and wise man could know—faugh! And to think of today in contrast, with such pale-pink brains that even a club of supposed artists gets shudders and convulsions if a picture goes beyond the feelings of a Beacon Street tea-table!

"The only saving grace of the present is that it's too damned stupid to question the past very closely. What do maps and records and guide-books really tell of the North End? Bah! At a guess I'll guarantee to lead you to thirty or forty alleys and networks of alleys north of Prince Street that aren't suspected by ten living beings outside of the foreigners that swarm them. And what do those Dagoes know of their meaning? No, Thurber, these ancient places are dreaming gorgeously and overflowing with wonder and terror and escape from the commonplace, and yet there's not a living soul to understand or profit by them. Or rather, there's only one living soul—for I haven't been digging around in the past for nothing!

"See here, you're interested in this sort of thing. What if I told you that I've got another studio up there, where I can catch the night-spirit of antique horror and paint things that I couldn't even think of in Newbury Street? Naturally I don't tell those cursed old maids at the club—with Reid, damn him, whispering even as it is that I'm a sort of monster bound down the toboggan of reverse evolution. Yes, Thurber, I decided long ago that one must paint terror as well as beauty from life, so I did some exploring in places where I had reason to know terror lives.

"I've got a place that I don't believe three living Nordic men besides myself have ever seen. It isn't so very far from the elevated as distance goes, but it's centuries away as the soul goes. I took it because of the queer old brick well in the cellar—one of the sort I told you about. The shack's almost tumbling down, so that nobody else would live there, and I'd hate to tell you how little I pay for it. The windows are boarded up, but I like that all the better, since I don't want daylight for what I do. I paint in the cellar, where the inspiration is thickest, but I've other rooms furnished on the ground floor. A Sicilian owns it, and I've hired it under the name of Peters.

"Now if you're game, I'll take you there tonight. I think you'd enjoy the pictures, for as I said, I've let myself go a bit there. It's no vast tour—I sometimes do it on foot, for I don't want to attract attention with a taxi in such a place. We can take the shuttle at the South Station for Battery Street, and after that the walk isn't much."

Well, Eliot, there wasn't much for me to do after that harangue but to keep myself from running instead of walking for the first vacant cab we could sight. We changed to the elevated at the South Station, and at about twelve o'clock had climbed down the steps at Battery Street and struck along the old waterfront past Constitution Wharf. I didn't keep track of the cross streets, and can't tell you yet which it was we turned up, but I know it wasn't Greenough Lane.

When we did turn, it was to climb through the deserted length of the oldest and dirtiest alley I ever saw in my life, with crumbling-looking gables, broken small-paned windows, and archaic chimneys that stood out half-disintegrated against the moonlit sky. I don't believe there were three houses in sight that hadn't been standing in Cotton Mather's time—certainly I glimpsed at least two with an overhang, and once I thought I saw a peaked roof-line of the almost forgotten pre-gambrel type, though antiquarians tell us there are none left in Boston.

From that alley, which had a dim light, we turned to the left into an equally silent and still narrower alley with no light at all; and in a minute made what I think was an obtuse-angled bend toward the right in the dark. Not long after this Pickman produced a flashlight and revealed an antediluvian ten-panelled door that looked damnably worm-eaten. Unlocking it, he ushered me into a barren hallway with what was once splendid dark-oak panelling—simple, of course, but thrillingly suggestive of the times of Andros and Phipps and the witchcraft. Then he took me through a door on the left, lighted an oil lamp, and told me to make myself at home.

Now, Eliot, I'm what the man in the street would call fairly "hard-boiled", but I'll confess that what I saw on the walls of that room gave me a bad turn. They were his pictures, you know—the ones he couldn't paint or even shew in Newbury Street—and he was right when he said he had "let himself go". Here—have another drink—I need one anyhow!

There's no use in my trying to tell you what they were like, because the awful, the blasphemous horror and the unbelievable loathsomeness and moral foetor came from simple touches quite beyond the power of words to classify. There was none of the exotic technique you see in Sidney Sime, none of the trans-Saturnian landscapes and lunar fungi that Clark Ashton Smith uses to freeze the blood. The backgrounds were mostly old churchyards, deep woods, cliffs by the sea, brick tunnels, ancient panelled rooms, or simple vaults of masonry. Copp's Hill Burying-Ground, which could not be many blocks away from this very house, was a favourite scene.

The madness and monstrosity lay in the figures in the foreground—for Pickman's morbid art was preëminently one of daemoniac portraiture. These figures were seldom completely human, but often approached humanity in varying degree. Most of the bodies, while roughly bipedal, had a forward-slumping and a vaguely canine cast. The texture of the majority was a kind of unpleasant rubberiness. Ugh! I can see them now! Their occupations—well, don't ask me to be too precise. They were usually feeding—I won't say on what. They were sometimes shewn in groups in cemeteries or underground passages, and often appeared to be in battle over their prey—or rather, their treasure-trove. And what damnable expressiveness Pickman sometimes gave the sightless faces of this charnel booty! Occasionally the things were shewn leaping through open windows at night, or squatting on the chests of sleepers, worrying at their throats. One canvas shewed a ring of them baying about a hanged witch on Gallows Hill, whose dead face held a close kinship to theirs.

But don't get the idea that it was all this hideous business of theme and setting which struck me faint. I'm not a three-year-old kid, and I'd seen much like this before. It was the *faces,* Eliot, those accursed *faces,* that leered and slavered out of the canvas with the very breath of life! By God, man, I verily believe they *were* alive! That nauseous wizard had waked the fires of hell in pigment, and his brush had been a nightmare-spawning wand. Give me that decanter, Eliot!

There was one thing called "The Lesson"—heaven pity me, that I ever saw it! Listen—can you fancy a squatting circle of nameless dog-like things in a churchyard teaching a small child how to feed like themselves? The price of a changeling, I suppose—you know the old myth about how the weird people leave their spawn in cradles in exchange for the human babes they steal. Pickman was shewing what happens to those stolen babes—how they grow up—and then I began to see a hideous relationship in the faces of the human and non-human figures. He was, in all his gradations of morbidity between the frankly non-human and the degradedly human, establishing a sardonic linkage and evolution. The dog-things were developed from mortals!

And no sooner had I wondered what he made of their own young as left with mankind in the form of changelings, than my eye caught a picture embodying that very thought. It was that of an ancient Puritan interior—a heavily beamed room with lattice windows, a settle, and clumsy seventeenth-century furniture, with the family sitting about while the father read from the Scriptures. Every face but one shewed nobility and reverence, but that one reflected the mockery of the pit. It was that of a young man in years, and no doubt belonged to a supposed son of that pious father, but in essence it was the kin of the unclean things. It was their changeling—and in a spirit of supreme irony Pickman had given the features a very perceptible resemblance to his own.

By this time Pickman had lighted a lamp in an adjoining room and was politely holding open the door for me, asking me if I would care to see his "modern studies". I hadn't been able to give him much of my opinions—I was too speechless with fright and loathing—but I think he fully understood and felt highly complimented. And now I want to assure you again, Eliot, that I'm no mollycoddle to scream at anything which shews a bit of departure from the usual. I'm not easily knocked out. Remember, too, that I'd just about recovered my wind and gotten used to those frightful pictures which turned colonial New England into a kind of annex of hell. Well, in spite of all this, that next room forced a real scream out of me, and I had to clutch at the doorway to keep from keeling over. The other chamber had shewn a pack of ghouls and witches overrunning the world of our forefathers, but this one brought the horror right into our own daily life!

Gad, how that man could paint! There was a study called "Subway Accident", in which a flock of the vile things were clambering up from some unknown catacomb through a crack in the floor of the Boylston Street subway and attacking a crowd of people on the platform. Another shewed a dance on Copp's Hill among the tombs with the background of today. Then there were any number of cellar views, with monsters creeping in through holes and rifts in the masonry and grinning as they squatted behind barrels or furnaces and waited for their first victim to descend the stairs.

One disgusting canvas seemed to depict a vast cross-section of Beacon Hill, with ant-like armies of the mephitic monsters squeezing themselves through burrows that honeycombed the ground. Dances in the modern cemeteries were freely pictured, and another conception somehow shocked me more than all the rest—a scene in an unknown vault, where scores of the beasts crowded about one who held a well-known Boston guide-book and was evidently reading aloud. All were pointing to a certain passage, and every face seemed so distorted with epileptic and reverberant laughter that I almost thought I heard the fiendish echoes. The title of the picture was, "Holmes, Lowell, and Longfellow Lie Buried in Mount Auburn".

As I gradually steadied myself and got readjusted to this second room of deviltry and morbidity, I began to analyse some of the points in my sickening loathing. In the first place, I said to myself, these things repelled because of the utter inhumanity and callous cruelty they shewed in Pickman. The fellow must be a relentless enemy of all mankind to take such glee in the torture of brain and flesh and the degradation of the mortal tenement. In the second place, they terrified because of their very greatness. Their art was the art that convinced—when we saw the pictures we saw the daemons themselves and were afraid of them. And the queer part was, that Pickman got none of his power from the use of selectiveness or bizarrerie. Nothing was blurred, distorted, or conventionalised; outlines were sharp and lifelike, and details were almost painfully defined. And the faces!

It was not any mere artist's interpretation that we saw; it was pandemonium itself, crystal clear in stark objectivity. That was it, by heaven! The man was not a fantaisiste or romanticist at all—he did not even try to give us the churning, prismatic ephemera of dreams, but coldly and sardonically reflected some stable, mechanistic, and well-established horror-world which he saw fully, brilliantly, squarely, and unfalteringly. God knows what that world can have been, or where he ever glimpsed the blasphemous shapes that loped and trotted and crawled through it; but whatever the baffling source of his images, one thing was plain. Pickman was in every sense—in conception and in execution—a thorough, painstaking, and almost scientific *realist.*

My host was now leading the way down-cellar to his actual studio, and I braced myself for some hellish effects among the unfinished canvases. As we reached the bottom of the damp stairs he turned his flashlight to a corner of the large open space at hand, revealing the circular brick curb of what was evidently a great well in the earthen floor. We walked nearer, and I saw that it must be five feet across, with walls a good foot thick and some six inches above the ground level—solid work of the seventeenth century, or I was much mistaken. That, Pickman said, was the kind of thing he had been talking about—an aperture of the network of tunnels that used to undermine the hill. I noticed idly that it did not seem to be bricked up, and that a heavy disc of wood formed the apparent cover. Thinking of the things this well must have been connected with if Pickman's wild hints had not been mere rhetoric, I shivered slightly; then turned to follow him up a step and through a narrow door into a room of fair size, provided with a wooden floor and furnished as a studio. An acetylene gas outfit gave the light necessary for work.

The unfinished pictures on easels or propped against the walls were as ghastly as the finished ones upstairs, and shewed the painstaking methods of the artist. Scenes were blocked out with extreme care, and pencilled guide-lines told of the minute exactitude which Pickman used in getting the right perspective and proportions. The man was great—I say it even now, knowing as much as I do. A large camera on a table excited my notice, and Pickman told me that he used it in taking scenes for backgrounds, so that he might paint them from photographs in the studio instead of carting his outfit around the town for this or that view. He thought a photograph quite as good as an actual scene or model for sustained work, and declared he employed them regularly.

There was something very disturbing about the nauseous sketches and half-finished monstrosities that leered around from every side of the room, and when Pickman suddenly unveiled a huge canvas on the side away from the light I could not for my life keep back a loud scream—the second I had emitted that night. It echoed and re-echoed through the dim vaultings of that ancient and nitrous cellar, and I had to choke back a flood of reaction that threatened to burst out as hysterical laughter. Merciful Creator, Eliot, but I don't know how much was real and how much was feverish fancy! It doesn't seem to me that earth can hold a dream like that!

It was a colossal and nameless blasphemy with glaring red eyes, and it held in bony claws a thing that had been a man, gnawing at the head as a child nibbles at a stick of candy. Its position was a kind of crouch, and as one looked one felt that at any moment it might drop its present prey and seek a juicier morsel. But damn it all, it wasn't even the fiendish subject that made it such an immortal fountain-head of all panic—not that, nor the dog face with its pointed ears, bloodshot eyes, flat nose, and drooling lips. It wasn't the scaly claws nor the mould-caked body nor the half-hooved feet—none of these, though any one of them might well have driven an excitable man to madness.

It was the technique, Eliot—the cursed, the impious, the unnatural technique! As I am a living being, I never elsewhere saw the actual breath of life so fused into a canvas. The monster was there—it glared and gnawed and gnawed and glared—and I knew that only a suspension of Nature's laws could ever let a man paint a thing like that without a model—without some glimpse of the nether world which no mortal unsold to the fiend has ever had.

Pinned with a thumb-tack to a vacant part of the canvas was a piece of paper, now badly curled up—probably, I thought, a photograph from which Pickman meant to paint a background as hideous as the nightmare it was to enhance. I reached out to uncurl and look at it, when suddenly I saw Pickman start as if shot. He had been listening with peculiar intensity ever since my shocked scream had waked unaccustomed echoes in the dark cellar, and now he seemed struck with a fright which, though not comparable to my own, had in it more of the physical than of the spiritual. He drew a revolver and motioned me to silence, then stepped out into the main cellar and closed the door behind him.

I think I was paralysed for an instant. Imitating Pickman's listening, I fancied I heard a faint scurrying sound somewhere, and a series of squeals or bleats in a direction I couldn't determine. I thought of huge rats and shuddered. Then there came a subdued sort of clatter which somehow set me all in gooseflesh—a furtive, groping kind of clatter, though I can't attempt to convey what I mean in words. It was like heavy wood falling on stone or brick—wood on brick—what did that make me think of?

It came again, and louder. There was a vibration as if the wood had fallen farther than it had fallen before. After that followed a sharp grating noise, a shouted gibberish from Pickman, and the deafening discharge of all six chambers of a revolver, fired spectacularly as a lion-tamer might fire in the air for effect. A muffled squeal or squawk, and a thud. Then more wood and brick grating, a pause, and the opening of the door—at which I'll confess I started violently. Pickman reappeared with his smoking weapon, cursing the bloated rats that infested the ancient well.

"The deuce knows what they eat, Thurber," he grinned, "for those archaic tunnels touched graveyard and witch-den and seacoast. But whatever it is, they must have run short, for they were devilish anxious to get out. Your yelling stirred them up, I fancy. Better be cautious in these old places—our rodent friends are the one drawback, though I sometimes think they're a positive asset by way of atmosphere and colour."

Well, Eliot, that was the end of the night's adventure. Pickman had promised to shew me the place, and heaven knows he had done it. He led me out of that tangle of alleys in another direction, it seems, for when we sighted a lamp post we were in a half-familiar street with monotonous rows of mingled tenement blocks and old houses. Charter Street, it turned out to be, but I was too flustered to notice just where we hit it. We were too late for the elevated, and walked back downtown through Hanover Street. I remember that walk. We switched from Tremont up Beacon, and Pickman left me at the corner of Joy, where I turned off. I never spoke to him again.

Why did I drop him? Don't be impatient. Wait till I ring for coffee. We've had enough of the other stuff, but I for one need something. No—it wasn't the paintings I saw in that place; though I'll swear they were enough to get him ostracised in nine-tenths of the homes and clubs of Boston, and I guess you won't wonder now why I have to steer clear of subways and cellars. It was—something I found in my coat the next morning. You know, the curled-up paper tacked to that frightful canvas in the cellar; the thing I thought was a photograph of some scene he meant to use as a background for that monster. That last scare had come while I was reaching to uncurl it, and it seems I had vacantly crumpled it into my pocket. But here's the coffee—take it black, Eliot, if you're wise.

Yes, that paper was the reason I dropped Pickman; Richard Upton Pickman, the greatest artist I have ever known—and the foulest being that ever leaped the bounds of life into the pits of myth and madness. Eliot, old Reid was right. He wasn't strictly human. Either he was born in strange shadow, or he'd found a way to unlock the forbidden gate. It's all the same now, for he's gone—back into the fabulous darkness he loved to haunt. Here, let's have the chandelier going.

Don't ask me to explain or even conjecture about what I burned. Don't ask me, either, what lay behind that mole-like scrambling Pickman was so keen to pass off as rats. There are secrets, you know, which might have come down from old Salem times, and Cotton Mather tells even stranger things. You know how damned lifelike Pickman's paintings were—how we all wondered where he got those faces.

Well—that paper wasn't a photograph of any background, after all. What it shewed was simply the monstrous being he was painting on that awful canvas. It was the model he was using—and its background was merely the wall of the cellar studio in minute detail. But by God, Eliot, *it was a photograph from life.*

THE SILVER KEY

When Randolph Carter was thirty he lost the key of the gate of dreams. Prior to that time he had made up for the prosiness of life by nightly excursions to strange and ancient cities beyond space, and lovely, unbelievable garden lands across ethereal seas; but as middle age hardened upon him he felt these liberties slipping away little by little, until at last he was cut off altogether. No more could his galleys sail up the river Oukranos past the gilded spires of Thran, or his elephant caravans tramp through perfumed jungles in Kled, where forgotten palaces with veined ivory columns sleep lovely and unbroken under the moon.

He had read much of things as they are, and talked with too many people. Well-meaning philosophers had taught him to look into the logical relations of things, and analyse the processes which shaped his thoughts and fancies. Wonder had gone away, and he had forgotten that all life is only a set of pictures in the brain, among which there is no difference betwixt those born of real things and those born of inward dreamings, and no cause to value the one above the other. Custom had dinned into his ears a superstitious reverence for that which tangibly and physically exists, and had made him secretly ashamed to dwell in visions. Wise men told him his simple fancies were inane and childish, and he believed it because he could see that they might easily be so. What he failed to recall was that the deeds of reality are just as inane and childish, and even more absurd because their actors persist in fancying them full of meaning and purpose as the blind cosmos grinds aimlessly on from nothing to something and from something back to nothing again, neither heeding nor knowing the wishes or existence of the minds that flicker for a second now and then in the darkness.

They had chained him down to things that are, and had then explained the workings of those things till mystery had gone out of the world. When he complained, and longed to escape into twilight realms where magic moulded all the little vivid fragments and prized associations of his mind into vistas of breathless expectancy and unquenchable delight, they turned him instead toward the new-found prodigies of science, bidding him find wonder in the atom's vortex and mystery in the sky's dimensions. And when he had failed to find these boons in things whose laws are known and measurable, they told him he lacked imagination, and was immature because he preferred dream-illusions to the illusions of our physical creation.

So Carter had tried to do as others did, and pretended that the common events and emotions of earthy minds were more important than the fantasies of rare and delicate souls. He did not dissent when they told him that the animal pain of a stuck pig or dyspeptic ploughman in real life is a greater thing than the peerless beauty of Narath with its hundred carven gates and domes of chalcedony, which he dimly remembered from his dreams; and under their guidance he cultivated a painstaking sense of pity and tragedy.

Once in a while, though, he could not help seeing how shallow, fickle, and meaningless all human aspirations are, and how emptily our real impulses contrast with those pompous ideals we profess to hold. Then he would have recourse to the polite laughter they had taught him to use against the extravagance and artificiality of dreams; for he saw that the daily life of our world is every inch as extravagant and artificial, and far less worthy of respect because of its poverty in beauty and its silly reluctance to admit its own lack of reason and purpose. In this way he became a kind of humorist, for he did not see that even humour is empty in a mindless universe devoid of any true standard of consistency or inconsistency.

In the first days of his bondage he had turned to the gentle churchly faith endeared to him by the naive trust of his fathers, for thence stretched mystic avenues which seemed to promise escape from life. Only on closer view did he mark the starved fancy and beauty, the stale and prosy triteness, and the owlish gravity and grotesque claims of solid truth which reigned boresomely and overwhelmingly among most of its professors; or feel to the full the awkwardness with which it sought to keep alive as literal fact the outgrown fears and guesses of a primal race confronting the unknown. It wearied Carter to see how solemnly people tried to make earthly reality out of old myths which every step of their boasted science confuted, and this misplaced seriousness killed the attachment he might have kept for the ancient creeds had they been content to offer the sonorous rites and emotional outlets in their true guise of ethereal fantasy.

But when he came to study those who had thrown off the old myths, he found them even more ugly than those who had not. They did not know that beauty lies in harmony, and that loveliness of life has no standard amidst an aimless cosmos save only its harmony with the dreams and the feelings which have gone before and blindly moulded our little spheres out of the rest of chaos. They did not see that good and evil and beauty and ugliness are only ornamental fruits of perspective, whose sole value lies in their linkage to what chance made our fathers think and feel, and whose finer details are different for every race and culture. Instead, they either denied these things altogether or transferred them to the crude, vague instincts which they shared with the beasts and peasants; so that their lives were dragged malodorously out in pain, ugliness, and disproportion, yet filled with a ludicrous pride at having escaped from something no more unsound than that which still held them. They had traded the false gods of fear and blind piety for those of licence and anarchy.

Carter did not taste deeply of these modern freedoms; for their cheapness and squalor sickened a spirit loving beauty alone, while his reason rebelled at the flimsy logic with which their champions tried to gild brute impulse with a sacredness stripped from the idols they had discarded. He saw that most of them, in common with their cast-off priestcraft, could not escape from the delusion that life has a meaning apart from that which men dream into it; and could not lay aside the crude notion of ethics and obligations beyond those of beauty, even when all Nature shrieked of its unconsciousness and impersonal unmorality in the light of their scientific discoveries. Warped and bigoted with preconceived illusions of justice, freedom, and consistency, they cast off the old lore and the old ways with the old beliefs; nor ever stopped to think that that lore and those ways were the sole makers of their present thoughts and judgments, and the sole guides and standards in a meaningless universe without fixed aims or stable points of reference. Having lost these artificial settings, their lives grew void of direction and dramatic interest; till at length they strove to drown their ennui in bustle and pretended usefulness, noise and excitement, barbaric display and animal sensation. When these things palled, disappointed, or grew nauseous through revulsion, they cultivated irony and bitterness, and found fault with the social order. Never could they realise that their brute foundations were as shifting and contradictory as the gods of their elders, and that the satisfaction of one moment is the bane of the next. Calm, lasting beauty comes only in dream, and this solace the world had thrown away when in its worship of the real it threw away the secrets of childhood and innocence.

Amidst this chaos of hollowness and unrest Carter tried to live as befitted a man of keen thought and good heritage. With his dreams fading under the ridicule of the age he could not believe in anything, but the love of harmony kept him close to the ways of his race and station. He walked impassive through the cities of men, and sighed because no vista seemed fully real; because every flash of yellow sunlight on tall roofs and every glimpse of balustraded plazas in the first lamps of evening served only to remind him of dreams he had once known, and to make him homesick for ethereal lands he no longer knew how to find. Travel was only a mockery; and even the Great War stirred him but little, though he served from the first in the Foreign Legion of France. For a while he sought friends, but soon grew weary of the crudeness of their emotions, and the sameness and earthiness of their visions. He felt vaguely glad that all his relatives were distant and out of touch with him, for they could not have understood his mental life. That is, none but his grandfather and great-uncle Christopher could, and they were long dead.

Then he began once more the writing of books, which he had left off when dreams first failed him. But here, too, was there no satisfaction or fulfilment; for the touch of earth was upon his mind, and he could not think of lovely things as he had done of yore. Ironic humour dragged down all the twilight minarets he reared, and the earthy fear of improbability blasted all the delicate and amazing flowers in his faery gardens. The convention of assumed pity spilt mawkishness on his characters, while the myth of an important reality and significant human events and emotions debased all his high fantasy into thin-veiled allegory and cheap social satire. His new novels were successful as his old ones had never been; and because he knew how empty they must be to please an empty herd, he burned them and ceased his writing. They were very graceful novels, in which he urbanely laughed at the dreams he lightly sketched; but he saw that their sophistication had sapped all their life away.

It was after this that he cultivated deliberate illusion, and dabbled in the notions of the bizarre and the eccentric as an antidote for the commonplace. Most of these, however, soon shewed their poverty and barrenness; and he saw that the popular doctrines of occultism are as dry and inflexible as those of science, yet without even the slender palliative of truth to redeem them. Gross stupidity, falsehood, and muddled thinking are not dream; and form no escape from life to a mind trained above their level. So Carter bought stranger books and sought out deeper and more terrible men of fantastic erudition; delving into arcana of consciousness that few have trod, and learning things about the secret pits of life, legend, and immemorial antiquity which disturbed him ever afterward. He decided to live on a rarer plane, and furnished his Boston home to suit his changing moods; one room for each, hung in appropriate colours, furnished with befitting books and objects, and provided with sources of the proper sensations of light, heat, sound, taste, and odour.

Once he heard of a man in the South who was shunned and feared for the blasphemous things he read in prehistoric books and clay tablets smuggled from India and Arabia. Him he visited, living with him and sharing his studies for seven years, till horror overtook them one midnight in an unknown and archaic graveyard, and only one emerged where two had entered. Then he went back to Arkham, the terrible witch-haunted old town of his forefathers in New England, and had experiences in the dark, amidst the hoary willows and tottering gambrel roofs, which made him seal for ever certain pages in the diary of a wild-minded ancestor. But these horrors took him only to the edge of reality, and were not of the true dream country he had known in youth; so that at fifty he despaired of any rest or contentment in a world grown too busy for beauty and too shrewd for dream.

Having perceived at last the hollowness and futility of real things, Carter spent his days in retirement, and in wistful disjointed memories of his dream-filled youth. He thought it rather silly that he bothered to keep on living at all, and got from a South American acquaintance a very curious liquid to take him to oblivion without suffering. Inertia and force of habit, however, caused him to defer action; and he lingered indecisively among thoughts of old times, taking down the strange hangings from his walls and refitting the house as it was in his early boyhood—purple panes, Victorian furniture, and all.

With the passage of time he became almost glad he had lingered, for his relics of youth and his cleavage from the world made life and sophistication seem very distant and unreal; so much so that a touch of magic and expectancy stole back into his nightly slumbers. For years those slumbers had known only such twisted reflections of every-day things as the commonest slumbers know, but now there returned a flicker of something stranger and wilder; something of vaguely awesome immanence which took the form of tensely clear pictures from his childhood days, and made him think of little inconsequential things he had long forgotten. He would often awake calling for his mother and grandfather, both in their graves a quarter of a century.

Then one night his grandfather reminded him of a key. The grey old scholar, as vivid as in life, spoke long and earnestly of their ancient line, and of the strange visions of the delicate and sensitive men who composed it. He spoke of the flame-eyed Crusader who learnt wild secrets of the Saracens that held him captive; and of the first Sir Randolph Carter who studied magic when Elizabeth was queen. He spoke, too, of that Edmund Carter who had just escaped hanging in the Salem witchcraft, and who had placed in an antique box a great silver key handed down from his ancestors. Before Carter awaked, the gentle visitant had told him where to find that box; that carved oak box of archaic wonder whose grotesque lid no hand had raised for two centuries.

In the dust and shadows of the great attic he found it, remote and forgotten at the back of a drawer in a tall chest. It was about a foot square, and its Gothic carvings were so fearful that he did not marvel no person since Edmund Carter had dared to open it. It gave forth no noise when shaken, but was mystic with the scent of unremembered spices. That it held a key was indeed only a dim legend, and Randolph Carter's father had never known such a box existed. It was bound in rusty iron, and no means was provided for working the formidable lock. Carter vaguely understood that he would find within it some key to the lost gate of dreams, but of where and how to use it his grandfather had told him nothing.

An old servant forced the carven lid, shaking as he did so at the hideous faces leering from the blackened wood, and at some unplaced familiarity. Inside, wrapped in a discoloured parchment, was a huge key of tarnished silver covered with cryptical arabesques; but of any legible explanation there was none. The parchment was voluminous, and held only the strange hieroglyphs of an unknown tongue written with an antique reed. Carter recognised the characters as those he had seen on a certain papyrus scroll belonging to that terrible scholar of the South who had vanished one midnight in a nameless cemetery. The man had always shivered when he read this scroll, and Carter shivered now.

But he cleaned the key, and kept it by him nightly in its aromatic box of ancient oak. His dreams were meanwhile increasing in vividness, and though shewing him none of the strange cities and incredible gardens of the old days, were assuming a definite cast whose purpose could not be mistaken. They were calling him back along the years, and with the mingled wills of all his fathers were pulling him toward some hidden and ancestral source. Then he knew he must go into the past and merge himself with old things, and day after day he thought of the hills to the north where haunted Arkham and the rushing Miskatonic and the lonely rustic homestead of his people lay.

In the brooding fire of autumn Carter took the old remembered way past graceful lines of rolling hill and stone-walled meadow, distant vale and hanging woodland, curving road and nestling farmstead, and the crystal windings of the Miskatonic, crossed here and there by rustic bridges of wood or stone. At one bend he saw the group of giant elms among which an ancestor had oddly vanished a century and a half before, and shuddered as the wind blew meaningly through them. Then there was the crumbling farmhouse of old Goody Fowler the witch, with its little evil windows and great roof sloping nearly to the ground on the north side. He speeded up his car as he passed it, and did not slacken till he had mounted the hill where his mother and her fathers before her were born, and where the old white house still looked proudly across the road at the breathlessly lovely panorama of rocky slope and verdant valley, with the distant spires of Kingsport on the horizon, and hints of the archaic, dream-laden sea in the farthest background.

Then came the steeper slope that held the old Carter place he had not seen in over forty years. Afternoon was far gone when he reached the foot, and at the bend half way up he paused to scan the outspread countryside golden and glorified in the slanting floods of magic poured out by a western sun. All the strangeness and expectancy of his recent dreams seemed present in this hushed and unearthly landscape, and he thought of the unknown solitudes of other planets as his eyes traced out the velvet and deserted lawns shining undulant between their tumbled walls, the clumps of faery forest setting off far lines of purple hills beyond hills, and the spectral wooded valley dipping down in shadow to dank hollows where trickling waters crooned and gurgled among swollen and distorted roots.

Something made him feel that motors did not belong in the realm he was seeking, so he left his car at the edge of the forest, and putting the great key in his coat pocket walked on up the hill. Woods now engulfed him utterly, though he knew the house was on a high knoll that cleared the trees except to the north. He wondered how it would look, for it had been left vacant and untended through his neglect since the death of his strange great-uncle Christopher thirty years before. In his boyhood he had revelled through long visits there, and had found weird marvels in the woods beyond the orchard.

Shadows thickened around him, for the night was near. Once a gap in the trees opened up to the right, so that he saw off across leagues of twilight meadow and spied the old Congregational steeple on Central Hill in Kingsport; pink with the last flush of day, the panes of the little round windows blazing with reflected fire. Then, when he was in deep shadow again, he recalled with a start that the glimpse must have come from childish memory alone, since the old white church had long been torn down to make room for the Congregational Hospital. He had read of it with interest, for the paper had told about some strange burrows or passages found in the rocky hill beneath.

Through his puzzlement a voice piped, and he started again at its familiarity after long years. Old Benijah Corey had been his Uncle Christopher's hired man, and was aged even in those far-off times of his boyhood visits. Now he must be well over a hundred, but that piping voice could come from no one else. He could distinguish no words, yet the tone was haunting and unmistakable. To think that "Old Benijy" should still be alive!

"Mister Randy! Mister Randy! Whar be ye? D'ye want to skeer yer Aunt Marthy plumb to death? Hain't she tuld ye to keep nigh the place in the arternoon an' git back afur dark? Randy! Ran … dee! … He's the beatin'est boy fer runnin' off in the woods I ever see; haff the time a-settin' moonin' raound that snake-den in the upper timber-lot! … Hey, yew, Ran … dee!"

Randolph Carter stopped in the pitch darkness and rubbed his hand across his eyes. Something was queer. He had been somewhere he ought not to be; had strayed very far away to places where he had not belonged, and was now inexcusably late. He had not noticed the time on the Kingsport steeple, though he could easily have made it out with his pocket telescope; but he knew his lateness was something very strange and unprecedented. He was not sure he had his little telescope with him, and put his hand in his blouse pocket to see. No, it was not there, but there was the big silver key he had found in a box somewhere. Uncle Chris had told him something odd once about an old unopened box with a key in it, but Aunt Martha had stopped the story abruptly, saying it was no kind of thing to tell a child whose head was already too full of queer fancies. He tried to recall just where he had found the key, but something seemed very confused. He guessed it was in the attic at home in Boston, and dimly remembered bribing Parks with half his week's allowance to help him open the box and keep quiet about it; but when he remembered this, the face of Parks came up very strangely, as if the wrinkles of long years had fallen upon the brisk little Cockney.

"Ran ... dee! Ran ... dee! Hi! Hi! Randy!"

A swaying lantern came around the black bend, and old Benijah pounced on the silent and bewildered form of the pilgrim.

"Durn ye, boy, so thar ye be! Ain't ye got a tongue in yer head, that ye can't answer a body? I ben callin' this haff hour, an' ye must a heerd me long ago! Dun't ye know yer Aunt Marthy's all a-fidget over yer being' off arter dark? Wait till I tell yer Uncle Chris when he gits hum! Ye'd orta know these here woods ain't no fitten place to be traipsin' this hour! They's things abroad what dun't do nobody no good, as my gran'sir' knowed afur me. Come, Mister Randy, or Hannah wun't keep supper no longer!"

So Randolph Carter was marched up the road where wondering stars glimmered through high autumn boughs. And dogs barked as the yellow light of small-paned windows shone out at the farther turn, and the Pleiades twinkled across the open knoll where a great gambrel roof stood black against the dim west. Aunt Martha was in the doorway, and did not scold too hard when Benijah shoved the truant in. She knew Uncle Chris well enough to expect such things of the Carter blood. Randolph did not shew his key, but ate his supper in silence and protested only when bedtime came. He sometimes dreamed better when awake, and he wanted to use that key.

In the morning Randolph was up early, and would have run off to the upper timber-lot if Uncle Chris had not caught him and forced him into his chair by the breakfast table. He looked impatiently around the low-pitched room with the rag carpet and exposed beams and corner-posts, and smiled only when the orchard boughs scratched at the little leaded panes of the rear window. The trees and the hills were close to him, and formed the gates of that timeless realm which was his true country.

Then, when he was free, he felt in his blouse pocket for the key; and being reassured, skipped off across the orchard to the rise beyond, where the wooded hill climbed again to heights above even the treeless knoll. The floor of the forest was mossy and mysterious, and great lichened rocks rose vaguely here and there in the dim light like Druid monoliths among the swollen and twisted trunks of a sacred grove. Once in his ascent Randolph crossed a rushing stream whose falls a little way off sang runic incantations to the lurking fauns and Ægipans and dryads.

Then he came to the strange cave in the forest slope, the dreaded "snake-den" which country folk shunned, and away from which Benijah had warned him again and again. It was deep; far deeper than anyone but Randolph suspected, for the boy had found a fissure in the farthermost black corner that led to a loftier grotto beyond—a haunting sepulchral place whose granite walls held a curious illusion of conscious artifice. On this occasion he crawled in as usual, lighting his way with matches filched from the sitting-room match-safe, and edging through the final crevice with an eagerness hard to explain even to himself. He could not tell why he approached the farther wall so confidently, or why he instinctively drew forth the great silver key as he did so. But on he went, and when he danced back to the house that night he offered no excuses for his lateness, nor heeded in the least the reproofs he gained for ignoring the noontide dinner-horn altogether.

Now it is agreed by all the distant relatives of Randolph Carter that something occurred to heighten his imagination in his tenth year. His cousin, Ernest B. Aspinwall, Esq., of Chicago, is fully ten years his senior; and distinctly recalls a change in the boy after the autumn of 1883. Randolph had looked on scenes of fantasy that few others can ever have beheld, and stranger still were some of the qualities which he shewed in relation to very mundane things. He seemed, in fine, to have picked up an odd gift of prophecy; and reacted unusually to things which, though at the time without meaning, were later found to justify the singular impressions. In subsequent decades as new inventions, new names, and new events appeared one by one in the book of history, people would now and then recall wonderingly how Carter had years before let fall some careless word of undoubted connexion with what was then far in the future. He did not himself understand these words, or know why certain things made him feel certain emotions; but fancied that some unremembered dream must be responsible. It was as early as 1897 that he turned pale when some traveller mentioned the French town of Belloy-en-Santerre, and friends remembered it when he was almost mortally wounded there in 1916, while serving with the Foreign Legion in the Great War.

Carter's relatives talk much of these things because he has lately disappeared. His little old servant Parks, who for years bore patiently with his vagaries, last saw him on the morning he drove off alone in his car with a key he had recently found. Parks had helped him get the key from the old box containing it, and had felt strangely affected by the grotesque carvings on the box, and by some other odd quality he could not name. When Carter left, he had said he was going to visit his old ancestral country around Arkham.

Half way up Elm Mountain, on the way to the ruins of the old Carter place, they found his motor set carefully by the roadside; and in it was a box of fragrant wood with carvings that frightened the countrymen who stumbled on it. The box held only a queer parchment whose characters no linguist or palaeographer has been able to decipher or identify. Rain had long effaced any possible footprints, though Boston investigators had something to say about evidences of disturbances among the fallen timbers of the Carter place. It was, they averred, as though someone had groped about the ruins at no distant period. A common white handkerchief found among forest rocks on the hillside beyond cannot be identified as belonging to the missing man.

There is talk of apportioning Randolph Carter's estate among his heirs, but I shall stand firmly against this course because I do not believe he is dead. There are twists of time and space, of vision and reality, which only a dreamer can divine; and from what I know of Carter I think he has merely found a way to traverse these mazes. Whether or not he will ever come back, I cannot say. He wanted the lands of dream he had lost, and yearned for the days of his childhood. Then he found a key, and I somehow believe he was able to use it to strange advantage.

I shall ask him when I see him, for I expect to meet him shortly in a certain dream-city we both used to haunt. It is rumoured in Ulthar, beyond the river Skai, that a new king reigns on the opal throne of Ilek-Vad, that fabulous town of turrets atop the hollow cliffs of glass overlooking the twilight sea wherein the bearded and finny Gnorri build their singular labyrinths, and I believe I know how to interpret this rumour. Certainly, I look forward impatiently to the sight of that great silver key, for in its cryptical arabesques there may stand symbolised all the aims and mysteries of a blindly impersonal cosmos.

THE STRANGE HIGH HOUSE IN THE MIST

In the morning mist comes up from the sea by the cliffs beyond Kingsport. White and feathery it comes from the deep to its brothers the clouds, full of dreams of dank pastures and caves of leviathan. And later, in still summer rains on the steep roofs of poets, the clouds scatter bits of those dreams, that men shall not live without rumour of old, strange secrets, and wonders that planets tell planets alone in the night. When tales fly thick in the grottoes of tritons, and conches in seaweed cities blow wild tunes learned from the Elder Ones, then great eager mists flock to heaven laden with lore, and oceanward eyes on the rocks see only a mystic whiteness, as if the cliff's rim were the rim of all earth, and the solemn bells of buoys tolled free in the aether of faery.

Now north of archaic Kingsport the crags climb lofty and curious, terrace on terrace, till the northernmost hangs in the sky like a grey frozen wind-cloud. Alone it is, a bleak point jutting in limitless space, for there the coast turns sharp where the great Miskatonic pours out of the plains past Arkham, bringing woodland legends and little quaint memories of New England's hills. The sea-folk in Kingsport look up at that cliff as other sea-folk look up at the pole-star, and time the night's watches by the way it hides or shews the Great Bear, Cassiopeia, and the Dragon. Among them it is one with the firmament, and truly, it is hidden from them when the mist hides the stars or the sun.

Some of the cliffs they love, as that whose grotesque profile they call Father Neptune, or that whose pillared steps they term The Causeway; but this one they fear because it is so near the sky. The Portuguese sailors coming in from a voyage cross themselves when they first see it, and the old Yankees believe it would be a much graver matter than death to climb it, if indeed that were possible. Nevertheless there is an ancient house on that cliff, and at evening men see lights in the small-paned windows.

The ancient house has always been there, and people say One dwells therein who talks with the morning mists that come up from the deep, and perhaps sees singular things oceanward at those times when the cliff's rim becomes the rim of all earth, and solemn buoys toll free in the white aether of faery. This they tell from hearsay, for that forbidding crag is always unvisited, and natives dislike to train telescopes on it. Summer boarders have indeed scanned it with jaunty binoculars, but have never seen more than the grey primeval roof, peaked and shingled, whose eaves come nearly to the grey foundations, and the dim yellow light of the little windows peeping out from under those eaves in the dusk. These summer people do not believe that the same One has lived in the ancient house for hundreds of years, but cannot prove their heresy to any real Kingsporter. Even the Terrible Old Man who talks to leaden pendulums in bottles, buys groceries with centuried Spanish gold, and keeps stone idols in the yard of his antediluvian cottage in Water Street can only say these things were the same when his grandfather was a boy, and that must have been inconceivable ages ago, when Belcher or Shirley or Pownall or Bernard was Governor of His Majesty's Province of the Massachusetts-Bay.

Then one summer there came a philosopher into Kingsport. His name was Thomas Olney, and he taught ponderous things in a college by Narragansett Bay. With stout wife and romping children he came, and his eyes were weary with seeing the same things for many years, and thinking the same well-disciplined thoughts. He looked at the mists from the diadem of Father Neptune, and tried to walk into their white world of mystery along the titan steps of The Causeway. Morning after morning he would lie on the cliffs and look over the world's rim at the cryptical aether beyond, listening to spectral bells and the wild cries of what might have been gulls. Then, when the mist would lift and the sea stand out prosy with the smoke of steamers, he would sigh and descend to the town, where he loved to thread the narrow olden lanes up and down hill, and study the crazy tottering gables and odd pillared doorways which had sheltered so many generations of sturdy sea-folk. And he even talked with the Terrible Old Man, who was not fond of strangers, and was invited into his fearsomely archaic cottage where low ceilings and wormy panelling hear the echoes of disquieting soliloquies in the dark small hours.

Of course it was inevitable that Olney should mark the grey unvisited cottage in the sky, on that sinister northward crag which is one with the mists and the firmament. Always over Kingsport it hung, and always its mystery sounded in whispers through Kingsport's crooked alleys. The Terrible Old Man wheezed a tale that his father had told him, of lightning that shot one night *up from* that peaked cottage to the clouds of higher heaven; and Granny Orne, whose tiny gambrel-roofed abode in Ship Street is all covered with moss and ivy, croaked over something her grandmother had heard at second-hand, about shapes that flapped out of the eastern mists straight into the narrow single door of that unreachable place—for the door is set close to the edge of the crag toward the ocean, and glimpsed only from ships at sea.

At length, being avid for new strange things and held back by neither the Kingsporter's fear nor the summer boarder's usual indolence, Olney made a very terrible resolve. Despite a conservative training—or because of it, for humdrum lives breed wistful longings for the unknown—he swore a great oath to scale that avoided northern cliff and visit the abnormally antique grey cottage in the sky. Very plausibly his saner self argued that the place must be tenanted by people who reached it from inland along the easier ridge beside the Miskatonic's estuary. Probably they traded in Arkham, knowing how little Kingsport liked their habitation, or perhaps being unable to climb down the cliff on the Kingsport side. Olney walked out along the lesser cliffs to where the great crag leaped insolently up to consort with celestial things, and became very sure that no human feet could mount it or descend it on that beetling southern slope. East and north it rose thousands of feet vertically from the water, so only the western side, inland and toward Arkham, remained.

One early morning in August Olney set out to find a path to the inaccessible pinnacle. He worked northwest along pleasant back roads, past Hooper's Pond and the old brick powder house to where the pastures slope up to the ridge above the Miskatonic and give a lovely vista of Arkham's white Georgian steeples across leagues of river and meadow. Here he found a shady road to Arkham, but no trail at all in the seaward direction he wished. Woods and fields crowded up to the high bank of the river's mouth, and bore not a sign of man's presence; not even a stone wall or a straying cow, but only the tall grass and giant trees and tangles of briers that the first Indian might have seen. As he climbed slowly east, higher and higher above the estuary on his left and nearer and nearer the sea, he found the way growing in difficulty; till he wondered how ever the dwellers in that disliked place managed to reach the world outside, and whether they came often to market in Arkham.

Then the trees thinned, and far below him on his right he saw the hills and antique roofs and spires of Kingsport. Even Central Hill was a dwarf from this height, and he could just make out the ancient graveyard by the Congregational Hospital, beneath which rumour said some terrible caves or burrows lurked. Ahead lay sparse grass and scrub blueberry bushes, and beyond them the naked rock of the crag and the thin peak of the dreaded grey cottage. Now the ridge narrowed, and Olney grew dizzy at his loneness in the sky. South of him the frightful precipice above Kingsport, north of him the vertical drop of nearly a mile to the river's mouth. Suddenly a great chasm opened before him, ten feet deep, so that he had to let himself down by his hands and drop to a slanting floor, and then crawl perilously up a natural defile in the opposite wall. So this was the way the folk of the uncanny house journeyed betwixt earth and sky!

When he climbed out of the chasm a morning mist was gathering, but he clearly saw the lofty and unhallowed cottage ahead; walls as grey as the rock, and high peak standing bold against the milky white of the seaward vapours. And he perceived that there was no door on this landward end, but only a couple of small lattice windows with dingy bull's-eye panes leaded in seventeenth-century fashion. All around him was cloud and chaos, and he could see nothing below but the whiteness of illimitable space. He was alone in the sky with this queer and very disturbing house; and when he sidled around to the front and saw that the wall stood flush with the cliff's edge, so that the single narrow door was not to be reached save from the empty aether, he felt a distinct terror that altitude could not wholly explain. And it was very odd that shingles so worm-eaten could survive, or bricks so crumbled still form a standing chimney.

As the mist thickened, Olney crept around to the windows on the north and west and south sides, trying them but finding them all locked. He was vaguely glad they were locked, because the more he saw of that house the less he wished to get in. Then a sound halted him. He heard a lock rattle and bolt shoot, and a long creaking follow as if a heavy door were slowly and cautiously opened. This was on the oceanward side that he could not see, where the narrow portal opened on blank space thousands of feet in the misty sky above the waves.

Then there was heavy, deliberate tramping in the cottage, and Olney heard the windows opening, first on the north side opposite him, and then on the west just around the corner. Next would come the south windows, under the great low eaves on the side where he stood; and it must be said that he was more than uncomfortable as he thought of the detestable house on one side and the vacancy of upper air on the other. When a fumbling came in the nearer casements he crept around to the west again, flattening himself against the wall beside the now opened windows. It was plain that the owner had come home; but he had not come from the land, nor from any balloon or airship that could be imagined. Steps sounded again, and Olney edged round to the north; but before he could find a haven a voice called softly, and he knew he must confront his host.

Stuck out of a west window was a great black-bearded face whose eyes were phosphorescent with the imprint of unheard-of sights. But the voice was gentle, and of a quaint olden kind, so that Olney did not shudder when a brown hand reached out to help him over the sill and into that low room of black oak wainscots and carved Tudor furnishings. The man was clad in very ancient garments, and had about him an unplaceable nimbus of sea-lore and dreams of tall galleons. Olney does not recall many of the wonders he told, or even who he was; but says that he was strange and kindly, and filled with the magic of unfathomed voids of time and space. The small room seemed green with a dim aqueous light, and Olney saw that the far windows to the east were not open, but shut against the misty aether with dull thick panes like the bottoms of old bottles.

That bearded host seemed young, yet looked out of eyes steeped in the elder mysteries; and from the tales of marvellous ancient things he related, it must be guessed that the village folk were right in saying he had communed with the mists of the sea and the clouds of the sky ever since there was any village to watch his taciturn dwelling from the plain below. And the day wore on, and still Olney listened to rumours of old times and far places, and heard how the Kings of Atlantis fought with the slippery blasphemies that wriggled out of rifts in ocean's floor, and how the pillared and weedy temple of Poseidonis is still glimpsed at midnight by lost ships, who know by its sight that they are lost. Years of the Titans were recalled, but the host grew timid when he spoke of the dim first age of chaos before the gods or even the Elder Ones were born, and when only *the other gods* came to dance on the peak of Hatheg-Kla in the stony desert near Ulthar, beyond the River Skai.

It was at this point that there came a knocking on the door; that ancient door of nail-studded oak beyond which lay only the abyss of white cloud. Olney started in fright, but the bearded man motioned him to be still, and tiptoed to the door to look out through a very small peep-hole. What he saw he did not like, so pressed his fingers to his lips and tiptoed around to shut and lock all the windows before returning to the ancient settle beside his guest. Then Olney saw lingering against the translucent squares of each of the little dim windows in succession a queer black outline as the caller moved inquisitively about before leaving; and he was glad his host had not answered the knocking. For there are strange objects in the great abyss, and the seeker of dreams must take care not to stir up or meet the wrong ones.

Then the shadows began to gather; first little furtive ones under the table, and then bolder ones in the dark panelled corners. And the bearded man made enigmatical gestures of prayer, and lit tall candles in curiously wrought brass candlesticks. Frequently he would glance at the door as if he expected someone, and at length his glance seemed answered by a singular rapping which must have followed some very ancient and secret code. This time he did not even glance through the peep-hole, but swung the great oak bar and shot the bolt, unlatching the heavy door and flinging it wide to the stars and the mist.

And then to the sound of obscure harmonies there floated into that room from the deep all the dreams and memories of earth's sunken Mighty Ones. And golden flames played about weedy locks, so that Olney was dazzled as he did them homage. Trident-bearing Neptune was there, and sportive tritons and fantastic nereids, and upon dolphins' backs was balanced a vast crenulate shell wherein rode the grey and awful form of primal Nodens, Lord of the Great Abyss. And the conches of the tritons gave weird blasts, and the nereids made strange sounds by striking on the grotesque resonant shells of unknown lurkers in black sea-caves. Then hoary Nodens reached forth a wizened hand and helped Olney and his host into the vast shell, whereat the conches and the gongs set up a wild and awesome clamour. And out into the limitless aether reeled that fabulous train, the noise of whose shouting was lost in the echoes of thunder.

All night in Kingsport they watched that lofty cliff when the storm and the mists gave them glimpses of it, and when toward the small hours the little dim windows went dark they whispered of dread and disaster. And Olney's children and stout wife prayed to the bland proper god of Baptists, and hoped that the traveller would borrow an umbrella and rubbers unless the rain stopped by morning. Then dawn swam dripping and mist-wreathed out of the sea, and the buoys tolled solemn in vortices of white aether. And at noon elfin horns rang over the ocean as Olney, dry and light-footed, climbed down from the cliffs to antique Kingsport with the look of far places in his eyes. He could not recall what he had dreamed in the sky-perched hut of that still nameless hermit, or say how he had crept down that crag untraversed by other feet. Nor could he talk of these matters at all save with the Terrible Old Man, who afterward mumbled queer things in his long white beard; vowing that the man who came down from that crag was not wholly the man who went up, and that somewhere under that grey peaked roof, or amidst inconceivable reaches of that sinister white mist, there lingered still the lost spirit of him who was Thomas Olney.

And ever since that hour, through dull dragging years of greyness and weariness, the philosopher has laboured and eaten and slept and done uncomplaining the suitable deeds of a citizen. Not any more does he long for the magic of farther hills, or sigh for secrets that peer like green reefs from a bottomless sea. The sameness of his days no longer gives him sorrow, and well-disciplined thoughts have grown enough for his imagination. His good wife waxes stouter and his children older and prosier and more useful, and he never fails to smile correctly with pride when the occasion calls for it. In his glance there is not any restless light, and if he ever listens for solemn bells or far elfin horns it is only at night when old dreams are wandering. He has never seen Kingsport again, for his family disliked the funny old houses, and complained that the drains were impossibly bad. They have a trim bungalow now at Bristol Highlands, where no tall crags tower, and the neighbours are urban and modern.

But in Kingsport strange tales are abroad, and even the Terrible Old Man admits a thing untold by his grandfather. For now, when the wind sweeps boisterous out of the north past the high ancient house that is one with the firmament, there is broken at last that ominous brooding silence ever before the bane of Kingsport's maritime cotters. And old folk tell of pleasing voices heard singing there, and of laughter that swells with joys beyond earth's joys; and say that at evening the little low windows are brighter than formerly. They say, too, that the fierce aurora comes oftener to that spot, shining blue in the north with visions of frozen worlds while the crag and the cottage hang black and fantastic against wild coruscations. And the mists of the dawn are thicker, and sailors are not quite so sure that all the muffled seaward ringing is that of the solemn buoys.

Worst of all, though, is the shrivelling of old fears in the hearts of Kingsport's young men, who grow prone to listen at night to the north wind's faint distant sounds. They swear no harm or pain can inhabit that high peaked cottage, for in the new voices gladness beats, and with them the tinkle of laughter and music. What tales the sea-mists may bring to that haunted and northernmost pinnacle they do not know, but they long to extract some hint of the wonders that knock at the cliff-yawning door when clouds are thickest. And patriarchs dread lest some day one by one they seek out that inaccessible peak in the sky, and learn what centuried secrets hide beneath the steep shingled roof which is part of the rocks and the stars and the ancient fears of Kingsport. That those venturesome youths will come back they do not doubt, but they think a light may be gone from their eyes, and a will from their hearts. And they do not wish quaint Kingsport with its climbing lanes and archaic gables to drag listless down the years while voice by voice the laughing chorus grows stronger and wilder in that unknown and terrible eyrie where mists and the dreams of mists stop to rest on their way from the sea to the skies.

They do not wish the souls of their young men to leave the pleasant hearths and gambrel-roofed taverns of old Kingsport, nor do they wish the laughter and song in that high rocky place to grow louder. For as the voice which has come has brought fresh mists from the sea and from the north fresh lights, so do they say that still other voices will bring more mists and more lights, till perhaps the olden gods (whose existence they hint only in whispers for fear the Congregational parson shall hear) may come out of the deep and from unknown Kadath in the cold waste and make their dwelling on that evilly appropriate crag so close to the gentle hills and valleys of quiet simple fisherfolk. This they do not wish, for to plain people things not of earth are unwelcome; and besides, the Terrible Old Man often recalls what Olney said about a knock that the lone dweller feared, and a shape seen black and inquisitive against the mist through those queer translucent windows of leaded bull's-eyes.

All these things, however, the Elder Ones only may decide; and meanwhile the morning mist still comes up by that lonely vertiginous peak with the steep ancient house, that grey low-eaved house where none is seen but where evening brings furtive lights while the north wind tells of strange revels. White and feathery it comes from the deep to its brothers the clouds, full of dreams of dank pastures and caves of leviathan. And when tales fly thick in the grottoes of tritons, and conches in seaweed cities blow wild tunes learned from the Elder Ones, then great eager vapours flock to heaven laden with lore; and Kingsport, nestling uneasy on its lesser cliffs below that awesome hanging sentinel of rock, sees oceanward only a mystic whiteness, as if the cliff's rim were the rim of all earth, and the solemn bells of the buoys tolled free in the aether of faery.

THE DREAM-QUEST OF UNKNOWN KADATH

Three times Randolph Carter dreamed of the marvellous city, and three times was he snatched away while still he paused on the high terrace above it. All golden and lovely it blazed in the sunset, with walls, temples, colonnades, and arched bridges of veined marble, silver-basined fountains of prismatic spray in broad squares and perfumed gardens, and wide streets marching between delicate trees and blossom-laden urns and ivory statues in gleaming rows; while on steep northward slopes climbed tiers of red roofs and old peaked gables harbouring little lanes of grassy cobbles. It was a fever of the gods; a fanfare of supernal trumpets and a clash of immortal cymbals. Mystery hung about it as clouds about a fabulous unvisited mountain; and as Carter stood breathless and expectant on that balustraded parapet there swept up to him the poignancy and suspense of almost-vanished memory, the pain of lost things, and the maddening need to place again what once had an awesome and momentous place.

He knew that for him its meaning must once have been supreme; though in what cycle or incarnation he had known it, or whether in dream or in waking, he could not tell. Vaguely it called up glimpses of a far, forgotten first youth, when wonder and pleasure lay in all the mystery of days, and dawn and dusk alike strode forth prophetick to the eager sound of lutes and song, unclosing faery gates toward further and surprising marvels. But each night as he stood on that high marble terrace with the curious urns and carven rail and looked off over that hushed sunset city of beauty and unearthly immanence, he felt the bondage of dream's tyrannous gods; for in no wise could he leave that lofty spot, or descend the wide marmoreal flights flung endlessly down to where those streets of elder witchery lay outspread and beckoning.

When for the third time he awaked with those flights still undescended and those hushed sunset streets still untraversed, he prayed long and earnestly to the hidden gods of dream that brood capricious above the clouds on unknown Kadath, in the cold waste where no man treads. But the gods made no answer and shewed no relenting, nor did they give any favouring sign when he prayed to them in dream, and invoked them sacrificially through the bearded priests Nasht and Kaman-Thah, whose cavern-temple with its pillar of flame lies not far from the gate of the waking world. It seemed, however, that his prayers must have been adversely heard, for after even the first of them he ceased wholly to behold the marvellous city; as if his three glimpses from afar had been mere accidents or oversights, and against some hidden plan or wish of the gods.

At length, sick with longing for those glittering sunset streets and cryptical hill lanes among ancient tiled roofs, nor able sleeping or waking to drive them from his mind, Carter resolved to go with bold entreaty whither no man had gone before, and dare the icy deserts through the dark to where unknown Kadath, veiled in cloud and crowned with unimagined stars, holds secret and nocturnal the onyx castle of the Great Ones.

In light slumber he descended the seventy steps to the cavern of flame and talked of this design to the bearded priests Nasht and Kaman-Thah. And the priests shook their pshent-bearing heads and vowed it would be the death of his soul. They pointed out that the Great Ones had shewn already their wish, and that it is not agreeable to them to be harassed by insistent pleas. They reminded him, too, that not only had no man ever been to unknown Kadath, but no man had ever suspected in what part of space it may lie; whether it be in the dreamlands around our world, or in those surrounding some unguessed companion of Fomalhaut or Aldebaran. If in our dreamland, it might conceivably be reached; but only three fully human souls since time began had ever crossed and re-crossed the black impious gulfs to other dreamlands, and of that three two had come back quite mad. There were, in such voyages, incalculable local dangers; as well as that shocking final peril which gibbers unmentionably outside the ordered universe, where no dreams reach; that last amorphous blight of nethermost confusion which blasphemes and bubbles at the centre of all infinity—the boundless daemon-sultan Azathoth, whose name no lips dare speak aloud, and who gnaws hungrily in inconceivable, unlighted chambers beyond time amidst the muffled, maddening beating of vile drums and the thin, monotonous whine of accursed flutes; to which detestable pounding and piping dance slowly, awkwardly, and absurdly the gigantic ultimate gods, the blind, voiceless, tenebrous, mindless Other Gods whose soul and messenger is the crawling chaos Nyarlathotep.

Of these things was Carter warned by the priests Nasht and Kaman-Thah in the cavern of flame, but still he resolved to find the gods on unknown Kadath in the cold waste, wherever that might be, and to win from them the sight and remembrance and shelter of the marvellous sunset city. He knew that his journey would be strange and long, and that the Great Ones would be against it; but being old in the land of dream he counted on many useful memories and devices to aid him. So asking a farewell blessing of the priests and thinking shrewdly on his course, he boldly descended the seven hundred steps to the Gate of Deeper Slumber and set out through the enchanted wood.

In the tunnels of that twisted wood, whose low prodigious oaks twine groping boughs and shine dim with the phosphorescence of strange fungi, dwell the furtive and secretive zoogs; who know many obscure secrets of the dream-world and a few of the waking world, since the wood at two places touches the lands of men, though it would be disastrous to say where. Certain unexplained rumours, events, and vanishments occur among men where the zoogs have access, and it is well that they cannot travel far outside the world of dream. But over the nearer parts of the dream-world they pass freely, flitting small and brown and unseen and bearing back piquant tales to beguile the hours around their hearths in the forest they love. Most of them live in burrows, but some inhabit the trunks of the great trees; and although they live mostly on fungi it is muttered that they have also a slight taste for meat, either physical or spiritual, for certainly many dreamers have entered that wood who have not come out. Carter, however, had no fear; for he was an old dreamer and had learnt their fluttering language and made many a treaty with them; having found through their help the splendid city of Celephaïs in Ooth-Nargai beyond the Tanarian Hills, where reigns half the year the great King Kuranes, a man he had known by another name in life. Kuranes was the one soul who had been to the star-gulfs and returned free from madness.

Threading now the low phosphorescent aisles between those gigantic trunks, Carter made fluttering sounds in the manner of the zoogs, and listened now and then for responses. He remembered one particular village of the creatures near the centre of the wood, where a circle of great mossy stones in what was once a clearing tells of older and more terrible dwellers long forgotten, and toward this spot he hastened. He traced his way by the grotesque fungi, which always seem better nourished as one approaches the dread circle where elder beings danced and sacrificed. Finally the greater light of those thicker fungi revealed a sinister green and grey vastness pushing up through the roof of the forest and out of sight. This was the nearest of the great ring of stones, and Carter knew he was close to the zoog village. Renewing his fluttering sound, he waited patiently; and was at length rewarded by an impression of many eyes watching him. It was the zoogs, for one sees their weird eyes long before one can discern their small, slippery brown outlines.

Out they swarmed, from hidden burrow and honeycombed tree, till the whole dim-litten region was alive with them. Some of the wilder ones brushed Carter unpleasantly, and one even nipped loathsomely at his ear; but these lawless spirits were soon restrained by their elders. The Council of Sages, recognising the visitor, offered a gourd of fermented sap from a haunted tree unlike the others, which had grown from a seed dropt down by someone on the moon; and as Carter drank it ceremoniously a very strange colloquy began. The zoogs did not, unfortunately, know where the peak of Kadath lies, nor could they even say whether the cold waste is in our dream-world or in another. Rumours of the Great Ones came equally from all points; and one might only say that they were likelier to be seen on high mountain peaks than in valleys, since on such peaks they dance reminiscently when the moon is above and the clouds beneath.

Then one very ancient zoog recalled a thing unheard-of by the others; and said that in Ulthar, beyond the river Skai, there still lingered the last copy of those inconceivably old Pnakotic Manuscripts made by waking men in forgotten boreal kingdoms and borne into the land of dreams when the hairy cannibal Gnophkehs overcame many-templed Olathoë and slew all the heroes of the land of Lomar. Those manuscripts, he said, told much of the gods; and besides, in Ulthar there were men who had seen the signs of the gods, and even one old priest who had scaled a great mountain to behold them dancing by moonlight. He had failed, though his companion had succeeded and perished namelessly.

So Randolph Carter thanked the zoogs, who fluttered amicably and gave him another gourd of moon-tree wine to take with him, and set out through the phosphorescent wood for the other side, where the rushing Skai flows down from the slopes of Lerion, and Hatheg and Nir and Ulthar dot the plain. Behind him, furtive and unseen, crept several of the curious zoogs; for they wished to learn what might befall him, and bear back the legend to their people. The vast oaks grew thicker as he pushed on beyond the village, and he looked sharply for a certain spot where they would thin somewhat, standing quite dead or dying among the unnaturally dense fungi and the rotting mould and mushy logs of their fallen brothers. There he would turn sharply aside, for at that spot a mighty slab of stone rests on the forest floor; and those who have dared approach it say that it bears an iron ring three feet wide. Remembering the archaic circle of great mossy rocks, and what it was possibly set up for, the zoogs do not pause near that expansive slab with its huge ring; for they realise that all which is forgotten need not necessarily be dead, and they would not like to see the slab rise slowly and deliberately.

Carter detoured at the proper place, and heard behind him the frightened fluttering of some of the more timid zoogs. He had known they would follow him, so he was not disturbed; for one grows accustomed to the anomalies of these prying creatures. It was twilight when he came to the edge of the wood, and the strengthening glow told him it was the twilight of morning. Over fertile plains rolling down to the Skai he saw the smoke of cottage chimneys, and on every hand were the hedges and ploughed fields and thatched roofs of a peaceful land. Once he stopped at a farmhouse well for a cup of water, and all the dogs barked affrightedly at the inconspicuous zoogs that crept through the grass behind. At another house, where people were stirring, he asked questions about the gods, and whether they danced often upon Lerion; but the farmer and his wife would only make the Elder Sign and tell him the way to Nir and Ulthar.

At noon he walked through the one broad high street of Nir, which he had once visited and which marked his farthest former travels in this direction; and soon afterward he came to the great stone bridge across the Skai, into whose central pier the masons had sealed a living human sacrifice when they built it thirteen-hundred years before. Once on the other side, the frequent presence of cats (who all arched their backs at the trailing zoogs) revealed the near neighbourhood of Ulthar; for in Ulthar, according to an ancient and significant law, no man may kill a cat. Very pleasant were the suburbs of Ulthar, with their little green cottages and neatly fenced farms; and still pleasanter was that quaint town itself, with its old peaked roofs and overhanging upper stories and numberless chimney-pots and narrow hill streets where one can see old cobbles whenever the graceful cats afford space enough. Carter, the cats being somewhat dispersed by the half-seen zoogs, picked his way directly to the modest Temple of the Elder Ones where the priests and old records were said to be; and once within that venerable circular tower of ivied stone—which crowns Ulthar's highest hill—he sought out the patriarch Atal, who had been up the forbidden peak Hatheg-Kla in the stony desert and had come down again alive.

Atal, seated on an ivory dais in a festooned shrine at the top of the temple, was fully three centuries old; but still very keen of mind and memory. From him Carter learned many things about the gods, but mainly that they are indeed only earth's gods, ruling feebly our own dreamland and having no power or habitation elsewhere. They might, Atal said, heed a man's prayer if in good humour; but one must not think of climbing to their onyx stronghold atop Kadath in the cold waste. It was lucky that no man knew where Kadath towers, for the fruits of ascending it would be very grave. Atal's companion Barzai the Wise had been drawn screaming into the sky for climbing merely the known peak of Hatheg-Kla. With unknown Kadath, if ever found, matters would be much worse; for although earth's gods may sometimes be surpassed by a wise mortal, they are protected by the Other Gods from Outside, whom it is better not to discuss. At least twice in the world's history the Other Gods set their seal upon earth's primal granite; once in antediluvian times, as guessed from a drawing in those parts of the Pnakotic Manuscripts too ancient to be read, and once on Hatheg-Kla when Barzai the Wise tried to see earth's gods dancing by moonlight. So, Atal said, it would be much better to let all gods alone except in tactful prayers.

Carter, though disappointed by Atal's discouraging advice and by the meagre help to be found in the Pnakotic Manuscripts and the Seven Cryptical Books of Hsan, did not wholly despair. First he questioned the old priest about that marvellous sunset city seen from the railed terrace, thinking that perhaps he might find it without the gods' aid; but Atal could tell him nothing. Probably, Atal said, the place belonged to his especial dream-world and not to the general land of vision that many know; and conceivably it might be on another planet. In that case earth's gods could not guide him if they would. But this was not likely, since the stopping of the dreams shewed pretty clearly that it was something the Great Ones wished to hide from him.

Then Carter did a wicked thing, offering his guileless host so many draughts of the moon-wine which the zoogs had given him that the old man became irresponsibly talkative. Robbed of his reserve, poor Atal babbled freely of forbidden things; telling of a great image reported by travellers as carved on the solid rock of the mountain Ngranek, on the isle of Oriab in the Southern Sea, and hinting that it may be a likeness which earth's gods once wrought of their own features in the days when they danced by moonlight on that mountain. And he hiccoughed likewise that the features of that image are very strange, so that one might easily recognise them, and that they are sure signs of the authentic race of the gods.

Now the use of all this in finding the gods became at once apparent to Carter. It is known that in disguise the younger among the Great Ones often espouse the daughters of men, so that around the borders of the cold waste wherein stands Kadath the peasants must all bear their blood. This being so, the way to find that waste must be to see the stone face on Ngranek and mark the features; then, having noted them with care, to search for such features among living men. Where they are plainest and thickest, there must the gods dwell nearest; and whatever stony waste lies back of the villages in that place must be that wherein stands Kadath.

Much of the Great Ones might be learnt in such regions, and those with their blood might inherit little memories very useful to a seeker. They might not know their parentage, for the gods so dislike to be known among men that none can be found who has seen their faces wittingly; a thing which Carter realised even as he sought to scale Kadath. But they would have queer lofty thoughts misunderstood by their fellows, and would sing of far places and gardens so unlike any known even in dreamland that common folk would call them fools; and from all this one could perhaps learn old secrets of Kadath, or gain hints of the marvellous sunset city which the gods held secret. And more, one might in certain cases seize some well-loved child of a god as hostage; or even capture some young god himself, disguised and dwelling amongst men with a comely peasant maiden as his bride.

Atal, however, did not know how to find Ngranek on its isle of Oriab; and recommended that Carter follow the singing Skai under its bridges down to the Southern Sea; where no burgess of Ulthar has ever been, but whence the merchants come in boats or with long caravans of mules and two-wheeled carts. There is a great city there, Dylath-Leen, but in Ulthar its reputation is bad because of the black three-banked galleys that sail to it with rubies from no clearly named shore. The traders that come from those galleys to deal with the jewellers are human, or nearly so, but the rowers are never beheld; and it is not thought wholesome in Ulthar that merchants should trade with black ships from unknown places whose rowers cannot be exhibited.

By the time he had given this information Atal was very drowsy, and Carter laid him gently on a couch of inlaid ebony and gathered his long beard decorously on his chest. As he turned to go, he observed that no suppressed fluttering followed him, and wondered why the zoogs had become so lax in their curious pursuit. Then he noticed all the sleek complacent cats of Ulthar licking their chops with unusual gusto, and recalled the spitting and caterwauling he had faintly heard in lower parts of the temple while absorbed in the old priest's conversation. He recalled, too, the evilly hungry way in which an especially impudent young zoog had regarded a small black kitten in the cobbled street outside. And because he loved nothing on earth more than small black kittens, he stooped and petted the sleek cats of Ulthar as they licked their chops, and did not mourn because those inquisitive zoogs would escort him no farther.

It was sunset now, so Carter stopped at an ancient inn on a steep little street overlooking the lower town. And as he went out on the balcony of his room and gazed down at the sea of red tiled roofs and cobbled ways and the pleasant fields beyond, all mellow and magical in the slanted light, he swore that Ulthar would be a very likely place to dwell in always, were not the memory of a greater sunset city ever goading one on toward unknown perils. Then twilight fell, and the pink walls of the plastered gables turned violet and mystic, and little yellow lights floated up one by one from old lattice windows. And sweet bells pealed in the temple tower above, and the first star winked softly above the meadows across the Skai. With the night came song, and Carter nodded as the lutanists praised ancient days from the filigreed balconies and tessellated courts of simple Ulthar. And there might have been sweetness even in the voices of Ulthar's many cats, but that they were mostly heavy and silent from strange feasting. Some of them stole off to those cryptical realms which are known only to cats and which villagers say are on the moon's dark side, whither the cats leap from tall housetops, but one small black kitten crept upstairs and sprang in Carter's lap to purr and play, and curled up near his feet when he lay down at last on the little couch whose pillows were stuffed with fragrant, drowsy herbs.

In the morning Carter joined a caravan of merchants bound for Dylath-Leen with the spun wool of Ulthar and the cabbages of Ulthar's busy farms. And for six days they rode with tinkling bells on the smooth road beside the Skai; stopping some nights at the inns of little quaint fishing towns, and on other nights camping under the stars while snatches of boatmen's songs came from the placid river. The country was very beautiful, with green hedges and groves and picturesque peaked cottages and octagonal windmills.

On the seventh day a blur of smoke arose on the horizon ahead, and then the tall black towers of Dylath-Leen, which is built mostly of basalt. Dylath-Leen with its thin angular towers looks in the distance like a bit of the Giants' Causeway, and its streets are dark and uninviting. There are many dismal sea-taverns near the myriad wharves, and all the town is thronged with the strange seamen of every land on earth and of a few which are said to be not on earth. Carter questioned the oddly robed men of that city about the peak of Ngranek on the isle of Oriab, and found that they knew of it well. Ships came from Baharna on that island, one being due to return thither in only a month, and Ngranek is but two days' zebra-ride from that port. But few had seen the stone face of the god, because it is on a very difficult side of Ngranek, which overlooks only sheer crags and a valley of sinister lava. Once the gods were angered with men on that side, and spoke of the matter to the Other Gods.

It was hard to get this information from the traders and sailors in Dylath-Leen's sea-taverns, because they mostly preferred to whisper of the black galleys. One of them was due in a week with rubies from its unknown shore, and the townsfolk dreaded to see it dock. The mouths of the men who came from it to trade were too wide, and the way their turbans were humped up in two points above their foreheads was in especially bad taste. And their shoes were the shortest and queerest ever seen in the Six Kingdoms. But worst of all was the matter of the unseen rowers. Those three banks of oars moved too briskly and accurately and vigorously to be comfortable, and it was not right for a ship to stay in port for weeks while the merchants traded, yet to give no glimpse of its crew. It was not fair to the tavern-keepers of Dylath-Leen, or to the grocers and butchers, either; for not a scrap of provisions was ever sent aboard. The merchants took only gold and stout black slaves from Parg across the river. That was all they ever took, those unpleasantly featured merchants and their unseen rowers; never anything from the butchers and grocers, but only gold and the fat black men of Parg whom they bought by the pound. And the odours from those galleys which the south wind blew in from the wharves are not to be described. Only by constantly smoking stong thagweed could even the hardiest denizen of the old sea-taverns bear them. Dylath-Leen would never have tolerated the black galleys had such rubies been obtainable elsewhere, but no mine in all earth's dreamland was known to produce their like.

Of these things Dylath-Leen's cosmopolitan folk chiefly gossiped whilst Carter waited patiently for the ship from Baharna, which might bear him to the isle whereon carven Ngranek towers lofty and barren. Meanwhile he did not fail to seek through the haunts of far travellers for any tales they might have concerning Kadath in the cold waste or a marvellous city of marble walls and silver fountains seen below terraces in the sunset. Of these things, however, he learned nothing; though he once thought that a certain old slant-eyed merchant looked queerly intelligent when the cold waste was spoken of. This man was reputed to trade with the horrible stone villages on the icy desert plateau of Leng, which no healthy folk visit and whose evil fires are seen at night from afar. He was even rumoured to have dealt with that high-priest not to be described, which wears a yellow silken mask over its face and dwells all alone in a prehistoric stone monastery. That such a person might well have had nibbling traffick with such beings as may conceivably dwell in the cold waste was not to be doubted, but Carter soon found that it was no use questioning him.

Then the black galley slipped into the harbour past the basalt mole and the tall lighthouse, silent and alien, and with a strange stench that the south wind drove into the town. Uneasiness rustled through the taverns along that waterfront, and after a while the dark wide-mouthed merchants with humped turbans and short feet clumped stealthily ashore to seek the bazaars of the jewellers. Carter observed them closely, and disliked them more the longer he looked at them. Then he saw them drive the stout black men of Parg up the gangplank grunting and sweating into that singular galley, and wondered in what lands—or if in any lands at all—those fat pathetic creatures might be destined to serve.

And on the third evening of that galley's stay one of the uncomfortable merchants spoke to him, smirking sinfully and hinting of what he had heard in the taverns of Carter's quest. He appeared to have knowledge too secret for public telling; and though the sound of his voice was unbearably hateful, Carter felt that the lore of so far a traveller must not be overlooked. He bade him therefore be his own guest in locked chambers above, and drew out the last of the zoogs' moon-wine to loosen his tongue. The strange merchant drank heavily, but smirked unchanged by the draught. Then he drew forth a curious bottle with wine of his own, and Carter saw that the bottle was a single hollowed ruby, grotesquely carved in patterns too fabulous to be comprehended. He offered his wine to his host, and though Carter took only the least sip, he felt the dizziness of space and the fever of unimagined jungles. All the while the guest had been smiling more and more broadly, and as Carter slipped into blankness the last thing he saw was that dark odious face convulsed with evil laughter, and something quite unspeakable where one of the two frontal puffs of that orange turban had become disarranged with the shakings of that epileptic mirth.

Carter next had consciousness amidst horrible odours beneath a tent-like awning on the deck of a ship, with the marvellous coasts of the Southern Sea flying by in unnatural swiftness. He was not chained, but three of the dark sardonic merchants stood grinning nearby, and the sight of those humps in their turbans made him almost as faint as did the stench that filtered up through the sinister hatches. He saw slip past him the glorious lands and cities of which a fellow-dreamer of earth—a lighthouse-keeper in ancient Kingsport—had often discoursed in the old days, and recognised the templed terraces of Zar, abode of forgotten dreams; the spires of infamous Thalarion, that daemon-city of a thousand wonders where the eidolon Lathi reigns; the charnel gardens of Xura, land of pleasures unattained, and the twin headlands of crystal, meeting above in a resplendent arch, which guard the harbour of Sona-Nyl, blessed land of fancy.

Past all these gorgeous lands the malodorous ship flew unwholesomely, urged by the abnormal strokes of those unseen rowers below. And before the day was done Carter saw that the steersman could have no other goal than the Basalt Pillars of the West, beyond which simple folk say splendid Cathuria lies, but which wise dreamers well know are the gates of a monstrous cataract wherein the oceans of earth's dreamland drop wholly to abysmal nothingness and shoot through the empty spaces toward other worlds and other stars and the awful voids outside the ordered universe where the daemon-sultan Azathoth gnaws hungrily in chaos amid pounding and piping and the hellish dancing of the Other Gods, blind, voiceless, tenebrous, and mindless, with their soul and messenger Nyarlathotep.

Meanwhile the three sardonic merchants would give no word of their intent, though Carter well knew that they must be leagued with those who wished to hold him from his quest. It is understood in the land of dream that the Other Gods have many agents moving among men; and all these agents, whether wholly human or slightly less than human, are eager to work the will of those blind and mindless things in return for the favour of their hideous soul and messenger, the crawling chaos Nyarlathotep. So Carter inferred that the merchants of the humped turbans, hearing of his daring search for the Great Ones in their castle on Kadath, had decided to take him away and deliver him to Nyarlathothep for whatever nameless bounty might be offered for such a prize. What might be the land of those merchants, in our known universe or in the eldritch spaces outside, Carter could not guess; nor could he imagine at what hellish trysting-place they would meet the crawling chaos to give him up and claim their reward. He knew, however, that no beings as nearly human as these would dare approach the ultimate nighted throne of the daemon Azathoth in the formless central void.

At the set of sun the merchants licked their excessively wide lips and glared hungrily, and one of them went below and returned from some hidden and offensive cabin with a pot and basket of plates. Then they squatted close together beneath the awning and ate the smoking meat that was passed around. But when they gave Carter a portion, he found something very terrible in the size and shape of it; so that he turned even paler than before and cast that portion into the sea when no eye was on him. And again he thought of those unseen rowers beneath, and of the suspicious nourishment from which their far too mechanical strength was derived.

It was dark when the galley passed betwixt the Basalt Pillars of the West and the sound of the ultimate cataract swelled portentous from ahead. And the spray of that cataract rose to obscure the stars, and the deck grew damp, and the vessel reeled in the surging current of the brink. Then with a queer whistle and plunge the leap was taken, and Carter felt the terrors of nightmare as earth fell away and the great boat shot silent and comet-like into planetary space. Never before had he known what shapeless black things lurk and caper and flounder all through the aether, leering and grinning at such voyagers as may pass, and sometimes feeling about with slimy paws when some moving object excites their curiosity. These are the nameless larvae of the Other Gods, and like them are blind and without mind, and possessed of singular hungers and thirsts.

But that offensive galley did not aim as far as Carter had feared, for he soon saw that the helmsman was steering a course directly for the moon. The moon was a crescent, shining larger and larger as they approached it, and shewing its singular craters and peaks uncomfortably. The ship made for the edge, and it soon became clear that its destination was that secret and mysterious side which is always turned away from the earth, and which no fully human person, save perhaps the dreamer Snireth-Ko, has ever beheld. The close aspect of the moon as the galley drew near proved very disturbing to Carter, and he did not like the size and shape of the ruins which crumbled here and there. The dead temples on the mountains were so placed that they could have glorified no wholesome or suitable gods, and in the symmetries of the broken columns there seemed to lurk some dark and inner meaning which did not invite solution. And what the structure and proportions of the olden worshippers could have been, Carter steadily refused to conjecture.

When the ship rounded the edge, and sailed over those lands unseen by man, there appeared in the queer landscape certain signs of life, and Carter saw many low, broad, round cottages in fields of grotesque whitish fungi. He noticed that these cottages had no windows, and thought that their shape suggested the huts of Esquimaux. Then he glimpsed the oily waves of a sluggish sea, and knew that the voyage was once more to be by water—or at least through some liquid. The galley struck the surface with a peculiar sound, and the odd elastic way the waves received it was very perplexing to Carter. They now slid along at great speed, once passing and hailing another galley of kindred form, but generally seeing nothing but that curious sea and a sky that was black and star-strown even though the sun shone scorchingly in it.

There presently rose ahead the jagged hills of a leprous-looking coast, and Carter saw the thick unpleasant grey towers of a city. The way they leaned and bent, the manner in which they were clustered, and the fact that they had no windows at all, was very disturbing to the prisoner; and he bitterly mourned the folly which had made him sip the curious wine of that merchant with the humped turban. As the coast drew nearer, and the hideous stench of that city grew stronger, he saw upon the jagged hills many forests, some of whose trees he recognised as akin to that solitary moon-tree in the enchanted wood of earth, from whose sap the small brown zoogs ferment their peculiar wine.

Carter could now distinguish moving figures on the noisome wharves ahead, and the better he saw them the worse he began to fear and detest them. For they were not men at all, or even approximately men, but great greyish-white slippery things which could expand and contract at will, and whose principal shape—though it often changed—was that of a sort of toad without any eyes, but with a curiously vibrating mass of short pink tentacles on the end of its blunt, vague snout. These objects were waddling busily about the wharves, moving bales and crates and boxes with preternatural strength, and now and then hopping on or off some anchored galley with long oars in their fore-paws. And now and then one would appear driving a herd of clumping slaves, which indeed were approximate human beings with wide mouths like those merchants who traded in Dylath-Leen; only these herds, being without turbans or shoes or clothing, did not seem so very human after all. Some of these slaves—the fatter ones, whom a sort of overseer would pinch experimentally—were unloaded from ships and nailed in crates which workers pushed into low warehouses or loaded on great lumbering vans.

Once a van was hitched up and driven off, and the fabulous thing which drew it was such that Carter gasped, even after having seen the other monstrosities of that hateful place. Now and then a small herd of slaves dressed and turbaned like the dark merchants would be driven aboard a galley, followed by a great crew of the slippery grey toad-things as officers, navigators, and rowers. And Carter saw that the almost-human creatures were reserved for the more ignominious kinds of servitude which required no strength, such as steering and cooking, fetching and carrying, and bargaining with men on the earth or other planets where they traded. These creatures must have been convenient on earth, for they were truly not unlike men when dressed and carefully shod and turbaned, and could haggle in the shops of men without embarrassment or curious explanations. But most of them, unless lean and ill-favoured, were unclothed and packed in crates and drawn off in lumbering lorries by fabulous things. Occasionally other beings were unloaded and crated; some very like these semi-humans, some not so similar, and some not similar at all. And he wondered if any of the poor stout black men of Parg were left to be unloaded and crated and shipped inland in those obnoxious drays.

When the galley landed at a greasy-looking quay of spongy rock a nightmare horde of toad-things wriggled out of the hatches, and two of them seized Carter and dragged him ashore. The smell and aspect of that city are beyond telling, and Carter held only scattered images of the tiled streets and black doorways and endless precipices of grey vertical walls without windows. At length he was dragged within a low doorway and made to climb infinite steps in pitch blackness. It was, apparently, all one to the toad-things whether it were light or dark. The odour of the place was intolerable, and when Carter was locked into a chamber and left alone he scarcely had strength to crawl around and ascertain its form and dimensions. It was circular, and about twenty feet across.

From then on time ceased to exist. At intervals food was pushed in, but Carter would not touch it. What his fate would be, he did not know; but he felt that he was held for the coming of that frightful soul and messenger of infinity's Other Gods, the crawling chaos Nyarlathotep. Finally, after an unguessed span of hours or days, the great stone door swung wide again and Carter was shoved down the stairs and out into the red-litten streets of that fearsome city. It was night on the moon, and all through the town were stationed slaves bearing torches.

In a destestable square a sort of procession was formed; ten of the toad-things and twenty-four almost-human torch-bearers, eleven on either side, and one each before and behind. Carter was placed in the middle of the line; five toad-things ahead and five behind, and one almost-human torch-bearer on each side of him. Certain of the toad-things produced disgustingly carven flutes of ivory and made loathsome sounds. To that hellish piping the column advanced out of the tiled streets and into nighted plains of obscene fungi, soon commencing to climb one of the lower and more gradual hills that lay behind the city. That on some frightful slope or blasphemous plateau the crawling chaos waited, Carter could not doubt; and he wished that the suspense might soon be over. The whining of those impious flutes was shocking, and he would have given worlds for some even half-normal sound; but these toad-things had no voices, and the slaves did not talk.

Then through that star-specked darkness there did come a normal sound. It rolled from the higher hills, and from all the jagged peaks around it was caught up and echoed in a swelling pandaemoniac chorus. It was the midnight yell of the cat, and Carter knew at last that the old village folk were right when they made low guesses about the cryptical realms which are known only to cats, and to which the elders among cats repair by stealth nocturnally, springing from high housetops. Verily, it is to the moon's dark side that they go to leap and gambol on the hills and converse with ancient shadows, and here amidst that column of foetid things Carter heard their homely, friendly cry, and thought of the steep roofs and warm hearths and little lighted windows of home.

Now much of the speech of cats was known to Randolph Carter, and in this far, terrible place he uttered the cry that was suitable. But that he need not have done, for even as his lips opened he heard the chorus wax and draw nearer, and saw swift shadows against the stars as small graceful shapes leaped from hill to hill in gathering legions. The call of the clan had been given, and before the foul procession had time even to be frightened a cloud of smothering fur and a phalanx of murderous claws were tidally and tempestuously upon it. The flutes stopped, and there were shrieks in the night. Dying almost-humans screamed, and cats spit and yowled and roared, but the toad-things made never a sound as their stinking green ichor oozed fatally onto that porous earth with the obscene fungi.

It was a stupendous sight while the torches lasted, and Carter had never before seen so many cats. Black, grey, and white; yellow, tiger, and mixed; common, Persian, and Manx; Thibetan, Angora, and Egyptian; all were there in the fury of battle, and there hovered over them some trace of that profound and inviolate sanctity which made their goddess great in the temples of Bubastis. They would leap seven strong at the throat of an almost-human or the pink tentacled snout of a toad-thing and drag it down savagely to the fungous plain, where myriads of their fellows would surge over it and into it with the frenzied claws and teeth of a divine battle-fury. Carter had seized a torch from a stricken slave, but was soon overborne by the surging waves of his loyal defenders. Then he lay in the utter blackness hearing the clangour of war and the shouts of the victors, and feeling the soft paws of his friends as they rushed to and fro over him in the fray.

At last awe and exhaustion closed his eyes, and when he opened them again it was upon a strange scene. The great shining disc of the earth, thirteen times greater than that of the moon as we see it, had risen with floods of weird light over the lunar landscape; and across all those leagues of wild plateau and ragged crest there squatted one endless sea of cats in orderly array. Circle on circle they reached, and two or three leaders out of the ranks were licking his face and purring to him consolingly. Of the dead slaves and toad-things there were not many signs, but Carter thought he saw one bone a little way off in the open space between him and the beginning of the solid circles of the warriors.

Carter now spoke with the leaders in the soft language of cats, and learned that his ancient friendship with the species was well known and often spoken of in the places where cats congregate. He had not been unmarked in Ulthar when he passed through, and the sleek old cats had remembered how he petted them after they had attended to the hungry zoogs who looked evilly at a small black kitten. And they recalled, too, how he had welcomed the very little kitten who came to see him at the inn, and how he had given it a saucer of rich cream in the morning before he left. The grandfather of that very little kitten was the leader of the army now assembled, for he had seen the evil procession from a far hill and recognised the prisoner as a sworn friend of his kind on earth and in the land of dream.

A yowl now came from a farther peak, and the old leader paused abruptly in his conversation. It was one of the army's outposts, stationed on the highest of the mountains to watch the one foe which earth's cats fear; the very large and peculiar cats from Saturn, who for some reason have not been oblivious of the charm of our moon's dark side. They are leagued by treaty with the evil toad-things, and are notoriously hostile to our earthly cats; so that at this juncture a meeting would have been a somewhat grave matter.

After a brief consultation of generals, the cats rose and assumed a closer formation, crowding protectingly around Carter and preparing to take the great leap through space back to the housetops of our earth and its dreamland. The old field-marshal advised Carter to let himself be borne along smoothly and passively in the massed ranks of furry leapers, and told him how to spring when the rest sprang and land gracefully when the rest landed. He also offered to deposit him in any spot he desired, and Carter decided on the city of Dylath-Leen whence the black galley had set out; for he wished to sail thence for Oriab and the carven crest of Ngranek, and also to warn the people of the city to have no more traffick with black galleys, if indeed that traffick could be tactfully and judiciously broken off. Then, upon a signal, the cats all leaped gracefully with their friend packed securely in their midst; while in a black cave on a far unhallowed summit of the moon-mountains still vainly waited the crawling chaos Nyarlathotep.

The leap of the cats through space was very swift; and being surrounded by his companions, Carter did not see this time the great black shapelessnesses that lurk and caper and flounder in the abyss. Before he fully realised what had happened he was back in his familiar room at the inn at Dylath-Leen, and the stealthy, friendly cats were pouring out of the window in streams. The old leader from Ulthar was the last to leave, and as Carter shook his paw he said he would be able to get home by cockcrow. When dawn came, Carter went downstairs and learned that a week had elapsed since his capture and leaving. There was still nearly a fortnight to wait for the ship bound toward Oriab, and during that time he said what he could against the black galleys and their infamous ways. Most of the townsfolk believed him; yet so fond were the jewellers of great rubies that none would wholly promise to cease trafficking with the wide-mouthed merchants. If aught of evil ever befalls Dylath-Leen through such traffick, it will not be his fault.

In about a week the desiderate ship put in by the black mole and tall lighthouse, and Carter was glad to see that she was a barque of wholesome men, with painted sides and yellow lateen sails and a grey captain in silken robes. Her cargo was the fragrant resin of Oriab's inner groves, and the delicate pottery baked by the artists of Baharna, and the strange little figures carved from Ngranek's ancient lava. For this they were paid in the wool of Ulthar and the iridescent textiles of Hatheg and the ivory that the black men carve across the river in Parg. Carter made arrangements with the captain to go to Baharna and was told that the voyage would take ten days. And during his week of waiting he talked much with that captain of Ngranek, and was told that very few have seen the carven face thereon; but that most travellers are content to learn its legends from old people and lava-gatherers and image-makers in Baharna and afterward say in their far homes that they have indeed beheld it. The captain was not even sure that any person now living had beheld that carven face, for the wrong side of Ngranek is very difficult and barren and sinister, and there are rumours of caves near the peak wherein dwell the night-gaunts. But the captain did not wish to say just what a night-gaunt might be like, since such cattle are known to haunt most persistently the dreams of those who think too often of them. Then Carter asked that captain about unknown Kadath in the cold waste, and the marvellous sunset city, but of these the good man could truly tell nothing.

Carter sailed out of Dylath-Leen one early morning when the tide turned, and saw the first rays of sunrise on the thin angular towers of that dismal basalt town. And for two days they sailed eastward in sight of green coasts, and saw often the pleasant fishing towns that climbed up steeply with their red roofs and chimney-pots from old dreaming wharves and beaches where nets lay drying. But on the third day they turned sharply south where the roll of the water was stronger, and soon passed from sight of any land. On the fifth day the sailors were nervous, but the captain apologised for their fears, saying that the ship was about to pass over the weedy walls and broken columns of a sunken city too old for memory, and that when the water was clear one could see so many moving shadows in that deep place that simple folk disliked it. He admitted, moreover, that many ships had been lost in that part of the sea; having been hailed when quite close to it, but never seen again.

That night the moon was very bright, and one could see a great way down in the water. There was so little wind that the ship could not move much, and the ocean was very calm. Looking over the rail Carter saw many fathoms deep the dome of a great temple, and in front of it an avenue of unnatural sphinxes leading to what was once a public square. Dolphins sported merrily in and out of the ruins, and porpoises revelled clumsily here and there, sometimes coming to the surface and leaping clear out of the sea. As the ship drifted on a little the floor of the ocean rose in hills, and one could clearly mark the lines of ancient climbing streets and the washed-down walls of myriad little houses.

Then the suburbs appeared, and finally a great lone building on a hill, of simpler architecture than the other structures, and in much better repair. It was dark and low and covered four sides of a square, with a tower at each corner, a paved court in the centre, and small curious round windows all over it. Probably it was of basalt, though weeds draped the greater part; and such was its lonely and impressive place on that far hill that it may have been a temple or a monastery. Some phosphorescent fish inside it gave the small round windows an aspect of shining, and Carter did not blame the sailors much for their fears. Then by the watery moonlight he noticed an odd high monolith in the middle of that central court, and saw that something was tied to it. And when after getting a telescope from the captain's cabin he saw that that bound thing was a sailor in the silk robes of Oriab, head downward and without any eyes, he was glad that a rising breeze soon took the ship ahead to more healthy parts of the sea.

The next day they spoke a ship with violet sails bound for Zar, in the land of forgotten dreams, with bulbs of strange coloured lilies for cargo. And on the evening of the eleventh day they came in sight of the isle of Oriab, with Ngranek rising jagged and snow-crowned in the distance. Oriab is a very great isle, and its port of Baharna a mighty city. The wharves of Baharna are of porphyry, and the city rises in great stone terraces behind them, having streets of steps that are frequently arched over by buildings and the bridges between buildings. There is a great canal which goes under the whole city in a tunnel with granite gates and leads to the inland lake of Yath, on whose farther shore are the vast clay-brick ruins of a primal city whose name is not remembered. As the ship drew into the harbour at evening the twin beacons Thon and Thal gleamed a welcome, and in all the million windows of Baharna's terraces mellow lights peeped out quietly and gradually as the stars peep out overhead in the dusk, till that steep and climbing seaport became a glittering constellation hung between the stars of heaven and the reflections of those stars in the still harbour.

The captain, after landing, made Carter a guest in his own small house on the shore of Yath where the rear of the town slopes down to it; and his wife and servants brought strange toothsome foods for the traveller's delight. And in the days after that Carter asked for rumours and legends of Ngranek in all the taverns and public places where lava-gatherers and image-makers meet, but could find no one who had been up the higher slopes or seen the carven face. Ngranek was a hard mountain with only an accursed valley behind it, and besides, one could never depend on the certainty that night-gaunts are altogether fabulous.

When the captain sailed back to Dylath-Leen Carter took quarters in an ancient tavern opening on an alley of steps in the original part of the town, which is built of brick and resembles the ruins on Yath's farther shore. Here he laid his plans for the ascent of Ngranek, and correlated all that he had learned from the lava-gatherers about the roads thither. The keeper of the tavern was a very old man, and had heard so many legends that he was a great help. He even took Carter to an upper room in that ancient house and shewed him a crude picture which a traveller had scratched on the clay wall in the olden days when men were bolder and less reluctant to visit Ngranek's higher slopes. The old tavern-keeper's great-grandfather had heard from his great-grandfather that the traveller who scratched that picture had climbed Ngranek and seen the carven face, here drawing it for others to behold; but Carter had very great doubts, since the large rough features on the wall were hasty and careless, and wholly overshadowed by a crowd of little companion shapes in the worst possible taste, with horns and wings and claws and curling tails.

At last, having gained all the information he was likely to gain in the taverns and public places of Baharna, Carter hired a zebra and set out one morning on the road by Yath's shore for those inland parts wherein towers stony Ngranek. On his right were rolling hills and pleasant orchards and neat little stone farmhouses, and he was much reminded of those fertile fields that flank the Skai. By evening he was near the nameless ancient ruins on Yath's farther shore, and though old lava-gatherers had warned him not to camp there at night, he tethered his zebra to a curious pillar before a crumbling wall and laid his blanket in a sheltered corner beneath some carvings whose meaning none could decipher. Around him he wrapped another blanket, for the nights are cold in Oriab; and when upon awaking once he thought he felt the wings of some insect brushing his face he covered his head altogether and slept in peace till roused by the magah birds in distant resin groves.

The sun had just come up over the great slope whereon leagues of primal brick foundations and worn walls and occasional cracked pillars and pedestals stretched down desolate to the shore of Yath, and Carter looked about for his tethered zebra. Great was his dismay to see that docile beast stretched prostrate beside the curious pillar to which it had been tied, and still greater was he vexed on finding that the steed was quite dead, with its blood all sucked away through a singular wound in its throat. His pack had been disturbed, and several shiny knick-knacks taken away, and all around on the dusty soil were great webbed footprints for which he could not in any way account. The legends and warnings of lava-gatherers occurred to him and he thought of what had brushed his face in the night. Then he shouldered his pack and strode on toward Ngranek, though not without a shiver when he saw close to him as the highway passed through the ruins a great gaping arch low in the wall of an old temple, with steps leading down into darkness farther than he could peer.

His course now led uphill through wilder and partly wooded country, and he saw only the huts of charcoal-burners and the camps of those who gathered resin from the groves. The whole air was fragrant with balsam, and all the magah birds sang blithely as they flashed their seven colours in the sun. Near sunset he came on a new camp of lava-gatherers returning with laden sacks from Ngranek's lower slopes; and here he also camped, listening to the songs and tales of the men, and overhearing what they whispered about a companion they had lost. He had climbed high to reach a mass of fine lava above him, and at nightfall did not return to his fellows. When they looked for him the next day they found only his turban, nor was there any sign on the crags below that he had fallen. They did not search any more, because the old men among them said it would be of no use. No one ever found what the night-gaunts took, though those beasts themselves were so uncertain as to be almost fabulous. Carter asked them if night-gaunts sucked blood and liked shiny things and left webbed footprints, but they all shook their heads negatively and seemed frightened at his making such an inquiry. When he saw how taciturn they had become he asked them no more, but went to sleep in his blanket.

The next day he rose with the lava-gatherers and exchanged farewells as they rode west and he rode east on a zebra he had bought of them. Their older men gave him blessings and warnings, and told him he had better not climb too high on Ngranek, but while he thanked them heartily he was in no wise dissuaded. For still did he feel that he must find the gods on unknown Kadath, and win from them a way to that haunting and marvellous city in the sunset. By noon, after a long uphill ride, he came upon some abandoned brick villages of the hill-people who had once dwelt thus close to Ngranek and carved images from its smooth lava. Here they had dwelt till the days of the old tavern-keeper's grandfather, but about that time they felt that their presence was disliked. Their homes had crept even up the mountain's slope, and the higher they built the more people they would miss when the sun rose. At last they decided it would be better to leave altogether, since things were sometimes glimpsed in the darkness which no one could interpret favourably; so in the end all of them went down to the sea and dwelt in Baharna, inhabiting a very old quarter and teaching their sons the old art of image-making which to this day they carry on. It was from these children of the exiled hill-people that Carter had heard the best tales about Ngranek when searching through Baharna's ancient taverns.

All this time the great gaunt side of Ngranek was looming up higher and higher as Carter approached it. There were sparse trees on the lower slope, and feeble shrubs above them, and then the bare hideous rock rose spectral into the sky to mix with frost and ice and eternal snow. Carter could see the rifts and ruggedness of that sombre stone, and did not welcome the prospect of climbing it. In places there were solid streams of lava, and scoriac heaps that littered slopes and ledges. Ninety aeons ago, before even the gods had danced upon its pointed peak, that mountain had spoken with fire and roared with the voices of the inner thunders. Now it towered all silent and sinister, bearing on the hidden side that secret titan image whereof rumour told. And there were caves in that mountain, which might be empty and alone with elder darkness, or might—if legend spoke truly—hold horrors of a form not to be surmised.

The ground sloped upward to the foot of Ngranek, thinly covered with scrub oaks and ash trees, and strown with bits of rock, lava, and ancient cinder. There were the charred embers of many camps, where the lava-gatherers were wont to stop, and several rude altars which they had built either to propitiate the Great Ones or to ward off what they dreamed of in Ngranek's high passes and labyrinthine caves. At evening Carter reached the farthermost pile of embers and camped for the night, tethering his zebra to a sapling and wrapping himself well in his blanket before going to sleep. And all through the night a voonith howled distantly from the shore of some hidden pool, but Carter felt no fear of that amphibious terror, since he had been told with certainty that not one of them dares even approach the slopes of Ngranek.

In the clear sunshine of morning Carter began the long ascent, taking his zebra as far as that useful beast could go, but tying it to a stunted ash tree when the floor of the thin road became too steep. Thereafter he scrambled up alone; first through the forest with its ruins of old villages in overgrown clearings, and then over the tough grass where anaemic shrubs grew here and there. He regretted coming clear of the trees, since the slope was very precipitous and the whole thing rather dizzying. At length he began to discern all the countryside spread out beneath him whenever he looked around; the deserted huts of the image-makers, the groves of resin trees and the camps of those who gathered from them, the woods where prismatic magahs nest and sing, and even a hint very far away of the shores of Yath and of those forbidding ancient ruins whose name is forgotten. He found it best not to look around, and kept on climbing and climbing till the shrubs became very sparse and there was often nothing but the tough grass to cling to.

Then the soil became meagre, with great patches of bare rock cropping out, and now and then the nest of a condor in a crevice. Finally there was nothing at all but the bare rock, and had it not been very rough and weathered, he could scarcely have ascended farther. Knobs, ledges, and pinnacles, however, helped greatly; and it was cheering to see occasionally the sign of some lava-gatherer scratched clumsily in the friable stone, and know that wholesome human creatures had been there before him. After a certain height the presence of man was further shewn by handholds and footholds hewn where they were needed, and by little quarries and excavations where some choice vein or stream of lava had been found. In one place a narrow ledge had been chopped artificially to an especially rich deposit far to the right of the main line of ascent. Once or twice Carter dared to look around, and was almost stunned by the spread of landscape below. All the island betwixt him and the coast lay open to his sight, with Baharna's stone terraces and the smoke of its chimneys mystical in the distance. And beyond that the illimitable Southern Sea with all its curious secrets.

Thus far there had not been much winding around the mountain, so that the farther and carven side was still hidden. Carter now saw a ledge running upward and to the left which seemed to head the way he wished, and this course he took in the hope that it might prove continuous. After ten minutes he saw it was indeed no cul-de-sac, but that it led steeply on in an arc which would, unless suddenly interrupted or deflected, bring him after a few hours' climbing to that unknown southern slope overlooking the desolate crags and the accursed valley of lava. As new country came into view below him he saw that it was bleaker and wilder than those seaward lands he had traversed. The mountain's side, too, was somewhat different; being here pierced by curious cracks and caves not found on the straighter route he had left. Some of these were above him and some beneath him, all opening on sheerly perpendicular cliffs and wholly unreachable by the feet of man. The air was very cold now, but so hard was the climbing that he did not mind it. Only the increasing rarity bothered him, and he thought that perhaps it was this which had turned the heads of other travellers and excited those absurd tales of night-gaunts whereby they explained the loss of such climbers as fell from these perilous paths. He was not much impressed by travellers' tales, but had a good curved scimitar in case of any trouble. All lesser thoughts were lost in the wish to see that carven face which might set him on the track of the gods atop unknown Kadath.

At last, in the fearsome iciness of upper space, he came round fully to the hidden side of Ngranek and saw in infinite gulfs below him the lesser crags and sterile abysses of lava which marked the olden wrath of the Great Ones. There was unfolded, too, a vast expanse of country to the south; but it was a desert land without fair fields or cottage chimneys, and seemed to have no ending. No trace of the sea was visible on this side, for Oriab is a great island. Black caverns and odd crevices were still numerous on the sheer vertical cliffs, but none of them was accessible to a climber. There now loomed aloft a great beetling mass which hampered the upward view, and Carter was for a moment shaken with doubt lest it prove impassable. Poised in windy insecurity miles above earth, with only space and death on one side and only slippery walls of rock on the other, he knew for a moment the fear that makes men shun Ngranek's hidden side. He could not turn round, yet the sun was already low. If there were no way aloft, the night would find him crouching there still, and the dawn would not find him at all.

But there was a way, and he saw it in due season. Only a very expert dreamer could have used those imperceptible footholds, yet to Carter they were sufficent. Surmounting now the outward-hanging rock, he found the slope above much easier than that below, since a great glacier's melting had left a generous space with loam and ledges. To the left a precipice dropped straight from unknown heights to unknown depths, with a cave's dark mouth just out of reach above him. Elsewhere, however, the mountain slanted back strongly, and even gave him space to lean and rest.

He felt from the chill that he must be near the snow line, and looked up to see what glittering pinnacles might be shining in that late ruddy sunlight. Surely enough, there was the snow uncounted thousands of feet above, and below it a great beetling crag like that he had just climbed; hanging there for ever in bold outline, black against the white of the frozen peak. And when he saw that crag he gasped and cried out aloud, and clutched at the jagged rock in awe; for the titan bulge had not stayed as earth's dawn had shaped it, but gleamed red and stupendous in the sunset with the carved and polished features of a god.

Stern and terrible shone that face that the sunset lit with fire. How vast it was no mind can ever measure, but Carter knew at once that man could never have fashioned it. It was a god chiselled by the hands of the gods, and it looked down haughty and majestic upon the seeker. Rumour had said it was strange and not to be mistaken, and Carter saw that it was indeed so; for those long narrow eyes and long-lobed ears, and that thin nose and pointed chin, all spoke of a race that is not of men but of gods. He clung overawed in that lofty and perilous eyrie, even though it was this which he had expected and come to find; for there is in a god's face more of marvel than prediction can tell, and when that face is vaster than a great temple and seen looking down at sunset in the cryptic silences of that upper world from whose dark lava it was divinely hewn of old, the marvel is so strong that none may escape it.

Here, too, was the added marvel of recognition; for although he had planned to search all dreamland over for those whose likeness to this face might mark them as the gods' children, he now knew that he need not do so. Certainly, the great face carven on that mountain was of no strange sort, but the kin of such as he had seen often in the taverns of the seaport Celephaïs which lies in Ooth-Nargai beyond the Tanarian Hills and is ruled over by that King Kuranes whom Carter once knew in waking life. Every year sailors with such a face came in dark ships from the north to trade their onyx for the carved jade and spun gold and little red singing birds of Celephaïs, and it was clear that these could be no others than the half-gods he sought. Where they dwelt, there must the cold waste lie close, and within it unknown Kadath and its onyx castle of the Great Ones. So to Celephaïs he must go, far distant from the isle of Oriab, and in such parts as would take him back to Dylath-Leen and up the Skai to the bridge by Nir, and again into the enchanted wood of the zoogs, whence the way would bend northward through the garden lands by Oukranos to the gilded spires of Thran, where he might find a galleon bound over the Cerenarian Sea.

But dusk was now thick, and the great carven face looked down even sterner in shadow. Perched on that ledge night found the seeker; and in the blackness he might neither go down nor go up, but only stand and cling and shiver in that narrow place till the day came, praying to keep awake lest sleep loose his hold and send him down the dizzy miles of air to the crags and sharp rocks of the accursed valley. The stars came out, but save for them there was only black nothingness in his eyes; nothingness leagued with death, against whose beckoning he might do no more than cling to the rocks and lean back away from an unseen brink. The last thing of earth that he saw in the gloaming was a condor soaring close to the westward precipice beside him, and darting screaming away when it came near the cave whose mouth yawned just out of reach.

Suddenly, without a warning sound in the dark, Carter felt his curved scimitar drawn stealthily out of his belt by some unseen hand. Then he heard it clatter down over the rocks below. And between him and the Milky Way he thought he saw a very terrible outline of something noxiously thin and horned and tailed and bat-winged. Other things, too, had begun to blot out patches of stars west of him, as if a flock of vague entities were flapping thickly and silently out of that inaccessible cave in the face of the precipice. Then a sort of cold rubbery arm seized his neck and something else seized his feet, and he was lifted inconsiderately up and swung about in space. Another minute and the stars were gone, and Carter knew that the night-gaunts had got him.

They bore him breathless into that cliffside cavern and through monstrous labyrinths beyond. When he struggled, as at first he did by instinct, they tickled him with deliberation. They made no sound at all themselves, and even their membraneous wings were silent. They were frightfully cold and damp and slippery, and their paws kneaded one detestably. Soon they were plunging hideously downward through inconceivable abysses in a whirling, giddying, sickening rush of dank, tomb-like air; and Carter felt they were shooting into the ultimate vortex of shrieking and daemonic madness. He screamed again and again, but whenever he did so the black paws tickled him with greater subtlety. Then he saw a sort of grey phosphorescence about, and guessed they were coming even to that inner world of subterrene horror of which dim legends tell, and which is litten only by the pale death-fire wherewith reeks the ghoulish air and the primal mists of the pits at earth's core.

At last far below him he saw faint lines of grey and ominous pinnacles which he knew must be the fabled Peaks of Thok. Awful and sinister they stand in the haunted dusk of sunless and eternal depths; higher than man may reckon, and guarding terrible valleys where the bholes crawl and burrow nastily. But Carter preferred to look at them than at his captors, which were indeed shocking and uncouth black beings with smooth, oily, whale-like surfaces, unpleasant horns that curved inward toward each other, bat-wings whose beating made no sound, ugly prehensile paws, and barbed tails that lashed needlessly and disquietingly. And worst of all, they never spoke or laughed, and never smiled because they had no faces at all to smile with, but only a suggestive blankness where a face ought to be. All they ever did was clutch and fly and tickle; that was the way of night-gaunts.

As the band flew lower the Peaks of Thok rose grey and towering on all sides, and one saw clearly that nothing lived on that austere and impassive granite of the endless twilight. At still lower levels the death-fires in the air gave out, and one met only the primal blackness of the void save aloft where the thin peaks stood out goblin-like. Soon the peaks were very far away, and nothing about but great rushing winds with the dankness of nethermost grottoes in them. Then in the end the night-gaunts landed on a floor of unseen things which felt like layers of bones, and left Carter all alone in that black valley. To bring him thither was the duty of the night-gaunts that guard Ngranek; and this done, they flapped away silently. When Carter tried to trace their flight he found he could not, since even the Peaks of Thok had faded out of sight. There was nothing anywhere but blackness and horror and silence and bones.

Now Carter knew from a certain source that he was in the vale of Pnath, where crawl and burrow the enormous bholes; but he did not know what to expect, because no one has ever seen a bhole or even guessed what such a thing may be like. Bholes are known only by dim rumour, from the rustling they make amongst mountains of bones and the slimy touch they have when they wriggle past one. They cannot be seen because they creep only in the dark. Carter did not wish to meet a bhole, so listened intently for any sound in the unknown depths of bones about him. Even in this fearsome place he had a plan and an objective, for whispers of Pnath and its approaches were not unknown to one with whom he had talked much in the old days. In brief, it seemed fairly likely that this was the spot into which all the ghouls of the waking world cast the refuse of their feastings; and that if he but had good luck he might stumble upon that mighty crag taller even than Thok's peaks which marks the edge of their domain. Showers of bones would tell him where to look, and once found he could call to a ghoul to let down a ladder; for strange to say, he had a very singular link with these terrible creatures.

A man he had known in Boston—a painter of strange pictures with a secret studio in an ancient and unhallowed alley near a graveyard—had actually made friends with the ghouls and had taught him to understand the simpler part of their disgusting meeping and glibbering. This man had vanished at last, and Carter was not sure but that he might find him now, and use for the first time in dreamland that far-away English of his dim waking life. In any case, he felt he could persuade a ghoul to guide him out of Pnath; and it would be better to meet a ghoul, which one can see, than a bhole, which one cannot see.

So Carter walked in the dark, and ran when he thought he heard something among the bones underfoot. Once he bumped into a stony slope, and knew it must be the base of one of Thok's peaks. Then at last he heard a monstrous rattling and clatter which reached far up in the air, and became sure he had come nigh the crag of the ghouls. He was not sure he could be heard from this valley miles below, but realised that the inner world has strange laws. As he pondered he was struck by a flying bone so heavy that it must have been a skull, and therefore realising his nearness to the fateful crag he sent up as best he might that meeping cry which is the call of the ghoul.

Sound travels slowly, so that it was some time before he heard an answering glibber. But it came at last, and before long he was told that a rope ladder would be lowered. The wait for this was very tense, since there was no telling what might not have been stirred up among those bones by his shouting. Indeed, it was not long before he actually did hear a vague rustling afar off. As this thoughtfully approached, he became more and more uncomfortable; for he did not wish to move away from the spot where the ladder would come. Finally the tension grew almost unbearable, and he was about to flee in panic when the thud of something on the newly heaped bones nearby drew his notice from the other sound. It was the ladder, and after a minute of groping he had it taut in his hands. But the other sound did not cease, and followed him even as he climbed. He had gone fully five feet from the ground when the rattling beneath waxed emphatic, and was a good ten feet up when something swayed the ladder from below. At a height which must have been fifteen or twenty feet he felt his whole side brushed by a great slippery length which grew alternately convex and concave with wriggling, and thereafter he climbed desperately to escape the unendurable nuzzling of that loathsome and overfed bhole whose form no man might see.

For hours he climbed with aching arms and blistered hands, seeing again the grey death-fire and Thok's uncomfortable pinnacles. At last he discerned above him the projecting edge of the great crag of the ghouls, whose vertical side he could not glimpse; and hours later he saw a curious face peering over it as a gargoyle peers over a parapet of Notre Dame. This almost made him lose his hold through faintness, but a moment later he was himself again; for his vanished friend Richard Pickman had once introduced him to a ghoul, and he knew well their canine faces and slumping forms and unmentionable idiosyncrasies. So he had himself well under control when that hideous thing pulled him out of the dizzy emptiness over the edge of the crag, and did not scream at the partly consumed refuse heaped at one side or at the squatting circles of ghouls who gnawed and watched curiously.

He was now on a dim-litten plain whose sole topographical features were great boulders and the entrances of burrows. The ghouls were in general respectful, even if one did attempt to pinch him while several others eyed his leanness speculatively. Through patient glibbering he made inquiries regarding his vanished friend, and found he had become a ghoul of some prominence in abysses nearer the waking world. A greenish elderly ghoul offered to conduct him to Pickman's present habitation, so despite a natural loathing he followed the creature into a capacious burrow and crawled after him for hours in the blackness of rank mould. They emerged on a dim plain strown with singular relics of earth—old gravestones, broken urns, and grotesque fragments of monuments—and Carter realised with some emotion that he was probably nearer the waking world than at any other time since he had gone down the seven hundred steps from the cavern of flame to the Gate of Deeper Slumber.

There, on a tombstone of 1768 stolen from the Granary Burying Ground in Boston, sat the ghoul which was once the artist Richard Upton Pickman. It was naked and rubbery, and had acquired so much of the ghoulish physiognomy that its human origin was already obscure. But it still remembered a little English, and was able to converse with Carter in grunts and monosyllables, helped out now and then by the glibbering of ghouls. When it learned that Carter wished to get to the enchanted wood and from there to the city Celephaïs in Ooth-Nargai beyond the Tanarian Hills, it seemed rather doubtful; for these ghouls of the waking world do no business in the graveyards of upper dreamland (leaving that to the web-footed wamps that are spawned in dead cities), and many things intervene betwixt their gulf and the enchanted wood, including the terrible kingdom of the gugs.

The gugs, hairy and gigantic, once reared stone circles in that wood and made strange sacrifices to the Other Gods and the crawling chaos Nyarlathotep, until one night an abomination of theirs reached the ears of earth's gods and they were banished to caverns below. Only a great trap-door of stone with an iron ring connects the abyss of the earth-ghouls with the enchanted wood, and this the gugs are afraid to open because of a curse. That a mortal dreamer could traverse their cavern realm and leave by that door is inconceivable; for mortal dreamers were their former food, and they have legends of the toothsomeness of such dreamers even though banishment has restricted their diet to the ghasts, those repulsive beings which die in the light, and which live in the vaults of Zin and leap on long hind legs like kangaroos.

So the ghoul that was Pickman advised Carter either to leave the abyss at Sarkomand, that deserted city in the valley below Leng where black nitrous stairways guarded by winged diorite lions lead down from dreamland to the lower gulfs, or to return through a churchyard to the waking world and begin the quest anew down the seventy steps of light slumber to the cavern of flame and the seven hundred steps to the Gate of Deeper Slumber and the enchanted wood. This, however, did not suit the seeker; for he knew nothing of the way from Leng to Ooth-Nargai, and was likewise reluctant to awake lest he forget all he had so far gained in this dream. It were disastrous to his quest to forget the august and celestial faces of those seamen from the north who traded onyx in Celephaïs, and who, being the sons of gods, must point the way to the cold waste and Kadath where the Great Ones dwell.

After much persuasion the ghoul consented to guide his guest inside the great wall of the gugs' kingdom. There was one chance that Carter might be able to steal through that twilight realm of circular stone towers at an hour when the giants would be all gorged and snoring indoors, and reach the central tower with the sign of Koth upon it, which has the stairs leading up to that stone trap-door in the enchanted wood. Pickman even consented to lend three ghouls to help with a tombstone lever in raising the stone door; for of ghouls the gugs are somewhat afraid, and they often flee from their own colossal graveyards when they see feasting there.

He also advised Carter to disguise as a ghoul himself; shaving the beard he had allowed to grow (for ghouls have none), wallowing naked in the mould to get the correct surface, and loping in the usual slumping way, with his clothing carried in a bundle as if it were a choice morsel from a tomb. They would reach the city of the gugs—which is coterminous with the whole kingdom—through the proper burrows, emerging in a cemetery not far from the stair-containing Tower of Koth. They must beware, however, of a large cave near the cemetery; for this is the mouth of the vaults of Zin, and the vindictive ghasts are always on watch there murderously for those denizens of the upper abyss who hunt and prey on them. The ghasts try to come out when the gugs sleep, and they attack ghouls as readily as gugs, for they cannot discriminate. They are very primitive, and eat one another. The gugs have a sentry at a narrow place in the vaults of Zin, but he is often drowsy and is sometimes surprised by a party of ghasts. Though ghasts cannot live in real light, they can endure the grey twilight of the abyss for hours.

So at length Carter crawled through endless burrows with three helpful ghouls bearing the slate gravestone of Col. Nehemiah Derby, obiit 1719, from the Charter Street Burying Ground in Salem. When they came again into open twilight they were in a forest of vast lichened monoliths reaching nearly as high as the eye could see and forming the modest gravestones of the gugs. On the right of the hole out of which they wriggled, and seen through aisles of monoliths, was a stupendous vista of Cyclopean round towers mounting up illimitably into the grey air of inner earth. This was the great city of the gugs, whose doorways are thirty feet high. Ghouls come here often, for a buried gug will feed a community for almost a year, and even with the added peril it is better to burrow for gugs than to bother with the graves of men. Carter now understood the occasional titan bones he had felt beneath him in the vale of Pnath.

Straight ahead, and just outside the cemetery, rose a sheer perpendicular cliff at whose base an immense and forbidding cavern yawned. This the ghouls told Carter to avoid as much as possible, since it was the entrance to the unhallowed vaults of Zin where gugs hunt ghasts in the darkness. And truly, that warning was soon well justified; for the moment a ghoul began to creep toward the towers to see if the hour of the gugs' resting had been rightly timed, there glowed in the gloom of that great cavern's mouth first one pair of yellowish-red eyes and then another, implying that the gugs were one sentry less, and that ghasts have indeed an excellent sharpness of smell. So the ghoul returned to the burrow and motioned his companions to be silent. It was best to leave the ghasts to their own devices, and there was a possibility that they might soon withdraw, since they must naturally be rather tired after coping with a gug sentry in the black vaults. After a moment something about the size of a small horse hopped out into the grey twilight, and Carter turned sick at the aspect of that scabrous and unwholesome beast, whose face is so curiously human despite the absence of a nose, a forehead, and other important particulars.

Presently three other ghasts hopped out to join their fellow, and a ghoul glibbered softly to Carter that their absence of battle-scars was a bad sign. It proved that they had not fought the gug sentry at all, but merely slipped past him as he slept, so that their strength and savagery were still unimpaired and would remain so till they had found and disposed of a victim. It was very unpleasant to see those filthy and disproportioned animals, which soon numbered about fifteen, grubbing about and making their kangaroo leaps in the grey twilight where titan towers and monoliths arose, but it was still more unpleasant when they spoke among themselves in the coughing gutturals of ghasts. And yet, horrible as they were, they were not so horrible as what presently came out of the cave after them with disconcerting suddenness.

It was a paw, fully two feet and a half across, and equipped with formidable talons. After it came another paw, and after that a great black-furred arm to which both of the paws were attached by short forearms. Then two pink eyes shone, and the head of the awakened gug sentry, large as a barrel, wobbled into view. The eyes jutted two inches from each side, shaded by bony protuberances overgrown with coarse hairs. But the head was chiefly terrible because of the mouth. That mouth had great yellow fangs and ran from the top to the bottom of the head, opening vertically instead of horizontally.

But before that unfortunate gug could emerge from the cave and rise to his full twenty feet, the vindictive ghasts were upon him. Carter feared for a moment that he would give an alarm and arouse all his kin, till a ghoul softly glibbered that gugs have no voice, but talk by means of facial expression. The battle which then ensued was truly a frightful one. From all sides the venomous ghasts rushed feverishly at the creeping gug, nipping and tearing with their muzzles, and mauling murderously with their hard pointed hooves. All the time they coughed excitedly, screaming when the great vertical mouth of the gug would occasionally bite into one of their number, so that the noise of the combat would surely have aroused the sleeping city had not the weakening of the sentry begun to transfer the action farther and farther within the cavern. As it was, the tumult soon receded altogether from sight in the blackness, with only occasional evil echoes to mark its continuance.

Then the most alert of the ghouls gave the signal for all to advance, and Carter followed the loping three out of the forest of monoliths and into the dark noisome streets of that awful city whose rounded towers of Cyclopean stone soared up beyond the sight. Silently they shambled over that rough rock pavement, hearing with disgust the abominable muffled snortings from great black doorways which marked the slumber of the gugs. Apprehensive of the ending of the rest hour, the ghouls set a somewhat rapid pace; but even so the journey was no brief one, for distances in that town of giants are on a great scale. At last, however, they came to a somewhat open space before a tower even vaster than the rest, above whose colossal doorway was fixed a monstrous symbol in bas-relief which made one shudder without knowing its meaning. This was the central tower with the sign of Koth, and those huge stone steps just visible through the dusk within were the beginning of the great flight leading to upper dreamland and the enchanted wood.

There now began a climb of interminable length in utter blackness; made almost impossible by the monstrous size of the steps, which were fashioned for gugs, and were therefore nearly a yard high. Of their number Carter could form no just estimate, for he soon became so worn out that the tireless and elastic ghouls were forced to aid him. All through the endless climb there lurked the peril of detection and pursuit; for though no gug dares lift the stone door to the forest because of the Great Ones' curse, there are no such restraints concerning the tower and the steps, and escaped ghasts are often chased even to the very top. So sharp are the ears of gugs, that the bare feet and hands of the climbers might readily be heard when the city awoke; and it would of course take but little time for the striding giants, accustomed from their ghast-hunts in the vaults of Zin to seeing without light, to overtake their smaller and slower quarry on those Cyclopean steps. It was very depressing to reflect that the silent pursuing gugs could not be heard at all, but would come very suddenly and shockingly in the dark upon the climbers. Nor could the traditional fear of gugs for ghouls be depended upon in that peculiar place where the advantages lay so heavily with the gugs. There was also some peril from the furtive and venomous ghasts, which frequently hopped up into the tower during the sleep hour of the gugs. If the gugs slept long, and the ghasts returned soon from their deed in the cavern, the scent of the climbers might easily be picked up by those loathsome and ill-disposed things; in which case it would almost be better to be eaten by a gug.

Then, after aeons of climbing, there came a cough from the darkness above; and matters assumed a very grave and unexpected turn. It was clear that a ghast, or perhaps even more, had strayed into that tower before the coming of Carter and his guides; and it was equally clear that this peril was very close. After a breathless second the leading ghoul pushed Carter to the wall and arranged his two kinsfolk in the best possible way, with the old slate tombstone raised for a crushing blow whenever the enemy might come in sight. Ghouls can see in the dark, so the party was not as badly off as Carter would have been alone. In another moment the clatter of hooves revealed the downward hopping of at least one beast, and the slab-bearing ghouls poised their weapon for a desperate blow. Presently two yellowish-red eyes flashed into view, and the panting of the ghast became audible above its clattering. As it hopped down to the step just above the ghouls, they wielded the ancient gravestone with prodigious force, so that there was only a wheeze and a choking before the victim collapsed in a noxious heap. There seemed to be only this one animal, and after a moment of listening the ghouls tapped Carter as a signal to proceed again. As before, they were obliged to aid him; and he was glad to leave that place of carnage where the ghast's uncouth remains sprawled invisible in the blackness.

At last the ghouls brought their companion to a halt; and feeling above him, Carter realised that the great stone trap-door was reached at last. To open so vast a thing completely was not to be thought of, but the ghouls hoped to get it up just enough to slip the gravestone under as a prop, and permit Carter to escape through the crack. They themselves planned to descend again and return through the city of the gugs, since their elusiveness was great, and they did not know the way overland to spectral Sarkomand with its lion-guarded gate to the abyss.

Mighty was the straining of those three ghouls at the stone of the door above them, and Carter helped push with as much strength as he had. They judged the edge next the top of the staircase to be the right one, and to this they bent all the force of their disreputably nourished muscles. After a few moments a crack of light appeared; and Carter, to whom that task had been entrusted, slipped the end of the old gravestone in the aperture. There now ensued a mighty heaving; but progress was very slow, and they had of course to return to their first position each time they failed to turn the slab and prop the portal open.

Suddenly their desperation was magnified a thousandfold by a sound on the steps below them. It was only the thumping and rattling of the slain ghast's hooved body as it rolled down to lower levels; but of all the possible causes of that body's dislodgment and rolling, none was in the least reassuring. Therefore, knowing the ways of gugs, the ghouls set to with something of a frenzy; and in a surprisingly short time had the door so high that they were able to hold it still whilst Carter turned the slab and left a generous opening. They now helped Carter through, letting him climb up to their rubbery shoulders and later guiding his feet as he clutched at the blessed soil of the upper dreamland outside. Another second and they were through themselves, knocking away the gravestone and closing the great trap-door while a panting became audible beneath. Because of the Great Ones' curse no gug might ever emerge from that portal, so with a deep relief and sense of repose Carter lay quietly on the thick grotesque fungi of the enchanted wood while his guides squatted near in the manner that ghouls rest.

Weird as was that enchanted wood through which he had fared so long ago, it was verily a haven and a delight after the gulfs he had now left behind. There was no living denizen about, for zoogs shun the mysterious door in fear, and Carter at once consulted with his ghouls about their future course. To return through the tower they no longer dared, and the waking world did not appeal to them when they learned that they must pass the priests Nasht and Kaman-Thah in the cavern of flame. So at length they decided to return through Sarkomand and its gate of the abyss, though of how to get there they knew nothing. Carter recalled that it lies in the valley below Leng, and recalled likewise that he had seen in Dylath-Leen a sinister, slant-eyed old merchant reputed to trade on Leng. Therefore he advised the ghouls to seek out Dylath-Leen, crossing the fields to Nir and the Skai and following the river to its mouth. This they at once resolved to do, and lost no time in loping off, since the thickening of the dusk promised a full night ahead for travel. And Carter shook the paws of those repulsive beasts, thanking them for their help and sending his gratitude to the beast which once was Pickman; but could not help sighing with pleasure when they left. For a ghoul is a ghoul, and at best an unpleasant companion for man. After that Carter sought a forest pool and cleansed himself of the mud of nether earth, thereupon reassuming the clothes he had so carefully carried.

It was now night in that redoubtable wood of monstrous trees, but because of the phosphorescence one might travel as well as by day; wherefore Carter set out upon the well-known route toward Celephaïs, in Ooth-Nargai beyond the Tanarian Hills. And as he went he thought of the zebra he had left tethered to an ash tree on Ngranek in far-away Oriab so many aeons ago, and wondered if any lava-gatherer had fed and released it. And he wondered, too, if he would ever return to Baharna and pay for the zebra that was slain by night in those ancient ruins by Yath's shore, and if the old tavern-keeper would remember him. Such were the thoughts that came to him in the air of the regained upper dreamland.

But presently his progress was halted by a sound from a very large hollow tree. He had avoided the great circle of stones, since he did not care to speak with zoogs just now; but it appeared from the singular fluttering in that huge tree that important councils were in session elsewhere. Upon drawing nearer he made out the accents of a tense and heated discussion; and before long became conscious of matters which he viewed with the greatest concern. For a war on the cats was under debate in that sovereign assembly of zoogs. It all came from the loss of the party which had sneaked after Carter to Ulthar, and which the cats had justly punished for unsuitable intentions. The matter had long rankled; and now, or within at least a month, the marshalled zoogs were about to strike the whole feline tribe in a series of surprise attacks, taking individual cats or groups of cats unawares, and giving not even the myriad cats of Ulthar a proper chance to drill and mobilise.

This was the plan of the zoogs, and Carter saw that he must foil it before leaving on his mighty quest.

Very quietly therefore did Randolph Carter steal to the edge of the wood and send the cry of the cat over the starlit fields. And a great grimalkin in a nearby cottage took up the burden and relayed it across leagues of rolling meadow to warriors large and small, black, grey, tiger, white, yellow, and mixed; and it echoed through Nir and beyond the Skai even into Ulthar, and Ulthar's numerous cats called in chorus and fell into a line of march. It was fortunate that the moon was not up, so that all the cats were on earth. Swiftly and silently leaping, they sprang from every hearth and housetop and poured in a great furry sea across the plains to the edge of the wood. Carter was there to greet them, and the sight of shapely, wholesome cats was indeed good for his eyes after the things he had seen and walked with in the abyss. He was glad to see his venerable friend and one-time rescuer at the head of Ulthar's detachment, a collar of rank around his sleek neck, and whiskers bristling at a martial angle. Better still, as a sub-lieutenant in that army was a brisk young fellow who proved to be none other than the very little kitten at the inn to whom Carter had given a saucer of rich cream on that long-vanished morning in Ulthar. He was a strapping and promising cat now, and purred as he shook hands with his friend. His grandfather said he was doing very well in the army, and that he might well expect a captaincy after one more campaign.

Carter now outlined the peril of the cat tribe, and was rewarded by deep-throated purrs of gratitude from all sides. Consulting with the generals, he prepared a plan of instant action which involved marching at once upon the zoog council and other known strongholds of zoogs; forestalling their surprise attacks and forcing them to terms before the mobilisation of their army of invasion. Thereupon without a moment's loss that great ocean of cats flooded the enchanted wood and surged around the council tree and the great stone circle. Flutterings rose to panic pitch as the enemy saw the newcomers, and there was very little resistance among the furtive and curious brown zoogs. They saw that they were beaten in advance, and turned from thoughts of vengeance to thoughts of present self-preservation.

Half the cats now seated themselves in a circular formation with the captured zoogs in the centre, leaving open a lane down which were marched the additional captives rounded up by the other cats in other parts of the wood. Terms were discussed at length, Carter acting as interpreter, and it was decided that the zoogs might remain a free tribe on condition of rendering to the cats a large annual tribute of grouse, quail, and pheasants from the less fabulous parts of their forest. Twelve young zoogs of noble families were taken as hostages to be kept in the Temple of the Cats at Ulthar, and the victors made it plain that any disappearances of cats on the borders of the zoog domain would be followed by consequences highly disastrous to zoogs. These matters disposed of, the assembled cats broke ranks and permitted the zoogs to slink off one by one to their respective homes, which they hastened to do with many a sullen backward glance.

The old cat general now offered Carter an escort through the forest to whatever border he wished to reach, deeming it likely that the zoogs would harbour dire resentment against him for the frustration of their warlike enterprise. This offer he welcomed with gratitude; not only for the safety it afforded, but because he liked the graceful companionship of cats. So in the midst of a pleasant and playful regiment, relaxed after the successful performance of its duty, Randolph Carter walked with dignity through that enchanted and phosphorescent wood of titan trees, talking of his quest with the old general and his grandson whilst others of the band indulged in fantastic gambols or chased fallen leaves that the wind drove among the fungi of the primeval floor. And the old cat said that he had heard much of unknown Kadath in the cold waste, but did not know where it was. As for the marvellous sunset city, he had not even heard of that, but would gladly relay to Carter anything he might later learn.

He gave the seeker some passwords of great value among the cats of dreamland, and commended him especially to the old chief of the cats in Celephaïs, whither he was bound. That old cat, already slightly known to Carter, was a dignified Maltese; and would prove highly influential in any transaction. It was dawn when they came to the proper edge of the wood, and Carter bade his friends a reluctant farewell. The young sub-lieutenant he had met as a small kitten would have followed him had not the old general forbidden it, but that austere patriarch insisted that the path of duty lay with the tribe and the army. So Carter set out alone over the golden fields that stretched mysterious beside a willow-fringed river, and the cats went back into the wood.

Well did the traveller know those garden lands that lie betwixt the wood and the Cerenarian Sea, and blithely did he follow the singing river Oukranos that marked his course. The sun rose higher over gentle slopes of grove and lawn, and heightened the colours of the thousand flowers that starred each knoll and dingle. A blessed haze lies upon all this region, wherein is held a little more of the sunlight than other places hold, and a little more of the summer's humming music of birds and bees; so that men walk through it as through a faery place, and feel greater joy and wonder than they ever afterward remember.

By noon Carter reached the jasper terraces of Kiran which slope down to the river's edge and bear that temple of loveliness wherein the King of Ilek-Vad comes from his far realm on the twilight sea once a year in a golden palanquin to pray to the god of Oukranos, who sang to him in youth when he dwelt in a cottage by its banks. All of jasper is that temple, and covering an acre of ground with its walls and courts, its seven pinnacled towers, and its inner shrine where the river enters through hidden channels and the god sings softly in the night. Many times the moon hears strange music as it shines on those courts and terraces and pinnacles, but whether that music be the song of the god or the chant of the cryptical priests, none but the King of Ilek-Vad may say; for only he has entered the temple or seen the priests. Now, in the drowsiness of day, that carven and delicate fane was silent, and Carter heard only the murmur of the great stream and the hum of the birds and bees as he walked onward under an enchanted sun.

All that afternoon the pilgrim wandered on through perfumed meadows and in the lee of gentle riverward hills bearing peaceful thatched cottages and the shrines of amiable gods carven from jasper or chrysoberyl. Sometimes he walked close to the bank of Oukranos and whistled to the sprightly and iridescent fish of that crystal stream, and at other times he paused amidst the whispering rushes and gazed at the great dark wood on the farther side, whose trees came down clear to the water's edge. In former dreams he had seen quaint lumbering buopoths come shyly out of that wood to drink, but now he could not glimpse any. Once in a while he paused to watch a carnivorous fish catch a fishing bird, which it lured to the water by shewing its tempting scales in the sun, and grasped by the beak with its enormous mouth as the winged hunter sought to dart down upon it.

Toward evening he mounted a low grassy rise and saw before him flaming in the sunset the thousand gilded spires of Thran. Lofty beyond belief are the alabaster walls of that incredible city, sloping inward toward the top and wrought in one solid piece by what means no man knows, for they are more ancient than memory. Yet lofty as they are with their hundred gates and two hundred turrets, the clustered towers within, all white beneath their golden spires, are loftier still; so that men on the plain around see them soaring into the sky, sometimes shining clear, sometimes caught at the top in tangles of cloud and mist, and sometimes clouded lower down with their utmost pinnacles blazing free above the vapours. And where Thran's gates open on the river are great wharves of marble, with ornate galleons of fragrant cedar and calamander riding gently at anchor, and strange bearded sailors sitting on casks and bales with the hieroglyphs of far places. Landward beyond the walls lies the farm country, where small white cottages dream between little hills, and narrow roads with many stone bridges wind gracefully among streams and gardens.

Down through this verdant land Carter walked at evening, and saw twilight float up from the river to the marvellous golden spires of Thran. And just at the hour of dusk he came to the southern gate, and was stopped by a red-robed sentry till he had told three dreams beyond belief, and proved himself a dreamer worthy to walk up Thran's steep mysterious streets and linger in bazaars where the wares of the ornate galleons were sold. Then into that incredible city he walked; through a wall so thick that the gate was a tunnel, and thereafter amidst curved and undulant ways winding deep and narrow between the heavenward towers. Lights shone through grated and balconied windows, and the sound of lutes and pipes stole timid from inner courts where marble fountains bubbled. Carter knew his way, and edged down through darker streets to the river, where at an old sea-tavern he found the captains and seamen he had known in myriad other dreams. There he bought his passage to Celephaïs on a great green galleon, and there he stopped for the night after speaking gravely to the venerable cat of that inn, who blinked dozing before an enormous hearth and dreamed of old wars and forgotten gods.

In the morning Carter boarded the galleon bound for Celephaïs, and sat in the prow as the ropes were cast off and the long sail down to the Cerenarian Sea began. For many leagues the banks were much as they were above Thran, with now and then a curious temple rising on the farther hills toward the right, and a drowsy village on the shore, with steep red roofs and nets spread in the sun. Mindful of his search, Carter questioned all the mariners closely about those whom they had met in the taverns of Celephaïs, asking the names and ways of the strange men with long, narrow eyes, long-lobed ears, thin noses, and pointed chins who came in dark ships from the north and traded onyx for the carved jade and spun gold and little red singing birds of Celephaïs. Of these men the sailors knew not much, save that they talked but seldom and spread a kind of awe about them.

Their land, very far away, was called Inganok, and not many people cared to go thither because it was a cold twilight land, and said to be close to unpleasant Leng; although high impassable mountains towered on the side where Leng was thought to lie, so that none might say whether this evil plateau with its horrible stone villages and unmentionable monastery were really there, or whether the rumour were only a fear that timid people felt in the night when those formidable barrier peaks loomed black against a rising moon. Certainly, men reached Leng from very different oceans. Of other boundaries of Inganok those sailors had no notion, nor had they heard of the cold waste and unknown Kadath save from vague unplaced report. And of the marvellous sunset city which Carter sought they knew nothing at all. So the traveller asked no more of far things, but bided his time till he might talk with those strange men from cold and twilight Inganok who are the seed of such gods as carved their features on Ngranek.

Late in the day the galleon reached those bends of the river which traverse the perfumed jungles of Kled. Here Carter wished he might disembark, for in those tropic tangles sleep wondrous palaces of ivory, lone and unbroken, where once dwelt fabulous monarchs of a land whose name is forgotten. Spells of the Elder Ones keep those palaces unharmed and undecayed, for it is written that there may one day be need of them again; and elephant caravans have glimpsed them from afar by moonlight, though none dares approach them closely because of the guardians to which their wholeness is due. But the ship swept on, and dusk hushed the hum of the day, and the first stars above blinked answers to the early fireflies on the banks as that jungle fell far behind, leaving only its fragrance as a memory that it had been. And all through the night that galleon floated on past mysteries unseen and unsuspected. Once a lookout reported fires on the hills to the east, but the sleepy captain said they had better not be looked at too much, since it was highly uncertain just who or what had lit them.

In the morning the river had broadened out greatly, and Carter saw by the houses along the banks that they were close to the vast trading city of Hlanith on the Cerenarian Sea. Here the walls are of rugged granite, and the houses peakedly fantastic with beamed and plastered gables. The men of Hlanith are more like those of the waking world than any others in dreamland; so that the city is not sought except for barter, but is prized for the solid work of its artisans. The wharves of Hlanith are of oak, and there the galleon made fast while the captain traded in the taverns. Carter also went ashore, and looked curiously upon the rutted streets where wooden ox-carts lumbered and feverish merchants cried their wares vacuously in the bazaars. The sea-taverns were all close to the wharves on cobbled lanes salt with the spray of high tides, and seemed exceedingly ancient with their low black-beamed ceilings and casements of greenish bull's-eye panes. Ancient sailors in those taverns talked much of distant ports, and told many stories of the curious men from twilight Inganok, but had little to add to what the seamen of the galleon had told. Then at last, after much unloading and loading, the ship set sail once more over the sunset sea, and the high walls and gables of Hlanith grew less as the last golden light of day lent them a wonder and beauty beyond any that men had given them.

Two nights and two days the galleon sailed over the Cerenarian Sea, sighting no land and speaking but one other vessel. Then near sunset of the second day there loomed up ahead the snowy peak of Aran with its gingko-trees swaying on the lower slopes, and Carter knew that they were come to the land of Ooth-Nargai and the marvellous city of Celephaïs. Swiftly there came into sight the glittering minarets of that fabulous town, and the untarnished marble walls with their bronze statues, and the great stone bridge where Naraxa joins the sea. Then rose the green gentle hills behind the town, with their groves and gardens of asphodels and the small shrines and cottages upon them; and far in the background the purple ridge of the Tanarians, potent and mystical, behind which lay forbidden ways into the waking world and toward other regions of dream.

The harbour was full of painted galleys, some of which were from the marble cloud-city of Serannian, that lies in ethereal space beyond where the sea meets the sky, and some of which were from more substantial ports on the oceans of dreamland. Among these the steersman threaded his way up to the spice-fragrant wharves, where the galleon made fast in the dusk as the city's million lights began to twinkle out over the water. Ever new seemed this deathless city of vision, for here time has no power to tarnish or destroy. As it has always been is still the turquoise temple of Nath-Horthath, and the eighty orchid-wreathed priests are the same who builded it ten thousand years ago. Shining still is the bronze of the great gates, nor are the onyx pavements ever worn or broken. And the great bronze statues on the walls look down on merchants and camel drivers older than fable, yet without one grey hair in their forked beards.

Carter did not at once seek out the temple or the palace or the citadel, but stayed by the seaward wall among traders and sailors. And when it was too late for rumours and legends he sought out an ancient tavern he knew well, and rested with dreams of the gods on unknown Kadath whom he sought. The next day he searched all along the quays for some of the strange mariners of Inganok, but was told that none were now in port, their galley not being due from the north for full two weeks. He found, however, one Thorabonian sailor who had been to Inganok and had worked in the onyx quarries of that twilight place; and this sailor said there was certainly a desert to the north of the peopled region, which everyone seemed to fear and shun. The Thorabonian opined that this desert led around the utmost rim of impassable peaks into Leng's horrible plateau, and that this was why men feared it; though he admitted there were other vague tales of evil presences and nameless sentinels. Whether or not this could be the fabled waste wherein unknown Kadath stands he did not know; but it seemed unlikely that those presences and sentinels, if indeed they truly existed, were stationed for naught.

On the following day Carter walked up the Street of the Pillars to the turquoise temple and talked with the high-priest. Though Nath-Horthath is chiefly worshipped in Celephaïs, all the Great Ones are mentioned in diurnal prayers; and the priest was reasonably versed in their moods. Like Atal in distant Ulthar, he strongly advised against any attempt to see them; declaring that they are testy and capricious, and subject to strange protection from the mindless Other Gods from Outside, whose soul and messenger is the crawling chaos Nyarlathotep. Their jealous hiding of the marvellous sunset city shewed clearly that they did not wish Carter to reach it, and it was doubtful how they would regard a quest whose object was to see them and plead before them. No man had ever found Kadath in the past, and it might be just as well if none ever found it in the future. Such rumours as were told about that onyx castle of the Great Ones were not by any means reassuring.

Having thanked the orchid-crowned high-priest, Carter left the temple and sought the bazaar of the sheep-butchers, where the old chief of Celephaïs' cats dwelt sleek and contented. That grey and dignified being was sunning himself on the onyx pavement, and extended a languid paw as his caller approached. But when Carter repeated the passwords and introductions furnished him by the old cat general of Ulthar, the furry patriach became very cordial and communicative; and told much of the secret lore known to cats on the seaward slopes of Ooth-Nargai. Best of all, he repeated several things told him furtively by the timid waterfront cats of Celephaïs about the men of Inganok, on whose dark ships no cat will go.

It seems that these men have an aura not of earth about them, though that is not the reason why no cat will sail on their ships. The reason for this is that Inganok holds shadows which no cat can endure, so that in all that cold twilight realm there is never a cheering purr or a homely mew. Whether it be because of things wafted over the impassable peaks from hypothetical Leng, or because of things filtering down from the chilly desert to the north, none may say; but it remains a fact that in that far land there broods a hint of outer space which cats do not like, and to which they are more sensitive than men. Therefore they will not go on the dark ships that seek the basalt quays of Inganok.

The old chief of the cats also told him where to find his friend King Kuranes, who in Carter's latter dreams had reigned alternately in the rose-crystal Palace of the Seventy Delights at Celephaïs and in the turreted cloud-castle of sky-floating Serannian. It seems that he could no more find content in those places, but had formed a mighty longing for the English cliffs and downlands of his boyhood; where in little dreaming villages England's old songs hover at evening behind lattice windows, and where grey church towers peep lovely through the verdure of distant valleys. He could not go back to these things in the waking world because his body was dead; but he had done the next best thing and dreamed a small tract of such countryside in the region east of the city, where meadows roll gracefully up from the sea-cliffs to the foot of the Tanarian Hills. There he dwelt in a grey Gothic manor-house of stone looking on the sea, and tried to think it was ancient Trevor Towers, where he was born and where thirteen generations of his forefathers had first seen the light. And on the coast nearby he had built a little Cornish fishing village with steep cobbled ways, settling therein such people as had the most English faces, and seeking ever to teach them the dear remembered accents of old Cornwall fishers. And in a valley not far off he had reared a great Norman Abbey whose tower he could see from his window, placing around it in the churchyard grey stones with the names of his ancestors carved thereon, and with a moss somewhat like Old England's moss. For though Kuranes was a monarch in the land of dream, with all imagined pomps and marvels, splendours and beauties, ecstasies and delights, novelties and excitements at his command, he would gladly have resigned for ever the whole of his power and luxury and freedom for one blessed day as a simple boy in that pure and quiet England, that ancient, beloved England which had moulded his being and of which he must always be immutably a part.

So when Carter bade that old grey chief of the cats adieu, he did not seek the terraced palace of rose-crystal but walked out the eastern gate and across the daisied fields toward a peaked gable which he glimpsed through the oaks of a park sloping up to the sea-cliffs. And in time he came to a great hedge and a gate with a little brick lodge, and when he rang the bell there hobbled to admit him no robed and anointed lackey of the palace, but a small stubbly old man in a smock who spoke as best he could in the quaint tones of far Cornwall. And Carter walked up the shady path between trees as near as possible to England's trees, and climbed the terraces among gardens set out as in Queen Anne's time. At the door, flanked by stone cats in the old way, he was met by a whiskered butler in suitable livery; and was presently taken to the library where Kuranes, Lord of Ooth-Nargai and the Sky around Serannian, sat pensive in a chair by the window looking on his little seacoast village and wishing that his old nurse would come in and scold him because he was not ready for that hateful lawn-party at the vicar's, with the carriage waiting and his mother nearly out of patience.

Kuranes, clad in a dressing-gown of the sort favoured by London tailors in his youth, rose eagerly to meet his guest; for the sight of an Anglo-Saxon from the waking world was very dear to him, even if it was a Saxon from Boston, Massachusetts, instead of from Cornwall. And for long they talked of old times, having much to say because both were old dreamers and well versed in the wonders of incredible places. Kuranes, indeed, had been out beyond the stars in the ultimate void, and was said to be the only one who had ever returned sane from such a voyage.

At length Carter brought up the subject of his quest, and asked of his host those questions he had asked of so many others. Kuranes did not know where Kadath was, or the marvellous sunset city; but he did know that the Great Ones were very dangerous creatures to seek out, and that the Other Gods had strange ways of protecting them from impertinent curiosity. He had learned much of the Other Gods in distant parts of space, especially in that region where form does not exist, and coloured gases study the innermost secrets. The violet gas S'ngac had told him terrible things of the crawling chaos Nyarlathotep, and had warned him never to approach the central void where the daemon-sultan Azathoth gnaws hungrily in the dark. Altogether, it was not well to meddle with the Elder Ones; and if they persistently denied all access to the marvellous sunset city, it were better not to seek that city.

Kuranes furthermore doubted whether his guest would profit aught by coming to the city even were he to gain it. He himself had dreamed and yearned long years for lovely Celephaïs and the land of Ooth-Nargai, and for the freedom and colour and high experience of life devoid of its chains, conventions, and stupidities. But now that he was come into that city and that land, and was the king thereof, he found the freedom and the vividness all too soon worn out, and monotonous for want of linkage with anything firm in his feelings and memories. He was a king in Ooth-Nargai, but found no meaning therein, and drooped always for the old familiar things of England that had shaped his youth. All his kingdom would he give for the sound of Cornish church bells over the downs, and all the thousand minarets of Celephaïs for the steep homely roofs of the village near his home. So he told his guest that the unknown sunset city might not hold quite the content he sought, and that perhaps it had better remain a glorious and half-remembered dream. For he had visited Carter often in the old waking days, and knew well the lovely New England slopes that had given him birth.

At the last, he was very certain, the seeker would long only for the early remembered scenes; the glow of Beacon Hill at evening, the tall steeples and winding hill streets of quaint Kingsport, the hoary gambrel roofs of ancient and witch-haunted Arkham, and the blessed miles of meads and valleys where stone walls rambled and white farmhouse gables peeped out from bowers of verdure. These things he told Randolph Carter, but still the seeker held to his purpose. And in the end they parted each with his own conviction, and Carter went back through the bronze gate into Celephaïs and down the Street of the Pillars to the old sea-wall, where he talked more with the mariners of far ports and waited for the dark ship from cold and twilight Inganok, whose strange-faced sailors and onyx-traders had in them the blood of the Great Ones.

One starlight evening when the Pharos shone splendid over the harbour the longed-for ship put in, and strange-faced sailors and traders appeared one by one and group by group in the ancient taverns along the sea-wall. It was very exciting to see again those living faces so like the godlike features on Ngranek, but Carter did not hasten to speak with the silent seamen. He did not know how much of pride and secrecy and dim supernal memory might fill those children of the Great Ones, and was sure it would not be wise to tell them of his quest or ask too closely of that cold desert stretching north of their twilight land. They talked little with the other folk in those ancient sea-taverns; but would gather in groups in remote corners and sing among themselves the haunting airs of unknown places, or chant long tales to one another in accents alien to the rest of dreamland. And so rare and moving were those airs and tales, that one might guess their wonders from the faces of those who listened, even though the words came to common ears only as strange cadence and obscure melody.

For a week the strange seamen lingered in the taverns and traded in the bazaars of Celephaïs, and before they sailed Carter had taken passage on their dark ship, telling them that he was an old onyx-miner and wishful to work in their quarries. That ship was very lovely and cunningly wrought, being of teakwood with ebony fittings and traceries of gold, and the cabin in which the traveller lodged had hangings of silk and velvet. One morning at the turn of the tide the sails were raised and the anchor lifted, and as Carter stood on the high stern he saw the sunrise-blazing walls and bronze statues and golden minarets of ageless Celephaïs sink into the distance, and the snowy peak of Mount Aran grow smaller and smaller. By noon there was nothing in sight save the gentle blue of the Cerenarian Sea, with one painted galley afar off bound for that cloud-hung realm of Serannian where the sea meets the sky.

And night came with gorgeous stars, and the dark ship steered for Charles' Wain and the Little Bear as they swung slowly round the pole. And the sailors sang strange songs of unknown places, and then stole off one by one to the forecastle while the wistful watchers murmured old chants and leaned over the rail to glimpse the luminous fish playing in bowers beneath the sea. Carter went to sleep at midnight, and rose in the glow of a young morning, marking that the sun seemed farther south than was its wont. And all through that second day he made progress in knowing the men of the ship, getting them little by little to talk of their cold twilight land, of their exquisite onyx city, and of their fear of the high and impassable peaks beyond which Leng was said to be. They told him how sorry they were that no cats would stay in the land of Inganok, and how they thought the hidden nearness of Leng was to blame for it. Only of the stony desert to the north they would not talk. There was something disquieting about that desert, and it was thought expedient not to admit its existence.

On later days they talked of the quarries in which Carter said he was going to work. There were many of them, for all the city of Inganok was builded of onyx, whilst great polished blocks of it were traded in Rinar, Ogrothan, and Celephaïs, and at home with the merchants of Thraa, Ilarnek, and Kadatheron, for the beautiful wares of those fabulous ports. And far to the north, almost in that cold desert whose existence the men of Inganok did not care to admit, there was an unused quarry greater than all the rest; from which had been hewn in forgotten times such prodigious lumps and blocks that the sight of their chiselled vacancies struck terror to all who beheld. Who had mined those incredible blocks, and whither they had been transported, no man might say; but it was thought best not to trouble that quarry, around which such inhuman memories might conceivably cling. So it was left all alone in the twilight, with only the raven and the rumoured shantak-bird to brood on its immensities. When Carter heard of this quarry he was moved to deep thought, for he knew from old tales that the Great Ones' castle atop unknown Kadath is of onyx.

Each day the sun wheeled lower and lower in the sky, and the mists overhead grew thicker and thicker. And in two weeks there was not any sunlight at all, but only a weird grey twilight shining through a dome of eternal cloud by day, and a cold starless phosphorescence from the under side of that cloud by night. On the twentieth day a great jagged rock in the sea was sighted from afar, the first land glimpsed since Aran's snowy peak had dwindled behind the ship. Carter asked the captain the name of that rock, but was told that it had no name and had never been sought by any vessel because of the sounds that came from it at night. And when, after dark, a dull and ceaseless howling arose from that jagged granite place, the traveller was glad that no stop had been made, and that the rock had no name. The seamen prayed and chanted till the noise was out of earshot, and Carter dreamed terrible dreams within dreams in the small hours.

Two mornings after that there loomed far ahead and to the east a line of great grey peaks whose tops were lost in the changeless clouds of that twilight world. And at the sight of them the sailors sang glad songs, and some knelt down on the deck to pray; so that Carter knew they were come to the land of Inganok and would soon be moored to the basalt quays of the great town bearing that land's name. Toward noon a dark coast-line appeared, and before three o'clock there stood out against the north the bulbous domes and fantastic spires of the onyx city. Rare and curious did that archaic city rise above its walls and quays, all of delicate black with scrolls, flutings, and arabesques of inlaid gold. Tall and many-windowed were the houses, and carved on every side with flowers and patterns whose dark symmetries dazzled the eye with a beauty more poignant than light. Some ended in swelling domes that tapered to a point, others in terraced pyramids whereon rose clustered minarets displaying every phase of strangeness and imagination. The walls were low, and pierced by frequent gates, each under a great arch rising high above the general level and capped by the head of a god chiselled with that same skill displayed in the monstrous face on distant Ngranek. On a hill in the centre rose a sixteen-angled tower greater than all the rest and bearing a high pinnacled belfry resting on a flattened dome. This, the seamen said, was the Temple of the Elder Ones, and was ruled by an old high-priest sad with inner secrets.

At intervals the clang of a strange bell shivered over the onyx city, answered each time by a peal of mystic music made up of horns, viols, and chanting voices. And from a row of tripods on a gallery round the high dome of the temple there burst flares of flame at certain moments; for the priests and people of that city were wise in the primal mysteries, and faithful in keeping the rhythms of the Great Ones as set forth in scrolls older than the Pnakotic Manuscripts. As the ship rode past the great basalt breakwater into the harbour the lesser noises of the city grew manifest, and Carter saw the slaves, sailors, and merchants on the docks. The sailors and merchants were of the strange-faced race of the gods, but the slaves were squat, slant-eyed folk said by rumour to have drifted somehow across or around the impassable peaks from valleys beyond Leng. The wharves reached wide outside the city wall and bore upon them all manner of merchandise from the galleys anchored there, while at one end were great piles of onyx both carved and uncarved awaiting shipment to the far markets of Rinar, Ogrothan, and Celephaïs.

It was not yet evening when the dark ship anchored beside a jutting quay of stone, and all the sailors and traders filed ashore and through the arched gate into the city. The streets of that city were paved with onyx, and some of them were wide and straight whilst others were crooked and narrow. The houses near the water were lower than the rest, and bore above their curiously arched doorways certain signs of gold said to be in honour of the respective small gods that favoured each. The captain of the ship took Carter to an old sea-tavern where flocked the mariners of quaint countries, and promised that he would next day shew him the wonders of the twilight city, and lead him to the taverns of the onyx-miners by the northern wall. And evening fell, and little bronze lamps were lighted, and the sailors in that tavern sang songs of remote places. But when from its high tower the great bell shivered over the city, and the peal of the horns and viols and voices rose cryptical in answer thereto, all ceased their songs or tales and bowed silent till the last echo died away. For there is a wonder and a strangeness on the twilight city of Inganok, and men fear to be lax in its rites lest a doom and a vengeance lurk unsuspectedly close.

Far in the shadows of that tavern Carter saw a squat form he did not like, for it was unmistakably that of the old slant-eyed merchant he had seen so long before in the taverns of Dylath-Leen, who was reputed to trade with the horrible stone villages of Leng which no healthy folk visit and whose evil fires are seen at night from afar, and even to have dealt with that high-priest not to be described, which wears a yellow silken mask over its face and dwells all alone in a prehistoric stone monastery. This man had seemed to shew a queer gleam of knowing when Carter asked the traders of Dylath-Leen about the cold waste and Kadath; and somehow his presence in dark and haunted Inganok, so close to the wonders of the north, was not a reassuring thing. He slipped wholly out of sight before Carter could speak to him, and sailors later said that he had come with a yak caravan from some point not well determined, bearing the colossal and rich-flavoured eggs of the rumoured shantak-bird to trade for the dexterous jade goblets that merchants brought from Ilarnek.

On the following morning the ship-captain led Carter through the onyx streets of Inganok, dark under their twilight sky. The inlaid doors and figured house-fronts, carven balconies and crystal-paned oriels all gleamed with a sombre and polished loveliness; and now and then a plaza would open out with black pillars, colonnades, and the statues of curious beings both human and fabulous. Some of the vistas down long and unbending streets, or through side alleys and over bulbous domes, spires, and arabesqued roofs, were weird and beautiful beyond words; and nothing was more splendid than the massive height of the great central Temple of the Elder Ones with its sixteen carven sides, its flattened dome, and its lofty pinnacled belfry, overtopping all else, and majestic whatever its foreground. And always to the east, far beyond the city walls and the leagues of pasture land, rose the gaunt grey sides of those topless and impassable peaks across which hideous Leng was said to lie.

The captain took Carter to the mighty temple, which is set with its walled garden in a great round plaza whence the streets go as spokes from a wheel's hub. The seven arched gates of that garden, each having over it a carven face like those on the city's gates, are always open; and the people roam reverently at will down the tiled paths and through the little lanes lined with grotesque termini and the shrines of modest gods. And there are fountains, pools, and basins there to reflect the frequent blaze of the tripods on the high balcony, all of onyx and having in them small luminous fish taken by divers from the lower bowers of ocean. When the deep clang from the temple's belfry shivers over the garden and the city, and the answer of the horns and viols and voices peals out from the seven lodges by the garden gates, there issue from the seven doors of the temple long columns of masked and hooded priests in black, bearing at arm's length before them great golden bowls from which a curious steam rises. And all the seven columns strut peculiarly in single file, legs thrown far forward without bending the knees, down the walks that lead to the seven lodges, wherein they disappear and do not appear again. It is said that subterrene paths connect the lodges with the temple, and that the long files of priests return through them; nor is it unwhispered that deep flights of onyx steps go down to mysteries that are never told. But only a few are those who hint that the priests in the masked and hooded columns are not human priests.

Carter did not enter the temple, because none but the Veiled King is permitted to do that. But before he left the garden the hour of the bell came, and he heard the shivering clang deafeningly above him, and the wailing of the horns and viols and voices loud from the lodges by the gates. And down the seven great walks stalked the long files of bowl-bearing priests in their singular way, giving to the traveller a fear which human priests do not often give. When the last of them had vanished he left that garden, noting as he did so a spot on the pavement over which the bowls had passed. Even the ship-captain did not like that spot, and hurried him on toward the hill whereon the Veiled King's palace rises many-domed and marvellous.

The ways to the onyx palace are steep and narrow, all but that broad curving one where the king and his companions ride on yaks or in yak-drawn chariots. Carter and his guide climbed up an alley that was all steps, between inlaid walls bearing strange signs in gold, and under balconies and oriels whence sometimes floated soft strains of music or breaths of exotic fragrance. Always ahead loomed those titan walls, mighty buttresses, and clustered and bulbous domes for which the Veiled King's palace is famous; and at length they passed under a great black arch and emerged in the gardens of the monarch's pleasure. There Carter paused in faintness at so much of beauty; for the onyx terraces and colonnaded walks, the gay parterres and delicate flowering trees espaliered to golden lattices, the brazen urns and tripods with cunning bas-reliefs, the pedestalled and almost breathing statues of veined black marble, the basalt-bottomed lagoons and tiled fountains with luminous fish, the tiny temples of iridescent singing birds atop carven columns, the marvellous scrollwork of the great bronze gates, and the blossoming vines trained along every inch of the polished walls all joined to form a sight whose loveliness was beyond reality, and half-fabulous even in the land of dream. There it shimmered like a vision under that grey twilight sky, with the domed and fretted magnificence of the palace ahead, and the fantastic silhouette of the distant impassable peaks on the right. And ever the small birds and the fountains sang, while the perfume of rare blossoms spread like a veil over that incredible garden. No other human presence was there, and Carter was glad it was so. Then they turned and descended again the onyx alley of steps, for the palace itself no visitor may enter; and it is not well to look too long and steadily at the great central dome, since it is said to house the archaic father of all the rumoured shantak-birds, and to send out queer dreams to the curious.

After that the captain took Carter to the north quarter of the town, near the Gate of the Caravans, where are the taverns of the yak-merchants and the onyx-miners. And there, in a low-ceiled inn of quarrymen, they said farewell; for business called the captain whilst Carter was eager to talk with miners about the north. There were many men in that inn, and the traveller was not long in speaking to some of them; saying that he was an old miner of onyx, and anxious to know somewhat of Inganok's quarries. But all that he learnt was not much more than he knew before, for the miners were timid and evasive about the cold desert to the north and the quarry that no man visits. They had fears of fabled emissaries from around the mountains where Leng is said to lie, and of evil presences and nameless sentinels far north among the scattered rocks. And they whispered also that the rumoured shantak-birds are no wholesome things; it being indeed for the best that no man has ever truly seen one (for that fabled father of shantaks in the king's dome is fed in the dark).

The next day, saying that he wished to look over all the various mines for himself and to visit the scattered farms and quaint onyx villages of Inganok, Carter hired a yak and stuffed great leathern saddle-bags for a journey. Beyond the Gate of the Caravans the road lay straight betwixt tilled fields, with many odd farmhouses crowned by low domes. At some of these houses the seeker stopped to ask questions; once finding a host so austere and reticent, and so full of an unplaced majesty like to that in the huge features on Ngranek, that he felt certain he had come at last upon one of the Great Ones themselves, or upon one with full nine-tenths of their blood, dwelling amongst men. And to that austere and reticent cotter he was careful to speak very well of the gods, and to praise all the blessings they had ever accorded him.

That night Carter camped in a roadside meadow beneath a great lygath-tree to which he tied his yak, and in the morning resumed his northward pilgrimage. At about ten o'clock he reached the small-domed village of Urg, where traders rest and miners tell their tales, and paused in its taverns till noon. It is here that the great caravan road turns west toward Selarn, but Carter kept on north by the quarry road. All the afternoon he followed that rising road, which was somewhat narrower than the great highway, and which now led through a region with more rocks than tilled fields. And by evening the low hills on his left had risen into sizeable black cliffs, so that he knew he was close to the mining country. All the while the great gaunt sides of the impassable mountains towered afar off at his right, and the farther he went, the worse tales he heard of them from the scattered farmers and traders and drivers of lumbering onyx-carts along the way.

On the second night he camped in the shadow of a large black crag, tethering his yak to a stake driven in the ground. He observed the greater phosphorescence of the clouds at this northerly point, and more than once thought he saw dark shapes outlined against them. And on the third morning he came in sight of the first onyx quarry, and greeted the men who there laboured with picks and chisels. Before evening he had passed eleven quarries; the land being here given over altogether to onyx cliffs and boulders, with no vegetation at all, but only great rocky fragments scattered about a floor of black earth, with the grey impassable peaks always rising gaunt and sinister on his right. The third night he spent in a camp of quarry men whose flickering fires cast weird reflections on the polished cliffs to the west. And they sang many songs and told many tales, shewing such strange knowledge of the olden days and the habits of gods that Carter could see they held many latent memories of their sires the Great Ones. They asked him whither he went, and cautioned him not to go too far to the north; but he replied that he was seeking new cliffs of onyx, and would take no more risks than were common among prospectors. In the morning he bade them adieu and rode on into the darkening north, where they had warned him he would find the feared and unvisited quarry whence hands older than men's hands had wrenched prodigious blocks. But he did not like it when, turning back to wave a last farewell, he thought he saw approaching the camp that squat and evasive old merchant with slanting eyes, whose conjectured traffick with Leng was the gossip of distant Dylath-Leen.

After two more quarries the inhabited part of Inganok seemed to end, and the road narrowed to a steeply rising yak-path among forbidding black cliffs. Always on the right towered the gaunt and distant peaks, and as Carter climbed farther and farther into this untraversed realm he found it grew darker and colder. Soon he perceived that there were no prints of feet or hooves on the black path beneath, and realised that he was indeed come into strange and deserted ways of elder time. Once in a while a raven would croak far overhead, and now and then a flapping behind some vast rock would make him think uncomfortably of the rumoured shantak-bird. But in the main he was alone with his shaggy steed, and it troubled him to observe that this excellent yak became more and more reluctant to advance, and more and more disposed to snort affrightedly at any small noise along the route.

The path now contracted between sable and glistening walls, and began to display an even greater steepness than before. It was a bad footing, and the yak often slipped on the stony fragments strown thickly about. In two hours Carter saw ahead a definite crest, beyond which was nothing but dull grey sky, and blessed the prospect of a level or downward course. To reach this crest, however, was no easy task; for the way had grown nearly perpendicular, and was perilous with loose black gravel and small stones. Eventually Carter dismounted and led his dubious yak; pulling very hard when the animal balked or stumbled, and keeping his own footing as best he might. Then sudddenly he came to the top and saw beyond, and gasped at what he saw.

The path indeed led straight ahead and slightly down, with the same lines of high natural walls as before; but on the left hand there opened out a monstrous space, vast acres in extent, where some archaic power had riven and rent the native cliffs of onyx in the form of a giants' quarry. Far back into the solid precipice ran that Cyclopean gouge, and deep down within earth's bowels its lower delvings yawned. It was no quarry of man, and the concave sides were scarred with great squares yards wide which told of the size of the blocks once hewn by nameless hands and chisels. High over its jagged rim huge ravens flapped and croaked, and vague whirrings in the unseen depths told of bats or urhags or less mentionable presences haunting the endless blackness. There Carter stood in the narrow way amidst the twilight with the rocky path sloping down before him; tall onyx cliffs on his right that led on as far as he could see, and tall cliffs on the left chopped off just ahead to make that terrible and unearthly quarry.

All at once the yak uttered a cry and burst from his control, leaping past him and darting on in a panic till it vanished down the narrow slope toward the north. Stones kicked by its flying hooves fell over the brink of the quarry and lost themselves in the dark without any sound of striking bottom; but Carter ignored the perils of that scanty path as he raced breathlessly after the flying steed. Soon the left-hand cliffs resumed their course, making the way once more a narrow lane; and still the traveller leaped on after the yak whose great wide prints told of its desperate flight.

Once he thought he heard the hoofbeats of the frightened beast, and doubled his speed from this encouragement. He was covering miles, and little by little the way was broadening in front till he knew he must soon emerge on the cold and dreaded desert to the north. The gaunt grey flanks of the distant impassable peaks were again visible above the right-hand crags, and ahead were the rocks and boulders of an open space which was clearly a foretaste of the dark and limitless plain. And once more those hoofbeats sounded in his ears, plainer than before, but this time giving terror instead of encouragement because he realised that they were not the frightened hoofbeats of his fleeing yak. These beats were ruthless and purposeful, and they were behind him.

Carter's pursuit of the yak became now a flight from an unseen thing, for though he dared not glance over his shoulder he felt that the presence behind him could be nothing wholesome or mentionable. His yak must have heard or felt it first, and he did not like to ask himself whether it had followed him from the haunts of men or had floundered up out of that black quarry pit. Meanwhile the cliffs had been left behind, so that the oncoming night fell over a great waste of sand and spectral rocks wherein all paths were lost. He could not see the hoofprints of his yak, but always from behind him there came that detestable clopping; mingled now and then with what he fancied were titantic flappings and whirrings. That he was losing ground seemed unhappily clear to him, and he knew he was hopelessly lost in this broken and blasted desert of meaningless rocks and untravelled sands. Only those remote and impassable peaks on the right gave him any sense of direction, and even they were less clear as the grey twilight waned and the sickly phosphorescene of the clouds took its place.

Then dim and misty in the darkling north before him he glimpsed a terrible thing. He had thought it for some moments a range of black mountains, but now he saw it was something more. The phosphorescence of the brooding clouds shewed it plainly, and even silhouetted parts of it as low vapours glowed behind. How distant it was he could not tell, but it must have been very far. It was thousands of feet high, stretching in a great concave arc from the grey impassable peaks to the unimagined westward spaces, and had once indeed been a ridge of mighty onyx hills. But now those hills were hills no more, for some hand greater than man's had touched them. Silent they squatted there atop the world like wolves or ghouls, crowned with clouds and mists and guarding the secrets of the north for ever. All in a great half circle they squatted, those dog-like mountains carven into monstrous watching statues, and their right hands were raised in menace against mankind.

It was only the flickering light of the clouds that made their mitred double heads seem to move, but as Carter stumbled on he saw arise from their shadowy laps great forms whose motions were no delusion. Winged and whirring, those forms grew larger each moment, and the traveller knew his stumbling was at an end. They were not any birds or bats known elsewhere on earth or in dreamland, for they were larger than elephants and had heads like a horse's. Carter knew that they must be the shantak-birds of ill rumour, and wondered no more what evil guardians and nameless sentinels made men avoid the boreal rock desert. And as he stopped in final resignation he dared at last to look behind him; where indeed was trotting the squat slant-eyed trader of evil legend, grinning astride a lean yak and leading on a noxious horde of leering shantaks to whose wings still clung the rime and nitre of the nether pits.

Trapped though he was by fabulous and hippocephalic winged nightmares that pressed around in great unholy circles, Randolph Carter did not lose consciousness. Lofty and horrible those titan gargoyles towered above him, while the slant-eyed merchant leaped down from his yak and stood grinning before the captive. Then the man motioned Carter to mount one of the repugnant shantaks, helping him up as his judgment struggled with his loathing. It was hard work ascending, for the shantak-bird has scales instead of feathers, and those scales are very slippery. Once he was seated, the slant-eyed man hopped up behind him, leaving the lean yak to be led away northward toward the ring of carven mountains by one of the incredible bird colossi.

There now followed a hideous whirl through frigid space, endlessly up and eastward toward the gaunt grey flanks of those impassable mountains beyond which Leng was said to lie. Far above the clouds they flew, till at last there lay beneath them those fabled summits which the folk of Inganok have never seen, and which lie always in high vortices of gleaming mist. Carter beheld them very plainly as they passed below, and saw upon their topmost peaks strange caves which made him think of those on Ngranek; but he did not question his captor about these things when he noticed that both the man and the horse-headed shantak appeared oddly fearful of them, hurrying past nervously and shewing great tension until they were left far in the rear.

The shantak now flew lower, revealing beneath the canopy of cloud a grey barren plain whereon at great distances shone little feeble fires. As they descended there appeared at intervals lone huts of granite and bleak stone villages whose tiny windows glowed with pallid light. And there came from those huts and villages a shrill droning of pipes and a nauseous rattle of crotala which proved at once that Inganok's people are right in their geographick rumours.

For travellers have heard such sounds before, and know that they float only from that cold desert plateau which healthy folk never visit; that haunted place of evil and mystery which is Leng.

Around the feeble fires dark forms were dancing, and Carter was curious as to what manner of beings they might be; for no healthy folk have ever been to Leng, and the place is known only by its fires and stone huts as seen from afar. Very slowly and awkwardly did those forms leap, and with an insane twisting and bending not good to behold; so that Carter did not wonder at the monstrous evil imputed to them by vague legend, or the fear in which all dreamland holds their abhorrent frozen plateau. As the shantak flew lower, the repulsiveness of the dancers became tinged with a certain hellish familiarity; and the prisoner kept straining his eyes and racking his memory for clues to where he had seen such creatures before.

They leaped as though they had hooves instead of feet, and seemed to wear a sort of wig or headpiece with small horns. Of other clothing they had none, but most of them were quite furry. Behind they had dwarfish tails, and when they glanced upward he saw the excessive width of their mouths. Then he knew what they were, and that they did not wear any wigs or headpieces after all. For the cryptic folk of Leng were of one race with the uncomfortable merchants of the black galleys that traded rubies at Dylath-Leen; those not quite human merchants who are the slaves of the monstrous moon-things! They were indeed the same dark folk who had shanghaied Carter on their noisome galley so long ago, and whose kith he had seen driven in herds about the unclean wharves of that accursed lunar city, with the leaner ones toiling and the fatter ones taken away in crates for other needs of their polypous and amorphous masters. Now he saw where such ambiguous creatures came from, and shuddered at the thought that Leng must be known to those formless abominations from the moon.

But the shantak flew on past the fires and the stone huts and the less than human dancers, and soared over sterile hills of grey granite and dim wastes of rock and ice and snow. Day came, and the phosphorescence of low clouds gave place to the misty twilight of that northern world, and still the vile bird winged meaningly through the cold and silence. At times the slant-eyed man talked with his steed in a hateful and guttural language, and the shantak would answer with tittering tones that rasped like the scratching of ground glass. All this while the land was getting higher, and finally they came to a windswept table-land which seemed the very roof of a blasted and tenantless world. There, all alone in the hush and the dusk and the cold, rose the uncouth stones of a squat windowless building, around which a circle of crude monoliths stood. In all this arrangement there was nothing human, and Carter surmised from old tales that he was indeed come to that most dreadful and legendary of all places, the remote and prehistoric monastery wherein dwells uncompanioned the high-priest not to be described, which wears a yellow silken mask over its face and prays to the Other Gods and their crawling chaos Nyarlathotep.

The loathsome bird now settled to the ground, and the slant-eyed man hopped down and helped his captive alight. Of the purpose of his seizure Carter now felt very sure; for clearly the slant-eyed merchant was an agent of the darker powers, eager to drag before his masters a mortal whose presumption had aimed at the finding of unknown Kadath and the saying of a prayer before the faces of the Great Ones in their onyx castle. It seemed likely that this merchant had caused his former capture by the slaves of the moon-things in Dylath-Leen, and that he now meant to do what the rescuing cats had baffled; taking the victim to some dread rendezvous with monstrous Nyarlathotep and telling with what boldness the seeking of unknown Kadath had been tried. Leng and the cold waste north of Inganok must be close to the Other Gods, and there the passes to Kadath are well guarded.

The slant-eyed man was small, but the great hippocephalic bird was there to see he was obeyed; so Carter followed where he led, and passed within the circle of standing rocks and into the low arched doorway of that windowless stone monastery. There were no lights inside, but the evil merchant lit a small clay lamp bearing morbid bas-reliefs and prodded his prisoner on through mazes of narrow winding corridors. On the walls of the corridors were painted frightful scenes older than history, and in a style unknown to the archaeologists of earth. After countless aeons their pigments were brillant still, for the cold and dryness of hideous Leng keep alive many primal things. Carter saw them fleetingly in the rays of that dim and moving lamp, and shuddered at the tale they told.

Through those archaic frescoes Leng's annals stalked; and the horned, hooved, and wide-mouthed almost-humans danced evilly amidst forgotten cities. There were scenes of old wars, wherein Leng's almost-humans fought with the bloated purple spiders of the neighbouring vales; and there were scenes also of the coming of the black galleys from the moon, and of the submission of Leng's people to the polypous and amorphous blasphemies that hopped and floundered and wriggled out of them. Those slippery greyish-white blasphemies they worshipped as gods, nor ever complained when scores of their best and fatted males were taken away in the black galleys. The monstrous moonbeasts made their camp on a jagged isle in the sea, and Carter could tell from the frescoes that this was none other than the lone nameless rock he had seen when sailing to Inganok; that grey accursed rock which Inganok's seamen shun, and from which vile howlings reverberate all through the night.

And in those frescoes was shewn the great seaport and capital of the almost-humans; proud and pillared betwixt the cliffs and the basalt wharves, and wondrous with high fanes and carven palaces. Great gardens and columned streets led from the cliffs and from each of the six sphinx-crowned gates to a vast central plaza, and in that plaza was a pair of winged colossal lions guarding the top of a subterrene staircase. Again and again were those huge winged lions shewn, their mighty flanks of diorite glistening in the grey twilight of the day and the cloudy phosphorescence of the night. And as Carter stumbled past their frequent and repeated pictures it came to him at last what indeed they were, and what city it was that the almost-humans had ruled so anciently before the coming of the black galleys. There could be no mistake, for the legends of dreamland are generous and profuse. Indubitably that primal city was no less a place than storied Sarkomand, whose ruins had bleached for a million years before the first true human saw the light, and whose twin titan lions guard eternally the steps that lead down from dreamland to the Great Abyss.

Other views shewed the gaunt grey peaks dividing Leng from Inganok, and the monstrous shantak-birds that build nests on the ledges half way up. And they shewed likewise the curious caves near the very topmost pinnacles, and how even the boldest of the shantaks fly screaming away from them. Carter had seen those caves when he passed over them, and had noticed their likeness to the caves on Ngranek. Now he knew that the likeness was more than a chance one, for in these pictures were shewn their fearsome denizens; and those bat-wings, curving horns, barbed tails, prehensile paws, and rubbery bodies were not strange to him. He had met those silent, flitting, and clutching creatures before; those mindless guardians of the Great Abyss whom even the Great Ones fear, and who own not Nyarlathotep but hoary Nodens as their lord. For they were the dreaded night-gaunts, who never laugh or smile because they have no faces, and who flap unendingly in the dark betwixt the Vale of Pnath and the passes to the outer world.

The slant-eyed merchant had now prodded Carter into a great domed space whose walls were carved in shocking bas-reliefs, and whose centre held a gaping circular pit surrounded by six malignly stained stone altars in a ring. There was no light in this vast and evil-smelling crypt, and the small lamp of the sinister merchant shone so feebly that one could grasp details only little by little. At the farther end was a high stone dais reached by five steps; and there on a golden throne sat a lumpish figure robed in yellow silk figured with red and having a yellow silken mask over its face. To this being the slant-eyed man made certain signs with his hands, and the lurker in the dark replied by raising a disgustingly carven flute of ivory in silk-covered paws and blowing certain loathsome sounds from beneath its flowing yellow mask. This colloquy went on for some time, and to Carter there was something sickeningly familiar in the sound of that flute and the stench of that malodorous place. It made him think of a frightful red-litten city and of the revolting procession that once filed through it; of that, and of an awful climb through lunar countryside beyond, before the rescuing rush of earth's friendly cats. He knew that the creature on the dais was without doubt the high-priest not to be described, of which legend whispers such fiendish and abnormal possibilities, but he feared to think just what that abhorred high-priest might be.

Then the figured silk slipped a trifle from one of the greyish-white paws, and Carter knew what the noisome high-priest was. And in that hideous second stark fear drove him to something his reason would never have dared attempt, for in all his shaken consciousness there was room only for one frantic will to escape from what squatted on that golden throne. He knew that hopeless labyrinths of stone lay betwixt him and the cold table-land outside, and that even on that table-land the noxious shantak still waited; yet in spite of all this there was in his mind only the instant need to get away from that wriggling, silk-robed monstrosity.

The slant-eyed man had set his curious lamp upon one of the high and wickedly stained altar-stones by the pit, and had moved forward somewhat to talk to the high-priest with his hands. Carter, hitherto wholly passive, now gave that man a terrific push with all the wild strength of fear, so that the victim toppled at once into that gaping well which rumour holds to reach down to the hellish Vaults of Zin where gugs hunt ghasts in the dark. In almost the same second he seized the lamp from the altar and dashed out into the frescoed labyrinths, racing this way and that as chance determined and trying not to think of the stealthy padding of shapeless paws on the stones behind him, or of the silent wrigglings and crawlings which must be going on back there in lightless corridors.

After a few moments he regretted his thoughtless haste, and wished he had tried to follow backward the frescoes he had passed on the way in. True, they were so confused and duplicated that they could not have done him much good, but he wished none the less he had made the attempt. Those he now saw were even more horrible than those he had seen then, and he knew he was not in the corridors leading outside. In time he became quite sure he was not followed, and slackened his pace somewhat; but scarce had he breathed in half relief when a new peril beset him. His lamp was waning, and he would soon be in pitch blackness with no means of sight or guidance.

When the light was all gone he groped slowly in the dark, and prayed to the Great Ones for such help as they might afford. At times he felt the stone floor sloping up or down, and once he stumbled over a step for which no reason seemed to exist. The farther he went the damper it seemed to be, and when he was able to feel a junction or the mouth of a side passage he always chose the way which sloped downward the least. He believed, though, that his general course was down; and the vault-like smell and incrustations on the greasy walls and floor alike warned him he was burrowing deep into Leng's unwholesome table-land. But there was not any warning of the thing which came at last; only the thing itself with its terror and shock and breath-taking chaos. One moment he was groping slowly over the slippery floor of an almost level place, and the next he was shooting dizzily downward in the dark through a burrow which must have been well-nigh vertical.

Of the length of that hideous sliding he could never be sure, but it seemed to take hours of delirious nausea and ecstatic frenzy. Then he realised he was still, with the phosphorescent clouds of a northern night shining sickly above him. All around were crumbling walls and broken columns, and the pavement on which he lay was pierced by straggling grass and wrenched asunder by frequent shrubs and roots. Behind him a basalt cliff rose topless and perpendicular; its dark side sculptured into repellent scenes, and pierced by an arched and carven entrance to the inner blacknesses out of which he had come. Ahead stretched double rows of pillars, and the fragments and pedestals of pillars, that spoke of a broad and bygone street; and from the urns and basins along the way he knew it had been a great street of gardens. Far off at its end the pillars spread to mark a vast round plaza, and in that open circle there loomed gigantic under the lurid night clouds a pair of monstrous things. Huge winged lions of diorite they were, with blackness and shadow between them. Full twenty feet they reared their grotesque and unbroken heads, and snarled derisive on the ruins around them. And Carter knew right well what they must be, for legend tells of only one such twain. They were the changeless guardians of the Great Abyss, and these dark ruins were in truth primordial Sarkomand.

Carter's first act was to close and barricade the archway in the cliff with fallen blocks and odd debris that lay around. He wished no follower from Leng's hateful monastery, for along the way ahead would lurk enough of other dangers. Of how to get from Sarkomand to the peopled parts of dreamland he knew nothing at all; nor could he gain much by descending to the grottoes of the ghouls, since he knew they were no better informed than he. The three ghouls which had helped him through the city of gugs to the outer world had not known how to reach Sarkomand in their journey back, but had planned to ask old traders in Dylath-Leen. He did not like to think of going again to the subterrene world of gugs and risking once more that hellish tower of Koth with its Cyclopean steps leading to the enchanted wood, yet he felt he might have to try this course if all else failed. Over Leng's plateau past the lone monastery he dared not go unaided; for the high-priest's emissaries must be many, while at the journey's end there would no doubt be the shantaks and perhaps other things to deal with. If he could get a boat he might sail back to Inganok past the jagged and hideous rock in the sea, for the primal frescoes in the monastery labyrinth had shewn that this frightful place lies not far from Sarkomand's basalt quays. But to find a boat in this aeon-deserted city was no probable thing, and it did not appear likely that he could ever make one.

Such were the thoughts of Randolph Carter when a new impression began beating upon his mind. All this while there had stretched before him the great corpse-like width of fabled Sarkomand with its black broken pillars and crumbling sphinx-crowned gates and titan stones and monstrous winged lions against the sickly glow of those luminous night clouds. Now he saw far ahead and on the right a glow that no clouds could account for, and knew he was not alone in the silence of that dead city. The glow rose and fell fitfully, flickering with a greenish tinge which did not reassure the watcher. And when he crept closer, down the littered street and through some narrow gaps between tumbled walls, he perceived that it was a campfire near the wharves with many vague forms clustered darkly around it, and a lethal odour hanging heavily over all. Beyond was the oily lapping of the harbour water with a great ship riding at anchor, and Carter paused in stark terror when he saw that the ship was indeed one of the dreaded black galleys from the moon.

Then, just as he was about to creep back from that destestable flame, he saw a stirring among the vague dark forms and heard a peculiar and unmistakable sound. It was the frightened meeping of a ghoul, and in a moment it had swelled to a veritable chorus of anguish. Secure as he was in the shadow of monstrous ruins, Carter allowed his curiosity to conquer his fear, and crept forward again instead of retreating. Once in crossing an open street he wriggled worm-like on his stomach, and in another place he had to rise to his feet to avoid making a noise among heaps of fallen marble. But always he succeeded in avoiding discovery, so that in a short time he had found a spot behind a titan pillar whence he could watch the whole green-litten scene of action. There, around a hideous fire fed by the obnoxious stems of lunar fungi, there squatted a stinking circle of the toad-like moonbeasts and their almost-human slaves. Some of these slaves were heating curious iron spears in the leaping flames, and at intervals applying their white-hot points to three tightly trussed prisoners that lay writhing before the leaders of the party. From the motions of their tentacles Carter could see that the blunt-snouted moonbeasts were enjoying the spectacle hugely, and vast was his horror when he suddenly recognised the frantic meeping and knew that the tortured ghouls were none other than the faithful trio which had guided him safely from the abyss and had thereafter set out from the enchanted wood to find Sarkomand and the gate to their native deeps.

The number of malodorous moonbeasts about that greenish fire was very great, and Carter saw that he could do nothing now to save his former allies. Of how the ghouls had been captured he could not guess; but fancied that the grey toad-like blasphemies had heard them inquire in Dylath-Leen concerning the way to Sarkomand and had not wished them to approach so closely the hateful plateau of Leng and the high-priest not to be described. For a moment he pondered on what he ought to do, and recalled how near he was to the gate of the ghouls' black kingdom. Clearly it was wisest to creep east to the plaza of twin lions and descend at once to the gulf, where assuredly he would meet no horrors worse than those above, and where he might soon find ghouls eager to rescue their brethren and perhaps to wipe out the moonbeasts from the black galley. It occured to him that the portal, like other gates to the abyss, might be guarded by flocks of night-gaunts; but he did not fear these faceless creatures now. He had learned that they are bound by solemn treaties with the ghouls, and the ghoul which was Pickman had taught him how to glibber a password they understood.

So Carter began another silent crawl through the ruins, edging slowly toward the great central plaza and the winged lions. It was ticklish work, but the moonbeasts were pleasantly busy and did not hear the slight noises which he twice made by accident among the scattered stones. At last he reached the open space and picked his way among the stunted trees and briers that had grown up therein. The gigantic lions loomed terrible above him in the sickly glow of the phosphorescent night clouds, but he manfully persisted toward them and presently crept round to their faces, knowing it was on that side he would find the mighty darkness which they guard. Ten feet apart crouched the mocking-faced beasts of diorite, brooding on Cyclopean pedestals whose sides were chiselled into fearsome bas-reliefs. Betwixt them was a tiled court with a central space which had once been railed with balusters of onyx. Midway in this space a black well opened, and Carter soon saw that he had indeed reached the yawning gulf whose crusted and mouldy stone steps lead down to the crypts of nightmare.

Terrible is the memory of that dark descent, in which hours wore themselves away whilst Carter wound sightlessly round and round down a fathomless spiral of steep and slippery stairs. So worn and narrow were the steps, and so greasy with the ooze of inner earth, that the climber never quite knew when to expect a breathless fall and hurtling down to the ultimate pits; and he was likewise uncertain just when or how the guardian night-gaunts would suddenly pounce upon him, if indeed there were any stationed in this primeval passage. All about him was a stifling odour of nether gulfs, and he felt that the air of these choking depths was not made for mankind. In time he became very numb and somnolent, moving more from automatic impulse than from reasoned will; nor did he realise any change when he stopped moving altogether as something quietly seized him from behind. He was flying very rapidly through the air before a malevolent tickling told him that the rubbery night-gaunts had performed their duty.

Awaked to the fact that he was in the cold, damp clutch of the faceless flutterers, Carter remembered the password of the ghouls and glibbered it as loudly as he could amidst the wind and chaos of flight. Mindless though night-gaunts are said to be, the effect was instantaneous; for all tickling stopped at once, and the creatures hastened to shift their captive to a more comfortable position. Thus encouraged, Carter ventured some explanations; telling of the seizure and torture of the three ghouls by the moonbeasts, and of the need of assembling a party to rescue them. The night-gaunts, though inarticulate, seemed to understand what was said;

and shewed greater haste and purpose in their flight. Suddenly the dense blackness gave place to the grey twilight of inner earth, and there opened up ahead one of those flat sterile plains on which ghouls love to squat and gnaw. Scattered tombstones and osseous fragments told of the denizens of that place; and as Carter gave a loud meep of urgent summons, a score of burrows emptied forth their leathery, dog-like tenants. The night-gaunts now flew low and set their passenger upon his feet, afterward withdrawing a little and forming a hunched semicircle on the ground while the ghouls greeted the newcomer.

Carter glibbered his message rapidly and explicitly to the grotesque company, and four of them at once departed through different burrows to spread the news to others and gather such troops as might be available for a rescue. After a long wait a ghoul of some importance appeared, and made significant signs to the night-gaunts, causing two of the latter to fly off into the dark. Thereafter there were constant accessions to the hunched flock of night-gaunts on the plain, till at length the slimy soil was fairly black with them. Meanwhile fresh ghouls crawled out of the burrows one by one, all glibbering excitedly and forming in crude battle array not far from the huddled night-gaunts. In time there appeared that proud and influential ghoul which was once the artist Richard Pickman of Boston, and to him Carter glibbered a very full account of what had occurred. The erstwhile Pickman, surprised to greet his ancient friend again, seemed very much impressed, and held a conference with other chiefs a little apart from the growing throng.

Finally, after scanning the ranks with care, the assembled chiefs all meeped in unison and began glibbering orders to the crowds of ghouls and night-gaunts. A large detachment of the horned flyers vanished at once, while the rest grouped themselves two by two on their knees with extended fore legs, awaiting the approach of the ghouls one by one. As each ghoul reached the pair of night-gaunts to which he was assigned, he was taken up and borne away into the blackness; till at last the whole throng had vanished save for Carter, Pickman, the other chiefs, and a few pairs of night-gaunts. Pickman explained that night-gaunts are the advance guard and battle steeds of the ghouls, and that the army was issuing forth to Sarkomand to deal with the moonbeasts. Then Carter and the ghoulish chiefs approached the waiting bearers and were taken up by the damp, slippery paws. Another moment and all were whirling in wind and darkness; endlessly up, up, up to the gate of the winged lions and the spectral ruins of primal Sarkomand.

When, after a great interval, Carter saw again the sickly light of Sarkomand's nocturnal sky, it was to behold the great central plaza swarming with militant ghouls and night-gaunts. Day, he felt sure, must be almost due; but so strong was the army that no surprise of the enemy would be needed. The greenish flare near the wharves still glimmered faintly, though the absence of ghoulish meeping shewed that the torture of the prisoners was over for the nonce. Softly glibbering directions to their steeds, and to the flock of riderless night-gaunts ahead, the ghouls presently rose in wide whirring columns and swept on over the bleak ruins toward the evil flame. Carter was now beside Pickman in the front rank of ghouls, and saw as they approached the noisome camp that the moonbeasts were totally unprepared. The three prisoners lay bound and inert beside the fire, while their toad-like captors slumped drowsily about in no certain order. The almost-human slaves were asleep, even the sentinels shirking a duty which in this realm must have seemed to them merely perfunctory.

The final swoop of the night-gaunts and mounted ghouls was very sudden, each of the greyish toad-like blasphemies and their almost-human slaves being seized by a group of night-gaunts before a sound was made. The moonbeasts, of course, were voiceless; and even the slaves had little chance to scream before rubbery paws choked them into silence. Horrible were the writhings of those great jellyish abnormalities as the sardonic night-gaunts clutched them, but nothing availed against the strength of those black prehensile talons. When a moonbeast writhed too violently, a night-gaunt would seize and pull its quivering pink tentacles; which seemed to hurt so much that the victim would cease its struggles. Carter expected to see much slaughter, but found that the ghouls were far subtler in their plans. They glibbered certain simple orders to the night-gaunts which held the captives, trusting the rest to instinct; and soon the hapless creatures were borne silently away into the Great Abyss, to be distributed impartially amongst the bholes, gugs, ghasts, and other dwellers in darkness whose modes of nourishment are not painless to their chosen victims. Meanwhile the three bound ghouls had been released and consoled by their conquering kinsfolk, whilst various parties searched the neighbourhood for possible remaining moonbeasts, and boarded the evil-smelling black galley at the wharf to make sure that nothing had escaped the general defeat. Surely enough, the capture had been thorough; for not a sign of further life could the victors detect. Carter, anxious to preserve a means of access to the rest of dreamland, urged them not to sink the anchored galley; and this request was freely granted out of gratitude for his act in reporting the plight of the captured trio. On the ship were found some very curious objects and decorations, some of which Carter cast at once into the sea.

Ghouls and night-gaunts now formed themselves in separate groups, the former questioning their rescued fellows anent past happenings. It appeared that the three had followed Carter's directions and proceeded from the enchanted wood to Dylath-Leen by way of Nir and the Skai, stealing human clothes at a lonely farmhouse and loping as closely as possible in the fashion of a man's walk. In Dylath-Leen's taverns their grotesque ways and faces had aroused much comment; but they had persisted in asking the way to Sarkomand until at last an old traveller was able to tell them. Then they knew that only a ship for Lelag-Leng would serve their purpose, and prepared to wait patiently for such a vessel.

But evil spies had doubtless reported much; for shortly a black galley put into port, and the wide-mouthed ruby merchants invited the ghouls to drink with them in a tavern. Wine was produced from one of those sinister bottles grotesquely carven from a single ruby, and after that the ghouls found themselves prisoners on the black galley as Carter had once found himself. This time, however, the unseen rowers steered not for the moon but for antique Sarkomand; bent evidently on taking their captives before the high-priest not to be described. They had touched at the jagged rock in the northern sea which Inganok's mariners shun, and the ghouls had there seen for the first time the real masters of the ship; being sickened despite their own callousness by such extremes of malign shapelessness and fearsome odour. There, too, were witnessed the nameless pastimes of the toad-like resident garrison—such pastimes as give rise to the night-howlings which men fear. After that had come the landing at ruined Sarkomand and the beginning of the tortures, whose continuance the present rescue had prevented.

Future plans were next discussed, the three rescued ghouls suggesting a raid on the jagged rock and the extermination of the toad-like garrison there. To this, however, the night-gaunts objected; since the prospect of flying over water did not please them. Most of the ghouls favoured the design, but were at a loss how to follow it without the help of the winged night-gaunts. Thereupon Carter, seeing that they could not navigate the anchored galley, offered to teach them the use of the great banks of oars; to which proposal they eagerly assented. Grey day had now come, and under that leaden northern sky a picked detachment of ghouls filed into the noisome ship and took their seats on the rowers' benches. Carter found them fairly apt at learning, and before night had risked several experimental trips around the harbour. Not till three days later, however, did he deem it safe to attempt the voyage of conquest. Then, the rowers trained and the night-gaunts safely stowed in the forecastle, the party set sail at last; Pickman and the other chiefs gathering on deck and discussing modes of approach and procedure.

On the very first night the howlings from the rock were heard. Such was their timbre that all the galley's crew shook visibly; but most of all trembled the three rescued ghouls who knew precisely what those howlings meant. It was not thought best to attempt an attack by night, so the ship lay to under the phosphorescent clouds to wait for the dawn of a greyish day. When the light was ample and the howlings still the rowers resumed their strokes, and the galley drew closer and closer to that jagged rock whose granite pinnacles clawed fantastically at the dull sky. The sides of the rock were very steep; but on ledges here and there could be seen the bulging walls of queer windowless dwellings, and the low railings guarding travelled high roads. No ship of men had ever come so near the place, or at least, had never come so near and departed again; but Carter and the ghouls were void of fear and kept inflexibly on, rounding the eastern face of the rock and seeking the wharves which the rescued trio described as being on the southern side within a harbour formed of steep headlands.

The headlands were prolongations of the island proper, and came so closely together that only one ship at a time might pass between them. There seemed to be no watchers on the outside, so the galley was steered boldly through the flume-like strait and into the stagnant foetid harbour beyond. Here, however, all was bustle and activity; with several ships lying at anchor along a forbidding stone quay, and scores of almost-human slaves and moonbeasts by the waterfront handling crates and boxes or driving nameless and fabulous horrors hitched to lumbering lorries. There was a small stone town hewn out of the vertical cliff above the wharves, with the start of a winding road that spiralled out of sight toward higher ledges of the rock. Of what lay inside that prodigious peak of granite none might say, but the things one saw on the outside were far from encouraging.

At sight of the incoming galley the crowds on the wharves displayed much eagerness; those with eyes staring intently, and those without eyes wriggling their pink tentacles expectantly. They did not, of course, realise that the black ship had changed hands; for ghouls look much like the horned and hooved almost-humans, and the night-gaunts were all out of sight below. By this time the leaders had fully formed a plan; which was to loose the night-gaunts as soon as the wharf was touched, and then to sail directly away, leaving matters wholly to the instincts of those almost mindless creatures. Marooned on the rock, the horned flyers would first of all seize whatever living things they found there, and afterward, quite helpless to think except in terms of the homing instinct, would forget their fear of water and fly swiftly back to the abyss; bearing their noisome prey to appropriate destinations in the dark, from which not much would emerge alive.

The ghoul that was Pickman now went below and gave the night-gaunts their simple instructions, while the ship drew very near to the ominous and malodorous wharves. Presently a fresh stir rose along the waterfront, and Carter saw that the motions of the galley had begun to excite suspicion. Evidently the steersman was not making for the right dock, and probably the watchers had noticed the difference between the hideous ghouls and the almost-human slaves whose places they were taking. Some silent alarm must have been given, for almost at once a horde of the mephitic moonbeasts began to pour from the little black doorways of the windowless houses and down the winding road at the right. A rain of curious javelins struck the galley as the prow hit the wharf, felling two ghouls and slightly wounding another; but at this point all the hatches were thrown open to emit a black cloud of whirring night-gaunts which swarmed over the town like a flock of horned and Cyclopean bats.

The jellyish moonbeasts had procured a great pole and were trying to push off the invading ship, but when the night-gaunts struck them they thought of such things no more. It was a very terrible spectacle to see those faceless and rubbery ticklers at their pastime, and tremendously impressive to watch the dense cloud of them spreading through the town and up the winding roadway to the reaches above. Sometimes a group of the black flutterers would drop a toad-like prisoner from aloft by mistake, and the manner in which the victim would burst was highly offensive to the sight and smell. When the last of the night-gaunts had left the galley the ghoulish leaders glibbered an order of withdrawal, and the rowers pulled quietly out of the harbour between the grey headlands while still the town was a chaos of battle and conquest.

The Pickman ghoul allowed several hours for the night-gaunts to make up their rudimentary minds and overcome their fear of flying over the sea, and kept the galley standing about a mile off the jagged rock while he waited and dressed the wounds of the injured. Night fell, and the grey twilight gave place to the sickly phosphorescence of low clouds, and all the while the leaders watched the high peaks of that accursed rock for signs of the night-gaunts' flight. Toward morning a black speck was seen hovering timidly over the topmost pinnacle, and shortly afterward the speck had become a swarm. Just before daybreak the swarm seemed to scatter, and within a quarter of an hour it had vanished wholly in the distance toward the northeast. Once or twice something seemed to fall from the thinning swarm into the sea; but Carter did not worry, since he knew from observation that the toad-like moonbeasts cannot swim. At length, when the ghouls were satisfied that all the night-gaunts had left for Sarkomand and the Great Abyss with their doomed burdens, the galley put back into the harbour betwixt the grey headlands; and all the hideous company landed and roamed curiously over that denuded rock with its towers and eyries and fortresses chiselled from the solid stone.

Frightful were the secrets uncovered in those evil and windowless crypts; for the remnants of unfinished pastimes were many, and in various stages of departure from their primal state. Carter put out of the way certain things which were after a fashion alive, and fled precipitately from a few other things about which he could not be very positive. The stench-filled houses were furnished mostly with grotesque stools and benches carven from moon-trees, and were painted inside with nameless and frantic designs. Countless weapons, implements, and ornaments lay about; including some large idols of solid ruby depicting singular beings not found on the earth. These latter did not, despite their material, invite either appropriation or long inspection; and Carter took the trouble to hammer five of them into very small pieces. The scattered spears and javelins he collected, and with Pickman's approval distributed among the ghouls. Such devices were new to the dog-like lopers, but their relative simplicity made them easy to master after a few concise hints.

The upper parts of the rock held more temples than private homes, and in numerous hewn chambers were found terrible carven altars and doubtfully stained fonts and shrines for the worship of things more monstrous than the mild gods atop Kadath. From the rear of one great temple stretched a low black passage which Carter followed far into the rock with a torch till he came to a lightless domed hall of vast porportions, whose vaultings were covered with daemoniac carvings and in whose centre yawned a foul and bottomless well like that in the hideous monastery of Leng where broods alone the high-priest not to be described. On the distant shadowy side, beyond the noisome well, he thought he discerned a small door of strangely wrought bronze; but for some reason he felt an unaccountable dread of opening it or even approaching it, and hastened back through the cavern to his unlovely allies as they shambled about with an ease and abandon he could scarcely feel. The ghouls had observed the unfinished pastimes of the moonbeasts, and had profited in their fashion. They had also found a hogshead of potent moon-wine, and were rolling it down to the wharves for removal and later use in diplomatic dealings, though the rescued trio, remembering its effect on them in Dylath-Leen, had warned their company to taste none of it. Of rubies from lunar mines there was a great store, both rough and polished, in one of the vaults near the water; but when the ghouls found they were not good to eat they lost all interest in them. Carter did not try to carry any away, since he knew too much about those which had mined them.

Suddenly there came an excited meeping from the sentries on the wharves, and all the loathsome foragers turned from their tasks to stare seaward and cluster round the waterfront. Betwixt the grey headlands a fresh black galley was rapidly advancing, and it could be but a moment before the almost-humans on deck would perceive the invasion of the town and give the alarm to the monstrous things below. Fortunately the ghouls still bore the spears and javelins which Carter had distributed amongst them; and at his command, sustained by the being that was Pickman, they now formed a line of battle and prepared to prevent the landing of the ship. Presently a burst of excitement on the galley told of the crew's discovery of the changed state of things, and the instant stoppage of the vessel proved that the superior numbers of the ghouls had been noted and taken into account. After a moment of hesitation the newcomers silently turned and passed out between the headlands again, but not for an instant did the ghouls imagine that the conflict was averted. Either the dark ship would seek reinforcements, or the crew would try to land elsewhere on the island; hence a party of scouts was at once sent up toward the pinnacle to see what the enemy's course would be.

In a very few minutes a ghoul returned breathless to say that the moonbeasts and almost-humans were landing on the outside of the more easterly of the rugged grey headlands, and ascending by hidden paths and ledges which a goat could scarcely tread in safety. Almost immediately afterward the galley was sighted again through the flume-like strait, but only for a second. Then, a few moments later, a second messenger panted down from aloft to say that another party was landing on the other headland; both being much more numerous than the size of the galley would seem to allow for. The ship itself, moving slowly with only one sparsely manned tier of oars, soon hove in sight betwixt the cliffs, and lay to in the foetid harbour as if to watch the coming fray and stand by for any possible use.

By this time Carter and Pickman had divided the ghouls into three parties, one to meet each of the two invading columns and one to remain in the town. The first two at once scrambled up the rocks in their respective directions, while the third was subdivided into a land party and a sea party. The sea party, commanded by Carter, boarded the anchored galley and rowed out to meet the undermanned galley of the newcomers; whereat the latter retreated through the strait to the open sea. Carter did not at once pursue it, for he knew he might be needed more acutely near the town.

Meanwhile the frightful detachments of the moonbeasts and almost-humans had lumbered up to the top of the headlands and were shockingly silhouetted on either side against the grey twilight sky. The thin hellish flutes of the invaders had now begun to whine, and the general effect of those hybrid, half-amorphous processions was as nauseating as the actual odour given off by the toad-like lunar blasphemies. Then the two parties of the ghouls swarmed into sight and joined the silhouetted panorama. Javelins began to fly from both sides, and the swelling meeps of the ghouls and the bestial howls of the almost-humans gradually joined the hellish whine of the flutes to form a frantick and indescribable chaos of daemon cacophony. Now and then bodies fell from the narrow ridges of the headlands into the sea outside or the harbour inside, in the latter case being sucked quickly under by certain submarine lurkers whose presence was indicated only by prodigious bubbles.

For half an hour this dual battle raged in the sky, till upon the west cliff the invaders were completely annihilated. On the east cliff, however, where the leader of the moonbeast party appeared to be present, the ghouls had not fared so well; and were slowly retreating to the slopes of the pinnacle proper. Pickman had quickly ordered reinforcements for this front from the party in the town, and these had helped greatly in the earlier stages of the combat. Then, when the western battle was over, the victorious survivors hastened across to the aid of their hard-pressed fellows; turning the tide and forcing the invaders back again along the narrow ridge of the headland. The almost-humans were by this time all slain, but the last of the toad-like horrors fought desperately with the great spears clutched in their powerful and disgusting paws. The time for javelins was now nearly past, and the fight became a hand-to-hand contest of what few spearmen could meet upon that narrow ridge.

As fury and recklessness increased, the number falling into the sea became very great. Those striking the harbour met nameless extinction from the unseen bubblers, but of those striking the open sea some were able to swim to the foot of the cliffs and land on tidal rocks, while the hovering galley of the enemy rescued several moonbeasts. The cliffs were unscalable except where the monsters had debarked, so that none of the ghouls on the rocks could rejoin their battle-line. Some were killed by javelins from the hostile galley or from the moonbeasts above, but a few survived to be rescued. When the security of the land parties seemed assured, Carter's galley sallied forth between the headlands and drove the hostile ship far out to sea; pausing to rescue such ghouls as were on the rocks or still swimming in the ocean. Several moonbeasts washed on rocks or reefs were speedily put out of the way.

Finally, the moonbeasts' galley being safely in the distance and the invading land army concentrated in one place, Carter landed a considerable force on the eastern headland in the enemy's rear; after which the fight was short-lived indeed. Attacked from both sides, the noisome flounderers were rapidly cut to pieces or pushed into the sea, till by evening the ghoulish chiefs agreed that the island was again clear of them. The hostile galley, meanwhile, had disappeared; and it was decided that the evil jagged rock had better be evacuated before any overwhelming horde of lunar horrors might be assembled and brought against the victors.

So by night Pickman and Carter assembled all the ghouls and counted them with care, finding that over a fourth had been lost in the day's battles. The wounded were placed on bunks in the galley, for Pickman always discouraged the old ghoulish custom of killing and eating one's own wounded, and the able-bodied troops were assigned to the oars or to such other places as they might most usefully fill. Under the low phosphorescent clouds of night the galley sailed, and Carter was not sorry to be departing from that island of unwholesome secrets, whose lightless domed hall with its bottomless well and repellent bronze door lingered restlessly in his fancy. Dawn found the ship in sight of Sarkomand's ruined quays of basalt, where a few night-gaunt sentries still waited, squatting like black horned gargoyles on the broken columns and crumbling sphinxes of that fearful city which lived and died before the years of man.

The ghouls made camp amongst the fallen stones of Sarkomand, despatching a messenger for enough night-gaunts to serve them as steeds. Pickman and the other chiefs were effusive in their gratitude for the aid Carter had lent them; and Carter now began to feel that his plans were indeed maturing well, and that he would be able to command the help of these fearsome allies not only in quitting this part of dreamland, but in pursuing his ultimate quest for the gods atop unknown Kadath, and the marvellous sunset city they so strangely withheld from his slumbers. Accordingly he spoke of these things to the ghoulish leaders; telling what he knew of the cold waste wherein Kadath stands and of the monstrous shantaks and the mountains carven into double-headed images which guard it. He spoke of the fear of shantaks for night-gaunts, and of how the vast hippocephalic birds fly screaming from the black burrows high up on the gaunt grey peaks that divide Inganok from hateful Leng. He spoke, too, of the things he had learnt concerning night-gaunts from the frescoes in the windowless monastery of the high-priest not to be described; how even the Great Ones fear them, and how their ruler is not the crawling chaos Nyarlathotep at all, but hoary and immemorial Nodens, Lord of the Great Abyss.

All these things Carter glibbered to the assembled ghouls, and presently outlined that request which he had in mind, and which he did not think extravagant considering the services he had so lately rendered the rubbery, dog-like lopers. He wished very much, he said, for the services of enough night-gaunts to bear him safely through the air past the realm of shantaks and carven mountains, and up into the cold waste beyond the returning tracks of any other mortal. He desired to fly to the onyx castle atop unknown Kadath in the cold waste to plead with the Great Ones for the sunset city they denied him, and felt sure that the night-gaunts could take him thither without trouble; high above the perils of the plain, and over the hideous double heads of those carven sentinel mountains that squat eternally in the grey dusk. For the horned and faceless creatures there could be no danger from aught of earth, since the Great Ones themselves dread them. And even were unexpected things to come from the Other Gods, who are prone to oversee the affairs of earth's milder gods, the night-gaunts need not fear; for the outer hells are indifferent matters to such silent and slippery flyers as own not Nyarlathotep for their master, but bow only to potent and archaic Nodens.

A flock of ten or fifteen night-gaunts, Carter glibbered, would surely be enough to keep any combination of shantaks at a distance; though perhaps it might be well to have some ghouls in the party to manage the creatures, their ways being better known to their ghoulish allies than to men. The party could land him at some convenient point within whatever walls that fabulous onyx citadel might have, waiting in the shadows for his return or his signal whilst he ventured inside the castle to give prayer to the gods of earth. If any ghouls chose to escort him into the throne-room of the Great Ones, he would be thankful, for their presence would add weight and importance to his plea. He would not, however, insist upon this but merely wished transportation to and from the castle atop unknown Kadath; the final journey being either to the marvellous sunset city itself, in case the gods proved favourable, or back to the earthward Gate of Deeper Slumber in the enchanted wood in case his prayers were fruitless.

Whilst Carter was speaking all the ghouls listened with great attention, and as the moments advanced the sky became black with clouds of those night-gaunts for which messengers had been sent. The winged horrors settled in a semicircle around the ghoulish army, waiting respectfully as the dog-like chieftains considered the wish of the earthly traveller. The ghoul that was Pickman glibbered gravely with its fellows, and in the end Carter was offered far more than he had at most expected. As he had aided the ghouls in their conquest of the moonbeasts, so would they aid him in his daring voyage to realms whence none had ever returned; lending him not merely a few of their allied night-gaunts, but their entire army as then encamped, veteran fighting ghouls and newly assembled night-gaunts alike, save only a small garrison for the captured black galley and such spoils as had come from the jagged rock in the sea. They would set out through the air whenever he might wish, and once arrived on Kadath a suitable train of ghouls would attend him in state as he placed his petition before earth's gods in their onyx castle.

Moved by a gratitude and satisfaction beyond words, Carter made plans with the ghoulish leaders for his audacious voyage. The army would fly high, they decided, over hideous Leng with its nameless monastery and wicked stone villages; stopping only at the vast grey peaks to confer with the shantak-frightening night-gaunts whose burrows honeycombed their summits. They would then, according to what advice they might receive from those denizens, choose their final course; approaching unknown Kadath either through the desert of carven mountains north of Inganok, or through the more northerly reaches of repulsive Leng itself. Dog-like and soulless as they are, the ghouls and night-gaunts had no dread of what those untrodden deserts might reveal; nor did they feel any deterring awe at the thought of Kadath towering lone with its onyx castle of mystery.

About midday the ghouls and night-gaunts prepared for flight, each ghoul selecting a suitable pair of horned steeds to bear him. Carter was placed well up toward the head of the column beside Pickman, and in front of the whole a double line of riderless night-gaunts was provided as a vanguard. At a brisk meep from Pickman the whole shocking army rose in a nightmare cloud above the broken columns and crumbling sphinxes of primordial Sarkomand; higher and higher, till even the great basalt cliff behind the town was cleared, and the cold, sterile table-land of Leng's outskirts laid open to sight. Still higher flew the black host, till even this table-land grew small beneath them; and as they worked northward over that windswept plateau of horror Carter saw once again with a shudder the circle of crude monoliths and the squat windowless building which he knew held that frightful silken-masked blasphemy from whose clutches he had so narrowly escaped. This time no descent was made as the army swept bat-like over the sterile landscape, passing the feeble fires of the unwholesome stone villages at a great altitude, and pausing not at all to mark the morbid twistings of the hooved, horned almost-humans that dance and pipe eternally therein. Once they saw a shantak-bird flying low over the plain, but when it saw them it screamed noxiously and flapped off to the north in grotesque panic.

At dusk they reached the jagged grey peaks that form the barrier of Inganok, and hovered about those strange caves near the summits which Carter recalled as so frightful to the shantaks. At the insistent meeping of the ghoulish leaders there issued forth from each lofty burrow a stream of horned black flyers; with which the ghouls and night-gaunts of the party conferred at length by means of ugly gestures. It soon became clear that the best course would be that over the cold waste north of Inganok, for Leng's northward reaches are full of unseen pitfalls that even the night-gaunts dislike; abysmal influences centreing in certain white hemispherical buildings on curious knolls, which common folklore associates unpleasantly with the Other Gods and their crawling chaos Nyarlathotep.

Of Kadath the flutterers of the peaks knew almost nothing, save that there must be some mighty marvel toward the north, over which the shantaks and the carven mountains stand guard. They hinted at rumoured abnormalities of proportion in those trackless leagues beyond, and recalled vague whispers of a realm where night broods eternally; but of definite data they had nothing to give. So Carter and his party thanked them kindly; and, crossing the topmost granite pinnacles to the skies of Inganok, dropped below the level of the phosphorescent night clouds and beheld in the distance those terrible squatting gargoyles that were mountains till some titan hand carved fright into their virgin rock.

There they squatted, in a hellish half-circle, their legs on the desert sand and their mitres piercing the luminous clouds; sinister, wolf-like, and double-headed, with faces of fury and right hands raised, dully and malignly watching the rim of man's world and guarding with horror the reaches of a cold northern world that is not man's. From their hideous laps rose evil shantaks of elephantine bulk, but these all fled with insane titters as the vanguard of night-gaunts was sighted in the misty sky. Northward above those gargoyle mountains the army flew, and over leagues of dim desert where never a landmark rose. Less and less luminous grew the clouds, till at length Carter could see only blackness around him; but never did the winged steeds falter, bred as they were in earth's blackest crypts, and seeing not with any eyes, but with the whole dank surface of their slippery forms. On and on they flew, past winds of dubious scent and sounds of dubious import; ever in thickest darkness, and covering such prodigious spaces that Carter wondered whether or not they could still be within earth's dreamland.

Then suddenly the clouds thinned and the stars shone spectrally above. All below was still black, but those pallid beacons in the sky seemed alive with a meaning and directiveness they had never possessed elsewhere. It was not that the figures of the constellations were different, but that the same familiar shapes now revealed a significance they had formerly failed to make plain. Everything focussed toward the north; every curve and asterism of the glittering sky became part of a vast design whose function was to hurry first the eye and then the whole observer onward to some secret and terrible goal of convergence beyond the frozen waste that stretched endlessly ahead. Carter looked toward the east where the great ridge of barrier peaks had towered along all the length of Inganok, and saw against the stars a jagged silhouette which told of its continued presence. It was more broken now, with yawning clefts and fantastically erratic pinnacles; and Carter studied closely the suggestive turns and inclinations of that grotesque outline, which seemed to share with the stars some subtle northward urge.

They were flying past at a tremendous speed, so that the watcher had to strain hard to catch details; when all at once he beheld just above the line of the topmost peaks a dark and moving object against the stars, whose course exactly paralleled that of his own bizarre party. The ghouls had likewise glimpsed it, for he heard their low glibbering all about him, and for a moment he fancied the object was a gigantic shantak, of a size vastly greater than that of the average specimen. Soon, however, he saw that this theory would not hold; for the shape of the thing above the mountains was not that of any hippocephalic bird. Its outline against the stars, necessarily vague as it was, resembled rather some huge mitred head or pair of heads infinitely magnified; and its rapid bobbing flight through the sky seemed most peculiarly a wingless one. Carter could not tell which side of the mountains it was on, but soon perceived that it had parts below the parts he had first seen, since it blotted out all the stars in places where the ridge was deeply cleft.

Then came a wide gap in the range, where the hideous reaches of transmontane Leng were joined to the cold waste on this side by a low pass through which the stars shone wanly. Carter watched this gap with intense care, knowing that he might see outlined against the sky beyond it the lower parts of the vast thing that flew undulantly above the pinnacles. The object had now floated ahead a trifle, and every eye of the party was fixed on the rift where it would presently appear in full-length silhouette. Gradually the huge thing above the peaks neared the gap, slightly slackening its speed as if conscious of having outdistanced the ghoulish army. For another minute suspense was keen, and then the brief instant of full silhouette and revelation came; bringing to the lips of the ghouls an awed and half-choked meep of cosmic fear, and to the soul of the traveller a chill that has never wholly left it. For the mammoth bobbing shape that overtopped the ridge was only a head—a mitred double head—and below it in terrible vastness loped the frightful swollen body that bore it; the mountain-high monstrosity that walked in stealth and silence; the hyaena-like distortion of a giant anthropoid shape that trotted blackly against the sky, its repulsive pair of cone-capped heads reaching half way to the zenith.

Carter did not lose consciousness or even scream aloud, for he was an old dreamer; but he looked behind him in horror and shuddered when he saw that there were other monstrous heads silhouetted above the level of the peaks, bobbing along stealthily after the first one. And straight in the rear were three of the mighty mountain shapes seen full against the southern stars, tiptoeing wolf-like and lumberingly, their tall mitres nodding thousands of feet in the air. The carven mountains, then, had not stayed squatting in that rigid semicircle north of Inganok with right hands uplifted. They had duties to perform, and were not remiss. But it was horrible that they never spoke, and never even made a sound in walking.

Meanwhile the ghoul that was Pickman had glibbered an order to the night-gaunts, and the whole army soared higher into the air. Up toward the stars the grotesque column shot, till nothing stood out any longer against the sky; neither the grey granite ridge that was still nor the carven and mitred mountains that walked. All was blackness beneath as the fluttering legions surged northward amidst rushing winds and invisible laughter in the aether, and never a shantak or less mentionable entity rose from the haunted wastes to pursue them. The farther they went, the faster they flew, till soon their dizzying speed seemed to pass that of a rifle ball and approach that of a planet in its orbit. Carter wondered how with such speed the earth could still stretch beneath them, but knew that in the land of dream dimensions have strange properties. That they were in a realm of eternal night he felt certain, and he fancied that the constellations overhead had subtly emphasised their northward focus; gathering themselves up as it were to cast the flying army into the void of the boreal pole, as the folds of a bag are gathered up to cast out the last bits of substance therein.

Then he noticed with terror that the wings of the night-gaunts were not flapping any more. The horned and faceless steeds had folded their membraneous appendages, and were resting quite passive in the chaos of wind that whirled and chuckled as it bore them on. A force not of earth had seized on the army, and ghouls and night-gaunts alike were powerless before a current which pulled madly and relentlessly into the north whence no mortal had ever returned. At length a lone pallid light was seen on the skyline ahead, thereafter rising steadily as they approached, and having beneath it a black mass that blotted out the stars. Carter saw that it must be some beacon on a mountain, for only a mountain could rise so vast as seen from so prodigious a height in the air.

Higher and higher rose the light and the blackness beneath it, till half the northern sky was obscured by the rugged conical mass. Lofty as the army was, that pale and sinister beacon rose above it, towering monstrous over all peaks and concernments of earth, and tasting the atomless aether where the cryptical moon and the mad planets reel. No mountain known of man was that which loomed before them. The high clouds far below were but a fringe for its foothills. The gasping dizziness of topmost air was but a girdle for its loins. Scornful and spectral climbed that bridge betwixt earth and heaven, black in eternal night, and crowned with a pshent of unknown stars whose awful and significant outline grew every moment clearer. Ghouls meeped in wonder as they saw it, and Carter shivered in fear lest all the hurtling army be dashed to pieces on the unyielding onyx of that Cyclopean cliff.

Higher and higher rose the light, till it mingled with the loftiest orbs of the zenith and winked down at the flyers with lurid mockery. All the north beneath it was blackness now; dread, stony blackness from infinite depths to infinite heights, with only that pale winking beacon perched unreachably at the top of all vision. Carter studied the light more closely, and saw at last what lines its inky background made against the stars. There were towers on that titan mountaintop; horrible domed towers in noxious and incalculable tiers and clusters beyond any dreamable workmanship of man; battlements and terraces of wonder and menace, all limned tiny and black and distant against the starry pshent that glowed malevolently at the uppermost rim of sight. Capping that most measureless of mountains was a castle beyond all mortal thought, and in it glowed the daemon-light. Then Randolph Carter knew that his quest was done, and that he saw above him the goal of all forbidden steps and audacious visions; the fabulous, the incredible home of the Great Ones atop unknown Kadath.

Even as he realised this thing, Carter noticed a change in the course of the helplessly wind-sucked party. They were rising abruptly now, and it was plain that the focus of their flight was the onyx castle where the pale light shone. So close was the great black mountain that its sides sped by them dizzily as they shot upward, and in the darkness they could discern nothing upon it. Vaster and vaster loomed the tenebrous towers of the nighted castle above, and Carter could see that it was well-nigh blasphemous in its immensity. Well might its stones have been quarried by nameless workmen in that horrible gulf rent out of the rock in the hill pass north of Inganok, for such was its size that a man on its threshold stood even as an ant on the steps of earth's loftiest fortress. The pshent of unknown stars above the myriad domed turrets glowed with a sallow, sickly flare, so that a kind of twilight hung about the murky walls of slippery onyx. The pallid beacon was now seen to be a single shining window high up in one of the loftiest towers, and as the helpless army neared the top of the mountain Carter thought he detected unpleasant shadows flitting across the feebly luminous expanse. It was a strangely arched window, of a design wholly alien to earth.

The solid rock now gave place to the giant foundations of the monstrous castle, and it seemed that the speed of the party was somewhat abated. Vast walls shot up, and there was a glimpse of a great gate through which the voyagers were swept. All was night in the titan courtyard, and then came the deeper blackness of inmost things as a huge arched portal engulfed the column. Vortices of cold wind surged dankly through sightless labyrinths of onyx, and Carter could never tell what Cyclopean stairs and corridors lay silent along the route of his endless aërial twisting. Always upward led the terrible plunge in darkness, and never a sound, touch, or glimpse broke the dense pall of mystery. Large as the army of ghouls and night-gaunts was, it was lost in the prodigious voids of that more than earthly castle. And when at last there suddenly dawned around him the lurid light of that single tower room whose lofty window had served as a beacon, it took Carter long to discern the far walls and high, distant ceiling, and to realise that he was indeed not again in the boundless air outside.

Randolph Carter had hoped to come into the throne-room of the Great Ones with poise and dignity, flanked and followed by impressive lines of ghouls in ceremonial order, and offering his prayer as a free and potent master among dreamers. He had known that the Great Ones themselves are not beyond a mortal's power to cope with, and had trusted to luck that the Other Gods and their crawling chaos Nyarlathotep would not happen to come to their aid at the crucial moment, as they had so often done before when men sought out earth's gods in their home or on their mountains. And with his hideous escort he had half hoped to defy even the Other Gods if need were, knowing as he did that ghouls have no masters, and that night-gaunts own not Nyarlathotep but only archaick Nodens for their lord. But now he saw that supernal Kadath in its cold waste is indeed girt with dark wonders and nameless sentinels, and that the Other Gods are of a surety vigilant in guarding the mild, feeble gods of earth. Void as they are of lordship over ghouls and night-gaunts, the mindless, shapeless blasphemies of outer space can yet control them when they must; so that it was not in state as a free and potent master of dreamers that Randolph Carter came into the Great Ones' throne-room with his ghouls. Swept and herded by nightmare tempests from the stars, and dogged by unseen horrors of the northern waste, all that army floated captive and helpless in the lurid light, dropping numbly to the onyx floor when by some voiceless order the winds of fright dissolved.

Before no golden dais had Randolph Carter come, nor was there any august circle of crowned and haloed beings with narrow eyes, long-lobed ears, thin nose, and pointed chin whose kinship to the carven face on Ngranek might stamp them as those to whom a dreamer might pray. Save for that one tower room the onyx castle atop Kadath was dark, and the masters were not there. Carter had come to unknown Kadath in the cold waste, but he had not found the gods. Yet still the lurid light glowed in that one tower room whose size was so little less than that of all outdoors, and whose distant walls and roof were so nearly lost to sight in thin, curling mists. Earth's gods were not there, it was true, but of subtler and less visible presences there could be no lack. Where the mild gods are absent, the Other Gods are not unrepresented; and certainly, the onyx castle of castles was far from tenantless. In what outrageous form or forms terror would next reveal itself, Carter could by no means imagine. He felt that his visit had been expected, and wondered how close a watch had all along been kept upon him by the crawling chaos Nyarlathotep. It is Nyarlathotep, horror of infinite shapes and dread soul and messenger of the Other Gods, that the fungous moonbeasts serve; and Carter thought of the black galley that had vanished when the tide of battle turned against the toad-like abnormalities on the jagged rock in the sea.

Reflecting upon these things, he was staggering to his feet in the midst of his nightmare company when there rang without warning through that pale-litten and limitless chamber the hideous blast of a daemon trumpet. Three times pealed that frightful brazen scream, and when the echoes of the third blast had died chucklingly away Randolph Carter saw that he was alone. Whither, why, and how the ghouls and night-gaunts had been snatched from sight was not for him to divine. He knew only that he was suddenly alone, and that whatever unseen powers lurked mockingly around him were no powers of earth's friendly dreamland. Presently from the chamber's uttermost reaches a new sound came. This, too, was a rhythmic trumpeting; but of a kind far removed from the three raucous blasts which had dissolved his grisly cohorts. In this low fanfare echoed all the wonder and melody of ethereal dream; exotic vistas of unimagined loveliness floating from each strange chord and subtly alien cadence. Odours of incense came to match the golden notes; and overhead a great light dawned, its colours changing in cycles unknown to earth's spectrum, and following the song of the trumpets in weird symphonic harmonies. Torches flared in the distance, and the beat of drums throbbed nearer amidst waves of tense expectancy.

Out of the thinning mists and the cloud of strange incense filed twin columns of giant black slaves with loin-cloths of iridescent silk. Upon their heads were strapped vast helmet-like torches of glittering metal, from which the fragrance of obscure balsams spread in fumous spirals. In their right hands were crystal wands whose tips were carven into leering chimaeras, while their left hands grasped long, thin silver trumpets which they blew in turn. Armlets and anklets of gold they had, and between each pair of anklets stretched a golden chain that held its wearer to a sober gait. That they were true black men of earth's dreamland was at once apparent, but it seemed less likely that their rites and postures were wholly things of our earth. Ten feet from Carter the columns stopped, and as they did so each trumpet flew abruptly to its bearer's thick lips. Wild and ecstatic was the blast that followed, and wilder still the cry that chorused just after from dark throats somehow made shrill by strange artifice.

Then down the wide lane betwixt the two columns a lone figure strode; a tall, slim figure with the young face of an antique Pharaoh, gay with prismatic robes and crowned with a golden pshent that glowed with inherent light. Close up to Carter strode that regal figure; whose proud carriage and swart features had in them the fascination of a dark god or fallen archangel, and around whose eyes there lurked the languid sparkle of caprious humour. It spoke, and in its mellow tones there rippled the mild music of Lethean streams.

"Randolph Carter," said the voice, "you have come to see the Great Ones whom it is unlawful for men to see. Watchers have spoken of this thing, and the Other Gods have grunted as they rolled and tumbled mindlessly to the sound of thin flutes in the black ultimate void where broods the daemon-sultan whose name no lips dare speak aloud.

"When Barzai the Wise climbed Hatheg-Kla to see the Great Ones dance and howl above the clouds in the moonlight he never returned. The Other Gods were there, and they did what was expected. Zenig of Aphorat sought to reach unknown Kadath in the cold waste, and his skull is now set in a ring on the little finger of one whom I need not name.

"But you, Randolph Carter, have braved all things of earth's dreamland, and burn still with the flame of quest. You came not as one curious, but as one seeking his due, nor have you failed ever in reverence toward the mild gods of earth. Yet have these gods kept you from the marvellous sunset city of your dreams, and wholly through their own small covetousness; for verily, they craved the weird loveliness of that which your fancy had fashioned, and vowed that henceforward no other spot should be their abode.

"They are gone from their castle on unknown Kadath to dwell in your marvellous city. All through its palaces of veined marble they revel by day, and when the sun sets they go out in the perfumed gardens and watch the golden glory on temples and colonnades, arched bridges and silver-basined fountains, and wide streets with blossom-laden urns and ivory statues in gleaming rows. And when night comes they climb tall terraces in the dew, and sit on carved benches of porphyry scanning the stars, or lean over pale balustrades to gaze at the town's steep northward slopes, where one by one the little windows in old peaked gables shine softly out with the calm yellow light of homely candles.

"The gods love your marvellous city, and walk no more in the ways of the gods. They have forgotten the high places of earth, and the mountains that knew their youth. The earth has no longer any gods that are gods, and only the Other Ones from outer space hold sway on unremembered Kadath. Far away in a valley of your own childhood, Randolph Carter, play the heedless Great Ones. You have dreamed too well, O wise arch-dreamer, for you have drawn dream's gods away from the world of all men's visions to that which is wholly yours; having builded out of your boyhood's small fancies a city more lovely than all the phantoms that have gone before.

"It is not well that earth's gods leave their thrones for the spider to spin on, and their realm for the Others to sway in the dark manner of Others. Fain would the powers from outside bring chaos and horror to you, Randolph Carter, who are the cause of their upsetting, but that they know it is by you alone that the gods may be sent back to their world. In that half-waking dreamland which is yours, no power of uttermost night may pursue; and only you can send the selfish Great Ones gently out of your marvellous sunset city, back through the northern twilight to their wonted place atop unknown Kadath in the cold waste.

"So, Randolph Carter, in the name of the Other Gods I spare you and charge you to serve my will. I charge you to seek that sunset city which is yours, and to send thence the drowsy truant gods for whom the dream-world waits. Not hard to find is that roseal fever of the gods, that fanfare of supernal trumpets and clash of immortal cymbals, that mystery whose place and meaning have haunted you through the halls of waking and the gulfs of dreaming, and tormented you with hints of vanished memory and the pain of lost things awesome and momentous. Not hard to find is that symbol and relic of your days of wonder, for truly, it is but the stable and eternal gem wherein all that wonder sparkles crystallised to light your evening path. Behold! It is not over unknown seas but back over well-known years that your quest must go; back to the bright strange things of infancy and the quick sun-drenched glimpses of magic that old scenes brought to wide young eyes.

"For know you, that your gold and marble city of wonder is only the sum of what you have seen and loved in youth. It is the glory of Boston's hillside roofs and western windows aflame with sunset; of the flower-fragrant Common and the great dome on the hill and the tangle of gables and chimneys in the violet valley where the many-bridged Charles flows drowsily. These things you saw, Randolph Carter, when your nurse first wheeled you out in the springtime, and they will be the last things you will ever see with eyes of memory and of love. And there is antique Salem with its brooding years, and spectral Marblehead scaling its rocky precipices into past centuries, and the glory of Salem's towers and spires seen afar from Marblehead's pastures across the harbour against the setting sun.

"There is Providence, quaint and lordly on its seven hills over the blue harbour, with terraces of green leading up to steeples and citadels of living antiquity, and Newport climbing wraith-like from its dreaming breakwater. Arkham is there, with its moss-grown gambrel roofs and the rocky rolling meadows behind it; and antediluvian Kingsport hoary with stacked chimneys and deserted quays and overhanging gables, and the marvel of high cliffs and the milky-misted ocean with tolling buoys beyond.

"Cool vales in Concord, cobbled lanes in Portsmouth, twilight bends of rustic New-Hampshire roads where giant elms half hide white farmhouse walls and creaking well-sweeps. Gloucester's salt wharves and Truro's windy willows. Vistas of distant steepled towns and hills beyond hills along the North Shore, hushed stony slopes and low ivied cottages in the lee of huge boulders in Rhode-Island's back country. Scent of the sea and fragrance of the fields; spell of the dark woods and joy of the orchards and gardens at dawn. These, Randolph Carter, are your city; for they are yourself. New-England bore you, and into your soul she poured a liquid loveliness which cannot die. This loveliness, moulded, crystallised, and polished by years of memory and dreaming, is your terraced wonder of elusive sunsets; and to find that marble parapet with curious urns and carven rail, and descend at last those endless balustraded steps to the city of broad squares and prismatic fountains, you need only to turn back to the thoughts and visions of your wistful boyhood.

"Look! through that window shine the stars of eternal night. Even now they are shining above the scenes you have known and cherished, drinking of their charm that they may shine more lovely over the gardens of dream. There is Antares—he is winking at this moment over the roofs of Tremont Street, and you could see him from your window on Beacon Hill. Out beyond those stars yawn the gulfs from whence my mindless masters have sent me. Some day you too may traverse them, but if you are wise you will beware such folly; for of those mortals who have been and returned, only one preserves a mind unshattered by the pounding, clawing horrors of the void. Terrors and blasphemies gnaw at one another for space, and there is more evil in the lesser ones than in the greater; even as you know from the deeds of those who sought to deliver you into my hands, whilst I myself harboured no wish to shatter you, and would indeed have helped you hither long ago had I not been elsewhere busy, and certain that you would yourself find the way. Shun, then, the outer hells, and stick to the calm, lovely things of your youth. Seek out your marvellous city and drive thence the recreant Great Ones, sending them back gently to those scenes which are of their own youth, and which wait uneasy for their return.

"Easier even than the way of dim memory is the way I will prepare for you. See! There comes hither a monstrous shantak, led by a slave who for your peace of mind had best keep invisible. Mount and be ready—there! Yogash the black will help you on the scaly horror. Steer for that brightest star just south of the zenith—it is Vega, and in two hours will be just above the terrace of your sunset city. Steer for it only till you hear a far-off singing in the high aether. Higher than that lurks madness, so rein your shantak when the first note lures. Look then back to earth, and you will see shining the deathless altar-flame of Ired-Naa from the sacred roof of a temple. That temple is in your desiderate sunset city, so steer for it before you heed the singing and are lost.

"When you draw nigh the city steer for the same high parapet whence of old you scanned the outspread glory, prodding the shantak till he cry aloud. That cry the Great Ones will hear and know as they sit on their perfumed terraces, and there will come upon them such a homesickness that all of your city's wonders will not console them for the absence of Kadath's grim castle and the pshent of eternal stars that crowns it.

"Then must you land amongst them with the shantak, and let them see and touch that noisome and hippocephalic bird; meanwhile discoursing to them of unknown Kadath, which you will so lately have left, and telling them how its boundless halls are lonely and unlighted, where of old they used to leap and revel in supernal radiance. And the shantak will talk to them in the manner of shantaks, but it will have no powers of persuasion beyond the recalling of elder days.

"Over and over must you speak to the wandering Great Ones of their home and youth, till at last they will weep and ask to be shewn the returning path they have forgotten. Thereat can you loose the waiting shantak, sending him skyward with the homing cry of his kind; hearing which the Great Ones will prance and jump with antique mirth, and forthwith stride after the loathly bird in the fashion of gods, through the deep gulfs of heaven to Kadath's familiar towers and domes.

"Then will the marvellous sunset city be yours to cherish and inhabit for ever, and once more will earth's gods rule the dreams of men from their accustomed seat. Go now—the casement is open and the stars await outside. Already your shantak wheezes and titters with impatience. Steer for Vega through the night, but turn when the singing sounds. Forget not this warning, lest horrors unthinkable suck you into the gulf of shrieking and ululant madness. Remember the Other Gods; they are great and mindless and terrible, and lurk in the outer voids. They are good gods to shun.

"*Hei! Aa-shanta 'nygh!* You are off! Send back earth's gods to their haunts on unknown Kadath, and pray to all space that you may never meet me in my thousand other forms. Farewell, Randolph Carter, and beware; *for I am Nyarlathotep, the Crawling Chaos!*"

And Randolph Carter, gasping and dizzy on his hideous shantak, shot screamingly into space toward the cold blue glare of boreal Vega; looking but once behind him at the clustered and chaotic turrets of the onyx nightmare wherein still glowed the lone lurid light of that window above the air and the clouds of earth's dreamland. Great polypous horrors slid darkly past, and unseen bat-wings beat multitudinous around him, but still he clung to the unwholesome mane of that loathly and hippocephalic scaled bird. The stars danced mockingly, almost shifting now and then to form pale signs of doom that one might wonder one had not seen and feared before; and ever the winds of aether howled of vague blackness and loneliness beyond the cosmos.

Then through the glittering vault ahead there fell a hush of portent, and all the winds and horrors slunk away as night things slink away before the dawn. Trembling in waves that golden wisps of nebula made weirdly visible, there rose a timid hint of far-off melody, droning in faint chords that our own universe of stars knows not. And as that music grew, the shantak raised its ears and plunged ahead, and Carter likewise bent to catch each lovely strain. It was a song, but not the song of any voice. Night and the spheres sang it, and it was old when space and Nyarlathotep and the Other Gods were born.

Faster flew the shantak, and lower bent the rider, drunk with the marvel of strange gulfs, and whirling in the crystal coils of outer magic. Then came too late the warning of the evil one, the sardonic caution of the daemon legate who had bidden the seeker beware the madness of that song. Only to taunt had Nyarlathotep marked out the way to safety and the marvellous sunset city; only to mock had that black messenger revealed the secret of those truant gods whose steps he could so easily lead back at will. For madness and the void's wild vengeance are Nyarlathotep's only gifts to the presumptuous; and frantick though the rider strove to turn his disgusting steed, that leering, tittering shantak coursed on impetuous and relentless, flapping its great slippery wings in malignant joy, and headed for those unhallowed pits whither no dreams reach; that last amorphous blight of nethermost confusion where bubbles and blasphemes at infinity's centre the mindless daemon-sultan Azathoth, whose name no lips dare speak aloud.

Unswerving and obedient to the foul legate's orders, that hellish bird plunged onward through shoals of shapeless lurkers and caperers in darkness, and vacuous herds of drifting entities that pawed and groped and groped and pawed; the nameless larvae of the Other Gods, that are like them blind and without mind, and possessed of singular hungers and thirsts.

Onward unswerving and relentless, and tittering hilariously to watch the chuckling and hysterics into which the siren song of night and the spheres had turned, that eldritch scaly monster bore its helpless rider; hurtling and shooting, cleaving the uttermost rim and spanning the outermost abysses; leaving behind the stars and the realms of matter, and darting meteor-like through stark formlessness toward those inconceivable, unlighted chambers beyond Time wherein black Azathoth gnaws shapeless and ravenous amidst the muffled, maddening beat of vile drums and the thin, monotonous whine of accursed flutes.

Onward—onward—through the screaming, cackling, and blackly populous gulfs—and then from some dim blessed distance there came an image and a thought to Randolph Carter the doomed. Too well had Nyarlathotep planned his mocking and his tantalising, for he had brought up that which no gusts of icy terror could quite efface. Home—New England—Beacon Hill—the waking world.

"For know you, that your gold and marble city of wonder is only the sum of what you have seen and loved in youth ... the glory of Boston's hillside roofs and western windows aflame with sunset; of the flower-fragrant Common and the great dome on the hill and the tangle of gables and chimneys in the violet valley where the many-bridged Charles flows drowsily ... this loveliness, moulded, crystallised, and polished by years of memory and dreaming, is your terraced wonder of elusive sunsets; and to find that marble parapet with curious urns and carven rail, and descend at last those endless balustraded steps to the city of broad squares and prismatic fountains, you need only to turn back to the thoughts and visions of your wistful boyhood."

Onward—onward—dizzily onward to ultimate doom through the blackness where sightless feelers pawed and slimy snouts jostled and nameless things tittered and tittered and tittered.

But the image and the thought had come, and Randolph Carter knew clearly that he was dreaming and only dreaming, and that somewhere in the background the world of waking and the city of his infancy still lay. Words came again—"You need only turn back to the thoughts and visions of your wistful boyhood." Turn—turn—blackness on every side, but Randolph Carter could turn.

Thick though the rushing nightmare that clutched his senses, Randolph Carter could turn and move. He could move, and if he chose he could leap off the evil shantak that bore him hurtlingly doomward at the orders of Nyarlathotep. He could leap off and dare those depths of night that yawned interminably down, those depths of fear whose terrors yet could not exceed the nameless doom that lurked waiting at chaos' core. He could turn and move and leap—he could—he would—he would—

Off that vast hippocephalic abomination leaped the doomed and desperate dreamer, and down through endless voids of sentient blackness he fell. Aeons reeled, universes died and were born again, stars became nebulae and nebulae became stars, and still Randolph Carter fell through those endless voids of sentient blackness.

Then in the slow creeping course of eternity the utmost cycle of the cosmos churned itself to another futile completion, and all things became again as they were unreckoned kalpas before. Matter and light were born anew as space once had known them; and comets, suns, and worlds sprang flaming into life, though nothing survived to tell that they had been and gone, been and gone, always and always, back to no first beginning.

And there was a firmament again, and a wind, and a glare of purple light in the eyes of a falling dreamer. There were gods and presences and wills; beauty and evil, and the shrieking of noxious night robbed of its prey. For through the unknown ultimate cycle had lived a thought and a vision of a dreamer's boyhood, and now there were re-made a waking world and an old cherished city to body and to justify these things. Out of the void S'ngac the violet gas had pointed the way, and archaic Nodens was bellowing his guidance from unhinted deeps.

Stars swelled to dawns, and dawns burst into fountains of gold, carmine, and purple, and still the dreamer fell. Cries rent the aether as ribbons of light beat back the fiends from outside. And hoary Nodens raised a howl of triumph when Nyarlathotep, close on his quarry, stopped baffled by a glare that seared his formless hunting-horrors to grey dust. Randolph Carter had indeed descended at last the wide marmoreal flights to his marvellous city, for he was come again to the fair New England world that had wrought him.

So to the organ chords of morning's myriad whistles, and dawn's blaze thrown dazzling through purple panes by the great gold dome of the State House on the hill, Randolph Carter leaped shoutingly awake within his Boston room. Birds sang in hidden gardens and the perfume of trellised vines came wistful from arbours his grandfather had reared. Beauty and light glowed from classic mantel and carven cornice and walls grotesquely figured, while a sleek black cat rose yawning from hearthside sleep that his master's start and shriek had disturbed. And vast infinities away, past the Gate of Deeper Slumber and the enchanted wood and the garden lands and the Cerenarian Sea and the twilight reaches of Inganok, the crawling chaos Nyarlathotep strode brooding into the onyx castle atop unknown Kadath in the cold waste, and taunted insolently the mild gods of earth whom he had snatched abruptly from their scented revels in the marvellous sunset city.

weldon**owen**

an imprint of Insight Editions
P.O. Box 3088
San Rafael, CA 94912
www.weldonowen.com

CEO *Raoul Goff*
VP Group Publisher *Jeff McLaughlin*
VP Publisher *Roger Shaw*
Publishing Director *Katie Killebrew*
Executive Editor *Jamie Thompson*
Managing Editor *Mary Beth Garhart*
Editorial Assistant *Jon Ellis*
VP Creative *Chrissy Kwasnik*
VP Manufacturing *Alix Nicholaeff*
Production Manager *Tiffani Patterson*

This edition published by Weldon Owen by arrangement with
The Book Shop, Ltd. and the H. P. Lovecraft Historical Society

Designed by Jon Pannier
Edited by Diane Namm

ISBN: 979-8-88674-233-6

This book is part of The H. P. Lovecraft Experience kit
and is not to be sold separately.

Manufactured in China by Insight Editions

10 9 8 7 6 5 4 3 2 1

ROOTS of PEACE REPLANTED PAPER

Insight Editions, in association with Roots of Peace, will plant two trees
for each tree used in the manufacturing of this book. Roots of Peace
is an internationally renowned humanitarian organization dedicated to
eradicating land mines worldwide and converting war-torn lands
into productive farms and wildlife habitats. Roots of Peace will plant
two million fruit and nut trees in Afghanistan and provide farmers there
with the skills and support necessary for sustainable land use.

THE COLLECTED FICTION OF
H. P. LOVECRAFT

Volume II

Howard P. Lovecraft collection, John Hay Library, Brown University

THE COLLECTED FICTION OF
H. P. LOVECRAFT

Volume II

weldonowen

CONTENTS

*The stories indicated are analyzed in detail in the companion *A Reader's Guide to Selected Works by H. P. Lovecraft.*

THE CASE OF CHARLES DEXTER WARD

"The essential Saltes of Animals may be so prepared and preserved, that an ingenious Man may have the whole Ark of Noah in his owne Studie, and raise the fine Shape of an Animal out of its Ashes at his Pleasure; and by the lyke Method from the essential Saltes of humane Dust, a Philosopher may, without any criminal Necromancy, call up the Shape of any dead Ancestour from the Dust whereinto his Bodie has been incinerated."

BORELLUS

I. *A Result and a Prologue*

1.

From a private hospital for the insane near Providence, Rhode Island, there recently disappeared an exceedingly singular person. He bore the name of Charles Dexter Ward, and was placed under restraint most reluctantly by the grieving father who had watched his aberration grow from a mere eccentricity to a dark mania involving both a possibility of murderous tendencies and a profound and peculiar change in the apparent contents of his mind. Doctors confess themselves quite baffled by his case, since it presented oddities of a general physiological as well as psychological character.

In the first place, the patient seemed oddly older than his twenty-six years would warrant. Mental disturbance, it is true, will age one rapidly; but the face of this young man had taken on a subtle cast which only the very aged usually acquire. In the second place, his organic processes shewed a certain queerness of proportion which nothing in medical experience can parallel. Respiration and heart action had a baffling lack of symmetry; the voice was lost, so that no sounds above a whisper were possible; digestion was incredibly prolonged and minimised, and neural reactions to standard stimuli bore no relation at all to anything heretofore recorded, either normal or pathological. The skin had a morbid chill and dryness, and the cellular structure of the tissue seemed exaggeratedly coarse and loosely knit. Even a large olive birthmark on the right hip had disappeared, whilst there had formed on the chest a very peculiar mole or blackish spot of which no trace existed before. In general, all physicians agree that in Ward the processes of metabolism had become retarded to a degree beyond precedent.

Psychologically, too, Charles Ward was unique. His madness held no affinity to any sort recorded in even the latest and most exhaustive of treatises, and was conjoined to a mental force which would have made him a genius or a leader had it not been twisted into strange and grotesque forms. Dr. Willett, who was Ward's family physician, affirms that the patient's gross mental capacity, as gauged by his response to matters outside the sphere of his insanity, had actually increased since the seizure. Ward, it is true, was always a scholar and an antiquarian; but even his most brilliant early work did not shew the prodigious grasp and insight displayed during his last examinations by the alienists. It was, indeed, a difficult matter to obtain a legal commitment to the hospital, so powerful and lucid did the youth's mind seem; and only on the evidence of others, and on the strength of many abnormal gaps in his stock of information as distinguished from his intelligence, was he finally placed in confinement. To the very moment of his vanishment he was an omnivorous reader and as great a conversationist as his poor voice permitted; and shrewd observers, failing to foresee his escape, freely predicted that he would not be long in gaining his discharge from custody.

Only Dr. Willett, who brought Charles Ward into the world and had watched his growth of body and mind ever since, seemed frightened at the thought of his future freedom. He had had a terrible experience and had made a terrible discovery which he dared not reveal to his sceptical colleagues. Willett, indeed, presents a minor mystery all his own in his connexion with the case. He was the last to see the patient before his flight, and emerged from that final conversation in a state of mixed horror and relief which several recalled when Ward's escape became known three hours later. That escape itself is one of the unsolved wonders of Dr. Waite's hospital. A window open above a sheer drop of sixty feet could hardly explain it, yet after that talk with Willett the youth was undeniably gone. Willett himself has no public explanations to offer, though he seems strangely easier in mind than before the escape. Many, indeed, feel that he would like to say more if he thought any considerable number would believe him. He had found Ward in his room, but shortly after his departure the attendants knocked in vain. When they opened the door the patient was not there, and all they found was the open window with a chill April breeze blowing in a cloud of fine bluish-grey dust that almost choked them. True, the dogs had howled some time before; but that was while Willett was still present, and they had caught nothing and shewn no disturbance later on. Ward's father was told at once over the telephone, but he seemed more saddened than surprised. By the time Dr. Waite called in person, Dr. Willett had been talking with him, and both disavowed any knowledge or complicity in the escape. Only from certain closely confidential friends of Willett and the senior Ward have any clues been gained, and even these are too wildly fantastic for general credence. The one fact which remains is that up to the present time no trace of the missing madman has been unearthed.

Charles Ward was an antiquarian from infancy, no doubt gaining his taste from the venerable town around him, and from the relics of the past which filled every corner of his parents' old mansion in Prospect Street on the crest of the hill. With the years his devotion to ancient things increased; so that history, genealogy, and the study of colonial architecture, furniture, and craftsmanship at length crowded everything else from his sphere of interests. These tastes are important to remember in considering his madness; for although they do not form its absolute nucleus, they play a prominent part in its superficial form. The gaps of information which the alienists noticed were all related to modern matters, and were invariably offset by a correspondingly excessive though outwardly concealed knowledge of bygone matters as brought out by adroit questioning; so that one would have fancied the patient literally transferred to a former age through some obscure sort of auto-hypnosis. The odd thing was that Ward seemed no longer interested in the antiquities he knew so well. He had, it appears, lost his regard for them through sheer familiarity; and all his final efforts were obviously bent toward mastering those common facts of the modern world which had been so totally and unmistakably expunged from his brain. That this wholesale deletion had occurred, he did his best to hide; but it was clear to all who watched him that his whole programme of reading and conversation was determined by a frantic wish to imbibe such knowledge of his own life and of the ordinary practical and cultural background of the twentieth century as ought to have been his by virtue of his birth in 1902 and his education in the schools of our own time. Alienists are now wondering how, in view of his vitally impaired range of data, the escaped patient manages to cope with the complicated world of today; the dominant opinion being that he is 'lying low' in some humble and unexacting position till his stock of modern information can be brought up to the normal.

The beginning of Ward's madness is a matter of dispute among alienists. Dr. Lyman, the eminent Boston authority, places it in 1919 or 1920, during the boy's last year at the Moses Brown School, when he suddenly turned from the study of the past to the study of the occult, and refused to qualify for college on the ground that he had individual researches of much greater importance to make. This is certainly borne out by Ward's altered habits at the time, especially by his continual search through town records and among old burying-grounds for a certain grave dug in 1771; the grave of an ancestor named Joseph Curwen, some of whose papers he professed to have found behind the panelling of a very old house in Olney Court, on Stampers' Hill, which Curwen was known to have built and occupied. It is, broadly speaking, undeniable that the winter of 1919–20 saw a great change in Ward; whereby he abruptly dropped his general antiquarian pursuits and embarked on a desperate delving into occult subjects both at home and abroad, varied only by this strangely persistent search for his forefather's grave.

From this opinion, however, Dr. Willett substantially dissents; basing his verdict on his close and continuous knowledge of the patient, and on certain frightful investigations and discoveries which he made toward the last. Those investigations and discoveries have left their mark upon him; so that his voice trembles when he tells them, and his hand trembles when he tries to write of them. Willett admits that the change of 1919–20 would ordinarily appear to mark the beginning of a progressive decadence which culminated in the horrible and uncanny alienation of 1928; but believes from personal observation that a finer distinction must be made. Granting freely that the boy was always ill-balanced temperamentally, and prone to be unduly susceptible and enthusiastic in his responses to phenomena around him, he refuses to concede that the early alteration marked the actual passage from sanity to madness; crediting instead Ward's own statement that he had discovered or rediscovered something whose effect on human thought was likely to be marvellous and profound. The true madness, he is certain, came with a later change; after the Curwen portrait and the ancient papers had been unearthed; after a trip to strange foreign places had been made, and some terrible invocations chanted under strange and secret circumstances; after certain *answers* to these invocations had been plainly indicated, and a frantic letter penned under agonising and inexplicable conditions; after the wave of vampirism and the ominous Pawtuxet gossip; and after the patient's memory commenced to exclude contemporary images whilst his voice failed and his physical aspect underwent the subtle modification so many subsequently noticed.

It was only about this time, Willett points out with much acuteness, that the nightmare qualities became indubitably linked with Ward; and the doctor feels shudderingly sure that enough solid evidence exists to sustain the youth's claim regarding his crucial discovery. In the first place, two workmen of high intelligence saw Joseph Curwen's ancient papers found. Secondly, the boy once shewed Dr. Willett those papers and a page of the Curwen diary, and each of the documents had every appearance of genuineness. The hole where Ward claimed to have found them was long a visible reality, and Willett had a very convincing final glimpse of them in surroundings which can scarcely be believed and can never perhaps be proved. Then there were the mysteries and coincidences of the Orne and Hutchinson letters, and the problem of the Curwen penmanship and of what the detectives brought to light about Dr. Allen; these things, and the terrible message in mediaeval minuscules found in Willett's pocket when he gained consciousness after his shocking experience.

And most conclusive of all, there are the two hideous *results* which the doctor obtained from a certain pair of formulae during his final investigations; results which virtually proved the authenticity of the papers and of their monstrous implications at the same time that those papers were borne for ever from human knowledge.

2.

One must look back at Charles Ward's earlier life as at something belonging as much to the past as the antiquities he loved so keenly. In the autumn of 1918, and with a considerable show of zest in the military training of the period, he had begun his junior year at the Moses Brown School, which lies very near his home. The old main building, erected in 1819, had always charmed his youthful antiquarian sense; and the spacious park in which the academy is set appealed to his sharp eye for landscape. His social activities were few; and his hours were spent mainly at home, in rambling walks, in his classes and drills, and in pursuit of antiquarian and genealogical data at the City Hall, the State House, the Public Library, the Athenaeum, the Historical Society, the John Carter Brown and John Hay Libraries of Brown University, and the newly opened Shepley Library in Benefit Street. One may picture him yet as he was in those days; tall, slim, and blond, with studious eyes and a slight stoop, dressed somewhat carelessly, and giving a dominant impression of harmless awkwardness rather than attractiveness.

His walks were always adventures in antiquity, during which he managed to recapture from the myriad relics of a glamorous old city a vivid and connected picture of the centuries before. His home was a great Georgian mansion atop the well-nigh precipitous hill that rises just east of the river; and from the rear windows of its rambling wings he could look dizzily out over all the clustered spires, domes, roofs, and skyscraper summits of the lower town to the purple hills of the countryside beyond. Here he was born, and from the lovely classic porch of the double-bayed brick facade his nurse had first wheeled him in his carriage; past the little white farmhouse of two hundred years before that the town had long ago overtaken, and on toward the stately colleges along the shady, sumptuous street, whose old square brick mansions and smaller wooden houses with narrow, heavy-columned Doric porches dreamed solid and exclusive amidst their generous yards and gardens.

He had been wheeled, too, along sleepy Congdon Street, one tier lower down on the steep hill, and with all its eastern homes on high terraces. The small wooden houses averaged a greater age here, for it was up this hill that the growing town had climbed; and in these rides he had imbibed something of the colour of a quaint colonial village. The nurse used to stop and sit on the benches of Prospect Terrace to chat with policemen; and one of the child's first memories is of the great westward sea of hazy roofs and domes and steeples and far hills which he saw one winter afternoon from that great railed embankment, all violet and mystic against a fevered, apocalyptic sunset of reds and golds and purples and curious greens. The vast marble dome of the State House stood out in massive silhouette, its crowning statue haloed fantastically by a break in one of the tinted stratus clouds that barred the flaming sky.

When he was larger his famous walks began; first with his impatiently dragged nurse, and then alone in dreamy meditation. Farther and farther down that almost perpendicular hill he would venture, each time reaching older and quainter levels of the ancient city. He would hesitate gingerly down vertical Jenckes Street with its bank walls and colonial gables to the shady Benefit Street corner, where before him was a wooden antique with an Ionic-pilastered pair of doorways, and beside him a prehistoric gambrel-roofer with a bit of primal farmyard remaining, and the great Judge Durfee house with its fallen vestiges of Georgian grandeur. It was getting to be a slum here; but the titan elms cast a restoring shadow over the place, and the boy used to stroll south past the long lines of pre-Revolutionary homes with their great central chimneys and classic portals. On the eastern side they were set high over basements with railed double flights of stone steps, and the young Charles could picture them as they were when the street was new, and red heels and periwigs set off the painted pediments whose signs of wear were now becoming so visible.

Westward the hill dropped almost as steeply as above, down to the old "Town Street" that the founders had laid out at the river's edge in 1636. Here ran innumerable little lanes with leaning, huddled houses of immense antiquity; and fascinated though he was, it was long before he dared to thread their archaic verticality for fear they would turn out a dream or a gateway to unknown terrors. He found it much less formidable to continue along Benefit Street past the iron fence of St. John's hidden churchyard and the rear of the 1761 Colony House and the mouldering bulk of the Golden Ball Inn where Washington stopped. At Meeting Street—the successive Gaol Lane and King Street of other periods—he would look upward to the east and see the arched flight of steps to which the highway had to resort in climbing the slope, and downward to the west, glimpsing the old brick colonial schoolhouse that smiles across the road at the ancient Sign of Shakespear's Head where the *Providence Gazette and Country-Journal* was printed before the Revolution. Then came the exquisite First Baptist Church of 1775, luxurious with its matchless Gibbs steeple, and the Georgian roofs and cupolas hovering by. Here and to the southward the neighbourhood became better, flowering at last into a marvellous group of early mansions; but still the little ancient lanes led off down the precipice to the west, spectral in their many-gabled archaism, and dipping to a riot of iridescent decay where the wicked old waterfront recalls its proud East India days amidst polyglot vice and squalor, rotting wharves, and blear-eyed ship-chandleries, with such surviving alley names as Packet, Bullion, Gold, Silver, Coin, Doubloon, Sovereign, Guilder, Dollar, Dime, and Cent.

Sometimes, as he grew taller and more adventurous, young Ward would venture down into this maelstrom of tottering houses, broken transoms, tumbling steps, twisted balustrades, swarthy faces, and nameless odours; winding from South Main to South Water, searching out the docks where the bay and sound steamers still touched, and returning northward at this lower level past the steep-roofed 1816 warehouses and the broad square at the Great Bridge, where the 1773 Market House still stands firm on its ancient arches. In that square he would pause to drink in the bewildering beauty of the old town as it rises on its eastward bluff, decked with its two Georgian spires and crowned by the vast new Christian Science dome as London is crowned by St. Paul's. He liked mostly to reach this point in the late afternoon, when the slanting sunlight touches the Market House and the ancient hill roofs and belfries with gold, and throws magic around the dreaming wharves where Providence Indiamen used to ride at anchor. After a long look he would grow almost dizzy with a poet's love for the sight, and then he would scale the slope homeward in the dusk past the old white church and up the narrow precipitous ways where yellow gleams would begin to peep out in small-paned windows and through fanlights set high over double flights of steps with curious wrought-iron railings.

At other times, and in later years, he would seek for vivid contrasts; spending half a walk in the crumbling colonial regions northwest of his home, where the hill drops to the lower eminence of Stampers' Hill with its ghetto and negro quarter clustering round the place where the Boston stage coach used to start before the Revolution, and the other half in the gracious southerly realm about George, Benevolent, Power, and Williams Streets, where the old slope holds unchanged the fine estates and bits of walled garden and steep green lane in which so many fragrant memories linger. These rambles, together with the diligent studies which accompanied them, certainly account for a large amount of the antiquarian lore which at last crowded the modern world from Charles Ward's mind; and illustrate the mental soil upon which fell, in that fateful winter of 1919–20, the seeds that came to such strange and terrible fruition.

Dr. Willett is certain that, up to this ill-omened winter of first change, Charles Ward's antiquarianism was free from every trace of the morbid. Graveyards held for him no particular attraction beyond their quaintness and historic value, and of anything like violence or savage instinct he was utterly devoid. Then, by insidious degrees, there appeared to develop a curious sequel to one of his genealogical triumphs of the year before; when he had discovered among his maternal ancestors a certain very long-lived man named Joseph Curwen, who had come from Salem in March of 1692, and about whom a whispered series of highly peculiar and disquieting stories clustered.

Ward's great-great-grandfather Welcome Potter had in 1785 married a certain "Ann Tillinghast, daughter of Mrs. Eliza, daughter to Capt. James Tillinghast", of whose paternity the family had preserved no trace. Late in 1918, whilst examining a volume of original town records in manuscript, the young genealogist encountered an entry describing a legal change of name, by which in 1772 a Mrs. Eliza Curwen, widow of Joseph Curwen, resumed, along with her seven-year-old daughter Ann, her maiden name of Tillinghast; on the ground 'that her Husband's name was become a publick Reproach by Reason of what was knowne after his Decease; the which confirming antient common Rumour, tho' not to be credited by a loyall Wife till so proven as to be wholely past Doubting'. This entry came to light upon the accidental separation of two leaves which had been carefully pasted together and treated as one by a laboured revision of the page numbers.

It was at once clear to Charles Ward that he had indeed discovered a hitherto unknown great-great-great-grandfather. The discovery doubly excited him because he had already heard vague reports and seen scattered allusions relating to this person; about whom there remained so few publicly available records, aside from those becoming public only in modern times, that it almost seemed as if a conspiracy had existed to blot him from memory. What did appear, moreover, was of such a singular and provocative nature that one could not fail to imagine curiously what it was the colonial recorders were so anxious to conceal and forget; or to suspect that the deletion had reasons all too valid.

Before this, Ward had been content to let his romancing about old Joseph Curwen remain in the idle stage; but having discovered his own relationship to this apparently "hushed-up" character, he proceeded to hunt out as systematically as possible whatever he might find concerning him. In this excited quest he eventually succeeded beyond his highest expectations; for old letters, diaries, and sheaves of unpublished memoirs in cobwebbed Providence garrets and elsewhere yielded many illuminating passages which their writers had not thought it worth their while to destroy. One important sidelight came from a point as remote as New York, where some Rhode Island colonial correspondence was stored in the Museum at Fraunces' Tavern. The really crucial thing, though, and what in Dr. Willett's opinion formed the definite source of Ward's undoing, was the matter found in August 1919 behind the panelling of the crumbling house in Olney Court. It was that, beyond a doubt, which opened up those black vistas whose end was deeper than the pit.

II. An Antecedent and a Horror

1.

Joseph Curwen, as revealed by the rambling legends embodied in what Ward heard and unearthed, was a very astonishing, enigmatic, and obscurely horrible individual. He had fled from Salem to Providence—that universal haven of the odd, the free, and the dissenting—at the beginning of the great witchcraft panic; being in fear of accusation because of his solitary ways and queer chemical or alchemical experiments. He was a colourless-looking man of about thirty, and was soon found qualified to become a freeman of Providence; thereafter buying a home lot just north of Gregory Dexter's at about the foot of Olney Street. His house was built on Stampers' Hill west of the Town Street, in what later became Olney Court; and in 1761 he replaced this with a larger one, on the same site, which is still standing.

Now the first odd thing about Joseph Curwen was that he did not seem to grow much older than he had been on his arrival. He engaged in shipping enterprises, purchased wharfage near Mile-End Cove, helped rebuild the Great Bridge in 1713, and in 1723 was one of the founders of the Congregational Church on the hill; but always did he retain the nondescript aspect of a man not greatly over thirty or thirty-five. As decades mounted up, this singular quality began to excite wide notice; but Curwen always explained it by saying that he came of hardy forefathers, and practiced a simplicity of living which did not wear him out. How such simplicity could be reconciled with the inexplicable comings and goings of the secretive merchant, and with the queer gleaming of his windows at all hours of night, was not very clear to the townsfolk; and they were prone to assign other reasons for his continued youth and longevity. It was held, for the most part, that Curwen's incessant mixings and boilings of chemicals had much to do with his condition. Gossip spoke of the strange substances he brought from London and the Indies on his ships or purchased in Newport, Boston, and New York; and when old Dr. Jabez

Bowen came from Rehoboth and opened his apothecary shop across the Great Bridge at the Sign of the Unicorn and Mortar, there was ceaseless talk of the drugs, acids, and metals that the taciturn recluse incessantly bought or ordered from him. Acting on the assumption that Curwen possessed a wondrous and secret medical skill, many sufferers of various sorts applied to him for aid; but though he appeared to encourage their belief in a non-committal way, and always gave them odd-coloured potions in response to their requests, it was observed that his ministrations to others seldom proved of benefit. At length, when over fifty years had passed since the stranger's advent, and without producing more than five years' apparent change in his face and physique, the people began to whisper more darkly; and to meet more than half way that desire for isolation which he had always shewn.

Private letters and diaries of the period reveal, too, a multitude of other reasons why Joseph Curwen was marvelled at, feared, and finally shunned like a plague. His passion for graveyards, in which he was glimpsed at all hours and under all conditions, was notorious; though no one had witnessed any deed on his part which could actually be termed ghoulish. On the Pawtuxet Road he had a farm, at which he generally lived during the summer, and to which he would frequently be seen riding at various odd times of the day or night. Here his only visible servants, farmers, and caretakers were a sullen pair of aged Narragansett Indians; the husband dumb and curiously scarred, and the wife of a very repulsive cast of countenance, probably due to a mixture of negro blood. In the lean-to of this house was the laboratory where most of the chemical experiments were conducted. Curious porters and teamers who delivered bottles, bags, or boxes at the small rear door would exchange accounts of the fantastic flasks, crucibles, alembics, and furnaces they saw in the low shelved room; and prophesied in whispers that the close-mouthed "chymist"—by which they meant *alchemist*—would not be long in finding the Philosopher's Stone. The nearest neighbours to this farm—the Fenners, a quarter of a mile away—had still queerer things to tell of certain sounds which they insisted came from the Curwen place in the night. There were cries, they said, and sustained howlings; and they did not like the large number of livestock which thronged the pastures, for no such amount was needed to keep a lone old man and a very few servants in meat, milk, and wool. The identity of the stock seemed to change from week to week as new droves were purchased from the Kingstown farmers. Then, too, there was something very obnoxious about a certain great stone outbuilding with only high narrow slits for windows.

Great Bridge idlers likewise had much to say of Curwen's town house in Olney Court; not so much the fine new one built in 1761, when the man must have been nearly a century old, but the first low gambrel-roofed one with the windowless attic and shingled sides, whose timbers he took the peculiar precaution of burning after its demolition. Here there was less mystery, it is true; but the hours at which lights were seen, the secretiveness of the two swarthy foreigners who comprised the only menservants, the hideous indistinct mumbling of the incredibly aged French housekeeper, the large amounts of food seen to enter a door within which only four persons lived, and the *quality* of certain voices often heard in muffled conversation at highly unseasonable times, all combined with what was known of the Pawtuxet farm to give the place a bad name.

In choicer circles, too, the Curwen home was by no means undiscussed; for as the newcomer had gradually worked into the church and trading life of the town, he had naturally made acquaintances of the better sort, whose company and conversation he was well fitted by education to enjoy. His birth was known to be good, since the Curwens or Corwins of Salem needed no introduction in New England. It developed that Joseph Curwen had travelled much in very early life, living for a time in England and making at least two voyages to the Orient; and his speech, when he deigned to use it, was that of a learned and cultivated Englishman. But for some reason or other Curwen did not care for society. Whilst never actually rebuffing a visitor, he always reared such a wall of reserve that few could think of anything to say to him which would not sound inane.

There seemed to lurk in his bearing some cryptic, sardonic arrogance, as if he had come to find all human beings dull through having moved among stranger and more potent entities. When Dr. Checkley the famous wit came from Boston in 1738 to be rector of King's Church, he did not neglect calling on one of whom he soon heard so much; but left in a very short while because of some sinister undercurrent he detected in his host's discourse. Charles Ward told his father, when they discussed Curwen one winter evening, that he would give much to learn what the mysterious old man had said to the sprightly cleric, but that all diarists agree concerning Dr. Checkley's reluctance to repeat anything he had heard. The good man had been hideously shocked, and could never recall Joseph Curwen without a visible loss of the gay urbanity for which he was famed.

More definite, however, was the reason why another man of taste and breeding avoided the haughty hermit. In 1746 Mr. John

Merritt, an elderly English gentleman of literary and scientific leanings, came from Newport to the town which was so rapidly overtaking it in standing, and built a fine country seat on the Neck in what is now the heart of the best residence section. He lived in considerable style and comfort, keeping the first coach and liveried servants in town, and taking great pride in his telescope, his microscope, and his well-chosen library of English and Latin books. Hearing of Curwen as the owner of the best library in Providence, Mr. Merritt early paid him a call, and was more cordially received than most other callers at the house had been. His admiration for his host's ample shelves, which besides the Greek, Latin, and English classics were equipped with a remarkable battery of philosophical, mathematical, and scientific works including Paracelsus, Agricola, Van Helmont, Sylvius, Glauber, Boyle, Boerhaave, Becher, and Stahl, led Curwen to suggest a visit to the farmhouse and laboratory whither he had never invited anyone before; and the two drove out at once in Mr. Merritt's coach.

Mr. Merritt always confessed to seeing nothing really horrible at the farmhouse, but maintained that the titles of the books in the special library of thaumaturgical, alchemical, and theological subjects which Curwen kept in a front room were alone sufficient to inspire him with a lasting loathing. Perhaps, however, the facial expression of the owner in exhibiting them contributed much of the prejudice. This bizarre collection, besides a host of standard works which Mr. Merritt was not too alarmed to envy, embraced nearly all the cabbalists, daemonologists, and magicians known to man; and was a treasure-house of lore in the doubtful realms of alchemy and astrology. Hermes Trismegistus in Mesnard's edition, the "Turba Philosophorum", Geber's "Liber Investigationis", and Artephius' "Key of Wisdom" all were there; with the cabbalistic "Zohar", Peter Jammy's set of Albertus Magnus, Raymond Lully's "Ars Magna et Ultima" in Zetzner's edition, Roger Bacon's "Thesaurus Chemicus", Fludd's "Clavis Alchimiae", and Trithemius' "De Lapide Philosophico" crowding them close. Mediaeval Jews and Arabs were represented in profusion, and Mr. Merritt turned pale when, upon taking down a fine volume conspicuously labelled as the "Qanoon-e-Islam", he found it was in truth the forbidden "Necronomicon" of the mad Arab Abdul Alhazred, of which he had heard such monstrous things whispered some years previously after the exposure of nameless rites at the strange little fishing village of Kingsport, in the Province of the Massachusetts-Bay.

But oddly enough, the worthy gentleman owned himself most impalpably disquieted by a mere minor detail. On the huge mahogany table there lay face downward a badly worn copy of Borellus, bearing many cryptical marginalia and interlineations in Curwen's hand. The book was open at about its middle, and one paragraph displayed such thick and tremulous pen-strokes beneath the lines of mystic black-letter that the visitor could not resist scanning it through. Whether it was the nature of the passage underscored, or the feverish heaviness of the strokes which formed the underscoring, he could not tell; but something in that combination affected him very badly and very peculiarly. He recalled it to the end of his days, writing it from memory in his diary and once trying to recite it to his close friend Dr. Checkley till he saw how greatly it disturbed the urbane rector. It read:

> "The essential Saltes of Animals may be so prepared and preserved, that an ingenious Man may have the whole Ark of Noah in his owne Studie, and raise the fine Shape of an Animal out of its Ashes at his Pleasure; and by the lyke Method from the essential Saltes of humane Dust, a Philosopher may, without any criminal Necromancy, call up the Shape of any dead Ancestour from the Dust whereinto his Bodie has been incinerated."

It was near the docks along the southerly part of the Town Street, however, that the worst things were muttered about Joseph Curwen. Sailors are superstitious folk; and the seasoned salts who manned the infinite rum, slave, and molasses sloops, the rakish privateers, and the great brigs of the Browns, Crawfords, and Tillinghasts, all made strange furtive signs of protection when they saw the slim, deceptively young-looking figure with its yellow hair and slight stoop entering the Curwen warehouse in Doubloon Street or talking with captains and supercargoes on the long quay where the Curwen ships rode restlessly. Curwen's own clerks and captains hated and feared him, and all his sailors were mongrel riff-raff from Martinique, St. Eustatius, Havana, or Port Royal. It was, in a way, the frequency with which these sailors were replaced which inspired the acutest and most tangible part of the fear in which the old man was held. A crew would be turned loose in the town on shore leave, some of its members perhaps charged with this errand or that; and when reassembled it would be almost sure to lack one or more men. That many of the errands had concerned the farm on the Pawtuxet Road, and that few of the sailors had ever been seen to return from that place, was not forgotten; so that in time it became exceedingly difficult for Curwen to keep his oddly assorted hands. Almost invariably several would desert soon after hearing the gossip of the Providence wharves, and their replacement in the West Indies became an increasingly great problem to the merchant.

By 1760 Joseph Curwen was virtually an outcast, suspected of vague horrors and daemoniac alliances which seemed all the more menacing because they could not be named, understood, or even proved to exist. The last straw may have come from the affair of the missing soldiers in 1758, for in March and April of that year two Royal regiments on their way to New France were quartered in Providence, and depleted by an inexplicable process far beyond the average rate of desertion. Rumour dwelt on the frequency with which Curwen was wont to be seen talking with the red-coated strangers; and as several of them began to be missed, people thought of the odd conditions among his own seamen. What would have happened if the regiments had not been ordered on, no one can tell.

Meanwhile the merchant's worldly affairs were prospering. He had a virtual monopoly of the town's trade in saltpetre, black pepper, and cinnamon, and easily led any other one shipping establishment save the Browns in his importation of brassware, indigo, cotton, woollens, salt, rigging, iron, paper, and English goods of every kind. Such shopkeepers as James Green, at the Sign of the Elephant in Cheapside, the Russells, at the Sign of the Golden Eagle across the Bridge, or Clark and Nightingale at the Frying-Pan and Fish near the New Coffee-House, depended almost wholly upon him for their stock; and his arrangements with the local distillers, the Narragansett dairymen and horse breeders, and the Newport candle-makers, made him one of the prime exporters of the Colony.

Ostracised though he was, he did not lack for civic spirit of a sort. When the Colony House burned down, he subscribed handsomely to the lotteries by which the new brick one—still standing at the head of its parade in the old main street—was built in 1761. In that same year, too, he helped rebuild the Great Bridge after the October gale. He replaced many of the books of the public library consumed in the Colony House fire, and bought heavily in the lottery that gave the muddy Market Parade and deep-rutted Town Street their pavement of great round stones with a brick footwalk or "causey" in the middle. About this time, also, he built the plain but excellent new house whose doorway is still such a triumph of carving. When the Whitefield adherents broke off from Dr. Cotton's hill church in 1743 and founded Deacon Snow's church across the Bridge, Curwen had gone with them; though his zeal and attendance soon abated. Now, however, he cultivated piety once more; as if to dispel the shadow which had thrown him into isolation and would soon begin to wreck his business fortunes if not sharply checked.

2.

The sight of this strange, pallid man, hardly middle-aged in aspect yet certainly not less than a full century old, seeking at last to emerge from a cloud of fright and detestation too vague to pin down or analyse, was at once a pathetic, a dramatic, and a contemptible thing. Such is the power of wealth and of surface gestures, however, that there came indeed a slight abatement in the visible aversion displayed toward him; especially after the rapid disappearances of his sailors abruptly ceased. He must likewise have begun to practice an extreme care and secrecy in his graveyard expeditions, for he was never again caught at such wanderings; whilst the rumours of uncanny sounds and manoeuvres at his Pawtuxet farm diminished in proportion. His rate of food consumption and cattle replacement remained abnormally high; but not until modern times, when Charles Ward examined a set of his accounts and invoices in the Shepley Library, did it occur to any person—save one embittered youth, perhaps—to make dark comparisons between the large number of Guinea blacks he imported until 1766, and the disturbingly small number for whom he could produce bona fide bills of sale either to slave-dealers at the Great Bridge or to the planters of the Narragansett Country. Certainly, the cunning and ingenuity of this abhorred character were uncannily profound, once the necessity for their exercise had become impressed upon him.

But of course the effect of all this belated mending was necessarily slight. Curwen continued to be avoided and distrusted, as indeed the one fact of his continued air of youth at a great age would have been enough to warrant; and he could see that in the end his fortunes would be likely to suffer. His elaborate studies and experiments, whatever they may have been, apparently required a heavy income for their maintenance; and since a change of environment would deprive him of the trading advantages he had gained, it would not have profited him to begin anew in a different region just then. Judgment demanded that he patch up his relations with the townsfolk of Providence, so that his presence might no longer be a signal for hushed conversation, transparent excuses of errands elsewhere, and a general atmosphere of constraint and uneasiness. His clerks, being now reduced to the shiftless and impecunious residue whom no one else would employ, were giving him much worry; and he held to his sea-captains and mates only by shrewdness in gaining some kind of ascendancy over them—a mortgage, a promissory note, or a bit of information very pertinent to their welfare. In many cases, diarists have recorded with some awe,

Curwen shewed almost the power of a wizard in unearthing family secrets for questionable use. During the final five years of his life it seemed as though only direct talks with the long-dead could possibly have furnished some of the data which he had so glibly at his tongue's end.

About this time the crafty scholar hit upon a last desperate expedient to regain his footing in the community. Hitherto a complete hermit, he now determined to contract an advantageous marriage; securing as a bride some lady whose unquestioned position would make all ostracism of his home impossible. It may be that he also had deeper reasons for wishing an alliance; reasons so far outside the known cosmic sphere that only papers found a century and a half after his death caused anyone to suspect them; but of this nothing certain can ever be learned. Naturally he was aware of the horror and indignation with which any ordinary courtship of his would be received, hence looked about for some likely candidate upon whose parents he might exert a suitable pressure. Such candidates, he found, were not at all easy to discover; since he had very particular requirements in the way of beauty, accomplishments, and social security. At length his survey narrowed down to the household of one of his best and oldest ship-captains, a widower of high birth and unblemished standing named Dutee Tillinghast, whose only daughter Eliza seemed dowered with every conceivable advantage save prospects as an heiress. Capt. Tillinghast was completely under the domination of Curwen; and consented, after a terrible interview in his cupolaed house on Power's Lane hill, to sanction the blasphemous alliance.

Eliza Tillinghast was at that time eighteen years of age, and had been reared as gently as the reduced circumstances of her father permitted. She had attended Stephen Jackson's school opposite the Court-House Parade; and had been diligently instructed by her mother, before the latter's death of smallpox in 1757, in all the arts and refinements of domestic life. A sampler of hers, worked in 1753 at the age of nine, may still be found in the rooms of the Rhode Island Historical Society. After her mother's death she had kept the house, aided only by one old black woman. Her arguments with her father concerning the proposed Curwen marriage must have been painful indeed; but of these we have no record. Certain it is that her engagement to young Ezra Weeden, second mate of the Crawford packet *Enterprise*, was dutifully broken off, and that her union with Joseph Curwen took place on the seventh of March, 1763, in the Baptist church, in the presence of one of the most distinguished assemblages which the town could boast; the ceremony being performed by the younger Samuel Winsor. The *Gazette* mentioned the event very briefly, and in most surviving copies the item in question seems to be cut or torn out. Ward found a single intact copy after much search in the archives of a private collector of note, observing with amusement the meaningless urbanity of the language:

> "Monday evening last, Mr. Joseph Curwen, of this Town, Merchant, was married to Miss Eliza Tillinghast, Daughter of Capt. Dutee Tillinghast, a young Lady who has real Merit, added to a beautiful Person, to grace the connubial State and perpetuate its Felicity."

The collection of Durfee-Arnold letters, discovered by Charles Ward shortly before his first reputed madness in the private collection of Melville F. Peters, Esq., of George St., and covering this and a somewhat antecedent period, throws vivid light on the outrage done to public sentiment by this ill-assorted match. The social influence of the Tillinghasts, however, was not to be denied; and once more Joseph Curwen found his house frequented by persons whom he could never otherwise have induced to cross his threshold. His acceptance was by no means complete, and his bride was socially the sufferer through her forced venture; but at all events the wall of utter ostracism was somewhat worn down. In his treatment of his wife the strange bridegroom astonished both her and the community by displaying an extreme graciousness and consideration. The new house in Olney Court was now wholly free from disturbing manifestations, and although Curwen was much absent at the Pawtuxet farm which his wife never visited, he seemed more like a normal citizen than at any other time in his long years of residence. Only one person remained in open enmity with him, this being the youthful ship's officer whose engagement to Eliza Tillinghast had been so abruptly broken. Ezra Weeden had frankly vowed vengeance; and though of a quiet and originally mild disposition, was now gaining a hate-bred, dogged purpose which boded no good to the usurping husband.

On the seventh of May, 1765, Curwen's only child Ann was born; and was christened by the Rev. John Graves of King's Church, of which both husband and wife had become communicants shortly after their marriage, in order to compromise between their respective Congregational and Baptist affiliations. The record of this birth, as well as that of the marriage two years before, was stricken from most copies of the church and town annals where it ought to appear; and Charles Ward located both with the greatest difficulty after his discovery of the widow's change of name had apprised him of his own relationship, and engendered the feverish interest which culminated in his madness. The birth entry, indeed, was found very curiously through correspondence with the heirs of the loyalist Dr. Graves, who had taken with him a duplicate set of records when he left his pastorate at the outbreak of the Revolution. Ward had tried this source because he knew that his great-great-grandmother Ann Tillinghast Potter had been an Episcopalian.

Shortly after the birth of his daughter, an event he seemed to welcome with a fervour greatly out of keeping with his usual coldness, Curwen resolved to sit for a portrait. This he had painted by a very gifted Scotsman named Cosmo Alexander, then a resident of Newport, and since famous as the early teacher of Gilbert Stuart. The likeness was said to have been executed on a wall-panel of the library of the house in Olney Court, but neither of the two old diaries mentioning it gave any hint of its ultimate disposition. At this period the erratic scholar shewed signs of unusual abstraction, and spent as much time as he possibly could at his farm on the Pawtuxet Road. He seemed, it was stated, in a condition of suppressed excitement or suspense; as if expecting some phenomenal thing or on the brink of some strange discovery. Chemistry or alchemy would appear to have played a great part, for he took from his house to the farm the greater number of his volumes on that subject.

His affectation of civic interest did not diminish, and he lost no opportunities for helping such leaders as Stephen Hopkins, Joseph Brown, and Benjamin West in their efforts to raise the cultural tone of the town, which was then much below the level of Newport in its patronage of the liberal arts. He had helped Daniel Jenckes found his bookshop in 1763, and was thereafter his best customer; extending aid likewise to the struggling *Gazette* that appeared each Wednesday at the Sign of Shakespear's Head. In politics he ardently supported Governor Hopkins against the Ward party whose prime strength was in Newport, and his really eloquent speech at Hacker's Hall in 1765 against the setting off of North Providence as a separate town with a pro-Ward vote in the General Assembly did more than any other one thing to wear down the prejudice against him. But Ezra Weeden, who watched him closely, sneered cynically at all this outward activity; and freely swore it was no more than a mask for some nameless traffick with the blackest gulfs of Tartarus. The revengeful youth began a systematic study of the man and his doings whenever he was in port; spending hours at night by the wharves with a dory in readiness when he saw lights in the Curwen warehouses, and following the small boat which would sometimes steal quietly off and down the bay. He also kept as close a watch as possible on the Pawtuxet farm, and was once severely bitten by the dogs the old Indian couple loosed upon him.

3.

In 1766 came the final change in Joseph Curwen. It was very sudden, and gained wide notice amongst the curious townsfolk; for the air of suspense and expectancy dropped like an old cloak, giving instant place to an ill-concealed exaltation of perfect triumph. Curwen seemed to have difficulty in restraining himself from public harangues on what he had found or learned or made; but apparently the need of secrecy was greater than the longing to share his rejoicing, for no explanation was ever offered by him. It was after this transition, which appears to have come early in July, that the sinister scholar began to astonish people by his possession of information which only their long-dead ancestors would seem to be able to impart.

But Curwen's feverish secret activities by no means ceased with this change. On the contrary, they tended rather to increase; so that more and more of his shipping business was handled by the captains whom he now bound to him by ties of fear as potent as those of bankruptcy had been. He altogether abandoned the slave trade, alleging that its profits were constantly decreasing. Every possible moment was spent at the Pawtuxet farm; though there were rumours now and then of his presence in places which, though not actually near graveyards, were yet so situated in relation to graveyards that thoughtful people wondered just how thorough the old merchant's change of habits really was. Ezra Weeden, though his periods of espionage were necessarily brief and intermittent on account of his sea voyaging, had a vindictive persistence which the bulk of the practical townsfolk and farmers lacked; and subjected Curwen's affairs to a scrutiny such as they had never had before.

Many of the odd manoeuvres of the strange merchant's vessels had been taken for granted on account of the unrest of the times, when every colonist seemed determined to resist the provisions of the Sugar Act which hampered a prominent traffick. Smuggling and evasion were the rule in Narragansett Bay, and nocturnal landings of illicit cargoes were continuous commonplaces. But Weeden, night after night following the lighters or small sloops which he saw steal off from the Curwen warehouses at the Town Street docks, soon felt assured that it was not merely His Majesty's armed ships which the sinister skulker was anxious to avoid. Prior to the change in 1766 these boats had for the most part contained chained negroes, who were carried down and across the bay and landed at an obscure point on the shore just north of Pawtuxet; being afterward driven up the bluff and across country to the Curwen farm, where they were locked in that enormous stone outbuilding which had only high narrow slits for windows. After that change, however, the whole programme was altered. Importation of slaves ceased at once, and for a time Curwen abandoned his midnight sailings. Then, about the spring of 1767, a new policy appeared. Once more the lighters grew wont to put out from the black, silent docks, and this time they would go down the bay some distance, perhaps as far as Namquit Point, where they would meet and receive cargo from strange ships of considerable size and widely varied appearance. Curwen's sailors would then deposit this cargo at the usual point on the shore, and transport it overland to the farm; locking it in the same cryptical stone building which had formerly received the negroes. The cargo consisted almost wholly of boxes and cases, of which a large proportion were oblong and heavy and disturbingly suggestive of coffins.

Weeden always watched the farm with unremitting assiduity; visiting it each night for long periods, and seldom letting a week go by without a sight except when the ground bore a footprint-revealing snow. Even then he would often walk as close as possible in the travelled road or on the ice of the neighbouring river to see what tracks others might have left. Finding his own vigils interrupted by nautical duties, he hired a tavern companion named Eleazar Smith to continue the survey during his absences; and between them the two could have set in motion some extraordinary rumours. That they did not do so was only because they knew the effect of publicity would be to warn their quarry and make further progress impossible. Instead, they wished to learn something definite before taking any action. What they did learn must have been startling indeed, and Charles Ward spoke many times to his parents of his regret at Weeden's later burning of his notebooks. All that can be told of their discoveries is what Eleazar Smith jotted down in a none too coherent diary, and what other diarists and letter writers have timidly repeated from the statements which they finally made—and according to which the farm was only the outer shell of some vast and revolting menace, of a scope and depth too profound and intangible for more than shadowy comprehension.

It is gathered that Weeden and Smith became early convinced that a great series of tunnels and catacombs, inhabited by a very sizeable staff of persons besides the old Indian and his wife, underlay the farm. The house was an old peaked relic of the middle seventeenth century with enormous stack chimney and diamond-paned lattice windows, the laboratory being in a lean-to toward the north, where the roof came nearly to the ground. This building stood clear of any other; yet judging by the different voices heard at odd times within, it must have been accessible through secret passages beneath. These voices, before 1766, were mere mumblings and negro whisperings and frenzied screams, coupled with curious chants or invocations. After that date, however, they assumed a very singular and terrible cast as they ran the gamut betwixt dronings of dull acquiescence and explosions of frantic pain or fury, rumblings of conversation and whines of entreaty, pantings of eagerness and shouts of protest. They appeared to be in different languages, all known to Curwen, whose rasping accents were frequently distinguishable in reply, reproof, or threatening. Sometimes it seemed that several persons must be in the house; Curwen, certain captives, and the guards of those captives. There were voices of a sort that neither Weeden nor Smith had ever heard before despite their wide knowledge of foreign parts, and many that they did seem to place as belonging to this or that nationality. The nature of the conversations seemed always a kind of catechism, as if Curwen were extorting some sort of information from terrified or rebellious prisoners.

Weeden had many verbatim reports of overheard scraps in his notebook, for English, French, and Spanish, which he knew, were frequently used; but of these nothing has survived. He did, however, say that besides a few ghoulish dialogues in which the past affairs of Providence families were concerned, most of the questions and answers he could understand were historical or scientific; occasionally pertaining to very remote places and ages. Once, for example, an alternately raging and sullen figure was questioned in French about the Black Prince's massacre at Limoges in 1370, as if there were some hidden reason which he ought to know. Curwen asked the prisoner—if prisoner it were—whether the order to slay was given because of the Sign of the Goat found on the altar in the ancient Roman crypt beneath the Cathedral, or whether the Dark Man of the Haute Vienne coven had spoken the Three Words. Failing to obtain replies, the inquisitor had seemingly resorted to extreme means; for there was a terrific shriek followed by silence and muttering and a bumping sound.

None of these colloquies were ever ocularly witnessed, since the windows were always heavily draped. Once, though, during a discourse in an unknown tongue, a shadow was seen on the curtain which startled Weeden exceedingly; reminding him of one of the puppets in a show he had seen in the autumn of 1764 in Hacker's Hall, when a man from Germantown, Pennsylvania, had given a clever mechanical spectacle advertised as a "View of the Famous City of Jerusalem, in which are represented Jerusalem, the Temple of Solomon, his Royal Throne, the noted Towers, and Hills, likewise the Sufferings of Our Saviour from the Garden of Gethsemane to the Cross on the Hill of Golgotha; an artful piece of Statuary, Worthy to be seen by the Curious." It was on this occasion that the listener, who had crept close to the window of the front room whence the speaking proceeded, gave a start which roused the old Indian pair and caused them to loose the dogs on him. After that no more conversations were ever heard in the house, and Weeden and Smith concluded that Curwen had transferred his field of action to regions below.

That such regions in truth existed, seemed amply clear from many things. Faint cries and groans unmistakably came up now and then from what appeared to be the solid earth in places far from any structure; whilst hidden in the bushes along the river-bank in the rear, where the high ground sloped steeply down to the valley of the Pawtuxet, there was found an arched oaken door in a frame of heavy masonry, which was obviously an entrance to caverns within the hill. When or how these catacombs could have been constructed, Weeden was unable to say; but he frequently pointed out how easily the place might have been reached by bands of unseen workmen from the river. Joseph Curwen put his mongrel seamen to diverse uses indeed! During the heavy spring rains of 1769 the two watchers kept a sharp eye on the steep river-bank to see if any subterrene secrets might be washed to light, and were rewarded by the sight of a profusion of both human and animal bones in places where deep gullies had been worn in the banks. Naturally there might be many explanations of such things in the rear of a stock farm, and in a locality where old Indian burying-grounds were common, but Weeden and Smith drew their own inferences.

It was in January 1770, whilst Weeden and Smith were still debating vainly on what, if anything, to think or do about the whole bewildering business, that the incident of the *Fortaleza* occurred. Exasperated by the burning of the revenue sloop *Liberty* at Newport during the previous summer, the customs fleet under Admiral Wallace had adopted an increased vigilance concerning strange vessels; and on this occasion His Majesty's armed schooner *Cygnet*, under Capt. Charles Leslie, captured after a short pursuit one early morning the snow *Fortaleza* of Barcelona, Spain, under

Capt. Manuel Arruda, bound according to its log from Grand Cairo, Egypt, to Providence. When searched for contraband material, this ship revealed the astonishing fact that its cargo consisted exclusively of Egyptian mummies, consigned to "Sailor A. B. C.", who would come to remove his goods in a lighter just off Namquit Point, and whose identity Capt. Arruda felt himself in honour bound not to reveal. The Vice-Admiralty Court at Newport, at a loss what to do in view of the non-contraband nature of the cargo on the one hand and of the unlawful secrecy of the entry on the other hand, compromised on Collector Robinson's recommendation by freeing the ship but forbidding it a port in Rhode Island waters. There were later rumours of its having been seen in Boston Harbour, though it never openly entered the Port of Boston.

This extraordinary incident did not fail of wide remark in Providence, and there were not many who doubted the existence of some connexion between the cargo of mummies and the sinister Joseph Curwen. His exotic studies and his curious chemical importations being common knowledge, and his fondness for graveyards being common suspicion; it did not take much imagination to link him with a freakish importation which could not conceivably have been destined for anyone else in the town. As if conscious of this natural belief, Curwen took care to speak casually on several occasions of the chemical value of the balsams found in mummies; thinking perhaps that he might make the affair seem less unnatural, yet stopping just short of admitting his participation. Weeden and Smith, of course, felt no doubt whatsoever of the significance of the thing; and indulged in the wildest theories concerning Curwen and his monstrous labours.

The following spring, like that of the year before, had heavy rains; and the watchers kept careful track of the river-bank behind the Curwen farm. Large sections were washed away, and a certain number of bones discovered; but no glimpse was afforded of any actual subterranean chambers or burrows. Something was rumoured, however, at the village of Pawtuxet about a mile below, where the river flows in falls over a rocky terrace to join the placid landlocked cove. There, where quaint old cottages climbed the hill from the rustic bridge, and fishing-smacks lay anchored at their sleepy docks, a vague report went round of things that were floating down the river and flashing into sight for a minute as they went over the falls. Of course the Pawtuxet is a long river which winds through many settled regions abounding in graveyards, and of course the spring rains had been very heavy; but the fisherfolk about the bridge did not like the wild way that one of the things stared as it shot down to the still water below, or the way that another half cried out although its condition had greatly departed from that of objects which normally cry out. That rumour sent Smith—for Weeden was just then at sea—in haste to the river-bank behind the farm; where surely enough there remained the evidences of an extensive cave-in. There was, however, no trace of a passage into the steep bank; for the miniature avalanche had left behind a solid wall of mixed earth and shrubbery from aloft. Smith went to the extent of some experimental digging, but was deterred by lack of success—or perhaps by fear of possible success. It is interesting to speculate on what the persistent and revengeful Weeden would have done had he been ashore at the time.

4.

By the autumn of 1770 Weeden decided that the time was ripe to tell others of his discoveries; for he had a large number of facts to link together, and a second eye-witness to refute the possible charge that jealousy and vindictiveness had spurred his fancy. As his first confidant he selected Capt. James Mathewson of the *Enterprise,* who on the one hand knew him well enough not to doubt his veracity, and on the other hand was sufficiently influential in the town to be heard in turn with respect. The colloquy took place in an upper room of Sabin's Tavern near the docks, with Smith present to corroborate virtually every statement; and it could be seen that Capt. Mathewson was tremendously impressed. Like nearly everyone else in the town, he had had black suspicions of his own anent Joseph Curwen; hence it needed only this confirmation and enlargement of data to convince him absolutely. At the end of the conference he was very grave, and enjoined strict silence upon the two younger men. He would, he said, transmit the information separately to some ten or so of the most learned and prominent citizens of Providence; ascertaining their views and following whatever advice they might have to offer. Secrecy would probably be essential in any case, for this was no matter that the town constables or militia could cope with; and above all else the excitable crowd must be kept in ignorance, lest there be enacted in these already troublous times a repetition of that frightful Salem panic of less than a century before which had first brought Curwen hither.

The right persons to tell, he believed, would be Dr. Benjamin West, whose pamphlet on the late transit of Venus proved him a scholar and keen thinker; Rev. James Manning, President of the College which had just moved up from Warren and was temporarily housed in the new King Street schoolhouse awaiting the completion of its building on the hill above Presbyterian-Lane; ex-Governor Stephen Hopkins, who had been a member of the Philosophical Society at Newport, and was a man of very broad perceptions; John Carter, publisher of the *Gazette*; all four of the Brown brothers, John, Joseph, Nicholas, and Moses, who formed the recognised local magnates, and of whom Joseph was an amateur scientist of parts; old Dr. Jabez Bowen, whose erudition was considerable, and who had much first-hand knowledge of Curwen's odd purchases; and Capt. Abraham Whipple, a privateersman of phenomenal boldness and energy who could be counted on to lead in any active measures needed. These men, if favourable, might eventually be brought together for collective deliberation; and with them would rest the responsibility of deciding whether or not to inform the Governor of the Colony, Joseph Wanton of Newport, before taking action.

The mission of Capt. Mathewson prospered beyond his highest expectations; for whilst he found one or two of the chosen confidants somewhat sceptical of the possible ghastly side of Weeden's tale, there was not one who did not think it necessary to take some sort of secret and coördinated action. Curwen, it was clear, formed a vague potential menace to the welfare of the town and Colony; and must be eliminated at any cost. Late in December 1770 a group of eminent townsmen met at the home of Stephen Hopkins and debated tentative measures. Weeden's notes, which he had given to Capt. Mathewson, were carefully read; and he and Smith were summoned to give testimony anent details. Something very like fear seized the whole assemblage before the meeting was over, though there ran through that fear a grim determination which Capt. Whipple's bluff and resonant profanity best expressed. They would not notify the Governor, because a more than legal course seemed necessary. With hidden powers of uncertain extent apparently at his disposal, Curwen was not a man who could safely be warned to leave town. Nameless reprisals might ensue, and even if the sinister creature complied, the removal would be no more than the shifting of an unclean burden to another place. The times were lawless, and men who had flouted the King's revenue forces for years were not the ones to balk at sterner things when duty impelled. Curwen must be surprised at his Pawtuxet farm by a large raiding party of seasoned privateersmen and given one decisive chance to explain himself. If he proved a madman, amusing himself with shrieks and imaginary conversations in different voices, he would be properly confined. If something graver appeared, and if the underground horrors indeed turned out to be real, he and all with him must die. It could be done quietly, and even the widow and her father need not be told how it came about.

While these serious steps were under discussion there occurred in the town an incident so terrible and inexplicable that for a time little else was mentioned for miles around. In the middle of a moonlight January night with heavy snow underfoot there resounded over the river and up the hill a shocking series of cries which brought sleepy heads to every window; and people around Weybosset Point saw a great white thing plunging frantically along the badly cleared space in front of the Turk's Head. There was a baying of dogs in the distance, but this subsided as soon as the clamour of the awakened town became audible. Parties of men with lanterns and muskets hurried out to see what was happening, but nothing rewarded their search. The next morning, however, a giant, muscular body, stark naked, was found on the jams of ice around the southern piers of the Great Bridge, where the Long Dock stretched out beside Abbott's distil-house, and the identity of this object became a theme for endless speculation and whispering. It was not so much the younger as the older folk who whispered, for only in the patriarchs did that rigid face with horror-bulging eyes strike any chord of memory. They, shaking as they did so, exchanged furtive murmurs of wonder and fear; for in those stiff, hideous features lay a resemblance so marvellous as to be almost an identity—and that identity was with a man who had died full fifty years before.

Ezra Weeden was present at the finding; and remembering the baying of the night before, set out along Weybosset Street and across Muddy Dock Bridge whence the sound had come. He had a curious expectancy, and was not surprised when, reaching the edge of the settled district where the street merged into the Pawtuxet Road, he came upon some very curious tracks in the snow. The naked giant had been pursued by dogs and many booted men, and the returning tracks of the hounds and their masters could be easily traced. They had given up the chase upon coming too near the town. Weeden smiled grimly, and as a perfunctory detail traced the footprints back to their source. It was the Pawtuxet farm of Joseph Curwen, as he well knew it would be; and he would have given much had the yard been less confusingly trampled. As it was, he dared not seem too interested in full daylight. Dr. Bowen, to whom Weeden went at once with his report, performed an autopsy on the strange corpse, and discovered peculiarities which baffled him utterly. The digestive tracts of the huge man seemed never to have been in use, whilst the whole skin had a coarse, loosely knit texture impossible to account for. Impressed by what the old men whispered of this body's likeness to the long-dead blacksmith Daniel Green, whose great-grandson Aaron Hoppin was a supercargo in Curwen's employ, Weeden asked casual questions till he found where Green was buried. That night a party of ten visited the old North Burying Ground opposite Herrenden's Lane and opened a grave. They found it vacant, precisely as they had expected.

Meanwhile arrangements had been made with the post riders to intercept Joseph Curwen's mail, and shortly before the incident of the naked body there was found a letter from one Jedediah Orne of Salem which made the coöperating citizens think deeply. Parts of it, copied and preserved in the private archives of the Smith family where Charles Ward found it, ran as follows:

> "I delight that you continue in ye Gett'g at Olde Matters in your Way, and doe not think better was done at Mr. Hutchinson's in Salem-Village. Certainely, there was Noth'g butt ye liveliest Awfullness in that which H. rais'd upp from What he cou'd gather onlie a part of. What you sente, did not Worke, whether because of Any Thing miss'g, or because ye Wordes were not Righte from my Speak'g or y^{r} Copy'g. I alone am at a Loss. I have not ye Chymicall art to followe Borellus, and owne my Self confounded by ye VII. Booke of ye Necronomicon that you recommende. But I wou'd have you Observe what was tolde to us aboute tak'g Care whom to calle up, for you are Sensible what Mr. Mather writ in ye Magnalia of ——, and can judge how truely that Horrendous thing is reported. I say to you againe, doe not call up Any that you can not put downe; by the Which I meane, Any that can in Turne call up somewhat against you, whereby your Powerfullest Devices may not be of use. Ask of the Lesser, lest the Greater shall not wish to Answer, and shall commande more than you. I was frighted when I read of your know'g what Ben Zariatnatmik hadde in his ebony Boxe, for I was conscious who must have tolde you. And againe I ask that you shalle write me as Jedediah and not Simon. In this Community a Man may not live too long, and you knowe my Plan by which I came back as my Son. I am desirous you will Acquaint me with what ye Blacke Man learnt from Sylvanus Cocidius in ye Vault, under ye Roman Wall, and will be oblig'd for ye Lend'g of ye MS. you speak of."

Another and unsigned letter from Philadelphia provoked equal thought, especially for the following passage:

> "I will observe what you say respecting the sending of Accounts only by y^{r} Vessels, but can not always be certain when to expect them. In the Matter spoke of, I require onlie one more thing; but wish to be sure I apprehend you exactly. You inform me, that no Part must be missing if the finest Effects are to be had, but you can not but know how hard it is to be sure. It seems a great Hazard and

> Burthen to take away the whole Box, and in Town (i.e. St. Peter's, St. Paul's, St. Mary's, or Christ Church) it can scarce be done at all. But I know what Imperfections were in the one I rais'd up October last, and how many live Specimens you were forc'd to imploy before you hit upon the right Mode in the year 1766; so will be guided by you in all Matters. I am impatient for y^{r} Brig, and inquire daily at Mr. Biddle's Wharf."

A third suspicious letter was in an unknown tongue and even an unknown alphabet. In the Smith diary found by Charles Ward a single oft-repeated combination of characters is clumsily copied; and authorities at Brown University have pronounced the alphabet Amharic or Abyssinian, although they do not recognise the word. None of these epistles was ever delivered to Curwen, though the disappearance of Jedediah Orne from Salem as recorded shortly afterward shewed that the Providence men took certain quiet steps. The Pennsylvania Historical Society also has some curious letters received by Dr. Shippen regarding the presence of an unwholesome character in Philadelphia. But more decisive steps were in the air, and it is in the secret assemblages of sworn and tested sailors and faithful old privateersmen in the Brown warehouses by night that we must look for the main fruits of Weeden's disclosures. Slowly and surely a plan of campaign was under development which would leave no trace of Joseph Curwen's noxious mysteries.

Curwen, despite all precautions, apparently felt that something was in the wind; for he was now remarked to wear an unusually worried look. His coach was seen at all hours in the town and on the Pawtuxet Road, and he dropped little by little the air of forced geniality with which he had latterly sought to combat the town's prejudice. The nearest neighbours to his farm, the Fenners, one night remarked a great shaft of light shooting into the sky from some aperture in the roof of that cryptical stone building with the high, excessively narrow windows; an event which they quickly communicated to John Brown in Providence. Mr. Brown had become the executive leader of the select group bent on Curwen's extirpation, and had informed the Fenners that some action was about to be taken. This he deemed needful because of the impossibility of their not witnessing the final raid; and he explained his course by saying that Curwen was known to be a spy of the customs officers at Newport, against whom the hand of every Providence shipper, merchant, and farmer was openly or clandestinely raised. Whether the ruse was wholly believed by neighbours who had seen so many queer things is not certain; but at any rate the Fenners were willing to connect any evil with a man of such queer ways. To them Mr. Brown had entrusted the duty of watching the Curwen farmhouse, and of regularly reporting every incident which took place there.

5.

The probability that Curwen was on guard and attempting unusual things, as suggested by the odd shaft of light, precipitated at last the action so carefully devised by the band of serious citizens. According to the Smith diary a company of about 100 men met at 10 p.m. on Friday, April 12th, 1771, in the great room of Thurston's Tavern at the Sign of the Golden Lion on Weybosset Point across the Bridge. Of the guiding group of prominent men in addition to the leader John Brown there were present Dr. Bowen, with his case of surgical instruments, President Manning without the great periwig (the largest in the Colonies) for which he was noted, Governor Hopkins, wrapped in a dark cloak and accompanied by his seafaring brother Esek, whom he had initiated at the last moment with the permission of the rest, John Carter, Capt. Mathewson, and Capt. Whipple, who was to lead the actual raiding party. These chiefs conferred apart in a rear chamber, after which Capt. Whipple emerged to the great room and gave the gathered seamen their last oaths and instructions. Eleazar Smith was with the leaders as they sat in the rear apartment awaiting the arrival of Ezra Weeden, whose duty was to keep track of Curwen and report the departure of his coach for the farm.

About 10:30 a heavy rumble was heard on the Great Bridge, followed by the sound of a coach in the street outside; and at that hour there was no need of waiting for Weeden in order to know that the doomed man had set out for his last night of unhallowed wizardry. A moment later, as the receding coach clattered faintly over the Muddy Dock Bridge, Weeden appeared; and the raiders fell silently into military order in the street, shouldering the firelocks, fowling-pieces, or whaling harpoons which they had with them. Weeden and Smith were with the party, and of the deliberating citizens there were present for active service Capt. Whipple, the leader, Capt. Esek Hopkins, John Carter, President Manning, Capt. Mathewson, and Dr. Bowen; together with Moses Brown, who had come up at the eleventh hour though absent from the preliminary session in the tavern. All these freemen and their hundred sailors began the long march without delay, grim and a trifle apprehensive as they left the Muddy Dock behind and mounted the gentle rise of Broad Street toward the Pawtuxet Road. Just beyond Elder Snow's church some of the men turned back to take a parting look at Providence lying outspread under the early spring stars. Steeples and gables rose dark and shapely, and salt breezes swept up gently from the cove north of the Bridge. Vega was climbing above the great hill across the water, whose crest of trees was broken by the roof-line of the unfinished College edifice. At the foot of that hill, and along the narrow mounting lanes of its side, the old town dreamed; Old Providence, for whose safety and sanity so monstrous and colossal a blasphemy was about to be wiped out.

An hour and a quarter later the raiders arrived, as previously agreed, at the Fenner farmhouse; where they heard a final report on their intended victim. He had reached his farm over half an hour before, and the strange light had soon afterward shot once into the sky. There were no lights in any visible windows, but this was always the case of late. Even as this news was given another great glare arose toward the south, and the party realised that they had indeed come close to the scene of awesome and unnatural wonders. Capt. Whipple now ordered his force to separate into three divisions; one of twenty men under Eleazar Smith to strike across to the shore and guard the landing-place against possible reinforcements for Curwen until summoned by a messenger for desperate service, a second of twenty men under Capt. Esek Hopkins to steal down into the river valley behind the Curwen farm and demolish with axes or gunpowder the oaken door in the high, steep bank, and the third to close in on the house and adjacent buildings themselves. Of this last division one third was to be led by Capt. Mathewson to the cryptical stone edifice with high narrow windows, another third to follow Capt. Whipple himself to the main farmhouse, and the remaining third to preserve a circle around the whole group of buildings until summoned by a final emergency signal.

The river party would break down the hillside door at the sound of a single whistle-blast, then waiting and capturing anything which might issue from the regions within. At the sound of two whistle-blasts it would advance through the aperture to oppose the enemy or join the rest of the raiding contingent. The party at the stone building would accept these respective signals in an analogous manner; forcing an entrance at the first, and at the second descending whatever passage into the ground might be discovered, and joining the general or focal warfare expected to take place within the caverns. A third or emergency signal of three blasts would summon the immediate reserve from its general guard duty; its twenty men dividing equally and entering the unknown depths through both farmhouse and stone building.

Capt. Whipple's belief in the existence of catacombs was absolute, and he took no alternative into consideration when making his plans. He had with him a whistle of great power and shrillness, and did not fear any missing or misunderstanding of signals. The final reserve at the landing, of course, was nearly out of the whistle's range; hence would require a special messenger if needed for help. Moses Brown and John Carter went with Capt. Hopkins to the river-bank, while Pres. Manning was detailed with Capt. Mathewson to the stone building. Dr. Bowen, with Ezra Weeden, remained in Capt. Whipple's party which was to storm the farmhouse itself. The attack was to begin as soon as a messenger from Capt. Hopkins had joined Capt. Whipple to notify him of the river party's readiness. The leader would then deliver the loud single blast, and the various advance parties would commence their simultaneous attack on three points. Shortly before 1 a.m. the three divisions left the Fenner farmhouse; one to guard the landing, another to seek the river valley and the hillside door, and the third to subdivide and attend to the actual buildings of the Curwen farm.

Eleazar Smith, who accompanied the shore-guarding party, records in his diary an uneventful march and a long wait on the bluff by the bay; broken once by what seemed to be the distant sound of the signal whistle and again by a peculiar muffled blend of roaring and crying and a powder blast which seemed to come from the same direction. Later on one man thought he caught some distant gunshots, and still later Smith himself felt the throb of titanic, thunderous words resounding in upper air. It was just before dawn that a single haggard messenger with wild eyes and a hideous unknown odour about his clothing appeared and told the detachment to disperse quietly to their homes and never again think or speak of the night's doings or of him who had been Joseph Curwen. Something about the bearing of the messenger carried a conviction which his mere words could never have conveyed; for though he was a seaman well known to many of them, there was something obscurely lost or gained in his soul which set him for evermore apart. It was the same later on when they met other old companions who had gone into that zone of horror. Most of them had lost or gained something imponderable and indescribable. They had seen or heard or felt something which was not for human creatures, and could not forget it. From them there was never any gossip, for to even the commonest of mortal instincts there are terrible boundaries. And from that single messenger the party at the shore caught a nameless awe which almost sealed their own lips. Very few are the rumours which ever came from any of them, and Eleazar Smith's diary is the only written record which has survived from that whole expedition which set forth from the Sign of the Golden Lion under the stars.

Charles Ward, however, discovered another vague sidelight in some Fenner correspondence which he found in New London, where he knew another branch of the family had lived. It seems that the Fenners, from whose house the doomed farm was distantly visible, had watched the departing columns of raiders; and had heard very clearly the angry barking of the Curwen dogs, followed by the first shrill blast which precipitated the attack. This blast had been followed by a repetition of the great shaft of light from the stone building, and in another moment, after a quick sounding of the second signal ordering a general invasion, there had come a subdued prattle of musketry followed by a horrible roaring cry which the correspondent Luke Fenner had represented in his epistle by the characters "*Waaaahrrrrr—R'waaahrrr*". This cry, however, had possessed a quality which no mere writing could convey, and the correspondent mentions that his mother fainted completely at the sound. It was later repeated less loudly, and further but more muffled evidences of gunfire ensued; together with a loud explosion of powder from the direction of the river. About an hour afterward all the dogs began to bay frightfully, and there were vague ground rumblings so marked that the candlesticks tottered on the mantelpiece. A strong smell of sulphur was noted; and Luke Fenner's father declared that he heard the third or emergency whistle signal, though the others failed to detect it. Muffled musketry sounded again, followed by a deep scream less piercing but even more horrible than those which had preceded it; a kind of throaty, nastily plastic cough or gurgle whose quality as a scream must have come more from its continuity and psychological import than from its actual acoustic value.

Then the flaming thing burst into sight at a point where the Curwen farm ought to lie, and the human cries of desperate and frightened men were heard. Muskets flashed and cracked, and the flaming thing fell to the ground. A second flaming thing appeared, and a shriek of human origin was plainly distinguished. Fenner wrote that he could even gather a few words belched in frenzy: "Almighty, protect thy lamb!" Then there were more shots, and the second flaming thing fell. After that came silence for about three-quarters of an hour; at the end of which time little Arthur Fenner, Luke's brother, exclaimed that he saw 'a red fog' going up to the stars from the accursed farm in the distance. No one but the child can testify to this, but Luke admits the significant coincidence implied by the panic of almost convulsive fright which at the same moment arched the backs and stiffened the fur of the three cats then within the room.

Five minutes later a chill wind blew up, and the air became suffused with such an intolerable stench that only the strong freshness of the sea could have prevented its being noticed by the shore party or by any wakeful souls in Pawtuxet village. This stench was nothing which any of the Fenners had ever encountered before, and produced a kind of clutching, amorphous fear beyond that of the tomb or the charnel-house. Close upon it came the awful voice which no hapless hearer will ever be able to forget. It thundered out of the sky like a doom, and windows rattled as its echoes died away. It was deep and musical; powerful as a bass organ, but evil as the forbidden books of the Arabs. What it said no man can tell, for it spoke in an unknown tongue, but this is the writing Luke Fenner set down to portray the daemoniac intonations: "DEESMEES—JESHET—BONE DOSEFE DUVEMA—ENITEMOSS." Not till the year 1919 did any soul link this crude transcript with anything else in mortal knowledge, but Charles Ward paled as he recognised what Mirandola had denounced in shudders as the ultimate horror among black magic's incantations.

An unmistakably human shout or deep chorused scream seemed to answer this malign wonder from the Curwen farm, after which the unknown stench grew complex with an added odour equally intolerable. A wailing distinctly different from the scream now burst out, and was protracted ululantly in rising and falling paroxysms. At times it became almost articulate, though no auditor could trace any definite words; and at one point it seemed to verge toward the confines of diabolic and hysterical laughter. Then a yell of utter, ultimate fright and stark madness wrenched from scores of human throats; a yell which came strong and clear despite the depth from which it must have burst; after which darkness and silence ruled all things. Spirals of acrid smoke ascended to blot out the stars, though no flames appeared, and no buildings were observed to be gone or injured on the following day.

Toward dawn two frightened messengers with monstrous and unplaceable odours saturating their clothing knocked at the Fenner door and requested a keg of rum, for which they paid very well indeed. One of them told the family that the affair of Joseph Curwen was over, and that the events of the night were not to be mentioned again. Arrogant as the order seemed, the aspect of him who gave it took away all resentment and lent it a fearsome authority; so that only these furtive letters of Luke Fenner, which he urged his Connecticut relative to destroy, remain to tell what was seen and heard. The non-compliance of that relative, whereby the letters were saved after all, has alone kept the matter from a merciful oblivion. Charles Ward had one detail to add as a result of a long canvass of Pawtuxet residents for ancestral traditions. Old Charles Slocum of that village said that there was known to his grandfather a queer rumour concerning a charred, distorted body found in the fields a week after the death of Joseph Curwen was announced. What kept the talk alive was the notion that this body, so far as could be seen in its burnt and twisted condition, was neither thoroughly human nor wholly allied to any animal which Pawtuxet folk had ever seen or read about.

6.

Not one man who participated in that terrible raid could ever be induced to say a word concerning it, and every fragment of the vague data which survives comes from those outside the final fighting party. There is something frightful in the care with which these actual raiders destroyed each scrap which bore the least allusion to the matter. Eight sailors had been killed, but although their bodies were not produced their families were satisfied with the statement that a clash with customs officers had occurred. The same statement also covered the numerous cases of wounds, all of which were extensively bandaged and treated only by Dr. Jabez Bowen, who had accompanied the party. Hardest to explain was the nameless odour clinging to all the raiders, a thing which was discussed for weeks. Of the citizen leaders, Capt. Whipple and Moses Brown were most severely hurt, and letters of their wives testify the bewilderment which their reticence and close guarding of their bandages produced. Psychologically every participant was aged, sobered, and shaken. It is fortunate that they were all strong men of action and simple, orthodox religionists, for with more subtle introspectiveness and mental complexity they would have fared ill indeed. President Manning was the most disturbed; but even he outgrew the darkest shadow, and smothered memories in prayers. Every man of those leaders had a stirring part to play in later years, and it is perhaps fortunate that this is so. Little more than a twelvemonth afterward Capt. Whipple led the mob who burnt the revenue ship *Gaspee*, and in this bold act we may trace one step in the blotting out of unwholesome images.

There was delivered to the widow of Joseph Curwen a sealed leaden coffin of curious design, obviously found ready on the spot when needed, in which she was told her husband's body lay. He had, it was explained, been killed in a customs battle about which it was not politic to give details. More than this no tongue ever uttered of Joseph Curwen's end, and Charles Ward had only a single hint wherewith to construct a theory. This hint was the merest thread—a shaky underscoring of a passage in Jedediah Orne's confiscated letter to Curwen, as partly copied in Ezra Weeden's handwriting. The copy was found in the possession of Smith's descendants; and we are left to decide whether Weeden gave it to his companion after the end, as a mute clue to the abnormality which had occurred, or whether, as is more probable, Smith had it before, and added the underscoring himself from what he had managed to extract from his friend by shrewd guessing and adroit cross-questioning. The underlined passage is merely this:

> *"I say to you againe, doe not call up Any that you can not put downe; by the Which I meane, Any that can in Turne call up somewhat against you, whereby your Powerfullest Devices may not be of use. Ask of the Lesser, lest the Greater shall not wish to Answer, and shall commande more than you."*

In the light of this passage, and reflecting on what last unmentionable allies a beaten man might try to summon in his direst extremity, Charles Ward may well have wondered whether any citizen of Providence killed Joseph Curwen.

The deliberate effacement of every memory of the dead man from Providence life and annals was vastly aided by the influence of the raiding leaders. They had not at first meant to be so thorough, and had allowed the widow and her father and child to remain in ignorance of the true conditions; but Capt. Tillinghast was an astute man, and soon uncovered enough rumours to whet his horror and cause him to demand that his daughter and granddaughter change their name, burn the library and all remaining papers, and chisel the inscription from the slate slab above Joseph Curwen's grave. He knew Capt. Whipple well, and probably extracted more hints from that bluff mariner than anyone else ever gained respecting the end of the accused sorcerer.

From that time on the obliteration of Curwen's memory became increasingly rigid, extending at last by common consent even to the town records and files of the *Gazette*. It can be compared in spirit only to the hush that lay on Oscar Wilde's name for a decade after his disgrace, and in extent only to the fate of that sinful King of Runazar in Lord Dunsany's tale, whom the Gods decided must not only cease to be, but must cease ever to have been.

Mrs. Tillinghast, as the widow became known after 1772, sold the house in Olney Court and resided with her father in Power's

Lane till her death in 1817. The farm at Pawtuxet, shunned by every living soul, remained to moulder through the years; and seemed to decay with unaccountable rapidity. By 1780 only the stone and brickwork were standing, and by 1800 even these had fallen to shapeless heaps. None ventured to pierce the tangled shrubbery on the river-bank behind which the hillside door may have lain, nor did any try to frame a definite image of the scenes amidst which Joseph Curwen departed from the horrors he had wrought.

Only robust old Capt. Whipple was heard by alert listeners to mutter once in a while to himself, "Pox on that ———, but he had no business to laugh while he screamed. 'Twas as though the damn'd ——— had some'at up his sleeve. For half a crown I'd burn his ———house."

III. A Search and an Evocation

1.

Charles Ward, as we have seen, first learned in 1918 of his descent from Joseph Curwen. That he at once took an intense interest in everything pertaining to the bygone mystery is not to be wondered at; for every vague rumour that he had heard of Curwen now became something vital to himself, in whom flowed Curwen's blood. No spirited and imaginative genealogist could have done otherwise than begin forthwith an avid and systematic collection of Curwen data.

In his first delvings there was not the slightest attempt at secrecy; so that even Dr. Lyman hesitates to date the youth's madness from any period before the close of 1919. He talked freely with his family—though his mother was not particularly pleased to own an ancestor like Curwen—and with the officials of the various museums and libraries he visited. In applying to private families for records thought to be in their possession he made no concealment of his object, and shared the somewhat amused scepticism with which the accounts of the old diarists and letter-writers were regarded. He often expressed a keen wonder as to what really had taken place a century and a half before at that Pawtuxet farmhouse whose site he vainly tried to find, and what Joseph Curwen really had been.

When he came across the Smith diary and archives and encountered the letter from Jedediah Orne he decided to visit Salem and look up Curwen's early activities and connexions there, which he did during the Easter vacation of 1919. At the Essex Institute, which was well known to him from former sojourns in the glamorous old town of crumbling Puritan gables and clustered gambrel roofs, he was very kindly received, and unearthed there a considerable amount of Curwen data. He found that his ancestor was born in Salem-Village, now Danvers, seven miles from town, on the eighteenth of February (O.S.) 1662–3; and that he had run away to sea at the age of fifteen, not appearing again for nine years, when he returned with the speech, dress, and manners of a native Englishman and settled in Salem proper. At that time he had little to do with his family, but spent most of his hours with the curious books he had brought from Europe, and the strange chemicals which came for him on ships from England, France, and Holland. Certain trips of his into the country were the objects of much local inquisitiveness, and were whisperingly associated with vague rumours of fires on the hills at night.

Curwen's only close friends had been one Edward Hutchinson of Salem-Village and one Simon Orne of Salem. With these men he was often seen in conference about the Common, and visits among them were by no means infrequent. Hutchinson had a house well out toward the woods, and it was not altogether liked by sensitive people because of the sounds heard there at night. He was said to entertain strange visitors, and the lights seen from his windows were not always of the same colour. The knowledge he displayed concerning long-dead persons and long-forgotten events was considered distinctly unwholesome, and he disappeared about the time the witchcraft panic began, never to be heard from again. At that time Joseph Curwen also departed, but his settlement in Providence was soon learned of. Simon Orne lived in Salem until 1720, when his failure to grow visibly old began to excite attention. He thereafter disappeared, though thirty years later his precise counterpart and self-styled son turned up to claim his property. The claim was allowed on the strength of documents in Simon Orne's known hand, and Jedediah Orne continued to dwell in Salem till 1771, when certain letters from Providence citizens to the Rev. Thomas Barnard and others brought about his quiet removal to parts unknown.

Certain documents by and about all of these strange characters were available at the Essex Institute, the Court House, and the Registry of Deeds, and included both harmless commonplaces such as land titles and bills of sale, and furtive fragments of a more provocative nature. There were four or five unmistakable allusions to them in the witchcraft trial records; as when one Hepzibah Lawson swore on July 16, 1692, at the Court of Oyer and Terminer under Judge Hathorne, that 'fortie Witches and the Blacke Man were wont to meete in the Woodes behind Mr. Hutchinson's house', and one Amity How declared at a session of August 8th before Judge Gedney that 'Mr. G. B. (Rev. George Burroughs) on that Nighte putt ye Divell his Marke upon Bridget S., Jonathan A., *Simon* O., Deliverance W., *Joseph* C., Susan P., Mehitable C., and Deborah B.' Then there was a catalogue of Hutchinson's uncanny library as found after his disappearance, and an unfinished manuscript in his handwriting, couched in a cipher none could read. Ward had a photostatic copy of this manuscript made, and began to work casually on the cipher as soon as it was delivered to him. After the following August his labours on the cipher became intense and feverish, and there is reason to believe from his speech and conduct that he hit upon the key before October or November. He never stated, though, whether or not he had succeeded.

But of greatest immediate interest was the Orne material. It took Ward only a short time to prove from identity of penmanship a thing he had already considered established from the text of the letter to Curwen; namely, that Simon Orne and his supposed son were one and the same person. As Orne had said to his correspondent, it was hardly safe to live too long in Salem, hence he resorted to a thirty-year sojourn abroad, and did not return to claim his lands except as a representative of a new generation. Orne had apparently been careful to destroy most of his correspondence, but the citizens who took action in 1771 found and preserved a few letters and papers which excited their wonder. There were cryptic formulae and diagrams in his and other hands which Ward now either copied with care or had photographed, and one extremely mysterious letter in a chirography that the searcher recognised from items in the Registry of Deeds as positively Joseph Curwen's.

This Curwen letter, though undated as to the year, was evidently not the one in answer to which Orne had written the confiscated missive; and from internal evidence Ward placed it not much later than 1750. It may not be amiss to give the text in full, as a sample of the style of one whose history was so dark and terrible. The recipient is addressed as "Simon", but a line (whether drawn by Curwen or Orne Ward could not tell) is run through the word.

Prouidence, I. May (Ut. vulgo)

Brother:—

My honour'd Antient ffriende, due Respects and earnest Wishes to Him whom we serve for y^r eternall Power. I am just come upon That which you ought to knowe, concern'g the Matter of the Laste Extremitie and what to doe regard'g yt. I am not dispos'd to followe you in go'g Away on acct. of my Yeares, for Prouidence hath not ye Sharpeness of ye Bay in hunt'g oute uncommon Things and bringinge to Tryall. I am ty'd up in Shippes and Goodes, and cou'd not doe as you did, besides the Whiche my ffarme at Patuxet hath under it What you Knowe, that wou'd not waite for my com'g Backe as an Other.

But I am not unreadie for harde ffortunes, as I haue tolde you, and haue longe work'd upon ye Way of get'g Backe after ye Laste. I laste Night strucke on ye Wordes that bringe up YOGGE-SOTHOTHE, and sawe for ye firste Time that fface spoke of by Ibn Schacabao in ye——. And IT said, that ye III Psalme in ye Liber-Damnatus holdes ye Clauicle. With Sunne in V House, Saturne in Trine, drawe ye Pentagram of Fire, and saye ye ninth Uerse thrice. This Uerse repeate eache Roodemas and Hallow's Eue, and ye Thing will breede in ye Outside Spheres.

And of ye Seede of Olde shal One be borne who shal looke Backe, tho' know'g not what he seekes.

Yett will this availe Nothing if there be no Heir, and if the Saltes, or the Way to make the Saltes, bee not Readie for his Hande; and here I will owne, I have not taken needed Stepps nor founde Much. Ye Process is plaguy harde to come neare; and it uses up such a Store of Specimens, I am harde putte to it to get Enough, notwithstand'g the Sailors I have from ye Indies. Ye People aboute are become curious, but I can stande them off. Ye Gentry are worse than ye Populace, be'g more Circumstantiall in their Accts. and more believ'd in what they tell. That Parson and Mr. Merritt have talk'd some, I am fearfull, but no Thing soe far is Dangerous. Ye Chymical substances are easie of get'g, there be'g II. goode Chymists in Towne, Dr. Bowen and Sam: Carew. I am foll'g oute what Borellus saith, and haue Helpe in Abdool Al-Hazred his VII. Booke. Whatever I gette, you shal haue. And in ye meane while, do not neglect to make use of ye Wordes I haue here giuen. I haue them Righte, but if you Desire to see HIM, imploy the Writinge on ye Piece of —— that I am putt'g in this Packet. Saye ye Uerses every Roodmas and Hallow's Eue; and if y^r Line runn not out, *one shal bee in yeares to come that shal looke backe and use what Saltes or Stuff for Saltes you shal leaue him.* Job XIV. XIV.

I rejoice you are again at Salem, and hope I may see you not longe hence. I have a goode Stallion, and am think'g of get'g a Coach, there be'g one (Mr. Merritt's) in Prouidence already, tho' ye Roades are bad. If you are dispos'd to Travel, doe not pass me bye. From Boston take ye Post Rd. thro' Dedham, Wrentham, and Attleborough, goode Taverns be'g at all these Townes. Stop at Mr. Bolcom's in Wrentham, where ye Beddes are finer than Mr. Hatch's, but eate at ye other House for their Cooke is better. Turne into Prou. by Patucket ffalls, and ye Rd. past Mr. Sayles's Tavern. My House opp. Mr. Epenetus Olney's Tavern off ye Towne Street, Ist on ye N. side of Olney's Court. Distance from Boston Stone abt. XLIV Miles.

Sir, I am y^r olde and true ffriend and Servt. in *Almousin-Metraton.*

Josephus C.

To Mr. Simon Orne,
William's-Lane, in Salem.

This letter, oddly enough, was what first gave Ward the exact location of Curwen's Providence home; for none of the records encountered up to that time had been at all specific. The discovery was doubly striking because it indicated, as the newer Curwen house built in 1761 on the site of the old, a dilapidated building still standing in Olney Court and well known to Ward in his antiquarian rambles over Stampers' Hill. The place was indeed only a few squares from his own home on the great hill's higher ground, and was now the abode of a negro family much esteemed for occasional washing, housecleaning, and furnace-tending services. To find, in distant Salem, such sudden proof of the significance of this familiar rookery in his own family history, was a highly impressive thing to Ward; and he resolved to explore the place immediately upon his return. The more mystical phases of the letter, which he took to be some extravagant kind of symbolism, frankly baffled him; though he noted with a thrill of curiosity that the Biblical passage referred to—Job 14, 14—was the familiar verse, "If a man die, shall he live again? All the days of my appointed time will I wait, till my change come."

2.

Young Ward came home in a state of pleasant excitement, and spent the following Saturday in a long and exhaustive study of the house in Olney Court. The place, now crumbling with age, had never been a mansion; but was a modest two-and-a-half story wooden town house of the familiar Providence colonial type, with plain peaked roof, large central chimney, and artistically carved doorway with rayed fanlight, triangular pediment, and trim Doric pilasters. It had suffered but little alteration externally, and Ward felt he was gazing on something very close to the sinister matters of his quest.

The present negro inhabitants were known to him, and he was very courteously shewn about the interior by old Asa and his stout wife Hannah. Here there was more change than the outside indicated, and Ward saw with regret that fully half of the fine scroll-and-urn overmantels and shell-carved cupboard linings were gone, whilst much of the fine wainscotting and bolection moulding was marked, hacked, and gouged, or covered up altogether with cheap wall paper. In general, the survey did not yield as much as Ward had somehow expected; but it was at least exciting to stand within the ancestral walls which had housed such a man of horror as Joseph Curwen. He saw with a thrill that a monogram had been very carefully effaced from the ancient brass knocker.

From then until after the close of school Ward spent his time on the photostatic copy of the Hutchinson cipher and the accumulation of local Curwen data. The former still proved unyielding; but of the latter he obtained so much, and so many clues to similar data elsewhere, that he was ready by July to make a trip to New London and New York to consult old letters whose presence in those places was indicated. This trip was very fruitful, for it brought him the Fenner letters with their terrible description of the Pawtuxet farmhouse raid, and the Nightingale-Talbot letters in which he learned of the portrait painted on a panel of the Curwen library. This matter of the portrait interested him particularly, since he would have given much to know just what Joseph Curwen looked like; and he decided to make a second search of the house in Olney Court to see if there might not be some trace of the ancient features beneath peeling coats of later paint or layers of mouldy wall-paper.

Early in August that search took place, and Ward went carefully over the walls of every room sizeable enough to have been by any possibility the library of the evil builder. He paid especial attention to the large panels of such overmantels as still remained; and was keenly excited after about an hour, when on a broad area above the fireplace in a spacious ground-floor room he became certain that the surface brought out by the peeling of several coats of paint was sensibly darker than any ordinary interior paint or the wood beneath it was likely to have been. A few more careful tests with a thin knife, and he knew that he had come upon an oil portrait of great extent. With truly scholarly restraint the youth did not risk the damage which an immediate attempt to uncover the hidden picture with the knife might have done, but just retired from the scene of his discovery to enlist expert help. In three days he returned with an artist of long experience, Mr. Walter C. Dwight, whose studio is near the foot of College Hill; and that accomplished restorer of paintings set to work at once with proper methods and chemical substances. Old Asa and his wife were duly excited over their strange visitors, and were properly reimbursed for this invasion of their domestic hearth.

As day by day the work of restoration progressed, Charles Ward looked on with growing interest at the lines and shades gradually unveiled after their long oblivion. Dwight had begun at the bottom; hence since the picture was a three-quarter-length one, the face did not come out for some time. It was meanwhile seen that the subject was a spare, well-shaped man with dark-blue coat, embroidered waistcoat, black satin small-clothes, and white silk stockings, seated in a carved chair against the background of a window with wharves and ships beyond. When the head came out it was observed to bear a neat Albemarle wig, and to possess a thin, calm, undistinguished face which seemed somehow familiar to both Ward and the artist. Only at the very last, though, did the restorer and his client begin to gasp with astonishment at the details of that lean, pallid visage, and to recognise with a touch of awe the dramatic trick which heredity had played. For it took the final bath of oil and the final stroke of the delicate scraper to bring out fully the expression which centuries had hidden; and to confront the bewildered Charles Dexter Ward, dweller in the past, with his own living features in the countenance of his horrible great-great-great-grandfather.

Ward brought his parents to see the marvel he had uncovered, and his father at once determined to purchase the picture despite its execution on stationary panelling. The resemblance to the boy, despite an appearance of rather greater age, was marvellous; and it could be seen that through some trick of atavism the physical contours of Joseph Curwen had found precise duplication after a century and a half. Mrs. Ward's resemblance to her ancestor was not at all marked, though she could recall relatives who had some of the facial characteristics shared by her son and the bygone Curwen. She did not relish the discovery, and told her husband that he had better burn the picture instead of bringing it home. There was, she averred, something unwholesome about it; not only intrinsically, but in its very resemblance to Charles. Mr. Ward, however, was a practical man of power and affairs—a cotton manufacturer with extensive mills at Riverpoint in the Pawtuxet Valley—and not one to listen to feminine scruples. The picture impressed him mightily with its likeness to his son, and he believed the boy deserved it as a present. In this opinion, it is needless to say, Charles most heartily concurred; and a few days later Mr. Ward located the owner of the house—a small rodent-featured person with a guttural accent—and obtained the whole mantel and overmantel bearing the picture at a curtly fixed price which cut short the impending torrent of unctuous haggling.

It now remained to take off the panelling and remove it to the Ward home, where provisions were made for its thorough restoration and installation with an electric mock-fireplace in Charles's third-floor study or library. To Charles was left the task of superintending this removal, and on the twenty-eighth of August he accompanied two expert workmen from the Crooker decorating firm to the house in Olney Court, where the mantel and portrait-bearing overmantel were detached with great care and precision for transportation in the company's motor truck. There was left a space of exposed brickwork marking the chimney's course, and in this young Ward observed a cubical recess about a foot square, which must have lain directly behind the head of the portrait. Curious as to what such a space might mean or contain, the youth approached and looked within; finding beneath the deep coatings of dust and soot some loose yellowed papers, a crude, thick copy-book, and a few mouldering textile shreds which may have formed the ribbon binding the rest together. Blowing away the bulk of the dirt and cinders, he took up the book and looked at the bold inscription on its cover. It was in a hand which he had learned to recognise at the Essex Institute, and proclaimed the volume as the "*Journall and Notes of Jos: Curwen, Gent., of Prouidence-Plantations, Late of Salem.*"

Excited beyond measure by his discovery, Ward shewed the book to the two curious workmen beside him. Their testimony is absolute as to the nature and genuineness of the finding, and Dr. Willett relies on them to help establish his theory that the youth was not mad when he began his major eccentricities. All the other papers were likewise in Curwen's handwriting, and one of them seemed especially portentous because of its inscription: "*To Him Who Shal Come After, & How He May Gett Beyonde Time & ye Spheres.*" Another was in a cipher; the same, Ward hoped, as the Hutchinson cipher which had hitherto baffled him. A third, and here the searcher rejoiced, seemed to be a key to the cipher; whilst the fourth and fifth were addressed respectively to "Edw: Hutchinson, Armiger" and "Jedediah Orne, Esq.", 'or Their Heir or Heirs, or Those Represent'g Them'. The sixth and last was inscribed: "*Joseph Curwen his Life and Travells Bet'n ye yeares 1678 and 1687: Of Whither He Voyag'd, Where He Stay'd, Whom He Sawe, and What He Learnt.*"

3.

We have now reached the point from which the more academic school of alienists date Charles Ward's madness. Upon his discovery the youth had looked immediately at a few of the inner pages of the book and manuscripts, and had evidently seen something which impressed him tremendously. Indeed, in shewing the titles to the workmen he appeared to guard the text itself with peculiar care, and to labour under a perturbation for which even the antiquarian and genealogical significance of the find could hardly account. Upon returning home he broke the news with an almost embarrassed air, as if he wished to convey an idea of its supreme importance without having to exhibit the evidence itself. He did not even shew the titles to his parents, but simply told them that he had found some documents in Joseph Curwen's handwriting, "mostly in cipher", which would have to be studied very carefully before yielding up their true meaning. It is unlikely that he would have shewn what he did to the workmen, had it not been for their unconcealed curiosity. As it was he doubtless wished to avoid any display of peculiar reticence which would increase their discussion of the matter.

That night Charles Ward sat up in his room reading the new-found book and papers, and when day came he did not desist. His meals, on his urgent request when his mother called to see what was amiss, were sent up to him; and in the afternoon he appeared only briefly when the men came to install the Curwen picture and mantelpiece in his study. The next night he slept in snatches in his clothes, meanwhile wrestling feverishly with the unravelling of the cipher manuscript. In the morning his mother saw that he was at work on the photostatic copy of the Hutchinson cipher, which he had frequently shewn her before; but in response to her query he said that the Curwen key could not be applied to it. That afternoon he abandoned his work and watched the men fascinatedly as they finished their installation of the picture with its woodwork above a cleverly realistic electric log, setting the mock-fireplace and overmantel a little out from the north wall as if a chimney existed, and boxing in the sides with panelling to match the room's. The front panel holding the picture was sawn and hinged to allow cupboard space behind it. After the workmen went he moved his work into the study and sat down before it with his eyes half on the cipher and half on the portrait which stared back at him like a year-adding and century-recalling mirror.

His parents, subsequently recalling his conduct at this period, give interesting details anent the policy of concealment which he practiced. Before servants he seldom hid any paper which he might be studying, since he rightly assumed that Curwen's intricate and archaic chirography would be too much for them. With his parents, however, he was more circumspect; and unless the manuscript in question were a cipher, or a mere mass of cryptic symbols and unknown ideographs (as that entitled "*To Him Who Shal Come After* etc." seemed to be), he would cover it with some convenient paper until his caller had departed. At night he kept the papers under lock and key in an antique cabinet of his, where he also placed them whenever he left the room. He soon resumed fairly regular hours and habits, except that his long walks and other outside interests seemed to cease. The opening of school, where he now began his senior year, seemed a great bore to him;

and he frequently asserted his determination never to bother with college. He had, he said, important special investigations to make, which would provide him with more avenues toward knowledge and the humanities than any university which the world could boast.

Naturally, only one who had always been more or less studious, eccentric, and solitary could have pursued this course for many days without attracting notice. Ward, however, was constitutionally a scholar and a hermit; hence his parents were less surprised than regretful at the close confinement and secrecy he adopted. At the same time, both his father and mother thought it odd that he would shew them no scrap of his treasure-trove, nor give any connected account of such data as he had deciphered. This reticence he explained away as due to a wish to wait until he might announce some connected revelation, but as the weeks passed without further disclosures there began to grow up between the youth and his family a kind of constraint; intensified in his mother's case by her manifest disapproval of all Curwen delvings.

During October Ward began visiting the libraries again, but no longer for the antiquarian matter of his former days. Witchcraft and magic, occultism and daemonology, were what he sought now; and when Providence sources proved unfruitful he would take the train for Boston and tap the wealth of the great library in Copley Square, the Widener Library at Harvard, or the Zion Research Library in Brookline, where certain rare works on Biblical subjects are available. He bought extensively, and fitted up a whole additional set of shelves in his study for newly acquired works on uncanny subjects; while during the Christmas holidays he made a round of out-of-town trips including one to Salem to consult certain records at the Essex Institute.

About the middle of January, 1920, there entered Ward's bearing an element of triumph which he did not explain, and he was no more found at work upon the Hutchinson cipher. Instead, he inaugurated a dual policy of chemical research and record-scanning; fitting up for the one a laboratory in the unused attic of the house, and for the latter haunting all the sources of vital statistics in Providence. Local dealers in drugs and scientific supplies, later questioned, give astonishingly queer and meaningless catalogues of the substances and instruments he purchased; but clerks at the State House, the City Hall, and the various libraries agree as to the definite object of his second interest. He was searching intensely and feverishly for the grave of Joseph Curwen, from whose slate slab an older generation had so wisely blotted the name.

Little by little there grew upon the Ward family the conviction that something was wrong. Charles had had freaks and changes of minor interests before, but this growing secrecy and absorption in strange pursuits was unlike even him. His school work was the merest pretence; and although he failed in no test, it could be seen that the old application had all vanished. He had other concernments now; and when not in his new laboratory with a score of obsolete alchemical books, could be found either poring over old burial records down town or glued to his volumes of occult lore in his study, where the startlingly—one almost fancied increasingly—similar features of Joseph Curwen stared blandly at him from the great overmantel on the north wall.

Late in March Ward added to his archive-searching a ghoulish series of rambles about the various ancient cemeteries of the city. The cause appeared later, when it was learned from City Hall clerks that he had probably found an important clue. His quest had suddenly shifted from the grave of Joseph Curwen to that of one Naphthali Field; and this shift was explained when, upon going over the files that he had been over, the investigators actually found a fragmentary record of Curwen's burial which had escaped the general obliteration, and which stated that the curious leaden coffin had been interred "10 ft. S. and 5 ft. W. of Naphthali Field's grave in y^{e} ———". The lack of a specified burying-ground in the surviving entry greatly complicated the search, and Naphthali Field's grave seemed as elusive as that of Curwen; but here no systematic effacement had existed, and one might reasonably be expected to stumble on the stone itself even if its record had perished. Hence the rambles—from which St. John's (the former King's) Churchyard and the ancient Congregational burying-ground in the midst of Swan Point Cemetery were excluded, since other statistics had shewn that the only Naphthali Field (obiit 1729) whose grave could have been meant had been a Baptist.

4.

It was toward May when Dr. Willett, at the request of the senior Ward and fortified with all the Curwen data which the family had gleaned from Charles in his non-secretive days, talked with the young man. The interview was of little value or conclusiveness, for Willett felt at every moment that Charles was thoroughly master of himself and in touch with matters of real importance; but it at least forced the secretive youth to offer some rational explanation of his recent demeanour. Of a pallid, impassive type not easily shewing embarrassment, Ward seemed quite ready to discuss his pursuits, though not to reveal their object. He stated that the papers of his ancestor had contained some remarkable secrets of early scientific knowledge, for the most part in cipher, of an apparent scope comparable only to the discoveries of Friar Bacon and perhaps surpassing even those. They were, however, meaningless except when correlated with a body of learning now wholly obsolete; so that their immediate presentation to a world equipped only with modern science would rob them of all impressiveness and dramatic significance. To take their vivid place in the history of human thought they must first be correlated by one familiar with the background out of which they evolved, and to this task of correlation Ward was now devoting himself. He was seeking to acquire as fast as possible those neglected arts of old which a true interpreter of the Curwen data must possess, and hoped in time to make a full announcement and presentation of the utmost interest to mankind and to the world of thought. Not even Einstein, he declared, could more profoundly revolutionise the current conception of things.

As to his graveyard search, whose object he freely admitted, but the details of whose progress he did not relate, he said he had reason to think that Joseph Curwen's mutilated headstone bore certain mystic symbols—carved from directions in his will and ignorantly spared by those who had effaced the name—which were absolutely essential to the final solution of his cryptic system. Curwen, he believed, had wished to guard his secret with care; and had consequently distributed the data in an exceedingly curious fashion. When Dr. Willett asked to see the mystic documents, Ward displayed much reluctance and tried to put him off with such things as the photostatic copies of the Hutchinson cipher and Orne formulae and diagrams; but finally shewed him the exteriors of some of the real Curwen finds—the "*Journall and Notes*", the cipher (title in cipher also), and the formula-filled message "*To Him Who Shal Come After*"—and let him glance inside such as were in obscure characters.

He also opened the diary at a page carefully selected for its innocuousness and gave Willett a glimpse of Curwen's connected handwriting in English. The doctor noted very closely the crabbed and complicated letters, and the general aura of the seventeenth century which clung round both penmanship and style despite the writer's survival into the eighteenth century, and became quickly certain that the document was genuine. The text itself was relatively trivial, and Willett recalled only a fragment:

> "Wedn. 16 Octr. 1754. My Sloope the *Wakeful* this Day putt in from London with XX newe Men pick'd up in ye Indies, Spaniards from Martineco and 2 Dutch Men from Surinam. Ye Dutch Men are like to Desert from have'g hearde Somewhat ill of these Ventures, but I will see to ye Inducing of them to Staye. ffor Mr. Knight Dexter at ye Boy and Book 120 Pieces Camblets, 100 Pieces Assrtd. Cambleteens, 20 Pieces blue Duffles, 100 Pieces Shalloons, 50 Pieces Calamancoes, 300 Pieces each, Shendsoy and Humhums. ffor Mr. Green at ye Elephant 50 Gallon Cyttles, 20 Warm'g Pannes, 15 Bake Cyttles, 10 pr. Smoke'g Tonges. ffor Mr. Perrigo 1 Sett of Awles. ffor Mr. Nightingale 50 Reames prime Foolscap. Say'd ye SABAOTH thrice last Nighte but None appear'd. I must heare more from Mr. H. in Transylvania, tho' it is Harde reach'g him and exceeding strange he can not give me the Use of what he hath so well us'd these hundred yeares. Simon hath not Writ these V. Weekes, but I expecte soon hear'g from him."

When upon reaching this point Dr. Willett turned the leaf he was quickly checked by Ward, who almost snatched the book from his grasp. All that the doctor had a chance to see on the newly opened page was a brief pair of sentences; but these, strangely enough, lingered tenaciously in his memory. They ran: "Ye Verse from Liber-Damnatus be'g spoke V Roodmasses and IV Hallows-Eves, I am Hopeful ye Thing is breed'g Outside ye Spheres. It will drawe One who is to Come, if I can make sure he shal bee, and he shal think on Past thinges and look back thro' all ye yeares, against ye which I must have ready ye Saltes or That to make 'em with."

Willett saw no more, but somehow this small glimpse gave a new and vague terror to the painted features of Joseph Curwen which stared blandly down from the overmantel. Ever after that he entertained the odd fancy—which his medical skill of course assured him was only a fancy—that the eyes of the portrait had a sort of wish, if not an actual tendency, to follow young Charles Ward as he moved about the room. He stopped before leaving to study the picture closely, marvelling at its resemblance to Charles and memorising every minute detail of the cryptical, colourless face, even down to a slight scar or pit in the smooth brow above the right eye. Cosmo Alexander, he decided, was a painter worthy of the Scotland that produced Raeburn, and a teacher worthy of his illustrious pupil Gilbert Stuart.

Assured by the doctor that Charles's mental health was in no danger, but that on the other hand he was engaged in researches which might prove of real importance, the Wards were more lenient than they might otherwise have been when during the following June the youth made positive his refusal to attend college. He had, he declared, studies of much more vital importance to pursue; and intimated a wish to go abroad the following year in order to avail himself of certain sources of data not existing in America. The senior Ward, while denying this latter wish as absurd for a boy of only eighteen, acquiesced regarding the university; so that after a none too brilliant graduation from the Moses Brown School there ensued for Charles a three-year period of intensive occult study and graveyard searching. He became recognised as an eccentric, and dropped even more completely from the sight of his family's friends than he had been before; keeping close to his work and only occasionally making trips to other cities to consult obscure records. Once he went south to talk with a strange old mulatto who dwelt in a swamp and about whom a newspaper had printed a curious article. Again he sought a small village in the Adirondacks whence reports of certain odd ceremonial practices had come. But still his parents forbade him the trip to the Old World which he desired.

Coming of age in April, 1923, and having previously inherited a small competence from his maternal grandfather, Ward determined at last to take the European trip hitherto denied him. Of his proposed itinerary he would say nothing save that the needs of his studies would carry him to many places, but he promised to write his parents fully and faithfully. When they saw he could not be dissuaded, they ceased all opposition and helped as best they could; so that in June the young man sailed for Liverpool with the farewell blessings of his father and mother, who accompanied him to Boston and waved him out of sight from the White Star pier in Charlestown. Letters soon told of his safe arrival, and of his securing good quarters in Great Russell Street, London; where he proposed to stay, shunning all family friends, till he had exhausted the resources of the British Museum in a certain direction. Of his daily life he wrote but little, for there was little to write. Study and experiment consumed all his time, and he mentioned a laboratory which he had established in one of his rooms. That he said nothing of antiquarian rambles in the glamorous old city with its luring skyline of ancient domes and steeples and its tangles of roads and alleys whose mystic convolutions and sudden vistas alternately beckon and surprise, was taken by his parents as a good index of the degree to which his new interests had engrossed his mind.

In June, 1924, a brief note told of his departure for Paris, to which he had before made one or two flying trips for material in the Bibliothèque Nationale. For three months thereafter he sent only postal cards, giving an address in the Rue St. Jacques and referring to a special search among rare manuscripts in the library of an unnamed private collector. He avoided acquaintances, and no tourists brought back reports of having seen him. Then came a silence, and in October the Wards received a picture card from Prague, Czecho-Slovakia, stating that Charles was in that ancient town for the purpose of conferring with a certain very aged man supposed to be the last living possessor of some very curious mediaeval information. He gave an address in the Neustadt, and announced no move till the following January; when he dropped several cards from Vienna telling of his passage through that city on the way toward a more easterly region whither one of his correspondents and fellow-delvers into the occult had invited him.

The next card was from Klausenburg in Transylvania, and told of Ward's progress toward his destination. He was going to visit a Baron Ferenczy, whose estate lay in the mountains east of Rakus; and was to be addressed at Rakus in the care of that nobleman. Another card from Rakus a week later, saying that his host's carriage had met him and that he was leaving the village for the mountains, was his last message for a considerable time; indeed, he did not reply to his parents' frequent letters until May, when he wrote to discourage the plan of his mother for a meeting in London, Paris, or Rome during the summer, when the elder Wards were planning to travel in Europe. His researches, he said, were such that he could not leave his present quarters; while the situation of Baron Ferenczy's castle did not favour visits. It was on a crag in the dark wooded mountains, and the region was so shunned by the country folk that normal people could not help feeling ill at ease. Moreover, the Baron was not a person likely to appeal to correct and conservative New England gentlefolk. His aspect and manners had idiosyncrasies, and his age was so great as to be disquieting. It would be better, Charles said, if his parents would wait for his return to Providence; which could scarcely be far distant.

That return did not, however, take place until May, 1926, when after a few heralding cards the young wanderer quietly slipped into New York on the *Homeric* and traversed the long miles to Providence by motor coach, eagerly drinking in the green rolling hills, the fragrant, blossoming orchards, and the white steepled towns of vernal Connecticut; his first taste of ancient New England in nearly four years. When the coach crossed the Pawcatuck and entered Rhode Island amidst the faery goldenness of a late spring afternoon his heart beat with quickened force, and the entry to Providence along Reservoir and Elmwood avenues was a breathless and wonderful thing despite the depths of forbidden lore to which he had delved. At the high square where Broad, Weybosset, and Empire Streets join, he saw before and below him in the fire of sunset the pleasant, remembered houses and domes and steeples of the old town; and his head swam curiously as the vehicle rolled down to the terminal behind the Biltmore, bringing into view the great dome and soft, roof-pierced greenery of the ancient hill across the river, and the tall colonial spire of the First Baptist Church limned pink in the magic evening light against the fresh springtime verdure of its precipitous background.

Old Providence! It was this place and the mysterious forces of its long, continuous history which had brought him into being, and which had drawn him back toward marvels and secrets whose boundaries no prophet might fix. Here lay the arcana, wondrous or dreadful as the case might be, for which all his years of travel and application had been preparing him. A taxicab whirled him through Post Office Square with its glimpse of the river, the old Market House, and the head of the bay, and up the steep curved slope of Waterman Street to Prospect, where the vast gleaming dome and sunset-flushed Ionic columns of the Christian Science Church beckoned northward. Then eight squares past the fine old estates his childish eyes had known, and the quaint brick sidewalks so often trodden by his youthful feet. And at last the little white overtaken farmhouse on the right, and on the left the classic Adam porch and stately bayed facade of the great brick house where he was born. It was twilight, and Charles Dexter Ward had come home.

5.

A school of alienists slightly less academic than Dr. Lyman's assign to Ward's European trip the beginning of his true madness. Admitting that he was sane when he started, they believe that his conduct upon returning implies a disastrous change. But even to this claim Dr. Willett refuses to accede. There was, he insists, something later; and the queernesses of the youth at this stage he attributes to the practice of rituals learned abroad—odd enough things, to be sure, but by no means implying mental aberration on the part of their celebrant. Ward himself, though visibly aged and hardened, was still normal in his general reactions; and in several talks with Willett displayed a balance which no madman—even an incipient one—could feign continuously for long. What elicited the notion of insanity at this period were the *sounds* heard at all hours from Ward's attic laboratory, in which he kept himself most of the time. There were chantings and repetitions, and thunderous declamations in uncanny rhythms; and although these sounds were always in Ward's own voice, there was something in the quality of that voice, and in the accents of the formulae it pronounced, which could not but chill the blood of every hearer. It was noticed that Nig, the venerable and beloved black cat of the household, bristled and arched his back perceptibly when certain of the tones were heard.

The odours occasionally wafted from the laboratory were likewise exceedingly strange. Sometimes they were very noxious, but more often they were aromatic, with a haunting, elusive quality which seemed to have the power of inducing fantastic images. People who smelled them had a tendency to glimpse momentary mirages of enormous vistas, with strange hills or endless avenues of sphinxes and hippogriffs stretching off into infinite distance. Ward did not resume his old-time rambles, but applied himself diligently to the strange books he had brought home, and to equally strange delvings within his quarters; explaining that European sources had greatly enlarged the possibilities of his work, and promising great revelations in the years to come. His older aspect increased to a startling degree his resemblance to the Curwen portrait in his library; and Dr. Willett would often pause by the latter after a call, marvelling at the virtual identity, and reflecting that only the small pit above the picture's right eye now remained to differentiate the long-dead wizard from the living youth. These calls of Willett's, undertaken at the request of the senior Wards, were curious affairs. Ward at no time repulsed the doctor, but the latter saw that he could never reach the young man's inner psychology. Frequently he noted peculiar things about; little wax images of grotesque design on the shelves or tables, and the half-erased remnants of circles, triangles, and pentagrams in chalk or charcoal on the cleared central space of the large room. And always in the night those rhythms and incantations thundered, till it became very difficult to keep servants or suppress furtive talk of Charles's madness.

In January, 1927, a peculiar incident occurred. One night about midnight, as Charles was chanting a ritual whose weird cadence echoed unpleasantly through the house below, there came a sudden gust of chill wind from the bay, and a faint, obscure trembling of the earth which everyone in the neighbourhood noted. At the same time the cat exhibited phenomenal traces of fright, while dogs bayed for as much as a mile around. This was the prelude to a sharp thunderstorm, anomalous for the season, which brought with it such a crash that Mr. and Mrs. Ward believed the house had been struck. They rushed upstairs to see what damage had been done, but Charles met them at the door to the attic; pale, resolute, and portentous, with an almost fearsome combination of triumph and seriousness on his face. He assured them that the house had not really been struck, and that the storm would soon be over. They paused, and looking through a window saw that he was indeed right; for the lightning flashed farther and farther off, whilst the trees ceased to bend in the strange frigid gust from the water. The thunder sank to a sort of dull mumbling chuckle and finally died away. Stars came out, and the stamp of triumph on Charles Ward's face crystallised into a very singular expression.

For two months or more after this incident Ward was less confined than usual to his laboratory. He exhibited a curious interest in the weather, and made odd inquiries about the date of the spring thawing of the ground. One night late in March he left the house after midnight, and did not return till almost morning; when his mother, being wakeful, heard a rumbling motor draw up to the carriage entrance. Muffled oaths could be distinguished, and Mrs. Ward, rising and going to the window, saw four dark figures removing a long, heavy box from a truck at Charles's direction and carrying it within by the side door. She heard laboured breathing and ponderous footfalls on the stairs, and finally a dull thumping in the attic; after which the footfalls descended again, and the four men reappeared outside and drove off in their truck.

The next day Charles resumed his strict attic seclusion, drawing down the dark shades of his laboratory windows and appearing to be working on some metal substance. He would open the door to no one, and steadfastly refused all proffered food. About noon a wrenching sound followed by a terrible cry and a fall were heard, but when Mrs. Ward rapped at the door her son at length answered faintly, and told her that nothing had gone amiss. The hideous and indescribable stench now welling out was absolutely harmless and unfortunately necessary. Solitude was the one prime essential, and he would appear later for dinner. That afternoon, after the conclusion of some odd hissing sounds which came from behind the locked portal, he did finally appear; wearing an extremely haggard aspect and forbidding anyone to enter the laboratory upon any pretext. This, indeed, proved the beginning of a new policy of secrecy; for never afterward was any other person permitted to visit either the mysterious garret workroom or the adjacent storeroom which he cleaned out, furnished roughly, and added to his inviolably private domain as a sleeping apartment. Here he lived, with books brought up from his library beneath, till the time he purchased the Pawtuxet bungalow and moved to it all his scientific effects.

In the evening Charles secured the paper before the rest of the family and damaged part of it through an apparent accident. Later on Dr. Willett, having fixed the date from statements by various members of the household, looked up an intact copy at the *Journal* office and found that in the destroyed section the following small item had occurred:

Nocturnal Diggers Surprised in
North Burial Ground

> Robert Hart, night watchman at the North Burial Ground, this morning discovered a party of several men with a motor truck in the oldest part of the cemetery, but apparently frightened them off before they had accomplished whatever their object may have been.
>
> The discovery took place at about four o'clock, when Hart's attention was attracted by the sound of a motor outside his shelter. Investigating, he saw a large truck on the main drive several rods away; but could not reach it before the sound of his feet on the gravel had revealed his approach. The men hastily placed a large box in the truck and drove away toward the street before they could be overtaken; and since no known grave was disturbed, Hart believes that this box was an object which they wished to bury.
>
> The diggers must have been at work for a long while before detection, for Hart found an enormous hole dug at a considerable distance back from the roadway in the lot of Amasa Field, where most of the old stones have long ago disappeared. The hole, a place as large and deep as a grave, was empty; and did not coincide with any interment mentioned in the cemetery records.
>
> Sergt. Riley of the Second Station viewed the spot and gave the opinion that the hole was dug by bootleggers rather gruesomely and ingeniously seeking a safe cache for liquor in a place not likely to be disturbed. In reply to questions Hart said he thought the escaping truck had headed up Rochambeau Avenue, though he could not be sure.

During the next few days Ward was seldom seen by his family. Having added sleeping quarters to his attic realm, he kept closely to himself there, ordering food brought to the door and not taking it in until after the servant had gone away. The droning of monotonous formulae and the chanting of bizarre rhythms recurred at intervals, while at other times occasional listeners could detect the sound of tinkling glass, hissing chemicals, running water, or roaring gas flames. Odours of the most unplaceable quality, wholly unlike any before noted, hung at times around the door; and the air of tension observable in the young recluse whenever he did venture briefly forth was such as to excite the keenest speculation. Once he made a hasty trip to the Athenaeum for a book he required, and again he hired a messenger to fetch him a highly obscure volume from Boston. Suspense was written portentously over the whole situation, and both the family and Dr. Willett confessed themselves wholly at a loss what to do or think about it.

6.

Then on the fifteenth of April a strange development occurred. While nothing appeared to grow different in kind, there was certainly a very terrible difference in degree; and Dr. Willett somehow attaches great significance to the change. The day was Good Friday, a circumstance of which the servants made much, but which others quite naturally dismiss as an irrelevant coincidence. Late in the afternoon young Ward began repeating a certain formula in a singularly loud voice, at the same time burning some substance so pungent that its fumes escaped over the entire house. The formula was so plainly audible in the hall outside the locked door that Mrs. Ward could not help memorising it as she waited and listened anxiously, and later on she was able to write it down at Dr. Willett's request. It ran as follows, and experts have told Dr. Willett that its very close analogue can be found in the mystic writings of "Eliphas Levi", that cryptic soul who crept through a crack in the forbidden door and glimpsed the frightful vistas of the void beyond:

> "Per Adonai Eloim, Adonai Jehova,
> Adonai Sabaoth, Metraton On Agla Mathon,
> verbum pythonicum, mysterium salamandrae,
> conventus sylvorum, antra gnomorum,
> daemonia Coeli Gad, Almousin, Gibor, Jehosua,
> Evam, Zariatnatmik, veni, veni, veni."

This had been going on for two hours without change or intermission when over all the neighbourhood a pandaemoniac howling of dogs set in. The extent of this howling can be judged from the space it received in the papers the next day, but to those in the Ward household it was overshadowed by the odour which instantly followed it; a hideous, all-pervasive odour which none of them had ever smelt before or have ever smelt since. In the midst of this mephitic flood there came a very perceptible flash like that of lightning, which would have been blinding and impressive but for the daylight around; and then was heard *the voice* that no listener can ever forget because of its thunderous remoteness, its incredible depth, and its eldritch dissimilarity to Charles Ward's voice. It shook the house, and was clearly heard by at least two neighbours above the howling of the dogs. Mrs. Ward, who had been listening in despair outside her son's locked laboratory, shivered as she recognised its hellish import; for Charles had told her of its evil fame in dark books, and of the manner in which it had thundered, according to the Fenner letters, above the doomed Pawtuxet farmhouse on the night of Joseph Curwen's annihilation. There was no mistaking that nightmare phrase, for Charles had described it too vividly in the old days when he had talked frankly of his Curwen investigations. And yet it was only this fragment of an archaic and forgotten language: "DIES MIES JESCHET BOENE DOESEF DOUVEMA ENITEMAUS."

Close upon this thundering there came a momentary darkening of the daylight, though sunset was still an hour distant, and then a puff of added odour different from the first but equally unknown and intolerable. Charles was chanting again now and his mother could hear syllables that sounded like "Yi-nash-Yog-Sothoth-he-lgeb-fi-throdog"—ending in a "Yah!" whose maniacal force mounted in an ear-splitting crescendo. A second later all previous memories were effaced by the wailing scream which burst out with frantic explosiveness and gradually changed form to a paroxysm of diabolic and hysterical laughter. Mrs. Ward, with the mingled fear and blind courage of maternity, advanced and knocked affrightedly at the concealing panels, but obtained no sign of recognition. She knocked again, but paused nervelessly as a second shriek arose, this one unmistakably in the familiar voice of her son, *and sounding concurrently with the still bursting cachinnations of that other voice.* Presently she fainted, although she is still unable to recall the precise and immediate cause. Memory sometimes makes merciful deletions.

Mr. Ward returned from the business section at about quarter past six; and not finding his wife downstairs, was told by the frightened servants that she was probably watching at Charles's door, from which the sounds had been far stranger than ever before. Mounting the stairs at once, he saw Mrs. Ward stretched at full length on the floor of the corridor outside the laboratory; and realising that she had fainted, hastened to fetch a glass of water from a set bowl in a neighbouring alcove. Dashing the cold fluid in her face, he was heartened to observe an immediate response on her part, and was watching the bewildered opening of her eyes when a chill shot through him and threatened to reduce him to the very state from which she was emerging. For the seemingly silent laboratory was not as silent as it had appeared to be, but held the murmurs of a tense, muffled conversation in tones too low for comprehension, yet of a quality profoundly disturbing to the soul.

It was not, of course, new for Charles to mutter formulae; but this muttering was definitely different. It was so palpably a dialogue, or imitation of a dialogue, with the regular alternation of inflections suggesting question and answer, statement and response. One voice was undisguisedly that of Charles, but the other had a depth and hollowness which the youth's best powers of ceremonial mimicry had scarcely approached before. There was something hideous, blasphemous, and abnormal about it, and but for a cry from his recovering wife which cleared his mind by arousing his protective instincts it is not likely that Theodore Howland Ward could have maintained for nearly a year more his old boast that he had never fainted. As it was, he seized his wife in his arms and bore her quickly downstairs before she could notice the voices which had so horribly disturbed him. Even so, however, he was not quick enough to escape catching something himself which caused him to stagger dangerously with his burden. For Mrs. Ward's cry had evidently been heard by others than he, and there had come in response to it from behind the locked door the first distinguishable words which that masked and terrible colloquy had yielded. They were merely an excited caution in Charles's own voice, but somehow their implications held a nameless fright for the father who overheard them. The phrase was just this: "*Sshh!—write!*"

Mr. and Mrs. Ward conferred at some length after dinner, and the former resolved to have a firm and serious talk with Charles that very night. No matter how important the object, such conduct could no longer be permitted; for these latest developments transcended every limit of sanity and formed a menace to the order and nervous well-being of the entire household. The youth must indeed have taken complete leave of his senses, since only downright madness could have prompted the wild screams and imaginary conversations in assumed voices which the present day had brought forth. All this must be stopped, or Mrs. Ward would be made ill and the keeping of servants become an impossibility.

Mr. Ward rose at the close of the meal and started upstairs for Charles's laboratory. On the third floor, however, he paused at the sounds which he heard proceeding from the now disused library of his son. Books were apparently being flung about and papers wildly rustled, and upon stepping to the door Mr. Ward beheld the youth within, excitedly assembling a vast armful of literary matter of every size and shape. Charles's aspect was very drawn and haggard, and he dropped his entire load with a start at the sound of his father's voice. At the elder man's command he sat down, and for some time listened to the admonitions he had so long deserved. There was no scene. At the end of the lecture he agreed that his father was right, and that his noises, mutterings, incantations, and chemical odours were indeed inexcusable nuisances. He agreed to a policy of greater quiet, though insisting on a prolongation of his extreme privacy. Much of his future work, he said, was in any case purely book research; and he could obtain quarters elsewhere for any such vocal rituals as might be necessary at a later stage. For the fright and fainting of his mother he expressed the keenest contrition, and explained that the conversation later heard was part of an elaborate symbolism designed to create a certain mental atmosphere. His use of abstruse technical terms somewhat bewildered Mr. Ward, but the parting impression was one of undeniable sanity and poise despite a mysterious tension of the utmost gravity. The interview was really quite inconclusive, and as Charles picked up his armful and left the room Mr. Ward hardly knew what to make of the entire business. It was as mysterious as the death of poor old Nig, whose stiffening form had been found an hour before in the basement, with staring eyes and fear-distorted mouth.

Driven by some vague detective instinct, the bewildered parent now glanced curiously at the vacant shelves to see what his son had taken up to the attic. The youth's library was plainly and rigidly classified, so that one might tell at a glance the books or at least the kind of books which had been withdrawn. On this occasion Mr. Ward was astonished to find that nothing of the occult or the antiquarian, beyond what had been previously removed, was missing. These new withdrawals were all modern items; histories, scientific treatises, geographies, manuals of literature, philosophic works, and certain contemporary newspapers and magazines. It was a very curious shift from Charles Ward's recent run of reading, and the father paused in a growing vortex of perplexity and an engulfing sense of strangeness. The strangeness was a very poignant sensation, and almost clawed at his chest as he strove to see just what was wrong around him. Something was indeed wrong, and tangibly as well as spiritually so. Ever since he had been in this room he had known that something was amiss, and at last it dawned upon him what it was.

On the north wall rose still the ancient carved overmantel from the house in Olney Court, but to the cracked and precariously restored oils of the large Curwen portrait disaster had come. Time and unequal heating had done their work at last, and at some time since the room's last cleaning the worst had happened. Peeling clear of the wood, curling tighter and tighter, and finally crumbling into small bits with what must have been malignly silent suddenness, the portrait of Joseph Curwen had resigned for ever its staring surveillance of the youth it so strangely resembled, and now lay scattered on the floor as a thin coating of fine bluish-grey dust.

IV. A Mutation and a Madness

1.

In the week following that memorable Good Friday Charles Ward was seen more often than usual, and was continually carrying books between his library and the attic laboratory. His actions were quiet and rational, but he had a furtive, hunted look which his mother did not like, and developed an incredibly ravenous appetite as gauged by his demands upon the cook. Dr. Willett had been told of those Friday noises and happenings, and on the following Tuesday had a long conversation with the youth in the library where the picture stared no more. The interview was, as always, inconclusive; but Willett is still ready to swear that the youth was sane and himself at the time. He held out promises of an early revelation, and spoke of the need of securing a laboratory elsewhere. At the loss of the portrait he grieved singularly little considering his first enthusiasm over it, but seemed to find something of positive humour in its sudden crumbling.

About the second week Charles began to be absent from the house for long periods, and one day when good old black Hannah came to help with the spring cleaning she mentioned his frequent visits to the old house in Olney Court, where he would come with a large valise and perform curious delvings in the cellar. He was always very liberal to her and to old Asa, but seemed more worried than he used to be; which grieved her very much, since she had watched him grow up from birth. Another report of his doings came from Pawtuxet, where some friends of the family saw him at a distance a surprising number of times. He seemed to haunt the resort and canoe-house of Rhodes-on-the-Pawtuxet, and subsequent inquiries by Dr. Willett at that place brought out the fact that his purpose was always to secure access to the rather hedged-in river-bank, along which he would walk toward the north, usually not reappearing for a very long while.

Late in May came a momentary revival of ritualistic sounds in the attic laboratory which brought a stern reproof from Mr. Ward and a somewhat distracted promise of amendment from Charles. It occurred one morning, and seemed to form a resumption of the imaginary conversation noted on that turbulent Good Friday. The youth was arguing or remonstrating hotly with himself, for there suddenly burst forth a perfectly distinguishable series of clashing shouts in differentiated tones like alternate demands and denials which caused Mrs. Ward to run upstairs and listen at the door. She could hear no more than a fragment whose only plain words were "must have it red for three months", and upon her knocking all sounds ceased at once. When Charles was later questioned by his father he said that there were certain conflicts of spheres of consciousness which only great skill could avoid, but which he would try to transfer to other realms.

About the middle of June a queer nocturnal incident occurred. In the early evening there had been some noise and thumping in the laboratory upstairs, and Mr. Ward was on the point of investigating when it suddenly quieted down. That midnight, after the family had retired, the butler was nightlocking the front door when according to his statement Charles appeared somewhat blunderingly and uncertainly at the foot of the stairs with a large suitcase and made signs that he wished egress. The youth spoke no word, but the worthy Yorkshireman caught one sight of his fevered eyes and trembled causelessly. He opened the door and young Ward went out, but in the morning he presented his resignation to Mrs. Ward. There was, he said, something unholy in the glance Charles had fixed on him. It was no way for a young gentleman to look at an honest person, and he could not possibly stay another night. Mrs. Ward allowed the man to depart, but she did not value his statement highly. To fancy Charles in a savage state that night was quite ridiculous, for as long as she had remained awake she had heard faint sounds from the laboratory above; sounds as if of sobbing and pacing, and of a sighing which told only of despair's profoundest depths. Mrs. Ward had grown used to listening for sounds in the night, for the mystery of her son was fast driving all else from her mind.

The next evening, much as on another evening nearly three months before, Charles Ward seized the newspaper very early and accidentally lost the main section. This matter was not recalled till later, when Dr. Willett began checking up loose ends and searching out missing links here and there. In the *Journal* office he found the section which Charles had lost, and marked two items as of possible significance. They were as follows:

More Cemetery Delving

It was this morning discovered by Robert Hart, night watchman at the North Burial Ground, that ghouls were again at work in the ancient portion of the cemetery. The grave of Ezra Weeden, who was born in 1740 and died in 1824 according to his uprooted and savagely splintered slate headstone, was found excavated and rifled, the work being evidently done with a spade stolen from an adjacent tool-shed.

Whatever the contents may have been after more than a century of burial, all was gone except a few slivers of decayed wood. There were no wheel tracks, but the police have measured a single set of footprints which they found in the vicinity, and which indicate the boots of a man of refinement.

Hart is inclined to link this incident with the digging discovered last March, when a party in a motor truck were frightened away after making a deep excavation; but Sergt. Riley of the Second Station discounts this theory and points to vital differences in the two cases. In March the digging had been in a spot where no grave was known; but this time a well-marked and cared-for grave had been rifled with every evidence of deliberate purpose, and with a conscious malignity expressed in the splintering of the slab which had been intact up to the day before.

Members of the Weeden family, notified of the happening, expressed their astonishment and regret; and were wholly unable to think of any enemy who would care to violate the grave of their ancestor. Hazard Weeden of 598 Angell Street recalls a family legend according to which Ezra Weeden was involved in some very peculiar circumstances, not dishonourable to himself, shortly before the Revolution; but of any modern feud or mystery he is frankly ignorant. Inspector Cunningham has been assigned to the case, and hopes to uncover some valuable clues in the near future.

Dogs Noisy in Pawtuxet

Residents of Pawtuxet were aroused about 3 a.m. today by a phenomenal baying of dogs which seemed to centre near the river just north of Rhodes-on-the-Pawtuxet. The volume and quality of the howling were unusually odd, according to most who heard it; and Fred Lemdin, night watchman at Rhodes, declares it was mixed with something very like the shrieks of a man in mortal terror and agony. A sharp and very brief thunderstorm, which seemed to strike somewhere near the bank of the river, put an end to the disturbance. Strange and unpleasant odours, probably from the oil tanks along the bay, are popularly linked with this incident; and may have had their share in exciting the dogs.

The aspect of Charles now became very haggard and hunted, and all agree in retrospect that he may have wished at this period to make some statement or confession from which sheer terror withheld him. The morbid listening of his mother in the night brought out the fact that he made frequent sallies abroad under cover of darkness, and most of the more academic alienists unite at present in charging him with the revolting cases of vampirism which the press so sensationally reported about this time, but which have not yet been definitely traced to any known perpetrator. These cases, too recent and celebrated to need detailed mention, involved victims of every age and type and seemed to cluster around two distinct localities; the residential hill and the North End, near the Ward home, and the suburban districts across the Cranston line near Pawtuxet. Both late wayfarers and sleepers with open windows were attacked, and those who lived to tell the tale spoke unanimously of a lean, lithe, leaping monster with burning eyes which fastened its teeth in the throat or upper arm and feasted ravenously.

Dr. Willett, who refuses to date the madness of Charles Ward as far back as even this, is cautious in attempting to explain these horrors. He has, he declares, certain theories of his own; and limits his positive statements to a peculiar kind of negation. "I will not," he says, "state who or what I believe perpetrated these attacks and murders, but I will declare that Charles Ward was innocent of them. I have reason to be sure he was ignorant of the taste of blood, as indeed his continued anaemic decline and increasing pallor prove better than any verbal argument. Ward meddled with terrible things, but he has paid for it, and he was never a monster or a villain. As for now—I don't like to think. A change came, and I'm content to believe that the old Charles Ward died with it. His soul did, anyhow, for that mad flesh that vanished from Waite's hospital had another."

Willett speaks with authority, for he was often at the Ward home attending Mrs. Ward, whose nerves had begun to snap under the strain. Her nocturnal listening had bred some morbid hallucinations which she confided to the doctor with hesitancy, and which he ridiculed in talking to her, although they made him ponder deeply when alone. These delusions always concerned the faint sounds which she fancied she heard in the attic laboratory and bedroom, and emphasised the occurrence of muffled sighs and sobbings at the most impossible times. Early in July Willett ordered Mrs. Ward to Atlantic City for an indefinite recuperative sojourn, and cautioned both Mr. Ward and the haggard and elusive Charles to write her only cheering letters. It is probably to this enforced and reluctant escape that she owes her life and continued sanity.

2.

Not long after his mother's departure Charles Ward began negotiating for the Pawtuxet bungalow. It was a squalid little wooden edifice with a concrete garage, perched high on the sparsely settled bank of the river slightly above Rhodes, but for some odd reason the youth would have nothing else. He gave the real-estate agencies no peace till one of them secured it for him at an exorbitant price from a somewhat reluctant owner, and as soon as it was vacant he took possession under cover of darkness, transporting in a great closed van the entire contents of his attic laboratory, including the books both weird and modern which he had borrowed from his study. He had this van loaded in the black small hours, and his father recalls only a drowsy realisation of stifled oaths and stamping feet on the night the goods were taken away. After that Charles moved back to his own old quarters on the third floor, and never haunted the attic again.

To the Pawtuxet bungalow Charles transferred all the secrecy with which he had surrounded his attic realm, save that he now appeared to have two sharers of his mysteries; a villainous-looking Portuguese half-caste from the South Main St. waterfront who acted as a servant, and a thin, scholarly stranger with dark glasses and a stubbly full beard of dyed aspect whose status was evidently that of a colleague. Neighbours vainly tried to engage these odd persons in conversation. The mulatto Gomes spoke very little English, and the bearded man, who gave his name as Dr. Allen, voluntarily followed his example. Ward himself tried to be more affable, but succeeded only in provoking curiosity with his rambling accounts of chemical research. Before long queer tales began to circulate regarding the all-night burning of lights; and somewhat later, after this burning had suddenly ceased, there rose still queerer tales of disproportionate orders of meat from the butcher's and of the muffled shouting, declamation, rhythmic chanting, and screaming supposed to come from some very deep cellar below the place. Most distinctly the new and strange household was bitterly disliked by the honest bourgeoisie of the vicinity, and it is not remarkable that dark hints were advanced connecting the hated establishment with the current epidemic of vampiristic attacks and murders; especially since the radius of that plague seemed now confined wholly to Pawtuxet and the adjacent streets of Edgewood.

Ward spent most of his time at the bungalow, but slept occasionally at home and was still reckoned a dweller beneath his father's roof. Twice he was absent from the city on week-long trips, whose destinations have not yet been discovered. He grew steadily paler and more emaciated even than before, and lacked some of his former assurance when repeating to Dr. Willett his old, old story of vital research and future revelations. Willett often waylaid him at his father's house, for the elder Ward was deeply worried and perplexed, and wished his son to get as much sound oversight as could be managed in the case of so secretive and independent an adult. The doctor still insists that the youth was sane even as late as this, and adduces many a conversation to prove his point.

About September the vampirism declined, but in the following January Ward almost became involved in serious trouble. For some time the nocturnal arrival and departure of motor trucks at the Pawtuxet bungalow had been commented upon, and at this juncture an unforeseen hitch exposed the nature of at least one item of their contents. In a lonely spot near Hope Valley had occurred one of the frequent sordid waylayings of trucks by "hi-jackers" in quest of liquor shipments, but this time the robbers had been destined to receive the greater shock. For the long cases they seized proved upon opening to contain some exceedingly gruesome things; so gruesome, in fact, that the matter could not be kept quiet amongst the denizens of the underworld. The thieves had hastily buried what they discovered, but when the State Police got wind of the matter a careful search was made. A recently arrested vagrant, under promise of immunity from prosecution on any additional charge, at last consented to guide a party of troopers to the spot; and there was found in that hasty cache a very hideous and shameful thing. It would not be well for the national—or even the international—sense of decorum if the public were ever to know what was uncovered by that awestruck party. There was no mistaking it, even by these far from studious officers; and telegrams to Washington ensued with feverish rapidity.

The cases were addressed to Charles Ward at his Pawtuxet bungalow, and State and Federal officials at once paid him a very forceful and serious call. They found him pallid and worried with his two odd companions, and received from him what seemed to be a valid explanation and evidence of innocence. He had needed certain anatomical specimens as part of a programme of research whose depth and genuineness anyone who had known him in the last decade could prove, and had ordered the required kind and number from agencies which he had thought as reasonably legitimate as such things can be. Of the *identity* of the specimens he had known absolutely nothing, and was properly shocked when the inspectors hinted at the monstrous effect on public sentiment and national dignity which a knowledge of the matter would produce. In this statement he was firmly sustained by his bearded colleague Dr. Allen, whose oddly hollow voice carried even more conviction than his own nervous tones; so that in the end the officials took no action, but carefully set down the

New York name and address which Ward gave them as a basis for a search which came to nothing. It is only fair to add that the specimens were quickly and quietly restored to their proper places, and that the general public will never know of their blasphemous disturbance.

On February 9, 1928, Dr. Willett received a letter from Charles Ward which he considers of extraordinary importance, and about which he has frequently quarrelled with Dr. Lyman. Lyman believes that this note contains positive proof of a well-developed case of *dementia praecox*, but Willett on the other hand regards it as the last perfectly sane utterance of the hapless youth. He calls especial attention to the normal character of the penmanship; which though shewing traces of shattered nerves, is nevertheless distinctly Ward's own. The text in full is as follows:

"100 Prospect St.
Providence, R.I.,
February 8, 1928.

"Dear Dr. Willett:—

"I feel that at last the time has come for me to make the disclosures which I have so long promised you, and for which you have pressed me so often. The patience you have shewn in waiting, and the confidence you have shewn in my mind and integrity, are things I shall never cease to appreciate.

"And now that I am ready to speak, I must own with humiliation that no triumph such as I dreamed of can ever be mine. Instead of triumph I have found terror, and my talk with you will not be a boast of victory but a plea for help and advice in saving both myself and the world from a horror beyond all human conception or calculation. You recall what those Fenner letters said of the old raiding party at Pawtuxet. That must all be done again, and quickly. Upon us depends more than can be put into words—all civilisation, all natural law, perhaps even the fate of the solar system and the universe. I have brought to light a monstrous abnormality, but I did it for the sake of knowledge. Now for the sake of all life and Nature you must help me thrust it back into the dark again.

"I have left that Pawtuxet place for ever, and we must extirpate everything existing there, alive or dead. I shall not go there again, and you must not believe it if you ever hear that I am there. I will tell you why I say this when I see you. I have come home for good, and wish you would call on me at the very first moment that you can spare five or six hours continuously to hear what I have to say. It will take that long—and believe me when I tell you that you never had a more genuine professional duty than this. My life and reason are the very least things which hang in the balance.

"I dare not tell my father, for he could not grasp the whole thing. But I have told him of my danger, and he has four men from a detective agency watching the house. I don't know how much good they can do, for they have against them forces which even you could scarcely envisage or acknowledge. So come quickly if you wish to see me alive and hear how you may help to save the cosmos from stark hell.

"Any time will do—I shall not be out of the house. Don't telephone ahead, for there is no telling who or what may try to intercept you. And let us pray to whatever gods there be that nothing may prevent this meeting.

"In utmost gravity and desperation,

"Charles Dexter Ward."

"P.S. Shoot Dr. Allen on sight *and dissolve his body in acid.* Don't burn it."

Dr. Willett received this note about 10:30 a.m., and immediately arranged to spare the whole late afternoon and evening for the momentous talk, letting it extend on into the night as long as might be necessary. He planned to arrive about four o'clock, and through all the intervening hours was so engulfed in every sort of wild speculation that most of his tasks were very mechanically performed. Maniacal as the letter would have sounded to a stranger, Willett had seen too much of Charles Ward's oddities to dismiss it as sheer raving. That something very subtle, ancient, and horrible was hovering about he felt quite sure, and the reference to Dr. Allen could almost be comprehended in view of what Pawtuxet gossip said of Ward's enigmatical colleague. Willett had never seen the man, but had heard much of his aspect and bearing, and could not but wonder what sort of eyes those much-discussed dark glasses might conceal.

Promptly at four Dr. Willett presented himself at the Ward residence, but found to his annoyance that Charles had not adhered to his determination to remain indoors. The guards were there, but said that the young man seemed to have lost part of his timidity. He had that morning done much apparently frightened arguing and protesting over the telephone, one of the detectives said, replying to some unknown voice with phrases such as "I am very tired and must rest a while", "I can't receive anyone for some time, you'll have to excuse me", "Please postpone decisive action till we can arrange some sort of compromise", or "I am very sorry, but I must take a complete vacation from everything; I'll talk with you later". Then, apparently gaining boldness through meditation, he had slipped out so quietly that no one had seen him depart or knew that he had gone until he returned about one o'clock and entered the house without a word. He had gone upstairs, where a bit of his fear must have surged back; for he was heard to cry out in a highly terrified fashion upon entering his library, afterward trailing off into a kind of choking gasp. When, however, the butler had gone to inquire what the trouble was, he had appeared at the door with a great show of boldness, and had silently gestured the man away in a manner that terrified him unaccountably. Then he had evidently done some rearranging of his shelves, for a great clattering and thumping and creaking ensued; after which he had reappeared and left at once. Willett inquired whether or not any message had been left, but was told that there was none. The butler seemed queerly disturbed about something in Charles's appearance and manner, and asked solicitously if there was much hope for a cure of his disordered nerves.

For almost two hours Dr. Willett waited vainly in Charles Ward's library, watching the dusty shelves with their wide gaps where books had been removed, and smiling grimly at the panelled overmantel on the north wall, whence a year before the suave features of old Joseph Curwen had looked mildly down. After a time the shadows began to gather, and the sunset cheer gave place to a vague growing terror which flew shadow-like before the night. Mr. Ward finally arrived, and shewed much surprise and anger at his son's absence after all the pains which had been taken to guard him. He had not known of Charles's appointment, and promised to notify Willett when the youth returned. In bidding the doctor goodnight he expressed his utter perplexity at his son's condition, and urged his caller to do all he could to restore the boy to normal poise. Willett was glad to escape from that library, for something frightful and unholy seemed to haunt it; as if the vanished picture had left behind a legacy of evil. He had never liked that picture; and even now, strong-nerved though he was, there lurked a quality in its vacant panel which made him feel an urgent need to get out into the pure air as soon as possible.

3.

The next morning Willett received a message from the senior Ward, saying that Charles was still absent. Mr. Ward mentioned that Dr. Allen had telephoned him to say that Charles would remain at Pawtuxet for some time, and that he must not be disturbed. This was necessary because Allen himself was suddenly called away for an indefinite period, leaving the researches in need of Charles's constant oversight. Charles sent his best wishes, and regretted any bother his abrupt change of plans might have caused. In listening to this message Mr. Ward heard Dr. Allen's voice for the first time, and it seemed to excite some vague and elusive memory which could not be actually placed, but which was disturbing to the point of fearfulness.

Faced by these baffling and contradictory reports, Dr. Willett was frankly at a loss what to do. The frantic earnestness of Charles's note was not to be denied, yet what could one think of its writer's immediate violation of his own expressed policy? Young Ward had written that his delvings had become blasphemous and menacing, that they and his bearded colleague must be extirpated at any cost, and that he himself would never return to their final scene; yet according to latest advices he had forgotten all this and was back in the thick of the mystery. Common sense bade one leave the youth alone with his freakishness, yet some deeper instinct would not permit the impression of that frenzied letter to subside. Willett read it over again, and could not make its essence sound as empty and insane as both its bombastic verbiage and its lack of fulfilment would seem to imply. Its terror was too profound and real, and in conjunction with what the doctor already knew evoked too vivid hints of monstrosities from beyond time and space to permit of any cynical explanation. There were nameless horrors abroad; and no matter how little one might be able to get at them, one ought to stand prepared for any sort of action at any time.

For over a week Dr. Willett pondered on the dilemma which seemed thrust upon him, and became more and more inclined to pay Charles a call at the Pawtuxet bungalow. No friend of the youth had ever ventured to storm this forbidden retreat, and even his father knew of its interior only from such descriptions as he chose to give; but Willett felt that some direct conversation with his patient was necessary. Mr. Ward had been receiving brief and non-committal typed notes from his son, and said that Mrs. Ward in her Atlantic City retirement had had no better word. So at length the doctor resolved to act; and despite a curious sensation inspired by old legends of Joseph Curwen, and by more recent revelations and warnings from Charles Ward, set boldly out for the bungalow on the bluff above the river.

Willett had visited the spot before through sheer curiosity, though of course never entering the house or proclaiming his presence; hence knew exactly the route to take. Driving out Broad Street one early afternoon toward the end of February in his small motor, he thought oddly of the grim party which had taken that selfsame road a hundred and fifty-seven years before on a terrible errand which none might ever comprehend.

The ride through the city's decaying fringe was short, and trim Edgewood and sleepy Pawtuxet presently spread out ahead.

Willett turned to the right down Lockwood Street and drove his car as far along that rural road as he could, then alighted and walked north to where the bluff towered above the lovely bends of the river and the sweep of misty downlands beyond. Houses were still few here, and there was no mistaking the isolated bungalow with its concrete garage on a high point of land at his left. Stepping briskly up the neglected gravel walk he rapped at the door with a firm hand, and spoke without a tremor to the evil Portuguese mulatto who opened it to the width of a crack.

He must, he said, see Charles Ward at once on vitally important business. No excuse would be accepted, and a repulse would mean only a full report of the matter to the elder Ward. The mulatto still hesitated, and pushed against the door when Willett attempted to open it; but the doctor merely raised his voice and renewed his demands. Then there came from the dark interior a husky whisper which somehow chilled the hearer through and through though he did not know why he feared it. "Let him in, Tony," it said, "we may as well talk now as ever." But disturbing as was the whisper, the greater fear was that which immediately followed. The floor creaked and the speaker hove in sight—and the owner of those strange and resonant tones was seen to be no other than Charles Dexter Ward.

The minuteness with which Dr. Willett recalled and recorded his conversation of that afternoon is due to the importance he assigns to this particular period. For at last he concedes a vital change in Charles Dexter Ward's mentality, and believes that the youth now spoke from a brain hopelessly alien to the brain whose growth he had watched for six and twenty years. Controversy with Dr. Lyman has compelled him to be very specific, and he definitely dates the madness of Charles Ward from the time the typewritten notes began to reach his parents. Those notes are not in Ward's normal style; not even in the style of that last frantic letter to Willett. Instead, they are strange and archaic, as if the snapping of the writer's mind had released a flood of tendencies and impressions picked up unconsciously through boyhood antiquarianism. There is an obvious effort to be modern, but the spirit and occasionally the language are those of the past.

The past, too, was evident in Ward's every tone and gesture as he received the doctor in that shadowy bungalow. He bowed, motioned Willett to a seat, and began to speak abruptly in that strange whisper which he sought to explain at the very outset.

"I am grown phthisical," he began, "from this cursed river air. You must excuse my speech. I suppose you are come from my father to see what ails me, and I hope you will say nothing to alarm him."

Willett was studying these scraping tones with extreme care, but studying even more closely the face of the speaker. Something, he felt, was wrong; and he thought of what the family had told him about the fright of that Yorkshire butler one night. He wished it were not so dark, but did not request that any blind be opened. Instead, he merely asked Ward why he had so belied the frantic note of little more than a week before.

"I was coming to that," the host replied. "You must know, I am in a very bad state of nerves, and do and say queer things I cannot account for. As I have told you often, I am on the edge of great matters; and the bigness of them has a way of making me light-headed. Any man might well be frighted of what I have found, but I am not to be put off for long. I was a dunce to have that guard and stick at home; for having gone this far, my place is here. I am not well spoke of by my prying neighbours, and perhaps I was led by weakness to believe myself what they say of me. There is no evil to any in what I do, so long as I do it rightly. Have the goodness to wait six months, and I'll shew you what will pay your patience well.

"You may as well know I have a way of learning old matters from things surer than books, and I'll leave you to judge the importance of what I can give to history, philosophy, and the arts by reason of the doors I have access to. My ancestor had all this when those witless peeping Toms came and murdered him. I now have it again, or am coming very imperfectly to have a part of it. This time nothing must happen, and least of all through any idiot fears of my own. Pray forget all I writ you, Sir, and have no fear of this place or any in it. Dr. Allen is a man of fine parts, and I owe him an apology for anything ill I have said of him. I wish I had no need to spare him, but there were things he had to do elsewhere. His zeal is equal to mine in all those matters, and I suppose that when I feared the work I feared him too as my greatest helper in it."

Ward paused, and the doctor hardly knew what to say or think. He felt almost foolish in the face of this calm repudiation of the letter; and yet there clung to him the fact that while the present discourse was strange and alien and indubitably mad, the note itself had been tragic in its naturalness and likeness to the Charles Ward he knew. Willett now tried to turn the talk on early matters, and recall to the youth some past events which would restore a familiar mood; but in this process he obtained only the most grotesque results. It was the same with all the alienists later on. Important sections of Charles Ward's store of mental images, mainly those touching modern times and his own personal life, had been unaccountably expunged; whilst all the massed antiquarianism of his youth had welled up from some profound subconsciousness to engulf the contemporary and the individual. The youth's intimate knowledge of elder things was abnormal and unholy, and he tried his best to hide it. When Willett would mention some favourite object of his boyhood archaistic studies he often shed by pure accident such a light as no normal mortal could conceivably be expected to possess, and the doctor shuddered as the glib allusion glided by.

It was not wholesome to know so much about the way the fat sheriff's wig fell off as he leaned over at the play in Mr. Douglass's Histrionick Academy in King Street on the eleventh of February, 1762, which fell on a Thursday; or about how the actors cut the text of Steele's *Conscious Lovers* so badly that one was almost glad the Baptist-ridden legislature closed the theatre a fortnight later. That Thomas Sabin's Boston coach was "damn'd uncomfortable" old letters may well have told; but what healthy antiquarian could recall how the creaking of Epenetus Olney's new signboard (the gaudy crown he set up after he took to calling his tavern the Crown Coffee House) was exactly like the first few notes of the new jazz piece all the radios in Pawtuxet were playing?

Ward, however, would not be quizzed long in this vein. Modern and personal topics he waved aside quite summarily, whilst regarding antique affairs he soon shewed the plainest boredom. What he wished clearly enough was only to satisfy his visitor enough to make him depart without the intention of returning. To this end he offered to shew Willett the entire house, and at once proceeded to lead the doctor through every room from cellar to attic. Willett looked sharply, but noted that the visible books were far too few and trivial ever to have filled the wide gaps on Ward's shelves at home, and that the meagre so-called "laboratory" was the flimsiest sort of a blind. Clearly, there were a library and a laboratory elsewhere; but just where, it was impossible to say. Essentially defeated in his quest for something he could not name, Willett returned to town before evening and told the senior Ward everything which had occurred. They agreed that the youth must be definitely out of his mind, but decided that nothing drastic need be done just then. Above all, Mrs. Ward must be kept in as complete an ignorance as her son's own strange typed notes would permit.

Mr. Ward now determined to call in person upon his son, making it wholly a surprise visit. Dr. Willett took him in his car one evening, guiding him to within sight of the bungalow and waiting patiently for his return. The session was a long one, and the father emerged in a very saddened and perplexed state. His reception had developed much like Willett's, save that Charles had been an excessively long time in appearing after the visitor had forced his way into the hall and sent the Portuguese away with an imperative demand; and in the bearing of the altered son there was no trace of filial affection. The lights had been dim, yet even so the youth had complained that they dazzled him outrageously. He had not spoken out loud at all, averring that his throat was in very poor condition; but in his hoarse whisper there was a quality so vaguely disturbing that Mr. Ward could not banish it from his mind.

Now definitely leagued together to do all they could toward the youth's mental salvation, Mr. Ward and Dr. Willett set about collecting every scrap of data which the case might afford. Pawtuxet gossip was the first item they studied, and this was relatively easy to glean since both had friends in that region. Dr. Willett obtained the most rumours because people talked more frankly to him than to a parent of the central figure, and from all he heard he could tell that young Ward's life had become indeed a strange one. Common tongues would not dissociate his household from the vampirism of the previous summer, while the nocturnal comings and goings of the motor trucks provided their share of dark speculation. Local tradesmen spoke of the queerness of the orders brought them by the evil-looking mulatto, and in particular of the inordinate amounts of meat and fresh blood secured from the two butcher shops in the immediate neighbourhood. For a household of only three, these quantities were quite absurd.

Then there was the matter of the sounds beneath the earth. Reports of these things were harder to pin down, but all the vague hints tallied in certain basic essentials. Noises of a ritual nature positively existed, and at times when the bungalow was dark. They might, of course, have come from the known cellar; but rumour insisted that there were deeper and more spreading crypts. Recalling the ancient tales of Joseph Curwen's catacombs, and assuming for granted that the present bungalow had been selected because of its situation on the old Curwen site as revealed in one or another of the documents found behind the picture, Willett and Mr. Ward gave this phase of the gossip much attention; and searched many times without success for the door in the river-bank which old manuscripts mentioned. As to popular opinions of the bungalow's various inhabitants, it was soon plain that the Brava Portuguese was loathed, the bearded and spectacled Dr. Allen feared, and the pallid young scholar disliked to a profound extent. During the last week or two Ward had obviously changed much, abandoning his attempts at affability and speaking only in hoarse but oddly repellent whispers on the few occasions that he ventured forth.

Such were the shreds and fragments gathered here and there; and over these Mr. Ward and Dr. Willett held many long and serious conferences. They strove to exercise deduction, induction, and constructive imagination to their utmost extent; and to correlate every known fact of Charles's later life, including the frantic letter which the doctor now shewed the father, with the meagre documentary evidence available concerning old Joseph Curwen. They would have given much for a glimpse of the papers Charles had found, for very clearly the key to the youth's madness lay in what he had learned of the ancient wizard and his doings.

4.

And yet, after all, it was from no step of Mr. Ward's or Dr. Willett's that the next move in this singular case proceeded. The father and the physician, rebuffed and confused by a shadow too shapeless and intangible to combat, had rested uneasily on their oars while the typed notes of young Ward to his parents grew fewer and fewer. Then came the first of the month with its customary financial adjustments, and the clerks at certain banks began a peculiar shaking of heads and telephoning from one to the other. Officials who knew Charles Ward by sight went down to the bungalow to ask why every cheque of his appearing at this juncture was a clumsy forgery, and were reassured less than they ought to have been when the youth hoarsely explained that his hand had lately been so much affected by a nervous shock as to make normal writing impossible. He could, he said, form no written characters at all except with great difficulty; and could prove it by the fact that he had been forced to type all his recent letters, even those to his father and mother, who would bear out the assertion.

What made the investigators pause in confusion was not this circumstance alone, for that was nothing unprecedented or fundamentally suspicious; nor even the Pawtuxet gossip, of which one or two of them had caught echoes. It was the muddled discourse of the young man which nonplussed them, implying as it did a virtually total loss of memory concerning important monetary matters which he had had at his fingertips only a month or two before. Something was wrong; for despite the apparent coherence and rationality of his speech, there could be no normal reason for this ill-concealed blankness on vital points. Moreover, although none of these men knew Ward well, they could not help observing the change in his language and manner. They had heard he was an antiquarian, but even the most hopeless antiquarians do not make daily use of obsolete phraseology and gestures. Altogether, this combination of hoarseness, palsied hands, bad memory, and altered speech and bearing must represent some disturbance or malady of genuine gravity, which no doubt formed the basis of the prevailing odd rumours; and after their departure the party of officials decided that a talk with the senior Ward was imperative.

So on the sixth of March, 1928, there was a long and serious conference in Mr. Ward's office, after which the utterly bewildered father summoned Dr. Willett in a kind of helpless resignation. Willett looked over the strained and awkward signatures of the cheques, and compared them in his mind with the penmanship of that last frantic note. Certainly, the change was radical and profound, and yet there was something damnably familiar about the new writing. It had crabbed and archaic tendencies of a very curious sort, and seemed to result from a type of stroke utterly different from that which the youth had always used. It was strange—but where had he seen it before? On the whole, it was obvious that Charles was insane. Of that there could be no doubt. And since it appeared unlikely that he could handle his property or continue to deal with the outside world much longer, something must quickly be done toward his oversight and possible cure. It was then that the alienists were called in, Drs. Peck and Waite of Providence and Dr. Lyman of Boston, to whom Mr. Ward and Dr. Willett gave the most exhaustive possible history of the case, and who conferred at length in the now unused library of their young patient, examining what books and papers of his were left in order to gain some further notion of his habitual mental cast. After scanning this material and examining the ominous note to Willett they all agreed that Charles Ward's studies had been enough to unseat or at least to warp any ordinary intellect, and wished most heartily that they could see his more intimate volumes and documents; but this latter they knew they could do, if at all, only after a scene at the bungalow itself. Willett now reviewed the whole case with febrile energy; it being at this time that he obtained the statements of the workmen who had seen Charles find the Curwen documents, and that he collated the incidents of the destroyed newspaper items, looking up the latter at the *Journal* office.

On Thursday, the eighth of March, Drs. Willett, Peck, Lyman, and Waite, accompanied by Mr. Ward, paid the youth their momentous call; making no concealment of their object and questioning the now acknowledged patient with extreme minuteness. Charles, though he was inordinately long in answering the summons and was still redolent of strange and noxious laboratory odours when he did finally make his agitated appearance, proved a far from recalcitrant subject; and admitted freely that his memory and balance had suffered somewhat from close application to abstruse studies. He offered no resistance when his removal to other quarters was insisted upon; and seemed, indeed, to display a high degree of intelligence as apart from mere memory. His conduct would have sent his interviewers away in bafflement had not the persistently archaic trend of his speech and the unmistakable replacement of modern by ancient ideas in his consciousness marked him out as one definitely removed from the normal. Of his work he would say no more to the group of doctors than he had formerly said to his family and to Dr. Willett, and his frantic note of the previous month he dismissed as mere nerves and hysteria. He insisted that the shadowy bungalow possessed no library or laboratory beyond the visible ones, and waxed abstruse in explaining the absence from the house of such odours as now saturated all his clothing. Neighbourhood gossip he attributed to nothing more than the cheap inventiveness of baffled curiosity. Of the whereabouts of Dr. Allen he said he did not feel at liberty to speak definitely, but assured his inquisitors that the bearded and spectacled man would return when needed. In paying off the stolid Brava who resisted all questioning by the visitors, and in closing the bungalow which still seemed to hold such nighted secrets, Ward shewed no sign of nervousness save a barely noticed tendency to pause as though listening for something very faint. He was apparently animated by a calmly philosophic resignation, as if his removal were the merest transient incident which would cause the least trouble if facilitated and disposed of once and for all. It was clear that he trusted to his obviously unimpaired keenness of absolute mentality to overcome all the embarrassments into which his twisted memory, his lost voice and handwriting, and his secretive and eccentric behaviour had led him. His mother, it was agreed, was not to be told of the change; his father supplying typed notes in his name. Ward was taken to the restfully and picturesquely situated private hospital maintained by Dr. Waite on Conanicut Island in the bay, and subjected to the closest scrutiny and questioning by all the physicians connected with the case. It was then that the physical oddities were noticed; the slackened metabolism, the altered skin, and the disproportionate neural reactions. Dr. Willett was the most perturbed of the various examiners, for he had attended

Ward all his life and could appreciate with terrible keenness the extent of his physical disorganisation. Even the familiar olive mark on his hip was gone, while on his chest was a great black mole or cicatrice which had never been there before, and which made Willett wonder whether the youth had ever submitted to any of the "witch markings" reputed to be inflicted at certain unwholesome nocturnal meetings in wild and lonely places. The doctor could not keep his mind off a certain transcribed witch-trial record from Salem which Charles had shewn him in the old non-secretive days, and which read: "Mr. G. B. on that Nighte putt ye Divell his Marke upon Bridget S., Jonathan A., Simon O., Deliverance W., Joseph C., Susan P., Mehitable C., and Deborah B." Ward's face, too, troubled him horribly, till at length he suddenly discovered why he was horrified. For above the young man's right eye was something which he had never previously noticed—a small scar or pit precisely like that in the crumbled painting of old Joseph Curwen, and perhaps attesting some hideous ritualistic inoculation to which both had submitted at a certain stage of their occult careers.

While Ward himself was puzzling all the doctors at the hospital a very strict watch was kept on all mail addressed either to him or to Dr. Allen, which Mr. Ward had ordered delivered at the family home. Willett had predicted that very little would be found, since any communications of a vital nature would probably have been exchanged by messenger; but in the latter part of March there did come a letter from Prague for Dr. Allen which gave both the doctor and the father deep thought. It was in a very crabbed and archaic hand; and though clearly not the effort of a foreigner, shewed almost as singular a departure from modern English as the speech of young Ward himself. It read:

Kleinstrasse 11,
Altstadt, Prague,
11th Feby. 1928.

Brother in Almousin-Metraton:—

I this day receiv'd y^r mention of what came up from the Salts I sent you. It was wrong, and meanes clearly that ye Headstones had been chang'd when Barnabas gott me the Specimen. It is often so, as you must be sensible of from the Thing you gott from ye Kings Chapell ground in 1769 and what H. gott from Olde Bury'g Point in 1690, that was like to ende him. I gott such a Thing in Aegypt 75 yeares gone, from the which came that Scar ye Boy saw on me here in 1924. As I told you longe ago, do not calle up That which you can not put downe; either from dead Saltes or out of ye Spheres beyond. Have ye Wordes for laying at all times readie, and stopp not to be sure when there is any Doubte of *Whom* you have. Stones are all

> chang'd now in Nine groundes out of 10. You are never sure till you question. I this day heard from H., who has had Trouble with the Soldiers. He is like to be sorry Transylvania is pass'd from Hungary to Roumania, and wou'd change his Seat if the Castel weren't so fulle of What we Knowe. But of this he hath doubtless writ you. In my next Send'g there will be Somewhat from a Hill tomb from ye East that will delight you greatly. Meanwhile forget not I am desirous of B. F. if you can possibly get him for me. You know G. in Philada. better than I. Have him up firste if you will, but doe not use him soe hard he will be Difficult, for I must speake to him in ye End.
>
> Yogg-Sothoth Neblod Zin
> Simon O.
>
> To Mr. J. C. in
> Providence.

Mr. Ward and Dr. Willett paused in utter chaos before this apparent bit of unrelieved insanity. Only by degrees did they absorb what it seemed to imply. So the absent Dr. Allen, and not Charles Ward, had come to be the leading spirit at Pawtuxet? That must explain the wild reference and denunciation in the youth's last frantic letter. And what of this addressing of the bearded and spectacled stranger as "Mr. J. C."? There was no escaping the inference, but there are limits to possible monstrosity. Who was "Simon O."; the old man Ward had visited in Prague four years previously? Perhaps, but in the centuries behind there had been another Simon O.—Simon Orne, alias Jedediah, of Salem, who vanished in 1771, *and whose peculiar handwriting Dr. Willett now unmistakably recognised from the photostatic copies of the Orne formulae which Charles had once shewn him.* What horrors and mysteries, what contradictions and contraventions of Nature, had come back after a century and a half to harass Old Providence with her clustered spires and domes?

The father and the old physician, virtually at a loss what to do or think, went to see Charles at the hospital and questioned him as delicately as they could about Dr. Allen, about the Prague visit, and about what he had learned of Simon or Jedediah Orne of Salem. To all these inquiries the youth was politely non-committal, merely barking in his hoarse whisper that he had found Dr. Allen to have a remarkable spiritual rapport with certain souls from the past, and that any correspondent the bearded man might have in Prague would probably be similarly gifted. When they left, Mr. Ward and Dr. Willett realised to their chagrin that they had really been the ones under catechism; and that without imparting anything vital himself, the confined youth had adroitly pumped them of everything the Prague letter had contained.

Drs. Peck, Waite, and Lyman were not inclined to attach much importance to the strange correspondence of young Ward's companion; for they knew the tendency of kindred eccentrics and monomaniacs to band together, and believed that Charles or Allen had merely unearthed an expatriated counterpart—perhaps one who had seen Orne's handwriting and copied it in an attempt to pose as the bygone character's reincarnation. Allen himself was perhaps a similar case, and may have persuaded the youth into accepting him as an avatar of the long-dead Curwen. Such things had been known before, and on the same basis the hard-headed doctors disposed of Willett's growing disquiet about Charles Ward's present handwriting, as studied from unpremeditated specimens obtained by various ruses. Willett thought he had placed its odd familiarity at last, and that what it vaguely resembled was the bygone penmanship of old Joseph Curwen himself; but this the other physicians regarded as a phase of imitativeness only to be expected in a mania of this sort, and refused to grant it any importance either favourable or unfavourable. Recognising this prosaic attitude in his colleagues, Willett advised Mr. Ward to keep to himself the letter which arrived for Dr. Allen on the second of April from Rakus, Transylvania, in a handwriting so intensely and fundamentally like that of the Hutchinson cipher that both father and physician paused in awe before breaking the seal. This read as follows:

Castle Ferenczy
7 March 1928.

> Dear C.:—Hadd a Squad of 20 Militia up to talk about what the Country Folk say. Must digg deeper and have less Hearde. These Roumanians plague me damnably, being officious and particular where you cou'd buy a Magyar off with a Drinke and ffood. Last monthe M. got me ye Sarcophagus of ye Five Sphinxes from ye Acropolis where He whome I call'd up say'd it wou'd be, and I have hadde 3 Talkes with *What was therein inhum'd.* It will go to S. O. in Prague directly, and thence to you. It is stubborn but you know ye Way with Such. You shew Wisdom in having lesse about than Before; for there was no Neede to keep the Guards in Shape and eat'g off their Heads, and it made Much to be founde in Case of Trouble, as you too welle know. *You* can now move and worke elsewhere with no Kill'g Trouble if needful, tho' I hope no Thing will soon force you to so Bothersome a Course. I rejoice that you traffick not so much with *Those Outside*; for there was ever a Mortall Peril in it, and you are sensible what it did when you ask'd Protection of One not dispos'd to give it. You excel me in gett'g ye fformulae so *another* may saye them with Success, but Borellus fancy'd it wou'd be so if just ye right Wordes were hadd. Does ye Boy use 'em often? I regret that he

> growes squeamish, as I fear'd he wou'd when I hadde him here nigh 15 Monthes, but am sensible you knowe how to deal with him. You can't saye him down with ye fformula, for that will Worke only upon such as ye other fformula hath call'd up from Saltes; but you still have strong Handes and Knife and Pistol, and Graves are not harde to digg, nor Acids loth to burne. O. sayes you have promis'd him B. F. I must have him after. B. goes to you soone, and may he give you what you wishe of that Darke Thing belowe Memphis. Imploy care in what you calle up, and beware of ye Boy. It will be ripe in a yeare's time to have up ye Legions from Underneath, and then there are no Boundes to what shal be oures. Have Confidence in what I saye, for you knowe O. and I have hadd these 150 yeares more than you to consulte these Matters in.
>
> Nephren-Ka nai Hadoth
> Edw: H.
>
> For J. Curwen, Esq.
> Providence.

But if Willett and Mr. Ward refrained from shewing this letter to the alienists, they did not refrain from acting upon it themselves. No amount of learned sophistry could controvert the fact that the strangely bearded and spectacled Dr. Allen, of whom Charles's frantic letter had spoken as such a monstrous menace, was in close and sinister correspondence with two inexplicable creatures whom Ward had visited in his travels and who plainly claimed to be survivals or avatars of Curwen's old Salem colleagues; that he was regarding himself as the reincarnation of Joseph Curwen, and that he entertained—or was at least advised to entertain—murderous designs against a "boy" who could scarcely be other than Charles Ward. There was organised horror afoot; and no matter who had started it, the missing Allen was by this time at the bottom of it. Therefore, thanking heaven that Charles was now safe in the hospital, Mr. Ward lost no time in engaging detectives to learn all they could of the cryptic bearded doctor; finding whence he had come and what Pawtuxet knew of him, and if possible discovering his current whereabouts. Supplying the men with one of the bungalow keys which Charles had yielded up, he urged them to explore Allen's vacant room which had been identified when the patient's belongings had been packed; obtaining what clues they could from any effects he might have left about. Mr. Ward talked with the detectives in his son's old library, and they felt a marked relief when they left it at last; for there seemed to hover about the place a vague aura of evil. Perhaps it was what they had heard of the infamous old wizard whose picture had once stared from the panelled overmantel, and perhaps it was something different and irrelevant; but in any case they all half sensed an intangible miasma which centred in that carven vestige of an older dwelling and which at times almost rose to the intensity of a material emanation.

V. A Nightmare and a Cataclysm

1.

And now swiftly followed that hideous experience which has left its indelible mark of fear on the soul of Marinus Bicknell Willett, and has added a decade to the visible age of one whose youth was even then far behind. Dr. Willett had conferred at length with Mr. Ward, and had come to an agreement with him on several points which both felt the alienists would ridicule. There was, they conceded, a terrible movement alive in the world, whose direct connexion with a necromancy even older than the Salem witchcraft could not be doubted. That at least two living men—and one other of whom they dared not think—were in absolute possession of minds or personalities which had functioned as early as 1690 or before was likewise almost unassailably proved even in the face of all known natural laws. What these horrible creatures—and Charles Ward as well—were doing or trying to do seemed fairly clear from their letters and from every bit of light both old and new which had filtered in upon the case. They were robbing the tombs of all the ages, including those of the world's wisest and greatest men, in the hope of recovering from the bygone ashes some vestige of the consciousness and lore which had once animated and informed them.

A hideous traffick was going on among these nightmare ghouls, whereby illustrious bones were bartered with the calm calculativeness of schoolboys swapping books; and from what was extorted from this centuried dust there was anticipated a power and a wisdom beyond anything which the cosmos had ever seen concentred in one man or group. They had found unholy ways to keep their brains alive, either in the same body or different bodies; and had evidently achieved a way of tapping the consciousness of the dead whom they gathered together. There had, it seems, been some truth in chimerical old Borellus when he wrote of preparing from even the most antique remains certain "Essential Saltes" from which the shade of a long-dead living thing might be raised up. There was a formula for evoking such a shade, and another for putting it down; and it had now been so perfected that it could be taught successfully. One must be careful about evocations, for the markers of old graves are not always accurate.

Willett and Mr. Ward shivered as they passed from conclusion to conclusion. Things—presences or voices of some sort—could be drawn down from unknown places as well as from the grave, and in this process also one must be careful. Joseph Curwen had indubitably evoked many forbidden things, and as for Charles—what might one think of him? What forces "outside the spheres" had reached him from Joseph Curwen's day and turned his mind on forgotten things? He had been led to find certain directions, and he had used them. He had talked with the man of horror in Prague and stayed long with the creature in the mountains of Transylvania. And he must have found the grave of Joseph Curwen at last. That newspaper item and what his mother had heard in the night were too significant to overlook. Then he had summoned something, and it must have come. That mighty voice aloft on Good Friday, and those *different* tones in the locked attic laboratory. What were they like, with their depth and hollowness? Was there not here some awful foreshadowing of the dreaded stranger Dr. Allen with his spectral bass? Yes, *that* was what Mr. Ward had felt with vague horror in his single talk with the man—if man it were—over the telephone!

What hellish consciousness or voice, what morbid shade or presence, had come to answer Charles Ward's secret rites behind that locked door? Those voices heard in argument—"must have it red for three months"—Good God! Was not that just before the vampirism broke out? The rifling of Ezra Weeden's ancient grave, and the cries later at Pawtuxet—whose mind had planned the vengeance and rediscovered the shunned seat of elder blasphemies? And then the bungalow and the bearded stranger, and the gossip, and the fear. The final madness of Charles neither father nor doctor could attempt to explain, but they did feel sure that the mind of Joseph Curwen had come to earth again and was following its ancient morbidities. Was daemoniac possession in truth a possibility? Allen had something to do with it, and the detectives must find out more about one whose existence menaced the young man's life. In the meantime, since the existence of some vast crypt beneath the bungalow seemed virtually beyond dispute, some effort must be made to find it. Willett and Mr. Ward, conscious of the sceptical attitude of the alienists, resolved during their final conference to undertake a joint secret exploration of unparalleled thoroughness; and agreed to meet at the bungalow on the following morning with valises and with certain tools and accessories suited to architectural search and underground exploration.

The morning of April 6th dawned clear, and both explorers were at the bungalow by ten o'clock. Mr. Ward had the key, and an entry and cursory survey were made. From the disordered condition of Dr. Allen's room it was obvious that the detectives had been there before, and the later searchers hoped that they had found some clue which might prove of value. Of course the main business lay in the cellar; so thither they descended without much delay, again making the circuit which each had vainly made before in the presence of the mad young owner. For a time everything seemed baffling, each inch of the earthen floor and stone walls having so solid and innocuous an aspect that the thought of a yawning aperture was scarcely to be entertained. Willett reflected that since the original cellar was dug without knowledge of any catacombs beneath, the beginning of the passage would represent the strictly modern delving of young Ward and his associates, where they had probed for the ancient vaults whose rumour could have reached them by no wholesome means.

The doctor tried to put himself in Charles's place to see how a delver would be likely to start, but could not gain much inspiration from this method. Then he decided on elimination as a policy, and went carefully over the whole subterranean surface both vertical and horizontal, trying to account for every inch separately. He was soon substantially narrowed down, and at last had nothing left but the small platform before the washtubs, which he had tried once before in vain. Now experimenting in every possible way, and exerting a double strength, he finally found that the top did indeed turn and slide horizontally on a corner pivot. Beneath it lay a trim concrete surface with an iron manhole, to which Mr. Ward at once rushed with excited zeal. The cover was not hard to lift, and the father had quite removed it when Willett noticed the queerness of his aspect. He was swaying and nodding dizzily, and in the gust of noxious air which swept up from the black pit beneath the doctor soon recognised ample cause.

In a moment Dr. Willett had his fainting companion on the floor above and was reviving him with cold water. Mr. Ward responded feebly, but it could be seen that the mephitic blast from the crypt had in some way gravely sickened him. Wishing to take no chances, Willett hastened out to Broad Street for a taxicab and had soon despatched the sufferer home despite his weak-voiced protests; after which he produced an electric torch, covered his nostrils with a band of sterile gauze, and descended once more to peer into the new-found depths.

The foul air had now slightly abated, and Willett was able to send a beam of light down the Stygian hole. For about ten feet, he saw, it was a sheer cylindrical drop with concrete walls and an iron ladder; after which the hole appeared to strike a flight of old stone steps which must originally have emerged to earth somewhat southwest of the present building.

2.

Willett freely admits that for a moment the memory of the old Curwen legends kept him from climbing down alone into that malodorous gulf. He could not help thinking of what Luke Fenner had reported on that last monstrous night. Then duty asserted itself and he made the plunge, carrying a great valise for the removal of whatever papers might prove of supreme importance. Slowly, as befitted one of his years, he descended the ladder and reached the slimy steps below. This was ancient masonry, his torch told him; and upon the dripping walls he saw the unwholesome moss of centuries. Down, down, ran the steps; not spirally, but in three abrupt turns; and with such narrowness that two men could have passed only with difficulty. He had counted about thirty when a sound reached him very faintly; and after that he did not feel disposed to count any more.

It was a godless sound; one of those low-keyed, insidious outrages of Nature which are not meant to be. To call it a dull wail, a doom-dragged whine, or a hopeless howl of chorused anguish and stricken flesh without mind would be to miss its most quintessential loathsomeness and soul-sickening overtones. Was it for this that Ward had seemed to listen on that day he was removed? It was the most shocking thing that Willett had ever heard, and it continued from no determinate point as the doctor reached the bottom of the steps and cast his torchlight around on lofty corridor walls surmounted by Cyclopean vaulting and pierced by numberless black archways. The hall in which he stood was perhaps fourteen feet high to the middle of the vaulting and ten or twelve feet broad. Its pavement was of large chipped flagstones, and its walls and roof were of dressed masonry. Its length he could not imagine, for it stretched ahead indefinitely into the blackness. Of the archways, some had doors of the old six-panelled colonial type, whilst others had none.

Overcoming the dread induced by the smell and the howling, Willett began to explore these archways one by one; finding beyond them rooms with groined stone ceilings, each of medium size and apparently of bizarre uses. Most of them had fireplaces, the upper courses of whose chimneys would have formed an interesting study in engineering. Never before or since had he seen such instruments or suggestions of instruments as here loomed up on every hand through the burying dust and cobwebs of a century and a half, in many cases evidently shattered as if by the ancient raiders. For many of the chambers seemed wholly untrodden by modern feet, and must have represented the earliest and most obsolete phases of Joseph Curwen's experimentation. Finally there came a room of obvious modernity, or at least of recent occupancy. There were oil heaters, bookshelves and tables, chairs and cabinets, and a desk piled high with papers of varying antiquity and contemporaneousness. Candlesticks and oil lamps stood about in several places; and finding a match-safe handy, Willett lighted such as were ready for use.

In the fuller gleam it appeared that this apartment was nothing less than the latest study or library of Charles Ward. Of the books the doctor had seen many before, and a good part of the furniture had plainly come from the Prospect Street mansion. Here and there was a piece well known to Willett, and the sense of familiarity became so great that he half forgot the noisomeness and the wailing, both of which were plainer here than they had been at the foot of the steps. His first duty, as planned long ahead, was to find and seize any papers which might seem of vital importance; especially those portentous documents found by Charles so long ago behind the picture in Olney Court. As he searched he perceived how stupendous a task the final unravelling would be; for file on file was stuffed with papers in curious hands and bearing curious designs, so that months or even years might be needed for a thorough deciphering and editing. Once he found large packets of letters with Prague and Rakus postmarks, and in writing clearly recognisable as Orne's and Hutchinson's; all of which he took with him as part of the bundle to be removed in his valise.

At last, in a locked mahogany cabinet once gracing the Ward home, Willett found the batch of old Curwen papers; recognising them from the reluctant glimpse Charles had granted him so many years ago. The youth had evidently kept them together very much as they had been when first he found them, since all the titles recalled by the workmen were present except the papers addressed to Orne and Hutchinson, and the cipher with its key. Willett placed the entire lot in his valise and continued his examination of the files. Since young Ward's immediate condition was the greatest matter at stake, the closest searching was done among the most obviously recent matter; and in this abundance of contemporary manuscript one very baffling oddity was noted. That oddity was the slight amount in Charles's normal writing, which indeed included nothing more recent than two months before. On the other hand, there were literally reams of symbols and formulae, historical notes and philosophical comment, in a crabbed penmanship absolutely identical with the ancient script of Joseph Curwen, though of undeniably modern dating. Plainly, a part of the latter-day programme had been a sedulous imitation of the old wizard's writing, which Charles seemed to have carried to a marvellous state of perfection. Of any third hand which might have been Allen's there was not a trace. If he had indeed come to be the leader, he must have forced young Ward to act as his amanuensis.

In this new material one mystic formula, or rather pair of formulae, recurred so often that Willett had it by heart before he had half finished his quest. It consisted of two parallel columns, the left-hand one surmounted by the archaic symbol called "Dragon's Head" and used in almanacks to indicate the ascending node, and the right-hand one headed by the corresponding sign of "Dragon's Tail" or descending node. The appearance of the whole was something like this, and almost unconsciously the doctor realised that the second half was no more than the first written syllabically backward with the exception of the final monosyllables and of the odd name *Yog-Sothoth,* which he had come to recognise under various spellings from other things he had seen in connexion with this horrible matter. The formulae were as follows—*exactly* so, as Willett is abundantly able to testify—and the first one struck an odd note of uncomfortable latent memory in his brain, which he recognised later when reviewing the events of that horrible Good Friday of the previous year.

☊	☋
Y'AI 'NG'NGAH,	OGTHROD AI'F
YOG-SOTHOTH	GEB'L—EE'H
H'EE—L'GEB	*YOG-SOTHOTH*
F'AI THRODOG	'NGAH'NG AI'Y
UAAAH	*ZHRO*

So haunting were these formulae, and so frequently did he come upon them, that before the doctor knew it he was repeating them under his breath. Eventually, however, he felt he had secured all the papers he could digest to advantage for the present; hence resolved to examine no more till he could bring the sceptical alienists en masse for an ampler and more systematic raid. He had still to find the hidden laboratory, so leaving his valise in the lighted room he emerged again into the black noisome corridor whose vaulting echoed ceaselessly with that dull and hideous whine.

The next few rooms he tried were all abandoned, or filled only with crumbling boxes and ominous-looking leaden coffins; but impressed him deeply with the magnitude of Joseph Curwen's original operations. He thought of the slaves and seamen who had disappeared, of the graves which had been violated in every part of the world, and of what that final raiding party must have seen; and then he decided it was better not to think any more. Once a great stone staircase mounted at his right, and he deduced that this must have reached to one of the Curwen outbuildings—perhaps the famous stone edifice with the high slit-like windows—provided the steps he had descended had led from the steep-roofed farmhouse. Suddenly the walls seemed to fall away ahead, and the stench and the wailing grew stronger. Willett saw that he had come upon a vast open space, so great that his torchlight would not carry across it; and as he advanced he encountered occasional stout pillars supporting the arches of the roof.

After a time he reached a circle of pillars grouped like the monoliths of Stonehenge, with a large carved altar on a base of three steps in the centre; and so curious were the carvings on that altar that he approached to study them with his electric light. But when he saw what they were he shrank away shuddering, and did not stop to investigate the dark stains which discoloured the upper surface and had spread down the sides in occasional thin lines. Instead, he found the distant wall and traced it as it swept round in a gigantic circle perforated by occasional black doorways and indented by a myriad of shallow cells with iron gratings and wrist and ankle bonds on chains fastened to the stone of the concave rear masonry. These cells were empty, but still the horrible odour and the dismal moaning continued, more insistent now than ever, and seemingly varied at times by a sort of slippery thumping.

3.

From that frightful smell and that uncanny noise Willett's attention could no longer be diverted. Both were plainer and more hideous in the great pillared hall than anywhere else, and carried a vague impression of being far below, even in this dark nether world of subterrene mystery. Before trying any of the black archways for steps leading further down, the doctor cast his beam of light about the stone-flagged floor. It was very loosely paved, and at irregular intervals there would occur a slab curiously pierced by small holes in no definite arrangement, while at one point there lay a very long ladder carelessly flung down. To this ladder, singularly enough, appeared to cling a particularly large amount of the frightful odour which encompassed everything. As he walked slowly about it suddenly occurred to Willett that both the noise and the odour seemed strongest directly above the oddly pierced slabs, as if they might be crude trap-doors leading down to some still deeper region of horror. Kneeling by one, he worked at it with his hands, and found that with extreme difficulty he could budge it. At his touch the moaning beneath ascended to a louder key, and only with vast trepidation did he persevere in the lifting of the heavy stone. A stench unnamable now rose from below, and the doctor's head reeled dizzily as he laid back the slab and turned his torch upon the exposed square yard of gaping blackness.

If he had expected a flight of steps to some wide gulf of ultimate abomination, Willett was destined to be disappointed; for amidst that foetor and cracked whining he discerned only the brick-faced top of a cylindrical well perhaps a yard and a half in diameter and devoid of any ladder or other means of descent. As the light shone down, the wailing changed suddenly to a series of horrible yelps; in conjunction with which there came again that sound of blind, futile scrambling and slippery thumping. The explorer trembled, unwilling even to imagine what noxious thing might be lurking in that abyss, but in a moment mustered up the courage to peer over the rough-hewn brink; lying at full length and holding the torch downward at arm's length to see what might lie below. For a second he could distinguish nothing but the slimy, moss-grown brick walls sinking illimitably into that half-tangible miasma of murk and foulness and anguished frenzy; and then he saw that something dark was leaping clumsily and frantically up and down at the bottom of the narrow shaft, which must have been from twenty to twenty-five feet below the stone floor where he lay. The torch shook in his hand, but he looked again to see what manner of living creature might be immured there in the darkness of that unnatural well; left starving by young Ward through all the long month since the doctors had taken him away, and clearly only one of a vast number prisoned in the kindred wells whose pierced stone covers so thickly studded the floor of the great vaulted cavern. Whatever the things were, they could not lie down in their cramped spaces; but must have crouched and whined and wailed and feebly leaped all those hideous weeks since their master had abandoned them unheeded.

But Marinus Bicknell Willett was sorry that he looked again; for surgeon and veteran of the dissecting-room though he was, he has not been the same since. It is hard to explain just how a single sight of a tangible object with measureable dimensions could so shake and change a man; and we may only say that there is about certain outlines and entities a power of symbolism and suggestion which acts frightfully on a sensitive thinker's perspective and whispers terrible hints of obscure cosmic relationships and unnamable realities behind the protective illusions of common vision. In that second look Willett saw such an outline or entity, for during the next few instants he was undoubtedly as stark mad as any inmate of Dr. Waite's private hospital. He dropped the electric torch from a hand drained of muscular power or nervous coördination, nor heeded the sound of crunching teeth which told of its fate at the bottom of the pit. He screamed and screamed and screamed in a voice whose falsetto panic no acquaintance of his would ever have recognised; and though he could not rise to his feet he crawled and rolled desperately away over the damp pavement where dozens of Tartarean wells poured forth their exhausted whining and yelping to answer his own insane cries. He tore his hands on the rough, loose stones, and many times bruised his head against the frequent pillars, but still he kept on. Then at last he slowly came to himself in the utter blackness and stench, and stopped his ears against the droning wail into which the burst of yelping had subsided. He was drenched with perspiration and without means of producing a light; stricken and unnerved in the abysmal blackness and horror, and crushed with a memory he never could efface. Beneath him dozens of those things still lived, and from one of the shafts the cover was removed. He knew that what he had seen could never climb up the slippery walls, yet shuddered at the thought that some obscure foothold might exist.

What the thing was, he would never tell. It was like some of the carvings on the hellish altar, but it was alive. Nature had never made it in this form, for it was too palpably *unfinished.* The deficiencies were of the most surprising sort, and the abnormalities of proportion could not be described. Willett consents only to say that this type of thing must have represented entities which Ward called up from *imperfect salts,* and which he kept for servile or ritualistic purposes. If it had not had a certain significance, its image would not have been carved on that damnable stone. It was not the worst thing depicted on that stone—but Willett never opened the other pits. At the time, the first connected idea in his mind was an idle paragraph from some of the old Curwen data he had digested long before; a phrase used by Simon or Jedediah Orne in that portentous confiscated letter to the bygone sorcerer: "Certainely, there was Noth'g butt ye liveliest Awfullness in that which H. rais'd upp from What he cou'd gather onlie a part of."

Then, horribly supplementing rather than displacing this image, there came a recollection of those ancient lingering rumours anent the burned, twisted thing found in the fields a week after the Curwen raid. Charles Ward had once told the doctor what old Slocum said of that object; that it was neither thoroughly human, nor wholly allied to any animal which Pawtuxet folk had ever seen or read about.

These words hummed in the doctor's mind as he rocked to and fro, squatting on the nitrous stone floor. He tried to drive them out, and repeated the Lord's Prayer to himself; eventually trailing off into a mnemonic hodge-podge like the modernistic "Waste Land" of Mr. T. S. Eliot and finally reverting to the oft-repeated dual formula he had lately found in Ward's underground library: "*Y'ai 'ng'ngah, Yog-Sothoth*", and so on till the final underlined "*Zhro*". It seemed to soothe him, and he staggered to his feet after a time; lamenting bitterly his fright-lost torch and looking wildly about for any gleam of light in the clutching inkiness of the chilly air. Think he would not; but he strained his eyes in every direction for some faint glint or reflection of the bright illumination he had left in the library. After a while he thought he detected a suspicion of a glow infinitely far away, and toward this he crawled in agonised caution on hands and knees amidst the stench and howling, always feeling ahead lest he collide with the numerous great pillars or stumble into the abominable pit he had uncovered.

Once his shaking fingers touched something which he knew must be the steps leading to the hellish altar, and from this spot he recoiled in loathing. At another time he encountered the pierced slab he had removed, and here his caution became almost pitiful. But he did not come upon the dread aperture after all, nor did anything issue from that aperture to detain him. What had been down there made no sound nor stir. Evidently its crunching of the fallen electric torch had not been good for it. Each time Willett's fingers felt a perforated slab he trembled. His passage over it would sometimes increase the groaning below, but generally it would produce no effect at all, since he moved very noiselessly. Several times during his progress the glow ahead diminished perceptibly, and he realised that the various candles and lamps he had left must be expiring one by one. The thought of being lost in utter darkness without matches amidst this underground world of nightmare labyrinths impelled him to rise to his feet and run, which he could safely do now that he had passed the open pit; for he knew that once the light failed, his only hope of rescue and survival would lie in whatever relief party Mr. Ward might send after missing him for a sufficient period. Presently, however, he emerged from the open space into the narrower corridor and definitely located the glow as coming from a door on his right.

In a moment he had reached it and was standing once more in young Ward's secret library, trembling with relief, and watching the sputterings of that last lamp which had brought him to safety.

4.

In another moment he was hastily filling the burned-out lamps from an oil supply he had previously noticed, and when the room was bright again he looked about to see if he might find a lantern for further exploration. For racked though he was with horror, his sense of grim purpose was still uppermost; and he was firmly determined to leave no stone unturned in his search for the hideous facts behind Charles Ward's bizarre madness. Failing to find a lantern, he chose the smallest of the lamps to carry; also filling his pockets with candles and matches, and taking with him a gallon can of oil, which he proposed to keep for reserve use in whatever hidden laboratory he might uncover beyond the terrible open space with its unclean altar and nameless covered wells. To traverse that space again would require his utmost fortitude, but he knew it must be done. Fortunately neither the frightful altar nor the opened shaft was near the vast cell-indented wall which bounded the cavern area, and whose black mysterious archways would form the next goals of a logical search.

So Willett went back to that great pillared hall of stench and anguished howling; turning down his lamp to avoid any distant glimpse of the hellish altar, or of the uncovered pit with the pierced stone slab beside it. Most of the black doorways led merely to small chambers, some vacant and some evidently used as storerooms; and in several of the latter he saw some very curious accumulations of various objects. One was packed with rotting and dust-draped bales of spare clothing, and the explorer thrilled when he saw that it was unmistakably the clothing of a century and a half before. In another room he found numerous odds and ends of modern clothing, as if gradual provisions were being made to equip a large body of men. But what he disliked most of all were the huge copper vats which occasionally appeared; these, and the sinister incrustations upon them. He liked them even less than the weirdly figured leaden bowls whose rims retained such obnoxious deposits and around which clung repellent odours perceptible above even the general noisomeness of the crypt. When he had completed about half the entire circuit of the wall he found another corridor like that from which he had come, and out of which many doors opened. This he proceeded to investigate; and after entering three rooms of medium size and of no significant contents, he came at last to a large oblong apartment whose business-like tanks and tables, furnaces and modern instruments, occasional books and endless shelves of jars and bottles proclaimed it indeed the long-sought laboratory of Charles Ward—and no doubt of old Joseph Curwen before him.

After lighting the three lamps which he found filled and ready, Dr. Willett examined the place and all its appurtenances with the keenest interest; noting from the relative quantities of various reagents on the shelves that young Ward's dominant concern must have been with some branch of organic chemistry. On the whole, little could be learned from the scientific ensemble, which included a gruesome-looking dissecting table; so that the room was really rather a disappointment. Among the books was a tattered old copy of Borellus in black-letter, and it was weirdly interesting to note that Ward had underlined the same passage whose marking had so perturbed good Mr. Merritt at Curwen's farmhouse more than a century and a half before. That older copy, of course, must have perished along with the rest of Curwen's occult library in the final raid. Three archways opened off the laboratory, and these the doctor proceeded to sample in turn. From his cursory survey he saw that two led merely to small storerooms; but these he canvassed with care, remarking the piles of coffins in various stages of damage and shuddering violently at two or three of the few coffin-plates he could decipher. There was much clothing also stored in these rooms, and several new and tightly nailed boxes which he did not stop to investigate. Most interesting of all, perhaps, were some odd bits which he judged to be fragments of old Joseph Curwen's laboratory appliances. These had suffered damage at the hands of the raiders, but were still partly recognisable as the chemical paraphernalia of the Georgian period.

The third archway led to a very sizeable chamber entirely lined with shelves and having in the centre a table bearing two lamps. These lamps Willett lighted, and in their brilliant glow studied the endless shelving which surrounded him. Some of the upper levels were wholly vacant, but most of the space was filled with small odd-looking leaden jars of two general types; one tall and without handles like a Grecian lekythos or oil-jug, and the other with a single handle and proportioned like a Phaleron jug. All had metal stoppers, and were covered with peculiar-looking symbols moulded in low relief. In a moment the doctor noticed that these jugs were classified with great rigidity; all the lekythoi being on one side of the room with a large wooden sign reading "Custodes" above them, and all the Phalerons on the other, correspondingly labelled with a sign reading "Materia". Each of the jars or jugs, except some on the upper shelves that turned out to be vacant, bore a cardboard tag with a number apparently referring to a catalogue; and Willett resolved to look for the latter presently. For the moment, however, he was more interested in the nature of the array as a whole; and experimentally opened several of the lekythoi and Phalerons at random with a view to a rough generalisation. The result was invariable. Both types of jar contained a small quantity of a single kind of substance; a fine dusty powder of very light weight and of many shades of dull, neutral colour. To the colours, which formed the only point of variation, there was no apparent method of disposal; and no distinction between what occurred in the lekythoi and what occurred in the Phalerons. A bluish-grey powder might be by the side of a pinkish-white one, and any one in a Phaleron might have its exact counterpart in a lekythos. The most individual feature about the powders was their non-adhesiveness. Willett would pour one into his hand, and upon returning it to its jug would find that no residue whatever remained on its palm.

The meaning of the two signs puzzled him, and he wondered why this battery of chemicals was separated so radically from those in glass jars on the shelves of the laboratory proper. "Custodes", "Materia"; that was the Latin for "Guards" and "Materials", respectively—and then there came a flash of memory as to where he had seen that word "Guards" before in connexion with this dreadful mystery. It was, of course, in the recent letter to Dr. Allen purporting to be from old Edward Hutchinson; and the phrase had read: "There was no Neede to keep the Guards in Shape and eat'g off their Heads, and it made Much to be founde in Case of Trouble, as you too welle know." What did this signify? But wait—was there not still *another* reference to "guards" in this matter which he had failed wholly to recall when reading the Hutchinson letter? Back in the old non-secretive days Ward had told him of the Eleazar Smith diary recording the spying of Smith and Weeden on the Curwen farm, and in that dreadful chronicle there had been a mention of conversations overheard before the old wizard betook himself wholly beneath the earth. There had been, Smith and Weeden insisted, terrible colloquies wherein figured Curwen, certain captives of his, *and the guards of those captives.* Those guards, according to Hutchinson or his avatar, had 'eaten their heads off', so that now Dr. Allen did not keep them *in shape.* And if not *in shape,* how save as the "salts" to which it appears this wizard band was engaged in reducing as many human bodies or skeletons as they could?

So *that* was what these lekythoi contained; the monstrous fruit of unhallowed rites and deeds, presumably won or cowed to such submission as to help, when called up by some hellish incantation, in the defence of their blasphemous master or the questioning of those who were not so willing? Willett shuddered at the thought of what he had been pouring in and out of his hands, and for a moment felt an impulse to flee in panic from that cavern of hideous shelves with their silent and perhaps watching sentinels. Then he thought of the "Materia"—in the myriad Phaleron jugs on the other side of the room. Salts too—and if not the salts of "guards", then the salts of what? God! Could it be possible that here lay the mortal relics of half the titan thinkers of all the ages; snatched by supreme ghouls from crypts where the world thought them safe, and subject to the beck and call of madmen who sought to drain their knowledge for some still wilder end whose ultimate effect would concern, as poor Charles had hinted in his frantic note, 'all civilisation, all natural law, perhaps even the fate of the solar system and the universe'? And Marinus Bicknell Willett had sifted their dust through his hands!

Then he noticed a small door at the farther end of the room, and calmed himself enough to approach it and examine the crude sign chiselled above. It was only a symbol, but it filled him with vague spiritual dread; for a morbid, dreaming friend of his had once drawn it on paper and told him a few of the things it means in the dark abyss of sleep. It was the sign of Koth, that dreamers see fixed above the archway of a certain black tower standing alone in twilight—and Willett did not like what his friend Randolph Carter had said of its powers. But a moment later he forgot the sign as he recognised a new acrid odour in the stench-filled air. This was a chemical rather than animal smell, and came clearly from the room beyond the door. And it was, unmistakably, the same odour which had saturated Charles Ward's clothing on the day the doctors had taken him away. So it was here that the youth had been interrupted by the final summons? He was wiser than old Joseph Curwen, for he had not resisted. Willett, boldly determined to penetrate every wonder and nightmare this nether realm might contain, seized the small lamp and crossed the threshold. A wave of nameless fright rolled out to meet him, but he yielded to no whim and deferred to no intuition. There was nothing alive here to harm him, and he would not be stayed in his piercing of the eldritch cloud which engulfed his patient.

The room beyond the door was of medium size, and had no furniture save a table, a single chair, and two groups of curious machines with clamps and wheels, which Willett recognised after a moment as mediaeval instruments of torture. On one side of the door stood a rack of savage whips, above which were some shelves bearing empty rows of shallow pedestalled cups of lead shaped like

Grecian kylikes. On the other side was the table; with a powerful Argand lamp, a pad and pencil, and two of the stoppered lekythoi from the shelves outside set down at irregular places as if temporarily or in haste. Willett lighted the lamp and looked carefully at the pad, to see what notes young Ward might have been jotting down when interrupted; but found nothing more intelligible than the following disjointed fragments in the crabbed Curwen chirography, which shed no light on the case as a whole:

"B. dy'd not. Escap'd into walls and founde Place below.
"Saw olde V. saye ye Sabaoth and learnt ye Way.
"Rais'd *Yog-Sothoth* thrice and was ye nexte Day deliver'd.
"F. soughte to wipe out all know'g howe to raise Those from Outside."

As the strong Argand blaze lit up the entire chamber the doctor saw that the wall opposite the door, between the two groups of torturing appliances in the corners, was covered with pegs from which hung a set of shapeless-looking robes of a rather dismal yellowish-white. But far more interesting were the two vacant walls, both of which were thickly covered with mystic symbols and formulae roughly chiselled in the smooth dressed stone. The damp floor also bore marks of carving; and with but little difficulty Willett deciphered a huge pentagram in the centre, with a plain circle about three feet wide half way between this and each corner. In one of these four circles, near where a yellowish robe had been flung carelessly down, there stood a shallow kylix of the sort found on the shelves above the whip-rack; and just outside the periphery was one of the Phaleron jugs from the shelves in the other room, its tag numbered 118. This was unstoppered, and proved upon inspection to be empty; but the explorer saw with a shiver that the kylix was not. Within its shallow area, and saved from scattering only by the absence of wind in this sequestered cavern, lay a small amount of a dry, dull-greenish, efflorescent powder which must have belonged in the jug; and Willett almost reeled at the implications that came sweeping over him as he correlated little by little the several elements and antecedents of the scene. The whips and the instruments of torture, the dust or salts from the jug of "Materia", the two lekythoi from the "Custodes" shelf, the robes, the formulae on the walls, the notes on the pad, the hints from letters and legends, and the thousand glimpses, doubts, and suppositions which had come to torment the friends and parents of Charles Ward—all these engulfed the doctor in a tidal wave of horror as he looked at that dry greenish powder outspread in the pedestalled leaden kylix on the floor.

With an effort, however, Willett pulled himself together and began studying the formulae chiselled on the walls. From the stained and incrusted letters it was obvious that they were carved in Joseph Curwen's time, and their text was such as to be vaguely familiar to one who had read much Curwen material or delved extensively into the history of magic. One the doctor clearly recognised as what Mrs. Ward heard her son chanting on that ominous Good Friday a year before, and what an authority had told him was a very terrible invocation addressed to secret gods outside the normal spheres. It was not spelled here exactly as Mrs. Ward had set it down from memory, nor yet as the authority had shewn it to him in the forbidden pages of "Eliphas Levi"; but its identity was unmistakable, and such words as *Sabaoth*, *Metraton*, *Almousin*, and *Zariatnatmik* sent a shudder of fright through the searcher who had seen and felt so much of cosmic abomination just around the corner.

This was on the left-hand wall as one entered the room. The right-hand wall was no less thickly inscribed, and Willett felt a start of recognition as he came upon the pair of formulae so frequently occurring in the recent notes in the library. They were, roughly speaking, the same; with the ancient symbols of "Dragon's Head" and "Dragon's Tail" heading them as in Ward's scribblings. But the spelling differed quite widely from that of the modern versions, as if old Curwen had had a different way of recording sound, or as if later study had evolved more powerful and perfected variants of the invocations in question. The doctor tried to reconcile the chiselled version with the one which still ran persistently in his head, and found it hard to do. Where the script he had memorised began "*Y'ai 'ng'ngah, Yog-Sothoth*", this epigraph started out as "*Aye, engengah, Yogge-Sothotha*"; which to his mind would seriously interfere with the syllabification of the second word.

Ground as the later text was into his consciousness, the discrepancy disturbed him; and he found himself chanting the first of the formulae aloud in an effort to square the sound he conceived with the letters he found carved. Weird and menacing in that abyss of antique blasphemy rang his voice; its accents keyed to a droning sing-song either through the spell of the past and the unknown, or through the hellish example of that dull, godless wail from the pits whose inhuman cadences rose and fell rhythmically in the distance through the stench and the darkness.

"Y'AI 'NG'NGAH,
YOG-SOTHOTH
H'EE—L'GEB
F'AI THRODOG
UAAAH!"

But what was this cold wind which had sprung into life at the very outset of the chant? The lamps were sputtering woefully, and the gloom grew so dense that the letters on the wall nearly faded from sight. There was smoke, too, and an acrid odour which quite drowned out the stench from the far-away wells; an odour like that he had smelt before, yet infinitely stronger and more pungent. He turned from the inscriptions to face the room with its bizarre contents, and saw that the kylix on the floor, in which the ominous efflorescent powder had lain, was giving forth a cloud of thick, greenish-black vapour of surprising volume and opacity. That powder—Great God! it had come from the shelf of "Materia"—what was it doing now, and what had started it? The formula he had been chanting—the first of the pair—Dragon's Head, *ascending node*—Blessed Saviour, could it be ...

The doctor reeled, and through his head raced wildly disjointed scraps from all he had seen, heard, and read of the frightful case of Joseph Curwen and Charles Dexter Ward. "I say to you againe, doe not call up Any that you can not put downe.... Have y[e] Wordes for laying at all times readie, and stopp not to be sure when there is any Doubte of *Whom* you have.... Three Talkes with *What was therein inhum'd* ..." *Mercy of heaven, what is that shape behind the parting smoke?*

5.

Marinus Bicknell Willett has no hope that any part of his tale will be believed except by certain sympathetic friends, hence he has made no attempt to tell it beyond his most intimate circle. Only a few outsiders have ever heard it repeated, and of these the majority laugh and remark that the doctor surely is getting old. He has been advised to take a long vacation and to shun future cases dealing with mental disturbance. But Mr. Ward knows that the veteran physician speaks only a horrible truth. Did not he himself see the noisome aperture in the bungalow cellar? Did not Willett send him home overcome and ill at eleven o'clock that portentous morning? Did he not telephone the doctor in vain that evening, and again the next day, and had he not driven to the bungalow itself on that following noon, finding his friend unconscious but unharmed on one of the beds upstairs? Willett had been breathing stertorously, and opened his eyes slowly when Mr. Ward gave him some brandy fetched from the car. Then he shuddered and screamed, crying out, "*That beard ... those eyes.... God, who are you?*" A very strange thing to say to a trim, blue-eyed, clean-shaven gentleman whom he had known from the latter's boyhood.

In the bright noon sunlight the bungalow was unchanged since the previous morning. Willett's clothing bore no disarrangement beyond certain smudges and worn places at the knees, and only a faint acrid odour reminded Mr. Ward of what he had smelt on his son that day he was taken to the hospital. The doctor's flashlight was missing, but his valise was safely there, as empty as when he had brought it. Before indulging in any explanations, and obviously with great moral effort, Willett staggered dizzily down to the cellar and tried the fateful platform before the tubs. It was unyielding. Crossing to where he had left his yet-unused tool satchel the day before, he obtained a chisel and began to pry up the stubborn planks one by one. Underneath the smooth concrete was still visible, but of any opening or perforation there was no longer a trace. Nothing yawned this time to sicken the mystified father who had followed the doctor downstairs; only the smooth concrete underneath the planks—no noisome well, no world of subterrene horrors, no secret library, no Curwen papers, no nightmare pits of stench and howling, no laboratory or shelves or chiselled formulae, no.... Dr. Willett turned pale, and clutched at the younger man. "Yesterday," he asked softly, "did you see it here ... and smell it?" And when Mr. Ward, himself transfixed with dread and wonder, found strength to nod an affirmative, the physician gave a sound half a sigh and half a gasp, and nodded in turn. "Then I will tell you," he said.

So for an hour, in the sunniest room they could find upstairs, the physician whispered his frightful tale to the wondering father. There was nothing to relate beyond the looming up of that form when the greenish-black vapour from the kylix parted, and Willett was too tired to ask himself what had really occurred. There were futile, bewildered head-shakings from both men, and once Mr. Ward ventured a hushed suggestion, "Do you suppose it would be of any use to dig?" The doctor was silent, for it seemed hardly fitting for any human brain to answer when powers of unknown spheres had so vitally encroached on this side of the Great Abyss. Again Mr. Ward asked, "But where did it go? It brought you here, you know, and it sealed up the hole somehow." And Willett again let silence answer for him.

But after all, this was not the final phase of the matter. Reaching for his handkerchief before rising to leave, Dr. Willett's fingers closed upon a piece of paper in his pocket which had not been there before, and which was companioned by the candles and matches he had seized in the vanished vault. It was a common sheet, torn obviously from the cheap pad in that fabulous room of horror somewhere underground, and the writing upon it was that of an ordinary lead pencil—doubtless the one which had lain beside the pad. It was folded very carelessly, and beyond the faint acrid scent of the cryptic chamber bore no print or mark of any world but this. But in the text itself it did indeed reek with wonder; for here was no script of any wholesome age, but the laboured strokes of mediaeval darkness, scarcely legible to the laymen who now strained over it, yet having combinations of symbols which seemed vaguely familiar. The briefly scrawled message was this, and its mystery lent purpose to the shaken pair, who forthwith walked steadily out to the Ward car and gave orders to be driven first to a quiet dining place and then to the John Hay Library on the hill.

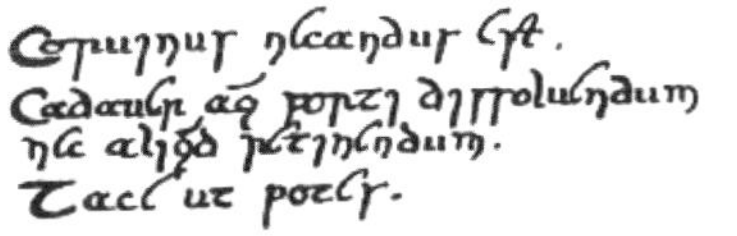

At the library it was easy to find good manuals of palaeography, and over these the two men puzzled till the lights of evening shone out from the great chandelier. In the end they found what was needed. The letters were indeed no fantastic invention, but the normal script of a very dark period. They were the pointed Saxon minuscules of the eighth or ninth century A.D., and brought with them memories of an uncouth time when under a fresh Christian veneer ancient faiths and ancient rites stirred stealthily, and the pale moon of Britain looked sometimes on strange deeds in the Roman ruins at Caerleon and Hexham, and by the towers along Hadrian's crumbling wall. The words were in such Latin as a barbarous age might remember—"*Corvinus necandus est. Cadaver aq(ua) forti dissolvendum, nec aliq(ui)d retinendum. Tace ut potes.*"—which may roughly be translated, "Curwen must be killed. The body must be dissolved in aqua fortis, nor must anything be retained. Keep silence as best you are able."

Willett and Mr. Ward were mute and baffled. They had met the unknown, and found that they lacked emotions to respond to it as they vaguely believed they ought. With Willett, especially, the capacity for receiving fresh impressions of awe was well-nigh exhausted; and both men sat still and helpless till the closing of the library forced them to leave. Then they drove listlessly to the Ward mansion in Prospect Street, and talked to no purpose into the night. The doctor rested toward morning, but did not go home. And he was still there Sunday noon when a telephone message came from the detectives who had been assigned to look up Dr. Allen.

Mr. Ward, who was pacing nervously about in a dressing-gown, answered the call in person; and told the men to come up early the next day when he heard their report was almost ready. Both Willett and he were glad that this phase of the matter was taking form, for whatever the origin of the strange minuscule message, it seemed certain that the "Curwen" who must be destroyed could be no other than the bearded and spectacled stranger. Charles had feared this man, and had said in the frantic note that he must be killed and dissolved in acid. Allen, moreover, had been receiving letters from the strange wizards in Europe under the name of Curwen, and palpably regarded himself as an avatar of the bygone necromancer. And now from a fresh and unknown source had come a message saying that "Curwen" must be killed and dissolved in acid. The linkage was too unmistakable to be factitious; and besides, was not Allen planning to murder young Ward upon the advice of the creature called Hutchinson? Of course, the letter they had seen had never reached the bearded stranger; but from its text they could see that Allen had already formed plans for dealing with the youth if he grew too 'squeamish'. Without doubt, Allen must be apprehended; and even if the most drastic directions were not carried out, he must be placed where he could inflict no harm upon Charles Ward.

That afternoon, hoping against hope to extract some gleam of information anent the inmost mysteries from the only available one capable of giving it, the father and the doctor went down the bay and called on young Charles at the hospital. Simply and gravely Willett told him all he had found, and noticed how pale he turned as each description made certain the truth of the discovery. The physician employed as much dramatic effect as he could, and watched for a wincing on Charles's part when he approached the matter of the covered pits and the nameless hybrids within. But Ward did not wince. Willett paused, and his voice grew indignant as he spoke of how the things were starving. He taxed the youth with shocking inhumanity, and shivered when only a sardonic laugh came in reply. For Charles, having dropped as useless his pretence that the crypt did not exist, seemed to see some ghastly jest in this affair; and chuckled hoarsely at something which amused him. Then he whispered, in accents doubly terrible because of the cracked voice he used, "Damn 'em, they *do* eat, but they *don't need to!* That's the rare part! A month, you say, without food? Lud, Sir, you be modest! D'ye know, that was the joke on poor old Whipple with his virtuous bluster! Kill everything off, would he? Why, damme, he was half-deaf with the noise from Outside and never saw or heard aught from the wells! He never dreamed they were there at all! Devil take ye, *those cursed things have been howling down there ever since Curwen was done for a hundred and fifty-seven years gone!*"

But no more than this could Willett get from the youth. Horrified, yet almost convinced against his will, he went on with his tale in the hope that some incident might startle his auditor out of the mad composure he maintained. Looking at the youth's face, the doctor could not but feel a kind of terror at the changes which recent months had wrought. Truly, the boy had drawn down nameless horrors from the skies. When the room with the formulae and the greenish dust was mentioned, Charles shewed his first sign of animation. A quizzical look overspread his face as he heard what Willett had read on the pad, and he ventured the mild statement that those notes were old ones, of no possible significance to anyone not deeply initiated in the history of magic. "But," he added, "had you but known the words to bring up that which I had out in the cup, you had not been here to tell me this. 'Twas Number 118, and I conceive you would have shook had you looked it up in my list in t'other room. 'Twas never raised by me, but I meant to have it up that day you came to invite me hither."

Then Willett told of the formula he had spoken and of the greenish-black smoke which had arisen; and as he did so he saw true fear dawn for the first time on Charles Ward's face. "It *came*, and you be here alive?" As Ward croaked the words his voice seemed almost to burst free of its trammels and sink to cavernous abysses of uncanny resonance. Willett, gifted with a flash of inspiration, believed he saw the situation, and wove into his reply a caution from a letter he remembered. "No. 118, you say? But don't forget that *stones are all changed now in nine grounds out of ten. You are never sure till you question!*" And then, without warning, he drew forth the minuscule message and flashed it before the patient's eyes. He could have wished no stronger result, for Charles Ward fainted forthwith.

All this conversation, of course, had been conducted with the greatest secrecy lest the resident alienists accuse the father and the physician of encouraging a madman in his delusions. Unaided, too, Dr. Willett and Mr. Ward picked up the stricken youth and placed him on the couch. In reviving, the patient mumbled many times of some word which he must get to Orne and Hutchinson at once; so when his consciousness seemed fully back the doctor told him that of those strange creatures at least one was his bitter enemy, and had given Dr. Allen advice for his assassination. This revelation produced no visible effect, and before it was made the visitors could see that their host had already the look of a hunted man. After that he would converse no more, so Willett and the father departed presently; leaving behind a caution against the bearded Allen, to which the youth only replied that this individual was very safely taken care of, and could do no one any harm even if he wished. This was said with an almost evil chuckle very painful to hear. They did not worry about any communications Charles might indite to that monstrous pair in Europe, since they knew that the hospital authorities seized all outgoing mail for censorship and would pass no wild or outré-looking missive.

There is, however, a curious sequel to the matter of Orne and Hutchinson, if such indeed the exiled wizards were. Moved by some vague presentiment amidst the horrors of that period, Willett arranged with an international press-cutting bureau for accounts of notable current crimes and accidents in Prague and in eastern Transylvania; and after six months believed that he had found two very significant things amongst the multifarious items he received and had translated. One was the total wrecking of a house by night in the oldest quarter of Prague, and the disappearance of the evil old man called Josef Nadek, who had dwelt in it alone ever since anyone could remember. The other was a titan explosion in the Transylvanian mountains east of Rakus, and the utter extirpation with all its inmates of the ill-regarded Castle Ferenczy, whose master was so badly spoken of by peasants and soldiery alike that he would shortly have been summoned to Bucharest for serious questioning had not this incident cut off a career already so long as to antedate all common memory. Willett maintains that the hand which wrote those minuscules was able to wield stronger weapons as well; and that while Curwen was left to him to dispose of, the writer felt able to find and deal with Orne and Hutchinson itself. Of what their fate may have been the doctor strives sedulously not to think.

6.

The following morning Dr. Willett hastened to the Ward home to be present when the detectives arrived. Allen's destruction or imprisonment—or Curwen's, if one might regard the tacit claim to reincarnation as valid—he felt must be accomplished at any cost, and he communicated this conviction to Mr. Ward as they sat waiting for the men to come. They were downstairs this time, for the upper parts of the house were beginning to be shunned because of a peculiar nauseousness which hung indefinitely about; a nauseousness which the older servants connected with some curse left by the vanished Curwen portrait.

At nine o'clock the three detectives presented themselves and immediately delivered all that they had to say. They had not, regrettably enough, located the Brava Tony Gomes as they had wished, nor had they found the least trace of Dr. Allen's source or present whereabouts; but they had managed to unearth a considerable number of local impressions and facts concerning the reticent stranger. Allen had struck Pawtuxet people as a vaguely unnatural being, and there was an universal belief that his thick Vandyke beard was either dyed or false—a belief conclusively upheld by the finding of such a false beard, together with a pair of dark glasses, in his room at the fateful bungalow. His voice, Mr. Ward could well testify from his one telephone conversation, had a depth and hollowness that could not be forgotten; and his glance seemed malign even through his smoked and horn-rimmed glasses. One shopkeeper, in the course of negotiations, had seen a specimen of his handwriting and declared it was very queer and crabbed; this being confirmed by pencilled notes of no clear meaning found in his room and identified by the merchant. In connexion with the vampirism rumours of the preceding summer, a majority of the gossips believed that Allen rather than Ward was the actual vampire. Statements were also obtained from the officials who had visited the bungalow after the unpleasant incident of the motor truck robbery. They had felt less of the sinister in Dr. Allen, but had recognised him as the dominant figure in the queer shadowy cottage. The place had been too dark for them to observe him clearly, but they would know him again if they saw him. His beard had looked odd, and they thought he had some slight scar above his dark spectacled right eye. As for the detectives' search of Allen's room, it yielded nothing definite save the beard and glasses, and several pencilled notes in a crabbed writing which Willett at once saw was identical with that shared by the old Curwen manuscripts and by the voluminous recent notes of young Ward found in the vanished catacombs of horror.

Dr. Willett and Mr. Ward caught something of a profound, subtle, and insidious cosmic fear from this data as it was gradually unfolded, and almost trembled in following up the vague, mad thought which had simultaneously reached their minds. The false beard and glasses—the crabbed Curwen penmanship—the old portrait and its tiny scar—*and the altered youth in the hospital with such a scar*—that deep, hollow voice on the telephone—was it not of this that Mr. Ward was reminded when his son barked forth those pitiable tones to which he now claimed to be reduced? Who had ever seen Charles and Allen together? Yes, the officials had once, but who later on? Was it not when Allen left that Charles suddenly lost his growing fright and began to live wholly at the bungalow? Curwen—Allen—Ward—in what blasphemous and abominable fusion had two ages and two persons become involved? That damnable resemblance of the picture to Charles—had it not used to stare and stare, and follow the boy around the room with its eyes? Why, too, did both Allen and Charles copy Joseph Curwen's handwriting, even when alone and off guard? And then the frightful work of those people—the lost crypt of horrors that had aged the doctor overnight; the starved monsters in the noisome pits; the awful formula which had yielded such nameless results; the message in minuscules found in Willett's pocket; the papers and the letters and all the talk of graves and "salts" and discoveries—whither did everything lead? In the end Mr. Ward did the most sensible thing. Steeling himself against any realisation of why he did it, he gave the detectives an article to be shewn to such Pawtuxet shopkeepers as had seen the portentous Dr. Allen. That article was a photograph of his luckless son, on which he now carefully drew in ink the pair of heavy glasses and the black pointed beard which the men had brought from Allen's room.

For two hours he waited with the doctor in the oppressive house where fear and miasma were slowly gathering as the empty panel in the upstairs library leered and leered and leered. Then the men returned. Yes. *The altered photograph was a very passable likeness of Dr. Allen.* Mr. Ward turned pale, and Willett wiped a suddenly dampened brow with his handkerchief. Allen—Ward—Curwen—it was becoming too hideous for coherent thought. What had the boy called out of the void, and what had it done to him? What, really, had happened from first to last? Who was this Allen who sought to kill Charles as too 'squeamish', and why had his destined victim said in the postscript to that frantic letter that he must be so completely obliterated in acid? Why, too, had the minuscule message, of whose origin no one dared think, said that "Curwen" must be likewise obliterated? What was the *change*, and when had the final stage occurred? That day when his frantic note was received—he had been nervous all the morning, then there was an alteration. He had slipped out unseen and swaggered boldly in past the men hired to guard him. That was the time, when he was out. But no—had he not cried out in terror as he entered his study—this very room? What had he found there? Or wait—*what had found him?* That simulacrum which brushed boldly in without having been seen to go—was that an alien shadow and a horror forcing itself upon a trembling figure which had never gone out at all? Had not the butler spoken of queer noises?

Willett rang for the man and asked him some low-toned questions. It had, surely enough, been a bad business. There had been noises—a cry, a gasp, a choking, and a sort of clattering or creaking or thumping, or all of these. And Mr. Charles was not the same when he stalked out without a word. The butler shivered as he spoke, and sniffed at the heavy air that blew down from some open window upstairs. Terror had settled definitely upon the house, and only the business-like detectives failed to imbibe a full measure of it. Even they were restless, for this case had held vague elements in the background which pleased them not at all. Dr. Willett was thinking deeply and rapidly, and his thoughts were terrible ones. Now and then he would almost break into muttering as he ran over in his head a new, appalling, and increasingly conclusive chain of nightmare happenings.

Then Mr. Ward made a sign that the conference was over, and everyone save him and the doctor left the room. It was noon now, but shadows as of coming night seemed to engulf the phantom-haunted mansion. Willett began talking very seriously to his host, and urged that he leave a great deal of the future investigation to him. There would be, he predicted, certain obnoxious elements which a friend could bear better than a relative. As family physician he must have a free hand, and the first thing he required was a period alone and undisturbed in the abandoned library upstairs, where the ancient overmantel had gathered about itself an aura of noisome horror more intense than when Joseph Curwen's features themselves glanced slyly down from the painted panel.

Mr. Ward, dazed by the flood of grotesque morbidities and unthinkably maddening suggestions that poured in upon him from every side, could only acquiesce; and half an hour later the doctor was locked in the shunned room with the panelling from Olney Court. The father, listening outside, heard fumbling sounds of moving and rummaging as the moments passed; and finally a wrench and a creak, as if a tight cupboard door were being opened. Then there was a muffled cry, a kind of snorting choke, and a hasty slamming of whatever had been opened. Almost at once the key rattled and Willett appeared in the hall, haggard and ghastly, and demanding wood for the real fireplace on the south wall of the room. The furnace was not enough, he said; and the electric log had little practical use. Longing yet not daring to ask questions, Mr. Ward gave the requisite orders and a man brought some stout pine logs, shuddering as he entered the tainted air of the library to place them in the grate. Willett meanwhile had gone up to the dismantled laboratory and brought down a few odds and ends not included in the moving of the July before. They were in a covered basket, and Mr. Ward never saw what they were.

Then the doctor locked himself in the library once more, and by the clouds of smoke which rolled down past the windows from the chimney it was known that he had lighted the fire. Later, after a great rustling of newspapers, that odd wrench and creaking were heard again; followed by a thumping which none of the eavesdroppers liked. Thereafter two suppressed cries of Willett's were heard, and hard upon these came a swishing rustle of indefinable hatefulness. Finally the smoke that the wind beat down from the chimney grew very dark and acrid, and everyone wished that the weather had spared them this choking and venomous inundation of peculiar fumes. Mr. Ward's head reeled, and the servants all clustered together in a knot to watch the horrible black smoke swoop down. After an age of waiting the vapours seemed to lighten, and half-formless sounds of scraping, sweeping, and other minor operations were heard behind the bolted door. And at last, after the slamming of some cupboard within, Willett made his appearance—sad, pale, and haggard, and bearing the cloth-draped basket he had taken from the upstairs laboratory. He had left the window open, and into that once accursed room was pouring a wealth of pure, wholesome air to mix with a queer new smell of disinfectants. The ancient overmantel still lingered; but it seemed robbed of malignity now, and rose as calm and stately in its white panelling as if it had never borne the picture of Joseph Curwen. Night was coming on, yet this time its shadows held no latent fright, but only a gentle melancholy. Of what he had done the doctor would never speak. To Mr. Ward he said, "I can answer no questions, but I will say that there are different kinds of magic. I have made a great purgation, and those in this house will sleep the better for it."

7.

That Dr. Willett's "purgation" had been an ordeal almost as nerve-racking in its way as his hideous wandering in the vanished crypt is shewn by the fact that the elderly physician gave out completely as soon as he reached home that evening. For three days he rested constantly in his room, though servants later muttered something about having heard him after midnight on Wednesday, when the outer door softly opened and closed with phenomenal softness. Servants' imaginations, fortunately, are limited, else comment might have been excited by an item in Thursday's *Evening Bulletin* which ran as follows:

North End Ghouls
Again Active

After a lull of ten months since the dastardly vandalism in the Weeden lot at the North Burial Ground, a nocturnal prowler was glimpsed early this morning in the same cemetery by Robert Hart, the night watchman. Happening to glance for a moment from his shelter at about 2 a.m., Hart observed the glow of a lantern or pocket torch not far to the northwest, and upon opening the door detected the figure of a man with a trowel very plainly silhouetted against a nearby electric light. At once starting in pursuit, he saw the figure dart hurriedly toward the main entrance, gaining the street and losing himself among the shadows before approach or capture was possible.

Like the first of the ghouls active during the past year, this intruder had done no real damage before detection. A vacant part of the Ward lot shewed signs of a little superficial digging, but nothing even nearly the size of a grave had been attempted, and no previous grave had been disturbed.

Hart, who cannot describe the prowler except as a small man probably having a full beard, inclines to the view that all three of the digging incidents have a common source; but police from the Second Station think otherwise on account of the savage nature of the second incident, where an ancient coffin was removed and its headstone violently shattered.

The first of the incidents, in which it is thought an attempt to bury something was frustrated, occurred a year ago last March, and has been attributed to bootleggers seeking a cache. It is possible, says Sergt. Riley, that this third affair is of similar nature. Officers at the Second Station are taking especial pains to capture the gang of miscreants responsible for these repeated outrages.

All day Thursday Dr. Willett rested as if recuperating from something past or nerving himself for something to come. In the evening he wrote a note to Mr. Ward, which was delivered the next morning and which caused the half-dazed parent to ponder long and deeply. Mr. Ward had not been able to go down to business since the shock of Monday with its baffling reports and its sinister "purgation", but he found something calming about the doctor's letter in spite of the despair it seemed to promise and the fresh mysteries it seemed to evoke.

"10 Barnes St.,
Providence, R.I.,
April 12, 1928

"Dear Theodore:—I feel that I must say a word to you before doing what I am going to do tomorrow. It will conclude the terrible business we have been going through (for I feel that no spade is ever likely to reach that monstrous place we know of), but I'm afraid it won't set your mind at rest unless I expressly assure you how very conclusive it is.

"You have known me ever since you were a small boy, so I think you will not distrust me when I hint that some matters are best left undecided and unexplored. It is better that you attempt no further speculation as to Charles's case, and almost imperative that you tell his mother nothing more than she already suspects. When I call on you tomorrow Charles will have escaped. That is all which need remain in anyone's mind. He was mad, and he escaped. You can tell his mother gently and gradually about the mad part when you stop sending the typed notes in his name. I'd advise you to join her in Atlantic City and take a rest yourself. God knows you need one after this shock, as I do myself. I am going south for a while to calm down and brace up.

"So don't ask me any questions when I call. It may be that something will go wrong, but I'll tell you if it does. I don't think it will. There will be nothing more to worry about, for Charles will be very, very safe. He is now—safer than you dream. You need hold no fears about Allen, and who or what he is. He forms as much a part of the past as Joseph Curwen's picture, and when I ring your doorbell you may feel certain that there is no such person. And what wrote that minuscule message will never trouble you or yours.

"But you must steel yourself to melancholy, and prepare your wife to do the same. I must tell you frankly that Charles's escape will not mean his restoration to you. He has been afflicted with a peculiar disease, as you must realise from the subtle physical as well as mental changes in him, and you must not hope to see him again. Have only this consolation—that he was never a fiend or even truly a madman, but only an eager, studious, and curious boy whose love of mystery and of the past was his undoing. He stumbled on things no mortal ought ever to know, and reached back through the years as no one ever should reach; and something came out of those years to engulf him.

"And now comes the matter in which I must ask you to trust me most of all. For there will be, indeed, no uncertainty about Charles's fate. In about a year, say, you can if you wish devise a suitable account of the end; for the boy will be no more. You can put up a stone in your lot at the North Burial Ground exactly ten feet west of your father's and facing the same way, and that will mark the true resting-place of your son. Nor need you fear that it will mark any abnormality or changeling. The ashes in that grave will be those of your own unaltered bone and sinew—of the real Charles Dexter Ward whose mind you watched from infancy—the real Charles with the olive-mark on his hip and without the black witch-mark on his chest or the pit on his forehead. The Charles who never did actual evil, and who will have paid with his life for his 'squeamishness'.

"That is all. Charles will have escaped, and a year from now you can put up his stone. Do not question me tomorrow. And believe that the honour of your ancient family remains untainted now, as it has been at all times in the past.

"With profoundest sympathy, and exhortations to fortitude, calmness, and resignation, I am ever

Sincerely your friend,
Marinus B. Willett"

So on the morning of Friday, April 13, 1928, Marinus Bicknell Willett visited the room of Charles Dexter Ward at Dr. Waite's private hospital on Conanicut Island. The youth, though making no attempt to evade his caller, was in a sullen mood; and seemed disinclined to open the conversation which Willett obviously desired. The doctor's discovery of the crypt and his monstrous experience therein had of course created a new source of embarrassment, so that both hesitated perceptibly after the interchange of a few strained formalities. Then a new element of constraint crept in, as Ward seemed to read behind the doctor's mask-like face a terrible purpose which had never been there before. The patient quailed, conscious that since the last visit there had been a change whereby the solicitous family physician had given place to the ruthless and implacable avenger.

Ward actually turned pale, and the doctor was the first to speak. "More," he said, "has been found out, and I must warn you fairly that a reckoning is due."

"Digging again, and coming upon more poor starving pets?" was the ironic reply. It was evident that the youth meant to shew bravado to the last.

"No," Willett slowly rejoined, "this time I did not have to dig. We have had men looking up Dr. Allen, and they found the false beard and spectacles in the bungalow."

"Excellent," commented the disquieted host in an effort to be wittily insulting, "and I trust they proved more becoming than the beard and glasses you now have on!"

"They would become you very well," came the even and studied response, "*as indeed they seem to have done.*"

As Willett said this, it almost seemed as though a cloud passed over the sun; though there was no change in the shadows on the floor. Then Ward ventured:

"And is this what asks so hotly for a reckoning? Suppose a man does find it now and then useful to be twofold?"

"No," said Willett gravely, "again you are wrong. It is no business of mine if any man seeks duality; *provided he has any right to exist at all, and provided he does not destroy what called him out of space.*"

Ward now started violently. "Well, Sir, what *have* ye found, and what d'ye want with me?"

The doctor let a little time elapse before replying, as if choosing his words for an effective answer.

"I have found," he finally intoned, "something in a cupboard behind an ancient overmantel where a picture once was, and I have burned it and buried the ashes where the grave of Charles Dexter Ward ought to be."

The madman choked and sprang from the chair in which he had been sitting:

"Damn ye, who did ye tell—and who'll believe it was he after these full two months, with me alive? What d'ye mean to do?"

Willett, though a small man, actually took on a kind of judicial majesty as he calmed the patient with a gesture.

"I have told no one. This is no common case—it is a madness out of time and a horror from beyond the spheres which no police or lawyers or courts or alienists could ever fathom or grapple with. Thank God some chance has left inside me the spark of imagination, that I might not go astray in thinking out this thing. *You cannot deceive me, Joseph Curwen, for I know that your accursed magic is true!*

"I know how you wove the spell that brooded outside the years and fastened on your double and descendant; I know how you drew him into the past and got him to raise you up from your detestable grave; I know how he kept you hidden in his laboratory while you studied modern things and roved abroad as a vampire by night, and how you later shewed yourself in beard and glasses that no one might wonder at your godless likeness to him; I know what you resolved to do when he balked at your monstrous rifling of the world's tombs, *and at what you planned afterward,* and I know how you did it.

"You left off your beard and glasses and fooled the guards around the house. They thought it was he who went in, and they thought it was he who came out when you had strangled and hidden him. But you hadn't reckoned on the different contents of two minds. You were a fool, Curwen, to fancy that a mere visual identity would be enough. Why didn't you think of the speech and the voice and the handwriting? It hasn't worked, you see, after all. You know better than I who or what wrote that message in minuscules, but I will warn you it was not written in vain. There are abominations and blasphemies which must be stamped out, and I believe that the writer of those words will attend to Orne and Hutchinson. One of those creatures wrote you once, 'do not call up any that you cannot put down'. You were undone once before, perhaps in that very way, and it may be that your own evil magic will undo you all again. Curwen, a man can't tamper with Nature beyond certain limits, and every horror you have woven will rise up to wipe you out."

But here the doctor was cut short by a convulsive cry from the creature before him. Hopelessly at bay, weaponless, and knowing that any show of physical violence would bring a score of attendants to the doctor's rescue, Joseph Curwen had recourse to his one ancient ally, and began a series of cabbalistic motions with his forefingers as his deep, hollow voice, now unconcealed by feigned hoarseness, bellowed out the opening words of a terrible formula.

"PER ADONAI ELOIM, ADONAI JEHOVA, ADONAI SABAOTH, METRATON...."

But Willett was too quick for him. Even as the dogs in the yard outside began to howl, and even as a chill wind sprang suddenly up from the bay, the doctor commenced the solemn and measured intonation of that which he had meant all along to recite. An eye for an eye—magic for magic—let the outcome shew how well the lesson of the abyss had been learned! So in a clear voice Marinus Bicknell Willett began the *second* of that pair of formulae whose first had raised the writer of those minuscules—the cryptic invocation whose heading was the Dragon's Tail, sign of the *descending node*—

"OGTHROD AI'F
GEB'L—EE'H
YOG-SOTHOTH
'NGAH'NG AI'Y
ZHRO!"

At the very first word from Willett's mouth the previously commenced formula of the patient stopped short. Unable to speak, the monster made wild motions with his arms until they too were arrested. When the awful name of *Yog-Sothoth* was uttered, the hideous change began. It was not merely a *dissolution*, but rather a *transformation* or *recapitulation*; and Willett shut his eyes lest he faint before the rest of the incantation could be pronounced.

But he did not faint, and that man of unholy centuries and forbidden secrets never troubled the world again. The madness out of time had subsided, and the case of Charles Dexter Ward was closed. Opening his eyes before staggering out of that room of horror, Dr. Willett saw that what he had kept in memory had not been kept amiss. There had, as he had predicted, been no need for acids. For like his accursed picture a year before, Joseph Curwen now lay scattered on the floor as a thin coating of fine bluish-grey dust.

THE COLOUR OUT OF SPACE

West of Arkham the hills rise wild, and there are valleys with deep woods that no axe has ever cut. There are dark narrow glens where the trees slope fantastically, and where thin brooklets trickle without ever having caught the glint of sunlight. On the gentler slopes there are farms, ancient and rocky, with squat, moss-coated cottages brooding eternally over old New England secrets in the lee of great ledges; but these are all vacant now, the wide chimneys crumbling and the shingled sides bulging perilously beneath low gambrel roofs.

The old folk have gone away, and foreigners do not like to live there. French-Canadians have tried it, Italians have tried it, and the Poles have come and departed. It is not because of anything that can be seen or heard or handled, but because of something that is imagined. The place is not good for the imagination, and does not bring restful dreams at night. It must be this which keeps the foreigners away, for old Ammi Pierce has never told them of anything he recalls from the strange days. Ammi, whose head has been a little queer for years, is the only one who still remains, or who ever talks of the strange days; and he dares to do this because his house is so near the open fields and the travelled roads around Arkham.

There was once a road over the hills and through the valleys, that ran straight where the blasted heath is now; but people ceased to use it and a new road was laid curving far toward the south.

Traces of the old one can still be found amidst the weeds of a returning wilderness, and some of them will doubtless linger even when half the hollows are flooded for the new reservoir. Then the dark woods will be cut down and the blasted heath will slumber far below blue waters whose surface will mirror the sky and ripple in the sun. And the secrets of the strange days will be one with the deep's secrets; one with the hidden lore of old ocean, and all the mystery of primal earth.

When I went into the hills and vales to survey for the new reservoir they told me the place was evil. They told me this in Arkham, and because that is a very old town full of witch legends I thought the evil must be something which grandams had whispered to children through centuries. The name "blasted heath" seemed to me very odd and theatrical, and I wondered how it had come into the folklore of a Puritan people. Then I saw that dark westward tangle of glens and slopes for myself, and ceased to wonder at anything beside its own elder mystery. It was morning when I saw it, but shadow lurked always there. The trees grew too thickly, and their trunks were too big for any healthy New England wood. There was too much silence in the dim alleys between them, and the floor was too soft with the dank moss and mattings of infinite years of decay.

In the open spaces, mostly along the line of the old road, there were little hillside farms; sometimes with all the buildings standing, sometimes with only one or two, and sometimes with only a lone chimney or fast-filling cellar. Weeds and briers reigned, and furtive wild things rustled in the undergrowth. Upon everything was a haze of restlessness and oppression; a touch of the unreal and the grotesque, as if some vital element of perspective or chiaroscuro were awry. I did not wonder that the foreigners would not stay, for this was no region to sleep in. It was too much like a landscape of Salvator Rosa; too much like some forbidden woodcut in a tale of terror.

But even all this was not so bad as the blasted heath. I knew it the moment I came upon it at the bottom of a spacious valley; for no other name could fit such a thing, or any other thing fit such a name. It was as if the poet had coined the phrase from having seen this one particular region. It must, I thought as I viewed it, be the outcome of a fire; but why had nothing new ever grown over those five acres of grey desolation that sprawled open to the sky like a great spot eaten by acid in the woods and fields? It lay largely to the north of the ancient road line, but encroached a little on the other side. I felt an odd reluctance about approaching, and did so at last only because my business took me through and past it.

There was no vegetation of any kind on that broad expanse, but only a fine grey dust or ash which no wind seemed ever to blow about. The trees near it were sickly and stunted, and many dead trunks stood or lay rotting at the rim. As I walked hurriedly by I saw the tumbled bricks and stones of an old chimney and cellar on my right, and the yawning black maw of an abandoned well whose stagnant vapours played strange tricks with the hues of the sunlight. Even the long, dark woodland climb beyond seemed welcome in contrast, and I marvelled no more at the frightened whispers of Arkham people. There had been no house or ruin near; even in the old days the place must have been lonely and remote. And at twilight, dreading to re-pass that ominous spot, I walked circuitously back to the town by the curving road on the south. I vaguely wished some clouds would gather, for an odd timidity about the deep skyey voids above had crept into my soul.

In the evening I asked old people in Arkham about the blasted heath, and what was meant by that phrase "strange days" which so many evasively muttered. I could not, however, get any good answers, except that all the mystery was much more recent than I had dreamed. It was not a matter of old legendry at all, but something within the lifetime of those who spoke. It had happened in the 'eighties, and a family had disappeared or was killed. Speakers would not be exact; and because they all told me to pay no attention to old Ammi Pierce's crazy tales, I sought him out the next morning, having heard that he lived alone in the ancient tottering cottage where the trees first begin to get very thick. It was a fearsomely archaic place, and had begun to exude the faint miasmal odour which clings about houses that have stood too long. Only with persistent knocking could I rouse the aged man, and when he shuffled timidly to the door I could tell he was not glad to see me. He was not so feeble as I had expected; but his eyes drooped in a curious way, and his unkempt clothing and white beard made him seem very worn and dismal. Not knowing just how he could best be launched on his tales, I feigned a matter of business; told him of my surveying, and asked vague questions about the district. He was far brighter and more educated than I had been led to think, and before I knew it had grasped quite as much of the subject as any man I had talked with in Arkham. He was not like other rustics I had known in the sections where reservoirs were to be. From him there were no protests at the miles of old wood and farmland to be blotted out, though perhaps there would have been had not his home lain outside the bounds of the future lake. Relief was all that he shewed; relief at the doom of the dark ancient valleys through which he had roamed all his life. They were better under water now—better under water since the strange days. And with this opening his husky voice sank low, while his body leaned forward and his right forefinger began to point shakily and impressively.

It was then that I heard the story, and as the rambling voice scraped and whispered on I shivered again and again despite the summer day. Often I had to recall the speaker from ramblings, piece out scientific points which he knew only by a fading parrot memory of professors' talk, or bridge over gaps where his sense of logic and continuity broke down. When he was done I did not wonder that his mind had snapped a trifle, or that the folk of Arkham would not speak much of the blasted heath. I hurried back before sunset to my hotel, unwilling to have the stars come out above me in the open; and the next day returned to Boston to give up my position. I could not go into that dim chaos of old forest and slope again, or face another time that grey blasted heath where the black well yawned deep beside the tumbled bricks and stones. The reservoir will soon be built now, and all those elder secrets will lie safe for ever under watery fathoms. But even then I do not believe I would like to visit that country by night—at least, not when the sinister stars are out; and nothing could bribe me to drink the new city water of Arkham.

It all began, old Ammi said, with the meteorite. Before that time there had been no wild legends at all since the witch trials, and even then these western woods were not feared half so much as the small island in the Miskatonic where the devil held court beside a curious stone altar older than the Indians. These were not haunted woods, and their fantastic dusk was never terrible till the strange days. Then there had come that white noontide cloud, that string of explosions in the air, and that pillar of smoke from the valley far in the wood. And by night all Arkham had heard of the great rock that fell out of the sky and bedded itself in the ground beside the well at the Nahum Gardner place. That was the house which had stood where the blasted heath was to come—the trim white Nahum Gardner house amidst its fertile gardens and orchards.

Nahum had come to town to tell people about the stone, and had dropped in at Ammi Pierce's on the way. Ammi was forty then, and all the queer things were fixed very strongly in his mind. He and his wife had gone with the three professors from Miskatonic University who hastened out the next morning to see the weird visitor from unknown stellar space, and had wondered why Nahum had called it so large the day before. It had shrunk, Nahum said as he pointed out the big brownish mound above the ripped earth and charred grass near the archaic well-sweep in his front yard; but the wise men answered that stones do not shrink. Its heat lingered persistently, and Nahum declared it had glowed faintly in the night. The professors tried it with a geologist's hammer and found it was oddly soft. It was, in truth, so soft as to be almost plastic; and they gouged rather than chipped a specimen to take back to the college for testing. They took it in an old pail borrowed from Nahum's kitchen, for even the small piece refused to grow cool. On the trip back they stopped at Ammi's to rest, and seemed thoughtful when Mrs. Pierce remarked that the fragment was growing smaller and burning the bottom of the pail. Truly, it was not large, but perhaps they had taken less than they thought.

The day after that—all this was in June of '82—the professors had trooped out again in a great excitement. As they passed Ammi's they told him what queer things the specimen had done, and how it had faded wholly away when they put it in a glass beaker. The beaker had gone, too, and the wise men talked of the strange stone's affinity for silicon. It had acted quite unbelievably in that well-ordered laboratory; doing nothing at all and shewing no occluded gases when heated on charcoal, being wholly negative in the borax bead, and soon proving itself absolutely non-volatile at any producible temperature, including that of the oxy-hydrogen blowpipe. On an anvil it appeared highly malleable, and in the dark its luminosity was very marked. Stubbornly refusing to grow cool, it soon had the college in a state of real excitement; and when upon heating before the spectroscope it displayed shining bands unlike any known colours of the normal spectrum there was much breathless talk of new elements, bizarre optical properties, and other things which puzzled men of science are wont to say when faced by the unknown.

Hot as it was, they tested it in a crucible with all the proper reagents. Water did nothing. Hydrochloric acid was the same. Nitric acid and even aqua regia merely hissed and spattered against its torrid invulnerability. Ammi had difficulty in recalling all these things, but recognised some solvents as I mentioned them in the usual order of use. There were ammonia and caustic soda, alcohol and ether, nauseous carbon disulphide and a dozen others; but although the weight grew steadily less as time passed, and the fragment seemed to be slightly cooling, there was no change in the solvents to shew that they had attacked the substance at all. It was a metal, though, beyond a doubt. It was magnetic, for one thing; and after its immersion in the acid solvents there seemed to be faint traces of the Widmanstätten figures found on meteoric iron. When the cooling had grown very considerable, the testing was carried on in glass; and it was in a glass beaker that they left all the chips made of the original fragment during the work. The next morning both chips and beaker were gone without trace, and only a charred spot marked the place on the wooden shelf where they had been.

All this the professors told Ammi as they paused at his door, and once more he went with them to see the stony messenger from the stars, though this time his wife did not accompany him. It had now most certainly shrunk, and even the sober professors could not doubt the truth of what they saw. All around the dwindling brown lump near the well was a vacant space, except where the earth had caved in; and whereas it had been a good seven feet across the day before, it was now scarcely five. It was still hot, and the sages studied its surface curiously as they detached another and larger piece with hammer and chisel. They gouged deeply this time, and as they pried away the smaller mass they saw that the core of the thing was not quite homogeneous.

They had uncovered what seemed to be the side of a large coloured globule imbedded in the substance. The colour, which resembled some of the bands in the meteor's strange spectrum, was almost impossible to describe; and it was only by analogy that they called it colour at all. Its texture was glossy, and upon tapping it appeared to promise both brittleness and hollowness. One of the professors gave it a smart blow with a hammer, and it burst with a nervous little pop. Nothing was emitted, and all trace of the thing vanished with the puncturing. It left behind a hollow spherical space about three inches across, and all thought it probable that others would be discovered as the enclosing substance wasted away.

Conjecture was vain; so after a futile attempt to find additional globules by drilling, the seekers left again with their new specimen—which proved, however, as baffling in the laboratory as its predecessor had been. Aside from being almost plastic, having heat, magnetism, and slight luminosity, cooling slightly in powerful acids, possessing an unknown spectrum, wasting away in air, and attacking silicon compounds with mutual destruction as a result, it presented no identifying features whatsoever; and at the end of the tests the college scientists were forced to own that they could not place it. It was nothing of this earth, but a piece of the great outside; and as such dowered with outside properties and obedient to outside laws.

That night there was a thunderstorm, and when the professors went out to Nahum's the next day they met with a bitter disappointment. The stone, magnetic as it had been, must have had some peculiar electrical property; for it had "drawn the lightning", as Nahum said, with a singular persistence. Six times within an hour the farmer saw the lightning strike the furrow in the front yard, and when the storm was over nothing remained but a ragged pit by the ancient well-sweep, half-choked with caved-in earth. Digging had borne no fruit, and the scientists verified the fact of the utter vanishment. The failure was total; so that nothing was left to do but go back to the laboratory and test again the disappearing fragment left carefully cased in lead. That fragment lasted a week, at the end of which nothing of value had been learned of it. When it had gone, no residue was left behind, and in time the professors felt scarcely sure they had indeed seen with waking eyes that cryptic vestige of the fathomless gulfs outside; that lone, weird message from other universes and other realms of matter, force, and entity.

As was natural, the Arkham papers made much of the incident with its collegiate sponsoring, and sent reporters to talk with Nahum Gardner and his family. At least one Boston daily also sent a scribe, and Nahum quickly became a kind of local celebrity. He was a lean, genial person of about fifty, living with his wife and three sons on the pleasant farmstead in the valley. He and Ammi exchanged visits frequently, as did their wives; and Ammi had nothing but praise for him after all these years. He seemed slightly proud of the notice his place had attracted, and talked often of the meteorite in the succeeding weeks. That July and August were hot, and Nahum worked hard at his haying in the ten-acre pasture across Chapman's Brook; his rattling wain wearing deep ruts in the shadowy lanes between. The labour tired him more than it had in other years, and he felt that age was beginning to tell on him.

Then fell the time of fruit and harvest. The pears and apples slowly ripened, and Nahum vowed that his orchards were prospering as never before. The fruit was growing to phenomenal size and unwonted gloss, and in such abundance that extra barrels were ordered to handle the future crop. But with the ripening came sore disappointment, for of all that gorgeous array of specious lusciousness not one single jot was fit to eat. Into the fine flavour of the pears and apples had crept a stealthy bitterness and sickishness, so that even the smallest of bites induced a lasting disgust. It was the same with the melons and tomatoes, and Nahum sadly saw that his entire crop was lost. Quick to connect events, he declared that the meteorite had poisoned the soil, and thanked heaven that most of the other crops were in the upland lot along the road.

Winter came early, and was very cold. Ammi saw Nahum less often than usual, and observed that he had begun to look worried. The rest of his family, too, seemed to have grown taciturn; and were far from steady in their churchgoing or their attendance at the various social events of the countryside. For this reserve or melancholy no cause could be found, though all the household confessed now and then to poorer health and a feeling of vague disquiet. Nahum himself gave the most definite statement of anyone when he said he was disturbed about certain footprints in the snow. They were the usual winter prints of red squirrels, white rabbits, and foxes, but the brooding farmer professed to see something not quite right about their nature and arrangement. He was never specific, but appeared to think that they were not as characteristic of the anatomy and habits of squirrels and rabbits and foxes as they ought to be. Ammi listened without interest to this talk until one night when he drove past Nahum's house in his sleigh on the way back from Clark's Corners. There had been a moon, and a rabbit had run across the road; and the leaps of that rabbit were longer than either Ammi or his horse liked. The latter, indeed, had almost run away when brought up by a firm rein. Thereafter Ammi gave Nahum's tales more respect, and wondered why the Gardner dogs seemed so cowed and quivering every morning. They had, it developed, nearly lost the spirit to bark.

In February the McGregor boys from Meadow Hill were out shooting woodchucks, and not far from the Gardner place bagged a very peculiar specimen. The proportions of its body seemed slightly altered in a queer way impossible to describe, while its face had taken on an expression which no one ever saw in a woodchuck before. The boys were genuinely frightened, and threw the thing away at once, so that only their grotesque tales of it ever reached the people of the countryside. But the shying of the horses near Nahum's house had now become an acknowledged thing, and all the basis for a cycle of whispered legend was fast taking form.

People vowed that the snow melted faster around Nahum's than it did anywhere else, and early in March there was an awed discussion in Potter's general store at Clark's Corners. Stephen Rice had driven past Gardner's in the morning, and had noticed the skunk-cabbages coming up through the mud by the woods across the road. Never were things of such size seen before, and they held strange colours that could not be put into any words. Their shapes were monstrous, and the horse had snorted at an odour which struck Stephen as wholly unprecedented. That afternoon several persons drove past to see the abnormal growth, and all agreed that plants of that kind ought never to sprout in a healthy world. The bad fruit of the fall before was freely mentioned, and it went from mouth to mouth that there was poison in Nahum's ground. Of course it was the meteorite; and remembering how strange the men from the college had found that stone to be, several farmers spoke about the matter to them.

One day they paid Nahum a visit; but having no love of wild tales and folklore were very conservative in what they inferred. The plants were certainly odd, but all skunk-cabbages are more or less odd in shape and odour and hue. Perhaps some mineral element from the stone had entered the soil, but it would soon be washed away. And as for the footprints and frightened horses—of course this was mere country talk which such a phenomenon as the aërolite would be certain to start. There was really nothing for serious men to do in cases of wild gossip, for superstitious rustics will say and believe anything. And so all through the strange days the professors stayed away in contempt. Only one of them, when given two phials of dust for analysis in a police job over a year and a half later, recalled that the queer colour of that skunk-cabbage had been very like one of the anomalous bands of light shewn by the meteor fragment in the college spectroscope, and like the brittle globule found imbedded in the stone from the abyss. The samples in this analysis case gave the same odd bands at first, though later they lost the property.

The trees budded prematurely around Nahum's, and at night they swayed ominously in the wind. Nahum's second son Thaddeus, a lad of fifteen, swore that they swayed also when there was no wind; but even the gossips would not credit this. Certainly, however, restlessness was in the air. The entire Gardner family developed the habit of stealthy listening, though not for any sound which they could consciously name. The listening was, indeed, rather a product of moments when consciousness seemed half to slip away. Unfortunately such moments increased week by week, till it became common speech that "something was wrong with all Nahum's folks". When the early saxifrage came out it had another strange colour; not quite like that of the skunk-cabbage, but plainly related and equally unknown to anyone who saw it. Nahum took some blossoms to Arkham and shewed them to the editor of the *Gazette*, but that dignitary did no more than write a humorous article about them, in which the dark fears of rustics were held up to polite ridicule. It was a mistake of Nahum's to tell a stolid city man about the way the great, overgrown mourning-cloak butterflies behaved in connexion with these saxifrages.

April brought a kind of madness to the country folk, and began that disuse of the road past Nahum's which led to its ultimate abandonment. It was the vegetation. All the orchard trees blossomed forth in strange colours, and through the stony soil of the yard and adjacent pasturage there sprang up a bizarre growth which only a botanist could connect with the proper flora of the region. No sane wholesome colours were anywhere to be seen except in the green grass and leafage; but everywhere those hectic and prismatic variants of some diseased, underlying primary tone without a place among the known tints of earth. The Dutchman's breeches became a thing of sinister menace, and the bloodroots grew insolent in their chromatic perversion. Ammi and the Gardners thought that most of the colours had a sort of haunting familiarity, and decided that they reminded one of the brittle globule in the meteor. Nahum ploughed and sowed the ten-acre pasture and the upland lot, but did nothing with the land around the house. He knew it would be of no use, and hoped that the summer's strange growths would draw all the poison from the soil. He was prepared for almost anything now, and had grown used to the sense of something near him waiting to be heard. The shunning of his house by neighbours told on him, of course; but it told on his wife more. The boys were better off, being at school each day; but they could not help being frightened by the gossip. Thaddeus, an especially sensitive youth, suffered the most.

In May the insects came, and Nahum's place became a nightmare of buzzing and crawling. Most of the creatures seemed not quite usual in their aspects and motions, and their nocturnal habits contradicted all former experience. The Gardners took to watching at night—watching in all directions at random for something … they could not tell what. It was then that they all owned that Thaddeus had been right about the trees. Mrs. Gardner was the next to see it from the window as she watched the swollen boughs of a maple against a moonlit sky. The boughs surely moved, and there was no wind. It must be the sap. Strangeness had come into everything growing now. Yet it was none of Nahum's family at all who made the next discovery. Familiarity had dulled them, and what they could not see was glimpsed by a timid windmill salesman from Bolton who drove by one night in ignorance of the country legends. What he told in Arkham was given a short paragraph in the *Gazette*; and it was there that all the farmers, Nahum included, saw it first. The night had been dark and the buggy-lamps faint, but around a farm in the valley which everyone knew from the account must be Nahum's the darkness had been less thick. A dim though distinct luminosity seemed to inhere in all the vegetation, grass, leaves, and blossoms alike, while at one moment a detached piece of the phosphorescence appeared to stir furtively in the yard near the barn.

The grass had so far seemed untouched, and the cows were freely pastured in the lot near the house, but toward the end of May the milk began to be bad. Then Nahum had the cows driven to the uplands, after which the trouble ceased. Not long after this the change in grass and leaves became apparent to the eye. All the verdure was going grey, and was developing a highly singular quality of brittleness. Ammi was now the only person who ever visited the place, and his visits were becoming fewer and fewer. When school closed the Gardners were virtually cut off from the world, and sometimes let Ammi do their errands in town. They were failing curiously both physically and mentally, and no one was surprised when the news of Mrs. Gardner's madness stole around.

It happened in June, about the anniversary of the meteor's fall, and the poor woman screamed about things in the air which she could not describe. In her raving there was not a single specific noun, but only verbs and pronouns. Things moved and changed and fluttered, and ears tingled to impulses which were not wholly sounds. Something was taken away—she was being drained of something—something was fastening itself on her that ought not to be—someone must make it keep off—nothing was ever still in the night—the walls and windows shifted. Nahum did not send her to the county asylum, but let her wander about the house as long as she was harmless to herself and others. Even when her expression changed he did nothing. But when the boys grew afraid of her, and Thaddeus nearly fainted at the way she made faces at him, he decided to keep her locked in the attic. By July she had ceased to speak and crawled on all fours, and before that month was over Nahum got the mad notion that she was slightly luminous in the dark, as he now clearly saw was the case with the nearby vegetation.

It was a little before this that the horses had stampeded. Something had aroused them in the night, and their neighing and kicking in their stalls had been terrible. There seemed virtually nothing to do to calm them, and when Nahum opened the stable door they all bolted out like frightened woodland deer. It took a week to track all four, and when found they were seen to be quite useless and unmanageable. Something had snapped in their brains, and each one had to be shot for its own good. Nahum borrowed a horse from Ammi for his haying, but found it would not approach the barn. It shied, balked, and whinnied, and in the end he could do nothing but drive it into the yard while the men used their own strength to get the heavy wagon near enough the hayloft for convenient pitching. And all the while the vegetation was turning grey and brittle. Even the flowers whose hues had been so strange were greying now, and the fruit was coming out grey and dwarfed and tasteless. The asters and goldenrod bloomed grey and distorted, and the roses and zinneas and hollyhocks in the front yard were such blasphemous-looking things that Nahum's oldest boy Zenas cut them down. The strangely puffed insects died about that time, even the bees that had left their hives and taken to the woods.

By September all the vegetation was fast crumbling to a greyish powder, and Nahum feared that the trees would die before the poison was out of the soil. His wife now had spells of terrific screaming, and he and the boys were in a constant state of nervous tension. They shunned people now, and when school opened the boys did not go. But it was Ammi, on one of his rare visits, who first realised that the well water was no longer good. It had an evil taste that was not exactly foetid nor exactly salty, and Ammi advised his friend to dig another well on higher ground to use till the soil was good again. Nahum, however, ignored the warning, for he had by that time become calloused to strange and unpleasant things. He and the boys continued to use the tainted supply, drinking it as listlessly and mechanically as they ate their meagre and ill-cooked meals and did their thankless and monotonous chores through the aimless days. There was something of stolid resignation about them all, as if they walked half in another world between lines of nameless guards to a certain and familiar doom.

Thaddeus went mad in September after a visit to the well. He had gone with a pail and had come back empty-handed, shrieking and waving his arms, and sometimes lapsing into an inane titter or a whisper about "the moving colours down there". Two in one family was pretty bad, but Nahum was very brave about it. He let the boy run about for a week until he began stumbling and hurting himself, and then he shut him in an attic room across the hall from his mother's. The way they screamed at each other from behind their locked doors was very terrible, especially to little Merwin, who fancied they talked in some horrible language that was not of earth. Merwin was getting frightfully imaginative, and his restlessness was worse after the shutting away of the brother who had been his greatest playmate.

Almost at the same time the mortality among the livestock commenced. Poultry turned greyish and died very quickly, their meat being found dry and noisome upon cutting. Hogs grew inordinately fat, then suddenly began to undergo loathsome changes which no one could explain. Their meat was of course useless, and Nahum was at his wit's end. No rural veterinary would approach his place, and the city veterinary from Arkham was openly baffled. The swine began growing grey and brittle and falling to pieces before they died, and their eyes and muzzles developed singular alterations. It was very inexplicable, for they had never been fed from the tainted vegetation. Then something struck the cows. Certain areas or sometimes the whole body would be uncannily shrivelled or compressed, and atrocious collapses or disintegrations were common. In the last stages—and death was always the result—there would be a greying and turning brittle like that which beset the hogs. There could be no question of poison, for all the cases occurred in a locked and undisturbed barn. No bites of prowling things could have brought the virus, for what live beast of earth can pass through solid obstacles? It must be only natural disease—yet what disease could wreak such results was beyond any mind's guessing. When the harvest came there was not an animal surviving on the place, for the stock and poultry were dead and the dogs had run away. These dogs, three in number, had all vanished one night and were never heard of again. The five cats had left some time before, but their going was scarcely noticed since there now seemed to be no mice, and only Mrs. Gardner had made pets of the graceful felines.

On the nineteenth of October Nahum staggered into Ammi's house with hideous news. The death had come to poor Thaddeus in his attic room, and it had come in a way which could not be told. Nahum had dug a grave in the railed family plot behind the farm, and had put therein what he found. There could have been nothing from outside, for the small barred window and locked door were intact; but it was much as it had been in the barn. Ammi and his wife consoled the stricken man as best they could, but shuddered as they did so. Stark terror seemed to cling round the Gardners and all they touched, and the very presence of one in the house was a breath from regions unnamed and unnamable. Ammi accompanied Nahum home with the greatest reluctance, and did what he might to calm the hysterical sobbing of little Merwin. Zenas needed no calming. He had come of late to do nothing but stare into space and obey what his father told him; and Ammi thought that his fate was very merciful. Now and then Merwin's screams were answered faintly from the attic, and in response to an inquiring look Nahum said that his wife was getting very feeble. When night approached, Ammi managed to get away; for not even friendship could make him stay in that spot when the faint glow of the vegetation began and the trees may or may not have swayed without wind. It was really lucky for

Ammi that he was not more imaginative. Even as things were, his mind was bent ever so slightly; but had he been able to connect and reflect upon all the portents around him he must inevitably have turned a total maniac. In the twilight he hastened home, the screams of the mad woman and the nervous child ringing horribly in his ears.

Three days later Nahum lurched into Ammi's kitchen in the early morning, and in the absence of his host stammered out a desperate tale once more, while Mrs. Pierce listened in a clutching fright. It was little Merwin this time. He was gone. He had gone out late at night with a lantern and pail for water, and had never come back. He'd been going to pieces for days, and hardly knew what he was about. Screamed at everything. There had been a frantic shriek from the yard then, but before the father could get to the door, the boy was gone. There was no glow from the lantern he had taken, and of the child himself no trace. At the time Nahum thought the lantern and pail were gone too; but when dawn came, and the man had plodded back from his all-night search of the woods and fields, he had found some very curious things near the well. There was a crushed and apparently somewhat melted mass of iron which had certainly been the lantern; while a bent bail and twisted iron hoops beside it, both half-fused, seemed to hint at the remnants of the pail. That was all. Nahum was past imagining, Mrs. Pierce was blank, and Ammi, when he had reached home and heard the tale, could give no guess. Merwin was gone, and there would be no use in telling the people around, who shunned all Gardners now. No use, either, in telling the city people at Arkham who laughed at everything. Thad was gone, and now Mernie was gone. Something was creeping and creeping and waiting to be seen and felt and heard. Nahum would go soon, and he wanted Ammi to look after his wife and Zenas if they survived him. It must all be a judgment of some sort; though he could not fancy what for, since he had always walked uprightly in the Lord's ways so far as he knew.

For over two weeks Ammi saw nothing of Nahum; and then, worried about what might have happened, he overcame his fears and paid the Gardner place a visit. There was no smoke from the great chimney, and for a moment the visitor was apprehensive of the worst. The aspect of the whole farm was shocking—greyish withered grass and leaves on the ground, vines falling in brittle wreckage from archaic walls and gables, and great bare trees clawing up at the grey November sky with a studied malevolence which Ammi could not but feel had come from some subtle change in the tilt of the branches. But Nahum was alive, after all. He was weak, and lying on a couch in the low-ceiled kitchen, but perfectly conscious and able to give simple orders to Zenas. The room was deadly cold; and as Ammi visibly shivered, the host shouted huskily to Zenas for more wood. Wood, indeed, was sorely needed; since the cavernous fireplace was unlit and empty, with a cloud of soot blowing about in the chill wind that came down the chimney. Presently Nahum asked him if the extra wood had made him any more comfortable, and then Ammi saw what had happened. The stoutest cord had broken at last, and the hapless farmer's mind was proof against more sorrow.

Questioning tactfully, Ammi could get no clear data at all about the missing Zenas. "In the well—he lives in the well—" was all that the clouded father would say. Then there flashed across the visitor's mind a sudden thought of the mad wife, and he changed his line of inquiry. "Nabby? Why, here she is!" was the surprised response of poor Nahum, and Ammi soon saw that he must search for himself. Leaving the harmless babbler on the couch, he took the keys from their nail beside the door and climbed the creaking stairs to the attic. It was very close and noisome up there, and no sound could be heard from any direction. Of the four doors in sight, only one was locked, and on this he tried various keys on the ring he had taken. The third key proved the right one, and after some fumbling Ammi threw open the low white door.

It was quite dark inside, for the window was small and half-obscured by the crude wooden bars; and Ammi could see nothing at all on the wide-planked floor. The stench was beyond enduring, and before proceeding further he had to retreat to another room and return with his lungs filled with breathable air. When he did enter he saw something dark in the corner, and upon seeing it more clearly he screamed outright. While he screamed he thought a momentary cloud eclipsed the window, and a second later he felt himself brushed as if by some hateful current of vapour. Strange colours danced before his eyes; and had not a present horror numbed him he would have thought of the globule in the meteor that the geologist's hammer had shattered, and of the morbid vegetation that had sprouted in the spring. As it was he thought only of the blasphemous monstrosity which confronted him, and which all too clearly had shared the nameless fate of young Thaddeus and the livestock. But the terrible thing about this horror was that it very slowly and perceptibly moved as it continued to crumble.

Ammi would give me no added particulars of this scene, but the shape in the corner does not reappear in his tale as a moving object. There are things which cannot be mentioned, and what is done in common humanity is sometimes cruelly judged by the law. I gathered that no moving thing was left in that attic room, and that to leave anything capable of motion there would have been a deed so monstrous as to damn any accountable being to eternal torment. Anyone but a stolid farmer would have fainted or gone mad, but Ammi walked conscious through that low doorway and locked the accursed secret behind him. There would be Nahum to deal with now; he must be fed and tended, and removed to some place where he could be cared for.

Commencing his descent of the dark stairs, Ammi heard a thud below him. He even thought a scream had been suddenly choked off, and recalled nervously the clammy vapour which had brushed by him in that frightful room above. What presence had his cry and entry started up? Halted by some vague fear, he heard still further sounds below. Indubitably there was a sort of heavy dragging, and a most detestably sticky noise as of some fiendish and unclean species of suction. With an associative sense goaded to feverish heights, he thought unaccountably of what he had seen upstairs. Good God! What eldritch dream-world was this into which he had blundered? He dared move neither backward nor forward, but stood there trembling at the black curve of the boxed-in staircase. Every trifle of the scene burned itself into his brain. The sounds, the sense of dread expectancy, the darkness, the steepness of the narrow steps—and merciful heaven! ... the faint but unmistakable luminosity of all the woodwork in sight; steps, sides, exposed laths, and beams alike!

Then there burst forth a frantic whinny from Ammi's horse outside, followed at once by a clatter which told of a frenzied runaway. In another moment horse and buggy had gone beyond earshot, leaving the frightened man on the dark stairs to guess what had sent them. But that was not all. There had been another sound out there. A sort of liquid splash—water—it must have been the well. He had left Hero untied near it, and a buggy-wheel must have brushed the coping and knocked in a stone. And still the pale phosphorescence glowed in that detestably ancient woodwork. God! how old the house was! Most of it built before 1670, and the gambrel roof not later than 1730.

A feeble scratching on the floor downstairs now sounded distinctly, and Ammi's grip tightened on a heavy stick he had picked up in the attic for some purpose. Slowly nerving himself, he finished his descent and walked boldly toward the kitchen. But he did not complete the walk, because what he sought was no longer there. It had come to meet him, and it was still alive after a fashion. Whether it had crawled or whether it had been dragged by any external force, Ammi could not say; but the death had been at it. Everything had happened in the last half-hour, but collapse, greying, and disintegration were already far advanced. There was a horrible brittleness, and dry fragments were scaling off. Ammi could not touch it, but looked horrifiedly into the distorted parody that had been a face. "What was it, Nahum—what was it?" he whispered, and the cleft, bulging lips were just able to crackle out a final answer.

"Nothin' … nothin' … the colour … it burns … cold an' wet, but it burns … it lived in the well … I seen it … a kind o' smoke … jest like the flowers last spring … the well shone at night … Thad an' Mernie an' Zenas … everything alive … suckin' the life out of everything … in that stone … it must a' come in that stone … pizened the whole place … dun't know what it wants … that round thing them men from the college dug outen the stone … they smashed it … it was that same colour … jest the same, like the flowers an' plants … must a' ben more of 'em … seeds … seeds … they growed … I seen it the fust time this week … must a' got strong on Zenas … he was a big boy, full o' life … it beats down your mind an' then gits ye … burns ye up … in the well water … you was right about that … evil water … Zenas never come back from the well … can't git away … draws ye … ye know summ'at's comin', but 'tain't no use … I seen it time an' agin senct Zenas was took … whar's Nabby, Ammi? … my head's no good … dun't know how long senct I fed her … it'll git her ef we ain't keerful … jest a colour … her face is gettin' to hev that colour sometimes towards night … an' it burns an' sucks … it come from some place whar things ain't as they is here … one o' them professors said so … he was right … look out, Ammi, it'll do suthin' more … sucks the life out…."

But that was all. That which spoke could speak no more because it had completely caved in. Ammi laid a red checked tablecloth over what was left and reeled out the back door into the fields. He climbed the slope to the ten-acre pasture and stumbled home by the north road and the woods. He could not pass that well from which his horse had run away. He had looked at it through the window, and had seen that no stone was missing from the rim. Then the lurching buggy had not dislodged anything after all—the splash had been something else—something which went into the well after it had done with poor Nahum….

When Ammi reached his house the horse and buggy had arrived before him and thrown his wife into fits of anxiety. Reassuring her without explanations, he set out at once for

Arkham and notified the authorities that the Gardner family was no more. He indulged in no details, but merely told of the deaths of Nahum and Nabby, that of Thaddeus being already known, and mentioned that the cause seemed to be the same strange ailment which had killed the livestock. He also stated that Merwin and Zenas had disappeared. There was considerable questioning at the police station, and in the end Ammi was compelled to take three officers to the Gardner farm, together with the coroner, the medical examiner, and the veterinary who had treated the diseased animals. He went much against his will, for the afternoon was advancing and he feared the fall of night over that accursed place, but it was some comfort to have so many people with him.

The six men drove out in a democrat-wagon, following Ammi's buggy, and arrived at the pest-ridden farmhouse about four o'clock. Used as the officers were to gruesome experiences, not one remained unmoved at what was found in the attic and under the red checked tablecloth on the floor below. The whole aspect of the farm with its grey desolation was terrible enough, but those two crumbling objects were beyond all bounds. No one could look long at them, and even the medical examiner admitted that there was very little to examine. Specimens could be analysed, of course, so he busied himself in obtaining them—and here it develops that a very puzzling aftermath occurred at the college laboratory where the two phials of dust were finally taken. Under the spectroscope both samples gave off an unknown spectrum, in which many of the baffling bands were precisely like those which the strange meteor had yielded in the previous year. The property of emitting this spectrum vanished in a month, the dust thereafter consisting mainly of alkaline phosphates and carbonates.

Ammi would not have told the men about the well if he had thought they meant to do anything then and there. It was getting toward sunset, and he was anxious to be away. But he could not help glancing nervously at the stony curb by the great sweep, and when a detective questioned him he admitted that Nahum had feared something down there—so much so that he had never even thought of searching it for Merwin or Zenas. After that nothing would do but that they empty and explore the well immediately, so Ammi had to wait trembling while pail after pail of rank water was hauled up and splashed on the soaking ground outside. The men sniffed in disgust at the fluid, and toward the last held their noses against the foetor they were uncovering. It was not so long a job as they had feared it would be, since the water was phenomenally low. There is no need to speak too exactly of what they found. Merwin and Zenas were both there, in part, though the vestiges were mainly skeletal. There were also a small deer and a large dog in about the same state, and a number of bones of smaller animals. The ooze and slime at the bottom seemed inexplicably porous and bubbling, and a man who descended on handholds with a long pole found that he could sink the wooden shaft to any depth in the mud of the floor without meeting any solid obstruction.

Twilight had now fallen, and lanterns were brought from the house. Then, when it was seen that nothing further could be gained from the well, everyone went indoors and conferred in the ancient sitting-room while the intermittent light of a spectral half-moon played wanly on the grey desolation outside. The men were frankly nonplussed by the entire case, and could find no convincing common element to link the strange vegetable conditions, the unknown disease of livestock and humans, and the unaccountable deaths of Merwin and Zenas in the tainted well. They had heard the common country talk, it is true; but could not believe that anything contrary to natural law had occurred. No doubt the meteor had poisoned the soil, but the illness of persons and animals who had eaten nothing grown in that soil was another matter. Was it the well water? Very possibly. It might be a good idea to analyse it. But what peculiar madness could have made both boys jump into the well? Their deeds were so similar—and the fragments shewed that they had both suffered from the grey brittle death. Why was everything so grey and brittle?

It was the coroner, seated near a window overlooking the yard, who first noticed the glow about the well. Night had fully set in, and all the abhorrent grounds seemed faintly luminous with more than the fitful moonbeams; but this new glow was something definite and distinct, and appeared to shoot up from the black pit like a softened ray from a searchlight, giving dull reflections in the little ground pools where the water had been emptied. It had a very queer colour, and as all the men clustered round the window Ammi gave a violent start. For this strange beam of ghastly miasma was to him of no unfamiliar hue. He had seen that colour before, and feared to think what it might mean. He had seen it in the nasty brittle globule in that aërolite two summers ago, had seen it in the crazy vegetation of the springtime, and had thought he had seen it for an instant that very morning against the small barred window of that terrible attic room where nameless things had happened. It had flashed there a second, and a clammy and hateful current of vapour had brushed past him—and then poor

Nahum had been taken by something of that colour. He had said so at the last—said it was like the globule and the plants. After that had come the runaway in the yard and the splash in the well—and now that well was belching forth to the night a pale insidious beam of the same daemoniac tint.

It does credit to the alertness of Ammi's mind that he puzzled even at that tense moment over a point which was essentially scientific. He could not but wonder at his gleaning of the same impression from a vapour glimpsed in the daytime, against a window opening on the morning sky, and from a nocturnal exhalation seen as a phosphorescent mist against the black and blasted landscape. It wasn't right—it was against Nature—and he thought of those terrible last words of his stricken friend, "It come from some place whar things ain't as they is here … one o' them professors said so…."

All three horses outside, tied to a pair of shrivelled saplings by the road, were now neighing and pawing frantically. The wagon driver started for the door to do something, but Ammi laid a shaky hand on his shoulder. "Dun't go out thar," he whispered. "They's more to this nor what we know. Nahum said somethin' lived in the well that sucks your life out. He said it must be some'at growed from a round ball like one we all seen in the meteor stone that fell a year ago June. Sucks an' burns, he said, an' is jest a cloud of colour like that light out thar now, that ye can hardly see an' can't tell what it is. Nahum thought it feeds on everything livin' an' gits stronger all the time. He said he seen it this last week. It must be somethin' from away off in the sky like the men from the college last year says the meteor stone was. The way it's made an' the way it works ain't like no way o' God's world. It's some'at from beyond."

So the men paused indecisively as the light from the well grew stronger and the hitched horses pawed and whinnied in increasing frenzy. It was truly an awful moment; with terror in that ancient and accursed house itself, four monstrous sets of fragments—two from the house and two from the well—in the woodshed behind, and that shaft of unknown and unholy iridescence from the slimy depths in front. Ammi had restrained the driver on impulse, forgetting how uninjured he himself was after the clammy brushing of that coloured vapour in the attic room, but perhaps it is just as well that he acted as he did. No one will ever know what was abroad that night; and though the blasphemy from beyond had not so far hurt any human of unweakened mind, there is no telling what it might not have done at that last moment, and with its seemingly increased strength and the special signs of purpose it was soon to display beneath the half-clouded moonlit sky.

All at once one of the detectives at the window gave a short, sharp gasp. The others looked at him, and then quickly followed his own gaze upward to the point at which its idle straying had been suddenly arrested. There was no need for words. What had been disputed in country gossip was disputable no longer, and it is because of the thing which every man of that party agreed in whispering later on that the strange days are never talked about in Arkham. It is necessary to premise that there was no wind at that hour of the evening. One did arise not long afterward, but there was absolutely none then. Even the dry tips of the lingering hedge-mustard, grey and blighted, and the fringe on the roof of the standing democrat-wagon were unstirred. And yet amid that tense, godless calm the high bare boughs of all the trees in the yard were moving. They were twitching morbidly and spasmodically, clawing in convulsive and epileptic madness at the moonlit clouds; scratching impotently in the noxious air as if jerked by some alien and bodiless line of linkage with subterrene horrors writhing and struggling below the black roots.

Not a man breathed for several seconds. Then a cloud of darker depth passed over the moon, and the silhouette of clutching branches faded out momentarily. At this there was a general cry; muffled with awe, but husky and almost identical from every throat. For the terror had not faded with the silhouette, and in a fearsome instant of deeper darkness the watchers saw wriggling at that treetop height a thousand tiny points of faint and unhallowed radiance, tipping each bough like the fire of St. Elmo or the flames that came down on the apostles' heads at Pentecost. It was a monstrous constellation of unnatural light, like a glutted swarm of corpse-fed fireflies dancing hellish sarabands over an accursed marsh; and its colour was that same nameless intrusion which Ammi had come to recognise and dread. All the while the shaft of phosphorescence from the well was getting brighter and brighter, bringing to the minds of the huddled men a sense of doom and abnormality which far outraced any image their conscious minds could form. It was no longer *shining* out; it was *pouring* out; and as the shapeless stream of unplaceable colour left the well it seemed to flow directly into the sky.

The veterinary shivered, and walked to the front door to drop the heavy extra bar across it. Ammi shook no less, and had to tug and point for lack of a controllable voice when he wished to draw notice to the growing luminosity of the trees. The neighing and stamping of the horses had become utterly frightful, but not a soul of that group in the old house would have ventured forth for any earthly reward. With the moments the shining of the trees increased, while their restless branches seemed to strain more and more toward verticality. The wood of the well-sweep was shining now, and presently a policeman dumbly pointed to some wooden sheds and bee-hives near the stone wall on the west. They were commencing to shine, too, though the tethered vehicles of the visitors seemed so far unaffected. Then there was a wild commotion and clopping in the road, and as Ammi quenched the lamp for better seeing they realised that the span of frantic greys had broken their sapling and run off with the democrat-wagon.

The shock served to loosen several tongues, and embarrassed whispers were exchanged. "It spreads on everything organic that's been around here," muttered the medical examiner. No one replied, but the man who had been in the well gave a hint that his long pole must have stirred up something intangible. "It was awful," he added. "There was no bottom at all. Just ooze and bubbles and the feeling of something lurking under there." Ammi's horse still pawed and screamed deafeningly in the road outside, and nearly drowned its owner's faint quaver as he mumbled his formless reflections. "It come from that stone … it growed down thar … it got everything livin' … it fed itself on 'em, mind and body … Thad an' Mernie, Zenas an' Nabby … Nahum was the last … they all drunk the water … it got strong on 'em … it come from beyond, whar things ain't like they be here … now it's goin' home…."

At this point, as the column of unknown colour flared suddenly stronger and began to weave itself into fantastic suggestions of shape which each spectator later described differently, there came from poor tethered Hero such a sound as no man before or since ever heard from a horse. Every person in that low-pitched sitting-room stopped his ears, and Ammi turned away from the window in horror and nausea. Words could not convey it—when Ammi looked out again the hapless beast lay huddled inert on the moonlit ground between the splintered shafts of the buggy. That was the last of Hero till they buried him next day. But the present was no time to mourn, for almost at this instant a detective silently called attention to something terrible in the very room with them. In the absence of the lamplight it was clear that a faint phosphorescence had begun to pervade the entire apartment. It glowed on the broad-planked floor and the fragment of rag carpet, and shimmered over the sashes of the small-paned windows. It ran up and down the exposed corner-posts, coruscated about the shelf and mantel, and infected the very doors and furniture. Each minute saw it strengthen, and at last it was very plain that healthy living things must leave that house.

Ammi shewed them the back door and the path up through the fields to the ten-acre pasture. They walked and stumbled as in a dream, and did not dare look back till they were far away on the high ground. They were glad of the path, for they could not have gone the front way, by that well. It was bad enough passing the glowing barn and sheds, and those shining orchard trees with their gnarled, fiendish contours; but thank heaven the branches did their worst twisting high up. The moon went under some very black clouds as they crossed the rustic bridge over Chapman's Brook, and it was blind groping from there to the open meadows.

When they looked back toward the valley and the distant Gardner place at the bottom they saw a fearsome sight. All the farm was shining with the hideous unknown blend of colour; trees, buildings, and even such grass and herbage as had not been wholly changed to lethal grey brittleness. The boughs were all straining skyward, tipped with tongues of foul flame, and lambent tricklings of the same monstrous fire were creeping about the ridgepoles of the house, barn, and sheds. It was a scene from a vision of Fuseli, and over all the rest reigned that riot of luminous amorphousness, that alien and undimensioned rainbow of cryptic poison from the well—seething, feeling, lapping, reaching, scintillating, straining, and malignly bubbling in its cosmic and unrecognisable chromaticism.

Then without warning the hideous thing shot vertically up toward the sky like a rocket or meteor, leaving behind no trail and disappearing through a round and curiously regular hole in the clouds before any man could gasp or cry out. No watcher can ever forget that sight, and Ammi stared blankly at the stars of Cygnus, Deneb twinkling above the others, where the unknown colour had melted into the Milky Way. But his gaze was the next moment called swiftly to earth by the crackling in the valley. It was just that. Only a wooden ripping and crackling, and not an explosion, as so many others of the party vowed. Yet the outcome was the same, for in one feverish, kaleidoscopic instant there burst up from that doomed and accursed farm a gleamingly eruptive cataclysm of unnatural sparks and substance; blurring the glance of the few who saw it, and sending forth to the zenith a bombarding cloudburst of such coloured and fantastic fragments as our universe must needs disown. Through quickly re-closing vapours they followed the great morbidity that had vanished, and in another second they had vanished too. Behind and below was only a darkness to which the men dared not return, and all about was a mounting wind which seemed to sweep down in black, frore gusts from interstellar space. It shrieked and howled, and lashed the fields and distorted woods in a mad cosmic frenzy, till soon the trembling party realised it would be no use waiting for the moon to shew what was left down there at Nahum's.

Too awed even to hint theories, the seven shaking men trudged back toward Arkham by the north road. Ammi was worse than his fellows, and begged them to see him inside his own kitchen, instead of keeping straight on to town. He did not wish to cross the nighted, wind-whipped woods alone to his home on the main road. For he had had an added shock that the others were spared, and was crushed for ever with a brooding fear he dared not even mention for many years to come. As the rest of the watchers on that tempestuous hill had stolidly set their faces toward the road, Ammi had looked back an instant at the shadowed valley of desolation so lately sheltering his ill-starred friend. And from that stricken, far-away spot he had seen something feebly rise, only to sink down again upon the place from which the great shapeless horror had shot into the sky. It was just a colour—but not any colour of our earth or heavens. And because Ammi recognised that colour, and knew that this last faint remnant must still lurk down there in the well, he has never been quite right since.

Ammi would never go near the place again. It is over half a century now since the horror happened, but he has never been there, and will be glad when the new reservoir blots it out. I shall be glad, too, for I do not like the way the sunlight changed colour around the mouth of that abandoned well I passed. I hope the water will always be very deep—but even so, I shall never drink it. I do not think I shall visit the Arkham country hereafter. Three of the men who had been with Ammi returned the next morning to see the ruins by daylight, but there were not any real ruins. Only the bricks of the chimney, the stones of the cellar, some mineral and metallic litter here and there, and the rim of that nefandous well. Save for Ammi's dead horse, which they towed away and buried, and the buggy which they shortly returned to him, everything that had ever been living had gone. Five eldritch acres of dusty grey desert remained, nor has anything ever grown there since. To this day it sprawls open to the sky like a great spot eaten by acid in the woods and fields, and the few who have ever dared glimpse it in spite of the rural tales have named it "the blasted heath".

The rural tales are queer. They might be even queerer if city men and college chemists could be interested enough to analyse the water from that disused well, or the grey dust that no wind seems ever to disperse. Botanists, too, ought to study the stunted flora on the borders of that spot, for they might shed light on the country notion that the blight is spreading—little by little, perhaps an inch a year. People say the colour of the neighbouring herbage is not quite right in the spring, and that wild things leave queer prints in the light winter snow. Snow never seems quite so heavy on the blasted heath as it is elsewhere. Horses—the few that are left in this motor age—grow skittish in the silent valley; and hunters cannot depend on their dogs too near the splotch of greyish dust.

They say the mental influences are very bad, too. Numbers went queer in the years after Nahum's taking, and always they lacked the power to get away. Then the stronger-minded folk all left the region, and only the foreigners tried to live in the crumbling old homesteads. They could not stay, though; and one sometimes wonders what insight beyond ours their wild, weird stores of whispered magic have given them. Their dreams at night, they protest, are very horrible in that grotesque country; and surely the very look of the dark realm is enough to stir a morbid fancy. No traveller has ever escaped a sense of strangeness in those deep ravines, and artists shiver as they paint thick woods whose mystery is as much of the spirit as of the eye. I myself am curious about the sensation I derived from my one lone walk before Ammi told me his tale. When twilight came I had vaguely wished some clouds would gather, for an odd timidity about the deep skyey voids above had crept into my soul.

Do not ask me for my opinion. I do not know—that is all. There was no one but Ammi to question; for Arkham people will not talk about the strange days, and all three professors who saw the aërolite and its coloured globule are dead. There were other globules—depend upon that. One must have fed itself and escaped, and probably there was another which was too late. No doubt it is still down the well—I know there was something wrong with the sunlight I saw above that miasmal brink. The rustics say the blight creeps an inch a year, so perhaps there is a kind of growth or nourishment even now. But whatever daemon hatchling is there, it must be tethered to something or else it would quickly spread. Is it fastened to the roots of those trees that claw the air? One of the current Arkham tales is about fat oaks that shine and move as they ought not to do at night.

What it is, only God knows. In terms of matter I suppose the thing Ammi described would be called a gas, but this gas obeyed laws that are not of our cosmos. This was no fruit of such worlds and suns as shine on the telescopes and photographic plates of our observatories. This was no breath from the skies whose motions and dimensions our astronomers measure or deem too vast to measure. It was just a colour out of space—a frightful messenger from unformed realms of infinity beyond all Nature as we know it; from realms whose mere existence stuns the brain and numbs us with the black extra-cosmic gulfs it throws open before our frenzied eyes.

I doubt very much if Ammi consciously lied to me, and I do not think his tale was all a freak of madness as the townsfolk had forewarned. Something terrible came to the hills and valleys on that meteor, and something terrible—though I know not in what proportion—still remains. I shall be glad to see the water come. Meanwhile I hope nothing will happen to Ammi. He saw so much of the thing—and its influence was so insidious. Why has he never been able to move away? How clearly he recalled those dying words of Nahum's—"can't git away ... draws ye ... ye know summ'at's comin', but 'tain't no use...." Ammi is such a good old man—when the reservoir gang gets to work I must write the chief engineer to keep a sharp watch on him. I would hate to think of him as the grey, twisted, brittle monstrosity which persists more and more in troubling my sleep.

THE DESCENDANT

In London there is a man who screams when the church bells ring. He lives all alone with his streaked cat in Gray's Inn, and people call him harmlessly mad. His room is filled with books of the tamest and most puerile kind, and hour after hour he tries to lose himself in their feeble pages. All he seeks from life is not to think. For some reason thought is very horrible to him, and anything which stirs the imagination he flees as a plague. He is thin and grey and wrinkled, but there are those who declare he is not nearly so old as he looks. Fear has its grisly claws upon him, and a sound will make him start with staring eyes and sweat-beaded forehead. Friends and companions he shuns, for he wishes to answer no questions. Those who once knew him as scholar and aesthete say it is very pitiful to see him now. He dropped them all years ago, and no one feels sure whether he left the country or merely sank from sight in some hidden byway. It is a decade now since he moved into Gray's Inn, and of where he had been he would say nothing till the night young Williams bought the "Necronomicon".

Williams was a dreamer, and only twenty-three, and when he moved into the ancient house he felt a strangeness and a breath of cosmic wind about the grey wizened man in the next room. He forced his friendship where old friends dared not force theirs, and marvelled at the fright that sat upon this gaunt, haggard watcher and listener. For that the man always watched and listened no one could doubt. He watched and listened with his mind more than with his eyes and ears, and strove every moment to drown something in his ceaseless poring over gay, insipid novels. And when the church bells rang he would stop his ears and scream, and the grey cat that dwelt with him would howl in unison till the last peal died reverberantly away.

But try as Williams would, he could not make his neighbour speak of anything profound or hidden. The old man would not live up to his aspect and manner, but would feign a smile and a light tone and prattle feverishly and frantically of cheerful trifles; his voice every moment rising and thickening till at last it would split in a piping and incoherent falsetto. That his learning was deep and thorough, his most trivial remarks made abundantly clear; and Williams was not surprised to hear that he had been to Harrow and Oxford. Later it developed that he was none other than Lord Northam, of whose ancient hereditary castle on the Yorkshire coast so many odd things were told; but when Williams tried to talk of the castle, and of its reputed Roman origin, he refused to admit that there was anything unusual about it. He even tittered shrilly when the subject of the supposed under crypts, hewn out of the solid crag that frowns on the North Sea, was brought up.

So matters went till that night when Williams brought home the infamous "Necronomicon" of the mad Arab Abdul Alhazred. He had known of the dreaded volume since his sixteenth year, when his dawning love of the bizarre had led him to ask queer questions of a bent old bookseller in Chandos Street; and he had always wondered why men paled when they spoke of it. The old bookseller had told him that only five copies were known to have survived the shocked edicts of priests and lawgivers against it and that all of these were locked up with frightened care by custodians who had ventured to begin a reading of the hateful black-letter. But now, at last, he had not only found an accessible copy but had made it his own at a ludicrously low figure. It was at a Jew's shop in the squalid precincts of Clare Market, where he had often bought strange things before, and he almost fancied the gnarled old Levite smiled amidst tangles of beard as the great discovery was made. The bulky leather cover with the brass clasp had been so prominently visible, and the price was so absurdly slight.

The one glimpse he had had of the title was enough to send him into transports, and some of the diagrams set in the vague Latin text excited the tensest and most disquieting recollections in his brain. He felt it was highly necessary to get the ponderous thing home and begin deciphering it, and bore it out of the shop with such precipitate haste that the old Jew chuckled disturbingly behind him. But when at last it was safe in his room he found the combination of black-letter and debased idiom too much for his powers as a linguist, and reluctantly called on his strange, frightened friend for help with the twisted, mediaeval Latin. Lord Northam was simpering inanities to his streaked cat, and started violently when the young man entered. Then he saw the volume and shuddered wildly, and fainted altogether when Williams uttered the title. It was when he regained his senses that he told his story; told his fantastic figment of madness in frantic whispers, lest his friend be not quick to burn the accursed book and give wide scattering to its ashes.

* * *

There must, Lord Northam whispered, have been something wrong at the start; but it would never have come to a head if he had not explored too far. He was the nineteenth Baron of a line whose beginnings went uncomfortably far back into the past—unbelievably far, if vague tradition could be heeded, for there were family tales of a descent from pre-Saxon times, when a certain Cnaeus Gabinius Capito, military tribune in the Third Augustan Legion then stationed at Lindum in Roman Britain, had been summarily expelled from his command for participation in certain rites unconnected with any known religion. Gabinius had, the rumour ran, come upon a cliffside cavern where strange folk met together and made the Elder Sign in the dark; strange folk whom the Britons knew not save in fear, and who were the last to survive from a great land in the west that had sunk, leaving only the islands with the raths and circles and shrines of which Stonehenge was the greatest. There was no certainty, of course, in the legend that Gabinius had built an impregnable fortress over the forbidden cave and founded a line which Pict and Saxon, Dane and Norman were powerless to obliterate; or in the tacit assumption that from this line sprang the bold companion and lieutenant of the Black Prince whom Edward Third created Baron of Northam. These things were not certain, yet they were often told; and in truth the stonework of Northam Keep did look alarmingly like the masonry of Hadrian's Wall. As a child Lord Northam had had peculiar dreams when sleeping in the older parts of the castle, and had acquired a constant habit of looking back through his memory for half-amorphous scenes and patterns and impressions which formed no part of his waking experience. He became a dreamer who found life tame and unsatisfying; a searcher for strange realms and relationships once familiar, yet lying nowhere in the visible regions of earth.

Filled with a feeling that our tangible world is only an atom in a fabric vast and ominous, and that unknown demesnes press on and permeate the sphere of the known at every point, Northam in youth and young manhood drained in turn the founts of formal religion and occult mystery. Nowhere, however, could he find ease and content; and as he grew older the staleness and limitations of life became more and more maddening to him. During the 'nineties he dabbled in Satanism, and at all times he devoured avidly any doctrine or theory which seemed to promise escape from the close vistas of science and the dully unvarying laws of Nature. Books like Ignatius Donnelly's chimerical account of Atlantis he absorbed with zest, and a dozen obscure precursors of Charles Fort enthralled him with their vagaries. He would travel leagues to follow up a furtive village tale of abnormal wonder, and once went into the desert of Araby to seek a Nameless City of faint report, which no man has ever beheld. There rose within him the tantalising faith that somewhere an easy gate existed, which if once found would admit him freely to those outer deeps whose echoes rattled so dimly at the back of his memory. It might be in the visible world, yet it might be only in his mind and soul. Perhaps he held within his own half-explored brain that cryptic link which would awaken him to elder and future lives in forgotten dimensions; which would bind him to the stars, and to the infinities and eternities beyond them.

HISTORY OF THE "NECRONOMICON"

Original title "Al Azif"—*azif* being the word used by the Arabs to designate that nocturnal sound (made by insects) suppos'd to be the howling of daemons.

Composed by Abdul Alhazred, a mad poet of Sanaá, in Yemen, who is said to have flourished during the period of the Ommiade caliphs, circa 700 A.D. He visited the ruins of Babylon and the subterranean secrets of Memphis and spent ten years alone in the great southern desert of Arabia—the Roba el Khaliyeh or "Empty Space" of the ancients—and "Dahna" or "Crimson" desert of the modern Arabs, which is held to be inhabited by protective evil spirits and monsters of death. Of this desert many strange and unbelievable marvels are told by those who pretend to have penetrated it. In his last years Alhazred dwelt in Damascus, where the "Necronomicon" ("Al Azif") was written, and of his final death or disappearance (738 A.D.) many terrible and conflicting things are told. He is said by Ebn Khallikan (12th cent. biographer) to have been seized by an invisible monster in broad daylight and devoured horribly before a large number of fright-frozen witnesses. Of his madness many things are told. He claimed to have seen the fabulous Irem, or City of Pillars, and to have found beneath the ruins of a certain nameless desert town the shocking annals and secrets of a race older than mankind. He was only an indifferent Moslem, worshipping unknown entities whom he called Yog-Sothoth and Cthulhu.

In A.D. 950 the "Azif", which had gained a considerable tho' surreptitious circulation amongst the philosophers of the age, was secretly translated into Greek by Theodorus Philetas of Constantinople under the title "Necronomicon". For a century it impelled certain experimenters to terrible attempts, when it was suppressed and burnt by the patriarch Michael. After this it is only heard of furtively, but (1228) Olaus Wormius made a Latin translation later in the Middle Ages, and the Latin text was printed twice—once in the fifteenth century in black-letter (evidently in Germany) and once in the seventeenth (prob. Spanish)—both editions being without identifying marks, and located as to time and place by internal typographical evidence only. The work both Latin and Greek was banned by Pope Gregory IX in 1232, shortly after its Latin translation, which called attention to it. The Arabic original was lost as early as Wormius' time, as indicated by his prefatory note (there is, however, a vague account of a secret copy appearing in San Francisco during the present century, but later perished in fire); and no sight of the Greek copy—which was printed in Italy between 1500 and 1550—has been reported since the burning of a certain Salem man's library in 1692. An English translation made by Dr. Dee was never printed, and exists only in fragments recovered from the original manuscript. Of the Latin texts now existing one (15th cent.) is known to be in the British Museum under lock and key, while another (17th cent.) is in the Bibliothèque Nationale at Paris. A seventeenth-century edition is in the Widener Library at Harvard, and in the library of Miskatonic University at Arkham; also in the library of the University of Buenos Ayres. Numerous other copies probably exist in secret, and a fifteenth-century one is persistently rumoured to form part of the collection of a celebrated American millionaire. A still vaguer rumour credits the preservation of a sixteenth-century Greek text in the Salem family of Pickman; but if it was so preserved, it vanished with the artist R. U. Pickman, who disappeared early in 1926. The book is rigidly suppressed by the authorities of most countries, and by all branches of organised ecclesiasticism. Reading leads to terrible consequences. It was from rumours of this book (of which relatively few of the general public know) that R. W. Chambers is said to have derived the idea of his early novel "The King in Yellow".

Chronology

Al Azif written circa 730 A.D. at Damascus by Abdul Alhazred
Tr. to Greek 950 A.D. as *Necronomicon* by Theodorus Philetas
Burnt by Patriarch Michael 1050 (i.e., Greek text). Arabic text now lost.
Olaus translates Greek to Latin 1228
1232—Latin ed. (and Greek) suppressed by Pope Gregory IX
14... Black-letter printed edition (Germany)
15... Greek text printed in Italy
16... Spanish reprint of Latin text

THE VERY OLD FOLK

I have myself been carried back to Roman times by my recent perusal of James Rhoades' Æneid, a translation never before read by me, & more faithful to P. Maro than any other version I have ever seen—including that of my late uncle Dr. Clark, which did not attain publication. This Virgilian diversion, together with the spectral thoughts incident to All Hallows' Eve with its Witch-Sabbaths on the hills, produced in me last Monday night a Roman dream of such supernal clearness & vividness, & such titanic adumbrations of hidden horror, that I verily believe I shall some day employ it in fiction. Roman dreams were no uncommon features of my youth—I used to follow the Divine Julius all over Gallia as a Tribunus Militum o'nights—but I had so long ceased to experience them, that the present one impressed me with extraordinary force.

It was a flaming sunset or late afternoon in the tiny provincial town of Pompelo, at the foot of the Pyrenees in Hispania Citerior. The year must have been in the late republic, for the province was still ruled by a senatorial proconsul instead of a praetorian legate of the Augustus, & the day was the first before the Kalends of November. The hills rose scarlet & gold to the north of the little town, & the westering sun shone ruddily & mystically on the crude new stone & plaster buildings of the dusty forum & the wooden walls of the circus some distance to the east. Groups of citizens—broad-browed Roman colonists & coarse-haired Romanised natives, together with obvious hybrids of the two strains, alike clad in cheap woollen togas—& sprinklings of helmeted legionaries & coarse-mantled, black-bearded tribesmen of the circumambient Vascones—all thronged the few paved streets & forum; moved by some vague & ill-defined uneasiness. I myself had just alighted from a litter, which the Illyrian bearers seemed to have brought in some haste from Calagurris, across the Iberus to the southward. It appeared that I was a provincial quaestor named L. Caelius Rufus, & that I had been summoned by the proconsul, P. Scribonius Libo, who had come from Tarraco some days before. The soldiers were the fifth cohort of the XIIth legion, under the military tribune Sex. Asellius; & the legatus of the whole legion, Cn. Balbutius, had also come from Calagurris, where the permanent station was. The cause of the conference was a horror that brooded on the hills. All the townsfolk were frightened, & had begged the presence of a cohort from Calagurris. It was the Terrible Season of the autumn, & the wild people in the mountains were preparing for the frightful ceremonies which only rumour told of in the towns. They were the very old folk who dwelt higher up in the hills & spoke a choppy language which the Vascones could not understand. One seldom saw them; but a few times a year they sent down little yellow squint-eyed messengers (who looked like Scythians) to trade with the merchants by means of gestures, & every spring & autumn they held the infamous rites on the peaks, their howlings & altar-fires throwing terror into the villages. Always the same—the night before the Kalends of Maius & the night before the Kalends of November. Townsfolk would disappear just before these nights, & never be heard of again. And there were whispers that the native shepherds & farmers were not ill-disposed toward the very old folk—that more than one thatched hut was vacant before midnight on the two hideous Sabbaths. This year the horror was very great, for the people knew that the wrath of the very old folk was upon Pompelo. Three months previously five of the little squint-eyed traders had come down from the hills, & in a market brawl three of them had been killed. The remaining two had gone back wordlessly to their mountains—*and this autumn not a single villager had disappeared.* There was a menace in this immunity. It was not like the very old folk to spare their victims at the Sabbath. It was too good to be normal, & the villagers were afraid. For many nights there had been a hollow drumming on the hills, & at last the aedile Tib. Annaeus Stilpo (half native in blood) had sent to Balbutius at Calagurris for a cohort to stamp out the Sabbath on the terrible night. Balbutius had carelessly refused, on the ground that the villagers' fears were empty, & that the loathsome rites of hill folk were of no concern to the Roman People unless our own citizens were menaced. I, however, who seemed to be a close friend of Balbutius, had disagreed with him; averring that I had studied deeply in the black forbidden lore, & that I believed the very old folk capable of visiting almost any nameless doom upon the town, which after all was a Roman settlement & contained a great number of our citizens. The complaining aedile's own mother Helvia was a pure Roman, the daughter of M. Helvius Cinna, who had come over with Scipio's army. Accordingly I had sent a slave—a nimble little Greek called Antipater—to the proconsul with letters, & Scribonius had heeded my plea & ordered Balbutius to send his fifth cohort, under Asellius, to Pompelo; entering the hills at dusk on the eve of November's Kalends & stamping out whatever nameless orgies he might find—bringing such prisoners as he might take to Tarraco for the next propraetor's court. Balbutius, however, had protested, so that more correspondence had ensued. I had written so much to the proconsul that he had become gravely interested, & had resolved to make a personal inquiry into the horror. He had at length proceeded to Pompelo with his lictors & attendants; there hearing enough rumours to be greatly impressed & disturbed, & standing firmly by his order for the Sabbath's extirpation. Desirous of conferring with one who had studied the subject, he ordered me to accompany Asellius' cohort—& Balbutius had also come along to press his adverse advice, for he honestly believed that drastic military action would stir up a dangerous sentiment of unrest among the Vascones both tribal & settled. So here we all were in the mystic sunset of the autumn hills—old Scribonius Libo in his toga praetexta, the golden light glancing on his shiny bald head & wrinkled hawk face, Balbutius with his gleaming helmet & breastplate, blue-shaven lips compressed in conscientiously dogged opposition, young Asellius with his polished greaves & superior sneer, & the curious throng of townsfolk, legionaries, tribesmen, peasants, lictors, slaves, & attendants. I myself seemed to wear a common toga, & to have no especially distinguishing characteristic. And everywhere horror brooded. The town & country folk scarcely dared speak aloud, & the men of Libo's entourage, who had been there nearly a week, seemed to have caught something of the nameless dread. Old Scribonius himself looked very grave, & the sharp voices of us later comers seemed to hold something of curious inappropriateness, as in a place of death or the temple of some mystic god. We entered the praetorium & held grave converse. Balbutius pressed his objections, & was sustained by Asellius, who appeared to hold all the natives in extreme contempt while at the same time deeming it inadvisable to excite them. Both soldiers maintained that we could better afford to antagonise the minority of colonists & civilised natives by inaction, than to antagonise a probable majority of tribesmen & cottagers by stamping out the dread rites. I, on the other hand, renewed my demand for action, & offered to accompany the cohort on any expedition it might undertake. I pointed out that the barbarous Vascones were at best turbulent & uncertain, so that skirmishes with them were inevitable sooner or later whichever course we might take; that they had not in the past proved dangerous adversaries to our legions, & that it would ill become the representatives of the Roman People to suffer barbarians to interfere with a course which the justice & prestige of the Republic demanded. That, on the other hand, the successful administration of a province depended primarily upon the safety & good-will of the civilised element in whose hands the local machinery of commerce & prosperity reposed, & in whose veins a large mixture of our own Italian blood coursed. These, though in numbers they might form a minority, were the stable element whose constancy might be relied on, & whose coöperation would most firmly bind the province to the Imperium of the Senate & the Roman People. It was at once a duty & an advantage to afford them the protection due to Roman citizens; even (& here I shot a sarcastic look at Balbutius & Asellius) at the expense of a little trouble & activity, & of a slight interruption of the draught-playing & cock-fighting at the camp in Calagurris. That the danger to the town and inhabitants of Pompelo was a real one, I could not from my studies doubt. I had read many scrolls out of Syria & Ægyptus, & the cryptic towns of Etruria, & had talked at length with the bloodthirsty priest of Diana Aricina in his temple in the woods bordering Lacus Nemorensis. There were shocking dooms that might be called out of the hills on the Sabbaths; dooms which ought not to exist within the territories of the Roman People; & to permit orgies of the kind known to prevail at Sabbaths would be but little in consonance with the customs of those whose forefathers, A. Postumius being consul, had executed so many Roman citizens for the practice of the Bacchanalia—a matter kept ever in memory by the Senatus Consultum de Bacchanalibus, graven upon bronze & set open to every eye. Checked in time, before the progress of the rites might evoke anything with which the iron of a Roman pilum might not be able to deal, the Sabbath would not be too much for the powers of a single cohort. Only participants need be apprehended, & the sparing of a great number of mere spectators would considerably lessen the resentment which any of the sympathising country folk might feel. In short, both principle & policy demanded stern action; & I could not doubt but that Publius Scribonius, bearing in mind the dignity & obligations of the Roman People, would adhere to his plan of despatching the cohort, me accompanying, despite such objections as Balbutius & Asellius—speaking indeed more like provincials than Romans—might see fit to offer & multiply. The slanting sun was now very low, & the whole town seemed draped in an unreal & malign glamour. Then P. Scribonius the proconsul signified his approval of my words, & stationed me with the cohort in the provisional capacity of a centurio primipilus; Balbutius & Asellius assenting, the former with better grace than the latter. As twilight fell on the wild autumnal slopes, a measured, hideous beating of strange drums floated down from afar in terrible rhythm. Some few of the legionarii shewed timidity, but sharp commands brought them into line, & the whole cohort was soon drawn up on the open plain east of the circus. Libo himself, as well as Balbutius, insisted on accompanying the cohort; but great difficulty was suffered in getting a native guide to point out the paths up the mountain. Finally a young man named Vercellius, the son of pure Roman parents, agreed to take us at least past the foothills. We began to march in the new dusk, with the thin silvern sickle of a young moon trembling over the woods on our left. That which disquieted us most was *the fact that the Sabbath was to be held at all.* Reports of the coming cohort must have reached the hills, & even the lack of a final decision could not make the rumour less alarming—yet there were the sinister drums as of yore, as if the celebrants had some peculiar reason to be indifferent whether or not the forces of the Roman People marched against them. The sound grew louder as we entered a rising gap in the hills, steep wooded banks enclosing us narrowly on either side, & displaying curiously fantastic tree-trunks in the light of our bobbing torches. All were afoot save Libo, Balbutius, Asellius, two or three of the centuriones, & myself, & at length the way became so steep & narrow that those who had horses were forced to leave them; a squad of ten men being left to guard them, though robber bands were not likely to be abroad on such a night of terror. Once in a while it seemed as though we detected a skulking form in the woods nearby, & after a half-hour's climb the steepness & narrowness of the way made the advance of so great a body of men—over 300, all told—exceedingly cumbrous & difficult. Then with utter & horrifying suddenness we heard a frightful sound from below. It was from the tethered horses—they had *screamed* .... not neighed, but *screamed* ..... & there was no light down there, nor the sound of any human thing, to shew why they had done so. At the same moment bonfires blazed out on all the peaks ahead, so that terror seemed to lurk equally before & behind us. Looking for the young Vercellius, our guide, we found only a crumpled heap weltering in a pool of blood. In his hand was a short sword snatched from the belt of D. Vibulanus, a subcenturio, & on his face was such a look of terror that the stoutest veterans turned pale at the sight. He had killed himself when the horses screamed .... he, who had been born & lived all his life in that region, & knew what men whispered about the hills. All the torches now began to dim, & the cries of frightened legionaries mingled with the unceasing screams of the tethered horses. The air grew perceptibly colder, more suddenly so than is usual at November's brink, & seemed stirred by terrible undulations which I could not help connecting with the beating of huge wings. The whole cohort now remained at a standstill, & as the torches faded I watched what I thought were fantastic shadows outlined in the sky by the spectral luminosity of the Via Lactea as it flowed through Perseus, Cassiopeia, Cepheus, & Cygnus. Then suddenly all the stars were blotted from the sky—even bright Deneb & Vega ahead, & the lone Altair & Fomalhaut behind us. And as the torches died out altogether, there remained above that stricken & shrieking cohort only the noxious & horrible altar-flames on the towering peaks; hellish & red, & now silhouetting the mad, leaping, & colossal forms of such nameless beasts as had never a Phrygian priest or Campanian grandam whispered of in the wildest of furtive tales. And above the nighted screaming of men & horses that daemoniac drumming rose to louder pitch, whilst an ice-cold wind of shocking sentience & deliberateness swept down from those forbidden heights & coiled about each man separately, till all the cohort was struggling & screaming in the dark, as if acting out the fate of Laocoön & his sons. Only old Scribonius Libo seemed resigned. He uttered words amidst the screaming, & they echo still in my ears. "*Malitia vetus—malitia vetus est ..... venit .... tandem venit....*"

And then I waked. It was the most vivid dream in years, drawing upon wells of the subconscious long untouched & forgotten. Of the fate of that cohort no record exists, but the town at least was saved—for encyclopaedias tell of the survival of Pompelo to this day, under the modern Spanish name of Pampelona. I shall have to look up Pampelona in some guidebook or travel volume, & see what its ancient tales & superstitions may be. But I shall never go near it on the night of All Hallows'—the night before the Kalends of November. In the genial summer it would be interesting to dig in those archaic hills, & to search a certain pass for the long-buried & encrusted eagles of a certain forgotten cohort.

IBID

("...—as Ibid says in his famous 'Lives of the Poets'."
—From a student theme.)

The erroneous idea that Ibid is the author of the "Lives" is so frequently met with, even among those pretending to a degree of culture, that it is worth correcting. It should be a matter of general knowledge that Cf. is responsible for this work. Ibid's masterpiece, on the other hand, was the famous "Op. Cit." wherein all the significant undercurrents of Graeco-Roman expression were crystallised once for all—and with admirable acuteness, notwithstanding the surprisingly late date at which Ibid wrote. There is a false report—very commonly reproduced in modern books prior to Von Schweinkopf's monumental "Geschichte der Ostrogothen in Italien"—that Ibid was a Romanised Visigoth of Ataulf's horde who settled in Placentia about 410 A.D. The contrary cannot be too strongly emphasised; for Von Schweinkopf, and since his time Littlewit[1] and Bêtenoir,[2] have shewn with irrefutable force that this strikingly isolated figure was a genuine Roman—or at least as genuine a Roman as that degenerate and mongrelised age could produce—of whom one might well say what Gibbon said of Boethius, "that he was the last whom Cato or Tully could have acknowledged

---

[1]*Rome and Byzantium: A Study in Survival* (Waukesha, 1869), Vol. XX, p. 598.
[2]*Influences Romains dans le Moyen Age* (Fond du Lac, 1877), Vol. XV, p. 720.

for their countryman." He was, like Boethius and nearly all the eminent men of his age, of the great Anician family, and traced his genealogy with much exactitude and self-satisfaction to all the heroes of the republic. His full name—long and pompous according to the custom of an age which had lost the trinomial simplicity of classic Roman nomenclature—is stated by Von Schweinkopf[3] to have been Caius Anicius Magnus Furius Camillus Æmilianus Cornelius Valerius Pompeius Julius Ibidus; though Littlewit[4] rejects *Æmilianus* and adds *Claudius Decius Junianus*; whilst Bêtenoir[5] differs radically, giving the full name as Magnus Furius Camillus Aurelius Antoninus Flavius Anicius Petronius Valentinianus Aegidius Ibidus.

The eminent critic and biographer was born in the year 486, shortly after the extinction of the Roman rule in Gaul by Clovis. Rome and Ravenna are rivals for the honour of his birth, though it is certain that he received his rhetorical and philosophical training in the schools of Athens—the extent of whose suppression by Theodosius a century before is grossly exaggerated by the superficial. In 512, under the benign rule of the Ostrogoth Theodoric, we behold him as a teacher of rhetoric at Rome, and in 516 he held the consulship together with Pompilius Numantius Bombastes Marcellinus Deodamnatus. Upon the death of Theodoric in 526, Ibidus retired from public life to compose his celebrated work (whose pure Ciceronian style is as remarkable a case of classic atavism as is the verse of Claudius Claudianus, who flourished a century before Ibidus); but he was later recalled to scenes of pomp to act as court rhetorician for Theodatus, nephew of Theodoric.

Upon the usurpation of Vitiges, Ibidus fell into disgrace and was for a time imprisoned; but the coming of the Byzantine-Roman army under Belisarius soon restored him to liberty and honours. Throughout the siege of Rome he served bravely in the army of the defenders, and afterward followed the eagles of Belisarius to Alba, Porto, and Centumcellae. After the Frankish siege of Milan, Ibidus was chosen to accompany the learned Bishop Datius to Greece, and resided with him at Corinth in the year 539. About 541 he removed to Constantinopolis, where he received every mark of imperial favour both from Justinianus and Justinus the Second. The Emperors Tiberius and Maurice did kindly honour to his old age, and contributed much to his

---

[3]Following Procopius, *Goth.* x..y..z.
[4]Following Jornandes, Codex Murat. xxj. 4144.
[5]After Pagi, 50–50.

immortality—especially Maurice, whose delight it was to trace his ancestry to old Rome notwithstanding his birth at Arabissus, in Cappadocia. It was Maurice who, in the poet's 101st year, secured the adoption of his work as a textbook in the schools of the empire, an honour which proved a fatal tax on the aged rhetorician's emotions, since he passed away peacefully at his home near the church of St. Sophia on the sixth day before the Kalends of September, A.D. 587, in the 102nd year of his age.

His remains, notwithstanding the troubled state of Italy, were taken to Ravenna for interment; but being interred in the suburb of Classe, were exhumed and ridiculed by the Lombard Duke of Spoleto, who took his skull to King Autharis for use as a wassail-bowl. Ibid's skull was proudly handed down from king to king of the Lombard line. Upon the capture of Pavia by Charlemagne in 774, the skull was seized from the tottering Desiderius and carried in the train of the Frankish conqueror. It was from this vessel, indeed, that Pope Leo administered the royal unction which made of the hero-nomad a Holy Roman Emperor. Charlemagne took Ibid's skull to his capital at Aix, soon afterward presenting it to his Saxon teacher Alcuin, upon whose death in 804 it was sent to Alcuin's kinsfolk in England.

William the Conqueror, finding it in an abbey niche where the pious family of Alcuin had placed it (believing it to be the skull of a saint[6] who had miraculously annihilated the Lombards by his prayers), did reverence to its osseous antiquity; and even the rough soldiers of Cromwell, upon destroying Ballylough Abbey in Ireland in 1650 (it having been secretly transported thither by a devout Papist in 1539, upon Henry VIII's dissolution of the English monasteries), declined to offer violence to a relic so venerable.

It was captured by the private solder Read-'em-and-Weep Hopkins, who not long after traded it to Rest-in-Jehovah Stubbs for a quid of the new Virginia weed. Stubbs, upon sending forth his son Zerubbabel to seek his fortune in New England in 1661 (for he thought ill of the Restoration atmosphere for a pious young yeoman), gave him St. Ibid's—or rather Brother Ibid's, for he abhorred all that was Popish—skull as a talisman. Upon landing in Salem Zerubbabel set it up in his cupboard beside the chimney, he having built a modest house near the town pump. However, he had not been wholly unaffected by the Restoration

[6]Not till the appearance of Von Schweinkopf's work in 1797 were St. Ibid and the rhetorician properly re-identified.

influence; and having become addicted to gaming, lost the skull to one Epenetus Dexter, a visiting freeman of Providence.

It was in the house of Dexter, in the northern part of the town near the present intersection of North Main and Olney Streets, on the occasion of Canonchet's raid of March 30, 1676, during King Philip's War; and the astute sachem, recognising it at once as a thing of singular venerableness and dignity, sent it as a symbol of alliance to a faction of the Pequots in Connecticut with whom he was negotiating. On April 4 he was captured by the colonists and soon after executed, but the austere head of Ibid continued on its wanderings.

The Pequots, enfeebled by a previous war, could give the now stricken Narragansetts no assistance; and in 1680 a Dutch fur-trader of Albany, Petrus van Schaack, secured the distinguished cranium for the modest sum of two guilders, he having recognised its value from the half-effaced inscription carved in Lombardic minuscules (palaeography, it might be explained, was one of the leading accomplishments of New-Netherland fur-traders of the seventeenth century).

From van Schaack, sad to say, the relic was stolen in 1683 by a French trader, Jean Grenier, whose Popish zeal recognised the features of one whom he had been taught at his mother's knee to revere as St. Ibide. Grenier, fired with virtuous rage at the possession of this holy symbol by a Protestant, crushed van Schaack's head one night with an axe and escaped to the north with his booty; soon, however, being robbed and slain by the half-breed voyageur Michel Savard, who took the skull—despite the illiteracy which prevented his recognising it—to add to a collection of similar but more recent material.

Upon his death in 1701 his half-breed son Pierre traded it among other things to some emissaries of the Sacs and Foxes, and it was found outside the chief's tepee a generation later by Charles de Langlade, founder of the trading post at Green Bay, Wisconsin. De Langlade regarded this sacred object with proper veneration and ransomed it at the expense of many glass beads; yet after his time it found itself in many other hands, being traded to settlements at the head of Lake Winnebago, to tribes around Lake Mendota, and finally, early in the nineteenth century, to one Solomon Juneau, a Frenchman, at the new trading post of Milwaukee on the Menominee River and the shore of Lake Michigan.

Later traded to Jacques Caboche, another settler, it was in 1850 lost in a game of chess or poker to a newcomer named Hans Zimmerman; being used by him as a beer-stein until one day, under the spell of its contents, he suffered it to roll from his front stoop to the prairie path before his home—where, falling into the burrow of a prairie-dog, it passed beyond his power of discovery or recovery upon his awaking.

So for generations did the sainted skull of Caius Anicius Magnus Furius Camillus Æmilianus Cornelius Valerius Pompeius Julius Ibidus, consul of Rome, favourite of emperors, and saint of the Romish church, lie hidden beneath the soil of a growing town. At first worshipped with dark rites by the prairie-dogs, who saw in it a deity sent from the upper world, it afterward fell into dire neglect as the race of simple, artless burrowers succumbed before the onslaught of the conquering Aryan. Sewers came, but they passed it by. Houses went up—2303 of them, and more—and at last one fateful night a titan thing occurred. Subtle Nature, convulsed with a spiritual ecstasy, like the froth of that region's quondam beverage, laid low the lofty and heaved high the humble—and behold! In the roseal dawn the burghers of Milwaukee rose to find a former prairie turned to a highland! Vast and far-reaching was the great upheaval. Subterrene arcana, hidden for years, came at last to the light. For there, full in the rifted roadway, lay bleached and tranquil in bland, saintly, and consular pomp the dome-like skull of Ibid!

THE DUNWICH HORROR

"Gorgons, and Hydras, and Chimaeras—dire stories of Celaeno and the Harpies—may reproduce themselves in the brain of superstition—*but they were there before.* They are transcripts, types—the archetypes are in us, and eternal. How else should the recital of that which we know in a waking sense to be false come to affect us at all? Is it that we naturally conceive terror from such objects, considered in their capacity of being able to inflict upon us bodily injury? O, least of all! *These terrors are of older standing. They date beyond body*—or without the body, they would have been the same.... That the kind of fear here treated is purely spiritual—that it is strong in proportion as it is objectless on earth, that it predominates in the period of our sinless infancy—are difficulties the solution of which might afford some probable insight into our ante-mundane condition, and a peep at least into the shadow-land of pre-existence."

—*Charles Lamb:* "Witches and Other Night-Fears"

I.

When a traveller in north central Massachusetts takes the wrong fork at the junction of the Aylesbury pike just beyond Dean's Corners he comes upon a lonely and curious country. The ground gets higher, and the brier-bordered stone walls press closer and closer against the ruts of the dusty, curving road. The trees of the frequent forest belts seem too large, and the wild weeds, brambles, and grasses attain a luxuriance not often found in settled regions. At the same time the planted fields appear singularly few and barren; while the sparsely scattered houses wear a surprisingly uniform aspect of age, squalor, and dilapidation. Without knowing why, one hesitates to ask directions from the gnarled, solitary figures spied now and then on crumbling doorsteps or on the sloping, rock-strown meadows. Those figures are so silent and furtive that one feels somehow confronted by forbidden things, with which it would be better to have nothing to do. When a rise in the road brings the mountains in view above the deep woods, the feeling of strange uneasiness is increased. The summits are too rounded and symmetrical to give a sense of comfort and naturalness, and sometimes the sky silhouettes with especial clearness the queer circles of tall stone pillars with which most of them are crowned.

Gorges and ravines of problematical depth intersect the way, and the crude wooden bridges always seem of dubious safety. When the road dips again there are stretches of marshland that one instinctively dislikes, and indeed almost fears at evening when unseen whippoorwills chatter and the fireflies come out in abnormal profusion to dance to the raucous, creepily insistent rhythms of stridently piping bull-frogs. The thin, shining line of the Miskatonic's upper reaches has an oddly serpent-like suggestion as it winds close to the feet of the domed hills among which it rises.

As the hills draw nearer, one heeds their wooded sides more than their stone-crowned tops. Those sides loom up so darkly and precipitously that one wishes they would keep their distance, but there is no road by which to escape them. Across a covered bridge one sees a small village huddled between the stream and the vertical slope of Round Mountain, and wonders at the cluster of rotting gambrel roofs bespeaking an earlier architectural period than that of the neighbouring region. It is not reassuring to see, on a closer glance, that most of the houses are deserted and falling to ruin, and that the broken-steepled church now harbours the one slovenly mercantile establishment of the hamlet. One dreads to trust the tenebrous tunnel of the bridge, yet there is no way to avoid it. Once across, it is hard to prevent the impression of a faint, malign odour about the village street, as of the massed mould and decay of centuries. It is always a relief to get clear of the place, and to follow the narrow road around the base of the hills and across the level country beyond till it rejoins the

Aylesbury pike. Afterward one sometimes learns that one has been through Dunwich.

Outsiders visit Dunwich as seldom as possible, and since a certain season of horror all the signboards pointing toward it have been taken down. The scenery, judged by any ordinary aesthetic canon, is more than commonly beautiful; yet there is no influx of artists or summer tourists. Two centuries ago, when talk of witch-blood, Satan-worship, and strange forest presences was not laughed at, it was the custom to give reasons for avoiding the locality. In our sensible age—since the Dunwich horror of 1928 was hushed up by those who had the town's and the world's welfare at heart—people shun it without knowing exactly why. Perhaps one reason—though it cannot apply to uninformed strangers—is that the natives are now repellently decadent, having gone far along that path of retrogression so common in many New England backwaters. They have come to form a race by themselves, with the well-defined mental and physical stigmata of degeneracy and inbreeding. The average of their intelligence is woefully low, whilst their annals reek of overt viciousness and of half-hidden murders, incests, and deeds of almost unnamable violence and perversity. The old gentry, representing the two or three armigerous families which came from Salem in 1692, have kept somewhat above the general level of decay; though many branches are sunk into the sordid populace so deeply that only their names remain as a key to the origin they disgrace. Some of the Whateleys and Bishops still send their eldest sons to Harvard and Miskatonic, though those sons seldom return to the mouldering gambrel roofs under which they and their ancestors were born.

No one, even those who have the facts concerning the recent horror, can say just what is the matter with Dunwich; though old legends speak of unhallowed rites and conclaves of the Indians, amidst which they called forbidden shapes of shadow out of the great rounded hills, and made wild orgiastic prayers that were answered by loud crackings and rumblings from the ground below. In 1747 the Reverend Abijah Hoadley, newly come to the Congregational Church at Dunwich Village, preached a memorable sermon on the close presence of Satan and his imps; in which he said:

> "It must be allow'd, that these Blasphemies of an infernall Train of Daemons are Matters of too common Knowledge to be deny'd; the cursed Voices of *Azazel* and *Buzrael*, of *Beelzebub* and *Belial*, being heard from under Ground by above a Score of credible Witnesses now living. I my self did not more than a Fortnight ago catch a very plain Discourse of evill Powers in the Hill behind

> my House; wherein there were a Rattling and Rolling, Groaning, Screeching, and Hissing, such as no Things of this Earth cou'd raise up, and which must needs have come from those Caves that only black Magick can discover, and only the Divell unlock."

Mr. Hoadley disappeared soon after delivering this sermon; but the text, printed in Springfield, is still extant. Noises in the hills continued to be reported from year to year, and still form a puzzle to geologists and physiographers.

Other traditions tell of foul odours near the hill-crowning circles of stone pillars, and of rushing airy presences to be heard faintly at certain hours from stated points at the bottom of the great ravines; while still others try to explain the Devil's Hop Yard—a bleak, blasted hillside where no tree, shrub, or grass-blade will grow. Then too, the natives are mortally afraid of the numerous whippoorwills which grow vocal on warm nights. It is vowed that the birds are psychopomps lying in wait for the souls of the dying, and that they time their eery cries in unison with the sufferer's struggling breath. If they can catch the fleeing soul when it leaves the body, they instantly flutter away chittering in daemoniac laughter; but if they fail, they subside gradually into a disappointed silence.

These tales, of course, are obsolete and ridiculous; because they come down from very old times. Dunwich is indeed ridiculously old—older by far than any of the communities within thirty miles of it. South of the village one may still spy the cellar walls and chimney of the ancient Bishop house, which was built before 1700; whilst the ruins of the mill at the falls, built in 1806, form the most modern piece of architecture to be seen. Industry did not flourish here, and the nineteenth-century factory movement proved short-lived. Oldest of all are the great rings of rough-hewn stone columns on the hilltops, but these are more generally attributed to the Indians than to the settlers. Deposits of skulls and bones, found within these circles and around the sizeable table-like rock on Sentinel Hill, sustain the popular belief that such spots were once the burial-places of the Pocumtucks; even though many ethnologists, disregarding the absurd improbability of such a theory, persist in believing the remains Caucasian.

II.

It was in the township of Dunwich, in a large and partly inhabited farmhouse set against a hillside four miles from the village and a mile and a half from any other dwelling, that Wilbur Whateley was born at 5 a.m. on Sunday, the second of February, 1913. This date was recalled because it was Candlemas, which people in Dunwich curiously observe under another name; and because the noises in the hills had sounded, and all the dogs of the countryside had barked persistently, throughout the night before. Less worthy of notice was the fact that the mother was one of the decadent Whateleys, a somewhat deformed, unattractive albino woman of thirty-five, living with an aged and half-insane father about whom the most frightful tales of wizardry had been whispered in his youth. Lavinia Whateley had no known husband, but according to the custom of the region made no attempt to disavow the child; concerning the other side of whose ancestry the country folk might—and did—speculate as widely as they chose. On the contrary, she seemed strangely proud of the dark, goatish-looking infant who formed such a contrast to her own sickly and pink-eyed albinism, and was heard to mutter many curious prophecies about its unusual powers and tremendous future.

Lavinia was one who would be apt to mutter such things, for she was a lone creature given to wandering amidst thunderstorms in the hills and trying to read the great odorous books which her father had inherited through two centuries of Whateleys, and which were fast falling to pieces with age and worm-holes. She had never been to school, but was filled with disjointed scraps of ancient lore that Old Whateley had taught her. The remote farmhouse had always been feared because of Old Whateley's reputation for black magic, and the unexplained death by violence of Mrs. Whateley when Lavinia was twelve years old had not helped to make the place popular. Isolated among strange influences, Lavinia was fond of wild and grandiose day-dreams and singular occupations; nor was her leisure much taken up by household cares in a home from which all standards of order and cleanliness had long since disappeared.

There was a hideous screaming which echoed above even the hill noises and the dogs' barking on the night Wilbur was born, but no known doctor or midwife presided at his coming. Neighbours knew nothing of him till a week afterward, when Old Whateley drove his sleigh through the snow into Dunwich Village and discoursed incoherently to the group of loungers at Osborn's general store. There seemed to be a change in the old man—an added element of furtiveness in the clouded brain which subtly transformed him from an object to a subject of fear—though he was not one to be perturbed by any common family event. Amidst it all he shewed some trace of the pride later noticed in his daughter, and what he said of the child's paternity was remembered by many of his hearers years afterward.

"I dun't keer what folks think—ef Lavinny's boy looked like his pa, he wouldn't look like nothin' ye expeck. Ye needn't think the only folks is the folks hereabaouts. Lavinny's read some, an' has seed some things the most o' ye only tell abaout. I calc'late her man is as good a husban' as ye kin find this side of Aylesbury; an' ef ye knowed as much abaout the hills as I dew, ye wouldn't ast no better church weddin' nor her'n. Let me tell ye suthin'—*some day yew folks'll hear a child o' Lavinny's a-callin' its father's name on the top o' Sentinel Hill!*"

The only persons who saw Wilbur during the first month of his life were old Zechariah Whateley, of the undecayed Whateleys, and Earl Sawyer's common-law wife, Mamie Bishop. Mamie's visit was frankly one of curiosity, and her subsequent tales did justice to her observations; but Zechariah came to lead a pair of Alderney cows which Old Whateley had bought of his son Curtis. This marked the beginning of a course of cattle-buying on the part of small Wilbur's family which ended only in 1928, when the Dunwich horror came and went; yet at no time did the ramshackle Whateley barn seem overcrowded with livestock. There came a period when people were curious enough to steal up and count the herd that grazed precariously on the steep hillside above the old farmhouse, and they could never find more than ten or twelve anaemic, bloodless-looking specimens. Evidently some blight or distemper, perhaps sprung from the unwholesome pasturage or the diseased fungi and timbers of the filthy barn, caused a heavy mortality amongst the Whateley animals. Odd wounds or sores, having something of the aspect of incisions, seemed to afflict the visible cattle; and once or twice during the earlier months certain callers fancied they could discern similar sores about the throats of the grey, unshaven old man and his slatternly, crinkly-haired albino daughter.

In the spring after Wilbur's birth Lavinia resumed her customary rambles in the hills, bearing in her misproportioned arms the swarthy child. Public interest in the Whateleys subsided after most of the country folk had seen the baby, and no one bothered to comment on the swift development which that newcomer seemed every day to exhibit. Wilbur's growth was indeed phenomenal, for within three months of his birth he had attained a size and muscular power not usually found in infants under a full year of age. His motions and even his vocal sounds shewed a restraint and deliberateness highly peculiar in an infant, and no one was really unprepared when, at seven months, he began to walk unassisted, with falterings which another month was sufficient to remove.

It was somewhat after this time—on Hallowe'en—that a great blaze was seen at midnight on the top of Sentinel Hill where the old table-like stone stands amidst its tumulus of ancient bones. Considerable talk was started when Silas Bishop—of the undecayed Bishops—mentioned having seen the boy running sturdily up that hill ahead of his mother about an hour before the blaze was remarked. Silas was rounding up a stray heifer, but he nearly forgot his mission when he fleetingly spied the two figures in the dim light of his lantern. They darted almost noiselessly through the underbrush, and the astonished watcher seemed to think they were entirely unclothed. Afterward he could not be sure about the boy, who may have had some kind of a fringed belt and a pair of dark trunks or trousers on. Wilbur was never subsequently seen alive and conscious without complete and tightly buttoned attire, the disarrangement or threatened disarrangement of which always seemed to fill him with anger and alarm. His contrast with his squalid mother and grandfather in this respect was thought very notable until the horror of 1928 suggested the most valid of reasons.

The next January gossips were mildly interested in the fact that "Lavinny's black brat" had commenced to talk, and at the age of only eleven months. His speech was somewhat remarkable both because of its difference from the ordinary accents of the region, and because it displayed a freedom from infantile lisping of which many children of three or four might well be proud. The boy was not talkative, yet when he spoke he seemed to reflect some elusive element wholly unpossessed by Dunwich and its denizens. The strangeness did not reside in what he said, or even in the simple idioms he used; but seemed vaguely linked with his intonation or with the internal organs that produced the spoken sounds. His facial aspect, too, was remarkable for its maturity; for though he shared his mother's and grandfather's chinlessness, his firm and precociously shaped nose united with the expression of his large, dark, almost Latin eyes to give him an air of quasi-adulthood and well-nigh preternatural intelligence. He was, however, exceedingly ugly despite his appearance of brilliancy; there being something almost goatish or animalistic about his thick lips, large-pored, yellowish skin, coarse crinkly hair, and oddly elongated ears. He was soon disliked even more decidedly than his mother and grandsire, and all conjectures about him were spiced with references to the bygone magic of Old Whateley, and how the hills once shook when he shrieked the dreadful name of *Yog-Sothoth* in the midst of a circle of stones with a great book open in his arms before him. Dogs abhorred the boy, and he was always obliged to take various defensive measures against their barking menace.

III.

Meanwhile Old Whateley continued to buy cattle without measurably increasing the size of his herd. He also cut timber and began to repair the unused parts of his house—a spacious, peaked-roofed affair whose rear end was buried entirely in the rocky hillside, and whose three least-ruined ground-floor rooms had always been sufficient for himself and his daughter. There must have been prodigious reserves of strength in the old man to enable him to accomplish so much hard labour; and though he still babbled dementedly at times, his carpentry seemed to shew the effects of sound calculation. It had really begun as soon as Wilbur was born, when one of the many tool-sheds had been put suddenly in order, clapboarded, and fitted with a stout fresh lock. Now, in restoring the abandoned upper story of the house, he was a no less thorough craftsman. His mania shewed itself only in his tight boarding-up of all the windows in the reclaimed section—though many declared that it was a crazy thing to bother with the reclamation at all. Less inexplicable was his fitting up of another downstairs room for his new grandson—a room which several callers saw, though no one was ever admitted to the closely boarded upper story. This chamber he lined with tall, firm shelving; along which he began gradually to arrange, in apparently careful order, all the rotting ancient books and parts of books which during his own day had been heaped promiscuously in odd corners of the various rooms.

"I made some use of 'em," he would say as he tried to mend a torn black-letter page with paste prepared on the rusty kitchen stove, "but the boy's fitten to make better use of 'em. He'd orter hev 'em as well sot as he kin, for they're goin' to be all of his larnin'."

When Wilbur was a year and seven months old—in September of 1914—his size and accomplishments were almost alarming. He had grown as large as a child of four, and was a fluent and incredibly intelligent talker. He ran freely about the fields and hills, and accompanied his mother on all her wanderings. At home he would pore diligently over the queer pictures and charts in his grandfather's books, while Old Whateley would instruct and catechise him through long, hushed afternoons. By this time the restoration of the house was finished, and those who watched it wondered why one of the upper windows had been made into a solid plank door. It was a window in the rear of the east gable end, close against the hill; and no one could imagine why a cleated wooden runway was built up to it from the ground. About the period of this work's completion people noticed that the old tool-house, tightly locked and windowlessly clapboarded since Wilbur's birth, had been abandoned again. The door swung listlessly open, and when Earl Sawyer once stepped within after a cattle-selling call on Old Whateley he was quite discomposed by the singular odour he encountered—such a stench, he averred, as he had never before smelt in all his life except near the Indian circles on the hills, and which could not come from anything sane or of this earth. But then, the homes and sheds of Dunwich folk have never been remarkable for olfactory immaculateness.

The following months were void of visible events, save that everyone swore to a slow but steady increase in the mysterious hill noises. On May-Eve of 1915 there were tremors which even the Aylesbury people felt, whilst the following Hallowe'en produced an underground rumbling queerly synchronised with bursts of flame—"them witch Whateleys' doin's"—from the summit of Sentinel Hill. Wilbur was growing up uncannily, so that he looked like a boy of ten as he entered his fourth year. He read avidly by himself now; but talked much less than formerly. A settled taciturnity was absorbing him, and for the first time people began to speak specifically of the dawning look of evil in his goatish face. He would sometimes mutter an unfamiliar jargon, and chant in bizarre rhythms which chilled the listener with a sense of unexplainable terror. The aversion displayed toward him by dogs had now become a matter of wide remark, and he was obliged to carry a pistol in order to traverse the countryside in safety. His occasional use of the weapon did not enhance his popularity amongst the owners of canine guardians.

The few callers at the house would often find Lavinia alone on the ground floor, while odd cries and footsteps resounded in the boarded-up second story. She would never tell what her father and the boy were doing up there, though once she turned pale and displayed an abnormal degree of fear when a jocose fish-peddler tried the locked door leading to the stairway. That peddler told the store loungers at Dunwich Village that he thought he heard a horse stamping on that floor above. The loungers reflected, thinking of the door and runway, and of the cattle that so swiftly disappeared. Then they shuddered as they recalled tales of Old Whateley's youth, and of the strange things that are called out of the earth when a bullock is sacrificed at the proper time to certain heathen gods. It had for some time been noticed that dogs had begun to hate and fear the whole Whateley place as violently as they hated and feared young Wilbur personally.

In 1917 the war came, and Squire Sawyer Whateley, as chairman of the local draft board, had hard work finding a quota of young Dunwich men fit even to be sent to a development camp.

The government, alarmed at such signs of wholesale regional decadence, sent several officers and medical experts to investigate; conducting a survey which New England newspaper readers may still recall. It was the publicity attending this investigation which set reporters on the track of the Whateleys, and caused the *Boston Globe* and *Arkham Advertiser* to print flamboyant Sunday stories of young Wilbur's precociousness, Old Whateley's black magic, the shelves of strange books, the sealed second story of the ancient farmhouse, and the weirdness of the whole region and its hill noises. Wilbur was four and a half then, and looked like a lad of fifteen. His lip and cheeks were fuzzy with a coarse dark down, and his voice had begun to break.

Earl Sawyer went out to the Whateley place with both sets of reporters and camera men, and called their attention to the queer stench which now seemed to trickle down from the sealed upper spaces. It was, he said, exactly like a smell he had found in the tool-shed abandoned when the house was finally repaired; and like the faint odours which he sometimes thought he caught near the stone circles on the mountains. Dunwich folk read the stories when they appeared, and grinned over the obvious mistakes. They wondered, too, why the writers made so much of the fact that Old Whateley always paid for his cattle in gold pieces of extremely ancient date. The Whateleys had received their visitors with ill-concealed distaste, though they did not dare court further publicity by a violent resistance or refusal to talk.

IV.

For a decade the annals of the Whateleys sink indistinguishably into the general life of a morbid community used to their queer ways and hardened to their May-Eve and All-Hallows orgies. Twice a year they would light fires on the top of Sentinel Hill, at which times the mountain rumblings would recur with greater and greater violence; while at all seasons there were strange and portentous doings at the lonely farmhouse. In the course of time callers professed to hear sounds in the sealed upper story even when all the family were downstairs, and they wondered how swiftly or how lingeringly a cow or bullock was usually sacrificed. There was talk of a complaint to the Society for the Prevention of Cruelty to Animals; but nothing ever came of it, since Dunwich folk are never anxious to call the outside world's attention to themselves.

About 1923, when Wilbur was a boy of ten whose mind, voice, stature, and bearded face gave all the impressions of maturity, a second great siege of carpentry went on at the old house. It was all inside the sealed upper part, and from bits of discarded lumber people concluded that the youth and his grandfather had knocked out all the partitions and even removed the attic floor, leaving only one vast open void between the ground story and the peaked roof. They had torn down the great central chimney, too, and fitted the rusty range with a flimsy outside tin stovepipe.

In the spring after this event Old Whateley noticed the growing number of whippoorwills that would come out of Cold Spring Glen to chirp under his window at night. He seemed to regard the circumstance as one of great significance, and told the loungers at Osborn's that he thought his time had almost come.

"They whistle jest in tune with my breathin' naow," he said, "an' I guess they're gittin' ready to ketch my soul. They know it's a-goin' aout, an' dun't calc'late to miss it. Yew'll know, boys, arter I'm gone, whether they git me er not. Ef they dew, they'll keep up a-singin' an' laffin' till break o' day. Ef they dun't, they'll kinder quiet daown like. I expeck them an' the souls they hunts fer hev some pretty tough tussles sometimes."

On Lammas Night, 1924, Dr. Houghton of Aylesbury was hastily summoned by Wilbur Whateley, who had lashed his one remaining horse through the darkness and telephoned from Osborn's in the village. He found Old Whateley in a very grave state, with a cardiac action and stertorous breathing that told of an end not far off. The shapeless albino daughter and oddly bearded grandson stood by the bedside, whilst from the vacant abyss overhead there came a disquieting suggestion of rhythmical surging or lapping, as of the waves on some level beach. The doctor, though, was chiefly disturbed by the chattering night birds outside; a seemingly limitless legion of whippoorwills that cried their endless message in repetitions timed diabolically to the wheezing gasps of the dying man. It was uncanny and unnatural—too much, thought Dr. Houghton, like the whole of the region he had entered so reluctantly in response to the urgent call.

Toward one o'clock Old Whateley gained consciousness, and interrupted his wheezing to choke out a few words to his grandson.

"More space, Willy, more space soon. Yew grows—an' *that* grows faster. It'll be ready to sarve ye soon, boy. Open up the gates to Yog-Sothoth with the long chant that ye'll find on page 751 *of the complete edition*, an' *then* put a match to the prison. Fire from airth can't burn it nohaow."

He was obviously quite mad. After a pause, during which the flock of whippoorwills outside adjusted their cries to the altered tempo while some indications of the strange hill noises came from afar off, he added another sentence or two.

"Feed it reg'lar, Willy, an' mind the quantity; but dun't let it grow too fast fer the place, fer ef it busts quarters or gits aout afore ye opens to Yog-Sothoth, it's all over an' no use. Only them from beyont kin make it multiply an' work.... Only them, the old uns as wants to come back...."

But speech gave place to gasps again, and Lavinia screamed at the way the whippoorwills followed the change. It was the same for more than an hour, when the final throaty rattle came. Dr. Houghton drew shrunken lids over the glazing grey eyes as the tumult of birds faded imperceptibly to silence. Lavinia sobbed, but Wilbur only chuckled whilst the hill noises rumbled faintly.

"They didn't git him," he muttered in his heavy bass voice.

Wilbur was by this time a scholar of really tremendous erudition in his one-sided way, and was quietly known by correspondence to many librarians in distant places where rare and forbidden books of old days are kept. He was more and more hated and dreaded around Dunwich because of certain youthful disappearances which suspicion laid vaguely at his door; but was always able to silence inquiry through fear or through use of that fund of old-time gold which still, as in his grandfather's time, went forth regularly and increasingly for cattle-buying. He was now tremendously mature of aspect, and his height, having reached the normal adult limit, seemed inclined to wax beyond that figure. In 1925, when a scholarly correspondent from Miskatonic University called upon him one day and departed pale and puzzled, he was fully six and three-quarters feet tall.

Through all the years Wilbur had treated his half-deformed albino mother with a growing contempt, finally forbidding her to go to the hills with him on May-Eve and Hallowmass; and in 1926 the poor creature complained to Mamie Bishop of being afraid of him.

"They's more abaout him as I knows than I kin tell ye, Mamie," she said, "an' naowadays they's more nor what I know myself. I vaow afur Gawd, I dun't know what he wants nor what he's a-tryin' to dew."

That Hallowe'en the hill noises sounded louder than ever, and fire burned on Sentinel Hill as usual; but people paid more attention to the rhythmical screaming of vast flocks of unnaturally belated whippoorwills which seemed to be assembled near the unlighted Whateley farmhouse. After midnight their shrill notes burst into a kind of pandaemoniac cachinnation which filled all the countryside, and not until dawn did they finally quiet down. Then they vanished, hurrying southward where they were fully a month overdue. What this meant, no one could quite be certain till later. None of the country folk seemed to have died—but poor Lavinia Whateley, the twisted albino, was never seen again.

In the summer of 1927 Wilbur repaired two sheds in the farmyard and began moving his books and effects out to them. Soon afterward Earl Sawyer told the loungers at Osborn's that more carpentry was going on in the Whateley farmhouse. Wilbur was closing all the doors and windows on the ground floor, and seemed to be taking out partitions as he and his grandfather had done upstairs four years before. He was living in one of the sheds, and Sawyer thought he seemed unusually worried and tremulous. People generally suspected him of knowing something about his mother's disappearance, and very few ever approached his neighbourhood now. His height had increased to more than seven feet, and shewed no signs of ceasing its development.

V.

The following winter brought an event no less strange than Wilbur's first trip outside the Dunwich region. Correspondence with the Widener Library at Harvard, the Bibliothèque Nationale in Paris, the British Museum, the University of Buenos Ayres, and the Library of Miskatonic University at Arkham had failed to get him the loan of a book he desperately wanted; so at length he set out in person, shabby, dirty, bearded, and uncouth of dialect, to consult the copy at Miskatonic, which was the nearest to him geographically. Almost eight feet tall, and carrying a cheap new valise from Osborn's general store, this dark and goatish gargoyle appeared one day in Arkham in quest of the dreaded volume kept under lock and key at the college library—the hideous *Necronomicon* of the mad Arab Abdul Alhazred in Olaus Wormius' Latin version, as printed in Spain in the seventeenth century. He had never seen a city before, but had no thought save to find his way to the university grounds; where, indeed, he passed heedlessly by the great white-fanged watchdog that barked with unnatural fury and enmity, and tugged frantically at its stout chain.

Wilbur had with him the priceless but imperfect copy of Dr. Dee's English version which his grandfather had bequeathed him, and upon receiving access to the Latin copy he at once began to collate the two texts with the aim of discovering a certain passage which would have come on the 751st page of his own defective volume. This much he could not civilly refrain from telling the librarian—the same erudite Henry Armitage (A.M. Miskatonic, Ph. D. Princeton, Litt. D. Johns Hopkins) who had once called at the farm, and who now politely plied him with questions. He was looking, he had to admit, for a kind of formula or incantation containing the frightful name *Yog-Sothoth*, and it puzzled him to find discrepancies, duplications, and ambiguities which made the matter of determination far from easy. As he copied the formula he finally chose, Dr. Armitage looked involuntarily over his shoulder at the open pages; the left-hand one of which, in the Latin version, contained such monstrous threats to the peace and sanity of the world.

> "Nor is it to be thought," ran the text as Armitage mentally translated it, "that man is either the oldest or the last of earth's masters, or that the common bulk of life and substance walks alone. The Old Ones were, the Old Ones are, and the Old Ones shall be. Not in the spaces we know, but *between* them, They walk serene and primal, undimensioned and to us unseen. *Yog-Sothoth* knows the gate. *Yog-Sothoth* is the gate. *Yog-Sothoth* is the key and guardian of the gate. Past, present, future, all are one in *Yog-Sothoth*. He knows where the Old Ones broke through of old, and where They shall break through again. He knows where They have trod earth's fields, and where They still tread them, and why no one can behold Them as They tread. By Their smell can men sometimes know Them near, but of Their semblance can no man know, *saving only in the features of those They have begotten on mankind*; and of those are there many sorts, differing in likeness from man's truest eidolon to that shape without sight or substance which is *Them*. They walk unseen and foul in lonely places where the Words have been spoken and the Rites howled through at their Seasons. The wind gibbers with Their voices, and the earth mutters with Their consciousness. They bend the forest and crush the city, yet may not forest or city behold the hand that smites. Kadath in the cold waste hath known Them, and what man knows Kadath? The ice desert of the South and the sunken isles of Ocean hold stones whereon Their seal is engraven, but who hath seen the deep frozen city or the sealed tower long garlanded with seaweed and barnacles? Great Cthulhu is Their cousin, yet can he spy Them only dimly. *Iä! Shub-Niggurath!* As a foulness shall ye know Them. Their hand is at your throats, yet ye see Them not; and Their habitation is even one with your guarded threshold. *Yog-Sothoth* is the key to the gate, whereby the spheres meet. Man rules now where They ruled once; They shall soon rule where man rules now. After summer is winter, and after winter summer. They wait patient and potent, for here shall They reign again."

Dr. Armitage, associating what he was reading with what he had heard of Dunwich and its brooding presences, and of Wilbur Whateley and his dim, hideous aura that stretched from a dubious birth to a cloud of probable matricide, felt a wave of fright as tangible as a draught of the tomb's cold clamminess. The bent, goatish giant before him seemed like the spawn of another planet or dimension; like something only partly of mankind, and linked to black gulfs of essence and entity that stretch like titan phantasms beyond all spheres of force and matter, space and time. Presently Wilbur raised his head and began speaking in that strange, resonant fashion which hinted at sound-producing organs unlike the run of mankind's.

"Mr. Armitage," he said, "I calc'late I've got to take that book home. They's things in it I've got to try under sarten conditions that I can't git here, an' it 'ud be a mortal sin to let a red-tape rule hold me up. Let me take it along, Sir, an' I'll swar they wun't nobody know the difference. I dun't need to tell ye I'll take good keer of it. It wa'n't me that put this Dee copy in the shape it is...."

He stopped as he saw firm denial on the librarian's face, and his own goatish features grew crafty. Armitage, half-ready to tell him he might make a copy of what parts he needed, thought suddenly of the possible consequences and checked himself. There was too much responsibility in giving such a being the key to such blasphemous outer spheres. Whateley saw how things stood, and tried to answer lightly.

"Wal, all right, ef ye feel that way abaout it. Maybe Harvard wun't be so fussy as yew be." And without saying more he rose and strode out of the building, stooping at each doorway.

Armitage heard the savage yelping of the great watchdog, and studied Whateley's gorilla-like lope as he crossed the bit of campus visible from the window. He thought of the wild tales he had heard, and recalled the old Sunday stories in the *Advertiser*; these things, and the lore he had picked up from Dunwich rustics and villagers during his one visit there. Unseen things not of earth—or at least not of tri-dimensional earth—rushed foetid and horrible through New England's glens, and brooded obscenely on the mountaintops. Of this he had long felt certain. Now he seemed to sense the close presence of some terrible part of the intruding horror, and to glimpse a hellish advance in the black dominion of the ancient and once passive nightmare. He locked away the "Necronomicon" with a shudder of disgust, but the room still reeked with an unholy and unidentifiable stench. "As a foulness shall ye know them," he quoted. Yes—the odour was the same as that which had sickened him at the Whateley farmhouse less than three years before. He thought of Wilbur, goatish and ominous, once again, and laughed mockingly at the village rumours of his parentage.

"Inbreeding?" Armitage muttered half-aloud to himself. "Great God, what simpletons! Shew them Arthur Machen's Great God Pan and they'll think it a common Dunwich scandal!

But what thing—what cursed shapeless influence on or off this three-dimensioned earth—was Wilbur Whateley's father? Born on Candlemas—nine months after May-Eve of 1912, when the talk about the queer earth noises reached clear to Arkham—What walked on the mountains that May-Night? What Roodmas horror fastened itself on the world in half-human flesh and blood?"

During the ensuing weeks Dr. Armitage set about to collect all possible data on Wilbur Whateley and the formless presences around Dunwich. He got in communication with Dr. Houghton of Aylesbury, who had attended Old Whateley in his last illness, and found much to ponder over in the grandfather's last words as quoted by the physician. A visit to Dunwich Village failed to bring out much that was new; but a close survey of the *Necronomicon*, in those parts which Wilbur had sought so avidly, seemed to supply new and terrible clues to the nature, methods, and desires of the strange evil so vaguely threatening this planet. Talks with several students of archaic lore in Boston, and letters to many others elsewhere, gave him a growing amazement which passed slowly through varied degrees of alarm to a state of really acute spiritual fear. As the summer drew on he felt dimly that something ought to be done about the lurking terrors of the upper Miskatonic valley, and about the monstrous being known to the human world as Wilbur Whateley.

VI.

The Dunwich horror itself came between Lammas and the equinox in 1928, and Dr. Armitage was among those who witnessed its monstrous prologue. He had heard, meanwhile, of Whateley's grotesque trip to Cambridge, and of his frantic efforts to borrow or copy from the *Necronomicon* at the Widener Library. Those efforts had been in vain, since Armitage had issued warnings of the keenest intensity to all librarians having charge of the dreaded volume. Wilbur had been shockingly nervous at Cambridge; anxious for the book, yet almost equally anxious to get home again, as if he feared the results of being away long.

Early in August the half-expected outcome developed, and in the small hours of the third Dr. Armitage was awakened suddenly by the wild, fierce cries of the savage watchdog on the college campus. Deep and terrible, the snarling, half-mad growls and barks continued; always in mounting volume, but with hideously significant pauses. Then there rang out a scream from a wholly different throat—such a scream as roused half the sleepers of Arkham and haunted their dreams ever afterward—such a scream as could come from no being born of earth, or wholly of earth.

Armitage, hastening into some clothing and rushing across the street and lawn to the college buildings, saw that others were ahead of him; and heard the echoes of a burglar-alarm still shrilling from the library. An open window shewed black and gaping in the moonlight. What had come had indeed completed its entrance; for the barking and the screaming, now fast fading into a mixed low growling and moaning, proceeded unmistakably from within. Some instinct warned Armitage that what was taking place was not a thing for unfortified eyes to see, so he brushed back the crowd with authority as he unlocked the vestibule door. Among the others he saw Professor Warren Rice and Dr. Francis Morgan, men to whom he had told some of his conjectures and misgivings; and these two he motioned to accompany him inside. The inward sounds, except for a watchful, droning whine from the dog, had by this time quite subsided; but Armitage now perceived with a sudden start that a loud chorus of whippoorwills among the shrubbery had commenced a damnably rhythmical piping, as if in unison with the last breaths of a dying man.

The building was full of a frightful stench which Dr. Armitage knew too well, and the three men rushed across the hall to the small genealogical reading-room whence the low whining came. For a second nobody dared to turn on the light, then Armitage summoned up his courage and snapped the switch. One of the three—it is not certain which—shrieked aloud at what sprawled before them among disordered tables and overturned chairs. Professor Rice declares that he wholly lost consciousness for an instant, though he did not stumble or fall.

The thing that lay half-bent on its side in a foetid pool of greenish-yellow ichor and tarry stickiness was almost nine feet tall, and the dog had torn off all the clothing and some of the skin. It was not quite dead, but twitched silently and spasmodically while its chest heaved in monstrous unison with the mad piping of the expectant whippoorwills outside. Bits of shoe-leather and fragments of apparel were scattered about the room, and just inside the window an empty canvas sack lay where it had evidently been thrown. Near the central desk a revolver had fallen, a dented but undischarged cartridge later explaining why it had not been fired. The thing itself, however, crowded out all other images at the time. It would be trite and not wholly accurate to say that no human pen could describe it, but one may properly say that it could not be vividly visualised by anyone whose ideas of aspect and contour are too closely bound up with the common life-forms of this planet and of the three known dimensions. It was partly human, beyond a doubt, with very man-like hands and head, and the goatish, chinless face had the stamp of the Whateleys upon it. But the torso and lower parts of the body were teratologically fabulous, so that only generous clothing could ever have enabled it to walk on earth unchallenged or uneradicated.

Above the waist it was semi-anthropomorphic; though its chest, where the dog's rending paws still rested watchfully, had the leathery, reticulated hide of a crocodile or alligator. The back was piebald with yellow and black, and dimly suggested the squamous covering of certain snakes. Below the waist, though, it was the worst; for here all human resemblance left off and sheer phantasy began. The skin was thickly covered with coarse black fur, and from the abdomen a score of long greenish-grey tentacles with red sucking mouths protruded limply. Their arrangement was odd, and seemed to follow the symmetries of some cosmic geometry unknown to earth or the solar system. On each of the hips, deep set in a kind of pinkish, ciliated orbit, was what seemed to be a rudimentary eye; whilst in lieu of a tail there depended a kind of trunk or feeler with purple annular markings, and with many evidences of being an undeveloped mouth or throat. The limbs, save for their black fur, roughly resembled the hind legs of prehistoric earth's giant saurians; and terminated in ridgy-veined pads that were neither hooves nor claws. When the thing breathed, its tail and tentacles rhythmically changed colour, as if from some circulatory cause normal to the non-human side of its ancestry. In the tentacles this was observable as a deepening of the greenish tinge, whilst in the tail it was manifest as a yellowish appearance which alternated with a sickly greyish-white in the spaces between the purple rings. Of genuine blood there was none; only the foetid greenish-yellow ichor which trickled along the painted floor beyond the radius of the stickiness, and left a curious discolouration behind it.

As the presence of the three men seemed to rouse the dying thing, it began to mumble without turning or raising its head. Dr. Armitage made no written record of its mouthings, but asserts confidently that nothing in English was uttered. At first the syllables defied all correlation with any speech of earth, but toward the last there came some disjointed fragments evidently taken from the "Necronomicon", that monstrous blasphemy in quest of which the thing had perished. These fragments, as Armitage recalls them, ran something like "*N'gai, n'gha'ghaa, bugg-shoggog, y'hah; Yog-Sothoth, Yog-Sothoth....*" They trailed off into nothingness as the whippoorwills shrieked in rhythmical crescendoes of unholy anticipation.

Then came a halt in the gasping, and the dog raised its head in a long, lugubrious howl. A change came over the yellow, goatish face of the prostrate thing, and the great black eyes fell in appallingly. Outside the window the shrilling of the whippoorwills had suddenly ceased, and above the murmurs of the gathering crowd there came the sound of a panic-struck whirring and fluttering. Against the moon vast clouds of feathery watchers rose and raced from sight, frantic at that which they had sought for prey.

All at once the dog started up abruptly, gave a frightened bark, and leaped nervously out of the window by which it had entered. A cry rose from the crowd, and Dr. Armitage shouted to the men outside that no one must be admitted till the police or medical examiner came. He was thankful that the windows were just too high to permit of peering in, and drew the dark curtains carefully down over each one. By this time two policemen had arrived; and Dr. Morgan, meeting them in the vestibule, was urging them for their own sakes to postpone entrance to the stench-filled reading-room till the examiner came and the prostrate thing could be covered up.

Meanwhile frightful changes were taking place on the floor. One need not describe the *kind* and *rate* of shrinkage and disintegration that occurred before the eyes of Dr. Armitage and Professor Rice; but it is permissible to say that, aside from the external appearance of face and hands, the really human element in Wilbur Whateley must have been very small. When the medical examiner came, there was only a sticky whitish mass on the painted boards, and the monstrous odour had nearly disappeared. Apparently Whateley had had no skull or bony skeleton; at least, in any true or stable sense. He had taken somewhat after his unknown father.

VII.

Yet all this was only the prologue of the actual Dunwich horror. Formalities were gone through by bewildered officials, abnormal details were duly kept from press and public, and men were sent to Dunwich and Aylesbury to look up property and notify any who might be heirs of the late Wilbur Whateley. They found the countryside in great agitation, both because of the growing rumblings beneath the domed hills, and because of the unwonted stench and the surging, lapping sounds which came increasingly from the great empty shell formed by Whateley's boarded-up farmhouse. Earl Sawyer, who tended the horse and cattle during Wilbur's absence, had developed a woefully acute case of nerves. The officials devised excuses not to enter the noisome boarded place; and were glad to confine their survey of the deceased's living quarters, the newly mended sheds, to a single visit. They filed a ponderous report at the court-house in Aylesbury, and litigations concerning heirship are said to be still in progress amongst the innumerable Whateleys, decayed and undecayed, of the upper Miskatonic valley.

An almost interminable manuscript in strange characters, written in a huge ledger and adjudged a sort of diary because of the spacing and the variations in ink and penmanship, presented a baffling puzzle to those who found it on the old bureau which served as its owner's desk. After a week of debate it was sent to Miskatonic University, together with the deceased's collection of strange books, for study and possible translation; but even the best linguists soon saw that it was not likely to be unriddled with ease. No trace of the ancient gold with which Wilbur and Old Whateley always paid their debts has yet been discovered.

It was in the dark of September 9th that the horror broke loose. The hill noises had been very pronounced during the evening, and dogs barked frantically all night. Early risers on the tenth noticed a peculiar stench in the air. About seven o'clock Luther Brown, the hired boy at George Corey's, between Cold Spring Glen and the village, rushed frenziedly back from his morning trip to Ten-Acre Meadow with the cows. He was almost convulsed with fright as he stumbled into the kitchen; and in the yard outside the no less frightened herd were pawing and lowing pitifully, having followed the boy back in the panic they shared with him. Between gasps Luther tried to stammer out his tale to Mrs. Corey.

"Up thar in the rud beyont the glen, Mis' Corey—they's suthin' ben thar! It smells like thunder, an' all the bushes an' little trees is pushed back from the rud like they'd a haouse ben moved along of it. An' that ain't the wust, nuther. They's *prints* in the rud, Mis' Corey—great raound prints as big as barrel-heads, all sunk daown deep like a elephant had ben along, *only they's a sight more nor four feet could make!* I looked at one or two afore I run, an' I see every one was covered with lines spreadin' aout from one place, like as if big palm-leaf fans—twict or three times as big as any they is—hed of ben paounded daown into the rud. An' the smell was awful, like what it is araound Wizard Whateley's ol' haouse...."

Here he faltered, and seemed to shiver afresh with the fright that had sent him flying home. Mrs. Corey, unable to extract more information, began telephoning the neighbours; thus starting on its rounds the overture of panic that heralded the major terrors. When she got Sally Sawyer, housekeeper at Seth Bishop's, the nearest place to Whateley's, it became her turn to listen instead of transmit; for Sally's boy Chauncey, who slept poorly, had been up on the hill toward Whateley's, and had dashed back in terror after one look at the place, and at the pasturage where Mr. Bishop's cows had been left out all night.

"Yes, Mis' Corey," came Sally's tremulous voice over the party wire, "Cha'ncey he just come back a-postin', and couldn't haff talk fer bein' scairt! He says Ol' Whateley's haouse is all blowed up, with the timbers scattered raound like they'd ben dynamite inside; only the bottom floor ain't through, but is all covered with a kind o' tar-like stuff that smells awful an' drips daown offen the aidges onto the graoun' whar the side timbers is blowed away. An' they's awful kinder marks in the yard, tew—great raound marks bigger raound than a hogshead, an' all sticky with stuff like is on the blowed-up haouse. Cha'ncey he says they leads off into the medders, whar a great swath wider'n a barn is matted daown, an' all the stun walls tumbled every whichway wherever it goes.

"An' he says, says he, Mis' Corey, as haow he sot to look fer Seth's caows, frighted ez he was; an' faound 'em in the upper pasture nigh the Devil's Hop Yard in an awful shape. Haff on 'em's clean gone, an' nigh haff o' them that's left is sucked most dry o' blood, with sores on 'em like they's ben on Whateley's cattle ever senct Lavinny's black brat was born. Seth he's gone aout naow to look at 'em, though I'll vaow he wun't keer ter git very nigh Wizard Whateley's! Cha'ncey didn't look keerful ter see whar the big matted-daown swath led arter it leff the pasturage, but he says he thinks it p'inted towards the glen rud to the village.

"I tell ye, Mis' Corey, they's suthin' abroad as hadn't orter be abroad, an' I for one think that black Wilbur Whateley, as come to the bad eend he desarved, is at the bottom of the breedin' of it. He wa'n't all human hisself, I allus says to everybody; an' I think he an' Ol' Whateley must a raised suthin' in that there nailed-up haouse as ain't even so human as he was. They's allus ben unseen things araound Dunwich—livin' things—as ain't human an' ain't good fer human folks.

"The graoun' was a-talkin' lass night, an' towards mornin' Cha'ncey he heerd the whippoorwills so laoud in Col' Spring Glen he couldn't sleep nun. Then he thought he heerd another faint-like saound over towards Wizard Whateley's—a kinder rippin' or tearin' o' wood, like some big box er crate was bein' opened fur off. What with this an' that, he didn't git to sleep at all till sunup, an' no sooner was he up this mornin', but he's got to go over to Whateley's an' see what's the matter. He see enough, I tell ye, Mis' Corey! This dun't mean no good, an' I think as all the menfolks ought to git up a party an' do suthin'. I know suthin' awful's abaout, an' feel my time is nigh, though only Gawd knows jest what it is.

"Did your Luther take accaount o' whar them big tracks led tew? No? Wal, Mis' Corey, ef they was on the glen rud this side o' the glen, an' ain't got to your haouse yet, I calc'late they must go into the glen itself. They would do that. I allus says Col' Spring Glen ain't no healthy nor decent place. The whippoorwills an' fireflies there never did act like they was creaters o' Gawd, an' they's them as says ye kin hear strange things a-rushin' an' a-talkin' in the air daown thar ef ye stand in the right place, atween the rock falls an' Bear's Den."

By that noon fully three-quarters of the men and boys of Dunwich were trooping over the roads and meadows between the new-made Whateley ruins and Cold Spring Glen; examining in horror the vast, monstrous prints, the maimed Bishop cattle, the strange, noisome wreck of the farmhouse, and the bruised, matted vegetation of the fields and roadsides. Whatever had burst loose upon the world had assuredly gone down into the great sinister ravine; for all the trees on the banks were bent and broken, and a great avenue had been gouged in the precipice-hanging underbrush. It was as though a house, launched by an avalanche, had slid down through the tangled growths of the almost vertical slope. From below no sound came, but only a distant, undefinable foetor; and it is not to be wondered at that the men preferred to stay on the edge and argue, rather than descend and beard the unknown Cyclopean horror in its lair. Three dogs that were with the party had barked furiously at first, but seemed cowed and reluctant when near the glen. Someone telephoned the news to the *Aylesbury Transcript*; but the editor, accustomed to wild tales from Dunwich, did no more than concoct a humorous paragraph about it; an item soon afterward reproduced by the Associated Press.

That night everyone went home, and every house and barn was barricaded as stoutly as possible. Needless to say, no cattle were allowed to remain in open pasturage. About two in the morning a frightful stench and the savage barking of the dogs awakened the household at Elmer Frye's, on the eastern edge of Cold Spring Glen, and all agreed that they could hear a sort of muffled swishing or lapping sound from somewhere outside. Mrs. Frye proposed telephoning the neighbours, and Elmer was about to agree when the noise of splintering wood burst in upon their deliberations. It came, apparently, from the barn; and was quickly followed by a hideous screaming and stamping amongst the cattle. The dogs slavered and crouched close to the feet of the fear-numbed family. Frye lit a lantern through force of habit, but knew it would be death to go out into that black farmyard. The children and the womenfolk whimpered, kept from screaming by some obscure, vestigial instinct of defence which told them their lives depended on silence. At last the noise of the cattle subsided to a pitiful moaning, and a great snapping, crashing, and crackling ensued. The Fryes, huddled together in the sitting-room, did not dare to move until the last echoes died away far down in Cold Spring Glen. Then, amidst the dismal moans from the stable and the daemoniac piping of late whippoorwills in the glen, Selina Frye tottered to the telephone and spread what news she could of the second phase of the horror.

The next day all the countryside was in a panic; and cowed, uncommunicative groups came and went where the fiendish thing had occurred. Two titan swaths of destruction stretched from the glen to the Frye farmyard, monstrous prints covered the bare patches of ground, and one side of the old red barn had completely caved in. Of the cattle, only about a quarter could be found and identified. Some of these were in curious fragments, and all that survived had to be shot. Earl Sawyer suggested that help be asked from Aylesbury or Arkham, but others maintained it would be of no use. Old Zebulon Whateley, of a branch that hovered about half way between soundness and decadence, made darkly wild suggestions about rites that ought to be practiced on the hilltops. He came of a line where tradition ran strong, and his memories of chantings in the great stone circles were not altogether connected with Wilbur and his grandfather.

Darkness fell upon a stricken countryside too passive to organise for real defence. In a few cases closely related families would band together and watch in the gloom under one roof; but in general there was only a repetition of the barricading of the night before, and a futile, ineffective gesture of loading muskets and setting pitchforks handily about. Nothing, however, occurred except some hill noises; and when the day came there were many who hoped that the new horror had gone as swiftly as it had come. There were even bold souls who proposed an offensive expedition down in the glen, though they did not venture to set an actual example to the still reluctant majority.

When night came again the barricading was repeated, though there was less huddling together of families. In the morning both the Frye and the Seth Bishop households reported excitement among the dogs and vague sounds and stenches from afar, while early explorers noted with horror a fresh set of the monstrous tracks in the road skirting Sentinel Hill. As before, the sides of the road shewed a bruising indicative of the blasphemously stupendous bulk of the horror; whilst the conformation of the tracks seemed to argue a passage in two directions, as if the moving mountain had come from Cold Spring Glen and returned to it along the same path. At the base of the hill a thirty-foot swath of crushed shrubbery and saplings led steeply upward, and the seekers gasped when they saw that even the most perpendicular places did not deflect the inexorable trail. Whatever the horror was, it could scale a sheer stony cliff of almost complete verticality; and as the investigators climbed around to the hill's summit by safer routes they saw that the trail ended—or rather, reversed—there.

It was here that the Whateleys used to build their hellish fires and chant their hellish rituals by the table-like stone on May-Eve and Hallowmass. Now that very stone formed the centre of a vast space thrashed around by the mountainous horror, whilst upon its slightly concave surface was a thick and foetid deposit of the same tarry stickiness observed on the floor of the ruined Whateley farmhouse when the horror escaped. Men looked at one another and muttered. Then they looked down the hill. Apparently the horror had descended by a route much the same as that of its ascent. To speculate was futile. Reason, logic, and normal ideas of motivation stood confounded. Only old Zebulon, who was not with the group, could have done justice to the situation or suggested a plausible explanation.

Thursday night began much like the others, but it ended less happily. The whippoorwills in the glen had screamed with such unusual persistence that many could not sleep, and about 3 a.m. all the party telephones rang tremulously. Those who took down their receivers heard a fright-mad voice shriek out, "Help, oh, my Gawd! ..." and some thought a crashing sound followed the breaking off of the exclamation. There was nothing more. No one dared do anything, and no one knew till morning whence the call came. Then those who had heard it called everyone on the line, and found that only the Fryes did not reply. The truth appeared an hour later, when a hastily assembled group of armed men trudged out to the Frye place at the head of the glen. It was horrible, yet hardly a surprise. There were more swaths and monstrous prints, but there was no longer any house. It had caved in like an egg-shell, and amongst the ruins nothing living or dead could be discovered. Only a stench and a tarry stickiness. The Elmer Fryes had been erased from Dunwich.

VIII.

In the meantime a quieter yet even more spiritually poignant phase of the horror had been blackly unwinding itself behind the closed door of a shelf-lined room in Arkham. The curious manuscript record or diary of Wilbur Whateley, delivered to Miskatonic University for translation, had caused much worry and bafflement among the experts in languages both ancient and modern; its very alphabet, notwithstanding a general resemblance to the heavily shaded Arabic used in Mesopotamia, being absolutely unknown to any available authority. The final conclusion of the linguists was that the text represented an artificial alphabet, giving the effect of a cipher; though none of the usual methods of cryptographic solution seemed to furnish any clue, even when applied on the basis of every tongue the writer might conceivably have used. The ancient books taken from Whateley's quarters, while absorbingly interesting and in several cases promising to open up new and terrible lines of research among philosophers and men of science, were of no assistance whatever in this matter. One of them, a heavy tome with an iron clasp, was in another unknown alphabet—this one of a very different cast, and resembling Sanscrit more than anything else. The old ledger was at length given wholly into the charge of Dr. Armitage, both because of his peculiar interest in the Whateley matter, and because of his wide linguistic learning and skill in the mystical formulae of antiquity and the Middle Ages.

Armitage had an idea that the alphabet might be something esoterically used by certain forbidden cults which have come down from old times, and which have inherited many forms and traditions from the wizards of the Saracenic world. That question, however, he did not deem vital; since it would be unnecessary to know the origin of the symbols if, as he suspected, they were used as a cipher in a modern language. It was his belief that, considering the great amount of text involved, the writer would scarcely have wished the trouble of using another speech than his own, save perhaps in certain special formulae and incantations. Accordingly he attacked the manuscript with the preliminary assumption that the bulk of it was in English.

Dr. Armitage knew, from the repeated failures of his colleagues, that the riddle was a deep and complex one; and that no simple mode of solution could merit even a trial. All through late August he fortified himself with the massed lore of cryptography; drawing upon the fullest resources of his own library, and wading night after night amidst the arcana of Trithemius' "Poligraphia", Giambattista Porta's "De Furtivis Literarum Notis", De Vigenère's "Traité des Chiffres", Falconer's "Cryptomenysis Patefacta", Davys' and Thicknesse's eighteenth-century treatises, and such fairly modern authorities as Blair, von Marten, and Klüber's "Kryptographik". He interspersed his study of the books with attacks on the manuscript itself, and in time became convinced that he had to deal with one of those subtlest and most ingenious of cryptograms, in which many separate lists of corresponding letters are arranged like the multiplication table, and the message built up with arbitrary key-words known only to the initiated. The older authorities seemed rather more helpful than the newer ones, and Armitage concluded that the code of the manuscript was one of great antiquity, no doubt handed down through a long line of mystical experimenters. Several times he seemed near daylight, only to be set back by some unforeseen obstacle. Then, as September approached, the clouds began to clear. Certain letters, as used in certain parts of the manuscript, emerged definitely and unmistakably; and it became obvious that the text was indeed in English.

On the evening of September 2nd the last major barrier gave way, and Dr. Armitage read for the first time a continuous passage of Wilbur Whateley's annals. It was in truth a diary, as all had thought; and it was couched in a style clearly shewing the mixed occult erudition and general illiteracy of the strange being who wrote it. Almost the first long passage that Armitage deciphered, an entry dated November 26, 1916, proved highly startling and disquieting. It was written, he remembered, by a child of three and a half who looked like a lad of twelve or thirteen.

> "Today learned the Aklo for the Sabaoth," it ran, "which did not like, it being answerable from the hill and not from the air. That upstairs more ahead of me than I had thought it would be, and is not like to have much earth brain. Shot Elam Hutchins's collie Jack when he went to bite me, and Elam says he would kill me if he dast. I guess he won't. Grandfather kept me saying the Dho formula last night, and I think I saw the inner city at the 2 magnetic poles. I shall go to those poles when the earth is cleared off, if I can't break through with the Dho-Hna formula when I commit it. They from the air told me at Sabbat that it will be years before I can clear off the earth, and I guess grandfather will be dead then, so I shall have to learn all the angles of the planes and all the formulas between the Yr and the Nhhngr. They from outside will help, but they cannot take body without human blood. That upstairs looks it will have the right cast. I can see it a little when I make the Voorish sign or blow the

powder of Ibn Ghazi at it, and it is near like them at May-Eve on the Hill. The other face may wear off some. I wonder how I shall look when the earth is cleared and there are no earth beings on it. He that came with the Aklo Sabaoth said I may be transfigured, there being much of outside to work on."

Morning found Dr. Armitage in a cold sweat of terror and a frenzy of wakeful concentration. He had not left the manuscript all night, but sat at his table under the electric light turning page after page with shaking hands as fast as he could decipher the cryptic text. He had nervously telephoned his wife he would not be home, and when she brought him a breakfast from the house he could scarcely dispose of a mouthful. All that day he read on, now and then halted maddeningly as a reapplication of the complex key became necessary. Lunch and dinner were brought him, but he ate only the smallest fraction of either. Toward the middle of the next night he drowsed off in his chair, but soon woke out of a tangle of nightmares almost as hideous as the truths and menaces to man's existence that he had uncovered.

On the morning of September 4th Professor Rice and Dr. Morgan insisted on seeing him for a while, and departed trembling and ashen-grey. That evening he went to bed, but slept only fitfully. Wednesday—the next day—he was back at the manuscript, and began to take copious notes both from the current sections and from those he had already deciphered. In the small hours of that night he slept a little in an easy-chair in his office, but was at the manuscript again before dawn. Some time before noon his physician, Dr. Hartwell, called to see him and insisted that he cease work. He refused; intimating that it was of the most vital importance for him to complete the reading of the diary, and promising an explanation in due course of time.

That evening, just as twilight fell, he finished his terrible perusal and sank back exhausted. His wife, bringing his dinner, found him in a half-comatose state; but he was conscious enough to warn her off with a sharp cry when he saw her eyes wander toward the notes he had taken. Weakly rising, he gathered up the scribbled papers and sealed them all in a great envelope, which he immediately placed in his inside coat pocket. He had sufficient strength to get home, but was so clearly in need of medical aid that Dr. Hartwell was summoned at once. As the doctor put him to bed he could only mutter over and over again, "*But what, in God's name, can we do?*"

Dr. Armitage slept, but was partly delirious the next day. He made no explanations to Hartwell, but in his calmer moments spoke of the imperative need of a long conference with Rice and Morgan. His wilder wanderings were very startling indeed, including frantic appeals that something in a boarded-up farmhouse be destroyed, and fantastic references to some plan for the extirpation of the entire human race and all animal and vegetable life from the earth by some terrible elder race of beings from another dimension. He would shout that the world was in danger, since the Elder Things wished to strip it and drag it away from the solar system and cosmos of matter into some other plane or phase of entity from which it had once fallen, vigintillions of aeons ago. At other times he would call for the dreaded *Necronomicon* and the *Daemonolatreia* of Remigius, in which he seemed hopeful of finding some formula to check the peril he conjured up.

"Stop them, stop them!" he would shout. "Those Whateleys meant to let them in, and the worst of all is left! Tell Rice and Morgan we must do something—it's a blind business, but I know how to make the powder.... It hasn't been fed since the second of August, when Wilbur came here to his death, and at that rate ..."

But Armitage had a sound physique despite his seventy-three years, and slept off his disorder that night without developing any real fever. He woke late Friday, clear of head, though sober with a gnawing fear and tremendous sense of responsibility. Saturday afternoon he felt able to go over to the library and summon Rice and Morgan for a conference, and the rest of that day and evening the three men tortured their brains in the wildest speculation and the most desperate debate. Strange and terrible books were drawn voluminously from the stack shelves and from secure places of storage; and diagrams and formulae were copied with feverish haste and in bewildering abundance. Of scepticism there was none. All three had seen the body of Wilbur Whateley as it lay on the floor in a room of that very building, and after that not one of them could feel even slightly inclined to treat the diary as a madman's raving.

Opinions were divided as to notifying the Massachusetts State Police, and the negative finally won. There were things involved which simply could not be believed by those who had not seen a sample, as indeed was made clear during certain subsequent investigations. Late at night the conference disbanded without having developed a definite plan, but all day Sunday Armitage was busy comparing formulae and mixing chemicals obtained from the college laboratory. The more he reflected on the hellish diary, the more he was inclined to doubt the efficacy of any material agent in stamping out the entity which Wilbur Whateley had left behind him—the earth-threatening entity which, unknown to him, was to burst forth in a few hours and become the memorable Dunwich horror.

Monday was a repetition of Sunday with Dr. Armitage, for the task in hand required an infinity of research and experiment. Further consultations of the monstrous diary brought about various changes of plan, and he knew that even in the end a large amount of uncertainty must remain. By Tuesday he had a definite line of action mapped out, and believed he would try a trip to Dunwich within a week. Then, on Wednesday, the great shock came. Tucked obscurely away in a corner of the *Arkham Advertiser* was a facetious little item from the Associated Press, telling what a record-breaking monster the bootleg whiskey of Dunwich had raised up. Armitage, half stunned, could only telephone for Rice and Morgan. Far into the night they discussed, and the next day was a whirlwind of preparation on the part of them all. Armitage knew he would be meddling with terrible powers, yet saw that there was no other way to annul the deeper and more malign meddling which others had done before him.

IX.

Friday morning Armitage, Rice, and Morgan set out by motor for Dunwich, arriving at the village about one in the afternoon. The day was pleasant, but even in the brightest sunlight a kind of quiet dread and portent seemed to hover about the strangely domed hills and the deep, shadowy ravines of the stricken region. Now and then on some mountaintop a gaunt circle of stones could be glimpsed against the sky. From the air of hushed fright at Osborn's store they knew something hideous had happened, and soon learned of the annihilation of the Elmer Frye house and family. Throughout that afternoon they rode around Dunwich; questioning the natives concerning all that had occurred, and seeing for themselves with rising pangs of horror the drear Frye ruins with their lingering traces of the tarry stickiness, the blasphemous tracks in the Frye yard, the wounded Seth Bishop cattle, and the enormous swaths of disturbed vegetation in various places. The trail up and down Sentinel Hill seemed to Armitage of almost cataclysmic significance, and he looked long at the sinister altar-like stone on the summit.

At length the visitors, apprised of a party of State Police which had come from Aylesbury that morning in response to the first telephone reports of the Frye tragedy, decided to seek out the officers and compare notes as far as practicable. This, however, they found more easily planned than performed; since no sign of the party could be found in any direction. There had been five of them in a car, but now the car stood empty near the ruins in the Frye yard. The natives, all of whom had talked with the policemen, seemed at first as perplexed as Armitage and his companions. Then old Sam Hutchins thought of something and turned pale, nudging Fred Farr and pointing to the dank, deep hollow that yawned close by.

"Gawd," he gasped, "I telled 'em not ter go daown into the glen, an' I never thought nobody'd dew it with them tracks an' that smell an' the whippoorwills a-screechin' daown thar in the dark o' noonday. . . ."

A cold shudder ran through natives and visitors alike, and every ear seemed strained in a kind of instinctive, unconscious listening. Armitage, now that he had actually come upon the horror and its monstrous work, trembled with the responsibility he felt to be his. Night would soon fall, and it was then that the mountainous blasphemy lumbered upon its eldritch course. *Negotium perambulans in tenebris. . . .* The old librarian rehearsed the formulae he had memorised, and clutched the paper containing the alternative ones he had not memorised. He saw that his electric flashlight was in working order. Rice, beside him, took from a valise a metal sprayer of the sort used in combating insects; whilst Morgan uncased the big-game rifle on which he relied despite his colleague's warnings that no material weapon would be of help.

Armitage, having read the hideous diary, knew painfully well what kind of a manifestation to expect; but he did not add to the fright of the Dunwich people by giving any hints or clues. He hoped that it might be conquered without any revelation to the world of the monstrous thing it had escaped. As the shadows gathered, the natives commenced to disperse homeward, anxious to bar themselves indoors despite the present evidence that all human locks and bolts were useless before a force that could bend trees and crush houses when it chose. They shook their heads at the visitors' plan to stand guard at the Frye ruins near the glen; and as they left, had little expectancy of ever seeing the watchers again.

There were rumblings under the hills that night, and the whippoorwills piped threateningly. Once in a while a wind, sweeping up out of Cold Spring Glen, would bring a touch of ineffable foetor to the heavy night air; such a foetor as all three of the watchers had smelled once before, when they stood above a dying thing that had passed for fifteen years and a half as a human being. But the looked-for terror did not appear. Whatever was down there in the glen was biding its time, and Armitage told his colleagues it would be suicidal to try to attack it in the dark.

Morning came wanly, and the night-sounds ceased. It was a grey, bleak day, with now and then a drizzle of rain; and heavier and heavier clouds seemed to be piling themselves up beyond the hills to the northwest. The men from Arkham were undecided what to do. Seeking shelter from the increasing rainfall beneath one of the few undestroyed Frye outbuildings, they debated the wisdom of waiting, or of taking the aggressive and going down into the glen in quest of their nameless, monstrous quarry. The downpour waxed in heaviness, and distant peals of thunder sounded from far horizons. Sheet lighting shimmered, and then a forky bolt flashed near at hand, as if descending into the accursed glen itself. The sky grew very dark, and the watchers hoped that the storm would prove a short, sharp one followed by clear weather.

It was still gruesomely dark when, not much over an hour later, a confused babel of voices sounded down the road. Another moment brought to view a frightened group of more than a dozen men, running, shouting, and even whimpering hysterically. Someone in the lead began sobbing out words, and the Arkham men started violently when those words developed a coherent form.

"Oh, my Gawd, my Gawd," the voice choked out. "It's a-goin' agin, *an' this time by day!* It's aout—it's aout an' a-movin' this very minute, an' only the Lord knows when it'll be on us all!"

The speaker panted into silence, but another took up his message.

"Nigh on a haour ago Zeb Whateley here heerd the 'phone a-ringin', an' it was Mis' Corey, George's wife, that lives daown by the junction. She says the hired boy Luther was aout drivin' in the caows from the storm arter the big bolt, when he see all the trees a-bendin' at the maouth o' the glen—opposite side ter this—an' smelt the same awful smell like he smelt when he faound the big tracks las' Monday mornin'. An' she says he says they was a swishin', lappin' saound, more nor what the bendin' trees an' bushes could make, an' all on a suddent the trees along the rud begun ter git pushed one side, an' they was a awful stompin' an' splashin' in the mud. But mind ye, Luther he didn't see nothin' at all, only jest the bendin' trees an' underbrush.

"Then fur ahead where Bishop's Brook goes under the rud he heerd a awful creakin' an' strainin' on the bridge, an' says he could tell the saound o' wood a-startin' to crack an' split. An' all the whiles he never see a thing, only them trees an' bushes a-bendin'. An' when the swishin' saound got very fur off—on the rud towards Wizard Whateley's an' Sentinel Hill—Luther he had the guts ter step up whar he'd heerd it fust an' look at the graound. It was all mud an' water, an' the sky was dark, an' the rain was wipin' aout all tracks abaout as fast as could be; but beginnin' at the glen maouth, whar the trees had moved, they was still some o' them awful prints big as bar'ls like he seen Monday."

At this point the first excited speaker interrupted.

"But *that* ain't the trouble naow—that was only the start. Zeb here was callin' folks up an' everybody was a-listenin' in when a call from Seth Bishop's cut in. His haousekeeper Sally was carryin' on fit ter kill—she'd jest seed the trees a-bendin' beside the rud, an' says they was a kind o' mushy saound, like a elephant puffin' an' treadin', a-headin' fer the haouse. Then she up an' spoke suddent of a fearful smell, an' says her boy Cha'ncey was a-screamin' as haow it was jest like what he smelt up to the Whateley rewins Monday mornin'. An' the dogs was all barkin' an' whinin' awful.

"An' then she let aout a turrible yell, an' says the shed daown the rud hed jest caved in like the storm hed blowed it over, only the wind wa'n't strong enough to dew that. Everybody was a-listenin', an' ye could hear lots o' folks on the wire a-gaspin'. All to onct Sally she yelled agin, an' says the front yard picket fence hed jest crumpled up, though they wa'n't no sign o' what done it. Then everybody on the line could hear Cha'ncey an' ol' Seth Bishop a-yellin' tew, an' Sally was shriekin' aout that suthin' heavy hed struck the haouse—not lightnin' nor nothin', but suthin' heavy agin' the front, that kep' a-launchin' itself agin an' agin, though ye couldn't see nothin' aout the front winders. An' then … an' then …"

Lines of fright deepened on every face; and Armitage, shaken as he was, had barely poise enough to prompt the speaker.

"An' then … Sally she yelled aout, 'O help, the haouse is a-cavin' in' … an' on the wire we could hear a turrible crashin', an' a hull flock o' screamin' … jest like when Elmer Frye's place was took, only wuss…."

The man paused, and another of the crowd spoke.

"That's all—not a saound nor squeak over the 'phone arter that. Jest still-like. We that heerd it got aout Fords an' wagons an' raounded up as many able-bodied menfolks as we could git, at Corey's place, an' come up here ter see what yew thought best ter dew. Not but what I think it's the Lord's jedgment fer our iniquities, that no mortal kin ever set aside."

Armitage saw that the time for positive action had come, and spoke decisively to the faltering group of frightened rustics.

"We must follow it, boys." He made his voice as reassuring as possible. "I believe there's a chance of putting it out of business.

You men know that those Whateleys were wizards—well, this thing is a thing of wizardry, and must be put down by the same means. I've seen Wilbur Whateley's diary and read some of the strange old books he used to read; and I think I know the right kind of a spell to recite to make the thing fade away. Of course, one can't be sure, but we can always take a chance. It's invisible—I knew it would be—but there's a powder in this long-distance sprayer that might make it shew up for a second. Later on we'll try it. It's a frightful thing to have alive, but it isn't as bad as what Wilbur would have let in if he'd lived longer. You'll never know what the world has escaped. Now we've only this one thing to fight, and it can't multiply. It can, though, do a lot of harm; so we mustn't hesitate to rid the community of it.

"We must follow it—and the way to begin is to go to the place that has just been wrecked. Let somebody lead the way—I don't know your roads very well, but I've an idea there might be a shorter cut across lots. How about it?"

The men shuffled about a moment, and then Earl Sawyer spoke softly, pointing with a grimy finger through the steadily lessening rain.

"I guess ye kin git to Seth Bishop's quickest by cuttin' acrost the lower medder here, wadin' the brook at the low place, an' climbin' through Carrier's mowin' an' the timber-lot beyont. That comes aout on the upper rud mighty nigh Seth's—a leetle t'other side."

Armitage, with Rice and Morgan, started to walk in the direction indicated; and most of the natives followed slowly. The sky was growing lighter, and there were signs that the storm had worn itself away. When Armitage inadvertently took a wrong direction, Joe Osborn warned him and walked ahead to shew the right one. Courage and confidence were mounting; though the twilight of the almost perpendicular wooded hill which lay toward the end of their short cut, and among whose fantastic ancient trees they had to scramble as if up a ladder, put these qualities to a severe test.

At length they emerged on a muddy road to find the sun coming out. They were a little beyond the Seth Bishop place, but bent trees and hideously unmistakable tracks shewed what had passed by. Only a few moments were consumed in surveying the ruins just around the bend. It was the Frye incident all over again, and nothing dead or living was found in either of the collapsed shells which had been the Bishop house and barn. No one cared to remain there amidst the stench and the tarry stickiness, but all turned instinctively to the line of horrible prints leading on toward the wrecked Whateley farmhouse and the altar-crowned slopes of Sentinel Hill.

As the men passed the site of Wilbur Whateley's abode they shuddered visibly, and seemed again to mix hesitancy with their zeal. It was no joke tracking down something as big as a house that one could not see, but that had all the vicious malevolence of a daemon. Opposite the base of Sentinel Hill the tracks left the road, and there was a fresh bending and matting visible along the broad swath marking the monster's former route to and from the summit.

Armitage produced a pocket telescope of considerable power and scanned the steep green side of the hill. Then he handed the instrument to Morgan, whose sight was keener. After a moment of gazing Morgan cried out sharply, passing the glass to Earl Sawyer and indicating a certain spot on the slope with his finger. Sawyer, as clumsy as most non-users of optical devices are, fumbled a while; but eventually focussed the lenses with Armitage's aid. When he did so his cry was less restrained than Morgan's had been.

"Gawd almighty, the grass an' bushes is a-movin'! It's a-goin' up—slow-like—creepin' up ter the top this minute, heaven only knows what fur!"

Then the germ of panic seemed to spread among the seekers. It was one thing to chase the nameless entity, but quite another to find it. Spells might be all right—but suppose they weren't? Voices began questioning Armitage about what he knew of the thing, and no reply seemed quite to satisfy. Everyone seemed to feel himself in close proximity to phases of Nature and of being utterly forbidden, and wholly outside the sane experience of mankind.

X.

In the end the three men from Arkham—old, white-bearded Dr. Armitage, stocky, iron-grey Professor Rice, and lean, youngish Dr. Morgan—ascended the mountain alone. After much patient instruction regarding its focussing and use, they left the telescope with the frightened group that remained in the road; and as they climbed they were watched closely by those among whom the glass was passed around. It was hard going, and Armitage had to be helped more than once. High above the toiling group the great swath trembled as its hellish maker re-passed with snail-like deliberateness. Then it was obvious that the pursuers were gaining.

Curtis Whateley—of the undecayed branch—was holding the telescope when the Arkham party detoured radically from the swath. He told the crowd that the men were evidently trying to get to a subordinate peak which overlooked the swath at a point considerably ahead of where the shrubbery was now bending. This, indeed, proved to be true; and the party were seen to gain the minor elevation only a short time after the invisible blasphemy had passed it.

Then Wesley Corey, who had taken the glass, cried out that Armitage was adjusting the sprayer which Rice held, and that something must be about to happen. The crowd stirred uneasily, recalling that this sprayer was expected to give the unseen horror a moment of visibility. Two or three men shut their eyes, but Curtis Whateley snatched back the telescope and strained his vision to the utmost. He saw that Rice, from the party's point of vantage above and behind the entity, had an excellent chance of spreading the potent powder with marvellous effect.

Those without the telescope saw only an instant's flash of grey cloud—a cloud about the size of a moderately large building—near the top of the mountain. Curtis, who had held the instrument, dropped it with a piercing shriek into the ankle-deep mud of the road. He reeled, and would have crumpled to the ground had not two or three others seized and steadied him. All he could do was moan half-inaudibly,

"Oh, oh, great Gawd … *that* … *that* …"

There was a pandemonium of questioning, and only Henry Wheeler thought to rescue the fallen telescope and wipe it clean of mud. Curtis was past all coherence, and even isolated replies were almost too much for him.

"Bigger'n a barn … all made o' squirmin' ropes … hull thing sort o' shaped like a hen's egg bigger'n anything, with dozens o' legs like hogsheads that haff shut up when they step … nothin' solid abaout it—all like jelly, an' made o' sep'rit wrigglin' ropes pushed clost together … great bulgin' eyes all over it … ten or twenty maouths or trunks a-stickin' aout all along the sides, big as stovepipes, an' all a-tossin' an' openin' an' shuttin' … all grey, with kinder blue or purple rings … *an' Gawd in heaven—that haff face on top! …*"

This final memory, whatever it was, proved too much for poor Curtis; and he collapsed completely before he could say more. Fred Farr and Will Hutchins carried him to the roadside and laid him on the damp grass. Henry Wheeler, trembling, turned the rescued telescope on the mountain to see what he might. Through the lenses were discernible three tiny figures, apparently running toward the summit as fast as the steep incline allowed. Only these—nothing more. Then everyone noticed a strangely unseasonable noise in the deep valley behind, and even in the underbrush of Sentinel Hill itself. It was the piping of unnumbered whippoorwills, and in their shrill chorus there seemed to lurk a note of tense and evil expectancy.

Earl Sawyer now took the telescope and reported the three figures as standing on the topmost ridge, virtually level with the altar-stone but at a considerable distance from it. One figure, he said, seemed to be raising its hands above its head at rhythmic intervals; and as Sawyer mentioned the circumstance the crowd seemed to hear a faint, half-musical sound from the distance, as if a loud chant were accompanying the gestures. The weird silhouette on that remote peak must have been a spectacle of infinite grotesqueness and impressiveness, but no observer was in a mood for aesthetic appreciation. "I guess he's sayin' the spell," whispered Wheeler as he snatched back the telescope. The whippoorwills were piping wildly, and in a singularly curious irregular rhythm quite unlike that of the visible ritual.

Suddenly the sunshine seemed to lessen without the intervention of any discernible cloud. It was a very peculiar phenomenon, and was plainly marked by all. A rumbling sound seemed brewing beneath the hills, mixed strangely with a concordant rumbling which clearly came from the sky. Lightning flashed aloft, and the wondering crowd looked in vain for the portents of storm. The chanting of the men from Arkham now became unmistakable, and Wheeler saw through the glass that they were all raising their arms in the rhythmic incantation. From some farmhouse far away came the frantic barking of dogs.

The change in the quality of the daylight increased, and the crowd gazed about the horizon in wonder. A purplish darkness, born of nothing more than a spectral deepening of the sky's blue, pressed down upon the rumbling hills. Then the lightning flashed again, somewhat brighter than before, and the crowd fancied that it had shewed a certain mistiness around the altar-stone on the distant height. No one, however, had been using the telescope at that instant. The whippoorwills continued their irregular pulsation, and the men of Dunwich braced themselves tensely against some imponderable menace with which the atmosphere seemed surcharged.

Without warning came those deep, cracked, raucous vocal sounds which will never leave the memory of the stricken group who heard them. Not from any human throat were they born, for the organs of man can yield no such acoustic perversions. Rather would one have said they came from the pit itself, had not their source been so unmistakably the altar-stone on the peak. It is almost erroneous to call them *sounds* at all, since so much of their ghastly, infra-bass timbre spoke to dim seats of consciousness and terror far subtler than the ear; yet one must do so, since their form was indisputably though vaguely that of half-articulate *words.* They were loud—loud as the rumblings and the thunder above which they echoed—yet did they come from no visible being. And because imagination might suggest a conjectural source in the world of non-visible beings, the huddled crowd at the mountain's base huddled still closer, and winced as if in expectation of a blow.

"*Ygnaiih ... ygnaiih ... thflthkh'ngha ... Yog-Sothoth ...*" rang the hideous croaking out of space. "*Y'bthnk ... h'ehye—n'grkdl'lh....*"

The speaking impulse seemed to falter here, as if some frightful psychic struggle were going on. Henry Wheeler strained his eye at the telescope, but saw only the three grotesquely silhouetted human figures on the peak, all moving their arms furiously in strange gestures as their incantation drew near its culmination. From what black wells of Acherontic fear or feeling, from what unplumbed gulfs of extra-cosmic consciousness or obscure, long-latent heredity, were those half-articulate thunder-croakings drawn? Presently they began to gather renewed force and coherence as they grew in stark, utter, ultimate frenzy.

"*Eh-ya-ya-ya-yahaah—e'yayayayaaaa ... ngh'aaaa ... ngh'aaaa* ... h'yuh ... h'yuh ... HELP! HELP! ... *ff—ff—ff*—FATHER! FATHER! YOG-SOTHOTH! ..."

But that was all. The pallid group in the road, still reeling at the *indisputably English* syllables that had poured thickly and thunderously down from the frantic vacancy beside that shocking altar-stone, were never to hear such syllables again. Instead, they jumped violently at the terrific report which seemed to rend the hills; the deafening, cataclysmic peal whose source, be it inner earth or sky, no hearer was ever able to place. A single lightning-bolt shot from the purple zenith to the altar-stone, and a great tidal wave of viewless force and indescribable stench swept down from the hill to all the countryside. Trees, grass, and underbrush were whipped into a fury; and the frightened crowd at the mountain's base, weakened by the lethal foetor that seemed about to asphyxiate them, were almost hurled off their feet. Dogs howled from the distance, green grass and foliage wilted to a curious, sickly yellow-grey, and over field and forest were scattered the bodies of dead whippoorwills.

The stench left quickly, but the vegetation never came right again. To this day there is something queer and unholy about the growths on and around that fearsome hill. Curtis Whateley was only just regaining consciousness when the Arkham men came slowly down the mountain in the beams of a sunlight once more brilliant and untainted. They were grave and quiet, and seemed shaken by memories and reflections even more terrible than those which had reduced the group of natives to a state of cowed quivering. In reply to a jumble of questions they only shook their heads and reaffirmed one vital fact.

"The thing has gone for ever," Armitage said. "It has been split up into what it was originally made of, and can never exist again. It was an impossibility in a normal world. Only the least fraction was really matter in any sense we know. It was like its father—and most of it has gone back to him in some vague realm or dimension outside our material universe; some vague abyss out of which only the most accursed rites of human blasphemy could ever have called him for a moment on the hills."

There was a brief silence, and in that pause the scattered senses of poor Curtis Whateley began to knit back into a sort of continuity; so that he put his hands to his head with a moan. Memory seemed to pick itself up where it had left off, and the horror of the sight that had prostrated him burst in upon him again.

"*Oh, oh, my Gawd, that haff face—that haff face on top of it ... that face with the red eyes an' crinkly albino hair, an' no chin, like the Whateleys.... It was a octopus, centipede, spider kind o' thing, but they was a haff-shaped man's face on top of it, an' it looked like Wizard Whateley's, only it was yards an' yards acrost....*"

He paused exhausted, as the whole group of natives stared in a bewilderment not quite crystallised into fresh terror. Only old Zebulon Whateley, who wanderingly remembered ancient things but who had been silent heretofore, spoke aloud.

"Fifteen year' gone," he rambled, "I heerd Ol' Whateley say as haow some day we'd hear a child o' Lavinny's a-callin' its father's name on the top o' Sentinel Hill...."

But Joe Osborn interrupted him to question the Arkham men anew.

"*What was it, anyhaow,* an' haowever did young Wizard Whateley call it aout o' the air it come from?"

Armitage chose his words very carefully.

"It was—well, it was mostly a kind of force that doesn't belong in our part of space; a kind of force that acts and grows and shapes itself by other laws than those of our sort of Nature. We have no business calling in such things from outside, and only very wicked people and very wicked cults ever try to. There was some of it in Wilbur Whateley himself—enough to make a devil and a precocious monster of him, and to make his passing out a pretty terrible sight. I'm going to burn his accursed diary, and if you men are wise you'll dynamite that altar-stone up there, and pull down all the rings of standing stones on the other hills. Things like that brought down the beings those Whateleys were so fond of—the beings they were going to let in tangibly to wipe out the human race and drag the earth off to some nameless place for some nameless purpose.

"But as to this thing we've just sent back—the Whateleys raised it for a terrible part in the doings that were to come. It grew fast and big from the same reason that Wilbur grew fast and big—but it beat him because it had a greater share of the *outsideness* in it. You needn't ask how Wilbur called it out of the air. He didn't call it out. *It was his twin brother, but it looked more like the father than he did.*"

THE WHISPERER IN DARKNESS

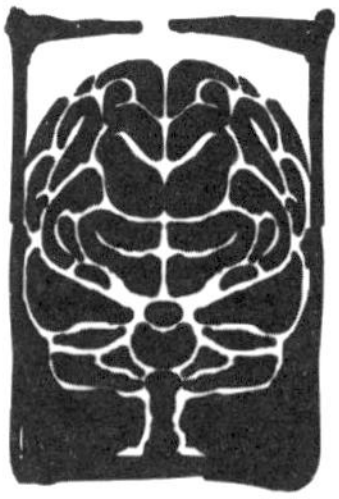

I.

Bear in mind closely that I did not see any actual visual horror at the end. To say that a mental shock was the cause of what I inferred—that last straw which sent me racing out of the lonely Akeley farmhouse and through the wild domed hills of Vermont in a commandeered motor at night—is to ignore the plainest facts of my final experience. Notwithstanding the deep extent to which I shared the information and speculations of Henry Akeley, the things I saw and heard, and the admitted vividness of the impression produced on me by these things, I cannot prove even now whether I was right or wrong in my hideous inference. For after all, Akeley's disappearance establishes nothing. People found nothing amiss in his house despite the bullet-marks on the outside and inside. It was just as though he had walked out casually for a ramble in the hills and failed to return. There was not even a sign that a guest had been there, or that those horrible cylinders and machines had been stored in the study. That he had mortally feared the crowded green hills and endless trickle of brooks among which he had been born and reared, means nothing at all, either; for thousands are subject to just such morbid fears. Eccentricity, moreover, could easily account for his strange acts and apprehensions toward the last.

The whole matter began, so far as I am concerned, with the historic and unprecedented Vermont floods of November 3, 1927. I was then, as now, an instructor of literature at Miskatonic University in Arkham, Massachusetts, and an enthusiastic amateur student of New England folklore. Shortly after the flood, amidst the varied reports of hardship, suffering, and organised relief which filled the press, there appeared certain odd stories of things found floating in some of the swollen rivers; so that many of my friends embarked on curious discussions and appealed to me to shed what light I could on the subject. I felt flattered at having my folklore study taken so seriously, and did what I could to belittle the wild, vague tales which seemed so clearly an outgrowth of old rustic superstitions. It amused me to find several persons of education who insisted that some stratum of obscure, distorted fact might underlie the rumours.

The tales thus brought to my notice came mostly through newspaper cuttings; though one yarn had an oral source and was repeated to a friend of mine in a letter from his mother in Hardwick, Vermont. The type of thing described was essentially the same in all cases, though there seemed to be three separate instances involved—one connected with the Winooski River near Montpelier, another attached to the West River in Windham County beyond Newfane, and a third centreing in the Passumpsic in Caledonia County above Lyndonville. Of course many of the stray items mentioned other instances, but on analysis they all seemed to boil down to these three. In each case country folk reported seeing one or more very bizarre and disturbing objects in the surging waters that poured down from the unfrequented hills, and there was a widespread tendency to connect these sights with a primitive, half-forgotten cycle of whispered legend which old people resurrected for the occasion.

What people thought they saw were organic shapes not quite like any they had ever seen before. Naturally, there were many human bodies washed along by the streams in that tragic period; but those who described these strange shapes felt quite sure that they were not human, despite some superficial resemblances in size and general outline. Nor, said the witnesses, could they have been any kind of animal known to Vermont. They were pinkish things about five feet long; with crustaceous bodies bearing vast pairs of dorsal fins or membraneous wings and several sets of articulated limbs, and with a sort of convoluted ellipsoid, covered with multitudes of very short antennae, where a head would ordinarily be. It was really remarkable how closely the reports from different sources tended to coincide; though the wonder was lessened by the fact that the old legends, shared at one time throughout the hill country, furnished a morbidly vivid picture which might well have coloured the imaginations of all the witnesses concerned. It was my conclusion that such witnesses—in every case naive and simple backwoods folk—had glimpsed the battered and bloated bodies of human beings or farm animals in the whirling currents; and had allowed the half-remembered folklore to invest these pitiful objects with fantastic attributes.

The ancient folklore, while cloudy, evasive, and largely forgotten by the present generation, was of a highly singular character, and obviously reflected the influence of still earlier Indian tales. I knew it well, though I had never been in Vermont, through the exceedingly rare monograph of Eli Davenport, which embraces material orally obtained prior to 1839 among the oldest people of the state. This material, moreover, closely coincided with tales which I had personally heard from elderly rustics in the mountains of New Hampshire. Briefly summarised, it hinted at a hidden race of monstrous beings which lurked somewhere among the remoter hills—in the deep woods of the highest peaks, and the dark valleys where streams trickle from unknown sources. These beings were seldom glimpsed, but evidences of their presence were reported by those who had ventured farther than usual up the slopes of certain mountains or into certain deep, steep-sided gorges that even the wolves shunned.

There were queer footprints or claw-prints in the mud of brook-margins and barren patches, and curious circles of stones, with the grass around them worn away, which did not seem to have been placed or entirely shaped by Nature. There were, too, certain caves of problematical depth in the sides of the hills; with mouths closed by boulders in a manner scarcely accidental, and with more than an average quota of the queer prints leading both toward and away from them—if indeed the direction of these prints could be justly estimated. And worst of all, there were the things which adventurous people had seen very rarely in the twilight of the remotest valleys and the dense perpendicular woods above the limits of normal hill-climbing.

It would have been less uncomfortable if the stray accounts of these things had not agreed so well. As it was, nearly all the rumours had several points in common; averring that the creatures were a sort of huge, light-red crab with many pairs of legs and with two great bat-like wings in the middle of the back. They sometimes walked on all their legs, and sometimes on the hindmost pair only, using the others to convey large objects of indeterminate nature. On one occasion they were spied in considerable numbers, a detachment of them wading along a shallow woodland watercourse three abreast in evidently disciplined formation. Once a specimen was seen flying—launching itself from the top of a bald, lonely hill at night and vanishing in the sky after its great flapping wings had been silhouetted an instant against the full moon.

These things seemed content, on the whole, to let mankind alone; though they were at times held responsible for the disappearance of venturesome individuals—especially persons who built houses too close to certain valleys or too high up on certain mountains. Many localities came to be known as inadvisable to settle in, the feeling persisting long after the cause was forgotten. People would look up at some of the neighbouring mountain-precipices with a shudder, even when not recalling how many settlers had been lost, and how many farmhouses burnt to ashes, on the lower slopes of those grim, green sentinels.

But while according to the earliest legends the creatures would appear to have harmed only those trespassing on their privacy; there were later accounts of their curiosity respecting men, and of their attempts to establish secret outposts in the human world. There were tales of the queer claw-prints seen around farmhouse windows in the morning, and of occasional disappearances in regions outside the obviously haunted areas. Tales, besides, of buzzing voices in imitation of human speech which made surprising offers to lone travellers on roads and cart-paths in the deep woods, and of children frightened out of their wits by things seen or heard where the primal forest pressed close upon their dooryards. In the final layer of legends—the layer just preceding the decline of superstition and the abandonment of close contact with the dreaded places—there are shocked references to hermits and remote farmers who at some period of life appeared to have undergone a repellent mental change, and who were shunned and whispered about as mortals who had sold themselves to the strange beings. In one of the northeastern counties it seemed to be a fashion about 1800 to accuse eccentric and unpopular recluses of being allies or representatives of the abhorred things.

As to what the things were—explanations naturally varied. The common name applied to them was "those ones", or "the old ones", though other terms had a local and transient use. Perhaps the bulk of the Puritan settlers set them down bluntly as familiars of the devil, and made them a basis of awed theological speculation. Those with Celtic legendry in their heritage—mainly the Scotch-Irish element of New Hampshire, and their kindred who had settled in Vermont on Governor Wentworth's colonial grants—linked them vaguely with the malign fairies and "little people" of the bogs and raths, and protected themselves with scraps of incantation handed down through many generations. But the Indians had the most fantastic theories of all. While different tribal legends differed, there was a marked consensus of belief in certain vital particulars; it being unanimously agreed that the creatures were not native to this earth.

The Pennacook myths, which were the most consistent and picturesque, taught that the Winged Ones came from the Great Bear in the sky, and had mines in our earthly hills whence they took a kind of stone they could not get on any other world. They did not live here, said the myths, but merely maintained outposts and flew back with vast cargoes of stone to their own stars in the north. They harmed only those earth-people who got too near them or spied upon them. Animals shunned them through instinctive hatred, not because of being hunted. They could not eat the things and animals of earth, but brought their own food from the stars. It was bad to get near them, and sometimes young hunters who went into their hills never came back. It was not good, either, to listen to what they whispered at night in the forest with voices like a bee's that tried to be like the voices of men. They knew the speech of all kinds of men—Pennacooks, Hurons, men of the Five Nations—but did not seem to have or need any speech of their own. They talked with their heads, which changed colour in different ways to mean different things.

All the legendry, of course, white and Indian alike, died down during the nineteenth century, except for occasional atavistical flareups. The ways of the Vermonters became settled; and once their habitual paths and dwellings were established according to a certain fixed plan, they remembered less and less what fears and avoidances had determined that plan, and even that there had been any fears or avoidances. Most people simply knew that certain hilly regions were considered as highly unhealthy, unprofitable, and generally unlucky to live in, and that the farther one kept from them the better off one usually was. In time the ruts of custom and economic interest became so deeply cut in approved places that there was no longer any reason for going outside them, and the haunted hills were left deserted by accident rather than by design. Save during infrequent local scares, only wonder-loving grandmothers and retrospective nonagenarians ever whispered of beings dwelling in those hills; and even such whisperers admitted that there was not much to fear from those things now that they were used to the presence of houses and settlements, and now that human beings let their chosen territory severely alone.

All this I had long known from my reading, and from certain folk-tales picked up in New Hampshire; hence when the flood-time rumours began to appear, I could easily guess what imaginative background had evolved them. I took great pains to explain this to my friends, and was correspondingly amused when several contentious souls continued to insist on a possible element of truth in the reports. Such persons tried to point out that the early legends had a significant persistence and uniformity, and that the virtually unexplored nature of the Vermont hills made it unwise to be dogmatic about what might or might not dwell among them; nor could they be silenced by my assurance that all the myths were of a well-known pattern common to most of mankind and determined by early phases of imaginative experience which always produced the same type of delusion.

It was of no use to demonstrate to such opponents that the Vermont myths differed but little in essence from those universal legends of natural personification which filled the ancient world with fauns and dryads and satyrs, suggested the *kallikanzari* of modern Greece, and gave to wild Wales and Ireland their dark hints of strange, small, and terrible hidden races of troglodytes and burrowers. No use, either, to point out the even more startlingly similar belief of the Nepalese hill tribes in the dreaded *Mi-Go* or "Abominable Snow-Men" who lurk hideously amidst the ice and rock pinnacles of the Himalayan summits. When I brought up this evidence, my opponents turned it against me by claiming that it must imply some actual historicity for the ancient tales; that it must argue the real existence of some queer elder earth-race, driven to hiding after the advent and dominance of mankind, which might very conceivably have survived in reduced numbers to relatively recent times—or even to the present.

The more I laughed at such theories, the more these stubborn friends asseverated them; adding that even without the heritage of legend the recent reports were too clear, consistent, detailed, and sanely prosaic in manner of telling, to be completely ignored. Two or three fanatical extremists went so far as to hint at possible meanings in the ancient Indian tales which gave the hidden beings a non-terrestrial origin; citing the extravagant books of Charles Fort with their claims that voyagers from other worlds and outer space have often visited the earth. Most of my foes, however, were merely romanticists who insisted on trying to transfer to real life the fantastic lore of lurking "little people" made popular by the magnificent horror-fiction of Arthur Machen.

II.

As was only natural under the circumstances, this piquant debating finally got into print in the form of letters to the *Arkham Advertiser*; some of which were copied in the press of those Vermont regions whence the flood-stories came. The *Rutland Herald* gave half a page of extracts from the letters on both sides, while the *Brattleboro Reformer* reprinted one of my long historical and mythological summaries in full, with some accompanying comments in "The Pendrifter's" thoughtful column which supported and applauded my sceptical conclusions. By the spring of 1928 I was almost a well-known figure in Vermont, notwithstanding the fact that I had never set foot in the state. Then came the challenging letters from Henry Akeley which impressed me so profoundly, and which took me for the first and last time to that fascinating realm of crowded green precipices and muttering forest streams.

Most of what I now know of Henry Wentworth Akeley was gathered by correspondence with his neighbours, and with his only son in California, after my experience in his lonely farmhouse. He was, I discovered, the last representative on his home soil of a long, locally distinguished line of jurists, administrators, and gentlemen-agriculturists. In him, however, the family mentality had veered away from practical affairs to pure scholarship; so that he had been a notable student of mathematics, astronomy, biology, anthropology, and folklore at the University of Vermont. I had never previously heard of him, and he did not give many autobiographical details in his communications; but from the first I saw he was a man of character, education, and intelligence, albeit a recluse with very little worldly sophistication.

Despite the incredible nature of what he claimed, I could not help at once taking Akeley more seriously than I had taken any of the other challengers of my views. For one thing, he was really close to the actual phenomena—visible and tangible—that he speculated so grotesquely about; and for another thing, he was amazingly willing to leave his conclusions in a tentative state like a true man of science. He had no personal preferences to advance, and was always guided by what he took to be solid evidence. Of course I began by considering him mistaken, but gave him credit for being intelligently mistaken; and at no time did I emulate some of his friends in attributing his ideas, and his fear of the lonely green hills, to insanity. I could see that there was a great deal to the man, and knew that what he reported must surely come from some strange circumstance deserving investigation, however little it might have to do with the fantastic causes he assigned. Later on I received from him certain material proofs which placed the matter on a somewhat different and bewilderingly bizarre basis.

I cannot do better than transcribe in full, so far as is possible, the long letter in which Akeley introduced himself, and which formed such an important landmark in my own intellectual history. It is no longer in my possession, but my memory holds almost every word of its portentous message; and again I affirm my confidence in the sanity of the man who wrote it. Here is the text—a text which reached me in the cramped, archaic-looking scrawl of one who had obviously not mingled much with the world during his sedate, scholarly life.

R.F.D. #2,
Townshend, Windham Co.,
Vermont.

May 5, 1928.

Albert N. Wilmarth, Esq.,
118 Saltonstall St.,
Arkham, Mass.,

My dear Sir:—

I have read with great interest the *Brattleboro Reformer's* reprint (Apr. 23, '28) of your letter on the recent stories of strange bodies seen floating in our flooded streams last fall, and on the curious folklore they so well agree with. It is easy to see why an outlander would take the position you take, and even why "Pendrifter" agrees with you. That is the attitude generally taken by educated persons both in and out of Vermont, and was my own attitude as a young man (I am now 57) before my studies, both general and in Davenport's book, led me to do some exploring in parts of the hills hereabouts not usually visited.

I was directed toward such studies by the queer old tales I used to hear from elderly farmers of the more ignorant sort, but now I wish I had let the whole matter alone. I might say, with all proper modesty, that the subject of anthropology and folklore is by no means strange to me. I took a good deal of it at college, and am familiar with most of the standard authorities such as Tylor, Lubbock, Frazer, Quatrefages, Murray, Osborn, Keith, Boule, G. Elliot Smith, and so on. It is no news to me that tales of hidden races are as old as all mankind. I have seen the reprints of letters from you, and those arguing with you, in the *Rutland Herald*, and guess I know about where your controversy stands at the present time.

What I desire to say now is, that I am afraid your adversaries are nearer right than yourself, even though all reason seems to be on your side. They are nearer right than they realise themselves—for of course they go only by theory, and cannot know what I know. If I knew as little of the matter as they, I would not feel justified in believing as they do. I would be wholly on your side.

You can see that I am having a hard time getting to the point, probably because I really dread getting to the point; but the upshot of the matter is that *I have certain evidence that monstrous things do indeed live in the woods on the high hills which nobody visits.* I have not seen any of the things floating in the rivers, as reported, *but I have seen things like them* under circumstances I dread to repeat. I have seen footprints, and of late have seen them nearer my own home (I live in the old Akeley place south of Townshend Village, on the side of Dark Mountain) than I dare tell you now. And I have overheard voices in the woods at certain points that I will not even begin to describe on paper.

At one place I heard them so much that I took a phonograph there—with a dictaphone attachment and wax blank—and I shall try to arrange to have you hear the record I got. I have run it on the machine for some of the old people up here, and one of the voices has nearly scared them paralysed by reason of its likeness to a certain voice (that buzzing voice in the woods which Davenport mentions) that their grandmothers have told about and mimicked for them. I know what most people think of a man who tells about "hearing voices"—but before you draw conclusions just listen to this record and ask some of the older backwoods people what they think of it. If you can account for it normally, very well; but there must be something behind it. *Ex nihilo nihil fit,* you know.

Now my object in writing you is not to start an argument, but to give you information which I think a man of your tastes will find deeply interesting. *This is private. Publicly I am on your side,* for certain things shew me that it does not do for people to know too much about these matters. My own studies are now wholly private, and I would not think of saying anything to attract people's attention and cause them to visit the places I have explored. It is true—terribly true—that there are *non-human creatures watching us all the time;* with spies among us gathering information. It is from a wretched man who, if he was sane (as I think he was), *was one of those spies,* that I got a large part of my clues to the matter. He later killed himself, but I have reason to think there are others now.

The things come from another planet, being able to live in interstellar space and fly through it on clumsy, powerful wings which have a way of resisting the ether but which are too poor at steering to be of much use in helping them about on earth. I will tell you about this later if you do not dismiss me at once as a madman. They come here to get metals from mines that go deep under the hills, *and I think I know where they come from.* They will not hurt us if we let them alone, but no one can say what will happen if we get too curious about them.

Of course a good army of men could wipe out their mining colony. That is what they are afraid of. But if that happened, more would come from *outside*—any number of them. They could easily conquer the earth, but have not tried so far because they have not needed to. They would rather leave things as they are to save bother.

I think they mean to get rid of me because of what I have discovered. There is a great black stone with unknown hieroglyphics half worn away which I found in the woods on Round Hill, east of here; and after I took it home everything became different. If they think I suspect too much they will either kill me *or take me off the earth to where they come from.* They like to take away men of learning once in a while, to keep informed on the state of things in the human world.

This leads me to my secondary purpose in addressing you—namely, to urge you to hush up the present debate rather than give it more publicity. *People must be kept away from these hills,* and in order to effect this, their curiosity ought not to be aroused any further. Heaven knows there is peril enough anyway, with promoters and real estate men flooding Vermont with herds of summer people to overrun the wild places and cover the hills with cheap bungalows.

I shall welcome further communication with you, and shall try to send you that phonograph record and black stone (which is so worn that photographs don't shew much) by express if you are willing. I say "try" because I think those creatures have a way of tampering with things around here. There is a sullen, furtive fellow named Brown, on a farm near the village, who I think is their spy. Little by little they are trying to cut me off from our world because I know too much about their world.

They have the most amazing way of finding out what I do. You may not even get this letter. I think I shall have to leave this part of the country and go to live with my son in San Diego, Cal., if things get any worse, but it is not easy to give up the place you were born in, and where your family has lived for six generations. Also, I would hardly dare sell this house to anybody now that the *creatures* have taken notice of it. They seem to be trying to get the black stone back and destroy the phonograph record, but I shall not let them if I can help it. My great police dogs always hold them back, for there are very few here as yet, and they are clumsy in getting about. As I have said, their wings are not much use for short flights on earth. I am on the very brink of deciphering that stone—in a very terrible way—and with your knowledge of folklore you may be able to supply missing links enough to help me. I suppose you know all about the fearful myths antedating the coming of man to the earth—the Yog-Sothoth and Cthulhu cycles—which are hinted at in the "Necronomicon". I had access to a copy of that once, and hear that you have one in your college library under lock and key.

To conclude, Mr. Wilmarth, I think that with our respective studies we can be very useful to each other. I don't wish to put you in any peril, and suppose I ought to warn you that possession of the

> stone and the record won't be very safe; but I think you will find any risks worth running for the sake of knowledge. I will drive down to Newfane or Brattleboro to send whatever you authorise me to send, for the express offices there are more to be trusted. I might say that I live quite alone now, since I can't keep hired help any more. They won't stay because of the things that try to get near the house at night, and that keep the dogs barking continually. I am glad I didn't get as deep as this into the business while my wife was alive, for it would have driven her mad.
>
> Hoping that I am not bothering you unduly, and that you will decide to get in touch with me rather than throw this letter into the waste basket as a madman's raving, I am
>
> Yrs. very truly,
>
> HENRY W. AKELEY
>
> P.S. I am making some extra prints of certain photographs taken by me, which I think will help to prove a number of the points I have touched on. The old people think they are monstrously true. I shall send you these very soon if you are interested. H. W. A.

It would be difficult to describe my sentiments upon reading this strange document for the first time. By all ordinary rules, I ought to have laughed more loudly at these extravagances than at the far milder theories which had previously moved me to mirth; yet something in the tone of the letter made me take it with paradoxical seriousness. Not that I believed for a moment in the hidden race from the stars which my correspondent spoke of; but that, after some grave preliminary doubts, I grew to feel oddly sure of his sanity and sincerity, and of his confrontation by some genuine though singular and abnormal phenomenon which he could not explain except in this imaginative way. It could not be as he thought it, I reflected, yet on the other hand it could not be otherwise than worthy of investigation. The man seemed unduly excited and alarmed about something, but it was hard to think that all cause was lacking. He was so specific and logical in certain ways—and after all, his yarn did fit in so perplexingly well with some of the old myths—even the wildest Indian legends.

That he had really overheard disturbing voices in the hills, and had really found the black stone he spoke about, was wholly possible despite the crazy inferences he made—inferences probably suggested by the man who had claimed to be a spy of the outer beings and had later killed himself. It was easy to deduce that this man must have been wholly insane, but that he probably had a streak of perverse outward logic which made the naive Akeley—already prepared for such things by his folklore studies—believe his tale. As for the latest developments—it appeared from his inability to keep hired help that Akeley's humbler rustic neighbours were as convinced as he that his house was besieged by uncanny things at night. The dogs really barked, too.

And then the matter of that phonograph record, which I could not but believe he had obtained in the way he said. It must mean something; whether animal noises deceptively like human speech, or the speech of some hidden, night-haunting human being decayed to a state not much above that of the lower animals. From this my thoughts went back to the black hieroglyphed stone, and to speculations upon what it might mean. Then, too, what of the photographs which Akeley said he was about to send, and which the old people had found so convincingly terrible?

As I re-read the cramped handwriting I felt as never before that my credulous opponents might have more on their side than I had conceded. After all, there might be some queer and perhaps hereditarily misshapen outcasts in those shunned hills, even though no such race of star-born monsters as folklore claimed. And if there were, then the presence of strange bodies in the flooded streams would not be wholly beyond belief. Was it too presumptuous to suppose that both the old legends and the recent reports had this much of reality behind them? But even as I harboured these doubts I felt ashamed that so fantastic a piece of bizarrerie as Henry Akeley's wild letter had brought them up.

In the end I answered Akeley's letter, adopting a tone of friendly interest and soliciting further particulars. His reply came almost by return mail; and contained, true to promise, a number of kodak views of scenes and objects illustrating what he had to tell. Glancing at these pictures as I took them from the envelope, I felt a curious sense of fright and nearness to forbidden things; for in spite of the vagueness of most of them, they had a damnably suggestive power which was intensified by the fact of their being genuine photographs—actual optical links with what they portrayed, and the product of an impersonal transmitting process without prejudice, fallibility, or mendacity.

The more I looked at them, the more I saw that my serious estimate of Akeley and his story had not been unjustified. Certainly, these pictures carried conclusive evidence of something in the Vermont hills which was at least vastly outside the radius of our common knowledge and belief. The worst thing of all was the footprint—a view taken where the sun shone on a mud patch somewhere in a deserted upland. This was no cheaply counterfeited thing, I could see at a glance; for the sharply defined pebbles and grass-blades in the field of vision gave a clear index of scale and left no possibility of a tricky double exposure. I have called the thing a "footprint", but "claw-print" would be a better term. Even now I can scarcely describe it save to say that it was hideously crab-like, and that there seemed to be some ambiguity about its direction. It was not a very deep or fresh print, but seemed to be about the size of an average man's foot. From a central pad, pairs of saw-toothed nippers projected in opposite directions—quite baffling as to function, if indeed the whole object were exclusively an organ of locomotion.

Another photograph—evidently a time-exposure taken in deep shadow—was of the mouth of a woodland cave, with a boulder of rounded regularity choking the aperture. On the bare ground in front of it one could just discern a dense network of curious tracks, and when I studied the picture with a magnifier I felt uneasily sure that the tracks were like the one in the other view. A third picture shewed a druid-like circle of standing stones on the summit of a wild hill. Around the cryptic circle the grass was very much beaten down and worn away, though I could not detect any footprints even with the glass. The extreme remoteness of the place was apparent from the veritable sea of tenantless mountains which formed the background and stretched away toward a misty horizon.

But if the most disturbing of all the views was that of the footprint, the most curiously suggestive was that of the great black stone found in the Round Hill woods. Akeley had photographed it on what was evidently his study table, for I could see rows of books and a bust of Milton in the background. The thing, as nearly as one might guess, had faced the camera vertically with a somewhat irregularly curved surface of one by two feet; but to say anything definite about that surface, or about the general shape of the whole mass, almost defies the power of language. What outlandish geometrical principles had guided its cutting—for artificially cut it surely was—I could not even begin to guess; and never before had I seen anything which struck me as so strangely and unmistakably alien to this world. Of the hieroglyphics on the surface I could discern very few, but one or two that I did see gave me rather a shock. Of course they might be fraudulent, for others besides myself had read the monstrous and abhorred *Necronomicon* of the mad Arab Abdul Alhazred; but it nevertheless made me shiver to recognise certain ideographs which study had taught me to link with the most blood-curdling and blasphemous whispers of things that had had a kind of mad half-existence before the earth and the other inner worlds of the solar system were made.

Of the five remaining pictures, three were of swamp and hill scenes which seemed to bear traces of hidden and unwholesome tenancy. Another was of a queer mark in the ground very near Akeley's house, which he said he had photographed the morning after a night on which the dogs had barked more violently than usual. It was very blurred, and one could really draw no certain conclusions from it; but it did seem fiendishly like that other mark or claw-print photographed on the deserted upland. The final picture was of the Akeley place itself; a trim white house of two stories and attic, about a century and a quarter old, and with a well-kept lawn and stone-bordered path leading up to a tastefully carved Georgian doorway. There were several huge police dogs on the lawn, squatting near a pleasant-faced man with a close-cropped grey beard whom I took to be Akeley himself—his own photographer, one might infer from the tube-connected bulb in his right hand.

From the pictures I turned to the bulky, closely written letter itself; and for the next three hours was immersed in a gulf of unutterable horror. Where Akeley had given only outlines before, he now entered into minute details; presenting long transcripts of words overheard in the woods at night, long accounts of monstrous pinkish forms spied in thickets at twilight on the hills, and a terrible cosmic narrative derived from the application of profound and varied scholarship to the endless bygone discourses of the mad self-styled spy who had killed himself. I found myself faced by names and terms that I had heard elsewhere in the most hideous of connexions—Yuggoth, Great Cthulhu, Tsathoggua, Yog-Sothoth, R'lyeh, Nyarlathotep, Azathoth, Hastur, Yian, Leng, the Lake of Hali, Bethmoora, the Yellow Sign, L'mur-Kathulos, Bran, and the Magnum Innominandum—and was drawn back through nameless aeons and inconceivable dimensions to worlds of elder, outer entity at which the crazed author of the *Necronomicon* had only guessed in the vaguest way. I was told of the pits of primal life, and of the streams that had trickled down therefrom; and finally, of the tiny rivulet from one of those streams which had become entangled with the destinies of our own earth.

My brain whirled; and where before I had attempted to explain things away, I now began to believe in the most abnormal and incredible wonders. The array of vital evidence was damnably vast and overwhelming; and the cool, scientific attitude of Akeley—an attitude removed as far as imaginable from the demented, the fanatical, the hysterical, or even the extravagantly speculative—had a tremendous effect on my thought and judgment. By the time I laid the frightful letter aside I could understand the fears he had come to entertain, and was ready to do anything in my power to keep people away from those wild, haunted hills. Even now, when time has dulled the impression and made me half question my own experience and horrible doubts, there are things in that letter of Akeley's which I would not quote, or even form into words on paper. I am almost glad that the letter and record and photographs are gone now—and I wish, for reasons I shall soon make clear, that the new planet beyond Neptune had not been discovered.

With the reading of that letter my public debating about the Vermont horror permanently ended. Arguments from opponents remained unanswered or put off with promises, and eventually the controversy petered out into oblivion. During late May and June I was in constant correspondence with Akeley; though once in a while a letter would be lost, so that we would have to retrace our ground and perform considerable laborious copying. What we were trying to do, as a whole, was to compare notes in matters of obscure mythological scholarship and arrive at a clearer correlation of the Vermont horrors with the general body of primitive world legend.

For one thing, we virtually decided that these morbidities and the hellish Himalayan *Mi-Go* were one and the same order of incarnated nightmare. There were also absorbing zo"logical conjectures, which I would have referred to Professor Dexter in my own college but for Akeley's imperative command to tell no one of the matter before us. If I seem to disobey that command now, it is only because I think that at this stage a warning about those farther Vermont hills—and about those Himalayan peaks which bold explorers are more and more determined to ascend—is more conducive to public safety than silence would be. One specific thing we were leading up to was a deciphering of the hieroglyphics on that infamous black stone—a deciphering which might well place us in possession of secrets deeper and more dizzying than any formerly known to man.

III.

Toward the end of June the phonograph record came—shipped from Brattleboro, since Akeley was unwilling to trust conditions on the branch line north of there. He had begun to feel an increased sense of espionage, aggravated by the loss of some of our letters; and said much about the insidious deeds of certain men whom he considered tools and agents of the hidden beings. Most of all he suspected the surly farmer Walter Brown, who lived alone on a run-down hillside place near the deep woods, and who was often seen loafing around corners in Brattleboro, Bellows Falls, Newfane, and South Londonderry in the most inexplicable and seemingly unmotivated way. Brown's voice, he felt convinced, was one of those he had overheard on a certain occasion in a very terrible conversation; and he had once found a footprint or claw-print near Brown's house which might possess the most ominous significance. It had been curiously near some of Brown's own footprints—footprints that faced toward it.

So the record was shipped from Brattleboro, whither Akeley drove in his Ford car along the lonely Vermont back roads. He confessed in an accompanying note that he was beginning to be afraid of those roads, and that he would not even go into Townshend for supplies now except in broad daylight. It did not pay, he repeated again and again, to know too much unless one were very remote from those silent and problematical hills. He would be going to California pretty soon to live with his son, though it was hard to leave a place where all one's memories and ancestral feelings centred.

Before trying the record on the commercial machine which I borrowed from the college administration building I carefully went over all the explanatory matter in Akeley's various letters. This record, he had said, was obtained about 1 a.m. on the first of May, 1915, near the closed mouth of a cave where the wooded west slope of Dark Mountain rises out of Lee's Swamp. The place had always been unusually plagued with strange voices, this being the reason he had brought the phonograph, dictaphone, and blank in expectation of results. Former experience had told him that May-Eve—the hideous Sabbat-night of underground European legend—would probably be more fruitful than any other date, and he was not disappointed. It was noteworthy, though, that he never again heard voices at that particular spot.

Unlike most of the overheard forest voices, the substance of the record was quasi-ritualistic, and included one palpably human voice which Akeley had never been able to place. It was not Brown's, but seemed to be that of a man of greater cultivation. The second voice, however, was the real crux of the thing—for this was the accursed *buzzing* which had no likeness to humanity despite the human words which it uttered in good English grammar and a scholarly accent.

The recording phonograph and dictaphone had not worked uniformly well, and had of course been at a great disadvantage because of the remote and muffled nature of the overheard ritual; so that the actual speech secured was very fragmentary. Akeley had given me a transcript of what he believed the spoken words to be, and I glanced through this again as I prepared the machine for action. The text was darkly mysterious rather than openly horrible, though a knowledge of its origin and manner of gathering gave it all the associative horror which any words could well possess. I will present it here in full as I remember it—and I am fairly confident that I know it correctly by heart, not only from reading the transcript, but from playing the record itself over and over again. It is not a thing which one might readily forget!

(INDISTINGUISHABLE SOUNDS)

(A CULTIVATED MALE HUMAN VOICE)

... is the Lord of the Wood, even to ... and the gifts of the men of Leng ... so from the wells of night to the gulfs of space, and from the gulfs of space to the wells of night, ever the praises of Great Cthulhu, of Tsathoggua, and of Him Who is not to be Named. Ever Their praises, and abundance to the Black Goat of the Woods. Iä! Shub-Niggurath! The Goat with a Thousand Young!

(A BUZZING IMITATION OF HUMAN SPEECH)

Iä! Shub-Niggurath! The Black Goat of the Woods
with a Thousand Young!

(HUMAN VOICE)

And it has come to pass that the Lord of the Woods, being ... seven and nine, down the onyx steps ... (tri)butes to Him in the Gulf, Azathoth, He of Whom Thou hast taught us marv(els) ... on the wings of night out beyond space, out beyond th ... to That whereof Yuggoth is the youngest child, rolling alone in black aether at the rim....

(BUZZING VOICE)

... go out among men and find the ways thereof, that He in the Gulf may know. To Nyarlathotep, Mighty Messenger, must all things be told. And He shall put on the semblance of men, the waxen mask and the robe that hides, and come down from the world of Seven Suns to mock....

(HUMAN VOICE)

... (Nyarl)athotep, Great Messenger, bringer of strange joy to Yuggoth through the void, Father of the Million Favoured Ones, Stalker among ...

(SPEECH CUT OFF BY END OF RECORD)

Such were the words for which I was to listen when I started the phonograph. It was with a trace of genuine dread and reluctance that I pressed the lever and heard the preliminary scratching of the sapphire point, and I was glad that the first faint, fragmentary words were in a human voice—a mellow, educated voice which seemed vaguely Bostonian in accent, and which was certainly not that of any native of the Vermont hills. As I listened to the tantalisingly feeble rendering, I seemed to find the speech identical with Akeley's carefully prepared transcript. On it chanted, in that mellow Bostonian voice … "Iä! Shub-Niggurath! The Goat with a Thousand Young! …"

And then I heard *the other voice.* To this hour I shudder retrospectively when I think of how it struck me, prepared though I was by Akeley's accounts. Those to whom I have since described the record profess to find nothing but cheap imposture or madness in it; but *could they have heard the accursed thing itself,* or read the bulk of Akeley's correspondence (especially that terrible and encyclopaedic second letter), I know they would think differently. It is, after all, a tremendous pity that I did not disobey Akeley and play the record for others—a tremendous pity, too, that all of his letters were lost. To me, with my first-hand impression of the actual sounds, and with my knowledge of the background and surrounding circumstances, the voice was a monstrous thing. It swiftly followed the human voice in ritualistic response, but in my imagination it was a morbid echo winging its way across unimaginable abysses from unimaginable outer hells. It is more than two years now since I last ran off that blasphemous waxen cylinder; but at this moment, and at all other moments, I can still hear that feeble, fiendish buzzing as it reached me for the first time.

"*Iä! Shub-Niggurath! The Black Goat of the Woods with a Thousand Young!*"

But though that voice is always in my ears, I have not even yet been able to analyse it well enough for a graphic description. It was like the drone of some loathsome, gigantic insect ponderously shaped into the articulate speech of an alien species, and I am perfectly certain that the organs producing it can have no resemblance to the vocal organs of man, or indeed to those of any of the mammalia. There were singularities in timbre, range, and overtones which placed this phenomenon wholly outside the sphere of humanity and earth-life. Its sudden advent that first time almost stunned me, and I heard the rest of the record through in a sort of abstracted daze. When the longer passage of buzzing came, there was a sharp intensification of that feeling of blasphemous infinity which had struck me during the shorter and earlier passage. At last the record ended abruptly, during an unusually clear speech of the human and Bostonian voice; but I sat stupidly staring long after the machine had automatically stopped.

I hardly need say that I gave that shocking record many another playing, and that I made exhaustive attempts at analysis and comment in comparing notes with Akeley. It would be both useless and disturbing to repeat here all that we concluded; but I may hint that we agreed in believing we had secured a clue to the source of some of the most repulsive primordial customs in the cryptic elder religions of mankind. It seemed plain to us, also, that there were ancient and elaborate alliances between the hidden outer creatures and certain members of the human race. How extensive these alliances were, and how their state today might compare with their state in earlier ages, we had no means of guessing; yet at best there was room for a limitless amount of horrified speculation. There seemed to be an awful, immemorial linkage in several definite stages betwixt man and nameless infinity. The blasphemies which appeared on earth, it was hinted, came from the dark planet Yuggoth, at the rim of the solar system; but this was itself merely the populous outpost of a frightful interstellar race whose ultimate source must lie far outside even the Einsteinian space-time continuum or greatest known cosmos.

Meanwhile we continued to discuss the black stone and the best way of getting it to Arkham—Akeley deeming it inadvisable to have me visit him at the scene of his nightmare studies. For some reason or other, Akeley was afraid to trust the thing to any ordinary or expected transportation route. His final idea was to take it across country to Bellows Falls and ship it on the Boston and Maine system through Keene and Winchendon and Fitchburg, even though this would necessitate his driving along somewhat lonelier and more forest-traversing hill roads than the main highway to Brattleboro. He said he had noticed a man around the express office at Brattleboro when he had sent the phonograph record, whose actions and expression had been far from reassuring. This man had seemed too anxious to talk with the clerks, and had taken the train on which the record was shipped. Akeley confessed that he had not felt strictly at ease about that record until he heard from me of its safe receipt.

About this time—the second week in July—another letter of mine went astray, as I learned through an anxious communication from Akeley. After that he told me to address him no more at Townshend, but to send all mail in care of the General Delivery at Brattleboro; whither he would make frequent trips either in his car or on the motor-coach line which had lately replaced passenger service on the lagging branch railway. I could see that he was getting more and more anxious, for he went into much detail about the increased barking of the dogs on moonless nights, and about the fresh claw-prints he sometimes found in the road and in the mud at the back of his farmyard when morning came. Once he told about a veritable army of prints drawn up in a line facing an equally thick and resolute line of dog-tracks, and sent a loathsomely disturbing kodak picture to prove it. That was after a night on which the dogs had outdone themselves in barking and howling.

On the morning of Wednesday, July 18, I received a telegram from Bellows Falls, in which Akeley said he was expressing the black stone over the B. & M. on Train No. 5508, leaving Bellows Falls at 12:15 p.m., standard time, and due at the North Station in Boston at 4:12 p.m. It ought, I calculated, to get up to Arkham at least by the next noon; and accordingly I stayed in all Thursday morning to receive it. But noon came and went without its advent, and when I telephoned down to the express office I was informed that no shipment for me had arrived. My next act, performed amidst a growing alarm, was to give a long-distance call to the express agent at the Boston North Station; and I was scarcely surprised to learn that my consignment had not appeared. Train No. 5508 had pulled in only 35 minutes late on the day before, but had contained no box addressed to me. The agent promised, however, to institute a searching inquiry; and I ended the day by sending Akeley a night-letter outlining the situation.

With commendable promptness a report came from the Boston office on the following afternoon, the agent telephoning as soon as he learned the facts. It seemed that the railway express clerk on No. 5508 had been able to recall an incident which might have much bearing on my loss—an argument with a very curious-voiced man, lean, sandy, and rustic-looking, when the train was waiting at Keene, N.H., shortly after one o'clock standard time.

The man, he said, was greatly excited about a heavy box which he claimed to expect, but which was neither on the train nor entered on the company's books. He had given the name of Stanley Adams, and had had such a queerly thick, droning voice, that it made the clerk abnormally dizzy and sleepy to listen to him. The clerk could not remember quite how the conversation had ended, but recalled starting into a fuller awakeness when the train began to move. The Boston agent added that this clerk was a young man of wholly unquestioned veracity and reliability, of known antecedents and long with the company.

That evening I went to Boston to interview the clerk in person, having obtained his name and address from the office. He was a frank, prepossessing fellow, but I saw that he could add nothing to his original account. Oddly, he was scarcely sure that he could even recognise the strange inquirer again. Realising that he had no more to tell, I returned to Arkham and sat up till morning writing letters to Akeley, to the express company, and to the police department and station agent in Keene. I felt that the strange-voiced man who had so queerly affected the clerk must have a pivotal place in the ominous business, and hoped that Keene station employes and telegraph-office records might tell something about him and about how he happened to make his inquiry when and where he did.

I must admit, however, that all my investigations came to nothing. The queer-voiced man had indeed been noticed around the Keene station in the early afternoon of July 18, and one lounger seemed to couple him vaguely with a heavy box; but he was altogether unknown, and had not been seen before or since. He had not visited the telegraph office or received any message so far as could be learned, nor had any message which might justly be considered a notice of the black stone's presence on No. 5508 come through the office for anyone. Naturally Akeley joined with me in conducting these inquiries, and even made a personal trip to Keene to question the people around the station; but his attitude toward the matter was more fatalistic than mine. He seemed to find the loss of the box a portentous and menacing fulfilment of inevitable tendencies, and had no real hope at all of its recovery. He spoke of the undoubted telepathic and hypnotic powers of the hill creatures and their agents, and in one letter hinted that he did not believe the stone was on this earth any longer. For my part, I was duly enraged, for I had felt there was at least a chance of learning profound and astonishing things from the old, blurred hieroglyphs. The matter would have rankled bitterly in my mind had not Akeley's immediately subsequent letters brought up a new phase of the whole horrible hill problem which at once seized all my attention.

IV.

The unknown things, Akeley wrote in a script grown pitifully tremulous, had begun to close in on him with a wholly new degree of determination. The nocturnal barking of the dogs whenever the moon was dim or absent was hideous now, and there had been attempts to molest him on the lonely roads he had to traverse by day. On the second of August, while bound for the village in his car, he had found a tree-trunk laid in his path at a point where the highway ran through a deep patch of woods; while the savage barking of the two great dogs he had with him told all too well of the things which must have been lurking near. What would have happened had the dogs not been there, he did not dare guess—but he never went out now without at least two of his faithful and powerful pack. Other road experiences had occurred on August 5th and 6th; a shot grazing his car on one occasion, and the barking of the dogs telling of unholy woodland presences on the other.

On August 15th I received a frantic letter which disturbed me greatly, and which made me wish Akeley could put aside his lonely reticence and call in the aid of the law. There had been frightful happenings on the night of the 12–13th, bullets flying outside the farmhouse, and three of the twelve great dogs being found shot dead in the morning. There were myriads of claw-prints in the road, with the human prints of Walter Brown among them. Akeley had started to telephone to Brattleboro for more dogs, but the wire had gone dead before he had a chance to say much. Later he went to Brattleboro in his car, and learned there that linemen had found the main telephone cable neatly cut at a point where it ran through the deserted hills north of Newfane. But he was about to start home with four fine new dogs, and several cases of ammunition for his big-game repeating rifle. The letter was written at the post office in Brattleboro, and came through to me without delay.

My attitude toward the matter was by this time quickly slipping from a scientific to an alarmedly personal one. I was afraid for Akeley in his remote, lonely farmhouse, and half afraid for myself because of my now definite connexion with the strange hill problem. The thing was *reaching out* so. Would it suck me in and engulf me? In replying to his letter I urged him to seek help, and hinted that I might take action myself if he did not. I spoke of visiting Vermont in person in spite of his wishes, and of helping him explain the situation to the proper authorities. In return, however, I received only a telegram from Bellows Falls which read thus:

> APPRECIATE YOUR POSITION BUT CAN DO NOTHING. TAKE NO ACTION YOURSELF FOR IT COULD ONLY HARM BOTH. WAIT FOR EXPLANATION.
>
> HENRY AKELY

But the affair was steadily deepening. Upon my replying to the telegram I received a shaky note from Akeley with the astonishing news that he had not only never sent the wire, but had not received the letter from me to which it was an obvious reply. Hasty inquiries by him at Bellows Falls had brought out that the message was deposited by a strange sandy-haired man with a curiously thick, droning voice, though more than this he could not learn. The clerk shewed him the original text as scrawled in pencil by the sender, but the handwriting was wholly unfamiliar. It was noticeable that the signature was misspelled—A-K-E-L-Y, without the second "E". Certain conjectures were inevitable, but amidst the obvious crisis he did not stop to elaborate upon them.

He spoke of the death of more dogs and the purchase of still others, and of the exchange of gunfire which had become a settled feature each moonless night. Brown's prints, and the prints of at least one or two more shod human figures, were now found regularly among the claw-prints in the road, and at the back of the farmyard. It was, Akeley admitted, a pretty bad business; and before long he would probably have to go to live with his California son whether or not he could sell the old place. But it was not easy to leave the only spot one could really think of as home. He must try to hang on a little longer; perhaps he could scare off the intruders—especially if he openly gave up all further attempts to penetrate their secrets.

Writing Akeley at once, I renewed my offers of aid, and spoke again of visiting him and helping him convince the authorities of his dire peril. In his reply he seemed less set against that plan than his past attitude would have led one to predict, but said he would like to hold off a little while longer—long enough to get his things in order and reconcile himself to the idea of leaving an almost morbidly cherished birthplace. People looked askance at his studies and speculations, and it would be better to get quietly off without setting the countryside in a turmoil and creating widespread doubts of his own sanity. He had had enough, he admitted, but he wanted to make a dignified exit if he could.

This letter reached me on the twenty-eighth of August, and I prepared and mailed as encouraging a reply as I could. Apparently the encouragement took effect, for Akeley had fewer terrors to report when he acknowledged my note. He was not very optimistic, though, and expressed the belief that it was only the full moon season which was holding the creatures off. He hoped there would not be many densely cloudy nights, and talked vaguely of boarding in Brattleboro when the moon waned. Again I wrote him encouragingly, but on September 5th there came a fresh communication which had obviously crossed my letter in the mails; and to this I could not give any such hopeful response.

In view of its importance I believe I had better give it in full—as best I can do from memory of the shaky script. It ran substantially as follows:

Monday.

Dear Wilmarth—

A rather discouraging P.S. to my last. Last night was thickly cloudy—though no rain—and not a bit of moonlight got through. Things were pretty bad, and I think the end is getting near, in spite of all we have hoped. After midnight something landed on the roof of the house, and the dogs all rushed up to see what it was. I could hear them snapping and tearing around, and then one managed to get on the roof by jumping from the low ell. There was a terrible fight up there, and I heard a frightful *buzzing* which I'll never forget. And then there was a shocking smell. About the same time bullets came through the window and nearly grazed me. I think the main line of the hill creatures had got close to the house when the dogs divided because of the roof business. What was up there I don't know yet, but I'm afraid the creatures are learning to steer better with their space wings. I put out the light and used the windows for loopholes, and raked all around the house with rifle fire aimed just high enough not to hit the dogs. That seemed to end the business, but in the morning I found great pools of blood in the yard, besides pools of a green sticky stuff that had the worst odour I have ever smelled. I climbed up on the roof and found more of the sticky stuff there. Five of the dogs were killed—I'm afraid I hit one myself by aiming too low, for he was shot in the back. Now I am setting the panes the shots broke, and am going to Brattleboro for more dogs. I guess the men at the kennels think I am crazy. Will drop another note later. Suppose I'll be ready for moving in a week or two, though it nearly kills me to think of it.

Hastily—
AKELEY

But this was not the only letter from Akeley to cross mine. On the next morning—September 6th—still another came; this time a frantic scrawl which utterly unnerved me and put me at a loss what to say or do next. Again I cannot do better than quote the text as faithfully as memory will let me.

Tuesday.

Clouds didn't break, so no moon again—and going into the wane anyhow. I'd have the house wired for electricity and put in a searchlight if I didn't know they'd cut the cables as fast as they could be mended.

I think I am going crazy. It may be that all I have ever written you is a dream or madness. It was bad enough before, but this time it is too much. *They talked to me last night*—talked in that cursed buzzing voice and told me things *that I dare not repeat to you.* I heard them plainly above the barking of the dogs, and once when they were drowned out *a human voice helped them.* Keep out of this, Wilmarth—it is worse than either you or I ever suspected. *They don't mean to let me get to California now—they want to take me off alive, or what theoretically and mentally amounts to alive*—not only to Yuggoth, but beyond that—away outside the galaxy *and possibly beyond the last curved rim of space.* I told them I wouldn't go where they wish, *or in the terrible way they propose to take me,* but I'm afraid it will be no use. My place is so far out that they may come by day as well as by night before long. Six more dogs killed, and I felt presences all along the wooded parts of the road when I drove into Brattleboro today.

It was a mistake for me to try to send you that phonograph record and black stone. Better smash the record before it's too late. Will drop you another line tomorrow if I'm still here. Wish I could arrange to get my books and things to Brattleboro and board there. I would run off without anything if I could, but something inside my mind holds me back. I can slip out to Brattleboro, where I ought to be safe, but I feel just as much a prisoner there as at the house. And I seem to know that I couldn't get much farther even if I dropped everything and tried. It is horrible—don't get mixed up in this.

Yrs—AKELEY

I did not sleep at all the night after receiving this terrible thing, and was utterly baffled as to Akeley's remaining degree of sanity. The substance of the note was wholly insane, yet the manner of expression—in view of all that had gone before—had a grimly potent quality of convincingness. I made no attempt to answer it, thinking it better to wait until Akeley might have time to reply to my latest communication. Such a reply indeed came on the following day, though the fresh material in it quite overshadowed any of the points brought up by the letter it nominally answered. Here is what I recall of the text, scrawled and blotted as it was in the course of a plainly frantic and hurried composition.

Wednesday.

W—

Yr letter came, but it's no use to discuss anything any more. I am fully resigned. Wonder that I have even enough will power left to fight them off. Can't escape even if I were willing to give up everything and run. They'll get me.

Had a letter from them yesterday—R.F.D. man brought it while I was at Brattleboro. Typed and postmarked Bellows Falls. Tells what they want to do with me—I can't repeat it. Look out for yourself, too! Smash that record. Cloudy nights keep up, and moon waning all the time. Wish I dared to get help—it might brace up my will power—but everyone who would dare to come at all would call me crazy unless there happened to be some proof. Couldn't ask people to come for no reason at all—am all out of touch with everybody and have been for years.

But I haven't told you the worst, Wilmarth. Brace up to read this, for it will give you a shock. I am telling the truth, though. It is this—*I have seen and touched one of the things, or part of one of the things.* God, man, but it's awful! It was dead, of course. One of the dogs had it, and I found it near the kennel this morning. I tried to save it in the woodshed to convince people of the whole thing, but it all evaporated in a few hours. Nothing left. You know, all those things in the rivers were seen only on the first morning after the flood. And here's the worst. I tried to photograph it for you, but when I developed the film *there wasn't anything visible except the woodshed.* What can the thing have been made of? I saw it and felt it, and they all leave footprints. It was surely made of matter—but what kind of matter? The shape can't be described. It was a great crab with a lot of pyramided fleshy rings or knots of thick, ropy stuff covered with feelers where a man's head would be. That green sticky stuff is its blood or juice. And there are more of them due on earth any minute.

Walter Brown is missing—hasn't been seen loafing around any of his usual corners in the villages hereabouts. I must have got him with one of my shots, though the creatures always seem to try to take their dead and wounded away.

Got into town this afternoon without any trouble, but am afraid they're beginning to hold off because they're sure of me. Am writing this in Brattleboro P.O. This may be goodbye—if it is, write my son George Goodenough Akeley, 176 Pleasant St., San Diego, Cal., *but don't come up here.* Write the boy if you don't hear from me in a week, and watch the papers for news.

I'm going to play my last two cards now—if I have the will power left. First to try poison gas on the things (I've got the right chemicals and have fixed up masks for myself and the dogs) and then if that doesn't work, tell the sheriff. They can lock me in a madhouse if they want to—it'll be better than what the *other creatures* would do. Perhaps I can get them to pay attention to the prints around the house—they are faint, but I can find them every morning. Suppose, though, police would say I faked them somehow; for they all think I'm a queer character.

Must try to have a state policeman spend a night here and see for himself—though it would be just like the creatures to learn about it and hold off that night. They cut my wires whenever I try to telephone in the night—the linemen think it is very queer, and may testify for me if they don't go and imagine I cut them myself. I haven't tried to keep them repaired for over a week now.

I could get some of the ignorant people to testify for me about the reality of the horrors, but everybody laughs at what they say, and anyway, they have shunned my place for so long that they don't know any of the new events. You couldn't get one of those run-down farmers to come within a mile of my house for love or money. The mail-carrier hears what they say and jokes me about it—God! If I only dared tell him how real it is! I think I'll try to get him to notice the prints, but he comes in the afternoon and they're usually about gone by that time. If I kept one by setting a box or pan over it, he'd think surely it was a fake or joke.

Wish I hadn't gotten to be such a hermit, so folks don't drop around as they used to. I've never dared shew the black stone or the kodak pictures, or play that record, to anybody but the ignorant people. The others would say I faked the whole business and do nothing but laugh. But I may yet try shewing the pictures. They give those claw-prints clearly, even if the things that made them can't be photographed. What a shame nobody else saw that *thing* this morning before it went to nothing!

But I don't know as I care. After what I've been through, a madhouse is as good a place as any. The doctors can help me make up my mind to get away from this house, and that is all that will save me.

Write my son George if you don't hear soon. Goodbye, smashthat record, and don't mix up in this.

Yrs—AKELEY

The letter frankly plunged me into the blackest of terror. I did not know what to say in answer, but scratched off some incoherent words of advice and encouragement and sent them by registered mail. I recall urging Akeley to move to Brattleboro at once, and place himself under the protection of the authorities; adding that I would come to that town with the phonograph record and help convince the courts of his sanity. It was time, too, I think I wrote, to alarm the people generally against this thing in their midst. It will be observed that at this moment of stress my own belief in all Akeley had told and claimed was virtually complete, though I did think his failure to get a picture of the dead monster was due not to any freak of Nature but to some excited slip of his own.

V.

Then, apparently crossing my incoherent note and reaching me Saturday afternoon, September 8th, came that curiously different and calming letter neatly typed on a new machine; that strange letter of reassurance and invitation which must have marked so prodigious a transition in the whole nightmare drama of the lonely hills. Again I will quote from memory—seeking for special reasons to preserve as much of the flavour of the style as I can. It was postmarked Bellows Falls, and the signature as well as the body of the letter was typed—as is frequent with beginners in typing. The text, though, was marvellously accurate for a tyro's work; and I concluded that Akeley must have used a machine at some previous period—perhaps in college. To say that the letter relieved me would be only fair, yet beneath my relief lay a substratum of uneasiness. If Akeley had been sane in his terror, was he now sane in his deliverance? And the sort of "improved rapport" mentioned ... what was it? The entire thing implied such a diametrical reversal of Akeley's previous attitude! But here is the substance of the text, carefully transcribed from a memory in which I take some pride.

Townshend, Vermont,
Thursday, Sept. 6, 1928.

My dear Wilmarth:—

It gives me great pleasure to be able to set you at rest regarding all the silly things I've been writing you. I say "silly", although by that I mean my frightened attitude rather than my descriptions of certain phenomena. Those phenomena are real and important enough; my mistake had been in establishing an anomalous attitude toward them.

I think I mentioned that my strange visitors were beginning to communicate with me, and to attempt such communication. Last night this exchange of speech became actual. In response to certain signals I admitted to the house a messenger from those outside—a fellow-human, let me hasten to say. He told me much that neither you nor I had even begun to guess, and shewed clearly how totally we had misjudged and misinterpreted the purpose of the Outer Ones in maintaining their secret colony on this planet.

It seems that the evil legends about what they have offered to men, and what they wish in connexion with the earth, are wholly the result of an ignorant misconception of allegorical speech—speech, of course, moulded by cultural backgrounds and thought-habits vastly different from anything we dream of. My own conjectures, I freely own, shot as widely past the mark as any of the guesses of illiterate farmers and savage Indians. What I had thought morbid and shameful and ignominious is in reality awesome and mind-expanding and even *glorious*—my previous estimate being merely a phase of man's eternal tendency to hate and fear and shrink from the *utterly different.*

Now I regret the harm I have inflicted upon these alien and incredible beings in the course of our nightly skirmishes. If only I had consented to talk peacefully and reasonably with them in the first place! But they bear me no grudge, their emotions being organised very differently from ours. It is their misfortune to have had as their human agents in Vermont some very inferior specimens—the late Walter Brown, for example. He prejudiced me vastly against them. Actually, they have never knowingly harmed men, but have often been cruelly wronged and spied upon by our species. There is a whole secret cult of evil men (a man of your mystical erudition will understand me when I link them with Hastur and the Yellow Sign) devoted to the purpose of tracking them down and injuring them on behalf of monstrous powers from other dimensions. It is against these aggressors—not against normal humanity—that the drastic precautions of the Outer Ones are directed. Incidentally, I learned that many of our lost letters were stolen not by the Outer Ones but by the emissaries of this malign cult.

All that the Outer Ones wish of man is peace and non-molestation and an increasing intellectual rapport. This latter is absolutely necessary now that our inventions and devices are expanding our knowledge and motions, and making it more and more impossible for the Outer Ones' necessary outposts to exist *secretly* on this planet. The alien beings desire to know mankind more fully, and to have a few of mankind's philosophic and scientific leaders know more about them. With such an exchange of knowledge all perils will pass, and a satisfactory *modus vivendi* be established. The very idea of any attempt to *enslave* or *degrade* mankind is ridiculous.

As a beginning of this improved rapport, the Outer Ones have naturally chosen me—whose knowledge of them is already so considerable—as their primary interpreter on earth. Much was told me last night—facts of the most stupendous and vista-opening nature—and more will be subsequently communicated to me both orally and in writing. I shall not be called upon to make any trip *outside* just yet, though I shall probably *wish* to do so later on—employing special means and transcending everything which we have hitherto been accustomed to regard as human experience. My house will be besieged no longer. Everything has reverted to normal, and the dogs will have no further occupation. In place of terror I have been given a rich boon of knowledge and intellectual adventure which few other mortals have ever shared.

The Outer Beings are perhaps the most marvellous organic things in or beyond all space and time—members of a cosmos-wide race of which all other life-forms are merely degenerate variants. They are more vegetable than animal, if these terms can be applied to the sort of matter composing them, and have a somewhat fungoid structure; though the presence of a chlorophyll-like substance and a very singular nutritive system differentiate them altogether from true cormophytic fungi. Indeed, the type is composed of a form of matter totally alien to our part of space—with electrons having a wholly different vibration-rate. That is why the beings cannot be photographed on the *ordinary* camera films and plates of our known universe, even though our eyes can see them. With proper knowledge, however, any good chemist could make a photographic emulsion which would record their images.

The genus is unique in its ability to traverse the heatless and airless interstellar void in full corporeal form, and some of its variants cannot do this without mechanical aid or curious surgical transpositions. Only a few species have the ether-resisting wings characteristic of the Vermont variety. Those inhabiting certain remote peaks in the Old World were brought in other ways. Their external resemblance to animal life, and to the sort of structure we understand as material, is a matter of parallel evolution rather than of close kinship. Their brain-capacity exceeds that of any other surviving life-form, although the winged types of our hill country are by no means the most highly developed. Telepathy is their usual means of discourse, though they have rudimentary vocal organs which, after a slight operation (for surgery is an incredibly expert and every-day thing among them), can roughly duplicate the speech of such types of organism as still use speech.

Their main *immediate* abode is a still undiscovered and almost lightless planet at the very edge of our solar system—beyond Neptune, and the ninth in distance from the sun. It is, as we have inferred, the object mystically hinted at as "Yuggoth" in certain ancient and forbidden writings; and it will soon be the scene of a strange focussing of thought upon our world in an effort to facilitate mental rapport. I would not be surprised if astronomers became sufficiently sensitive to these thought-currents to discover Yuggoth when the Outer Ones wish them to do so. But Yuggoth, of course, is only the stepping-stone. The main body of the beings inhabits strangely organised abysses wholly beyond the utmost reach of any human imagination. The space-time globule which we recognise as the totality of all cosmic entity is only an atom in the genuine infinity which is theirs. *And as much of this infinity as any human brain can hold is eventually to be opened up to me, as it has been to not more than fifty other men since the human race has existed.*

You will probably call this raving at first, Wilmarth, but in time you will appreciate the titanic opportunity I have stumbled upon. I want you to share as much of it as is possible, and to that end must tell you thousands of things that won't go on paper. In the past I have warned you not to come to see me. Now that all is safe, I take pleasure in rescinding that warning and inviting you.

Can't you make a trip up here before your college term opens? It would be marvellously delightful if you could. Bring along the phonograph record and all my letters to you as consultative data—we shall need them in piecing together the whole tremendous story. You might bring the kodak prints, too, since I seem to have mislaid the negatives and my own prints in all this recent excitement. But what a wealth of facts I have to add to all this groping and tentative material—*and what a stupendous device I have to supplement my additions!*

Don't hesitate—I am free from espionage now, and you will not meet anything unnatural or disturbing. Just come along and let my car meet you at the Brattleboro station—prepare to stay as long as you can, and expect many an evening of discussion of things beyond all human conjecture. Don't tell anyone about it, of course—for this matter must not get to the promiscuous public.

The train service to Brattleboro is not bad—you can get a time-table in Boston. Take the B. & M. to Greenfield, and then change for the brief remainder of the way. I suggest your taking the convenient 4:10 p.m.—standard—from Boston. This gets into Greenfield at 7:35, and at 9:19 a train leaves there which reaches Brattleboro at

10:01. That is week-days. Let me know the date and I'll have my car on hand at the station.

Pardon this typed letter, but my handwriting has grown shaky of late, as you know, and I don't feel equal to long stretches of script. I got this new Corona in Brattleboro yesterday—it seems to work very well.

Awaiting word, and hoping to see you shortly with the phonograph record and all my letters—and the kodak prints—

I am

Yours in anticipation,

HENRY W. AKELEY.

To Albert N. Wilmarth, Esq.,
Miskatonic University,
Arkham, Mass.

The complexity of my emotions upon reading, re-reading, and pondering over this strange and unlooked-for letter is past adequate description. I have said that I was at once relieved and made uneasy, but this expresses only crudely the overtones of diverse and largely subconscious feelings which comprised both the relief and the uneasiness. To begin with, the thing was so antipodally at variance with the whole chain of horrors preceding it—the change of mood from stark terror to cool complacency and even exultation was so unheralded, lightning-like, and complete! I could scarcely believe that a single day could so alter the psychological perspective of one who had written that final frenzied bulletin of Wednesday, no matter what relieving disclosures that day might have brought. At certain moments a sense of conflicting unrealities made me wonder whether this whole distantly reported drama of fantastic forces were not a kind of half-illusory dream created largely within my own mind. Then I thought of the phonograph record and gave way to still greater bewilderment.

The letter seemed so unlike anything which could have been expected! As I analysed my impression, I saw that it consisted of two distinct phases. First, granting that Akeley had been sane before and was still sane, the indicated change in the situation itself was so swift and unthinkable. And secondly, the change in Akeley's own manner, attitude, and language was so vastly beyond the normal or the predictable. The man's whole personality seemed to have undergone an insidious mutation—a mutation so deep that one could scarcely reconcile his two aspects with the supposition that both represented equal sanity. Word-choice, spelling—all were subtly different. And with my academic sensitiveness to prose style, I could trace profound divergences in his commonest reactions and rhythm-responses. Certainly, the emotional cataclysm or revelation which could produce so radical an overturn must be an extreme one indeed! Yet in another way the letter seemed quite characteristic of Akeley. The same old passion for infinity—the same old scholarly inquisitiveness. I could not for a moment—or more than a moment—credit the idea of spuriousness or malign substitution. Did not the invitation—the willingness to have me test the truth of the letter in person—prove its genuineness?

I did not retire Saturday night, but sat up thinking of the shadows and marvels behind the letter I had received. My mind, aching from the quick succession of monstrous conceptions it had been forced to confront during the last four months, worked upon this startling new material in a cycle of doubt and acceptance which repeated most of the steps experienced in facing the earlier wonders; till long before dawn a burning interest and curiosity had begun to replace the original storm of perplexity and uneasiness. Mad or sane, metamorphosed or merely relieved, the chances were that Akeley had actually encountered some stupendous change of perspective in his hazardous research; some change at once diminishing his danger—real or fancied—and opening dizzy new vistas of cosmic and superhuman knowledge. My own zeal for the unknown flared up to meet his, and I felt myself touched by the contagion of the morbid barrier-breaking. To shake off the maddening and wearying limitations of time and space and natural law—to be linked with the vast *outside*—to come close to the nighted and abysmal secrets of the infinite and the ultimate—surely such a thing was worth the risk of one's life, soul, and sanity! And Akeley had said there was no longer any peril—he had invited me to visit him instead of warning me away as before. I tingled at the thought of what he might now have to tell me—there was an almost paralysing fascination in the thought of sitting in that lonely and lately beleaguered farmhouse with a man who had talked with actual emissaries from outer space; sitting there with the terrible record and the pile of letters in which Akeley had summarised his earlier conclusions.

So late Sunday morning I telegraphed Akeley that I would meet him in Brattleboro on the following Wednesday—September 12th—if that date were convenient for him. In only one respect did I depart from his suggestions, and that concerned the choice of a train. Frankly, I did not feel like arriving in that haunted Vermont region late at night; so instead of accepting the train he chose I telephoned the station and devised another arrangement. By rising early and taking the 8:07 a.m. (standard) into Boston,

I could catch the 9:25 for Greenfield; arriving there at 12:22 noon. This connected exactly with a train reaching Brattleboro at 1:08 p.m.—a much more comfortable hour than 10:01 for meeting Akeley and riding with him into the close-packed, secret-guarding hills.

I mentioned this choice in my telegram, and was glad to learn in the reply which came toward evening that it had met with my prospective host's endorsement. His wire ran thus:

> ARRANGEMENT SATISFACTORY. WILL MEET 1:08 TRAIN WEDNESDAY. DON'T FORGET RECORD AND LETTERS AND PRINTS. KEEP DESTINATION QUIET. EXPECT GREAT REVELATIONS.
> AKELEY.

Receipt of this message in direct response to one sent to Akeley—and necessarily delivered to his house from the Townshend station either by official messenger or by a restored telephone service—removed any lingering subconscious doubts I may have had about the authorship of the perplexing letter. My relief was marked—indeed, it was greater than I could account for at the time; since all such doubts had been rather deeply buried. But I slept soundly and long that night, and was eagerly busy with preparations during the ensuing two days.

VI.

On Wednesday I started as agreed, taking with me a valise full of simple necessities and scientific data, including the hideous phonograph record, the kodak prints, and the entire file of Akeley's correspondence. As requested, I had told no one where I was going; for I could see that the matter demanded utmost privacy, even allowing for its most favourable turns. The thought of actual mental contact with alien, outside entities was stupefying enough to my trained and somewhat prepared mind; and this being so, what might one think of its effect on the vast masses of uninformed laymen? I do not know whether dread or adventurous expectancy was uppermost in me as I changed trains at Boston and began the long westward run out of familiar regions into those I knew less thoroughly. Waltham—Concord—Ayer—Fitchburg—Gardner—Athol—

My train reached Greenfield seven minutes late, but the northbound connecting express had been held. Transferring in haste, I felt a curious breathlessness as the cars rumbled on through the early afternoon sunlight into territories I had always read of but had never before visited. I knew I was entering an altogether older-fashioned and more primitive New England than the mechanised, urbanised coastal and southern areas where all my life had been spent; an unspoiled, ancestral New England without the foreigners and factory-smoke, billboards and concrete roads, of the sections which modernity has touched. There would be odd survivals of that continuous native life whose deep roots make it the one authentic outgrowth of the landscape—the continuous native life which keeps alive strange ancient memories, and fertilises the soil for shadowy, marvellous, and seldom-mentioned beliefs.

Now and then I saw the blue Connecticut River gleaming in the sun, and after leaving Northfield we crossed it. Ahead loomed green and cryptical hills, and when the conductor came around I learned that I was at last in Vermont. He told me to set my watch back an hour, since the northern hill country will have no dealings with new-fangled daylight time schemes. As I did so it seemed to me that I was likewise turning the calender back a century.

The train kept close to the river, and across in New Hampshire I could see the approaching slope of steep Wantastiquet, about which singular old legends cluster. Then streets appeared on my left, and a green island shewed in the stream on my right. People rose and filed to the door, and I followed them. The cars stopped, and I alighted beneath the long train-shed of the Brattleboro station.

Looking over the line of waiting motors I hesitated a moment to see which one might turn out to be the Akeley Ford, but my identity was divined before I could take the initiative. And yet it was clearly not Akeley himself who advanced to meet me with an outstretched hand and a mellowly phrased query as to whether I was indeed Mr. Albert N. Wilmarth of Arkham. This man bore no resemblance to the bearded, grizzled Akeley of the snapshot; but was a younger and more urban person, fashionably dressed, and wearing only a small, dark moustache. His cultivated voice held an odd and almost disturbing hint of vague familiarity, though I could not definitely place it in my memory.

As I surveyed him I heard him explaining that he was a friend of my prospective host's who had come down from Townshend in his stead. Akeley, he declared, had suffered a sudden attack of some asthmatic trouble, and did not feel equal to making a trip in the outdoor air. It was not serious, however, and there was to be no change in plans regarding my visit. I could not make out just how much this Mr. Noyes—as he announced himself—knew of Akeley's researches and discoveries, though it seemed to me that his casual manner stamped him as a comparative outsider. Remembering what a hermit Akeley had been, I was a trifle surprised at the ready availability of such a friend; but did not let my puzzlement deter me from entering the motor to which he gestured me. It was not the small ancient car I had expected from Akeley's descriptions, but a large and immaculate specimen of recent pattern—apparently Noyes's own, and bearing Massachusetts licence plates with the amusing "sacred codfish" device of that year. My guide, I concluded, must be a summer transient in the Townshend region.

Noyes climbed into the car beside me and started it at once. I was glad that he did not overflow with conversation, for some peculiar atmospheric tensity made me feel disinclined to talk. The town seemed very attractive in the afternoon sunlight as we swept up an incline and turned to the right into the main street. It drowsed like the older New England cities which one remembers from boyhood, and something in the collocation of roofs and steeples and chimneys and brick walls formed contours touching deep viol-strings of ancestral emotion. I could tell that I was at the gateway of a region half-bewitched through the piling-up of unbroken time-accumulations; a region where old, strange things have had a chance to grow and linger because they have never been stirred up.

As we passed out of Brattleboro my sense of constraint and foreboding increased, for a vague quality in the hill-crowded countryside with its towering, threatening, close-pressing green and granite slopes hinted at obscure secrets and immemorial survivals which might or might not be hostile to mankind. For a time our course followed a broad, shallow river which flowed down from unknown hills in the north, and I shivered when my companion told me it was the West River. It was in this stream, I recalled from newspaper items, that one of the morbid crab-like beings had been seen floating after the floods.

Gradually the country around us grew wilder and more deserted. Archaic covered bridges lingered fearsomely out of the past in pockets of the hills, and the half-abandoned railway track paralleling the river seemed to exhale a nebulously visible air of desolation. There were awesome sweeps of vivid valley where great cliffs rose, New England's virgin granite shewing grey and austere through the verdure that scaled the crests. There were gorges where untamed streams leaped, bearing down toward the river the unimagined secrets of a thousand pathless peaks. Branching away now and then were narrow, half-concealed roads that bored their way through solid, luxuriant masses of forest among whose primal trees whole armies of elemental spirits might well lurk. As I saw these I thought of how Akeley had been molested by unseen agencies on his drives along this very route, and did not wonder that such things could be.

The quaint, sightly village of Newfane, reached in less than an hour, was our last link with that world which man can definitely call his own by virtue of conquest and complete occupancy. After that we cast off all allegiance to immediate, tangible, and time-touched things, and entered a fantastic world of hushed unreality in which the narrow, ribbon-like road rose and fell and curved with an almost sentient and purposeful caprice amidst the tenantless green peaks and half-deserted valleys. Except for the sound of the motor, and the faint stir of the few lonely farms we passed at infrequent intervals, the only thing that reached my ears was the gurgling, insidious trickle of strange waters from numberless hidden fountains in the shadowy woods.

The nearness and intimacy of the dwarfed, domed hills now became veritably breath-taking. Their steepness and abruptness were even greater than I had imagined from hearsay, and suggested nothing in common with the prosaic objective world we know. The dense, unvisited woods on those inaccessible slopes seemed to harbour alien and incredible things, and I felt that the very outline of the hills themselves held some strange and aeon-forgotten meaning, as if they were vast hieroglyphs left by a rumoured titan race whose glories live only in rare, deep dreams. All the legends of the past, and all the stupefying imputations of Henry Akeley's letters and exhibits, welled up in my memory to heighten the atmosphere of tension and growing menace. The purpose of my visit, and the frightful abnormalities it postulated, struck at me all at once with a chill sensation that nearly overbalanced my ardour for strange delvings.

My guide must have noticed my disturbed attitude; for as the road grew wilder and more irregular, and our motion slower and more jolting, his occasional pleasant comments expanded into a steadier flow of discourse. He spoke of the beauty and weirdness of the country, and revealed some acquaintance with the folklore studies of my prospective host. From his polite questions it was obvious that he knew I had come for a scientific purpose, and that I was bringing data of some importance; but he gave no sign of appreciating the depth and awfulness of the knowledge which Akeley had finally reached.

His manner was so cheerful, normal, and urbane that his remarks ought to have calmed and reassured me; but oddly enough, I felt only the more disturbed as we bumped and veered onward into the unknown wilderness of hills and woods. At times it seemed as if he were pumping me to see what I knew of the monstrous secrets of the place, and with every fresh utterance that vague, teasing, baffling *familiarity* in his voice increased. It was not an ordinary or healthy familiarity despite the thoroughly wholesome and cultivated nature of the voice. I somehow linked it with forgotten nightmares, and felt that I might go mad if I recognised it. If any good excuse had existed, I think I would have turned back from my visit. As it was, I could not well do so—and it occurred to me that a cool, scientific conversation with Akeley himself after my arrival would help greatly to pull me together.

Besides, there was a strangely calming element of cosmic beauty in the hypnotic landscape through which we climbed and plunged fantastically. Time had lost itself in the labyrinths behind, and around us stretched only the flowering waves of faery and the recaptured loveliness of vanished centuries—the hoary groves, the untainted pastures edged with gay autumnal blossoms, and at vast intervals the small brown farmsteads nestling amidst huge trees beneath vertical precipices of fragrant brier and meadow-grass. Even the sunlight assumed a supernal glamour, as if some special atmosphere or exhalation mantled the whole region. I had seen nothing like it before save in the magic vistas that sometimes form the backgrounds of Italian primitives. Sodoma and Leonardo conceived such expanses, but only in the distance, and through the vaultings of Renaissance arcades. We were now burrowing bodily through the midst of the picture, and I seemed to find in its necromancy a thing I had innately known or inherited, and for which I had always been vainly searching.

Suddenly, after rounding an obtuse angle at the top of a sharp ascent, the car came to a standstill. On my left, across a well-kept lawn which stretched to the road and flaunted a border of whitewashed stones, rose a white, two-and-a-half-story house of unusual size and elegance for the region, with a congeries of contiguous or arcade-linked barns, sheds, and windmill behind and to the right. I recognised it at once from the snapshot I had received, and was not surprised to see the name of Henry Akeley on the galvanised-iron mail-box near the road. For some distance back of the house a level stretch of marshy and sparsely wooded land extended, beyond which soared a steep, thickly forested hillside ending in a jagged leafy crest. This latter, I knew, was the summit of Dark Mountain, half way up which we must have climbed already.

Alighting from the car and taking my valise, Noyes asked me to wait while he went in and notified Akeley of my advent.

He himself, he added, had important business elsewhere, and could not stop for more than a moment. As he briskly walked up the path to the house I climbed out of the car myself, wishing to stretch my legs a little before settling down to a sedentary conversation. My feeling of nervousness and tension had risen to a maximum again now that I was on the actual scene of the morbid beleaguering described so hauntingly in Akeley's letters, and I honestly dreaded the coming discussions which were to link me with such alien and forbidden worlds.

Close contact with the utterly bizarre is often more terrifying than inspiring, and it did not cheer me to think that this very bit of dusty road was the place where those monstrous tracks and that foetid green ichor had been found after moonless nights of fear and death. Idly I noticed that none of Akeley's dogs seemed to be about. Had he sold them all as soon as the Outer Ones had made peace with him? Try as I might, I could not have the same confidence in the depth and sincerity of that peace which appeared in Akeley's final and queerly different letter. After all, he was a man of much simplicity and with little worldly experience. Was there not, perhaps, some deep and sinister undercurrent beneath the surface of the new alliance?

Led by my thoughts, my eyes turned downward to the powdery road surface which had held such hideous testimonies. The last few days had been dry, and tracks of all sorts cluttered the rutted, irregular highway despite the unfrequented nature of the district. With a vague curiosity I began to trace the outlines of some of the heterogeneous impressions, trying meanwhile to curb the flights of macabre fancy which the place and its memories suggested. There was something menacing and uncomfortable in the funereal stillness, in the muffled, subtle trickle of distant brooks, and in the crowding green peaks and black-wooded precipices that choked the narrow horizon.

And then an image shot into my consciousness which made those vague menaces and flights of fancy seem mild and insignificant indeed. I have said that I was scanning the miscellaneous prints in the road with a kind of idle curiosity—but all at once that curiosity was shockingly snuffed out by a sudden and paralysing gust of active terror. For though the dust tracks were in general confused and overlapping, and unlikely to arrest any casual gaze, my restless vision had caught certain details near the spot where the path to the house joined the highway; and had recognised beyond doubt or hope the frightful significance of those details. It was not for nothing, alas, that I had pored for hours over the kodak views of the Outer Ones' claw-prints which Akeley had sent. Too well did I know the marks of those loathsome nippers, and that hint of ambiguous direction which stamped the horrors as no creatures of this planet. No chance had been left me for merciful mistake. Here, indeed, in objective form before my own eyes, and surely made not many hours ago, were at least three marks which stood out blasphemously among the surprising plethora of blurred footprints leading to and from the Akeley farmhouse. *They were the hellish tracks of the living fungi from Yuggoth.*

I pulled myself together in time to stifle a scream. After all, what more was there than I might have expected, assuming that I had really believed Akeley's letters? He had spoken of making peace with the things. Why, then, was it strange that some of them had visited his house? But the terror was stronger than the reassurance. Could any man be expected to look unmoved for the first time upon the claw-marks of animate beings from outer depths of space? Just then I saw Noyes emerge from the door and approach with a brisk step. I must, I reflected, keep command of myself, for the chances were that this genial friend knew nothing of Akeley's profoundest and most stupendous probings into the forbidden.

Akeley, Noyes hastened to inform me, was glad and ready to see me; although his sudden attack of asthma would prevent him from being a very competent host for a day or two. These spells hit him hard when they came, and were always accompanied by a debilitating fever and general weakness. He never was good for much while they lasted—had to talk in a whisper, and was very clumsy and feeble in getting about. His feet and ankles swelled, too, so that he had to bandage them like a gouty old beef-eater. Today he was in rather bad shape, so that I would have to attend very largely to my own needs; but he was none the less eager for conversation. I would find him in the study at the left of the front hall—the room where the blinds were shut. He had to keep the sunlight out when he was ill, for his eyes were very sensitive.

As Noyes bade me adieu and rode off northward in his car I began to walk slowly toward the house. The door had been left ajar for me; but before approaching and entering I cast a searching glance around the whole place, trying to decide what had struck me as so intangibly queer about it. The barns and sheds looked trimly prosaic enough, and I noticed Akeley's battered Ford in its capacious, unguarded shelter. Then the secret of the queerness reached me. It was the total silence. Ordinarily a farm is at least moderately murmurous from its various kinds of livestock, but here all signs of life were missing. What of the hens and the hogs?

The cows, of which Akeley had said he possessed several, might conceivably be out to pasture, and the dogs might possibly have been sold; but the absence of any trace of cackling or grunting was truly singular.

I did not pause long on the path, but resolutely entered the open house door and closed it behind me. It had cost me a distinct psychological effort to do so, and now that I was shut inside I had a momentary longing for precipitate retreat. Not that the place was in the least sinister in visual suggestion; on the contrary, I thought the graceful late-colonial hallway very tasteful and wholesome, and admired the evident breeding of the man who had furnished it. What made me wish to flee was something very attenuated and indefinable. Perhaps it was a certain odd odour which I thought I noticed—though I well knew how common musty odours are in even the best of ancient farmhouses.

VII.

Refusing to let these cloudy qualms overmaster me, I recalled Noyes's instructions and pushed open the six-panelled, brass-latched white door on my left. The room beyond was darkened, as I had known before; and as I entered it I noticed that the queer odour was stronger there. There likewise appeared to be some very faint, half-imaginary rhythm or vibration in the air. For a moment the closed blinds allowed me to see very little, but then a kind of apologetic hacking or whispering sound drew my attention to a great easy-chair in the farther, darker corner of the room. Within its shadowy depths I saw the white blur of a man's face and hands; and in a moment I had crossed to greet the figure who had tried to speak. Dim though the light was, I perceived that this was indeed my host. I had studied the kodak picture repeatedly, and there could be no mistake about this firm, weather-beaten face with the cropped, grizzled beard.

But as I looked again my recognition was mixed with sadness and anxiety; for certainly, this face was that of a very sick man. I felt that there must be something more than asthma behind that strained, rigid, immobile expression and unwinking glassy stare; and realised how terribly the strain of his frightful experiences must have told on him. Was it not enough to break any human being—even a younger man than this intrepid delver into the forbidden? The strange and sudden relief, I feared, had come too late to save him from something like a general breakdown. There was a touch of the pitiful in the limp, lifeless way his lean hands rested in his lap. He had on a loose dressing-gown, and was swathed around the head and high around the neck with a vivid yellow scarf or hood.

And then I saw that he was trying to talk in the same hacking whisper with which he had greeted me. It was a hard whisper to catch at first, since the grey moustache concealed all movements of the lips, and something in its timbre disturbed me greatly; but by concentrating my attention I could soon make out its purport surprisingly well. The accent was by no means a rustic one, and the language was even more polished than correspondence had led me to expect.

"Mr. Wilmarth, I presume? You must pardon my not rising. I am quite ill, as Mr. Noyes must have told you; but I could not resist having you come just the same. You know what I wrote in my last letter—there is so much to tell you tomorrow when I shall feel better. I can't say how glad I am to see you in person after all our many letters. You have the file with you, of course? And the kodak prints and record? Noyes put your valise in the hall—I suppose you saw it. For tonight I fear you'll have to wait on yourself to a great extent. Your room is upstairs—the one over this—and you'll see the bathroom door open at the head of the staircase. There's a meal spread for you in the dining-room—right through this door at your right—which you can take whenever you feel like it. I'll be a better host tomorrow—but just now weakness leaves me helpless.

"Make yourself at home—you might take out the letters and pictures and record and put them on the table here before you go upstairs with your bag. It is here that we shall discuss them—you can see my phonograph on that corner stand.

"No, thanks—there's nothing you can do for me. I know these spells of old. Just come back for a little quiet visiting before night, and then go to bed when you please. I'll rest right here—perhaps sleep here all night as I often do. In the morning I'll be far better able to go into the things we must go into. You realise, of course, the utterly stupendous nature of the matter before us. To us, as to only a few men on this earth, there will be opened up gulfs of time and space and knowledge beyond anything within the conception of human science or philosophy.

"Do you know that Einstein is wrong, and that certain objects and forces *can* move with a velocity greater than that of light? With proper aid I expect to go backward and forward in time, and actually *see* and *feel* the earth of remote past and future epochs. You can't imagine the degree to which those beings have carried science. There is nothing they can't do with the mind and body of living organisms. I expect to visit other planets, and even other stars and galaxies. The first trip will be to Yuggoth, the nearest world fully peopled by the beings. It is a strange dark orb at the very rim of our solar system—unknown to earthly astronomers as yet. But I must have written you about this. At the proper time, you know, the beings there will direct thought-currents toward us and cause it to be discovered—or perhaps let one of their human allies give the scientists a hint.

"There are mighty cities on Yuggoth—great tiers of terraced towers built of black stone like the specimen I tried to send you. That came from Yuggoth. The sun shines there no brighter than a star, but the beings need no light. They have other, subtler senses, and put no windows in their great houses and temples. Light even hurts and hampers and confuses them, for it does not exist at all in the black cosmos outside time and space where they came from originally. To visit Yuggoth would drive any weak man mad—yet I am going there. The black rivers of pitch that flow under those mysterious Cyclopean bridges—things built by some elder race extinct and forgotten before the beings came to Yuggoth from the ultimate voids—ought to be enough to make any man a Dante or Poe if he can keep sane long enough to tell what he has seen.

"But remember—that dark world of fungoid gardens and windowless cities isn't really terrible. It is only to us that it would seem so. Probably this world seemed just as terrible to the beings when they first explored it in the primal age. You know they were here long before the fabulous epoch of Cthulhu was over, and remember all about sunken R'lyeh when it was above the waters. They've been inside the earth, too—there are openings which human beings know nothing of—some of them in these very Vermont hills—and great worlds of unknown life down there; blue-litten K'n-yan, red-litten Yoth, and black, lightless N'kai. It's from N'kai that frightful Tsathoggua came—you know, the amorphous, toad-like god-creature mentioned in the Pnakotic Manuscripts and the 'Necronomicon' and the Commoriom myth-cycle preserved by the Atlantean high-priest Klarkash-Ton.

"But we will talk of all this later on. It must be four or five o'clock by this time. Better bring the stuff from your bag, take a bite, and then come back for a comfortable chat."

Very slowly I turned and began to obey my host; fetching my valise, extracting and depositing the desired articles, and finally ascending to the room designated as mine. With the memory of that roadside claw-print fresh in my mind, Akeley's whispered paragraphs had affected me queerly; and the hints of familiarity with this unknown world of fungous life—forbidden Yuggoth—made my flesh creep more than I cared to own. I was tremendously sorry about Akeley's illness, but had to confess that his hoarse whisper had a hateful as well as pitiful quality. If only he wouldn't *gloat* so about Yuggoth and its black secrets!

My room proved a very pleasant and well-furnished one, devoid alike of the musty odour and disturbing sense of vibration; and after leaving my valise there I descended again to greet Akeley and take the lunch he had set out for me. The dining-room was just beyond the study, and I saw that a kitchen ell extended still farther in the same direction. On the dining-table an ample array of sandwiches, cake, and cheese awaited me, and a Thermos-bottle beside a cup and saucer testified that hot coffee had not been forgotten. After a well-relished meal I poured myself a liberal cup of coffee, but found that the culinary standard had suffered a lapse in this one detail. My first spoonful revealed a faintly unpleasant acrid taste, so that I did not take more. Throughout the lunch I thought of Akeley sitting silently in the great chair in the darkened next room. Once I went in to beg him to share the repast, but he whispered that he could eat nothing as yet. Later on, just before he slept, he would take some malted milk—all he ought to have that day.

After lunch I insisted on clearing the dishes away and washing them in the kitchen sink—incidentally emptying the coffee which I had not been able to appreciate. Then returning to the darkened study I drew up a chair near my host's corner and prepared for such conversation as he might feel inclined to conduct. The letters, pictures, and record were still on the large centre-table, but for the nonce we did not have to draw upon them. Before long I forgot even the bizarre odour and curious suggestions of vibration.

I have said that there were things in some of Akeley's letters—especially the second and most voluminous one—which I would not dare to quote or even form into words on paper. This hesitancy applies with still greater force to the things I heard whispered that evening in the darkened room among the lonely haunted hills. Of the extent of the cosmic horrors unfolded by that raucous voice I cannot even hint. He had known hideous things before, but what he had learned since making his pact with the Outside Things was almost too much for sanity to bear. Even now I absolutely refuse to believe what he implied about the constitution of ultimate infinity, the juxtaposition of dimensions, and the frightful position of our known cosmos of space and time in the unending chain of linked cosmos-atoms which makes up the immediate super-cosmos of curves, angles, and material and semi-material electronic organisation.

Never was a sane man more dangerously close to the arcana of basic entity—never was an organic brain nearer to utter annihilation in the chaos that transcends form and force and symmetry. I learned whence Cthulhu *first* came, and why half the great temporary stars of history had flared forth. I guessed—from hints which made even my informant pause timidly—the secret behind the Magellanic Clouds and globular nebulae, and the black truth veiled by the immemorial allegory of Tao. The nature of the Doels was plainly revealed, and I was told the essence (though not the source) of the Hounds of Tindalos. The legend of Yig, Father of Serpents, remained figurative no longer, and I started with loathing when told of the monstrous nuclear chaos beyond angled space which the *Necronomicon* had mercifully cloaked under the name of Azathoth. It was shocking to have the foulest nightmares of secret myth cleared up in concrete terms whose stark, morbid hatefulness exceeded the boldest hints of ancient and mediaeval mystics. Ineluctably I was led to believe that the first whisperers of these accursed tales must have had discourse with Akeley's Outer Ones, and perhaps have visited outer cosmic realms as Akeley now proposed visiting them.

I was told of the Black Stone and what it implied, and was glad that it had not reached me. My guesses about those hieroglyphs had been all too correct! And yet Akeley now seemed reconciled to the whole fiendish system he had stumbled upon; reconciled and eager to probe farther into the monstrous abyss. I wondered what beings he had talked with since his last letter to me, and whether many of them had been as human as that first emissary he had mentioned. The tension in my head grew insufferable, and I built up all sorts of wild theories about that queer, persistent odour and those insidious hints of vibration in the darkened room.

Night was falling now, and as I recalled what Akeley had written me about those earlier nights I shuddered to think there would be no moon. Nor did I like the way the farmhouse nestled in the lee of that colossal forested slope leading up to Dark Mountain's unvisited crest. With Akeley's permission I lighted a small oil lamp, turned it low, and set it on a distant bookcase beside the ghostly bust of Milton; but afterward I was sorry I had done so, for it made my host's strained, immobile face and listless hands look damnably abnormal and corpse-like. He seemed half-incapable of motion, though I saw him nod stiffly once in a while.

After what he had told, I could scarcely imagine what profounder secrets he was saving for the morrow; but at last it developed that his trip to Yuggoth and beyond—*and my own possible participation in it*—was to be the next day's topic. He must have been amused by the start of horror I gave at hearing a cosmic voyage on my part proposed, for his head wabbled violently when I shewed my fear. Subsequently he spoke very gently of how human beings might accomplish—and several times had accomplished—the seemingly impossible flight across the interstellar void. It seemed *that complete human bodies did not indeed make the trip,* but that the prodigious surgical, biological, chemical, and mechanical skill of the Outer Ones had found a way to convey human brains without their concomitant physical structure.

There was a harmless way to extract a brain, and a way to keep the organic residue alive during its absence. The bare, compact cerebral matter was then immersed in an occasionally replenished fluid within an ether-tight cylinder of a metal mined in Yuggoth, certain electrodes reaching through and connecting at will with elaborate instruments capable of duplicating the three vital faculties of sight, hearing, and speech. For the winged fungus-beings to carry the brain-cylinders intact through space was an easy matter. Then, on every planet covered by their civilisation, they would find plenty of adjustable faculty-instruments capable of being connected with the encased brains; so that after a little fitting these travelling intelligences could be given a full sensory and articulate life—albeit a bodiless and mechanical one—at each stage of their journeying through and beyond the space-time continuum. It was as simple as carrying a phonograph record about and playing it wherever a phonograph of the corresponding make exists. Of its success there could be no question. Akeley was not afraid. Had it not been brilliantly accomplished again and again?

For the first time one of the inert, wasted hands raised itself and pointed stiffly to a high shelf on the farther side of the room. There, in a neat row, stood more than a dozen cylinders of a metal I had never seen before—cylinders about a foot high and somewhat less in diameter, with three curious sockets set in an isosceles triangle over the front convex surface of each. One of them was linked at two of the sockets to a pair of singular-looking machines that stood in the background. Of their purport I did not need to be told, and I shivered as with ague. Then I saw the hand point to a much nearer corner where some intricate instruments with attached cords and plugs, several of them much like the two devices on the shelf behind the cylinders, were huddled together.

"There are four kinds of instruments here, Wilmarth," whispered the voice. "Four kinds—three faculties each—makes twelve pieces in all. You see there are four different sorts of beings represented in those cylinders up there. Three humans, six fungoid beings who can't navigate space corporeally, two beings from Neptune (God! if you could see the body this type has on its own planet!), and the rest entities from the central caverns of an especially interesting dark star beyond the galaxy. In the principal outpost inside Round Hill you'll now and then find more cylinders and machines—cylinders of extra-cosmic brains with different senses from any we know—allies and explorers from the uttermost Outside—and special machines for giving them impressions and expression in the several ways suited at once to them and to the comprehensions of different types of listeners. Round Hill, like most of the beings' main outposts all through the various universes, is a very cosmopolitan place! Of course, only the more common types have been lent to me for experiment.

"Here—take the three machines I point to and set them on the table. That tall one with the two glass lenses in front—then the box with the vacuum tubes and sounding-board—and now the one with the metal disc on top. Now for the cylinder with the label 'B-67' pasted on it. Just stand in that Windsor chair to reach the shelf. Heavy? Never mind! Be sure of the number—B-67. Don't bother that fresh, shiny cylinder joined to the two testing instruments—the one with my name on it. Set B-67 on the table near where you've put the machines—and see that the dial switch on all three machines is jammed over to the extreme left.

"Now connect the cord of the lens machine with the upper socket on the cylinder—there! Join the tube machine to the lower left-hand socket, and the disc apparatus to the other socket. Now move all the dial switches on the machines over to the extreme right—first the lens one, then the disc one, and then the tube one. That's right. I might as well tell you that this is a human being—just like any of us. I'll give you a taste of some of the others tomorrow."

To this day I do not know why I obeyed those whispers so slavishly, or whether I thought Akeley was mad or sane. After what had gone before, I ought to have been prepared for anything; but this mechanical mummery seemed so like the typical vagaries of crazed inventors and scientists that it struck a chord of doubt which even the preceding discourse had not excited. What the whisperer implied was beyond all human belief—yet were not the other things still farther beyond, and less preposterous only because of their remoteness from tangible concrete proof?

As my mind reeled amidst this chaos, I became conscious of a mixed grating and whirring from all three of the machines lately linked to the cylinder—a grating and whirring which soon subsided into a virtual noiselessness. What was about to happen? Was I to hear a voice? And if so, what proof would I have that it was not some cleverly concocted radio device talked into by a concealed but closely watching speaker? Even now I am unwilling to swear just what I heard, or just what phenomenon really took place before me. But something certainly seemed to take place.

To be brief and plain, the machine with the tubes and sound-box suddenly began to speak, and with a point and intelligence which left no doubt that the speaker was actually present and observing us. The voice was loud, metallic, lifeless, and plainly mechanical in every detail of its production. It was incapable of inflection or expressiveness, but scraped and rattled on with a deadly precision and deliberation.

"Mr. Wilmarth," it said, "I hope I do not startle you. I am a human being like yourself, though my body is now resting safely under proper vitalising treatment inside Round Hill, about a mile and a half east of here. I myself am here with you—my brain is in that cylinder and I see, hear, and speak through these electronic vibrators. In a week I am going across the void as I have been many times before, and I expect to have the pleasure of Mr. Akeley's company. I wish I might have yours as well; for I know you by sight and reputation, and have kept close track of your correspondence with our friend. I am, of course, one of the men who have become allied with the outside beings visiting our planet. I met them first in the Himalayas, and have helped them in various ways. In return they have given me experiences such as few men have ever had.

"Do you realise what it means when I say I have been on thirty-seven different celestial bodies—planets, dark stars, and less definable objects—including eight outside our galaxy and two outside the curved cosmos of space and time? All this has not harmed me in the least. My brain has been removed from my body by fissions so adroit that it would be crude to call the operation surgery. The visiting beings have methods which make these extractions easy and almost normal—and one's body never ages when the brain is out of it. The brain, I may add, is virtually immortal with its mechanical faculties and a limited nourishment supplied by occasional changes of the preserving fluid.

"Altogether, I hope most heartily that you will decide to come with Mr. Akeley and me. The visitors are eager to know men of knowledge like yourself, and to shew them the great abysses that most of us have had to dream about in fanciful ignorance. It may seem strange at first to meet them, but I know you will be above minding that. I think Mr. Noyes will go along, too—the man who doubtless brought you up here in his car. He has been one of us for years—I suppose you recognised his voice as one of those on the record Mr. Akeley sent you."

At my violent start the speaker paused a moment before concluding.

"So, Mr. Wilmarth, I will leave the matter to you; merely adding that a man with your love of strangeness and folklore ought never to miss such a chance as this. There is nothing to fear. All transitions are painless, and there is much to enjoy in a wholly mechanised state of sensation. When the electrodes are disconnected, one merely drops off into a sleep of especially vivid and fantastic dreams.

"And now, if you don't mind, we might adjourn our session till tomorrow. Good night—just turn all the switches back to the left; never mind the exact order, though you might let the lens machine be last. Good night, Mr. Akeley—treat our guest well! Ready now with those switches?"

That was all. I obeyed mechanically and shut off all three switches, though dazed with doubt of everything that had occurred. My head was still reeling as I heard Akeley's whispering voice telling me that I might leave all the apparatus on the table just as it was. He did not essay any comment on what had happened, and indeed no comment could have conveyed much to my burdened faculties. I heard him telling me I could take the lamp to use in my room, and deduced that he wished to rest alone in the dark. It was surely time he rested, for his discourse of the afternoon and evening had been such as to exhaust even a vigorous man. Still dazed, I bade my host good night and went upstairs with the lamp, although I had an excellent pocket flashlight with me.

I was glad to be out of that downstairs study with the queer odour and vague suggestions of vibration, yet could not of course escape a hideous sense of dread and peril and cosmic abnormality as I thought of the place I was in and the forces I was meeting. The wild, lonely region, the black, mysteriously forested slope towering so close behind the house, the footprints in the road, the sick, motionless whisperer in the dark, the hellish cylinders and machines, and above all the invitations to strange surgery and stranger voyagings—these things, all so new and in such sudden succession, rushed in on me with a cumulative force which sapped my will and almost undermined my physical strength.

To discover that my guide Noyes was the human celebrant in that monstrous bygone Sabbat-ritual on the phonograph record was a particular shock, though I had previously sensed a dim, repellent familiarity in his voice. Another special shock came from my own attitude toward my host whenever I paused to analyse it; for much as I had instinctively liked Akeley as revealed in his correspondence, I now found that he filled me with a distinct repulsion. His illness ought to have excited my pity; but instead, it gave me a kind of shudder. He was so rigid and inert and corpse-like—and that incessant whispering was so hateful and unhuman!

It occurred to me that this whispering was different from anything else of the kind I had ever heard; that, despite the curious motionlessness of the speaker's moustache-screened lips, it had a latent strength and carrying-power remarkable for the wheezings of an asthmatic. I had been able to understand the speaker when wholly across the room, and once or twice it had seemed to me that the faint but penetrant sounds represented not so much weakness as deliberate repression—for what reason I could not guess. From the first I had felt a disturbing quality in their timbre. Now, when I tried to weigh the matter, I thought I could trace this impression to a kind of subconscious familiarity like that which had made Noyes's voice so hazily ominous. But when or where I had encountered the thing it hinted at, was more than I could tell.

One thing was certain—I would not spend another night here. My scientific zeal had vanished amidst fear and loathing, and I felt nothing now but a wish to escape from this net of morbidity and unnatural revelation. I knew enough now. It must indeed be true that strange cosmic linkages do exist—but such things are surely not meant for normal human beings to meddle with.

Blasphemous influences seemed to surround me and press chokingly upon my senses. Sleep, I decided, would be out of the question; so I merely extinguished the lamp and threw myself on the bed fully dressed. No doubt it was absurd, but I kept ready for some unknown emergency; gripping in my right hand the revolver I had brought along, and holding the pocket flashlight in my left. Not a sound came from below, and I could imagine how my host was sitting there with cadaverous stiffness in the dark.

Somewhere I heard a clock ticking, and was vaguely grateful for the normality of the sound. It reminded me, though, of another thing about the region which disturbed me—the total absence of animal life. There were certainly no farm beasts about, and now I realised that even the accustomed night-noises of wild living things were absent. Except for the sinister trickle of distant unseen waters, that stillness was anomalous—interplanetary—and I wondered what star-spawned, intangible blight could be hanging over the region. I recalled from old legends that dogs and other beasts had always hated the Outer Ones, and thought of what those tracks in the road might mean.

VIII.

Do not ask me how long my unexpected lapse into slumber lasted, or how much of what ensued was sheer dream. If I tell you that I awaked at a certain time, and heard and saw certain things, you will merely answer that I did not wake then; and that everything was a dream until the moment when I rushed out of the house, stumbled to the shed where I had seen the old Ford, and seized that ancient vehicle for a mad, aimless race over the haunted hills which at last landed me—after hours of jolting and winding through forest-threatened labyrinths—in a village which turned out to be Townshend.

You will also, of course, discount everything else in my report; and declare that all the pictures, record-sounds, cylinder-and-machine sounds, and kindred evidences were bits of pure deception practiced on me by the missing Henry Akeley. You will even hint that he conspired with other eccentrics to carry out a silly and elaborate hoax—that he had the express shipment removed at Keene, and that he had Noyes make that terrifying wax record. It is odd, though, that Noyes has not even yet been identified; that he was unknown at any of the villages near Akeley's place, though he must have been frequently in the region. I wish I had stopped to memorise the licence-number of his car—or perhaps it is better after all that I did not. For I, despite all you can say, and despite all I sometimes try to say to myself, know that loathsome outside influences must be lurking there in the half-unknown hills—and that those influences have spies and emissaries in the world of men. To keep as far as possible from such influences and such emissaries is all that I ask of life in future.

When my frantic story sent a sheriff's posse out to the farmhouse, Akeley was gone without leaving a trace. His loose dressing-gown, yellow scarf, and foot-bandages lay on the study floor near his corner easy-chair, and it could not be decided whether any of his other apparel had vanished with him. The dogs and livestock were indeed missing, and there were some curious bullet-holes both on the house's exterior and on some of the walls within; but beyond this nothing unusual could be detected. No cylinders or machines, none of the evidences I had brought in my valise, no queer odour or vibration-sense, no footprints in the road, and none of the problematical things I glimpsed at the very last.

I stayed a week in Brattleboro after my escape, making inquiries among people of every kind who had known Akeley; and the results convince me that the matter is no figment of dream or delusion. Akeley's queer purchases of dogs and ammunition and chemicals, and the cutting of his telephone wires, are matters of record; while all who knew him—including his son in California—concede that his occasional remarks on strange studies had a certain consistency. Solid citizens believe he was mad, and unhesitatingly pronounce all reported evidences mere hoaxes devised with insane cunning and perhaps abetted by eccentric associates; but the lowlier country folk sustain his statements in every detail. He had shewed some of these rustics his photographs and black stone, and had played the hideous record for them; and they all said the footprints and buzzing voice were like those described in ancestral legends.

They said, too, that suspicious sights and sounds had been noticed increasingly around Akeley's house after he found the black stone, and that the place was now avoided by everybody except the mail man and other casual, tough-minded people. Dark Mountain and Round Hill were both notoriously haunted spots, and I could find no one who had ever closely explored either. Occasional disappearances of natives throughout the district's history were well attested, and these now included the semi-vagabond Walter Brown, whom Akeley's letters had mentioned. I even came upon one farmer who thought he had personally glimpsed one of the queer bodies at flood-time in the swollen West River, but his tale was too confused to be really valuable.

When I left Brattleboro I resolved never to go back to Vermont, and I feel quite certain I shall keep my resolution. Those wild hills are surely the outpost of a frightful cosmic race—as I doubt all the less since reading that a new ninth planet has been glimpsed beyond Neptune, just as those influences had said it would be glimpsed. Astronomers, with a hideous appropriateness they little suspect, have named this thing "Pluto". I feel, beyond question, that it is nothing less than nighted Yuggoth—and I shiver when I try to figure out the real reason *why* its monstrous denizens wish it to be known in this way at this especial time. I vainly try to assure myself that these daemoniac creatures are not gradually leading up to some new policy hurtful to the earth and its normal inhabitants.

But I have still to tell of the ending of that terrible night in the farmhouse. As I have said, I did finally drop into a troubled doze; a doze filled with bits of dream which involved monstrous landscape-glimpses. Just what awaked me I cannot yet say, but that I did indeed awake at this given point I feel very certain. My first confused impression was of stealthily creaking floor-boards in the hall outside my door, and of a clumsy, muffled fumbling at the latch. This, however, ceased almost at once; so that my really clear impressions begin with the voices heard from the study below. There seemed to be several speakers, and I judged that they were controversially engaged.

By the time I had listened a few seconds I was broad awake, for the nature of the voices was such as to make all thought of sleep ridiculous. The tones were curiously varied, and no one who had listened to that accursed phonograph record could harbour any doubts about the nature of at least two of them. Hideous though the idea was, I knew that I was under the same roof with nameless things from abysmal space; for those two voices were unmistakably the blasphemous buzzings which the Outside Beings used in their communication with men. The two were individually different—different in pitch, accent, and tempo—but they were both of the same damnable general kind.

A third voice was indubitably that of a mechanical utterance-machine connected with one of the detached brains in the cylinders. There was as little doubt about that as about the buzzings; for the loud, metallic, lifeless voice of the previous evening, with its inflectionless, expressionless scraping and rattling, and its impersonal precision and deliberation, had been utterly unforgettable. For a time I did not pause to question whether the intelligence behind the scraping was the identical one which had formerly talked to me; but shortly afterward I reflected that *any* brain would emit vocal sounds of the same quality if linked to the same mechanical speech-producer; the only possible differences being in language, rhythm, speed, and pronunciation. To complete the eldritch colloquy there were two actually human voices—one the crude speech of an unknown and evidently rustic man, and the other the suave Bostonian tones of my erstwhile guide Noyes.

As I tried to catch the words which the stoutly fashioned floor so bafflingly intercepted, I was also conscious of a great deal of stirring and scratching and shuffling in the room below; so that I could not escape the impression that it was full of living beings—many more than the few whose speech I could single out. The exact nature of this stirring is extremely hard to describe, for very few good bases of comparison exist. Objects seemed now and then to move across the room like conscious entities; the sound of their footfalls having something about it like a loose, hard-surfaced clattering—as of the contact of ill-coördinated surfaces of horn or hard rubber. It was, to use a more concrete but less accurate comparison, as if people with loose, splintery wooden shoes were shambling and rattling about on the polished board floor. On the nature and appearance of those responsible for the sounds, I did not care to speculate.

Before long I saw that it would be impossible to distinguish any connected discourse. Isolated words—including the names of Akeley and myself—now and then floated up, especially when uttered by the mechanical speech-producer; but their true significance was lost for want of continuous context. Today I refuse to form any definite deductions from them, and even their frightful effect on me was one of *suggestion* rather than of *revelation.* A terrible and abnormal conclave, I felt certain, was assembled below me; but for what shocking deliberations I could not tell. It was curious how this unquestioned sense of the malign and the blasphemous pervaded me despite Akeley's assurances of the Outsiders' friendliness.

With patient listening I began to distinguish clearly between voices, even though I could not grasp much of what any of the voices said. I seemed to catch certain typical emotions behind some of the speakers. One of the buzzing voices, for example, held an unmistakable note of authority; whilst the mechanical voice, notwithstanding its artificial loudness and regularity, seemed to be in a position of subordination and pleading. Noyes's tones exuded a kind of conciliatory atmosphere. The others I could make no attempt to interpret. I did not hear the familiar whisper of Akeley, but well knew that such a sound could never penetrate the solid flooring of my room.

I will try to set down some of the few disjointed words and other sounds I caught, labelling the speakers of the words as best I know how. It was from the speech-machine that I first picked up a few recognisable phrases.

(THE SPEECH-MACHINE)

> "... brought it on myself ... sent back the letters and the record ... end on it ... taken in ... seeing and hearing ... damn you ... impersonal force, after all ... fresh, shiny cylinder ... great God...."

(FIRST BUZZING VOICE)

> "... time we stopped ... small and human ... Akeley ... brain ... saying ..."

(SECOND BUZZING VOICE)

> "... Nyarlathotep ... Wilmarth ... record and letters ... cheap imposture...."

(NOYES)

"... (an unpronounceable word or name, possibly *N'gah-Kthun*) ... harmless ... peace ... couple of weeks ... theatrical ... told you that before...."

(FIRST BUZZING VOICE)

"... no reason ... original plan ... effects ... Noyes can watch ... Round Hill ... fresh cylinder ... Noyes's car...."

(NOYES)

"... well ... all yours ... down here ... rest ... place...."

(SEVERAL VOICES AT ONCE IN INDISTINGUISHABLE SPEECH)

(MANY FOOTSTEPS, INCLUDING THE PECULIAR LOOSE STIRRING OR CLATTERING)

(A CURIOUS SORT OF FLAPPING SOUND)

(THE SOUND OF AN AUTOMOBILE STARTING AND RECEDING)

(SILENCE)

That is the substance of what my ears brought me as I lay rigid upon that strange upstairs bed in the haunted farmhouse among the daemoniac hills—lay there fully dressed, with a revolver clenched in my right hand and a pocket flashlight gripped in my left. I became, as I have said, broad awake; but a kind of obscure paralysis nevertheless kept me inert till long after the last echoes of the sounds had died away. I heard the wooden, deliberate ticking of the ancient Connecticut clock somewhere far below, and at last made out the irregular snoring of a sleeper. Akeley must have dozed off after the strange session, and I could well believe that he needed to do so.

Just what to think or what to do was more than I could decide. After all, what *had* I heard beyond things which previous information might have led me to expect? Had I not known that the nameless Outsiders were now freely admitted to the farmhouse? No doubt Akeley had been surprised by an unexpected visit from them. Yet something in that fragmentary discourse had chilled me immeasurably, raised the most grotesque and horrible doubts, and made me wish fervently that I might wake up and prove everything a dream. I think my subconscious mind must have caught something which my consciousness has not yet recognised. But what of Akeley? Was he not my friend, and would he not have protested if any harm were meant me? The peaceful snoring below seemed to cast ridicule on all my suddenly intensified fears.

Was it possible that Akeley had been imposed upon and used as a lure to draw me into the hills with the letters and pictures and phonograph record? Did those beings mean to engulf us both in a common destruction because we had come to know too much? Again I thought of the abruptness and unnaturalness of that change in the situation which must have occurred between Akeley's penultimate and final letters. Something, my instinct told me, was terribly wrong. All was not as it seemed. That acrid coffee which I refused—had there not been an attempt by some hidden, unknown entity to drug it? I must talk to Akeley at once, and restore his sense of proportion. They had hypnotised him with their promises of cosmic revelations, but now he must listen to reason. We must get out of this before it would be too late. If he lacked the will power to make the break for liberty, I would supply it. Or if I could not persuade him to go, I could at least go myself. Surely he would let me take his Ford and leave it in a garage at Brattleboro. I had noticed it in the shed—the door being left unlocked and open now that peril was deemed past—and I believed there was a good chance of its being ready for instant use. That momentary dislike of Akeley which I had felt during and after the evening's conversation was all gone now. He was in a position much like my own, and we must stick together. Knowing his indisposed condition, I hated to wake him at this juncture, but I knew that I must. I could not stay in this place till morning as matters stood.

At last I felt able to act, and stretched myself vigorously to regain command of my muscles. Arising with a caution more impulsive than deliberate, I found and donned my hat, took my valise, and started downstairs with the flashlight's aid. In my nervousness I kept the revolver clutched in my right hand, being able to take care of both valise and flashlight with my left. Why I exerted these precautions I do not really know, since I was even then on my way to awaken the only other occupant of the house.

As I half tiptoed down the creaking stairs to the lower hall I could hear the sleeper more plainly, and noticed that he must be in the room on my left—the living-room I had not entered. On my right was the gaping blackness of the study in which I had heard the voices. Pushing open the unlatched door of the living-room I traced a path with the flashlight toward the source of the snoring, and finally turned the beams on the sleeper's face. But in the next second I hastily turned them away and commenced a cat-like retreat to the hall, my caution this time springing from reason as well as from instinct. For the sleeper on the couch was not Akeley at all, but my quondam guide Noyes.

Just what the real situation was, I could not guess; but common sense told me that the safest thing was to find out as much as possible before arousing anybody. Regaining the hall, I silently closed and latched the living-room door after me; thereby lessening the chances of awaking Noyes. I now cautiously entered the dark study, where I expected to find Akeley, whether asleep or awake, in the great corner chair which was evidently his favourite resting-place. As I advanced, the beams of my flashlight caught the great centre-table, revealing one of the hellish cylinders with sight and hearing machines attached, and with a speech-machine standing close by, ready to be connected at any moment. This, I reflected, must be the encased brain I had heard talking during the frightful conference; and for a second I had a perverse impulse to attach the speech-machine and see what it would say.

It must, I thought, be conscious of my presence even now; since the sight and hearing attachments could not fail to disclose the rays of my flashlight and the faint creaking of the floor beneath my feet. But in the end I did not dare meddle with the thing. I idly saw that it was the fresh, shiny cylinder with Akeley's name on it, which I had noticed on the shelf earlier in the evening and which my host had told me not to bother. Looking back at that moment, I can only regret my timidity and wish that I had boldly caused the apparatus to speak. God knows what mysteries and horrible doubts and questions of identity it might have cleared up! But then, it may be merciful that I let it alone.

From the table I turned my flashlight to the corner where I thought Akeley was, but found to my perplexity that the great easy-chair was empty of any human occupant asleep or awake. From the seat to the floor there trailed voluminously the familiar old dressing-gown, and near it on the floor lay the yellow scarf and the huge foot-bandages I had thought so odd. As I hesitated, striving to conjecture where Akeley might be, and why he had so suddenly discarded his necessary sick-room garments, I observed that the queer odour and sense of vibration were no longer in the room. What had been their cause? Curiously it occurred to me that I had noticed them only in Akeley's vicinity. They had been strongest where he sat, and wholly absent except in the room with him or just outside the doors of that room. I paused, letting the flashlight wander about the dark study and racking my brain for explanations of the turn affairs had taken.

Would to heaven I had quietly left the place before allowing that light to rest again on the vacant chair. As it turned out, I did not leave quietly; but with a muffled shriek which must have disturbed, though it did not quite awake, the sleeping sentinel across the hall. That shriek, and Noyes's still-unbroken snore, are the last sounds I ever heard in that morbidity-choked farmhouse beneath the black-wooded crest of a haunted mountain—that focus of trans-cosmic horror amidst the lonely green hills and curse-muttering brooks of a spectral rustic land.

It is a wonder that I did not drop flashlight, valise, and revolver in my wild scramble, but somehow I failed to lose any of these. I actually managed to get out of that room and that house without making any further noise, to drag myself and my belongings safely into the old Ford in the shed, and to set that archaic vehicle in motion toward some unknown point of safety in the black, moonless night. The ride that followed was a piece of delirium out of Poe or Rimbaud or the drawings of Doré, but finally I reached Townshend. That is all. If my sanity is still unshaken, I am lucky. Sometimes I fear what the years will bring, especially since that new planet Pluto has been so curiously discovered.

As I have implied, I let my flashlight return to the vacant easy-chair after its circuit of the room; then noticing for the first time the presence of certain objects in the seat, made inconspicuous by the adjacent loose folds of the empty dressing-gown. These are the objects, three in number, which the investigators did not find when they came later on. As I said at the outset, there was nothing of actual visual horror about them. The trouble was in what they led one to infer. Even now I have my moments of half-doubt—moments in which I half accept the scepticism of those who attribute my whole experience to dream and nerves and delusion.

The three things were damnably clever constructions of their kind, and were furnished with ingenious metallic clamps to attach them to organic developments of which I dare not form any conjecture. I hope—devoutly hope—that they were the waxen products of a master artist, despite what my inmost fears tell me. Great God! That whisperer in darkness with its morbid odour and vibrations! Sorcerer, emissary, changeling, outsider … that hideous repressed buzzing … and all the time in that fresh, shiny cylinder on the shelf … poor devil … "prodigious surgical, biological, chemical, and mechanical skill" …

For the things in the chair, perfect to the last, subtle detail of microscopic resemblance—or identity—were the face and hands of Henry Wentworth Akeley.

AT THE MOUNTAINS OF MADNESS

I.

I am forced into speech because men of science have refused to follow my advice without knowing why. It is altogether against my will that I tell my reasons for opposing this contemplated invasion of the antarctic—with its vast fossil-hunt and its wholesale boring and melting of the ancient ice-cap—and I am the more reluctant because my warning may be in vain. Doubt of the real facts, as I must reveal them, is inevitable; yet if I suppressed what will seem extravagant and incredible there would be nothing left. The hitherto withheld photographs, both ordinary and aërial, will count in my favour; for they are damnably vivid and graphic. Still, they will be doubted because of the great lengths to which clever fakery can be carried. The ink drawings, of course, will be jeered at as obvious impostures; notwithstanding a strangeness of technique which art experts ought to remark and puzzle over.

In the end I must rely on the judgment and standing of the few scientific leaders who hav e, on the one hand, sufficient independence of thought to weigh my data on its own hideously convincing merits or in the light of certain primordial and highly baffling myth-cycles; and on the other hand, sufficient influence to deter the exploring world in general from any rash and overambitious programme in the region of those mountains of madness. It is an unfortunate fact that relatively obscure men like myself and my associates, connected only with a small university, have little chance of making an impression where matters of a wildly bizarre or highly controversial nature are concerned.

It is further against us that we are not, in the strictest sense, specialists in the fields which came primarily to be concerned. As a geologist my object in leading the Miskatonic University Expedition was wholly that of securing deep-level specimens of rock and soil from various parts of the antarctic continent, aided by the remarkable drill devised by Prof. Frank H. Pabodie of our engineering department. I had no wish to be a pioneer in any other field than this; but I did hope that the use of this new mechanical appliance at different points along previously explored paths would bring to light materials of a sort hitherto unreached by the ordinary methods of collection. Pabodie's drilling apparatus, as the public already knows from our reports, was unique and radical in its lightness, portability, and capacity to combine the ordinary artesian drill principle with the principle of the small circular rock drill in such a way as to cope quickly with strata of varying hardness. Steel head, jointed rods, gasoline motor, collapsible wooden derrick, dynamiting paraphernalia, cording, rubbish-removal auger, and sectional piping for bores five inches wide and up to 1000 feet deep all formed, with needed accessories, no greater load than three seven-dog sledges could carry; this being made possible by the clever aluminum alloy of which most of the metal objects were fashioned. Four large Dornier aëroplanes, designed especially for the tremendous altitude flying necessary on the antarctic plateau and with added fuel-warming and quick-starting devices worked out by Pabodie, could transport our entire expedition from a base at the edge of the great ice barrier to various suitable inland points, and from these points a sufficient quota of dogs would serve us.

We planned to cover as great an area as one antarctic season—or longer, if absolutely necessary—would permit, operating mostly in the mountain ranges and on the plateau south of Ross Sea; regions explored in varying degree by Shackleton, Amundsen, Scott, and Byrd. With frequent changes of camp, made by aëroplane and involving distances great enough to be of geological significance, we expected to unearth a quite unprecedented amount of material; especially in the pre-Cambrian strata of which so narrow a range of antarctic specimens had previously been secured. We wished also to obtain as great as possible a variety of the upper fossiliferous rocks, since the primal life-history of this bleak realm of ice and death is of the highest importance to our knowledge of the earth's past. That the antarctic continent was once temperate and even tropical, with a teeming vegetable and animal life of which the lichens, marine fauna, arachnida, and penguins of the northern edge are the only survivals, is a matter of common information; and we hoped to expand that information in variety, accuracy, and detail. When a simple boring revealed fossiliferous signs, we would enlarge the aperture by blasting in order to get specimens of suitable size and condition.

Our borings, of varying depth according to the promise held out by the upper soil or rock, were to be confined to exposed or nearly exposed land surfaces—these inevitably being slopes and ridges because of the mile or two-mile thickness of solid ice overlying the lower levels. We could not afford to waste drilling depth on any considerable amount of mere glaciation, though Pabodie had worked out a plan for sinking copper electrodes in thick clusters of borings and melting off limited areas of ice with current from a gasoline-driven dynamo. It is this plan—which we could not put into effect except experimentally on an expedition such as ours—that the coming Starkweather-Moore Expedition proposes to follow despite the warnings I have issued since our return from the antarctic.

The public knows of the Miskatonic Expedition through our frequent wireless reports to the *Arkham Advertiser* and Associated Press, and through the later articles by Pabodie and myself. We consisted of four men from the University—Pabodie, Lake of the biology department, Atwood of the physics department (also a meteorologist), and I representing geology and having nominal command—besides sixteen assistants; seven graduate students from Miskatonic and nine skilled mechanics. Of these sixteen, twelve were qualified aëroplane pilots, all but two of whom were competent wireless operators. Eight of them understood navigation with compass and sextant, as did Pabodie, Atwood, and I. In addition, of course, our two ships—wooden ex-whalers, reinforced for ice conditions and having auxiliary steam—were fully manned. The Nathaniel Derby Pickman Foundation, aided by a few special contributions, financed the expedition; hence our preparations were extremely thorough despite the absence of great publicity. The dogs, sledges, machines, camp materials, and unassembled parts of our five planes were delivered in Boston, and there our ships were loaded. We were marvellously well-equipped for our specific purposes, and in all matters pertaining to supplies, regimen, transportation, and camp construction we profited by the excellent example of our many recent and exceptionally brilliant predecessors. It was the unusual number and fame of these predecessors which made our own expedition—ample though it was—so little noticed by the world at large.

As the newspapers told, we sailed from Boston Harbour on September 2, 1930; taking a leisurely course down the coast and through the Panama Canal, and stopping at Samoa and Hobart, Tasmania, at which latter place we took on final supplies. None of our exploring party had ever been in the polar regions before, hence we all relied greatly on our ship captains—J. B. Douglas, commanding the brig *Arkham*, and serving as commander of the sea party, and Georg Thorfinnssen, commanding the barque *Miskatonic*—both veteran whalers in antarctic waters. As we left the inhabited world behind the sun sank lower and lower in the north, and stayed longer and longer above the horizon each day. At about 62° South Latitude we sighted our first icebergs—table-like objects with vertical sides—and just before reaching the Antarctic Circle, which we crossed on October 20th with appropriately quaint ceremonies, we were considerably troubled with field ice. The falling temperature bothered me considerably after our long voyage through the tropics, but I tried to brace up for the worse rigours to come. On many occasions the curious atmospheric effects enchanted me vastly; these including a strikingly vivid mirage—the first I had ever seen—in which distant bergs became the battlements of unimaginable cosmic castles.

Pushing through the ice, which was fortunately neither extensive nor thickly packed, we regained open water at South Latitude 67°, East Longitude 175°. On the morning of October 26th a strong "land blink" appeared on the south, and before noon we all felt a thrill of excitement at beholding a vast, lofty, and snow-clad mountain chain which opened out and covered the whole vista ahead. At last we had encountered an outpost of the great unknown continent and its cryptic world of frozen death. These peaks were obviously the Admiralty Range discovered by Ross, and it would now be our task to round Cape Adare and sail down the east coast of Victoria Land to our contemplated base on the shore of McMurdo Sound at the foot of the volcano Erebus in South Latitude 77° 9′.

The last lap of the voyage was vivid and fancy-stirring, great barren peaks of mystery looming up constantly against the west as the low northern sun of noon or the still lower horizon-grazing southern sun of midnight poured its hazy reddish rays over the white snow, bluish ice and water lanes, and black bits of exposed granite slope. Through the desolate summits swept raging intermittent gusts of the terrible antarctic wind; whose cadences sometimes held vague suggestions of a wild and half-sentient musical piping, with notes extending over a wide range, and which for some subconscious mnemonic reason seemed to me disquieting and even dimly terrible. Something about the scene reminded me of the strange and disturbing Asian paintings of Nicholas Roerich, and of the still stranger and more disturbing descriptions of the evilly fabled plateau of Leng which occur in the dreaded "Necronomicon" of the mad Arab Abdul Alhazred. I was rather sorry, later on, that I had ever looked into that monstrous book at the college library.

On the seventh of November, sight of the westward range having been temporarily lost, we passed Franklin Island; and the next day descried the cones of Mts. Erebus and Terror on Ross Island ahead, with the long line of the Parry Mountains beyond. There now stretched off to the east the low, white line of the great ice barrier; rising perpendicularly to a height of 200 feet like the rocky cliffs of Quebec, and marking the end of southward navigation. In the afternoon we entered McMurdo Sound and stood off the coast in the lee of smoking Mt. Erebus. The scoriac peak towered up some 12,700 feet against the eastern sky, like a Japanese print of the sacred Fujiyama; while beyond it rose the white, ghost-like height of Mt. Terror, 10,900 feet in altitude, and now extinct as a volcano. Puffs of smoke from Erebus came intermittently, and one of the graduate assistants—a brilliant young fellow named Danforth—pointed out what looked like lava on the snowy slope; remarking that this mountain, discovered in 1840, had undoubtedly been the source of Poe's image when he wrote seven years later of

> "—the lavas that restlessly roll
> Their sulphurous currents down Yaanek
> In the ultimate climes of the pole—
> That groan as they roll down Mount Yaanek
> In the realms of the boreal pole."

Danforth was a great reader of bizarre material, and had talked a good deal of Poe. I was interested myself because of the antarctic scene of Poe's only long story—the disturbing and enigmatical "Arthur Gordon Pym". On the barren shore, and on the lofty ice barrier in the background, myriads of grotesque penguins squawked and flapped their fins; while many fat seals were visible on the water, swimming or sprawling across large cakes of slowly drifting ice.

Using small boats, we effected a difficult landing on Ross Island shortly after midnight on the morning of the 9th, carrying a line of cable from each of the ships and preparing to unload supplies by means of a breeches-buoy arrangement. Our sensations on first treading antarctic soil were poignant and complex, even though at this particular point the Scott and Shackleton expeditions had preceded us. Our camp on the frozen shore below the volcano's slope was only a provisional one; headquarters being kept aboard the *Arkham*. We landed all our drilling apparatus, dogs, sledges, tents, provisions, gasoline tanks, experimental ice-melting outfit, cameras both ordinary and aërial, aëroplane parts, and other accessories, including three small portable wireless outfits (besides those in the planes) capable of communicating with the *Arkham's* large outfit from any part of the antarctic continent that we would be likely to visit. The ship's outfit, communicating with the outside world, was to convey press reports to the *Arkham Advertiser's* powerful wireless station on Kingsport Head, Mass. We hoped to complete our work during a single antarctic summer; but if this proved impossible we would winter on the *Arkham*, sending the *Miskatonic* north before the freezing of the ice for another summer's supplies.

I need not repeat what the newspapers have already published about our early work: of our ascent of Mt. Erebus; our successful mineral borings at several points on Ross Island and the singular speed with which Pabodie's apparatus accomplished them, even through solid rock layers; our provisional test of the small ice-melting equipment; our perilous ascent of the great barrier with sledges and supplies; and our final assembling of five huge aëroplanes at the camp atop the barrier. The health of our land party—twenty men and 55 Alaskan sledge dogs—was remarkable, though of course we had so far encountered no really destructive temperatures or windstorms. For the most part, the thermometer varied between zero and 20° or 25° above, and our experience with New England winters had accustomed us to rigours of this sort. The barrier camp was semi-permanent, and destined to be a storage cache for gasoline, provisions, dynamite, and other supplies. Only four of our planes were needed to carry the actual exploring material, the fifth being left with a pilot and two men from the ships at the storage cache to form a means of reaching us from the *Arkham* in case all our exploring planes were lost. Later, when not using all the other planes for moving apparatus, we would employ one or two in a shuttle transportation service between this cache and another permanent base on the great plateau from 600 to 700 miles southward, beyond Beardmore Glacier. Despite the almost unanimous accounts of appalling winds and tempests that pour down from the plateau, we determined to dispense with intermediate bases, taking our chances in the interest of economy and probable efficiency.

Wireless reports have spoken of the breath-taking four-hour non-stop flight of our squadron on November 21st over the lofty shelf ice, with vast peaks rising on the west, and the unfathomed silences echoing to the sound of our engines. Wind troubled us only moderately, and our radio compasses helped us through the one opaque fog we encountered. When the vast rise loomed ahead, between Latitudes 83° and 84°, we knew we had reached Beardmore Glacier, the largest valley glacier in the world, and that the frozen sea was now giving place to a frowning and mountainous coast-line. At last we were truly entering the white, aeon-dead world of the ultimate south, and even as we realised it we saw the peak of Mt. Nansen in the eastern distance, towering up to its height of almost 15,000 feet.

The successful establishment of the southern base above the glacier in Latitude 86° 7′, East Longitude 174° 23′, and the phenomenally rapid and effective borings and blastings made at various points reached by our sledge trips and short aëroplane flights, are matters of history; as is the arduous and triumphant ascent of Mt. Nansen by Pabodie and two of the graduate students—Gedney and Carroll—on December 13–15th. We were some 8500 feet above sea-level, and when experimental drillings revealed solid ground only twelve feet down through the snow and ice at certain points, we made considerable use of the small melting apparatus and sunk bores and performed dynamiting at many places where no previous explorer had ever thought of securing mineral specimens. The pre-Cambrian granites and beacon sandstones thus obtained confirmed our belief that this plateau was homogeneous with the great bulk of the continent to the west, but somewhat different from the parts lying eastward below South America—which we then thought to form a separate and smaller continent divided from the larger one by a frozen junction of Ross and Weddell Seas, though Byrd has since disproved the hypothesis.

In certain of the sandstones, dynamited and chiselled after boring revealed their nature, we found some highly interesting fossil markings and fragments—notably ferns, seaweeds, trilobites, crinoids, and such molluscs as linguellae and gasteropods—all of which seemed of real significance in connexion with the region's primordial history. There was also a queer triangular, striated marking about a foot in greatest diameter which Lake pieced together from three fragments of slate brought up from a deep-blasted aperture. These fragments came from a point to the westward, near the Queen Alexandra Range; and Lake, as a biologist, seemed to find their curious marking unusually puzzling and provocative, though to my geological eye it looked not unlike some of the ripple effects reasonably common in the sedimentary rocks. Since slate is no more than a metamorphic formation into which a sedimentary stratum is pressed, and since the pressure itself produces odd distorting effects on any markings which may exist, I saw no reason for extreme wonder over the striated depression.

On January 6, 1931, Lake, Pabodie, Danforth, all six of the students, four mechanics, and myself flew directly over the south pole in two of the great planes, being forced down once by a sudden high wind which fortunately did not develop into a typical storm. This was, as the papers have stated, one of several observation flights; during others of which we tried to discern new topographical features in areas unreached by previous explorers. Our early flights were disappointing in this latter respect; though they afforded us some magnificent examples of the richly fantastic and deceptive mirages of the polar regions, of which our sea voyage had given us some brief foretastes. Distant mountains floated in the sky as enchanted cities, and often the whole white world would dissolve into a gold, silver, and scarlet land of Dunsanian dreams and adventurous expectancy under the magic of the low midnight sun. On cloudy days we had considerable trouble in flying, owing to the tendency of snowy earth and sky to merge into one mystical opalescent void with no visible horizon to mark the junction of the two.

At length we resolved to carry out our original plan of flying 500 miles eastward with all four exploring planes and establishing a fresh sub-base at a point which would probably be on the smaller continental division, as we mistakenly conceived it. Geological specimens obtained there would be desirable for purposes of comparison. Our health so far had remained excellent; lime-juice well offsetting the steady diet of tinned and salted food, and temperatures generally above zero enabling us to do without our thickest furs. It was now midsummer, and with haste and care we might be able to conclude work by March and avoid a tedious wintering through the long antarctic night. Several savage windstorms had burst upon us from the west, but we had escaped damage through the skill of Atwood in devising rudimentary aëroplane shelters and windbreaks of heavy snow blocks, and in reinforcing the principal camp buildings with snow. Our good luck and efficiency had indeed been almost uncanny.

The outside world knew, of course, of our programme, and was told also of Lake's strange and dogged insistence on a westward—or rather, northwestward—prospecting trip before our radical shift to the new base. It seems that he had pondered a great deal, and with alarmingly radical daring, over that triangular striated marking in the slate; reading into it certain contradictions in Nature and geological period which whetted his curiosity to the utmost, and made him avid to sink more borings and blastings in the west-stretching formation to which the exhumed fragments evidently belonged. He was strangely convinced that the marking was the print of some bulky, unknown, and radically unclassifiable organism of considerably advanced evolution, notwithstanding that the rock which bore it was of so vastly ancient a date—Cambrian if not actually pre-Cambrian—as to preclude the probable existence not only of all highly evolved life, but of any life at all above the unicellular or at most the trilobite stage. These fragments, with their odd marking, must have been 500 million to a thousand million years old.

II.

Popular imagination, I judge, responded actively to our wireless bulletins of Lake's start northwestward into regions never trodden by human foot or penetrated by human imagination; though we did not mention his wild hopes of revolutionising the entire sciences of biology and geology. His preliminary sledging and boring journey of January 11–18th with Pabodie and five others—marred by the loss of two dogs in an upset when crossing one of the great pressure-ridges in the ice—had brought up more and more of the archaean slate; and even I was interested by the singular profusion of evident fossil markings in that unbelievably ancient stratum. These markings, however, were of very primitive life-forms involving no great paradox except that any life-forms should occur in rock as definitely pre-Cambrian as this seemed to be; hence I still failed to see the good sense of Lake's demand for an interlude in our time-saving programme—an interlude requiring the use of all four planes, many men, and the whole of the expedition's mechanical apparatus. I did not, in the end, veto the plan; though I decided not to accompany the northwestward party despite Lake's plea for my geological advice. While they were gone, I would remain at the base with Pabodie and five men and work out final plans for the eastward shift. In preparation for this transfer one of the planes had begun to move up a good gasoline supply from McMurdo Sound; but this could wait temporarily. I kept with me one sledge and nine dogs, since it is unwise to be at any time without possible transportation in an utterly tenantless world of aeon-long death.

Lake's sub-expedition into the unknown, as everyone will recall, sent out its own reports from the short-wave transmitters on the planes; these being simultaneously picked up by our apparatus at the southern base and by the *Arkham* at McMurdo Sound, whence they were relayed to the outside world on wave-lengths up to 50 metres. The start was made January 22 at 4 a.m.; and the first wireless message we received came only two hours later, when Lake spoke of descending and starting a small-scale ice-melting and bore at a point some 300 miles away from us. Six hours after that a second and very excited message told of the frantic, beaver-like work whereby a shallow shaft had been sunk and blasted; culminating in the discovery of slate fragments with several markings approximately like the one which had caused the original puzzlement.

Three hours later a brief bulletin announced the resumption of the flight in the teeth of a raw and piercing gale; and when I despatched a message of protest against further hazards, Lake replied curtly that his new specimens made any hazard worth taking. I saw that his excitement had reached the point of mutiny, and that I could do nothing to check this headlong risk of the whole expedition's success; but it was appalling to think of his plunging deeper and deeper into that treacherous and sinister white immensity of tempests and unfathomed mysteries which stretched off for some 1500 miles to the half-known, half-suspected coast-line of Queen Mary and Knox Lands.

Then, in about an hour and a half more, came that doubly excited message from Lake's moving plane which almost reversed my sentiments and made me wish I had accompanied the party.

> "10:05 p.m. On the wing. After snowstorm, have spied mountain range ahead higher than any hitherto seen. May equal Himalayas allowing for height of plateau. Probable Latitude 76° 15′, Longitude 113° 10′ E. Reaches far as can see to right and left. Suspicion of two smoking cones. All peaks black and bare of snow. Gale blowing off them impedes navigation."

After that Pabodie, the men, and I hung breathlessly over the receiver. Thought of this titanic mountain rampart 700 miles away inflamed our deepest sense of adventure; and we rejoiced that our expedition, if not ourselves personally, had been its discoverers. In half an hour Lake called us again.

> "Moulton's plane forced down on plateau in foothills, but nobody hurt and perhaps can repair. Shall transfer essentials to other three for return or further moves if necessary, but no more heavy plane travel needed just now. Mountains surpass anything

> in imagination. Am going up scouting in Carroll's plane, with all weight out. You can't imagine anything like this. Highest peaks must go over 35,000 feet. Everest out of the running. Atwood to work out height with theodolite while Carroll and I go up. Probably wrong about cones, for formations look stratified. Possibly pre-Cambrian slate with other strata mixed in. Queer skyline effects—regular sections of cubes clinging to highest peaks. Whole thing marvellous in red-gold light of low sun. Like land of mystery in a dream or gateway to forbidden world of untrodden wonder. Wish you were here to study."

Though it was technically sleeping-time, not one of us listeners thought for a moment of retiring. It must have been a good deal the same at McMurdo Sound, where the supply cache and the *Arkham* were also getting the messages; for Capt. Douglas gave out a call congratulating everybody on the important find, and Sherman, the cache operator, seconded his sentiments. We were sorry, of course, about the damaged aëroplane; but hoped it could be easily mended. Then, at 11 p.m., came another call from Lake.

> "Up with Carroll over highest foothills. Don't dare try really tall peaks in present weather, but shall later. Frightful work climbing, and hard going at this altitude, but worth it. Great range fairly solid, hence can't get any glimpses beyond. Main summits exceed Himalayas, and very queer. Range looks like pre-Cambrian slate, with plain signs of many other upheaved strata. Was wrong about volcanism. Goes farther in either direction than we can see. Swept clear of snow above about 21,000 feet. Odd formations on slopes of highest mountains. Great low square blocks with exactly vertical sides, and rectangular lines of low vertical ramparts, like the old Asian castles clinging to steep mountains in Roerich's paintings. Impressive from distance. Flew close to some, and Carroll thought they were formed of smaller separate pieces, but that is probably weathering. Most edges crumbled and rounded off as if exposed to storms and climate changes for millions of years. Parts, especially upper parts, seem to be of lighter-coloured rock than any visible strata on slopes proper, hence an evidently crystalline origin. Close flying shews many cave-mouths, some unusually regular in outline, square or semicircular. You must come and investigate. Think I saw rampart squarely on top of one peak. Height seems about 30,000 to 35,000 feet. Am up 21,500 myself, in devilish gnawing cold. Wind whistles and pipes through passes and in and out of caves, but no flying danger so far."

From then on for another half-hour Lake kept up a running fire of comment, and expressed his intention of climbing some of the peaks on foot. I replied that I would join him as soon as he could send a plane, and that Pabodie and I would work out the best gasoline plan—just where and how to concentrate our supply in view of the expedition's altered character. Obviously, Lake's boring operations, as well as his aëroplane activities, would need a great deal delivered at the new base which he was to establish at the foot of the mountains; and it was possible that the eastward flight might not be made after all this season. In connexion with this business I called Capt. Douglas and asked him to get as much as possible out of the ships and up the barrier with the single dog-team we had left there. A direct route across the unknown region between Lake and McMurdo Sound was what we really ought to establish.

Lake called me later to say that he had decided to let the camp stay where Moulton's plane had been forced down, and where repairs had already progressed somewhat. The ice-sheet was very thin, with dark ground here and there visible, and he would sink some borings and blasts at that very point before making any sledge trips or climbing expeditions. He spoke of the ineffable majesty of the whole scene, and the queer state of his sensations at being in the lee of vast silent pinnacles whose ranks shot up like a wall reaching the sky at the world's rim. Atwood's theodolite observations had placed the height of the five tallest peaks at from 30,000 to 34,000 feet. The windswept nature of the terrain clearly disturbed Lake, for it argued the occasional existence of prodigious gales violent beyond anything we had so far encountered. His camp lay a little more than five miles from where the higher foothills abruptly rose. I could almost trace a note of subconscious alarm in his words—flashed across a glacial void of 700 miles—as he urged that we all hasten with the matter and get the strange new region disposed of as soon as possible. He was about to rest now, after a continuous day's work of almost unparalleled speed, strenuousness, and results.

In the morning I had a three-cornered wireless talk with Lake and Capt. Douglas at their widely separated bases; and it was agreed that one of Lake's planes would come to my base for Pabodie, the five men, and myself, as well as for all the fuel it could carry. The rest of the fuel question, depending on our decision about an easterly trip, could wait for a few days; since Lake had enough for immediate camp heat and borings. Eventually the old southern base ought to be restocked; but if we postponed the easterly trip we would not use it till the next summer, and meanwhile Lake must send a plane to explore a direct route between his new mountains and McMurdo Sound.

Pabodie and I prepared to close our base for a short or long period, as the case might be. If we wintered in the antarctic we would probably fly straight from Lake's base to the *Arkham* without returning to this spot. Some of our conical tents had already been reinforced by blocks of hard snow, and now we decided to complete the job of making a permanent Esquimau village. Owing to a very liberal tent supply, Lake had with him all that his base would need even after our arrival. I wirelessed that Pabodie and I would be ready for the northwestward move after one day's work and one night's rest.

Our labours, however, were not very steady after 4 p.m.; for about that time Lake began sending in the most extraordinary and excited messages. His working day had started unpropitiously; since an aëroplane survey of the nearly exposed rock surfaces shewed an entire absence of those archaean and primordial strata for which he was looking, and which formed so great a part of the colossal peaks that loomed up at a tantalising distance from the camp. Most of the rocks glimpsed were apparently Jurassic and Comanchian sandstones and Permian and Triassic schists, with now and then a glossy black outcropping suggesting a hard and slaty coal. This rather discouraged Lake, whose plans all hinged on unearthing specimens more than 500 million years older. It was clear to him that in order to recover the archaean slate vein in which he had found the odd markings, he would have to make a long sledge trip from these foothills to the steep slopes of the gigantic mountains themselves.

He had resolved, nevertheless, to do some local boring as part of the expedition's general programme; hence set up the drill and put five men to work with it while the rest finished settling the camp and repairing the damaged aëroplane. The softest visible rock—a sandstone about a quarter of a mile from the camp—had been chosen for the first sampling; and the drill made excellent progress without much supplementary blasting. It was about three hours afterward, following the first really heavy blast of the operation, that the shouting of the drill crew was heard; and that young Gedney—the acting foreman—rushed into the camp with the startling news.

They had struck a cave. Early in the boring the sandstone had given place to a vein of Comanchian limestone full of minute fossil cephalopods, corals, echini, and spirifera, and with occasional suggestions of siliceous sponges and marine vertebrate bones—the latter probably of teliosts, sharks, and ganoids. This in itself was important enough, as affording the first vertebrate fossils the expedition had yet secured; but when shortly afterward the drill-head dropped through the stratum into apparent vacancy, a wholly new and doubly intense wave of excitement spread among the excavators. A good-sized blast had laid open the subterrene secret; and now, through a jagged aperture perhaps five feet across and three feet thick, there yawned before the avid searchers a section of shallow limestone hollowing worn more than fifty million years ago by the trickling ground waters of a bygone tropic world.

The hollowed layer was not more than seven or eight feet deep, but extended off indefinitely in all directions and had a fresh, slightly moving air which suggested its membership in an extensive subterranean system. Its roof and floor were abundantly equipped with large stalactites and stalagmites, some of which met in columnar form; but important above all else was the vast deposit of shells and bones which in places nearly choked the passage. Washed down from unknown jungles of Mesozoic tree-ferns and fungi, and forests of Tertiary cycads, fan-palms, and primitive angiosperms, this osseous medley contained representatives of more Cretaceous, Eocene, and other animal species than the greatest palaeontologist could have counted or classified in a year. Molluscs, crustacean armour, fishes, amphibians, reptiles, birds, and early mammals—great and small, known and unknown. No wonder Gedney ran back to the camp shouting, and no wonder everyone else dropped work and rushed headlong through the biting cold to where the tall derrick marked a new-found gateway to secrets of inner earth and vanished aeons.

When Lake had satisfied the first keen edge of his curiosity he scribbled a message in his notebook and had young Moulton run back to the camp to despatch it by wireless. This was my first word of the discovery, and it told of the identification of early shells, bones of ganoids and placoderms, remnants of labyrinthodonts and thecodonts, great mososaur skull fragments, dinosaur vertebrae and armour-plates, pterodactyl teeth and wing-bones, archaeopteryx debris, Miocene sharks' teeth, primitive bird-skulls, and skulls, vertebrae, and other bones of archaic mammals such as palaeotheres, xiphodons, dinocerases, eohippi, oreodons, and titanotheres. There was nothing as recent as a mastodon, elephant, true camel, deer, or bovine animal; hence Lake concluded that the last deposits had occurred during the Oligocene age, and that the hollowed stratum had lain in its present dried, dead, and inaccessible state for at least thirty million years.

On the other hand, the prevalence of very early life-forms was singular in the highest degree. Though the limestone formation was, on the evidence of such typical imbedded fossils as ventriculites, positively and unmistakably Comanchian and not a particle earlier; the free fragments in the hollow space included a surprising proportion from organisms hitherto considered as peculiar to far older periods—even rudimentary fishes, molluscs, and corals as remote as the Silurian or Ordovician. The inevitable inference was that in this part of the world there had been a remarkable and unique degree of continuity between the life of over 300 million years ago and that of only thirty million years ago. How far this continuity had extended beyond the Oligocene age when the cavern was closed, was of course past all speculation. In any event, the coming of the frightful ice in the Pleistocene some 500,000 years ago—a mere yesterday as compared with the age of this cavity—must have put an end to any of the primal forms which had locally managed to outlive their common terms.

Lake was not content to let his first message stand, but had another bulletin written and despatched across the snow to the camp before Moulton could get back. After that Moulton stayed at the wireless in one of the planes; transmitting to me—and to the *Arkham* for relaying to the outside world—the frequent postscripts which Lake sent him by a succession of messengers. Those who followed the newspapers will remember the excitement created among men of science by that afternoon's reports—reports which have finally led, after all these years, to the organisation of that very Starkweather-Moore Expedition which I am so anxious to dissuade from its purposes. I had better give the messages literally as Lake sent them, and as our base operator McTighe translated them from his pencil shorthand.

> "Fowler makes discovery of highest importance in sandstone and limestone fragments from blasts. Several distinct triangular striated prints like those in archaean slate, proving that source survived from over 600 million years ago to Comanchian times without more than moderate morphological changes and decrease in average size. Comanchian prints apparently more primitive or decadent, if anything, than older ones. Emphasise importance of discovery in press. Will mean to biology what Einstein has meant to mathematics and physics. Joins up with my previous work and amplifies conclusions. Appears to indicate, as I suspected, that earth has seen whole cycle or cycles of organic life before known one that begins with archaeozoic cells. Was evolved and specialised not later than thousand million years ago, when planet was young and recently uninhabitable for any life-forms of normal protoplasmic structure. Question arises when, where, and how development took place."

> "Later. Examining certain skeletal fragments of large land and marine saurians and primitive mammals, find singular local wounds or injuries to bony structure not attributable to any known

predatory or carnivorous animal of any period. Of two sorts—straight, penetrant bores, and apparently hacking incisions. One or two cases of cleanly severed bone. Not many specimens affected. Am sending to camp for electric torches. Will extend search area underground by hacking away stalactites."

"Still later. Have found peculiar soapstone fragment about six inches across and an inch and a half thick, wholly unlike any visible local formation. Greenish, but no evidences to place its period. Has curious smoothness and regularity. Shaped like five-pointed star with tips broken off, and signs of other cleavage at inward angles and in centre of surface. Small, smooth depression in centre of unbroken surface. Arouses much curiosity as to source and weathering. Probably some freak of water action. Carroll, with magnifier, thinks he can make out additional markings of geologic significance. Groups of tiny dots in regular patterns. Dogs growing uneasy as we work, and seem to hate this soapstone. Must see if it has any peculiar odour. Will report again when Mills gets back with light and we start on underground area."

"10:15 p.m. Important discovery. Orrendorf and Watkins, working underground at 9:45 with light, found monstrous barrel-shaped fossil of wholly unknown nature; probably vegetable unless overgrown specimen of unknown marine radiata. Tissue evidently preserved by mineral salts. Tough as leather, but astonishing flexibility retained in places. Marks of broken-off parts at ends and around sides. Six feet end to end, 3.5 feet central diameter, tapering to 1 foot at each end. Like a barrel with five bulging ridges in place of staves. Lateral breakages, as of thinnish stalks, are at equator in middle of these ridges. In furrows between ridges are curious growths. Combs or wings that fold up and spread out like fans. All greatly damaged but one, which gives almost 7-foot wing spread. Arrangement reminds one of certain monsters of primal myth, especially fabled Elder Things in *Necronomicon*. These wings seem to be membraneous, stretched on framework of glandular tubing. Apparent minute orifices in frame tubing at wing tips. Ends of body shrivelled, giving no clue to interior or to what has been broken off there. Must dissect when we get back to camp. Can't decide whether vegetable or animal. Many features obviously of almost incredible primitiveness. Have set all hands cutting stalactites and looking for further specimens. Additional scarred bones found, but these must wait. Having trouble with dogs. They can't endure the new specimen, and would probably tear it to pieces if we didn't keep it at a distance from them."

"11:30 p.m. Attention, Dyer, Pabodie, Douglas. Matter of highest—I might say transcendent—importance. *Arkham* must relay to Kingsport Head Station at once. Strange barrel growth is the archaean thing that left prints in rocks. Mills, Boudreau, and Fowler discover cluster of thirteen more at underground point forty feet from aperture. Mixed with curiously rounded and configured soapstone fragments smaller than one previously found—star-shaped but no marks of breakage except at some of the points. Of organic specimens, eight apparently perfect, with all appendages. Have brought all to surface, leading off dogs to distance. They cannot stand the things. Give close attention to description and repeat back for accuracy. Papers must get this right.

"Objects are eight feet long all over. Six-foot five-ridged barrel torso 3.5 feet central diameter, 1 foot end diameters. Dark grey, flexible, and infinitely tough. Seven-foot membraneous wings of same colour, found folded, spread out of furrows between ridges. Wing framework tubular or glandular, of lighter grey, with orifices at wing tips. Spread wings have serrated edge. Around equator, one at central apex of each of the five vertical, stave-like ridges, are five systems of light-grey flexible arms or tentacles found tightly folded to torso but expansible to maximum length of over 3 feet. Like arms of primitive crinoid. Single stalks 3 inches diameter branch after 6 inches into five sub-stalks, each of which branches after 8 inches into five small, tapering tentacles or tendrils, giving each stalk a total of 25 tentacles.

"At top of torso blunt bulbous neck of lighter grey with gill-like suggestions holds yellowish five-pointed starfish-shaped apparent head covered with 3-inch wiry cilia of various prismatic colours. Head thick and puffy, about 2 feet point to point, with 3-inch flexible yellowish tubes projecting from each point. Slit in exact centre of top probably breathing aperture. At end of each tube is spherical expansion where yellowish membrane rolls back on handling to reveal glassy, red-irised globe, evidently an eye. Five slightly longer reddish tubes start from inner angles of starfish-shaped head and end in sac-like swellings of same colour which upon pressure open to bell-shaped orifices 2 inches maximum diameter and lined with sharp white tooth-like projections. Probable mouths. All these tubes, cilia, and points of starfish-head found folded tightly down; tubes and points clinging to bulbous neck and torso. Flexibility surprising despite vast toughness.

"At bottom of torso rough but dissimilarly functioning counterparts of head arrangements exist. Bulbous light-grey pseudo-neck, without gill suggestions, holds greenish five-pointed starfish-arrangement. Tough, muscular arms 4 feet long and tapering from 7 inches diameter at base to about 2.5 at point. To each point is attached small end of a greenish five-veined membraneous triangle 8 inches long and 6 wide at farther end. This is the paddle, fin, or pseudo-foot which has made prints in rocks from a thousand million to 50 or 60 million years old. From inner angles of starfish-arrangement project 2-foot reddish tubes tapering from 3 inches diameter at base to 1 at tip. Orifices at tips. All these parts infinitely tough and leathery, but extremely flexible. Four-foot arms with paddles undoubtedly used for locomotion of some sort, marine or otherwise. When moved, display suggestions of exaggerated muscularity. As found, all these projections tightly folded over pseudo-neck and end of torso, corresponding to projections at other end.

"Cannot yet assign positively to animal or vegetable kingdom, but odds now favour animal. Probably represents incredibly advanced evolution of radiata without loss of certain primitive features. Echinoderm resemblances unmistakable despite local contradictory evidences. Wing structure puzzles in view of probable marine habitat, but may have use in water navigation. Symmetry is curiously vegetable-like, suggesting vegetable's essentially up-and-down structure rather than animal's fore-and-aft structure. Fabulously early date of evolution, preceding even simplest archaean protozoa hitherto known, baffles all conjecture as to origin.

"Complete specimens have such uncanny resemblance to certain creatures of primal myth that suggestion of ancient existence outside antarctic becomes inevitable. Dyer and Pabodie have read *Necronomicon* and seen Clark Ashton Smith's nightmare paintings based on text, and will understand when I speak of Elder Things supposed to have created all earth-life as jest or mistake. Students have always thought conception formed from morbid imaginative treatment of very ancient tropical radiata. Also like prehistoric folklore things Wilmarth has spoken of—Cthulhu cult appendages, etc.

"Vast field of study opened. Deposits probably of late Cretaceous or early Eocene period, judging from associated specimens. Massive stalagmites deposited above them. Hard work hewing out, but toughness prevented damage. State of preservation miraculous, evidently owing to limestone action. No more found so far, but will resume search later. Job now to get fourteen huge specimens to camp without dogs, which bark furiously and can't be trusted near them. With nine men—three left to guard the dogs—we ought to manage the three sledges fairly well, though wind is bad. Must establish plane communication with McMurdo Sound and begin shipping material. But I've got to dissect one of these things before we take any rest. Wish I had a real laboratory here. Dyer better kick himself for having tried to stop my westward trip. First the world's greatest mountains, and then this. If this last isn't the high spot of the expedition, I don't know what is. We're made scientifically. Congrats, Pabodie, on the drill that opened up the cave. Now will *Arkham* please repeat description?"

The sensations of Pabodie and myself at receipt of this report were almost beyond description, nor were our companions much behind us in enthusiasm. McTighe, who had hastily translated a few high spots as they came from the droning receiving set, wrote out the entire message from his shorthand version as soon as Lake's operator signed off. All appreciated the epoch-making significance of the discovery, and I sent Lake congratulations as soon as the *Arkham's* operator had repeated back the descriptive parts as requested; and my example was followed by Sherman from his station at the McMurdo Sound supply cache, as well as by Capt. Douglas of the *Arkham*. Later, as head of the expedition, I added some remarks to be relayed through the *Arkham* to the outside world. Of course, rest was an absurd thought amidst this excitement; and my only wish was to get to Lake's camp as quickly as I could. It disappointed me when he sent word that a rising mountain gale made early aërial travel impossible.

But within an hour and a half interest again rose to banish disappointment. Lake was sending more messages, and told of the completely successful transportation of the fourteen great specimens to the camp. It had been a hard pull, for the things were surprisingly heavy; but nine men had accomplished it very neatly. Now some of the party were hurriedly building a snow corral at a safe distance from the camp, to which the dogs could be brought for greater convenience in feeding. The specimens were laid out on the hard snow near the camp, save for one on which Lake was making crude attempts at dissection.

This dissection seemed to be a greater task than had been expected; for despite the heat of a gasoline stove in the newly raised laboratory tent, the deceptively flexible tissues of the chosen specimen—a powerful and intact one—lost nothing of their more than leathery toughness. Lake was puzzled as to how he might make the requisite incisions without violence destructive enough to upset all the structural niceties he was looking for. He had, it is true, seven more perfect specimens; but these were too few to use up recklessly unless the cave might later yield an unlimited supply. Accordingly he removed the specimen and dragged in one which, though having remnants of the starfish-arrangements at both ends, was badly crushed and partly disrupted along one of the great torso furrows.

Results, quickly reported over the wireless, were baffling and provocative indeed. Nothing like delicacy or accuracy was possible with instruments hardly able to cut the anomalous tissue, but the little that was achieved left us all awed and bewildered. Existing biology would have to be wholly revised, for this thing was no product of any cell-growth science knows about. There had been scarcely any mineral replacement, and despite an age of perhaps forty million years the internal organs were wholly intact. The leathery, undeteriorative, and almost indestructible quality was an inherent attribute of the thing's form of organisation; and pertained to some palaeogean cycle of invertebrate evolution utterly beyond our powers of speculation. At first all that Lake found was dry, but as the heated tent produced its thawing effect, organic moisture of pungent and offensive odour was encountered toward the thing's uninjured side. It was not blood, but a thick, dark-green fluid apparently answering the same purpose. By the time Lake reached this stage all 37 dogs had been brought to the still uncompleted corral near the camp; and even at that distance set up a savage barking and show of restlessness at the acrid, diffusive smell.

Far from helping to place the strange entity, this provisional dissection merely deepened its mystery. All guesses about its external members had been correct, and on the evidence of these one could hardly hesitate to call the thing animal; but internal inspection brought up so many vegetable evidences that Lake was left hopelessly at sea. It had digestion and circulation, and eliminated waste matter through the reddish tubes of its starfish-shaped base. Cursorily, one would say that its respiratory apparatus handled oxygen rather than carbon dioxide; and there were odd evidences of air-storage chambers and methods of shifting respiration from the external orifice to at least two other fully developed breathing-systems—gills and pores. Clearly, it was amphibian and probably adapted to long airless hibernation-periods as well. Vocal organs seemed present in connexion with the main respiratory system, but they presented anomalies beyond immediate solution. Articulate speech, in the sense of syllable-utterance, seemed barely conceivable; but musical piping notes covering a wide range were highly probable. The muscular system was almost preternaturally developed.

The nervous system was so complex and highly developed as to leave Lake aghast. Though excessively primitive and archaic in some respects, the thing had a set of ganglial centres and connectives arguing the very extremes of specialised development. Its five-lobed brain was surprisingly advanced; and there were signs of a sensory equipment, served in part through the wiry cilia of the head, involving factors alien to any other terrestrial organism. Probably it had more than five senses, so that its habits could not be predicted from any existing analogy. It must, Lake thought, have been a creature of keen sensitiveness and delicately differentiated functions in its primal world; much like the ants and bees of today. It reproduced like the vegetable cryptogams, especially the pteridophytes; having spore-cases at the tips of the wings and evidently developing from a thallus or prothallus.

But to give it a name at this stage was mere folly. It looked like a radiate, but was clearly something more. It was partly vegetable, but had three-fourths of the essentials of animal structure. That it was marine in origin, its symmetrical contour and certain other attributes clearly indicated; yet one could not be exact as to the limit of its later adaptations. The wings, after all, held a persistent suggestion of the aërial. How it could have undergone its tremendously complex evolution on a new-born earth in time to leave prints in archaean rocks was so far beyond conception as to make Lake whimsically recall the primal myths about Great Old Ones who filtered down from the stars and concocted earth-life as a joke or mistake; and the wild tales of cosmic hill things from Outside told by a folklorist colleague in Miskatonic's English department.

Naturally, he considered the possibility of the pre-Cambrian prints' having been made by a less evolved ancestor of the present specimens; but quickly rejected this too facile theory upon considering the advanced structural qualities of the older fossils. If anything, the later contours shewed decadence rather than higher evolution. The size of the pseudo-feet had decreased, and the whole morphology seemed coarsened and simplified. Moreover, the nerves and organs just examined all held singular suggestions of retrogression from forms still more complex. Atrophied and vestigial parts were surprisingly prevalent. Altogether, little could be said to have been solved; and Lake fell back on mythology for a provisional name—jocosely dubbing his finds "The Elder Ones".

At about 2:30 a.m., having decided to postpone further work and get a little rest, he covered the dissected organism with a tarpaulin, emerged from the laboratory tent, and studied the intact specimens with renewed interest. The ceaseless antarctic sun had begun to limber up their tissues a trifle, so that the head-points and tubes of two or three shewed signs of unfolding; but Lake did not believe there was any danger of immediate decomposition in the almost sub-zero air. He did, however, move all the undissected specimens closer together and throw a spare tent over them in order to keep off the direct solar rays. That would also help to keep their possible scent away from the dogs, whose hostile unrest was really becoming a problem even at their substantial distance and behind the higher and higher snow walls which an increased quota of the men were hastening to raise around their quarters. He had to weight down the corners of the tent-cloth with heavy blocks of snow to hold it in place amidst the rising gale, for the titan mountains seemed about to deliver some gravely severe blasts. Early apprehensions about sudden antarctic winds were revived, and under Atwood's supervision precautions were taken to bank the tents, new dog-corral, and crude aëroplane shelters with snow on the mountainward side. These latter shelters, begun with hard snow blocks during odd moments, were by no means as high as they should have been; and Lake finally detached all hands from other tasks to work on them.

It was after four when Lake at last prepared to sign off and advised us all to share the rest period his outfit would take when the shelter walls were a little higher. He held some friendly chat with Pabodie over the ether, and repeated his praise of the really marvellous drills that had helped him make his discovery. Atwood also sent greetings and praises. I gave Lake a warm word of congratulation, owning up that he was right about the western trip; and we all agreed to get in touch by wireless at ten in the morning. If the gale was then over, Lake would send a plane for the party at my base. Just before retiring I despatched a final message to the *Arkham* with instructions about toning down the day's news for the outside world, since the full details seemed radical enough to rouse a wave of incredulity until further substantiated.

III.

None of us, I imagine, slept very heavily or continuously that morning; for both the excitement of Lake's discovery and the mounting fury of the wind were against such a thing. So savage was the blast, even where we were, that we could not help wondering how much worse it was at Lake's camp, directly under the vast unknown peaks that bred and delivered it. McTighe was awake at ten o'clock and tried to get Lake on the wireless, as agreed, but some electrical condition in the disturbed air to the westward seemed to prevent communication. We did, however, get the *Arkham*, and Douglas told me that he had likewise been vainly trying to reach Lake. He had not known about the wind, for very little was blowing at McMurdo Sound despite its persistent rage where we were.

Throughout the day we all listened anxiously and tried to get Lake at intervals, but invariably without results. About noon a positive frenzy of wind stampeded out of the west, causing us to fear for the safety of our camp; but it eventually died down, with only a moderate relapse at 2 p.m. After three o'clock it was very quiet, and we redoubled our efforts to get Lake. Reflecting that he had four planes, each provided with an excellent short-wave outfit, we could not imagine any ordinary accident capable of crippling all his wireless equipment at once. Nevertheless the stony silence continued; and when we thought of the delirious force the wind must have had in his locality we could not help making the most direful conjectures.

By six o'clock our fears had become intense and definite, and after a wireless consultation with Douglas and Thorfinnssen I resolved to take steps toward investigation. The fifth aëroplane, which we had left at the McMurdo Sound supply cache with Sherman and two sailors, was in good shape and ready for instant use; and it seemed that the very emergency for which it had been saved was now upon us. I got Sherman by wireless and ordered him to join me with the plane and the two sailors at the southern base as quickly as possible; the air conditions being apparently highly favourable. We then talked over the personnel of the coming investigation party; and decided that we would include all hands, together with the sledge and dogs which I had kept with me. Even so great a load would not be too much for one of the huge planes built to our especial orders for heavy machinery transportation. At intervals I still tried to reach Lake with the wireless, but all to no purpose.

Sherman, with the sailors Gunnarsson and Larsen, took off at 7:30; and reported a quiet flight from several points on the wing. They arrived at our base at midnight, and all hands at once discussed the next move. It was risky business sailing over the antarctic in a single aëroplane without any line of bases, but no one drew back from what seemed like the plainest necessity. We turned in at two o'clock for a brief rest after some preliminary loading of the plane, but were up again in four hours to finish the loading and packing.

At 7:15 a.m., January 25th, we started flying northwestward under McTighe's pilotage with ten men, seven dogs, a sledge, a fuel and food supply, and other items including the plane's wireless outfit. The atmosphere was clear, fairly quiet, and relatively mild in temperature; and we anticipated very little trouble in reaching the latitude and longitude designated by Lake as the site of his camp. Our apprehensions were over what we might find, or fail to find, at the end of our journey; for silence continued to answer all calls despatched to the camp.

Every incident of that four-and-a-half-hour flight is burned into my recollection because of its crucial position in my life. It marked my loss, at the age of fifty-four, of all that peace and balance which the normal mind possesses through its accustomed conception of external Nature and Nature's laws. Thenceforward the ten of us—but the student Danforth and myself above all others—were to face a hideously amplified world of lurking horrors which nothing can erase from our emotions, and which we would refrain from sharing with mankind in general if we could. The newspapers have printed the bulletins we sent from the moving plane; telling of our non-stop course, our two battles with treacherous upper-air gales, our glimpse of the broken surface where Lake had sunk his mid-journey shaft three days before, and our sight of a group of those strange fluffy snow-cylinders noted by Amundsen and Byrd as rolling in the wind across the endless leagues of frozen plateau. There came a point, though, when our sensations could not be conveyed in any words the press would understand; and a later point when we had to adopt an actual rule of strict censorship.

The sailor Larsen was first to spy the jagged line of witch-like cones and pinnacles ahead, and his shouts sent everyone to the windows of the great cabined plane. Despite our speed, they were very slow in gaining prominence; hence we knew that they must be infinitely far off, and visible only because of their abnormal height. Little by little, however, they rose grimly into the western sky; allowing us to distinguish various bare, bleak, blackish summits, and to catch the curious sense of phantasy which they inspired as seen in the reddish antarctic light against the provocative background of iridescent ice-dust clouds. In the whole spectacle there was a persistent, pervasive hint of stupendous secrecy and potential revelation; as if these stark, nightmare spires marked the pylons of a frightful gateway into forbidden spheres of dream, and complex gulfs of remote time, space, and ultra-dimensionality. I could not help feeling that they were evil things—mountains of madness whose farther slopes looked out over some accursed ultimate abyss. That seething, half-luminous cloud-background held ineffable suggestions of a vague, ethereal *beyondness* far more than terrestrially spatial; and gave appalling reminders of the utter remoteness, separateness, desolation, and aeon-long death of this untrodden and unfathomed austral world.

It was young Danforth who drew our notice to the curious regularities of the higher mountain skyline—regularities like clinging fragments of perfect cubes, which Lake had mentioned in his messages, and which indeed justified his comparison with the dream-like suggestions of primordial temple-ruins on cloudy Asian mountaintops so subtly and strangely painted by Roerich. There was indeed something hauntingly Roerich-like about this whole unearthly continent of mountainous mystery. I had felt it in October when we first caught sight of Victoria Land, and I felt it afresh now. I felt, too, another wave of uneasy consciousness of archaean mythical resemblances; of how disturbingly this lethal realm corresponded to the evilly famed plateau of Leng in the primal writings. Mythologists have placed Leng in Central Asia; but the racial memory of man—or of his predecessors—is long, and it may well be that certain tales have come down from lands and mountains and temples of horror earlier than Asia and earlier than any human world we know. A few daring mystics have hinted at a pre-Pleistocene origin for the fragmentary Pnakotic Manuscripts, and have suggested that the devotees of Tsathoggua were as alien to mankind as Tsathoggua itself. Leng, wherever in space or time it might brood, was not a region I would care to be in or near; nor did I relish the proximity of a world that had ever bred such ambiguous and archaean monstrosities as those Lake had just mentioned. At the moment I felt sorry that I had ever read the abhorred "Necronomicon", or talked so much with that unpleasantly erudite folklorist Wilmarth at the university.

This mood undoubtedly served to aggravate my reaction to the bizarre mirage which burst upon us from the increasingly opalescent zenith as we drew near the mountains and began to make out the cumulative undulations of the foothills. I had seen dozens of polar mirages during the preceding weeks, some of them quite as uncanny and fantastically vivid as the present sample; but this one had a wholly novel and obscure quality of menacing symbolism, and I shuddered as the seething labyrinth of fabulous walls and towers and minarets loomed out of the troubled ice-vapours above our heads.

The effect was that of a Cyclopean city of no architecture known to man or to human imagination, with vast aggregations of night-black masonry embodying monstrous perversions of geometrical laws and attaining the most grotesque extremes of sinister bizarrerie. There were truncated cones, sometimes terraced or fluted, surmounted by tall cylindrical shafts here and there bulbously enlarged and often capped with tiers of thinnish scalloped discs; and strange, beetling, table-like constructions suggesting piles of multitudinous rectangular slabs or circular plates or five-pointed stars with each one overlapping the one beneath. There were composite cones and pyramids either alone or surmounting cylinders or cubes or flatter truncated cones and pyramids, and occasional needle-like spires in curious clusters of five. All of these febrile structures seemed knit together by tubular bridges crossing from one to the other at various dizzy heights, and the implied scale of the whole was terrifying and oppressive in its sheer giganticism. The general type of mirage was not unlike some of the wilder forms observed and drawn by the arctic whaler Scoresby in 1820; but at this time and place, with those dark, unknown mountain peaks soaring stupendously ahead, that anomalous elder-world discovery in our minds, and the pall of probable disaster enveloping the greater part of our expedition, we all seemed to find in it a taint of latent malignity and infinitely evil portent.

I was glad when the mirage began to break up, though in the process the various nightmare turrets and cones assumed distorted temporary forms of even vaster hideousness. As the whole illusion dissolved to churning opalescence we began to look earthward again, and saw that our journey's end was not far off. The unknown mountains ahead rose dizzyingly up like a fearsome rampart of giants, their curious regularities shewing with startling clearness even without a field-glass. We were over the lowest foothills now, and could see amidst the snow, ice, and bare patches of their main plateau a couple of darkish spots which we took to be Lake's camp and boring. The higher foothills shot up between five and six miles away, forming a range almost distinct from the terrifying line of more than Himalayan peaks beyond them. At length Ropes—the student who had relieved McTighe at the controls—began to head downward toward the left-hand dark spot whose size marked it as the camp. As he did so, McTighe sent out the last uncensored wireless message the world was to receive from our expedition.

Everyone, of course, has read the brief and unsatisfying bulletins of the rest of our antarctic sojourn. Some hours after our landing we sent a guarded report of the tragedy we found, and reluctantly announced the wiping out of the whole Lake party by the frightful wind of the preceding day, or of the night before that. Eleven known dead, young Gedney missing. People pardoned our hazy lack of details through realisation of the shock the sad event must have caused us, and believed us when we explained that the mangling action of the wind had rendered all eleven bodies unsuitable for transportation outside. Indeed, I flatter myself that even in the midst of our distress, utter bewilderment, and soul-clutching horror, we scarcely went beyond the truth in any specific instance. The tremendous significance lies in what we dared not tell—what I would not tell now but for the need of warning others off from nameless terrors.

It is a fact that the wind had wrought dreadful havoc. Whether all could have lived through it, even without the other thing, is gravely open to doubt. The storm, with its fury of madly driven ice-particles, must have been beyond anything our expedition had encountered before. One aëroplane shelter—all, it seems, had been left in a far too flimsy and inadequate state—

was nearly pulverised; and the derrick at the distant boring was entirely shaken to pieces. The exposed metal of the grounded planes and drilling machinery was bruised into a high polish, and two of the small tents were flattened despite their snow banking. Wooden surfaces left out in the blast were pitted and denuded of paint, and all signs of tracks in the snow were completely obliterated. It is also true that we found none of the archaean biological objects in a condition to take outside as a whole. We did gather some minerals from a vast tumbled pile, including several of the greenish soapstone fragments whose odd five-pointed rounding and faint patterns of grouped dots caused so many doubtful comparisons; and some fossil bones, among which were the most typical of the curiously injured specimens.

None of the dogs survived, their hurriedly built snow enclosure near the camp being almost wholly destroyed. The wind may have done that, though the greater breakage on the side next the camp, which was not the windward one, suggests an outward leap or break of the frantic beasts themselves. All three sledges were gone, and we have tried to explain that the wind may have blown them off into the unknown. The drill and ice-melting machinery at the boring were too badly damaged to warrant salvage, so we used them to choke up that subtly disturbing gateway to the past which Lake had blasted. We likewise left at the camp the two most shaken-up of the planes; since our surviving party had only four real pilots—Sherman, Danforth, McTighe, and Ropes—in all, with Danforth in a poor nervous shape to navigate. We brought back all the books, scientific equipment, and other incidentals we could find, though much was rather unaccountably blown away. Spare tents and furs were either missing or badly out of condition.

It was approximately 4 p.m., after wide plane cruising had forced us to give Gedney up for lost, that we sent our guarded message to the *Arkham* for relaying; and I think we did well to keep it as calm and non-committal as we succeeded in doing. The most we said about agitation concerned our dogs, whose frantic uneasiness near the biological specimens was to be expected from poor Lake's accounts. We did not mention, I think, their display of the same uneasiness when sniffing around the queer greenish soapstones and certain other objects in the disordered region; objects including scientific instruments, aëroplanes, and machinery both at the camp and at the boring, whose parts had been loosened, moved, or otherwise tampered with by winds that must have harboured singular curiosity and investigativeness.

About the fourteen biological specimens we were pardonably indefinite. We said that the only ones we discovered were damaged, but that enough was left of them to prove Lake's description wholly and impressively accurate. It was hard work keeping our personal emotions out of this matter—and we did not mention numbers or say exactly how we had found those which we did find. We had by that time agreed not to transmit anything suggesting madness on the part of Lake's men, and it surely looked like madness to find six imperfect monstrosities carefully buried upright in nine-foot snow graves under five-pointed mounds punched over with groups of dots in patterns exactly like those on the queer greenish soapstones dug up from Mesozoic or Tertiary times. The eight perfect specimens mentioned by Lake seemed to have been completely blown away.

We were careful, too, about the public's general peace of mind; hence Danforth and I said little about that frightful trip over the mountains the next day. It was the fact that only a radically lightened plane could possibly cross a range of such height which mercifully limited that scouting tour to the two of us. On our return at 1 a.m. Danforth was close to hysterics, but kept an admirably stiff upper lip. It took no persuasion to make him promise not to shew our sketches and the other things we brought away in our pockets, not to say anything more to the others than what we had agreed to relay outside, and to hide our camera films for private development later on; so that part of my present story will be as new to Pabodie, McTighe, Ropes, Sherman, and the rest as it will be to the world in general. Indeed—Danforth is closer-mouthed than I; for he saw—or thinks he saw—one thing he will not tell even me.

As all know, our report included a tale of a hard ascent; a confirmation of Lake's opinion that the great peaks are of archaean slate and other very primal crumpled strata unchanged since at least middle Comanchian times; a conventional comment on the regularity of the clinging cube and rampart formations; a decision that the cave-mouths indicate dissolved calcareous veins; a conjecture that certain slopes and passes would permit of the scaling and crossing of the entire range by seasoned mountaineers; and a remark that the mysterious other side holds a lofty and immense super-plateau as ancient and unchanging as the mountains themselves—20,000 feet in elevation, with grotesque rock formations protruding through a thin glacial layer and with low gradual foothills between the general plateau surface and the sheer precipices of the highest peaks.

This body of data is in every respect true so far as it goes, and it completely satisfied the men at the camp. We laid our absence of sixteen hours—a longer time than our announced flying, landing, reconnoitring, and rock-collecting programme called for—to a long mythical spell of adverse wind conditions; and told truly of our landing on the farther foothills. Fortunately our tale sounded realistic and prosaic enough not to tempt any of the others into emulating our flight. Had any tried to do that, I would have used every ounce of my persuasion to stop them—and I do not know what Danforth would have done. While we were gone, Pabodie, Sherman, Ropes, McTighe, and Williamson had worked like beavers over Lake's two best planes; fitting them again for use despite the altogether unaccountable juggling of their operative mechanism.

We decided to load all the planes the next morning and start back for our old base as soon as possible. Even though indirect, that was the safest way to work toward McMurdo Sound; for a straight-line flight across the most utterly unknown stretches of the aeon-dead continent would involve many additional hazards. Further exploration was hardly feasible in view of our tragic decimation and the ruin of our drilling machinery; and the doubts and horrors around us—which we did not reveal—made us wish only to escape from this austral world of desolation and brooding madness as swiftly as we could.

As the public knows, our return to the world was accomplished without further disasters. All planes reached the old base on the evening of the next day—January 27th—after a swift non-stop flight; and on the 28th we made McMurdo Sound in two laps, the one pause being very brief, and occasioned by a faulty rudder in the furious wind over the ice-shelf after we had cleared the great plateau. In five days more the *Arkham* and *Miskatonic*, with all hands and equipment on board, were shaking clear of the thickening field ice and working up Ross Sea with the mocking mountains of Victoria Land looming westward against a troubled antarctic sky and twisting the wind's wails into a wide-ranged musical piping which chilled my soul to the quick. Less than a fortnight later we left the last hint of polar land behind us, and thanked heaven that we were clear of a haunted, accursed realm where life and death, space and time, have made black and blasphemous alliances in the unknown epochs since matter first writhed and swam on the planet's scarce-cooled crust.

Since our return we have all constantly worked to discourage antarctic exploration, and have kept certain doubts and guesses to ourselves with splendid unity and faithfulness. Even young Danforth, with his nervous breakdown, has not flinched or babbled to his doctors—indeed, as I have said, there is one thing he thinks he alone saw which he will not tell even me, though I think it would help his psychological state if he would consent to do so. It might explain and relieve much, though perhaps the thing was no more than the delusive aftermath of an earlier shock. That is the impression I gather after those rare irresponsible moments when he whispers disjointed things to me—things which he repudiates vehemently as soon as he gets a grip on himself again.

It will be hard work deterring others from the great white south, and some of our efforts may directly harm our cause by drawing inquiring notice. We might have known from the first that human curiosity is undying, and that the results we announced would be enough to spur others ahead on the same age-long pursuit of the unknown. Lake's reports of those biological monstrosities had aroused naturalists and palaeontologists to the highest pitch; though we were sensible enough not to shew the detached parts we had taken from the actual buried specimens, or our photographs of those specimens as they were found. We also refrained from shewing the more puzzling of the scarred bones and greenish soapstones; while Danforth and I have closely guarded the pictures we took or drew on the super-plateau across the range, and the crumpled things we smoothed, studied in terror, and brought away in our pockets. But now that Starkweather-Moore party is organising, and with a thoroughness far beyond anything our outfit attempted. If not dissuaded, they will get to the innermost nucleus of the antarctic and melt and bore till they bring up that which may end the world we know. So I must break through all reticences at last—even about that ultimate nameless thing beyond the mountains of madness.

IV.

It is only with vast hesitancy and repugnance that I let my mind go back to Lake's camp and what we really found there—and to that other thing beyond the frightful mountain wall. I am constantly tempted to shirk the details, and to let hints stand for actual facts and ineluctable deductions. I hope I have said enough already to let me glide briefly over the rest; the rest, that is, of the horror at the camp. I have told of the wind-ravaged terrain, the damaged shelters, the disarranged machinery, the varied uneasinesses of our dogs, the missing sledges and other items, the deaths of men and dogs, the absence of Gedney, and the six insanely buried biological specimens, strangely sound in texture for all their structural injuries, from a world forty million years dead. I do not recall whether I mentioned that upon checking up the canine bodies we found one dog missing. We did not think much about that till later—indeed, only Danforth and I have thought of it at all.

The principal things I have been keeping back relate to the bodies, and to certain subtle points which may or may not lend a hideous and incredible kind of rationale to the apparent chaos. At the time I tried to keep the men's minds off those points; for it was so much simpler—so much more normal—to lay everything to an outbreak of madness on the part of some of Lake's party. From the look of things, that daemon mountain wind must have been enough to drive any man mad in the midst of this centre of all earthly mystery and desolation.

The crowning abnormality, of course, was the condition of the bodies—men and dogs alike. They had all been in some terrible kind of conflict, and were torn and mangled in fiendish and altogether inexplicable ways. Death, so far as we could judge, had in each case come from strangulation or laceration. The dogs had evidently started the trouble, for the state of their ill-built corral bore witness to its forcible breakage from within. It had been set some distance from the camp because of the hatred of the animals for those hellish archaean organisms, but the precaution seemed to have been taken in vain. When left alone in that monstrous wind behind flimsy walls of insufficient height they must have stampeded—whether from the wind itself, or from some subtle, increasing odour emitted by the nightmare specimens, one could not say. Those specimens, of course, had been covered with a tent-cloth; yet the low antarctic sun had beat steadily upon that cloth, and Lake had mentioned that solar heat tended to make the strangely sound and tough tissues of the things relax and expand. Perhaps the wind had whipped the cloth from over them, and jostled them about in such a way that their more pungent olfactory qualities became manifest despite their unbelievable antiquity.

But whatever had happened, it was hideous and revolting enough. Perhaps I had better put squeamishness aside and tell the worst at last—though with a categorical statement of opinion, based on the first-hand observations and most rigid deductions of both Danforth and myself, that the then missing Gedney was in no way responsible for the loathsome horrors we found. I have said that the bodies were frightfully mangled. Now I must add that some were incised and subtracted from in the most curious, cold-blooded, and inhuman fashion. It was the same with dogs and men. All the healthier, fatter bodies, quadrupedal or bipedal, had had their most solid masses of tissue cut out and removed, as by a careful butcher; and around them was a strange sprinkling of salt—taken from the ravaged provision-chests on the planes—which conjured up the most horrible associations. The thing had occurred in one of the crude aëroplane shelters from which the plane had been dragged out, and subsequent winds had effaced all tracks which could have supplied any plausible theory. Scattered bits of clothing, roughly slashed from the human incision-subjects, hinted no clues. It is useless to bring up the half-impression of certain faint snow-prints in one shielded corner of the ruined enclosure—because that impression did not concern human prints at all, but was clearly mixed up with all the talk of fossil prints which poor Lake had been giving throughout the preceding weeks. One had to be careful of one's imagination in the lee of those overshadowing mountains of madness.

As I have indicated, Gedney and one dog turned out to be missing in the end. When we came on that terrible shelter we had missed two dogs and two men; but the fairly unharmed dissecting tent, which we entered after investigating the monstrous graves, had something to reveal. It was not as Lake had left it, for the covered parts of the primal monstrosity had been removed from the improvised table. Indeed, we had already realised that one of the six imperfect and insanely buried things we had found—the one with the trace of a peculiarly hateful odour—must represent the collected sections of the entity which Lake had tried to analyse. On and around that laboratory table were strown other things, and it did not take long for us to guess that those things were the carefully though oddly and inexpertly dissected parts of one man and one dog. I shall spare the feelings of survivors by omitting mention of the man's identity. Lake's anatomical instruments were missing, but there were evidences of their careful cleansing. The gasoline stove was also gone, though around it we found a curious litter of matches. We buried the human parts beside the other ten men, and the canine parts with the other 35 dogs. Concerning the bizarre smudges on the laboratory table, and on the jumble of roughly handled illustrated books scattered near it, we were much too bewildered to speculate.

This formed the worst of the camp horror, but other things were equally perplexing. The disappearance of Gedney, the one dog, the eight uninjured biological specimens, the three sledges, and certain instruments, illustrated technical and scientific books, writing materials, electric torches and batteries, food and fuel, heating apparatus, spare tents, fur suits, and the like, was utterly beyond sane conjecture; as were likewise the spatter-fringed ink-blots on certain pieces of paper, and the evidences of curious alien fumbling and experimentation around the planes and all other mechanical devices both at the camp and at the boring. The dogs seemed to abhor this oddly disordered machinery. Then, too, there was the upsetting of the larder, the disappearance of certain staples, and the jarringly comical heap of tin cans pried open in the most unlikely ways and at the most unlikely places. The profusion of scattered matches, intact, broken, or spent, formed another minor enigma; as did the two or three tent-cloths and fur suits which we found lying about with peculiar and unorthodox slashings conceivably due to clumsy efforts at unimaginable adaptations. The maltreatment of the human and canine bodies, and the crazy burial of the damaged archaean specimens, were all of a piece with this apparent disintegrative madness. In view of just such an eventuality as the present one, we carefully photographed all the main evidences of insane disorder at the camp; and shall use the prints to buttress our pleas against the departure of the proposed Starkweather-Moore Expedition.

Our first act after finding the bodies in the shelter was to photograph and open the row of insane graves with the five-pointed snow mounds. We could not help noticing the resemblance of these monstrous mounds, with their clusters of grouped dots, to poor Lake's descriptions of the strange greenish soapstones; and when we came on some of the soapstones themselves in the great mineral pile we found the likeness very close indeed. The whole general formation, it must be made clear, seemed abominably suggestive of the starfish-head of the archaean entities; and we agreed that the suggestion must have worked potently upon the sensitised minds of Lake's overwrought party. Our own first sight of the actual buried entities formed a horrible moment, and sent the imaginations of Pabodie and myself back to some of the shocking primal myths we had read and heard. We all agreed that the mere sight and continued presence of the things must have coöperated with the oppressive polar solitude and daemon mountain wind in driving Lake's party mad.

For madness—centreing in Gedney as the only possible surviving agent—was the explanation spontaneously adopted by everybody so far as spoken utterance was concerned; though I will not be so naive as to deny that each of us may have harboured wild guesses which sanity forbade him to formulate completely. Sherman, Pabodie, and McTighe made an exhaustive aëroplane cruise over all the surrounding territory in the afternoon, sweeping the horizon with field-glasses in quest of Gedney and of the various missing things; but nothing came to light. The party reported that the titan barrier range extended endlessly to right and left alike, without any diminution in height or essential structure. On some of the peaks, though, the regular cube and rampart formations were bolder and plainer; having doubly fantastic similitudes to Roerich-painted Asian hill ruins. The distribution of cryptical cave-mouths on the black snow-denuded summits seemed roughly even as far as the range could be traced.

In spite of all the prevailing horrors we were left with enough sheer scientific zeal and adventurousness to wonder about the unknown realm beyond those mysterious mountains. As our guarded messages stated, we rested at midnight after our day of terror and bafflement; but not without a tentative plan for one or more range-crossing altitude flights in a lightened plane with aërial camera and geologist's outfit, beginning the following morning. It was decided that Danforth and I try it first, and we awaked at 7 a.m. intending an early trip; though heavy winds—mentioned in our brief bulletin to the outside world—delayed our start till nearly nine o'clock.

I have already repeated the non-committal story we told the men at camp—and relayed outside—after our return sixteen hours later. It is now my terrible duty to amplify this account by filling in the merciful blanks with hints of what we really saw in that hidden trans-montane world—hints of the revelations which have finally driven Danforth to a nervous collapse. I wish he would add a really frank word about the thing which he alone thinks he saw—even though it was probably a nervous delusion—and which was perhaps the last straw that put him where he is; but he is firm against that. All I can do is to repeat his later disjointed whispers about what set him shrieking as the plane soared back through the wind-tortured mountain pass after that real and tangible shock which I shared. This will form my last word. If the plain signs of surviving elder horrors in what I disclose be not enough to keep others from meddling with the inner antarctic—or at least from prying too deeply beneath the surface of that ultimate waste of forbidden secrets and unhuman, aeon-cursed desolation—the responsibility for unnamable and perhaps immensurable evils will not be mine.

Danforth and I, studying the notes made by Pabodie in his afternoon flight and checking up with a sextant, had calculated that the lowest available pass in the range lay somewhat to the right of us, within sight of camp, and about 23,000 or 24,000 feet above sea-level. For this point, then, we first headed in the lightened plane as we embarked on our flight of discovery. The camp itself, on foothills which sprang from a high continental plateau, was some 12,000 feet in altitude; hence the actual height increase necessary was not so vast as it might seem. Nevertheless we were acutely conscious of the rarefied air and intense cold as we rose; for on account of visibility conditions we had to leave the cabin windows open. We were dressed, of course, in our heaviest furs.

As we drew near the forbidding peaks, dark and sinister above the line of crevasse-riven snow and interstitial glaciers, we noticed more and more the curiously regular formations clinging to the slopes; and thought again of the strange Asian paintings of Nicholas Roerich. The ancient and wind-weathered rock strata fully verified all of Lake's bulletins, and proved that these hoary pinnacles had been towering up in exactly the same way since a surprisingly early time in earth's history—perhaps over fifty million years. How much higher they had once been, it was futile to guess; but everything about this strange region pointed to obscure atmospheric influences unfavourable to change, and calculated to retard the usual climatic processes of rock disintegration.

But it was the mountainside tangle of regular cubes, ramparts, and cave-mouths which fascinated and disturbed us most. I studied them with a field-glass and took aërial photographs whilst Danforth drove; and at times relieved him at the controls—though my aviation knowledge was purely an amateur's—in order to let him use the binoculars. We could easily see that much of the material of the things was a lightish archaean quartzite, unlike any formation visible over broad areas of the general surface; and that their regularity was extreme and uncanny to an extent which poor Lake had scarcely hinted.

As he had said, their edges were crumbled and rounded from untold aeons of savage weathering; but their preternatural solidity and tough material had saved them from obliteration. Many parts, especially those closest to the slopes, seemed identical in substance with the surrounding rock surface. The whole arrangement looked like the ruins of Machu Picchu in the Andes, or the primal foundation-walls of Kish as dug up by the Oxford–Field Museum Expedition in 1929; and both Danforth and I obtained that occasional impression of *separate Cyclopean blocks* which Lake had attributed to his flight-companion Carroll. How to account for such things in this place was frankly beyond me, and I felt queerly humbled as a geologist. Igneous formations often have strange regularities—like the famous Giants' Causeway in Ireland—but this stupendous range, despite Lake's original suspicion of smoking cones, was above all else non-volcanic in evident structure.

The curious cave-mouths, near which the odd formations seemed most abundant, presented another albeit a lesser puzzle because of their regularity of outline. They were, as Lake's bulletin had said, often approximately square or semicircular; as if the natural orifices had been shaped to greater symmetry by some magic hand. Their numerousness and wide distribution were remarkable, and suggested that the whole region was honeycombed with tunnels dissolved out of limestone strata. Such glimpses as we secured did not extend far within the caverns, but we saw that they were apparently clear of stalactites and stalagmites. Outside, those parts of the mountain slopes adjoining the apertures seemed invariably smooth and regular; and Danforth thought that the slight cracks and pittings of the weathering tended toward unusual patterns. Filled as he was with the horrors and strangenesses discovered at the camp, he hinted that the pittings vaguely resembled those baffling groups of dots sprinkled over the primeval greenish soapstones, so hideously duplicated on the madly conceived snow mounds above those six buried monstrosities.

We had risen gradually in flying over the higher foothills and along toward the relatively low pass we had selected. As we advanced we occasionally looked down at the snow and ice of the land route, wondering whether we could have attempted the trip with the simpler equipment of earlier days. Somewhat to our surprise we saw that the terrain was far from difficult as such things go; and that despite the crevasses and other bad spots it would not have been likely to deter the sledges of a Scott, a Shackleton, or an Amundsen. Some of the glaciers appeared to lead up to wind-bared passes with unusual continuity, and upon reaching our chosen pass we found that its case formed no exception.

Our sensations of tense expectancy as we prepared to round the crest and peer out over an untrodden world can hardly be described on paper; even though we had no cause to think the regions beyond the range essentially different from those already seen and traversed. The touch of evil mystery in these barrier mountains, and in the beckoning sea of opalescent sky glimpsed betwixt their summits, was a highly subtle and attenuated matter not to be explained in literal words. Rather was it an affair of vague psychological symbolism and aesthetic association—a thing mixed up with exotic poetry and paintings, and with archaic myths lurking in shunned and forbidden volumes. Even the wind's burden held a peculiar strain of conscious malignity; and for a second it seemed that the composite sound included a bizarre musical whistling or piping over a wide range as the blast swept in and out of the omnipresent and resonant cave-mouths. There was a cloudy note of reminiscent repulsion in this sound, as complex and unplaceable as any of the other dark impressions.

We were now, after a slow ascent, at a height of 23,570 feet according to the aneroid; and had left the region of clinging snow definitely below us. Up here were only dark, bare rock slopes and the start of rough-ribbed glaciers—but with those provocative cubes, ramparts, and echoing cave-mouths to add a portent of the unnatural, the fantastic, and the dream-like. Looking along the line of high peaks, I thought I could see the one mentioned by poor Lake, with a rampart exactly on top. It seemed to be half-lost in a queer antarctic haze; such a haze, perhaps, as had been responsible for Lake's early notion of volcanism. The pass loomed directly before us, smooth and windswept between its jagged and malignly frowning pylons. Beyond it was a sky fretted with swirling vapours and lighted by the low polar sun—the sky of that mysterious farther realm upon which we felt no human eye had ever gazed.

A few more feet of altitude and we would behold that realm. Danforth and I, unable to speak except in shouts amidst the howling, piping wind that raced through the pass and added to the noise of the unmuffled engines, exchanged eloquent glances. And then, having gained those last few feet, we did indeed stare across the momentous divide and over the unsampled secrets of an elder and utterly alien earth.

V.

I think that both of us simultaneously cried out in mixed awe, wonder, terror, and disbelief in our own senses as we finally cleared the pass and saw what lay beyond. Of course we must have had some natural theory in the back of our heads to steady our faculties for the moment. Probably we thought of such things as the grotesquely weathered stones of the Garden of the Gods in Colorado, or the fantastically symmetrical wind-carved rocks of the Arizona desert. Perhaps we even half thought the sight a mirage like that we had seen the morning before on first approaching those mountains of madness. We must have had some such normal notions to fall back upon as our eyes swept that limitless, tempest-scarred plateau and grasped the almost endless labyrinth of colossal, regular, and geometrically eurhythmic stone masses which reared their crumbled and pitted crests above a glacial sheet not more than 40 or 50 feet deep at its thickest, and in places obviously thinner.

The effect of the monstrous sight was indescribable, for some fiendish violation of known natural law seemed certain at the outset. Here, on a hellishly ancient table-land fully 20,000 feet high, and in a climate deadly to habitation since a pre-human age not less than 500,000 years ago, there stretched nearly to the vision's limit a tangle of orderly stone which only the desperation of mental self-defence could possibly attribute to any but a conscious and artificial cause. We had previously dismissed, so far as serious thought was concerned, any theory that the cubes and ramparts of the mountainsides were other than natural in origin. How could they be otherwise, when man himself could scarcely have been differentiated from the great apes at the time when this region succumbed to the present unbroken reign of glacial death?

Yet now the sway of reason seemed irrefutably shaken, for this Cyclopean maze of squared, curved, and angled blocks had features which cut off all comfortable refuge. It was, very clearly, the blasphemous city of the mirage in stark, objective, and ineluctable reality. That damnable portent had had a material basis after all—there had been some horizontal stratum of ice-dust in the upper air, and this shocking stone survival had projected its image across the mountains according to the simple laws of reflection. Of course the phantom had been twisted and exaggerated, and had contained things which the real source did not contain; yet now, as we saw that real source, we thought it even more hideous and menacing than its distant image.

Only the incredible, unhuman massiveness of these vast stone towers and ramparts had saved the frightful thing from utter annihilation in the hundreds of thousands—perhaps millions—of years it had brooded there amidst the blasts of a bleak upland. "Corona Mundi … Roof of the World …" All sorts of fantastic phrases sprang to our lips as we looked dizzily down at the unbelievable spectacle. I thought again of the eldritch primal myths that had so persistently haunted me since my first sight of this dead antarctic world—of the daemoniac plateau of Leng, of the Mi-Go, or Abominable Snow-Men of the Himalayas, of the Pnakotic Manuscripts with their pre-human implications, of the Cthulhu cult, of the *Necronomicon*, and of the Hyperborean legends of formless Tsathoggua and the worse than formless star-spawn associated with that semi-entity.

For boundless miles in every direction the thing stretched off with very little thinning; indeed, as our eyes followed it to the right and left along the base of the low, gradual foothills which separated it from the actual mountain rim, we decided that we could see no thinning at all except for an interruption at the left of the pass through which we had come. We had merely struck, at random, a limited part of something of incalculable extent. The foothills were more sparsely sprinkled with grotesque stone structures, linking the terrible city to the already familiar cubes and ramparts which evidently formed its mountain outposts. These latter, as well as the queer cave-mouths, were as thick on the inner as on the outer sides of the mountains.

The nameless stone labyrinth consisted, for the most part, of walls from 10 to 150 feet in ice-clear height, and of a thickness varying from five to ten feet. It was composed mostly of prodigious blocks of dark primordial slate, schist, and sandstone—blocks in many cases as large as 4 × 6 × 8 feet—though in several places it seemed to be carved out of a solid, uneven bed-rock of pre-Cambrian slate. The buildings were far from equal in size; there being innumerable honeycomb-arrangements of enormous extent as well as smaller separate structures. The general shape of these things tended to be conical, pyramidal, or terraced; though there were many perfect cylinders, perfect cubes, clusters of cubes, and other rectangular forms, and a peculiar sprinkling of angled edifices whose five-pointed ground plan roughly suggested modern fortifications. The builders had made constant and expert use of the principle of the arch, and domes had probably existed in the city's heyday.

The whole tangle was monstrously weathered, and the glacial surface from which the towers projected was strown with fallen blocks and immemorial debris. Where the glaciation was transparent we could see the lower parts of the gigantic piles, and noticed the ice-preserved stone bridges which connected the different towers at varying distances above the ground. On the exposed walls we could detect the scarred places where other and higher bridges of the same sort had existed. Closer inspection revealed countless largish windows; some of which were closed with shutters of a petrified material originally wood, though most gaped open in a sinister and menacing fashion. Many of the ruins, of course, were roofless, and with uneven though wind-rounded upper edges; whilst others, of a more sharply conical or pyramidal model or else protected by higher surrounding structures, preserved intact outlines despite the omnipresent crumbling and pitting. With the field-glass we could barely make out what seemed to be sculptural decorations in horizontal bands—decorations including those curious groups of dots whose presence on the ancient soapstones now assumed a vastly larger significance.

In many places the buildings were totally ruined and the ice-sheet deeply riven from various geologic causes. In other places the stonework was worn down to the very level of the glaciation. One broad swath, extending from the plateau's interior to a cleft in the foothills about a mile to the left of the pass we had traversed, was wholly free from buildings; and probably represented, we concluded, the course of some great river which in Tertiary times—millions of years ago—had poured through the city and into some prodigious subterranean abyss of the great barrier range. Certainly, this was above all a region of caves, gulfs, and underground secrets beyond human penetration.

Looking back to our sensations, and recalling our dazedness at viewing this monstrous survival from aeons we had thought pre-human, I can only wonder that we preserved the semblance of equilibrium which we did. Of course we knew that something—chronology, scientific theory, or our own consciousness—was woefully awry; yet we kept enough poise to guide the plane, observe many things quite minutely, and take a careful series of photographs which may yet serve both us and the world in good stead. In my case, ingrained scientific habit may have helped; for above all my bewilderment and sense of menace there burned a dominant curiosity to fathom more of this age-old secret—to know what sort of beings had built and lived in this incalculably gigantic place, and what relation to the general world of its time or of other times so unique a concentration of life could have had.

For this place could be no ordinary city. It must have formed the primary nucleus and centre of some archaic and unbelievable chapter of earth's history whose outward ramifications, recalled only dimly in the most obscure and distorted myths, had vanished utterly amidst the chaos of terrene convulsions long before any human race we know had shambled out of apedom. Here sprawled a palaeogean megalopolis compared with which the fabled Atlantis and Lemuria, Commoriom and Uzuldaroum, and Olathoë in the land of Lomar are recent things of today—not even of yesterday; a megalopolis ranking with such whispered pre-human blasphemies as Valusia, R'lyeh, Ib in the land of Mnar, and the Nameless City of Arabia Deserta. As we flew above that tangle of stark titan towers my imagination sometimes escaped all bounds and roved aimlessly in realms of fantastic associations—even weaving links betwixt this lost world and some of my own wildest dreams concerning the mad horror at the camp.

The plane's fuel-tank, in the interest of greater lightness, had been only partly filled; hence we now had to exert caution in our explorations. Even so, however, we covered an enormous extent of ground—or rather, air—after swooping down to a level where the wind became virtually negligible. There seemed to be no limit to the mountain range, or to the length of the frightful stone city which bordered its inner foothills. Fifty miles of flight in each direction shewed no major change in the labyrinth of rock and masonry that clawed up corpse-like through the eternal ice. There were, though, some highly absorbing diversifications; such as the carvings on the canyon where that broad river had once pierced the foothills and approached its sinking-place in the great range. The headlands at the stream's entrance had been boldly carved into Cyclopean pylons; and something about the ridgy, barrel-shaped designs stirred up oddly vague, hateful, and confusing semi-remembrances in both Danforth and me.

We also came upon several star-shaped open spaces, evidently public squares; and noted various undulations in the terrain. Where a sharp hill rose, it was generally hollowed out into some sort of rambling stone edifice; but there were at least two exceptions. Of these latter, one was too badly weathered to disclose what had been on the jutting eminence, while the other still bore a fantastic conical monument carved out of the solid rock and roughly resembling such things as the well-known Snake Tomb in the ancient valley of Petra.

Flying inland from the mountains, we discovered that the city was not of infinite width, even though its length along the foothills seemed endless. After about thirty miles the grotesque stone buildings began to thin out, and in ten more miles we came to an unbroken waste virtually without signs of sentient artifice. The course of the river beyond the city seemed marked by a broad depressed line; while the land assumed a somewhat greater ruggedness, seeming to slope slightly upward as it receded in the mist-hazed west.

So far we had made no landing, yet to leave the plateau without an attempt at entering some of the monstrous structures would have been inconceivable. Accordingly we decided to find a smooth place on the foothills near our navigable pass, there grounding the plane and preparing to do some exploration on foot. Though these gradual slopes were partly covered with a scattering of ruins, low flying soon disclosed an ample number of possible landing-places. Selecting that nearest to the pass, since our next flight would be across the great range and back to camp, we succeeded about 12:30 p.m. in coming down on a smooth, hard snowfield wholly devoid of obstacles and well adapted to a swift and favourable takeoff later on.

It did not seem necessary to protect the plane with a snow banking for so brief a time and in so comfortable an absence of high winds at this level; hence we merely saw that the landing skis were safely lodged, and that the vital parts of the mechanism were guarded against the cold. For our foot journey we discarded the heaviest of our flying furs, and took with us a small outfit consisting of pocket compass, hand camera, light provisions, voluminous notebooks and paper, geologist's hammer and chisel, specimen-bags, coil of climbing rope, and powerful electric torches with extra batteries; this equipment having been carried in the plane on the chance that we might be able to effect a landing, take ground pictures, make drawings and topographical sketches, and obtain rock specimens from some bare slope, outcropping, or mountain cave. Fortunately we had a supply of extra paper to tear up, place in a spare specimen-bag, and use on the ancient principle of hare-and-hounds for marking our course in any interior mazes we might be able to penetrate. This had been brought in case we found some cave system with air quiet enough to allow such a rapid and easy method in place of the usual rock-chipping method of trail-blazing.

Walking cautiously downhill over the crusted snow toward the stupendous stone labyrinth that loomed against the opalescent west, we felt almost as keen a sense of imminent marvels as we had felt on approaching the unfathomed mountain pass four hours previously. True, we had become visually familiar with the incredible secret concealed by the barrier peaks; yet the prospect of actually entering primordial walls reared by conscious beings perhaps millions of years ago—before any known race of men could have existed—was none the less awesome and potentially terrible in its implications of cosmic abnormality. Though the thinness of the air at this prodigious altitude made exertion somewhat more difficult than usual; both Danforth and I found ourselves bearing up very well, and felt equal to almost any task which might fall to our lot. It took only a few steps to bring us to a shapeless ruin worn level with the snow, while ten or fifteen rods farther on there was a huge roofless rampart still complete in its gigantic five-pointed outline and rising to an irregular height of ten or eleven feet. For this latter we headed; and when at last we were able actually to touch its weathered Cyclopean blocks, we felt that we had established an unprecedented and almost blasphemous link with forgotten aeons normally closed to our species.

This rampart, shaped like a star and perhaps 300 feet from point to point, was built of Jurassic sandstone blocks of irregular size, averaging 6 × 8 feet in surface. There was a row of arched loopholes or windows about four feet wide and five feet high; spaced quite symmetrically along the points of the star and at its inner angles, and with the bottoms about four feet from the glaciated surface. Looking through these, we could see that the masonry was fully five feet thick, that there were no partitions remaining within, and that there were traces of banded carvings or bas-reliefs on the interior walls; facts we had indeed guessed before, when flying low over this rampart and others like it. Though lower parts must have originally existed, all traces of such things were now wholly obscured by the deep layer of ice and snow at this point.

We crawled through one of the windows and vainly tried to decipher the nearly effaced mural designs, but did not attempt to disturb the glaciated floor. Our orientation flights had indicated that many buildings in the city proper were less ice-choked, and that we might perhaps find wholly clear interiors leading down to the true ground level if we entered those structures still roofed at the top. Before we left the rampart we photographed it carefully, and studied its mortarless Cyclopean masonry with complete bewilderment. We wished that Pabodie were present, for his engineering knowledge might have helped us guess how such titanic blocks could have been handled in that unbelievably remote age when the city and its outskirts were built up.

The half-mile walk downhill to the actual city, with the upper wind shrieking vainly and savagely through the skyward peaks in the background, was something whose smallest details will always remain engraved on my mind. Only in fantastic nightmares could any human beings but Danforth and me conceive such optical effects. Between us and the churning vapours of the west lay that monstrous tangle of dark stone towers; its outré and incredible forms impressing us afresh at every new angle of vision. It was a mirage in solid stone, and were it not for the photographs I would still doubt that such a thing could be. The general type of masonry was identical with that of the rampart we had examined; but the extravagant shapes which this masonry took in its urban manifestations were past all description.

Even the pictures illustrate only one or two phases of its infinite bizarrerie, endless variety, preternatural massiveness, and utterly alien exoticism. There were geometrical forms for which an Euclid could scarcely find a name—cones of all degrees of irregularity and truncation; terraces of every sort of provocative disproportion; shafts with odd bulbous enlargements; broken columns in curious groups; and five-pointed or five-ridged arrangements of mad grotesqueness. As we drew nearer we could see beneath certain transparent parts of the ice-sheet, and detect some of the tubular stone bridges that connected the crazily sprinkled structures at various heights. Of orderly streets there seemed to be none, the only broad open swath being a mile to the left, where the ancient river had doubtless flowed through the town into the mountains.

Our field-glasses shewed the external horizontal bands of nearly effaced sculptures and dot-groups to be very prevalent, and we could half imagine what the city must once have looked like—even though most of the roofs and tower-tops had necessarily perished. As a whole, it had been a complex tangle of twisted lanes and alleys; all of them deep canyons, and some little better than tunnels because of the overhanging masonry or overarching bridges. Now, outspread below us, it loomed like a dream-phantasy against a westward mist through whose northern end the low, reddish antarctic sun of early afternoon was struggling to shine; and when for a moment that sun encountered a denser obstruction and plunged the scene into temporary shadow, the effect was subtly menacing in a way I can never hope to depict. Even the faint howling and piping of the unfelt wind in the great mountain passes behind us took on a wilder note of purposeful malignity. The last stage of our descent to the town was unusually steep and abrupt, and a rock outcropping at the edge where the grade changed led us to think that an artificial terrace had once existed there. Under the glaciation, we believed, there must be a flight of steps or its equivalent.

When at last we plunged into the labyrinthine town itself, clambering over fallen masonry and shrinking from the oppressive nearness and dwarfing height of omnipresent crumbling and pitted walls, our sensations again became such that I marvel at the amount of self-control we retained. Danforth was frankly jumpy, and began making some offensively irrelevant speculations about the horror at the camp—which I resented all the more because I could not help sharing certain conclusions forced upon us by many features of this morbid survival from nightmare antiquity. The speculations worked on his imagination, too; for in one place—where a debris-littered alley turned a sharp corner—he insisted that he saw faint traces of ground markings which he did not like; whilst elsewhere he stopped to listen to a subtle imaginary sound from some undefined point—a muffled musical piping, he said, not unlike that of the wind in the mountain caves yet somehow disturbingly different. The ceaseless *five-pointedness* of the surrounding architecture and of the few distinguishable mural arabesques had a dimly sinister suggestiveness we could not escape; and gave us a touch of terrible subconscious certainty concerning the primal entities which had reared and dwelt in this unhallowed place.

Nevertheless our scientific and adventurous souls were not wholly dead; and we mechanically carried out our programme of chipping specimens from all the different rock types represented in the masonry. We wished a rather full set in order to draw better conclusions regarding the age of the place. Nothing in the great outer walls seemed to date from later than the Jurassic and Comanchian periods, nor was any piece of stone in the entire place of a greater recency than the Pliocene age. In stark certainty, we were wandering amidst a death which had reigned at least 500,000 years, and in all probability even longer.

As we proceeded through this maze of stone-shadowed twilight we stopped at all available apertures to study interiors and investigate entrance possibilities. Some were above our reach, whilst others led only into ice-choked ruins as unroofed and barren as the rampart on the hill. One, though spacious and inviting, opened on a seemingly bottomless abyss without visible means of descent. Now and then we had a chance to study the petrified wood of a surviving shutter, and were impressed by the fabulous antiquity implied in the still discernible grain. These things had come from Mesozoic gymnosperms and conifers—especially Cretaceous cycads—and from fan-palms and early angiosperms of plainly Tertiary date. Nothing definitely later than the Pliocene could be discovered. In the placing of these shutters—whose edges shewed the former presence of queer and long-vanished hinges—usage seemed to be varied; some being on the outer and some on the inner side of the deep embrasures. They seemed to have become wedged in place, thus surviving the rusting of their former and probably metallic fixtures and fastenings.

After a time we came across a row of windows—in the bulges of a colossal five-ridged cone of undamaged apex—which led into a vast, well-preserved room with stone flooring; but these were too high in the room to permit of descent without a rope. We had a rope with us, but did not wish to bother with this twenty-foot drop unless obliged to—especially in this thin plateau air where great demands were made upon the heart action. This enormous room was probably a hall or concourse of some sort, and our electric torches shewed bold, distinct, and potentially startling sculptures arranged round the walls in broad, horizontal bands separated by equally broad strips of conventional arabesques. We took careful note of this spot, planning to enter here unless a more easily gained interior were encountered.

Finally, though, we did encounter exactly the opening we wished; an archway about six feet wide and ten feet high, marking the former end of an aërial bridge which had spanned an alley about five feet above the present level of glaciation. These archways, of course, were flush with upper-story floors; and in this case one of the floors still existed. The building thus accessible was a series of rectangular terraces on our left facing westward. That across the alley, where the other archway yawned, was a decrepit cylinder with no windows and with a curious bulge about ten feet above the aperture. It was totally dark inside, and the archway seemed to open on a well of illimitable emptiness.

Heaped debris made the entrance to the vast left-hand building doubly easy, yet for a moment we hesitated before taking advantage of the long-wished chance. For though we had penetrated into this tangle of archaic mystery, it required fresh resolution to carry us actually inside a complete and surviving building of a fabulous elder world whose nature was becoming more and more hideously plain to us. In the end, however, we made the plunge; and scrambled up over the rubble into the gaping embrasure. The floor beyond was of great slate slabs, and seemed to form the outlet of a long, high corridor with sculptured walls.

Observing the many inner archways which led off from it, and realising the probable complexity of the nest of apartments within, we decided that we must begin our system of hare-and-hound trail-blazing. Hitherto our compasses, together with frequent glimpses of the vast mountain range between the towers in our rear, had been enough to prevent our losing our way; but from now on, the artificial substitute would be necessary. Accordingly we reduced our extra paper to shreds of suitable size, placed these in a bag to be carried by Danforth, and prepared to use them as economically as safety would allow. This method would probably gain us immunity from straying, since there did not appear to be any strong air-currents inside the primordial masonry. If such should develop, or if our paper supply should give out, we could of course fall back on the more secure though more tedious and retarding method of rock-chipping.

Just how extensive a territory we had opened up, it was impossible to guess without a trial. The close and frequent connexion of the different buildings made it likely that we might cross from one to another on bridges underneath the ice except where impeded by local collapses and geologic rifts, for very little glaciation seemed to have entered the massive constructions. Almost all the areas of transparent ice had revealed the submerged windows as tightly shuttered, as if the town had been left in that uniform state until the glacial sheet came to crystallise the lower part for all succeeding time. Indeed, one gained a curious impression that this place had been deliberately closed and deserted in some dim, bygone aeon, rather than overwhelmed by any sudden calamity or even gradual decay. Had the coming of the ice been foreseen, and had a nameless population left en masse to seek a less doomed abode? The precise physiographic conditions attending the formation of the ice-sheet at this point would have to wait for later solution. It had not, very plainly, been a grinding drive. Perhaps the pressure of accumulated snows had been responsible; and perhaps some flood from the river, or from the bursting of some ancient glacial dam in the great range, had helped to create the special state now observable. Imagination could conceive almost anything in connexion with this place.

VI.

It would be cumbrous to give a detailed, consecutive account of our wanderings inside that cavernous, aeon-dead honeycomb of primal masonry; that monstrous lair of elder secrets which now echoed for the first time, after uncounted epochs, to the tread of human feet. This is especially true because so much of the horrible drama and revelation came from a mere study of the omnipresent mural carvings. Our flashlight photographs of those carvings will do much toward proving the truth of what we are now disclosing, and it is lamentable that we had not a larger film supply with us. As it was, we made crude notebook sketches of certain salient features after all our films were used up.

The building which we had entered was one of great size and elaborateness, and gave us an impressive notion of the architecture of that nameless geologic past. The inner partitions were less massive than the outer walls, but on the lower levels were excellently preserved. Labyrinthine complexity, involving curiously irregular differences in floor levels, characterised the entire arrangement; and we should certainly have been lost at the very outset but for the trail of torn paper left behind us. We decided to explore the more decrepit upper parts first of all, hence climbed aloft in the maze for a distance of some 100 feet, to where the topmost tier of chambers yawned snowily and ruinously open to the polar sky. Ascent was effected over the steep, transversely ribbed stone ramps or inclined planes which everywhere served in lieu of stairs. The rooms we encountered were of all imaginable shapes and proportions, ranging from five-pointed stars to triangles and perfect cubes. It might be safe to say that their general average was about 30 × 30 feet in floor area, and 20 feet in height; though many larger apartments existed. After thoroughly examining the upper regions and the glacial level we descended story by story into the submerged part, where indeed we soon saw we were in a continuous maze of connected chambers and passages probably leading over unlimited areas outside this particular building. The Cyclopean massiveness and giganticism of everything about us became curiously oppressive; and there was something vaguely but deeply unhuman in all the contours, dimensions, proportions, decorations, and constructional nuances of the blasphemously archaic stonework. We soon realised from what the carvings revealed that this monstrous city was many million years old.

We cannot yet explain the engineering principles used in the anomalous balancing and adjustment of the vast rock masses, though the function of the arch was clearly much relied on. The rooms we visited were wholly bare of all portable contents, a circumstance which sustained our belief in the city's deliberate desertion. The prime decorative feature was the almost universal system of mural sculpture; which tended to run in continuous horizontal bands three feet wide and arranged from floor to ceiling in alternation with bands of equal width given over to geometrical arabesques. There were exceptions to this rule of arrangement, but its preponderance was overwhelming. Often, however, a series of smooth cartouches containing oddly patterned groups of dots would be sunk along one of the arabesque bands.

The technique, we soon saw, was mature, accomplished, and aesthetically evolved to the highest degree of civilised mastery; though utterly alien in every detail to any known art tradition of the human race. In delicacy of execution no sculpture I have ever seen could approach it. The minutest details of elaborate vegetation, or of animal life, were rendered with astonishing vividness despite the bold scale of the carvings; whilst the conventional designs were marvels of skilful intricacy. The arabesques displayed a profound use of mathematical principles, and were made up of obscurely symmetrical curves and angles based on the quantity of five. The pictorial bands followed a highly formalised tradition, and involved a peculiar treatment of perspective; but had an artistic force that moved us profoundly notwithstanding the intervening gulf of vast geologic periods. Their method of design hinged on a singular juxtaposition of the cross-section with the two-dimensional silhouette, and embodied an analytical psychology beyond that of any known race of antiquity. It is useless to try to compare this art with any represented in our museums. Those who see our photographs will probably find its closest analogue in certain grotesque conceptions of the most daring futurists.

The arabesque tracery consisted altogether of depressed lines whose depth on unweathered walls varied from one to two inches. When cartouches with dot-groups appeared—evidently as inscriptions in some unknown and primordial language and alphabet—the depression of the smooth surface was perhaps an inch and a half, and of the dots perhaps a half-inch more. The pictorial bands were in counter-sunk low relief, their background being depressed about two inches from the original wall surface. In some specimens marks of a former colouration could be detected, though for the most part the untold aeons had disintegrated and banished any pigments which may have been applied. The more one studied the marvellous technique the more one admired the things. Beneath their strict conventionalisation one could grasp the minute and accurate observation and graphic skill of the artists; and indeed, the very conventions themselves served to symbolise and accentuate the real essence or vital differentiation of every object delineated. We felt, too, that besides these recognisable excellences there were others lurking just beyond the reach of our perceptions. Certain touches here and there gave vague hints of latent symbols and stimuli which another mental and emotional background, and a fuller or different sensory equipment, might have made of profound and poignant significance to us.

The subject-matter of the sculptures obviously came from the life of the vanished epoch of their creation, and contained a large proportion of evident history. It is this abnormal historic-mindedness of the primal race—a chance circumstance operating, through coincidence, miraculously in our favour—which made the carvings so awesomely informative to us, and which caused us to place their photography and transcription above all other considerations. In certain rooms the dominant arrangement was varied by the presence of maps, astronomical charts, and other scientific designs on an enlarged scale—these things giving a naive and terrible corroboration to what we gathered from the pictorial friezes and dados. In hinting at what the whole revealed, I can only hope that my account will not arouse a curiosity greater than sane caution on the part of those who believe me at all. It would be tragic if any were to be allured to that realm of death and horror by the very warning meant to discourage them.

Interrupting these sculptured walls were high windows and massive twelve-foot doorways; both now and then retaining the petrified wooden planks—elaborately carved and polished—of the actual shutters and doors. All metal fixtures had long ago vanished, but some of the doors remained in place and had to be forced aside as we progressed from room to room. Window-frames with odd transparent panes—mostly elliptical—survived here and there, though in no considerable quantity. There were also frequent niches of great magnitude, generally empty, but once in a while containing some bizarre object carved from green soapstone which was either broken or perhaps held too inferior to warrant removal. Other apertures were undoubtedly connected with bygone mechanical facilities—heating, lighting, and the like—of a sort suggested in many of the carvings. Ceilings tended to be plain, but had sometimes been inlaid with green soapstone or other tiles, mostly fallen now. Floors were also paved with such tiles, though plain stonework predominated.

As I have said, all furniture and other moveables were absent; but the sculptures gave a clear idea of the strange devices which had once filled these tomb-like, echoing rooms. Above the glacial sheet the floors were generally thick with detritus, litter, and debris; but farther down this condition decreased. In some of the lower chambers and corridors there was little more than gritty dust or ancient incrustations, while occasional areas had an uncanny air of newly swept immaculateness. Of course, where rifts or collapses had occurred, the lower levels were as littered as the upper ones. A central court—as in other structures we had seen from the air—saved the inner regions from total darkness; so that we seldom had to use our electric torches in the upper rooms except when studying sculptural details. Below the ice-cap, however, the twilight deepened; and in many parts of the tangled ground level there was an approach to absolute blackness.

To form even a rudimentary idea of our thoughts and feelings as we penetrated this aeon-silent maze of unhuman masonry one must correlate a hopelessly bewildering chaos of fugitive moods, memories, and impressions. The sheer appalling antiquity and lethal desolation of the place were enough to overwhelm almost any sensitive person, but added to these elements were the recent unexplained horror at the camp, and the revelations all too soon effected by the terrible mural sculptures around us. The moment we came upon a perfect section of carving, where no ambiguity of interpretation could exist, it took only a brief study to give us the hideous truth—a truth which it would be naive to claim Danforth and I had not independently suspected before, though we had carefully refrained from even hinting it to each other. There could now be no further merciful doubt about the nature of the beings which had built and inhabited this monstrous dead city millions of years ago, when man's ancestors were primitive archaic mammals, and vast dinosaurs roamed the tropical steppes of Europe and Asia.

We had previously clung to a desperate alternative and insisted—each to himself—that the omnipresence of the five-pointed motif meant only some cultural or religious exaltation of the archaean natural object which had so patently embodied the quality of five-pointedness; as the decorative motifs of Minoan Crete exalted the sacred bull, those of Egypt the scarabaeus, those of Rome the wolf and the eagle, and those of various savage tribes some chosen totem-animal. But this lone refuge was now stripped from us, and we were forced to face definitely the reason-shaking realisation which the reader of these pages has doubtless long ago anticipated. I can scarcely bear to write it down in black and white even now, but perhaps that will not be necessary.

The things once rearing and dwelling in this frightful masonry in the age of dinosaurs were not indeed dinosaurs, but far worse. Mere dinosaurs were new and almost brainless objects—but the builders of the city were wise and old, and had left certain traces in rocks even then laid down well-nigh a thousand million years … rocks laid down before the true life of earth had advanced beyond plastic groups of cells … rocks laid down before the true life of earth had existed at all. They were the makers and enslavers of that life, and above all doubt the originals of the fiendish elder myths which things like the Pnakotic Manuscripts and the "Necronomicon" affrightedly hint about. They were the Great Old Ones that had filtered down from the stars when earth was young—the beings whose substance an alien evolution had shaped, and whose powers were such as this planet had never bred. And to think that only the day before Danforth and I had actually looked upon fragments of their millennially fossilised substance … and that poor Lake and his party had seen their complete outlines….

It is of course impossible for me to relate in proper order the stages by which we picked up what we know of that monstrous chapter of pre-human life. After the first shock of the certain revelation we had to pause a while to recuperate, and it was fully three o'clock before we got started on our actual tour of systematic research. The sculptures in the building we entered were of relatively late date—perhaps two million years ago—as checked up by geological, biological, and astronomical features; and embodied an art which would be called decadent in comparison with that of specimens we found in older buildings after crossing bridges under the glacial sheet. One edifice hewn from the solid rock seemed to go back forty or possibly even fifty million years—to the lower Eocene or upper Cretaceous—and contained bas-reliefs of an artistry surpassing anything else, with one tremendous exception, that we encountered. That was, we have since agreed, the oldest domestic structure we traversed.

Were it not for the support of those flashlights soon to be made public, I would refrain from telling what I found and inferred, lest I be confined as a madman. Of course, the infinitely early parts of the patchwork tale—representing the pre-terrestrial life of the star-headed beings on other planets, in other galaxies, and in other universes—can readily be interpreted as the fantastic mythology of those beings themselves; yet such parts sometimes involved designs and diagrams so uncannily close to the latest findings of mathematics and astrophysics that I scarcely know what to think. Let others judge when they see the photographs I shall publish.

Naturally, no one set of carvings which we encountered told more than a fraction of any connected story; nor did we even begin to come upon the various stages of that story in their proper order. Some of the vast rooms were independent units so far as their designs were concerned, whilst in other cases a continuous chronicle would be carried through a series of rooms and corridors. The best of the maps and diagrams were on the walls of a frightful abyss below even the ancient ground level—a cavern perhaps 200 feet square and 60 feet high, which had almost undoubtedly been an educational centre of some sort. There were many provoking repetitions of the same material in different rooms and buildings; since certain chapters of experience, and certain summaries or phases of racial history, had evidently been favourites with different decorators or dwellers. Sometimes, though, variant versions of the same theme proved useful in settling debatable points and filling in gaps.

I still wonder that we deduced so much in the short time at our disposal. Of course, we even now have only the barest outline; and much of that was obtained later on from a study of the photographs and sketches we made. It may be the effect of this later study—the revived memories and vague impressions acting in conjunction with his general sensitiveness and with that final supposed horror-glimpse whose essence he will not reveal even to me—which has been the immediate source of Danforth's present breakdown. But it had to be; for we could not issue our warning intelligently without the fullest possible information, and the issuance of that warning is a prime necessity. Certain lingering influences in that unknown antarctic world of disordered time and alien natural law make it imperative that further exploration be discouraged.

VII.

The full story, so far as deciphered, will eventually appear in an official bulletin of Miskatonic University. Here I shall sketch only the salient high lights in a formless, rambling way. Myth or otherwise, the sculptures told of the coming of those star-headed things to the nascent, lifeless earth out of cosmic space—their coming, and the coming of many other alien entities such as at certain times embark upon such spatial pioneering. They seemed able to traverse the interstellar ether on their vast membraneous wings—thus oddly confirming some curious hill folklore long ago told me by an antiquarian colleague. They had lived under the sea a good deal, building fantastic cities and fighting terrific battles with nameless adversaries by means of intricate devices employing unknown principles of energy. Evidently their scientific and mechanical knowledge far surpassed man's today, though they made use of its more widespread and elaborate forms only when obliged to. Some of the sculptures suggested that they had passed through a stage of mechanised life on other planets, but had receded upon finding its effects emotionally unsatisfying. Their preternatural toughness of organisation and simplicity of natural wants made them peculiarly able to live on a high plane without the more specialised fruits of artificial manufacture, and even without garments except for occasional protection against the elements.

It was under the sea, at first for food and later for other purposes, that they first created earth-life—using available substances according to long-known methods. The more elaborate experiments came after the annihilation of various cosmic enemies. They had done the same thing on other planets; having manufactured not only necessary foods, but certain multicellular protoplasmic masses capable of moulding their tissues into all sorts of temporary organs under hypnotic influence and thereby forming ideal slaves to perform the heavy work of the community. These viscous masses were without doubt what Abdul Alhazred whispered about as the "shoggoths" in his frightful "Necronomicon", though even that mad Arab had not hinted that any existed on earth except in the dreams of those who had chewed a certain alkaloidal herb. When the star-headed Old Ones on this planet had synthesised their simple food forms and bred a good supply of shoggoths, they allowed other cell-groups to develop into other forms of animal and vegetable life for sundry purposes; extirpating any whose presence became troublesome.

With the aid of the shoggoths, whose expansions could be made to lift prodigious weights, the small, low cities under the sea grew to vast and imposing labyrinths of stone not unlike those which later rose on land. Indeed, the highly adaptable Old Ones had lived much on land in other parts of the universe, and probably retained many traditions of land construction. As we studied the architecture of all these sculptured palaeogean cities, including that whose aeon-dead corridors we were even then traversing, we were impressed by a curious coincidence which we have not yet tried to explain, even to ourselves. The tops of the buildings, which in the actual city around us had of course been weathered into shapeless ruins ages ago, were clearly displayed in the bas-reliefs; and shewed vast clusters of needle-like spires, delicate finials on certain cone and pyramid apexes, and tiers of thin, horizontal scalloped discs capping cylindrical shafts. And this was exactly what we had seen in that monstrous and portentous mirage, cast by a dead city whence such skyline features had been absent for thousands and tens of thousands of years, which loomed on our ignorant eyes across the unfathomed mountains of madness as we first approached poor Lake's ill-fated camp.

Of the life of the Old Ones, both under the sea and after part of them migrated to land, volumes could be written. Those in shallow water had continued the fullest use of the eyes at the ends of their five main head tentacles, and had practiced the arts of sculpture and of writing in quite the usual way—the writing accomplished with a stylus on waterproof waxen surfaces. Those lower down in the ocean depths, though they used a curious phosphorescent organism to furnish light, pieced out their vision with obscure special senses operating through the prismatic cilia on their heads—senses which rendered all the Old Ones partly independent of light in emergencies. Their forms of sculpture and writing had changed curiously during the descent, embodying certain apparently chemical coating processes—probably to secure phosphorescence—which the bas-reliefs could not make clear to us. The beings moved in the sea partly by swimming—using the lateral crinoid arms—and partly by wriggling with the lower tier of tentacles containing the pseudo-feet. Occasionally they accomplished long swoops with the auxiliary use of two or more sets of their fan-like folding wings. On land they locally used the pseudo-feet, but now and then flew to great heights or over long distances with their wings. The many slender tentacles into which the crinoid arms branched were infinitely delicate, flexible, strong, and accurate in muscular-nervous coördination; ensuring the utmost skill and dexterity in all artistic and other manual operations.

The toughness of the things was almost incredible. Even the terrific pressures of the deepest sea-bottoms appeared powerless to harm them. Very few seemed to die at all except by violence, and their burial-places were very limited. The fact that they covered their vertically inhumed dead with five-pointed inscribed mounds set up thoughts in Danforth and me which made a fresh pause and recuperation necessary after the sculptures revealed it. The beings multiplied by means of spores—like vegetable pteridophytes as Lake had suspected—but owing to their prodigious toughness and longevity, and consequent lack of replacement needs, they did not encourage the large-scale development of new prothalli except when they had new regions to colonise. The young matured swiftly, and received an education evidently beyond any standard we can imagine. The prevailing intellectual and aesthetic life was highly evolved, and produced a tenaciously enduring set of customs and institutions which I shall describe more fully in my coming monograph. These varied slightly according to sea or land residence, but had the same foundations and essentials.

Though able, like vegetables, to derive nourishment from inorganic substances; they vastly preferred organic and especially animal food. They ate uncooked marine life under the sea, but cooked their viands on land. They hunted game and raised meat herds—slaughtering with sharp weapons whose odd marks on certain fossil bones our expedition had noted. They resisted all ordinary temperatures marvellously; and in their natural state could live in water down to freezing. When the great chill of the Pleistocene drew on, however—nearly a million years ago—the land dwellers had to resort to special measures including artificial heating; until at last the deadly cold appears to have driven them back into the sea. For their prehistoric flights through cosmic space, legend said, they had absorbed certain chemicals and become almost independent of eating, breathing, or heat conditions; but by the time of the great cold they had lost track of the method. In any case they could not have prolonged the artificial state indefinitely without harm.

Being non-pairing and semi-vegetable in structure, the Old Ones had no biological basis for the family phase of mammal life; but seemed to organise large households on the principles of comfortable space-utility and—as we deduced from the pictured occupations and diversions of co-dwellers—congenial mental association. In furnishing their homes they kept everything in the centre of the huge rooms, leaving all wall spaces free for decorative treatment. Lighting, in the case of the land inhabitants, was accomplished by a device probably electro-chemical in nature. Both on land and under water they used curious tables, chairs, and couches like cylindrical frames—for they rested and slept upright with folded-down tentacles—and racks for the hinged sets of dotted surfaces forming their books.

Government was evidently complex and probably socialistic, though no certainties in this regard could be deduced from the sculptures we saw. There was extensive commerce, both local and between different cities; certain small, flat counters, five-pointed and inscribed, serving as money. Probably the smaller of the various greenish soapstones found by our expedition were pieces of such currency. Though the culture was mainly urban, some agriculture and much stock-raising existed. Mining and a limited amount of manufacturing were also practiced. Travel was very frequent, but permanent migration seemed relatively rare except for the vast colonising movements by which the race expanded. For personal locomotion no external aid was used; since in land, air, and water movement alike the Old Ones seemed to possess excessively vast capacities for speed. Loads, however, were drawn by beasts of burden—shoggoths under the sea, and a curious variety of primitive vertebrates in the later years of land existence.

These vertebrates, as well as an infinity of other life-forms—animal and vegetable, marine, terrestrial, and aërial—were the products of unguided evolution acting on life-cells made by the Old Ones but escaping beyond their radius of attention. They had been suffered to develop unchecked because they had not come in conflict with the dominant beings. Bothersome forms, of course, were mechanically exterminated. It interested us to see in some of the very last and most decadent sculptures a shambling primitive mammal, used sometimes for food and sometimes as an amusing buffoon by the land dwellers, whose vaguely simian and human foreshadowings were unmistakable. In the building of land cities the huge stone blocks of the high towers were generally lifted by vast-winged pterodactyls of a species heretofore unknown to palaeontology.

The persistence with which the Old Ones survived various geologic changes and convulsions of the earth's crust was little short of miraculous. Though few or none of their first cities seem to have remained beyond the archaean age, there was no interruption in their civilisation or in the transmission of their records. Their original place of advent to the planet was the Antarctic Ocean, and it is likely that they came not long after the matter forming the moon was wrenched from the neighbouring South Pacific. According to one of the sculptured maps, the whole globe was then under water, with stone cities scattered farther and farther from the antarctic as aeons passed. Another map shews a vast bulk of dry land around the south pole, where it is evident that some of the beings made experimental settlements though their main centres were transferred to the nearest sea-bottom. Later maps, which display this land mass as cracking and drifting, and sending certain detached parts northward, uphold in a striking way the theories of continental drift lately advanced by Taylor, Wegener, and Joly.

With the upheaval of new land in the South Pacific tremendous events began. Some of the marine cities were hopelessly shattered, yet that was not the worst misfortune. Another race—a land race of beings shaped like octopi and probably corresponding to the fabulous pre-human spawn of Cthulhu—soon began filtering down from cosmic infinity and precipitated a monstrous war which for a time drove the Old Ones wholly back to the sea—a colossal blow in view of the increasing land settlements. Later peace was made, and the new lands were given to the Cthulhu spawn whilst the Old Ones held the sea and the older lands. New land cities were founded—the greatest of them in the antarctic, for this region of first arrival was sacred. From then on, as before, the antarctic remained the centre of the Old Ones' civilisation, and all the discoverable cities built there by the Cthulhu spawn were blotted out. Then suddenly the lands of the Pacific sank again, taking with them the frightful stone city of R'lyeh and all the cosmic octopi, so that the Old Ones were again supreme on the planet except for one shadowy fear about which they did not like to speak. At a rather later age their cities dotted all the land and water areas of the globe—hence the recommendation in my coming monograph that some archaeologist make systematic borings with Pabodie's type of apparatus in certain widely separated regions.

The steady trend down the ages was from water to land; a movement encouraged by the rise of new land masses, though the ocean was never wholly deserted. Another cause of the landward movement was the new difficulty in breeding and managing the shoggoths upon which successful sea-life depended. With the march of time, as the sculptures sadly confessed, the art of creating new life from inorganic matter had been lost; so that the Old Ones had to depend on the moulding of forms already in existence. On land the great reptiles proved highly tractable; but the shoggoths of the sea, reproducing by fission and acquiring a dangerous degree of accidental intelligence, presented for a time a formidable problem.

They had always been controlled through the hypnotic suggestion of the Old Ones, and had modelled their tough plasticity into various useful temporary limbs and organs; but now their self-modelling powers were sometimes exercised independently, and in various imitative forms implanted by past suggestion. They had, it seems, developed a semi-stable brain whose separate and occasionally stubborn volition echoed the will of the Old Ones without always obeying it. Sculptured images of these shoggoths filled Danforth and me with horror and loathing. They were normally shapeless entities composed of a viscous jelly which looked like an agglutination of bubbles; and each averaged about fifteen feet in diameter when a sphere. They had, however, a constantly shifting shape and volume; throwing out temporary developments or forming apparent organs of sight, hearing, and speech in imitation of their masters, either spontaneously or according to suggestion.

They seem to have become peculiarly intractable toward the middle of the Permian age, perhaps 150 million years ago, when a veritable war of re-subjugation was waged upon them by the marine Old Ones. Pictures of this war, and of the headless, slime-coated fashion in which the shoggoths typically left their slain victims, held a marvellously fearsome quality despite the intervening abyss of untold ages. The Old Ones had used curious weapons of molecular disturbance against the rebel entities, and in the end had achieved a complete victory. Thereafter the sculptures shewed a period in which shoggoths were tamed and broken by armed Old Ones as the wild horses of the American west were tamed by cowboys. Though during the rebellion the shoggoths had shewn an ability to live out of water, this transition was not encouraged; since their usefulness on land would hardly have been commensurate with the trouble of their management.

During the Jurassic age the Old Ones met fresh adversity in the form of a new invasion from outer space—this time by half-fungous, half-crustacean creatures from a planet identifiable as the remote and recently discovered Pluto; creatures undoubtedly the same as those figuring in certain whispered hill legends of the north, and remembered in the Himalayas as the Mi-Go, or Abominable Snow-Men. To fight these beings the Old Ones attempted, for the first time since their terrene advent, to sally forth again into the planetary ether; but despite all traditional preparations found it no longer possible to leave the earth's atmosphere. Whatever the old secret of interstellar travel had been, it was now definitely lost to the race. In the end the Mi-Go drove the Old Ones out of all the northern lands, though they were powerless to disturb those in the sea. Little by little the slow retreat of the elder race to their original antarctic habitat was beginning.

It was curious to note from the pictured battles that both the Cthulhu spawn and the Mi-Go seem to have been composed of matter more widely different from that which we know than was the substance of the Old Ones. They were able to undergo transformations and reintegrations impossible for their adversaries, and seem therefore to have originally come from even remoter gulfs of cosmic space. The Old Ones, but for their abnormal toughness and peculiar vital properties, were strictly material, and must have had their absolute origin within the known space-time continuum; whereas the first sources of the other beings can only be guessed at with bated breath. All this, of course, assuming that the non-terrestrial linkages and the anomalies ascribed to the invading foes are not pure mythology. Conceivably, the Old Ones might have invented a cosmic framework to account for their occasional defeats; since historical interest and pride obviously formed their chief psychological element. It is significant that their annals failed to mention many advanced and potent races of beings whose mighty cultures and towering cities figure persistently in certain obscure legends.

The changing state of the world through long geologic ages appeared with startling vividness in many of the sculptured maps and scenes. In certain cases existing science will require revision, while in other cases its bold deductions are magnificently confirmed. As I have said, the hypothesis of Taylor, Wegener, and Joly that all the continents are fragments of an original antarctic land mass which cracked from centrifugal force and drifted apart over a technically viscous lower surface—an hypothesis suggested by such things as the complementary outlines of Africa and South America, and the way the great mountain chains are rolled and shoved up—receives striking support from this uncanny source.

Maps evidently shewing the Carboniferous world of a hundred million or more years ago displayed significant rifts and chasms destined later to separate Africa from the once continuous realms of Europe (then the Valusia of hellish primal legend), Asia, the Americas, and the antarctic continent. Other charts—and most significantly one in connexion with the founding fifty million years ago of the vast dead city around us—shewed all the present continents well differentiated. And in the latest discoverable specimen—dating perhaps from the Pliocene age—the approximate world of today appeared quite clearly despite the linkage of Alaska with Siberia, of North America with Europe through Greenland, and of South America with the antarctic continent through Graham Land. In the Carboniferous map the whole globe—ocean floor and rifted land mass alike—bore symbols of the Old Ones' vast stone cities, but in the later charts the gradual recession toward the antarctic became very plain.

The final Pliocene specimen shewed no land cities except on the antarctic continent and the tip of South America, nor any ocean cities north of the fiftieth parallel of South Latitude. Knowledge and interest in the northern world, save for a study of coast-lines probably made during long exploration flights on those fan-like membraneous wings, had evidently declined to zero among the Old Ones.

Destruction of cities through the upthrust of mountains, the centrifugal rending of continents, the seismic convulsions of land or sea-bottom, and other natural causes was a matter of common record; and it was curious to observe how fewer and fewer replacements were made as the ages wore on. The vast dead megalopolis that yawned around us seemed to be the last general centre of the race; built early in the Cretaceous age after a titanic earth-buckling had obliterated a still vaster predecessor not far distant. It appeared that this general region was the most sacred spot of all, where reputedly the first Old Ones had settled on a primal sea-bottom. In the new city—many of whose features we could recognise in the sculptures, but which stretched fully a hundred miles along the mountain range in each direction beyond the farthest limits of our aërial survey—there were reputed to be preserved certain sacred stones forming part of the first sea-bottom city, which were thrust up to light after long epochs in the course of the general crumpling of strata.

VIII.

Naturally, Danforth and I studied with especial interest and a peculiarly personal sense of awe everything pertaining to the immediate district in which we were. Of this local material there was naturally a vast abundance; and on the tangled ground level of the city we were lucky enough to find a house of very late date whose walls, though somewhat damaged by a neighbouring rift, contained sculptures of decadent workmanship carrying the story of the region much beyond the period of the Pliocene map whence we derived our last general glimpse of the pre-human world. This was the last place we examined in detail, since what we found there gave us a fresh immediate objective.

Certainly, we were in one of the strangest, weirdest, and most terrible of all the corners of earth's globe. Of all existing lands it was infinitely the most ancient; and the conviction grew upon us that this hideous upland must indeed be the fabled nightmare plateau of Leng which even the mad author of the "Necronomicon" was reluctant to discuss. The great mountain chain was tremendously long—starting as a low range at Luitpold

Land on the coast of Weddell Sea and virtually crossing the entire continent. The really high part stretched in a mighty arc from about Latitude 82°, E. Longitude 60° to Latitude 70°, E. Longitude 115°, with its concave side toward our camp and its seaward end in the region of that long, ice-locked coast whose hills were glimpsed by Wilkes and Mawson at the Antarctic Circle.

Yet even more monstrous exaggerations of Nature seemed disturbingly close at hand. I have said that these peaks are higher than the Himalayas, but the sculptures forbid me to say that they are earth's highest. That grim honour is beyond doubt reserved for something which half the sculptures hesitated to record at all, whilst others approached it with obvious repugnance and trepidation. It seems that there was one part of the ancient land—the first part that ever rose from the waters after the earth had flung off the moon and the Old Ones had seeped down from the stars—which had come to be shunned as vaguely and namelessly evil. Cities built there had crumbled before their time, and had been found suddenly deserted. Then when the first great earth-buckling had convulsed the region in the Comanchian age, a frightful line of peaks had shot suddenly up amidst the most appalling din and chaos—and earth had received her loftiest and most terrible mountains.

If the scale of the carvings was correct, these abhorred things must have been much over 40,000 feet high—radically vaster than even the shocking mountains of madness we had crossed. They extended, it appeared, from about Latitude 77°, E. Longitude 70° to Latitude 70°, E. Longitude 100°—less than 300 miles away from the dead city, so that we would have spied their dreaded summits in the dim western distance had it not been for that vague opalescent haze. Their northern end must likewise be visible from the long Antarctic Circle coast-line at Queen Mary Land.

Some of the Old Ones, in the decadent days, had made strange prayers to those mountains; but none ever went near them or dared to guess what lay beyond. No human eye had ever seen them, and as I studied the emotions conveyed in the carvings I prayed that none ever might. There are protecting hills along the coast beyond them—Queen Mary and Kaiser Wilhelm Lands—and I thank heaven no one has been able to land and climb those hills. I am not as sceptical about old tales and fears as I used to be, and I do not laugh now at the pre-human sculptor's notion that lightning paused meaningfully now and then at each of the brooding crests, and that an unexplained glow shone from one of those terrible pinnacles all through the long polar night. There may be a very real and very monstrous meaning in the old Pnakotic whispers about Kadath in the Cold Waste.

But the terrain close at hand was hardly less strange, even if less namelessly accursed. Soon after the founding of the city the great mountain range became the seat of the principal temples, and many carvings shewed what grotesque and fantastic towers had pierced the sky where now we saw only the curiously clinging cubes and ramparts. In the course of ages the caves had appeared, and had been shaped into adjuncts of the temples. With the advance of still later epochs all the limestone veins of the region were hollowed out by ground waters, so that the mountains, the foothills, and the plains below them were a veritable network of connected caverns and galleries. Many graphic sculptures told of explorations deep underground, and of the final discovery of the Stygian sunless sea that lurked at earth's bowels.

This vast nighted gulf had undoubtedly been worn by the great river which flowed down from the nameless and horrible westward mountains, and which had formerly turned at the base of the Old Ones' range and flowed beside that chain into the Indian Ocean between Budd and Totten Lands on Wilkes's coast-line. Little by little it had eaten away the limestone hill base at its turning, till at last its sapping currents reached the caverns of the ground waters and joined with them in digging a deeper abyss. Finally its whole bulk emptied into the hollow hills and left the old bed toward the ocean dry. Much of the later city as we now found it had been built over that former bed. The Old Ones, understanding what had happened, and exercising their always keen artistic sense, had carved into ornate pylons those headlands of the foothills where the great stream began its descent into eternal darkness.

This river, once crossed by scores of noble stone bridges, was plainly the one whose extinct course we had seen in our aëroplane survey. Its position in different carvings of the city helped us to orient ourselves to the scene as it had been at various stages of the region's age-long, aeon-dead history; so that we were able to sketch a hasty but careful map of the salient features—squares, important buildings, and the like—for guidance in further explorations. We could soon reconstruct in fancy the whole stupendous thing as it was a million or ten million or fifty million years ago, for the sculptures told us exactly what the buildings and mountains and squares and suburbs and landscape setting and luxuriant Tertiary vegetation had looked like. It must have had a marvellous and mystic beauty, and as I thought of it I almost forgot the clammy sense of sinister oppression with which the city's inhuman age and massiveness and deadness and remoteness and glacial twilight had choked and weighed on my spirit. Yet according to certain carvings the denizens of that city had themselves known the clutch of oppressive terror; for there was a sombre and recurrent type of scene in which the Old Ones were shewn in the act of recoiling affrightedly from some object—never allowed to appear in the design—found in the great river and indicated as having been washed down through waving, vine-draped cycad-forests from those horrible westward mountains.

It was only in the one late-built house with the decadent carvings that we obtained any foreshadowing of the final calamity leading to the city's desertion. Undoubtedly there must have been many sculptures of the same age elsewhere, even allowing for the slackened energies and aspirations of a stressful and uncertain period; indeed, very certain evidence of the existence of others came to us shortly afterward. But this was the first and only set we directly encountered. We meant to look farther later on; but as I have said, immediate conditions dictated another present objective. There would, though, have been a limit—for after all hope of a long future occupancy of the place had perished among the Old Ones, there could not but have been a complete cessation of mural decoration. The ultimate blow, of course, was the coming of the great cold which once held most of the earth in thrall, and which has never departed from the ill-fated poles—the great cold that, at the world's other extremity, put an end to the fabled lands of Lomar and Hyperborea.

Just when this tendency began in the antarctic it would be hard to say in terms of exact years. Nowadays we set the beginning of the general glacial periods at a distance of about 500,000 years from the present, but at the poles the terrible scourge must have commenced much earlier. All quantitative estimates are partly guesswork; but it is quite likely that the decadent sculptures were made considerably less than a million years ago, and that the actual desertion of the city was complete long before the conventional opening of the Pleistocene—500,000 years ago—as reckoned in terms of the earth's whole surface.

In the decadent sculptures there were signs of thinner vegetation everywhere, and of a decreased country life on the part of the Old Ones. Heating devices were shewn in the houses, and winter travellers were represented as muffled in protective fabrics. Then we saw a series of cartouches (the continuous band arrangement being frequently interrupted in these late carvings) depicting a constantly growing migration to the nearest refuges of greater warmth—some fleeing to cities under the sea off the far-away coast, and some clambering down through networks of limestone caverns in the hollow hills to the neighbouring black abyss of subterrene waters.

In the end it seems to have been the neighbouring abyss which received the greatest colonisation. This was partly due, no doubt, to the traditional sacredness of this especial region; but may have been more conclusively determined by the opportunities it gave for continuing the use of the great temples on the honeycombed mountains, and for retaining the vast land city as a place of summer residence and base of communication with various mines. The linkage of old and new abodes was made more effective by means of several gradings and improvements along the connecting routes, including the chiselling of numerous direct tunnels from the ancient metropolis to the black abyss—sharply down-pointing tunnels whose mouths we carefully drew, according to our most thoughtful estimates, on the guide map we were compiling. It was obvious that at least two of these tunnels lay within a reasonable exploring distance of where we were; both being on the mountainward edge of the city, one less than a quarter-mile toward the ancient rivercourse, and the other perhaps twice that distance in the opposite direction.

The abyss, it seems, had shelving shores of dry land at certain places; but the Old Ones built their new city under water—no doubt because of its greater certainty of uniform warmth. The depth of the hidden sea appears to have been very great, so that the earth's internal heat could ensure its habitability for an indefinite period. The beings seem to have had no trouble in adapting themselves to part-time—and eventually, of course, whole-time—residence under water; since they had never allowed their gill systems to atrophy. There were many sculptures which shewed how they had always frequently visited their submarine kinsfolk elsewhere, and how they had habitually bathed on the deep bottom of their great river. The darkness of inner earth could likewise have been no deterrent to a race accustomed to long antarctic nights.

Decadent though their style undoubtedly was, these latest carvings had a truly epic quality where they told of the building of the new city in the cavern sea. The Old Ones had gone about it scientifically; quarrying insoluble rocks from the heart of the honeycombed mountains, and employing expert workers from the nearest submarine city to perform the construction according to the best methods. These workers brought with them all that was necessary to establish the new venture—shoggoth-tissue from which to breed stone-lifters and subsequent beasts of burden for the cavern city, and other protoplasmic matter to mould into phosphorescent organisms for lighting purposes.

At last a mighty metropolis rose on the bottom of that Stygian sea; its architecture much like that of the city above, and its workmanship displaying relatively little decadence because of the precise mathematical element inherent in building operations. The newly bred shoggoths grew to enormous size and singular intelligence, and were represented as taking and executing orders with marvellous quickness. They seemed to converse with the Old Ones by mimicking their voices—a sort of musical piping over a wide range, if poor Lake's dissection had indicated aright—and to work more from spoken commands than from hypnotic suggestions as in earlier times. They were, however, kept in admirable control. The phosphorescent organisms supplied light with vast effectiveness, and doubtless atoned for the loss of the familiar polar auroras of the outer-world night.

Art and decoration were pursued, though of course with a certain decadence. The Old Ones seemed to realise this falling off themselves; and in many cases anticipated the policy of Constantine the Great by transplanting especially fine blocks of ancient carving from their land city, just as the emperor, in a similar age of decline, stripped Greece and Asia of their finest art to give his new Byzantine capital greater splendours than its own people could create. That the transfer of sculptured blocks had not been more extensive, was doubtless owing to the fact that the land city was not at first wholly abandoned. By the time total abandonment did occur—and it surely must have occurred before the polar Pleistocene was far advanced—the Old Ones had perhaps become satisfied with their decadent art—or had ceased to recognise the superior merit of the older carvings. At any rate, the aeon-silent ruins around us had certainly undergone no wholesale sculptural denudation; though all the best separate statues, like other moveables, had been taken away.

The decadent cartouches and dados telling this story were, as I have said, the latest we could find in our limited search. They left us with a picture of the Old Ones shuttling back and forth betwixt the land city in summer and the sea-cavern city in winter, and sometimes trading with the sea-bottom cities off the antarctic coast. By this time the ultimate doom of the land city must have been recognised, for the sculptures shewed many signs of the cold's malign encroachments. Vegetation was declining, and the terrible snows of the winter no longer melted completely even in midsummer. The saurian livestock were nearly all dead, and the mammals were standing it none too well. To keep on with the work of the upper world it had become necessary to adapt some of the amorphous and curiously cold-resistant shoggoths to land life; a thing the Old Ones had formerly been reluctant to do. The great river was now lifeless, and the upper sea had lost most of its denizens except the seals and whales. All the birds had flown away, save only the great, grotesque penguins.

What had happened afterward we could only guess. How long had the new sea-cavern city survived? Was it still down there, a stony corpse in eternal blackness? Had the subterranean waters frozen at last? To what fate had the ocean-bottom cities of the outer world been delivered? Had any of the Old Ones shifted north ahead of the creeping ice-cap? Existing geology shews no trace of their presence. Had the frightful Mi-Go been still a menace in the outer land world of the north? Could one be sure of what might or might not linger even to this day in the lightless and unplumbed abysses of earth's deepest waters? Those things had seemingly been able to withstand any amount of pressure—and men of the sea have fished up curious objects at times. And has the killer-whale theory really explained the savage and mysterious scars on antarctic seals noticed a generation ago by Borchgrevingk?

The specimens found by poor Lake did not enter into these guesses, for their geologic setting proved them to have lived at what must have been a very early date in the land city's history. They were, according to their location, certainly not less than thirty million years old; and we reflected that in their day the sea-cavern city, and indeed the cavern itself, had had no existence. They would have remembered an older scene, with lush Tertiary vegetation everywhere, a younger land city of flourishing arts around them, and a great river sweeping northward along the base of the mighty mountains toward a far-away tropic ocean.

And yet we could not help thinking about these specimens—especially about the eight perfect ones that were missing from Lake's hideously ravaged camp. There was something abnormal about that whole business—the strange things we had tried so hard to lay to somebody's madness—those frightful graves—the amount *and nature* of the missing material—Gedney—the unearthly toughness of those archaic monstrosities, and the queer vital freaks the sculptures now shewed the race to have.... Danforth and I had seen a good deal in the last few hours, and were prepared to believe and keep silent about many appalling and incredible secrets of primal Nature.

IX.

I have said that our study of the decadent sculptures brought about a change in our immediate objective. This of course had to do with the chiselled avenues to the black inner world, of whose existence we had not known before, but which we were now eager to find and traverse. From the evident scale of the carvings we deduced that a steeply descending walk of about a mile through either of the neighbouring tunnels would bring us to the brink of the dizzy sunless cliffs above the great abyss; down whose side adequate paths, improved by the Old Ones, led to the rocky shore of the hidden and nighted ocean. To behold this fabulous gulf in stark reality was a lure which seemed impossible of resistance once we knew of the thing—yet we realised we must begin the quest at once if we expected to include it on our present flight.

It was now 8 p.m., and we had not enough battery replacements to let our torches burn on for ever. We had done so much of our studying and copying below the glacial level that our battery supply had had at least five hours of nearly continuous use; and despite the special dry cell formula would obviously be good for only about four more, though by keeping one torch unused, except for especially interesting or difficult places, we might manage to eke out a safe margin beyond that. It would not do to be without a light in these Cyclopean catacombs, hence in order to make the abyss trip we must give up all further mural deciphering. Of course we intended to revisit the place for days and perhaps weeks of intensive study and photography—curiosity having long ago got the better of horror—but just now we must hasten. Our supply of trail-blazing paper was far from unlimited, and we were reluctant to sacrifice spare notebooks or sketching paper to augment it; but we did let one large notebook go. If worst came to worst, we could resort to rock-chipping—and of course it would be possible, even in case of really lost direction, to work up to full daylight by one channel or another if granted sufficient time for plentiful trial and error. So at last we set off eagerly in the indicated direction of the nearest tunnel.

According to the carvings from which we had made our map, the desired tunnel-mouth could not be much more than a quarter of a mile from where we stood; the intervening space shewing solid-looking buildings quite likely to be penetrable still at a sub-glacial level. The opening itself would be in the basement—on the angle nearest the foothills—of a vast five-pointed structure of evidently public and perhaps ceremonial nature, which we tried to identify from our aërial survey of the ruins. No such structure came to our minds as we recalled our flight, hence we concluded that its upper parts had been greatly damaged, or that it had been totally shattered in an ice-rift we had noticed. In the latter case the tunnel would probably turn out to be choked, so that we would have to try the next nearest one—the one less than a mile to the north. The intervening rivercourse prevented our trying any of the more southerly tunnels on this trip; and indeed, if both of the neighbouring ones were choked it was doubtful whether our batteries would warrant an attempt on the next northerly one—about a mile beyond our second choice.

As we threaded our dim way through the labyrinth with the aid of map and compass—traversing rooms and corridors in every stage of ruin or preservation, clambering up ramps, crossing upper floors and bridges and clambering down again, encountering choked doorways and piles of debris, hastening now and then along finely preserved and uncannily immaculate stretches, taking false leads and retracing our way (in such cases removing the blind paper trail we had left), and once in a while striking the bottom of an open shaft through which daylight poured or trickled down—we were repeatedly tantalised by the sculptured walls along our route. Many must have told tales of immense historical importance, and only the prospect of later visits reconciled us to the need of passing them by. As it was, we slowed down once in a while and turned on our second torch. If we had had more films we would certainly have paused briefly to photograph certain bas-reliefs, but time-consuming hand copying was clearly out of the question.

I now come once more to a place where the temptation to hesitate, or to hint rather than state, is very strong. It is necessary, however, to reveal the rest in order to justify my course in discouraging further exploration. We had wormed our way very close to the computed site of the tunnel's mouth—having crossed a second-story bridge to what seemed plainly the tip of a pointed wall, and descended to a ruinous corridor especially rich in decadently elaborate and apparently ritualistic sculptures of late workmanship—when, about 8:30 p.m., Danforth's keen young nostrils gave us the first hint of something unusual. If we had had a dog with us, I suppose we would have been warned before. At first we could not precisely say what was wrong with the formerly crystal-pure air, but after a few seconds our memories reacted only too definitely. Let me try to state the thing without flinching. There was an odour—and that odour was vaguely, subtly, and unmistakably akin to what had nauseated us upon opening the insane grave of the horror poor Lake had dissected.

Of course the revelation was not as clearly cut at the time as it sounds now. There were several conceivable explanations, and we did a good deal of indecisive whispering. Most important of all, we did not retreat without further investigation; for having come this far, we were loath to be balked by anything short of certain disaster. Anyway, what we must have suspected was altogether too wild to believe. Such things did not happen in any normal world. It was probably sheer irrational instinct which made us dim our single torch—tempted no longer by the decadent and sinister sculptures that leered menacingly from the oppressive walls—and which softened our progress to a cautious tiptoeing and crawling over the increasingly littered floor and heaps of debris.

Danforth's eyes as well as nose proved better than mine, for it was likewise he who first noticed the queer aspect of the debris after we had passed many half-choked arches leading to chambers and corridors on the ground level. It did not look quite as it ought after countless thousands of years of desertion, and when we cautiously turned on more light we saw that a kind of swath seemed to have been lately tracked through it. The irregular nature of the litter precluded any definite marks, but in the smoother places there were suggestions of the dragging of heavy objects. Once we thought there was a hint of parallel tracks, as if of runners. This was what made us pause again.

It was during that pause that we caught—simultaneously this time—the other odour ahead. Paradoxically, it was both a less frightful and a more frightful odour—less frightful intrinsically, but infinitely appalling in this place under the known circumstances ... unless, of course, Gedney.... For the odour was the plain and familiar one of common petrol—every-day gasoline.

Our motivation after that is something I will leave to psychologists. We knew now that some terrible extension of the camp horrors must have crawled into this nighted burial-place of the aeons, hence could not doubt any longer the existence of nameless conditions—present or at least recent—just ahead. Yet in the end we did let sheer burning curiosity—or anxiety—or auto-hypnotism—or vague thoughts of responsibility toward Gedney—or what not—drive us on. Danforth whispered again of the print he thought he had seen at the alley-turning in the ruins above; and of the faint musical piping—potentially of tremendous significance in the light of Lake's dissection report despite its close resemblance to the cave-mouth echoes of the windy peaks—which he thought he had shortly afterward half heard from unknown depths below. I, in my turn, whispered of how the camp was left—of what had disappeared, and of how the madness of a lone survivor might have conceived the inconceivable—a wild trip across the monstrous mountains and a descent into the unknown primal masonry—

But we could not convince each other, or even ourselves, of anything definite. We had turned off all light as we stood still, and vaguely noticed that a trace of deeply filtered upper day kept the blackness from being absolute. Having automatically begun to move ahead, we guided ourselves by occasional flashes from our torch. The disturbed debris formed an impression we could not shake off, and the smell of gasoline grew stronger. More and more ruin met our eyes and hampered our feet, until very soon we saw that the forward way was about to cease. We had been all too correct in our pessimistic guess about that rift glimpsed from the air. Our tunnel quest was a blind one, and we were not even going to be able to reach the basement out of which the abyssward aperture opened.

The torch, flashing over the grotesquely carven walls of the blocked corridor in which we stood, shewed several doorways in various states of obstruction; and from one of them the gasoline odour—quite submerging that other hint of odour—came with especial distinctness. As we looked more steadily, we saw that beyond a doubt there had been a slight and recent clearing away of debris from that particular opening. Whatever the lurking horror might be, we believed the direct avenue toward it was now plainly manifest. I do not think anyone will wonder that we waited an appreciable time before making any further motion.

And yet, when we did venture inside that black arch, our first impression was one of anticlimax. For amidst the littered expanse of that sculptured crypt—a perfect cube with sides of about twenty feet—there remained no recent object of instantly discernible size; so that we looked instinctively, though in vain, for a farther doorway. In another moment, however, Danforth's sharp vision had descried a place where the floor debris had been disturbed; and we turned on both torches full strength. Though what we saw in that light was actually simple and trifling, I am none the less reluctant to tell of it because of what it implied. It was a rough levelling of the debris, upon which several small objects lay carelessly scattered, and at one corner of which a considerable amount of gasoline must have been spilled lately enough to leave a strong odour even at this extreme super-plateau altitude. In other words, it could not be other than a sort of camp—a camp made by questing beings who like us had been turned back by the unexpectedly choked way to the abyss.

Let me be plain. The scattered objects were, so far as substance was concerned, all from Lake's camp; and consisted of tin cans as queerly opened as those we had seen at that ravaged place, plus many spent matches, three illustrated books more or less curiously smudged, an empty ink bottle with its pictorial and instructional carton, a broken fountain pen, some oddly snipped fragments of fur and tent-cloth, a used electric battery with circular of directions, a folder that came with our type of tent-heater, and a sprinkling of crumpled papers. It was all bad enough, but when we smoothed out the papers and looked at what was on them we felt we had come to the worst. We had found certain inexplicably blotted papers at the camp which might have prepared us, yet the effect of the sight down there in the pre-human vaults of a nightmare city was almost too much to bear.

A mad Gedney might have made the groups of dots in imitation of those found on the greenish soapstones, just as the dots on those insane five-pointed grave-mounds might have been made; and he might conceivably have prepared rough, hasty sketches—varying in their accuracy or lack of it—which outlined the neighbouring parts of the city and traced the way from a circularly represented place outside our previous route—a place we identified as a great cylindrical tower in the carvings and as a vast circular gulf glimpsed in our aërial survey—to the present five-pointed structure and the tunnel-mouth therein. He might, I repeat, have prepared such sketches; for those before us were quite obviously compiled as our own had been from late sculptures somewhere in the glacial labyrinth, though not from the ones which we had seen and used. But what this art-blind bungler could never have done was to execute those sketches in a strange and assured technique perhaps superior, despite haste and carelessness, to any of the decadent carvings from which they were taken—the characteristic and unmistakable technique of the Old Ones themselves in the dead city's heyday.

There are those who will say Danforth and I were utterly mad not to flee for our lives after that; since our conclusions were now—notwithstanding their wildness—completely fixed, and of a nature I need not even mention to those who have read my account as far as this. Perhaps we were mad—for have I not said those horrible peaks were mountains of madness? But I think I can detect something of the same spirit—albeit in a less extreme form—in the men who stalk deadly beasts through African jungles to photograph them or study their habits. Half-paralysed with terror though we were, there was nevertheless fanned within us a blazing flame of awe and curiosity which triumphed in the end.

Of course we did not mean to face that—or those—which we knew had been there, but we felt that they must be gone by now. They would by this time have found the other neighbouring entrance to the abyss, and have passed within to whatever night-black fragments of the past might await them in the ultimate gulf—the ultimate gulf they had never seen. Or if that entrance, too, was blocked, they would have gone on to the north seeking another. They were, we remembered, partly independent of light.

Looking back to that moment, I can scarcely recall just what precise form our new emotions took—just what change of immediate objective it was that so sharpened our sense of expectancy. We certainly did not mean to face what we feared—yet I will not deny that we may have had a lurking, unconscious wish to spy certain things from some hidden vantage-point. Probably we had not given up our zeal to glimpse the abyss itself, though there was interposed a new goal in the form of that great circular place shewn on the crumpled sketches we had found. We had at once recognised it as a monstrous cylindrical tower figuring in the very earliest carvings, but appearing only as a prodigious round aperture from above. Something about the impressiveness of its rendering, even in these hasty diagrams, made us think that its sub-glacial levels must still form a feature of peculiar importance. Perhaps it embodied architectural marvels as yet unencountered by us. It was certainly of incredible age according to the sculptures in which it figured—being indeed among the first things built in the city. Its carvings, if preserved, could not but be highly significant. Moreover, it might form a good present link with the upper world—a shorter route than the one we were so carefully blazing, and probably that by which those others had descended.

At any rate, the thing we did was to study the terrible sketches—which quite perfectly confirmed our own—and start back over the indicated course to the circular place; the course which our nameless predecessors must have traversed twice before us. The other neighbouring gate to the abyss would lie beyond that. I need not speak of our journey—during which we continued to leave an economical trail of paper—for it was precisely the same in kind as that by which we had reached the cul-de-sac; except that it tended to adhere more closely to the ground level and even descend to basement corridors. Every now and then we could trace certain disturbing marks in the debris or litter or detritus under foot; and after we had passed outside the radius of the gasoline scent we were again faintly conscious—spasmodically—of that more hideous and more persistent scent. After the way had branched from our former course we sometimes gave the rays of our single torch a furtive sweep along the walls; noting in almost every case the well-nigh omnipresent sculptures, which indeed seem to have formed a main aesthetic outlet for the Old Ones.

About 9:30 p.m., while traversing a vaulted corridor whose increasingly glaciated floor seemed somewhat below the ground level and whose roof grew lower as we advanced, we began to see strong daylight ahead and were able to turn off our torch. It appeared that we were coming to the vast circular place, and that our distance from the upper air could not be very great. The corridor ended in an arch surprisingly low for these megalithic ruins, but we could see much through it even before we emerged. Beyond there stretched a prodigious round space—fully 200 feet in diameter—strown with debris and containing many choked archways corresponding to the one we were about to cross. The walls were—in available spaces—boldly sculptured into a spiral band of heroic proportions; and displayed, despite the destructive weathering caused by the openness of the spot, an artistic splendour far beyond anything we had encountered before. The littered floor was quite heavily glaciated, and we fancied that the true bottom lay at a considerably lower depth.

But the salient object of the place was the titanic stone ramp which, eluding the archways by a sharp turn outward into the open floor, wound spirally up the stupendous cylindrical wall like an inside counterpart of those once climbing outside the monstrous towers or ziggurats of antique Babylon. Only the rapidity of our flight, and the perspective which confounded the descent with the tower's inner wall, had prevented our noticing this feature from the air, and thus caused us to seek another avenue to the sub-glacial level. Pabodie might have been able to tell what sort of engineering held it in place, but Danforth and I could merely admire and marvel. We could see mighty stone corbels and pillars here and there, but what we saw seemed inadequate to the function performed. The thing was excellently preserved up to the present top of the tower—a highly remarkable circumstance in view of its exposure—and its shelter had done much to protect the bizarre and disturbing cosmic sculptures on the walls.

As we stepped out into the awesome half-daylight of this monstrous cylinder-bottom—fifty million years old, and without doubt the most primally ancient structure ever to meet our eyes—we saw that the ramp-traversed sides stretched dizzily up to a height of fully sixty feet. This, we recalled from our aërial survey, meant an outside glaciation of some forty feet; since the yawning gulf we had seen from the plane had been at the top of an approximately twenty-foot mound of crumbled masonry, somewhat sheltered for three-fourths of its circumference by the massive curving walls of a line of higher ruins. According to the sculptures the original tower had stood in the centre of an immense circular plaza; and had been perhaps 500 or 600 feet high, with tiers of horizontal discs near the top, and a row of needle-like spires along the upper rim. Most of the masonry had obviously toppled outward rather than inward—a fortunate happening, since otherwise the ramp might have been shattered and the whole interior choked. As it was, the ramp shewed sad battering; whilst the choking was such that all the archways at the bottom seemed to have been recently half-cleared.

It took us only a moment to conclude that this was indeed the route by which those others had descended, and that this would be the logical route for our own ascent despite the long trail of paper we had left elsewhere. The tower's mouth was no farther from the foothills and our waiting plane than was the great terraced building we had entered, and any further sub-glacial exploration we might make on this trip would lie in this general region. Oddly, we were still thinking about possible later trips—even after all we had seen and guessed. Then as we picked our way cautiously over the debris of the great floor, there came a sight which for the time excluded all other matters.

It was the neatly huddled array of three sledges in that farther angle of the ramp's lower and outward-projecting course which had hitherto been screened from our view. There they were—the three sledges missing from Lake's camp—shaken by a hard usage which must have included forcible dragging along great reaches of snowless masonry and debris, as well as much hand portage over utterly unnavigable places. They were carefully and intelligently packed and strapped, and contained things memorably familiar enough—the gasoline stove, fuel cans, instrument cases, provision tins, tarpaulins obviously bulging with books, and some bulging with less obvious contents—everything derived from Lake's equipment. After what we had found in that other room, we were in a measure prepared for this encounter. The really great shock came when we stepped over and undid one tarpaulin whose outlines had peculiarly disquieted us. It seems that others as well as Lake had been interested in collecting typical specimens; for there were two here, both stiffly frozen, perfectly preserved, patched with adhesive plaster where some wounds around the neck had occurred, and wrapped with patent care to prevent further damage. They were the bodies of young Gedney and the missing dog.

X.

Many people will probably judge us callous as well as mad for thinking about the northward tunnel and the abyss so soon after our sombre discovery, and I am not prepared to say that we would have immediately revived such thoughts but for a specific circumstance which broke in upon us and set up a whole new train of speculations. We had replaced the tarpaulin over poor Gedney and were standing in a kind of mute bewilderment when the sounds finally reached our consciousness—the first sounds we had heard since descending out of the open where the mountain wind whined faintly from its unearthly heights. Well known and mundane though they were, their presence in this remote world of death was more unexpected and unnerving than any grotesque or fabulous tones could possibly have been—since they gave a fresh upsetting to all our notions of cosmic harmony.

Had it been some trace of that bizarre musical piping over a wide range which Lake's dissection report had led us to expect in those others—and which, indeed, our overwrought fancies had been reading into every wind-howl we had heard since coming on the camp horror—it would have had a kind of hellish congruity with the aeon-dead region around us. A voice from other epochs belongs in a graveyard of other epochs. As it was, however, the noise shattered all our profoundly seated adjustments—all our tacit acceptance of the inner antarctic as a waste as utterly and irrevocably void of every vestige of normal life as the sterile disc of the moon. What we heard was not the fabulous note of any buried blasphemy of elder earth from whose supernal toughness an age-denied polar sun had evoked a monstrous response. Instead, it was a thing so mockingly normal and so unerringly familiarised by our sea days off Victoria Land and our camp days at McMurdo Sound that we shuddered to think of it here, where such things ought not to be. To be brief—it was simply the raucous squawking of a penguin.

The muffled sound floated from sub-glacial recesses nearly opposite to the corridor whence we had come—regions manifestly in the direction of that other tunnel to the vast abyss. The presence of a living water-bird in such a direction—in a world whose surface was one of age-long and uniform lifelessness—could lead to only one conclusion; hence our first thought was to verify the objective reality of the sound. It was, indeed, repeated; and seemed at times to come from more than one throat. Seeking its source, we entered an archway from which much debris had been cleared; resuming our trail-blazing—with an added paper-supply taken with curious repugnance from one of the tarpaulin bundles on the sledges—when we left daylight behind.

As the glaciated floor gave place to a litter of detritus, we plainly discerned some curious dragging tracks; and once Danforth found a distinct print of a sort whose description would be only too superfluous. The course indicated by the penguin cries was precisely what our map and compass prescribed as an approach to the more northerly tunnel-mouth, and we were glad to find that a bridgeless thoroughfare on the ground and basement levels seemed open. The tunnel, according to the chart, ought to start from the basement of a large pyramidal structure which we seemed vaguely to recall from our aërial survey as remarkably well preserved. Along our path the single torch shewed a customary profusion of carvings, but we did not pause to examine any of these.

Suddenly a bulky white shape loomed up ahead of us, and we flashed on the second torch. It is odd how wholly this new quest had turned our minds from earlier fears of what might lurk near. Those other ones, having left their supplies in the great circular place, must have planned to return after their scouting trip toward or into the abyss; yet we had now discarded all caution concerning them as completely as if they had never existed. This white, waddling thing was fully six feet high, yet we seemed to realise at once that it was not one of those others. They were larger and dark, and according to the sculptures their motion over land surfaces was a swift, assured matter despite the queerness of their sea-born tentacle equipment. But to say that the white thing did not profoundly frighten us would be vain. We were indeed clutched for an instant by a primitive dread almost sharper than the worst of our reasoned fears regarding those others. Then came a flash of anticlimax as the white shape sidled into a lateral archway to our left to join two others of its kind which had summoned it in raucous tones. For it was only a penguin—albeit of a huge, unknown species larger than the greatest of the known king penguins, and monstrous in its combined albinism and virtual eyelessness.

When we had followed the thing into the archway and turned both our torches on the indifferent and unheeding group of three we saw that they were all eyeless albinos of the same unknown and gigantic species. Their size reminded us of some of the archaic penguins depicted in the Old Ones' sculptures, and it did not take us long to conclude that they were descended from the same stock—undoubtedly surviving through a retreat to some warmer inner region whose perpetual blackness had destroyed their pigmentation and atrophied their eyes to mere useless slits. That their present habitat was the vast abyss we sought, was not for a moment to be doubted; and this evidence of the gulf's continued warmth and habitability filled us with the most curious and subtly perturbing fancies.

We wondered, too, what had caused these three birds to venture out of their usual domain. The state and silence of the great dead city made it clear that it had at no time been an habitual seasonal rookery, whilst the manifest indifference of the trio to our presence made it seem odd that any passing party of those others should have startled them. Was it possible that those others had taken some aggressive action or tried to increase their meat supply? We doubted whether that pungent odour which the dogs had hated could cause an equal antipathy in these penguins; since their ancestors had obviously lived on excellent terms with the Old Ones—an amicable relationship which must have survived in the abyss below as long as any of the Old Ones remained. Regretting—in a flareup of the old spirit of pure science—that we could not photograph these anomalous creatures, we shortly left them to their squawking and pushed on toward the abyss whose openness was now so positively proved to us, and whose exact direction occasional penguin tracks made clear.

Not long afterward a steep descent in a long, low, doorless, and peculiarly sculptureless corridor led us to believe that we were approaching the tunnel-mouth at last. We had passed two more penguins, and heard others immediately ahead. Then the corridor ended in a prodigious open space which made us gasp involuntarily—a perfect inverted hemisphere, obviously deep underground; fully a hundred feet in diameter and fifty feet high, with low archways opening around all parts of the circumference but one, and that one yawning cavernously with a black arched aperture which broke the symmetry of the vault to a height of nearly fifteen feet. It was the entrance to the great abyss.

In this vast hemisphere, whose concave roof was impressively though decadently carved to a likeness of the primordial celestial dome, a few albino penguins waddled—aliens there, but indifferent and unseeing. The black tunnel yawned indefinitely off at a steep descending grade, its aperture adorned with grotesquely chiselled jambs and lintel. From that cryptical mouth we fancied a current of slightly warmer air and perhaps even a suspicion of vapour proceeded; and we wondered what living entities other than penguins the limitless void below, and the contiguous honeycombings of the land and the titan mountains, might conceal. We wondered, too, whether the trace of mountaintop smoke at first suspected by poor Lake, as well as the odd haze we had ourselves perceived around the rampart-crowned peak, might not be caused by the tortuous-channelled rising of some such vapour from the unfathomed regions of earth's core.

Entering the tunnel, we saw that its outline was—at least at the start—about fifteen feet each way; sides, floor, and arched roof composed of the usual megalithic masonry. The sides were sparsely decorated with cartouches of conventional designs in a late, decadent style; and all the construction and carving were marvellously well preserved. The floor was quite clear, except for a slight detritus bearing outgoing penguin tracks and the inward tracks of those others. The farther one advanced, the warmer it became; so that we were soon unbuttoning our heavy garments. We wondered whether there were any actually igneous manifestations below, and whether the waters of that sunless sea were hot. After a short distance the masonry gave place to solid rock, though the tunnel kept the same proportions and presented the same aspect of carved regularity. Occasionally its varying grade became so steep that grooves were cut in the floor. Several times we noted the mouths of small lateral galleries not recorded in our diagrams; none of them such as to complicate the problem of our return, and all of them welcome as possible refuges in case we met unwelcome entities on their way back from the abyss. The nameless scent of such things was very distinct. Doubtless it was suicidally foolish to venture into that tunnel under the known conditions, but the lure of the unplumbed is stronger in certain persons than most suspect—indeed, it was just such a lure which had brought us to this unearthly polar waste in the first place. We saw several penguins as we passed along, and speculated on the distance we would have to traverse. The carvings had led us to expect a steep downhill walk of about a mile to the abyss, but our previous wanderings had shewn us that matters of scale were not wholly to be depended on.

After about a quarter of a mile that nameless scent became greatly accentuated, and we kept very careful track of the various lateral openings we passed. There was no visible vapour as at the mouth, but this was doubtless due to the lack of contrasting cooler air. The temperature was rapidly ascending, and we were not surprised to come upon a careless heap of material shudderingly familiar to us. It was composed of furs and tent-cloths taken from Lake's camp, and we did not pause to study the bizarre forms into which the fabrics had been slashed. Slightly beyond this point we noticed a decided increase in the size and number of the side-galleries, and concluded that the densely honeycombed region beneath the higher foothills must now have been reached. The nameless scent was now curiously mixed with another and scarcely less offensive odour—of what nature we could not guess, though we thought of decaying organisms and perhaps unknown subterrene fungi. Then came a startling expansion of the tunnel for which the carvings had not prepared us—a broadening and rising into a lofty, natural-looking elliptical cavern with a level floor; some 75 feet long and 50 broad, and with many immense side-passages leading away into cryptical darkness.

Though this cavern was natural in appearance, an inspection with both torches suggested that it had been formed by the artificial destruction of several walls between adjacent honeycombings. The walls were rough, and the high vaulted roof was thick with stalactites; but the solid rock floor had been smoothed off, and was free from all debris, detritus, or even dust to a positively abnormal extent. Except for the avenue through which we had come, this was true of the floors of all the great galleries opening off from it; and the singularity of the condition was such as to set us vainly puzzling. The curious new foetor which had supplemented the nameless scent was excessively pungent here; so much so that it destroyed all trace of the other. Something about this whole place, with its polished and almost glistening floor, struck us as more vaguely baffling and horrible than any of the monstrous things we had previously encountered.

The regularity of the passage immediately ahead, as well as the larger proportion of penguin-droppings there, prevented all confusion as to the right course amidst this plethora of equally great cave-mouths. Nevertheless we resolved to resume our paper trail-blazing if any further complexity should develop; for dust tracks, of course, could no longer be expected. Upon resuming our direct progress we cast a beam of torchlight over the tunnel walls—and stopped short in amazement at the supremely radical change which had come over the carvings in this part of the passage. We realised, of course, the great decadence of the Old Ones' sculpture at the time of the tunnelling; and had indeed noticed the inferior workmanship of the arabesques in the stretches behind us. But now, in this deeper section beyond the cavern, there was a sudden difference wholly transcending explanation—a difference in basic nature as well as in mere quality, and involving so profound and calamitous a degradation of skill that nothing in the hitherto observed rate of decline could have led one to expect it.

This new and degenerate work was coarse, bold, and wholly lacking in delicacy of detail. It was counter-sunk with exaggerated depth in bands following the same general line as the sparse cartouches of the earlier sections, but the height of the reliefs did not reach the level of the general surface. Danforth had the idea that it was a second carving—a sort of palimpsest formed after the obliteration of a previous design. In nature it was wholly decorative and conventional; and consisted of crude spirals and angles roughly following the quintile mathematical tradition of the Old Ones, yet seeming more like a parody than a perpetuation of that tradition. We could not get it out of our minds that some subtly but profoundly alien element had been added to the aesthetic feeling behind the technique—an alien element, Danforth guessed, that was responsible for the manifestly laborious substitution. It was like, yet disturbingly unlike, what we had come to recognise as the Old Ones' art; and I was persistently reminded of such hybrid things as the ungainly Palmyrene sculptures fashioned in the Roman manner. That others had recently noticed this belt of carving was hinted by the presence of a used torch battery on the floor in front of one of the most characteristic designs.

Since we could not afford to spend any considerable time in study, we resumed our advance after a cursory look; though frequently casting beams over the walls to see if any further decorative changes developed. Nothing of the sort was perceived, though the carvings were in places rather sparse because of the numerous mouths of smooth-floored lateral tunnels. We saw and heard fewer penguins, but thought we caught a vague suspicion of an infinitely distant chorus of them somewhere deep within the earth. The new and inexplicable odour was abominably strong, and we could detect scarcely a sign of that other nameless scent. Puffs of visible vapour ahead bespoke increasing contrasts in temperature, and the relative nearness of the sunless sea-cliffs of the great abyss. Then, quite unexpectedly, we saw certain obstructions on the polished floor ahead—obstructions which were quite definitely not penguins—and turned on our second torch after making sure that the objects were quite stationary.

XI.

Still another time have I come to a place where it is very difficult to proceed. I ought to be hardened by this stage; but there are some experiences and intimations which scar too deeply to permit of healing, and leave only such an added sensitiveness that memory reinspires all the original horror. We saw, as I have said, certain obstructions on the polished floor ahead; and I may add that our nostrils were assailed almost simultaneously by a very curious intensification of the strange prevailing foetor, now quite plainly mixed with the nameless stench of those others which had gone before us. The light of the second torch left no doubt of what the obstructions were, and we dared approach them only because we could see, even from a distance, that they were quite as past all harming power as had been the six similar specimens unearthed from the monstrous star-mounded graves at poor Lake's camp.

They were, indeed, as lacking in completeness as most of those we had unearthed—though it grew plain from the thick, dark-green pool gathering around them that their incompleteness was of infinitely greater recency. There seemed to be only four of them, whereas Lake's bulletins would have suggested no less than eight as forming the group which had preceded us. To find them in this state was wholly unexpected, and we wondered what sort of monstrous struggle had occurred down here in the dark.

Penguins, attacked in a body, retaliate savagely with their beaks; and our ears now made certain the existence of a rookery far beyond. Had those others disturbed such a place and aroused murderous pursuit? The obstructions did not suggest it, for penguin beaks against the tough tissues Lake had dissected could hardly account for the terrible damage our approaching glance was beginning to make out. Besides, the huge blind birds we had seen appeared to be singularly peaceful.

Had there, then, been a struggle among those others, and were the absent four responsible? If so, where were they? Were they close at hand and likely to form an immediate menace to us? We glanced anxiously at some of the smooth-floored lateral passages as we continued our slow and frankly reluctant approach. Whatever the conflict was, it had clearly been that which had frightened the penguins into their unaccustomed wandering. It must, then, have arisen near that faintly heard rookery in the incalculable gulf beyond, since there were no signs that any birds had normally dwelt here. Perhaps, we reflected, there had been a hideous running fight, with the weaker party seeking to get back to the cached sledges when their pursuers finished them. One could picture the daemoniac fray between namelessly monstrous entities as it surged out of the black abyss with great clouds of frantic penguins squawking and scurrying ahead.

I say that we approached those sprawling and incomplete obstructions slowly and reluctantly. Would to heaven we had never approached them at all, but had run back at top speed out of that blasphemous tunnel with the greasily smooth floors and the degenerate murals aping and mocking the things they had superseded—run back, before we had seen what we did see, and before our minds were burned with something which will never let us breathe easily again!

Both of our torches were turned on the prostrate objects, so that we soon realised the dominant factor in their incompleteness. Mauled, compressed, twisted, and ruptured as they were, their chief common injury was total decapitation. From each one the tentacled starfish-head had been removed; and as we drew near we saw that the manner of removal looked more like some hellish tearing or suction than like any ordinary form of cleavage. Their noisome dark-green ichor formed a large, spreading pool; but its stench was half overshadowed by that newer and stranger stench, here more pungent than at any other point along our route. Only when we had come very close to the sprawling obstructions could we trace that second, unexplainable foetor to any immediate source—and the instant we did so Danforth, remembering certain very vivid sculptures of the Old Ones' history in the Permian age 150 million years ago, gave vent to a nerve-tortured cry which echoed hysterically through that vaulted and archaic passage with the evil palimpsest carvings.

I came only just short of echoing his cry myself; for I had seen those primal sculptures, too, and had shudderingly admired the way the nameless artist had suggested that hideous slime-coating found on certain incomplete and prostrate Old Ones—those whom the frightful shoggoths had characteristically slain and sucked to a ghastly headlessness in the great war of re-subjugation. They were infamous, nightmare sculptures even when telling of age-old, bygone things; for shoggoths and their work ought not to be seen by human beings or portrayed by any beings. The mad author of the *Necronomicon* had nervously tried to swear that none had been bred on this planet, and that only drugged dreamers had ever conceived them. Formless protoplasm able to mock and reflect all forms and organs and processes—viscous agglutinations of bubbling cells—rubbery fifteen-foot spheroids infinitely plastic and ductile—slaves of suggestion, builders of cities—more and more sullen, more and more intelligent, more and more amphibious, more and more imitative—Great God! What madness made even those blasphemous Old Ones willing to use and to carve such things?

And now, when Danforth and I saw the freshly glistening and reflectively iridescent black slime which clung thickly to those headless bodies and stank obscenely with that new unknown odour whose cause only a diseased fancy could envisage—clung to those bodies and sparkled less voluminously on a smooth part of the accursedly re-sculptured wall *in a series of grouped dots*—we understood the quality of cosmic fear to its uttermost depths. It was not fear of those four missing others—for all too well did we suspect they would do no harm again. Poor devils! After all, they were not evil things of their kind. They were the men of another age and another order of being. Nature had played a hellish jest on them—as it will on any others that human madness, callousness, or cruelty may hereafter drag up in that hideously dead or sleeping polar waste—and this was their tragic homecoming.

They had not been even savages—for what indeed had they done? That awful awakening in the cold of an unknown epoch—perhaps an attack by the furry, frantically barking quadrupeds, and a dazed defence against them and the equally frantic white simians with the queer wrappings and paraphernalia ... poor Lake, poor Gedney ... and poor Old Ones! Scientists to the last—what had they done that we would not have done in their place? God, what intelligence and persistence! What a facing of the incredible, just as those carven kinsmen and forbears had faced things only a little less incredible! Radiates, vegetables, monstrosities, star-spawn—whatever they had been, they were men!

They had crossed the icy peaks on whose templed slopes they had once worshipped and roamed among the tree-ferns. They had found their dead city brooding under its curse, and had read its carven latter days as we had done. They had tried to reach their living fellows in fabled depths of blackness they had never seen—and what had they found? All this flashed in unison through the thoughts of Danforth and me as we looked from those headless, slime-coated shapes to the loathsome palimpsest sculptures and the diabolical dot-groups of fresh slime on the wall beside them—looked and understood what must have triumphed and survived down there in the Cyclopean water-city of that nighted, penguin-fringed abyss, whence even now a sinister curling mist had begun to belch pallidly as if in answer to Danforth's hysterical scream.

The shock of recognising that monstrous slime and headlessness had frozen us into mute, motionless statues, and it is only through later conversations that we have learned of the complete identity of our thoughts at that moment. It seemed aeons that we stood there, but actually it could not have been more than ten or fifteen seconds. That hateful, pallid mist curled forward as if veritably driven by some remoter advancing bulk—and then came a sound which upset much of what we had just decided, and in so doing broke the spell and enabled us to run like mad past squawking, confused penguins over our former trail back to the city, along ice-sunken megalithic corridors to the great open circle, and up that archaic spiral ramp in a frenzied automatic plunge for the sane outer air and light of day.

The new sound, as I have intimated, upset much that we had decided; because it was what poor Lake's dissection had led us to attribute to those we had just judged dead. It was, Danforth later told me, precisely what he had caught in infinitely muffled form when at that spot beyond the alley-corner above the glacial level; and it certainly had a shocking resemblance to the wind-pipings we had both heard around the lofty mountain caves. At the risk of seeming puerile I will add another thing, too; if only because of the surprising way Danforth's impression chimed with mine. Of course common reading is what prepared us both to make the interpretation, though Danforth has hinted at queer notions about unsuspected and forbidden sources to which Poe may have had access when writing his "Arthur Gordon Pym" a century ago. It will be remembered that in that fantastic tale there is a word of unknown but terrible and prodigious significance connected with the antarctic and screamed eternally by the gigantic, spectrally snowy birds of that malign region's core. "*Tekeli-li! Tekeli-li!*" That, I may admit, is exactly what we thought we heard conveyed by that sudden sound behind the advancing white mist—that insidious musical piping over a singularly wide range.

We were in full flight before three notes or syllables had been uttered, though we knew that the swiftness of the Old Ones would enable any scream-roused and pursuing survivor of the slaughter to overtake us in a moment if it really wished to do so. We had a vague hope, however, that non-aggressive conduct and a display of kindred reason might cause such a being to spare us in case of capture; if only from scientific curiosity. After all, if such an one had nothing to fear for itself it would have no motive in harming us. Concealment being futile at this juncture, we used our torch for a running glance behind, and perceived that the mist was thinning. Would we see, at last, a complete and living specimen of those others? Again came that insidious musical piping—"*Tekeli-li! Tekeli-li!*"

Then, noting that we were actually gaining on our pursuer, it occurred to us that the entity might be wounded. We could take no chances, however, since it was very obviously approaching in answer to Danforth's scream rather than in flight from any other entity. The timing was too close to admit of doubt. Of the whereabouts of that less conceivable and less mentionable nightmare—that foetid, unglimpsed mountain of slime-spewing protoplasm whose race had conquered the abyss and sent land pioneers to re-carve and squirm through the burrows of the hills—we could form no guess; and it cost us a genuine pang to leave this probably crippled Old One—perhaps a lone survivor—to the peril of recapture and a nameless fate.

Thank heaven we did not slacken our run. The curling mist had thickened again, and was driving ahead with increased speed; whilst the straying penguins in our rear were squawking and screaming and displaying signs of a panic really surprising in view of their relatively minor confusion when we had passed them. Once more came that sinister, wide-ranged piping—"*Tekeli-*

li! Tekeli-li!" We had been wrong. The thing was not wounded, but had merely paused on encountering the bodies of its fallen kindred and the hellish slime inscription above them. We could never know what that daemon message was—but those burials at Lake's camp had shewn how much importance the beings attached to their dead. Our recklessly used torch now revealed ahead of us the large open cavern where various ways converged, and we were glad to be leaving those morbid palimpsest sculptures—almost felt even when scarcely seen—behind.

Another thought which the advent of the cave inspired was the possibility of losing our pursuer at this bewildering focus of large galleries. There were several of the blind albino penguins in the open space, and it seemed clear that their fear of the oncoming entity was extreme to the point of unaccountability. If at that point we dimmed our torch to the very lowest limit of travelling need, keeping it strictly in front of us, the frightened squawking motions of the huge birds in the mist might muffle our footfalls, screen our true course, and somehow set up a false lead. Amidst the churning, spiralling fog the littered and unglistening floor of the main tunnel beyond this point, as differing from the other morbidly polished burrows, could hardly form a highly distinguishing feature; even, so far as we could conjecture, for those indicated special senses which made the Old Ones partly though imperfectly independent of light in emergencies. In fact, we were somewhat apprehensive lest we go astray ourselves in our haste. For we had, of course, decided to keep straight on toward the dead city; since the consequences of loss in those unknown foothill honeycombings would be unthinkable.

The fact that we survived and emerged is sufficient proof that the thing did take a wrong gallery whilst we providentially hit on the right one. The penguins alone could not have saved us, but in conjunction with the mist they seem to have done so. Only a benign fate kept the curling vapours thick enough at the right moment, for they were constantly shifting and threatening to vanish. Indeed, they did lift for a second just before we emerged from the nauseously re-sculptured tunnel into the cave; so that we actually caught one first and only half-glimpse of the oncoming entity as we cast a final, desperately fearful glance backward before dimming the torch and mixing with the penguins in the hope of dodging pursuit. If the fate which screened us was benign, that which gave us the half-glimpse was infinitely the opposite; for to that flash of semi-vision can be traced a full half of the horror which has ever since haunted us.

Our exact motive in looking back again was perhaps no more than the immemorial instinct of the pursued to gauge the nature and course of its pursuer; or perhaps it was an automatic attempt to answer a subconscious question raised by one of our senses. In the midst of our flight, with all our faculties centred on the problem of escape, we were in no condition to observe and analyse details; yet even so our latent brain-cells must have wondered at the message brought them by our nostrils. Afterward we realised what it was—that our retreat from the foetid slime-coating on those headless obstructions, and the coincident approach of the pursuing entity, had not brought us the exchange of stenches which logic called for. In the neighbourhood of the prostrate things that new and lately unexplainable foetor had been wholly dominant; but by this time it ought to have largely given place to the nameless stench associated with those others. This it had not done—for instead, the newer and less bearable smell was now virtually undiluted, and growing more and more poisonously insistent each second.

So we glanced back—simultaneously, it would appear; though no doubt the incipient motion of one prompted the imitation of the other. As we did so we flashed both torches full strength at the momentarily thinned mist; either from sheer primitive anxiety to see all we could, or in a less primitive but equally unconscious effort to dazzle the entity before we dimmed our light and dodged among the penguins of the labyrinth-centre ahead. Unhappy act! Not Orpheus himself, or Lot's wife, paid much more dearly for a backward glance. And again came that shocking, wide-ranged piping—"*Tekeli-li! Tekeli-li!*"

I might as well be frank—even if I cannot bear to be quite direct—in stating what we saw; though at the time we felt that it was not to be admitted even to each other. The words reaching the reader can never even suggest the awfulness of the sight itself. It crippled our consciousness so completely that I wonder we had the residual sense to dim our torches as planned, and to strike the right tunnel toward the dead city. Instinct alone must have carried us through—perhaps better than reason could have done; though if that was what saved us, we paid a high price. Of reason we certainly had little enough left. Danforth was totally unstrung, and the first thing I remember of the rest of the journey was hearing him light-headedly chant an hysterical formula in which I alone of mankind could have found anything but insane irrelevance. It reverberated in falsetto echoes among the squawks of the penguins; reverberated through the vaultings ahead, and—thank God—through the now empty vaultings behind. He could not have begun it at once—else we would not have been alive and blindly racing. I shudder to think of what a shade of difference in his nervous reactions might have brought.

"South Station Under—Washington Under—Park Street Under—Kendall—Central—Harvard...." The poor fellow was chanting the familiar stations of the Boston-Cambridge tunnel that burrowed through our peaceful native soil thousands of miles away in New England, yet to me the ritual had neither irrelevance nor home-feeling. It had only horror, because I knew unerringly the monstrous, nefandous analogy that had suggested it. We had expected, upon looking back, to see a terrible and incredible moving entity if the mists were thin enough; but of that entity we had formed a clear idea. What we did see—for the mists were indeed all too malignly thinned—was something altogether different, and immeasurably more hideous and detestable. It was the utter, objective embodiment of the fantastic novelist's 'thing that should not be'; and its nearest comprehensible analogue is a vast, onrushing subway train as one sees it from a station platform—the great black front looming colossally out of infinite subterraneous distance, constellated with strangely coloured lights and filling the prodigious burrow as a piston fills a cylinder.

But we were not on a station platform. We were on the track ahead as the nightmare plastic column of foetid black iridescence oozed tightly onward through its fifteen-foot sinus; gathering unholy speed and driving before it a spiral, re-thickening cloud of the pallid abyss-vapour. It was a terrible, indescribable thing vaster than any subway train—a shapeless congeries of protoplasmic bubbles, faintly self-luminous, and with myriads of temporary eyes forming and unforming as pustules of greenish light all over the tunnel-filling front that bore down upon us, crushing the frantic penguins and slithering over the glistening floor that it and its kind had swept so evilly free of all litter. Still came that eldritch, mocking cry—"*Tekeli-li! Tekeli-li!*" And at last we remembered that the daemoniac shoggoths—given life, thought, and plastic organ-patterns solely by the Old Ones, and having no language save that which the dot-groups expressed—*had likewise no voice save the imitated accents of their bygone masters.*

XII.

Danforth and I have recollections of emerging into the great sculptured hemisphere and of threading our back trail through the Cyclopean rooms and corridors of the dead city; yet these are purely dream-fragments involving no memory of volition, details, or physical exertion. It was as if we floated in a nebulous world or dimension without time, causation, or orientation. The grey half-daylight of the vast circular space sobered us somewhat; but we did not go near those cached sledges or look again at poor

Gedney and the dog. They have a strange and titanic mausoleum, and I hope the end of this planet will find them still undisturbed.

It was while struggling up the colossal spiral incline that we first felt the terrible fatigue and short breath which our race through the thin plateau air had produced; but not even the fear of collapse could make us pause before reaching the normal outer realm of sun and sky. There was something vaguely appropriate about our departure from those buried epochs; for as we wound our panting way up the sixty-foot cylinder of primal masonry we glimpsed beside us a continuous procession of heroic sculptures in the dead race's early and undecayed technique—a farewell from the Old Ones, written fifty million years ago.

Finally scrambling out at the top, we found ourselves on a great mound of tumbled blocks; with the curved walls of higher stonework rising westward, and the brooding peaks of the great mountains shewing beyond the more crumbled structures toward the east. The low antarctic sun of midnight peered redly from the southern horizon through rifts in the jagged ruins, and the terrible age and deadness of the nightmare city seemed all the starker by contrast with such relatively known and accustomed things as the features of the polar landscape. The sky above was a churning and opalescent mass of tenuous ice-vapours, and the cold clutched at our vitals. Wearily resting the outfit-bags to which we had instinctively clung throughout our desperate flight, we rebuttoned our heavy garments for the stumbling climb down the mound and the walk through the aeon-old stone maze to the foothills where our aëroplane waited. Of what had set us fleeing from the darkness of earth's secret and archaic gulfs we said nothing at all.

In less than a quarter of an hour we had found the steep grade to the foothills—the probable ancient terrace—by which we had descended, and could see the dark bulk of our great plane amidst the sparse ruins on the rising slope ahead. Half way uphill toward our goal we paused for a momentary breathing-spell, and turned to look again at the fantastic palaeogean tangle of incredible stone shapes below us—once more outlined mystically against an unknown west. As we did so we saw that the sky beyond had lost its morning haziness; the restless ice-vapours having moved up to the zenith, where their mocking outlines seemed on the point of settling into some bizarre pattern which they feared to make quite definite or conclusive.

There now lay revealed on the ultimate white horizon behind the grotesque city a dim, elfin line of pinnacled violet whose needle-pointed heights loomed dream-like against the beckoning rose-colour of the western sky. Up toward this shimmering rim sloped the ancient table-land, the depressed course of the bygone river traversing it as an irregular ribbon of shadow. For a second we gasped in admiration of the scene's unearthly cosmic beauty, and then vague horror began to creep into our souls. For this far violet line could be nothing else than the terrible mountains of the forbidden land—highest of earth's peaks and focus of earth's evil; harbourers of nameless horrors and archaean secrets; shunned and prayed to by those who feared to carve their meaning; untrodden by any living thing of earth, but visited by the sinister lightnings and sending strange beams across the plains in the polar night—beyond doubt the unknown archetype of that dreaded Kadath in the Cold Waste beyond abhorrent Leng, whereof unholy primal legends hint evasively. We were the first human beings ever to see them—and I hope to God we may be the last.

If the sculptured maps and pictures in that pre-human city had told truly, these cryptic violet mountains could not be much less than 300 miles away; yet none the less sharply did their dim elfin essence jut above that remote and snowy rim, like the serrated edge of a monstrous alien planet about to rise into unaccustomed heavens. Their height, then, must have been tremendous beyond all known comparison—carrying them up into tenuous atmospheric strata peopled by such gaseous wraiths as rash flyers have barely lived to whisper of after unexplainable falls. Looking at them, I thought nervously of certain sculptured hints of what the great bygone river had washed down into the city from their accursed slopes—and wondered how much sense and how much folly had lain in the fears of those Old Ones who carved them so reticently. I recalled how their northerly end must come near the coast at Queen Mary Land, where even at that moment Sir Douglas Mawson's expedition was doubtless working less than a thousand miles away; and hoped that no evil fate would give Sir Douglas and his men a glimpse of what might lie beyond the protecting coastal range. Such thoughts formed a measure of my overwrought condition at the time—and Danforth seemed to be even worse.

Yet long before we had passed the great star-shaped ruin and reached our plane our fears had become transferred to the lesser but vast enough range whose re-crossing lay ahead of us. From these foothills the black, ruin-crusted slopes reared up starkly and hideously against the east, again reminding us of those strange Asian paintings of Nicholas Roerich; and when we thought of the damnable honeycombings inside them, and of the frightful amorphous entities that might have pushed their foetidly squirming way even to the topmost hollow pinnacles, we could not face without panic the prospect of again sailing by those suggestive skyward cave-mouths where the wind made sounds like an evil musical piping over a wide range. To make matters worse, we saw distinct traces of local mist around several of the summits—as poor Lake must have done when he made that early mistake about volcanism—and thought shiveringly of that kindred mist from which we had just escaped; of that, and of the blasphemous, horror-fostering abyss whence all such vapours came.

All was well with the plane, and we clumsily hauled on our heavy flying furs. Danforth got the engine started without trouble, and we made a very smooth takeoff over the nightmare city. Below us the primal Cyclopean masonry spread out as it had done when first we saw it—so short, yet infinitely long, a time ago—and we began rising and turning to test the wind for our crossing through the pass. At a very high level there must have been great disturbance, since the ice-dust clouds of the zenith were doing all sorts of fantastic things; but at 24,000 feet, the height we needed for the pass, we found navigation quite practicable. As we drew close to the jutting peaks the wind's strange piping again became manifest, and I could see Danforth's hands trembling at the controls. Rank amateur though I was, I thought at that moment that I might be a better navigator than he in effecting the dangerous crossing between pinnacles; and when I made motions to change seats and take over his duties he did not protest. I tried to keep all my skill and self-possession about me, and stared at the sector of reddish farther sky betwixt the walls of the pass—resolutely refusing to pay attention to the puffs of mountaintop vapour, and wishing that I had wax-stopped ears like Ulysses' men off the Sirens' coast to keep that disturbing wind-piping from my consciousness.

But Danforth, released from his piloting and keyed up to a dangerous nervous pitch, could not keep quiet. I felt him turning and wriggling about as he looked back at the terrible receding city, ahead at the cave-riddled, cube-barnacled peaks, sidewise at the bleak sea of snowy, rampart-strown foothills, and upward at the seething, grotesquely clouded sky. It was then, just as I was trying to steer safely through the pass, that his mad shrieking brought us so close to disaster by shattering my tight hold on myself and causing me to fumble helplessly with the controls for a moment. A second afterward my resolution triumphed and we made the crossing safely—yet I am afraid that Danforth will never be the same again.

I have said that Danforth refused to tell me what final horror made him scream out so insanely—a horror which, I feel sadly sure, is mainly responsible for his present breakdown. We had snatches of shouted conversation above the wind's piping and the engine's buzzing as we reached the safe side of the range and swooped slowly down toward the camp, but that had mostly to do with the pledges of secrecy we had made as we prepared to leave the nightmare city. Certain things, we had agreed, were not for people to know and discuss lightly—and I would not speak of them now but for the need of heading off that Starkweather-Moore Expedition, and others, at any cost. It is absolutely necessary, for the peace and safety of mankind, that some of earth's dark, dead corners and unplumbed depths be let alone; lest sleeping abnormalities wake to resurgent life, and blasphemously surviving nightmares squirm and splash out of their black lairs to newer and wider conquests.

All that Danforth has ever hinted is that the final horror was a mirage. It was not, he declares, anything connected with the cubes and caves of echoing, vaporous, wormily honeycombed mountains of madness which we crossed; but a single fantastic, daemoniac glimpse, among the churning zenith-clouds, of what lay back of those other violet westward mountains which the Old Ones had shunned and feared. It is very probable that the thing was a sheer delusion born of the previous stresses we had passed through, and of the actual though unrecognised mirage of the dead transmontane city experienced near Lake's camp the day before; but it was so real to Danforth that he suffers from it still.

He has on rare occasions whispered disjointed and irresponsible things about "the black pit", "the carven rim", "the proto-shoggoths", "the windowless solids with five dimensions", "the nameless cylinder", "the elder pharos", "Yog-Sothoth", "the primal white jelly", "the colour out of space", "the wings", "the eyes in darkness", "the moon-ladder", "the original, the eternal, the undying", and other bizarre conceptions; but when he is fully himself he repudiates all this and attributes it to his curious and macabre reading of earlier years. Danforth, indeed, is known to be among the few who have ever dared go completely through that worm-riddled copy of the *Necronomicon* kept under lock and key in the college library.

The higher sky, as we crossed the range, was surely vaporous and disturbed enough; and although I did not see the zenith I can well imagine that its swirls of ice-dust may have taken strange forms. Imagination, knowing how vividly distant scenes can sometimes be reflected, refracted, and magnified by such layers of restless cloud, might easily have supplied the rest—and of course Danforth did not hint any of those specific horrors till after his memory had had a chance to draw on his bygone reading. He could never have seen so much in one instantaneous glance.

At the time his shrieks were confined to the repetition of a single mad word of all too obvious source:

"*Tekeli-li! Tekeli-li!*"

THE SHADOW OVER INNSMOUTH

I.

During the winter of 1927–28 officials of the Federal government made a strange and secret investigation of certain conditions in the ancient Massachusetts seaport of Innsmouth. The public first learned of it in February, when a vast series of raids and arrests occurred, followed by the deliberate burning and dynamiting—under suitable precautions—of an enormous number of crumbling, worm-eaten, and supposedly empty houses along the abandoned waterfront. Uninquiring souls let this occurrence pass as one of the major clashes in a spasmodic war on liquor.

Keener news-followers, however, wondered at the prodigious number of arrests, the abnormally large force of men used in making them, and the secrecy surrounding the disposal of the prisoners. No trials, or even definite charges, were reported; nor were any of the captives seen thereafter in the regular gaols of the nation. There were vague statements about disease and concentration camps, and later about dispersal in various naval and military prisons, but nothing positive ever developed. Innsmouth itself was left almost depopulated, and is even now only beginning to shew signs of a sluggishly revived existence.

Complaints from many liberal organisations were met with long confidential discussions, and representatives were taken on trips to certain camps and prisons. As a result, these societies became surprisingly passive and reticent. Newspaper men were harder to manage, but seemed largely to coöperate with the government in the end. Only one paper—a tabloid always discounted because of its wild policy—mentioned the deep-diving submarine that discharged torpedoes downward in the marine abyss just beyond Devil Reef. That item, gathered by chance in a haunt of sailors, seemed indeed rather far-fetched; since the low, black reef lies a full mile and a half out from Innsmouth Harbour.

People around the country and in the nearby towns muttered a great deal among themselves, but said very little to the outer world. They had talked about dying and half-deserted Innsmouth for nearly a century, and nothing new could be wilder or more hideous than what they had whispered and hinted years before. Many things had taught them secretiveness, and there was now no need to exert pressure on them. Besides, they really knew very little; for wide salt marshes, desolate and unpeopled, keep neighbours off from Innsmouth on the landward side.

But at last I am going to defy the ban on speech about this thing. Results, I am certain, are so thorough that no public harm save a shock of repulsion could ever accrue from a hinting of what was found by those horrified raiders at Innsmouth. Besides, what was found might possibly have more than one explanation. I do not know just how much of the whole tale has been told even to me, and I have many reasons for not wishing to probe deeper. For my contact with this affair has been closer than that of any other layman, and I have carried away impressions which are yet to drive me to drastic measures.

It was I who fled frantically out of Innsmouth in the early morning hours of July 16, 1927, and whose frightened appeals for government inquiry and action brought on the whole reported episode. I was willing enough to stay mute while the affair was fresh and uncertain; but now that it is an old story, with public interest and curiosity gone, I have an odd craving to whisper about those few frightful hours in that ill-rumoured and evilly shadowed seaport of death and blasphemous abnormality. The mere telling helps me to restore confidence in my own faculties; to reassure myself that I was not simply the first to succumb to a contagious nightmare hallucination. It helps me, too, in making up my mind regarding a certain terrible step which lies ahead of me.

I never heard of Innsmouth till the day before I saw it for the first and—so far—last time. I was celebrating my coming of age by a tour of New England—sightseeing, antiquarian, and genealogical—and had planned to go directly from ancient

Newburyport to Arkham, whence my mother's family was derived. I had no car, but was travelling by train, trolley, and motor coach, always seeking the cheapest possible route. In Newburyport they told me that the steam train was the thing to take to Arkham; and it was only at the station ticket-office, when I demurred at the high fare, that I learned about Innsmouth. The stout, shrewd-faced agent, whose speech shewed him to be no local man, seemed sympathetic toward my efforts at economy, and made a suggestion that none of my other informants had offered.

"You *could* take that old bus, I suppose," he said with a certain hesitation, "but it ain't thought much of hereabouts. It goes through Innsmouth—you may have heard about that—and so the people don't like it. Run by an Innsmouth fellow—Joe Sargent—but never gets any custom from here, or Arkham either, I guess. Wonder it keeps running at all. I s'pose it's cheap enough, but I never see more'n two or three people in it—nobody but those Innsmouth folks. Leaves the Square—front of Hammond's Drug Store—at 10 a.m. and 7 p.m. unless they've changed lately. Looks like a terrible rattletrap—I've never ben on it."

That was the first I ever heard of shadowed Innsmouth. Any reference to a town not shewn on common maps or listed in recent guide-books would have interested me, and the agent's odd manner of allusion roused something like real curiosity. A town able to inspire such dislike in its neighbours, I thought, must be at least rather unusual, and worthy of a tourist's attention. If it came before Arkham I would stop off there—and so I asked the agent to tell me something about it. He was very deliberate, and spoke with an air of feeling slightly superior to what he said.

"Innsmouth? Well, it's a queer kind of a town down at the mouth of the Manuxet. Used to be almost a city—quite a port before the War of 1812—but all gone to pieces in the last hundred years or so. No railroad now—B. & M. never went through, and the branch line from Rowley was given up years ago.

"More empty houses than there are people, I guess, and no business to speak of except fishing and lobstering. Everybody trades mostly either here or in Arkham or Ipswich. Once they had quite a few mills, but nothing's left now except one gold refinery running on the leanest kind of part time.

"That refinery, though, used to be a big thing, and Old Man Marsh, who owns it, must be richer'n Croesus. Queer old duck, though, and sticks mighty close in his home. He's supposed to have developed some skin disease or deformity late in life that makes him keep out of sight. Grandson of Captain Obed Marsh, who founded the business. His mother seems to've ben some kind of foreigner—they say a South Sea islander—so everybody raised Cain when he married an Ipswich girl fifty years ago. They always do that about Innsmouth people, and folks here and hereabouts always try to cover up any Innsmouth blood they have in 'em. But Marsh's children and grandchildren look just like anybody else so far's I can see. I've had 'em pointed out to me here—though, come to think of it, the elder children don't seem to be around lately. Never saw the old man.

"And why is everybody so down on Innsmouth? Well, young fellow, you mustn't take too much stock in what people around here say. They're hard to get started, but once they do get started they never let up. They've ben telling things about Innsmouth—whispering 'em, mostly—for the last hundred years, I guess, and I gather they're more scared than anything else. Some of the stories would make you laugh—about old Captain Marsh driving bargains with the devil and bringing imps out of hell to live in Innsmouth, or about some kind of devil-worship and awful sacrifices in some place near the wharves that people stumbled on around 1845 or thereabouts—but I come from Panton, Vermont, and that kind of story don't go down with me.

"You ought to hear, though, what some of the old-timers tell about the black reef off the coast—Devil Reef, they call it. It's well above water a good part of the time, and never much below it, but at that you could hardly call it an island. The story is that there's a whole legion of devils seen sometimes on that reef—sprawled about, or darting in and out of some kind of caves near the top. It's a rugged, uneven thing, a good bit over a mile out, and toward the end of shipping days sailors used to make big detours just to avoid it.

"That is, sailors that didn't hail from Innsmouth. One of the things they had against old Captain Marsh was that he was supposed to land on it sometimes at night when the tide was right. Maybe he did, for I dare say the rock formation was interesting, and it's just barely possible he was looking for pirate loot and maybe finding it; but there was talk of his dealing with daemons there. Fact is, I guess on the whole it was really the Captain that gave the bad reputation to the reef.

"That was before the big epidemic of 1846, when over half the folks in Innsmouth was carried off. They never did quite figure out what the trouble was, but it was probably some foreign kind of disease brought from China or somewhere by the shipping. It surely was bad enough—there was riots over it, and all sorts of ghastly doings that I don't believe ever got outside of town—and it left the place in awful shape. Never came back—there can't be more'n 300 or 400 people living there now.

"But the real thing behind the way folks feel is simply race prejudice—and I don't say I'm blaming those that hold it. I hate those Innsmouth folks myself, and I wouldn't care to go to their town. I s'pose you know—though I can see you're a Westerner by your talk—what a lot our New England ships used to have to do with queer ports in Africa, Asia, the South Seas, and everywhere else, and what queer kinds of people they sometimes brought back with 'em. You've probably heard about the Salem man that came home with a Chinese wife, and maybe you know there's still a bunch of Fiji Islanders somewhere around Cape Cod.

"Well, there must be something like that back of the Innsmouth people. The place always was badly cut off from the rest of the country by marshes and creeks, and we can't be sure about the ins and outs of the matter; but it's pretty clear that old Captain Marsh must have brought home some odd specimens when he had all three of his ships in commission back in the twenties and thirties. There certainly is a strange kind of a streak in the Innsmouth folks today—I don't know how to explain it, but it sort of makes you crawl. You'll notice a little in Sargent if you take his bus. Some of 'em have queer narrow heads with flat noses and bulgy, stary eyes that never seem to shut, and their skin ain't quite right. Rough and scabby, and the sides of their necks are all shrivelled or creased up. Get bald, too, very young. The older fellows look the worst—fact is, I don't believe I've ever seen a very old chap of that kind. Guess they must die of looking in the glass! Animals hate 'em—they used to have lots of horse trouble before autos came in.

"Nobody around here or in Arkham or Ipswich will have anything to do with 'em, and they act kind of offish themselves when they come to town or when anybody tries to fish on their grounds. Queer how fish are always thick off Innsmouth Harbour when there ain't any anywhere else around—but just try to fish there yourself and see how the folks chase you off! Those people used to come here on the railroad—walking and taking the train at Rowley after the branch was dropped—but now they use that bus.

"Yes, there's a hotel in Innsmouth—called the Gilman House—but I don't believe it can amount to much. I wouldn't advise you to try it. Better stay over here and take the ten o'clock bus tomorrow morning; then you can get an evening bus there for Arkham at eight o'clock. There was a factory inspector who stopped at the Gilman a couple of years ago, and he had a lot of unpleasant hints about the place. Seems they get a queer crowd there, for this fellow heard voices in other rooms—though most of 'em was empty—that gave him the shivers. It was foreign talk, he thought, but he said the bad thing about it was the kind of voice that sometimes spoke. It sounded so unnatural—slopping-like, he said—that he didn't dare undress and go to sleep. Just waited up and lit out the first thing in the morning. The talk went on most all night.

"This fellow—Casey, his name was—had a lot to say about how the Innsmouth folks watched him and seemed kind of on guard. He found the Marsh refinery a queer place—it's in an old mill on the lower falls of the Manuxet. What he said tallied up with what I'd heard. Books in bad shape, and no clear account of any kind of dealings. You know it's always ben a kind of mystery where the Marshes get the gold they refine. They've never seemed to do much buying in that line, but years ago they shipped out an enormous lot of ingots.

"Used to be talk of a queer foreign kind of jewellery that the sailors and refinery men sometimes sold on the sly, or that was seen once or twice on some of the Marsh womenfolks. People allowed maybe old Captain Obed traded for it in some heathen port, especially since he was always ordering stacks of glass beads and trinkets such as seafaring men used to get for native trade. Others thought and still think he'd found an old pirate cache out on Devil Reef. But here's a funny thing. The old Captain's ben dead these sixty years, and there ain't ben a good-sized ship out of the place since the Civil War; but just the same the Marshes still keep on buying a few of those native trade things—mostly glass and rubber gewgaws, they tell me. Maybe the Innsmouth folks like 'em to look at themselves—Gawd knows they've gotten to be about as bad as South Sea cannibals and Guinea savages.

"That plague of '46 must have taken off the best blood in the place. Anyway, they're a doubtful lot now, and the Marshes and other rich folks are as bad as any. As I told you, there probably ain't more'n 400 people in the whole town in spite of all the streets they say there are. I guess they're what they call 'white trash' down South—lawless and sly, and full of secret doings. They get a lot of fish and lobsters and do exporting by truck. Queer how the fish swarm right there and nowhere else.

"Nobody can ever keep track of those people, and state school officials and census men have a devil of a time. You can bet that prying strangers ain't welcome around Innsmouth. I've heard personally of more'n one business or government man that's disappeared there, and there's loose talk of one who went crazy and is out at Danvers now. They must have fixed up some awful scare for that fellow.

"That's why I wouldn't go at night if I was you. I've never ben there and have no wish to go, but I guess a daytime trip couldn't hurt you—even though the people hereabouts will advise you not to make it. If you're just sightseeing, and looking for old-time stuff, Innsmouth ought to be quite a place for you."

And so I spent part of that evening at the Newburyport Public Library looking up data about Innsmouth. When I had tried to question natives in the shops, the lunch room, the garages, and the fire station, I had found them even harder to get started than the ticket-agent had predicted; and realised that I could not spare the time to overcome their first instinctive reticences. They had a kind of obscure suspiciousness, as if there were something amiss with anyone too much interested in Innsmouth. At the Y.M.C.A., where I was stopping, the clerk merely discouraged my going to such a dismal, decadent place; and the people at the library shewed much the same attitude. Clearly, in the eyes of the educated, Innsmouth was merely an exaggerated case of civic degeneration.

The Essex County histories on the library shelves had very little to say, except that the town was founded in 1643, noted for shipbuilding before the Revolution, a seat of great marine prosperity in the early nineteenth century, and later a minor factory centre using the Manuxet as power. The epidemic and riots of 1846 were very sparsely treated, as if they formed a discredit to the county.

References to decline were few, though the significance of the later record was unmistakable. After the Civil War all industrial life was confined to the Marsh Refining Company, and the marketing of gold ingots formed the only remaining bit of major commerce aside from the eternal fishing. That fishing paid less and less as the price of the commodity fell and large-scale corporations offered competition, but there was never a dearth of fish around Innsmouth Harbour. Foreigners seldom settled there, and there was some discreetly veiled evidence that a number of Poles and Portuguese who had tried it had been scattered in a peculiarly drastic fashion.

Most interesting of all was a glancing refererence to the strange jewellery vaguely associated with Innsmouth. It had evidently impressed the whole countryside more than a little, for mention was made of specimens in the museum of Miskatonic University at Arkham, and in the display room of the Newburyport Historical Society. The fragmentary descriptions of these things were bald and prosaic, but they hinted to me an undercurrent of persistent strangeness. Something about them seemed so odd and provocative that I could not put them out of my mind, and despite the relative lateness of the hour I resolved to see the local sample—said to be a large, queerly proportioned thing evidently meant for a tiara—if it could possibly be arranged.

The librarian gave me a note of introduction to the curator of the Society, a Miss Anna Tilton, who lived nearby, and after a brief explanation that ancient gentlewoman was kind enough to pilot me into the closed building, since the hour was not outrageously late. The collection was a notable one indeed, but in my present mood I had eyes for nothing but the bizarre object which glistened in a corner cupboard under the electric lights.

It took no excessive sensitiveness to beauty to make me literally gasp at the strange, unearthly splendour of the alien, opulent phantasy that rested there on a purple velvet cushion. Even now I can hardly describe what I saw, though it was clearly enough a sort of tiara, as the description had said. It was tall in front, and with a very large and curiously irregular periphery, as if designed for a head of almost freakishly elliptical outline. The material seemed to be predominantly gold, though a weird lighter lustrousness hinted at some strange alloy with an equally beautiful and scarcely identifiable metal. Its condition was almost perfect, and one could have spent hours in studying the striking and puzzlingly untraditional designs—some simply geometrical, and some plainly marine—chased or moulded in high relief on its surface with a craftsmanship of incredible skill and grace.

The longer I looked, the more the thing fascinated me; and in this fascination there was a curiously disturbing element hardly to be classified or accounted for. At first I decided that it was the queer other-worldly quality of the art which made me uneasy. All other art objects I had ever seen either belonged to some known racial or national stream, or else were consciously modernistic defiances of every recognised stream. This tiara was neither. It clearly belonged to some settled technique of infinite maturity and perfection, yet that technique was utterly remote from any—Eastern or Western, ancient or modern—which I had ever heard of or seen exemplified. It was as if the workmanship were that of another planet.

However, I soon saw that my uneasiness had a second and perhaps equally potent source residing in the pictorial and mathematical suggestions of the strange designs. The patterns all hinted of remote secrets and unimaginable abysses in time and space, and the monotonously aquatic nature of the reliefs became almost sinister. Among these reliefs were fabulous monsters of abhorrent grotesqueness and malignity—half ichthyic and half batrachian in suggestion—which one could not dissociate from a certain haunting and uncomfortable sense of pseudo-memory, as if they called up some image from deep cells and tissues whose retentive functions are wholly primal and awesomely ancestral. At times I fancied that every contour of these blasphemous fish-frogs was overflowing with the ultimate quintessence of unknown and inhuman evil.

In odd contrast to the tiara's aspect was its brief and prosy history as related by Miss Tilton. It had been pawned for a ridiculous sum at a shop in State Street in 1873, by a drunken Innsmouth man shortly afterward killed in a brawl. The Society had acquired it directly from the pawnbroker, at once giving it a display worthy of its quality. It was labelled as of probable East-Indian or Indo-Chinese provenance, though the attribution was frankly tentative.

Miss Tilton, comparing all possible hypotheses regarding its origin and its presence in New England, was inclined to believe that it formed part of some exotic pirate hoard discovered by old Captain Obed Marsh. This view was surely not weakened by the insistent offers of purchase at a high price which the Marshes began to make as soon as they knew of its presence, and which they repeated to this day despite the Society's unvarying determination not to sell.

As the good lady shewed me out of the building she made it clear that the pirate theory of the Marsh fortune was a popular one among the intelligent people of the region. Her own attitude toward shadowed Innsmouth—which she had never seen—was one of disgust at a community slipping far down the cultural scale, and she assured me that the rumours of devil-worship were partly justified by a peculiar secret cult which had gained force there and engulfed all the orthodox churches.

It was called, she said, "The Esoteric Order of Dagon", and was undoubtedly a debased, quasi-pagan thing imported from the East a century before, at a time when the Innsmouth fisheries seemed to be going barren. Its persistence among a simple people was quite natural in view of the sudden and permanent return of abundantly fine fishing, and it soon came to be the greatest influence on the town, replacing Freemasonry altogether and taking up headquarters in the old Masonic Hall on New Church Green.

All this, to the pious Miss Tilton, formed an excellent reason for shunning the ancient town of decay and desolation; but to me it was merely a fresh incentive. To my architectural and historical anticipations was now added an acute anthropological zeal, and I could scarcely sleep in my small room at the "Y" as the night wore away.

II.

Shortly before ten the next morning I stood with my one small valise in front of Hammond's Drug Store in old Market Square waiting for the Innsmouth bus. As the hour for its arrival drew near I noticed a general drift of the loungers to other places up the street, or to the Ideal Lunch across the square. Evidently the ticket-agent had not exaggerated the dislike which local people bore toward Innsmouth and its denizens. In a few moments a small motor coach of extreme decrepitude and dirty grey colour rattled down State Street, made a turn, and drew up at the curb beside me. I felt immediately that it was the right one; a guess which the half-illegible sign on the windshield—"*Arkham-Innsmouth-Newb'port*"—soon verified.

There were only three passengers—dark, unkempt men of sullen visage and somewhat youthful cast—and when the vehicle stopped they clumsily shambled out and began walking up State Street in a silent, almost furtive fashion. The driver also alighted, and I watched him as he went into the drug store to make some purchase. This, I reflected, must be the Joe Sargent mentioned by the ticket-agent; and even before I had noticed any details there spread over me a wave of spontaneous aversion which could be neither checked nor explained. It suddenly struck me as very natural that the local people should not wish to ride on a bus owned and driven by this man, or to visit any oftener than possible the habitat of such a man and his kinsfolk.

When the driver came out of the store I looked at him more carefully and tried to determine the source of my evil impression. He was a thin, stoop-shouldered man not much under six feet tall, dressed in shabby blue civilian clothes and wearing a frayed grey golf cap. His age was perhaps thirty-five, but the odd, deep creases in the sides of his neck made him seem older when one did not study his dull, expressionless face. He had a narrow head, bulging, watery blue eyes that seemed never to wink, a flat nose, a receding forehead and chin, and singularly undeveloped ears. His long, thick lip and coarse-pored, greyish cheeks seemed almost beardless except for some sparse yellow hairs that straggled and curled in irregular patches; and in places the surface seemed queerly irregular, as if peeling from some cutaneous disease. His hands were large and heavily veined, and had a very unusual greyish-blue tinge. The fingers were strikingly short in proportion to the rest of the structure, and seemed to have a tendency to curl closely into the huge palm. As he walked toward the bus I observed his peculiarly shambling gait and saw that his feet were inordinately immense. The more I studied them the more I wondered how he could buy any shoes to fit them.

A certain greasiness about the fellow increased my dislike. He was evidently given to working or lounging around the fish docks, and carried with him much of their characteristic smell. Just what foreign blood was in him I could not even guess. His oddities certainly did not look Asiatic, Polynesian, Levantine, or negroid, yet I could see why the people found him alien. I myself would have thought of biological degeneration rather than alienage.

I was sorry when I saw that there would be no other passengers on the bus. Somehow I did not like the idea of riding alone with this driver. But as the leaving time obviously approached I conquered my qualms and followed the man aboard, extending him a dollar bill and murmuring the single word "Innsmouth". He looked curiously at me for a second as he returned forty cents change without speaking. I took a seat far behind him, but on the same side of the bus, since I wished to watch the shore during the journey.

At length the decrepit vehicle started with a jerk, and rattled noisily past the old brick buildings of State Street amidst a cloud of vapour from the exhaust. Glancing at the people on the sidewalks, I thought I detected in them a curious wish to avoid looking at the bus—or at least a wish to avoid seeming to look at it. Then we turned to the left into High Street, where the going was smoother; flying by stately old mansions of the early republic and still older colonial farmhouses, passing the Lower Green and Parker River, and finally emerging into a long, monotonous stretch of open shore country.

The day was warm and sunny, but the landscape of sand, sedge-grass, and stunted shrubbery became more and more desolate as we proceeded. Out the window I could see the blue water and the sandy line of Plum Island, and we presently drew very near the beach as our narrow road veered off from the main highway to Rowley and Ipswich. There were no visible houses, and I could tell by the state of the road that traffic was very light hereabouts. The small, weather-worn telephone poles carried only two wires. Now and then we crossed crude wooden bridges over tidal creeks that wound far inland and promoted the general isolation of the region.

Once in a while I noticed dead stumps and crumbling foundation-walls above the drifting sand, and recalled the old tradition quoted in one of the histories I had read, that this was once a fertile and thickly settled countryside. The change, it was said, came simultaneously with the Innsmouth epidemic of 1846, and was thought by simple folk to have a dark connexion with hidden forces of evil. Actually, it was caused by the unwise cutting of woodlands near the shore, which robbed the soil of its best protection and opened the way for waves of wind-blown sand.

At last we lost sight of Plum Island and saw the vast expanse of the open Atlantic on our left. Our narrow course began to climb steeply, and I felt a singular sense of disquiet in looking at the lonely crest ahead where the rutted roadway met the sky. It was as if the bus were about to keep on in its ascent, leaving the sane earth altogether and merging with the unknown arcana of upper air and cryptical sky. The smell of the sea took on ominous implications, and the silent driver's bent, rigid back and narrow head became more and more hateful. As I looked at him I saw that the back of his head was almost as hairless as his face, having only a few straggling yellow strands upon a grey scabrous surface.

Then we reached the crest and beheld the outspread valley beyond, where the Manuxet joins the sea just north of the long line of cliffs that culminate in Kingsport Head and veer off toward Cape Ann. On the far, misty horizon I could just make out the dizzy profile of the Head, topped by the queer ancient house of which so many legends are told; but for the moment all my attention was captured by the nearer panorama just below me. I had, I realised, come face to face with rumour-shadowed Innsmouth.

It was a town of wide extent and dense construction, yet one with a portentous dearth of visible life. From the tangle of chimney-pots scarcely a wisp of smoke came, and the three tall steeples loomed stark and unpainted against the seaward horizon. One of them was crumbling down at the top, and in that and another there were only black gaping holes where clock-dials should have been. The vast huddle of sagging gambrel roofs and peaked gables conveyed with offensive clearness the idea of wormy decay, and as we approached along the now descending road I could see that many roofs had wholly caved in. There were some large square Georgian houses, too, with hipped roofs, cupolas, and railed "widow's walks". These were mostly well back from the water, and one or two seemed to be in moderately sound condition. Stretching inland from among them I saw the rusted, grass-grown line of the abandoned railway, with leaning telegraph-poles now devoid of wires, and the half-obscured lines of the old carriage roads to Rowley and Ipswich.

The decay was worst close to the waterfront, though in its very midst I could spy the white belfry of a fairly well-preserved brick structure which looked like a small factory. The harbour, long clogged with sand, was enclosed by an ancient stone breakwater; on which I could begin to discern the minute forms of a few seated fishermen, and at whose end were what looked like the foundations of a bygone lighthouse. A sandy tongue had formed inside this barrier, and upon it I saw a few decrepit cabins, moored dories, and scattered lobster-pots. The only deep water seemed to be where the river poured out past the belfried structure and turned southward to join the ocean at the breakwater's end.

Here and there the ruins of wharves jutted out from the shore to end in indeterminate rottenness, those farthest south seeming the most decayed. And far out at sea, despite a high tide, I glimpsed a long, black line scarcely rising above the water yet carrying a suggestion of odd latent malignancy. This, I knew, must be Devil Reef. As I looked, a subtle, curious sense of beckoning seemed superadded to the grim repulsion; and oddly enough, I found this overtone more disturbing than the primary impression.

We met no one on the road, but presently began to pass deserted farms in varying stages of ruin. Then I noticed a few inhabited houses with rags stuffed in the broken windows and shells and dead fish lying about the littered yards. Once or twice I saw listless-looking people working in barren gardens or digging clams on the fishy-smelling beach below, and groups of dirty, simian-visaged children playing around weed-grown doorsteps. Somehow these people seemed more disquieting than the dismal buildings, for almost every one had certain peculiarities of face and motions which I instinctively disliked without being able to define or comprehend them. For a second I thought this typical physique suggested some picture I had seen, perhaps in a book, under circumstances of particular horror or melancholy; but this pseudo-recollection passed very quickly.

As the bus reached a lower level I began to catch the steady note of a waterfall through the unnatural stillness. The leaning, unpainted houses grew thicker, lined both sides of the road, and displayed more urban tendencies than did those we were leaving behind. The panorama ahead had contracted to a street scene, and in spots I could see where a cobblestone pavement and stretches of brick sidewalk had formerly existed. All the houses were apparently deserted, and there were occasional gaps where tumbledown chimneys and cellar walls told of buildings that had collapsed. Pervading everything was the most nauseous fishy odour imaginable.

Soon cross streets and junctions began to appear; those on the left leading to shoreward realms of unpaved squalor and decay, while those on the right shewed vistas of departed grandeur. So far I had seen no people in the town, but there now came signs of a sparse habitation—curtained windows here and there, and an occasional battered motor-car at the curb. Pavement and sidewalks were increasingly well defined, and though most of the houses were quite old—wood and brick structures of the early nineteenth century—they were obviously kept fit for habitation. As an amateur antiquarian I almost lost my olfactory disgust and my feeling of menace and repulsion amidst this rich, unaltered survival from the past.

But I was not to reach my destination without one very strong impression of poignantly disagreeable quality. The bus had come to a sort of open concourse or radial point with churches on two sides and the bedraggled remains of a circular green in the centre, and I was looking at a large pillared hall on the right-hand junction ahead. The structure's once white paint was now grey and peeling, and the black and gold sign on the pediment was so faded that I could only with difficulty make out the words "Esoteric Order of Dagon". This, then, was the former Masonic Hall now given over to a degraded cult. As I strained to decipher this inscription my notice was distracted by the raucous tones of a cracked bell across the street, and I quickly turned to look out the window on my own side of the coach.

The sound came from a squat-towered stone church of manifestly later date than most of the houses, built in a clumsy Gothic fashion and having a disproportionately high basement with shuttered windows. Though the hands of its clock were missing on the side I glimpsed, I knew that those hoarse strokes were telling the hour of eleven. Then suddenly all thoughts of time were blotted out by an onrushing image of sharp intensity and unaccountable horror which had seized me before I knew what it really was. The door of the church basement was open, revealing a rectangle of blackness inside. And as I looked, a certain object crossed or seemed to cross that dark rectangle; burning into my brain a momentary conception of nightmare which was all the more maddening because analysis could not shew a single nightmarish quality in it.

It was a living object—the first except the driver that I had seen since entering the compact part of the town—and had I been in a steadier mood I would have found nothing whatever of terror in it. Clearly, as I realised a moment later, it was the pastor; clad in some peculiar vestments doubtless introduced since the Order of Dagon had modified the ritual of the local churches. The thing which had probably caught my first subconscious glance and supplied the touch of bizarre horror was the tall tiara he wore; an almost exact duplicate of the one Miss Tilton had shewn me the previous evening. This, acting on my imagination, had supplied namelessly sinister qualities to the indeterminate face and robed, shambling form beneath it. There was not, I soon decided, any reason why I should have felt that shuddering touch of evil pseudo-memory. Was it not natural that a local mystery cult should adopt among its regimentals an unique type of head-dress made familiar to the community in some strange way—perhaps as treasure-trove?

A very thin sprinkling of repellent-looking youngish people now became visible on the sidewalks—lone individuals, and silent knots of two or three. The lower floors of the crumbling houses sometimes harboured small shops with dingy signs, and I noticed a parked truck or two as we rattled along. The sound of waterfalls became more and more distinct, and presently I saw a fairly deep river-gorge ahead, spanned by a wide, iron-railed highway bridge beyond which a large square opened out. As we clanked over the bridge I looked out on both sides and observed some factory buildings on the edge of the grassy bluff or part way down. The water far below was very abundant, and I could see two vigorous sets of falls upstream on my right and at least one downstream on my left. From this point the noise was quite deafening. Then we rolled into the large semicircular square across the river and drew up on the right-hand side in front of a tall, cupola-crowned building with remnants of yellow paint and with a half-effaced sign proclaiming it to be the Gilman House.

I was glad to get out of that bus, and at once proceeded to check my valise in the shabby hotel lobby. There was only one person in sight—an elderly man without what I had come to call the "Innsmouth look"—and I decided not to ask him any of the questions which bothered me; remembering that odd things had been noticed in this hotel. Instead, I strolled out on the square, from which the bus had already gone, and studied the scene minutely and appraisingly.

One side of the cobblestoned open space was the straight line of the river; the other was a semicircle of slant-roofed brick buildings of about the 1800 period, from which several streets radiated away to the southeast, south, and southwest. Lamps were depressingly few and small—all low-powered incandescents—and I was glad that my plans called for departure before dark, even though I knew the moon would be bright. The buildings were all in fair condition, and included perhaps a dozen shops in current operation; of which one was a grocery of the First National chain, others a dismal restaurant, a drug store, and a wholesale fish-dealer's office, and still another, at the eastern extremity of the square near the river, an office of the town's only industry—the Marsh Refining Company. There were perhaps ten people visible, and four or five automobiles and motor trucks stood scattered about. I did not need to be told that this was the civic centre of Innsmouth. Eastward I could catch blue glimpses of the harbour, against which rose the decaying remains of three once beautiful Georgian steeples. And toward the shore on the opposite bank of the river I saw the white belfry surmounting what I took to be the Marsh refinery.

For some reason or other I chose to make my first inquiries at the chain grocery, whose personnel was not likely to be native to Innsmouth. I found a solitary boy of about seventeen in charge, and was pleased to note the brightness and affability which promised cheerful information. He seemed exceptionally eager to talk, and I soon gathered that he did not like the place, its fishy smell, or its furtive people. A word with any outsider was a relief to him. He hailed from Arkham, boarded with a family who came from Ipswich, and went back home whenever he got a moment off. His family did not like him to work in Innsmouth, but the chain had transferred him there and he did not wish to give up his job.

There was, he said, no public library or chamber of commerce in Innsmouth, but I could probably find my way about. The street I had come down was Federal. West of that were the fine old residence streets—Broad, Washington, Lafayette, and Adams—and east of it were the shoreward slums. It was in these slums—along Main Street—that I would find the old Georgian churches, but they were all long abandoned. It would be well not to make oneself too conspicuous in such neighbourhoods—especially north of the river—since the people were sullen and hostile. Some strangers had even disappeared.

Certain spots were almost forbidden territory, as he had learned at considerable cost. One must not, for example, linger much around the Marsh refinery, or around any of the still used churches, or around the pillared Order of Dagon Hall at New Church Green. Those churches were very odd—all violently disavowed by their respective denominations elsewhere, and apparently using the queerest kind of ceremonials and clerical vestments. Their creeds were heterodox and mysterious, involving hints of certain marvellous transformations leading to bodily immortality—of a sort—on this earth. The youth's own pastor—Dr. Wallace of Asbury M. E. Church in Arkham—had gravely urged him not to join any church in Innsmouth.

As for the Innsmouth people—the youth hardly knew what to make of them. They were as furtive and seldom seen as animals that live in burrows, and one could hardly imagine how they passed the time apart from their desultory fishing. Perhaps—judging from the quantities of bootleg liquor they consumed—they lay for most of the daylight hours in an alcoholic stupor. They seemed sullenly banded together in some sort of fellowship and understanding—despising the world as if they had access to other and preferable spheres of entity. Their appearance—especially those staring, unwinking eyes which one never saw shut—was certainly shocking enough; and their voices were disgusting. It was awful to hear them chanting in their churches at night, and especially during their main festivals or revivals, which fell twice a year on April 30th and October 31st.

They were very fond of the water, and swam a great deal in both river and harbour. Swimming races out to Devil Reef were very common, and everyone in sight seemed well able to share in this arduous sport. When one came to think of it, it was generally only rather young people who were seen about in public, and of these the oldest were apt to be the most tainted-looking. When exceptions did occur, they were mostly persons with no trace of aberrancy, like the old clerk at the hotel. One wondered what became of the bulk of the older folk, and whether the "Innsmouth look" were not a strange and insidious disease-phenomenon which increased its hold as years advanced.

Only a very rare affliction, of course, could bring about such vast and radical anatomical changes in a single individual after maturity—changes involving osseous factors as basic as the shape of the skull—but then, even this aspect was no more baffling and unheard-of than the visible features of the malady as a whole. It would be hard, the youth implied, to form any real conclusions regarding such a matter; since one never came to know the natives personally no matter how long one might live in Innsmouth.

The youth was certain that many specimens even worse than the worst visible ones were kept locked indoors in some places. People sometimes heard the queerest kind of sounds. The tottering waterfront hovels north of the river were reputedly connected by hidden tunnels, being thus a veritable warren of unseen abnormalities. What kind of foreign blood—if any—these beings had, it was impossible to tell. They sometimes kept certain especially repulsive characters out of sight when government agents and others from the outside world came to town.

It would be of no use, my informant said, to ask the natives anything about the place. The only one who would talk was a very aged but normal-looking man who lived at the poorhouse on the north rim of the town and spent his time walking about or lounging around the fire station. This hoary character, Zadok Allen, was ninety-six years old and somewhat touched in the head, besides being the town drunkard. He was a strange, furtive creature who constantly looked over his shoulder as if afraid of something, and when sober could not be persuaded to talk at all with strangers. He was, however, unable to resist any offer of his favourite poison; and once drunk would furnish the most astonishing fragments of whispered reminiscence.

After all, though, little useful data could be gained from him; since his stories were all insane, incomplete hints of impossible marvels and horrors which could have no source save in his own disordered fancy. Nobody ever believed him, but the natives did not like him to drink and talk with strangers; and it was not always safe to be seen questioning him. It was probably from him that some of the wildest popular whispers and delusions were derived.

Several non-native residents had reported monstrous glimpses from time to time, but between old Zadok's tales and the malformed denizens it was no wonder such illusions were current. None of the non-natives ever stayed out late at night, there being a widespread impression that it was not wise to do so. Besides, the streets were loathsomely dark.

As for business—the abundance of fish was certainly almost uncanny, but the natives were taking less and less advantage of it. Moreover, prices were falling and competition was growing. Of course the town's real business was the refinery, whose commercial office was on the square only a few doors east of where we stood. Old Man Marsh was never seen, but sometimes went to the works in a closed, curtained car.

There were all sorts of rumours about how Marsh had come to look. He had once been a great dandy, and people said he still wore the frock-coated finery of the Edwardian age, curiously adapted to certain deformities. His sons had formerly conducted the office in the square, but latterly they had been keeping out of sight a good deal and leaving the brunt of affairs to the younger generation. The sons and their sisters had come to look very queer, especially the elder ones; and it was said that their health was failing.

One of the Marsh daughters was a repellent, reptilian-looking woman who wore an excess of weird jewellery clearly of the same exotic tradition as that to which the strange tiara belonged. My informant had noticed it many times, and had heard it spoken of as coming from some secret hoard, either of pirates or of daemons. The clergymen—or priests, or whatever they were called nowadays—also wore this kind of ornament as a head-dress; but one seldom caught glimpses of them. Other specimens the youth had not seen, though many were rumoured to exist around Innsmouth.

The Marshes, together with the other three gently bred families of the town—the Waites, the Gilmans, and the Eliots—were all very retiring. They lived in immense houses along Washington Street, and several were reputed to harbour in concealment certain living kinsfolk whose personal aspect forbade public view, and whose deaths had been reported and recorded.

Warning me that most of the street signs were down, the youth drew for my benefit a rough but ample and painstaking sketch map of the town's salient features. After a moment's study I felt sure that it would be of great help, and pocketed it with profuse thanks. Disliking the dinginess of the single restaurant I had seen, I bought a fair supply of cheese crackers and ginger wafers to serve as a lunch later on. My programme, I decided, would be to thread the principal streets, talk with any non-natives I might encounter, and catch the eight o'clock coach for Arkham. The town, I could see, formed a significant and exaggerated example of communal decay; but being no sociologist I would limit my serious observations to the field of architecture.

Thus I began my systematic though half-bewildered tour of Innsmouth's narrow, shadow-blighted ways. Crossing the bridge and turning toward the roar of the lower falls, I passed close to the Marsh refinery, which seemed oddly free from the noise of industry. This building stood on the steep river bluff near a bridge and an open confluence of streets which I took to be the earliest civic centre, displaced after the Revolution by the present Town Square.

Re-crossing the gorge on the Main Street bridge, I struck a region of utter desertion which somehow made me shudder. Collapsing huddles of gambrel roofs formed a jagged and fantastic skyline, above which rose the ghoulish, decapitated steeple of an ancient church. Some houses along Main Street were tenanted, but most were tightly boarded up. Down unpaved side streets I saw the black, gaping windows of deserted hovels, many of which leaned at perilous and incredible angles through the sinking of part of the foundations. Those windows stared so spectrally that it took courage to turn eastward toward the waterfront. Certainly, the terror of a deserted house swells in geometrical rather than arithmetical progression as houses mutiply to form a city of stark desolation. The sight of such endless avenues of fishy-eyed vacancy and death, and the thought of such linked infinities of black, brooding compartments given over to cobwebs and memories and the conqueror worm, start up vestigial fears and aversions that not even the stoutest philosophy can disperse.

Fish Street was as deserted as Main, though it differed in having many brick and stone warehouses still in excellent shape. Water Street was almost its duplicate, save that there were great seaward gaps where wharves had been. Not a living thing did I see, except for the scattered fishermen on the distant breakwater, and not a sound did I hear save the lapping of the harbour tides and the roar of the falls in the Manuxet. The town was getting more and more on my nerves, and I looked behind me furtively as I picked my way back over the tottering Water Street bridge. The Fish Street bridge, according to the sketch, was in ruins.

North of the river there were traces of squalid life—active fish-packing houses in Water Street, smoking chimneys and patched roofs here and there, occasional sounds from indeterminate sources, and infrequent shambling forms in the dismal streets and unpaved lanes—but I seemed to find this even more oppressive than the southerly desertion. For one thing, the people were more hideous and abnormal than those near the centre of the town; so that I was several times evilly reminded of something utterly fantastic which I could not quite place. Undoubtedly the alien strain in the Innsmouth folk was stronger here than farther inland—unless, indeed, the "Innsmouth look" were a disease rather than a blood strain, in which case this district might be held to harbour the more advanced cases.

One detail that annoyed me was the *distribution* of the few faint sounds I heard. They ought naturally to have come wholly from the visibly inhabited houses, yet in reality were often strongest inside the most rigidly boarded-up facades. There were creakings, scurryings, and hoarse doubtful noises; and I thought uncomfortably about the hidden tunnels suggested by the grocery boy. Suddenly I found myself wondering what the voices of those denizens would be like. I had heard no speech so far in this quarter, and was unaccountably anxious not to do so.

Pausing only long enough to look at two fine but ruinous old churches at Main and Church Streets, I hastened out of that vile waterfront slum. My next logical goal was New Church Green, but somehow or other I could not bear to re-pass the church in whose basement I had glimpsed the inexplicably frightening form of that strangely diademmed priest or pastor. Besides, the grocery youth had told me that the churches, as well as the Order of Dagon Hall, were not advisable neighbourhoods for strangers.

Accordingly I kept north along Main to Martin, then turning inland, crossing Federal Street safely north of the Green, and entering the decayed patrician neighbourhood of northern Broad, Washington, Lafayette, and Adams Streets. Though these stately old avenues were ill-surfaced and unkempt, their elm-shaded dignity had not entirely departed. Mansion after mansion claimed my gaze, most of them decrepit and boarded up amidst neglected grounds, but one or two in each street shewing signs of occupancy. In Washington Street there was a row of four or five in excellent repair and with finely tended lawns and gardens. The most sumptuous of these—with wide terraced parterres extending back the whole way to Lafayette Street—I took to be the home of Old Man Marsh, the afflicted refinery owner.

In all these streets no living thing was visible, and I wondered at the complete absence of cats and dogs from Innsmouth. Another thing which puzzled and disturbed me, even in some of the best-preserved mansions, was the tightly shuttered condition of many third-story and attic windows. Furtiveness and secretiveness seemed universal in this hushed city of alienage and death, and I could not escape the sensation of being watched from ambush on every hand by sly, staring eyes that never shut.

I shivered as the cracked stroke of three sounded from a belfry on my left. Too well did I recall the squat church from which those notes came. Following Washington Street toward the river, I now faced a new zone of former industry and commerce; noting the ruins of a factory ahead, and seeing others, with the traces of an old railway station and covered railway bridge beyond, up the gorge on my right.

The uncertain bridge now before me was posted with a warning sign, but I took the risk and crossed again to the south bank where traces of life reappeared. Furtive, shambling creatures stared cryptically in my direction, and more normal faces eyed me coldly and curiously. Innsmouth was rapidly becoming intolerable, and I turned down Paine Street toward the Square in the hope of getting some vehicle to take me to Arkham before the still-distant starting-time of that sinister bus.

It was then that I saw the tumbledown fire station on my left, and noticed the red-faced, bushy-bearded, watery-eyed old man in nondescript rags who sat on a bench in front of it talking with a pair of unkempt but not abnormal-looking firemen. This, of course, must be Zadok Allen, the half-crazed, liquorish nonagenarian whose tales of old Innsmouth and its shadow were so hideous and incredible.

III.

It must have been some imp of the perverse—or some sardonic pull from dark, hidden sources—which made me change my plans as I did. I had long before resolved to limit my observations to architecture alone, and I was even then hurrying toward the Square in an effort to get quick transportation out of this festering city of death and decay; but the sight of old Zadok Allen set up new currents in my mind and made me slacken my pace uncertainly.

I had been assured that the old man could do nothing but hint at wild, disjointed, and incredible legends, and I had been warned that the natives made it unsafe to be seen talking with him; yet the thought of this aged witness to the town's decay, with memories going back to the early days of ships and factories, was a lure that no amount of reason could make me resist. After all, the strangest and maddest of myths are often merely symbols or allegories based upon truth—and old Zadok must have seen everything which went on around Innsmouth for the last ninety years. Curiosity flared up beyond sense and caution, and in my youthful egotism I fancied I might be able to sift a nucleus of real history from the confused, extravagant outpouring I would probably extract with the aid of raw whiskey.

I knew that I could not accost him then and there, for the firemen would surely notice and object. Instead, I reflected, I would prepare by getting some bootleg liquor at a place where the grocery boy had told me it was plentiful. Then I would loaf near the fire station in apparent casualness, and fall in with old Zadok after he had started on one of his frequent rambles. The youth had said that he was very restless, seldom sitting around the station for more than an hour or two at a time.

A quart bottle of whiskey was easily, though not cheaply, obtained in the rear of a dingy variety-store just off the Square in Eliot Street. The dirty-looking fellow who waited on me had a touch of the staring "Innsmouth look", but was quite civil in his way; being perhaps used to the custom of such convivial strangers—truckmen, gold-buyers, and the like—as were occasionally in town.

Reëntering the Square I saw that luck was with me; for—shuffling out of Paine Street around the corner of the Gilman

House—I glimpsed nothing less than the tall, lean, tattered form of old Zadok Allen himself. In accordance with my plan, I attracted his attention by brandishing my newly purchased bottle; and soon realised that he had begun to shuffle wistfully after me as I turned into Waite Street on my way to the most deserted region I could think of.

I was steering my course by the map the grocery boy had prepared, and was aiming for the wholly abandoned stretch of southern waterfront which I had previously visited. The only people in sight there had been the fishermen on the distant breakwater; and by going a few squares south I could get beyond the range of these, finding a pair of seats on some abandoned wharf and being free to question old Zadok unobserved for an indefinite time. Before I reached Main Street I could hear a faint and wheezy "Hey, Mister!" behind me, and I presently allowed the old man to catch up and take copious pulls from the quart bottle.

I began putting out feelers as we walked along to Water Street and turned southward amidst the omnipresent desolation and crazily tilted ruins, but found that the aged tongue did not loosen as quickly as I had expected. At length I saw a grass-grown opening toward the sea between crumbling brick walls, with the weedy length of an earth-and-masonry wharf projecting beyond. Piles of moss-covered stones near the water promised tolerable seats, and the scene was sheltered from all possible view by a ruined warehouse on the north. Here, I thought, was the ideal place for a long secret colloquy; so I guided my companion down the lane and picked out spots to sit in among the mossy stones. The air of death and desertion was ghoulish, and the smell of fish almost insufferable; but I was resolved to let nothing deter me.

About four hours remained for conversation if I were to catch the eight o'clock coach for Arkham, and I began to dole out more liquor to the ancient tippler; meanwhile eating my own frugal lunch. In my donations I was careful not to overshoot the mark, for I did not wish Zadok's vinous garrulousness to pass into a stupor. After an hour his furtive taciturnity shewed signs of disappearing, but much to my disappointment he still sidetracked my questions about Innsmouth and its shadow-haunted past. He would babble of current topics, revealing a wide acquaintance with newspapers and a great tendency to philosophise in a sententious village fashion.

Toward the end of the second hour I feared my quart of whiskey would not be enough to produce results, and was wondering whether I had better leave old Zadok and go back for more. Just then, however, chance made the opening which my questions had been unable to make; and the wheezing ancient's rambling took a turn that caused me to lean forward and listen alertly. My back was toward the fishy-smelling sea, but he was facing it, and something or other had caused his wandering gaze to light on the low, distant line of Devil Reef, then shewing plainly and almost fascinatingly above the waves. The sight seemed to displease him, for he began a series of weak curses which ended in a confidential whisper and a knowing leer. He bent toward me, took hold of my coat lapel, and hissed out some hints that could not be mistaken.

"Thar's whar it all begun—that cursed place of all wickedness whar the deep water starts. Gate o' hell—sheer drop daown to a bottom no saoundin'-line kin tech. Ol' Cap'n Obed done it—him that faound aout more'n was good fer him in the Saouth Sea islands.

"Everybody was in a bad way them days. Trade fallin' off, mills losin' business—even the new ones—an' the best of our menfolks kilt a-privateerin' in the War of 1812 or lost with the *Elizy* brig an' the *Ranger* snow—both on 'em Gilman venters. Obed Marsh he had three ships afloat—brigantine *Columby*, brig *Hetty*, an' barque *Sumatry Queen*. He was the only one as kep' on with the East-Injy an' Pacific trade, though Esdras Martin's barkentine *Malay Pride* made a venter as late as 'twenty-eight.

"Never was nobody like Cap'n Obed—old limb o' Satan! Heh, heh! I kin mind him a-tellin' abaout furren parts, an' callin' all the folks stupid fer goin' to Christian meetin' an' bearin' their burdens meek an' lowly. Says they'd orter git better gods like some o' the folks in the Injies—gods as ud bring 'em good fishin' in return fer their sacrifices, an' ud reely answer folks's prayers.

"Matt Eliot, his fust mate, talked a lot, too, only he was agin' folks's doin' any heathen things. Told abaout an island east of Otaheité whar they was a lot o' stone ruins older'n anybody knew anything abaout, kind o' like them on Ponape, in the Carolines, but with carvin's of faces that looked like the big statues on Easter Island. They was a little volcanic island near thar, too, whar they was other ruins with diff'rent carvin's—ruins all wore away like they'd ben under the sea onct, an' with picters of awful monsters all over 'em.

"Wal, Sir, Matt he says the natives araound thar had all the fish they cud ketch, an' sported bracelets an' armlets an' head rigs made aout of a queer kind o' gold an' covered with picters o' monsters jest like the ones carved over the ruins on the little island—sorter fish-like frogs or frog-like fishes that was drawed in all kinds o' positions like they was human bein's. Nobody cud git aout o' them whar they got all the stuff, an' all the other natives wondered haow they managed to find fish in plenty even when the very next islands had lean pickin's. Matt he got to wonderin' too, an' so did Cap'n Obed. Obed he notices, besides, that lots of the han'some young folks ud drop aout o' sight fer good from year to year, an' that they wa'n't many old folks araound. Also, he thinks some of the folks looks durned queer even fer Kanakys.

"It took Obed to git the truth aout o' them heathen. I dun't know haow he done it, but he begun by tradin' fer the gold-like things they wore. Ast 'em whar they come from, an' ef they cud git more, an' finally wormed the story aout o' the old chief—Walakea, they called him. Nobody but Obed ud ever a believed the old yeller devil, but the Cap'n cud read folks like they was books. Heh, heh! Nobody never believes me naow when I tell 'em, an' I dun't s'pose you will, young feller—though come to look at ye, ye hev kind o' got them sharp-readin' eyes like Obed had."

The old man's whisper grew fainter, and I found myself shuddering at the terrible and sincere portentousness of his intonation, even though I knew his tale could be nothing but drunken phantasy.

"Wal, Sir, Obed he larnt that they's things on this arth as most folks never heerd abaout—an' wouldn't believe ef they did hear. It seems these Kanakys was sacrificin' heaps o' their young men an' maidens to some kind o' god-things that lived under the sea, an' gittin' all kinds o' favours in return. They met the things on the little islet with the queer ruins, an' it seems them awful picters o' frog-fish monsters was supposed to be picters o' these things. Mebbe they was the kind o' critters as got all the mermaid stories an' sech started. They had all kinds o' cities on the sea-bottom, an' this island was heaved up from thar. Seems they was some of the things alive in the stone buildin's when the island come up sudden to the surface. That's haow the Kanakys got wind they was daown thar. Made sign-talk as soon as they got over bein' skeert, an' pieced up a bargain afore long.

"Them things liked human sacrifices. Had had 'em ages afore, but lost track o' the upper world arter a time. What they done to the victims it ain't fer me to say, an' I guess Obed wa'n't none too sharp abaout askin'. But it was all right with the heathens, because they'd ben havin' a hard time an' was desp'rate abaout everything. They give a sarten number o' young folks to the sea-things twict every year—May-Eve an' Hallowe'en—reg'lar as cud be. Also give some o' the carved knick-knacks they made. What the things agreed to give in return was a plenty o' fish—they druv 'em in from all over the sea—an' a few gold-like things naow an' then.

"Wal, as I says, the natives met the things on the little volcanic islet—goin' thar in canoes with the sacrifices et cet'ry, and bringin' back any of the gold-like jools as was comin' to 'em. At fust the things didn't never go onto the main island, but arter a time they come to want to. Seems they hankered arter mixin' with the folks, an' havin' j'int ceremonies on the big days—May-Eve an' Hallowe'en. Ye see, they was able to live both in an' aout o' water—what they call amphibians, I guess. The Kanakys told 'em as haow folks from the other islands might wanta wipe 'em aout ef they got wind o' their bein' thar, but they says they dun't keer much, because they cud wipe aout the hull brood o' humans ef they was willin' to bother—that is, any as didn't hev sarten signs sech as was used onct by the lost Old Ones, whoever they was. But not wantin' to bother, they'd lay low when anybody visited the island.

"When it come to matin' with them toad-lookin' fishes, the Kanakys kind o' balked, but finally they larnt something as put a new face on the matter. Seems that human folks has got a kind o' relation to sech water-beasts—that everything alive come aout o' the water onct, an' only needs a little change to go back agin. Them things told the Kanakys that ef they mixed bloods there'd be children as ud look human at fust, but later turn more'n more like the things, till finally they'd take to the water an' jine the main lot o' things daown thar. An' this is the important part, young feller—them as turned into fish things an' went into the water *wouldn't never die*. Them things never died excep' they was kilt violent.

"Wal, Sir, it seems by the time Obed knowed them islanders they was all full o' fish blood from them deep-water things. When they got old an' begun to shew it, they was kep' hid until they felt like takin' to the water an' quittin' the place. Some was more teched than others, an' some never did change quite enough to take to the water; but mostly they turned aout jest the way them things said. Them as was born more like the things changed arly, but them as was nearly human sometimes stayed on the island till they was past seventy, though they'd usually go daown under fer trial trips afore that. Folks as had took to the water gen'rally come back a good deal to visit, so's a man ud often be a-talkin' to his own five-times-great-grandfather, who'd left the dry land a couple o' hundred years or so afore.

"Everybody got aout o' the idee o' dyin'—excep' in canoe wars with the other islanders, or as sacrifices to the sea-gods daown below, or from snake-bite or plague or sharp gallopin' ailments or somethin' afore they cud take to the water—but simply looked forrad to a kind o' change that wa'n't a bit horrible arter a while. They thought what they'd got was well wuth all they'd had to give up—an' I guess Obed kind o' come to think the same hisself when he'd chewed over old Walakea's story a bit. Walakea, though, was one of the few as hadn't got none of the fish blood—bein' of a royal line that intermarried with royal lines on other islands.

"Walakea he shewed Obed a lot o' rites an' incantations as had to do with the sea-things, an' let him see some o' the folks in the village as had changed a lot from human shape. Somehaow or other, though, he never would let him see one of the reg'lar things from right aout o' the water. In the end he give him a funny kind o' thingumajig made aout o' lead or something, that he said ud bring up the fish things from any place in the water whar they might be a nest of 'em. The idee was to drop it daown with the right kind o' prayers an' sech. Walakea allaowed as the things was scattered all over the world, so's anybody that looked abaout cud find a nest an' bring 'em up ef they was wanted.

"Matt he didn't like this business at all, an' wanted Obed shud keep away from the island; but the Cap'n was sharp fer gain, an' faound he cud git them gold-like things so cheap it ud pay him to make a specialty of 'em. Things went on that way fer years, an' Obed got enough o' that gold-like stuff to make him start the refinery in Waite's old run-daown fullin' mill. He didn't dass sell the pieces like they was, fer folks ud be all the time askin' questions. All the same his crews ud git a piece an' dispose of it naow and then, even though they was swore to keep quiet; an' he let his womenfolks wear some o' the pieces as was more human-like than most.

"Wal, come abaout 'thutty-eight—when I was seven year' old—Obed he faound the island people all wiped aout between v'yages. Seems the other islanders had got wind o' what was goin' on, an' had took matters into their own hands. S'pose they must a had, arter all, them old magic signs as the sea-things says was the only things they was afeard of. No tellin' what any o' them Kanakys will chance to git a holt of when the sea-bottom throws up some island with ruins older'n the deluge. Pious cusses, these was—they didn't leave nothin' standin' on either the main island or the little volcanic islet excep' what parts of the ruins was too big to knock daown. In some places they was little stones strowed abaout—like charms—with somethin' on 'em like what ye call a swastika naowadays. Prob'ly them was the Old Ones' signs. Folks all wiped aout, no trace o' no gold-like things, an' none o' the nearby Kanakys ud breathe a word abaout the matter. Wouldn't even admit they'd ever ben any people on that island.

"That naturally hit Obed pretty hard, seein' as his normal trade was doin' very poor. It hit the whole of Innsmouth, too, because in seafarin' days what profited the master of a ship gen'lly profited the crew proportionate. Most o' the folks araound the taown took the hard times kind o' sheep-like an' resigned, but they was in bad shape because the fishin' was peterin' aout an' the mills wa'n't doin' none too well.

"Then's the time Obed he begun a-cursin' at the folks fer bein' dull sheep an' prayin' to a Christian heaven as didn't help 'em none. He told 'em he'd knowed of folks as prayed to gods that give somethin' ye reely need, an' says ef a good bunch o' men ud stand by him, he cud mebbe git a holt o' sarten paowers as ud bring plenty o' fish an' quite a bit o' gold. O' course them as sarved on the *Sumatry Queen* an' seed the island knowed what he meant, an' wa'n't none too anxious to git clost to sea-things like they'd heerd tell on, but them as didn't know what 'twas all abaout got kind o' swayed by what Obed had to say, an' begun to ast him what he cud do to set 'em on the way to the faith as ud bring 'em results."

Here the old man faltered, mumbled, and lapsed into a moody and apprehensive silence; glancing nervously over his shoulder and then turning back to stare fascinatedly at the distant black reef. When I spoke to him he did not answer, so I knew I would have to let him finish the bottle. The insane yarn I was hearing interested me profoundly, for I fancied there was contained within it a sort of crude allegory based upon the strangenesses of Innsmouth and elaborated by an imagination at once creative and full of scraps of exotic legend. Not for a moment did I believe that the tale had any really substantial foundation; but none the less the account held a hint of genuine terror, if only because it brought in references to strange jewels clearly akin to the malign tiara I had seen at Newburyport. Perhaps the ornaments had, after all, come from some strange island; and possibly the wild stories were lies of the bygone Obed himself rather than of this antique toper.

I handed Zadok the bottle, and he drained it to the last drop. It was curious how he could stand so much whiskey, for not even a trace of thickness had come into his high, wheezy voice. He licked the nose of the bottle and slipped it into his pocket, then beginning to nod and whisper softly to himself. I bent close to catch any articulate words he might utter, and thought I saw a sardonic smile behind the stained, bushy whiskers. Yes—he was really forming words, and I could grasp a fair proportion of them.

"Poor Matt—Matt he allus was agin' it—tried to line up the folks on his side, an' had long talks with the preachers—no use—they run the Congregational parson aout o' taown, an' the Methodist feller quit—never did see Resolved Babcock, the Baptist parson, agin—Wrath o' Jehovy—I was a mighty little critter, but I heerd what I heerd an' seen what I seen—Dagon an' Ashtoreth—Belial an' Beëlzebub—Golden Caff an' the idols o' Canaan an' the Philistines—Babylonish abominations—*Mene, mene, tekel, upharsin*—"

He stopped again, and from the look in his watery blue eyes I feared he was close to a stupor after all. But when I gently shook his shoulder he turned on me with astonishing alertness and snapped out some more obscure phrases.

"Dun't believe me, hey? Heh, heh, heh—then jest tell me, young feller, why Cap'n Obed an' twenty odd other folks used to row aout to Devil Reef in the dead o' night an' chant things so laoud ye cud hear 'em all over taown when the wind was right? Tell me that, hey? An' tell me why Obed was allus droppin' heavy things daown into the deep water t'other side o' the reef whar the bottom shoots daown like a cliff lower'n ye kin saound? Tell me what he done with that funny-shaped lead thingumajig as Walakea give him? Hey, boy? An' what did they all haowl on May-Eve, an' agin the next Hallowe'en? An' why'd the new church parsons—fellers as used to be sailors—wear them queer robes an' cover theirselves with them gold-like things Obed brung? Hey?"

The watery blue eyes were almost savage and maniacal now, and the dirty white beard bristled electrically. Old Zadok probably saw me shrink back, for he began to cackle evilly.

"Heh, heh, heh, heh! Beginnin' to see, hey? Mebbe ye'd like to a ben me in them days, when I seed things at night aout to sea from the cupalo top o' my haouse. Oh, I kin tell ye, little pitchers hev big ears, an' I wa'n't missin' nothin' o' what was gossiped abaout Cap'n Obed an' the folks aout to the reef! Heh, heh, heh! Haow abaout the night I took my pa's ship's glass up to the cupalo an' seed the reef a-bristlin' thick with shapes that dove off quick soon's the moon riz? Obed an' the folks was in a dory, but them shapes dove off the far side into the deep water an' never come up.... Haow'd ye like to be a little shaver alone up in a cupalo a-watchin' shapes *as wa'n't human shapes?* ... Hey? ... Heh, heh, heh, heh...."

The old man was getting hysterical, and I began to shiver with a nameless alarm. He laid a gnarled claw on my shoulder, and it seemed to me that its shaking was not altogether that of mirth.

"S'pose one night ye seed somethin' heavy heaved offen Obed's dory beyond the reef, an' then larned nex' day a young feller was missin' from home? Hey? Did anybody ever see hide or hair o' Hiram Gilman agin? Did they? An' Nick Pierce, an' Luelly Waite, an' Adoniram Saouthwick, an' Henry Garrison? Hey? Heh, heh, heh, heh.... Shapes talkin' sign language with their hands ... them as had reel hands....

"Wal, Sir, that was the time Obed begun to git on his feet agin. Folks see his three darters a-wearin' gold-like things as nobody'd never see on 'em afore, an' smoke started comin' aout o' the refin'ry chimbly. Other folks was prosp'rin', too—fish begun to swarm into the harbour fit to kill, an' heaven knows what sized cargoes we begun to ship aout to Newb'ryport, Arkham, an' Boston. 'Twas then Obed got the ol' branch railrud put through. Some Kingsport fishermen heerd abaout the ketch an' come up in sloops, but they was all lost. Nobody never see 'em agin. An' jest then our folks organised the Esoteric Order o' Dagon, an' bought Masonic Hall offen Calvary Commandery for it ... heh, heh, heh! Matt Eliot was a Mason an' agin' the sellin', but he dropped aout o' sight jest then.

"Remember, I ain't sayin' Obed was set on hevin' things jest like they was on that Kanaky isle. I dun't think he aimed at fust to do no mixin', nor raise no younguns to take to the water an' turn into fishes with eternal life. He wanted them gold things, an' was willin' to pay heavy, an' I guess the *others* was satisfied fer a while....

"Come in 'forty-six the taown done some lookin' an' thinkin' fer itself. Too many folks missin'—too much wild preachin' at meetin' of a Sunday—too much talk abaout that reef. I guess I done a bit by tellin' Selectman Mowry what I see from the cupalo. They was a party one night as follered Obed's craowd aout to the reef, an' I heerd shots betwixt the dories. Nex' day Obed an' thutty-two others was in gaol, with everybody a-wonderin' jest what was afoot an' jest what charge agin' 'em cud be got to holt. God, ef anybody'd looked ahead ... a couple o' weeks later, when nothin' had ben throwed into the sea fer that long...."

Zadok was shewing signs of fright and exhaustion, and I let him keep silence for a while, though glancing apprehensively at my watch. The tide had turned and was coming in now, and the sound of the waves seemed to arouse him. I was glad of that tide, for at high water the fishy smell might not be so bad. Again I strained to catch his whispers.

"That awful night ... I seed 'em ... I was up in the cupalo ... hordes of 'em ... swarms of 'em ... all over the reef an' swimmin' up the harbour into the Manuxet.... God, what happened in the streets of Innsmouth that night ... they rattled our door, but pa wouldn't open ... then he clumb aout the kitchen winder with his musket to find Selectman Mowry an' see what he cud do.... Maounds o' the dead an' the dyin' ... shots an' screams ... shaoutin' in Ol' Squar an' Taown Squar an' New Church Green ... gaol throwed open ... proclamation ... treason ... called it the plague when folks come in an' faound haff our people missin' ... nobody left but them as ud jine in with Obed an' them things or else keep quiet ... never heerd o' my pa no more...."

The old man was panting, and perspiring profusely. His grip on my shoulder tightened.

"Everything cleaned up in the mornin'—but they was *traces*.... Obed he kinder takes charge an' says things is goin' to be changed ... *others'll* worship with us at meetin'-time, an' sarten haouses hez got to entertain *guests* ... *they* wanted to mix like they done with the Kanakys, an' he fer one didn't feel baound to stop 'em. Far gone, was Obed ... jest like a crazy man on the subjeck. He says they brung us fish an' treasure, an' shud hev what they hankered arter....

"Nothin' was to be diff'runt on the aoutside, only we was to keep shy o' strangers ef we knowed what was good fer us. We all hed to take the Oath o' Dagon, an' later on they was secon' an' third Oaths that some on us took. Them as ud help special, ud git special rewards—gold an' sech— No use balkin', fer they was millions of 'em daown thar. They'd ruther not start risin' an' wipin' aout humankind, but ef they was gave away an' forced to, they cud do a lot toward jest that. We didn't hev them old charms to cut 'em off like folks in the Saouth Sea did, an' them Kanakys wudn't never give away their secrets.

"Yield up enough sacrifices an' savage knick-knacks an' harbourage in the taown when they wanted it, an' they'd let well enough alone. Wudn't bother no strangers as might bear tales aoutside—that is, withaout they got pryin'. All in the band of the faithful—Order o' Dagon—an' the children shud never die, but go back to the Mother Hydra an' Father Dagon what we all come from onct—*Iä! Iä! Cthulhu fhtagn! Ph'nglui mglw'nafh Cthulhu R'lyeh wgah-nagl fhtagn*—"

Old Zadok was fast lapsing into stark raving, and I held my breath. Poor old soul—to what pitiful depths of hallucination had his liquor, plus his hatred of the decay, alienage, and disease around him, brought that fertile, imaginative brain! He began to moan now, and tears were coursing down his channelled cheeks into the depths of his beard.

"God, what I seen senct I was fifteen year' old—*Mene, mene, tekel, upharsin!*—the folks as was missin', an' them as kilt theirselves—them as told things in Arkham or Ipswich or sech places was all called crazy, like you're a-callin' me right naow—but God, what I seen— They'd a kilt me long ago fer what I know, only I'd took the fust an' secon' Oaths o' Dagon offen Obed, so was pertected unlessen a jury of 'em proved I told things knowin' an' delib'rit ... but I wudn't take the third Oath—I'd a died ruther'n take that—

"It got wuss araound Civil War time, *when children born senct 'forty-six begun to grow up*—some of 'em, that is. I was afeard—never did no pryin' arter that awful night, an' never see one o'—*them*—clost to in all my life. That is, never no full-blooded one. I went to the war, an' ef I'd a had any guts or sense I'd a never come back, but settled away from here. But folks wrote me things wa'n't so bad. That, I s'pose, was because gov'munt draft men was in taown arter 'sixty-three. Arter the war it was jest as bad agin. People begun to fall off—mills an' shops shet daown—shippin' stopped an' the harbour choked up—railrud give up—but *they* ... they never stopped swimmin' in an' aout o' the river from that cursed reef o' Satan—an' more an' more attic winders got a-boarded up, an' more an' more noises was heerd in haouses as wa'n't s'posed to hev nobody in 'em....

"Folks aoutside hev their stories abaout us—s'pose you've heerd a plenty on 'em, seein' what questions ye ast—stories abaout things they've seed naow an' then, an' abaout that queer joolry as still comes in from somewhars an' ain't quite all melted up—but nothin' never gits def'nite. Nobody'll believe nothin'. They call them gold-like things pirate loot, an' allaow the Innsmouth folks hez furren blood or is distempered or somethin'. Besides, them that lives here shoo off as many strangers as they kin, an' encourage the rest not to git very cur'ous, specially raound night time. Beasts balk at the critters—hosses wuss'n mules—but when they got autos that was all right.

"In 'forty-six Cap'n Obed took a second wife *that nobody in the taown never see*—some says he didn't want to, but was made to by them as he'd called in—had three children by her—two as disappeared young, but one gal as looked like anybody else an' was eddicated in Europe. Obed finally got her married off by a trick to an Arkham feller as didn't suspect nothin'. But nobody aoutside'll hev nothin' to do with Innsmouth folks naow. Barnabas Marsh that runs the refin'ry naow is Obed's grandson by his fust wife—son of Onesiphorus, his eldest son, *but his mother was another o' them as wa'n't never seed aoutdoors.*

"Right naow Barnabas is abaout changed. Can't shet his eyes no more, an' is all aout o' shape. They say he still wears clothes, but he'll take to the water soon. Mebbe he's tried it already—they do sometimes go daown fer little spells afore they go fer good. Ain't ben seed abaout in public fer nigh on ten year'. Dun't know haow his poor wife kin feel—she come from Ipswich, an' they nigh lynched Barnabas when he courted her fifty odd year' ago. Obed he died in 'seventy-eight, an' all the next gen'ration is gone naow—the fust wife's children dead, an' the rest ... God knows...."

The sound of the incoming tide was now very insistent, and little by little it seemed to change the old man's mood from maudlin tearfulness to watchful fear. He would pause now and then to renew those nervous glances over his shoulder or out toward the reef, and despite the wild absurdity of his tale, I could not help beginning to share his vague apprehensiveness. Zadok now grew shriller, and seemed to be trying to whip up his courage with louder speech.

"Hey, yew, why dun't ye say somethin'? Haow'd ye like to be livin' in a taown like this, with everything a-rottin' an' a-dyin', an' boarded-up monsters crawlin' an' bleatin' an' barkin' an' hoppin' araoun' black cellars an' attics every way ye turn? Hey? Haow'd ye like to hear the haowlin' night arter night from the churches an' Order o' Dagon Hall, *an' know what's doin' part o' the haowlin'*? Haow'd ye like to hear what comes from that awful reef every May-Eve an' Hallowmass? Hey? Think the old man's crazy, eh? Wal, Sir, *let me tell ye that ain't the wust!*"

Zadok was really screaming now, and the mad frenzy of his voice disturbed me more than I care to own.

"Curse ye, dun't set thar a-starin' at me with them eyes—I tell Obed Marsh he's in hell, an' hez got to stay thar! Heh, heh ... in hell, I says! Can't git me—I hain't done nothin' nor told nobody nothin'—

"Oh, you, young feller? Wal, even ef I hain't told nobody nothin' yet, I'm a-goin' to naow! You jest set still an' listen to me, boy—this is what I ain't never told nobody.... I says I didn't do no pryin' arter that night—*but I faound things aout jest the same!*

"Yew want to know what the reel horror is, hey? Wal, it's this—it ain't what them fish devils *hez done, but what they're a-goin' to do!* They're a-bringin' things up aout o' whar they come from into the taown—ben doin' it fer years, an' slackenin' up lately. Them haouses north o' the river betwixt Water an' Main Streets is full of 'em—them devils *an' what they brung*—an' when they git ready.... I say, *when they git ready* ... ever hear tell of a *shoggoth?* ...

"Hey, d'ye hear me? I tell ye *I know what them things be—I seen 'em one night when* … EH-AHHHH—AH! E'YAAHHHH…."

The hideous suddenness and inhuman frightfulness of the old man's shriek almost made me faint. His eyes, looking past me toward the malodorous sea, were positively starting from his head; while his face was a mask of fear worthy of Greek tragedy. His bony claw dug monstrously into my shoulder, and he made no motion as I turned my head to look at whatever he had glimpsed.

There was nothing that I could see. Only the incoming tide, with perhaps one set of ripples more local than the long-flung line of breakers. But now Zadok was shaking me, and I turned back to watch the melting of that fear-frozen face into a chaos of twitching eyelids and mumbling gums. Presently his voice came back—albeit as a trembling whisper.

"*Git aout o' here!* Git aout o' here! *They seen us*—git aout fer your life! Dun't wait fer nothin'—*they know naow*— Run fer it—quick—*aout o' this taown*—"

Another heavy wave dashed against the loosening masonry of the bygone wharf, and changed the mad ancient's whisper to another inhuman and blood-curdling scream.

"E—YAAAHHHH! … YHAAAAAAAA! …"

Before I could recover my scattered wits he had relaxed his clutch on my shoulder and dashed wildly inland toward the street, reeling northward around the ruined warehouse wall.

I glanced back at the sea, but there was nothing there. And when I reached Water Street and looked along it toward the north there was no remaining trace of Zadok Allen.

IV.

I can hardly describe the mood in which I was left by this harrowing episode—an episode at once mad and pitiful, grotesque and terrifying. The grocery boy had prepared me for it, yet the reality left me none the less bewildered and disturbed. Puerile though the story was, old Zadok's insane earnestness and horror had communicated to me a mounting unrest which joined with my earlier sense of loathing for the town and its blight of intangible shadow.

Later I might sift the tale and extract some nucleus of historic allegory; just now I wished to put it out of my head. The hour had grown perilously late—my watch said 7:15, and the Arkham bus left Town Square at eight—so I tried to give my thoughts as neutral and practical a cast as possible, meanwhile walking rapidly through the deserted streets of gaping roofs and leaning houses toward the hotel where I had checked my valise and would find my bus.

Though the golden light of late afternoon gave the ancient roofs and decrepit chimneys an air of mystic loveliness and peace, I could not help glancing over my shoulder now and then. I would surely be very glad to get out of malodorous and fear-shadowed Innsmouth, and wished there were some other vehicle than the bus driven by that sinister-looking fellow Sargent. Yet I did not hurry too precipitately, for there were architectural details worth viewing at every silent corner; and I could easily, I calculated, cover the necessary distance in a half-hour.

Studying the grocery youth's map and seeking a route I had not traversed before, I chose Marsh Street instead of State for my approach to Town Square. Near the corner of Fall Street I began to see scattered groups of furtive whisperers, and when I finally reached the Square I saw that almost all the loiterers were congregated around the door of the Gilman House. It seemed as if many bulging, watery, unwinking eyes looked oddly at me as I claimed my valise in the lobby, and I hoped that none of these unpleasant creatures would be my fellow-passengers on the coach.

The bus, rather early, rattled in with three passengers somewhat before eight, and an evil-looking fellow on the sidewalk muttered a few indistinguishable words to the driver. Sargent threw out a mail-bag and a roll of newspapers, and entered the hotel; while the passengers—the same men whom I had seen arriving in Newburyport that morning—shambled to the sidewalk and exchanged some faint guttural words with a loafer in a language I could have sworn was not English. I boarded the empty coach and took the same seat I had taken before, but was hardly settled before Sargent reappeared and began mumbling in a throaty voice of peculiar repulsiveness.

I was, it appeared, in very bad luck. There had been something wrong with the engine, despite the excellent time made from Newburyport, and the bus could not complete the journey to Arkham. No, it could not possibly be repaired that night, nor was there any other way of getting transportation out of Innsmouth, either to Arkham or elsewhere. Sargent was sorry, but I would have to stop over at the Gilman. Probably the clerk would make the price easy for me, but there was nothing else to do. Almost dazed by this sudden obstacle, and violently dreading the fall of night in this decaying and half-unlighted town, I left the bus and reëntered the hotel lobby; where the sullen, queer-looking night clerk told me I could have Room 428 on next the top floor—large, but without running water—for a dollar.

Despite what I had heard of this hotel in Newburyport, I signed the register, paid my dollar, let the clerk take my valise, and followed that sour, solitary attendant up three creaking flights of stairs past dusty corridors which seemed wholly devoid of life. My room, a dismal rear one with two windows and bare, cheap furnishings, overlooked a dingy courtyard otherwise hemmed in by low, deserted brick blocks, and commanded a view of decrepit westward-stretching roofs with a marshy countryside beyond. At the end of the corridor was a bathroom—a discouraging relique with ancient marble bowl, tin tub, faint electric light, and musty wooden panelling around all the plumbing fixtures.

It being still daylight, I descended to the Square and looked around for a dinner of some sort; noticing as I did so the strange glances I received from the unwholesome loafers. Since the grocery was closed, I was forced to patronise the restaurant I had shunned before; a stooped, narrow-headed man with staring, unwinking eyes, and a flat-nosed wench with unbelievably thick, clumsy hands being in attendance. The service was all of the counter type, and it relieved me to find that much was evidently served from cans and packages. A bowl of vegetable soup with crackers was enough for me, and I soon headed back for my cheerless room at the Gilman; getting an evening paper and a flyspecked magazine from the evil-visaged clerk at the rickety stand beside his desk.

As twilight deepened I turned on the one feeble electric bulb over the cheap, iron-framed bed, and tried as best I could to continue the reading I had begun. I felt it advisable to keep my mind wholesomely occupied, for it would not do to brood over the abnormalities of this ancient, blight-shadowed town while I was still within its borders. The insane yarn I had heard from the aged drunkard did not promise very pleasant dreams, and I felt I must keep the image of his wild, watery eyes as far as possible from my imagination.

Also, I must not dwell on what that factory inspector had told the Newburyport ticket-agent about the Gilman House and the voices of its nocturnal tenants—not on that, nor on the face beneath the tiara in the black church doorway; the face for whose horror my conscious mind could not account. It would perhaps have been easier to keep my thoughts from disturbing topics had the room not been so gruesomely musty. As it was, the lethal mustiness blended hideously with the town's general fishy odour and persistently focussed one's fancy on death and decay.

Another thing that disturbed me was the absence of a bolt on the door of my room. One had been there, as marks clearly shewed, but there were signs of recent removal. No doubt it had become out of order, like so many other things in this decrepit edifice. In my nervousness I looked around and discovered a bolt on the clothespress which seemed to be of the same size, judging from the marks, as the one formerly on the door. To gain a partial relief from the general tension I busied myself by transferring this hardware to the vacant place with the aid of a handy three-in-one device including a screw-driver which I kept on my key-ring. The bolt fitted perfectly, and I was somewhat relieved when I knew that I could shoot it firmly upon retiring. Not that I had any real apprehension of its need, but that any symbol of security was welcome in an environment of this kind. There were adequate bolts on the two lateral doors to connecting rooms, and these I proceeded to fasten.

I did not undress, but decided to read till I was sleepy and then lie down with only my coat, collar, and shoes off. Taking a pocket flashlight from my valise, I placed it in my trousers, so that I could read my watch if I woke up later in the dark. Drowsiness, however, did not come; and when I stopped to analyse my thoughts I found to my disquiet that I was really unconsciously listening for something—listening for something which I dreaded but could not name. That inspector's story must have worked on my imagination more deeply than I had suspected. Again I tried to read, but found that I made no progress.

After a time I seemed to hear the stairs and corridors creak at intervals as if with footsteps, and wondered if the other rooms were beginning to fill up. There were no voices, however, and it struck me that there was something subtly furtive about the creaking. I did not like it, and debated whether I had better try to sleep at all. This town had some queer people, and there had undoubtedly been several disappearances. Was this one of those inns where travellers were slain for their money? Surely I had no look of excessive prosperity. Or were the townsfolk really so resentful about curious visitors? Had my obvious sightseeing, with its frequent map-consultations, aroused unfavourable notice? It occurred to me that I must be in a highly nervous state to let a few random creakings set me off speculating in this fashion—but I regretted none the less that I was unarmed.

At length, feeling a fatigue which had nothing of drowsiness in it, I bolted the newly outfitted hall door, turned off the light, and threw myself down on the hard, uneven bed—coat, collar, shoes, and all. In the darkness every faint noise of the night seemed magnified, and a flood of doubly unpleasant thoughts swept over me. I was sorry I had put out the light, yet was too tired to rise and turn it on again. Then, after a long, dreary interval, and prefaced by a fresh creaking of stairs and corridor, there came that soft, damnably unmistakable sound which seemed like a malign fulfilment of all my apprehensions. Without the least shadow of a doubt, the lock on my hall door was being tried—cautiously, furtively, tentatively—with a key.

My sensations upon recognising this sign of actual peril were perhaps less rather than more tumultuous because of my previous vague fears. I had been, albeit without definite reason, instinctively on my guard—and that was to my advantage in the new and real crisis, whatever it might turn out to be. Nevertheless the change in the menace from vague premonition to immediate reality was a profound shock, and fell upon me with the force of a genuine blow. It never once occurred to me that the fumbling might be a mere mistake. Malign purpose was all I could think of, and I kept deathly quiet, awaiting the would-be intruder's next move.

After a time the cautious rattling ceased, and I heard the room to the north entered with a pass-key. Then the lock of the connecting door to my room was softly tried. The bolt held, of course, and I heard the floor creak as the prowler left the room. After a moment there came another soft rattling, and I knew that the room to the south of me was being entered. Again a furtive trying of a bolted connecting door, and again a receding creaking. This time the creaking went along the hall and down the stairs, so I knew that the prowler had realised the bolted condition of my doors and was giving up his attempt for a greater or lesser time, as the future would shew.

The readiness with which I fell into a plan of action proves that I must have been subconsciously fearing some menace and considering possible avenues of escape for hours. From the first I felt that the unseen fumbler meant a danger not to be met or dealt with, but only to be fled from as precipitately as possible. The one thing to do was to get out of that hotel alive as quickly as I could, and through some channel other than the front stairs and lobby.

Rising softly and throwing my flashlight on the switch, I sought to light the bulb over my bed in order to choose and pocket some belongings for a swift, valiseless flight. Nothing, however, happened; and I saw that the power had been cut off. Clearly, some cryptic, evil movement was afoot on a large scale—just what, I could not say. As I stood pondering with my hand on the now useless switch I heard a muffled creaking on the floor below, and thought I could barely distinguish voices in conversation. A moment later I felt less sure that the deeper sounds were voices, since the apparent hoarse barkings and loose-syllabled croakings bore so little resemblance to recognised human speech. Then I thought with renewed force of what the factory inspector had heard in the night in this mouldering and pestilential building.

Having filled my pockets with the flashlight's aid, I put on my hat and tiptoed to the windows to consider chances of descent. Despite the state's safety regulations there was no fire escape on this side of the hotel, and I saw that my windows commanded only a sheer three-story drop to the cobbled courtyard. On the right and left, however, some ancient brick business blocks abutted on the hotel; their slant roofs coming up to a reasonable jumping distance from my fourth-story level. To reach either of these lines of buildings I would have to be in a room two doors from my own—in one case on the north and in the other case on the south—and my mind instantly set to work calculating what chances I had of making the transfer.

I could not, I decided, risk an emergence into the corridor; where my footsteps would surely be heard, and where the difficulties of entering the desired room would be insuperable. My progress, if it was to be made at all, would have to be through the less solidly built connecting doors of the rooms; the locks and bolts of which I would have to force violently, using my shoulder as a battering-ram whenever they were set against me. This, I thought, would be possible owing to the rickety nature of the house and its fixtures; but I realised I could not do it noiselessly. I would have to count on sheer speed, and the chance of getting to a window before any hostile forces became coördinated enough to open the right door toward me with a pass-key. My own outer door I reinforced by pushing the bureau against it—little by little, in order to make a minimum of sound.

I perceived that my chances were very slender, and was fully prepared for any calamity. Even getting to another roof would not solve the problem, for there would then remain the task of reaching the ground and escaping from the town. One thing in my favour was the deserted and ruinous state of the abutting buildings, and the number of skylights gaping blackly open in each row.

Gathering from the grocery boy's map that the best route out of town was southward, I glanced first at the connecting door on the south side of the room. It was designed to open in my direction, hence I saw—after drawing the bolt and finding other fastenings in place—it was not a favourable one for forcing. Accordingly abandoning it as a route, I cautiously moved the bedstead against it to hamper any attack which might be made on it later from the next room. The door on the north was hung to open away from me, and this—though a test proved it to be locked or bolted from the other side—I knew must be my route. If I could gain the roofs of the buildings in Paine Street and descend successfully to the ground level, I might perhaps dart through the courtyard and the adjacent or opposite buildings to Washington or Bates—or else emerge in Paine and edge around southward into Washington. In any case, I would aim to strike Washington somehow and get quickly out of the Town Square region. My preference would be to avoid Paine, since the fire station there might be open all night.

As I thought of these things I looked out over the squalid sea of decaying roofs below me, now brightened by the beams of a moon not much past full. On the right the black gash of the river-gorge clove the panorama; abandoned factories and railway station clinging barnacle-like to its sides. Beyond it the rusted railway and the Rowley road led off through a flat, marshy terrain dotted with islets of higher and dryer scrub-grown land. On the left the creek-threaded countryside was nearer, the narrow road to Ipswich gleaming white in the moonlight. I could not see from my side of the hotel the southward route toward Arkham which I had determined to take.

I was irresolutely speculating on when I had better attack the northward door, and on how I could least audibly manage it, when I noticed that the vague noises underfoot had given place to a fresh and heavier creaking of the stairs. A wavering flicker of light shewed through my transom, and the boards of the corridor began to groan with a ponderous load. Muffled sounds of possible vocal origin approached, and at length a firm knock came at my outer door.

For a moment I simply held my breath and waited. Eternities seemed to elapse, and the nauseous fishy odour of my environment seemed to mount suddenly and spectacularly. Then the knocking was repeated—continuously, and with growing insistence. I knew that the time for action had come, and forthwith drew the bolt of the northward connecting door, bracing myself for the task of battering it open. The knocking waxed louder, and I hoped that its volume would cover the sound of my efforts. At last beginning my attempt, I lunged again and again at the thin panelling with my left shoulder, heedless of shock or pain. The door resisted even more than I had expected, but I did not give in. And all the while the clamour at the outer door increased.

Finally the connecting door gave, but with such a crash that I knew those outside must have heard. Instantly the outside knocking became a violent battering, while keys sounded ominously in the hall doors of the rooms on both sides of me. Rushing through the newly opened connexion, I succeeded in bolting the northerly hall door before the lock could be turned; but even as I did so I heard the hall door of the third room—the one from whose window I had hoped to reach the roof below—being tried with a pass-key.

For an instant I felt absolute despair, since my trapping in a chamber with no window egress seemed complete. A wave of almost abnormal horror swept over me, and invested with a terrible but unexplainable singularity the flashlight-glimpsed dust prints made by the intruder who had lately tried my door from this room. Then, with a dazed automatism which persisted despite hopelessness, I made for the next connecting door and performed the blind motion of pushing at it in an effort to get through and—granting that fastenings might be as providentially intact as in this second room—bolt the hall door beyond before the lock could be turned from outside.

Sheer fortunate chance gave me my reprieve—for the connecting door before me was not only unlocked but actually ajar. In a second I was through, and had my right knee and shoulder against a hall door which was visibly opening inward. My pressure took the opener off guard, for the thing shut as I pushed, so that I could slip the well-conditioned bolt as I had done with the other door. As I gained this respite I heard the battering at the two other doors abate, while a confused clatter came from the connecting door I had shielded with the bedstead. Evidently the bulk of my assailants had entered the southerly room and were massing in a lateral attack. But at the same moment a pass-key sounded in the next door to the north, and I knew that a nearer peril was at hand.

The northward connecting door was wide open, but there was no time to think about checking the already turning lock in the hall. All I could do was to shut and bolt the open connecting door, as well as its mate on the opposite side—pushing a bedstead against the one and a bureau against the other, and moving a washstand in front of the hall door. I must, I saw, trust to such makeshift barriers to shield me till I could get out the window and on the roof of the Paine Street block. But even in this acute moment my chief horror was something apart from the immediate weakness of my defences. I was shuddering because not one of my pursuers, despite some hideous pantings, gruntings, and subdued barkings at odd intervals, was uttering an unmuffled or intelligible vocal sound.

As I moved the furniture and rushed toward the windows I heard a frightful scurrying along the corridor toward the room north of me, and perceived that the southward battering had ceased. Plainly, most of my opponents were about to concentrate against the feeble connecting door which they knew must open directly on me. Outside, the moon played on the ridgepole of the block below, and I saw that the jump would be desperately hazardous because of the steep surface on which I must land.

Surveying the conditions, I chose the more southerly of the two windows as my avenue of escape; planning to land on the inner slope of the roof and make for the nearest skylight. Once inside one of the decrepit brick structures I would have to reckon with pursuit; but I hoped to descend and dodge in and out of yawning doorways along the shadowed courtyard, eventually getting to Washington Street and slipping out of town toward the south.

The clatter at the northerly connecting door was now terrific, and I saw that the weak panelling was beginning to splinter. Obviously, the besiegers had brought some ponderous object into play as a battering-ram. The bedstead, however, still held firm; so that I had at least a faint chance of making good my escape. As I opened the window I noticed that it was flanked by heavy velour draperies suspended from a pole by brass rings, and also that there was a large projecting catch for the shutters on the exterior. Seeing a possible means of avoiding the dangerous jump, I yanked at the hangings and brought them down, pole and all; then quickly hooking two of the rings in the shutter catch and flinging the drapery outside. The heavy folds reached fully to the abutting roof, and I saw that the rings and catch would be likely to bear my weight. So, climbing out of the window and down the improvised rope ladder, I left behind me for ever the morbid and horror-infested fabric of the Gilman House.

I landed safely on the loose slates of the steep roof, and succeeded in gaining the gaping black skylight without a slip. Glancing up at the window I had left, I observed it was still dark, though far across the crumbling chimneys to the north I could see lights ominously blazing in the Order of Dagon Hall, the Baptist church, and the Congregational church which I recalled so shiveringly. There had seemed to be no one in the courtyard below, and I hoped there would be a chance to get away before the spreading of a general alarm. Flashing my pocket lamp into the skylight, I saw that there were no steps down. The distance was slight, however, so I clambered over the brink and dropped; striking a dusty floor littered with crumbling boxes and barrels.

The place was ghoulish-looking, but I was past minding such impressions and made at once for the staircase revealed by my flashlight—after a hasty glance at my watch, which shewed the hour to be 2 a.m. The steps creaked, but seemed tolerably sound;

and I raced down past a barn-like second story to the ground floor. The desolation was complete, and only echoes answered my footfalls. At length I reached the lower hall, at one end of which I saw a faint luminous rectangle marking the ruined Paine Street doorway. Heading the other way, I found the back door also open; and darted out and down five stone steps to the grass-grown cobblestones of the courtyard.

The moonbeams did not reach down here, but I could just see my way about without using the flashlight. Some of the windows on the Gilman House side were faintly glowing, and I thought I heard confused sounds within. Walking softly over to the Washington Street side I perceived several open doorways, and chose the nearest as my route out. The hallway inside was black, and when I reached the opposite end I saw that the street door was wedged immovably shut. Resolved to try another building, I groped my way back toward the courtyard, but stopped short when close to the doorway.

For out of an opened door in the Gilman House a large crowd of doubtful shapes was pouring—lanterns bobbing in the darkness, and horrible croaking voices exchanging low cries in what was certainly not English. The figures moved uncertainly, and I realised to my relief that they did not know where I had gone; but for all that they sent a shiver of horror through my frame. Their features were indistinguishable, but their crouching, shambling gait was abominably repellent. And worst of all, I perceived that one figure was strangely robed, and unmistakably surmounted by a tall tiara of a design altogether too familiar. As the figures spread throughout the courtyard, I felt my fears increase. Suppose I could find no egress from this building on the street side? The fishy odour was detestable, and I wondered I could stand it without fainting. Again groping toward the street, I opened a door off the hall and came upon an empty room with closely shuttered but sashless windows. Fumbling in the rays of my flashlight, I found I could open the shutters; and in another moment had climbed outside and was carefully closing the aperture in its original manner.

I was now in Washington Street, and for the moment saw no living thing nor any light save that of the moon. From several directions in the distance, however, I could hear the sound of hoarse voices, of footsteps, and of a curious kind of pattering which did not sound quite like footsteps. Plainly I had no time to lose. The points of the compass were clear to me, and I was glad that all the street-lights were turned off, as is often the custom on strongly moonlit nights in unprosperous rural regions.

Some of the sounds came from the south, yet I retained my design of escaping in that direction. There would, I knew, be plenty of deserted doorways to shelter me in case I met any person or group who looked like pursuers.

I walked rapidly, softly, and close to the ruined houses. While hatless and dishevelled after my arduous climb, I did not look especially noticeable; and stood a good chance of passing unheeded if forced to encounter any casual wayfarer. At Bates Street I drew into a yawning vestibule while two shambling figures crossed in front of me, but was soon on my way again and approaching the open space where Eliot Street obliquely crosses Washington at the intersection of South. Though I had never seen this space, it had looked dangerous to me on the grocery youth's map; since the moonlight would have free play there. There was no use trying to evade it, for any alternative course would involve detours of possibly disastrous visibility and delaying effect. The only thing to do was to cross it boldly and openly; imitating the typical shamble of the Innsmouth folk as best I could, and trusting that no one—or at least no pursuer of mine—would be there.

Just how fully the pursuit was organised—and indeed, just what its purpose might be—I could form no idea. There seemed to be unusual activity in the town, but I judged that the news of my escape from the Gilman had not yet spread. I would, of course, soon have to shift from Washington to some other southward street; for that party from the hotel would doubtless be after me. I must have left dust prints in that last old building, revealing how I had gained the street.

The open space was, as I had expected, strongly moonlit; and I saw the remains of a park-like, iron-railed green in its centre. Fortunately no one was about, though a curious sort of buzz or roar seemed to be increasing in the direction of Town Square. South Street was very wide, leading directly down a slight declivity to the waterfront and commanding a long view out at sea; and I hoped that no one would be glancing up it from afar as I crossed in the bright moonlight.

My progress was unimpeded, and no fresh sound arose to hint that I had been spied. Glancing about me, I involuntarily let my pace slacken for a second to take in the sight of the sea, gorgeous in the burning moonlight at the street's end. Far out beyond the breakwater was the dim, dark line of Devil Reef, and as I glimpsed it I could not help thinking of all the hideous legends I had heard in the last thirty-four hours—legends which portrayed this ragged rock as a veritable gateway to realms of unfathomed horror and inconceivable abnormality.

Then, without warning, I saw the intermittent flashes of light on the distant reef. They were definite and unmistakable, and awaked in my mind a blind horror beyond all rational proportion. My muscles tightened for panic flight, held in only by a certain unconscious caution and half-hypnotic fascination. And to make matters worse, there now flashed forth from the lofty cupola of the Gilman House, which loomed up to the northeast behind me, a series of analogous though differently spaced gleams which could be nothing less than an answering signal.

Controlling my muscles, and realising afresh how plainly visible I was, I resumed my brisker and feignedly shambling pace; though keeping my eyes on that hellish and ominous reef as long as the opening of South Street gave me a seaward view. What the whole proceeding meant, I could not imagine; unless it involved some strange rite connected with Devil Reef, or unless some party had landed from a ship on that sinister rock. I now bent to the left around the ruinous green; still gazing toward the ocean as it blazed in the spectral summer moonlight, and watching the cryptical flashing of those nameless, unexplainable beacons.

It was then that the most horrible impression of all was borne in upon me—the impression which destroyed my last vestige of self-control and set me running frantically southward past the yawning black doorways and fishily staring windows of that deserted nightmare street. For at a closer glance I saw that the moonlit waters between the reef and the shore were far from empty. They were alive with a teeming horde of shapes swimming inward toward the town; and even at my vast distance and in my single moment of perception I could tell that the bobbing heads and flailing arms were alien and aberrant in a way scarcely to be expressed or consciously formulated.

My frantic running ceased before I had covered a block, for at my left I began to hear something like the hue and cry of organised pursuit. There were footsteps and guttural sounds, and a rattling motor wheezed south along Federal Street. In a second all my plans were utterly changed—for if the southward highway were blocked ahead of me, I must clearly find another egress from Innsmouth. I paused and drew into a gaping doorway, reflecting how lucky I was to have left the moonlit open space before these pursuers came down the parallel street.

A second reflection was less comforting. Since the pursuit was down another street, it was plain that the party was not following me directly. It had not seen me, but was simply obeying a general plan of cutting off my escape. This, however, implied that all roads leading out of Innsmouth were similarly patrolled;

for the denizens could not have known what route I intended to take. If this were so, I would have to make my retreat across country away from any road; but how could I do that in view of the marshy and creek-riddled nature of all the surrounding region? For a moment my brain reeled—both from sheer hopelessness and from a rapid increase in the omnipresent fishy odour.

Then I thought of the abandoned railway to Rowley, whose solid line of ballasted, weed-grown earth still stretched off to the northwest from the crumbling station on the edge of the river-gorge. There was just a chance that the townsfolk would not think of that; since its brier-choked desertion made it half-impassable, and the unlikeliest of all avenues for a fugitive to choose. I had seen it clearly from my hotel window, and knew about how it lay. Most of its earlier length was uncomfortably visible from the Rowley road, and from high places in the town itself; but one could perhaps crawl inconspicuously through the undergrowth. At any rate, it would form my only chance of deliverance, and there was nothing to do but try it.

Drawing inside the hall of my deserted shelter, I once more consulted the grocery boy's map with the aid of the flashlight. The immediate problem was how to reach the ancient railway; and I now saw that the safest course was ahead to Babson Street, then west to Lafayette—there edging around but not crossing an open space homologous to the one I had traversed—and subsequently back northward and westward in a zigzagging line through Lafayette, Bates, Adams, and Bank Streets—the latter skirting the river-gorge—to the abandoned and dilapidated station I had seen from my window. My reason for going ahead to Babson was that I wished neither to re-cross the earlier open space nor to begin my westward course along a cross street as broad as South.

Starting once more, I crossed the street to the right-hand side in order to edge around into Babson as inconspicuously as possible. Noises still continued in Federal Street, and as I glanced behind me I thought I saw a gleam of light near the building through which I had escaped. Anxious to leave Washington Street, I broke into a quiet dog-trot, trusting to luck not to encounter any observing eye. Next the corner of Babson Street I saw to my alarm that one of the houses was still inhabited, as attested by curtains at the window; but there were no lights within, and I passed it without disaster.

In Babson Street, which crossed Federal and might thus reveal me to the searchers, I clung as closely as possible to the sagging, uneven buildings; twice pausing in a doorway as the noises behind me momentarily increased. The open space ahead shone wide and desolate under the moon, but my route would not force me to cross it. During my second pause I began to detect a fresh distribution of the vague sounds; and upon looking cautiously out from cover beheld a motor-car darting across the open space, bound outward along Eliot Street, which there intersects both Babson and Lafayette.

As I watched—choked by a sudden rise in the fishy odour after a short abatement—I saw a band of uncouth, crouching shapes loping and shambling in the same direction; and knew that this must be the party guarding the Ipswich road, since that highway forms an extension of Eliot Street. Two of the figures I glimpsed were in voluminous robes, and one wore a peaked diadem which glistened whitely in the moonlight. The gait of this figure was so odd that it sent a chill through me—for it seemed to me the creature was almost *hopping*.

When the last of the band was out of sight I resumed my progress; darting around the corner into Lafayette Street, and crossing Eliot very hurriedly lest stragglers of the party be still advancing along that thoroughfare. I did hear some croaking and clattering sounds far off toward Town Square, but accomplished the passage without disaster. My greatest dread was in re-crossing broad and moonlit South Street—with its seaward view—and I had to nerve myself for the ordeal. Someone might easily be looking, and possible Eliot Street stragglers could not fail to glimpse me from either of two points. At the last moment I decided I had better slacken my trot and make the crossing as before in the shambling gait of an average Innsmouth native.

When the view of the water again opened out—this time on my right—I was half-determined not to look at it at all. I could not, however, resist; but cast a sidelong glance as I carefully and imitatively shambled toward the protecting shadows ahead. There was no ship visible, as I had half expected there would be. Instead, the first thing which caught my eye was a small rowboat pulling in toward the abandoned wharves and laden with some bulky, tarpaulin-covered object. Its rowers, though distantly and indistinctly seen, were of an especially repellent aspect. Several swimmers were still discernible; while on the far black reef I could see a faint, steady glow unlike the winking beacon visible before, and of a curious colour which I could not precisely identify. Above the slant roofs ahead and to the right there loomed the tall cupola of the Gilman House, but it was completely dark. The fishy odour, dispelled for a moment by some merciful breeze, now closed in again with maddening intensity.

I had not quite crossed the street when I heard a muttering band advancing along Washington from the north. As they reached the broad open space where I had had my first disquieting glimpse of the moonlit water I could see them plainly only a block away—and was horrified by the bestial abnormality of their faces and the dog-like sub-humanness of their crouching gait. One man moved in a positively simian way, with long arms frequently touching the ground; while another figure—robed and tiaraed—seemed to progress in an almost hopping fashion. I judged this party to be the one I had seen in the Gilman's courtyard—the one, therefore, most closely on my trail. As some of the figures turned to look in my direction I was transfixed with fright, yet managed to preserve the casual, shambling gait I had assumed. To this day I do not know whether they saw me or not. If they did, my stratagem must have deceived them, for they passed on across the moonlit space without varying their course—meanwhile croaking and jabbering in some hateful guttural patois I could not identify.

Once more in shadow, I resumed my former dog-trot past the leaning and decrepit houses that stared blankly into the night. Having crossed to the western sidewalk I rounded the nearest corner into Bates Street, where I kept close to the buildings on the southern side. I passed two houses shewing signs of habitation, one of which had faint lights in upper rooms, yet met with no obstacle. As I turned into Adams Street I felt measurably safer, but received a shock when a man reeled out of a black doorway directly in front of me. He proved, however, too hopelessly drunk to be a menace; so that I reached the dismal ruins of the Bank Street warehouses in safety.

No one was stirring in that dead street beside the river-gorge, and the roar of the waterfalls quite drowned my footsteps. It was a long dog-trot to the ruined station, and the great brick warehouse walls around me seemed somehow more terrifying than the fronts of private houses. At last I saw the ancient arcaded station—or what was left of it—and made directly for the tracks that started from its farther end.

The rails were rusty but mainly intact, and not more than half the ties had rotted away. Walking or running on such a surface was very difficult; but I did my best, and on the whole made very fair time. For some distance the line kept on along the gorge's brink, but at length I reached the long covered bridge where it crossed the chasm at a dizzy height. The condition of this bridge would determine my next step. If humanly possible, I would use it; if not, I would have to risk more street wandering and take the nearest intact highway bridge.

The vast, barn-like length of the old bridge gleamed spectrally in the moonlight, and I saw that the ties were safe for at least a few feet within. Entering, I began to use my flashlight, and was almost knocked down by the cloud of bats that flapped past me. About half way across there was a perilous gap in the ties which I feared for a moment would halt me; but in the end I risked a desperate jump which fortunately succeeded.

I was glad to see the moonlight again when I emerged from that macabre tunnel. The old tracks crossed River Street at grade, and at once veered off into a region increasingly rural and with less and less of Innsmouth's abhorrent fishy odour. Here the dense growth of weeds and briers hindered me and cruelly tore my clothes, but I was none the less glad that they were there to give me concealment in case of peril. I knew that much of my route must be visible from the Rowley road.

The marshy region began very shortly, with the single track on a low, grassy embankment where the weedy growth was somewhat thinner. Then came a sort of island of higher ground, where the line passed through a shallow open cut choked with bushes and brambles. I was very glad of this partial shelter, since at this point the Rowley road was uncomfortably near according to my window view. At the end of the cut it would cross the track and swerve off to a safer distance; but meanwhile I must be exceedingly careful. I was by this time thankfully certain that the railway itself was not patrolled.

Just before entering the cut I glanced behind me, but saw no pursuer. The ancient spires and roofs of decaying Innsmouth gleamed lovely and ethereal in the magic yellow moonlight, and I thought of how they must have looked in the old days before the shadow fell. Then, as my gaze circled inland from the town, something less tranquil arrested my notice and held me immobile for a second.

What I saw—or fancied I saw—was a disturbing suggestion of undulant motion far to the south; a suggestion which made me conclude that a very large horde must be pouring out of the city along the level Ipswich road. The distance was great, and I could distinguish nothing in detail; but I did not at all like the look of that moving column. It undulated too much, and glistened too brightly in the rays of the now westering moon. There was a suggestion of sound, too, though the wind was blowing the other way—a suggestion of bestial scraping and bellowing even worse than the muttering of the parties I had lately overheard.

All sorts of unpleasant conjectures crossed my mind. I thought of those very extreme Innsmouth types said to be hidden in crumbling, centuried warrens near the waterfront. I thought, too, of those nameless swimmers I had seen. Counting the parties so far glimpsed, as well as those presumably covering other roads, the number of my pursuers must be strangely large for a town as depopulated as Innsmouth.

Whence could come the dense personnel of such a column as I now beheld? Did those ancient, unplumbed warrens teem with a twisted, uncatalogued, and unsuspected life? Or had some unseen ship indeed landed a legion of unknown outsiders on that hellish reef? Who were they? Why were they here? And if such a column of them was scouring the Ipswich road, would the patrols on the other roads be likewise augmented?

I had entered the brush-grown cut and was struggling along at a very slow pace when that damnable fishy odour again waxed dominant. Had the wind suddenly changed eastward, so that it blew in from the sea and over the town? It must have, I concluded, since I now began to hear shocking guttural murmurs from that hitherto silent direction. There was another sound, too—a kind of wholesale, colossal flopping or pattering which somehow called up images of the most detestable sort. It made me think illogically of that unpleasantly undulating column on the far-off Ipswich road.

And then both stench and sounds grew stronger, so that I paused shivering and grateful for the cut's protection. It was here, I recalled, that the Rowley road drew so close to the old railway before crossing westward and diverging. Something was coming along that road, and I must lie low till its passage and vanishment in the distance. Thank heaven these creatures employed no dogs for tracking—though perhaps that would have been impossible amidst the omnipresent regional odour. Crouched in the bushes of that sandy cleft I felt reasonably safe, even though I knew the searchers would have to cross the track in front of me not much more than a hundred yards away. I would be able to see them, but they could not, except by a malign miracle, see me.

All at once I began dreading to look at them as they passed. I saw the close moonlit space where they would surge by, and had curious thoughts about the irredeemable pollution of that space. They would perhaps be the worst of all Innsmouth types—something one would not care to remember.

The stench waxed overpowering, and the noises swelled to a bestial babel of croaking, baying, and barking without the least suggestion of human speech. Were these indeed the voices of my pursuers? Did they have dogs after all? So far I had seen none of the lower animals in Innsmouth. That flopping or pattering was monstrous—I could not look upon the degenerate creatures responsible for it. I would keep my eyes shut till the sounds receded toward the west. The horde was very close now—the air foul with their hoarse snarlings, and the ground almost shaking with their alien-rhythmed footfalls. My breath nearly ceased to come, and I put every ounce of will power into the task of holding my eyelids down.

I am not even yet willing to say whether what followed was a hideous actuality or only a nightmare hallucination. The later action of the government, after my frantic appeals, would tend to confirm it as a monstrous truth; but could not an hallucination have been repeated under the quasi-hypnotic spell of that ancient, haunted, and shadowed town? Such places have strange properties, and the legacy of insane legend might well have acted on more than one human imagination amidst those dead, stench-cursed streets and huddles of rotting roofs and crumbling steeples. Is it not possible that the germ of an actual contagious madness lurks in the depths of that shadow over Innsmouth? Who can be sure of reality after hearing things like the tale of old Zadok Allen? The government men never found poor Zadok, and have no conjectures to make as to what became of him. Where does madness leave off and reality begin? Is it possible that even my latest fear is sheer delusion?

But I must try to tell what I thought I saw that night under the mocking yellow moon—saw surging and hopping down the Rowley road in plain sight in front of me as I crouched among the wild brambles of that desolate railway cut. Of course my resolution to keep my eyes shut had failed. It was foredoomed to failure—for who could crouch blindly while a legion of croaking, baying entities of unknown source flopped noisomely past, scarcely more than a hundred yards away?

I thought I was prepared for the worst, and I really ought to have been prepared considering what I had seen before. My other pursuers had been accursedly abnormal—so should I not have been ready to face a *strengthening* of the abnormal element; to look upon forms in which there was no mixture of the normal at all? I did not open my eyes until the raucous clamour came loudly from a point obviously straight ahead. Then I knew that a long section of them must be plainly in sight where the sides of the cut flattened out and the road crossed the track—and I could no longer keep myself from sampling whatever horror that leering yellow moon might have to shew.

It was the end, for whatever remains to me of life on the surface of this earth, of every vestige of mental peace and confidence in the integrity of Nature and of the human mind. Nothing that I could have imagined—nothing, even, that I could have gathered had I credited old Zadok's crazy tale in the most literal way—would be in any way comparable to the daemoniac, blasphemous reality that I saw—or believe I saw. I have tried to hint what it was in order to postpone the horror of writing it down baldly. Can it be possible that this planet has actually spawned such things; that human eyes have truly seen, as objective flesh, what man has hitherto known only in febrile phantasy and tenuous legend?

And yet I saw them in a limitless stream—flopping, hopping, croaking, bleating—surging inhumanly through the spectral moonlight in a grotesque, malignant saraband of fantastic nightmare. And some of them had tall tiaras of that nameless whitish-gold metal … and some were strangely robed … and one, who led the way, was clad in a ghoulishly humped black coat and striped trousers, and had a man's felt hat perched on the shapeless thing that answered for a head….

I think their predominant colour was a greyish-green, though they had white bellies. They were mostly shiny and slippery, but the ridges of their backs were scaly. Their forms vaguely suggested the anthropoid, while their heads were the heads of fish, with prodigious bulging eyes that never closed. At the sides of their necks were palpitating gills, and their long paws were webbed. They hopped irregularly, sometimes on two legs and sometimes on four. I was somehow glad that they had no more than four limbs. Their croaking, baying voices, clearly used for articulate speech, held all the dark shades of expression which their staring faces lacked.

But for all of their monstrousness they were not unfamiliar to me. I knew too well what they must be—for was not the memory of that evil tiara at Newburyport still fresh? They were the blasphemous fish-frogs of the nameless design—living and horrible—and as I saw them I knew also of what that humped, tiaraed priest in the black church basement had so fearsomely reminded me. Their number was past guessing. It seemed to me that there were limitless swarms of them—and certainly my momentary glimpse could have shewn only the least fraction. In another instant everything was blotted out by a merciful fit of fainting; the first I had ever had.

V.

It was a gentle daylight rain that awaked me from my stupor in the brush-grown railway cut, and when I staggered out to the roadway ahead I saw no trace of any prints in the fresh mud. The fishy odour, too, was gone. Innsmouth's ruined roofs and toppling steeples loomed up greyly toward the southeast, but not a living creature did I spy in all the desolate salt marshes around. My watch was still going, and told me that the hour was past noon.

The reality of what I had been through was highly uncertain in my mind, but I felt that something hideous lay in the background. I must get away from evil-shadowed Innsmouth—and accordingly I began to test my cramped, wearied powers of locomotion. Despite weakness, hunger, horror, and bewilderment I found myself after a time able to walk; so started slowly along the muddy road to Rowley. Before evening I was in the village, getting a meal and providing myself with presentable clothes. I caught the night train to Arkham, and the next day talked long and earnestly with government officials there; a process I later repeated in Boston. With the main result of these colloquies the public is now familiar—and I wish, for normality's sake, there were nothing more to tell. Perhaps it is madness that is overtaking me—yet perhaps a greater horror—or a greater marvel—is reaching out.

As may well be imagined, I gave up most of the foreplanned features of the rest of my tour—the scenic, architectural, and antiquarian diversions on which I had counted so heavily. Nor did I dare look for that piece of strange jewellery said to be in the Miskatonic University Museum. I did, however, improve my stay in Arkham by collecting some genealogical notes I had long wished to possess; very rough and hasty data, it is true, but capable of good use later on when I might have time to collate and codify them. The curator of the historical society there—Mr. E. Lapham Peabody—was very courteous about assisting me, and expressed unusual interest when I told him I was a grandson of Eliza Orne of Arkham, who was born in 1867 and had married James Williamson of Ohio at the age of seventeen.

It seemed that a maternal uncle of mine had been there many years before on a quest much like my own; and that my grandmother's family was a topic of some local curiosity. There had, Mr. Peabody said, been considerable discussion about the marriage of her father, Benjamin Orne, just after the Civil War; since the ancestry of the bride was peculiarly puzzling. That bride was understood to have been an orphaned Marsh of New Hampshire—a cousin of the Essex County Marshes—but her education had been in France and she knew very little of her family. A guardian had deposited funds in a Boston bank to maintain her and her French governess; but that guardian's name was unfamiliar to Arkham people, and in time he dropped out of sight, so that the governess assumed his role by court appointment. The Frenchwoman—now long dead—was very taciturn, and there were those who said she could have told more than she did.

But the most baffling thing was the inability of anyone to place the recorded parents of the young woman—Enoch and Lydia (Meserve) Marsh—among the known families of New Hampshire. Possibly, many suggested, she was the natural daughter of some Marsh of prominence—she certainly had the true Marsh eyes. Most of the puzzling was done after her early death, which took place at the birth of my grandmother—her only child. Having formed some disagreeable impressions connected with the name of Marsh, I did not welcome the news that it belonged on my own ancestral tree; nor was I pleased by Mr. Peabody's suggestion that I had the true Marsh eyes myself. However, I was grateful for data which I knew would prove valuable; and took copious notes and lists of book references regarding the well-documented Orne family.

I went directly home to Toledo from Boston, and later spent a month at Maumee recuperating from my ordeal. In September I entered Oberlin for my final year, and from then till the next June was busy with studies and other wholesome activities—reminded of the bygone terror only by occasional official visits from government men in connexion with the campaign which my pleas and evidence had started. Around the middle of July—just a year after the Innsmouth experience—I spent a week with my late mother's family in Cleveland; checking some of my new genealogical data with the various notes, traditions, and bits of heirloom material in existence there, and seeing what kind of a connected chart I could construct.

I did not exactly relish this task, for the atmosphere of the Williamson home had always depressed me. There was a strain of morbidity there, and my mother had never encouraged my visiting her parents as a child, although she always welcomed her father when he came to Toledo. My Arkham-born grandmother had seemed strange and almost terrifying to me, and I do not think I grieved when she disappeared. I was eight years old then, and it was said that she had wandered off in grief after the suicide of my uncle Douglas, her eldest son. He had shot himself after a trip to New England—the same trip, no doubt, which had caused him to be recalled at the Arkham Historical Society.

This uncle had resembled her, and I had never liked him either. Something about the staring, unwinking expression of both of them had given me a vague, unaccountable uneasiness. My mother and uncle Walter had not looked like that. They were like their father, though poor little cousin Lawrence—Walter's son—had been an almost perfect duplicate of his grandmother before his condition took him to the permanent seclusion of a sanitarium at Canton. I had not seen him in four years, but my uncle once implied that his state, both mental and physical, was very bad. This worry had probably been a major cause of his mother's death two years before.

My grandfather and his widowed son Walter now comprised the Cleveland household, but the memory of older times hung thickly over it. I still disliked the place, and tried to get my researches done as quickly as possible. Williamson records and traditions were supplied in abundance by my grandfather; though for Orne material I had to depend on my uncle Walter, who put at my disposal the contents of all his files, including notes, letters, cuttings, heirlooms, photographs, and miniatures.

It was in going over the letters and pictures on the Orne side that I began to acquire a kind of terror of my own ancestry. As I have said, my grandmother and uncle Douglas had always disturbed me. Now, years after their passing, I gazed at their pictured faces with a measurably heightened feeling of repulsion and alienation. I could not at first understand the change, but gradually a horrible sort of *comparison* began to obtrude itself on my unconscious mind despite the steady refusal of my consciousness to admit even the least suspicion of it. It was clear that the typical expression of these faces now suggested something it had not suggested before—something which would bring stark panic if too openly thought of.

But the worst shock came when my uncle shewed me the Orne jewellery in a downtown safe-deposit vault. Some of the items were delicate and inspiring enough, but there was one box of strange old pieces descended from my mysterious great-grandmother which my uncle was almost reluctant to produce. They were, he said, of very grotesque and almost repulsive design, and had never to his knowledge been publicly worn; though my grandmother used to enjoy looking at them. Vague legends of bad luck clustered around them, and my great-grandmother's French governess had said they ought not to be worn in New England, though it would be quite safe to wear them in Europe.

As my uncle began slowly and grudgingly to unwrap the things he urged me not to be shocked by the strangeness and frequent hideousness of the designs. Artists and archaeologists who had seen them pronounced their workmanship superlatively and exotically exquisite, though no one seemed able to define their exact material or assign them to any specific art tradition. There were two armlets, a tiara, and a kind of pectoral; the latter having in high relief certain figures of almost unbearable extravagance.

During this description I had kept a tight rein on my emotions, but my face must have betrayed my mounting fears. My uncle looked concerned, and paused in his unwrapping to study my countenance. I motioned to him to continue, which he did with renewed signs of reluctance. He seemed to expect some demonstration when the first piece—the tiara—became visible, but I doubt if he expected quite what actually happened. I did not expect it, either, for I thought I was thoroughly forewarned regarding what the jewellery would turn out to be. What I did was to faint silently away, just as I had done in that brier-choked railway cut a year before.

From that day on my life has been a nightmare of brooding and apprehension, nor do I know how much is hideous truth and how much madness. My great-grandmother had been a Marsh of unknown source whose husband lived in Arkham—and did not old Zadok say that the daughter of Obed Marsh by a monstrous mother was married to an Arkham man through a trick? What was it the ancient toper had muttered about the likeness of my eyes to Captain Obed's? In Arkham, too, the curator had told me I had the true Marsh eyes. Was Obed Marsh my own great-great-grandfather? Who—or *what*—then, was my great-great-grandmother? But perhaps this was all madness. Those whitish-gold ornaments might easily have been bought from some Innsmouth sailor by the father of my great-grandmother, whoever he was. And that look in the staring-eyed faces of my grandmother and self-slain uncle might be sheer fancy on my part—sheer fancy, bolstered up by the Innsmouth shadow which had so darkly coloured my imagination. But why had my uncle killed himself after an ancestral quest in New England?

For more than two years I fought off these reflections with partial success. My father secured me a place in an insurance office, and I buried myself in routine as deeply as possible. In the winter of 1930–31, however, the dreams began. They were very sparse and insidious at first, but increased in frequency and vividness as the weeks went by. Great watery spaces opened out before me, and I seemed to wander through titanic sunken porticos and labyrinths of weedy Cyclopean walls with grotesque fishes as my companions. Then the *other shapes* began to appear, filling me with nameless horror the moment I awoke. But during the dreams they did not horrify me at all—I was one with them; wearing their unhuman trappings, treading their aqueous ways, and praying monstrously at their evil sea-bottom temples.

There was much more than I could remember, but even what I did remember each morning would be enough to stamp me as a madman or a genius if ever I dared write it down. Some frightful influence, I felt, was seeking gradually to drag me out of the sane world of wholesome life into unnamable abysses of blackness and alienage; and the process told heavily on me. My health and appearance grew steadily worse, till finally I was forced to give up my position and adopt the static, secluded life of an invalid. Some odd nervous affliction had me in its grip, and I found myself at times almost unable to shut my eyes.

It was then that I began to study the mirror with mounting alarm. The slow ravages of disease are not pleasant to watch, but in my case there was something subtler and more puzzling in the background. My father seemed to notice it, too, for he began looking at me curiously and almost affrightedly. What was taking place in me? Could it be that I was coming to resemble my grandmother and uncle Douglas?

One night I had a frightful dream in which I met my grandmother under the sea. She lived in a phosphorescent palace of many terraces, with gardens of strange leprous corals and grotesque brachiate efflorescences, and welcomed me with a warmth that may have been sardonic. She had changed—as those who take to the water change—and told me she had never died. Instead, she had gone to a spot her dead son had learned about, and had leaped to a realm whose wonders—destined for him as well—he had spurned with a smoking pistol. This was to be my realm, too—I could not escape it. I would never die, but would live with those who had lived since before man ever walked the earth.

I met also that which had been her grandmother. For eighty thousand years Pth'thya-l'yi had lived in Y'ha-nthlei, and thither she had gone back after Obed Marsh was dead. Y'ha-nthlei was not destroyed when the upper-earth men shot death into the sea. It was hurt, but not destroyed. The Deep Ones could never be destroyed, even though the palaeogean magic of the forgotten Old Ones might sometimes check them. For the present they would rest; but some day, if they remembered, they would rise again for the tribute Great Cthulhu craved. It would be a city greater than Innsmouth next time. They had planned to spread, and had brought up that which would help them, but now they must wait once more. For bringing the upper-earth men's death I must do a penance, but that would not be heavy. This was the dream in which I saw a *shoggoth* for the first time, and the sight set me awake in a frenzy of screaming. That morning the mirror definitely told me I had acquired *the Innsmouth look.*

So far I have not shot myself as my uncle Douglas did. I bought an automatic and almost took the step, but certain dreams deterred me. The tense extremes of horror are lessening, and I feel queerly drawn toward the unknown sea-deeps instead of fearing them. I hear and do strange things in sleep, and awake with a kind of exaltation instead of terror. I do not believe I need to wait for the full change as most have waited. If I did, my father would probably shut me up in a sanitarium as my poor little cousin is shut up. Stupendous and unheard-of splendours await me below, and I shall seek them soon. *Iä-R'lyeh! Cthulhu fhtagn! Iä! Iä!* No, I shall not shoot myself—I cannot be made to shoot myself!

I shall plan my cousin's escape from that Canton madhouse, and together we shall go to marvel-shadowed Innsmouth. We shall swim out to that brooding reef in the sea and dive down through black abysses to Cyclopean and many-columned Y'ha-nthlei, and in that lair of the Deep Ones we shall dwell amidst wonder and glory for ever.

THE DREAMS IN THE WITCH HOUSE

Whether the dreams brought on the fever or the fever brought on the dreams Walter Gilman did not know. Behind everything crouched the brooding, festering horror of the ancient town, and of the mouldy, unhallowed garret gable where he wrote and studied and wrestled with figures and formulae when he was not tossing on the meagre iron bed. His ears were growing sensitive to a preternatural and intolerable degree, and he had long ago stopped the cheap mantel clock whose ticking had come to seem like a thunder of artillery. At night the subtle stirring of the black city outside, the sinister scurrying of rats in the wormy partitions, and the creaking of hidden timbers in the centuried house, were enough to give him a sense of strident pandemonium. The darkness always teemed with unexplained sound—and yet he sometimes shook with fear lest the noises he heard should subside and allow him to hear certain other, fainter noises which he suspected were lurking behind them.

He was in the changeless, legend-haunted city of Arkham, with its clustering gambrel roofs that sway and sag over attics where witches hid from the King's men in the dark, olden days of the Province. Nor was any spot in that city more steeped in macabre memory than the gable room which harboured him—for it was this house and this room which had likewise harboured old Keziah Mason, whose flight from Salem Gaol at the last no one was ever able to explain. That was in 1692—the gaoler had gone mad and babbled of a small, white-fanged furry thing which scuttled out of Keziah's cell, and not even Cotton Mather could explain the curves and angles smeared on the grey stone walls with some red, sticky fluid.

Possibly Gilman ought not to have studied so hard. Non-Euclidean calculus and quantum physics are enough to stretch any brain; and when one mixes them with folklore, and tries to trace a strange background of multi-dimensional reality behind the ghoulish hints of the Gothic tales and the wild whispers of the chimney-corner, one can hardly expect to be wholly free from mental tension. Gilman came from Haverhill, but it was only after he had entered college in Arkham that he began to connect his mathematics with the fantastic legends of elder magic. Something in the air of the hoary town worked obscurely on his imagination. The professors at Miskatonic had urged him to slacken up, and had voluntarily cut down his course at several points. Moreover, they had stopped him from consulting the dubious old books on forbidden secrets that were kept under lock and key in a vault at the university library. But all these precautions came late in the day, so that Gilman had some terrible hints from the dreaded "Necronomicon" of Abdul Alhazred, the fragmentary "Book of Eibon", and the suppressed "Unaussprechlichen Kulten" of von Junzt to correlate with his abstract formulae on the properties of space and the linkage of dimensions known and unknown.

He knew his room was in the old Witch House—that, indeed, was why he had taken it. There was much in the Essex County records about Keziah Mason's trial, and what she had admitted under pressure to the Court of Oyer and Terminer had fascinated Gilman beyond all reason. She had told Judge Hathorne of lines and curves that could be made to point out directions leading through the walls of space to other spaces beyond, and had implied that such lines and curves were frequently used at certain midnight meetings in the dark valley of the white stone beyond Meadow Hill and on the unpeopled island in the river. She had spoken also of the Black Man, of her oath, and of her new secret name of Nahab. Then she had drawn those devices on the walls of her cell and vanished.

Gilman believed strange things about Keziah, and had felt a queer thrill on learning that her dwelling was still standing after more than 235 years. When he heard the hushed Arkham whispers about Keziah's persistent presence in the old house and the narrow streets, about the irregular human tooth-marks left on certain sleepers in that and other houses, about the childish cries heard near May-Eve and Hallowmass, about the stench often noted in the old house's attic just after those dreaded seasons, and about the small, furry, sharp-toothed thing which haunted the mouldering structure and the town and nuzzled people curiously in the black hours before dawn, he resolved to live in the place at any cost. A room was easy to secure; for the house was unpopular, hard to rent, and long given over to cheap lodgings. Gilman could not have told what he expected to find there, but he knew he wanted to be in the building where some circumstance had more or less suddenly given a mediocre old woman of the seventeenth century an insight into mathematical depths perhaps beyond the utmost modern delvings of Planck, Heisenberg, Einstein, and de Sitter.

He studied the timber and plaster walls for traces of cryptic designs at every accessible spot where the paper had peeled, and within a week managed to get the eastern attic room where Keziah was held to have practiced her spells. It had been vacant from the first—for no one had ever been willing to stay there long—but the Polish landlord had grown wary about renting it. Yet nothing whatever happened to Gilman till about the time of the fever. No ghostly Keziah flitted through the sombre halls and chambers, no small furry thing crept into his dismal eyrie to nuzzle him, and no record of the witch's incantations rewarded his constant search. Sometimes he would take walks through shadowy tangles of unpaved musty-smelling lanes where eldritch brown houses of unknown age leaned and tottered and leered mockingly through narrow, small-paned windows. Here he knew strange things had happened once, and there was a faint suggestion behind the surface that everything of that monstrous past might not—at least in the darkest, narrowest, and most intricately crooked alleys—have utterly perished. He also rowed out twice to the ill-regarded island in the river, and made a sketch of the singular angles described by the moss-grown rows of grey standing stones whose origin was so obscure and immemorial.

Gilman's room was of good size but queerly irregular shape; the north wall slanting perceptibly inward from the outer to the inner end, while the low ceiling slanted gently downward in the same direction. Aside from an obvious rat-hole and the signs of other stopped-up ones, there was no access—nor any appearance of a former avenue of access—to the space which must have existed between the slanting wall and the straight outer wall on the house's north side, though a view from the exterior shewed where a window had been boarded up at a very remote date. The loft above the ceiling—which must have had a slanting floor—was likewise inaccessible. When Gilman climbed up a ladder to the cobwebbed level loft above the rest of the attic he found vestiges of a bygone aperture tightly and heavily covered with ancient planking and secured by the stout wooden pegs common in colonial carpentry. No amount of persuasion, however, could induce the stolid landlord to let him investigate either of these two closed spaces.

As time wore along, his absorption in the irregular wall and ceiling of his room increased; for he began to read into the odd angles a mathematical significance which seemed to offer vague clues regarding their purpose. Old Keziah, he reflected, might have had excellent reasons for living in a room with peculiar angles; for was it not through certain angles that she claimed to have gone outside the boundaries of the world of space we know? His interest gradually veered away from the unplumbed voids beyond the slanting surfaces, since it now appeared that the purpose of those surfaces concerned the side he was already on.

The touch of brain-fever and the dreams began early in February. For some time, apparently, the curious angles of Gilman's room had been having a strange, almost hypnotic effect on him; and as the bleak winter advanced he had found himself staring more and more intently at the corner where the down-slanting ceiling met the inward-slanting wall. About this period his inability to concentrate on his formal studies worried him considerably, his apprehensions about the mid-year examinations being very acute. But the exaggerated sense of hearing was scarcely less annoying. Life had become an insistent and almost unendurable cacophony, and there was that constant, terrifying impression of *other* sounds—perhaps from regions beyond life—trembling on the very brink of audibility. So far as concrete noises went, the rats in the ancient partitions were the worst. Sometimes their scratching seemed not only furtive but deliberate. When it came from beyond the slanting north wall it was mixed with a sort of dry rattling—and when it came from the century-closed loft above the slanting ceiling Gilman always braced himself as if expecting some horror which only bided its time before descending to engulf him utterly.

The dreams were wholly beyond the pale of sanity, and Gilman felt that they must be a result, jointly, of his studies in mathematics and in folklore. He had been thinking too much about the vague regions which his formulae told him must lie beyond the three dimensions we know, and about the possibility that old Keziah Mason—guided by some influence past all conjecture—had actually found the gate to those regions. The yellowed county records containing her testimony and that of her accusers were so damnably suggestive of things beyond human experience—and the descriptions of the darting little furry object which served as her familiar were so painfully realistic despite their incredible details.

That object—no larger than a good-sized rat and quaintly called by the townspeople "Brown Jenkin"—seemed to have been the fruit of a remarkable case of sympathetic herd-delusion, for in 1692 no less than eleven persons had testified to glimpsing it. There were recent rumours, too, with a baffling and disconcerting amount of agreement. Witnesses said it had long hair and the shape of a rat, but that its sharp-toothed, bearded face was evilly human while its paws were like tiny human hands. It took messages betwixt old Keziah and the devil, and was nursed on the witch's blood—which it sucked like a vampire. Its voice was a kind of loathsome titter, and it could speak all languages. Of all the bizarre monstrosities in Gilman's dreams, nothing filled him with greater panic and nausea than this blasphemous and diminutive hybrid, whose image flitted across his vision in a form a thousandfold more hateful than anything his waking mind had deduced from the ancient records and the modern whispers.

Gilman's dreams consisted largely in plunges though limitless abysses of inexplicably coloured twilight and bafflingly disordered sound; abysses whose material and gravitational properties, and whose relation to his own entity, he could not even begin to explain. He did not walk or climb, fly or swim, crawl or wriggle; yet always experienced a mode of motion partly voluntary and partly involuntary. Of his own condition he could not well judge, for sight of his arms, legs, and torso seemed always cut off by some odd disarrangement of perspective; but he felt that his physical organisation and faculties were somehow marvellously transmuted and obliquely projected—though not without a certain grotesque relationship to his normal proportions and properties.

The abysses were by no means vacant, being crowded with indescribably angled masses of alien-hued substance, some of which appeared to be organic while others seemed inorganic. A few of the organic objects tended to awake vague memories in the back of his mind, though he could form no conscious idea of what they mockingly resembled or suggested. In the later dreams he began to distinguish separate categories into which the organic objects appeared to be divided, and which seemed to involve in each case a radically different species of conduct-pattern and basic motivation. Of these categories one seemed to him to include objects slightly less illogical and irrelevant in their motions than the members of the other categories.

All the objects—organic and inorganic alike—were totally beyond description or even comprehension. Gilman sometimes compared the inorganic masses to prisms, labyrinths, clusters of cubes and planes, and Cyclopean buildings; and the organic things struck him variously as groups of bubbles, octopi, centipedes, living Hindoo idols, and intricate Arabesques roused into a kind of ophidian animation. Everything he saw was unspeakably menacing and horrible; and whenever one of the organic entities appeared by its motions to be noticing him, he felt a stark, hideous fright which generally jolted him awake. Of how the organic entities moved, he could tell no more than of how he moved himself. In time he observed a further mystery—the tendency of certain entities to appear suddenly out of empty space, or to disappear totally with equal suddenness. The shrieking, roaring confusion of sound which permeated the abysses was past all analysis as to pitch, timbre, or rhythm; but seemed to be synchronous with vague visual changes in all the indefinite objects, organic and inorganic alike. Gilman had a constant sense of dread that it might rise to some unbearable degree of intensity during one or another of its obscure, relentlessly inevitable fluctuations.

But it was not in these vortices of complete alienage that he saw Brown Jenkin. That shocking little horror was reserved for certain lighter, sharper dreams which assailed him just before he dropped into the fullest depths of sleep. He would be lying in the dark fighting to keep awake when a faint lambent glow would seem to shimmer around the centuried room, shewing in a violet mist the convergence of angled planes which had seized his brain so insidiously. The horror would appear to pop out of the rat-hole in the corner and patter toward him over the sagging, wide-planked floor with evil expectancy in its tiny, bearded human face—but mercifully, this dream always melted away before the object got close enough to nuzzle him. It had hellishly long, sharp, canine teeth. Gilman tried to stop up the rat-hole every day, but each night the real tenants of the partitions would gnaw away the obstruction, whatever it might be. Once he had the landlord nail tin over it, but the next night the rats gnawed a fresh hole—in making which they pushed or dragged out into the room a curious little fragment of bone.

Gilman did not report his fever to the doctor, for he knew he could not pass the examinations if ordered to the college infirmary when every moment was needed for cramming. As it was, he failed in Calculus D and Advanced General Psychology, though not without hope of making up lost ground before the end of the term. It was in March when the fresh element entered his lighter preliminary dreaming, and the nightmare shape of Brown Jenkin began to be companioned by the nebulous blur which grew more and more to resemble a bent old woman. This addition disturbed him more than he could account for, but finally he decided that it was like an ancient crone whom he had twice actually encountered in the dark tangle of lanes near the abandoned wharves. On those occasions the evil, sardonic, and seemingly unmotivated stare of the beldame had set him almost shivering—especially the first time, when an overgrown rat darting across the shadowed mouth of a neighbouring alley had made him think irrationally of Brown Jenkin. Now, he reflected, those nervous fears were being mirrored in his disordered dreams.

That the influence of the old house was unwholesome, he could not deny; but traces of his early morbid interest still held him there. He argued that the fever alone was responsible for his nightly phantasies, and that when the touch abated he would be free from the monstrous visions. Those visions, however, were of abhorrent vividness and convincingness; and whenever he awaked he retained a vague sense of having undergone much more than he remembered. He was hideously sure that in unrecalled dreams he had talked with both Brown Jenkin and the old woman, and that they had been urging him to go somewhere with them and to meet a third being of greater potency.

Toward the end of March he began to pick up in his mathematics, though other studies bothered him increasingly. He was getting an intuitive knack for solving Riemannian equations, and astonished Professor Upham by his comprehension of fourth-dimensional and other problems which had floored all the rest of the class. One afternoon there was a discussion of possible freakish curvatures in space, and of theoretical points of approach or even contact between our part of the cosmos and various other regions as distant as the farthest stars or the trans-galactic gulfs themselves—or even as fabulously remote as the tentatively conceivable cosmic units beyond the whole Einsteinian space-time continuum. Gilman's handling of this theme filled everyone with admiration, even though some of his hypothetical illustrations caused an increase in the always plentiful gossip about his nervous and solitary eccentricity. What made the students shake their heads was his sober theory that a man might—given mathematical knowledge admittedly beyond all likelihood of human acquirement—step deliberately from the earth to any other celestial body which might lie at one of an infinity of specific points in the cosmic pattern.

Such a step, he said, would require only two stages; first, a passage out of the three-dimensional sphere we know, and second, a passage back to the three-dimensional sphere at another point, perhaps one of infinite remoteness. That this could be accomplished without loss of life was in many cases conceivable. Any being from any part of three-dimensional space could probably survive in the fourth dimension; and its survival of the second stage would depend upon what alien part of three-dimensional space it might select for its re-entry. Denizens of some planets might be able to live on certain others—even planets belonging to other galaxies, or to similar-dimensional phases of other space-time continua—though of course there must be vast numbers of mutually uninhabitable even though mathematically juxtaposed bodies or zones of space.

It was also possible that the inhabitants of a given dimensional realm could survive entry to many unknown and incomprehensible realms of additional or indefinitely multiplied dimensions—be they within or outside the given space-time continuum—and that the converse would be likewise true. This was a matter for speculation, though one could be fairly certain that the type of mutation involved in a passage from any given dimensional plane to the next higher plane would not be destructive of biological integrity as we understand it. Gilman could not be very clear about his reasons for this last assumption, but his haziness here was more than overbalanced by his clearness on other complex points. Professor Upham especially liked his demonstration of the kinship of higher mathematics to certain phases of magical lore transmitted down the ages from an ineffable antiquity—human or pre-human—whose knowledge of the cosmos and its laws was greater than ours.

Around the first of April Gilman worried considerably because his slow fever did not abate. He was also troubled by what some of his fellow-lodgers said about his sleep-walking. It seemed that he was often absent from his bed, and that the creaking of his floor at certain hours of the night was remarked by the man in the room below. This fellow also spoke of hearing the tread of shod feet in the night; but Gilman was sure he must have been mistaken in this, since shoes as well as other apparel were always precisely in place in the morning. One could develop all sorts of aural delusions in this morbid old house—for did not Gilman himself, even in daylight, now feel certain that noises other than rat-scratchings came from the black voids beyond the slanting wall and above the slanting ceiling? His pathologically sensitive ears began to listen for faint footfalls in the immemorially sealed loft overhead, and sometimes the illusion of such things was agonisingly realistic.

However, he knew that he had actually become a somnambulist; for twice at night his room had been found vacant, though with all his clothing in place. Of this he had been assured by Frank Elwood, the one fellow-student whose poverty forced him to room in this squalid and unpopular house. Elwood had been studying in the small hours and had come up for help on a differential equation, only to find Gilman absent. It had been rather presumptuous of him to open the unlocked door after knocking had failed to rouse a response, but he had needed the help very badly and thought that his host would not mind a gentle prodding awake. On neither occasion, though, had Gilman been there—and when told of the matter he wondered where he could have been wandering, barefoot and with only his night-clothes on. He resolved to investigate the matter if reports of his sleep-walking continued, and thought of sprinkling flour on the floor of the corridor to see where his footsteps might lead. The door was the only conceivable egress, for there was no possible foothold outside the narrow window.

As April advanced Gilman's fever-sharpened ears were disturbed by the whining prayers of a superstitious loomfixer named Joe Mazurewicz, who had a room on the ground floor. Mazurewicz had told long, rambling stories about the ghost of old Keziah and the furry, sharp-fanged, nuzzling thing, and had said he was so badly haunted at times that only his silver crucifix—given him for the purpose by Father Iwanicki of St. Stanislaus' Church—could bring him relief. Now he was praying because the Witches' Sabbath was drawing near. May-Eve was Walpurgis-Night, when hell's blackest evil roamed the earth and all the slaves of Satan gathered for nameless rites and deeds. It was always a very bad time in Arkham, even though the fine folks up in Miskatonic Avenue and High and Saltonstall Streets pretended to know nothing about it. There would be bad doings—and a child or two would probably be missing. Joe knew about such things, for his grandmother in the old country had heard tales from her grandmother. It was wise to pray and count one's beads at this season. For three months Keziah and Brown Jenkin had not been near Joe's room, nor near Paul Choynski's room, nor anywhere else—and it meant no good when they held off like that. They must be up to something.

Gilman dropped in at a doctor's office on the sixteenth of the month, and was surprised to find his temperature was not as high as he had feared. The physician questioned him sharply, and advised him to see a nerve specialist. On reflection, he was glad he had not consulted the still more inquisitive college doctor. Old Waldron, who had curtailed his activities before, would have made him take a rest—an impossible thing now that he was so close to great results in his equations. He was certainly near the boundary between the known universe and the fourth dimension, and who could say how much farther he might go?

But even as these thoughts came to him he wondered at the source of his strange confidence. Did all of this perilous sense of imminence come from the formulae on the sheets he covered day by day? The soft, stealthy, imaginary footsteps in that sealed loft above were unnerving. And now, too, there was a growing feeling that somebody was constantly persuading him to do something terrible which he could not do. How about the somnambulism? Where did he go sometimes in the night? And what was that faint suggestion of sound which once in a while seemed to trickle through the maddening confusion of identifiable sounds even in broad daylight and full wakefulness? Its rhythm did not correspond to anything on earth, unless perhaps to the cadence of one or two unmentionable Sabbat-chants, and sometimes he feared it corresponded to certain attributes of the vague shrieking or roaring in those wholly alien abysses of dream.

The dreams were meanwhile getting to be atrocious. In the lighter preliminary phase the evil old woman was now of fiendish distinctness, and Gilman knew she was the one who had frightened him in the slums. Her bent back, long nose, and shrivelled chin were unmistakable, and her shapeless brown garments were like those he remembered. The expression on her face was one of hideous malevolence and exultation, and when he awaked he could recall a croaking voice that persuaded and threatened. He must meet the Black Man, and go with them all to the throne of Azathoth at the centre of ultimate Chaos. That was what she said. He must sign in his own blood the book of Azathoth and take a new secret name now that his independent delvings had gone so far. What kept him from going with her and Brown Jenkin and the other to the throne of Chaos where the thin flutes pipe mindlessly was the fact that he had seen the name "Azathoth" in the "Necronomicon", and knew it stood for a primal evil too horrible for description.

The old woman always appeared out of thin air near the corner where the downward slant met the inward slant. She seemed to crystallise at a point closer to the ceiling than to the floor, and every night she was a little nearer and more distinct before the dream shifted. Brown Jenkin, too, was always a little nearer at the last, and its yellowish-white fangs glistened shockingly in that unearthly violet phosphorescence. Its shrill loathsome tittering stuck more and more in Gilman's head, and he could remember in the morning how it had pronounced the words "Azathoth" and "Nyarlathotep".

In the deeper dreams everything was likewise more distinct, and Gilman felt that the twilight abysses around him were those of the fourth dimension. Those organic entities whose motions seemed least flagrantly irrelevant and unmotivated were probably projections of life-forms from our own planet, including human beings. What the others were in their own dimensional sphere or spheres he dared not try to think. Two of the less irrelevantly moving things—a rather large congeries of iridescent, prolately spheroidal bubbles and a very much smaller polyhedron of unknown colours and rapidly shifting surface angles—seemed to take notice of him and follow him about or float ahead as he changed position among the titan prisms, labyrinths, cube-and-plane clusters, and quasi-buildings; and all the while the vague shrieking and roaring waxed louder and louder, as if approaching some monstrous climax of utterly unendurable intensity.

During the night of April 19–20th the new development occurred. Gilman was half-involuntarily moving about in the twilight abysses with the bubble-mass and the small polyhedron floating ahead, when he noticed the peculiarly regular angles formed by the edges of some gigantic neighbouring prism-clusters. In another second he was out of the abyss and standing tremulously on a rocky hillside bathed in intense, diffused green light. He was barefooted and in his night-clothes, and when he tried to walk discovered that he could scarcely lift his feet. A swirling vapour hid everything but the immediate sloping terrain from sight, and he shrank from the thought of the sounds that might surge out of that vapour.

Then he saw the two shapes laboriously crawling toward him—the old woman and the little furry thing. The crone strained up to her knees and managed to cross her arms in a singular fashion, while Brown Jenkin pointed in a certain direction with a horribly anthropoid fore-paw which it raised with evident difficulty. Spurred by an impulse he did not originate, Gilman dragged himself forward along a course determined by the angle of the old woman's arms and the direction of the small monstrosity's paw, and before he had shuffled three steps he was back in the twilight abysses. Geometrical shapes seethed around him, and he fell dizzily and interminably. At last he woke in his bed in the crazily angled garret of the eldritch old house.

He was good for nothing that morning, and stayed away from all his classes. Some unknown attraction was pulling his eyes in a seemingly irrelevant direction, for he could not help staring at a certain vacant spot on the floor. As the day advanced the focus of his unseeing eyes changed position, and by noon he had conquered the impulse to stare at vacancy. About two o'clock he went out for lunch, and as he threaded the narrow lanes of the city he found himself turning always to the southeast. Only an effort halted him at a cafeteria in Church Street, and after the meal he felt the unknown pull still more strongly.

He would have to consult a nerve specialist after all—perhaps there was a connexion with his somnambulism—but meanwhile he might at least try to break the morbid spell himself. Undoubtedly he could still manage to walk away from the pull; so with great resolution he headed against it and dragged himself deliberately north along Garrison Street. By the time he had reached the bridge over the Miskatonic he was in a cold perspiration, and he clutched at the iron railing as he gazed upstream at the ill-regarded island whose regular lines of ancient standing stones brooded sullenly in the afternoon sunlight.

Then he gave a start. For there was a clearly visible living figure on that desolate island, and a second glance told him it was certainly the strange old woman whose sinister aspect had worked itself so disastrously into his dreams. The tall grass near her was moving, too, as if some other living thing were crawling close to the ground. When the old woman began to turn toward him he fled precipitately off the bridge and into the shelter of the town's labyrinthine waterfront alleys. Distant though the island was, he felt that a monstrous and invincible evil could flow from the sardonic stare of that bent, ancient figure in brown.

The southeastward pull still held, and only with tremendous resolution could Gilman drag himself into the old house and up the rickety stairs. For hours he sat silent and aimless, with his eyes shifting gradually westward. About six o'clock his sharpened ears caught the whining prayers of Joe Mazurewicz two floors below, and in desperation he seized his hat and walked out into the sunset-golden streets, letting the now directly southward pull carry him where it might. An hour later darkness found him in the open fields beyond Hangman's Brook, with the glimmering spring stars shining ahead. The urge to walk was gradually changing to an urge to leap mystically into space, and suddenly he realised just where the source of the pull lay.

It was in the sky. A definite point among the stars had a claim on him and was calling him. Apparently it was a point somewhere between Hydra and Argo Navis, and he knew that he had been urged toward it ever since he had awaked soon after dawn. In the morning it had been underfoot; afternoon found it rising in the southeast, and now it was roughly south but wheeling toward the west. What was the meaning of this new thing? Was he going mad? How long would it last? Again mustering his resolution, Gilman turned and dragged himself back to the sinister old house.

Mazurewicz was waiting for him at the door, and seemed both anxious and reluctant to whisper some fresh bit of superstition. It was about the witch light. Joe had been out celebrating the night before—it was Patriots' Day in Massachusetts—and had come home after midnight. Looking up at the house from outside, he had thought at first that Gilman's window was dark; but then he had seen the faint violet glow within. He wanted to warn the gentleman about that glow, for everybody in Arkham knew it was Keziah's witch light which played near Brown Jenkin and the ghost of the old crone herself. He had not mentioned this before, but now he must tell about it because it meant that Keziah and her long-toothed familiar were haunting the young gentleman. Sometimes he and Paul Choynski and Landlord Dombrowski thought they saw that light seeping out of cracks in the sealed loft above the young gentleman's room, but they had all agreed not to talk about that. However, it would be better for the gentleman to take another room and get a crucifix from some good priest like Father Iwanicki.

As the man rambled on Gilman felt a nameless panic clutch at his throat. He knew that Joe must have been half drunk when he came home the night before, yet this mention of a violet light in the garret window was of frightful import. It was a lambent glow of this sort which always played about the old woman and the small furry thing in those lighter, sharper dreams which prefaced his plunge into unknown abysses, and the thought that a wakeful second person could see the dream-luminance was utterly beyond sane harbourage. Yet where had the fellow got such an odd notion? Had he himself talked as well as walked around the house in his sleep? No, Joe said, he had not—but he must check up on this. Perhaps Frank Elwood could tell him something, though he hated to ask.

Fever—wild—dreams—somnambulism—illusions of sounds—a pull toward a point in the sky—and now a suspicion of insane sleep-talking! He must stop studying, see a nerve specialist, and take himself in hand. When he climbed to the second story he paused at Elwood's door but saw that the other youth was out. Reluctantly he continued up to his garret room and sat down in the dark. His gaze was still pulled to the southwest, but he also found himself listening intently for some sound in the closed loft above, and half imagining that an evil violet light seeped down through an infinitesimal crack in the low, slanting ceiling.

That night as Gilman slept the violet light broke upon him with heightened intensity, and the old witch and small furry thing—getting closer than ever before—mocked him with inhuman squeals and devilish gestures. He was glad to sink into the vaguely roaring twilight abysses, though the pursuit of that iridescent bubble-congeries and that kaleidoscopic little polyhedron was menacing and irritating. Then came the shift as vast converging planes of a slippery-looking substance loomed above and below him—a shift which ended in a flash of delirium and a blaze of unknown, alien light in which yellow, carmine, and indigo were madly and inextricably blended.

He was half lying on a high, fantastically balustraded terrace above a boundless jungle of outlandish, incredible peaks, balanced planes, domes, minarets, horizontal discs poised on pinnacles, and numberless forms of still greater wildness—some of stone and some of metal—which glittered gorgeously in the mixed, almost blistering glare from a polychromatic sky. Looking upward he saw three stupendous discs of flame, each of a different hue, and at a different height above an infinitely distant curving horizon of low mountains. Behind him tiers of higher terraces towered aloft as far as he could see. The city below stretched away to the limits of vision, and he hoped that no sound would well up from it.

The pavement from which he easily raised himself was of a veined, polished stone beyond his power to identify, and the tiles were cut in bizarre-angled shapes which struck him as less asymmetrical than based on some unearthly symmetry whose laws he could not comprehend. The balustrade was chest-high, delicate, and fantastically wrought, while along the rail were ranged at short intervals little figures of grotesque design and exquisite workmanship. They, like the whole balustrade, seemed to be made of some sort of shining metal whose colour could not be guessed in this chaos of mixed effulgences; and their nature utterly defied conjecture. They represented some ridged, barrel-shaped object with thin horizontal arms radiating spoke-like from a central ring, and with vertical knobs or bulbs projecting from the head and base of the barrel. Each of these knobs was the hub of a system of five long, flat, triangularly tapering arms arranged around it like the arms of a starfish—nearly horizontal, but curving slightly away from the central barrel. The base of the bottom knob was fused to the long railing with so delicate a point of contact that several figures had been broken off and were missing. The figures were about four and a half inches in height, while the spiky arms gave them a maximum diameter of about two and a half inches.

When Gilman stood up the tiles felt hot to his bare feet. He was wholly alone, and his first act was to walk to the balustrade and look dizzily down at the endless, Cyclopean city almost two thousand feet below. As he listened he thought a rhythmic confusion of faint musical pipings covering a wide tonal range welled up from the narrow streets beneath, and he wished he might discern the denizens of the place. The sight turned him giddy after a while, so that he would have fallen to the pavement had he not clutched instinctively at the lustrous balustrade. His right hand fell on one of the projecting figures, the touch seeming to steady him slightly. It was too much, however, for the exotic delicacy of the metal-work, and the spiky figure snapped off under his grasp. Still half-dazed, he continued to clutch it as his other hand seized a vacant space on the smooth railing.

But now his oversensitive ears caught something behind him, and he looked back across the level terrace. Approaching him softly though without apparent furtiveness were five figures, two of which were the sinister old woman and the fanged, furry little animal. The other three were what sent him unconscious—for they were living entities about eight feet high, shaped precisely like the spiky images on the balustrade, and propelling themselves by a spider-like wriggling of their lower set of starfish-arms.

Gilman awaked in his bed, drenched by a cold perspiration and with a smarting sensation in his face, hands, and feet. Springing to the floor, he washed and dressed in frantic haste, as if it were necessary for him to get out of the house as quickly as possible. He did not know where he wished to go, but felt that once more he would have to sacrifice his classes. The odd pull toward that spot in the sky between Hydra and Argo had abated, but another of even greater strength had taken its place. Now he felt that he must go north—infinitely north. He dreaded to cross the bridge that gave a view of the desolate island in the Miskatonic, so went over the Peabody Avenue bridge. Very often he stumbled, for his eyes and ears were chained to an extremely lofty point in the blank blue sky.

After about an hour he got himself under better control, and saw that he was far from the city. All around him stretched the bleak emptiness of salt marshes, while the narrow road ahead led to Innsmouth—that ancient, half-deserted town which Arkham people were so curiously unwilling to visit. Though the northward pull had not diminished, he resisted it as he had resisted the other pull, and finally found that he could almost balance the one against the other. Plodding back to town and getting some coffee at a soda fountain, he dragged himself into the public library and browsed aimlessly among the lighter magazines. Once he met some friends who remarked how oddly sunburned he looked, but he did not tell them of his walk. At three o'clock he took some lunch at a restaurant, noting meanwhile that the pull had either lessened or divided itself. After that he killed the time at a cheap cinema show, seeing the inane performance over and over again without paying any attention to it.

About nine at night he drifted homeward and stumbled into the ancient house. Joe Mazurewicz was whining unintelligible prayers, and Gilman hastened up to his own garret chamber without pausing to see if Elwood was in. It was when he turned on the feeble electric light that the shock came. At once he saw there was something on the table which did not belong there, and a second look left no room for doubt. Lying on its side—for it could not stand up alone—was the exotic spiky figure which in his monstrous dream he had broken off the fantastic balustrade. No detail was missing. The ridged, barrel-shaped centre, the thin, radiating arms, the knobs at each end, and the flat, slightly outward-curving starfish-arms spreading from those knobs—all were there. In the electric light the colour seemed to be a kind of iridescent grey veined with green, and Gilman could see amidst his horror and bewilderment that one of the knobs ended in a jagged break corresponding to its former point of attachment to the dream-railing.

Only his tendency toward a dazed stupor prevented him from screaming aloud. This fusion of dream and reality was too much to bear. Still dazed, he clutched at the spiky thing and staggered downstairs to Landlord Dombrowski's quarters. The whining prayers of the superstitious loomfixer were still sounding through the mouldy halls, but Gilman did not mind them now. The landlord was in, and greeted him pleasantly. No, he had not seen that thing before and did not know anything about it. But his wife had said she found a funny tin thing in one of the beds when she fixed the rooms at noon, and maybe that was it. Dombrowski called her, and she waddled in. Yes, that was the thing. She had found it in the young gentleman's bed—on the side next the wall. It had looked very queer to her, but of course the young gentleman had lots of queer things in his room—books and curios and pictures and markings on paper. She certainly knew nothing about it.

So Gilman climbed upstairs again in a mental turmoil, convinced that he was either still dreaming or that his somnambulism had run to incredible extremes and led him to depredations in unknown places. Where had he got this outr, thing? He did not recall seeing it in any museum in Arkham. It must have been somewhere, though; and the sight of it as he snatched it in his sleep must have caused the odd dream-picture of the balustraded terrace. Next day he would make some very guarded inquiries—and perhaps see the nerve specialist.

Meanwhile he would try to keep track of his somnambulism. As he went upstairs and across the garret hall he sprinkled about some flour which he had borrowed—with a frank admission as to its purpose—from the landlord. He had stopped at Elwood's door on the way, but had found all dark within. Entering his room, he placed the spiky thing on the table, and lay down in complete mental and physical exhaustion without pausing to undress. From the closed loft above the slanting ceiling he thought he heard a faint scratching and padding, but he was too disorganised even to mind it. That cryptical pull from the north was getting very strong again, though it seemed now to come from a lower place in the sky.

In the dazzling violet light of dream the old woman and the fanged, furry thing came again and with greater distinctness than on any former occasion. This time they actually reached him, and he felt the crone's withered claws clutching at him. He was pulled out of bed and into empty space, and for a moment he heard a rhythmic roaring and saw the twilight amorphousness of the vague abysses seething around him. But that moment was very brief, for presently he was in a crude, windowless little space with rough beams and planks rising to a peak just above his head, and with a curious slanting floor underfoot. Propped level on that floor were low cases full of books of every degree of antiquity and disintegration, and in the centre were a table and bench, both apparently fastened in place. Small objects of unknown shape and nature were ranged on the tops of the cases, and in the flaming violet light Gilman thought he saw a counterpart of the spiky image which had puzzled him so horribly. On the left the floor fell abruptly away, leaving a black triangular gulf out of which, after a second's dry rattling, there presently climbed the hateful little furry thing with the yellow fangs and bearded human face.

The evilly grinning beldame still clutched him, and beyond the table stood a figure he had never seen before—a tall, lean man of dead black colouration but without the slightest sign of negroid features; wholly devoid of either hair or beard, and wearing as his only garment a shapeless robe of some heavy black fabric. His feet were indistinguishable because of the table and bench, but he must have been shod, since there was a clicking whenever he changed position. The man did not speak, and bore no trace of expression on his small, regular features. He merely pointed to a book of prodigious size which lay open on the table, while the beldame thrust a huge grey quill into Gilman's right hand. Over everything was a pall of intense, maddening fear, and the climax was reached when the furry thing ran up the dreamer's clothing to his shoulders and then down his left arm, finally biting him sharply in the wrist just below his cuff. As the blood spurted from this wound Gilman lapsed into a faint.

He awaked on the morning of the 22nd with a pain in his left wrist, and saw that his cuff was brown with dried blood. His recollections were very confused, but the scene with the black man in the unknown space stood out vividly. The rats must have bitten him as he slept, giving rise to the climax of that frightful dream. Opening the door, he saw that the flour on the corridor floor was undisturbed except for the huge prints of the loutish fellow who roomed at the other end of the garret. So he had not been sleep-walking this time. But something would have to be done about those rats. He would speak to the landlord about them. Again he tried to stop up the hole at the base of the slanting wall, wedging in a candlestick which seemed of about the right size. His ears were ringing horribly, as if with the residual echoes of some horrible noise heard in dreams.

As he bathed and changed clothes he tried to recall what he had dreamed after the scene in the violet-litten space, but nothing definite would crystallise in his mind. That scene itself must have corresponded to the sealed loft overhead, which had begun to attack his imagination so violently, but later impressions were faint and hazy. There were suggestions of the vague, twilight abysses, and of still vaster, blacker abysses beyond them—abysses in which all fixed suggestions of form were absent. He had been taken there by the bubble-congeries and the little polyhedron which always dogged him; but they, like himself, had changed to wisps of milky, barely luminous mist in this farther void of ultimate blackness. Something else had gone on ahead—a larger wisp which now and then condensed into nameless approximations of form—and he thought that their progress had not been in a straight line, but rather along the alien curves and spirals of some ethereal vortex which obeyed laws unknown to the physics and mathematics of any conceivable cosmos. Eventually there had been a hint of vast, leaping shadows, of a monstrous, half-acoustic pulsing, and of the thin, monotonous piping of an unseen flute—but that was all. Gilman decided he had picked up that last conception from what he had read in the "Necronomicon" about the mindless entity Azathoth, which rules all time and space from a curiously environed black throne at the centre of Chaos.

When the blood was washed away the wrist wound proved very slight, and Gilman puzzled over the location of the two tiny punctures. It occurred to him that there was no blood on the bedspread where he had lain—which was very curious in view of the amount on his skin and cuff. Had he been sleep-walking within his room, and had the rat bitten him as he sat in some chair or paused in some less rational position? He looked in every corner for brownish drops or stains, but did not find any. He had better, he thought, sprinkle flour within the room as well as outside the door—though after all no further proof of his sleep-walking was needed. He knew he did walk—and the thing to do now was to stop it. He must ask Frank Elwood for help. This morning the strange pulls from space seemed lessened, though they were replaced by another sensation even more inexplicable. It was a vague, insistent impulse to fly away from his present situation, but held not a hint of the specific direction in which he wished to fly. As he picked up the strange spiky image on the table he thought the older northward pull grew a trifle stronger; but even so, it was wholly overruled by the newer and more bewildering urge.

He took the spiky image down to Elwood's room, steeling himself against the whines of the loomfixer which welled up from the ground floor. Elwood was in, thank heaven, and appeared to be stirring about. There was time for a little conversation before leaving for breakfast and college, so Gilman hurriedly poured forth an account of his recent dreams and fears. His host was very sympathetic, and agreed that something ought to be done. He was shocked by his guest's drawn, haggard aspect, and noticed the queer, abnormal-looking sunburn which others had remarked during the past week. There was not much, though, that he could say. He had not seen Gilman on any sleep-walking expedition, and had no idea what the curious image could be. He had, though, heard the French-Canadian who lodged just under Gilman talking to Mazurewicz one evening. They were telling each other how badly they dreaded the coming of Walpurgis-Night, now only a few days off; and were exchanging pitying comments about the poor, doomed young gentleman. Desrochers, the fellow under Gilman's room, had spoken of nocturnal footsteps both shod and unshod, and of the violet light he saw one night when he had stolen fearfully up to peer through Gilman's keyhole. He had not dared to peer, he told Mazurewicz, after he had glimpsed that light through the cracks around the door. There had been soft talking, too—and as he began to describe it his voice had sunk to an inaudible whisper.

Elwood could not imagine what had set these superstitious creatures gossiping, but supposed their imaginations had been roused by Gilman's late hours and somnolent walking and talking on the one hand, and by the nearness of traditionally feared May-Eve on the other hand. That Gilman talked in his sleep was plain, and it was obviously from Desrochers' keyhole-listenings that the delusive notion of the violet dream-light had got abroad. These simple people were quick to imagine they had seen any odd thing they had heard about. As for a plan of action—Gilman had better move down to Elwood's room and avoid sleeping alone. Elwood would, if awake, rouse him whenever he began to talk or rise in his sleep. Very soon, too, he must see the specialist. Meanwhile they would take the spiky image around to the various museums and to certain professors; seeking identification and stating that it had been found in a public rubbish-can. Also, Dombrowski must attend to the poisoning of those rats in the walls.

Braced up by Elwood's companionship, Gilman attended classes that day. Strange urges still tugged at him, but he could sidetrack them with considerable success. During a free period he shewed the queer image to several professors, all of whom were intensely interested, though none of them could shed any light upon its nature or origin. That night he slept on a couch which Elwood had had the landlord bring to the second-story room, and for the first time in weeks was wholly free from disquieting dreams. But the feverishness still hung on, and the whines of the loomfixer were an unnerving influence.

During the next few days Gilman enjoyed an almost perfect immunity from morbid manifestations. He had, Elwood said, shewed no tendency to talk or rise in his sleep; and meanwhile the landlord was putting rat-poison everywhere. The only disturbing element was the talk among the superstitious foreigners, whose imaginations had become highly excited. Mazurewicz was always trying to make him get a crucifix, and finally forced one upon him which he said had been blessed by the good Father Iwanicki. Desrochers, too, had something to say—in fact, he insisted that cautious steps had sounded in the now vacant room above him on the first and second nights of Gilman's absence from it. Paul Choynski thought he heard sounds in the halls and on the stairs at night, and claimed that his door had been softly tried, while

Mrs. Dombrowski vowed she had seen Brown Jenkin for the first time since All-Hallows. But such naive reports could mean very little, and Gilman let the cheap metal crucifix hang idly from a knob on his host's dresser.

For three days Gilman and Elwood canvassed the local museums in an effort to identify the strange spiky image, but always without success. In every quarter, however, interest was intense; for the utter alienage of the thing was a tremendous challenge to scientific curiosity. One of the small radiating arms was broken off and subjected to chemical analysis, and the result is still talked about in college circles. Professor Ellery found platinum, iron, and tellurium in the strange alloy; but mixed with these were at least three other apparent elements of high atomic weight which chemistry was absolutely powerless to classify. Not only did they fail to correspond with any known element, but they did not even fit the vacant places reserved for probable elements in the periodic system. The mystery remains unsolved to this day, though the image is on exhibition at the museum of Miskatonic University.

On the morning of April 27th a fresh rat-hole appeared in the room where Gilman was a guest, but Dombrowski tinned it up during the day. The poison was not having much effect, for scratchings and scurryings in the walls were virtually undiminished. Elwood was out late that night, and Gilman waited up for him. He did not wish to go to sleep in a room alone—especially since he thought he had glimpsed in the evening twilight the repellent old woman whose image had become so horribly transferred to his dreams. He wondered who she was, and what had been near her rattling the tin cans in a rubbish-heap at the mouth of a squalid courtyard. The crone had seemed to notice him and leer evilly at him—though perhaps this was merely his imagination.

The next day both youths felt very tired, and knew they would sleep like logs when night came. In the evening they drowsily discussed the mathematical studies which had so completely and perhaps harmfully engrossed Gilman, and speculated about the linkage with ancient magic and folklore which seemed so darkly probable. They spoke of old Keziah Mason, and Elwood agreed that Gilman had good scientific grounds for thinking she might have stumbled on strange and significant information. The hidden cults to which these witches belonged often guarded and handed down surprising secrets from elder, forgotten aeons; and it was by no means impossible that Keziah had actually mastered the art of passing through dimensional gates. Tradition emphasises the uselessness of material barriers in halting a witch's motions, and who can say what underlies the old tales of broomstick rides through the night?

Whether a modern student could ever gain similar powers from mathematical research alone, was still to be seen. Success, Gilman added, might lead to dangerous and unthinkable situations; for who could foretell the conditions pervading an adjacent but normally inaccessible dimension? On the other hand, the picturesque possibilities were enormous. Time could not exist in certain belts of space, and by entering and remaining in such a belt one might preserve one's life and age indefinitely; never suffering organic metabolism or deterioration except for slight amounts incurred during visits to one's own or similar planes. One might, for example, pass into a timeless dimension and emerge at some remote period of the earth's history as young as before.

Whether anybody had ever managed to do this, one could hardly conjecture with any degree of authority. Old legends are hazy and ambiguous, and in historic times all attempts at crossing forbidden gaps seem complicated by strange and terrible alliances with beings and messengers from outside. There was the immemorial figure of the deputy or messenger of hidden and terrible powers—the "Black Man" of the witch-cult, and the "Nyarlathotep" of the "Necronomicon". There was, too, the baffling problem of the lesser messengers or intermediaries—the quasi-animals and queer hybrids which legend depicts as witches' familiars. As Gilman and Elwood retired, too sleepy to argue further, they heard Joe Mazurewicz reel into the house half-drunk, and shuddered at the desperate wildness of his whining prayers.

That night Gilman saw the violet light again. In his dream he had heard a scratching and gnawing in the partitions, and thought that someone fumbled clumsily at the latch. Then he saw the old woman and the small furry thing advancing toward him over the carpeted floor. The beldame's face was alight with inhuman exultation, and the little yellow-toothed morbidity tittered mockingly as it pointed at the heavily sleeping form of Elwood on the other couch across the room. A paralysis of fear stifled all attempts to cry out. As once before, the hideous crone seized Gilman by the shoulders, yanking him out of bed and into empty space. Again the infinitude of the shrieking twilight abysses flashed past him, but in another second he thought he was in a dark, muddy, unknown alley of foetid odours, with the rotting walls of ancient houses towering up on every hand.

Ahead was the robed black man he had seen in the peaked space in the other dream, while from a lesser distance the old woman was beckoning and grimacing imperiously. Brown Jenkin was rubbing itself with a kind of affectionate playfulness around the ankles of the black man, which the deep mud largely concealed. There was a dark open doorway on the right, to which the black man silently pointed. Into this the grimacing crone started, dragging Gilman after her by his pajama sleeve. There were evil-smelling staircases which creaked ominously, and on which the old woman seemed to radiate a faint violet light; and finally a door leading off a landing. The crone fumbled with the latch and pushed the door open, motioning to Gilman to wait and disappearing inside the black aperture.

The youth's oversensitive ears caught a hideous strangled cry, and presently the beldame came out of the room bearing a small, senseless form which she thrust at the dreamer as if ordering him to carry it. The sight of this form, and the expression on its face, broke the spell. Still too dazed to cry out, he plunged recklessly down the noisome staircase and into the mud outside; halting only when seized and choked by the waiting black man. As consciousness departed he heard the faint, shrill tittering of the fanged, rat-like abnormality.

On the morning of the 29th Gilman awaked into a maelstrom of horror. The instant he opened his eyes he knew something was terribly wrong, for he was back in his old garret room with the slanting wall and ceiling, sprawled on the now unmade bed. His throat was aching inexplicably, and as he struggled to a sitting posture he saw with growing fright that his feet and pajama-bottoms were brown with caked mud. For the moment his recollections were hopelessly hazy, but he knew at least that he must have been sleep-walking. Elwood had been lost too deeply in slumber to hear and stop him. On the floor were confused muddy prints, but oddly enough they did not extend all the way to the door. The more Gilman looked at them, the more peculiar they seemed; for in addition to those he could recognise as his there were some smaller, almost round markings—such as the legs of a large chair or table might make, except that most of them tended to be divided into halves. There were also some curious muddy rat-tracks leading out of a fresh hole and back into it again. Utter bewilderment and the fear of madness racked Gilman as he staggered to the door and saw that there were no muddy prints outside. The more he remembered of his hideous dream the more terrified he felt, and it added to his desperation to hear Joe Mazurewicz chanting mournfully two floors below.

Descending to Elwood's room he roused his still-sleeping host and began telling of how he had found himself, but Elwood could form no idea of what might really have happened. Where Gilman could have been, how he got back to his room without making tracks in the hall, and how the muddy, furniture-like prints came to be mixed with his in the garret chamber, were wholly beyond conjecture. Then there were those dark, livid marks on his throat, as if he had tried to strangle himself. He put his hands up to them, but found that they did not even approximately fit. While they were talking Desrochers dropped in to say that he had heard a terrific clattering overhead in the dark small hours. No, there had been no one on the stairs after midnight—though just before midnight he had heard faint footfalls in the garret, and cautiously descending steps he did not like. It was, he added, a very bad time of year for Arkham. The young gentleman had better be sure to wear the crucifix Joe Mazurewicz had given him. Even the daytime was not safe, for after dawn there had been strange sounds in the house—especially a thin, childish wail hastily choked off.

Gilman mechanically attended classes that morning, but was wholly unable to fix his mind on his studies. A mood of hideous apprehension and expectancy had seized him, and he seemed to be awaiting the fall of some annihilating blow. At noon he lunched at the University Spa, picking up a paper from the next seat as he waited for dessert. But he never ate that dessert; for an item on the paper's first page left him limp, wild-eyed, and able only to pay his check and stagger back to Elwood's room.

There had been a strange kidnapping the night before in Orne's Gangway, and the two-year-old child of a clod-like laundry worker named Anastasia Wolejko had completely vanished from sight. The mother, it appeared, had feared this event for some time; but the reasons she assigned for her fear were so grotesque that no one took them seriously. She had, she said, seen Brown Jenkin about the place now and then ever since early in March, and knew from its grimaces and titterings that little Ladislas must be marked for sacrifice at the awful Sabbat on Walpurgis-Night. She had asked her neighbour Mary Czanek to sleep in the room and try to protect the child, but Mary had not dared. She could not tell the police, for they never believed such things. Children had been taken that way every year ever since she could remember. And her friend Pete Stowacki would not help because he wanted the child out of the way anyhow.

But what threw Gilman into a cold perspiration was the report of a pair of revellers who had been walking past the mouth of the gangway just after midnight. They admitted they had been drunk, but both vowed they had seen a crazily dressed trio furtively entering the dark passageway. There had, they said, been a huge robed negro, a little old woman in rags, and a young white man in his night-clothes. The old woman had been dragging the youth, while around the feet of the negro a tame rat was rubbing and weaving in the brown mud.

Gilman sat in a daze all the afternoon, and Elwood—who had meanwhile seen the papers and formed terrible conjectures from them—found him thus when he came home. This time neither could doubt but that something hideously serious was closing in around them. Between the phantasms of nightmare and the realities of the objective world a monstrous and unthinkable relationship was crystallising, and only stupendous vigilance could avert still more direful developments. Gilman must see a specialist sooner or later, but not just now, when all the papers were full of this kidnapping business.

Just what had really happened was maddeningly obscure, and for a moment both Gilman and Elwood exchanged whispered theories of the wildest kind. Had Gilman unconsciously succeeded better than he knew in his studies of space and its dimensions? Had he actually slipped outside our sphere to points unguessed and unimaginable? Where—if anywhere—had he been on those nights of daemoniac alienage? The roaring twilight abysses—the green hillside—the blistering terrace—the pulls from the stars—the ultimate black vortex—the black man—the muddy alley and the stairs—the old witch and the fanged, furry horror—the bubble-congeries and the little polyhedron—the strange sunburn—the wrist wound—the unexplained image—the muddy feet—the throat-marks—the tales and fears of the superstitious foreigners—what did all this mean? To what extent could the laws of sanity apply to such a case?

There was no sleep for either of them that night, but next day they both cut classes and drowsed. This was April 30th, and with the dusk would come the hellish Sabbat-time which all the foreigners and the superstitious old folk feared. Mazurewicz came home at six o'clock and said people at the mill were whispering that the Walpurgis-revels would be held in the dark ravine beyond Meadow Hill where the old white stone stands in a place queerly void of all plant-life. Some of them had even told the police and advised them to look there for the missing Wolejko child, but they did not believe anything would be done. Joe insisted that the poor young gentleman wear his nickel-chained crucifix, and Gilman put it on and dropped it inside his shirt to humour the fellow.

Late at night the two youths sat drowsing in their chairs, lulled by the rhythmical praying of the loomfixer on the floor below. Gilman listened as he nodded, his preternaturally sharpened hearing seeming to strain for some subtle, dreaded murmur beyond the noises in the ancient house. Unwholesome recollections of things in the "Necronomicon" and the Black Book welled up, and he found himself swaying to infandous rhythms said to pertain to the blackest ceremonies of the Sabbat and to have an origin outside the time and space we comprehend.

Presently he realised what he was listening for—the hellish chant of the celebrants in the distant black valley. How did he know so much about what they expected? How did he know the time when Nahab and her acolyte were due to bear the brimming bowl which would follow the black cock and the black goat? He saw that Elwood had dropped asleep, and tried to call out and waken him. Something, however, closed his throat. He was not his own master. Had he signed the black man's book after all?

Then his fevered, abnormal hearing caught the distant, wind-borne notes. Over miles of hill and field and alley they came, but he recognised them none the less. The fires must be lit, and the dancers must be starting in. How could he keep himself from going? What was it that had enmeshed him? Mathematics—folklore—the house—old Keziah—Brown Jenkin ... and now he saw that there was a fresh rat-hole in the wall near his couch. Above the distant chanting and the nearer praying of Joe Mazurewicz came another sound—a stealthy, determined scratching in the partitions. He hoped the electric lights would not go out. Then he saw the fanged, bearded little face in the rat-hole—the accursed little face which he at last realised bore such a shocking, mocking resemblance to old Keziah's—and heard the faint fumbling at the door.

The screaming twilight abysses flashed before him, and he felt himself helpless in the formless grasp of the iridescent bubble-congeries. Ahead raced the small, kaleidoscopic polyhedron, and all through the churning void there was a heightening and acceleration of the vague tonal pattern which seemed to foreshadow some unutterable and unendurable climax. He seemed to know what was coming—the monstrous burst of Walpurgis-rhythm in whose cosmic timbre would be concentrated all the primal, ultimate space-time seethings which lie behind the massed spheres of matter and sometimes break forth in measured reverberations that penetrate faintly to every layer of entity and give hideous significance throughout the worlds to certain dreaded periods.

But all this vanished in a second. He was again in the cramped, violet-litten peaked space with the slanting floor, the low cases of ancient books, the bench and table, the queer objects, and the triangular gulf at one side. On the table lay a small white figure—an infant boy, unclothed and unconscious—while on the other side stood the monstrous, leering old woman with a gleaming, grotesque-hafted knife in her right hand, and a queerly proportioned pale metal bowl covered with curiously chased designs and having delicate lateral handles in her left. She was intoning some croaking ritual in a language which Gilman could not understand, but which seemed like something guardedly quoted in the "Necronomicon".

As the scene grew clear he saw the ancient crone bend forward and extend the empty bowl across the table—and unable to control his own motions, he reached far forward and took it in both hands, noticing as he did so its comparative lightness. At the same moment the disgusting form of Brown Jenkin scrambled up over the brink of the triangular black gulf on his left. The crone now motioned him to hold the bowl in a certain position while she raised the huge, grotesque knife above the small white victim as high as her right hand could reach. The fanged, furry thing began tittering a continuation of the unknown ritual, while the witch croaked loathsome responses. Gilman felt a gnawing, poignant abhorrence shoot through his mental and emotional paralysis, and the light metal bowl shook in his grasp. A second later the downward motion of the knife broke the spell completely, and he dropped the bowl with a resounding bell-like clangour while his hands darted out frantically to stop the monstrous deed.

In an instant he had edged up the slanting floor around the end of the table and wrenched the knife from the old woman's claws; sending it clattering over the brink of the narrow triangular gulf. In another instant, however, matters were reversed; for those murderous claws had locked themselves tightly around his own throat, while the wrinkled face was twisted with insane fury. He felt the chain of the cheap crucifix grinding into his neck, and in his peril wondered how the sight of the object itself would affect the evil creature. Her strength was altogether superhuman, but as she continued her choking he reached feebly in his shirt and drew out the metal symbol, snapping the chain and pulling it free.

At sight of the device the witch seemed struck with panic, and her grip relaxed long enough to give Gilman a chance to break it entirely. He pulled the steel-like claws from his neck, and would have dragged the beldame over the edge of the gulf had not the claws received a fresh access of strength and closed in again. This time he resolved to reply in kind, and his own hands reached out for the creature's throat. Before she saw what he was doing he had the chain of the crucifix twisted about her neck, and a moment later he had tightened it enough to cut off her breath. During her last struggle he felt something bite at his ankle, and saw that Brown Jenkin had come to her aid. With one savage kick he sent the morbidity over the edge of the gulf and heard it whimper on some level far below.

Whether he had killed the ancient crone he did not know, but he let her rest on the floor where she had fallen. Then, as he turned away, he saw on the table a sight which nearly snapped the last thread of his reason. Brown Jenkin, tough of sinew and with four tiny hands of daemoniac dexterity, had been busy while the witch was throttling him, and his efforts had been in vain. What he had prevented the knife from doing to the victim's chest, the yellow fangs of the furry blasphemy had done to a wrist—and the bowl so lately on the floor stood full beside the small lifeless body.

In his dream-delirium Gilman heard the hellish, alien-rhythmed chant of the Sabbat coming from an infinite distance, and knew the black man must be there. Confused memories mixed themselves with his mathematics, and he believed his subconscious mind held the angles which he needed to guide him back to the normal world—alone and unaided for the first time. He felt sure he was in the immemorially sealed loft above his own room, but whether he could ever escape through the slanting floor or the long-stopped egress he doubted greatly. Besides, would not an escape from a dream-loft bring him merely into a dream-house—an abnormal projection of the actual place he sought? He was wholly bewildered as to the relation betwixt dream and reality in all his experiences.

The passage through the vague abysses would be frightful, for the Walpurgis-rhythm would be vibrating, and at last he would have to hear that hitherto veiled cosmic pulsing which he so mortally dreaded. Even now he could detect a low, monstrous shaking whose tempo he suspected all too well. At Sabbat-time it always mounted and reached through to the worlds to summon the initiate to nameless rites. Half the chants of the Sabbat were patterned on this faintly overheard pulsing which no earthly ear could endure in its unveiled spatial fulness. Gilman wondered, too, whether he could trust his instinct to take him back to the right part of space. How could he be sure he would not land on that green-litten hillside of a far planet, on the tessellated terrace above the city of tentacled monsters somewhere beyond the galaxy, or in the spiral black vortices of that ultimate void of Chaos wherein reigns the mindless daemon-sultan Azathoth?

Just before he made the plunge the violet light went out and left him in utter blackness. The witch—old Keziah—Nahab—that must have meant her death. And mixed with the distant chant of the Sabbat and the whimpers of Brown Jenkin in the gulf below he thought he heard another and wilder whine from unknown depths. Joe Mazurewicz—the prayers against the Crawling Chaos now turning to an inexplicably triumphant shriek—worlds of sardonic actuality impinging on vortices of febrile dream—Iä! Shub-Niggurath! The Goat with a Thousand Young....

They found Gilman on the floor of his queerly angled old garret room long before dawn, for the terrible cry had brought Desrochers and Choynski and Dombrowski and Mazurewicz at once, and had even wakened the soundly sleeping Elwood in his chair. He was alive, and with open, staring eyes, but seemed largely unconscious. On his throat were the marks of murderous hands, and on his left ankle was a distressing rat-bite. His clothing was badly rumpled, and Joe's crucifix was missing. Elwood trembled, afraid even to speculate on what new form his friend's sleep-walking had taken. Mazurewicz seemed half-dazed because of a "sign" he said he had had in response to his prayers, and he crossed himself frantically when the squealing and whimpering of a rat sounded from beyond the slanting partition.

When the dreamer was settled on his couch in Elwood's room they sent for Dr. Malkowski—a local practitioner who would repeat no tales where they might prove embarrassing—and he gave Gilman two hypodermic injections which caused him to relax in something like natural drowsiness. During the day the patient regained consciousness at times and whispered his newest dream disjointedly to Elwood. It was a painful process, and at its very start brought out a fresh and disconcerting fact.

Gilman—whose ears had so lately possessed an abnormal sensitiveness—was now stone deaf. Dr. Malkowski, summoned again in haste, told Elwood that both ear-drums were ruptured, as if by the impact of some stupendous sound intense beyond all human conception or endurance. How such a sound could have been heard in the last few hours without arousing all the Miskatonic Valley was more than the honest physician could say.

Elwood wrote his part of the colloquy on paper, so that a fairly easy communication was maintained. Neither knew what to make of the whole chaotic business, and decided it would be better if they thought as little as possible about it. Both, though, agreed that they must leave this ancient and accursed house as soon as it could be arranged. Evening papers spoke of a police raid on some curious revellers in a ravine beyond Meadow Hill just before dawn, and mentioned that the white stone there was an object of age-long superstitious regard. Nobody had been caught, but among the scattering fugitives had been glimpsed a huge negro. In another column it was stated that no trace of the missing child Ladislas Wolejko had been found.

The crowning horror came that very night. Elwood will never forget it, and was forced to stay out of college the rest of the term because of the resulting nervous breakdown. He had thought he heard rats in the partitions all the evening, but paid little attention to them. Then, long after both he and Gilman had retired, the atrocious shrieking began. Elwood jumped up, turned on the lights, and rushed over to his guest's couch. The occupant was emitting sounds of veritably inhuman nature, as if racked by some torment beyond description. He was writhing under the bedclothes, and a great red stain was beginning to appear on the blankets.

Elwood scarcely dared to touch him, but gradually the screaming and writhing subsided. By this time Dombrowski, Choynski, Desrochers, Mazurewicz, and the top-floor lodger were all crowding into the doorway, and the landlord had sent his wife back to telephone for Dr. Malkowski. Everybody shrieked when a large rat-like form suddenly jumped out from beneath the ensanguined bedclothes and scuttled across the floor to a fresh, open hole close by. When the doctor arrived and began to pull down those frightful covers Walter Gilman was dead.

It would be barbarous to do more than suggest what had killed Gilman. There had been virtually a tunnel through his body—something had eaten his heart out. Dombrowski, frantic at the failure of his constant rat-poisoning efforts, cast aside all thought of his lease and within a week had moved with all his older lodgers to a dingy but less ancient house in Walnut Street. The worst thing for a while was keeping Joe Mazurewicz quiet; for the brooding loomfixer would never stay sober, and was constantly whining and muttering about spectral and terrible things.

It seems that on that last hideous night Joe had stooped to look at the crimson rat-tracks which led from Gilman's couch to the nearby hole. On the carpet they were very indistinct, but a piece of open flooring intervened between the carpet's edge and the base-board. There Mazurewicz had found something monstrous—or thought he had, for no one else could quite agree with him despite the undeniable queerness of the prints. The tracks on the flooring were certainly vastly unlike the average prints of a rat, but even Choynski and Desrochers would not admit that they were like the prints of four tiny human hands.

The house was never rented again. As soon as Dombrowski left it the pall of its final desolation began to descend, for people shunned it both on account of its old reputation and because of the new foetid odour. Perhaps the ex-landlord's rat-poison had worked after all, for not long after his departure the place became a neighbourhood nuisance. Health officials traced the smell to the closed spaces above and beside the eastern garret room, and agreed that the number of dead rats must be enormous. They decided, however, that it was not worth their while to hew open and disinfect the long-sealed spaces; for the foetor would soon be over, and the locality was not one which encouraged fastidious standards. Indeed, there were always vague local tales of unexplained stenches upstairs in the Witch House just after May-Eve and Hallowmass. The neighbours grumblingly acquiesced in the inertia—but the foetor none the less formed an additional count against the place. Toward the last the house was condemned as an habitation by the building inspector.

Gilman's dreams and their attendant circumstances have never been explained. Elwood, whose thoughts on the entire episode are sometimes almost maddening, came back to college the next autumn and graduated in the following June. He found the spectral gossip of the town much diminished, and it is indeed a fact that—notwithstanding certain reports of a ghostly tittering in the deserted house which lasted almost as long as that edifice itself—no fresh appearances either of old Keziah or of Brown Jenkin have been muttered of since Gilman's death. It is rather fortunate that Elwood was not in Arkham in that later year when certain events abruptly renewed the local whispers about elder horrors. Of course he heard about the matter afterward and suffered untold torments of black and bewildered speculation; but even that was not as bad as actual nearness and several possible sights would have been.

In March, 1931, a gale wrecked the roof and great chimney of the vacant Witch House, so that a chaos of crumbling bricks, blackened, moss-grown shingles, and rotting planks and timbers crashed down into the loft and broke through the floor beneath. The whole attic story was choked with debris from above, but no one took the trouble to touch the mess before the inevitable razing of the decrepit structure. That ultimate step came in the following December, and it was when Gilman's old room was cleared out by reluctant, apprehensive workmen that the gossip began.

Among the rubbish which had crashed through the ancient slanting ceiling were several things which made the workmen pause and call in the police. Later the police in turn called in the coroner and several professors from the university. There were bones—badly crushed and splintered, but clearly recognisable as human—whose manifestly modern date conflicted puzzlingly with the remote period at which their only possible lurking-place, the low, slant-floored loft overhead, had supposedly been sealed from all human access. The coroner's physician decided that some belonged to a small child, while certain others—found mixed with shreds of rotten brownish cloth—belonged to a rather undersized, bent female of advanced years. Careful sifting of debris also disclosed many tiny bones of rats caught in the collapse, as well as older rat-bones gnawed by small fangs in a fashion now and then highly productive of controversy and reflection.

Other objects found included the mingled fragments of many books and papers, together with a yellowish dust left from the total disintegration of still older books and papers. All, without exception, appeared to deal with black magic in its most advanced and horrible forms; and the evidently recent date of certain items is still a mystery as unsolved as that of the modern human bones. An even greater mystery is the absolute homogeneity of the crabbed, archaic writing found on a wide range of papers whose conditions and watermarks suggest age differences of at least 150 to 200 years. To some, though, the greatest mystery of all is the variety of utterly inexplicable objects—objects whose shapes, materials, types of workmanship, and purposes baffle all conjecture—found scattered amidst the wreckage in evidently diverse states of injury. One of these things—which excited several Miskatonic professors profoundly—is a badly damaged monstrosity plainly resembling the strange image which Gilman gave to the college museum, save that it is larger, wrought of some peculiar bluish stone instead of metal, and possessed of a singularly angled pedestal with undecipherable hieroglyphics.

Archaeologists and anthropologists are still trying to explain the bizarre designs chased on a crushed bowl of light metal whose inner side bore ominous brownish stains when found. Foreigners and credulous grandmothers are equally garrulous about the modern nickel crucifix with broken chain mixed in the rubbish and shiveringly identified by Joe Mazurewicz as that which he had given poor Gilman many years before. Some believe this crucifix was dragged up to the sealed loft by rats, while others think it must have been on the floor in some corner of Gilman's old room all the time. Still others, including Joe himself, have theories too wild and fantastic for sober credence.

When the slanting wall of Gilman's room was torn out, the once sealed triangular space between that partition and the house's north wall was found to contain much less structural debris, even in proportion to its size, than the room itself; though it had a ghastly layer of older materials which paralysed the wreckers with horror. In brief, the floor was a veritable ossuary of the bones of small children—some fairly modern, but others extending back in infinite gradations to a period so remote that crumbling was almost complete. On this deep bony layer rested a knife of great size, obvious antiquity, and grotesque, ornate, and exotic design—above which the debris was piled.

In the midst of this debris, wedged between a fallen plank and a cluster of cemented bricks from the ruined chimney, was an object destined to cause more bafflement, veiled fright, and openly superstitious talk in Arkham than anything else discovered in the haunted and accursed building. This object was the partly crushed skeleton of a huge, diseased rat, whose abnormalities of form are still a topic of debate and source of singular reticence among the members of Miskatonic's department of comparative anatomy. Very little concerning this skeleton has leaked out, but the workmen who found it whisper in shocked tones about the long, brownish hairs with which it was associated.

The bones of the tiny paws, it is rumoured, imply prehensile characteristics more typical of a diminutive monkey than of a rat; while the small skull with its savage yellow fangs is of the utmost anomalousness, appearing from certain angles like a miniature, monstrously degraded parody of a human skull. The workmen crossed themselves in fright when they came upon this blasphemy, but later burned candles of gratitude in St. Stanislaus' Church because of the shrill, ghostly tittering they felt they would never hear again.

THROUGH THE GATES OF THE SILVER KEY

(with E. Hoffmann Price)

I.

In a vast room hung with strangely figured arras and carpeted with Bokhara rugs of impressive age and workmanship four men were sitting around a document-strown table. From the far corners, where odd tripods of wrought-iron were now and then replenished by an incredibly aged negro in sombre livery, came the hypnotic fumes of olibanum; while in a deep niche on one side there ticked a curious coffin-shaped clock whose dial bore baffling hieroglyphs and whose four hands did not move in consonance with any time-system known on this planet. It was a singular and disturbing room, but well fitted to the business now at hand. For here, in the New Orleans home of this continent's greatest mystic, mathematician, and orientalist, there was being settled at last the estate of a scarcely less great mystic, scholar, author, and dreamer who had vanished from the face of the earth four years before.

Randolph Carter, who had all his life sought to escape from the tedium and limitations of waking reality in the beckoning vistas of dreams and the fabled avenues of other dimensions, disappeared from the sight of man on the seventh of October, 1928, at the age of fifty-four. His career had been a strange and lonely one, and there were those who inferred from his curious novels many episodes more bizarre than any in his recorded history. His association with Harley Warren, the South Carolina dreamer whose studies in the primal Naacal language of the Himalayan priests had led to such outrageous conclusions, had been close. Indeed, it was he who—one mist-mad, terrible night in an ancient graveyard—had seen Warren descend into a dank and nitrous vault, never to emerge. Carter lived in Boston, but it was from the wild, haunted hills behind hoary and witch-accursed Arkham that all his forbears had come. And it was amid those ancient, cryptically brooding hills that he had ultimately vanished.

His old servant Parks—who died early in 1930—had spoken of the strangely aromatic and hideously carven box he had found in the attic, and of the undecipherable parchments and queerly figured silver key which that box had contained; matters of which Carter had also written to others. Carter, he said, had told him that this key had come down from his ancestors, and that it would help him to unlock the gate to his lost boyhood, and to strange dimensions and fantastic realms which he had hitherto visited only in vague, brief, and elusive dreams. Then one day Carter took the box and its contents and rode away in his car, never to return.

Later on people found the car at the side of an old, grass-grown road in the hills behind crumbling Arkham—the hills where Carter's forbears had once dwelt, and where the ruined cellar of the great Carter homestead still gaped to the sky. It was in a grove of tall elms nearby that another of the Carters had mysteriously vanished in 1781, and not far away was the half-rotted cottage where Goody Fowler the witch had brewed her ominous potions still earlier. The region had been settled in 1692 by fugitives from the witchcraft trials in Salem, and even now it bore a name for vaguely ominous things scarcely to be envisaged. Edmund Carter had fled from the shadow of Gallows Hill just in time, and the tales of his sorceries were many. Now, it seemed, his lone descendant had gone somewhere to join him.

In the car they found the hideously carved box of fragrant wood, and the parchment which no man could read. The Silver Key was gone—presumably with Carter. Further than that there was no certain clue. Detectives from Boston said that the fallen timbers of the old Carter place seemed oddly disturbed, and somebody found a handkerchief on the rock-ridged, sinisterly wooded slope behind the ruins near the dreaded cave called the "Snake-Den". It was then that the country legends about the Snake-Den gained a new vitality. Farmers whispered of the blasphemous uses to which old Edmund Carter the wizard had put that horrible grotto, and added later tales about the fondness which Randolph Carter himself had had for it when a boy. In

Carter's boyhood the venerable gambrel-roofed homestead was still standing and tenanted by his great-uncle Christopher. He had visited there often, and had talked singularly about the Snake-Den. People remembered what he had said about a deep fissure and an unknown inner cave beyond, and speculated on the change he had shewn after spending one whole memorable day in the cavern when he was nine. That was in October, too—and ever after that he had seemed to have an uncanny knack at prophesying future events.

It had rained late in the night that Carter vanished, and no one was quite able to trace his footprints from the car. Inside the Snake-Den all was amorphous liquid mud owing to copious seepage. Only the ignorant rustics whispered about the prints they thought they spied where the great elms overhang the road, and on the sinister hillside near the Snake-Den, where the handkerchief was found. Who could pay attention to whispers that spoke of stubby little tracks like those which Randolph Carter's square-toed boots made when he was a small boy? It was as crazy a notion as that other whisper—that the tracks of old Benijah Corey's peculiar heel-less boots had met the stubby little tracks in the road. Old Benijah had been the Carters' hired man when Randolph was young—but he had died thirty years ago.

It must have been these whispers—plus Carter's own statement to Parks and others that the queerly arabesqued Silver Key would help him to unlock the gate of his lost boyhood—which caused a number of mystical students to declare that the missing man had actually doubled back on the trail of time and returned through forty-five years to that other October day in 1883 when he had stayed in the Snake-Den as a small boy. When he came out that night, they argued, he had somehow made the whole trip to 1928 and back—for did he not thereafter know of things which were to happen later? And yet he had never spoken of anything to happen after 1928.

One student—an elderly eccentric of Providence, Rhode Island, who had enjoyed a long and close correspondence with Carter—had a still more elaborate theory, and believed that Carter had not only returned to boyhood, but achieved a further liberation, roving at will through the prismatic vistas of boyhood dream. After a strange vision this man published a tale of Carter's vanishing, in which he hinted that the lost one now reigned as king on the opal throne of Ilek-Vad, that fabulous town of turrets atop the hollow cliffs of glass overlooking the twilight sea wherein the bearded and finny Gnorri build their singular labyrinths.

It was this old man, Ward Phillips, who pleaded most loudly against the apportionment of Carter's estate to his heirs—all distant cousins—on the ground that he was still alive in another time-dimension and might well return some day. Against him was arrayed the legal talent of one of the cousins, Ernest B. Aspinwall of Chicago, a man ten years Carter's senior, but keen as a youth in forensic battles. For four years the contest had raged, but now the time for apportionment had come, and this vast, strange room in New Orleans was to be the scene of the arrangements.

It was the home of Carter's literary and financial executor—the distinguished Creole student of mysteries and Eastern antiquities, Etienne-Laurent de Marigny. Carter had met de Marigny during the war, when they both served in the French Foreign Legion, and had at once cleaved to him because of their similar tastes and outlook. When, on a memorable joint furlough, the learned young Creole had taken the wistful Boston dreamer to Bayonne, in the south of France, and had shewn him certain terrible secrets in the nighted and immemorial crypts that burrow beneath that brooding, aeon-weighted city, the friendship was for ever sealed. Carter's will had named de Marigny as executor, and now that vivid scholar was reluctantly presiding over the settlement of the estate. It was sad work for him, for like the old Rhode-Islander he did not believe that Carter was dead. But what weight have the dreams of mystics against the harsh wisdom of the world?

Around the table in that strange room in the old French quarter sat the men who claimed an interest in the proceedings. There had been the usual legal advertisements of the conference in papers wherever Carter heirs were thought to live, yet only four now sat listening to the abnormal ticking of that coffin-shaped clock which told no earthly time, and to the bubbling of the courtyard fountain beyond half-curtained, fanlighted windows. As the hours wore on the faces of the four were half-shrouded in the curling fumes from the tripods, which, piled recklessly with fuel, seemed to need less and less attention from the silently gliding and increasingly nervous old negro.

There was Etienne de Marigny himself—slim, dark, handsome, moustached, and still young. Aspinwall, representing the heirs, was white-haired, apoplectic-faced, side-whiskered, and portly. Phillips, the Providence mystic, was lean, grey, long-nosed, clean-shaven, and stoop-shouldered. The fourth man was non-committal in age—lean, and with a dark, bearded, singularly immobile face of very regular contour, bound with the turban of a high-caste Brahmin and having night-black, burning, almost irisless eyes which seemed to gaze out from a vast distance behind the features. He had announced himself as the Swami Chandraputra, an adept from Benares with important information to give; and both de Marigny and Phillips—who had corresponded with him—had been quick to recognise the genuineness of his mystical acquirements. His speech had an oddly forced, hollow, metallic quality, as if the use of English taxed his vocal apparatus; yet his language was as easy, correct, and idiomatic as any native Anglo-Saxon's. In general attire he was the normal European civilian, but his loose clothes sat peculiarly badly on him, while his bushy black beard, Eastern turban, and large white mittens gave him an air of exotic eccentricity.

De Marigny, fingering the parchment found in Carter's car, was speaking.

"No, I have not been able to make anything of the parchment. Mr. Phillips, here, also gives it up. Col. Churchward declares it is not Naacal, and it looks nothing at all like the hieroglyphs on that Easter Island wooden club. The carvings on that box, though, do strongly suggest Easter Island images. The nearest thing I can recall to these parchment characters—notice how all the letters seem to hang down from horizontal word-bars—is the writing in a book poor Harley Warren once had. It came from India while Carter and I were visiting him in 1919, and he never would tell us anything about it. Said it would be better if we didn't know, and hinted that it might have come originally from some place other than the earth. He took it with him in December when he went down into the vault in that old graveyard—but neither he nor the book ever came to the surface again. Some time ago I sent our friend here—the Swami Chandraputra—a memory-sketch of some of those letters, and also a photostatic copy of the Carter parchment. He believes he may be able to shed light on them after certain references and consultations.

"But the key—Carter sent me a photograph of that. Its curious arabesques were not letters, but seem to have belonged to the same culture-tradition as the hieroglyphs on the parchment. Carter always spoke of being on the point of solving the mystery, though he never gave details. Once he grew almost poetic about the whole business. That antique Silver Key, he said, would unlock the successive doors that bar our free march down the mighty corridors of space and time to the very Border which no man has crossed since Shaddad with his terrific genius built and concealed in the sands of Arabia Petraea the prodigious domes and uncounted minarets of thousand-pillared Irem. Half-starved dervishes—wrote Carter—and thirst-crazed nomads have returned to tell of that monumental portal, and of the Hand that is sculptured above the keystone of the arch, but no man has passed and returned to say that his footprints on the garnet-strown sands within bear witness to his visit. The key, he surmised, was that for which the Cyclopean sculptured Hand vainly grasps.

"Why Carter didn't take the parchment as well as the key, we cannot say. Perhaps he forgot it—or perhaps he forbore to take it through recollection of one who had taken a book of like characters into a vault and never returned. Or perhaps it was really immaterial to what he wished to do."

As de Marigny paused, old Mr. Phillips spoke in a harsh, shrill voice.

"We can know of Randolph Carter's wandering only what we dream. I have been to many strange places in dreams, and have heard many strange and significant things in Ulthar, beyond the river Skai. It does not appear that the parchment was needed, for certainly, Carter reëntered the world of his boyhood dreams, and is now a king in Ilek-Vad."

Mr. Aspinwall grew doubly apoplectic-looking as he sputtered.

"Can't somebody shut that old fool up? We've had enough of these moonings. The problem is to divide the property, and it's about time we got to it."

For the first time Swami Chandraputra spoke in his queerly alien voice.

"Gentlemen, there is more to this matter than you think. Mr. Aspinwall does not do well to laugh at the evidence of dreams. Mr. Phillips has taken an incomplete view—perhaps because he has not dreamed enough. I, myself, have done much dreaming—we in India have always done that, just as all the Carters seem to have done it. You, Mr. Aspinwall, as a maternal cousin, are naturally not a Carter. My own dreams, and certain other sources of information, have told me a great deal which you still find obscure. For example, Randolph Carter forgot that parchment—which he couldn't then decipher—yet it would have been well for him had he remembered to take it. You see, I really have learned pretty much what happened to Carter after he left his car with the Silver Key at sunset on that seventh of October four years ago."

Aspinwall audibly sneered, but the others sat up with heightened interest. The smoke from the tripods increased, and the crazy ticking of that coffin-shaped clock seemed to fall into bizarre patterns like the dots and dashes of some alien and insoluble telegraph message from outer space. The Hindoo leaned back, half closed his eyes, and continued in that oddly laboured yet idiomatic voice, while before his audience there began to float a picture of what had happened to Randolph Carter.

II.

The hills behind Arkham are full of a strange magic—something, perhaps, which the old wizard Edmund Carter called down from the stars and up from the crypts of nether earth when he fled there from Salem in 1692. As soon as Randolph Carter was back among them he knew that he was close to one of the gates which a few audacious, abhorred, and alien-souled men have blasted through the titan walls betwixt the world and the outside absolute. Here, he felt, and on this day of the year, he could carry out with success the message he had deciphered months before from the arabesques of that tarnished and incredibly ancient Silver Key. He knew now how it must be rotated, how it must be held up to the setting sun, and what syllables of ceremony must be intoned into the void at the ninth and last turning. In a spot as close to a dark polarity and induced gate as this, it could not fail in its primary function. Certainly, he would rest that night in the lost boyhood for which he had never ceased to mourn.

He got out of the car with the key in his pocket, walking uphill deeper and deeper into the shadowy core of that brooding, haunted countryside of winding road, vine-grown stone wall, black woodland, gnarled, neglected orchard, gaping-windowed, deserted farmhouse, and nameless ruin. At the sunset hour, when the distant spires of Kingsport gleamed in the ruddy blaze, he took out the key and made the needed turnings and intonations. Only later did he realise how soon the ritual had taken effect.

Then in the deepening twilight he had heard a voice out of the past. Old Benijah Corey, his great-uncle's hired man. Had not old Benijah been dead for thirty years? Thirty years before when? What was time? Where had he been? Why was it strange that Benijah should be calling him on this seventh of October, 1883? Was he not out later than Aunt Martha had told him to stay? What was this key in his blouse pocket, where his little telescope—given him by his father on his ninth birthday two months before—ought to be? Had he found it in the attic at home? Would it unlock the mystic pylon which his sharp eye had traced amidst the jagged rocks at the back of that inner cave behind the Snake-Den on the hill? That was the place they always coupled with old Edmund Carter the wizard. People wouldn't go there, and nobody but he had ever noticed or squirmed through the root-choked fissure to that great black inner chamber with the pylon. Whose hands had carved that hint of a pylon out of the living rock? Old Wizard

Edmund's—or *others* that he had conjured up and commanded? That evening little Randolph ate supper with Uncle Chris and Aunt Martha in the old gambrel-roofed farmhouse.

Next morning he was up early, and out through the twisted-boughed apple orchard to the upper timber-lot where the mouth of the Snake-Den lurked black and forbidding amongst grotesque, overnourished oaks. A nameless expectancy was upon him, and he did not even notice the loss of his handkerchief as he fumbled in his blouse pocket to see if the queer Silver Key was safe. He crawled through the dark orifice with tense, adventurous assurance, lighting his way with matches taken from the sitting-room. In another moment he had wriggled through the root-choked fissure at the farther end, and was in the vast, unknown inner grotto whose ultimate rock wall seemed half like a monstrous and consciously shapen pylon. Before that dank, dripping wall he stood silent and awestruck, lighting one match after another as he gazed. Was that stony bulge above the keystone of the imagined arch really a gigantic sculptured hand? Then he drew forth the Silver Key, and made motions and intonations whose source he could only dimly remember. Was anything forgotten? He knew only that he wished to cross the barrier to the untrammelled land of his dreams and the gulfs where all dimensions dissolve in the absolute.

III.

What happened then is scarcely to be described in words. It is full of those paradoxes, contradictions, and anomalies which have no place in waking life, but which fill our more fantastic dreams, and are taken as matters of course till we return to our narrow, rigid, objective world of limited causation and tri-dimensional logic. As the Hindoo continued his tale, he had difficulty in avoiding what seemed—even more than the notion of a man transferred through the years to boyhood—an air of trivial, puerile extravagance. Mr. Aspinwall, in disgust, gave an apoplectic snort and virtually stopped listening.

For the rite of the Silver Key, as practiced by Randolph Carter in that black, haunted cave within a cave, did not prove unavailing. From the first gesture and syllable an aura of strange, awesome mutation was apparent—a sense of incalculable disturbance and confusion in time and space, yet one which held no hint of what we recognise as motion and duration. Imperceptibly, such things as age and location ceased to have any significance whatever. The day before, Randolph Carter had miraculously leaped a gulf of years. Now there was no distinction between boy and man. There was only the entity Randolph Carter, with a certain store of images which had lost all connexion with terrestrial scenes and circumstances of acquisition. A moment before, there had been an inner cave with vague suggestions of a monstrous arch and gigantic sculptured hand on the farther wall. Now there was neither cave nor absence of cave; neither wall nor absence of wall. There was only a flux of impressions not so much visual as cerebral, amidst which the entity that was Randolph Carter experienced perceptions or registrations of all that his mind revolved on, yet without any clear consciousness of the way in which he received them.

By the time the rite was over Carter knew that he was in no region whose place could be told by earth's geographers, and in no age whose date history could fix. For the nature of what was happening was not wholly unfamiliar to him. There were hints of it in the cryptical Pnakotic fragments, and a whole chapter in the forbidden *Necronomicon* of the mad Arab Abdul Alhazred had taken on significance when he had deciphered the designs graven on the Silver Key. A gate had been unlocked—not indeed the Ultimate Gate, but one leading from earth and time to that extension of earth which is outside time, and from which in turn the Ultimate Gate leads fearsomely and perilously to the Last Void which is outside all earths, all universes, and all matter.

There would be a Guide—and a very terrible one; a Guide who had been an entity of earth millions of years before, when man was undreamed of, and when forgotten shapes moved on a steaming planet building strange cities among whose last, crumbling ruins the earliest mammals were to play. Carter remembered what the monstrous "Necronomicon" had vaguely and disconcertingly adumbrated concerning that Guide.

"And while there are those," the mad Arab had written, "who have dared to seek glimpses beyond the Veil, and to accept HIM as a Guide, they would have been more prudent had they avoided commerce with HIM; for it is written in the Book of Thoth how terrific is the price of a single glimpse. Nor may those who pass ever return, for in the Vastnesses transcending our world are Shapes of darkness that seize and bind. The Affair that shambleth about in the night, the Evil that defieth the Elder Sign, the Herd that stand watch at the secret portal each tomb is known to have, and that thrive on that which groweth out of the tenants within—all these Blacknesses are lesser than HE Who guardeth the Gateway; HE Who will guide the rash one beyond all the worlds into the Abyss of unnamable Devourers. For HE is 'UMR AT-TAWIL, the Most Ancient One, that the scribe rendereth as THE PROLONGED OF LIFE."

Memory and imagination shaped dim half-pictures with uncertain outlines amidst the seething chaos, but Carter knew that they were of memory and imagination only. Yet he felt that it was not chance which built these things in his consciousness, but rather some vast reality, ineffable and undimensioned, which surrounded him and strove to translate itself into the only symbols he was capable of grasping. For no mind of earth may grasp the extensions of shape which interweave in the oblique gulfs outside time and the dimensions we know.

There floated before Carter a cloudy pageantry of shapes and scenes which he somehow linked with earth's primal, aeon-forgotten past. Monstrous living things moved deliberately through vistas of fantastic handiwork that no sane dream ever held, and landscapes bore incredible vegetation and cliffs and mountains and masonry of no human pattern. There were cities under the sea, and denizens thereof; and towers in great deserts where globes and cylinders and nameless winged entities shot off into space or hurtled down out of space. All this Carter grasped, though the images bore no fixed relation to one another or to him. He himself had no stable form or position, but only such shifting hints of form and position as his whirling fancy supplied.

He had wished to find the enchanted regions of his boyhood dreams, where galleys sail up the river Oukranos past the gilded spires of Thran, and elephant caravans tramp through perfumed jungles in Kled beyond forgotten palaces with veined ivory columns that sleep lovely and unbroken under the moon. Now, intoxicated with wider visions, he scarcely knew what he sought. Thoughts of infinite and blasphemous daring rose in his mind, and he knew he would face the dreaded Guide without fear, asking monstrous and terrible things of him.

All at once the pageant of impressions seemed to achieve a vague kind of stabilisation. There were great masses of towering stone, carven into alien and incomprehensible designs and disposed according to the laws of some unknown, inverse geometry. Light filtered down from a sky of no assignable colour in baffling, contradictory directions, and played almost sentiently over what seemed to be a curved line of gigantic hieroglyphed pedestals more hexagonal than otherwise and surmounted by cloaked, ill-defined Shapes.

There was another Shape, too, which occupied no pedestal, but which seemed to glide or float over the cloudy, floor-like lower level. It was not exactly permanent in outline, but held transient suggestions of something remotely preceding or paralleling the human form, though half as large again as an ordinary man. It seemed to be heavily cloaked, like the Shapes on the pedestals, with some neutral-coloured fabric; and Carter could not detect any eye-holes through which it might gaze. Probably it did not need to gaze, for it seemed to belong to an order of being far outside the merely physical in organisation and faculties.

A moment later Carter knew that this was so, for the Shape had spoken to his mind without sound or language. And though the name it uttered was a dreaded and terrible one, Randolph Carter did not flinch in fear. Instead, he spoke back, equally without sound or language, and made those obeisances which the hideous "Necronomicon" had taught him to make. For this Shape was nothing less than that which all the world has feared since Lomar rose out of the sea and the Winged Ones came to earth to teach the Elder Lore to man. It was indeed the frightful Guide and Guardian of the Gate—'Umr at-Tawil, the Most Ancient One, that the scribe rendereth the Prolonged of Life.

The Guide knew, as he knew all things, of Carter's quest and coming, and that this seeker of dreams and secrets stood before him unafraid. There was no horror or malignity in what he radiated, and Carter wondered for a moment whether the mad Arab's terrific, blasphemous hints, and extracts from the Book of Thoth, might not have come from envy and a baffled wish to do what was now about to be done. Or perhaps the Guide reserved his horror and malignity for those who feared. As the radiations continued, Carter mentally interpreted them in the form of words.

"I am indeed that Most Ancient One," said the Guide, "of whom you know. We have awaited you—the Ancient Ones and I. You are welcome, even though long delayed. You have the Key, and have unlocked the First Gate. Now the Ultimate Gate is ready for your trial. If you fear, you need not advance. You may still go back unharmed the way you came. But if you choose to advance …"

The pause was ominous, but the radiations continued to be friendly. Carter hesitated not a moment, for a burning curiosity drove him on.

"I will advance," he radiated back, "and I accept you as my Guide."

At this reply the Guide seemed to make a sign by certain motions of his robe which may or may not have involved the lifting of an arm or some homologous member. A second sign followed, and from his well-learnt lore Carter knew that he was at last very close to the Ultimate Gate. The light now changed to another inexplicable colour, and the Shapes on the quasi-hexagonal pedestals became more clearly defined. As they sat more erect, their outlines became more like those of men, though Carter knew that they could not be men. Upon their cloaked heads there now seemed to rest tall, uncertainly coloured mitres, strangely suggestive of those on certain nameless figures chiselled by a forgotten sculptor along the living cliffs of a high, forbidden mountain in Tartary; while grasped in certain folds of their swathings were long sceptres whose carven heads bodied forth a grotesque and archaic mystery.

Carter guessed what they were, whence they came, and Whom they served; and guessed, too, the price of their service. But he was still content, for at one mighty venture he was to learn all. Damnation, he reflected, is but a word bandied about by those whose blindness leads them to condemn all who can see, even with a single eye. He wondered at the vast conceit of those who had babbled of the *malignant* Ancient Ones, as if They could pause from their everlasting dreams to wreak a wrath upon mankind. As well, he thought, might a mammoth pause to visit frantic vengeance on an angleworm. Now the whole assemblage on the vaguely hexagonal pillars was greeting him with a gesture of those oddly carven sceptres, and radiating a message which he understood:

"We salute you, Most Ancient One, and you, Randolph Carter, whose daring has made you one of us."

Carter saw now that one of the pedestals was vacant, and a gesture of the Most Ancient One told him it was reserved for him. He saw also another pedestal, taller than the rest, and at the centre of the oddly curved line (neither semicircle nor ellipse, parabola nor hyperbola) which they formed. This, he guessed, was the Guide's own throne. Moving and rising in a manner hardly definable, Carter took his seat; and as he did so he saw that the Guide had likewise seated himself.

Gradually and mistily it became apparent that the Most Ancient One was holding something—some object clutched in the outflung folds of his robe as if for the sight, or what answered for sight, of the cloaked Companions. It was a large sphere or apparent sphere of some obscurely iridescent metal, and as the Guide put it forward a low, pervasive half-impression of *sound* began to rise and fall in intervals which seemed to be rhythmic even though they followed no rhythm of earth. There was a suggestion of chanting—or what human imagination might interpret as chanting. Presently the quasi-sphere began to grow luminous, and as it gleamed up into a cold, pulsating light of unassignable colour Carter saw that its flickerings conformed to the alien rhythm of the chant. Then all the mitred, sceptre-bearing Shapes on the pedestals commenced a slight, curious swaying in the same inexplicable rhythm, while nimbuses of unclassifiable light—resembling that of the quasi-sphere—played round their shrouded heads.

The Hindoo paused in his tale and looked curiously at the tall, coffin-shaped clock with the four hands and hieroglyphed dial, whose crazy ticking followed no known rhythm of earth.

"You, Mr. de Marigny," he suddenly said to his learned host, "do not need to be told the particular alien rhythm to which those cowled Shapes on the hexagonal pillars chanted and nodded. You are the only one else—in America—who has had a taste of the outer extension. That clock—I suppose it was sent you by the Yogi poor Harley Warren used to talk about—the seer who said that he alone of living men had been to Yian-Ho, the hidden legacy of sinister, aeon-old Leng, and had borne certain things away from that dreadful and forbidden city. I wonder how many of its subtler properties you know? If my dreams and readings be correct, it was made by those who knew much of the First Gateway. But let me go on with my tale."

At last, continued the Swami, the swaying and the suggestion of chanting ceased, the lambent nimbuses around the now drooping and motionless heads faded away, while the cloaked Shapes slumped curiously on their pedestals. The quasi-sphere, however, continued to pulsate with inexplicable light. Carter felt that the Ancient Ones were sleeping as they had been when he first saw them, and he wondered out of what cosmic dreams his coming had wakened them. Slowly there filtered into his mind the truth that this strange chanting ritual had been one of instruction, and that the Companions had been chanted by the Most Ancient One into a new and peculiar kind of sleep, in order that their dreams might open the Ultimate Gate to which the Silver Key was a passport. He knew that in the profundity of this deep sleep they were contemplating unplumbed vastnesses of utter and absolute Outsideness with which the earth has nothing to do, and that they were to accomplish that which his presence had demanded.

The Guide did not share this sleep, but seemed still to be giving instructions in some subtle, soundless way. Evidently he was implanting images of those things which he wished the Companions to dream; and Carter knew that as each of the Ancient Ones pictured the prescribed thought, there would be born the nucleus of a manifestation visible to his own earthly eyes. When the dreams of all the Shapes had achieved a oneness, that manifestation would occur, and everything he required would be materialised, through concentration. He had seen such things on earth—in India, where the combined, projected will of a circle of adepts can make a thought take tangible substance, and in hoary Atlaanât, of which few men dare speak.

Just what the Ultimate Gate was, and how it was to be passed, Carter could not be certain; but a feeling of tense expectancy surged over him. He was conscious of having a kind of body, and of holding the fateful Silver Key in his hand. The masses of towering stone opposite him seemed to possess the evenness of a wall, toward the centre of which his eyes were irresistibly drawn. And then suddenly he felt the mental currents of the Most Ancient One cease to flow forth.

For the first time Carter realised how terrific utter silence, mental and physical, may be. The earlier moments had never failed to contain some perceptible rhythm, if only the faint, cryptical pulse of the earth's dimensional extension, but now the hush of the abyss seemed to fall upon everything. Despite his intimations of body, he had no audible breath; and the glow of 'Umr at-Tawil's quasi-sphere had grown petrifiedly fixed and unpulsating. A potent nimbus, brighter than those which had played round the heads of the Shapes, blazed frozenly over the shrouded skull of the terrible Guide.

A dizziness assailed Carter, and his sense of lost orientation waxed a thousandfold. The strange lights seemed to hold the quality of the most impenetrable blacknesses heaped upon blacknesses, while about the Ancient Ones, so close on their pseudo-hexagonal thrones, there hovered an air of the most stupefying remoteness. Then he felt himself wafted into immeasurable depths, with waves of perfumed warmth lapping against his face. It was as if he floated in a torrid, rose-tinctured sea; a sea of drugged wine whose waves broke foaming against shores of brazen fire. A great fear clutched him as he half saw that vast expanse of surging sea lapping against its far-off coast. But the moment of silence was broken—the surgings were speaking to him in a language that was not of physical sound or articulate words.

"The man of Truth is beyond good and evil," intoned a voice that was not a voice. "The man of Truth has ridden to All-Is-One. The man of Truth has learnt that Illusion is the only reality, and that substance is an impostor."

And now, in that rise of masonry to which his eyes had been so irresistibly drawn, there appeared the outline of a titanic arch not unlike that which he thought he had glimpsed so long ago in that cave within a cave, on the far, unreal surface of the three-dimensioned earth. He realised that he had been using the Silver Key—moving it in accord with an unlearnt and instinctive ritual closely akin to that which had opened the Inner Gate. That rose-drunken sea which lapped his cheeks was, he realised, no more or less than the adamantine mass of the solid wall yielding before his spell, and the vortex of thought with which the Ancient Ones had aided his spell. Still guided by instinct and blind determination, he floated forward—and through the Ultimate Gate.

IV.

Randolph Carter's advance through that Cyclopean bulk of abnormal masonry was like a dizzy precipitation through the measureless gulfs between the stars. From a great distance he felt triumphant, godlike surges of deadly sweetness, and after that the rustling of great wings, and impressions of sound like the chirpings and murmurings of objects unknown on earth or in the solar system. Glancing backward, he saw not one gate alone, but a multiplicity of gates, at some of which clamoured Forms he strove not to remember.

And then, suddenly, he felt a greater terror than that which any of the Forms could give—a terror from which he could not flee because it was connected with himself. Even the First Gateway had taken something of stability from him, leaving him uncertain about his bodily form and about his relationship to the mistily defined objects around him, but it had not disturbed his sense of unity. He had still been Randolph Carter, a fixed point in the dimensional seething. Now, beyond the Ultimate Gateway, he realised in a moment of consuming fright that he was not one person, but many persons.

He was in many places at the same time. On earth, on October 7, 1883, a little boy named Randolph Carter was leaving the Snake-Den in the hushed evening light and running down the rocky slope and through the twisted-boughed orchard toward his Uncle Christopher's house in the hills behind Arkham—yet at that same moment, which was also somehow in the earthly year of 1928, a vague shadow not less Randolph Carter was sitting on a pedestal among the Ancient Ones in earth's trans-dimensional extension. Here, too, was a third Randolph Carter in the unknown and formless cosmic abyss beyond the Ultimate Gate. And elsewhere, in a chaos of scenes whose infinite multiplicity and monstrous diversity brought him close to the brink of madness, were a limitless confusion of beings which he knew were as much himself as the local manifestation now beyond the Ultimate Gate.

There were "Carters" in settings belonging to every known and suspected age of earth's history, and to remoter ages of earthly entity transcending knowledge, suspicion, and credibility. "Carters" of forms both human and non-human, vertebrate and invertebrate, conscious and mindless, animal and vegetable. And more, there were "Carters" having nothing in common with earthly life, but moving outrageously amidst backgrounds of other planets and systems and galaxies and cosmic continua. Spores of eternal life drifting from world to world, universe to universe, yet all equally himself. Some of the glimpses recalled dreams—both faint and vivid, single and persistent—which he had had through the long years since he first began to dream, and a few possessed a haunting, fascinating, and almost horrible familiarity which no earthly logic could explain.

Faced with this realisation, Randolph Carter reeled in the clutch of supreme horror—horror such as had not been hinted even at the climax of that hideous night when two had ventured into an ancient and abhorred necropolis under a waning moon and only one had emerged. No death, no doom, no anguish can arouse the surpassing despair which flows from a loss of *identity*. Merging with nothingness is peaceful oblivion; but to be aware of existing and yet to know that one is no longer a definite being distinguished from other beings—that one no longer has a *self*—that is the nameless summit of agony and dread.

He knew that there had been a Randolph Carter of Boston, yet could not be sure whether he—the fragment or facet of an entity beyond the Ultimate Gate—had been that one or some other. His *self* had been annihilated; and yet he—if indeed there could, in view of that utter nullity of individual existence, be such a thing as *he*—was equally aware of being in some inconceivable way a legion of selves. It was as though his body had been suddenly transformed into one of those many-limbed and many-headed effigies sculptured in Indian temples, and he contemplated the aggregation in a bewildered attempt to discern which was the original and which the additions—if indeed (supremely monstrous thought) there *were* any original as distinguished from other embodiments.

Then, in the midst of these devastating reflections, Carter's beyond-the-gate fragment was hurled from what had seemed the nadir of horror to black, clutching pits of a horror still more profound. This time it was largely external—a force or personality which at once confronted and surrounded and pervaded him, and which in addition to its local presence, seemed also to be a part of himself, and likewise to be coexistent with all time and coterminous with all space. There was no visual image, yet the sense of entity and the awful concept of combined localism, identity, and infinity lent a paralysing terror beyond anything which any Carter-fragment had hitherto deemed capable of existing.

In the face of that awful wonder, the quasi-Carter forgot the horror of destroyed individuality. It was an All-in-One and One-in-All of limitless being and self—not merely a thing of one Space-Time continuum, but allied to the ultimate animating essence of existence's whole unbounded sweep—the last, utter sweep which has no confines and which outreaches fancy and mathematics alike. It was perhaps that which certain secret cults of earth have whispered of as YOG-SOTHOTH, and which has been a deity under other names; that which the crustaceans of Yuggoth worship as the Beyond-One, and which the vaporous brains of the spiral nebulae know by an untranslatable Sign—yet in a flash the Carter-facet realised how slight and fractional all these conceptions are.

And now the BEING was addressing the Carter-facet in prodigious waves that smote and burned and thundered—a concentration of energy that blasted its recipient with well-nigh unendurable violence, and that followed, with certain definite variations, the singular unearthly rhythm which had marked the chanting and swaying of the Ancient Ones, and the flickering of the monstrous lights, in that baffling region beyond the First Gate. It was as though suns and worlds and universes had converged upon one point whose very position in space they had conspired to annihilate with an impact of resistless fury. But amidst the greater terror one lesser terror was diminished; for the searing waves appeared somehow to isolate the beyond-the-gate Carter from his infinity of duplicates—to restore, as it were, a certain amount of the illusion of identity. After a time the hearer began to translate the waves into speech-forms known to him, and his sense of horror and oppression waned. Fright became pure awe, and what had seemed blasphemously abnormal seemed now only ineffably majestic.

"Randolph Carter," IT seemed to say, "MY manifestations on your planet's extension, the Ancient Ones, have sent you as one who would lately have returned to small lands of dream which he had lost, yet who with greater freedom has risen to greater and nobler desires and curiosities. You wished to sail up golden Oukranos, to search out forgotten ivory cities in orchid-heavy Kled, and to reign on the opal throne of Ilek-Vad, whose fabulous towers and numberless domes rise mighty toward a single red star in a firmament alien to your earth and to all matter. Now, with the passing of two Gates, you wish loftier things. You would not flee like a child from a scene disliked to a dream beloved, but would plunge like a man into that last and inmost of secrets which lies behind all scenes and dreams.

"What you wish, I have found good; and I am ready to grant that which I have granted eleven times only to beings of your planet—five times only to those you call men, or those resembling them. I am ready to shew you the Ultimate Mystery, to look on which is to blast a feeble spirit. Yet before you gaze full at that last and first of secrets you may still wield a free choice, and return if you will through the two Gates with the Veil still unrent before your eyes."

V.

A sudden shutting-off of the waves left Carter in a chilling and awesome silence full of the spirit of desolation. On every hand pressed the illimitable vastness of the void, yet the seeker knew that the BEING was still there. After a moment he thought of words whose mental substance he flung into the abyss:

"I accept. I will not retreat."

The waves surged forth again, and Carter knew that the BEING had heard. And now there poured from that limitless MIND a flood of knowledge and explanation which opened new vistas to the seeker, and prepared him for such a grasp of the cosmos as he had never hoped to possess. He was told how childish and limited is the notion of a tri-dimensional world, and what an infinity of directions there are besides the known directions of up-down, forward-backward, and right-left. He was shewn the smallness and tinsel emptiness of the little gods of earth, with their petty human interests and connexions—their hatreds, rages, loves, and vanities; their craving for praise and sacrifice, and their demands for faiths contrary to Nature and reason.

While most of the impressions translated themselves to Carter as words, there were others to which other senses gave interpretation. Perhaps with eyes and perhaps with imagination he perceived that he was in a region of dimensions beyond those conceivable to the eye and brain of man. He saw now, in the brooding shadows of that which had been first a vortex of power and then an illimitable void, a sweep of creation that dizzied his senses. From some inconceivable vantage-point he looked upon prodigious forms whose multiple extensions transcended any conception of being, size, and boundaries which his mind had hitherto been able to hold, despite a lifetime of cryptical study. He began to understand dimly why there could exist at the same time the little boy Randolph Carter in the Arkham farmhouse in 1883, the misty form on the vaguely hexagonal pillar beyond the First Gate, the fragment now facing the PRESENCE in the limitless abyss, and all the other "Carters" his fancy or perception envisaged.

Then the waves increased in strength, and sought to improve his understanding, reconciling him to the multiform entity of which his present fragment was an infinitesimal part. They told him that every figure of space is but the result of the intersection by a plane of some corresponding figure of one more dimension—as a square is cut from a cube or a circle from a sphere. The cube and sphere, of three dimensions, are thus cut from corresponding forms of four dimensions that men know only through guesses and dreams; and these in turn are cut from forms of five dimensions, and so on up to the dizzy and reachless heights of archetypal infinity. The world of men and of the gods of men is merely an infinitesimal phase of an infinitesimal thing—the three-dimensional phase of that small wholeness reached by the First Gate, where 'Umr at-Tawil dictates dreams to the Ancient Ones. Though men hail it as reality and brand thoughts of its many-dimensioned original as unreality, it is in truth the very opposite. That which we call substance and reality is shadow and illusion, and that which we call shadow and illusion is substance and reality.

Time, the waves went on, is motionless, and without beginning or end. That it has motion, and is the cause of change, is an illusion. Indeed, it is itself really an illusion, for except to the narrow sight of beings in limited dimensions there are no such things as past, present, and future. Men think of time only because of what they call change, yet that too is illusion. All that was, and is, and is to be, exists simultaneously.

These revelations came with a godlike solemnity which left Carter unable to doubt. Even though they lay almost beyond his comprehension, he felt that they must be true in the light of that final cosmic reality which belies all local perspectives and narrow partial views; and he was familiar enough with profound speculations to be free from the bondage of local and partial conceptions. Had his whole quest not been based upon a faith in the unreality of the local and the partial?

After an impressive pause the waves continued, saying that what the denizens of few-dimensioned zones call change is merely a function of their consciousness, which views the external world from various cosmic angles. As the shapes produced by the cutting of a cone seem to vary with the angles of cutting—being circle, ellipse, parabola, or hyperbola according to that angle, yet without any change in the cone itself—so do the local aspects of an unchanged and endless reality seem to change with the cosmic angle of regarding. To this variety of angles of consciousness the feeble beings of the inner worlds are slaves, since with rare exceptions they cannot learn to control them. Only a few students of forbidden things have gained inklings of this control, and have thereby conquered time and change. But the entities outside the Gates command all angles, and view the myriad parts of the cosmos in terms of fragmentary, change-involving perspective, or of the changeless totality beyond perspective, in accordance with their will.

As the waves paused again, Carter began to comprehend, vaguely and terrifiedly, the ultimate background of that riddle of lost individuality which had at first so horrified him. His intuition pieced together the fragments of revelation, and brought him closer and closer to a grasp of the secret. He understood that much of the frightful revelation would have come upon him—splitting up his ego amongst myriads of earthly counterparts—inside the First Gate, had not the magic of 'Umr at-Tawil kept it from him in order that he might use the Silver Key with precision for the Ultimate Gate's opening. Anxious for clearer knowledge, he sent out waves of thought, asking more of the exact relationship between his various facets—the fragment now beyond the Ultimate Gate, the fragment still on the quasi-hexagonal pedestal beyond the First Gate, the boy of 1883, the man of 1928, the various ancestral beings who had formed his heritage and the bulwark of his ego, and the nameless denizens of other aeons and other worlds which that first hideous flash of ultimate perception had identified with him. Slowly the waves of the BEING surged out in reply, trying to make plain what was almost beyond the reach of an earthly mind.

All descended lines of beings of the finite dimensions, continued the waves, and all stages of growth in each one of these beings, are merely manifestations of one archetypal and eternal being in the space outside dimensions. Each local being—son, father, grandfather, and so on—and each stage of individual being—infant, child, boy, young man, old man—is merely one of the infinite phases of that same archetypal and eternal being, caused by a variation in the angle of the consciousness-plane which cuts it. Randolph Carter at all ages; Randolph Carter and all his ancestors both human and pre-human, terrestrial and pre-terrestrial; all these were only phases of one ultimate, eternal "Carter" outside space and time—phantom projections differentiated only by the angle at which the plane of consciousness happened to cut the eternal archetype in each case.

A slight change of angle could turn the student of today into the child of yesterday; could turn Randolph Carter into that wizard Edmund Carter who fled from Salem to the hills behind Arkham in 1692, or that Pickman Carter who in the year 2169 would use strange means in repelling the Mongol hordes from Australia; could turn a human Carter into one of those earlier entities which had dwelt in primal Hyperborea and worshipped black, plastic Tsathoggua after flying down from Kythanil, the double planet that once revolved round Arcturus; could turn a terrestrial Carter to a remotely ancestral and doubtfully shaped dweller on Kythanil itself, or a still remoter creature of trans-galactic Shonhi, or a four-dimensioned gaseous consciousness in an older space-time continuum, or a vegetable brain of the future on a dark, radio-active comet of inconceivable orbit—and so on, in the endless cosmic circle.

The archetypes, throbbed the waves, are the people of the ultimate abyss—formless, ineffable, and guessed at only by rare dreamers on the low-dimensioned worlds. Chief among such was this informing BEING Itself ... *which indeed was Carter's own archetype.* The glutless zeal of Carter and all his forbears for forbidden cosmic secrets was a natural result of derivation from the SUPREME ARCHETYPE. On every world all great wizards, all great thinkers, all great artists, are facets of IT.

Almost stunned with awe, and with a kind of terrifying delight, Randolph Carter's consciousness did homage to that transcendent ENTITY from which it was derived. As the waves paused again he pondered in the mighty silence, thinking of strange tributes, stranger questions, and still stranger requests. Curious concepts flowed conflictingly through a brain dazed with unaccustomed vistas and unforeseen disclosures. It occurred to him that, if those disclosures were literally true, he might *bodily* visit all those infinitely distant ages and parts of the universe which he had hitherto known only in dreams, could he but command the magic to change the angle of his consciousness-plane. And did not the Silver Key supply that magic? Had it not first changed him from a man in 1928 to a boy in 1883, and then to something quite outside time? Oddly, despite his present apparent absence of body, he knew that the Key was still with him.

While the silence still lasted, Randolph Carter radiated forth the thoughts and questions which assailed him. He knew that in this ultimate abyss he was equidistant from every facet of his archetype—human or non-human, earthly or extra-earthly, galactic or trans-galactic; and his curiosity regarding the other phases of his being—especially those phases which were farthest from an earthly 1928 in time and space, or which had most persistently haunted his dreams throughout life—was at fever heat. He felt that his archetypal ENTITY could at will send him bodily to any of these phases of bygone and distant life by changing his consciousness-plane, and despite the marvels he had undergone he burned for the further marvel of walking in the flesh through those grotesque and incredible scenes which visions of the night had fragmentarily brought him.

Without definite intention he was asking the PRESENCE for access to a dim, fantastic world whose five multi-coloured suns, alien constellations, dizzy black crags, clawed, tapir-snouted denizens, bizarre metal towers, unexplained tunnels, and cryptical floating cylinders had intruded again and again upon his slumbers. That world, he felt vaguely, was in all the conceivable cosmos the one most freely in touch with others; and he longed to explore the vistas whose beginnings he had glimpsed, and to embark through space to those still remoter worlds with which the clawed, snouted denizens trafficked. There was no time for fear. As at all crises of his strange life, sheer cosmic curiosity triumphed over everything else.

When the waves resumed their awesome pulsing Carter knew that his terrible request was granted. The BEING was telling him of the nighted gulfs through which he would have to pass, of the unknown quintuple star in an unsuspected galaxy around which the alien world revolved, and of the burrowing inner horrors against which the clawed, snouted race of that world perpetually fought. IT told him, too, of how the angle of his personal consciousness-plane, and the angle of his consciousness-plane regarding the space-time elements of the sought-for world, would have to be tilted simultaneously in order to restore to that world the Carter-facet which had dwelt there.

The PRESENCE warned him to be sure of his symbols if he wished ever to return from the remote and alien world he had chosen, and he radiated back an impatient affirmation; confident that the Silver Key, which he felt was with him and which he knew had tilted both world and personal planes in throwing him back to 1883, contained those symbols which were meant. And now the BEING, grasping his impatience, signified Its readiness to accomplish the monstrous precipitation. The waves abruptly ceased, and there supervened a momentary stillness tense with nameless and dreadful expectancy.

Then, without warning, came a whirring and drumming that swelled to a terrific thundering. Once again Carter felt himself the focal point of an intense concentration of energy which smote and hammered and seared unbearably in the now-familiar alien rhythm of outer space, and which he could not classify as either the blasting heat of a blazing star or the all-petrifying cold of the ultimate abyss. Bands and rays of colour utterly foreign to any spectrum of our universe played and wove and interlaced before him, and he was conscious of a frightful velocity of motion. He caught one fleeting glimpse of a figure sitting *alone* upon a cloudy throne more hexagonal than otherwise....

VI.

As the Hindoo paused in his story he saw that de Marigny and Phillips were watching him absorbedly. Aspinwall pretended to ignore the narrative, and kept his eyes ostentatiously on the papers before him. The alien-rhythmed ticking of the coffin-shaped clock took on a new and portentous meaning, while the fumes from the choked, neglected tripods wove themselves into fantastic and inexplicable shapes, and formed disturbing combinations with the grotesque figures of the draught-swayed tapestries. The old negro who had tended them was gone—perhaps some growing tension had frightened him out of the house. An almost apologetic hesitancy hampered the speaker as he resumed in his oddly laboured yet idiomatic voice.

"You have found these things of the abyss hard to believe," he said, "but you will find the tangible and material things ahead still harder. That is the way of our minds. Marvels are doubly incredible when brought into three dimensions from the vague regions of possible dream. I shall not try to tell you much—that would be another and very different story. I will tell only what you absolutely have to know."

Carter, after that final vortex of alien and polychromatic rhythm, had found himself in what for a moment he thought was his old insistent dream. He was, as many a night before, walking amidst throngs of clawed, snouted beings through the streets of a labyrinth of inexplicably fashioned metal under a blaze of diverse solar colour; and as he looked down he saw that his body was like those of the others—rugose, partly squamous, and curiously articulated in a fashion mainly insect-like yet not without a caricaturish resemblance to the human outline. The Silver Key was still in his grasp—though held by a noxious-looking claw.

In another moment the dream-sense vanished, and he felt rather as one just awaked from a dream. The ultimate abyss—the BEING—an entity of absurd, outlandish race called "Randolph Carter" on a world of the future not yet born—some of these things were parts of the persistent, recurrent dreams of the wizard Zkauba on the planet Yaddith. They were too persistent—they interfered with his duties in weaving spells to keep the frightful Dholes in their burrows, and became mixed up with his recollections of the myriad real worlds he had visited in his light-beam envelope. And now they had become quasi-real as never before. This heavy, material Silver Key in his right upper claw, exact image of one he had dreamt about, meant no good. He must rest and reflect, and consult the Tablets of Nhing for advice on what to do. Climbing a metal wall in a lane off the main concourse, he entered his apartment and approached the rack of tablets.

Seven day-fractions later Zkauba squatted on his prism in awe and half-despair, for the truth had opened up a new and conflicting set of memories. Nevermore could he know the peace of being one entity. For all time and space he was two—Zkauba the Wizard of Yaddith, disgusted with the thought of the repellent earth-mammal Carter that he was to be and had been, and Randolph Carter, of Boston on the earth, shivering with fright at the clawed, snouted thing which he had once been, and had become again.

The time-units spent on Yaddith, croaked the Swami—whose laboured voice was beginning to shew signs of fatigue—made a tale in themselves which could not be related in brief compass. There were trips to Shonhi and Mthura and Kath, and other worlds in the twenty-eight galaxies accessible to the light-beam envelopes of the creatures of Yaddith, and trips back and forth through aeons of time with the aid of the Silver Key and various other symbols known to Yaddith's wizards. There were hideous struggles with the bleached, viscous Dholes in the primal tunnels that honeycombed the planet. There were awed sessions in libraries amongst the massed lore of ten thousand worlds living and dead. There were tense conferences with other minds of Yaddith, including that of the Arch-Ancient Buo. Zkauba told no one of what had befallen his personality, but when the Randolph Carter facet was uppermost he would study furiously every possible means of returning to the earth and to human form, and would desperately practice human speech with the buzzing, alien throat-organs so ill adapted to it.

The Carter-facet had soon learned with horror that the Silver Key was unable to effect his return to human form. It was, as he deduced too late from things he remembered, things he dreamed, and things he inferred from the lore of Yaddith, a product of Hyperborea on the earth; with power over the personal consciousness-angles of human beings alone. It could, however, change the planetary angle and send the user at will through time in an unchanged body. There had been an added spell which gave it the limitless powers it otherwise lacked; but this, too, was a human discovery—peculiar to a spatially unreachable region, and not to be duplicated by the wizards of Yaddith. It had been written on the undecipherable parchment in the hideously carven box with the Silver Key, and Carter bitterly lamented that he had left it behind. The now inaccessible BEING of the abyss had warned him to be sure of his symbols, and had doubtless thought he lacked nothing.

As time wore on he strove harder and harder to utilise the monstrous lore of Yaddith in finding a way back to the abyss and the omnipotent ENTITY. With his new knowledge he could have done much toward reading the cryptic parchment; but that power, under present conditions, was merely ironic. There were times, however, when the Zkauba-facet was uppermost, and when he strove to erase the conflicting Carter-memories which troubled him.

Thus long spaces of time wore on—ages longer than the brain of man could grasp, since the beings of Yaddith die only after prolonged cycles. After many hundred revolutions the Carter-facet seemed to gain on the Zkauba-facet, and would spend vast periods calculating the distance of Yaddith in space and time from the human earth that was to be. The figures were staggering—aeons and light-years beyond counting—but the immemorial lore of Yaddith fitted Carter to grasp such things. He cultivated the power of dreaming himself momentarily earthward, and learned many things about our planet that he had never known before. But he could not dream the needed formula on the missing parchment.

Then at last he conceived a wild plan of escape from Yaddith—which began when he found a drug that would keep his Zkauba-facet always dormant, yet without dissolution of the knowledge and memories of Zkauba. He thought that his calculations would let him perform a voyage with a light-wave envelope such as no being of Yaddith had ever performed—a *bodily* voyage through nameless aeons and across incredible galactic reaches to the solar system and the earth itself. Once on earth, though in the body of a clawed, snouted thing, he might be able somehow to find—and finish deciphering—the strangely hieroglyphed parchment he had left in the car at Arkham; and with its aid—and the Key's—resume his normal terrestrial semblance.

He was not blind to the perils of the attempt. He knew that when he had brought the planet-angle to the right aeon (a thing impossible to do while hurtling through space), Yaddith would be a dead world dominated by the triumphant Dholes, and that his escape in the light-wave envelope would be a matter of grave doubt. Likewise was he aware of how he must achieve suspended animation, in the manner of an adept, to endure the aeon-long flight through fathomless abysses. He knew, too, that—assuming his voyage succeeded—he must immunise himself to the bacterial and other earthly conditions hostile to a body from Yaddith. Furthermore, he must provide a way of feigning human shape on earth till he might recover and decipher the parchment and resume that shape in truth. Otherwise he would probably be discovered and destroyed by the people in horror as a thing that should not be. And there must be some gold—luckily obtainable on Yaddith—to tide him over that period of quest.

Slowly Carter's plans went forward. He provided a light-wave envelope of abnormal toughness, able to stand both the prodigious time-transition and the unexampled flight through space. He tested all his calculations, and sent forth his earthward dreams again and again, bringing them as close as possible to 1928. He practiced suspended animation with marvellous success. He discovered just the bacterial agent he needed, and worked out the varying gravity-stress to which he must become used. He artfully fashioned a waxen mask and loose costume enabling him to pass among men as a human being of a sort, and devised a doubly potent spell with which to hold back the Dholes at the moment of his starting from the black, dead Yaddith of the inconceivable future. He took care, too, to assemble a large supply of the drugs—unobtainable on earth—which would keep his Zkauba-facet in abeyance till he might shed the Yaddith body, nor did he neglect a small store of gold for earthly use.

The starting-day was a time of doubt and apprehension. Carter climbed up to his envelope-platform, on the pretext of sailing for the triple star Nython, and crawled into the sheath of shining metal. He had just room to perform the ritual of the Silver Key, and as he did so he slowly started the levitation of his envelope. There was an appalling seething and darkening of the day, and a hideous racking of pain. The cosmos seemed to reel irresponsibly, and the other constellations danced in a black sky.

All at once Carter felt a new equilibrium. The cold of interstellar gulfs gnawed at the outside of his envelope, and he could see that he floated free in space—the metal building from which he had started having decayed ages before. Below him the ground was festering with gigantic Dholes; and even as he looked, one reared up several hundred feet and levelled a bleached, viscous end at him. But his spells were effective, and in another moment he was falling away from Yaddith unharmed.

VII.

In that bizarre room in New Orleans, from which the old black servant had instinctively fled, the odd voice of Swami Chandraputra grew hoarser still.

"Gentlemen," he continued, "I will not ask you to believe these things until I have shewn you special proof. Accept it, then, as a myth, when I tell you of the *thousands of light-years—thousands of years of time, and uncounted billions of miles*—that Randolph Carter hurtled through space as a nameless, alien entity in a thin envelope of electron-activated metal. He timed his period of suspended animation with utmost care, planning to have it end only a few years before the time of landing on the earth in or near 1928.

"He will never forget that awakening. Remember, gentlemen, that before that aeon-long sleep *he had lived consciously for thousands of terrestrial years amidst the alien and horrible wonders of Yaddith.* There was a hideous gnawing of cold, a cessation of menacing dreams, and a glance through the eye-plates of the envelope. Stars, clusters, nebulae, on every hand—*and at last their outlines bore some kinship to the constellations of earth that he knew.*

"Some day his descent into the solar system may be told. He saw Kynarth and Yuggoth on the rim, passed close to Neptune and glimpsed the hellish white fungi that spot it, learned an untellable secret from the close-glimpsed mists of Jupiter and saw the horror on one of the satellites, and gazed at the Cyclopean ruins that sprawl over Mars' ruddy disc. When the earth drew near he saw it as a thin crescent which swelled alarmingly in size. He slackened speed, though his sensations of homecoming made him wish to lose not a moment. I will not try to tell you of those sensations as I learned them from Carter.

"Well, toward the last Carter hovered about in the earth's upper air waiting till daylight came over the western hemisphere. He wanted to land where he had left—near the Snake-Den in the hills behind Arkham. If any of you have been away from home long—and I know one of you has—I leave it to you how the sight of New England's rolling hills and great elms and gnarled orchards and ancient stone walls must have affected him.

"He came down at dawn in the lower meadow of the old Carter place, and was thankful for the silence and solitude. It was autumn, as when he had left, and the smell of the hills was balm to his soul. He managed to drag the metal envelope up the slope of the timber-lot into the Snake-Den, though it would not go through the weed-choked fissure to the inner cave. It was there also that he covered his alien body with the human clothing and waxen mask which would be necessary. He kept the envelope here for over a year, till certain circumstances made a new hiding-place necessary.

"He walked to Arkham—incidentally practicing the management of his body in human posture and against terrestrial gravity—and got his gold changed to money at a bank. He also made some inquiries—posing as a foreigner ignorant of much English—and found that the year was 1930, only two years after the goal he had aimed at.

"Of course his position was horrible. Unable to assert his identity, forced to live on guard every moment, with certain difficulties regarding food, and with a need to conserve the alien drug which kept his Zkauba-facet dormant, he felt that he must act as quickly as possible. Going to Boston and taking a room in the decaying West End, where he could live cheaply and inconspicuously, he at once established inquiries concerning Randolph Carter's estate and effects. It was then that he learned how anxious Mr. Aspinwall, here, was to have the estate divided, and how valiantly Mr. de Marigny and Mr. Phillips were striving to keep it intact."

The Hindoo bowed, though no expression crossed his dark, tranquil, and thickly bearded face.

"Indirectly," he continued, "Carter secured a good copy of the missing parchment and began work on its deciphering. I am glad to say that I was able to help in all this—for he appealed to me quite early, and through me came in touch with other mystics throughout the world. I went to live with him in Boston—a wretched place in Chambers St. As for the parchment—I am pleased to help Mr. de Marigny in his perplexity. To him let me say that the language of those hieroglyphics is not Naacal but R'lyehian, which was brought to earth by the spawn of Cthulhu countless cycles ago. It is, of course, a translation—there was an Hyperborean original millions of years earlier in the primal tongue of Tsath-yo.

"There was more to decipher than Carter had looked for, but at no time did he give up hope. Early this year he made great strides through a book he imported from Nepal, and there is no question but that he will win before long. Unfortunately, however, one handicap has developed—the exhaustion of the alien drug which keeps the Zkauba-facet dormant. This is not, however, as great a calamity as was feared. Carter's personality is gaining in the body, and when Zkauba comes uppermost—for shorter and shorter periods, and now only when evoked by some unusual excitement—he is generally too dazed to undo any of Carter's work. He cannot find the metal envelope that would take him back to Yaddith, for although he almost did once, Carter hid it anew at a time when the Zkauba-facet was wholly latent. All the harm he has done is to frighten a few people and create certain nightmare rumours among the Poles and Lithuanians of Boston's West End. So far, he has never injured the careful disguise prepared by the Carter-facet, though he sometimes throws it off so that parts have to be replaced. I have seen what lies beneath—and it is not good to see.

"A month ago Carter saw the advertisement of this meeting, and knew that he must act quickly to save his estate. He could not wait to decipher the parchment and resume his human form. Consequently he deputed me to act for him, and in that capacity I am here.

"Gentlemen, I say to you that Randolph Carter is not dead; that he is temporarily in an anomalous condition, but that within two or three months at the outside he will be able to appear in proper form and demand the custody of his estate. I am prepared to offer proof if necessary. Therefore I beg that you will adjourn this meeting for an indefinite period."

VIII.

De Marigny and Phillips stared at the Hindoo as if hypnotised, while Aspinwall emitted a series of snorts and bellows. The old attorney's disgust had by now surged into open rage, and he pounded the table with an apoplectically veined fist. When he spoke, it was in a kind of bark.

"How long is this foolery to be borne? I've listened an hour to this madman—this faker—and now he has the damned effrontery to say Randolph Carter is alive—to ask us to postpone the settlement for no good reason! Why don't you throw the scoundrel out, de Marigny? Do you mean to make us all the butts of a charlatan or idiot?"

De Marigny quietly raised his hand and spoke softly.

"Let us think slowly and clearly. This has been a very singular tale, and there are things in it which I, as a mystic not altogether ignorant, recognise as far from irresponsible. Furthermore—since 1930 I have received letters from the Swami which tally with this account."

As he paused, old Mr. Phillips ventured a word.

"Swami Chandraputra spoke of proofs. I, too, recognise

much that is significant in this story, and I have myself had many oddly corroborative letters from the Swami during the last two years; but some of these statements are very extreme. Is there not something tangible which can be shewn?"

At last the impassive-faced Swami replied, slowly and hoarsely, and drawing an object from the pocket of his loose coat as he spoke.

"While none of you here has ever *seen* the Silver Key itself, Messrs. de Marigny and Phillips have seen photographs of it. *Does this look familiar to you?*"

He fumblingly laid on the table, with his large, white-mittened hand, a heavy key of tarnished silver—nearly five inches long, of unknown and utterly exotic workmanship, and covered from end to end with hieroglyphs of the most bizarre description. De Marigny and Phillips gasped.

"That's it!" cried de Marigny. "The camera doesn't lie. I couldn't be mistaken!"

But Aspinwall had already launched a reply.

"Fools! What does it prove? If that's the real key that belonged to my cousin, it's up to this foreigner—this damned nigger—to explain how he got it! Randolph vanished with the key four years ago. How do we know he wasn't robbed and murdered? He was half-crazy himself, and in touch with still crazier people.

"Look here, you nigger—where did you get that key? Did you kill Randolph Carter?"

The Swami's features, abnormally placid, did not change; but the remote, irisless black eyes behind them blazed dangerously. He spoke with great difficulty.

"Please control yourself, Mr. Aspinwall. There is another form of proof that I *could* give, but its effect upon everybody would not be pleasant. Let us be reasonable. Here are some papers obviously written since 1930, and in the unmistakable style of Randolph Carter."

He clumsily drew a long envelope from inside his loose coat and handed it to the sputtering attorney as de Marigny and Phillips watched with chaotic thoughts and a dawning feeling of supernal wonder.

"Of course the handwriting is almost illegible—but remember that Randolph Carter now has no hands well adapted to forming human script."

Aspinwall looked through the papers hurriedly, and was visibly perplexed, but he did not change his demeanour. The room was tense with excitement and nameless dread, and the alien rhythm of the coffin-shaped clock had an utterly diabolic sound to de Marigny and Phillips—though the lawyer seemed affected not at all. Aspinwall spoke again.

"These look like clever forgeries. If they aren't, they may mean that Randolph has been brought under the control of people with no good purpose. There's only one thing to do—have this faker arrested. De Marigny, will you telephone for the police?"

"Let us wait," answered their host. "I do not think this case calls for the police. I have a certain idea. Mr. Aspinwall, this gentleman is a mystic of real attainments. He says he is in the confidence of Randolph Carter. Will it satisfy you if he can answer certain questions which could be answered only by one in such confidence? I know Carter, and can ask such questions. Let me get a book which I think will make a good test."

He turned toward the door to the library, Phillips dazedly following in a kind of automatic way. Aspinwall remained where he was, studying closely the Hindoo who confronted him with abnormally impassive face. Suddenly, as Chandraputra clumsily restored the Silver Key to his pocket, the lawyer emitted a guttural shout which stopped de Marigny and Phillips in their tracks.

"Hey, by God, I've got it! This rascal is in disguise. I don't believe he's an East Indian at all. That face—it isn't a face, but a *mask!* I guess his story put that into my head, but it's true. It never moves, and that turban and beard hide the edges. This fellow's a common crook! He isn't even a foreigner—I've been watching his language. He's a Yankee of some sort. And look at those mittens—he knows his fingerprints could be spotted. Damn you, I'll pull that thing off—"

"Stop!" The hoarse, oddly alien voice of the Swami held a tone beyond all mere earthly fright. "I told you there was *another form of proof which I could give if necessary,* and I warned you not to provoke me to it. This red-faced old meddler is right—I'm not really an East Indian. *This face is a mask, and what it covers is not human.* You others have guessed—I felt that minutes ago. It wouldn't be pleasant if I took that mask off—let it alone, Ernest. I may as well tell you that *I am Randolph Carter.*"

No one moved. Aspinwall snorted and made vague motions. De Marigny and Phillips, across the room, watched the workings of his red face and studied the back of the turbaned figure that confronted him. The clock's abnormal ticking was hideous, and the tripod fumes and swaying arras danced a dance of death. The half-choking lawyer broke the silence.

"No you don't, you crook—you can't scare me! You've reasons of your own for not wanting that mask off. Maybe we'd know who you are. Off with it—"

As he reached forward, the Swami seized his hand with one of his own clumsily mittened members, evoking a curious cry of mixed pain and surprise. De Marigny started toward the two, but paused confused as the pseudo-Hindoo's shout of protest changed to a wholly inexplicable rattling and buzzing sound. Aspinwall's red face was furious, and with his free hand he made another lunge at his opponent's bushy beard. This time he succeeded in getting a hold, and at his frantic tug the whole waxen visage came loose from the turban and clung to the lawyer's apoplectic fist.

As it did so, Aspinwall uttered a frightful gurgling cry, and Phillips and de Marigny saw his face convulsed with a wilder, deeper, and more hideous epilepsy of stark panic than ever they had seen on human countenance before. The pseudo-Swami had meanwhile released his other hand and was standing as if dazed, making buzzing noises of a most abnormal quality. Then the turbaned figure slumped oddly into a posture scarcely human, and began a curious, fascinated sort of shuffle toward the coffin-shaped clock that ticked out its cosmic and abnormal rhythm. His now uncovered face was turned away, and de Marigny and Phillips could not see what the lawyer's act had disclosed. Then their attention was turned to Aspinwall, who was sinking ponderously to the floor. The spell was broken—but when they reached the old man he was dead.

Turning quickly to the shuffling Swami's receding back, de Marigny saw one of the great white mittens drop listlessly off a dangling arm. The fumes of the olibanum were thick, and all that could be glimpsed of the revealed hand was something long and black. Before the Creole could reach the retreating figure, old Mr. Phillips laid a restraining hand on his shoulder.

"Don't!" he whispered. "We don't know what we're up against—that other facet, you know—Zkauba, the Wizard of Yaddith...."

The turbaned figure had now reached the abnormal clock, and the watchers saw through the dense fumes a blurred black claw fumbling with the tall, hieroglyphed door. The fumbling made a queer clicking sound. Then the figure entered the coffin-shaped case and pulled the door shut after it.

De Marigny could no longer be restrained, but when he reached and opened the clock it was empty. The abnormal ticking went on, beating out the dark cosmic rhythm which underlies all mystical gate-openings. On the floor the great white mitten, and the dead man with a bearded mask clutched in his hand, had nothing further to reveal.

A year has passed, and nothing has been heard of Randolph Carter. His estate is still unsettled. The Boston address from which one "Swami Chandraputra" sent inquiries to various mystics in 1930–31–32 was indeed tenanted by a strange Hindoo, but he left shortly before the date of the New Orleans conference and has never been seen since. He was said to be dark, expressionless, and bearded, and his landlord thinks the swarthy mask—which was duly exhibited—looks very like him. He was never, however, suspected of any connexion with the nightmare apparitions whispered of by local Slavs. The hills behind Arkham were searched for the "metal envelope", but nothing of the sort was ever found. However, a clerk in Arkham's First National Bank does recall a queer turbaned man who cashed an odd bit of gold bullion in October, 1930.

De Marigny and Phillips scarcely know what to make of the business. After all, what was proved? There was a story. There was a key which might have been forged from one of the pictures Carter had freely distributed in 1928. There were papers—all indecisive. There was a masked stranger, but who now living saw behind the mask? Amidst the strain and the olibanum fumes that act of vanishing in the clock might easily have been a dual hallucination. Hindoos know much of hypnotism. Reason proclaims the "Swami" a criminal with designs on Randolph Carter's estate. But the autopsy said that Aspinwall had died of a sudden shock. Was it rage *alone* which caused it? And some things in that story …

In a vast room hung with strangely figured arras and filled with olibanum fumes, Etienne-Laurent de Marigny often sits listening with vague sensations to the abnormal rhythm of that hieroglyphed, coffin-shaped clock.

THE THING ON THE DOORSTEP

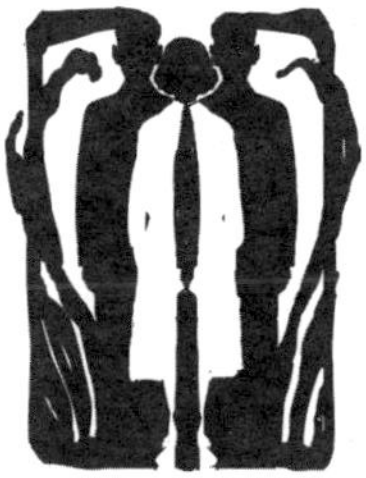

I.

It is true that I have sent six bullets through the head of my best friend, and yet I hope to shew by this statement that I am not his murderer. At first I shall be called a madman—madder than the man I shot in his cell at the Arkham Sanitarium. Later some of my readers will weigh each statement, correlate it with the known facts, and ask themselves how I could have believed otherwise than as I did after facing the evidence of that horror—that thing on the doorstep.

Until then I also saw nothing but madness in the wild tales I have acted on. Even now I ask myself whether I was misled—or whether I am not mad after all. I do not know—but others have strange things to tell of Edward and Asenath Derby, and even the stolid police are at their wits' ends to account for that last terrible visit. They have tried weakly to concoct a theory of a ghastly jest or warning by discharged servants, yet they know in their hearts that the truth is something infinitely more terrible and incredible.

So I say that I have not murdered Edward Derby. Rather have I avenged him, and in so doing purged the earth of a horror whose survival might have loosed untold terrors on all mankind. There are black zones of shadow close to our daily paths, and now and then some evil soul breaks a passage through. When that happens, the man who knows must strike before reckoning the consequences.

I have known Edward Pickman Derby all his life. Eight years my junior, he was so precocious that we had much in common from the time he was eight and I sixteen. He was the most phenomenal child scholar I have ever known, and at seven was writing verse of a sombre, fantastic, almost morbid cast which astonished the tutors surrounding him. Perhaps his private education and coddled seclusion had something to do with his premature flowering. An only child, he had organic weaknesses which startled his doting parents and caused them to keep him closely chained to their side. He was never allowed out without his nurse, and seldom had a chance to play unconstrainedly with other children. All this doubtless fostered a strange, secretive inner life in the boy, with imagination as his one avenue of freedom.

At any rate, his juvenile learning was prodigious and bizarre; and his facile writings such as to captivate me despite my greater age. About that time I had leanings toward art of a somewhat grotesque cast, and I found in this younger child a rare kindred spirit. What lay behind our joint love of shadows and marvels was, no doubt, the ancient, mouldering, and subtly fearsome town in which we lived—witch-cursed, legend-haunted Arkham, whose huddled, sagging gambrel roofs and crumbling Georgian balustrades brood out the centuries beside the darkly muttering Miskatonic.

As time went by I turned to architecture and gave up my design of illustrating a book of Edward's daemoniac poems, yet our comradeship suffered no lessening. Young Derby's odd genius developed remarkably, and in his eighteenth year his collected nightmare-lyrics made a real sensation when issued under the title "Azathoth and Other Horrors". He was a close correspondent of the notorious Baudelairean poet Justin Geoffrey, who wrote "The People of the Monolith" and died screaming in a madhouse in 1926 after a visit to a sinister, ill-regarded village in Hungary.

In self-reliance and practical affairs, however, Derby was greatly retarded because of his coddled existence. His health had improved, but his habits of childish dependence were fostered by overcareful parents; so that he never travelled alone, made independent decisions, or assumed responsibilities. It was early seen that he would not be equal to a struggle in the business or professional arena, but the family fortune was so ample that this formed no tragedy. As he grew to years of manhood he retained a deceptive aspect of boyishness. Blond and blue-eyed, he had the fresh complexion of a child; and his attempts to raise a moustache were discernible only with difficulty. His voice was soft and light, and his pampered, unexercised life gave him a juvenile chubbiness rather than the paunchiness of premature middle age. He was of good height, and his handsome face would have made him a notable gallant had not his shyness held him to seclusion and bookishness.

Derby's parents took him abroad every summer, and he was quick to seize on the surface aspects of European thought and expression. His Poe-like talents turned more and more toward the decadent, and other artistic sensitivenesses and yearnings were half-aroused in him. We had great discussions in those days. I had been through Harvard, had studied in a Boston architect's office, had married, and had finally returned to Arkham to practice my profession—settling in the family homestead in Saltonstall St., since my father had moved to Florida for his health. Edward used to call almost every evening, till I came to regard him as one of the household. He had a characteristic way of ringing the doorbell or sounding the knocker that grew to be a veritable code signal, so that after dinner I always listened for the familiar three brisk strokes followed by two more after a pause. Less frequently I would visit at his house and note with envy the obscure volumes in his constantly growing library.

Derby went through Miskatonic University in Arkham, since his parents would not let him board away from them. He entered at sixteen and completed his course in three years, majoring in English and French literature and receiving high marks in everything but mathematics and the sciences. He mingled very little with the other students, though looking enviously at the "daring" or "Bohemian" set—whose superficially "smart" language and meaninglessly ironic pose he aped, and whose dubious conduct he wished he dared adopt.

What he did do was to become an almost fanatical devotee of subterranean magical lore, for which Miskatonic's library was and is famous. Always a dweller on the surface of phantasy and strangeness, he now delved deep into the actual runes and riddles left by a fabulous past for the guidance or puzzlement of posterity. He read things like the frightful "Book of Eibon", the "Unaussprechlichen Kulten" of von Junzt, and the forbidden "Necronomicon" of the mad Arab Adbul Alhazred, though he did not tell his parents he had seen them. Edward was twenty when my son and only child was born, and seemed pleased when I named the newcomer Edward Derby Upton, after him.

By the time he was twenty-five Edward Derby was a prodigiously learned man and a fairly well-known poet and fantaisiste, though his lack of contacts and responsibilities had slowed down his literary growth by making his products derivative and overbookish. I was perhaps his closest friend—finding him an inexhaustible mine of vital theoretical topics, while he relied on me for advice in whatever matters he did not wish to refer to his parents. He remained single—more through shyness, inertia, and parental protectiveness than through inclination—and moved in society only to the slightest and most perfunctory extent. When the war came both health and ingrained timidity kept him at home. I went to Plattsburg for a commission, but never got overseas.

So the years wore on. Edward's mother died when he was thirty-four, and for months he was incapacitated by some odd psychological malady. His father took him to Europe, however, and he managed to pull out of his trouble without visible effects. Afterward he seemed to feel a sort of grotesque exhilaration, as if of partial escape from some unseen bondage. He began to mingle in the more "advanced" college set despite his middle age, and was present at some extremely wild doings—on one occasion paying heavy blackmail (which he borrowed of me) to keep his presence at a certain affair from his father's notice. Some of the whispered rumours about the wild Miskatonic set were extremely singular. There was even talk of black magic and of happenings utterly beyond credibility.

II.

Edward was thirty-eight when he met Asenath Waite. She was, I judge, about twenty-three at the time; and was taking a special course in mediaeval metaphysics at Miskatonic. The daughter of a friend of mine had met her before—in the Hall School at Kingsport—and had been inclined to shun her because of her odd reputation. She was dark, smallish, and very good-looking except for overprotuberant eyes; but something in her expression alienated extremely sensitive people. It was, however, largely her origin and conversation which caused average folk to avoid her. She was one of the Innsmouth Waites, and dark legends have clustered for generations about crumbling, half-deserted Innsmouth and its people. There are tales of horrible bargains about the year 1850, and of a strange element "not quite human" in the ancient families of the run-down fishing port—tales such as only old-time Yankees can devise and repeat with proper awesomeness.

Asenath's case was aggravated by the fact that she was Ephraim Waite's daughter—the child of his old age by an unknown wife who always went veiled. Ephraim lived in a half-decayed mansion in Washington Street, Innsmouth, and those who had seen the place (Arkham folk avoid going to Innsmouth whenever they can) declared that the attic windows were always boarded, and that strange sounds sometimes floated from within as evening drew on. The old man was known to have been a prodigious magical student in his day, and legend averred that he could raise or quell storms at sea according to his whim. I had seen him one or twice in my youth as he came to Arkham to consult forbidden tomes at the college library, and had hated his wolfish, saturnine face with its tangle of iron-grey beard. He had died insane—under rather queer circumstances—just before his daughter (by his will made a nominal ward of the principal) entered the Hall School, but she had been his morbidly avid pupil and looked fiendishly like him at times.

The friend whose daughter had gone to school with Asenath Waite repeated many curious things when the news of Edward's acquaintance with her began to spread about. Asenath, it seemed, had posed as a kind of magician at school; and had really seemed able to accomplish some highly baffling marvels. She professed to be able to raise thunderstorms, though her seeming success was generally laid to some uncanny knack at prediction. All animals markedly disliked her, and she could make any dog howl by certain motions of her right hand. There were times when she displayed snatches of knowledge and language very singular—and very shocking—for a young girl; when she would frighten her schoolmates with leers and winks of an inexplicable kind, and would seem to extract an obscene and zestful irony from her present situation.

Most unusual, though, were the well-attested cases of her influence over other persons. She was, beyond question, a genuine hypnotist. By gazing peculiarly at a fellow-student she would often give the latter a distinct feeling of *exchanged personality*—as if the subject were placed momentarily in the magician's body and able to stare half across the room at her real body, whose eyes blazed and protruded with an alien expression. Asenath often made wild claims about the nature of consciousness and about its independence of the physical frame—or at least from the life-processes of the physical frame. Her crowning rage, however, was that she was not a man; since she believed a male brain had certain unique and far-reaching cosmic powers. Given a man's brain, she declared, she could not only equal but surpass her father in mastery of unknown forces.

Edward met Asenath at a gathering of "intelligentsia" held in one of the students' rooms, and could talk of nothing else when he came to see me the next day. He had found her full of the interests and erudition which engrossed him most, and was in addition wildly taken with her appearance. I had never seen the young woman, and recalled casual references only faintly, but I knew who she was. It seemed rather regrettable that Derby should become so upheaved about her; but I said nothing to discourage him, since infatuation thrives on opposition. He was not, he said, mentioning her to his father.

In the next few weeks I heard of very little but Asenath from young Derby. Others now remarked Edward's autumnal gallantry, though they agreed that he did not look even nearly his actual age, or seem at all inappropriate as an escort for his bizarre divinity. He was only a trifle paunchy despite his indolence and self-indulgence, and his face was absolutely without lines. Asenath, on the other hand, had the premature crow's feet which come from the exercise of an intense will.

About this time Edward brought the girl to call on me, and I at once saw that his interest was by no means one-sided. She eyed him continually with an almost predatory air, and I perceived that their intimacy was beyond untangling. Soon afterward I had a visit from old Mr. Derby, whom I had always admired and respected. He had heard the tales of his son's new friendship, and had wormed the whole truth out of "the boy". Edward meant to marry Asenath, and had even been looking at houses in the suburbs. Knowing my usually great influence with his son, the father wondered if I could help to break the ill-advised affair off; but I regretfully expressed my doubts. This time it was not a question of Edward's weak will but of the woman's strong will. The perennial child had transferred his dependence from the parental image to a new and stronger image, and nothing could be done about it.

The wedding was performed a month later—by a justice of the peace, according to the bride's request. Mr. Derby, at my advice, offered no opposition; and he, my wife, my son, and I attended the brief ceremony—the other guests being wild young people from the college. Asenath had bought the old Crowninshield place in the country at the end of High Street, and they proposed to settle there after a short trip to Innsmouth, whence three servants and some books and household goods were to be brought. It was probably not so much consideration for Edward and his father as a personal wish to be near the college, its library, and its crowd of "sophisticates", that made Asenath settle in Arkham instead of returning permanently home.

When Edward called on me after the honeymoon I thought he looked slightly changed. Asenath had made him get rid of the undeveloped moustache, but there was more than that. He looked soberer and more thoughtful, his habitual pout of childish rebelliousness being exchanged for a look almost of genuine sadness. I was puzzled to decide whether I liked or disliked the change. Certainly, he seemed for the moment more normally adult than ever before. Perhaps the marriage was a good thing—might not the *change* of dependence form a start toward actual *neutralisation*, leading ultimately to responsible independence? He came alone, for Asenath was very busy. She had brought a vast store of books and apparatus from Innsmouth (Derby shuddered as he spoke the name), and was finishing the restoration of the Crowninshield house and grounds.

Her home in—that town—was a rather disquieting place, but certain objects in it had taught him some surprising things. He was progressing fast in esoteric lore now that he had Asenath's guidance. Some of the experiments she proposed were very daring and radical—he did not feel at liberty to describe them—but he had confidence in her powers and intentions. The three servents were very queer—an incredibly aged couple who had been with old Ephraim and referred occasionally to him and to Asenath's dead mother in a cryptic way, and a swarthy young wench who had marked anomalies of feature and seemed to exude a perpetual odour of fish.

III.

For the next two years I saw less and less of Derby. A fortnight would sometimes slip by without the familiar three-and-two strokes at the front door; and when he did call—or when, as happened with increasing infrequency, I called on him—he was very little disposed to converse on vital topics. He had become secretive about those occult studies which he used to describe and discuss so minutely, and preferred not to talk of his wife. She had aged tremendously since her marriage, till now—oddly enough—she seemed the elder of the two. Her face held the most concentratedly determined expression I had ever seen, and her whole aspect seemed to gain a vague, unplaceable repulsiveness. My wife and son noticed it as much as I, and we all ceased gradually to call on her—for which, Edward admitted in one of his boyishly tactless moments, she was unmitigatedly grateful. Occasionally the Derbys would go on long trips—ostensibly to Europe, though Edward sometimes hinted at obscurer destinations.

It was after the first year that people began talking about the change in Edward Derby. It was very casual talk, for the change was purely psychological; but it brought up some interesting points. Now and then, it seemed, Edward was observed to wear an expression and to do things wholly incompatible with his usual flabby nature. For example—although in the old days he could not drive a car, he was now seen occasionally to dash into or out of the old Crowninshield driveway with Asenath's powerful Packard, handling it like a master, and meeting traffic entanglements with a skill and determination utterly alien to his accustomed nature. In such cases he seemed always to be just back from some trip or just starting on one—what sort of trip, no one could guess, although he mostly favoured the Innsmouth road.

Oddly, the metamorphosis did not seem altogether pleasing. People said he looked too much like his wife, or like old Ephraim Waite himself, in these moments—or perhaps these moments seemed unnatural because they were so rare. Sometimes, hours after starting out in this way, he would return listlessly sprawled on the rear seat of the car while an obviously hired chauffeur or mechanic drove. Also, his preponderant aspect on the streets or during his decreasing round of social contacts (including, I may say, his calls on me) was the old-time indecisive one—its irresponsible childishness even more marked than in the past. While Asenath's face aged, Edward's—aside from those exceptional occasions—actually relaxed into a kind of exaggerated immaturity, save when a trace of the new sadness or understanding would flash across it. It was really very puzzling. Meanwhile the Derbys almost dropped out of the gay college circle—not through their own disgust, we heard, but because something about their present studies shocked even the most callous of the other decadents.

It was in the third year of the marriage that Edward began to hint openly to me of a certain fear and dissatisfaction. He would let fall remarks about things 'going too far', and would talk darkly about the need of 'saving his identity'. At first I ignored such references, but in time I began to question him guardedly, remembering what my friend's daughter had said about Asenath's hypnotic influence over the other girls at school—the cases where students had thought they were in her body looking across the room at themselves. This questioning seemed to make him at once alarmed and grateful, and once he mumbled something about having a serious talk with me later.

About this time old Mr. Derby died, for which I was afterward very thankful. Edward was badly upset, though by no means disorganised. He had seen astonishingly little of his parent since his marriage, for Asenath had concentrated in herself all his vital sense of family linkage. Some called him callous in his loss—especially since those jaunty and confident moods with the car began to increase. He now wished to move back into the old Derby mansion, but Asenath insisted on staying in the Crowninshield house, to which she had become well adjusted.

Not long afterward my wife heard a curious thing from a friend—one of the few who had not dropped the Derbys. She had been out to the end of High St. to call on the couple, and had seen a car shoot briskly out of the drive with Edward's oddly confident and almost sneering face above the wheel. Ringing the bell, she had been told by the repulsive wench that Asenath was also out; but had chanced to look up at the house in leaving. There, at one of Edward's library windows, she had glimpsed a hastily withdrawn face—a face whose expression of pain, defeat, and wistful hopelessness was poignant beyond description. It was—incredibly enough in view of its usual domineering cast—Asenath's; yet the caller had vowed that in that instant the sad, muddled eyes of poor Edward were gazing out from it.

Edward's calls now grew a trifle more frequent, and his hints occasionally became concrete. What he said was not to be believed, even in centuried and legend-haunted Arkham; but he threw out his dark lore with a sincerity and convincingness which made one fear for his sanity. He talked about terrible meetings in lonely places, of Cyclopean ruins in the heart of the Maine woods beneath which vast staircases lead down to abysses of nighted secrets, of complex angles that lead through invisible walls to other regions of space and time, and of hideous exchanges of personality that permit explorations in remote and forbidden places, on other worlds, and in different space-time continua.

He would now and then back up certain crazy hints by exhibiting objects which utterly nonplussed me—elusively coloured and bafflingly textured objects like nothing ever heard of on earth, whose insane curves and surfaces answered no conceivable purpose and followed no conceivable geometry. These things, he said, came 'from outside'; and his wife knew how to get them. Sometimes—but always in frightened and ambiguous whispers—he would suggest things about old Ephraim Waite, whom he had seen occasionally at the college library in the old days. These adumbrations were never specific, but seemed to revolve around some especially horrible doubt as to whether the old wizard were really dead—in a spiritual as well as corporeal sense.

At times Derby would halt abruptly in his revelations, and I wondered whether Asenath could possibly have divined his speech at a distance and cut him off through some unknown sort of telepathic mesmerism—some power of the kind she had displayed at school. Certainly, she suspected that he told me things, for as the weeks passed she tried to stop his visits with words and glances of a most inexplicable potency. Only with difficulty could he get to see me, for although he would pretend to be going somewhere else, some invisible force would generally clog his motions or make him forget his destination for the time being. His visits usually came when Asenath was away—'away in her own body', as he once oddly put it. She always found out later—the servants watched his goings and comings—but evidently she thought it inexpedient to do anything drastic.

IV.

Derby had been married more than three years on that August day when I got the telegram from Maine. I had not seen him for two months, but had heard he was away "on business". Asenath was supposed to be with him, though watchful gossips declared there was someone upstairs in the house behind the doubly curtained windows. They had watched the purchases made by the servants. And now the town marshal of Chesuncook had wired of the draggled madman who stumbled out of the woods with delirious ravings and screamed to me for protection. It was Edward—and he had been just able to recall his own name and my name and address.

Chesuncook is close to the wildest, deepest, and least explored forest belt in Maine, and it took a whole day of feverish jolting through fantastic and forbidding scenery to get there in a car. I found Derby in a cell at the town farm, vacillating between frenzy and apathy. He knew me at once, and began pouring out a meaningless, half-incoherent torrent of words in my direction.

"Dan—for God's sake! The pit of the shoggoths! Down the six thousand steps … the abomination of abominations … I never would let her take me, and then I found myself there…. Iä! Shub-Niggurath! … The shape rose up from the altar, and there were 500 that howled…. The Hooded Thing bleated 'Kamog! Kamog!'—that was old Ephraim's secret name in the coven…. I was there, where she promised she wouldn't take me…. A minute before I was locked in the library, and then I was there where she had gone with my body—in the place of utter blasphemy, the unholy pit where the black realm begins and the watcher guards the gate…. I saw a shoggoth—it changed shape…. I can't stand it…. I won't stand it…. I'll kill her if she ever sends me there again…. I'll kill that entity … her, him, it … I'll kill it! I'll kill it with my own hands!"

It took me an hour to quiet him, but he subsided at last. The next day I got him decent clothes in the village, and set out with him for Arkham. His fury of hysteria was spent, and he was inclined to be silent; though he began muttering darkly to himself when the car passed through Augusta—as if the sight of a city aroused unpleasant memories. It was clear that he did not wish to go home; and considering the fantastic delusions he seemed to have about his wife—delusions undoubtedly springing from some actual hypnotic ordeal to which he had been subjected—I thought it would be better if he did not. I would, I resolved, put him up myself for a time; no matter what unpleasantness it would make with Asenath. Later I would help him get a divorce, for most assuredly there were mental factors which made this marriage suicidal for him. When we struck open country again Derby's muttering faded away, and I let him nod and drowse on the seat beside me as I drove.

During our sunset dash through Portland the muttering commenced again, more distinctly than before, and as I listened I caught a stream of utterly insane drivel about Asenath. The extent to which she had preyed on Edward's nerves was plain, for he had woven a whole set of hallucinations around her. His present predicament, he mumbled furtively, was only one of a long series. She was getting hold of him, and he knew that some day she would never let go. Even now she probably let him go only when she had to, because she couldn't hold on long at a time. She constantly took his body and went to nameless places for nameless rites, leaving him in her body and locking him upstairs—but sometimes she couldn't hold on, and he would find himself suddenly in his own body again in some far-off, horrible, and perhaps unknown place. Sometimes she'd get hold of him again and sometimes she couldn't. Often he was left stranded somewhere as I had found him … time and again he had to find his way home from frightful distances, getting somebody to drive the car after he found it.

The worst thing was that she was holding on to him longer and longer at a time. She wanted to be a man—to be fully human—that was why she got hold of him. She had sensed the mixture of fine-wrought brain and weak will in him. Some day she would crowd him out and disappear with his body—disappear to become a great magician like her father and leave him marooned in that female shell that wasn't even quite human. Yes, he knew about the Innsmouth blood now. There had been traffick with things from the sea—it was horrible.... And old Ephraim—he had known the secret, and when he grew old did a hideous thing to keep alive … he wanted to live for ever … Asenath would succeed—one successful demonstration had taken place already.

As Derby muttered on I turned to look at him closely, verifying the impression of change which an earlier scrutiny had given me. Paradoxically, he seemed in better shape than usual—harder, more normally developed, and without the trace of sickly flabbiness caused by his indolent habits. It was as if he had been really active and properly exercised for the first time in his coddled life, and I judged that Asenath's force must have pushed him into unwonted channels of motion and alertness. But just now his mind was in a pitiable state; for he was mumbling wild extravagances about his wife, about black magic, about old Ephraim, and about some revelation which would convince even me. He repeated names which I recognised from bygone browsings in forbidden volumes, and at times made me shudder with a certain thread of mythological consistency—of convincing coherence—which ran through his maundering. Again and again he would pause, as if to gather courage for some final and terrible disclosure.

"Dan, Dan, don't you remember him—the wild eyes and the unkempt beard that never turned white? He glared at me once, and I never forgot it. Now *she* glares that way. *And I know why!* He found it in the 'Necronomicon'—the formula. I don't dare tell you the page yet, but when I do you can read and understand. Then you will know what has engulfed me. On, on, on, on—body to body to body—he means never to die. The life-glow—he knows how to break the link … it can flicker on a while even when the body is dead. I'll give you hints, and maybe you'll guess. Listen, Dan—do you know why my wife always takes such pains with that silly backhand writing? Have you ever seen a manuscript of old Ephraim's? Do you want to know why I shivered when I saw some hasty notes Asenath had jotted down?

"Asenath … *is there such a person?* Why did they half think there was poison in old Ephraim's stomach? Why do the Gilmans whisper about the way he shrieked—like a frightened child—when he went mad and Asenath locked him up in the padded attic room where—the other—had been? *Was it old Ephraim's soul that was locked in? Who locked in whom?* Why had he been looking for months for someone with a fine mind and a weak will? Why did he curse that his daughter wasn't a son? Tell me, Daniel Upton—*what devilish exchange was perpetrated in the house of horror where that blasphemous monster had his trusting, weak-willed, half-human child at his mercy?* Didn't he make it permanent—as she'll do in the end with me? Tell me why that thing that calls itself Asenath writes differently when off guard, *so that you can't tell its script from …*"

Then the thing happened. Derby's voice was rising to a thin treble scream as he raved, when suddenly it was shut off with an almost mechanical click. I thought of those other occasions at my home when his confidences had abruptly ceased—when I had half fancied that some obscure telepathic wave of Asenath's mental force was intervening to keep him silent. This, though, was something altogether different—and, I felt, infinitely more horrible. The face beside me was twisted almost unrecognisably for a moment, while through the whole body there passed a shivering motion—as if all the bones, organs, muscles, nerves, and glands were readjusting themselves to a radically different posture, set of stresses, and general personality.

Just where the supreme horror lay, I could not for my life tell; yet there swept over me such a swamping wave of sickness and repulsion—such a freezing, petrifying sense of utter alienage and abnormality—that my grasp of the wheel grew feeble and uncertain. The figure beside me seemed less like a lifelong friend than like some monstrous intrusion from outer space—some damnable, utterly accursed focus of unknown and malign cosmic forces.

I had faltered only a moment, but before another moment was over my companion had seized the wheel and forced me to change places with him. The dusk was now very thick, and the lights of Portland far behind, so I could not see much of his face. The blaze of his eyes, though, was phenomenal; and I knew that he must now be in that queerly energised state—so unlike his usual self—which so many people had noticed. It seemed odd and incredible that listless Edward Derby—he who could never assert himself, and who had never learned to drive—should be ordering me about and taking the wheel of my own car, yet that was precisely what had happened. He did not speak for some time, and in my inexplicable horror I was glad he did not.

In the lights of Biddeford and Saco I saw his firmly set mouth, and shivered at the blaze of his eyes. The people were right—he did look damnably like his wife and like old Ephraim when in these moods. I did not wonder that the moods were disliked—there was certainly something unnatural and diabolic in them, and I felt the sinister element all the more because of the wild ravings I had been hearing. This man, for all my lifelong knowledge of Edward Pickman Derby, was a stranger—an intrusion of some sort from the black abyss.

He did not speak until we were on a dark stretch of road, and when he did his voice seemed utterly unfamiliar. It was deeper, firmer, and more decisive than I had ever known it to be; while its accent and pronunciation were altogether changed—though vaguely, remotely, and rather disturbingly recalling something

I could not quite place. There was, I thought, a trace of very profound and very genuine irony in the timbre—not the flashy, meaninglessly jaunty pseudo-irony of the callow "sophisticate", which Derby had habitually affected, but something grim, basic, pervasive, and potentially evil. I marvelled at the self-possession so soon following the spell of panic-struck muttering.

"I hope you'll forget my attack back there, Upton," he was saying. "You know what my nerves are, and I guess you can excuse such things. I'm enormously grateful, of course, for this lift home.

"And you must forget, too, any crazy things I may have been saying about my wife—and about things in general. That's what comes from overstudy in a field like mine. My philosophy is full of bizarre concepts, and when the mind gets worn out it cooks up all sorts of imaginary concrete applications. I shall take a rest from now on—you probably won't see me for some time, and you needn't blame Asenath for it.

"This trip was a bit queer, but it's really very simple. There are certain Indian relics in the north woods—standing stones, and all that—which mean a good deal in folklore, and Asenath and I are following that stuff up. It was a hard search, so I seem to have gone off my head. I must send somebody for the car when I get home. A month's relaxation will put me back on my feet."

I do not recall just what my own part of the conversation was, for the baffling alienage of my seatmate filled all my consciousness. With every moment my feeling of elusive cosmic horror increased, till at length I was in a virtual delirium of longing for the end of the drive. Derby did not offer to relinquish the wheel, and I was glad of the speed with which Portsmouth and Newburyport flashed by.

At the junction where the main highway runs inland and avoids Innsmouth I was half-afraid my driver would take the bleak shore road that goes through that damnable place. He did not, however, but darted rapidly past Rowley and Ipswich toward our destination. We reached Arkham before midnight, and found the lights still on at the old Crowninshield house. Derby left the car with a hasty repetition of his thanks, and I drove home alone with a curious feeling of relief. It had been a terrible drive—all the more terrible because I could not quite tell why—and I did not regret Derby's forecast of a long absence from my company.

V.

The next two months were full of rumours. People spoke of seeing Derby more and more in his new energised state, and Asenath was scarcely ever in to her few callers. I had only one visit from Edward, when he called briefly in Asenath's car—duly reclaimed from wherever he had left it in Maine—to get some books he had lent me. He was in his new state, and paused only long enough for some evasively polite remarks. It was plain that he had nothing to discuss with me when in this condition—and I noticed that he did not even trouble to give the old three-and-two signal when ringing the doorbell. As on that evening in the car, I felt a faint, infinitely deep horror which I could not explain; so that his swift departure was a prodigious relief.

In mid-September Derby was away for a week, and some of the decadent college set talked knowingly of the matter—hinting at a meeting with a notorious cult-leader, lately expelled from England, who had established headquarters in New York. For my part I could not get that strange ride from Maine out of my head. The transformation I had witnessed had affected me profoundly, and I caught myself again and again trying to account for the thing—and for the extreme horror it had inspired in me.

But the oddest rumours were those about the sobbing in the old Crowninshield house. The voice seemed to be a woman's, and some of the younger people thought it sounded like Asenath's. It was heard only at rare intervals, and would sometimes be choked off as if by force. There was talk of an investigation, but this was dispelled one day when Asenath appeared in the streets and chatted in a sprightly way with a large number of acquaintances—apologising for her recent absences and speaking incidentally about the nervous breakdown and hysteria of a guest from Boston. The guest was never seen, but Asenath's appearance left nothing to be said. And then someone complicated matters by whispering that the sobs had once or twice been in a man's voice.

One evening in mid-October I heard the familiar three-and-two ring at the front door. Answering it myself, I found Edward on the steps, and saw in a moment that his personality was the old one which I had not encountered since the day of his ravings on that terrible ride from Chesuncook. His face was twitching with a mixture of odd emotions in which fear and triumph seemed to share dominion, and he looked furtively over his shoulder as I closed the door behind him.

Following me clumsily to the study, he asked for some whiskey to steady his nerves. I forbore to question him, but waited till he felt like beginning whatever he wanted to say. At length he ventured some information in a choking voice.

"Asenath has gone, Dan. We had a long talk last night while the servants were out, and I made her promise to stop preying on me. Of course I had certain—certain occult defences I never told you about. She had to give in, but got frightfully angry. Just packed up and started for New York—walked right out to catch the 8:20 in to Boston. I suppose people will talk, but I can't help that. You needn't mention that there was any trouble—just say she's gone on a long research trip.

"She's probably going to stay with one of her horrible groups of devotees. I hope she'll go west and get a divorce—anyhow, I've made her promise to keep away and let me alone. It was horrible, Dan—she was stealing my body—crowding me out—making a prisoner of me. I lay low and pretended to let her do it, but I had to be on the watch. I could plan if I was careful, for she can't read my mind literally, or in detail. All she could read of my planning was a sort of general mood of rebellion—and she always thought I was helpless. Never thought I could get the best of her … but I had a spell or two that worked."

Derby looked over his shoulder and took some more whiskey.

"I paid off those damned servants this morning when they got back. They were ugly about it, and asked questions, but they went. They're her kind—Innsmouth people—and were hand and glove with her. I hope they'll let me alone—I didn't like the way they laughed when they walked away. I must get as many of Dad's old servants again as I can. I'll move back home now.

"I suppose you think I'm crazy, Dan—but Arkham history ought to hint at things that back up what I've told you—and what I'm going to tell you. You've seen one of the changes, too—in your car after I told you about Asenath that day coming from Maine. That was when she got me—drove me out of my body. The last thing of the ride I remember was when I was all worked up trying to tell you *what that she-devil is.* Then she got me, and in a flash I was back at the house—in the library where those damned servants had me locked up—and in that cursed fiend's body … that isn't even human…. You know, it was she you must have ridden home with … that preying wolf in my body…. You ought to have known the difference!"

I shuddered as Derby paused. Surely, I *had* known the difference—yet could I accept an explanation as insane as this? But my distracted caller was growing even wilder.

"I had to save myself—I had to, Dan! She'd have got me for good at Hallowmass—they hold a Sabbat up there beyond Chesuncook, and the sacrifice would have clinched things. She'd have got me for good … she'd have been I, and I'd have been she … for ever … too late…. My body'd have been hers for good…. She'd have been a man, and fully human, just as she wanted to be…. I suppose she'd have put me out of the way—killed her own ex-body with me in it, damn her, *just as she did before*—just as she, he, or it did before...."

Edward's face was now atrociously distorted, and he bent it uncomfortably close to mine as his voice fell to a whisper.

"You must know what I hinted in the car—*that she isn't Asenath at all, but really old Ephraim himself.* I suspected it a year and a half ago, and I know it now. Her handwriting shews it when she's off guard—sometimes she jots down a note in writing that's just like her father's manuscripts, stroke for stroke—and sometimes she says things that nobody but an old man like Ephraim could say. He changed forms with her when he felt death coming—she was the only one he could find with the right kind of brain and a weak enough will—he got her body permanently, just as she almost got mine, and then poisoned the old body he'd put her into. Haven't you seen old Ephraim's soul glaring out of that she-devil's eyes dozens of times ... and out of mine when she had control of my body?"

The whisperer was panting, and paused for breath. I said nothing, and when he resumed his voice was nearer normal. This, I reflected, was a case for the asylum, but I would not be the one to send him there. Perhaps time and freedom from Asenath would do its work. I could see that he would never wish to dabble in morbid occultism again.

"I'll tell you more later—I must have a long rest now. I'll tell you something of the forbidden horrors she led me into—something of the age-old horrors that even now are festering in out-of-the-way corners with a few monstrous priests to keep them alive. Some people know things about the universe that nobody ought to know, and can do things that nobody ought to be able to do. I've been in it up to my neck, but that's the end. Today I'd burn that damned 'Necronomicon' and all the rest if I were librarian at Miskatonic.

"But she can't get me now. I must get out of that accursed house as soon as I can, and settle down at home. You'll help me, I know, if I need help. Those devilish servants, you know ... and if people should get too inquisitive about Asenath. You see, I can't give them her address.... Then there are certain groups of searchers—certain cults, you know—that might misunderstand our breaking up ... some of them have damnably curious ideas and methods. I know you'll stand by me if anything happens—even if I have to tell you a lot that will shock you...."

I had Edward stay and sleep in one of the guest-chambers that night, and in the morning he seemed calmer. We discussed certain possible arrangements for his moving back into the Derby mansion, and I hoped he would lose no time in making the change. He did not call the next evening, but I saw him frequently during the ensuing weeks. We talked as little as possible about strange and unpleasant things, but discussed the renovation of the old Derby house, and the travels which Edward promised to take with my son and me the following summer.

Of Asenath we said almost nothing, for I saw that the subject was a peculiarly disturbing one. Gossip, of course, was rife; but that was no novelty in connexion with the strange menage at the old Crowninshield house. One thing I did not like was what Derby's banker let fall in an overexpansive mood at the Miskatonic Club—about the cheques Edward was sending regularly to a Moses and Abigail Sargent and a Eunice Babson in Innsmouth. That looked as if those evil-faced servants were extorting some kind of tribute from him—yet he had not mentioned the matter to me.

I wished that the summer—and my son's Harvard vacation—would come, so that we could get Edward to Europe. He was not, I soon saw, mending as rapidly as I had hoped he would; for there was something a bit hysterical in his occasional exhilaration, while his moods of fright and depression were altogether too frequent. The old Derby house was ready by December, yet Edward constantly put off moving. Though he hated and seemed to fear the Crowninshield place, he was at the same time queerly enslaved by it. He could not seem to begin dismantling things, and invented every kind of excuse to postpone action. When I pointed this out to him he appeared unaccountably frightened. His father's old butler—who was there with other reacquired family servants—told me one day that Edward's occasional prowlings about the house, and especially down cellar, looked odd and unwholesome to him. I wondered if Asenath had been writing disturbing letters, but the butler said there was no mail which could have come from her.

VI.

It was about Christmas that Derby broke down one evening while calling on me. I was steering the conversation toward next summer's travels when he suddenly shrieked and leaped up from his chair with a look of shocking, uncontrollable fright—a cosmic panic and loathing such as only the nether gulfs of nightmare could bring to any sane mind.

"My brain! My brain! God, Dan—it's tugging—from beyond—knocking—clawing—that she-devil—even now—Ephraim—Kamog! Kamog!—The pit of the shoggoths—Iä! Shub-Niggurath! The Goat with a Thousand Young! …

"The flame—the flame … beyond body, beyond life … in the earth … oh, God! …"

I pulled him back to his chair and poured some wine down his throat as his frenzy sank to a dull apathy. He did not resist, but kept his lips moving as if talking to himself. Presently I realised that he was trying to talk to me, and bent my ear to his mouth to catch the feeble words.

" … again, again … she's trying … I might have known … nothing can stop that force; not distance, nor magic, nor death … it comes and comes, mostly in the night … I can't leave … it's horrible … oh, God, Dan, *if you only knew as I do just how horrible it is….*"

When he had slumped down into a stupor I propped him with pillows and let normal sleep overtake him. I did not call a doctor, for I knew what would be said of his sanity, and wished to give nature a chance if I possibly could. He waked at midnight, and I put him to bed upstairs, but he was gone by morning. He had let himself quietly out of the house—and his butler, when called on the wire, said he was at home pacing restlessly about the library.

Edward went to pieces rapidly after that. He did not call again, but I went daily to see him. He would always be sitting in his library, staring at nothing and having an air of abnormal *listening.* Sometimes he talked rationally, but always on trivial topics. Any mention of his trouble, of future plans, or of Asenath would send him into a frenzy. His butler said he had frightful seizures at night, during which he might eventually do himself harm.

I had a long talk with his doctor, banker, and lawyer, and finally took the physician with two specialist colleagues to visit him. The spasms that resulted from the first questions were violent and pitiable—and that evening a closed car took his poor struggling body to the Arkham Sanitarium. I was made his guardian and called on him twice weekly—almost weeping to hear his wild shrieks, awesome whispers, and dreadful, droning repetitions of such phrases as "I had to do it—I had to do it … it'll get me … it'll get me … down there … down there in the dark…. Mother, mother! Dan! Save me … save me…."

How much hope of recovery there was, no one could say; but I tried my best to be optimistic. Edward must have a home if he emerged, so I transferred his servants to the Derby mansion, which would surely be his sane choice. What to do about the Crowninshield place with its complex arrangements and collections of utterly inexplicable objects I could not decide, so left it momentarily untouched—telling the Derby housemaid to go over and dust the chief rooms once a week, and ordering the furnace man to have a fire on those days.

The final nightmare came before Candlemas—heralded, in cruel irony, by a false gleam of hope. One morning late in January the sanitarium telephoned to report that Edward's reason had suddenly come back. His continuous memory, they said, was badly impaired; but sanity itself was certain. Of course he must remain some time for observation, but there could be little doubt of the outcome. All going well, he would surely be free in a week.

I hastened over in a flood of delight, but stood bewildered when a nurse took me to Edward's room. The patient rose to greet me, extending his hand with a polite smile; but I saw in an instant that he bore the strangely energised personality which had seemed so foreign to his own nature—the competent personality I had found so vaguely horrible, and which Edward himself had once vowed was the intruding soul of his wife. There was the same blazing vision—so like Asenath's and old Ephraim's—and the same firm mouth; and when he spoke I could sense the same grim, pervasive irony in his voice—the deep irony so redolent of potential evil. This was the person who had driven my car through the night five months before—the person I had not seen since that brief call when he had forgotten the old-time doorbell signal and stirred such nebulous fears in me—and now he filled me with the same dim feeling of blasphemous alienage and ineffable cosmic hideousness.

He spoke affably of arrangements for release—and there was nothing for me to do but assent, despite some remarkable gaps in his recent memories. Yet I felt that something was terribly, inexplicably wrong and abnormal. There were horrors in this thing that I could not reach. This was a sane person—but was it indeed the Edward Derby I had known? If not, who or what was it—*and where was Edward?* Ought it to be free or confined … or ought it to be extirpated from the face of the earth? There was a hint of the abysmally sardonic in everything the creature said—the Asenath-like eyes lent a special and baffling mockery to certain words about the 'early liberty earned by an *especially close confinement*'. I must have behaved very awkwardly, and was glad to beat a retreat.

All that day and the next I racked my brain over the problem. What had happened? What sort of mind looked out through those alien eyes in Edward's face? I could think of nothing but this dimly terrible enigma, and gave up all efforts to perform my usual work. The second morning the hospital called up to say that the recovered patient was unchanged, and by evening I was close to a nervous collapse—a state I admit, though others will vow it coloured my subsequent vision. I have nothing to say on this point except that no madness of mine could account for *all* the evidence.

VII.

It was in the night—after that second evening—that stark, utter horror burst over me and weighted my spirit with a black, clutching panic from which it can never shake free. It began with a telephone call just before midnight. I was the only one up, and sleepily took down the receiver in the library. No one seemed to be on the wire, and I was about to hang up and go to bed when my ear caught a very faint suspicion of sound at the other end. Was someone trying under great difficulties to talk? As I listened I thought I heard a sort of half-liquid bubbling noise—"*glub ... glub ... glub*"—which had an odd suggestion of inarticulate, unintelligible word and syllable divisions. I called "Who is it?" But the only answer was "*glub-glub ... glub-glub*". I could only assume that the noise was mechanical; but fancying that it might be a case of a broken instrument able to receive but not to send, I added, "I can't hear you. Better hang up and try Information." Immediately I heard the receiver go on the hook at the other end.

This, I say, was just before midnight. When that call was traced afterward it was found to come from the old Crowninshield house, though it was fully half a week from the housemaid's day to be there. I shall only hint what was found at that house—the upheaval in a remote cellar storeroom, the tracks, the dirt, the hastily rifled wardrobe, the baffling marks on the telephone, the clumsily used stationery, and the detestable stench lingering over everything. The police, poor fools, have their smug little theories, and are still searching for those sinister discharged servants—who have dropped out of sight amidst the present furore. They speak of a ghoulish revenge for things that were done, and say I was included because I was Edward's best friend and adviser.

Idiots!—do they fancy those brutish clowns could have forged that handwriting? Do they fancy they could have brought what later came? Are they blind to the changes in that body that was Edward's? As for me, *I now believe all that Edward Derby ever told me.* There are horrors beyond life's edge that we do not suspect, and once in a while man's evil prying calls them just within our range. Ephraim—Asenath—that devil called them in, and they engulfed Edward as they are engulfing me.

Can I be sure that I am safe? Those powers survive the life of the physical form. The next day—in the afternoon, when I pulled out of my prostration and was able to walk and talk coherently—I went to the madhouse and shot him dead for Edward's and the world's sake, but can I be sure till he is cremated? They are keeping the body for some silly autopsies by different doctors—but I say he must be cremated. *He must be cremated—he who was not Edward Derby when I shot him.* I shall go mad if he is not, for I may be the next. But my will is not weak—and I shall not let it be undermined by the terrors I know are seething around it. One life—Ephraim, Asenath, and Edward—who now? I *will not* be driven out of my body … I *will not* change souls with that bullet-ridden lich in the madhouse!

But let me try to tell coherently of that final horror. I will not speak of what the police persistently ignored—the tales of that dwarfed, grotesque, malodorous thing met by at least three wayfarers in High St. just before two o'clock, and the nature of the single footprints in certain places. I will say only that just about two the doorbell and knocker waked me—doorbell and knocker both, plied alternately and uncertainly in a kind of weak desperation, *and each trying to keep to Edward's old signal of three-and-two strokes.*

Roused from sound sleep, my mind leaped into a turmoil. Derby at the door—and remembering the old code! That new personality had not remembered it … was Edward suddenly back in his rightful state? Why was he here in such evident stress and haste? Had he been released ahead of time, or had he escaped? Perhaps, I thought as I flung on a robe and bounded downstairs, his return to his old self had brought raving and violence, revoking his discharge and driving him to a desperate dash for freedom. Whatever had happened, he was good old Edward again, and I would help him!

When I opened the door into the elm-arched blackness a gust of insufferably foetid wind almost flung me prostrate. I choked in nausea, and for a second scarcely saw the dwarfed, humped figure on the steps. The summons had been Edward's, but who was this foul, stunted parody? Where had Edward had time to go? His ring had sounded only a second before the door opened.

The caller had on one of Edward's overcoats—its bottom almost touching the ground, and its sleeves rolled back yet still covering the hands. On the head was a slouch hat pulled low, while a black silk muffler concealed the face. As I stepped unsteadily forward, the figure made a semi-liquid sound like that I had heard over the telephone—"*glub … glub …*"—and thrust at me a large, closely written paper impaled on the end of a long pencil. Still reeling from the morbid and unaccountable foetor, I seized this paper and tried to read it in the light from the doorway.

Beyond question, it was in Edward's script. But why had he written when he was close enough to ring—and why was the script so awkward, coarse, and shaky? I could make out nothing in the dim half light, so edged back into the hall, the dwarf figure clumping mechanically after but pausing on the inner door's threshold. The odour of this singular messenger was really appalling, and I hoped (not in vain, thank God!) that my wife would not wake and confront it.

Then, as I read the paper, I felt my knees give under me and my vision go black. I was lying on the floor when I came to, that accursed sheet still clutched in my fear-rigid hand. This is what it said.

> "Dan—go to the sanitarium and kill it. Exterminate it. It isn't Edward Derby any more. She got me—it's Asenath—*and she has been dead three months and a half.* I lied when I said she had gone away. I killed her. I had to. It was sudden, but we were alone and I was in my right body. I saw a candlestick and smashed her head in. She would have got me for good at Hallowmass.
>
> "I buried her in the farther cellar storeroom under some old boxes and cleaned up all the traces. The servants suspected next morning, but they have such secrets that they dare not tell the police. I sent them off, but God knows what they—and others of the cult—will do.
>
> "I thought for a while I was all right, and then I felt the tugging at my brain. I knew what it was—I ought to have remembered. A soul like hers—or Ephraim's—is half detached, and keeps right on after death as long as the body lasts. She was getting me—making me change bodies with her—*seizing my body and putting me in that corpse of hers buried in the cellar.*
>
> "I knew what was coming—that's why I snapped and had to go to the asylum. Then it came—I found myself choked in the dark—in Asenath's rotting carcass down there in the cellar under the boxes where I put it. And I knew she must be in my body at the sanitarium—*permanently,* for it was after Hallowmass, and the sacrifice would work even without her being there—sane, and ready for release as a menace to the world. I was desperate, *and in spite of everything I clawed my way out.*
>
> "I'm too far gone to talk—I couldn't manage to telephone—but I can still write. I'll get fixed up somehow and bring you this last word and warning. *Kill that fiend* if you value the peace and comfort of the world. *See that it is cremated.* If you don't, it will live on and on, body to body for ever, and I can't tell you what it will do. Keep clear of black magic, Dan, it's the devil's business. Goodbye—you've been a great friend. Tell the police whatever they'll believe—and I'm damnably sorry to drag all this on you. I'll be at peace before long—this thing won't hold together much more. Hope you can read this. *And kill that thing—kill it.*
>
> Yours—Ed."

It was only afterward that I read the last half of this paper, for I had fainted at the end of the third paragraph. I fainted again when I saw and smelled what cluttered up the threshold where the warm air had struck it. The messenger would not move or have consciousness any more.

The butler, tougher-fibred than I, did not faint at what met him in the hall in the morning. Instead, he telephoned the police. When they came I had been taken upstairs to bed, but the—other mass—lay where it had collapsed in the night. The men put handkerchiefs to their noses.

What they finally found inside Edward's oddly assorted clothes was mostly liquescent horror. There were bones, too—and a crushed-in skull. Some dental work positively identified the skull as Asenath's.

THE EVIL CLERGYMAN

I was shewn into the attic chamber by a grave, intelligent-looking man with quiet clothes and an iron-grey beard, who spoke to me in this fashion:

"Yes, *he* lived here—but I don't advise your doing anything. Your curiosity makes you irresponsible. *We* never come here at night, and it's only because of *his* will that we keep it this way. You know what *he* did. That abominable society took charge at last, and we don't know where *he* is buried. There was no way the law or anything else could reach the society.

"I hope you won't stay till after dark. And I beg of you to let that thing on the table—the thing that looks like a match box—alone. We don't know what it is, but we suspect it has something to do with what *he* did. *We* even avoid looking at it very steadily."

After a time the man left me alone in the attic room. It was very dingy and dusty, and only primitively furnished, but it had a neatness which shewed it was not a slum-denizen's quarters. There were shelves full of theological and classical books, and another bookcase containing treatises on magic—Paracelsus, Albertus Magnus, Trithemius, Hermes Trismegistus, Borellus, and others in strange alphabets whose titles I could not decipher. The furniture was very plain. There was a door, but it led only into a closet. The only egress was the aperture in the floor up to which the crude, steep staircase led. The windows were of bull's-eye pattern, and the black oak beams bespoke unbelievable antiquity. Plainly, this house was of the Old World. I seemed to know where I was, but cannot recall what I then knew. Certainly the town was *not* London. My impression is of a small seaport.

The small object on the table fascinated me intensely. I seemed to know what to do with it, for I drew a pocket electric light—or what looked like one—out of my pocket and nervously tested its flashes. The light was not white but violet, and seemed less like true light than like some radio-active bombardment. I recall that I did not regard it as a common flashlight—indeed, I *had* a common flashlight in another pocket.

It was getting dark, and the ancient roofs and chimney-pots outside looked very queer through the bull's-eye window-panes. Finally I summoned up courage and propped the small object up on the table against a book—then turned the rays of the peculiar violet light upon it. The light seemed now to be more like a rain or hail of small violet particles than like a continuous beam. As the particles struck the glassy surface at the centre of the strange device, they seemed to produce a crackling noise like the sputtering of a vacuum tube through which sparks are passed. The dark glassy surface displayed a pinkish glow, and a vague white shape seemed to be taking form at its centre. Then I noticed that I was not alone in the room—and put the ray-projector back in my pocket.

But the newcomer did not speak—nor did I hear any sound whatever during all the immediately following moments. Everything was shadowy pantomime, as if seen at a vast distance through some intervening haze—although on the other hand the newcomer and all subsequent comers loomed large and close, as if both near and distant, according to some abnormal geometry.

The newcomer was a thin, dark man of medium height attired in the clerical garb of the Anglican church. He was apparently about thirty years old, with a sallow, olive complexion and fairly good features, but an abnormally high forehead. His black hair was well cut and neatly brushed, and he was clean-shaven though blue-chinned with a heavy growth of beard. He wore rimless spectacles with steel bows. His build and lower facial features were like other clergymen I had seen, but he had a vastly higher forehead, and was darker and more intelligent-looking—also more subtly and concealedly *evil*-looking. At the present moment—having just lighted a faint oil lamp—he looked nervous, and before I knew it he was casting all his magical books into a fireplace on the window side of the room (where the wall slanted sharply) which I had not noticed before. The flames devoured the volumes greedily—leaping up in strange colours and emitting indescribably hideous odours as the strangely hieroglyphed leaves and wormy bindings succumbed to the devastating element. All at once I saw there were others in the room—grave-looking men in clerical costume, one of whom wore the bands and knee-breeches of a bishop. Though I could hear nothing, I could see that they were bringing a decision of vast import to the first-comer. They seemed to hate and fear him at the same time, and he seemed to return these sentiments. His face set itself into a grim expression, but I could see his right hand shaking as he tried to grip the back of a chair. The bishop pointed to the empty case and to the fireplace (where the flames had died down amidst a charred, non-committal mass), and seemed filled with a peculiar loathing. The first-comer then gave a wry smile and reached out with his left hand toward the small object on the table. Everyone then seemed frightened. The procession of clerics began filing down the steep stairs through the trap-door in the floor, turning and making menacing gestures as they left. The bishop was last to go.

The first-comer now went to a cupboard on the inner side of the room and extracted a coil of rope. Mounting a chair, he attached one end of the rope to a hook in the great exposed central beam of black oak, and began making a noose with the other end. Realising he was about to hang himself, I started forward to dissuade or save him. He saw me and ceased his preparations, looking at me with a kind of *triumph* which puzzled and disturbed me. He slowly stepped down from the chair and began gliding toward me with a positively wolfish grin on his dark, thin-lipped face.

I felt somehow in deadly peril, and drew out the peculiar ray-projector as a weapon of defence. Why I thought it could help me, I do not know. I turned it on—full in his face, and saw the sallow features glow first with violet and then with pinkish light. His expression of wolfish exultation began to be crowded aside by a look of profound fear—which did not, however, wholly displace the exultation. He stopped in his tracks—then, flailing his arms wildly in the air, began to stagger backward. I saw he was edging toward the open stair-well in the floor, and tried to shout a warning, but he did not hear me. In another instant he had lurched backward through the opening and was lost to view.

I found difficulty in moving toward the stair-well, but when I did get there I found no crushed body on the floor below. Instead there was a clatter of people coming up with lanterns, for the spell of phantasmal silence had broken, and I once more heard sounds and saw figures as normally tri-dimensional. Something had evidently drawn a crowd to this place. Had there been a noise I had not heard? Presently the two people (simple villagers, apparently) farthest in the lead saw me—and stood paralysed. One of them shrieked loudly and reverberently:

"Ahrrrh! … It be 'ee, zur? Again?"

Then they all turned and fled frantically. All, that is, but one. When the crowd was gone I saw the grave-bearded man who had brought me to this place—standing alone with a lantern. He was gazing at me gaspingly and fascinatedly, but did not seem afraid. Then he began to ascend the stairs, and joined me in the attic. He spoke:

"So you *didn't* let it alone! I'm sorry. I know what has happened. It happened once before, but the man got frightened and shot himself. You ought not to have made *him* come back. You know what *he* wants. But you mustn't get frightened like the other man he got. Something very strange and terrible has happened to you, but it didn't get far enough to hurt your mind and personality. If you'll keep cool, and accept the need for making certain radical readjustments in your life, you can keep right on enjoying the world, and the fruits of your scholarship. But you can't live here—and I don't think you'll wish to go back to London. I'd advise America.

"You mustn't try anything more with that—thing. Nothing can be put back now. It would only make matters worse to do—or summon—anything. You are not as badly off as you might be—but you must get out of here at once and stay away. You'd better thank heaven it didn't go further….

"I'm going to prepare you as bluntly as I can. There's been a certain change—in your personal appearance. *He* always causes that. But in a new country you can get used to it. There's a mirror up at the other end of the room, and I'm going to take you to it. You'll get a shock—though you will see nothing repulsive."

I was now shaking with a deadly fear, and the bearded man almost had to hold me up as he walked me across the room to the mirror, the faint lamp (i.e., that formerly on the table, not the still fainter lantern he had brought) in his free hand. This is what I saw in the glass:

A thin, dark man of medium stature attired in the clerical garb of the Anglican church, apparently about thirty, and with rimless, steel-bowed glasses glistening beneath a sallow, olive forehead of abnormal height.

It was the silent first-comer who had burned his books.

For all the rest of my life, in outward form, I was to be that man!

THE BOOK

My memories are very confused. There is even much doubt as to where they begin; for at times I feel appalling vistas of years stretching behind me, while at other times it seems as if the present moment were an isolated point in a grey, formless infinity. I am not even certain how I am communicating this message. While I know I am speaking, I have a vague impression that some strange and perhaps terrible mediation will be needed to bear what I say to the points where I wish to be heard. My identity, too, is bewilderingly cloudy. I seem to have suffered a great shock—perhaps from some utterly monstrous outgrowth of my cycles of unique, incredible experience.

These cycles of experience, of course, all stem from that worm-riddled book. I remember when I found it—in a dimly lighted place near the black, oily river where the mists always swirl. That place was very old, and the ceiling-high shelves full of rotting volumes reached back endlessly through windowless inner rooms and alcoves. There were, besides, great formless heaps of books on the floor and in crude bins; and it was in one of these heaps that I found the thing. I never learned its title, for the early pages were missing; but it fell open toward the end and gave me a glimpse of something which sent my senses reeling.

There was a formula—a sort of list of things to say and do—which I recognised as something black and forbidden; something which I had read of before in furtive paragraphs of mixed abhorrence and fascination penned by those strange ancient delvers into the universe's guarded secrets whose decaying texts I loved to absorb. It was a key—a guide—to certain gateways and transitions of which mystics have dreamed and whispered since the race was young, and which lead to freedoms and discoveries beyond the three dimensions and realms of life and matter that we know. Not for centuries had any man recalled its vital substance or known where to find it, but this book was very old indeed. No printing-press, but the hand of some half-crazed monk, had traced these ominous Latin phrases in uncials of awesome antiquity.

I remember how the old man leered and tittered, and made a curious sign with his hand when I bore it away. He had refused to take pay for it, and only long afterward did I guess why. As I hurried home through those narrow, winding, mist-choked waterfront streets I had a frightful impression of being stealthily followed by softly padding feet. The centuried, tottering houses on both sides seemed alive with a fresh and morbid malignity—as if some hitherto closed channel of evil understanding had abruptly been opened. I felt that those walls and overhanging gables of mildewed brick and fungous plaster and timber—with fishy, eye-like, diamond-paned windows that leered—could hardly desist from advancing and crushing me … yet I had read only the least fragment of that blasphemous rune before closing the book and bringing it away.

I remember how I read the book at last—white-faced, and locked in the attic room that I had long devoted to strange searchings. The great house was very still, for I had not gone up till after midnight. I think I had a family then—though the details are very uncertain—and I know there were many servants. Just what the year was, I cannot say; for since then I have known many ages and dimensions, and have had all my notions of time dissolved and refashioned. It was by the light of candles that I read—I recall the relentless dripping of the wax—and there were chimes that came every now and then from distant belfries. I seemed to keep track of those chimes with a peculiar intentness, as if I feared to hear some very remote, intruding note among them.

Then came the first scratching and fumbling at the dormer window that looked out high above the other roofs of the city. It came as I droned aloud the ninth verse of that primal lay, and I knew amidst my shudders what it meant. For he who passes the gateways always wins a shadow, and never again can he be alone. I had evoked—and the book was indeed all I had suspected. That night I passed the gateway to a vortex of twisted time and vision, and when morning found me in the attic room I saw in the walls and shelves and fittings that which I had never seen before.

Nor could I ever after see the world as I had known it. Mixed with the present scene was always a little of the past and a little of the future, and every once-familiar object loomed alien in the new perspective brought by my widened sight. From then on I walked in a fantastic dream of unknown and half-known shapes; and with each new gateway crossed, the less plainly could I recognise the things of the narrow sphere to which I had so long been bound. What I saw about me none else saw; and I grew doubly silent and aloof lest I be thought mad. Dogs had a fear of me, for they felt the outside shadow which never left my side. But still I read more—in hidden, forgotten books and scrolls to which my new vision led me—and pushed through fresh gateways of space and being and life-patterns toward the core of the unknown cosmos.

I remember the night I made the five concentric circles of fire on the floor, and stood in the innermost one chanting that monstrous litany the messenger from Tartary had brought. The walls melted away, and I was swept by a black wind through gulfs of fathomless grey with the needle-like pinnacles of unknown mountains miles below me. After a while there was utter blackness, and then the light of myriad stars forming strange, alien constellations. Finally I saw a green-litten plain far below me, and discerned on it the twisted towers of a city built in no fashion I had ever known or read of or dreamed of. As I floated closer to that city I saw a great square building of stone in an open space, and felt a hideous fear clutching at me. I screamed and struggled, and after a blankness was again in my attic room, sprawled flat over the five phosphorescent circles on the floor. In that night's wandering there was no more of strangeness than in many a former night's wandering; but there was more of terror because I knew I was closer to those outside gulfs and worlds than I had ever been before. Thereafter I was more cautious with my incantations, for I had no wish to be cut off from my body and from the earth in unknown abysses whence I could never return.

THE SHADOW OUT OF TIME

I.

After twenty-two years of nightmare and terror, saved only by a desperate conviction of the mythical source of certain impressions, I am unwilling to vouch for the truth of that which I think I found in Western Australia on the night of July 17–18, 1935. There is reason to hope that my experience was wholly or partly an hallucination—for which, indeed, abundant causes existed. And yet, its realism was so hideous that I sometimes find hope impossible. If the thing did happen, then man must be prepared to accept notions of the cosmos, and of his own place in the seething vortex of time, whose merest mention is paralysing. He must, too, be placed on guard against a specific lurking peril which, though it will never engulf the whole race, may impose monstrous and unguessable horrors upon certain venturesome members of it. It is for this latter reason that I urge, with all the force of my being, a final abandonment of all attempts at unearthing those fragments of unknown, primordial masonry which my expedition set out to investigate.

Assuming that I was sane and awake, my experience on that night was such as has befallen no man before. It was, moreover, a frightful confirmation of all I had sought to dismiss as myth and dream. Mercifully there is no proof, for in my fright I lost the awesome object which would—if real and brought out of that noxious abyss—have formed irrefutable evidence. When I came upon the horror I was alone—and I have up to now told no one about it. I could not stop the others from digging in its direction, but chance and the shifting sand have so far saved them from finding it. Now I must formulate some definitive statement—not only for the sake of my own mental balance, but to warn such others as may read it seriously.

These pages—much in whose earlier parts will be familiar to close readers of the general and scientific press—are written in the cabin of the ship that is bringing me home. I shall give them to my son, Prof. Wingate Peaslee of Miskatonic University—the only member of my family who stuck to me after my queer amnesia of long ago, and the man best informed on the inner facts of my case. Of all living persons, he is least likely to ridicule what I shall tell of that fateful night. I did not enlighten him orally before sailing, because I think he had better have the revelation in written form. Reading and re-reading at leisure will leave with him a more convincing picture than my confused tongue could hope to convey. He can do as he thinks best with this account—shewing it, with suitable comment, to any quarters where it will be likely to accomplish good. It is for the sake of such readers as are unfamiliar with the earlier phases of my case that I am prefacing the revelation itself with a fairly ample summary of its background.

My name is Nathaniel Wingate Peaslee, and those who recall the newspaper tales of a generation back—or the letters and articles in psychological journals six or seven years ago—will know who and what I am. The press was filled with details of my strange amnesia in 1908–13, and much was made of the traditions of horror, madness, and witchcraft which lurk behind the ancient Massachusetts town then and now forming my place of residence. Yet I would have it known that there is nothing whatever of the mad or sinister in my heredity and early life. This is a highly important fact in view of the shadow which fell so suddenly upon me from *outside* sources. It may be that centuries of dark brooding had given to crumbling, whisper-haunted Arkham a peculiar vulnerability as regards such shadows—though even this seems doubtful in the light of those other cases which I later came to study. But the chief point is that my own ancestry and background are altogether normal. What came, came from *somewhere else*—where, I even now hesitate to assert in plain words.

I am the son of Jonathan and Hannah (Wingate) Peaslee, both of wholesome old Haverhill stock. I was born and reared in Haverhill—at the old homestead in Boardman Street near

Golden Hill—and did not go to Arkham till I entered Miskatonic University at the age of eighteen. That was in 1889. After my graduation I studied economics at Harvard, and came back to Miskatonic as Instructor of Political Economy in 1895. For thirteen years more my life ran smoothly and happily. I married Alice Keezar of Haverhill in 1896, and my three children, Robert K., Wingate, and Hannah, were born in 1898, 1900, and 1903, respectively. In 1898 I became an associate professor, and in 1902 a full professor. At no time had I the least interest in either occultism or abnormal psychology.

It was on Thursday, May 14, 1908, that the queer amnesia came. The thing was quite sudden, though later I realised that certain brief, glimmering visions of several hours previous—chaotic visions which disturbed me greatly because they were so unprecedented—must have formed premonitory symptoms. My head was aching, and I had a singular feeling—altogether new to me—that someone else was trying to get possession of my thoughts.

The collapse occurred about 10:20 a.m., while I was conducting a class in Political Economy VI—history and present tendencies of economics—for juniors and a few sophomores. I began to see strange shapes before my eyes, and to feel that I was in a grotesque room other than the classroom. My thoughts and speech wandered from my subject, and the students saw that something was gravely amiss. Then I slumped down unconscious in my chair, in a stupor from which no one could arouse me. Nor did my rightful faculties again look out upon the daylight of our normal world for five years, four months, and thirteen days.

It is, of course, from others that I have learned what followed. I shewed no sign of consciousness for sixteen and a half hours, though removed to my home at 27 Crane Street and given the best of medical attention. At 3 a.m. May 15 my eyes opened and I began to speak, but before long the doctors and my family were thoroughly frightened by the trend of my expression and language. It was clear that I had no remembrance of my identity or of my past, though for some reason I seemed anxious to conceal this lack of knowledge. My eyes gazed strangely at the persons around me, and the flexions of my facial muscles were altogether unfamiliar.

Even my speech seemed awkward and foreign. I used my vocal organs clumsily and gropingly, and my diction had a curiously stilted quality, as if I had laboriously learned the English language from books. The pronunciation was barbarously alien, whilst the idiom seemed to include both scraps of curious archaism and expressions of a wholly incomprehensible cast. Of the latter one in particular was very potently—even terrifiedly—recalled by the youngest of the physicians twenty years afterward. For at that late period such a phrase began to have an actual currency—first in England and then in the United States—and though of much complexity and indisputable newness, it reproduced in every least particular the mystifying words of the strange Arkham patient of 1908.

Physical strength returned at once, although I required an odd amount of re-education in the use of my hands, legs, and bodily apparatus in general. Because of this and other handicaps inherent in the mnemonic lapse, I was for some time kept under strict medical care. When I saw that my attempts to conceal the lapse had failed, I admitted it openly, and became eager for information of all sorts. Indeed, it seemed to the doctors that I lost interest in my proper personality as soon as I found the case of amnesia accepted as a natural thing. They noticed that my chief efforts were to master certain points in history, science, art, language, and folklore—some of them tremendously abstruse, and some childishly simple—which remained, very oddly in many cases, outside my consciousness.

At the same time they noticed that I had an inexplicable command of many almost unknown sorts of knowledge—a command which I seemed to wish to hide rather than display. I would inadvertently refer, with casual assurance, to specific events in dim ages outside the range of accepted history—passing off such references as a jest when I saw the surprise they created. And I had a way of speaking of the future which two or three times caused actual fright. These uncanny flashes soon ceased to appear, though some observers laid their vanishment more to a certain furtive caution on my part than to any waning of the strange knowledge behind them. Indeed, I seemed anomalously avid to absorb the speech, customs, and perspectives of the age around me; as if I were a studious traveller from a far, foreign land.

As soon as permitted, I haunted the college library at all hours; and shortly began to arrange for those odd travels, and special courses at American and European universities, which evoked so much comment during the next few years. I did not at any time suffer from a lack of learned contacts, for my case had a mild celebrity among the psychologists of the period. I was lectured upon as a typical example of secondary personality—even though I seemed to puzzle the lecturers now and then with some bizarre symptom or some queer trace of carefully veiled mockery.

Of real friendliness, however, I encountered little. Something in my aspect and speech seemed to excite vague fears and aversions in everyone I met, as if I were a being infinitely removed from all that is normal and healthful. This idea of a black, hidden horror connected with incalculable gulfs of some sort of *distance* was oddly widespread and persistent. My own family formed no exception. From the moment of my strange waking my wife had regarded me with extreme horror and loathing, vowing that I was some utter alien usurping the body of her husband. In 1910 she obtained a legal divorce, nor would she ever consent to see me even after my return to normalcy in 1913. These feelings were shared by my elder son and my small daughter, neither of whom I have ever since seen.

Only my second son Wingate seemed able to conquer the terror and repulsion which my change aroused. He indeed felt that I was a stranger, but though only eight years old held fast to a faith that my proper self would return. When it did return he sought me out, and the courts gave me his custody. In succeeding years he helped me with the studies to which I was driven, and today at thirty-five he is a professor of psychology at Miskatonic. But I do not wonder at the horror I caused—for certainly, the mind, voice, and facial expression of the being that awaked on May 15, 1908 were not those of Nathaniel Wingate Peaslee.

I will not attempt to tell much of my life from 1908 to 1913, since readers may glean all the outward essentials—as I largely had to do—from files of old newspapers and scientific journals. I was given charge of my funds, and spent them slowly and on the whole wisely, in travel and in study at various centres of learning. My travels, however, were singular in the extreme; involving long visits to remote and desolate places. In 1909 I spent a month in the Himalayas, and in 1911 aroused much attention through a camel trip into the unknown deserts of Arabia. What happened on those journeys I have never been able to learn. During the summer of 1912 I chartered a ship and sailed in the arctic north of Spitzbergen, afterward shewing signs of disappointment. Later in that year I spent weeks alone beyond the limits of previous or subsequent exploration in the vast limestone cavern systems of western Virginia—black labyrinths so complex that no retracing of my steps could even be considered.

My sojourns at the universities were marked by abnormally rapid assimilation, as if the secondary personality had an intelligence enormously superior to my own. I have found, also, that my rate of reading and solitary study was phenomenal. I could master every detail of a book merely by glancing over it as fast as I could turn the leaves; while my skill at interpreting complex figures in an instant was veritably awesome. At times there appeared almost ugly reports of my power to influence the thoughts and acts of others, though I seemed to have taken care to minimise displays of this faculty.

Other ugly reports concerned my intimacy with leaders of occultist groups, and scholars suspected of connexion with nameless bands of abhorrent elder-world hierophants. These rumours, though never proved at the time, were doubtless stimulated by the known tenor of some of my reading—for the consultation of rare books at libraries cannot be effected secretly. There is tangible proof—in the form of marginal notes—that I went minutely through such things as the Comte d'Erlette's "Cultes des Goules", Ludvig Prinn's "De Vermis Mysteriis", the "Unaussprechlichen Kulten" of von Junzt, the surviving fragments of the puzzling "Book of Eibon", and the dreaded "Necronomicon" of the mad Arab Abdul Alhazred. Then, too, it is undeniable that a fresh and evil wave of underground cult activity set in about the time of my odd mutation.

In the summer of 1913 I began to display signs of ennui and flagging interest, and to hint to various associates that a change might soon be expected in me. I spoke of returning memories of my earlier life—though most auditors judged me insincere, since all the recollections I gave were casual, and such as might have been learned from my old private papers. About the middle of August I returned to Arkham and reopened my long-closed house in Crane Street. Here I installed a mechanism of the most curious aspect, constructed piecemeal by different makers of scientific apparatus in Europe and America, and guarded carefully from the sight of anyone intelligent enough to analyse it. Those who did see it—a workman, a servant, and the new housekeeper—say that it was a queer mixture of rods, wheels, and mirrors, though only about two feet tall, one foot wide, and one foot thick. The central mirror was circular and convex. All this is borne out by such makers of parts as can be located.

On the evening of Friday, September 26, I dismissed the housekeeper and the maid till noon of the next day. Lights burned in the house till late, and a lean, dark, curiously foreign-looking man called in an automobile. It was about 1 a.m. that the lights were last seen. At 2:15 a.m. a policeman observed the place in darkness, but with the stranger's motor still at the curb. By four o'clock the motor was certainly gone. It was at six that a hesitant, foreign voice on the telephone asked Dr. Wilson to call at my house and bring me out of a peculiar faint. This call—a long-distance one—was later traced to a public booth in the North Station in Boston, but no sign of the lean foreigner was ever unearthed.

When the doctor reached my house he found me unconscious in the sitting-room—in an easy-chair with a table drawn up before it. On the polished table-top were scratches shewing where some heavy object had rested. The queer machine was gone, nor was anything afterward heard of it. Undoubtedly the dark, lean foreigner had taken it away. In the library grate were abundant ashes evidently left from the burning of every remaining scrap of paper on which I had written since the advent of the amnesia. Dr. Wilson found my breathing very peculiar, but after an hypodermic injection it became more regular.

At 11:15 a.m., September 27, I stirred vigorously, and my hitherto mask-like face began to shew signs of expression. Dr. Wilson remarked that the expression was not that of my secondary personality, but seemed much like that of my normal self. About 11:30 I muttered some very curious syllables—syllables which seemed unrelated to any human speech. I appeared, too, to struggle against something. Then, just after noon—the housekeeper and maid having meanwhile returned—I began to mutter in English.

"… of the orthodox economists of that period, Jevons typifies the prevailing trend toward scientific correlation. His attempt to link the commercial cycle of prosperity and depression with the physical cycle of the solar spots forms perhaps the apex of …"

Nathaniel Wingate Peaslee had come back—a spirit in whose time-scale it was still that Thursday morning in 1908, with the economics class gazing up at the battered desk on the platform.

II.

My reabsorption into normal life was a painful and difficult process. The loss of over five years creates more complications than can be imagined, and in my case there were countless matters to be adjusted. What I heard of my actions since 1908 astonished and disturbed me, but I tried to view the matter as philosophically as I could. At last regaining custody of my second son Wingate, I settled down with him in the Crane Street house and endeavoured to resume teaching—my old professorship having been kindly offered me by the college.

I began work with the February, 1914, term, and kept at it just a year. By that time I realised how badly my experience had shaken me. Though perfectly sane—I hoped—and with no flaw in my original personality, I had not the nervous energy of the old days. Vague dreams and queer ideas continually haunted me, and when the outbreak of the world war turned my mind to history I found myself thinking of periods and events in the oddest possible fashion. My conception of *time*—my ability to distinguish between consecutiveness and simultaneousness—seemed subtly disordered; so that I formed chimerical notions about living in one age and casting one's mind all over eternity for knowledge of past and future ages.

The war gave me strange impressions of *remembering* some of its far-off *consequences*—as if I knew how it was coming out and could look *back* upon it in the light of future information. All such quasi-memories were attended with much pain, and with a feeling that some artificial psychological barrier was set against them. When I diffidently hinted to others about my impressions I met with varied responses. Some persons looked uncomfortably at me, but men in the mathematics department spoke of new developments in those theories of relativity—then discussed only in learned circles—which were later to become so famous. Dr. Albert Einstein, they said, was rapidly reducing *time* to the status of a mere dimension.

But the dreams and disturbed feelings gained on me, so that I had to drop my regular work in 1915. Certain of the impressions were taking an annoying shape—giving me the persistent notion that my amnesia had formed some unholy sort of *exchange*; that the secondary personality had indeed been an intruding force from unknown regions, and that my own personality had suffered displacement. Thus I was driven to vague and frightful speculations concerning the whereabouts of my true self during the years that another had held my body. The curious knowledge and strange conduct of my body's late tenant troubled me more and more as I learned further details from persons, papers, and magazines. Queernesses which had baffled others seemed to harmonise terribly with some background of black knowledge which festered in the chasms of my subconsciousness. I began to search feverishly for every scrap of information bearing on the studies and travels of *that other one* during the dark years.

Not all of my troubles were as semi-abstract as this. There were the dreams—and these seemed to grow in vividness and concreteness. Knowing how most would regard them, I seldom mentioned them to anyone but my son or certain trusted psychologists, but eventually I commenced a scientific study of other cases in order to see how typical or non-typical such visions might be among amnesia victims. My results, aided by psychologists, historians, anthropologists, and mental specialists of wide experience, and by a study which included all records of split personalities from the days of daemoniac-possession legends to the medically realistic present, at first bothered me more than they consoled me.

I soon found that my dreams had indeed no counterpart in the overwhelming bulk of true amnesia cases. There remained, however, a tiny residue of accounts which for years baffled and shocked me with their parallelism to my own experience. Some of them were bits of ancient folklore; others were case-histories in the annals of medicine; one or two were anecdotes obscurely buried in standard histories. It thus appeared that, while my special kind of affliction was prodigiously rare, instances of it had occurred at long intervals ever since the beginning of man's annals. Some centuries might contain one, two, or three cases; others none—or at least none whose record survived.

The essence was always the same—a person of keen thoughtfulness seized with a strange secondary life and leading for a greater or lesser period an utterly alien existence typified at first by vocal and bodily awkwardness, and later by a wholesale acquisition of scientific, historic, artistic, and anthropological knowledge; an acquisition carried on with feverish zest and with a wholly abnormal absorptive power. Then a sudden return of the rightful consciousness, intermittently plagued ever after with vague, unplaceable dreams suggesting fragments of some hideous memory elaborately blotted out. And the close resemblance of those nightmares to my own—even in some of the smallest particulars—left no doubt in my mind of their significantly typical nature. One or two of the cases had an added ring of faint, blasphemous familiarity, as if I had heard of them before through some cosmic channel too morbid and frightful to contemplate. In three instances there was specific mention of such an unknown machine as had been in my house before the second change.

Another thing that cloudily worried me during my investigation was the somewhat greater frequency of cases where a brief, elusive glimpse of the typical nightmares was afforded to persons not visited with well-defined amnesia. These persons were largely of mediocre mind or less—some so primitive that they could scarcely be thought of as vehicles for abnormal scholarship and preternatural mental acquisitions. For a second they would be fired with alien force—then a backward lapse and a thin, swift-fading memory of unhuman horrors.

There had been at least three such cases during the past half-century—one only fifteen years before. Had something been *groping blindly through time* from some unsuspected abyss in

Nature? Were these faint cases monstrous, sinister *experiments* of a kind and authorship utterly beyond sane belief? Such were a few of the formless speculations of my weaker hours—fancies abetted by myths which my studies uncovered. For I could not doubt but that certain persistent legends of immemorial antiquity, apparently unknown to the victims and physicians connected with recent amnesia cases, formed a striking and awesome elaboration of memory-lapses such as mine.

Of the nature of the dreams and impressions which were growing so clamorous I still almost fear to speak. They seemed to savour of madness, and at times I believed I was indeed going mad. Was there a special type of delusion afflicting those who had suffered lapses of memory? Conceivably, the efforts of the subconscious mind to fill up a perplexing blank with pseudo-memories might give rise to strange imaginative vagaries. This, indeed (though an alternative folklore theory finally seemed to me more plausible), was the belief of many of the alienists who helped me in my search for parallel cases, and who shared my puzzlement at the exact resemblances sometimes discovered. They did not call the condition true insanity, but classed it rather among neurotic disorders. My course in trying to track it down and analyse it, instead of vainly seeking to dismiss or forget it, they heartily endorsed as correct according to the best psychological principles. I especially valued the advice of such physicians as had studied me during my possession by the other personality.

My first disturbances were not visual at all, but concerned the more abstract matters which I have mentioned. There was, too, a feeling of profound and inexplicable horror concerning *myself.* I developed a queer fear of seeing my own form, as if my eyes would find it something utterly alien and inconceivably abhorrent. When I did glance down and behold the familiar human shape in quiet grey or blue clothing I always felt a curious relief, though in order to gain this relief I had to conquer an infinite dread. I shunned mirrors as much as possible, and was always shaved at the barber's.

It was a long time before I correlated any of these disjointed feelings with the fleeting visual impressions which began to develop. The first such correlation had to do with the odd sensation of an external, artificial restraint on my memory. I felt that the snatches of sight I experienced had a profound and terrible meaning, and a frightful connexion with myself, but that some purposeful influence held me from grasping that meaning and that connexion. Then came that queerness about the element of *time,* and with it desperate efforts to place the fragmentary dream-glimpses in the chronological and spatial pattern.

The glimpses themselves were at first merely strange rather than horrible. I would seem to be in an enormous vaulted chamber whose lofty stone groinings were well-nigh lost in the shadows overhead. In whatever time or place this scene might be, the principle of the arch was known as fully and used as extensively as by the Romans. There were colossal round windows and high arched doors, and pedestals or tables each as tall as the height of an ordinary room. Vast shelves of dark wood lined the walls, holding what seemed to be volumes of immense size with strange hieroglyphs on their backs. The exposed stonework held curious carvings, always in curvilinear mathematical designs, and there were chiselled inscriptions in the same characters that the huge books bore. The dark granite masonry was of a monstrous megalithic type, with lines of convex-topped blocks fitting the concave-bottomed courses which rested upon them. There were no chairs, but the tops of the vast pedestals were littered with books, papers, and what seemed to be writing materials—oddly figured jars of a purplish metal, and rods with stained tips. Tall as the pedestals were, I seemed at times able to view them from above. On some of them were great globes of luminous crystal serving as lamps, and inexplicable machines formed of vitreous tubes and metal rods. The windows were glazed, and latticed with stout-looking bars. Though I dared not approach and peer out them, I could see from where I was the waving tops of singular fern-like growths. The floor was of massive octagonal flagstones, while rugs and hangings were entirely lacking.

Later I had visions of sweeping through Cyclopean corridors of stone, and up and down gigantic inclined planes of the same monstrous masonry. There were no stairs anywhere, nor any passage way less than thirty feet wide. Some of the structures through which I floated must have towered into the sky for thousands of feet. There were multiple levels of black vaults below, and never-opened trap-doors sealed down with metal bands and holding dim suggestions of some special peril. I seemed to be a prisoner, and horror hung broodingly over everything I saw. I felt that the mocking curvilinear hieroglyphs on the walls would blast my soul with their message were I not guarded by a merciful ignorance.

Still later my dreams included vistas from the great round windows, and from the titanic flat roof, with its curious gardens, wide barren area, and high, scalloped parapet of stone, to which the topmost of the inclined planes led. There were almost endless leagues of giant buildings, each in its garden, and ranged along paved roads fully 200 feet wide. They differed greatly in aspect, but few were less than 500 feet square or a thousand feet high. Many seemed so limitless that they must have had a frontage of several thousand feet, while some shot up to mountainous altitudes in the grey, steamy heavens. They seemed to be mainly of stone or concrete, and most of them embodied the oddly curvilinear type of masonry noticeable in the building that held me. Roofs were flat and garden-covered, and tended to have scalloped parapets. Sometimes there were terraces and higher levels, and wide cleared spaces amidst the gardens. The great roads held hints of motion, but in the earlier visions I could not resolve this impression into details.

In certain places I beheld enormous dark cylindrical towers which climbed far above any of the other structures. These appeared to be of a totally unique nature, and shewed signs of prodigious age and dilapidation. They were built of a bizarre type of square-cut basalt masonry, and tapered slightly toward their rounded tops. Nowhere in any of them could the least traces of windows or other apertures save huge doors be found. I noticed also some lower buildings—all crumbling with the weathering of aeons—which resembled these dark cylindrical towers in basic architecture. Around all these aberrant piles of square-cut masonry there hovered an inexplicable aura of menace and concentrated fear, like that bred by the sealed trap-doors.

The omnipresent gardens were almost terrifying in their strangeness, with bizarre and unfamiliar forms of vegetation nodding over broad paths lined with curiously carven monoliths. Abnormally vast fern-like growths predominated; some green, and some of a ghastly, fungoid pallor. Among them rose great spectral things resembling calamites, whose bamboo-like trunks towered to fabulous heights. Then there were tufted forms like fabulous cycads, and grotesque dark-green shrubs and trees of coniferous aspect. Flowers were small, colourless, and unrecognisable, blooming in geometrical beds and at large among the greenery. In a few of the terrace and roof-top gardens were larger and more vivid blossoms of almost offensive contours and seeming to suggest artificial breeding. Fungi of inconceivable size, outlines, and colours speckled the scene in patterns bespeaking some unknown but well-established horticultural tradition. In the larger gardens on the ground there seemed to be some attempt to preserve the irregularities of Nature, but on the roofs there was more selectiveness, and more evidences of the topiary art.

The skies were almost always moist and cloudy, and sometimes I would seem to witness tremendous rains. Once in a while, though, there would be glimpses of the sun—which looked abnormally large—and of the moon, whose markings held a touch of difference from the normal that I could never quite fathom. When—very rarely—the night sky was clear to any extent, I beheld constellations which were nearly beyond recognition. Known outlines were sometimes approximated, but seldom duplicated; and from the position of the few groups I could recognise, I felt I must be in the earth's southern hemisphere, near the Tropic of Capricorn. The far horizon was always steamy and indistinct, but I could see that great jungles of unknown tree-ferns, calamites, lepidodendra, and sigillaria lay outside the city, their fantastic frondage waving mockingly in the shifting vapours. Now and then there would be suggestions of motion in the sky, but these my early visions never resolved.

By the autumn of 1914 I began to have infrequent dreams of strange floatings over the city and and through the regions around it. I saw interminable roads through forests of fearsome growths with mottled, fluted, and banded trunks, and past other cities as strange as the one which persistently haunted me. I saw monstrous constructions of black or iridescent stone in glades and clearings where perpetual twilight reigned, and traversed long causeways over swamps so dark that I could tell but little of their moist, towering vegetation. Once I saw an area of countless miles strown with age-blasted basaltic ruins whose architecture had been like that of the few windowless, round-topped towers in the haunting city. And once I saw the sea—a boundless steamy expanse beyond the colossal stone piers of an enormous town of domes and arches. Great shapeless suggestions of shadow moved over it, and here and there its surface was vexed with anomalous spoutings.

III.

As I have said, it was not immediately that these wild visions began to hold their terrifying quality. Certainly, many persons have dreamed intrinsically stranger things—things compounded of unrelated scraps from daily life, pictures, and reading, and arranged in fantastically novel forms by the unchecked caprices of sleep. For some time I accepted the visions as natural, even though I had never before been an extravagant dreamer. Many of the vague anomalies, I argued, must have come from trivial sources too numerous to track down; while others seemed to reflect a common text-book knowledge of the plants and other conditions of the primitive world of a hundred and fifty million years ago—the world of the Permian or Triassic age. In the course of some months, however, the element of terror did figure with accumulating force. This was when the dreams began so unfailingly to have the aspect of *memories,* and when my mind began to link them with my growing abstract disturbances—the feeling of mnemonic restraint, the curious impressions regarding *time,* the sense of a loathsome exchange with my secondary personality of 1908–13, and, considerably later, the inexplicable loathing of my own person.

As certain definite details began to enter the dreams, their horror increased a thousandfold—until by October, 1915, I felt I must do something. It was then that I began an intensive study of other cases of amnesia and visions, feeling that I might thereby objectivise my trouble and shake clear of its emotional grip. However, as before mentioned, the result was at first almost exactly opposite. It disturbed me vastly to find that my dreams had been so closely duplicated; especially since some of the accounts were too early to admit of any geological knowledge—and therefore of any idea of primitive landscapes—on the subjects' part. What is more, many of these accounts supplied very horrible details and explanations in connexion with the visions of great buildings and jungle gardens—and other things. The actual sights and vague impressions were bad enough, but what was hinted or asserted by some of the other dreamers savoured of madness and blasphemy. Worst of all, my own pseudo-memory was aroused to wilder dreams and hints of coming revelations. And yet most doctors deemed my course, on the whole, an advisable one.

I studied psychology systematically, and under the prevailing stimulus my son Wingate did the same—his studies leading eventually to his present professorship. In 1917 and 1918 I took special courses at Miskatonic. Meanwhile my examination of medical, historical, and anthropological records became indefatigable; involving travels to distant libraries, and finally including even a reading of the hideous books of forbidden elder lore in which my secondary personality had been so disturbingly interested. Some of the latter were the actual copies I had consulted in my altered state, and I was greatly disturbed by certain marginal notations and ostensible *corrections* of the hideous text in a script and idiom which somehow seemed oddly unhuman.

These markings were mostly in the respective languages of the various books, all of which the writer seemed to know with equal though obviously academic facility. One note appended to von Junzt's "Unaussprechlichen Kulten", however, was alarmingly otherwise. It consisted of certain curvilinear hieroglyphs in the same ink as that of the German corrections, but following no recognised human pattern. And these hieroglyphs were closely and unmistakably akin to the characters constantly met with in my dreams—characters whose meaning I would sometimes momentarily fancy I knew or was just on the brink of recalling. To complete my black confusion, many librarians assured me that, in view of previous examinations and records of consultation of the volumes in question, all of these notations must have been made by myself in my secondary state. This despite the fact that I was and still am ignorant of three of the languages involved.

Piecing together the scattered records, ancient and modern, anthropological and medical, I found a fairly consistent mixture of myth and hallucination whose scope and wildness left me utterly dazed. Only one thing consoled me—the fact that the myths were of such early existence. What lost knowledge could have brought pictures of the Palaeozoic or Mesozoic landscape into these primitive fables, I could not even guess, but the pictures had been there. Thus a basis existed for the formation of a fixed type of delusion. Cases of amnesia no doubt created the general myth-pattern—but afterward the fanciful accretions of the myths must have reacted on amnesia sufferers and coloured their pseudo-memories. I myself had read and heard all the early tales during my memory-lapse—my quest had amply proved that. Was it not natural, then, for my subsequent dreams and emotional impressions to become coloured and moulded by what my memory subtly held over from my secondary state? A few of the myths had significant connexions with other cloudy legends of the pre-human world, especially those Hindoo tales involving stupefying gulfs of time and forming part of the lore of modern theosophists.

Primal myth and modern delusion joined in their assumption that mankind is only one—perhaps the least—of the highly evolved and dominant races of this planet's long and largely unknown career. Things of inconceivable shape, they implied, had reared great towers to the sky and delved into every secret of Nature before the first amphibian forbear of man had crawled out of the hot sea three hundred million years ago. Some had come down from the stars; a few were as old as the cosmos itself; others had risen swiftly from terrene germs as far behind the first germs of our life-cycle as those germs are behind ourselves. Spans of thousands of millions of years, and linkages with other galaxies and universes, were freely spoken of. Indeed, there was no such thing as time in its humanly accepted sense.

But most of the tales and impressions concerned a relatively late race, of a queer and intricate shape resembling no life-form known to science, which had lived till only fifty million years before the advent of man. This, they indicated, was the greatest race of all; because it alone had conquered the secret of time. It had learned all things that ever were known *or ever would be known* on the earth, through the power of its keener minds to project themselves into the past and future, even through gulfs of millions of years, and study the lore of every age. From the accomplishments of this race arose all legends of *prophets,* including those in human mythology.

In its vast libraries were volumes of text and pictures holding the whole of earth's annals—histories and descriptions of every species that had ever been or that ever would be, with full records of their arts, their achievements, their languages, and their psychologies. With this aeon-embracing knowledge, the Great Race chose from every era and life-form such thoughts, arts, and processes as might suit its own nature and situation. Knowledge of the past, secured through a kind of mind-casting outside the recognised senses, was harder to glean than knowledge of the future.

In the latter case the course was easier and more material. With suitable mechanical aid a mind would project itself forward in time, feeling its dim, extra-sensory way till it approached the desired period. Then, after preliminary trials, it would seize on the best discoverable representative of the highest of that period's life-forms; entering the organism's brain and setting up therein its own vibrations while the displaced mind would strike back to the period of the displacer, remaining in the latter's body till a reverse process was set up. The projected mind, in the body of the organism of the future, would then pose as a member of the race whose outward form it wore; learning as quickly as possible all that could be learned of the chosen age and its massed information and techniques.

Meanwhile the displaced mind, thrown back to the displacer's age and body, would be carefully guarded. It would be kept from harming the body it occupied, and would be drained of all its knowledge by trained questioners. Often it could be questioned in its own language, when previous quests into the future had brought back records of that language. If the mind came from a body whose language the Great Race could not physically reproduce, clever machines would be made, on which the alien speech could be played as on a musical instrument. The Great Race's members were immense rugose cones ten feet high, and with head and other organs attached to foot-thick, distensible limbs spreading from the apexes. They spoke by the clicking or scraping of huge paws or claws attached to the end of two of their four limbs, and walked by the expansion and contraction of a viscous layer attached to their vast ten-foot bases.

When the captive mind's amazement and resentment had worn off, and when (assuming that it came from a body vastly different from the Great Race's) it had lost its horror at its unfamiliar temporary form, it was permitted to study its new environment and experience a wonder and wisdom approximating that of its displacer. With suitable precautions, and in exchange for suitable services, it was allowed to rove all over the habitable world in titan airships or on the huge boat-like atomic-engined vehicles which traversed the great roads, and to delve freely into the libraries containing the records of the planet's past and future. This reconciled many captive minds to their lot; since none were other than keen, and to such minds the unveiling of hidden mysteries of earth—closed chapters of inconceivable pasts and dizzying vortices of future time which include the years ahead of their own natural ages—forms always, despite the abysmal horrors often unveiled, the supreme experience of life.

Now and then certain captives were permitted to meet other captive minds seized from the future—to exchange thoughts with consciousnesses living a hundred or a thousand or a million years before or after their own ages. And all were urged to write copiously in their own languages of themselves and their respective periods; such documents to be filed in the great central archives.

It may be added that there was one sad special type of captive whose privileges were far greater than those of the majority. These were the dying *permanent* exiles, whose bodies in the future had been seized by keen-minded members of the Great Race who, faced with death, sought to escape mental extinction. Such melancholy exiles were not as common as might be expected, since the longevity of the Great Race lessened its love of life—especially among those superior minds capable of projection. From cases of the permanent projection of elder minds arose many of those lasting changes of personality noticed in later history—including mankind's.

As for the ordinary cases of exploration—when the displacing mind had learned what it wished in the future, it would build an apparatus like that which had started its flight and reverse the process of projection. Once more it would be in its own body in its own age, while the lately captive mind would return to that body of the future to which it properly belonged. Only when one or the other of the bodies had died during the exchange was this restoration impossible. In such cases, of course, the exploring mind had—like those of the death-escapers—to live out an alien-bodied life in the future; or else the captive mind—like the dying permanent exiles—had to end its days in the form and past age of the Great Race.

This fate was least horrible when the captive mind was also of the Great Race—a not infrequent occurrence, since in all its periods that race was intensely concerned with its own future. The number of dying permanent exiles of the Great Race was very slight—largely because of the tremendous penalties attached to displacements of future Great Race minds by the moribund. Through projection, arrangements were made to inflict these penalties on the offending minds in their new future bodies—and sometimes forced re-exchanges were effected. Complex cases of the displacement of exploring or already captive minds by minds in various regions of the past had been known and carefully rectified. In every age since the discovery of mind-projection, a minute but well-recognised element of the population consisted of Great Race minds from past ages, sojourning for a longer or shorter while.

When a captive mind of alien origin was returned to its own body in the future, it was purged by an intricate mechanical hypnosis of all it had learned in the Great Race's age—this because of certain troublesome consequences inherent in the general carrying forward of knowledge in large quantities. The few existing instances of clear transmission had caused, and would cause at known future times, great disasters. And it was largely in consequence of two cases of the kind (said the old myths) that mankind had learned what it had concerning the Great Race. Of all things surviving *physically and directly* from that aeon-distant world, there remained only certain ruins of great stones in far places and under the sea, and parts of the text of the frightful Pnakotic Manuscripts.

Thus the returning mind reached its own age with only the faintest and most fragmentary visions of what it had undergone since its seizure. All memories that could be eradicated were eradicated, so that in most cases only a dream-shadowed blank stretched back to the time of the first exchange. Some minds recalled more than others, and the chance joining of memories had at rare times brought hints of the forbidden past to future ages. There probably never was a time when groups or cults did not secretly cherish certain of these hints. In the "Necronomicon" the presence of such a cult among human beings was suggested—a cult that sometimes gave aid to minds voyaging down the aeons from the days of the Great Race.

And meanwhile the Great Race itself waxed well-nigh omniscient, and turned to the task of setting up exchanges with the minds of other planets, and of exploring their pasts and futures. It sought likewise to fathom the past years and origin of that black, aeon-dead orb in far space whence its own mental heritage had come—for the mind of the Great Race was older than its bodily form. The beings of a dying elder world, wise with the ultimate secrets, had looked ahead for a new world and species wherein they might have long life; and had sent their minds en masse into that future race best adapted to house them—the cone-shaped things that peopled our earth a billion years ago. Thus the Great Race came to be, while the myriad minds sent backward were left to die in the horror of strange shapes. Later the race would again face death, yet would live through another forward migration of its best minds into the bodies of others who had a longer physical span ahead of them.

Such was the background of intertwined legend and hallucination. When, around 1920, I had my researches in coherent shape, I felt a slight lessening of the tension which their earlier stages had increased. After all, and in spite of the fancies prompted by blind emotions, were not most of my phenomena readily explainable? Any chance might have turned my mind to dark studies during the amnesia—and then I read the forbidden legends and met the members of ancient and ill-regarded cults. That, plainly, supplied the material for the dreams and disturbed feelings which came after the return of memory. As for the marginal notes in dream-hieroglyphs and languages unknown to me, but laid at my door by librarians—I might easily have picked up a smattering of the tongues during my secondary state, while the hieroglyphs were doubtless coined by my fancy from descriptions in old legends, and *afterward* woven into my dreams. I tried to verify certain points through conversation with known cult-leaders, but never succeeded in establishing the right connexions.

At times the parallelism of so many cases in so many distant ages continued to worry me as it had at first, but on the other hand I reflected that the excitant folklore was undoubtedly more universal in the past than in the present. Probably all the other victims whose cases were like mine had had a long and familiar knowledge of the tales I had learned only when in my secondary state. When these victims had lost their memory, they had associated themselves with the creatures of their household myths—the fabulous invaders supposed to displace men's minds—and had thus embarked upon quests for knowledge which they thought they could take back to a fancied non-human past. Then when their memory returned, they reversed the associative process and thought of themselves as the former captive minds instead of as the displacers. Hence the dreams and pseudo-memories following the conventional myth-pattern.

Despite the seeming cumbrousness of these explanations, they came finally to supersede all others in my mind—largely because of the greater weakness of any rival theory. And a substantial number of eminent psychologists and anthropologists gradually agreed with me. The more I reflected, the more convincing did my reasoning seem; till in the end I had a really effective bulwark against the visions and impressions which still assailed me. Suppose I did see strange things at night? These were only what I had heard and read of. Suppose I did have odd loathings and perspectives and pseudo-memories? These, too, were only echoes of myths absorbed in my secondary state. Nothing that I might dream, nothing that I might feel, could be of any actual significance.

Fortified by this philosophy, I greatly improved in nervous equilibrium, even though the visions (rather than the abstract impressions) steadily became more frequent and more disturbingly detailed. In 1922 I felt able to undertake regular work again, and put my newly gained knowledge to practical use by accepting an instructorship in psychology at the university. My old chair of political economy had long been adequately filled—besides which, methods of teaching economics had changed greatly since my heyday. My son was at this time just entering on the post-graduate studies leading to his present professorship, and we worked together a great deal.

IV.

I continued, however, to keep a careful record of the outré dreams which crowded upon me so thickly and vividly. Such a record, I argued, was of genuine value as a psychological document. The glimpses still seemed damnably like *memories*, though I fought off this impression with a goodly measure of success. In writing, I treated the phantasms as things seen; but at all other times I brushed them aside like any gossamer illusions of the night. I had never mentioned such matters in common conversation; though reports of them, filtering out as such things will, had aroused sundry rumours regarding my mental health. It is amusing to reflect that these rumours were confined wholly to laymen, without a single champion among physicians or psychologists.

Of my visions after 1914 I will here mention only a few, since fuller accounts and records are at the disposal of the serious student. It is evident that with time the curious inhibitions somewhat waned, for the scope of my visions vastly increased. They have never, though, become other than disjointed fragments seemingly without clear motivation. Within the dreams I seemed gradually to acquire a greater and greater freedom of wandering. I floated through many strange buildings of stone, going from one to the other along mammoth underground passages which seemed to form the common avenues of transit. Sometimes I encountered those gigantic sealed trap-doors in the lowest level, around which such an aura of fear and forbiddenness clung. I saw tremendous tessellated pools, and rooms of curious and inexplicable utensils of myriad sorts. Then there were colossal caverns of intricate machinery whose outlines and purpose were wholly strange to me, and whose *sound* manifested itself only after many years of dreaming. I may here remark that sight and sound are the only senses I have ever exercised in the visionary world.

The real horror began in May, 1915, when I first saw the *living things.* This was before my studies had taught me what, in view of the myths and case histories, to expect. As mental barriers wore down, I beheld great masses of thin vapour in various parts of the building and in the streets below. These steadily grew more solid and distinct, till at last I could trace their monstrous outlines with uncomfortable ease. They seemed to be enormous iridescent cones, about ten feet high and ten feet wide at the base, and made up of some ridgy, scaly, semi-elastic matter. From their apexes projected four flexible, cylindrical members, each a foot thick, and of a ridgy substance like that of the cones themselves. These members were sometimes contracted almost to nothing, and sometimes extended to any distance up to about ten feet. Terminating two of them were enormous claws or nippers. At the end of a third were four red, trumpet-like appendages. The fourth terminated in an irregular yellowish globe some two feet in diameter and having three great dark eyes ranged along its central circumference. Surmounting this head were four slender grey stalks bearing flower-like appendages, whilst from its nether side dangled eight greenish antennae or tentacles. The great base of the central cone was fringed with a rubbery grey substance which moved the whole entity through expansion and contraction.

Their actions, though harmless, horrified me even more than their appearance—for it is not wholesome to watch monstrous objects doing what one has known only human beings to do. These objects moved intelligently around the great rooms, getting books from the shelves and taking them to the great tables, or vice versa, and sometimes writing diligently with a pen-like rod gripped in the greenish head-tentacles. The huge nippers were used in carrying books and in conversation—speech consisting of a kind of clicking and scraping. The objects had no clothing, but wore satchels or knapsacks suspended from the top of the conical trunk. They commonly carried their head and its supporting member at the level of the cone top, though it was frequently raised or lowered. The other three great members tended to rest downward on the sides of the cone, contracted to about five feet each, when not in use. From their rate of reading, writing, and operating their machines (those on the tables seemed somehow connected with thought) I concluded that their intelligence was enormously greater than man's.

Afterward I saw them everywhere; swarming in all the great chambers and corridors, tending monstrous machines in vaulted crypts, and racing along the vast roads in gigantic boat-shaped cars. I ceased to be afraid of them, for they seemed to form supremely natural parts of their environment. Individual differences amongst them began to be manifest, and a few appeared to be under some kind of restraint. These latter, though shewing no physical variation, had a diversity of gestures and habits which marked them off not only from the majority, but very largely from one another. They wrote a great deal in what seemed to my cloudy vision a vast variety of characters—never the typical curvilinear hieroglyphs of the majority. A few, I fancied, used our own familiar alphabet. Most of them worked much more slowly than the general mass of the entities.

All this time *my own part* in the dreams seemed to be that of a disembodied consciousness with a range of vision wider than the normal; floating freely about, yet confined to the ordinary avenues and speeds of travel. Not until August, 1915, did any suggestions of bodily existence begin to harass me. I say *harass*, because the first phase was a purely abstract though infinitely terrible association of my previously noted body-loathing with the scenes of my visions. For a while my chief concern during dreams was to avoid looking down at myself, and I recall how grateful I was for the total absence of large mirrors in the strange rooms. I was mightily troubled by the fact that I always saw the great tables—whose height could not be under ten feet—from a level not below that of their surfaces.

And then the morbid temptation to look down at myself became greater and greater, till one night I could not resist it. At first my downward glance revealed nothing whatever. A moment later I perceived that this was because my head lay at the end of a flexible neck of enormous length. Retracting this neck and gazing down very sharply, I saw the scaly, rugose, iridescent bulk of a vast cone ten feet tall and ten feet wide at the base. That was when I waked half of Arkham with my screaming as I plunged madly up from the abyss of sleep.

Only after weeks of hideous repetition did I grow half-reconciled to these visions of myself in monstrous form. In the dreams I now moved bodily among the other unknown entities, reading terrible books from the endless shelves and writing for hours at the great tables with a stylus managed by the green tentacles that hung down from my head. Snatches of what I read and wrote would linger in my memory. There were horrible annals of other worlds and other universes, and of stirrings of formless life outside all universes. There were records of strange orders of beings which had peopled the world in forgotten pasts, and frightful chronicles of grotesque-bodied intelligences which would people it millions of years after the death of the last human being. And I learned of chapters in human history whose existence no scholar of today has ever suspected. Most of these writings were in the language of the hieroglyphs; which I studied in a queer way with the aid of droning machines, and which was evidently an agglutinative speech with root systems utterly unlike any found in human languages. Other volumes were in other unknown tongues learned in the same queer way. A very few were in languages I knew. Extremely clever pictures, both inserted in the records and forming separate collections, aided me immensely. And all the time I seemed to be setting down a history of my own age in English. On waking, I could recall only minute and meaningless scraps of the unknown tongues which my dream-self had mastered, though whole phrases of the history stayed with me.

I learned—even before my waking self had studied the parallel cases or the old myths from which the dreams doubtless sprang—that the entities around me were of the world's greatest race, which had conquered time and had sent exploring minds into every age. I knew, too, that I had been snatched from my age while *another* used my body in that age, and that a few of the other strange forms housed similarly captured minds. I seemed to talk, in some odd language of claw-clickings, with exiled intellects from every corner of the solar system.

There was a mind from the planet we know as Venus, which would live incalculable epochs to come, and one from an outer moon of Jupiter six million years in the past. Of earthly minds there were some from the winged, star-headed, half-vegetable race of palaeogean Antarctica; one from the reptile people of fabled Valusia; three from the furry pre-human Hyperborean worshippers of Tsathoggua; one from the wholly abominable Tcho-Tchos; two from the arachnid denizens of earth's last age; five from the hardy coleopterous species immediately following mankind, to which the Great Race was some day to transfer its keenest minds en masse in the face of horrible peril; and several from different branches of humanity.

I talked with the mind of Yiang-Li, a philosopher from the cruel empire of Tsan-Chan, which is to come in A.D. 5000; with that of a general of the great-headed brown people who held South Africa in B.C. 50,000; with that of a twelfth-century Florentine monk named Bartolomeo Corsi; with that of a king of Lomar who had ruled that terrible polar land 100,000 years before the squat, yellow Inutos came from the west to engulf it; with that of Nug-Soth, a magician of the dark conquerors of A.D. 16,000; with that of a Roman named Titus Sempronius Blaesus, who had been a quaestor in Sulla's time; with that of Khephnes, an Egyptian of the 14th Dynasty who told me the hideous secret of Nyarlathotep; with that of a priest of Atlantis' middle kingdom; with that of a Suffolk gentleman of Cromwell's day, James Woodville; with that of a court astronomer of pre-Inca Peru; with that of the Australian physicist Nevil Kingston-Brown, who will die in A.D. 2518; with that of an archimage of vanished Yhe in the Pacific; with that of Theodotides, a Graeco-Bactrian official of B.C. 200; with that of an aged Frenchman of Louis XIII's time named Pierre-Louis Montmagny; with that of Crom-Ya, a Cimmerian chieftain of B.C. 15,000; and with so many others that my brain cannot hold the shocking secrets and dizzying marvels I learned from them.

I awaked each morning in a fever, sometimes frantically trying to verify or discredit such information as fell within the range of modern human knowledge. Traditional facts took on new and doubtful aspects, and I marvelled at the dream-fancy which could invent such surprising addenda to history and science. I shivered at the mysteries the past may conceal, and trembled at the menaces the future may bring forth. What was hinted in the speech of post-human entities of the fate of mankind produced such an effect on me that I will not set it down here. After man there would be the mighty beetle civilisation, the bodies of whose members the cream of the Great Race would seize when the monstrous doom overtook the elder world. Later, as the earth's span closed, the transferred minds would again migrate through time and space—to another stopping-place in the bodies of the bulbous vegetable entities of Mercury. But there would be races after them, clinging pathetically to the cold planet and burrowing to its horror-filled core, before the utter end.

Meanwhile, in my dreams, I wrote endlessly in that history of my own age which I was preparing—half voluntarily and half through promises of increased library and travel opportunities—for the Great Race's central archives. The archives were in a colossal subterranean structure near the city's centre, which I came to know well through frequent labours and consultations. Meant to last as long as the race, and to withstand the fiercest of earth's convulsions, this titan repository surpassed all other buildings in the massive, mountain-like firmness of its construction.

The records, written or printed on great sheets of a curiously tenacious cellulose fabric, were bound into books that opened from the top, and were kept in individual cases of a strange, extremely light rustless metal of greyish hue, decorated with mathematical designs and bearing the title in the Great Race's curvilinear hieroglyphs. These cases were stored in tiers of rectangular vaults—like closed, locked shelves—wrought of the same rustless metal and fastened by knobs with intricate turnings. My own history was assigned a specific place in the vaults of the lowest or vertebrate level—the section devoted to the cultures of mankind and of the furry and reptilian races immediately preceding it in terrestrial dominance.

But none of the dreams ever gave me a full picture of daily life. All were the merest misty, disconnected fragments, and it is certain that these fragments were not unfolded in their rightful sequence. I have, for example, a very imperfect idea of my own living arrangements in the dream-world; though I seem to have possessed a great stone room of my own. My restrictions as a prisoner gradually disappeared, so that some of the visions included vivid travels over the mighty jungle roads, sojourns in strange cities, and explorations of some of the vast dark windowless ruins from which the Great Race shrank in curious fear. There were also long sea-voyages in enormous, many-decked boats of incredible swiftness, and trips over wild regions in closed, projectile-like airships lifted and moved by electrical repulsion. Beyond the wide, warm ocean were other cities of the Great Race, and on one far continent I saw the crude villages of the black-snouted, winged creatures who would evolve as a dominant stock after the Great Race had sent its foremost minds into the future to escape the creeping horror. Flatness and exuberant green life were always the keynote of the scene. Hills were low and sparse, and usually displayed signs of volcanic forces.

Of the animals I saw, I could write volumes. All were wild; for the Great Race's mechanised culture had long since done away with domestic beasts, while food was wholly vegetable or synthetic. Clumsy reptiles of great bulk floundered in steaming morasses, fluttered in the heavy air, or spouted in the seas and lakes; and among these I fancied I could vaguely recognise lesser, archaic prototypes of many forms—dinosaurs, pterodactyls, ichthyosaurs, labyrinthodonts, rhamphorhynci, plesiosaurs, and the like—made familiar through palaeontology. Of birds or mammals there were none that I could discern.

The ground and swamps were constantly alive with snakes, lizards, and crocodiles, while insects buzzed incessantly amidst the lush vegetation. And far out at sea unspied and unknown monsters spouted mountainous columns of foam into the vaporous sky. Once I was taken under the ocean in a gigantic submarine vessel with searchlights, and glimpsed some living horrors of awesome magnitude. I saw also the ruins of incredible sunken cities, and the wealth of crinoid, brachiopod, coral, and ichthyic life which everywhere abounded.

Of the physiology, psychology, folkways, and detailed history of the Great Race my visions preserved but little information, and many of the scattered points I here set down were gleaned from my study of old legends and other cases rather than from my own dreaming. For in time, of course, my reading and research caught up with and passed the dreams in many phases; so that certain dream-fragments were explained in advance, and formed verifications of what I had learned. This consolingly established my belief that similar reading and research, accomplished by my secondary self, had formed the source of the whole terrible fabric of pseudo-memories.

The period of my dreams, apparently, was one somewhat less than 150,000,000 years ago, when the Palaeozoic age was giving place to the Mesozoic. The bodies occupied by the Great Race represented no surviving—or even scientifically known—line of terrestrial evolution, but were of a peculiar, closely homogeneous, and highly specialised organic type inclining as much to the vegetable as to the animal state. Cell-action was of an unique sort almost precluding fatigue, and wholly eliminating the need of sleep. Nourishment, assimilated through the red trumpet-like appendages on one of the great flexible limbs, was always semi-fluid and in many aspects wholly unlike the food of existing animals. The beings had but two of the senses which we recognise—sight and hearing, the latter accomplished through the flower-like appendages on the grey stalks above their heads—but of other and incomprehensible senses (not, however, well utilisable by alien captive minds inhabiting their bodies) they possessed many. Their three eyes were so situated as to give them a range of vision wider than the normal. Their blood was a sort of deep-greenish ichor of great thickness. They had no sex, but reproduced through seeds or spores which clustered on their bases and could be developed only under water. Great, shallow tanks were used for the growth of their young—which were, however, reared only in small numbers on account of the longevity of individuals; four or five thousand years being the common life span.

Markedly defective individuals were quietly disposed of as soon as their defects were noticed. Disease and the approach of death were, in the absence of a sense of touch or of physical pain, recognised by purely visual symptoms. The dead were incinerated with dignified ceremonies. Once in a while, as before mentioned, a keen mind would escape death by forward projection in time; but such cases were not numerous. When one did occur, the exiled mind from the future was treated with the utmost kindness till the dissolution of its unfamiliar tenement.

The Great Race seemed to form a single loosely knit nation or league, with major institutions in common, though there were four definite divisions. The political and economic system of each unit was a sort of fascistic socialism, with major resources rationally distributed, and power delegated to a small governing board elected by the votes of all able to pass certain educational and psychological tests. Family organisation was not overstressed, though ties among persons of common descent were recognised, and the young were generally reared by their parents.

Resemblances to human attitudes and institutions were, of course, most marked in those fields where on the one hand highly abstract elements were concerned, or where on the other hand there was a dominance of the basic, unspecialised urges common to all organic life. A few added likenesses came through conscious adoption as the Great Race probed the future and copied what it liked. Industry, highly mechanised, demanded but little time from each citizen; and the abundant leisure was filled with intellectual and aesthetic activities of various sorts. The sciences were carried to an unbelievable height of development, and art was a vital part of life, though at the period of my dreams it had passed its crest and meridian. Technology was enormously stimulated through the constant struggle to survive, and to keep in existence the physical fabric of great cities, imposed by the prodigious geologic upheavals of those primal days.

Crime was surprisingly scanty, and was dealt with through highly efficient policing. Punishments ranged from privilege-deprivation and imprisonment to death or major emotion-wrenching, and were never administered without a careful study of the criminal's motivations. Warfare, largely civil for the last few millennia though sometimes waged against reptilian and octopodic invaders, or against the winged, star-headed Old Ones who centred in the antarctic, was infrequent though infinitely devastating. An enormous army, using camera-like weapons which produced tremendous electrical effects, was kept on hand for purposes seldom mentioned, but obviously connected with the ceaseless fear of the dark, windowless elder ruins and of the great sealed trap-doors in the lowest subterrene levels.

This fear of the basalt ruins and trap-doors was largely a matter of unspoken suggestion—or, at most, of furtive quasi-whispers. Everything specific which bore on it was significantly absent from such books as were on the common shelves. It was the one subject lying altogether under a taboo among the Great Race, and seemed to be connected alike with horrible bygone struggles, and with that future peril which would some day force the race to send its keener minds ahead en masse in time. Imperfect and fragmentary as were the other things presented by dreams and legends, this matter was still more bafflingly shrouded. The vague old myths avoided it—or perhaps all allusions had for some reason been excised. And in the dreams of myself and others, the hints were peculiarly few. Members of the Great Race never intentionally referred to the matter, and what could be gleaned came only from some of the more sharply observant captive minds.

According to these scraps of information, the basis of the fear was a horrible elder race of half-polypous, utterly alien entities which had come through space from immeasurably distant universes and had dominated the earth and three other solar planets about six hundred million years ago. They were only partly material—as we understand matter—and their type of consciousness and media of perception differed wholly from those of terrestrial organisms. For example, their senses did not include that of sight; their mental world being a strange, non-visual pattern of impressions. They were, however, sufficiently material to use implements of normal matter when in cosmic areas containing it; and they required housing—albeit of a peculiar kind. Though their *senses* could penetrate all material barriers, their *substance* could not; and certain forms of electrical energy could wholly destroy them. They had the power of aërial motion despite the absence of wings or any other visible means of levitation. Their minds were of such texture that no exchange with them could be effected by the Great Race.

When these things had come to the earth they had built mighty basalt cities of windowless towers, and had preyed horribly upon the beings they found. Thus it was when the minds of the Great Race sped across the void from that obscure trans-galactic world known in the disturbing and debatable Eltdown Shards as Yith. The newcomers, with the instruments they created, had found it easy to subdue the predatory entities and drive them down to those caverns of inner earth which they had already joined to their abodes and begun to inhabit. Then they had sealed the entrances and left them to their fate, afterward occupying most of their great cities and preserving certain important buildings for reasons connected more with superstition than with indifference, boldness, or scientific and historical zeal.

But as the aeons passed, there came vague, evil signs that the Elder Things were growing strong and numerous in the inner world. There were sporadic irruptions of a particularly hideous character in certain small and remote cities of the Great Race, and in some of the deserted elder cities which the Great Race had not peopled—places where the paths to the gulfs below had not been properly sealed or guarded. After that greater precautions were taken, and many of the paths were closed for ever—though a few were left with sealed trap-doors for strategic use in fighting the Elder Things if ever they broke forth in unexpected places; fresh rifts caused by that selfsame geologic change which had choked some of the paths and had slowly lessened the number of outer-world structures and ruins surviving from the conquered entities.

The irruptions of the Elder Things must have been shocking beyond all description, since they had permanently coloured the psychology of the Great Race. Such was the fixed mood of horror that the very *aspect* of the creatures was left unmentioned—at no time was I able to gain a clear hint of what they looked like. There were veiled suggestions of a monstrous *plasticity*, and of temporary *lapses of visibility*, while other fragmentary whispers referred to their control and military use of *great winds*. Singular *whistling* noises, and colossal footprints made up of five circular toe-marks, seemed also to be associated with them.

It was evident that the coming doom so desperately feared by the Great Race—the doom that was one day to send millions of keen minds across the chasm of time to strange bodies in the safer future—had to do with a final successful irruption of the Elder Beings. Mental projections down the ages had clearly foretold such a horror, and the Great Race had resolved that none who could escape should face it. That the foray would be a matter of vengeance, rather than an attempt to reoccupy the outer world, they knew from the planet's later history—for their projections shewed the coming and going of subsequent races untroubled by the monstrous entities. Perhaps these entities had come to prefer earth's inner abysses to the variable, storm-ravaged surface, since light meant nothing to them. Perhaps, too, they were slowly weakening with the aeons. Indeed, it was known that they would be quite dead in the time of the post-human beetle race which the fleeing minds would tenant. Meanwhile the Great Race maintained its cautious vigilance, with potent weapons ceaselessly ready despite the horrified banishing of the subject from common speech and visible records. And always the shadow of nameless fear hung about the sealed trap-doors and the dark, windowless elder towers.

V.

That is the world of which my dreams brought me dim, scattered echoes every night. I cannot hope to give any true idea of the horror and dread contained in such echoes, for it was upon a wholly intangible quality—the sharp sense of *pseudo-memory*—that such feelings mainly depended. As I have said, my studies gradually gave me a defence against these feelings, in the form of rational psychological explanations; and this saving influence was augmented by the subtle touch of accustomedness which comes with the passage of time. Yet in spite of everything the vague, creeping terror would return momentarily now and then. It did not, however, engulf me as it had before; and after 1922 I lived a very normal life of work and recreation.

In the course of years I began to feel that my experience—together with the kindred cases and the related folklore—ought to be definitely summarised and published for the benefit of serious students; hence prepared a series of articles briefly covering the whole ground and illustrated with crude sketches of some of the shapes, scenes, decorative motifs, and hieroglyphs remembered from the dreams. These appeared at various times during 1928 and 1929 in the *Journal of the American Psychological Society*, but did not attract much attention. Meanwhile I continued to record my dreams with the minutest care, even though the growing stack of reports attained troublesomely vast proportions.

On July 10, 1934, there was forwarded to me by the Psychological Society the letter which opened the culminating and most horrible phase of the whole mad ordeal. It was postmarked Pilbarra, Western Australia, and bore the signature of one whom I found, upon inquiry, to be a mining engineer of considerable prominence. Enclosed were some very curious snapshots. I will reproduce the text in its entirety, and no reader can fail to understand how tremendous an effect it and the photographs had upon me.

I was, for a time, almost stunned and incredulous; for although I had often thought that some basis of fact must underlie certain phases of the legends which had coloured my dreams, I was none the less unprepared for anything like a tangible survival from a lost world remote beyond all imagination. Most devastating of all were the photographs—for here, in cold, incontrovertible realism, there stood out against a background of sand certain worn-down, water-ridged, storm-weathered blocks of stone whose slightly convex tops and slightly concave bottoms told their own story. And when I studied them with a magnifying glass I could see all too plainly, amidst the batterings and pittings, the traces of those vast curvilinear designs and occasional hieroglyphs whose significance had become so hideous to me. But here is the letter, which speaks for itself:

49, Dampier Str.,
Pilbarra, W. Australia,
18 May, 1934.

Prof. N. W. Peaslee,
c/o Am. Psychol. Society,
30, E. 41st Str.,
N. Y. City, U.S.A.

My dear Sir:—

A recent conversation with Dr. E. M. Boyle of Perth, and some papers with your articles which he has just sent me, make it advisable for me to tell you about certain things I have seen in the Great Sandy Desert east of our gold field here. It would seem, in view of the peculiar legends about old cities with huge stonework and strange designs and hieroglyphs which you describe, that I have come upon something very important.

The blackfellows have always been full of talk about "great stones with marks on them", and seem to have a terrible fear of such things. They connect them in some way with their common racial legends about Buddai, the gigantic old man who lies asleep for ages underground with his head on his arm, and who will some day awake and eat up the world. There are some very old and half-forgotten tales of enormous underground huts of great stones, where passages lead down and down, and where horrible things have happened. The blacks claim that once some warriors, fleeing in battle, went down into one and never came back, but that frightful winds began to blow from the place soon after they went down. However, there usually isn't much in what these natives say.

But what I have to tell is more than this. Two years ago, when I was prospecting about 500 miles east in the desert, I came on a lot of queer pieces of dressed stone perhaps 3 × 2 × 2 feet in size, and weathered and pitted to the very limit. At first I couldn't find any of the marks the blackfellows told about, but when I looked close enough I could make out some deeply carved lines in spite of the weathering. They were peculiar curves, just like what the blacks had tried to describe. I imagine there must have been 30 or 40 blocks, some nearly buried in the sand, and all within a circle perhaps a quarter of a mile's diameter.

When I saw some, I looked around closely for more, and made a careful reckoning of the place with my instruments. I also took pictures of 10 or 12 of the most typical blocks, and will enclose the prints for you to see. I turned my information and pictures over to the government at Perth, but they have done nothing with them. Then I met Dr. Boyle, who had read your articles in the *Journal of the American Psychological Society*, and in time happened to mention the stones. He was enormously interested, and became quite excited when I shewed him my snapshots, saying that the stones and markings were just like those of the masonry you had dreamed about and seen described in legends. He meant to write you, but was delayed. Meanwhile he sent me most of the magazines with your articles, and I saw at once from your drawings and descriptions that my stones are certainly the kind you mean. You can appreciate this from the enclosed prints. Later on you will hear directly from Dr. Boyle.

Now I can understand how important all this will be to you. Without question we are faced with the remains of an unknown civilisation older than any dreamed of before, and forming a basis for your legends. As a mining engineer I have some knowledge of geology, and can tell you that these blocks are so ancient they frighten me. They are mostly sandstone and granite, though one is almost certainly made of a queer sort of *cement* or *concrete*. They bear evidence of water action, as if this part of the world had been submerged and come up again after long ages—all since these blocks were made and used. It is a matter of hundreds of thousands of years—or heaven knows how much more. I don't like to think about it.

In view of your previous diligent work in tracking down the legends and everything connected with them, I cannot doubt but that you will want to lead an expedition to the desert and make some archaeological excavations. Both Dr. Boyle and I are prepared to coöperate in such work if you—or organisations known to you—can furnish the funds. I can get together a dozen miners for the heavy digging—the blacks would be of no use, for I've found that they have an almost maniacal fear of this particular spot. Boyle and I are saying nothing to others, for you very obviously ought to have precedence in any discoveries or credit.

The place can be reached from Pilbarra in about 4 days by motor tractor—which we'd need for our apparatus. It is somewhat west and south of Warburton's path of 1873, and 100 miles southeast of Joanna Spring. We could float things up the De Grey River instead of starting from Pilbarra—but all that can be talked over later. Roughly, the stones lie at a point about 22° 3′ 14″ South Latitude, 125° 0′ 39″ East Longitude. The climate is tropical, and the desert conditions are trying. Any expedition had better be made in winter—June or July or August. I shall welcome further correspondence on this subject, and am indeed keenly eager to assist in any plan you may devise. After studying your articles, I am deeply impressed with the profound significance of the whole matter. Dr. Boyle will write later. When rapid communication is needed, a cable to Perth can be relayed by wireless.

Hoping profoundly for an early message,

Believe me,
Most faithfully yours,
Robert B. F. Mackenzie.

Of the immediate aftermath of this letter, much can be learned from the press. My good fortune in securing the backing of Miskatonic University was great, and both Mr. Mackenzie and Dr. Boyle proved invaluable in arranging matters at the Australian end. We were not too specific with the public about our objects, since the whole matter would have lent itself unpleasantly to sensational and jocose treatment by the cheaper newspapers. As a result, printed reports were sparing; but enough appeared to tell of our quest for reported Australian ruins and to chronicle our various preparatory steps.

Professors William Dyer of the college's geology department (leader of the Miskatonic Antarctic Expedition of 1930–31), Ferdinand C. Ashley of the department of ancient history, and Tyler M. Freeborn of the department of anthropology—together with my son Wingate—accompanied me. My correspondent Mackenzie came to Arkham early in 1935 and assisted in our final preparations. He proved to be a tremendously competent and affable man of about fifty, admirably well-read, and deeply familiar with all the conditions of Australian travel. He had tractors waiting at Pilbarra, and we chartered a tramp steamer of sufficiently light draught to get up the river to that point. We were prepared to excavate in the most careful and scientific fashion, sifting every particle of sand, and disturbing nothing which might seem to be in or near its original situation.

Sailing from Boston aboard the wheezy *Lexington* on March 28, 1935, we had a leisurely trip across the Atlantic and Mediterranean, through the Suez Canal, down the Red Sea, and across the Indian Ocean to our goal. I need not tell how the sight of the low, sandy West Australian coast depressed me, and how I detested the crude mining town and dreary gold fields where the tractors were given their last loads. Dr. Boyle, who met us, proved to be elderly, pleasant, and intelligent—and his knowledge of psychology led him into many long discussions with my son and me.

Discomfort and expectancy were oddly mingled in most of us when at length our party of eighteen rattled forth over the arid leagues of sand and rock. On Friday, May 31st, we forded a branch of the De Grey and entered the realm of utter desolation. A certain positive terror grew on me as we advanced to this actual site of the elder world behind the legends—a terror of course abetted by the fact that my disturbing dreams and pseudo-memories still beset me with unabated force.

It was on Monday, June 3, that we saw the first of the half-buried blocks. I cannot describe the emotions with which I actually touched—in objective reality—a fragment of Cyclopean masonry in every respect like the blocks in the walls of my dream-buildings. There was a distinct trace of carving—and my hands trembled as I recognised part of a curvilinear decorative scheme made hellish to me through years of tormenting nightmare and baffling research.

A month of digging brought a total of some 1250 blocks in varying stages of wear and disintegration. Most of these were carven megaliths with curved tops and bottoms. A minority were smaller, flatter, plain-surfaced, and square or octagonally cut—like those of the floors and pavements in my dreams—while a few were singularly massive and curved or slanted in such a manner as to suggest use in vaulting or groining, or as parts of arches or round window casings. The deeper—and the farther north and east—we dug, the more blocks we found; though we still failed to discover any trace of arrangement among them. Prof. Dyer was appalled at the measureless age of the fragments, and Freeborn found traces of symbols which fitted darkly into certain Papuan and Polynesian legends of infinite antiquity. The condition and scattering of the blocks told mutely of vertiginous cycles of time and geologic upheavals of cosmic savagery.

We had an aëroplane with us, and my son Wingate would often go up to different heights and scan the sand-and-rock waste for signs of dim, large-scale outlines—either differences of level or trails of scattered blocks. His results were virtually negative; for whenever he would one day think he had glimpsed some significant trend, he would on his next trip find the impression replaced by another equally insubstantial—a result of the shifting, wind-blown sand. One or two of these ephemeral suggestions, though, affected me queerly and disagreeably. They seemed, after a fashion, to dovetail horribly with something which I had dreamed or read, but which I could no longer remember. There was a terrible *pseudo-familiarity* about them—which somehow made me look furtively and apprehensively over the abominable, sterile terrain toward the north and northeast.

Around the first week in July I developed an unaccountable set of mixed emotions about that general northeasterly region. There was horror, and there was curiosity—but more than that, there was a persistent and perplexing illusion of *memory.* I tried all sorts of psychological expedients to get these notions out of my head, but met with no success. Sleeplessness also gained upon me, but I almost welcomed this because of the resultant shortening of my dream-periods. I acquired the habit of taking long, lone walks in the desert late at night—usually to the north or northeast, whither the sum of my strange new impulses seemed subtly to pull me.

Sometimes on these walks, I would stumble over nearly buried fragments of the ancient masonry. Though there were fewer visible blocks here than where we had started, I felt sure that there must be a vast abundance beneath the surface. The ground was less level than at our camp, and the prevailing high winds now and then piled the sand into fantastic temporary hillocks—exposing some traces of the elder stones while it covered other traces. I was queerly anxious to have the excavations extend to this territory, yet at the same time dreaded what might be revealed. Obviously, I was getting into a rather bad state—all the worse because I could not account for it.

An indication of my poor nervous health can be gained from my response to an odd discovery which I made on one of my nocturnal rambles. It was on the evening of July 11th, when a gibbous moon flooded the mysterious hillocks with a curious pallor. Wandering somewhat beyond my usual limits, I came upon a great stone which seemed to differ markedly from any we had yet encountered. It was almost wholly covered, but I stooped and cleared away the sand with my hands, later studying the object carefully and supplementing the moonlight with my electric torch. Unlike the other very large blocks, this one was perfectly square-cut, with no convex or concave surface. It seemed, too, to be of a dark basaltic substance wholly dissimilar to the granite and sandstone and occasional concrete of the now familiar fragments.

Suddenly I rose, turned, and ran for the camp at top speed. It was a wholly unconscious and irrational flight, and only when I was close to my tent did I fully realise why I had run. Then it came to me. The queer dark stone was something which I had dreamed and read about, and which was linked with the uttermost horrors of the aeon-old legendry. It was one of the blocks of that basaltic elder masonry which the fabled Great Race held in such fear—the tall, windowless ruins left by those brooding, half-material, alien Things that festered in earth's nether abysses and against whose wind-like, invisible forces the trap-doors were sealed and the sleepless sentinels posted.

I remained awake all that night, but by dawn realised how silly I had been to let the shadow of a myth upset me. Instead of being frightened, I should have had a discoverer's enthusiasm. The next forenoon I told the others about my find, and Dyer, Freeborn, Boyle, my son, and I set out to view the anomalous block. Failure, however, confronted us. I had formed no clear idea of the stone's location, and a late wind had wholly altered the hillocks of shifting sand.

VI.

I come now to the crucial and most difficult part of my narrative—all the more difficult because I cannot be quite certain of its reality. At times I feel uncomfortably sure that I was not dreaming or deluded; and it is this feeling—in view of the stupendous implications which the objective truth of my experience would raise—which impels me to make this record. My son—a trained psychologist with the fullest and most sympathetic knowledge of my whole case—shall be the primary judge of what I have to tell.

First let me outline the externals of the matter, as those at the camp know them. On the night of July 17–18, after a windy day, I retired early but could not sleep. Rising shortly before eleven, and afflicted as usual with that strange feeling regarding the northeastward terrain, I set out on one of my typical nocturnal walks; seeing and greeting only one person—an Australian miner named Tupper—as I left our precincts. The moon, slightly past full, shone from a clear sky and drenched the ancient sands with a white, leprous radiance which seemed to me somehow infinitely evil. There was no longer any wind, nor did any return for nearly five hours, as amply attested by Tupper and others who did not sleep through the night. The Australian last saw me walking rapidly across the pallid, secret-guarding hillocks toward the northeast.

About 3:30 a.m. a violent wind blew up, waking everyone in camp and felling three of the tents. The sky was unclouded, and the desert still blazed with that leprous moonlight. As the party saw to the tents my absence was noted, but in view of my previous walks this circumstance gave no one alarm. And yet as many as three men—all Australians—seemed to feel something sinister in the air. Mackenzie explained to Prof. Freeborn that this was a fear picked up from blackfellow folklore—the natives having woven a curious fabric of malignant myth about the high winds which at long intervals sweep across the sands under a clear sky. Such winds, it is whispered, blow out of great stone huts under the ground where terrible things have happened—and are never felt except near places where the big marked stones are scattered. Close to four the gale subsided as suddenly as it had begun, leaving the sand hills in new and unfamiliar shapes.

It was just past five, with the bloated, fungoid moon sinking in the west, when I staggered into camp—hatless, tattered, features scratched and ensanguined, and without my electric torch. Most of the men had returned to bed, but Prof. Dyer was smoking a pipe in front of his tent. Seeing my winded and almost frenzied state, he called Dr. Boyle, and the two of them got me on my cot and made me comfortable. My son, roused by the stir, soon joined them, and they all tried to force me to lie still and attempt sleep.

But there was no sleep for me. My psychological state was very extraordinary—different from anything I had previously suffered. After a time I insisted on talking—nervously and elaborately explaining my condition. I told them I had become fatigued, and had lain down in the sand for a nap. There had, I said, been dreams even more frightful than usual—and when I was awaked by the sudden high wind my overwrought nerves had snapped. I had fled in panic, frequently falling over half-buried stones and thus gaining my tattered and bedraggled aspect. I must have slept long—hence the hours of my absence.

Of anything strange either seen or experienced I hinted absolutely nothing—exercising the greatest self-control in that respect. But I spoke of a change of mind regarding the whole work of the expedition, and earnestly urged a halt in all digging toward the northeast. My reasoning was patently weak—for I mentioned a dearth of blocks, a wish not to offend the superstitious miners, a possible shortage of funds from the college, and other things either untrue or irrelevant. Naturally, no one paid the least attention to my new wishes—not even my son, whose concern for my health was very obvious.

The next day I was up and around the camp, but took no part in the excavations. Seeing that I could not stop the work, I decided to return home as soon as possible for the sake of my nerves, and made my son promise to fly me in the plane to Perth—a thousand miles to the southwest—as soon as he had surveyed the region I wished let alone. If, I reflected, the thing I had seen was still visible, I might decide to attempt a specific warning even at the cost of ridicule. It was just conceivable that the miners who knew the local folklore might back me up. Humouring me, my son made the survey that very afternoon; flying over all the terrain my walk could possibly have covered. Yet nothing of what I had found remained in sight. It was the case of the anomalous basalt block all over again—the shifting sand had wiped out every trace. For an instant I half regretted having lost a certain awesome object in my stark fright—but now I know that the loss was merciful. I can still believe my whole experience an illusion—especially if, as I devoutly hope, that hellish abyss is never found.

Wingate took me to Perth July 20, though declining to abandon the expedition and return home. He stayed with me till the 25th, when the steamer for Liverpool sailed. Now, in the cabin of the *Empress,* I am pondering long and frantically on the entire matter, and have decided that my son at least must be informed. It shall rest with him whether to diffuse the matter more widely. In order to meet any eventuality I have prepared this summary of the background—as already known in a scattered way to others—and will now tell as briefly as possible what seemed to happen during my absence from the camp that hideous night.

Nerves on edge, and whipped into a kind of perverse eagerness by that inexplicable, dread-mingled, pseudo-mnemonic urge toward the northeast, I plodded on beneath the evil, burning moon. Here and there I saw, half-shrouded by the sand, those primal Cyclopean blocks left from nameless and forgotten aeons. The incalculable age and brooding horror of this monstrous waste began to oppress me as never before, and I could not keep from thinking of my maddening dreams, of the frightful legends which lay behind them, and of the present fears of natives and miners concerning the desert and its carven stones.

And yet I plodded on as if to some eldritch rendezvous—more and more assailed by bewildering fancies, compulsions, and pseudo-memories. I thought of some of the possible contours of the lines of stones as seen by my son from the air, and wondered why they seemed at once so ominous and so familiar. Something was fumbling and rattling at the latch of my recollection, while another unknown force sought to keep the portal barred.

The night was windless, and the pallid sand curved upward and downward like frozen waves of the sea. I had no goal, but somehow ploughed along as if with fate-bound assurance. My dreams welled up into the waking world, so that each sand-embedded megalith seemed part of endless rooms and corridors of pre-human masonry, carved and hieroglyphed with symbols that I knew too well from years of custom as a captive mind of the Great Race. At moments I fancied I saw those omniscient conical horrors moving about at their accustomed tasks, and I feared to look down lest I find myself one with them in aspect. Yet all the while I saw the sand-covered blocks as well as the rooms and corridors; the evil, burning moon as well as the lamps of luminous crystal; the endless desert as well as the waving ferns and cycads beyond the windows. I was awake and dreaming at the same time.

I do not know how long or how far—or indeed, in just what direction—I had walked when I first spied the heap of blocks bared by the day's wind. It was the largest group in one place that I had so far seen, and so sharply did it impress me that the visions of fabulous aeons faded suddenly away. Again there were only the desert and the evil moon and the shards of an unguessed past. I drew close and paused, and cast the added light of my electric torch over the tumbled pile. A hillock had blown away, leaving a low, irregularly round mass of megaliths and smaller fragments some forty feet across and from two to eight feet high.

From the very outset I realised that there was some utterly unprecedented quality about these stones. Not only was the mere number of them quite without parallel, but something in the sand-worn traces of design arrested me as I scanned them under the mingled beams of the moon and my torch. Not that any one differed essentially from the earlier specimens we had found. It was something subtler than that. The impression did not come when I looked at one block alone, but only when I ran my eye over several almost simultaneously. Then, at last, the truth dawned on me. The curvilinear patterns on many of these blocks were *closely related*—parts of one vast decorative conception. For the first time in this aeon-shaken waste I had come upon a mass of masonry in its old position—tumbled and fragmentary, it is true, but none the less existing in a very definite sense.

Mounting at a low place, I clambered laboriously over the heap; here and there clearing away the sand with my fingers, and constantly striving to interpret varieties of size, shape, and style, and relationships of design. After a while I could vaguely guess at the nature of the bygone structure, and at the designs which had once stretched over the vast surfaces of the primal masonry. The perfect identity of the whole with some of my dream-glimpses appalled and unnerved me. This was once a Cyclopean corridor thirty feet wide and thirty feet tall, paved with octagonal blocks and solidly vaulted overhead. There would have been rooms opening off on the right, and at the farther end one of those strange inclined planes would have wound down to still lower depths.

I started violently as these conceptions occurred to me, for there was more in them than the blocks themselves had supplied. How did I know that this level should have been far underground? How did I know that the plane leading upward should have been behind me? How did I know that the long subterrene passage to the Square of Pillars ought to lie on the left one level above me? How did I know that the room of machines, and the rightward-leading tunnel to the central archives, ought to lie two levels below? How did I know that there would be one of those horrible, metal-banded trap-doors at the very bottom, four levels down? Bewildered by this intrusion from the dream-world, I found myself shaking and bathed in a cold perspiration.

Then, as a last, intolerable touch, I felt that faint, insidious stream of cool air trickling upward from a depressed place near the centre of the huge heap. Instantly, as once before, my visions faded, and I saw again only the evil moonlight, the brooding desert, and the spreading tumulus of palaeogean masonry. Something real and tangible, yet fraught with infinite suggestions of nighted mystery, now confronted me. For that stream of air could argue but one thing—a hidden gulf of great size beneath the disordered blocks on the surface.

My first thought was of the sinister blackfellow legends of vast underground huts among the megaliths where horrors happen and great winds are born. Then thoughts of my own dreams came back, and I felt dim pseudo-memories tugging at my mind. What manner of place lay below me? What primal, inconceivable source of age-old myth-cycles and haunting nightmares might I be on the brink of uncovering? It was only for a moment that I hesitated, for more than curiosity or scientific zeal was driving me on and working against my growing fear.

I seemed to move almost automatically, as if in the clutch of some compelling fate. Pocketing my torch, and struggling with a strength I had not thought I possessed, I wrenched aside first one titan fragment of stone and then another, till there welled up a strong draught whose dampness contrasted oddly with the desert's dry air. A black rift began to yawn, and at length—when I had pushed away every fragment small enough to budge—the leprous moonlight blazed on an aperture of ample width to admit me.

I drew out my torch and cast a brilliant beam into the opening. Below me was a chaos of tumbled masonry, sloping roughly down toward the north at an angle of about forty-five degrees, and evidently the result of some bygone collapse from above. Between its surface and the ground level was a gulf of impenetrable blackness at whose upper edge were signs of gigantic, stress-heaved vaulting. At this point, it appeared, the desert's sands lay directly upon a floor of some titan structure of earth's youth—how preserved through aeons of geologic convulsion I could not then and cannot now even attempt to guess.

In retrospect, the barest idea of a sudden, lone descent into such a doubtful abyss—and at a time when one's whereabouts were unknown to any living soul—seems like the utter apex of insanity. Perhaps it was—yet that night I embarked without hesitancy upon such a descent. Again there was manifest that lure and driving of fatality which had all along seemed to direct my course. With torch flashing intermittently to save the battery, I commenced a mad scramble down the sinister, Cyclopean incline below the opening—sometimes facing forward as I found good hand and foot holds, and at other times turning to face the heap of megaliths as I clung and fumbled more precariously. In two directions beside me, distant walls of carven, crumbling masonry loomed dimly under the direct beams of my torch. Ahead, however, was only unbroken blackness.

I kept no track of time during my downward scramble. So seething with baffling hints and images was my mind, that all objective matters seemed withdrawn to incalculable distances. Physical sensation was dead, and even fear remained as a wraith-like, inactive gargoyle leering impotently at me. Eventually I reached a level floor strown with fallen blocks, shapeless fragments of stone, and sand and detritus of every kind. On either side—perhaps thirty feet apart—rose massive walls culminating in huge groinings. That they were carved I could just discern, but the nature of the carvings was beyond my perception. What held me most was the vaulting overhead. The beam from my torch could not reach the roof, but the lower parts of the monstrous arches stood out distinctly. And so perfect was their identity with what I had seen in countless dreams of the elder world, that I trembled actively for the first time.

Behind and high above, a faint luminous blur told of the distant moonlit world outside. Some vague shred of caution warned me that I should not let it out of my sight, lest I have no guide for my return. I now advanced toward the wall on my left, where the traces of carving seemed plainest. The littered floor was nearly as hard to traverse as the downward heap had been, but I managed to pick my difficult way. At one place I heaved aside some blocks and kicked away the detritus to see what the pavement was like, and shuddered at the utter, fateful familiarity of the great octagonal stones whose buckled surface still held roughly together.

Reaching a convenient distance from the wall, I cast the torchlight slowly and carefully over its worn remnants of carving. Some bygone influx of water seemed to have acted on the sandstone surface, while there were curious incrustations which I could not explain. In places the masonry was very loose and distorted, and I wondered how many aeons more this primal, hidden edifice could keep its remaining traces of form amidst earth's heavings.

But it was the carvings themselves which excited me most. Despite their time-crumbled state, they were relatively easy to trace at close range; and the complete, intimate familiarity of every detail almost stunned my imagination. That the major attributes of this hoary masonry should be familiar, was not beyond normal credibility. Powerfully impressing the weavers of certain myths, they had become embodied in a stream of cryptic lore which, somehow coming to my notice during the amnesic period, had evoked vivid images in my subconscious mind. But how could I explain the exact and minute fashion in which each line and spiral of these strange designs tallied with what I had dreamt for more than a score of years? What obscure, forgotten iconography could have reproduced each subtle shading and nuance which so persistently, exactly, and unvaryingly besieged my sleeping vision night after night?

For this was no chance or remote resemblance. Definitely and absolutely, the millennially ancient, aeon-hidden corridor in which I stood was the original of something I knew in sleep as intimately as I knew my own house in Crane Street, Arkham. True, my dreams shewed the place in its undecayed prime; but the identity was no less utter on that account. I was wholly and horribly oriented. The particular structure I was in was known to me. Known, too, was its place in that terrible elder city of dream. That I could visit unerringly any point in that structure or in that city which had escaped the changes and devastations of uncounted ages, I realised with hideous and instinctive certainty. What in God's name could all this mean? How had I come to know what I knew? And what awful reality could lie behind those antique tales of the beings which had dwelt in this labyrinth of primordial stone?

Words can convey only fractionally the welter of dread and bewilderment which ate at my spirit. I knew this place. I knew what lay below me, and what had lain overhead before the myriad towering stories had fallen to dust and debris and the desert. No need now, I thought with a shudder, to keep that faint blur of moonlight in view. I was torn betwixt a longing to flee and a feverish mixture of burning curiosity and driving fatality. What had happened to this monstrous megalopolis of eld in the millions of years since the time of my dreams? Of the subterrene mazes which had underlain the city and linked all its titan towers, how much had still survived the writhings of earth's crust?

Had I come upon a whole buried world of unholy archaism? Could I find still the house of the writing-master, and the tower where S'gg'ha, a captive mind from the star-headed vegetable carnivores of Antarctica, had chiselled certain pictures on the blank spaces of the walls? Would the passage at the second level down, to the hall of the alien minds, be still unchoked and traversable? In that hall the captive mind of an incredible entity—a half-plastic denizen of the hollow interior of an unknown trans-Plutonian planet eighteen million years in the future—had kept a certain thing which it had modelled from clay.

I shut my eyes and put my hand to my head in a vain, pitiful effort to drive these insane dream-fragments from my consciousness. Then, for the first time, I felt acutely the coolness, motion, and dampness of the surrounding air. Shuddering, I realised that a vast chain of aeon-dead black gulfs must indeed be yawning somewhere beyond and below me. I thought of the frightful chambers and corridors and inclines as I recalled them from my dreams. Would the way to the central archives still be open? Again that driving fatality tugged insistently at my brain as I recalled the awesome records that once lay cased in those rectangular vaults of rustless metal.

There, said the dreams and legends, had reposed the whole history, past and future, of the cosmic space-time continuum—written by captive minds from every orb and every age in the solar system. Madness, of course—but had I not now stumbled into a nighted world as mad as I? I thought of the locked metal shelves, and of the curious knob-twistings needed to open each one. My own came vividly into my consciousness. How often had I gone through that intricate routine of varied turns and pressures in the terrestrial vertebrate section on the lowest level! Every detail was fresh and familiar. If there were such a vault as I had dreamed of, I could open it in a moment. It was then that madness took me utterly. An instant later, and I was leaping and stumbling over the rocky debris toward the well-remembered incline to the depths below.

VII.

From that point forward my impressions are scarcely to be relied on—indeed, I still possess a final, desperate hope that they all form parts of some daemoniac dream—or illusion born of delirium. A fever raged in my brain, and everything came to me through a kind of haze—sometimes only intermittently. The rays of my torch shot feebly into the engulfing blackness, bringing phantasmal flashes of hideously familiar walls and carvings, all blighted with the decay of ages. In one place a tremendous mass of vaulting had fallen, so that I had to clamber over a mighty mound of stones reaching almost to the ragged, grotesquely stalactited roof. It was all the ultimate apex of nightmare, made worse by that blasphemous tug of pseudo-memory. One thing only was unfamiliar, and that was my own size in relation to the monstrous masonry. I felt oppressed by a sense of unwonted smallness, as if the sight of these towering walls from a mere human body were something wholly new and abnormal. Again and again I looked nervously down at myself, vaguely disturbed by the human form I possessed.

Onward through the blackness of the abyss I leaped, plunged, and staggered—often falling and bruising myself, and once nearly shattering my torch. Every stone and corner of that daemoniac gulf was known to me, and at many points I stopped to cast beams of light through choked and crumbling yet familiar archways. Some rooms had totally collapsed; others were bare or debris-filled. In a few I saw masses of metal—some fairly intact, some broken, and some crushed or battered—which I recognised as the colossal pedestals or tables of my dreams. What they could in truth have been, I dared not guess.

I found the downward incline and began its descent—though after a time halted by a gaping, ragged chasm whose narrowest point could not be much less than four feet across. Here the stonework had fallen through, revealing incalculable inky depths beneath. I knew there were two more cellar levels in this titan edifice, and trembled with fresh panic as I recalled the metal-clamped trap-door on the lowest one. There would be no guards now—for what had lurked beneath had long since done its hideous work and sunk into its long decline. By the time of the post-human beetle race it would be quite dead. And yet, as I thought of the native legends, I trembled anew.

It cost me a terrible effort to vault that yawning chasm, since the littered floor prevented a running start—but madness drove me on. I chose a place close to the left-hand wall—where the rift was least wide and the landing-spot reasonably clear of dangerous debris—and after one frantic moment reached the other side in safety. At last gaining the lower level, I stumbled on past the archway of the room of machines, within which were fantastic ruins of metal half-buried beneath fallen vaulting. Everything was where I knew it would be, and I climbed confidently over the heaps which barred the entrance of a vast transverse corridor. This, I realised, would take me under the city to the central archives.

Endless ages seemed to unroll as I stumbled, leaped, and crawled along that debris-cluttered corridor. Now and then I could make out carvings on the age-stained walls—some familiar, others seemingly added since the period of my dreams. Since this was a subterrene house-connecting highway, there were no archways save when the route led through the lower levels of various buildings. At some of these intersections I turned aside long enough to look down well-remembered corridors and into well-remembered rooms. Twice only did I find any radical changes from what I had dreamed of—and in one of these cases I could trace the sealed-up outlines of the archway I remembered.

I shook violently, and felt a curious surge of retarding weakness, as I steered a hurried and reluctant course through the crypt of one of those great windowless ruined towers whose alien basalt masonry bespoke a whispered and horrible origin. This primal vault was round and fully 200 feet across, with nothing carved upon the dark-hued stonework. The floor was here free from anything save dust and sand, and I could see the apertures leading upward and downward. There were no stairs or inclines—indeed, my dreams had pictured those elder towers as wholly untouched by the fabulous Great Race. Those who had built them had not needed stairs or inclines. In the dreams, the downward aperture had been tightly sealed and nervously guarded. Now it lay open—black and yawning, and giving forth a current of cool, damp air. Of what limitless caverns of eternal night might brood below, I would not permit myself to think.

Later, clawing my way along a badly heaped section of the corridor, I reached a place where the roof had wholly caved in. The debris rose like a mountain, and I climbed up over it, passing through a vast empty space where my torchlight could reveal neither walls nor vaulting. This, I reflected, must be the cellar of the house of the metal-purveyors fronting the third square not far from the archives. What had happened to it I could not conjecture.

I found the corridor again beyond the mountain of detritus and stones, but after a short distance encountered a wholly choked place where the fallen vaulting almost touched the perilously sagging ceiling. How I managed to wrench and tear aside enough blocks to afford a passage, and how I dared disturb the tightly packed fragments when the least shift of equilibrium might have brought down all the tons of superincumbent masonry to crush me to nothingness, I do not know. It was sheer madness that impelled and guided me—if, indeed, my whole underground adventure was not—as I hope—a hellish delusion or phase of dreaming. But I did make—or dream that I made—a passage that I could squirm through. As I wriggled over the mound of debris—my torch, switched continuously on, thrust deeply within my mouth—I felt myself torn by the fantastic stalactites of the jagged floor above me.

I was now close to the great underground archival structure which seemed to form my goal. Sliding and clambering down the farther side of the barrier, and picking my way along the remaining stretch of corridor with hand-held, intermittently flashing torch, I came at last to a low, circular crypt with arches—still in a marvellous state of preservation—opening off on every side. The walls, or such parts of them as lay within reach of my torchlight, were densely hieroglyphed and chiselled with typical curvilinear symbols—some added since the period of my dreams.

This, I realised, was my fated destination, and I turned at once through a familiar archway on my left. That I could find a clear passage up and down the incline to all the surviving levels, I had oddly little doubt. This vast, earth-protected pile, housing the annals of all the solar system, had been built with supernal skill and strength to last as long as that system itself. Blocks of stupendous size, poised with mathematical genius and bound with cements of incredible toughness, had combined to form a mass as firm as the planet's rocky core. Here, after ages more prodigious than I could sanely grasp, its buried bulk still stood in all its essential contours; the vast, dust-drifted floors scarce sprinkled with the litter elsewhere so dominant.

The relatively easy walking from this point onward went curiously to my head. All the frantic eagerness hitherto frustrated by obstacles now took itself out in a kind of febrile speed, and I literally raced along the low-roofed, monstrously well-remembered aisles beyond the archway. I was past being astonished by the familiarity of what I saw. On every hand the great hieroglyphed metal shelf-doors loomed monstrously; some yet in place, others sprung open, and still others bent and buckled under bygone geologic stresses not quite strong enough to shatter the titan masonry. Here and there a dust-covered heap below a gaping empty shelf seemed to indicate where cases had been shaken down by earth-tremors. On occasional pillars were great symbols or letters proclaiming classes and sub-classes of volumes.

Once I paused before an open vault where I saw some of the accustomed metal cases still in position amidst the omnipresent gritty dust. Reaching up, I dislodged one of the thinner specimens with some difficulty, and rested it on the floor for inspection. It was titled in the prevailing curvilinear hieroglyphs, though something in the arrangement of the characters seemed subtly unusual. The odd mechanism of the hooked fastener was perfectly well known to me, and I snapped up the still rustless and workable lid and drew out the book within. The latter, as expected, was some 20 × 15 inches in area, and two inches thick; the thin metal covers opening at the top. Its tough cellulose pages seemed unaffected by the myriad cycles of time they had lived through, and I studied the queerly pigmented, brush-drawn letters of the text—symbols utterly unlike either the usual curved hieroglyphs or any alphabet known to human scholarship—with a haunting, half-aroused memory. It came to me that this was the language used by a captive mind I had slightly known in my dreams—a mind from a large asteroid on which had survived much of the archaic life and lore of the primal planet whereof it formed a fragment. At the same time I recalled that this level of the archives was devoted to volumes dealing with the non-terrestrial planets.

As I ceased poring over this incredible document I saw that the light of my torch was beginning to fail, hence quickly inserted the extra battery I always had with me. Then, armed with the stronger radiance, I resumed my feverish racing through unending tangles of aisles and corridors—recognising now and then some familiar shelf, and vaguely annoyed by the acoustic conditions which made my footfalls echo incongruously in these catacombs of aeon-long death and silence. The very prints of my shoes behind me in the millennially untrodden dust made me shudder. Never before, if my mad dreams held anything of truth, had human feet pressed upon those immemorial pavements. Of the particular goal of my insane racing, my conscious mind held no hint. There was, however, some force of evil potency pulling at my dazed will and buried recollections, so that I vaguely felt I was not running at random.

I came to a downward incline and followed it to profounder depths. Floors flashed by me as I raced, but I did not pause to explore them. In my whirling brain there had begun to beat a certain rhythm which set my right hand twitching in unison. I wanted to unlock something, and felt that I knew all the intricate twists and pressures needed to do it. It would be like a modern safe with a combination lock. Dream or not, I had once known and still knew. How any dream—or any scrap of unconsciously absorbed legend—could have taught me a detail so minute, so intricate, and so complex, I did not attempt to explain to myself. I was beyond all coherent thought. For was not this whole experience—this shocking familiarity with a set of unknown ruins, and this monstrously exact identity of everything before me with what only dreams and scraps of myth could have suggested—a horror beyond all reason? Probably it was my basic conviction then—as it is now during my saner moments—that I was not awake at all, and that the entire buried city was a fragment of febrile hallucination.

Eventually I reached the lowest level and struck off to the right of the incline. For some shadowy reason I tried to soften my steps, even though I lost speed thereby. There was a space I was afraid to cross on this last, deeply buried floor, and as I drew near it I recalled what thing in that space I feared. It was merely one of the metal-barred and closely guarded trap-doors. There would be no guards now, and on that account I trembled and tiptoed as I had done in passing through that black basalt vault where a similar trap-door had yawned. I felt a current of cool, damp air, as I had felt there, and wished that my course led in another direction. Why I had to take the particular course I was taking, I did not know.

When I came to the space I saw that the trap-door yawned widely open. Ahead the shelves began again, and I glimpsed on the floor before one of them a heap very thinly covered with dust, where a number of cases had recently fallen. At the same moment a fresh wave of panic clutched me, though for some time I could not discover why. Heaps of fallen cases were not uncommon, for all through the aeons this lightless labyrinth had been racked by the heavings of earth and had echoed at intervals to the deafening clatter of toppling objects. It was only when I was nearly across the space that I realised why I shook so violently.

Not the heap, but something about the dust of the level floor was troubling me. In the light of my torch it seemed as if that dust were not as even as it ought to be—there were places where it looked thinner, as if it had been disturbed not many months before. I could not be sure, for even the apparently thinner places were dusty enough; yet a certain suspicion of regularity in the fancied unevenness was highly disquieting. When I brought the torchlight close to one of the queer places I did not like what I saw—for the illusion of regularity became very great. It was as if there were regular lines of composite impressions—impressions that went in threes, each slightly over a foot square and consisting of five nearly circular three-inch prints, one in advance of the other four.

These possible lines of foot-square impressions appeared to lead in two directions, as if something had gone somewhere and returned. They were of course very faint, and may have been illusions or accidents; but there was an element of dim, fumbling terror about the way I thought they ran. For at one end of them was the heap of cases which must have clattered down not long before, while at the other end was the ominous trap-door with the cool, damp wind, yawning unguarded down to abysses past imagination.

VIII.

That my strange sense of compulsion was deep and overwhelming is shewn by its conquest of my fear. No rational motive could have drawn me on after that hideous suspicion of prints and the creeping dream-memories it excited. Yet my right hand, even as it shook with fright, still twitched rhythmically in its eagerness to turn a lock it hoped to find. Before I knew it I was past the heap of lately fallen cases and running on tiptoe through aisles of utterly unbroken dust toward a point which I seemed to know morbidly, horribly well. My mind was asking itself questions whose origin and relevancy I was only beginning to guess. Would the shelf be reachable by a human body? Could my human hand master all the aeon-remembered motions of the lock? Would the lock be undamaged and workable? And what would I do—what dare I do—with what (as I now commenced to realise) I both hoped and feared to find? Would it prove the awesome, brain-shattering truth of something past normal conception, or shew only that I was dreaming?

The next I knew I had ceased my tiptoe racing and was standing still, staring at a row of maddeningly familiar hieroglyphed shelves. They were in a state of almost perfect preservation, and only three of the doors in this vicinity had sprung open. My feelings toward these shelves cannot be described—so utter and insistent was the sense of old acquaintance. I was looking high up, at a row near the top and wholly out of my reach, and wondering how I could climb to best advantage. An open door four rows from the bottom would help, and the locks of the closed doors formed possible holds for hands and feet. I would grip the torch between my teeth as I had in other places where both hands were needed. Above all, I must make no noise. How to get down what I wished to remove would be difficult, but I could probably hook its movable fastener in my coat collar and carry it like a knapsack. Again I wondered whether the lock would be undamaged. That I could repeat each familiar motion I had not the least doubt. But I hoped the thing would not scrape or creak—and that my hand could work it properly.

Even as I thought these things I had taken the torch in my mouth and begun to climb. The projecting locks were poor supports; but as I had expected, the opened shelf helped greatly. I used both the difficultly swinging door and the edge of the aperture itself in my ascent, and managed to avoid any loud creaking. Balanced on the upper edge of the door, and leaning far to my right, I could just reach the lock I sought. My fingers, half-numb from climbing, were very clumsy at first; but I soon saw that they were anatomically adequate. And the memory-rhythm was strong in them. Out of unknown gulfs of time the intricate secret motions had somehow reached my brain correctly in every detail—for after less than five minutes of trying there came a click whose familiarity was all the more startling because I had not consciously anticipated it. In another instant the metal door was slowly swinging open with only the faintest grating sound.

Dazedly I looked over the row of greyish case-ends thus exposed, and felt a tremendous surge of some wholly inexplicable emotion. Just within reach of my right hand was a case whose curving hieroglyphs made me shake with a pang infinitely more complex than one of mere fright. Still shaking, I managed to dislodge it amidst a shower of gritty flakes, and ease it over toward myself without any violent noise. Like the other case I had handled, it was slightly more than 20 × 15 inches in size, with curved mathematical designs in low relief. In thickness it just exceeded three inches. Crudely wedging it between myself and the surface I was climbing, I fumbled with the fastener and finally got the hook free. Lifting the cover, I shifted the fairly heavy object to my back, and let the hook catch hold of my collar. Hands now free, I awkwardly clambered down to the dusty floor, and prepared to inspect my prize.

Kneeling in the gritty dust, I swung the case around and rested it in front of me. My hands shook, and I dreaded to draw out the book within almost as much as I longed—and felt compelled—to do so. It had very gradually become clear to me what I ought to find, and this realisation nearly paralysed my faculties. If the thing were there—and if I were not dreaming—the implications would be quite beyond the power of the human spirit to bear. What tormented me most was my momentary inability to feel that my surroundings were a dream. The sense of reality was hideous—and again becomes so as I recall the scene.

At length I tremblingly pulled the book from its container and stared fascinatedly at the well-known hieroglyphs on the cover. It seemed to be in prime condition, and the curvilinear letters of the title held me in almost as hypnotised a state as if I could read them. Indeed, I cannot swear that I did not actually read them in some transient and terrible access of abnormal memory. I do not know how long it was before I dared to lift that thin metal cover. I temporised and made excuses to myself. I took the torch from my mouth and shut it off to save the battery. Then, in the dark, I screwed up my courage—finally lifting the cover without turning on the light. Last of all I did indeed flash the torch upon the exposed page—steeling myself in advance to suppress any sound no matter what I should find.

I looked for an instant, then almost collapsed. Clenching my teeth, however, I kept silence. I sank wholly to the floor and put a hand to my forehead amidst the engulfing blackness. What I dreaded and expected was there. Either I was dreaming, or time and space had become a mockery. I must be dreaming—but I would test the horror by carrying this thing back and shewing it to my son if it were indeed a reality. My head swam frightfully, even though there were no visible objects in the unbroken gloom to swirl around me. Ideas and images of the starkest terror—excited by the vistas which my glimpse had opened up—began to throng in upon me and cloud my senses.

I thought of those possible prints in the dust, and trembled at the sound of my own breathing as I did so. Once again I flashed on the light and looked at the page as a serpent's victim may look at his destroyer's eyes and fangs. Then, with clumsy fingers in the dark, I closed the book, put it in its container, and snapped the lid and the curious hooked fastener. This was what I must carry back to the outer world if it truly existed—if the whole abyss truly existed—if I, and the world itself, truly existed.

Just when I tottered to my feet and commenced my return I cannot be certain. It comes to me oddly—as a measure of my sense of separation from the normal world—that I did not even once look at my watch during those hideous hours underground. Torch in hand, and with the ominous case under one arm, I eventually found myself tiptoeing in a kind of silent panic past the draught-giving abyss and those lurking suggestions of prints. I lessened my precautions as I climbed up the endless inclines, but could not shake off a shadow of apprehension which I had not felt on the downward journey.

I dreaded having to re-pass through that black basalt crypt that was older than the city itself, where cold draughts welled up from unguarded depths. I thought of that which the Great Race had feared, and of what might still be lurking—be it ever so weak and dying—down there. I thought of those possible five-circle prints and of what my dreams had told me of such prints—and of strange winds and whistling noises associated with them. And I thought of the tales of the modern blacks, wherein the horror of great winds and nameless subterrene ruins was dwelt upon.

I knew from a carven wall symbol the right floor to enter, and came at last—after passing that other book I had examined—to the great circular space with the branching archways. On my right, and at once recognisable, was the arch through which I had arrived. This I now entered, conscious that the rest of my course would be harder because of the tumbled state of the masonry outside the archive building. My new metal-cased burden weighed upon me, and I found it harder and harder to be quiet as I stumbled among debris and fragments of every sort.

Then I came to the ceiling-high mound of debris through which I had wrenched a scanty passage. My dread at wriggling through again was infinite; for my first passage had made some noise, and I now—after seeing those possible prints—dreaded sound above all things. The case, too, doubled the problem of traversing the narrow crevice. But I clambered up the barrier as best I could, and pushed the case through the aperture ahead of me. Then, torch in mouth, I scrambled through myself—my back torn as before by stalactites. As I tried to grasp the case again, it fell some distance ahead of me down the slope of the debris, making a disturbing clatter and arousing echoes which sent me into a cold perspiration. I lunged for it at once, and regained it without further noise—but a moment afterward the slipping of blocks under my feet raised a sudden and unprecedented din.

That din was my undoing. For, falsely or not, I thought I heard it answered in a terrible way from spaces far behind me. I thought I heard a shrill, whistling sound, like nothing else on earth, and beyond any adequate verbal description. It may have been only my imagination. If so, what followed has a certain grim irony—since, save for the panic of this thing, the second thing might never have happened.

As it was, my frenzy was absolute and unrelieved. Taking my torch in my hand and clutching feebly at the case, I leaped and bounded wildly ahead with no idea in my brain beyond a mad desire to race out of these nightmare ruins to the waking world of desert and moonlight which lay so far above. I hardly knew it when I reached the mountain of debris which towered into the vast blackness beyond the caved-in roof, and bruised and cut myself repeatedly in scrambling up its steep slope of jagged blocks and fragments. Then came the great disaster. Just as I blindly crossed the summit, unprepared for the sudden dip ahead, my feet slipped utterly and I found myself involved in a mangling avalanche of sliding masonry whose cannon-loud uproar split the black cavern air in a deafening series of earth-shaking reverberations.

I have no recollection of emerging from this chaos, but a momentary fragment of consciousness shews me as plunging and tripping and scrambling along the corridor amidst the clangour—case and torch still with me. Then, just as I approached that primal basalt crypt I had so dreaded, utter madness came. For as the echoes of the avalanche died down, there became audible a repetition of that frightful, alien whistling I thought I had heard before. This time there was no doubt about it—and what was worse, it came from a point not behind but *ahead of me.*

Probably I shrieked aloud then. I have a dim picture of myself as flying through the hellish basalt vault of the Elder Things, and hearing that damnable alien sound piping up from the open, unguarded door of limitless nether blacknesses. There was a wind, too—not merely a cool, damp draught, but a violent, purposeful blast belching savagely and frigidly from that abominable gulf whence the obscene whistling came.

There are memories of leaping and lurching over obstacles of every sort, with that torrent of wind and shrieking sound growing moment by moment, and seeming to curl and twist purposefully around me as it struck out wickedly from the spaces behind and beneath. Though in my rear, that wind had the odd effect of hindering instead of aiding my progress; as if it acted like a noose or lasso thrown around me. Heedless of the noise I made, I clattered over a great barrier of blocks and was again in the structure that led to the surface. I recall glimpsing the archway to the room of machines and almost crying out as I saw the incline leading down to where one of those blasphemous trap-doors must be yawning two levels below. But instead of crying out I muttered over and over to myself that this was all a dream from which I must soon wake. Perhaps I was in camp—perhaps I was at home in Arkham. As these hopes bolstered up my sanity I began to mount the incline to the higher level.

I knew, of course, that I had the four-foot cleft to re-cross, yet was too racked by other fears to realise the full horror until I came almost upon it. On my descent, the leap across had been easy—but could I clear the gap as readily when going uphill, and hampered by fright, exhaustion, the weight of the metal case, and the anomalous backward tug of that daemon wind? I thought of these things at the last moment, and thought also of the nameless entities which might be lurking in the black abysses below the chasm.

My wavering torch was growing feeble, but I could tell by some obscure memory when I neared the cleft. The chill blasts of wind and the nauseous whistling shrieks behind me were for the moment like a merciful opiate, dulling my imagination to the horror of the yawning gulf ahead. And then I became aware of the added blasts and whistling *in front of me*—tides of abomination surging up through the cleft itself from depths unimagined and unimaginable.

Now, indeed, the essence of pure nightmare was upon me. Sanity departed—and ignoring everything except the animal impulse of flight, I merely struggled and plunged upward over the incline's debris as if no gulf had existed. Then I saw the chasm's edge, leaped frenziedly with every ounce of strength I possessed, and was instantly engulfed in a pandaemoniac vortex of loathsome sound and utter, materially tangible blackness.

That is the end of my experience, so far as I can recall. Any further impressions belong wholly to the domain of phantasmagoric delirium. Dream, madness, and memory merged wildly together in a series of fantastic, fragmentary delusions which can have no relation to anything real. There was a hideous fall through incalculable leagues of viscous, sentient darkness, and a babel of noises utterly alien to all that we know of the earth and its organic life. Dormant, rudimentary senses seemed to start into vitality within me, telling of pits and voids peopled by floating horrors and leading to sunless crags and oceans and teeming cities of windowless basalt towers upon which no light ever shone.

Secrets of the primal planet and its immemorial aeons flashed through my brain without the aid of sight or sound, and there were known to me things which not even the wildest of my former dreams had ever suggested. And all the while cold fingers of damp vapour clutched and picked at me, and that eldritch, damnable whistling shrieked fiendishly above all the alternations of babel and silence in the whirlpools of darkness around.

Afterward there were visions of the Cyclopean city of my dreams—not in ruins, but just as I had dreamed of it. I was in my conical, non-human body again, and mingled with crowds of the Great Race and the captive minds who carried books up and down the lofty corridors and vast inclines. Then, superimposed upon these pictures, were frightful momentary flashes of a non-visual consciousness involving desperate struggles, a writhing free from clutching tentacles of whistling wind, an insane, bat-like flight through half-solid air, a feverish burrowing through the cyclone-whipped dark, and a wild stumbling and scrambling over fallen masonry.

Once there was a curious, intrusive flash of half-sight—a faint, diffuse suspicion of bluish radiance far overhead. Then there came a dream of wind-pursued climbing and crawling—of wriggling into a blaze of sardonic moonlight through a jumble of debris which slid and collapsed after me amidst a morbid hurricane. It was the evil, monotonous beating of that maddening moonlight which at last told me of the return of what I had once known as the objective, waking world.

I was clawing prone through the sands of the Australian desert, and around me shrieked such a tumult of wind as I had never before known on our planet's surface. My clothing was in rags, and my whole body was a mass of bruises and scratches. Full consciousness returned very slowly, and at no time could I tell just where true memory left off and delirious dream began. There had seemed to be a mound of titan blocks, an abyss beneath it, a monstrous revelation from the past, and a nightmare horror at the end—but how much of this was real? My flashlight was gone, and likewise any metal case I may have discovered. Had there been such a case—or any abyss—or any mound? Raising my head, I looked behind me, and saw only the sterile, undulant sands of the waste.

The daemon wind died down, and the bloated, fungoid moon sank reddeningly in the west. I lurched to my feet and began to stagger southwestward toward the camp. What in truth had happened to me? Had I merely collapsed in the desert and dragged a dream-racked body over miles of sand and buried blocks? If not, how could I bear to live any longer? For in this new doubt all my faith in the myth-born unreality of my visions dissolved once more into the hellish older doubting. If that abyss was real, then the Great Race was real—and its blasphemous reachings and seizures in the cosmos-wide vortex of time were no myths or nightmares, but a terrible, soul-shattering actuality.

Had I, in full hideous fact, been drawn back to a pre-human world of a hundred and fifty million years ago in those dark, baffling days of the amnesia? Had my present body been the vehicle of a frightful alien consciousness from palaeogean gulfs of time? Had I, as the captive mind of those shambling horrors, indeed known that accursed city of stone in its primordial heyday, and wriggled down those familiar corridors in the loathsome shape of my captor? Were those tormenting dreams of more than twenty years the offspring of stark, monstrous *memories?* Had I once veritably talked with minds from reachless corners of time and space, learned the universe's secrets past and to come, and written the annals of my own world for the metal cases of those titan archives? And were those others—those shocking Elder Things of the mad winds and daemon pipings—in truth a lingering, lurking menace, waiting and slowly weakening in black abysses while varied shapes of life drag out their multimillennial courses on the planet's age-racked surface?

I do not know. If that abyss and what it held were real, there is no hope. Then, all too truly, there lies upon this world of man a mocking and incredible shadow out of time. But mercifully, there is no proof that these things are other than fresh phases of my myth-born dreams. I did not bring back the metal case that would have been a proof, and so far those subterrene corridors have not been found. If the laws of the universe are kind, they will never be found. But I must tell my son what I saw or thought I saw, and let him use his judgment as a psychologist in gauging the reality of my experience, and communicating this account to others.

I have said that the awful truth behind my tortured years of dreaming hinges absolutely upon the actuality of what I thought I saw in those Cyclopean buried ruins. It has been hard for me literally to set down the crucial revelation, though no reader can have failed to guess it. Of course it lay in that book within the metal case—the case which I pried out of its forgotten lair amidst the undisturbed dust of a million centuries. No eye had seen, no hand had touched that book since the advent of man to this planet. And yet, when I flashed my torch upon it in that frightful megalithic abyss, I saw that the queerly pigmented letters on the brittle, aeon-browned cellulose pages were not indeed any nameless hieroglyphs of earth's youth. They were, instead, the letters of our familiar alphabet, spelling out the words of the English language in my own handwriting.

THE HAUNTER OF THE DARK

(Dedicated to Robert Bloch)

I have seen the dark universe yawning
    Where the black planets roll without aim—
Where they roll in their horror unheeded,
    Without knowledge or lustre or name.

—*Nemesis.*

Cautious investigators will hesitate to challenge the common belief that Robert Blake was killed by lightning, or by some profound nervous shock derived from an electrical discharge. It is true that the window he faced was unbroken, but Nature has shewn herself capable of many freakish performances. The expression on his face may easily have arisen from some obscure muscular source unrelated to anything he saw, while the entries in his diary are clearly the result of a fantastic imagination aroused by certain local superstitions and by certain old matters he had uncovered. As for the anomalous conditions at the deserted church on Federal Hill—the shrewd analyst is not slow in attributing them to some charlatanry, conscious or unconscious, with at least some of which Blake was secretly connected.

For after all, the victim was a writer and painter wholly devoted to the field of myth, dream, terror, and superstition, and avid in his quest for scenes and effects of a bizarre, spectral sort. His earlier stay in the city—a visit to a strange old man as deeply given to occult and forbidden lore as he—had ended amidst death and flame, and it must have been some morbid instinct which drew him back from his home in Milwaukee. He may have known of the old stories despite his statements to the contrary in the diary, and his death may have nipped in the bud some stupendous hoax destined to have a literary reflection.

Among those, however, who have examined and correlated all this evidence, there remain several who cling to less rational and commonplace theories. They are inclined to take much of Blake's diary at its face value, and point significantly to certain facts such as the undoubted genuineness of the old church record, the verified existence of the disliked and unorthodox Starry Wisdom sect prior to 1877, the recorded disappearance of an inquisitive reporter named Edwin M. Lillibridge in 1893, and—above all—the look of monstrous, transfiguring fear on the face of the young writer when he died. It was one of these believers who, moved to fanatical extremes, threw into the bay the curiously angled stone and its strangely adorned metal box found in the old church steeple—the black windowless steeple, and not the tower where Blake's diary said those things originally were. Though widely censured both officially and unofficially, this man—a reputable physician with a taste for odd folklore—averred that he had rid the earth of something too dangerous to rest upon it.

Between these two schools of opinion the reader must judge for himself. The papers have given the tangible details from a sceptical angle, leaving for others the drawing of the picture as Robert Blake saw it—or thought he saw it—or pretended to see it. Now, studying the diary closely, dispassionately, and at leisure, let us summarise the dark chain of events from the expressed point of view of their chief actor.

Young Blake returned to Providence in the winter of 1934–5, taking the upper floor of a venerable dwelling in a grassy court off College Street—on the crest of the great eastward hill near the Brown University campus and behind the marble John Hay Library. It was a cosy and fascinating place, in a little garden oasis of village-like antiquity where huge, friendly cats sunned themselves atop a convenient shed. The square Georgian house had a monitor roof, classic doorway with fan carving, small-paned windows, and all the other earmarks of early nineteenth-century workmanship. Inside were six-panelled doors, wide floor-boards, a curving colonial staircase, white Adam-period mantels, and a rear set of rooms three steps below the general level.

Blake's study, a large southwest chamber, overlooked the front garden on one side, while its west windows—before one of which he had his desk—faced off from the brow of the hill and commanded a splendid view of the lower town's outspread roofs and of the mystical sunsets that flamed behind them. On the far horizon were the open countryside's purple slopes. Against these, some two miles away, rose the spectral hump of Federal Hill, bristling with huddled roofs and steeples whose remote outlines wavered mysteriously, taking fantastic forms as the smoke of the city swirled up and enmeshed them. Blake had a curious sense that he was looking upon some unknown, ethereal world which might or might not vanish in dream if ever he tried to seek it out and enter it in person.

Having sent home for most of his books, Blake bought some antique furniture suitable to his quarters and settled down to write and paint—living alone, and attending to the simple housework himself. His studio was in a north attic room, where the panes of the monitor roof furnished admirable lighting. During that first winter he produced five of his best-known short stories—"The Burrower Beneath", "The Stairs in the Crypt", "Shaggai", "In the Vale of Pnath", and "The Feaster from the Stars"—and painted seven canvases; studies of nameless, unhuman monsters, and profoundly alien, non-terrestrial landscapes.

At sunset he would often sit at his desk and gaze dreamily off at the outspread west—the dark towers of Memorial Hall just below, the Georgian court-house belfry, the lofty pinnacles of the downtown section, and that shimmering, spire-crowned mound in the distance whose unknown streets and labyrinthine gables so potently provoked his fancy. From his few local acquaintances he learned that the far-off slope was a vast Italian quarter, though most of the houses were remnants of older Yankee and Irish days. Now and then he would train his field-glasses on that spectral, unreachable world beyond the curling smoke; picking out individual roofs and chimneys and steeples, and speculating upon the bizarre and curious mysteries they might house. Even with optical aid Federal Hill seemed somehow alien, half fabulous, and linked to the unreal, intangible marvels of Blake's own tales and pictures. The feeling would persist long after the hill had faded into the violet, lamp-starred twilight, and the court-house floodlights and the red Industrial Trust beacon had blazed up to make the night grotesque.

Of all the distant objects on Federal Hill, a certain huge, dark church most fascinated Blake. It stood out with especial distinctness at certain hours of the day, and at sunset the great tower and tapering steeple loomed blackly against the flaming sky. It seemed to rest on especially high ground; for the grimy facade, and the obliquely seen north side with sloping roof and the tops of great pointed windows, rose boldly above the tangle of surrounding ridgepoles and chimney-pots. Peculiarly grim and austere, it appeared to be built of stone, stained and weathered with the smoke and storms of a century and more. The style, so far as the glass could shew, was that earliest experimental form of Gothic revival which preceded the stately Upjohn period and held over some of the outlines and proportions of the Georgian age. Perhaps it was reared around 1810 or 1815.

As months passed, Blake watched the far-off, forbidding structure with an oddly mounting interest. Since the vast windows were never lighted, he knew that it must be vacant. The longer he watched, the more his imagination worked, till at length he began to fancy curious things. He believed that a vague, singular aura of desolation hovered over the place, so that even the pigeons and swallows shunned its smoky eaves. Around other towers and belfries his glass would reveal great flocks of birds, but here they never rested. At least, that is what he thought and set down in his diary. He pointed the place out to several friends, but none of them had even been on Federal Hill or possessed the faintest notion of what the church was or had been.

In the spring a deep restlessness gripped Blake. He had begun his long-planned novel—based on a supposed survival of the witch-cult in Maine—but was strangely unable to make progress with it. More and more he would sit at his westward window and gaze at the distant hill and the black, frowning steeple shunned by the birds. When the delicate leaves came out on the garden boughs the world was filled with a new beauty, but Blake's restlessness was merely increased. It was then that he first thought of crossing the city and climbing bodily up that fabulous slope into the smoke-wreathed world of dream.

Late in April, just before the aeon-shadowed Walpurgis time, Blake made his first trip into the unknown. Plodding through the endless downtown streets and the bleak, decayed squares beyond, he came finally upon the ascending avenue of century-worn steps, sagging Doric porches, and blear-paned cupolas which he felt must lead up to the long-known, unreachable world beyond the mists. There were dingy blue-and-white street signs which meant nothing to him, and presently he noted the strange, dark faces of the drifting crowds, and the foreign signs over curious shops in brown, decade-weathered buildings. Nowhere could he find any of the objects he had seen from afar; so that once more he half fancied that the Federal Hill of that distant view was a dream-world never to be trod by living human feet.

Now and then a battered church facade or crumbling spire came in sight, but never the blackened pile that he sought. When he asked a shopkeeper about a great stone church the man smiled and shook his head, though he spoke English freely. As Blake climbed higher, the region seemed stranger and stranger, with bewildering mazes of brooding brown alleys leading eternally off to the south. He crossed two or three broad avenues, and once thought he glimpsed a familiar tower. Again he asked a merchant about the massive church of stone, and this time he could have sworn that the plea of ignorance was feigned. The dark man's face had a look of fear which he tried to hide, and Blake saw him make a curious sign with his right hand.

Then suddenly a black spire stood out against the cloudy sky on his left, above the tiers of brown roofs lining the tangled southerly alleys. Blake knew at once what it was, and plunged toward it through the squalid, unpaved lanes that climbed from the avenue. Twice he lost his way, but he somehow dared not ask any of the patriarchs or housewives who sat on their doorsteps, or any of the children who shouted and played in the mud of the shadowy lanes.

At last he saw the tower plain against the southwest, and a huge stone bulk rose darkly at the end of an alley. Presently he stood in a windswept open square, quaintly cobblestoned, with a high bank wall on the farther side. This was the end of his quest; for upon the wide, iron-railed, weed-grown plateau which the wall supported—a separate, lesser world raised fully six feet above the surrounding streets—there stood a grim, titan bulk whose identity, despite Blake's new perspective, was beyond dispute.

The vacant church was in a state of great decrepitude. Some of the high stone buttresses had fallen, and several delicate finials lay half lost among the brown, neglected weeds and grasses. The sooty Gothic windows were largely unbroken, though many of the stone mullions were missing. Blake wondered how the obscurely painted panes could have survived so well, in view of the known habits of small boys the world over. The massive doors were intact and tightly closed. Around the top of the bank wall, fully enclosing the grounds, was a rusty iron fence whose gate—at the head of a flight of steps from the square—was visibly padlocked. The path from the gate to the building was completely overgrown. Desolation and decay hung like a pall above the place, and in the birdless eaves and black, ivyless walls Blake felt a touch of the dimly sinister beyond his power to define.

There were very few people in the square, but Blake saw a policeman at the northerly end and approached him with questions about the church. He was a great wholesome Irishman, and it seemed odd that he would do little more than make the sign of the cross and mutter that people never spoke of that building. When Blake pressed him he said very hurriedly that the Italian priests warned everybody against it, vowing that a monstrous evil had once dwelt there and left its mark. He himself had heard dark whispers of it from his father, who recalled certain sounds and rumours from his boyhood.

There had been a bad sect there in the ould days—an outlaw sect that called up awful things from some unknown gulf of night. It had taken a good priest to exorcise what had come, though there did be those who said that merely the light could do it. If Father O'Malley were alive there would be many the thing he could tell. But now there was nothing to do but let it alone. It hurt nobody now, and those that owned it were dead or far away. They had run away like rats after the threatening talk in '77, when people began to mind the way folks vanished now and then in the neighbourhood. Some day the city would step in and take the property for lack of heirs, but little good would come of anybody's touching it. Better it be left alone for the years to topple, lest things be stirred that ought to rest for ever in their black abyss.

After the policeman had gone Blake stood staring at the sullen steepled pile. It excited him to find that the structure seemed as sinister to others as to him, and he wondered what grain of truth might lie behind the old tales the bluecoat had repeated. Probably they were mere legends evoked by the evil look of the place, but even so, they were like a strange coming to life of one of his own stories.

The afternoon sun came out from behind dispersing clouds, but seemed unable to light up the stained, sooty walls of the old temple that towered on its high plateau. It was odd that the green of spring had not touched the brown, withered growths in the raised, iron-fenced yard. Blake found himself edging nearer the raised area and examining the bank wall and rusted fence for possible avenues of ingress. There was a terrible lure about the blackened fane which was not to be resisted. The fence had no opening near the steps, but around on the north side were some missing bars. He could go up the steps and walk around on the narrow coping outside the fence till he came to the gap. If the people feared the place so wildly, he would encounter no interference.

He was on the embankment and almost inside the fence before anyone noticed him. Then, looking down, he saw the few people in the square edging away and making the same sign with their right hands that the shopkeeper in the avenue had made. Several windows were slammed down, and a fat woman darted into the street and pulled some small children inside a rickety, unpainted house. The gap in the fence was very easy to pass through, and before long Blake found himself wading amidst the rotting, tangled growths of the deserted yard. Here and there the worn stump of a headstone told him that there had once been burials in this field; but that, he saw, must have been very long ago. The sheer bulk of the church was oppressive now that he was close to it, but he conquered his mood and approached to try the three great doors in the facade. All were securely locked, so he began a circuit of the Cyclopean building in quest of some minor and more penetrable opening. Even then he could not be sure that he wished to enter that haunt of desertion and shadow, yet the pull of its strangeness dragged him on automatically.

A yawning and unprotected cellar window in the rear furnished the needed aperture. Peering in, Blake saw a subterrene gulf of cobwebs and dust faintly litten by the western sun's filtered rays. Debris, old barrels, and ruined boxes and furniture of numerous sorts met his eye, though over everything lay a shroud of dust which softened all sharp outlines. The rusted remains of a hot-air furnace shewed that the building had been used and kept in shape as late as mid-Victorian times.

Acting almost without conscious initiative, Blake crawled through the window and let himself down to the dust-carpeted and debris-strown concrete floor. The vaulted cellar was a vast one, without partitions; and in a corner far to the right, amid dense shadows, he saw a black archway evidently leading upstairs. He felt a peculiar sense of oppression at being actually within the great spectral building, but kept it in check as he cautiously scouted about—finding a still-intact barrel amid the dust, and rolling it over to the open window to provide for his exit. Then, bracing himself, he crossed the wide, cobweb-festooned space toward the arch. Half choked with the omnipresent dust, and covered with ghostly gossamer fibres, he reached and began to climb the worn stone steps which rose into the darkness. He had no light, but groped carefully with his hands. After a sharp turn he felt a closed door ahead, and a little fumbling revealed its ancient latch. It opened inward, and beyond it he saw a dimly illumined corridor lined with worm-eaten panelling.

Once on the ground floor, Blake began exploring in a rapid fashion. All the inner doors were unlocked, so that he freely passed from room to room. The colossal nave was an almost eldritch place with its drifts and mountains of dust over box pews, altar, hour-glass pulpit, and sounding-board, and its titanic ropes of cobweb stretching among the pointed arches of the gallery and entwining the clustered Gothic columns. Over all this hushed desolation played a hideous leaden light as the declining afternoon sun sent its rays through the strange, half-blackened panes of the great apsidal windows.

The paintings on those windows were so obscured by soot that Blake could scarcely decipher what they had represented, but from the little he could make out he did not like them. The designs were largely conventional, and his knowledge of obscure symbolism told him much concerning some of the ancient patterns. The few saints depicted bore expressions distinctly open to criticism, while one of the windows seemed to shew merely a dark space with spirals of curious luminosity scattered about in it. Turning away from the windows, Blake noticed that the cobwebbed cross above the altar was not of the ordinary kind, but resembled the primordial ankh or crux ansata of shadowy Egypt.

In a rear vestry room beside the apse Blake found a rotting desk and ceiling-high shelves of mildewed, disintegrating books. Here for the first time he received a positive shock of objective horror, for the titles of those books told him much. They were the black, forbidden things which most sane people have never even heard of, or have heard of only in furtive, timorous whispers; the banned and dreaded repositories of equivocal secrets and immemorial formulae which have trickled down the stream of time from the days of man's youth, and the dim, fabulous days before man was. He had himself read many of them—a Latin version of the abhorred "Necronomicon", the sinister "Liber Ivonis", the infamous "Cultes des Goules" of Comte d'Erlette, the "Unaussprechlichen Kulten" of von Junzt, and old Ludvig Prinn's hellish "De Vermis Mysteriis". But there were others he had known merely by reputation or not at all—the Pnakotic Manuscripts, the "Book of Dzyan", and a crumbling volume in wholly unidentifiable characters yet with certain symbols and diagrams shudderingly recognisable to the occult student. Clearly, the lingering local rumours had not lied. This place had once been the seat of an evil older than mankind and wider than the known universe.

In the ruined desk was a small leather-bound record-book filled with entries in some odd cryptographic medium. The manuscript writing consisted of the common traditional symbols used today in astronomy and anciently in alchemy, astrology, and other dubious arts—the devices of the sun, moon, planets, aspects, and zodiacal signs—here massed in solid pages of text, with divisions and paragraphings suggesting that each symbol answered to some alphabetical letter.

In the hope of later solving the cryptogram, Blake bore off this volume in his coat pocket. Many of the great tomes on the shelves fascinated him unutterably, and he felt tempted to borrow them at some later time. He wondered how they could have remained undisturbed so long. Was he the first to conquer the clutching, pervasive fear which had for nearly sixty years protected this deserted place from visitors?

Having now thoroughly explored the ground floor, Blake ploughed again through the dust of the spectral nave to the front vestibule, where he had seen a door and staircase presumably leading up to the blackened tower and steeple—objects so long familiar to him at a distance. The ascent was a choking experience, for dust lay thick, while the spiders had done their worst in this constricted place. The staircase was a spiral with high, narrow wooden treads, and now and then Blake passed a clouded window looking dizzily out over the city. Though he had seen no ropes below, he expected to find a bell or peal of bells in the tower whose narrow, louver-boarded lancet windows his field-glass had studied so often. Here he was doomed to disappointment; for when he attained the top of the stairs he found the tower chamber vacant of chimes, and clearly devoted to vastly different purposes.

The room, about fifteen feet square, was faintly lighted by four lancet windows, one on each side, which were glazed within their screening of decayed louver-boards. These had been further fitted with tight, opaque screens, but the latter were now largely rotted away. In the centre of the dust-laden floor rose a curiously angled stone pillar some four feet in height and two in average diameter, covered on each side with bizarre, crudely incised, and wholly unrecognisable hieroglyphs. On this pillar rested a metal box of peculiarly asymmetrical form; its hinged lid thrown back, and its interior holding what looked beneath the decade-deep dust to be an egg-shaped or irregularly spherical object some four inches through. Around the pillar in a rough circle were seven high-backed Gothic chairs still largely intact, while behind them, ranging along the dark-panelled walls, were seven colossal images of crumbling, black-painted plaster, resembling more than anything else the cryptic carven megaliths of mysterious Easter Island. In one corner of the cobwebbed chamber a ladder was built into the wall, leading up to the closed trap-door of the windowless steeple above.

As Blake grew accustomed to the feeble light he noticed odd bas-reliefs on the strange open box of yellowish metal. Approaching, he tried to clear the dust away with his hands and handkerchief, and saw that the figurings were of a monstrous and utterly alien kind; depicting entities which, though seemingly alive, resembled no known life-form ever evolved on this planet.

The four-inch seeming sphere turned out to be a nearly black, red-striated polyhedron with many irregular flat surfaces; either a very remarkable crystal of some sort, or an artificial object of carved and highly polished mineral matter. It did not touch the bottom of the box, but was held suspended by means of a metal band around its centre, with seven queerly designed supports extending horizontally to angles of the box's inner wall near the top. This stone, once exposed, exerted upon Blake an almost alarming fascination. He could scarcely tear his eyes from it, and as he looked at its glistening surfaces he almost fancied it was transparent, with half-formed worlds of wonder within. Into his mind floated pictures of alien orbs with great stone towers, and other orbs with titan mountains and no mark of life, and still remoter spaces where only a stirring in vague blacknesses told of the presence of consciousness and will.

When he did look away, it was to notice a somewhat singular mound of dust in the far corner near the ladder to the steeple. Just why it took his attention he could not tell, but something in its contours carried a message to his unconscious mind. Ploughing toward it, and brushing aside the hanging cobwebs as he went, he began to discern something grim about it. Hand and handkerchief soon revealed the truth, and Blake gasped with a baffling mixture of emotions. It was a human skeleton, and it must have been there for a very long time. The clothing was in shreds, but some buttons and fragments of cloth bespoke a man's grey suit. There were other bits of evidence—shoes, metal clasps, huge buttons for round cuffs, a stickpin of bygone pattern, a reporter's badge with the name of the old *Providence Telegram*, and a crumbling leather pocketbook. Blake examined the latter with care, finding within it several bills of antiquated issue, a celluloid advertising calendar for 1893, some cards with the name "Edwin M. Lillibridge", and a paper covered with pencilled memoranda.

This paper held much of a puzzling nature, and Blake read it carefully at the dim westward window. Its disjointed text included such phrases as the following:

> "Prof. Enoch Bowen home from Egypt May 1844—buys old Free-Will Church in July—his archaeological work & studies in occult well known."
>
> "Dr. Drowne of 4th Baptist warns against Starry Wisdom in sermon Dec. 29, 1844."
>
> "Congregation 97 by end of '45."
>
> "1846—3—disappearances—first mention of Shining Trapezohedron."
>
> "7 disappearances 1848—stories of blood sacrifice begin."

> "Investigation 1853 comes to nothing—stories of sounds."
>
> "Fr. O'Malley tells of devil-worship with box found in great Egyptian ruins—says they call up something that can't exist in light. Flees a little light, and banished by strong light. Then has to be summoned again. Probably got this from deathbed confession of Francis X. Feeney, who had joined Starry Wisdom in '49. These people say the Shining Trapezohedron shews them heaven & other worlds, & that the Haunter of the Dark tells them secrets in some way."
>
> "Story of Orrin B. Eddy 1857. They call it up by gazing at the crystal, & have a secret language of their own."
>
> "200 or more in cong. 1863, exclusive of men at front."
>
> "Irish boys mob church in 1869 after Patrick Regan's disappearance."
>
> "Veiled article in J. March 14, '72, but people don't talk about it."
>
> "6 disappearances 1876—secret committee calls on Mayor Doyle."
>
> "Action promised Feb. 1877—church closes in April."
>
> "Gang—Federal Hill Boys—threaten Dr. ——— and vestrymen in May."
>
> "181 persons leave city before end of '77—mention no names."
>
> "Ghost stories begin around 1880—try to ascertain truth of report that no human being has entered church since 1877."
>
> "Ask Lanigan for photograph of place taken 1851." …

Restoring the paper to the pocketbook and placing the latter in his coat, Blake turned to look down at the skeleton in the dust. The implications of the notes were clear, and there could be no doubt but that this man had come to the deserted edifice forty-two years before in quest of a newspaper sensation which no one else had been bold enough to attempt. Perhaps no one else had known of his plan—who could tell? But he had never returned to his paper. Had some bravely suppressed fear risen to overcome him and bring on sudden heart-failure? Blake stooped over the gleaming bones and noted their peculiar state. Some of them were badly scattered, and a few seemed oddly *dissolved* at the ends. Others were strangely yellowed, with vague suggestions of charring. This charring extended to some of the fragments of clothing. The skull was in a very peculiar state—stained yellow, and with a charred aperture in the top as if some powerful acid had eaten through the solid bone. What had happened to the skeleton during its four decades of silent entombment here Blake could not imagine.

Before he realised it, he was looking at the stone again, and letting its curious influence call up a nebulous pageantry in his mind. He saw processions of robed, hooded figures whose outlines were not human, and looked on endless leagues of desert lined with carved, sky-reaching monoliths. He saw towers and walls in nighted depths under the sea, and vortices of space where wisps of black mist floated before thin shimmerings of cold purple haze. And beyond all else he glimpsed an infinite gulf of sheer darkness, where solid and semi-solid forms were known only by their windy stirrings, and cloudy patterns of force seemed to superimpose order on chaos and hold forth a key to all the paradoxes and arcana of the worlds we know.

Then all at once the spell was broken by an access of gnawing, indeterminate panic fear. Blake choked and turned away from the stone, conscious of some formless alien presence close to him and watching him with horrible intentness. He felt entangled with something—something which was not in the stone, but which had looked through it at him—something which would ceaselessly follow him with a cognition that was not physical sight. Plainly, the place was getting on his nerves—as well it might in view of his gruesome find. The light was waning, too, and since he had no illuminant with him he knew he would have to be leaving soon.

It was then, in the gathering twilight, that he thought he saw a faint trace of luminosity in the crazily angled stone. He had tried to look away from it, but some obscure compulsion drew his eyes back. Was there a subtle phosphorescence of radio-activity about the thing? What was it that the dead man's notes had said concerning a *Shining Trapezohedron?* What, anyway, was this abandoned lair of cosmic evil? What had been done here, and what might still be lurking in the bird-shunned shadows? It seemed now as if an elusive touch of foetor had arisen somewhere close by, though its source was not apparent. Blake seized the cover of the long-open box and snapped it down. It moved easily on its alien hinges, and closed completely over the unmistakably glowing stone.

At the sharp click of that closing a soft stirring sound seemed to come from the steeple's eternal blackness overhead, beyond the trap-door. Rats, without question—the only living things to reveal their presence in this accursed pile since he had entered it. And yet that stirring in the steeple frightened him horribly, so that he plunged almost wildly down the spiral stairs, across the ghoulish nave, into the vaulted basement, out amidst the gathering dusk of the deserted square, and down through the teeming, fear-haunted alleys and avenues of Federal Hill toward the sane central streets and the home-like brick sidewalks of the college district.

During the days which followed, Blake told no one of his expedition. Instead, he read much in certain books, examined long years of newspaper files downtown, and worked feverishly at the cryptogram in that leather volume from the cobwebbed vestry room. The cipher, he soon saw, was no simple one; and after a long period of endeavour he felt sure that its language could not be English, Latin, Greek, French, Spanish, Italian, or German. Evidently he would have to draw upon the deepest wells of his strange erudition.

Every evening the old impulse to gaze westward returned, and he saw the black steeple as of yore amongst the bristling roofs of a distant and half-fabulous world. But now it held a fresh note of terror for him. He knew the heritage of evil lore it masked, and with the knowledge his vision ran riot in queer new ways. The birds of spring were returning, and as he watched their sunset flights he fancied they avoided the gaunt, lone spire as never before. When a flock of them approached it, he thought, they would wheel and scatter in panic confusion—and he could guess at the wild twitterings which failed to reach him across the intervening miles.

It was in June that Blake's diary told of his victory over the cryptogram. The text was, he found, in the dark Aklo language used by certain cults of evil antiquity, and known to him in a halting way through previous researches. The diary is strangely reticent about what Blake deciphered, but he was patently awed and disconcerted by his results. There are references to a Haunter of the Dark awaked by gazing into the Shining Trapezohedron, and insane conjectures about the black gulfs of chaos from which it was called. The being is spoken of as holding all knowledge, and demanding monstrous sacrifices. Some of Blake's entries shew fear lest the thing, which he seemed to regard as summoned, stalk abroad; though he adds that the street-lights form a bulwark which cannot be crossed.

Of the Shining Trapezohedron he speaks often, calling it a window on all time and space, and tracing its history from the days it was fashioned on dark Yuggoth, before ever the Old Ones brought it to earth. It was treasured and placed in its curious box by the crinoid things of Antarctica, salvaged from their ruins by the serpent-men of Valusia, and peered at aeons later in Lemuria by the first human beings. It crossed strange lands and stranger seas, and sank with Atlantis before a Minoan fisher meshed it in his net and sold it to swarthy merchants from nighted Khem. The Pharaoh Nephren-Ka built around it a temple with a windowless crypt, and did that which caused his name to be stricken from all monuments and records. Then it slept in the ruins of that evil fane which the priests and the new Pharaoh destroyed, till the delver's spade once more brought it forth to curse mankind.

Early in July the newspapers oddly supplement Blake's entries, though in so brief and casual a way that only the diary has called general attention to their contribution. It appears that a new fear had been growing on Federal Hill since a stranger had entered the dreaded church. The Italians whispered of unaccustomed stirrings and bumpings and scrapings in the dark windowless steeple, and called on their priests to banish an entity which haunted their dreams. Something, they said, was constantly watching at a door to see if it were dark enough to venture forth. Press items mentioned the long-standing local superstitions, but failed to shed much light on the earlier background of the horror. It was obvious that the young reporters of today are no antiquarians. In writing of these things in his diary, Blake expresses a curious kind of remorse, and talks of the duty of burying the Shining Trapezohedron and of banishing what he had evoked by letting daylight into the hideous jutting spire. At the same time, however, he displays the dangerous extent of his fascination, and admits a morbid longing—pervading even his dreams—to visit the accursed tower and gaze again into the cosmic secrets of the glowing stone.

Then something in the *Journal* on the morning of July 17 threw the diarist into a veritable fever of horror. It was only a variant of the other half-humorous items about the Federal Hill restlessness, but to Blake it was somehow very terrible indeed. In the night a thunderstorm had put the city's lighting-system out of commission for a full hour, and in that black interval the Italians had nearly gone mad with fright. Those living near the dreaded church had sworn that the thing in the steeple had taken advantage of the street-lamps' absence and gone down into the body of the church, flopping and bumping around in a viscous, altogether dreadful way. Toward the last it had bumped up to the tower, where there were sounds of the shattering of glass. It could go wherever the darkness reached, but light would always send it fleeing.

When the current blazed on again there had been a shocking commotion in the tower, for even the feeble light trickling through the grime-blackened, louver-boarded windows was too much for the thing. It had bumped and slithered up into its tenebrous steeple just in time—for a long dose of light would have sent it back into the abyss whence the crazy stranger had called it. During the dark hour praying crowds had clustered round the church in the rain with lighted candles and lamps somehow shielded with folded papers and umbrellas—a guard of light to save the city from the nightmare that stalks in darkness. Once, those nearest the church declared, the outer door had rattled hideously.

But even this was not the worst. That evening in the *Bulletin* Blake read of what the reporters had found. Aroused at last to the whimsical news value of the scare, a pair of them had defied the frantic crowds of Italians and crawled into the church through the cellar window after trying the doors in vain. They found the dust of the vestibule and of the spectral nave ploughed up in a singular way, with bits of rotted cushions and satin pew-linings scattered curiously around. There was a bad odour everywhere, and here and there were bits of yellow stain and patches of what looked like charring. Opening the door to the tower, and pausing a moment at the suspicion of a scraping sound above, they found the narrow spiral stairs wiped roughly clean.

In the tower itself a similarly half-swept condition existed. They spoke of the heptagonal stone pillar, the overturned Gothic chairs, and the bizarre plaster images; though strangely enough the metal box and the old mutilated skeleton were not mentioned. What disturbed Blake the most—except for the hints of stains and charring and bad odours—was the final detail that explained the crashing glass. Every one of the tower's lancet windows was broken, and two of them had been darkened in a crude and hurried way by the stuffing of satin pew-linings and cushion-horsehair into the spaces between the slanting exterior louver-boards. More satin fragments and bunches of horsehair lay scattered around the newly swept floor, as if someone had been interrupted in the act of restoring the tower to the absolute blackness of its tightly curtained days.

Yellowish stains and charred patches were found on the ladder to the windowless spire, but when a reporter climbed up, opened the horizontally sliding trap-door, and shot a feeble flashlight beam into the black and strangely foetid space, he saw nothing but darkness, and an heterogeneous litter of shapeless fragments near the aperture. The verdict, of course, was charlatanry. Somebody had played a joke on the superstitious hill-dwellers, or else some fanatic had striven to bolster up their fears for their own supposed good. Or perhaps some of the younger and more sophisticated dwellers had staged an elaborate hoax on the outside world. There was an amusing aftermath when the police sent an officer to verify the reports. Three men in succession found ways of evading the assignment, and the fourth went very reluctantly and returned very soon without adding to the account given by the reporters.

From this point onward Blake's diary shews a mounting tide of insidious horror and nervous apprehension. He upbraids himself for not doing something, and speculates wildly on the consequences of another electrical breakdown. It has been verified that on three occasions—during thunderstorms—he telephoned the electric light company in a frantic vein and asked that desperate precautions against a lapse of power be taken. Now and then his entries shew concern over the failure of the reporters to find the metal box and stone, and the strangely marred old skeleton, when they explored the shadowy tower room. He assumed that these things had been removed—whither, and by whom or what, he could only guess. But his worst fears concerned himself, and the kind of unholy rapport he felt to exist between his mind and that lurking horror in the distant steeple—that monstrous thing of night which his rashness had called out of the ultimate black spaces. He seemed to feel a constant tugging at his will, and callers of that period remember how he would sit abstractedly at his desk and stare out the west window at that far-off, spire-bristling mound beyond the swirling smoke of the city. His entries dwell monotonously on certain terrible dreams, and of a strengthening of the unholy rapport in his sleep. There is mention of a night when he awaked to find himself fully dressed, outdoors, and headed automatically down College Hill toward the west. Again and again he dwells on the fact that the thing in the steeple knows where to find him.

The week following July 30 is recalled as the time of Blake's partial breakdown. He did not dress, and ordered all his food by telephone. Visitors remarked the cords he kept near his bed, and he said that sleep-walking had forced him to bind his ankles every night with knots which would probably hold or else waken him with the labour of untying.

In his diary he told of the hideous experience which had brought the collapse. After retiring on the night of the 30th he had suddenly found himself groping about in an almost black space. All he could see were short, faint, horizontal streaks of bluish light, but he could smell an overpowering foetor and hear a curious jumble of soft, furtive sounds above him. Whenever he moved he stumbled over something, and at each noise there would come a sort of answering sound from above—a vague stirring, mixed with the cautious sliding of wood on wood.

Once his groping hands encountered a pillar of stone with a vacant top, whilst later he found himself clutching the rungs of a ladder built into the wall, and fumbling his uncertain way upward toward some region of intenser stench where a hot, searing blast beat down against him. Before his eyes a kaleidoscopic range of phantasmal images played, all of them dissolving at intervals into the picture of a vast, unplumbed abyss of night wherein whirled suns and worlds of an even profounder blackness. He thought of the ancient legends of Ultimate Chaos, at whose centre sprawls the blind idiot god Azathoth, Lord of All Things, encircled by his flopping horde of mindless and amorphous dancers, and lulled by the thin monotonous piping of a daemoniac flute held in nameless paws.

Then a sharp report from the outer world broke through his stupor and roused him to the unutterable horror of his position. What it was, he never knew—perhaps it was some belated peal from the fireworks heard all summer on Federal Hill as the dwellers hail their various patron saints, or the saints of their native villages in Italy. In any event he shrieked aloud, dropped frantically from the ladder, and stumbled blindly across the obstructed floor of the almost lightless chamber that encompassed him.

He knew instantly where he was, and plunged recklessly down the narrow spiral staircase, tripping and bruising himself at every turn. There was a nightmare flight through a vast cobwebbed nave whose ghostly arches reached up to realms of leering shadow, a sightless scramble through a littered basement, a climb to regions of air and street-lights outside, and a mad racing down a spectral hill of gibbering gables, across a grim, silent city of tall black towers, and up the steep eastward precipice to his own ancient door.

On regaining consciousness in the morning he found himself lying on his study floor fully dressed. Dirt and cobwebs covered him, and every inch of his body seemed sore and bruised. When he faced the mirror he saw that his hair was badly scorched, while a trace of strange, evil odour seemed to cling to his upper outer clothing. It was then that his nerves broke down. Thereafter, lounging exhaustedly about in a dressing-gown, he did little but stare from his west window, shiver at the threat of thunder, and make wild entries in his diary.

The great storm broke just before midnight on August 8th. Lightning struck repeatedly in all parts of the city, and two remarkable fireballs were reported. The rain was torrential, while a constant fusillade of thunder brought sleeplessness to thousands. Blake was utterly frantic in his fear for the lighting system, and tried to telephone the company around 1 a.m., though by that time service had been temporarily cut off in the interest of safety. He recorded everything in his diary—the large, nervous, and often undecipherable hieroglyphs telling their own story of growing frenzy and despair, and of entries scrawled blindly in the dark.

He had to keep the house dark in order to see out the window, and it appears that most of his time was spent at his desk, peering anxiously through the rain across the glistening miles of downtown roofs at the constellation of distant lights marking Federal Hill. Now and then he would fumblingly make an entry in his diary, so that detached phrases such as "The lights must not go"; "It knows where I am"; "I must destroy it"; and "It is calling to me, but perhaps it means no injury this time" are found scattered down two of the pages.

Then the lights went out all over the city. It happened at 2:12 a.m. according to power-house records, but Blake's diary gives no indication of the time. The entry is merely, "Lights out—God help me." On Federal Hill there were watchers as anxious as he, and rain-soaked knots of men paraded the square and alleys around the evil church with umbrella-shaded candles, electric flashlights, oil lanterns, crucifixes, and obscure charms of the many sorts common to southern Italy. They blessed each flash of lightning, and made cryptical signs of fear with their right hands when a turn in the storm caused the flashes to lessen and finally to cease altogether. A rising wind blew out most of the candles, so that the scene grew threateningly dark. Someone roused Father Merluzzo of Spirito Santo Church, and he hastened to the dismal square to pronounce whatever helpful syllables he could. Of the restless and curious sounds in the blackened tower, there could be no doubt whatever.

For what happened at 2:35 we have the testimony of the priest, a young, intelligent, and well-educated person; of Patrolman William J. Monahan of the Central Station, an officer of the highest reliability who had paused at that part of his beat to inspect the crowd; and of most of the seventy-eight men who had gathered around the church's high bank wall—especially those in the square where the eastward facade was visible. Of course there was nothing which can be proved as being outside the order of Nature. The possible causes of such an event are many. No one can speak with certainty of the obscure chemical processes arising in a vast, ancient, ill-aired, and long-deserted building of heterogeneous contents. Mephitic vapours—spontaneous combustion—pressure of gases born of long decay—any one of numberless phenomena might be responsible. And then, of course, the factor of conscious charlatanry can by no means be excluded. The thing was really quite simple in itself, and covered less than three minutes of actual time. Father Merluzzo, always a precise man, looked at his watch repeatedly.

It started with a definite swelling of the dull fumbling sounds inside the black tower. There had for some time been a vague exhalation of strange, evil odours from the church, and this had now become emphatic and offensive. Then at last there was a sound of splintering wood, and a large, heavy object crashed down in the yard beneath the frowning easterly facade. The tower was invisible now that the candles would not burn, but as the object neared the ground the people knew that it was the smoke-grimed louver-boarding of that tower's east window.

Immediately afterward an utterly unbearable foetor welled forth from the unseen heights, choking and sickening the trembling watchers, and almost prostrating those in the square. At the same time the air trembled with a vibration as of flapping wings, and a sudden east-blowing wind more violent than any previous blast snatched off the hats and wrenched the dripping umbrellas of the crowd. Nothing definite could be seen in the candleless night, though some upward-looking spectators thought they glimpsed a great spreading blur of denser blackness against the inky sky—something like a formless cloud of smoke that shot with meteor-like speed toward the east.

That was all. The watchers were half numbed with fright, awe, and discomfort, and scarcely knew what to do, or whether to do anything at all. Not knowing what had happened, they did not relax their vigil; and a moment later they sent up a prayer as a sharp flash of belated lightning, followed by an ear-splitting crash of sound, rent the flooded heavens. Half an hour later the rain stopped, and in fifteen minutes more the street-lights sprang on again, sending the weary, bedraggled watchers relievedly back to their homes.

The next day's papers gave these matters minor mention in connexion with the general storm reports. It seems that the great lightning flash and deafening explosion which followed the Federal Hill occurrence were even more tremendous farther east, where a burst of the singular foetor was likewise noticed. The phenomenon was most marked over College Hill, where the crash awaked all the sleeping inhabitants and led to a bewildered round of speculations. Of those who were already awake only a few saw the anomalous blaze of light near the top of the hill, or noticed the inexplicable upward rush of air which almost stripped the leaves from the tees and blasted the plants in the gardens. It was agreed that the lone, sudden lightning-bolt must have struck somewhere in this neighbourhood, though no trace of its striking could afterward be found. A youth in the Tau Omega fraternity house thought he saw a grotesque and hideous mass of smoke in the air just as the preliminary flash burst, but his observation has not been verified. All of the few observers, however, agree as to the violent gust from the west and the flood of intolerable stench which preceded the belated stroke; whilst evidence concerning the momentary burned odour after the stroke is equally general.

These points were discussed very carefully because of their probable connexion with the death of Robert Blake. Students in the Psi Delta house, whose upper rear windows looked into Blake's study, noticed the blurred white face at the westward window on the morning of the 9th, and wondered what was wrong with the expression. When they saw the same face in the same position that evening, they felt worried, and watched for the lights to come up in his apartment. Later they rang the bell of the darkened flat, and finally had a policeman force the door.

The rigid body sat bolt upright at the desk by the window, and when the intruders saw the glassy, bulging eyes, and the marks of stark, convulsive fright on the twisted features, they turned away in sickened dismay. Shortly afterward the coroner's physician made an examination, and despite the unbroken window reported electrical shock, or nervous tension induced by an electrical discharge, as the cause of death. The hideous expression he ignored altogether, deeming it a not improbable result of the profound shock as experienced by a person of such abnormal imagination and unbalanced emotions. He deduced these latter qualities from the books, paintings, and manuscripts found in the apartment, and from the blindly scrawled entries in the diary on the desk. Blake had prolonged his frenzied jottings to the last, and the broken-pointed pencil was found clutched in his spasmodically contracted right hand.

The entries after the failure of the lights were highly disjointed, and legible only in part. From them certain investigators have drawn conclusions differing greatly from the materialistic official verdict, but such speculations have little chance for belief among the conservative. The case of these imaginative theorists has not been helped by the action of superstitious Dr. Dexter, who threw the curious box and angled stone—an object certainly self-luminous as seen in the black windowless steeple where it was found—into the deepest channel of Narragansett Bay. Excessive imagination and neurotic unbalance on Blake's part, aggravated by knowledge of the evil bygone cult whose startling traces he had uncovered, form the dominant interpretation given those final frenzied jottings. These are the entries—or all that can be made of them.

"Lights still out—must be five minutes now. Everything depends on lightning. Yaddith grant it will keep up! ... Some influence seems beating through it.... Rain and thunder and wind deafen.... The thing is taking hold of my mind....

"Trouble with memory. I see things I never knew before. Other worlds and other galaxies ... Dark ... The lightning seems dark and the darkness seems light....

"It cannot be the real hill and church that I see in the pitch-darkness. Must be retinal impression left by flashes. Heaven grant the Italians are out with their candles if the lightning stops!

"What am I afraid of? Is it not an avatar of Nyarlathotep, who in antique and shadowy Khem even took the form of man? I remember Yuggoth, and more distant Shaggai, and the ultimate void of the black planets....

"The long, winging flight through the void ... cannot cross the universe of light ... re-created by the thoughts caught in the Shining Trapezohedron ... send it through the horrible abysses of radiance....

"My name is Blake—Robert Harrison Blake of 620 East Knapp Street, Milwaukee, Wisconsin.... I am on this planet....

"Azathoth have mercy!—the lightning no longer flashes—horrible—I can see everything with a monstrous sense that is not sight—light is dark and dark is light ... those people on the hill ... guard ... candles and charms ... their priests ...

"Sense of distance gone—far is near and near is far. No light—no glass—see that steeple—that tower—window—can hear—Roderick Usher—am mad or going mad—the thing is stirring and fumbling in the tower—I am it and it is I—I want to get out ... must get out and unify the forces.... It knows where I am....

"I am Robert Blake, but I see the tower in the dark. There is a monstrous odour ... senses transfigured ... boarding at that tower window cracking and giving way.... Iä ... ngai ... ygg....

"I see it—coming here—hell-wind—titan blur—black wings—Yog-Sothoth save me—the three-lobed burning eye...."

APPENDIX: JUVENILIA (1897–1902)

The Little Glass Bottle

"Heave to, there's something floating to the leeward" the speaker was a short stockily built man whose name was William Jones. he was the captain of a small cat boat in which he & a party of men were sailing at the time the story opens.

"Aye aye sir" answered John Towers & the boat was brought to a stand still Captain Jones reached out his hand for the object which he now discerned to be a glass bottle "Nothing but a rum flask that the men on a passing boat threw over" he said but from an impulse of curiosity he reached out for it. it was a rum flask & he was about to throw it away when he noticed a piece of paper in it. He pulled it out & on it read the following

> Jan 1 1864
> I am John Jones who writes this letter my ship is fast sinking with a treasure on board I am where it is marked * on the enclosed chart

Captain Jones turned the sheet over & the other side was a chart

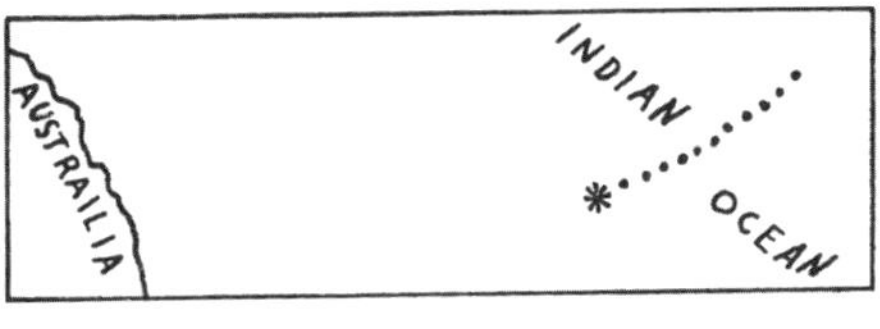

on the edge were written these words

> dotted lines represent course we took

"Towers" Said Capt. Jones excitedly "read this" Towers did as he was directed "I think it would pay to go" said Capt. Jones "do you"? "Just as you say" replied Towers. "We'll charter a schooner this very day" said the exited captain "All right" said Towers so they hired a boat and started off govnd by the dotted lines of they chart in 4 weeks the reached the place where directed & the divers went down and came up with an iron bottle they found in it the following lines scribbled on a piece of brown paper

> Dec 3 1880
>
> Dear Searcher excuse me for the practical joke I have played on you but it serves you right to find nothing for your foolish act—
>
> "Well it does" said Capt Jones "go on"
>
> However I will defray your expenses to & from the place you found your bottle I think it will be $25.0.00 so that amount you will find in an Iron box I know where you found the bottle because I put this bottle here & the iron box & then found a good place to put the second bottle hoping the enclosed money will defray your expenses some I close—Anonymus"

"I'd like to kick his head off" said Capt Jones "Here diver go & get the $25.0.00 in a minute the diver came up bearing an iron box inside it was found $25.0.00 It defrayed their expenses but I hardly think that they will ever go to a mysterious place as directed by a mysterious bottle

THE SECRET CAVE

or John Lees adventure

"Now be good children" Said Mrs. Lee "While I am away & dont get into mischief". Mr. & Mrs. Lee were going off for the day & To leave The Two children John 10 yrs old & Alice 2 yrs old "Yes" replied John

As Soon as The Elder Lees were away the younger Lees went down cellar & began to rummage among the rubbish little alice leaned against the wall watching John. As John was making a boat of barrel staves the Little girl gave a piercing cry as the bricks behind her crumbled away he rushed up to her & Lifted her out screaming loudly as soon as her screams subsided she said "the wall went away" John went up & saw that there was a passage he said to the little girl "lets come & see what this is" "Yes" she said the entered the place they could stand up it the passage was farther than they could see they John went back upstairs & went to the kitchen drawer & got 2 candles & some matches & then they went back to the cellar passage. the two once more entered there was plastering on the walls ceiling & floor nothing was visible but a box this was for a seat nevertheless they examined it & found it to contain nothing the walked on farther & pretty soon the plastering left off & they were in a cave Little alice was frightened at first but at her brothers assurance that it was "all right" she allayed her fears. soon they came to a small box which John took up & carried within pretty soon they came on a *boat* in it were two oars he dragged it with difficulty along with him soon they found the passage came to an abrupt stop he pulled the obstacle away & to his dismay water rushed in in torrents John was an expert swimmer & long breathed he had Just taken a breath so he tried to rise but with the box & his sister he found it quite impossible then he caught sight of the boat rising he grasped it....

The next he knew he was on the surface clinging tightly to the body of his sister & the mysterious box he could not imagine how the water got in but a new peril menaced them if the water continued rising it would rise to the top suddenly a thought presented itself. he could shut off the water he speedily did this & lifting the now lifeless body of his sister into the boat he himself climbed in & sailed down the passage it was gruesome & uncanny absolutely dark his candle being put out by the flood & a dead body lying near he did not gaze about him but rowed for his life when he did look up he was floating in his own cellar he quickly rushed up stairs with the body, to find his parents had come home He told them the story

* * * * * *

The funeral of alice occupied so much time that John quite forgot about the box—but when they *did* open it they found it to be a *solid gold* chunk worth about $10,000 enough to pay for any thing but the death of his sister.

End

THE MYSTERY OF THE GRAVE-YARD

or "A Dead Man's Revenge"

A Detective Story,
By *H. P. Lovecraft.*

Chapter I
The Burns's Tomb.

It was noon in the Little village of Mainville, and a sorrowful group of people were standing around the Burns's Tomb. Joseph Burns was dead. (when dying, he had given the following strange orders:—"Before you put my body in the tomb, drop this ball onto the floor, at a spot marked "A"." he then handed a small golden ball to the rector.) The people greatly regretted his death. After The funeral services were finished, Mr Dobson (the rector) said, "My friends, I will now gratify the last wishes of the deceased. So saying, he descended into the tomb. (to lay the ball on the spot marked "A") Soon the funeral party Began to be impatient, and after a time Mr. Cha's. Greene (the Lawyer) descended to make a search. Soon he came up with a frightened face, and said, "Mr Dobson is *not there*"!

Chapter II
Mysterious Mr. Bell.

It was 3.10 o'clock in ye afternoone whenne The door bell of the Dobson mansion rang loudly, and the servant on going to the door, found an elderly man, with black hair, and side whiskers.

He asked to see Miss Dobson. Upon arriving in her presence he said, "Miss Dobson, I know where your father is, and for £10,000 I will restore him. My name is Mr. Bell." "Mr. Bell," said Miss Dobson, "will you excuse me from the room a moment?" "Certainly". replied Mr Bell. In a short time she returned, and said, "Mr. Bell, I understand you. You have abducted my father, and hold him for a ransom"

Chapter III
At The Police Station.

It was 3.20 o'clock in the afternoon when the telephone bell at the North End Police Station rang furiously, and Gibson, (the telephone Man) Inquired what was the matter,

"Have found out about fathers dissapearance"! a womans voice said. "Im Miss Dobson, and father has been abducted, "Send King John"! King John was a famous western detective. Just then a man rushed in, and shouted, "Oh! Terrors! Come To the Graveyard!"

Chapter IV
The West Window.

Now let us return to the Dobson Mansion. Mr Bell was rather taken aback by Miss Dobson's plain speaking, but when he recovered his speech he said, "Don't put it quite so plain, Miss Dobson, for I—" He was interrupted by the entrance of King John, who with a brace of revolvers in his hands, barred all egress by the doorway. But quicker than thought Bell sprang to a west window,—and jumped.

Chapter V
The Secret of The grave.

Now let us return to the station house. After the exited visitor had calmed somewhat, he could tell his story straighter. He had seen three men in the graveyard shouting "Bell! Bell! where are you old man!?" and acting very suspiciously. He then followed them, and *they entered The Burns's Tomb!* He then followed them in and they touched a spring at a point marked "A" and then Dissapeared". "I wish king John were here", Said Gibson, "What's your name,"? "John Spratt". replied the visitor.

Chapter VI
The chase for Bell.

Now let us return To the Dobson Mansion again:—King John was utterly confounded at the Sudden movement of Bell, but when he recovered from his surprise, his first thought was of chase. Accordingly, he started in pursuit of the abductor. He tracked him down to the R. R. Station and found to his dismay that he had taken the train for Kent, a large city toward the south, and between which and Mainville there existed no telegraph or telephone. The train had Just Started!

Chapter VII
The Negro Hackman.

The Kent train started at 10.35, and about 10.36 an exited, dusty, and tired man[1] rushed into the Mainville hack. office and said to a negro hackman who was standing by the door—"If you can take me to Kent in 15 minutes I will give you a dollar". "I doan' see how I'm ter git there", said the negro "I hab'n't got a decent pair of hosses an' I hab—" "Two Dollars"! Shouted The Traveller, "all right" said the Hackman.

[1]King John.

Chapter VIII (*Long.*)
Bells Surprise.

It was 11 o'clock at Kent, all of the stores were closed but one, a dingy, dirty, little shop, down at the west end. It lay between Kent Harbour, & the Kent & Mainville R.R. In the Front room a shabbily dressed person of doubtful age was conversing with a middle aged woman with gray haire, "I have agreed to do the job, Lindy," he said, "Bell will arrive at 11.30 and the carraige is ready to take him down to the wharf, where a ship for Africa sails tonighte".

"But If King John were to come?" queried "Lindy"

"Then we'd get nabbed, an' Bell would be hung" Replied The man.

Just then a rap sounded at the door "Are you Bell"? inquired Lindy "Yes" was the response, "And I caught the 10.35 and King John got Left, so we are all right". At 11.40 the party reached The Landing, and saw a ship Loom up in the darkness. "The Kehdive" "of Africa" was painted on the hull, and Just as they were to step on board, a man stepped forward in the darkness and said "John Bell, I arrest you in the Queen's name"!

It was King John.

Chapter IX
The Trial.

The daye of The Trial had arrived, and a crowd of people had gathered around the Little grove, (which served for a court house in summer) To hear the trial of John Bell on the charge of kid-napping. "Mr. Bell," said the judge "what is the secret of the Burns's tomb"

"I well tell you this much" said Bell, "If you go into the tomb and touch a certain spot marked "A" you will find out"

"Now where is Mr Dobson"? queried the judge, "Here"! said a voice behind them, and The *figure of Mr Dobson HIMSELF* loomed up in the doorway.

"How did you get here"! &c was chorused. "'Tis a long story," said Dobson.

Chapter X
Dobson's Story.

"When I went down into the tomb," Said Dobson, "Everything was darkness, I could see nothing. but Finally I discerned the letter "A" printed in white on the onyx floor, I dropped the ball on the Letter, and immediately a trap-door opened and a man sprang up. It was this man, here," (he said (pointing at Bell, who stood Trembling on the prisoner's docke) "and he pulled me down into a brilliantly lighted, and palatial apartment where I have Lived until to-day. One day a young man rushed in and exclaimed "The secret Is revealed!" and was gone. He did not see me. Once Bell left his key behind, and I took the impression in wax, and the next day was spent in filing keys to fit the Lock. The next day my key fitted. and the next day (which is to-day) I escaped."

Chapter XI
The Mystery unveiled.

"Why did the late J. Burns, ask you to put the ball there"? (at "A"?) queried the Judge? "To get me into trouble" replied Dobson "He, and Francis Burns, (his brother) have plotted against me for years, and I knew not, in what way they would harm me". "Sieze Francis Burns"! yelled the Judge.

Chapter XII
Conclusion.

Francis Burns, and John Bell, were sent to prison for life. Mr Dobson was cordially welcomed by his daughter, who, by the way had become Mrs King John. "Lindy" and her accomplice were sent to Newgate for 30 days as aidors and abbettors of a criminal escape.

The End.

Price 25¢

THE MYSTERIOVS SHIP

[short version]

BY
HOWARD PHILLIPS LOVECRAFT.

THE ROYAL PRESS.
1902.

Chapter 1.

In the spring of 1847, the little village of Ruralville was thrown into a state of exitement by the arrival of a strange brig in the harbour. It carried no flag, & everything about it was such as would exite suspicion. It had no name. Its captain was named Manuel Ruello. The exitement increased however when John Griggs dissapeared from his home. This was Oct. 4. on Oct. 5 the brig was gone.

Chapter 2.

The brig, in leaving, was met by a U. S. Frigate and a sharp fight ensued. When over, they[1] missed a man named Henry Johns.

[1](The Frigate.)

Chapter 3.

The brig continued its course in the direction of Madagascar, upon its arrival, The natives fled in all directions. When they came together on the other side of the island, one was missing. His name was Dahabea.

Chapter 4.

At length it was decided that something must be done. A reward of £5,000 was offered for the capture of Manuel Ruello, When startling news came, a nameless brig was wrecked on the Florida Keys.

Chapter 5.

A ship was sent to Florida, and the mystery was solved. In the exitement of the fight they would launch a sub-marine boat and take what they wanted. there it lay, tranquilly rocking on the waters of the Atlantic when someone called out "John Brown has dissapeared." And sure enough John Brown was gone.

Chapter 6.

The finding of the sub-marine boat, and the dissapearance of John Brown, cause renewed exitement amongst the people, when a new discovery was made. In transcribing this discovery it is necessary to relate a geographical fact. At the N. Pole there exists a vast continent composed of volcanic soil, a portion of which is open to explorers. It is called "No-Mans Land."

Chapter 7.

In the extreme southern part of No-Mans Land, there was found a hvt, and several other signs of human habitation. they promptly entered, and, chained to the floor, lay Griggs, Johns, & Dahabea. They, upon arriving in London, separated, Griggs going to Ruralville, Johns to the Frigate, & Dahabea to Madagascar.

Chapter 8.

But the mystery of John Brown was still unsolved, so they kept strict watch over the port at No-Mans Land, and when the sub-marine boat arrived, and the pirates, one by one, and headed by Manuel Ruello, left the ship, they were met by a rapid fire. After the fight brown was recovered.

Chapter 9.

Griggs was royally received at Ruralville, & a dinner was given in honour of Henry Johns, Dahabea was made King of Madagascar, & Brown was made Captain of his ship.

THE END.

THE MYSTERIOUS SHIP

[long version]

by Anonymus

In the Spring of 1847, the little village of Ruralville was thrown into a state of excitement by the landing of a strange Brig in the harbour. It carried no flag, and no name was painted on its side, and everything about it was such as would excite suspicion. It was from Tripoli, Africa, and the captain was named Manuel Ruello. The Excitement increased, however; when John Griggs, (The magnate of the villiage) suddenly disappeared from his home. This was the night of October 4th—on October 5th the Brig left.

Chapter II

It was 8 bells on the U.S. Frigate "Constitution" when Commander Farragut sighted a strange brig to the westward. It carried no flag, and no name was painted on its side, and everything about it was such as would excite suspicion. On hailing it put up the Pirates Flag. Farragut ordered a gun fired and no sooner did he fire, than the pirate ship gave them a broadside when the Fight was over Commander Farragut Missed one man named Henry F. Johns.

Chapter III

It was Summer on the Island of Madagascar. And Natives were picking corn, when one cried "Companions! I sight a ship!

with no flag and with no name printed on the side and with eveything about it such as would excite Suspicion!" And The Natives fled in all directions when They came together on The other side of The Island one was missing his name was Dahabea.

Chapter IV

At length it was Decided Something must be done, Notes were compared. Three abductions were found to have taken place Dissapearance of John Griggs, Henry John, & Dahabea, were recalled. Finally Advertisements were issued offering £5000 reward for the capture of Manuel Ruello, Ship, Prisoners, & crew. When exciting News reached London! An unknown Brig with no name was wrecked of The Florida Keys in America!

Chapter V

The People Hurried to Florida and Beheld———. A steel spindle shaped object Lay placidly on the water Beside the shattered wreck of The brig. "A Submarine Boat"! shouted one "Yes!" shouted another "The mystery is cleared" said a wise looking man. "In the excitement of the fight they launch the submarine boat and take as many as they wish, unseen. And——." "John Brown has dissapeared"! shouted a voice from the deck. Sure enough John Brown was gone!

Chapter VI

The Finding of The Submarine boat and the dissapearance of John Brown caused renewed excitement among the People. and a new discovery was made. In relating this discovery It is necessary to relate a geographical Fact:—At the North Pole there is supposed to exist a vast continent composed of volcanic soil, a portion is open to travellers and explorers but it is barren and unfruitful. and thus absolutely Impassable. It is called "No-Mans Land".

Chapter VII

In the Extreme southern part of No-Mans Land There was found a wharf and a hut &c and every sign of former human habitation. A rusty door-plate was nailed to the hut inscribed in old English "M. Ruello". This, then, was the home of Manuel Ruello. the house brought to light a note book belonging to John Griggs, and The Log of the "Constitution" taken from Henry Johns, and the Madagascar Reaper belong To Dahabea.

Chapter VIII

When about to leave, they Observed a spring on the side of the hut. They pressed it.—A hole appeared in the side of the hut which they promptly entered. They were in a subterranean cavern. the beach ran down to the edge of a black, murky, sea. on the sea lay a dark oblong object—viz another Submarine boat which they entered. There bound to the cabin Floor Lay Griggs, Johns, and Dahabea, all alive and well. They, when arriving in London, separated, Griggs going to Ruralville, Johns, To the Constitution and Dahabea to Madagascar.

Chapter IX

But The mystery of John Brown lay still unsolved. So They Kept strict watch over the port at no-mans Land, Hoping The Submarine Boat would arrive. At length, however, it did arrive bearing with it John Brown. They Fixed upon the 5th of October For the Attack. They ranged along the shore and Formed Bodies. Finally one by one and Headed by Manuel Ruello The Pirates left the Boat, They were (to their astonishment) Met By a Rapid Fire.

Chapter X Conclusion

The Pirates were at Length defeated and a search was made for Brown. At Length he (the aforesaid Brown) was found. John Gregg was royally received at Ruralville and a dinner was

Dahabea was made King of Madagascar, and Manuel Ruello was Executed at Newgate Prison.

The End

DISCARDED DRAFT OF "THE SHADOW OVER INNSMOUTH"

[pp. 1–6:]

It was in the summer of 1927 that I suddenly cut short my sightseeing tour of New England and returned to Cleveland under a nervous strain. I have seldom mentioned the particulars of this trip, and hardly know why I do so now except that a recent newspaper cutting has somehow relieved the tension which formerly existed. A sweeping fire, it appears, has wiped out most of the empty ancient houses along the deserted Innsmouth waterfront as well as a certain number of buildings farther inland; while a singularly simultaneous explosion, heard for many miles around, has destroyed to a vast depth the great black reef a mile and a half out from shore where the sea-bottom abruptly falls to form an incalculable abyss. For certain reasons I take great satisfaction in these occurrences, even the first of which seems to me a blessing rather than a disaster. Especially am I glad that the old brick jewellery factory and the pillared Order of Dagon Hall have gone along with the rest. There is talk of incendiarism, and I suppose old Father Iwanicki could tell much if he chose; but what I know gives a very unusual angle to my opinion.

I never heard of Innsmouth till the day before I saw it for the first and last time. It does not seem to be mentioned on any modern map, and I was planning to go directly from Newburyport to Arkham, and thence to Gloucester, if I could find transportation. I had no car, but was travelling by motor coach, train, and trolley, always seeking the cheapest possible route. In Newburyport they told me that the steam train was the thing to take to Arkham; and it was only at the station ticket office, when I demurred at the high fare, that I heard about Innsmouth. The agent, whose speech shewed him to be no local man, seemed sympathetic toward my efforts at economy, and made a suggestion that none of my other informants had offered,

"You could take that old bus, I suppose," he said with a certain hesitation, "but it isn't thought much of hereabouts. It goes through Innsmouth—you may have heard about that—and so the people don't like it. Run by an Innsmouth man—Joe Sargent—but never gets any custom from here, or from Arkham either, I guess. Wonder it keeps running at all. I suppose it's cheap enough, but I never see more than two or three people in it—nobody but those Innsmouth folks. Leaves the Square—front of Hammond's Drug Store—at 10 a.m. and 7 p.m. unless they've changed lately. Looks like a terrible rattletrap—I've never been on it."

That was the first I ever heard of Innsmouth. Any reference to a town not listed in the guidebooks would have interested me, and the agent's odd manner of allusion roused something like real curiosity. A town able to inspire such dislike in its neighbours, I thought, must be at least rather unusual, and worthy of a sightseer's attention. If it came before Arkham I would stop off there—and so I asked the agent to tell me something about it.

He was very deliberate, and spoke with an air of feeling somewhat superior to what he said.

"Innsmouth? Well, it's a queer kind of a town down at the mouth of the Manuxet. It used to be almost a city—quite a seaport before the War of 1812—but the place has all gone to pieces in the last hundred years or so. No railroad now—the B & M never went through there, and the branch line from Rowley was given up years ago. More empty houses than there are people, I guess, and no business to speak of. Everybody trades either here or in Arkham or Ipswich. At one time they had quite a number of mills there, but nothing's left now but one jewellery refinery.

"That's a pretty prominent proposition, though—all the travelling salesmen seem to know about it. Makes a special kind of fancy jewellery out of a secret alloy that nobody can analyse very well. They say it's platinum, silver, and gold—but these people sell it so cheap that you can hardly believe it. Guess they have a corner on that kind of goods.

"Old man Marsh, who owns the thing, must be richer than Croesus. Queer old duck, though, and sticks pretty close around the town. He's the grandson of Capt. Obed Marsh, who founded the business. His mother was some kind of foreigner—they say a South Sea native—so everybody raised Cain when he married an Ipswich girl fifty years ago. They always do that about Innsmouth people. But his children and grandchildren look just like anybody else so far as I can see. I've had 'em pointed out to me here. Never saw the old man.

"And why is everybody so down on Innsmouth? Well—you mustn't take too much stock in what people around here say. They're hard to get started, but once they do get started they never stop. They've been telling things about Innsmouth—whispering 'em, mostly—for the last hundred years, I guess, and I gather they're more scared than anything else. Some of the stories would make you laugh—about old Captain Marsh driving bargains with the devil and bringing imps out of hell to live in Innsmouth, or about some kind of devil-worship and awful sacrifices in some place near the wharves that people stumbled on around 1850 or thereabouts—but I come from Panton, Vermont, and that kind of story doesn't go down with me.

"The real thing behind all this is simply race prejudice—and I don't say I'm blaming those that hold it. I hate those Innsmouth folks myself, and I wouldn't care to go to their town. I suppose you know—though I can see you're a Westerner by the way you talk—what a lot our New England ships used to have to do with queer ports in Asia, Africa, the South Seas, and everywhere else, and what queer kinds of people they sometimes brought back with them. You've probably heard about the Salem man that came back with a Chinese wife, and maybe you know there's still a colony of Fiji Islanders somewhere around Cape Cod.

"Well, there must be something like that back of the Innsmouth people. The place was always badly cut off from the rest of the country by salt marshes and inlets, and we can't be sure about the ins and outs of the matter, but it's pretty plain that old Captain Marsh must have brought home some odd specimens when he had all three of his ships in commission back in the 1830's and 1840's. There certainly is a strange kind of a streak in the Innsmouth folks today—I don't know how to express it, but it sort of makes me crawl. You'll notice it a little in Joe Sargent if you take that bus. Some of them have flat noses, big mouths, weak retreating chins, and a funny kind of rough grey skin. The sides of their necks are sort of shrivelled or creased up, and they get bald very young. Nobody around here or in Arkham will have anything to do with them, and they act kind of offish themselves when they come to town. They used to ride on the railroad, walking and taking the train at Rowley or Ipswich, but now they use that bus.

"Yes, there's a hotel in Innsmouth—called the Gilman House—but I don't believe it can amount to much. I wouldn't advise you to try it. Better stay over here and take the ten o'clock bus tomorrow morning. Then you can get an evening bus there for Arkham at 8 o'clock. There was a factory inspector who stopped at the Gilman a couple of years ago, and he had a lot of unpleasant hints about the place. It seems they get a queer crowd there, for this fellow heard voices in other rooms that gave him the shivers. It was foreign talk, but he said the bad thing about it was the kind of voice that sometimes spoke. It sounded so unnatural—slopping-like, he said—that he didn't dare go to sleep. Just kept dressed and lit out early in the morning. The talk went on most of the night.

"This man—Casey, his name was—had a lot to say about the old Marsh factory, and what he said fitted in very well with some of the wild stories. The books were in no kind of shape, and the machinery looked old and almost abandoned, as if it hadn't been run a great deal. The place still used water power from the Lower Falls of the Manuxet. There were only a few employees, and they didn't seem to be doing much. It made me think, when he told me, about the local rumours that Marsh doesn't actually make the stuff he sells. Many people say he doesn't get enough factory supplies to be really running the place, and that he must be importing those queer ornaments from somewhere—heaven knows where. I don't believe that, though. The Marshes have been selling those outlandish rings and armlets and tiaras and things for nearly a hundred years; and if there were anywhere else where they got 'em, the general public would have found out all about it by this time. Then, too, there's no shipping or in-bound trucking around Innsmouth that would account for such imports. What does get imported is the queerest kind of glass and rubber trinkets—makes you think of what they used to buy in the old days to trade with savages. But it's a straight fact that all inspectors run up against queer things at the plant. Twenty odd years ago one of them disappeared at Innsmouth—never heard of again—and I myself knew George Cole, who went insane down there one night, and had to be lugged away by two men from the Danvers asylum, where he is now. He talks of some kind of sound and shrieks things about 'scaly water-devils'.

"And that makes me think of another of the old stories—about the black reef off the coast. Devil's Reef, they call it. It's almost above water a good part of the time, but at that you could hardly call it a real island. The story is that there's a whole legion of devils seen sometimes on that reef—sprawled about, or darting in and out of some kind of caves near the top. It's a rugged, uneven thing, a good bit over a mile out, and sailors used to make great detours just to avoid it. One of the things they had against Captain Marsh was that he used to land on it sometimes when it was fairly dry. Probably the rock formation interested him, but there was talk about his having dealings with demons. That was before the big epidemic of 1846, when over half the people in Innsmouth were carried off. They never did quite figure out what the trouble was, but it was probably some foreign kind of disease brought from China or somewhere by the shipping.

"Maybe that plague took off the best blood in Innsmouth. Anyway, they're a doubtful lot now—and there can't be more than 500 or 600 of them. The rich Marshes are as bad as any. I guess they're all what people call 'white trash' down South—lawless and sly, and full of secret doings. Lobster fishermen, mostly—exporting by truck. Nobody can ever keep track of 'em, and state school officials and census people have a devil of a time. That's why I wouldn't go at night if I were you. I've never been there and have no wish to go, but I guess a daytime trip wouldn't hurt you—even though the people here will advise you not to take it. If you're just sightseeing, Innsmouth ought to be quite a place for you."

And so I spent that evening at the Newburyport Public Library looking up data about Innsmouth. When I had tried to question natives in the shops, the lunch room, and the fire station I had found them even harder to get started that the ticket agent had predicted, and realised that I could not spare the time to overcome their first instinctive reticence. They had a kind of obscure suspiciousness. At the YMCA the clerk merely discouraged my going to such a dismal, decadent place, and the people at the library shewed much the same attitude, holding Innsmouth to be merely an exaggerated case of civic degeneration.

The Essex County histories on the shelves had very little to say, except that the town was founded in 1643, noted for shipbuilding before the Revolution, a seat of great marine prosperity in the early nineteenth century, and later on a minor factory centre using the Manuxet as power. References to decline were very few, though the signfiicance of the later records was unmistakable. After the Civil War all industrial life centred in the Marsh Refining Company at the Lower Falls, and the marketing of its products formed the only remaining bit of major commerce. There were very few foreigners; mostly Poles and Portuguese on the southern fringe of the town. Local finances were very bad, and but for the Marsh factory the place would have been bankrupt.

I saw a good many booklets and catalogues and advertising calendars of the Marsh Refining Company in the business department of the library, and began to realise what a striking thing that lone industry was. The jewels and ornaments it sold were of the finest possible artistry and the most extreme originality; so delicately wrought, indeed, that one could not doubt but that handicraft played a large part in at least their final stages of manufacture. Some of the half-tone pictures of them interested me profoundly, for the strangeness and beauty of the designs seemed to my eye indicative of a profound and exotic genius—a genius so spectacular and bizarre that one could not help wondering whence the inspiration had come. It was easy to credit the boast of one of the booklets that this jewellery was a favourite with persons of sophisticated taste, and that several specimens were exhibited in museums of modern craftsmanship.

Large pieces predominated—armlets, tiaras, and elaborate pendants—but rings and lesser items were numerous. The raised or incised designs—partly conventional and partly with a curious marine motif—were wrought in a style of tremendous distinctiveness and of utter dissimilarity to the art traditions of any race or epoch I knew about. This other-worldly character was emphasised by the oddness of the precious alloy, whose general effect was suggested in several colour-plates. Something about these pictured things fascinated me intensely—almost disproportionately—and I resolved to see as many original specimens as possible both at Innsmouth and in shops and museums elsewhere. Yet there was a distinct element of repulsion mixed with the fascination; proceeding, perhaps, from the evil and silly old legends about the founder of the business which the ticket agent had told me.

[p. 17:]

The door of the Marsh retail office was open, and I walked in with considerable expectancy. The interior was shabby and ill-lighted, but contained a large number of display cases of solid and capable workmanship. A youngish man came forward to meet me, and as I studied his face a fresh wave of disturbance passed over me. He was not unhandsome, but there was something subtly bizarre and aberrant about his features and vocal timbre. I could not stifle a keen sudden aversion, and acquired an unexplained reluctance to seem like any sort of curious investigator. Before I knew it I found myself telling the fellow that I was a jewellery buyer for a Cleveland firm, and preparing myself to shew a merely professional interest in what I should see.

It was hard, though, to carry out this policy. The clerk switched on more lights and began to lead me from case to case, but when I beheld the glittering marvels before me I could scarcely walk steadily or talk coherently. It took no excessive sensivitiveness to beauty to make one literally gasp at the strange, alien loveliness of these opulent objects, and as I gazed fascinatedly I saw how little justice even the colour-plates had done them. Even now I can hardly describe what I saw—though those who own such pieces or have seen them in shops and museums can supply the missing data. The massed effect of so many elaborate examples was what produced my especial feeling of awe and unrest. For somehow or other, these singular grotesques and arabesques did not seem to be the product of any earthly handiwork—least of all a factory only a stone's throw away. The patterns and traceries all hinted of remote spaces and unimaginable abysses, and the aquatic nature of the occasional pictorial items added to the general unearthliness. Some of the fabulous monsters filled me with an uncomfortable sense of dark pseudo-memory which I tried

[p. 21:]
the taint and blasphemy of furtive Innsmouth. He, like me, was a normal being outside the pall of decay and normally terrified by it. But because he was so inextricably close to the thing, he had been broken in a way that I was not yet broken.

Shaking off the hands of the firemen who sought to detain him, the ancient rose to hsi feet and greeted me as if I were an acquaintance. The grocery youth had told me where most of Uncle Zadok's liquor was obtained, and without a word I began leading him in that direction—through the Square and around into Eliot Street. His step was astonishingly brisk for one of his age and bibulousness, and I marvelled at the original strength of his constitution. My haste to leave Innsmouth had abated for the moment, and I felt instead a queer curiosity to dip into this mumbling patriarch's chaotic store of extravagant myth.

When we had bought a quart of whiskey in the rear of a dismal variety store, I led Uncle Zadok along South Street to the utterly abandoned section of the waterfront, and still farther southward to a point where even the fishermen on the distant breakwater could not see us, where I knew we could talk undisturbed. For some reason or other he seemed to dislike this arrangement—casting nervous glances out to sea in the direction of Devil Reef—but the lure of the whiskey was too strong for him to resist. After we had found a seat on the edge of a rotting wharf I gave him a pull at the bottle and waited for it to take effect. Naturally I graduated the doses very carefully, for I did not wish the old man's loquacity to turn into a stupor. As he grew more mellow, I began to venture some remarks and inquiries about Innsmouth, and was really startled by the terrible and sincere portentousness of his lowered voice. He did not seem as crazy as his wild tales would indicate, and I found myself shuddering even when I could not believe his fantastic inventions. I hardly wondered at the naive credulity of superstitious Father Iwanicki.

weldon**owen**

an imprint of Insight Editions

P.O. Box 3088
San Rafael, CA 94912
www.weldonowen.com

CEO *Raoul Goff*
VP Group Publisher *Jeff McLaughlin*
VP Publisher *Roger Shaw*
Publishing Director *Katie Killebrew*
Executive Editor *Jamie Thompson*
Managing Editor *Mary Beth Garhart*
Editorial Assistant *Jon Ellis*
VP Creative *Chrissy Kwasnik*
VP Manufacturing *Alix Nicholaeff*
Production Manager *Tiffani Patterson*

This edition published by Weldon Owen by arrangement with
The Book Shop, Ltd. and the H. P. Lovecraft Historical Society

Designed by Jon Pannier
Edited by Diane Namm

ISBN: 979-8-88674-233-6

This book is part of The H. P. Lovecraft Experience kit
and is not to be sold separately.

Manufactured in China by Insight Editions

10 9 8 7 6 5 4 3 2 1

ROOTS of PEACE   REPLANTED PAPER

Insight Editions, in association with Roots of Peace, will plant two trees
for each tree used in the manufacturing of this book. Roots of Peace
is an internationally renowned humanitarian organization dedicated to
eradicating land mines worldwide and converting war-torn lands
into productive farms and wildlife habitats. Roots of Peace will plant
two million fruit and nut trees in Afghanistan and provide farmers there
with the skills and support necessary for sustainable land use.

A READER'S GUIDE TO SELECTED WORKS BY
H. P. LOVECRAFT

LEE MOYER

A READER'S GUIDE TO SELECTED WORKS BY H. P. LOVECRAFT

Sean Branney and Andrew Leman

Founders, The H. P. Lovecraft Historical Society

weldon**owen**

CONTENTS

Howard P. Lovecraft collection, John Hay Library, Brown University

INTRODUCTION

Nameless monstrosities emerge from the vast depths of space. Ancient evils awaken. Fantastic adventures occur beyond the walls of sleep. People experience fear so intense that their minds collapse into madness. Welcome to the world of H. P. Lovecraft.

H. P. Lovecraft's literary legacy, steeped in the uncanny and the arcane, has left an indelible mark on the genres of horror and science fiction, establishing him as the preeminent architect of cosmic dread and mortal terror. Though largely ignored in his own lifetime, his stories have inspired generations of artists, musicians, filmmakers, and authors and have won him a legion of devoted fans across the globe. For readers who are new to Lovecraft, or those interested in taking a deeper dive into what he's all about, we've prepared this *Reader's Guide*. We've selected ten of his most impactful stories, and we'll explore them in depth. All these tales are printed in full in the companion volumes, but the information in this guide will highlight the most noteworthy elements of these stories. Some find Lovecraft highly controversial, and we'll address these misgivings as well.

We, the founders of the H. P. Lovecraft Historical Society (HPLHS), have been reading Lovecraft for more than forty years; we've adapted his work into motion pictures, stage musicals, games, audiobooks, radio dramas, and even Christmas carols. In addition to simply being enjoyable as literature, H. P. Lovecraft's work has inspired us. We hope you, too, will find a wealth of material to ponder and enjoy as you read it yourself.

Because we have included Lovecraft's biographical information in the introduction to the companion volumes, this book will focus on ten of his most iconic stories. In addition to his fiction, Lovecraft wrote an estimated 90,000 letters—believed to be more than anyone else in American history. Through these letters, we have learned a great deal about his life and works, and we have included quotes from them throughout to provide extra context to the stories.

Lovecraft's fiction consists of two novellas and more than sixty short stories, many of which feature persistent themes. Collectively, these themes, along with Lovecraft's antique and prolix literary style, when applied in a literary manner, give us the adjective "Lovecraftian."

Lovecraftian Themes

The Hereditary Curse

The notion of the hereditary curse is that one is predetermined to suffer disastrous consequences resulting from one's lineage. The curse is an ill fate that is due to scientific forces (genetics), rather than destiny or the whims of the gods. Both of Lovecraft's parents died in a mental asylum, so it's not surprising that a fear of what might lurk buried in his own genes emerged as a theme that haunted him.

Dreams and Madness

Lovecraft was a vivid dreamer, and he mostly enjoyed the visions and experiences conjured by his unconscious mind. On numerous occasions, he wondered whether dream lives are of greater significance than waking lives, and many of his tales are directly based on his own dreams. Although Lovecraft's tales of cosmic horror and science fiction tend to be the most popular, he also wrote several stories set in fantastical "dreamlands" inspired by the works of Lord Dunsany, an Anglo-Irish writer and dramatist.

Lovecraft appreciated the fragility of the human psyche, and many of his tales involve characters whose sanity is destroyed by the terrors they witness or the discoveries they make. He was aware of the theories of Sigmund Freud and other cutting-edge psychiatrists of his day, but he didn't think very highly of them. He recognized Freud as an important thinker, but described his theories as "puerile," apparently because they placed so much emphasis on libido and sexual development, topics the prudish Lovecraft tended to disregard. Psychiatry and psychology were fledgling fields in his day and did not command the wide academic respect of traditional hard sciences, such as astronomy, chemistry, and mathematics. Lovecraft generally steered clear of new sciences, though he was keenly interested in the latest developments in established disciplines.

Science

Some readers are surprised to learn that an author with such a vivid imagination was a strict scientific materialist. Lovecraft studied chemistry and astronomy in his youth, and he wrote columns on both subjects for the *Providence Journal*. Some of his stories are outright science fiction, written when that genre was in its infancy, and others even anticipate real scientific discoveries. At the HPLHS, we like to quip that many of Lovecraft's works are "based on a true story."

Superstition and Cults

Although Lovecraft was an atheist committed to rational thought and empirical evidence, he well understood that magic, superstition, and religion were age-old ways for humans to cope with primal fears and instincts and could be used to create compelling fiction. He was not afraid to mine the "lunatic fringe" for story ideas.

Knowledge Equals Danger

One of Lovecraft's favorite scientific disciplines was astronomy, and his knowledge of the subject led him to grasp the profound scale of both the size and age of the universe. As a result, he believed that human beings are highly limited in what they can perceive, and that, if they were able to understand their true place in the vast scope of the universe, they would be terrified by their insignificance. The more we know, the more we imperil our own wellbeing.

Nihilism and Cosmicism

Lovecraft's personal outlook on life could be bleakly nihilistic. He believed man is utterly insignificant in the vastness of the cosmos, free will is an illusion, and in the end nothing matters. But if that's all there was to it, his stories wouldn't be much fun to read. His view of the world also contained wonder and mystery and awe, and the possibility of magic and tantalizing suggestions of ancient truth that fire the reader's imagination. He sometimes found great beauty in his cosmic vision and describes it in rhapsodic and occasionally moving terms that verge on poetry.

Who Are the Monsters?

Numerous Lovecraft stories feature alien creatures that, from a human perspective, are monstrous. But seen from the detached Lovecraftian point of view, some of them are not so monstrous at all. For example, Deep Ones, Mi-Go, the Elder Things, and even the mysterious Colour Out of Space behave in fully rational, if incomprehensible, ways, and simply pursue the objectives of their own kind. It is sadly ironic that Lovecraft saw humanity in his monsters, but not always in his fellow humans.

Enduring Creations

Lovecraft has given us many great, enduring characters and locations in his stories, and some of these are interwoven throughout his tales to create a comprehensive backdrop that adds to their verisimilitude. In the decades since Lovecraft's death, these creations have been adopted by other authors and have taken on lives of their own.

Arkham, Massachusetts

First mentioned in passing in the 1920 story "The Picture in the House," this fictional New England town was concieved of as an analogue of Salem, with a long and haunted history of witchcraft panic, Puritan folly, and numerous examples of the colonial architecture that Lovecraft adored. He avoided specifying its exact location, but he describes it as being near the coast somewhere in Essex County. The town is bisected by the fictional Miskatonic River, which feeds into the Atlantic, making Arkham a functioning port. Not too big and not too small, the town provides a rich setting for fiction (appearing in ten of Lovecraft's stories) and for role-playing games. Like Miskatonic University, Arkham has been fleshed out in tremendous detail by subsequent writers. Authors of DC Comics in the 1970s named the infamous Arkham Asylum in the Batman comics after this town.

Miskatonic University

First appearing in the 1921 story "Herbert West—Reanimator," this fictitious institution is located in the fictional city of Arkham, Massachusetts. Inspired largely by Brown University, located in Lovecraft's hometown of Providence, Rhode Island, Miskatonic is the fantasy university that Lovecraft would have loved to have attended. It enjoys the prestige of an Ivy League institution, and it is the soul of the surrounding community. Its faculty members are experts in their fields, and the university is sufficiently endowed to dispatch expeditions to remote corners of the globe.

The university is also home to the Orne Library, an idealized college library, with a legendary restricted section that houses an uncommonly rich collection of rare occult volumes. As an embodiment of the organized human quest for knowledge, Miskatonic proves a perfect backdrop for many Lovecraftian tales. His use of this locale will be explored in greater depth in our later discussions of the Miskatonic-based stories. Many well-educated Lovecraft fans note with some irony that they possess more memorabilia from Miskatonic than they do from the schools they actually attended.

The *Necronomicon*

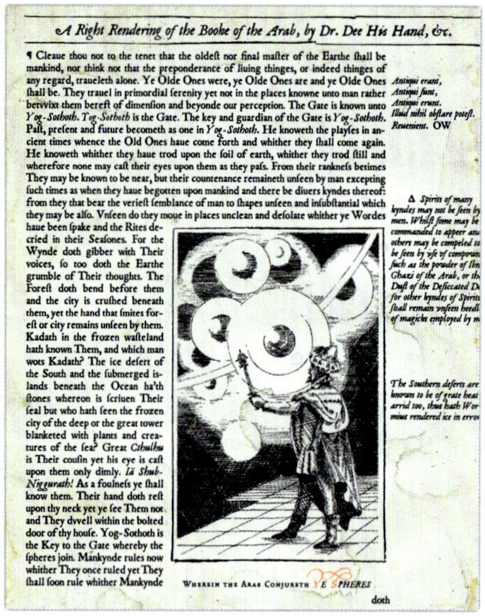

A Right Rendering of the Booke of the Arab, by Dr. Dee His Hand, &c.

¶ Cleaue thou not to the tenet that the oldeſt nor final maſter of the Earthe ſhall be mankind, nor think not that the preponderance of liuing thinges, or indeed thinges of any regard, traueleth alone. Ye Olde Ones were, ye Olde Ones are and ye Olde Ones ſhall be. They trauel in primordial ſerenity yet not in the places knowne unto man rather betvvixt them bereſt of dimenſion and beyonde our perception. The Gate is known unto *Yog-Sothoth*. *Yog-Sothoth* is the Gate. The key and guardian of the Gate is *Yog-Sothoth*. Paſt, preſent and future becometh as one in *Yog-Sothoth*. He knoweth the playſes in ancient times whence the Old Ones haue come forth and whither they ſhall come again. He knoweth whither they haue trod upon the ſoil of earth, whither they trod ſtill and wherefore none may caſt their eyes upon them as they paſs. From their rankneſs betimes They may be known to be near, but their countenance remaineth unſeen by man excepting ſuch times as when they haue begotten upon mankind and there be diuers kyndes thereof: from they that bear the verieſt ſemblance of man to ſhapes unſeen and inſubſtantial which they may be alſo. Vnſeen do they moue in places unclean and deſolate whither ye Wordes haue been ſpake and the Rites decried in their Seaſones. For the Wynde doth gibber with Their voices, ſo too doth the Earthe grumble of Their thoughts. The Foreſt doth bend before them and the city is cruſhed beneath them, yet the hand that ſmites foreſt or city remains unſeen by them. Kadath in the frozen waſteland hath known Them, and which man wots Kadath? The ice deſert of the South and the ſubmerged iſlands beneath the Ocean ha'th ſtones whereon is ſcriuen Their ſeal but who hath ſeen the frozen city of the deep or the great tower blanketed with plants and creatures of the ſea? Great *Cthulhu* is Their couſin yet his eye is caſt upon them only dimly. *Iä Shub-Niggurath!* As a foulneſs ye ſhall know them. Their hand doth reſt upon thy neck yet ye ſee Them not and They dvvell within the bolted door of thy houſe. Yog-Sothoth is the Key to the Gate whereby the ſpheres join. Mankynde rules now whither They once ruled yet They ſhall ſoon rule whither Mankynde doth

Antiqui erant, Antiqui ſunt, Antiqui erunt. Illud nihil obſtare poteſt. Reuenient. OW

Δ *Spirits of many kyndes may not be ſeen by men. Whilſt ſome may be commanded to appeer and others may be compeled to be ſeen by vſe of compoun ſuch as the powder of Ibn Ghazi of the Arab, or the Duſt of the Deſiccated D for other kyndes of Spirits ſhall remain vnſeen heedl of magicks employed by m*

The Southern deſerts are known to be of grate heat arrid too, thus hath Wor mius rendered ice in erro

WHEREIN THE ARAB CONJURETH YE SPHERES

A page from the Necronomicon
PROP CREATED FOR *DARK ADVENTURE RADIO THEATRE®*: "THE DUNWICH HORROR"

Conceived as the greatest and most dangerous book of arcane lore and black magic ever written, the *Necronomicon* first appears in the 1922 story "The Hound." Lovecraft returned to it so frequently that he developed a detailed faux history in 1927 so he could keep his own references consistent. This history (some have called it a hoax) left many people convinced the book was genuine, and it has been picked up by numerous other authors, artists, and filmmakers.

According to Lovecraft's history, the *Necronomicon* was written by Abdul Alhazred (one of Lovecraft's own childhood alter egos) sometime in the eighth century under the original title Al Azif, an allusion to the nocturnal sound of demons. He quoted several passages from it in various stories, but later warned a friend it was better not to get too specific about it. "If anyone were to try to write the *Necronomicon*," he wrote, "it would disappoint all those who have shuddered at cryptic references to it." Several people have been unable to resist the temptation, however, and there have been a fair number of *Necronomicons* produced by other writers over the decades. (The HPLHS has made its own small contribution to the lore of the *Necronomicon* in a Miskatonic University monograph.)

The Cthulhu Mythos

A term never actually used by Lovecraft himself, the Cthulhu Mythos refers to an overarching mythology of ancient gods and monstrous beings that is woven through some of his tales. Lovecraft used the term "Yog-Sothothery," generally doing so in a playful manner with his correspondents when referring to the interconnected mythology of his own works. He never took any of it seriously, and the Yog-Sothothery is even self-contradictory in some places, since he made it up as he went along. It was not his intention to build a cohesive mythology, a fact that has been lost on some modern-day scholars and fans.

Lovecraft's friend, colleague, and publisher, August Derleth, claimed that Lovecraft summed up his thoughts this way:

> All my stories, unconnected as they may be… are based on the fundamental lore or legend that this world was inhabited at one time by another race who, in practising black magic, lost their foothold and were expelled, yet live on outside ever ready to take possession of this earth again.
>
> *Tales of the Cthulhu Mythos, p. vii*

This famous passage, however, is not in Lovecraft's own words. Rather, it is Derleth's paraphrasing of a recollection by Lovecraft's friend Harold Farnese, who said Lovecraft had written words to this effect in a letter that has since been lost. Much effort has gone into trying to systematize Lovecraft's pantheon and to correlate some of his creations to elements such as fire, air, and water, or to the Judeo-Christian framework of good and evil. Ultimately, however, attempts to categorize Lovecraft's fictional worlds only minimize and terrestrialize HPL's staggering imagination. The potency of cosmic fear comes from the vastness of the cosmos and its incomprehensible dissimilarity to the world that we know and inhabit.

Enduring Controversy

It is undeniable that Lovecraft wrote offensively racist things in his private correspondence and public essays and held bigoted views that come through in many of his stories. The HPLHS rejects that worldview and chooses to focus its attention on Lovecraft's significant contributions to horror and science fiction literature instead. We believe that separating creators from their creations is a better alternative than "canceling" artists outright. Those who would enjoy Lovecraft's works must reconcile qualms about the man with appreciation for his artistic creations. In this volume, we'll discuss some of the ways racism is manifested in his tales.

Spoiler Alert!

If you've read this far, we're delighted by your enthusiasm to know more about H. P. Lovecraft. If you're new to his stories, we urge you to put this book down and turn your attention, instead, to the *Collected Fiction of H. P. Lovecraft* included in this set and read the stories before you read our analysis. In this *Reader's Guide*, you'll find in-depth discussions of ten of Lovecraft's most important and influential stories—and many of the great surprises in store for you will be spoiled if you read the guide before the stories.

For each story included in this guide, we cover the tale's origin and impact, the plot, the characters, the settings, the themes, and the symbols / motifs used in that story. We point out noteworthy quotations and discuss their significance. Finally, we toss out some discussion questions that are interesting to explore. We hope we've added some clarity, insights, and context to help you better enjoy Lovecraft's works.

H. P. Lovecraft can be a challenging read, as he was the first to admit. In May of 1923, when he first submitted some of his stories to *Weird Tales* magazine, he included a cover letter to editor Edwin Baird that read:

> I have no idea that these things will be found suitable, for I pay no attention to the demands of commercial writing. My object is such pleasure as I can obtain from the creation of certain bizarre pictures, situations, or atmospheric effects; and the only reader I hold in mind is myself.

It is, in part, because he stuck so pertinaciously to his own idiosyncratic visions and ideals that his work is still read today, while so much of the rest of the material published in the pulp magazines of his day was quickly forgotten. A century later, Lovecraft continues to find a new, passionate, global audience. The works of H. P. Lovecraft have brought us a tremendous amount of enjoyment over the past forty years. We hope you'll find the stories fun, thought-provoking, and more than a little creepy. *Ludo fore putavimus!*

A READER'S GUIDE TO SELECTED WORKS BY H. P. LOVECRAFT

THE OUTSIDER

OVERVIEW

This 2,620-word tale was written in the first half of 1921 and represents the early stages of Lovecraft's development as an author. This story was also written around the time of the death of Lovecraft's mother, Sarah Susan Phillips Lovecraft.

The early stories were heavily influenced by the works of his favorite author, Edgar Allan Poe. "The Outsider" embraces a vague, Poe-like setting—a Gothic castle, which is unpeopled except for a strange, possibly undead narrator who haunts its halls. Unable to endure the solitude any longer, the narrator, through great toil, makes his way out into the world of the living.

Is the narrator Lovecraft himself? Clearly, he thought of himself as an outsider. In a March 29, 1926, letter to his aunt, Lillian D. Clark, Lovecraft wrote:

> I am essentially a recluse who will have very little to do with people wherever he may be. I think that most people only make me nervous ... It makes no difference how well they mean or how cordial they are—they simply get on my nerves unless they chance to represent a peculiarly similar combination of tastes, experiences, & heritages ... My life lies not among people but among scenes—my local affections are not personal, but topographical & architectural. No one in Providence—family aside—has any especial bond of interest with me ... The question is that of which roofs & chimneys & doorways & trees & street vistas I love the best; which hills & woods, which roads & meadows, which farmhouses & views of distant white steeples in green valleys. I am always an outsider—to all scenes & all people—but outsiders have their sentimental preferences in visual environment.

This passage demonstrates a duality present in the author's nature. He both is and is not the recluse he describes here. While it's true that one would not consider him a "social" person for much of his life, both Lovecraft's correspondence and many biographies depict a man very much at home in social situations, someone who enjoys travel and is eager to spend time with friends. The more time a reader spends with Lovecraft, the more these apparent self-contradictions reveal themselves.

As with many of his stories, he was quite critical of "The Outsider." Ten years after completing it, on June 19, 1931, he wrote in a letter to J. Vernon Shea:

> To my mind, this tale—written a decade ago—is too glibly mechanical in its climactic effect, & almost comic in the bombastic pomposity of its language. As I re-read it, I can hardly understand how I could have let myself be tangled up in such baroque & windy rhetoric as recently as ten years ago. It represents my literal though unconscious imitation of Poe at its very height.

ART BY VIRGIL FINLAY. PUBLISHED BY ARKHAM HOUSE, 1939

The story was first published in *Weird Tales* magazine in 1926. No collection of Lovecraft's stories was published during his lifetime, but he had discussed a possible anthology with *Weird Tales* editor, Farnsworth Wright, and suggested the title *The Outsider and Others.* Following Lovecraft's death in 1937, his friends and colleagues August Derleth and Donald Wandrei assembled a collection of his stories and submitted it to several publishers. None accepted the manuscript, so the two men formed their own publishing company, Arkham House. Its first book was entitled *The Outsider and Others,* and had a print run of 1,268 copies, priced at $5 each. This volume is now highly sought by collectors and, when one appears on the market, it typically sells for $7,500 or more.

STORY SUMMARY

An unnamed enigmatic figure describes his life of solitude in an ancient, moldering castle. After enduring apparently lifelong loneliness, he decides to seek out light in the tallest tower of the castle. A perilous climb takes him up the tower and through a grate, where he beholds the full moon. The sight fills him with a sense of joy and déjà vu. Then, stunned, he discovers that he is not looking out from a lofty tower but, instead, he has journeyed only as far as ground level. Seemingly, what he thought was a castle was, in fact, a crypt.

The Outsider then explores his surroundings, haunted by a sense that everything is "maddeningly familiar." He emerges from the castle into a cemetery, where he wanders the countryside. Hearing the sound of revelry in a distant castle, he goes there and sees the partygoers through a window. As he enters the room, the revelers flee in terror. The Outsider moves through the ballroom searching for the source of the horror only to find himself face to face with the monster that so terrified the crowd. When the Outsider reaches out to touch the terrifying figure, his outstretched fingers touch the polished surface of a mirror. In horror, he recognizes it is his own reflection.

CHARACTERS/KEY FIGURES

The Outsider

There is only one real character in this story, and it is challenging to make literal sense of him. He seems to be dead, yet he's alive. There's a suggestion that the castle is familiar to him, yet he seems to have been entombed in isolation beneath it without any recollection of his death or his reanimation. He vaguely recalls an unhappy childhood in the place where he currently lives. He has recollections of trees and groves, yet ostensibly lives far underground. Lovecraft doesn't attempt to make sense of these inconsistencies. He focuses solely on creating mood and atmosphere in the character's world.

SETTING

A Gothic Castle

Lovecraft credited Poe with being the first author to bring a sense of artistry to the backdrop of a Gothic setting. In his essay "Supernatural Horror in Literature," published in 1927, Lovecraft described the trappings of the Gothic castle thus: "... the Gothic castle, with its awesome antiquity, vast distances and ramblings, deserted or ruined wings, damp corridors, unwholesome hidden catacombs, and galaxy of ghosts and appalling legends, as a nucleus of suspense and daemoniac fright."

The setting of "The Outsider" is all of this and more. Leaning heavily into his love for Poe's works, Lovecraft created a place the likes of which hadn't been seen since Poe's "The Fall of the House of Usher," and the finale is reminiscent of Poe's "The Masque of the Red Death." He never gives the reader an explanation of the nature or purpose of the apparently underground tower structure. As with many of his early stories, his focus is entirely on creating an atmosphere.

THEMES

One of These Things Is Not Like the Others

Lovecraft was aware that his proclivities, interests, and actions set him apart from most of humankind. Lovecraft was an only child. Indeed, the only other family member of his generation was a cousin who died of tuberculosis at the age of eighteen, five years before "The Outsider" was written. Although young Lovecraft had playmates his own age during the intermittent years he had formal schooling, his upbringing was one of unusual isolation.

Most of the time, Lovecraft seems to have enjoyed feeling above his contemporaries in interests and pursuits, considering himself to be better and more refined than others. He was quite successful at insulating himself from many of the elements of life that he found disagreeable, and for much of his youth, he was able to live in relative solitude, filling his days with reading and writing. This began to change when he joined the world of amateur journalism, and began the epistolary friendships that would sustain him for the rest of his life.

Familial Curse

The narrator appears to be the lone, surviving member of an ancient family, and the creepy nature of his surroundings suggests some kind of doom that is never explained. In many of Lovecraft's letters, he recounts tales from his childhood, and he consistently represents most of the first decade of his life at 598 Angell Street as an idyllic time spent in a wonderful household surrounded by an affluent, adoring family and a devoted staff. However, in 1904, the death of his grandfather, Whipple Van Buren Phillips, precipitated a swift, unexpected, and devastating drop in the family's fortunes.

A Poor Self-Image

Although Lovecraft considered himself superior to others in most respects, one wonders if that was a coping mechanism for a fundamentally poor self-image. There is an account of his mother having referred to her son as "hideous"; if that report is true, such disparaging remarks would have helped shape his negative view of himself. During the brief time he was married to Sonia Davis, Lovecraft told her he found his mother's comments "devastating." Throughout his life, he often referred to his looks in self-deprecating terms. In correspondence with his Aunt Lillian, he complained of his persistent difficulties with ingrown facial hairs. And hardly anyone can look at a portrait of Lovecraft without noting his uncommonly prognathic jaw. Thus, we're left to wonder if the monstrosity seen in the mirror in "The Outsider" is actually a reflection of the way Lovecraft saw himself.

SYMBOLS AND MOTIFS

Gothic Style

Setting aside the influence of Edgar Allan Poe for a moment, in "Supernatural Horror in Literature," Lovecraft explores in detail the history of the gothic literary tradition, tracing its evolution from eighteenth-century novels to works written during his own lifetime. In particular, he extolls the virtues of Charlotte Brontë's *Wuthering Heights* (1847). Rather than a love story, the novel was for Lovecraft "a tense expression of man's shuddering reaction to the unknown." After "The Outsider," Lovecraft no longer wrote stories steeped in the gothic tradition, the exception being his remarkable 1923 tale "The Rats in the Walls."

Poe Without Girls

While Lovecraft wrote many tales in the style of Poe, he never embraced one key element that is prominent in Poe's works. Female characters are central to many of Poe's horror tales, and they are often either dying or dead. The protagonists in these stories are driven by strange compulsions in their romantic relationships. Almost invariably, the stories' endings are tinged with a macabre sense of grief and loss. Lovecraft, however, was not remotely interested in sexuality—nor human feelings in general. He never focused on or explored romantic love in a meaningful way in his fiction. Where Lovecraft cleaves to Poe's settings and language, his stories never mirror the emotional core so common in many of Poe's tales.

The Italicized Shocker

"The Outsider" features an early example of one of Lovecraft's stylistic hallmarks: a shocking final sentence emphasized with italics. At least it's meant to be shocking. He spends so much time on the buildup to that final sentence that a modern reader can often see it coming from quite a distance, and there are times when the italics have the opposite of the intended effect. At its most successful, italicizing the last sentence serves to confirm a conclusion the reader has often long suspected, but sometimes it is merely an awkward recapitulation of the obvious. More than a few post-Lovecraft writers have parodied and lampooned this technique.

NOTABLE QUOTES

"I know always that I am an outsider; a stranger in this century and among those who are still men."

This quotation is often interpreted as Lovecraft describing himself. In many ways, it's true: Lovecraft always yearned to have been an English gentleman living in New England during the 18th century colonial age.

"Unhappy is he to whom the memories of childhood bring only fear and sadness."

This opening to "The Outsider" kicks off the story on an uncommonly personal note. Many people assume the quote to be autobiographical and are surprised to learn that Lovecraft cherished his own early childhood.

"I cannot even hint what it was like, for it was a compound of all that is unclean, uncanny, unwelcome, abnormal, and detestable. It was the ghoulish shade of decay, antiquity, and desolation; the putrid, dripping eidolon of unwholesome revelation; the awful baring of that which the merciful earth should always hide."

Here, the Outsider describes his own image in gloriously overwrought, prolix, sesquipedalian Lovecraftian verbiage. If this is Lovecraft describing himself, he sure is hard on the old boy.

Pay no charges to messenger

H P LOVECRAFT
598 ANGELL STREET
PROVIDENCE R I

For quick service, reply by bearer

URGENT: DELIVER WITHOUT DELAY

RECEIVER'S NUMBER 163212138

DATE 21 JUN 1921

TIME FILED 8:35 P.M.

CHECK 170 S=1

SENDING STATION: LEXINGTON

TELEGRAM

The World Wide Electrical Printing Telegraph Co. Ltd.

This is a full-rate telegram or electric lettergram unless its deferred character is indicated by a suitable symbol above or preceding the address. The filing time shown in the date line on telegrams and cablegrams is STANDARD TIME at point of origin. FORM HPLHS-001

SYMBOLS: DL=DAY LETTER NL=NIGHT LETTER LC=DEFERRED CABLE NLT=CABLE NIGHT LETTER SR=SHIP RADIOGRAM

DISCUSSION TOPICS

- Is the narrator's exile from the world of the living self-imposed? Is this the life he's chosen for himself, or is he a victim of his own ancestry or upbringing? Do you think the story is intended to evoke shock or pity?
- Do the apparent self-contradictions of the narrator's descriptions undermine his reliability in general? Can we trust anything he says? Is he even alive?
- Alienation from oneself and from others has been a major preoccupation of philosophers and sociologists from classical times, and it is one of the overriding themes of twentieth-century literature in general. Where do you think Lovecraft fits in among other writers of his era who handled this subject, like Franz Kafka, Fyodor Dostoevsky, and T. S. Eliot?
- Lovecraft ends many of his stories with a bold statement of an idea the reader already suspects. By the time the last sentence of "The Outsider" rolls around, most readers will have figured out what's happening. What are the advantages of this storytelling technique?

THE CALL OF CTHULHU

OVERVIEW

"The Call of Cthulhu" is perhaps Lovecraft's most important and iconic tale. He wrote this 12,000-word story in the autumn of 1926, shortly after returning to his hometown of Providence, Rhode Island, following two unhappy years of living in New York and the dissolution of his marriage. It was first published in the February 1928 issue of *Weird Tales* and kicked off the most productive and successful period of his weird-fiction career.

The story was inspired, at least in part, by actual dreams Lovecraft had in 1919 and 1920, which he described in letters to his friends. He wrote the following note in his Commonplace Book around that time:

> Man visits museum of antiquities—asks that it accept a bas-relief he has just made—old and learned curator laughs and says he cannot accept anything so modern. Man says that "dreams are older than brooding Egypt or the contemplative Sphinx or garden-girdled Babylonia" and that he had fashioned the sculpture in his dreams. Curator bids him shew his product, and when he does so, curator shews horror. Asks who the man may be. He tells modern name. "No—before that" says curator. Man does not remember except in dreams. Then curator offers high price, but man fears he means to destroy sculpture. Asks fabulous price—curator will consult directors. Add good development and describe nature of bas-relief.

Lovecraft's dreams form the nucleus of the first part of the story, and Lovecraft plotted out the rest of it in the autumn of 1925. He was also influenced by Guy de Maupassant's "The Horla" (1887), about an invisible presence that drives men mad, which Lovecraft read sometime around 1922; and by Arthur Machen's "The Novel of the Black Seal" (1895), which features a professor who pieces together evidence of supernatural creatures. He was also likely influenced by "The Kraken," an 1830 sonnet by Alfred, Lord Tennyson, which speaks of an ancient monster that sleeps beneath the waves and will one day return to the surface.

HOWARD P. LOVECRAFT COLLECTION, JOHN HAY LIBRARY, BROWN UNIVERSITY

"The Call of Cthulu" is notable for its anonymous first-person point of view and its nested story-within-a-story structure. Lovecraft presents the tale as a "found document," allowing the reader to suspend disbelief and imagine that the events that transpire in the story are all true. It features a prime example of one of his most notorious storytelling strategies: to declare something is "indescribable" while simultaneously describing it so indirectly and evocatively that the reader forms a strong mental image of it. It is multilayered, complex, philosophical, epic in scope, and ends in rip-roaring adventure. It is arguably Lovecraft's most famous and influential work, and the title character has been the subject of countless artistic depictions, beginning with sketches drawn by Lovecraft himself. This story has been adapted for film and as an internationally popular tabletop role-playing game.

The Impact of "The Call of Cthulhu"

Weird Tales magazine editor Farnsworth Wright rejected the story when it was first submitted for publication. It was only because Lovecraft's friend Donald Wandrei told him that it was going to be published elsewhere that Wright changed his mind.

"The Call of Cthulhu" made a relatively minor splash when it first appeared in *Weird Tales* in February 1928: In fact, "The Ghost Table," a story about a haunted piece of furniture, was featured on the cover of that issue. But there's something about the dreaded, tentacle-faced titular monstrosity that has attracted an ever-growing number of fans over the ensuing century. Cthulhu, alongside the *Necronomicon* and Miskatonic University, are surely Lovecraft's most enduring creations.

The story received an additional bump in its fame and popularity when, in 1982, the game company Chaosium, Inc., published a new role-playing game set in a Lovecraftian milieu. Titled Call of Cthulhu®, it is not exclusively related to the story, but rather uses Lovecraft's work as a setting, much the same way the game Dungeons & Dragons™ uses the works of J. R. R. Tolkien. The Call of Cthulhu® game has enjoyed tremendous global success over the past forty years. The song "Call of Ktulu" by Metallica has sold millions of copies. Fans around the world enjoy video games and a motion picture, all with the celebrated title *The Call of Cthulhu.*

Cthulhu has crept up from its watery slumber in R'lyeh to make appearances on *South Park* and *The Simpsons*. Its image can be found on untold numbers of T-shirts, bumper stickers, coffee mugs, and fluffy slippers. It has even been proposed as a US presidential candidate several times: "Why vote for the lesser evil?" At this point, Cthulhu's fame far exceeds that of its creator.

STORY SUMMARY

"The Call of Cthulhu" is structured in three distinct parts. Each ends up providing its own unique layer to the collective narrative, cumulatively building upon the events of the preceding chapter.

I. The Horror in Clay

A man inherits his great-uncle's estate and, in going through his papers, discovers that his uncle was investigating a mystery. The uncle, George Gammell Angell, was a professor of Semitic languages at Brown University. In 1926, he was approached by a young artist named Henry Wilcox, who was eager to show him a clay tablet he'd sculpted, inspired by a dream that followed a recent earthquake. The tablet depicted a strange creature with wings and a tentacled face in front of a bizarre architectural backdrop, accompanied by strange hieroglyphic writing. The piece bore the name "Cthulhu." Wilcox had only dreamed the thing, and he had no idea what the word meant, but he hoped Professor Angell could help decipher it. Angell found the object fascinating, and the two continued to meet to discuss the artist's dreams. Angell also made inquiries among numerous friends and colleagues, amassing a large file of other dream accounts, as well as newspaper clippings about strange dreams and other anomalous events worldwide. In late April of that year, the artist fell ill and was hospitalized in a delirium. Two weeks later, he awoke with no recollection of his strange dreams.

II. The Narrative of Inspector Legrasse

The significance of his uncle's account eludes the nephew until he discovers older papers in the files: The Narrative of Inspector Legrasse. Here, the uncle describes having met with a police inspector from New Orleans in 1908 at a convention of archeologists. In the hopes of deciphering its meaning, Inspector Legrasse attended the convention to show the assembled experts a strange artifact that he'd recovered while working on a case. The artifact bore striking similarities to the clay tablet sculpted by Henry Wilcox, which is what had fascinated Professor Angell and inspired his expanded investigation.

Inspector Legrasse related how a community of backwoods folks in the Louisiana swamps had come to the police with tales of animals, women, and children having gone missing deep in the bayou country. The inspector organized a raid, and he and his men were horrified to find a crazed cult conducting hellish rituals, including the sacrifice of humans, deep in the swamp. The police recovered an idol of a bizarre, tentacled creature from the cultists. They captured and questioned one of the cult's participants, a man called Castro. Under interrogation, Castro revealed that the idol was of a being called Cthulhu, one of the "Great Old Ones" that had come from the stars untold aeons ago. Further, Castro confessed that the cult carried out its monstrous rituals in Cthulhu's name. Castro told of ancient lore, quoting a passage from a book called the *Necronomicon*: "That is not dead which can eternal lie, and with strange aeons even death may die." He hinted that the cult to which he belonged is ancient and worldwide, and that Cthulhu spoke to humans through their dreams.

In yet another nested layer of the narrative, one of the other archeologists attending the convention, Professor William Channing Webb, revealed that decades earlier he had encountered a similar idol and cult among "Esquimaux" in Greenland. The similar experiences of Inspector Legrasse and Professor Webb made a deep impression on Professor Angell, so when Henry Wilcox presented a comparable depiction based on his dreams, Angell began to gather data on the subject. His nephew suspects that this investigation led to Angell's death, but the nephew is now sufficiently intrigued to want to interview Wilcox, whom he finds at an artist's studio in Providence. The nephew leaves this meeting convinced of Wilcox's sincerity, and increasingly disturbed by the prospect of a worldwide cult of Cthulhu.

III. The Madness from the Sea

In the third part of the story, the narrator himself takes up his dead uncle's investigation. While visiting a friend who is a curator of geology at a natural history museum, the narrator notices, among rock specimens wrapped in newspaper, a photograph of another idol matching the descriptions of the three idols previously encountered. The accompanying newspaper article describes the misadventure of the crew of the *Emma*, a New Zealand schooner, which was thrown off course by stormy seas in the South Pacific at the same time Wilcox was hospitalized with delirium. The *Emma* was attacked by the "queer and evil-looking crew of Kanakas and half-castes" of a steam yacht called the *Alert*, which they encountered in the storm. In the ensuing battle, the men of the *Emma* killed the *Alert*'s crew and commandeered their yacht, while the *Emma* sank. The newspaper account further reports that the captain of the *Emma* and his first mate were killed in the fighting, and the surviving sailors, now led by second mate Gustaf Johansen, landed on an unknown island, where all but two members of the ship's crew died before being rescued and towed back to New Zealand. Johansen himself is the only survivor who made it back to port.

The Alert Idol
SCULPTED BY ANDREW LEMAN FOR THE MOTION PICTURE *THE CALL OF CTHULHU*. PHOTO BY STEPHANIE MOREY

Gripped by the similarities to his uncle's previous encounters, as well as by the coincidental timing, the nephew now decides to devote himself to investigating the mystery. He travels to New Zealand and Australia to follow up on the newspaper story, and then goes to Oslo in the hope of interviewing Gustaf Johansen. He learns from Johansen's wife that her husband died under mysterious circumstances not long after returning from sea, but that he left behind a detailed account of what really happened on that strange island. Johansen wrote his account in English, so his wife would not accidentally read the horrible tale.

The narrator reads Johansen's account and learns that the island was a piece of the "nightmare corpse city of R'lyeh" that sank into the ocean eons ago, imprisoning the undead Cthulhu in its depths. The city was brought to the surface somehow by the earthquake and storm, and when the sailors of the *Emma* landed on it, they explored it and inadvertently released Cthulhu from its ancient prison. All but two of the sailors were killed, leaving only Johansen and his companion, Briden, to escape back to the *Alert* and sail away. Cthulhu pursued them, and Johansen turned the ship into a battering ram to attack the gigantic creature. Cthulhu was temporarily damaged by the ship and gave up pursuit, enabling Johansen to escape. As he fled in the *Alert*, Johansen saw Cthulhu re-forming. Briden went insane and died.

The narrator puts Johansen's account alongside the rest of his uncle's evidence and abandons the investigation, concluding that it would have been better if he had never investigated in the first place, and he hopes no one else will ever discover what he has learned.

CHARACTERS/KEY FIGURES

Francis Wayland Thurston

In this tale, Lovecraft never refers to the protagonist by name and provides no details of his personal life save for his relationship to his great-uncle. We only learn the nephew's name through the story's subtitle, "Found Among the Papers of the Late Francis Wayland Thurston, of Boston." In keeping this story's protagonist anonymous, Lovecraft creates an Everyman. These events happen to Thurston, but they could happen to any of us, if only we were able to correlate the myriad horrific facts that surround us. We are protected only by our ignorance, which, ironically, we no longer possess by virtue of having read Thurston's account. The subtitle tells us at the very beginning that Thurston is dead, but we never learn when or how he met his demise. It is implied that his death was a consequence of the secrets he unearthed, secrets that we ourselves learn by reading his story. Through Thurston, Lovecraft draws the reader into the ongoing mystery, implying that the reader may even become the cult's next victim.

George Gammell Angell

Professor Angell is an archetypal Lovecraftian character: old, wise, and possessing a deep knowledge of antiquity. It is the pursuit of even greater knowledge that precipitates his death. Like many a Lovecraftian protagonist, Professor Angell is a truth seeker by nature, ready and eager to go to great lengths to find answers to a lingering mystery. The character's name is inspired by people and places in Lovecraft's life. His own uncle was Edward Francis Gamwell, a newspaper editor. Lovecraft's cherished childhood home was on Angell Street in Providence.

Henry Anthony Wilcox

Page from Wilcox's sketchbook
PROP FROM THE MOTION PICTURE *THE CALL OF CTHULHU*

Wilcox is a young man from a prominent family whose artistic temperament makes him susceptible to the dream influence of Cthulhu. Lovecraft includes artists as prominent characters in other stories as well, regarding them as special people possessed of great sensitivity and imagination. However, because his own tastes in fine art were very conservative, he also felt ambivalence toward artists and expressed disdain for anything he considered to be a pose. Lovecraft describes Wilcox as "of a type, at once slightly affected and slightly ill-mannered, which I could never like; but I was willing enough now to admit both his genius and his honesty." Lovecraft considered himself a literary artist, never compromising his vision or catering to the tastes of the public or magazine editors. Like Wilcox, Lovecraft was powerfully influenced by his dreams and used his dreams as inspiration for his work. Wilcox is, on some level, a stand-in for Lovecraft himself.

John Raymond Legrasse

Serving as the point-of-view character in the second section of this tale, Inspector Legrasse is as close to an action hero as one finds in Lovecraft's tales. When confronted with the diabolism of the cult, he does his best to shut it down and restore order. Like Wilcox, he seeks the advice of learned experts to better understand what he has witnessed, but Legrasse's actions are ultimately meaningless against the greater threat posed by Cthulhu and his kind. Even the most stalwart action hero is no match for the cosmic forces at work here.

Castro

Castro is a specific embodiment of the numerous other nameless cultists in the story, and he is a typical Lovecraftian villain. He is depicted as of mixed race, highlighting Lovecraft's fear, suspicion, and ignorance of anyone "foreign." We don't learn much about who Castro is and how he came to be involved with the cult, because, to Lovecraft, none of that is important. What is important is that Castro can provide extensive exposition to hint at some of the basic tenets of the cult and the monstrosities they worship. Castro is a pawn serving at the behest of Cthulhu and its kind; his actions, like Legrasse's, are fundamentally of little consequence. No human actions are ultimately of significant consequence in this story.

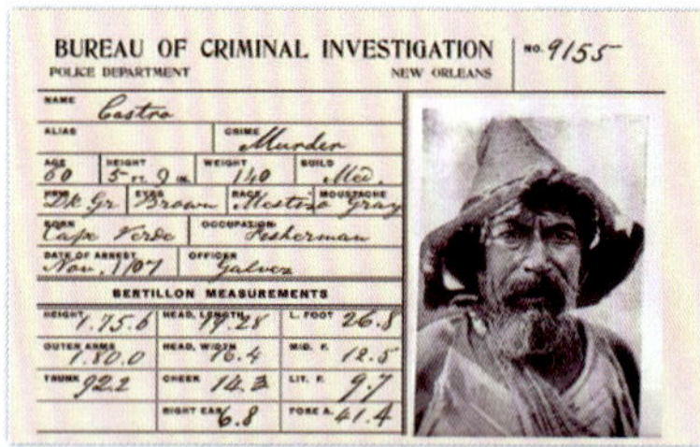

Castro's police record
PROP FROM *DARK ADVENTURE RADIO THEATRE*®: "THE CALL OF CTHULHU"

Gustaf Johansen

Like Legrasse, Johansen provides us with a "man of action" who responds boldly under dire circumstances. Unlike Legrasse, he does not long survive his brush with the Great Old Ones, and like Thurston himself, tells his part of the story from beyond the grave. Johansen is of a heroic Nordic type that Lovecraft greatly admired. He is the only character in the story not depicted as unusually intelligent or well educated, but as a stolid working-class hero.

Cthulhu

This gigantic ancient cosmic alien entity dwells beneath the Pacific Ocean, combining the features of a dragon, an octopus, and an anthropoid monstrosity. One of the "Great Old Ones," Cthulhu came to this planet from somewhere very far away, vigintillions of years ago, roaming free until black magic trapped it in R'lyeh. Since then, Cthulhu has slumbered and communicated to the "fleshly minds of mammals" through their dreams, inspiring generations of insane cultists to worship in anticipation of the day when the "stars are right," and it will return to the surface.

Lovecraft deliberately made the name impossible to pronounce properly and easy to misspell. He may well have been inspired by the Greek word "chthonic," meaning "of the earth" or "underground," but ultimately it is not meant to be a human word. Lovecraft himself gave conflicting accounts of how it should be pronounced, but he advised in a letter: "The first syllable pronounced gutturally and very thickly. The 'u' is about like that in 'full,' and the first syllable is not unlike 'klul' in sound, hence the 'h' represents the guttural thickness." Virtually nobody follows Lovecraft's advice, however, and most people use the pronunciation "kuh-THOO-loo." Cthulhu has resonated strongly with readers since the story was first published.

THEMES

"The Call of Cthulhu" is among the most iconically thematic of Lovecraft's tales. This story contains one of Lovecraft's most emblematic quotes:

> The most merciful thing in the world, I think, is the inability of the human mind to correlate all its contents. We live on a placid island of ignorance in the midst of black seas of infinity, and it was not meant that we should voyage far. The sciences, each straining in its own direction, have hitherto harmed us little; but some day the piecing together of dissociated knowledge will open up such terrifying vistas of reality, and of our frightful position therein, that we shall either go mad from the revelation or flee from the light into the peace and safety of a new dark age.

This quotation is often rightly used to encapsulate Lovecraft's view of cosmic horror. The universe is vast and the whole experience of mankind is irrelevant in the grand scheme of things. The quote also embodies the concept that knowledge is a dangerous thing, an idea that Lovecraft revisits in many of his stories.

This story, among others, was inspired by dreams Lovecraft had, and dreaming is a key concept in the tale. Cthulhu communicates from his slumber by invading the dreams of sensitive humans. Lovecraft was known to be a vivid dreamer who often retained a clear memory of his dreams. In other tales, he speculates that the dream life is more real than what we experience when awake. This story also features characters who are driven insane by what they experience, and madness is a recurring theme in his life and work. Lovecraft often calls into question the very nature of reality, and our perception of it, leaving the reader with much to contemplate.

SETTING AND MOTIFS

Cthulhu and the Great Old Ones

The events of "The Call of Cthulhu" span decades and continents. Lovecraft does this purposefully to create a sense that Cthulhu and the Great Old Ones are all around us, and it is only human inattentiveness that protects us from perceiving them. Some of the story takes place in Lovecraft's beloved hometown of Providence, Rhode Island, with its familiar locales of Brown University and the still-extant Fleur de Lys building. The second part of the story takes place in New Orleans and adjacent Louisiana swamp country, though it was written before Lovecraft had ever visited the region.

R'lyeh

Lovecraft does a remarkable job of painting a picture of the monstrous corpse city of R'lyeh, with its impossible angles and non-Euclidean geometry. It is a setting that should not be feasible, and his descriptions of it challenge the reader to imagine a space where the known laws of physics are routinely violated. He specifies its location very precisely: 47°9′ S; 126°43′ W, in the middle of a truly vast expanse of empty ocean near what is now known as the pole of inaccessibility, dubbed Point Nemo in 1992. It is the point on the planet farthest from any inhabited landmass, and various space agencies now use the area as a satellite reentry site to reduce the risk of injuring people. The International Space Station is scheduled to crash there in 2031.

Newspaper Articles as Storytelling Device

Lovecraft often uses newspaper articles as a storytelling device in his fiction, and "The Call of Cthulhu" features a lengthy item supposedly from the *Sydney Bulletin.* The *Bulletin* was a real weekly journal published in Sydney starting in 1880. It was more of a magazine than a newspaper, and its news coverage was slanted and sensational. It featured prominently, and controversially, in the literary life of Australia. Professor Angell employs press-clipping bureaus to gather newspaper items from all over the world, documenting events that may be related to Cthulhu's rise. In the days before electronic media, these bureaus would scan numerous newspapers, physically cutting out items to satisfy the interests of their clients. The first such service was instituted in London in 1852, when a newsagent noticed that various actors and artists were interested in seeing press notices about themselves. He realized he could make a profitable business by catering to their vanity, and he began selling just the clippings that clients were interested in reading, rather than entire newspapers.

Prosaic Reality

Lovecraft felt strongly that prosaic reality was a vital ingredient of any weird tale, using it to make the "weird" thing as believable as possible. He often incorporated real people, events, and publications into his fiction, and "The Call of Cthulhu" features several examples of this storytelling strategy. The earthquake mentioned in the first section of the story, which prompted Wilcox's strange dreams of Cthulhu, was an actual event that took place on March 28, 1925. The epicenter was in Canada, but it was felt as far south as Virginia. It was covered with a three-column headline in the *New York Times*, among many other publications. Lovecraft cites *The Story of Atlantis* and the *Lost Lemuria* (1925) by W. Scott-Elliot, *The Witch-Cult in Western Europe* (1921) by Margaret Murray, and *The Golden Bough* (1890) by Sir James George Frazer, all real books of anthropology or theosophical lore. By weaving in the names of real books, Lovecraft makes his reference to his own fictional *Necronomicon* seem that much more credible.

The Sydney Bulletin
PROP FROM THE MOTION PICTURE
THE CALL OF CTHULHU

Lovecraft was part of a very amiable circle of fellow writers, and he often found ways to nod to them in his fiction. In this story, the "learned friend in Paterson, New Jersey; the curator of a local museum and a mineralogist of note," is a description of his friend and colleague James F. Morton. The artistic works of Henry Wilcox are explicitly compared to those of Clark Ashton Smith, another of Lovecraft's friends. Even in the middle of a horror tale, Lovecraft found ways to wink at those in the know.

The Necronomicon

The *Necronomicon*, one of Lovecraft's other most famous creations, makes a cameo appearance in this story when it is quoted by Castro as he is interrogated.

Yog-Sothothery ~ Great Cthulhu and More

"The Call of Cthulhu" is one of Lovecraft's greatest stories making use of the Cthulhu Mythos. Through Castro, Lovecraft lays out the basic ground rules about Cthulhu and the Great Old Ones and their effect upon humankind. He gives some ominous, vague hints about other less-described Great Old Ones that lurk unseen. He also provides shadowy suggestions about the "Black Winged Ones" that were responsible for killing the victims in the swamp. The story is seminal in laying the groundwork for the Cthulhu Mythos.

NOTABLE QUOTES

"That is not dead which can eternal lie, And with strange aeons even death may die."

This famous couplet is a quote within a quote—Lovecraft used it in a previous story, "The Nameless City," written in 1921. In that tale, Lovecraft attributes the lines to Abdul Alhazred but does not mention the *Necronomicon*.

"Ph'nglui mglw'nafh Cthulhu R'lyeh wgah'nagl fhtagn."

This bit of fictional language is designed, like Cthulhu's name, to be unpronounceable. It's quoted by Professor Webb as something he heard from "a singular tribe or cult of degenerate Esquimaux" in Greenland. Legrasse, having heard the same phrase from the deranged swamp cultists, offers the following translation: "In his house at R'lyeh dead Cthulhu waits dreaming."

Part of what makes this story so impactful and enduring is the way it engages the reader. In the original tongue, the quote piques our imagination with its alien nature. The poetic simplicity of the translation has a similar effect.

"He had said that the geometry of the dream-place he saw was abnormal, non-Euclidean, and loathsomely redolent of spheres and dimensions apart from ours."

Lovecraft was fascinated by non-Euclidean geometry, and he developed the idea further in other stories, particularly in "The Dreams in the Witch House" in 1932. It is a wonderful hybrid space—half scientific and half magical—in which anything can happen. He uses it to great effect, and it has become one of his hallmarks.

Legrasse recounts the information gathered from Castro, the swamp cultist:

"They worshipped, so they said, the Great Old Ones who lived ages before there were any men, and who came to the young world out of the sky. Those Old Ones were gone now, inside the earth and under the sea; but their dead bodies had told their secrets in dreams to the first men, who formed a cult which had never died."

In this passage, Lovecraft economically sums up centuries of insane beliefs. He was prone to use formal and sometimes flowery language, but this passage is remarkably simple and clear. In contrast, the following passage showcases Lovecraft at his archaic and prolix best:

"The Thing cannot be described—there is no language for such abysms of shrieking and immemorial lunacy, such eldritch contradictions of all matter, force, and cosmic order. A mountain walked or stumbled."

This passage features Lovecraft's classic one-two punch, first saying that something cannot be described, and then describing it in vague, but evocative, terms. Many critics deride Lovecraft for his tendency to describe things as "indescribable" or "unnameable," but he often goes on to find more specific articulations of the otherworldly horrors he's depicting.

"There was a bursting as of an exploding bladder, a slushy nastiness as of a cloven sunfish, a stench as of a thousand opened graves, and a sound that the chronicler would not put on paper."

The "slushy nastiness as of a cloven sunfish," is such an odd and specific description that it stands out even among Lovecraft's other vivid turns of phrase. Lovecraft was well known for his aversion to seafood and sea creatures, but it's not clear what he meant to convey by this description. "Sunfish" is a name applied to a couple of different species, but while most of them are very large and rather strange, none of them is any nastier when you cleave it than any other kind of fish would be. Then again, the diet of sunfish consists mostly of jellyfish, so maybe that's what he was getting at. Perhaps Lovecraft had seen a rotting sunfish on one of his oceanside rambles, and that's why the comparison came to mind.

The story concludes with the following quote, effectively disconnecting this story from the characters who have told it, and laying future horrors at the feet of the reader:

"Who knows the end? What has risen may sink, and what has sunk may rise. Loathsomeness waits and dreams in the deep, and decay spreads over the tottering cities of men. A time will come—but I must not and cannot think!"

H P LOVECRAFT
10 BARNES STREET
PROVIDENCE R I

Pay no charges to messenger | *For quick service, reply by bearer*

URGENT: DELIVER WITHOUT DELAY

RECEIVER'S NUMBER 941321151ER
DATE 3 SEP 1926
TIME FILED 11:55 A.M.
CHECK 192 S=1

TELEGRAM

The World Wide Electrical Printing Telegraph Co. Ltd.

This is a full-rate telegram or electric lettergram unless its deferred character is indicated by a suitable symbol above or preceding the address. The filing time shown in the date line on telegrams and cablegrams is STANDARD TIME at point of origin. FORM HPLHS-001

SENDING STATION: POINT NEMO

SYMBOLS: DL=DAY LETTER NL=NIGHT LETTER LC=DEFERRED CABLE NLT=CABLE NIGHT LETTER SR=SHIP RADIOGRAM

DISCUSSION TOPICS

- Cthulhu remains one of Lovecraft's most enduring creations. Why do you think that is? Is it due purely to the anthropomorphic form with the octopoid head, or is it connected to the subtle and insidious nature of Cthulhu's impact on humanity?
- Thurston posits that knowledge is dangerous, and that mankind is better off in ignorance. Do you think he's right? When and in what circumstances would you opt for ignorance over knowledge?
- Some cultures place tremendous significance on dreams; others dismiss them outright. Does the notion of external horrors creeping into human minds via dreams make the story more or less frightening to you?
- In his essay "Supernatural Horror in Literature," Lovecraft discusses the very first gothic novel, *The Castle of Otranto*, written by Horace Walpole in 1764. Lovecraft (with just cause) thought it was terrible, but like "The Call of Cthulhu," it is presented as a "found document." "Found footage" has been used in numerous successful horror films in recent decades. Do you think it's an effective storytelling strategy? Is it better suited to "weird" fiction than other kinds? Was it better suited to Lovecraft's day than to our own?

THE CASE OF CHARLES DEXTER WARD

OVERVIEW

This is Lovecraft's longest work of horror fiction, a novella of 51,000 words. Written early in 1927, the ambitious story combines many of Lovecraft's favorite elements: a Providence setting, an ancestral curse, reanimation, eighteenth-century gentlemen, and an occult horror. It was never published during his lifetime—indeed, the original manuscript was never even typed. It literally languished in a drawer in his desk.

It seems likely that he found inspiration for this story in 1926 when he read Walter de la Mare's novel *The Return*, in which a character undergoes a mental possession after sleeping on the grave of an eighteenth-century pirate. Lovecraft singled out the novel in his 1927 essay "Supernatural Horror in Literature."

The titular Charles is a stand-in for young Lovecraft. While Charles is not the story's protagonist, the tale does revolve around him. He's a Providence antiquarian, a precocious and enthusiastic student, and he's enthralled by the dark history of his own family. Again, we see an ancestral curse at work—although here, it is not an ancestral genetic trait that affects Charles, but rather the malicious ancestor himself. Lovecraft touches on another theme that appears in several of his tales: the cost of the pursuit of knowledge.

In general, his works at this point in his career include more elements of science fiction than appear in his earlier stories. In this novella, he eschews science in favor of a small amount of Yog-Sothothery, some creative alchemy, and more traditional horror tropes, including vampirism. Lovecraft was ultimately very critical of both *The Case of Charles Dexter Ward* and the novella that preceded it, *The Dream-Quest of Unknown Kadath.* In a March 1934 letter to Robert H. Barlow, Lovecraft wrote, "Kadath is a puerile hash of imitation Dunsany conceptions, while 'Charles Dexter Ward' is a cumbrous creaking bit of self-conscious antiquarianism. I've expunged both from my acknowledged list of writings…"

Despite its author's low opinion of the tale, many fans consider this to be their favorite Lovecraft story. It was first adapted as a motion picture in 1963 by the famed B-movie filmmaker Roger Corman with the title *The Haunted Palace* (it was thought that naming it after a Poe poem might provide more box office draw). It received another, better, motion picture adaptation in Dan O'Bannon's 1991 film *The Resurrected.*

STORY SUMMARY

I. A Result and a Prologue

A young man named Charles Dexter Ward disappears from a mental hospital near Providence. He was attended to by his family physician, Dr. Marinus Bicknell Willett. Charles is a history buff, and in his extensive research, he learns about Joseph Curwen, an obscure ancestor of his who emigrated to Providence from Salem, dogged by rumors of his dubious nature and implications of witchcraft.

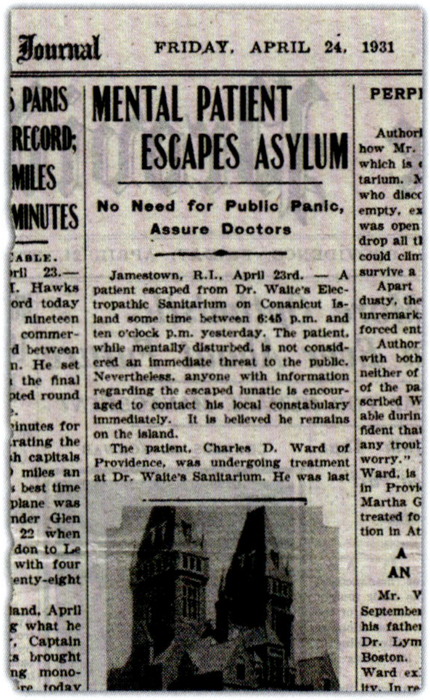

Journal — FRIDAY, APRIL 24, 1931

MENTAL PATIENT ESCAPES ASYLUM

No Need for Public Panic, Assure Doctors

Jamestown, R.I., April 23rd. — A patient escaped from Dr. Waite's Electropathic Sanitarium on Conanicut Island some time between 6:45 p.m. and ten o'clock p.m. yesterday. The patient, while mentally disturbed, is not considered an immediate threat to the public. Nevertheless, anyone with information regarding the escaped lunatic is encouraged to contact his local constabulary immediately. It is believed he remains on the island.

The patient, Charles D. Ward of Providence, was undergoing treatment at Dr. Waite's Sanitarium. He was last

Charles Dexter Ward escapes!

PROP FROM *DARK ADVENTURE RADIO THEATRE®: THE CASE OF CHARLES DEXTER WARD*

II. An Antecedent and a Horror

In a flashback to the eighteenth century, rumors about Curwen suggested that he practiced alchemy and evidenced a disturbing failure to age. To get into the good graces of Providence society, Curwen invested his fortune in the town. Still unable to shake his bad reputation, Curwen tried to marry his way to respectability by wedding Eliza Tillinghast, daughter of a sea captain. He bought a fine home in Olney Court and divided his time between his home and a farm outside of town on the Pawtuxet Road.

Citizens of Providence found Curwen's behavior suspicious, and a mounting cry arose within the community to investigate his shady activities. A committee of Providence's leading citizens gathered evidence about Curwen and his nefarious practices, resulting in an elaborately coordinated assault on Curwen's farm. It turned into a bloody affair, and witnesses reported bizarre supernatural noises and weird lights. Curwen was killed in the raid and entombed in a special lead-sealed casket. The raiders agreed never to speak publicly about the terrible events that took place on the farm, and they subsequently attempted to systematically erase Curwen from the town's history.

III. A Search and an Evocation

In the present day, Charles's fixation on his ancestor grows. He discovers correspondence between Curwen and two associates, Hutchinson and Orne. They seemed to be conspiring in some kind of occult experiments.

Charles visits Curwen's former house in Olney Court and finds a painted-over portrait of Curwen, who looks strikingly like Charles. Behind the portrait, he finds documents written by Curwen, apparently intended for discovery by one of his descendants in the future. One of the documents is written in a cipher. Charles is thrilled, and he works tirelessly to decipher the message. He also embarks on studies of witchcraft, magic, occultism, and demonology, and explores some of Providence's oldest cemeteries. Worried by their son's erratic behavior, the Wards ask Dr. Willett to meet with Charles. Willett determines that Charles is eccentric, but not insane.

Charles comes of age and uses his inheritance to travel to London, Paris, and Transylvania. Upon his return, Charles conducts secret alchemical experiments in an attic laboratory, and he becomes increasingly furtive. Newspaper reports describe diggers vandalizing the North Burying Ground. The Ward home is shaken by Charles performing some kind of occult ritual in his laboratory. His worried parents attempt to learn what he's up to. Charles insists they not disturb his research.

IV. A Mutation and a Madness

Charles adds dozens of books on a variety of topics to his attic library. The Wards hear him behaving oddly—apparently having arguments with himself. Charles is haggard and evasive, and avoids questions from his parents and Dr. Willett.

In deference to his mother's growing agitation, Charles rents a bungalow on the old Pawtuxet Road and moves his laboratory there. He orders a great deal of obscure equipment to be shipped to the laboratory, and he begins to work with a new colleague named Dr. Allen. Dr. Willett receives a letter from Charles, begging for help, warning him to shoot Dr. Allen on sight if he approaches him. Willett goes to meet Charles at his parents' home, but the young man does not appear. Servants at the Ward house report having heard a struggle upstairs, after which Charles left. Willett concludes that Charles has truly gone mad.

Willett and Mr. Ward visit Charles at the Pawtuxet bungalow. They find Charles much changed in his manner, speaking in a hoarse whisper. He uses old-fashioned vocabulary and displays an eerie knowledge of the past. He shows them his laboratory, which suspiciously contains only a fraction of the equipment that had been in Charles's old attic laboratory. They conclude something is very wrong.

Ward intercepts letters, apparently from Orne and Hutchinson, describing occult conversations with the dead. Willett and Ward, joined by several alienists, visit Charles again at the bungalow. All conclude he is insane and should be institutionalized. Charles smugly surrenders.

V. A Nightmare and a Cataclysm

Willett and Ward arrive at the conclusion that perhaps Joseph Curwen has been somehow brought back from the dead and is still in cahoots with Orne and Hutchinson. They return to the bungalow, which they believe is connected to Curwen's original eighteenth-century farm, to investigate more thoroughly. In the cellar, they discover a secret tunnel leading further underground. A dreadful stench emanates from the passageway. Ward swoons, and Willett enters the tunnel alone.

In the ancient tunnels beneath the bungalow, Willett discovers Charles's real library and laboratory in Curwen's catacombs. He spies an incantation used by Curwen and his diabolical colleagues to reconstitute the dead from their "essential saltes." Nearby, Willett finds a vast room with many deep pits from which he hears dreadful howling noises.

Removing a lid from one of these pits, Willett discovers a hellish, half-formed remnant of a human being, squealing piteously. The sight causes a temporary bout of madness in Willett, who then stumbles into a room containing countless jars of saltes, torture equipment, and Curwen's transcripts of his conversations with the dead. In a bold move, Willett speaks the incantation over the saltes marked 118, and then, as an apparition begins to form, he faints.

Willett awakes in the bungalow and finds a note in his pocket. He meets with Ward and learns that the note, written in Latin, urges him to kill Curwen. The pair decides to speak to Charles in the asylum. Charles, still cultivating an eighteenth-century persona, seems unimpressed with their discoveries from beneath the bungalow, but he becomes palpably frightened by Willett's revelation that he conjured up saltes 118.

Unable to determine what has become of Dr. Allen, Ward and Willett realize no one has ever seen Charles and Allen together—they recognize that, if they removed Allen's beard and sunglasses, he would look exactly like Charles. They fear that perhaps Curwen really has come back from the dead! Willett then locks himself in Charles's old study in the Ward house. Eavesdropping through the study door, Ward hears Willett moving things around in the room and lighting a massive fire in the fireplace.

Later, Willett sends Ward a kindly note stating that Charles is no more. He was a curious boy, caught up in matters beyond his control. The public will be led to believe that Charles escaped from the asylum, and in a year's time, the Wards should put up a headstone for Charles in the graveyard. It is implied that Willett found Charles's dead body in the attic and cremated it. The person who has been posing as Charles for the last several months is, in fact, the magically resurrected Joseph Curwen.

Willett returns to the asylum for a final confrontation with Joseph Curwen. In a magical showdown, Willett uses an incantation to reduce the dangerous sorcerer to his saltes—a fine, blue-gray dust.

Portrait of Joseph Curwen
ILLUSTRATION BY DARRELL TUTCHTON

CHARACTERS/KEY FIGURES

Marinus Bicknell Willett

Dr. Willett is a strong Lovecraftian protagonist who is more than up to the challenge of doing battle with supernatural horrors. He's well educated and able to employ his erudition to great effect. Willett is introduced as the lifelong physician of Charles Dexter Ward. He clearly feels a deep affinity for his patient and does his utmost to provide sensitive and devoted care for the entire Ward family throughout this weird journey. Willett's display of compassion and sympathy are character traits that seldom appear in Lovecraft stories. Willett arrives in the story relatively late for a protagonist, but he drives the plot of the final two-thirds of the tale. Willett ultimately succeeds by reversing the resurrection spell and using it against the dreadful forces he confronts.

Charles Dexter Ward

Charles is, perhaps, the young adult that Lovecraft wished he had been. From his place in the upper echelon of society, Charles is a dyed-in-the-wool antiquarian, fond of taking long walks through Providence. He's an amateur scientist with a keen interest in chemistry and history, much like the young Lovecraft. However, while Lovecraft strongly believed that late-colonial New England was a golden age, Charles's experience is quite different, having had a very unpleasant brush with an emissary from that time—his ancestor Joseph Curwen. Charles is seduced into reincarnating his ancestor, for whom Charles ultimately proves to be no match.

Portrait of Charles Dexter Ward
ILLUSTRATION BY DARRELL TUTCHTON

Theodore Howland Ward

When you think of Lovecraft's personal history, it's not surprising that his stories feature many avuncular and grandfatherly characters but few actual fathers. Theodore Ward fills the role of father admirably, though, always doing his best to care for his son, even though he doesn't understand how to help him as circumstances spin wildly out of control. He joins forces with Dr. Willett, and the two men eventually piece together the fact that Curwen has returned, and that Charles is his intended victim. Theodore Ward is spared the most grisly aspects of Charles's demise when Dr. Willett breaks the unhappy news to him as gently as possible.

Joseph Curwen/Dr. Allen

Curwen is probably Lovecraft's most badass human villain: smart, powerful, and malevolent. Lovecraft used the Salem witchcraft panic as backstory for Curwen, who fled the town in 1692 (when things were looking decidedly bad for witches). Curwen then arrived in Providence—"that universal haven of the odd, the free, and the dissenting"—and promptly continued his black magic practices. Curwen and his evil friends figured out how to prevent themselves from aging, and each developed a different strategy to avoid alarming neighbors. Lovecraft withholds the details, but somehow Curwen succeeds in preserving his spirit in such a manner that he could be physically reconstituted in a future age. However improbable, Curwen's plot works marvelously well, and Charles manages to exhume his remains and, using ancient sorceries, bring Curwen back to life in 1920s Providence. By creating an alter ego named Dr. Allen, who is ostensibly Charles's assistant, Curwen successfully positions himself to kill Charles and take over his life.

The story doesn't precisely clarify Curwen's ultimate ambition. He and his cohorts, Orne and Hutchinson, rob graves and perform acts of occultism to learn the secrets of the world's greatest minds by reanimating their bodies and torturing them. We are left to guess what Curwen's ultimate aspiration might be, but clearly, he and his friends are up to no good.

Dr. Allen is Joseph Curwen in disguise. His costume, consisting of a false beard and sunglasses, is clearly convincing, as it deceives several ostensibly smart characters for a surprisingly long time.

Hutchinson and Orne

Although we never really encounter them in the story except through the letters they write, Edward Hutchinson and Simon Orne were Curwen's coconspirators in Salem during the age of the witch trials. Hutchinson seems to have survived the centuries via black magic, and by 1922, he is living in Transylvania under the name Baron Ferenczy. As part of Charles's induction into the occult, he goes to Transylvania to study with Hutchinson.

Orne left Salem around 1720, after his apparent "failure to grow old" drew unwanted attention. Thirty years later, a person named Jedediah Orne returned to Salem, claiming to be Simon Orne's son. During Charles's lifetime, Orne was living in Prague and was likely visited by Charles during his European tour.

It is implied that the mysterious and apparently powerful entity 118, raised by Willett from saltes in Curwen's catacombs, somehow found and defeated Hutchinson and Orne in the same way that Willett defeated Curwen.

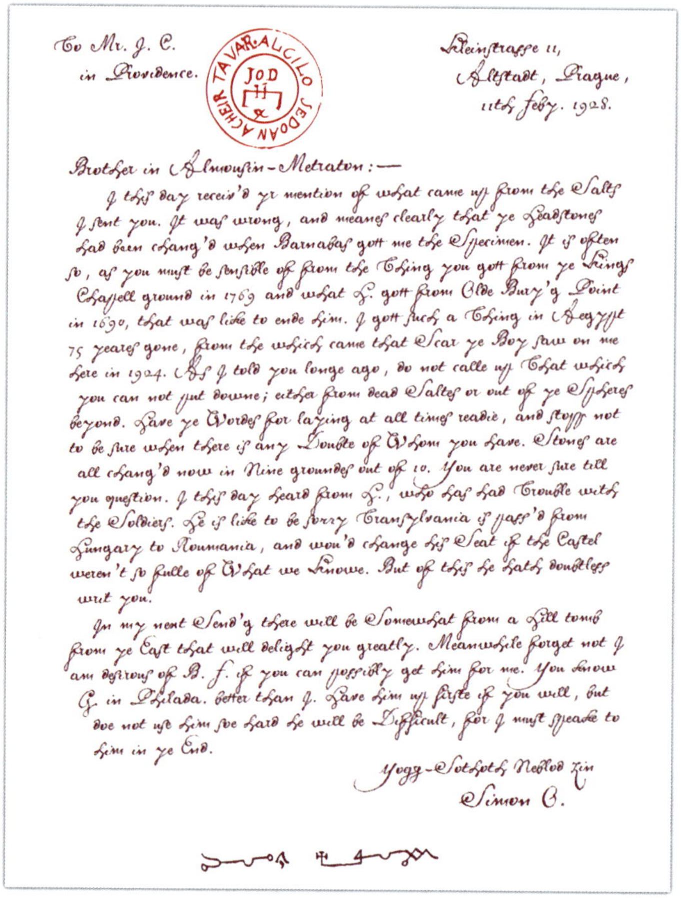

To Mr. J. C.
in Providence.

Kleinstrasse 11,
Altstadt, Prague,
11th Feby. 1928.

Brother in Almonsin-Metraton:—

I this day receiv'd yr mention of what came up from the Salts I sent you. It was wrong, and meanes clearly that ye Headstones had been chang'd when Barnabas gott me the Specimen. It is often so, as you must be sensible of from the Thing you gott from ye Kings Chapell ground in 1769 and what H. gott from Olde Bury'g Point in 1690, that was like to ende him. I gott such a Thing in Aegypt 75 yeares gone, from the which came that Scar ye Boy saw on me here in 1924. As I told you longe ago, do not calle up That which you can not put downe; either from dead Saltes or out of ye Spheres beyond. Have ye Wordes for laying at all times readie, and stopp not to be sure when there is any Doubte of Whom you have. Stones are all chang'd now in Nine groundes out of 10. You are never sure till you question. I this day heard from H., who has had Trouble with the Soldiers. He is like to be sorry Transylvania is pass'd from Hungary to Roumania, and wou'd change his Seat if the Castel weren't so fulle of What we Knowe. But of this he hath doubtless writ you.

In my next Send'g there will be Somewhat from a Hill tomb from ye East that will delight you greatly. Meanwhile forget not I am desirous of B. F. if you can possibly get him for me. You know G. in Philada. better than I. Have him up firste if you will, but doe not use him soe hard he will be Difficult, for I must speake to him in ye End.

Yogg-Sothoth Neblod Zin
Simon O.

The correspondence of Hutchinson and Orne

PROP FROM *DARK ADVENTURE RADIO THEATRE®: THE CASE OF CHARLES DEXTER WARD*

Captain Abraham Whipple

The captain (1733–1819) was a real-world privateer famed for his service in the Continental Navy. He was an indirect ancestor of Lovecraft's, related to his beloved, maternal grandfather, Whipple Phillips. In this story, he joins in the enterprise to destroy Joseph Curwen.

THEMES

Generational Curse

The dangers that one's ancestors may pose manifest themselves differently in this tale than they do in his other stories. Here, Curwen plots to manipulate, use, and destroy his descendant during his own lifetime, hundreds of years before that descendant would even be born. And Charles is more than simply a descendant of Curwen's: the two are (a bit conveniently) all but identical in appearance. One is left to wonder whether Curwen's powers were such that Charles's subsequent life decisions weren't decisions at all, but a matter of fate, set in motion by Curwen. Either way, as in Lovecraft's other stories where familial curses are an issue, the recipient of the curse is left in a powerless position, unable to do anything more than suffer the consequences of destructive genetics.

Knowledge Is Dangerous

Charles's undoing is mainly a result of his relentless curiosity. Perhaps there is an element of fate or manipulation at work, but if Charles had, at any point, abandoned his inquiries into Joseph Curwen, the matter would never have led to Curwen's return and everything that happened as a result. Certainly, Dr. Willett sees Charles as a victim of his own curiosity.

The Past Is Alive

H. P. Lovecraft was a man out of time. He never felt at home in the era into which he was born. He idealized eighteenth-century New England and enjoyed imagining himself as an English gentleman, wearing a periwig and frock coat. No piece of Lovecraftian fiction embraces that age as vigorously as this tale. Lovecraft not only created an antagonist who modelled Lovecraft's ideal, but he wrote an extended flashback sequence that takes the reader to that cherished era. This gave Lovecraft a chance to re-create the Providence he knew from history, and to people it with the types of characters he found fascinating.

He also kept the past alive by keeping the character Joseph Curwen alive and inserting him into Providence in the 1920s. Curwen appears to adjust to the modern age with surprisingly little difficulty, not being overly impressed with any of the advances made in the intervening centuries. Like Lovecraft, Curwen is underwhelmed by modernity. Given Lovecraft's penchant for this age and thorough knowledge of its history, it is rather surprising that he never attempted another piece of historical fiction set in eighteenth-century Providence. His 1925 tale "He" does touch on this theme, but it is not one of Lovecraft's more successful stories.

SETTING AND MOTIFS

Alchemy

Lovecraft was a strict scientific materialist. He did not believe in the supernatural, religion, gods, or devils, or think that occult practices were truly effective. Alchemy, however, is a slightly different discipline. The precursor to modern chemistry, alchemy represented the first historical efforts to manipulate physical elements to change their fundamental nature. While famed for the pursuit of "turning lead into gold," most alchemists saw the practice as a spiritual pursuit. They believed that learning how to transmute base metals into gold would lead them to discover how to transfigure the base human soul into godliness. The alchemy practiced in this story is attributed to the real seventeenth-century alchemist Pierre Borel (whose name is Latinized as "Borellus"). Borellus was quoted by Cotton Mather in *Magnalia Christi Americana*, a book that Lovecraft had in his personal library. Ultimately, Lovecraft's use of alchemy and necromancy provides him with an effective plot device draped in the trappings of the history of early New England.

H. P. Lovecraft as Charles Dexter Ward

Charles Dexter Ward is, in many ways, an echo of the young H. P. Lovecraft. Charles's parents give him free rein to follow all kinds of intellectual pursuits. As an antiquarian, he studied the architecture and history of his beloved Providence, just like Lovecraft. S. T. Joshi and David E. Schultz, Lovecraft scholars, have argued that Charles is based on William Mauran, a young man in Providence whom Lovecraft might have known and who resided for some time in the Halsey mansion (the basis for the Ward home). Mauran's family also had a farmhouse in nearby Pawtuxet. But, since Charles is hunted by a nefarious ancestor, it's hard not to conclude that Charles is an embodiment of Lovecraft's own fear of being visited by an ancestral curse.

Madness

Madness is a theme that Lovecraft revisits time and again in his tales. The very concept of insanity has a long and complex history—attributed at various times to the gods, to the devil, to witches, to the conditions of childhood, to personal failure, and to neurochemistry. The care and treatment of the mentally ill have likewise varied greatly over time and across cultures. In some places, such people have been revered, believed to be touched by the divine. More often, though, they have been locked away as shameful nuisances. Some insane asylums lived up to their names and provided genuine care for their inmates. Many were little more than horrific prisons. Both of Lovecraft's parents languished in Butler Hospital, and his personal experience with asylums was such that the prospect of insanity clearly troubled him. It's worth noting that, in several instances, Lovecraft's afflicted characters are not actually mad, but are instead the victims of supernatural or cosmic forces.

The fact that there are several psychiatrists in this story, none of whom is effective in diagnosing or treating Charles's illness, might well reflect the author's thoughts about psychiatry. Charles is involuntarily admitted to an asylum, but he is not mad at all. Nor, in fact, is he Charles. The person being institutionalized is actually Joseph Curwen, who would appear to be more evil than he is insane.

In multiple instances in this story, characters undergo experiences beyond what they can deal with. Mrs. Ward, while only a minor character, is unable to cope with her son's growing eccentricities, so eventually she must be sent off on a sojourn to a sanitarium—a fashionable form of recuperation at that time. Later, after Dr. Willett conjures the saltes of 118 into existence, he apparently swoons and awakens in a bed in the Pawtuxet bungalow. Fortunately, Lovecraft spares us what must have been a strange and awkward scene in which 118 writes his note in Latin and then tucks Dr. Willett into bed.

Providence

While Lovecraft wrote many horror stories, he set only a few in his beloved Providence—most notably "The Shunned House," "The Haunter of the Dark," and *The Case of Charles Dexter Ward*. Dexter was a prominent name in the city, coming from a nineteenth-century merchant named Ebenezer Knight Dexter. At his death in 1824, Dexter left his forty-acre farm to the city, on the condition that it be used to build an asylum for the poor and the insane. The Dexter Asylum was still in operation when Lovecraft wrote this story, although it was, by then, a bleak place. In every story that Lovecraft set in Providence, the unique character of his beloved hometown shines through, the supernatural forces at work are ultimately vanquished, and matters are restored in the end to a state of normalcy.

Yog-Sothothery ~ Yog-Sothoth Itself

Yog-Sothoth is referred to numerous times in this tale, but in a manner that is interestingly vague. It is depicted as some kind of supernatural entity that can be called upon, and its name appears to be a key part of some of the magical incantations that the characters invoke. But Yog is not anthropomorphized here and never appears as a character. The story's villains invoke Yog's name as a sort of oath of fealty in the conclusions of their letters.

While much of the ritual language used in this story was cribbed by Lovecraft from *The Mysteries of Magic* by Eliphas Levi, translated by A. E. Waite, the diabolical Simon Orne provides excellent original safety advice to any aspiring occultists dealing with the forces of the Cthulhu Mythos. (See Notable Quotes.)

NOTABLE QUOTES

"... he was never a fiend or even truly a madman, but only an eager, studious, and curious boy whose love of mystery and of the past was his undoing. He stumbled on things no mortal ought ever to know, and reached back through the years as no one ever should reach; and something came out of those years to engulf him."

This quotation from Dr. Willett about Charles sums up the hubris that was Charles's undoing. The quote also contains an echo of the persistent sense of dread that burdened Lovecraft, a fear of the incipient madness that was in both his parents' bloodlines, and which he feared would someday be his own undoing.

"Do not call up that which you cannot put down."

Sound advice for the aspiring occultist. When summoning demons and other extra-dimensional monstrosities, the prudent practitioner should always ensure that any entity thus summoned is not too powerful, and he or she should have a backup plan for when things invariably go horribly wrong.

"God! Could it be possible that here lay the mortal relics of half the titan thinkers of all the ages; snatched by supreme ghouls from crypts where the world thought them safe, and subject to the beck and call of madmen who sought to drain their knowledge for some still wilder end…"

Lovecraft was entranced by the notion of an enduring repository of knowledge, a kind of library with sources impractical in the real world. The idea is embodied in the Mi-Go's collection of brains from a variety of species in *The Whisperer in Darkness*, the trans-temporal library of the Great Race in *The Shadow Out of Time*, and in the collected jars of essential saltes of the world's greatest minds in *The Case of Charles Dexter Ward*.

"There seemed to lurk in his bearing some cryptic, sardonic arrogance, as if he had come to find all human beings dull through having moved among stranger and more potent entities."

Many of Lovecraft's antagonists perceive themselves as having transcended their human origins by trafficking with eldritch powers: Old Whateley, Ephraim Waite, Obed Marsh. Clearly, the powers unleashed through such arcane practices are prone to corrupt one's humanity while boosting one's self-esteem.

"From a private hospital for the insane near Providence, Rhode Island, there recently disappeared an exceedingly singular person. He bore the name of Charles Dexter Ward…"

If Lovecraft's final sentences often fail to deliver the dramatic impact he hoped for, his opening sentences frequently provide a very effective hook that entices the reader immediately to delve further into the story.

"… that man of unholy centuries and forbidden secrets never troubled the world again. The madness out of time had subsided, and the case of Charles Dexter Ward was closed."

For this story title, he considered "The Madness Out of Time." Clearly, he liked the ring of it since he later used the title *The Shadow Out of Time*.

H P LOVECRAFT
10 BARNES STREET
PROVIDENCE R I

Pay no charges to messenger

For quick service, reply by bearer

URGENT: DELIVER WITHOUT DELAY

RECEIVER'S NUMBER 25716341
DATE 1 MAR 1927
TIME FILED 2:27 P.M.
CHECK 257 0=25
SENDING STATION: PRAGUE

TELEGRAM

The World Wide Electrical Printing Telegraph Co. Ltd.

This is a full-rate telegram or electric lettergram unless its deferred character is indicated by a suitable symbol above or preceding the address. The filing time shown in the date line on telegrams and cablegrams is STANDARD TIME at point of origin. FORM HPLHS-001

SYMBOLS: DL=DAY LETTER NL=NIGHT LETTER LC=DEFERRED CABLE NLT=CABLE NIGHT LETTER SR=SHIP RADIOGRAM

DISCUSSION TOPICS

- When Dr. Willett investigates the basement beneath the bungalow, he does so alone, and the “omniscient” third-person narration of the story is very much from Willett’s point of view. Do you feel he remains a reliable narrator for the remainder of the tale? How does it change your perspective of the story if Dr. Willet is “believable” compared to if he is “unreliable”?
- Some of Lovecraft’s stories contain a story within the story, like this one’s protracted flashback to the raid on the Curwen farm. Does such a departure from the story’s main narrative distract you from the main throughline, or do you find the excursion makes the return to the main story even more enjoyable? Why?
- Do you perceive Charles as a victim of a genetic/temporal doom, or do you think he brings about his own demise through his unrelenting curiosity?
- Orne, Hutchinson, and Curwen sought to wrest secrets from the distinguished minds of deceased experts in various fields. What do you think they were trying to learn? If you could call up someone from their saltes, whom would you call, and what would you want to ask?
- The very concept of “insanity” is fraught with complications, and there are some people—even some psychiatrists—who question whether such a thing as insanity even exists. Apart from a handful of specifically identifiable brain diseases, “mental illness” can be seen as an entirely metaphorical construct to help us deal with problematical people. Do you think insanity is real? Is the idea of it useful or harmful?

THE COLOUR OUT OF SPACE

OVERVIEW

This 12,000-word story was written in the spring of 1927 and proved to be Lovecraft's favorite of his tales. It is certainly one of his most understated and subtle stories, in which the horror is presented with little explanation. Its human characters are wholly ineffectual, but the plight of the family whose lives are destroyed is uncommonly poignant. His aspiration to create a cosmic horror, a threat well outside human experience or understanding, shines here. It was first published in the September 1927 issue of *Amazing Stories*, but he received only $25 in payment, which, even in 1927, was a pittance. Lovecraft grew to detest the magazine's editor, Hugo Gernsback.

In his evolution as a writer, Lovecraft went through phases where he produced works largely inspired by Edgar Allan Poe, and later by the writings of Lord Dunsany. But at this point in his career, he had found his own voice and was writing tales that were truly "Lovecraftian." Many of these later stories are as much science fiction as they are horror. Lovecraft himself preferred the blanket term "weird tales." "The Colour Out of Space" is a superb example of his writing at the apex of his career.

> I have just finished one new tale which I'll send you in my next. This one has little flashes of the quasi-poetic, but is for the most part realistic; with a homely country setting "West of Arkham." Something falls from the sky and terror broods.
>
> *H. P. Lovecraft to Bernard Austin Dwyer, March 26, 1927*

STORY SUMMARY

A surveyor working on a new reservoir discovers a strangely barren patch of land in the backwoods of rural Massachusetts called the "Blasted Heath." He questions a local farmer named Ammi Pierce, who shares the history of the heath. It was once the Gardner Farm, which was struck by a meteorite in 1882. Scientists from Miskatonic University hurried to the crater, eager to collect a sample from the huge specimen. Back in their laboratory, under a spectroscope, the sample revealed colors no one had ever seen before. Mysteriously, the sample diminished in size, and by the following day, it had disappeared entirely, along with the beaker it was in.

Returning to the farm, the scientists prepared to take another sample. On striking the meteorite with a rock hammer, they revealed a glassy globule that, when broken open, appeared to be empty inside. An electrical storm struck the farm that night, with multiple lightning strikes hitting the meteorite. By morning, the once-sizable rock was gone.

Ammi visited the farm throughout the summer and saw incredible plant growth. Crops grew fast and large, but everything was inedible. As winter set in, animals on the farm and local wildlife displayed odd mutations, and the Gardners themselves began acting peculiarly. By spring, plants on the farm became a strange color, which no one could quite identify. Trees glowed and swayed slightly, even when there was no wind. Nahum Gardner sought help, but no one at the university or the newspaper showed any interest.

The change took its toll on the Gardner family. Nahum's wife, Nabby, showed signs of insanity, and Nahum was forced to lock her in their attic. The livestock behaved erratically, seeming to decay in much the same way as the farm's crops had earlier. Ammi continued to visit the family, and over time, bore witness to a slow madness and a pervasive apathy that overtook them all. Eventually, Nahum Gardner, like everything and everyone else on the farm, crumbled to dust before Ammi's eyes.

Panicked, Ammi returned to Arkham to seek help from the authorities. Three policemen, the coroner, and the medical examiner accompanied him to the farm, and their investigation turned up many disturbing details, including the remains of the boys Zenas and Merwin at the bottom of the Gardners' well. Night set in, and they beheld a weird glow moving over all the buildings on the farm. Even the tips of the tree branches glowed with an unearthly light. As their horses neighed in terror, the men witnessed the strange "Colour" rising out of the well, shooting back into the night sky.

After that, nothing ever grew on the land around the Gardner Farm. It became known as the Blasted Heath, and it was soon flooded with water for a new reservoir.

CHARACTERS/KEY FIGURES

The Unnamed Narrator

The story is told almost entirely in the form of a flashback within a frame narrative, and the narrator largely remains one step removed from the events he relates. The unnamed character is a surveyor working on a project to build a new reservoir. His discovery of the Blasted Heath, and his inquiry into it, reveal a series of strange events that took place there decades earlier.

The narrator shows compassion for Ammi Pierce, a local farmer who describes the events to the narrator, expressing his hope that Ammi does not meet the same fate as the Gardners. Yet, he also displays an ecological shortsightedness typical of the early twentieth century. The meteorite has poisoned the Gardner land with something unknown and horrible, but the narrator does not suggest that anything be done to protect the water (and drinking water, at that!) in the proposed reservoir from contamination. Rather, he blithely hopes that inundating the region will somehow make things better: "Something terrible came to the hills and valleys on that meteor, and something terrible—though I know not in what proportion—still remains. I shall be glad to see the water come." The HPLHS does not condone the practice of drinking from water sources tainted with alien meteorites.

Ammi Pierce

A rustic farmer and neighbor to the Gardners, Ammi relates the story of the "strange days" to the surveyor. His tale constitutes the bulk of the narrative, but the narrator has been warned that Ammi is old and possibly crazy, so he's not sure whether to believe him or not. Ammi expresses his fondness and compassion for his neighbors' plight, doing what little he can to help them in the face of a cosmic challenge. In the end, he bears the torch of knowledge, being the last one who remembers what took place. Without Ammi's story, no one would know the horror submerged beneath the reservoir.

Nahum Gardner

Poor Nahum is a well-intended and good-natured farmer who bears the brunt of a horrible accident. A meteorite falls to the ground on his property, slowly consuming his farm, his family, his sanity, and his health—all inexorably carried out with a cruel randomness.

Abigail "Nabby" Gardner

Nabby meets a similar fate to Nahum's, although her decline is fiercer and more rapid. It's hard not to wonder if there are echoes of Lovecraft's mother's madness at work in the depiction of this character.

Zenas, Thaddeus, and Merwin Gardner

The Gardners' children are also destroyed. First, Thaddeus goes mad, like his mother. Zenas and Merwin are drawn to the strange Colour in the well, which is where they meet their demise.

The Colour

Alien and indefinable, the Colour is one of Lovecraft's more compelling creations, in part because we simply cannot understand it. Is it alive? Is it intelligent? Lovecraft's predilection for British spellings pays off here by adding to the foreignness of the entity and giving it a hint of personality.

THEMES

Cosmic Indifference

A traditional trope in horror fiction is that something is coming to get the protagonist. Maybe it's a zombie, or a ghost, or a diabolical ex-girlfriend. This antagonist typically has a comprehensible motive, such as revenge, hunger, or a similar drive. Lovecraft takes such ideas entirely out of the equation here. The Colour appears to have shown up wholly by chance. It looks to be completely unaware of its victims. Its arrival, its actions, and even its eventual departure seem to be driven either by chance or a motive outside human comprehension. The Colour is propelled by no motive we can understand, and it is indifferent to the humans it impacts. This notion is at the core of the concept of "cosmic horror." Humans don't matter, and no action they take will affect or eliminate the cosmic forces at work.

Collateral Damage

The Gardner Farm, its animals, and its people never appear to be the intended victims of the Colour. They are all completely innocent. We never understand whether the Colour was meant to arrive on Earth at all, or if the impact of the meteorite was some kind of mistake. The Gardners pay a horrible price, but they are merely senseless collateral damage.

SETTINGS AND MOTIFS

The Blasted Heath

Lovecraft begins the story by evoking the image of the wild, dense, virgin forests of the rural Massachusetts countryside. He immediately contrasts this with his description of the "Blasted Heath": "… five acres of grey desolation that sprawled open to the sky like a great spot eaten by acid… There was no vegetation of any kind on that broad expanse, but only a fine grey dust or ash which no wind seemed ever to blow about."

The reader, like the narrator of the story, is left to conclude that something terrible happened in this place. The heath is seemingly a permanent result of the destruction wrought by the Colour.

The Reservoir

The reservoir in the story is fictional, but it was inspired by a couple of real reservoirs in Massachusetts. The damming of the Swift River for the construction of the Quabbin

Reservoir, which supplies Boston with drinking water to this day, was a massive civil engineering project in Lovecraft's time. It required the relocation of numerous cemeteries and the flooding of many small towns and villages. In a letter dated October 13, 1935, Lovecraft wrote to Richard Ely Morse: "Tragedy always attends the blotting-out of an ancient countryside where generations have dwelt & left the accumulated memories & tangible monuments of their long continuous presence."

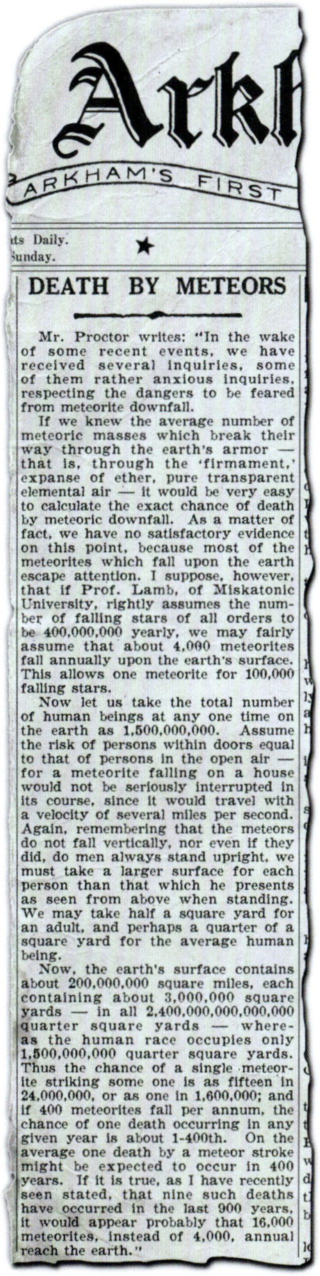

Arkh

ARKHAM'S FIRST

nts Daily.
Sunday.

DEATH BY METEORS

Mr. Proctor writes: "In the wake of some recent events, we have received several inquiries, some of them rather anxious inquiries, respecting the dangers to be feared from meteorite downfall.

If we knew the average number of meteoric masses which break their way through the earth's armor — that is, through the 'firmament,' expanse of ether, pure transparent elemental air — it would be very easy to calculate the exact chance of death by meteoric downfall. As a matter of fact, we have no satisfactory evidence on this point, because most of the meteorites which fall upon the earth escape attention. I suppose, however, that if Prof. Lamb, of Miskatonic University, rightly assumes the number of falling stars of all orders to be 400,000,000 yearly, we may fairly assume that about 4,000 meteorites fall annually upon the earth's surface. This allows one meteorite for 100,000 falling stars.

Now let us take the total number of human beings at any one time on the earth as 1,500,000,000. Assume the risk of persons within doors equal to that of persons in the open air — for a meteorite falling on a house would not be seriously interrupted in its course, since it would travel with a velocity of several miles per second. Again, remembering that the meteors do not fall vertically, nor even if they did, do men always stand upright, we must take a larger surface for each person than that which he presents as seen from above when standing. We may take half a square yard for an adult, and perhaps a quarter of a square yard for the average human being.

Now, the earth's surface contains about 200,000,000 square miles, each containing about 3,000,000 square yards — in all 2,400,000,000,000,000 quarter square yards — whereas the human race occupies only 1,500,000,000 quarter square yards. Thus the chance of a single meteorite striking some one is as fifteen in 24,000,000, or as one in 1,600,000; and if 400 meteorites fall per annum, the chance of one death occurring in any given year is about 1-400th. On the average one death by a meteor stroke might be expected to occur in 400 years. If it is true, as I have recently seen stated, that nine such deaths have occurred in the last 900 years, it would appear probably that 16,000 meteorites, instead of 4,000, annual reach the earth."

Miskatonic in the news
PROP FROM *DARK ADVENTURE RADIO THEATRE*®

Miskatonic University

The depiction of Lovecraft's favorite university here is an inverse of its depiction in "The Dunwich Horror." In the latter story, the powers of academia are marshaled against an otherworldly horror, and human intellect prevails. Here, the university's best minds study the Colour, and they walk away utterly perplexed by its impenetrability: The most advanced scientific methods they can apply are useless.

Radiation Poisoning

Many readers have noted the similarities between the afflictions suffered by the Gardners and radiation poisoning. Lovecraft was keenly interested in science and took pride in keeping abreast of the scientific developments of his day. Certainly, he would have been aware of Marie Curie's Nobel Prize for Chemistry in 1911 for the discovery and production of radium, a highly radioactive element. Industry was slow to perceive the dangers of radium and, in the 1920s, household cleaning supplies and even condoms were augmented with radium. Lovecraft owned a spinthariscope, a household device for observing individual nuclear disintegrations caused by the interaction of ionizing radiation with a phosphor.

The most common symptoms of radiation poisoning are nausea, headache, diarrhea, and fever. Exposure to radiation can also cause burn-like symptoms, genetic damage, and a host of other issues. Radiation is decidedly bad for you. So, of course, is having a Colour Out of Space land on your farm! Although Lovecraft might have appreciated that radiation can be perilous, there is no firm evidence to indicate his Colour was radioactive. He did succeed in creating something similar, nonetheless—an entity that damages all living things by its mere proximity to them.

Yog-Sothothery ~ Yes and No

Lovecraft shares so little information about the Colour that it is hard to discern whether it has any connection to the greater mythology that he wove into most of his later tales. And that's part of the fun of this story—the reader is left wondering whether the Gardners were visited by some kind of mythos monstrosity, or whether it was just a random meteorite that caused dire consequences.

NOTABLE QUOTES

"West of Arkham the hills rise wild, and there are valleys with deep woods that no axe has ever cut."

This simple quotation paints a picture of a remote New England world where humans have yet to make any kind of mark. It is, of course, ironic, as humans will be unable to make a mark against the Colour.

"It was just a colour out of space—a frightful messenger from unformed realms of infinity beyond all Nature as we know it; from realms whose mere existence stuns the brain and numbs us with the black extra-cosmic gulfs it throws open before our frenzied eyes."

Wow! This one's a doozy. Some may find it wordy and challengingly complex. But, if you're reading this book, we're going to wager that you're the kind of person who will read a forty-three-word sentence like this and think, "This guy rocks!"

"The way they screamed at each other from behind their locked doors was very terrible, especially to little Merwin, who fancied they talked in some terrible language that was not of Earth."

After they go mad, Nabby and Thaddeus are locked away in the attic. Lovecraft was never really interested in the human characters in his stories, but part of what makes this story so powerful is his vivid and truly heartbreaking descriptions of what happens to the members of the Gardner family.

"… over all the rest reigned that riot of luminous amorphousness, that alien and undimensioned rainbow of cryptic poison from the well—seething, feeling, lapping, reaching, scintillating, straining, and malignly bubbling in its cosmic and unrecognisable chromaticism."

Here, Lovecraft heightens the horror by deploying a series of verbs (note a similarly constructed string of four verbs in the Notable Quotes for *The Shadow over Innsmouth*). His Colour, already well established as visually disturbing, here becomes active and comes to disconcerting life.

H P LOVECRAFT
10 BARNES STREET
PROVIDENCE R I

Pay no charges to messenger

For quick service, reply by bearer

URGENT: DELIVER WITHOUT DELAY

RECEIVER'S NUMBER
82525112621 1521

DATE
28 MAR 1927

TIME FILED
1:52 P.M.

CHECK
168 X=6

TELEGRAM

The World Wide Electrical Printing Telegraph Co. Ltd.

This is a full-rate telegram or electric lettergram unless its deferred character is indicated by a suitable symbol above or preceding the address. The filing time shown in the date line on telegrams and cablegrams is STANDARD TIME at point of origin.

FORM HPLHS-001

SENDING STATION:
AMHERST

SYMBOLS: DL=DAY LETTER NL=NIGHT LETTER LC=DEFERRED CABLE NLT=CABLE NIGHT LETTER SR=SHIP RADIOGRAM

DISCUSSION TOPICS

- The horror in this story does not appear to be supernatural at all, but rather a natural phenomenon simply from beyond previous human experience. Does this make it more frightening or less frightening than a supernatural menace (for example, a ghost or vampire) with an agenda?
- The Colour departs but leaves behind its residue in an area soon to be flooded for a reservoir. Do you think the story is an intentional expression of environmentalism on Lovecraft's part (i.e., beware of what goes in our water)? Or do you think he uses the concept of the reservoir to give the Colour a means of threatening the reader (i.e., you might be drinking the monster right now)?
- This story has two layers: It's the surveyor's present-day story and a retelling of the story he heard from Ammi, the last surviving eyewitness. Why do you think Lovecraft used that frame narrative? If Ammi or Nahum had been the sole narrator, how do you think the story would be different?

THE DUNWICH HORROR

OVERVIEW

This 17,000-word story was written in August of 1928 and promptly saw publication in the April 1929 issue of *Weird Tales* magazine. As he did in an earlier tale, "The Picture in the House," Lovecraft set out to capture some of the atmospheric terror he found in the decaying farm country of rural Massachusetts.

"The Dunwich Horror" departs from many of Lovecraft's works by using an omniscient third-person narrator. Lovecraft was fond of telling his stories from the point of view of the person experiencing them; deviation from his storytelling norm gives "The Dunwich Horror" a different tone. It is also a departure insofar as the story is presented as a tale of good versus evil, in which good, somehow, emerges victorious. Rather than being driven mad by his knowledge of arcane subjects, Professor Armitage successfully deploys his knowledge to defeat the Whateleys.

The first half of the story is typically Lovecraftian in that he provides a complex and plausible setup for a problem that will emerge later. Once it becomes clear that the problem is the titular Dunwich Horror itself, the tale becomes a quasi kaiju story of a great, invisible rampaging monster. There's an implication that the "Horror" may somehow pose a threat to all of humanity but, more immediately, the challenge is to keep it from destroying all the farms and farmers around Dunwich. Armitage's knowledge connects it to the greater cosmic horror of the Cthulhu Mythos. The actions taken by Armitage and his colleagues successfully thwart the Horror, but they do nothing to address the enduring threat of Yog-Sothoth and its kind.

The tale is unusually cinematic, complete with human character arcs, dialogue, and action set pieces. It was, in fact, adapted into a feature film in 1970, produced by Roger Corman and starring none other than 1950s *Gidget* sweetheart Sandra Dee, in a career-ending performance. Although the movie version strays considerably from the original story—including, for example, a very sexy and conspicuously short Wilbur Whateley played by Dean Stockwell—it was the first Hollywood production to credit Lovecraft by name. We can assert with total confidence that he would have hated it.

STORY SUMMARY

Chapters I—II

The story begins in a small town in rural Massachusetts. Dunwich is shrouded in a strange history and, nearby, a ring of standing stones from ancient times crowns Sentinel Hill. The Whateley family lives in a farmhouse just outside of town. Lavinia, a middle-aged albino woman, lives with her father, Old Whateley, reputed to be a practitioner of black magic. Lavinia gives birth to a bastard child named Wilbur, a strange "goatish" boy who matures at an alarming rate. His grandfather boasts to neighbors that the child is destined for greatness.

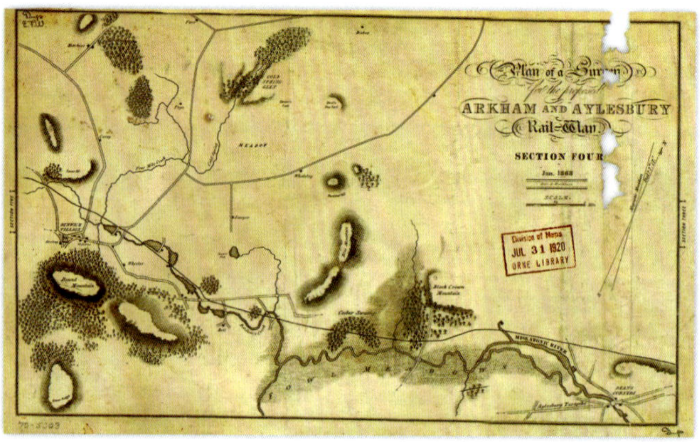

Fictional map of rural Massachusetts
PROP FROM *DARK ADVENTURE RADIO THEATRE*®: "THE DUNWICH HORROR"

Chapter III

Wilbur continues his strangely accelerated growth while Old Whateley buys more cows than his small family would seem to require. The local draft board visits Dunwich, seeking men for the Great War, and finds the Whateley household an alarming mystery. Neighbors wonder what might be afoot at the odd farmhouse.

Chapter IV

By 1923, when Wilbur is ten years old, he appears to be a grown man. His mother, Lavinia, confesses to neighbors that she is terrified of what he has become and, shortly thereafter, she is never heard from again. Old Whateley's health declines, and he gives Wilbur some odd and troubling deathbed advice, ominously mentioning "the complete edition." Wilbur follows his grandfather's instructions, making peculiar modifications to the farmhouse.

Chapter V

Wilbur, now grown into a "dark and goatish gargoyle" over eight feet tall, ventures to Miskatonic's Orne Library to compare his English copy of the *Necronomicon* with the library's complete Latin edition. Head librarian Dr. Henry Armitage intercepts Wilbur and, although the two discuss passages in the dread-filled book, Armitage denies Wilbur's request to borrow it and sends him away. Alarmed by Wilbur's interest, Armitage begins a private investigation.

Chapter VI

Wilbur returns to Miskatonic, breaks into the library, attempts to steal the *Necronomicon*, and is killed by a watchdog. Armitage and his colleagues, Rice and Morgan, arrive to see the dying Wilbur, a barely human monstrosity, disintegrating on the floor. Wilbur, apparently, took after his unknown father.

Chapter VII

Weeks later, farms around Dunwich are attacked by a great, invisible presence. Fences are smashed, cattle devoured, and whole farmhouses are destroyed along with their occupants by an enormous but unseen thing that makes terrifying noises and smells ghastly. Whatever the thing is, it seems to lumber off into a hiding place in nearby Cold Spring Glen.

Chapter VIII

Armitage receives an old ledger recovered from the now abandoned Whateley house and toils to break its arcane code. He hears reports of strange destruction in Dunwich and concludes the Whateleys must have succeeded in using the *Necronomicon* to summon an extra-dimensional being that is responsible for the rampage. He gathers his colleagues, who realize desperate action is required, and the trio sets off for Dunwich.

Chapter IX

The professors arrive to discover the invisible menace is continuing to attack farms in Dunwich. They finally track its ascent up Sentinel Hill by following a swath of foliage as it is destroyed by the gigantic unseen force. Local farmers lead the academics in their pursuit.

Chapter X

Armitage, Rice, and Morgan ascend Sentinel Hill for a final showdown with the thing. They're armed with an alchemical powder capable of rendering the menace visible, and an occult ritual intended to vanquish it. From a distance, the farmers watch the scene unfold. Armitage's plan is successful, and the creature is at last revealed to be a colossal mass of tentacles and hooved feet with a giant face that resembles the Whateleys. It cries out pitifully to Yog-Sothoth before Armitage's ritual sends it back to whence it came. Armitage explains to the farmers that it was Wilbur's half-brother, although it looked more like the father than Wilbur did.

CHARACTERS/KEY FIGURES

Henry Armitage

Henry Armitage is one of Lovecraft's most iconic protagonists and, in many ways, he differs from Lovecraft's other leading men. Henry is superbly well educated, with several degrees—an MA from Miskatonic University, a PhD from Princeton, and a doctor of letters degree from Johns Hopkins. Unlike Lovecraft's other stories, where knowledge and investigation lead characters to their undoing, in "The Dunwich Horror," it is Armitage's erudition that saves the day. By putting his mind to the challenge of Wilbur's cipher, Armitage concocts a plan whereby he and his colleagues can deploy the same ritual magic to defeat the Dunwich Horror that the Whateleys used to summon the thing in the first place. The story ends with a triumphant Armitage and the citizens of Dunwich saved.

Wilbur Whateley

Wilbur is the monstrous offspring created through the union of Lavinia Whateley and Yog-Sothoth. Alarmingly precocious, Wilbur could speak at eleven months of age. By the time he was four years old, he "looked like a lad of fifteen." But Wilbur only appeared to be a human being. In fact, his body was constituted of matter unlike that of earthly organisms:

PROP FROM *DARK ADVENTURE RADIO THEATRE®*: "THE DUNWICH HORROR"

> The thing that lay half-bent on its side in a foetid pool of greenish-yellowichorand tarry stickiness was almost nine feet tall, and the dog had torn off all the clothing and some of the skin.... It was partly human, beyond a doubt, with very manlike hands and head, and the goatish, chinless face had the stamp of the Whateleys upon it. But the torso and lower parts of the body were teratologically fabulous, so that only generous clothing could ever have enabled it to walk on earth unchallenged or uneradicated.

Old Whateley

Wizard Whately prostitutes his daughter to cosmic gods, becoming Wilbur's grandfather and mentor in the occult arts, and doing what he can to prepare Wilbur to care for his brother and carry out his sinister plan: "... some plan for the extirpation of the entire human race and all animal and vegetable life from the Earth by some terrible elder race of beings from another dimension."

Old Whateley is an interesting villain while putting his evil plan in motion, but then he dies off and has little to do with the plan's execution. Lovecraft made good use of New England folklore about whippoorwills consuming the souls of the deceased, as the birds flock to Wizard Whateley in his death throes.

Lavinia Whately

Lovecraft shows little love for the albino Lavinia, describing her as sickly, slatternly, and malformed. He characterizes her as deranged, running about on mountaintops during electrical storms and, most remarkably, somehow procreating with Yog-Sothoth. Like many other of Lovecraft's female characters, he uses Lavinia in a purely functional manner, although there is a bit of pathos in her final confession. Her implied murder by her son is barely acknowledged in the tale.

The entire Whateley family—complete with book-loving, tutor grandfather; flighty, whiter-than-white mother; mysterious, absent father; and precocious monster child older than his years—is a hillbilly funhouse-mirror reflection of Lovecraft's own family.

Dr. Francis Morgan & Professor Warren Rice

Lovecraft provides Armitage with a couple of colleagues to help with his investigation but gives them little in the way of actual personality. The most distinctive thing about Rice is that his beard is "iron-grey," while Morgan's main quality is that he brings a gun to a monster fight.

The Dunwich Horror

This invisible monstrosity is Wilbur's brother. Much of the fun surrounding this creature is how little Lovecraft tells us about it. We never exactly understand what compulsion drives it to return to Sentinel Hill for the story's climax, where for a fleeting instant it is made visible by Armitage and his friends, who spray it with the powder of Ibn Ghazi. Its heart-wrenching cries for its father are rather poignant, if you don't get hung up on the fact that its father will wipe out all life on Earth. This could be seen as another case of a sympathetic monster.

Lovecraft took inspiration from several other "invisible monster" stories that he enjoyed, notably Guy de Maupassant's "The Horla," Fitz-James O'Brien's "What Was It?," and Algernon Blackwood's "The Wendigo." He freely takes inspiration (and gives credit for it) from Arthur Machen's "The Great God Pan."

Yog-Sothoth

Yog-Sothoth is one of the most prominent gods in the Lovecraftian pantheon, so much so that Lovecraft himself referred lightheartedly to his mythology as Yog-Sothothery. While this entity is first named in Lovecraft's novella *The Case of Charles Dexter Ward*, most of what we learn about Yog-Sothoth appears in this story, namely in text quoted from the *Necronomicon*. In his collaboration with Hazel Heald, "The Horror in the Museum," Lovecraft describes the entity as follows: "Imagination called up the shocking form of fabulous Yog-Sothoth—only a congeries of iridescent globes, yet stupendous in its malign suggestiveness." Weird, right? Lovecraft is more effective in this story, though, describing the monstrousness of Wilbur's brother by saying, "It looked more like the father [Yog-Sothoth] than he did."

THEMES

Cosmic Horror ~ Humanity Wins! What?

A central tenet behind cosmic horror is that human beings are of no consequence to the universe at large. As a result, the actions taken by humans typically have no meaningful impact on the forces at work in Lovecraft's stories. "The Dunwich Horror" stands out as a rare example of the contrary. This tale may well have the "happiest ending" of any of Lovecraft's major works, and it's easy to see how it could inspire movie and gaming adaptations.

Cursed Genes

This is another example of Lovecraft's exploration of an ancestral curse and how its horror manifests itself through, let us say, "malgenics." Old Whateley is viewed as descending from the "decayed" side of his family. Lovecraft doesn't explain what he means by the term; presumably, it's indicative of at least moral decay, if not something more literal. Lavinia is born into a cursed ancestral line and openly exhibits (to Lovecraft, at least) genetic defects. Lavinia's selection of a mate (if, indeed, she selected him at all) increases the likelihood that the family curse will be visited upon her son, Wilbur. All we know about Lavinia's mother is that she died by violence when Lavinia was twelve, and we're left to presume that Old Wizard Whateley was responsible for her death, possibly by trying to force her to procreate with Yog-Sothoth first, before Lavinia did. Lovecraft never even suggests how Wilbur is conceived, but it couldn't have been natural, and it well might not have been voluntary on Lavinia's part.

Knowledge Is Power ~ For Good

In most of Lovecraft's stories, knowledge comes at a terrible price, often leading to death and madness, but this story stands in defiance of that trend. Here, it's precisely Armitage's knowledge, which he wields like a weapon, that enables him and his colleagues to fight the horror. While the process is taxing for him, it is ultimately not destructive, and it leads to the salvation of Dunwich and the surrounding farms.

SETTINGS AND MOTIFS

Dunwich

The notion of decay and degeneration weighed heavily on Lovecraft. Outside his familiar environment of Providence, the sense of decay in the New England countryside provided a dark thrill.

> But the true epicure in the terrible … esteems most of all the ancient, lonely farmhouses of backwoods New England; for there the dark elements of strength, solitude, grotesqueness, and ignorance combine to form the perfection of the hideous.
>
> *H. P. Lovecraft, "The Picture in the House"*

In creating Dunwich, he took the atmosphere of backwoods rusticity and peopled it with a degenerated family, even going so far as to overtly refer to the "decayed" and "undecayed" branches of the Whateley and Bishop families. Lovecraft imagined that in such communities, a family like the Whateleys would have had the freedom to conduct their unholy rites among the standing stones on Sentinel Hill and to pass along a tradition of black magic without drawing unwanted attention from the outside world.

Miskatonic University

Miskatonic provides the backdrop for only one portion of the narrative, but that portion of the story has an outsized impact on the reader's conception of Miskatonic University. We get a glimpse of the campus, the students, a few members of the faculty, and even the valiant guard dog. But our view is primarily driven by the character of Henry Armitage. As the university's head librarian, Armitage is practically the embodiment of all human virtue. When the disturbing Wilbur Whateley calls to consult the *Necronomicon*, Armitage could have simply slammed the door on him. Instead, he engages with Wilbur in an effort to understand what he's up to, and even shares some information from the infamous book before ultimately denying his request. Armitage's capability and resolve demonstrate what Miskatonic is ultimately all about. It's an institution of esoteric learning where members of the faculty are willing and able to shake off the bonds of conventional academic thinking and use their esoteric knowledge to emerge victorious against the world's darkest threats.

The Necronomicon

No single story by Lovecraft provides as much information about his celebrated fictional grimoire as "The Dunwich Horror." Here, he references both the Latin edition by Olaus Wormius, as well as the even rarer English translation by John Dee. In addition to providing a protracted and disturbing direct quote from the book, he gives us an extra shudder with a subtle reference to the book's size when Old Whateley refers to a chant on page 751, suggesting the occult tome must be a massive collection of ungodly secrets (and raising the bar for those reckless souls who have tried to produce a complete version).

Yog-Sothothery ~ Yog & Son

"The Dunwich Horror" is another tale that substantively expands what readers can learn about Lovecraft's evolving mythology. Here, Yog-Sothoth is anthropomorphized, at least to the extent that it can "father" a child with a human being—and later be called upon by its son. But its interaction with humans would seem to be planned as a short-term relationship, as the greater plan seems to be the extirpation of all life on Earth.

This story's lengthy quotations from the *Necronomicon* provide the reader with a generous amount of information about what the Great Old Ones are and how they operate.

NOTABLE QUOTES

"Let me tell ye suthin'—some day yew folks'll hear a child o' Lavinny's a-callin' its father's name on the top o' Sentinel Hill!"

Wizard Whateley sets up the story's climax with this strange prognostication made early in the tale. It's the kind of prophecy that seems meaningless until a very specific set of circumstances are met. Much of the story's abundant dialogue is written in this kind of phonetic backwoods Yankee patois.

"The Old Ones were, the Old Ones are, and the Old Ones shall be. Not in the spaces we know, but between them. They walk serene and primal, undimensioned and to us unseen."

Lovecraft's celebrated *Necronomicon* makes its most substantive appearance in "The Dunwich Horror." These passages, ostensibly written by the "mad Arab" Abdul Alhazred centuries ago, have inspired generations of readers to reject the notion that the *Necronomicon* is a fictitious book created by Lovecraft; instead, it has galvanized them to believe this storied occult tome is real.

"Man rules now where They ruled once; They shall soon rule where man rules now. After summer is winter, and after winter summer. They wait patient and potent, for here shall They reign again."

We have elsewhere discussed inaccurate quotes regarding the Cthulhu Mythos and how the mythology was purported to have worked. This quotation from the *Necronomicon* would appear to corroborate those ideas, but it's essential to understand that, here, Lovecraft is not opining about his own work. Rather, he is attempting to create the sort of language one would find in an occult grimoire. If you hear an echo of *Game of Thrones* in this quote ("winter is coming"), you're not wrong. George R. R. Martin is an enthusiastic Lovecraft fan.

"Yog-Sothoth knows the gate. Yog-Sothoth is the gate. Yog-Sothoth is the key and guardian of the gate. Past, present, future, all are one in Yog-Sothoth."

"Yog-Sothothery" in action! Many of the passages ostensibly quoted from the *Necronomicon* are filled with such delightful occult-tinged mumbo-jumbo.

"... it was mostly a kind of force that doesn't belong in our part of space; a kind of force that acts and grows and shapes itself by other laws than those of our sort of Nature. We have no business calling in such things from outside, and only very wicked people and very wicked cults ever try to."

The story concludes as Professor Armitage attempts to interpret for the terrified farmers the horror they've just witnessed. It isn't a simple thing to explain.

H P LOVECRAFT
10 BARNES STREET
PROVIDENCE R I

Pay no charges to messenger

For quick service, reply by bearer

URGENT: DELIVER WITHOUT DELAY

RECEIVER'S NUMBER
14214451625

DATE
5 AUG 1928

TIME FILED
10:15 A.M.

CHECK
140 H3

SENDING STATION:
WILBRAHAM

TELEGRAM

The World Wide Electrical Printing Telegraph Co. Ltd.

This is a full-rate telegram or electric lettergram unless its deferred character is indicated by a suitable symbol above or preceding the address. The filing time shown in the date line on telegrams and cablegrams is STANDARD TIME at point of origin.

FORM HPLHS-001

SYMBOLS: DL=DAY LETTER NL=NIGHT LETTER LC=DEFERRED CABLE NLT=CABLE NIGHT LETTER SR=SHIP RADIOGRAM

DISCUSSION TOPICS

- This is a rare instance of a Lovecraft story in which humans prevail over quasi-cosmic forces. Does its "happy" ending make you like the story more or less?
- This story utilizes the occult and magic as supernatural elements that occur in the natural world. Does that make it more or less effective for you than stories that happen completely within the "normal" boundaries of the natural world? Do you see "magic" as an undiscovered part of the natural world, something supernatural, or something else?
- Sentinel Hill, with its Stonehenge-like ring of ancient standing stones, is a prominent location in this story. Such megalithic structures are not uncommon in New England, and some of them are thousands of years old. Is Lovecraft using the stones of Sentinel Hill as pure set dressing, or do you think they have actual story significance?

THE WHISPERER IN DARKNESS

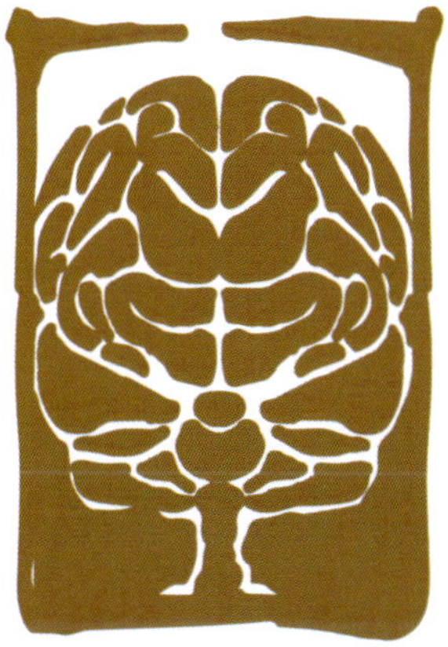

OVERVIEW

This 26,000-word story was written in the spring and summer of 1930 and first published in the August 1931 issue of *Weird Tales*. The story was principally inspired by visits Lovecraft made to the Green Mountain region of southern Vermont, first in 1927 and then again in the summer of 1928. His visits made a powerful impression on him (see "The Wilds of Vermont" entry in Setting/Motifs). When southern Vermont suffered flooding of historic levels in November 1927, he incorporated the floods into his tale.

> In my unfinished "Whisperer in Darkness" I have the idea of transplanted brains kept in metal cylinders for interplanetary transportation, and connected with speaking machines when arrived at their destinations… Thus a person becomes like a phonograph record… I must whip this yarn into final shape soon.
>
> *H. P. Lovecraft to Clark Ashton Smith, September 11, 1930*

While generally considered a horror story, *The Whisperer in Darkness* is also a seminal work of science fiction, using several tropes that would become hallmarks of the genre: alien invaders, disembodied human brains, and weird science. The reveal made by Wilmarth in the story's final sentence is a technique used by Lovecraft on several occasions. Ample foreshadowing helps most readers figure out what is to come. Lovecraft's "revelation" in the final sentence is not intended to be a surprise to the reader, but rather to chill the reader by confirming a conclusion already reached.

STORY SUMMARY

Chapter I

Following extensive flooding in Vermont in 1927, newspapers report a number of sightings of strange creatures—giant, pinkish, crab-like things—washing up in river debris. Albert Wilmarth, a professor of folklore at Miskatonic University, writes to newspapers explaining that a long tradition of folklore in the region is responsible for what these farmers think they are seeing in the floodwaters. He believes there is a perfectly natural explanation for everything.

Chapter II

A farmer from the region, Henry Akeley, sends a long private letter to Wilmarth explaining, in detail, that the creatures are real, and he has collected substantial evidence, including photos of their strange footprints. More letters from Akeley, combined with the photos, pique Wilmarth's curiosity, and he begins to think there might be more to these sightings than he presumed.

Chapter III

Akeley laments that locals, like the farmer Walter Brown, have been conspiring with the creatures and interfering with his mail. Akeley arranges to send Wilmarth a wax-cylinder recording he made of the creatures having a conversation with a refined-sounding gentleman. It is all very strange. Akeley also attempts to send Wilmarth a ritual stone belonging to the creatures. The shipment is apparently interfered with and never arrives in Arkham.

Chapter IV

More letters from Akeley describe that he is under siege now from the hill creatures who regularly attack his guard dogs and cut his phone lines. There have been actual exchanges of gunfire. Akeley urgently warns Wilmarth not to get involved any further in the matter.

Chapter V

A new letter from Akeley (typed, not handwritten) begs Wilmarth to forget about all the "silly" things he has been writing. The creatures, rather than being terrifying, are misunderstood and wondrous. In a conspicuous reversal of attitude, Akeley encourages Wilmarth to pay him a visit in Vermont and to bring the evidence along so they can discuss it together. Wilmarth notices that Akeley misspells his own name at the end of the letter, but chalks it up to him being unused to a typewriter.

Chapter VI

Wilmarth accepts Akeley's invitation and travels by train to Vermont. At the station, he is met by a Mr. Noyes, who identifies himself as a friend of Akeley's. Noyes explains that Akeley is unwell and was unable to make the drive to the station. Noyes drives Wilmarth out to the lonely Akeley farmhouse. After going in first to make sure Akeley is ready, he tells Wilmarth to let himself in, as Akeley is expecting him, and Noyes leaves. Alone, Wilmarth enters the farmhouse.

Chapter VII

Wilmarth at last meets the sickly-looking Akeley, who is seated in a chair in his dim living room, strangely wrapped up in a dressing gown and scarf. Akeley whispers a greeting to his guest and claims he has terrible asthma, which requires him to stay cloaked in the dark, but says he looks forward to their chat. Wilmarth takes a break to unpack and have a snack, then returns to the living room. There, Akeley reveals the true nature of the hill creatures: They are a scientifically advanced extraterrestrial species, more like a fungus than any other form of Earth life. They originate from outside our solar system but have a base on an as-yet-undiscovered planet out past Neptune called Yuggoth. Akeley says now that he understands them, they have his respect and admiration. In his strange whispering voice, he reveals numerous awesome cosmic secrets he has learned from the creatures.

When Wilmarth has trouble believing Akeley's tale, Akeley points to a hutch in the room on which there are several metal cylinders and some strange machinery. At Akeley's direction, Wilmarth hooks up a cylinder labeled "B-67," and he activates the equipment. He is startled to hear a strange, mechanical voice speak. The voice claims to be that of a human brain, removed from its body and stored in the cylinder. In this condition, it can live forever and join the creatures on incredible journeys to the farthest reaches of the universe. The voice says there are many such cylinders in a nearby cave where the creatures live, including some that contain brains of nonhuman intelligence. Akeley confirms all this and says he plans to let the creatures put his own brain in a cylinder so he can also share their travels. He hopes Wilmarth will join them. Rattled, Wilmarth turns off the equipment and returns to his bedroom upstairs to think.

Chapter VIII

Wilmarth describes his hasty, terrified flight from the Akeley farm. He also tells of the discovery of a new planet out past Neptune, which the astronomers call Pluto. He then recounts the events that precipitated his terrified departure.

From his room, Wilmarth had been awakened by a whispered conversation downstairs between Akeley, the mechanical-cylinder voice, Mr. Noyes (whom he recognized as the voice on the wax-cylinder recording), and other strange buzzing voices, all apparently plotting his demise. Once the voices stopped, Wilmarth snuck downstairs and discovered Noyes asleep on a couch. He returned to the living room, expecting to find Akeley, but in his place on the chair was what appeared to be Akeley's face and hands, cast aside along with the wrappings. The whisperer in darkness had not been Henry Akeley at all. Wilmarth fled into the night.

CHARACTERS/KEY FIGURES

Albert Wilmarth

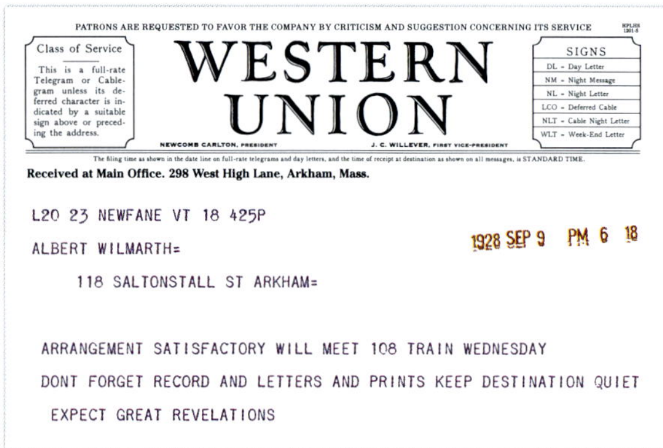
PATRONS ARE REQUESTED TO FAVOR THE COMPANY BY CRITICISM AND SUGGESTION CONCERNING ITS SERVICE

Class of Service

This is a full-rate Telegram or Cablegram unless its deferred character is indicated by a suitable sign above or preceding the address.

WESTERN UNION

NEWCOMB CARLTON, PRESIDENT J. C. WILLEVER, FIRST VICE-PRESIDENT

SIGNS

DL - Day Letter
NM - Night Message
NL - Night Letter
LCO - Deferred Cable
NLT - Cable Night Letter
WLT - Week-End Letter

The filing time as shown in the date line on full-rate telegrams and day letters, and the time of receipt at destination as shown on all messages, is STANDARD TIME.

Received at Main Office. 298 West High Lane, Arkham, Mass.

L20 23 NEWFANE VT 18 425P

ALBERT WILMARTH= 1928 SEP 9 PM 6 18

118 SALTONSTALL ST ARKHAM=

ARRANGEMENT SATISFACTORY WILL MEET 108 TRAIN WEDNESDAY
DONT FORGET RECORD AND LETTERS AND PRINTS KEEP DESTINATION QUIET
EXPECT GREAT REVELATIONS

Telegram from Albert Wilmarth
PROP FROM THE MOTION PICTURE *THE WHISPERER IN DARKNESS*

Wilmarth maintains the tradition of Lovecraftian first-person narrators. He is an intellectual, a professor of folklore at Arkham's celebrated Miskatonic University. Like Lovecraft, he is both intelligent and well-read but lacks experience in the world outside his scholarly realm. His intelligence and erudition seem to work against him at times, as he tends to rationalize away warning signs that are obvious to the reader. He enters the story as a staunch skeptic, and the events he experiences both terrify him and profoundly shake his conception of the universe. Wilmarth is a classic Lovecraftian "dubious narrator." Much of the story's horror is experienced by him alone; there are no witnesses and there's little material evidence to corroborate his story. It is possible that the horror of the story exists solely in Wilmarth's imagination, not in objective reality.

Henry Wentworth Akeley

Henry Akeley seems to be the perfect correspondent for Albert Wilmarth. Introduced as a farmer in rural Vermont, Akeley quickly demonstrates that he's well educated, intelligent, and thoughtful. The fact that Akeley is seemingly rational, as evidenced by his correspondence with Wilmarth, is a key reason that Wilmarth chooses to engage him in an epistolary conversation. As the horrors close in around him, Akeley is unwilling to leave his family farm, clinging to the last bits of his heritage. Ultimately, he is a tragic figure and a casualty of the alien occupation unfolding around him. His fate remains somewhat ambiguous. While it's all but certain that his brain has been removed by the Mi-Go (see "The Hill Creatures" Key Figures entry on the following page) and placed in a cylinder, it's not clear when that happened, or whether he consented to it. The face and hands left behind on the chair might be his actual remains, but they might be cunning replicas.

Mr. Noyes and Walter Brown

The hill creatures have human allies who work with them, for reasons or rewards we aren't given to understand. The sinister Noyes is one such ally, with a refined Bostonian accent. (The fact that his name is a homophone for the word "noise" may be merely a coincidence.) As henchmen go, Noyes proves ultimately ineffective, literally falling asleep on the job. Walter Brown is another collaborator, a Vermont mountain rustic who keeps Akeley under surveillance and interferes with his attempts to communicate with Wilmarth. When Akeley no longer sees Brown loafing about in nearby towns, he assumes that he killed Brown during one of their gunfire exchanges. This seems to be confirmed by the letter from "Akley," which refers to "the late Walter Brown." Like Noyes, Brown is an unimpressive lackey.

Cylinder B-67

A disembodied, allegedly human brain that communicates with Wilmarth and Akeley, B-67 makes the case on behalf of the extraterrestrials for how glorious it is to be separated from one's body, enabling travel to distant corners of the universe. Its clear and polite manner makes its pitch convincing, but there's something unsettling, too, in its mechanical, emotionless delivery. The reader now faces the same conundrum as Wilmarth: Is a disembodied brain trustworthy?

The Hill Creatures

This species of flying fungi is among Lovecraft's most fascinating creations. Most Lovecraft fans refer to them as "Mi-Go," because they are likened to Himalayan abominable snowmen with the same name. But he never actually names them in the story. They are neither "monsters" nor supernatural in any way—they are a species of beings from another part of the universe who visit Earth. Like the Deep Ones in *The Shadow over Innsmouth*, the Mi-Go seem to seek the status quo: "They will not hurt us if we let them alone, but no one can say what will happen if we get too curious about them."

Lovecraft was contemptuous of the more simplistic anthropoid extraterrestrials that appeared in pulp stories by other writers. He depicts his creatures as both crab-like and fungal, encouraging the reader to envision something very alien indeed. The extraterrestrials seem to have both their own culture and religion, apparently worshipping Shub-Niggurath.

THEMES

Folklore Arises from Truth

Lovecraft frequently explores the notion that folklore has its roots in a distant, all-but-forgotten reality. "The Call of Cthulhu," for example, begins with an epigraph from Algernon Blackwood's novel *The Centaur*:

> Of such great powers or beings there may be conceivably a survival … a survival of a hugely remote period when … consciousness was manifested, perhaps, in shapes in forms long since withdrawn before the tide of advancing humanity … forms of which poetry and legend alone have caught a flying memory and called them gods, monsters, mythical beings of all sorts and kinds ….

In *The Whisperer in Darkness*, the fictional folklorist Eli Davenport collects legends of the hill creatures going back to the indigenous Pennacook tribe. It's worth pointing out that Lovecraft was enthusiastic about the verisimilitude that this notion brought to a story, however, he did not believe it himself.

Ignorance Is Bliss

Many a Lovecraftian protagonist meets his demise as a result of an investigation: whatever else they may discover, the investigators often die or sink into madness. Wilmarth escapes from his investigation relatively unscathed, perhaps because his training as a folklorist has inured him to strange revelations or perhaps because he simply runs away before it's too late. Akeley (not to mention an alarmingly high number of his guard dogs) is destroyed by his encounter with the Mi-Go, which is ironic, since it is Akeley who begs Wilmarth not to investigate the matter. It should be noted that, as with the roots of folklore discussed above, this notion that knowledge leads to destruction is a literary device that Lovecraft used on many occasions but not one of his personal beliefs. He was a big fan of intellectual curiosity and scientific inquiry of all kinds.

The Limits of Human Perception

Lovecraft appreciated that everything humans know about the world around them is distilled through five highly limited senses. As technologies developed, even before Lovecraft's birth, they unveiled different kinds of matter and energy previously unknown to us. Thus, he concluded, it is folly to assume the universe consists only of the things we currently perceive. As a man of both science and imagination, he enjoyed exploring ideas of what other "senses" could exist and what things those senses might perceive. He describes the Mi-Go outpost in Round Hill as having "cylinders of extra-cosmic brains with different senses from any we know." The full set of sensory add-ons to the Mi-Go's brain-cylinder equipment might be extensive indeed. Readers interested in this notion would likely enjoy Lovecraft's short story "From Beyond."

SETTING AND MOTIFS

The Wilds of Vermont

The setting in the Vermont woods is an essential element of the story. Lovecraft lived his entire life in Providence, apart from a brief stint in New York. When he first visited Vermont, he was stunned by the setting:

> It is truly our own ancestral land, without the intrusion of any blood, customs, or devices alien to primal New England. The hills are high and green, the roads narrow and rutted, and the foliage rich and untainted. Everything modern and decadent is left behind as one enters this Arcadian and time-defying elder world, and it is almost possible to imagine a special magical quality in the air, and a deeper, purer blue in the sky ... It is, in truth, a complete realisation of everything I have ever sought in idyllic life and scenery.
>
> *H. P. Lovecraft to Frank Belknap Long, August 1927*

On a literary level, the verdant hills of Vermont were menacing abodes of diabolical backwoods forces, and Lovecraft was eager to include the locale and the locals in a piece of fiction. In 1928 he returned to Vermont, spending two weeks outside of Brattleboro with his friend Vrest Orton. On this trip, he witnessed the damage wrought by the floods of the preceding winter. During his stay, he met with Bert Akley and Arthur Henry Goodenough, locals whose names he incorporated into this story.

Pen Pals

Like Bram Stoker's *Dracula* and Mary Shelley's *Frankenstein*, this tale partly takes the form of an epistolary novel. Much of the story is told via letters between Wilmarth and Akeley. Lovecraft was America's most voluminous epistolarian. Letter writing was a vital part of his life, and some of his missives were seventy or more handwritten pages. A collection of just nine of his letters recently sold at auction for more than $52,000. Lovecraft had many prominent pen pals he never met in person, including Clark Ashton Smith and Robert E. Howard. It's striking to think that when Wilmarth finally meets his pen pal, Akeley, he's really meeting an alien.

The Mind Unencumbered by a Body

Although not the first story about a brain kept alive in a jar of some kind, this tale was an early and influential presentation of that idea. For Lovecraft, the achievements of mankind's intellect were humanity's highest calling. He showed little interest in what people (including himself) did or felt during their lives, believing that ideas and thoughts were the most significant accomplishments. So, for him, there was a very real allure to the Mi-Go's ability to separate a brain from its biological needs and frailties. As a further bonus, Lovecraft imagined that, when a brain is disconnected from its sensory apparatus, it "drops off into a sleep of especially vivid and fantastic dreams." He regularly described having potent and spectacular dreams. The appeal of an existence tied solely to ideas and dreams might horrify most of us, but the notion was uniquely appealing to Lovecraft.

Scientific Immortality

In a few tales, Lovecraft creates characters who are keen to achieve immortality. The immortality they seek, however, is neither supernatural nor spiritual, but practical and scientific. In "Herbert West—Reanimator," a mad scientist tries to preserve life indefinitely via chemistry. In *The Shadow over Innsmouth*, Olmstead is enticed by the notion of becoming a Deep One, a species of creatures that live forever unless killed by violent means. Likewise, when the Mi-Go extract brains and place them in cylinders, they bestow on those individuals an immortality of sorts. According to the disembodied brain B-67, "The brain … is virtually immortal with its mechanical faculties and a limited nourishment supplied by occasional changes of the preserving fluid."

Yuggoth and the Discovery of Pluto

As early as the mid-nineteenth century, astronomers suspected that there might be another planet in our solar system beyond the orbit of Neptune. On February 18, 1930, astronomer Clyde Tombaugh spotted the sought-after planet. Lovecraft was thrilled, describing it as:

> … a thing which excites me more than any other happening of recent times … I have always wished I could live to see such a thing come to light—& here it is! The first real planet to be discovered since 1846, & only the third in the history of the human race! One wonders what it is like, & what dim-litten fungi may sprout coldly on its frozen surface! I think I shall suggest its being named Yuggoth!
>
> *H. P. Lovecraft to Elizabeth Toldridge, April 1, 1930*

He did just that in this story, making Pluto / Yuggoth a local outpost for the Mi-Go.

Not only did Lovecraft honor astronomy, astronomers honored Lovecraft. Following the 2015 discovery of a prominent surface feature on Pluto, NASA conducted an online poll to name it. The winning name? Cthulhu Regio, in honor of Lovecraft. Sadly, the name didn't stick: The feature was subsequently officially renamed Belton Regio in honor of its discoverer, astronomer Michael J. Belton.

Yog-Sothothery ~ Shub and Nyarly

This tale is packed with references to other elements of the Cthulhu Mythos, Shub-Niggurath, in particular. This entity is often considered to be a god by readers of Lovecraftian fiction, but Lovecraft provides very little information about it. He first refers to it in a 1928 collaboration with Adolphe de Castro called "The Last Test," wherein a character proclaims "Iä Shub-Niggurath." Later in 1928, in "The Dunwich Horror," he included a quotation from the *Necronomicon*, again, only saying "Iä Shub-Niggurath." In this story, he is a bit more expansive, including a quotation from an occult rite in which Shub-Niggurath is referred to as "the black goat of the woods with a thousand young." His stories "The Dreams in the Witch House" and "The Thing on the Doorstep" have similar shout-outs to this entity.

Lovecraft incorporated Shub-Niggurath into several of his collaboration stories as well. In an interesting departure, in the story "The Mound," he refers to Shub-Niggurath as "the All-mother," attributing human gender to what is presumably a cosmic entity unlikely to share gender or gender roles used by humanity. Does it matter? Ultimately, perhaps not; the entities of the Cthulhu Mythos were not conceived to be part of a formalized, structured pantheon. Rather, they were created by Lovecraft on a largely ad hoc basis and then deployed in subsequent stories. Further, the characters who engage with Shub-Niggurath and her ilk tend to be deranged cultists whose understanding of the cosmic nature of the beings they worship is limited at best.

In addition to Shub-Niggurath, Lovecraft makes provocative mention of Nyarlathotep, another Cthulhu Mythos fan favorite. This cosmic god was first described in an eponymous short story, written in 1920, and revisited frequently thereafter. His strange, pseudo-Egyptian name comes up on the wax-cylinder recording Akeley sends to Wilmarth: "To Nyarlathotep, Mighty Messenger, must all things be told. And He shall put on the semblance of men, the waxen mask and the robe that hides, and come down from the world of Seven Suns to mock ... " Although its name makes use of the ancient Egyptian suffix "hotep" meaning "peace" or "contentment," the name has no literal meaning in ancient Egyptian. In fact, ancient Egyptians did not use the phoneme "L." Lovecraft said the name came to him in a dream.

"Akeley," whispering in darkness, also mentions Cthulhu and R'lyeh, Yog-Sothoth, Azathoth, the *Necronomicon* and the Pnakotic Manuscripts, and K'n-yan and N'kai, as well as elements from works by Lovecraft's friends, including Hastur (Ambrose Bierce), Tsathoggua, Bran, and L'mur Kathulos (Robert E. Howard), Bethmoora (Lord Dunsany), and the Yellow Sign (Robert W. Chambers). He also drops the name of the Atlantean high priest Klarkash-Ton, a nod to his friend Clark Ashton Smith. This story is a cornucopia of Yog-Sothothery!

NOTABLE QUOTES

"Bear in mind closely that I did not see any actual visual horror at the end."

Lovecraftian protagonists are nagged by self-doubt. Unable to come to terms with the reality of the cosmic horrors they've encountered, they often look for ways to rationalize the mind-blasting things they've witnessed, or at least express them in equivocal terms to give the reader plausible deniability.

"People must be kept away from these hills, and in order to effect this, their curiosity ought not to be aroused any further."

The reader will hear this thought echoed in *At the Mountains of Madness* in Professor Dyer's plea that future scientists avoid Antarctic exploration. It is, of course, a completely self-defeating sentiment. If Lovecraft's characters didn't want to arouse people's curiosity, they should probably just keep their mouths shut completely. But where's the fun in that?

"It gives me great pleasure to be able to set you at rest regarding all the silly things I've been writing you. I say "silly," although by that I mean my frightened attitude rather than my descriptions of certain phenomena."

This is one of Lovecraft's most successful deployments of dramatic irony. Wilmarth reads Akeley's reversal of attitude and finds some comfort in it. For the reader, though, the reversal sets off alarm bells, confirming our fear that all is not what it seems with Mr. "Akley."

"Do you know that Einstein is wrong, and that certain objects and forces can move with a velocity greater than that of light? With proper aid I expect to go backward and forward in time, and actually see and feel the earth of remote past and future epochs."

Einstein published his theory of general relativity in 1915, and, as a science enthusiast, Lovecraft was fascinated by it. Einstein presented a new articulation of the rules that govern the universe, one that challenged the laws of Newtonian physics that preceded it. Lovecraft was eager to violate Einstein's new rules.

"Two or three fanatical extremists went so far as to hint at possible meanings in the ancient Indian tales, which gave the hidden beings a non-terrestrial origin; citing the extravagant books of Charles Fort with their claims that voyagers from other worlds and outer space have often visited earth."

Charles Fort (1874–1932) was a fascinating and difficult-to-understand writer. He wrote four books chronicling weird real-world phenomena, mostly culled from newspaper accounts. He didn't necessarily claim that extraterrestrials had visited Earth, but he didn't rule it out. Whether he was gullible or skeptical, he had a huge impact on lots of speculative fiction.

"Great God! That whisperer in darkness with its morbid odor and vibrations! Sorcerer, emissary, changeling, outsider … that hideous repressed buzzing … and all the time in that fresh, shiny cylinder on the shelf … poor devil…."

Lovecraft had a penchant for the quadripartite description. He uses a similar pattern in describing the Old Ones in *At the Mountains of Madness*—radiates, vegetables, monstrosities, star spawn.

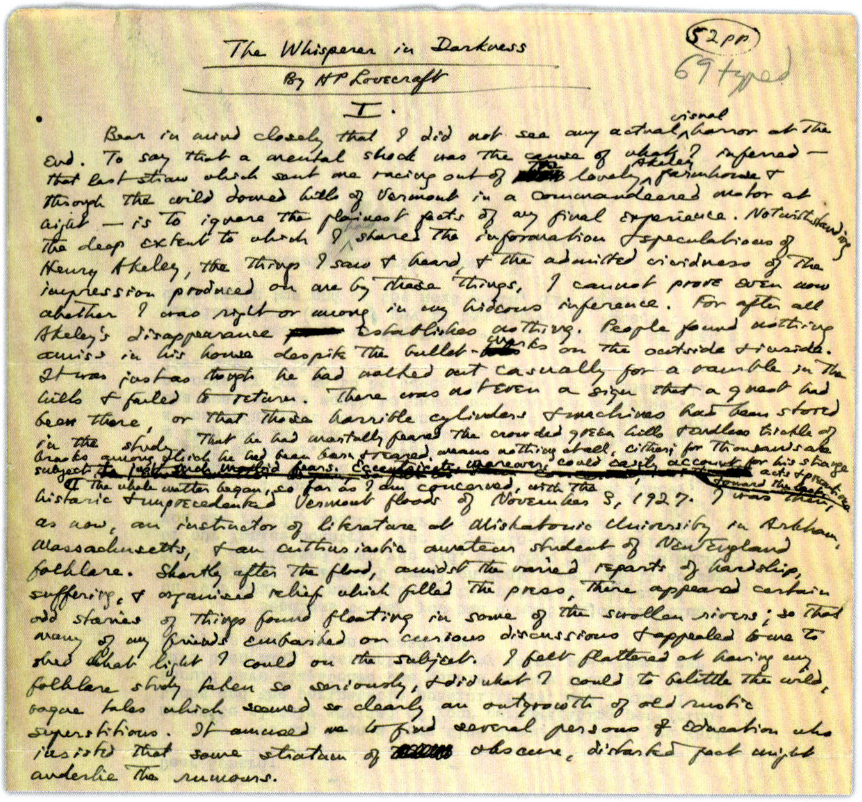

The Whisperer in Darkness

By H P Lovecraft

52 pp.

69 typed

I.

Bear in mind closely that I did not see any actual visual horror at the end. To say that a mental shock was the cause of what I inferred—that last straw which sent me racing out of the lonely Akeley farmhouse & through the wild domed hills of Vermont in a commandeered motor at night—is to ignore the plainest facts of my final experience. Notwithstanding the deep extent to which I shared the information & speculations of Henry Akeley, the things I saw & heard, & the admitted vividness of the impression produced on me by these things, I cannot prove even now whether I was right or wrong in my hideous inference. For after all Akeley's disappearance establishes nothing. People found nothing amiss in his house despite the bullet-marks on the outside & inside. It was just as though he had walked out casually for a ramble in the hills & failed to return. There was not even a sign that a guest had been there, or that those horrible cylinders & machines had been stored in the study. That he had mortally feared the crowded green hills & endless trickle of brooks among which he had been born & reared, means nothing at all, either; for thousands are subject to just such morbid fears. Eccentricity, moreover, could easily account for his strange acts & apprehensions toward the last.

The whole matter began, so far as I am concerned, with the historic & unprecedented Vermont floods of November 3, 1927. I was then, as now, an instructor of literature at Miskatonic University in Arkham, Massachusetts, & an enthusiastic amateur student of New England folklore. Shortly after the flood, amidst the varied reports of hardship, suffering, & organised relief which filled the press, there appeared certain odd stories of things found floating in some of the swollen rivers; so that many of my friends embarked on curious discussions & appealed to me to shed what light I could on the subject. I felt flattered at having my folklore study taken so seriously, & did what I could to belittle the wild, vague tales which seemed so clearly an outgrowth of old rustic superstitions. It amused me to find several persons of education who insisted that some stratum of obscure, distorted fact might underlie the rumours.

Portion of a handwritten Lovecraft manuscript

HOWARD P. LOVECRAFT COLLECTION, JOHN HAY LIBRARY, BROWN UNIVERSITY

Pay no charges to messenger

H P LOVECRAFT
10 BARNES STREET
PROVIDENCE R I

URGENT: DELIVER WITHOUT DELAY

For quick service, reply by bearer

RECEIVER'S NUMBER 26251311264

DATE 26 SEP 1930

TIME FILED 4:19 P.M.

CHECK 248 22M

SENDING STATION: BELLOWS FALLS

TELEGRAM

The World Wide Electrical Printing Telegraph Co. Ltd.

This is a full-rate telegram or electric lettergram unless its deferred character is indicated by a suitable symbol above or preceding the address. The filing time shown in the date line on telegrams and cablegrams is STANDARD TIME at point of origin. FORM HPLHS-001

SYMBOLS: DL=DAY LETTER NL=NIGHT LETTER LC=DEFERRED CABLE NLT=CABLE NIGHT LETTER SR=SHIP RADIOGRAM

DISCUSSION TOPICS

- Is B-67 onto something? Could life as a disembodied brain be as terrific as he makes it sound? Given the opportunity to accept a similar offer, would you opt for immortality as a disembodied brain? Why or why not?
- Do you believe that folklore has its roots in some kind of truth? Or is it the other way around: Do we perceive truth through the filter of myths and folktales we invent?
- Do you think the Mi-Go are a "misunderstood" species of creatures, and that perhaps human interaction with them could be positive? Are you inclined to think they are just manipulating humans to get what they want? Why do you think that?
- Like a lot of Lovecraft characters, Wilmarth starts his account by warning us we'll never believe it, or we shouldn't believe it. Does that make us more inclined to believe it? If we didn't get that warning, would the story seem more plausible, or less so?
- Do you have any pen pals? Have you ever met them in person? Did they turn out to be different in the flesh than they seemed on paper?
- So, what exactly was the "Whisperer in Darkness" that spoke to Wilmarth? Was it a Mi-Go disguised as Akeley? Was it the god Nyarlathotep himself, donning "the waxen mask and the robe that hides"? Whoever/whatever it was, it went to a lot of trouble to have a chat with Wilmarth. Why do you suppose it let him get away?

AT THE MOUNTAINS OF MADNESS

OVERVIEW

Lovecraft's third-longest work, *At the Mountains of Madness* is a 41,500-word novella written in early 1931. This heady tale of a polar expedition gone horribly awry is considered one of his greatest literary achievements, masterfully blending science and fiction in an innovative and unsettling manner. He spends much of his storytelling effort creating atmosphere and cultivating a sense of history rather than developing characters or action sequences.

Lovecraft was a lifelong devotee of Edgar Allan Poe, and this tale pays some homage to Poe's works, including the novel *The Narrative of Arthur Gordon Pym,* a tale of a whaling ship headed to the polar south. Lovecraft was also keenly interested in real scientific explorations of the Antarctic and was inspired by the expeditions of Admiral Richard Byrd, and others. The descriptions of the sociological and political organization of the Elder civilization seem to be inspired by Oswald Spengler's massive work *The Decline of the West,* the first volume of which Lovecraft had read in 1927.

> There is no field other than the weird in which I have any aptitude or inclination for fictional composition. Life has never interested me so much as the escape from life. However—there is a region on the border betwixt weirdness and "scientification" in which I might conceivably experiment. Indeed, the "Mountains of Madness" belongs largely to this type.
>
> *H. P. Lovecraft to J. Vernon Shea, August 7, 1931*

Never one to waste paper, Lovecraft carefully mapped out the plot of *At the Mountains of Madness*, complete with sketches of an Elder Thing, on the inside and outside of a disassembled envelope he pulled from his stack of incoming mail. The story, like many of his others, was written in longhand on the blank back sides of letters he had received.

Lovecraft knew that the story was probably too long to be published in its entirety in a single issue of *Weird Tales*, and expected it to be cut into two parts. When editor Farnsworth Wright rejected it completely, he was bitterly disappointed and let the typescript sit in a drawer for four years. It was Julius Schwartz, acting as the author's agent, who submitted it to the competing magazine *Astounding Stories*, where it was finally published in three parts in early 1936. Although the story got star treatment, including a great cover illustration and interior art by Howard V. Brown, the text was mangled with numerous editorial cuts and typographical errors that so enraged Lovecraft that he later referred to editor F. Orlin Tremaine as "that god-damn'd dung of a hyaena." It would be another fifty years before it was fully corrected by S. T. Joshi and published as Lovecraft intended by Arkham House. This corrected text is used in the companion volumes.

Two years after the original publication of Lovecraft's novella, *Astounding Stories* printed another arresting tale of Antarctic scientists destroyed by a revived ancient shapeshifting creature. Entitled "Who Goes There?" and written by John W. Campbell, this story was later adapted into the classic 1982 horror film *The Thing*, and although there's little evidence Lovecraft's story was a direct influence, *The Thing* remains a remarkably "Lovecraftian" film.

A big-budget motion picture adaptation of *At the Mountains of Madness* has long been the ambition of horror auteur Guillermo del Toro. No studio has yet given the project a green light, despite many A-list people having been attached to it over the years.

STORY SUMMARY

Chapter I

The tale begins with Professor Dyer making a public appeal that a proposed expedition to the Antarctic be canceled. Dyer, a survivor of the ill-fated Miskatonic University expedition, warns that such an expedition poses dangers to humankind. He goes on to provide a full account of the strange and terrible discoveries made by his team on the frozen continent. In Dyer's accounting, the Miskatonic Expedition traveled to Antarctica and set up a base camp. Preliminary excavations using innovative machinery led the team to discover a series of fossils, some of which were particularly puzzling to Professor Lake, the team's lead biologist. With other scientists and graduate students, Lake used two of the team's airplanes to detour to an advance camp to investigate an unexplored region.

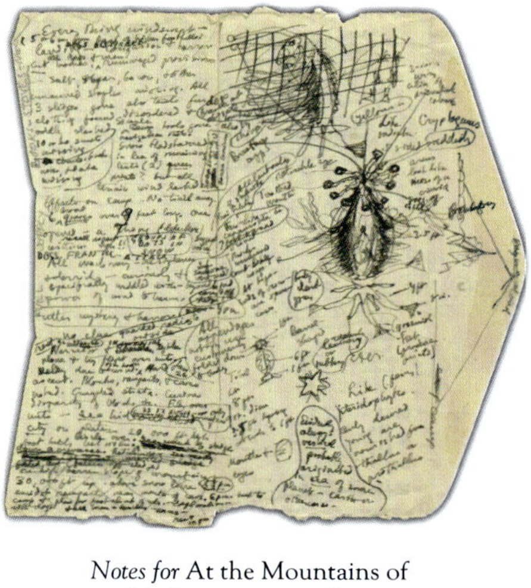

Notes for At the Mountains of Madness *on an envelope*
HOWARD P. LOVECRAFT COLLECTION, JOHN HAY LIBRARY, BROWN UNIVERSITY

Chapter II

Lake arrived at his advance camp on a glacier in the foothills of what might be the tallest mountains on Earth. He sent radio transmissions to his colleagues describing the team's astonishing discovery of a cave containing a seemingly impossible assortment of fossils from many different geologic eras. Among the fossils were strange, leathery, barrel-shaped ones of a species hitherto unknown to man. The entire expedition team was thrilled and amazed.

Chapter III

Unable to reach Lake's camp by radio, Dyer's team mounted a rescue expedition. They arrived at the massive mountains and found the remains of Lake's camp. Everything had been destroyed, and the scientists and sled dogs were dead, save for one of each that was missing. The would-be rescue team decided to report minimal information about the disaster.

Chapter IV

At this point, Dyer begins to reveal facts previously concealed from the public, and the story takes on aspects of a murder mystery. The bodies of the men and dogs had been torn and mangled. From some, chunks of flesh had been cut from the corpses and salted like meat. In Lake's dissection tent, one man and one dog had been methodically dismembered. Supplies and a sled were missing. The damaged fossils of the Elder Ones were buried upright in the snow and marked with curious five-pointed stones. The unburied ones were nowhere to be found. Dyer and graduate student Danforth took the plane up to look for Gedney, the missing man, whom they presumed had gone insane and murdered everyone else. They flew toward the mountains, which appeared to have odd cube-like formations on them, where they heard strange piping sounds. They decided to fly over a pass to view a never-before-seen part of the world.

Chapter V

From their airplane, Dyer and Danforth beheld a vast labyrinth of stone towers and buildings, miles wide, which could only be the remains of a city more ancient than anything previously imagined by mortals. They reconnoitered from the air, taking photographs and keeping sufficient poise to make numerous detailed observations. Then they landed the plane on a smooth snowfield, grabbed some gear, and ventured into the city itself.

Chapters VI—VIII

The quest for the missing Gedney is interrupted by a detailed description of the city of the Elder Things and the mind-blowing bas-reliefs that appear throughout. The history of the Elder Things was told through these complex sculptures, which were of an extremely sophisticated yet utterly alien design. With his geological expertise, Dyer could tell that the stones of the city date from the Jurassic Period—they are roughly 180 million years old. Dyer and Danforth came to realize that the city was built by an intelligent alien species far older than the dinosaurs. The bas-reliefs reveal that all normal terrestrial life, including human life, was created as an accident, or a joke, by these Old Ones. These superintelligent alien creatures bioengineered sentient protoplasm into ideal slave organisms, called "shoggoths," which were enormously strong and capable of changing size and shape to accomplish any needed task. The city itself, and a comparable one in the ocean, were built using the slave labor of the shoggoths. The sculptures chronicled the long decline of the Elder civilization and the rebellion of the shoggoths.

Chapters IX—X

Dyer and Danforth noticed the smell of gasoline and followed it to a chamber of the ancient city, where they discovered supplies from Lake's camp along with sketches that no human being could have made. They came to believe that the missing "fossilized" creatures were not dead at all, but they had been revived and were now roaming the city somewhere ahead of them. The sketches pointed the way to the center of the ancient city, and while attempting to follow them, Dyer and Danforth came across the dead bodies of Gedney and the missing dog, apparently preserved for food.

Chapter XI

The men continued and encountered giant albino penguins living deep below the city. They then discovered the decapitated remains of the living Elder Things and realized that some other monstrous entity must still survive in the city. Suddenly, they heard a terrible piping sound and the strange words "tekeli-li," and a huge shoggoth emerged from a tunnel and bore down on them. They fled in terror.

Chapter XII

As they fled in their plane, they experienced one last horror: the sight of a range of mountains even bigger than the ones they'd seen already and the sounds of more strange piping noises. These were the mountains even the Elder Things and the shoggoths feared. Danforth was driven mad, and the two vowed never to speak of the horrors they witnessed in the ancient city. They returned to Arkham, and Danforth was put in psychiatric care. Dyer made the decision to break his vow in the hopes of preventing another expedition from blundering into the mind-shattering realm of the mountains of madness.

CHARACTERS/KEY FIGURES

Professor Dyer

In typical Lovecraftian style, the character development of our protagonist is virtually nonexistent. Professor Dyer isn't even given a first name (although Lovecraft brought the character back in his 1935 story *The Shadow Out of Time*, where he reveals Dyer's first name as William). Dyer, a professor from Miskatonic University's Geology Department, narrates the story in the hopes of dissuading future expeditions. His role in the story is almost entirely perfunctory; he is there solely to narrate the events. Dyer's expertise in geology proves useful as he grasps the shocking timeframe of the Elder Things, but as a human being, we see very little in his behavior that differentiates him from any other character in the story. We do see one interesting moment of emotional reversal in the story. Initially, Dyer is eager to explore the alien city, while Danforth is reticent. Later, Danforth displays an eagerness to explore, and it is Dyer who gets the proverbial cold feet.

Danforth

Danforth is a graduate assistant at Miskatonic University. Like the professors he works for, he remains a largely undeveloped character, and, like them, he is not given a first name. He is described as "brilliant" and a "great reader of bizarre material," including both the *Necronomicon* and the works of Edgar Allan Poe, and he could be considered a nod to Lovecraft's own young protegé Frank Belknap Long. At the story's end, he attempts to cope with the horrors he has witnessed by mumbling to himself the names of the stops on Boston's subway system. The character gains a degree of human specificity only through the symptoms of his incipient insanity.

Professor Lake

Lake is the expedition's co-leader and head biologist. His numerous breathless radio reports of discoveries raise the excitement of all the members of the expedition, but he pays the ultimate price for the knowledge he gains.

Professor Frank H. Pabodie

Professor Pabodie, a member of Miskatonic's Engineering Department, developed a special ice-melting drill for the expedition. For whatever reason, he is the only character in this story who has a first name.

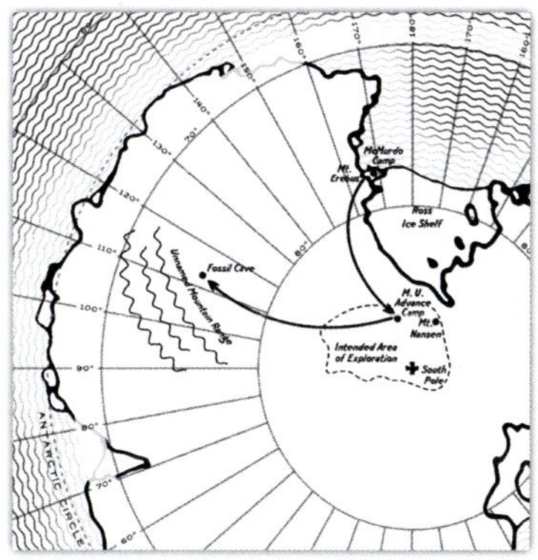

Map of Antarctica

PROP FROM *DARK ADVENTURE RADIO THEATRE®: AT THE MOUNTAINS OF MADNESS*

Gedney

While most of the other characters in the story are vaguely sketched, poor Gedney is little more than a prop. He is killed in the conflict with the Elder Things at Lake's camp, and then neatly butchered and packed on a sledge for future use as food. The discovery of his body provides a potent confirmation of the reader's fear about his fate.

Elder Things

Also somewhat confusingly referred to as "Old Ones," these aliens are among the most fascinating of Lovecraft's creatures. He felt it was important to move away from the idea of aliens being "little green men" or any kind of anthropomorphic entities. His solution was to create bizarre, barrel-shaped creatures with starfish-like appendages at their top and bottom, wings, and a myriad of crinoid-like tentacles to use as "arms." The Elder Things are capable of flight and can live both undersea and upon the land.

But interestingly, Lovecraft gave the Elder Things numerous humanlike psychological traits. They're curious, intellectual, and aesthetically refined. Like humans, they live in cities, make art, and have furniture. Their society is the kind of idealized socialism that Lovecraft admired. And, troublingly, like some human societies, the Old Ones have slaves/servants, here depicted in the form of the loathsome black shoggoths who eventually rebel. It's not much of an intellectual leap to see this relationship between the idealized Old Ones and their rebellious servants as an echo of Lovecraft's own racist views about what he perceived to be the superiority of the Nordic race and his fears of the black "working class" race. The ultimate plight of the Old Ones is a metaphor for

Lovecraft's intolerant fears about the doom facing his own race and class. He was deeply afraid that the place of "his people" would be subsumed by strong, dark races. He bitterly resented the transformation of Providence by immigrants, clinging to an idealized notion that the eighteenth-century world of the English colonists was the pinnacle of history. Of course, Lovecraft always imagined himself as a plantation owner with ample leisure time to pursue his artistic interests, and never as a slave working in the fields. Lovecraft clearly felt great sympathy for his Elder Things, and has Dyer declaring in a moment of insight, "... they were men!"

Shoggoths

The dreaded shoggoths rank among Lovecraft fans as one of his most frightening creations—train-sized blobs of angry sentient protoplasm, capable of generating limbs, eyes, and mouths at will. Made by the Elder Ones, this race of creatures then turned upon their former masters, unleashing violence upon them. While there's no evidence to suggest that Lovecraft intended them to be symbolic, it's easy to imagine that they, in some ways, represented a warped sociological fear on his part. Although shoggoths were subjugated and victimized, Lovecraft's sympathy for aliens does not appear to extend to the shoggoths.

PROP FROM *DARK ADVENTURE RADIO THEATRE*®: *AT THE MOUNTAINS OF MADNESS*

Giant Blind Albino Penguins

The blind albino penguins appear only briefly near the end of the story, and at first blush they can seem a little goofy. But it is interesting to note that in 2017, more than eighty years after Lovecraft wrote this novella, fifty-million-year-old fossils of gorilla-sized penguins *(Kumimanu fordycei)* were discovered in New Zealand. It is a testament to both Lovecraft's imagination and his devotion to science that he accurately foresaw the possibility of such animals, and it offers one more example of why we often say his works are "based on a true story."

THEMES

Cosmic Horror

At the Mountains of Madness proves to be one of Lovecraft's most effective embodiments of cosmic horror. Here, an alien species colonized Earth in a past so distant that almost no trace of it remains. These beings "filtered down from the stars and concocted Earth-life as a joke or mistake"—all life that's ever existed on this planet is a by-product of their tinkering, a mere afterthought.

Utopia

In many ways, the society of the Old Ones represents what Lovecraft himself imagined an ideal society to be. To him, the idyllic society was one where the basic needs of life were met by the government, and citizens were left with ample leisure time for thought and artistic pursuits. Who counts as a "citizen" of this utopia is a thorny question. Lovecraft was not a fan of the concept of democracy, believing that, for government to be successful, decisions and policies needed to be made by experts, not by the ill-educated public.

Universality

The Old Ones are not "monsters" at all. They are, for all practical purposes, human.

Degeneration

Ultimately, the great horror is not the Old Ones but their rebellious servants who now lurk unseen, ready to lash out. This is a manifestation of Lovecraft's fear of the collapse of the order of his idealized eighteenth-century world. In discovering the city of the Elder Things, Dyer and Danforth enter the ultimate physical embodiment of a great society degenerated into ruin. He believed that Western civilization was undergoing a similar degeneration and was heading rapidly toward collapse.

Knowledge Leads to Disaster

There are secrets (lots of them) that humankind is best not knowing.

> We might have known from the first that human curiosity is undying, and that the results we announced would be enough to spur others ahead on the same age-long pursuit of the unknown.... If not dissuaded, they will

> get to the innermost nucleus of the antarctic and melt and bore till they bring up that which may end the world we know. So I must break through all reticences at last—even about that ultimate nameless thing beyond the mountains of madness.

Many Lovecraftian protagonists come to rue the knowledge they have acquired or the price they have paid to acquire it. Lovecraft frequently lets curiosity kill the metaphorical cat (or at least drive it insane).

The Things That Monsters Fear

As with the Flying Polyps in *The Shadow Out of Time*, Lovecraft here shows us monsters and affrightedly hints at the things (shoggoths) and the places (the violet pinnacles) that the Elder Things fear. While he endeavors to build an atmosphere of dread throughout the story, this technique lets him easily suggest, no matter how dreadful the reader may find the scene unfolding, something even worse awaits just beyond.

SETTINGS AND MOTIFS

Antarctica

When this story was written, in the era before satellites and deep-sea submersibles, there were still huge regions of our planet that no human had ever seen, and the interior of Antarctica was one of them. The continent was romanticized somewhat due to the dramatic accounts of the Shackleton and Scott expeditions of the 1910s. American Admiral Richard E. Byrd had concluded his first Antarctic expedition (1928–1930) less than a year before Lovecraft wrote this story. The remote setting gave him a locale where things like Earth's tallest mountains or a vast ancient city in the ice could be plausible.

The Outer Ruins
PROP FROM *DARK ADVENTURE RADIO THEATRE®: AT THE MOUNTAINS OF MADNESS*

The Lost City

The City of the Old Ones is remarkable for the extensive detail in which Lovecraft describes it. He had a passion for both architecture and ancient civilizations, and here he has taken the opportunity to create a fictionalized city of unfathomable antiquity. He paints elaborate images of the Cyclopean stonework, bridges, and domes that once made this incredibly alien place a living and breathing city. The "Cyclopean" stonework to which he refers does not merely mean big; it refers to a specific style of non-mortared stonework best exemplified by the Mycenaean and Inca cultures. We see glimpses of other ancient/alien cities in the Lovecraft stories *The Shadow over Innsmouth*, *The Shadow Out of Time*, "The Mound," and "The Nameless City."

Real Science

In the first third of the story, Lovecraft goes to great pains to introduce many geological and paleontological terms. While some readers (and magazine editors) can find them cumbrous, he believed it was essential to use as much real science as possible to reinforce the story's sense of authenticity and plausibility. It is only after convincing the reader of the reality of the story's events that he begins to factor in stranger and more fantastic elements. Among other cutting-edge science specifically cited by Lovecraft is the theory of continental drift. Although now generally acknowledged, in 1931 this was a relatively new and highly controversial idea.

Real Art

Lovecraft repeatedly compares Antarctic mountain scenery to the paintings of Nicholas Roerich (1874–1947), a prominent expatriate Russian painter of architecture and theosophical subjects. Roerich traveled on an expedition through the Himalayas (1925–29), and Lovecraft was especially captivated by Roerich's paintings of the high mountain region.

Yog-Sothothery ~ Shoggoths and Beyond

Lovecraft loads this story with references and allusions to other fictional works of his own and of his friends. He mentions the *Necronomicon* repeatedly, as well as the Pnakotic Manuscripts, which he first created for the story "Polaris" in 1918. He refers to the *Arkham Advertiser*, one of the daily newspapers of his fictional town. He mentions Kadath, Lomar, and the Plateau of Leng, all fictional places from his various Dreamlands tales. He also mentions Hyperborea, a fictional place from the works of his friends Clark Ashton Smith and Robert E. Howard. He name-checks Albert Wilmarth, the protagonist of *The Whisperer in Darkness*, the story he had written just a year earlier, and he alludes to the Mi-Go that appear in it. He drops the names of Cthulhu, Yog-Sothoth, and even the Colour Out of Space. The story ends with bizarre words lifted directly from Edgar Allan Poe's *Narrative of Arthur Gordon Pym*: "Tekeli-li!"

The most enduring contributions to the Cthulhu Mythos from this story are his unflappable Elder Things and their rebellious servitors, the dread shoggoths. Shoggoths, in particular, have been a fan favorite, appearing in numerous Lovecraftian homages.

NOTABLE QUOTES

"... there are some experiences and intimations which scar too deeply to permit of healing and leave only such an added sensitiveness that memory reinspires all the original horror."

As his characters struggle to grasp the wonders and terrors they have seen, Lovecraft describes the psychology at work in a way that calls to mind post-traumatic stress disorder. A psychological condition that would not be officially named nor diagnosed until 1980, PTSD affects persons who have undergone "a catastrophic stressor that was outside the range of usual human experience." During his lifetime, Lovecraft would have seen the brutalizing effects of the Great War upon soldiers returning home; perhaps his characters' revisiting of previous mental trauma is a callback to shell-shocked war veterans.

"Radiates, vegetables, monstrosities, star spawn—whatever they had been, they were men!"

Dyer recounts the moment when he understands that the "monsters" he's been pursuing through the ancient city are not truly monstrous at all. They are scientists and adventurers, like himself. This idea of depicting ourselves in the monster and recognizing the monster in ourselves was portrayed effectively in Mary Shelley's novel, *Frankenstein*.

"The effect was that of a Cyclopean city of no architecture known to man or to human imagination, with vast aggregations of night-black masonry embodying monstrous perversions of geometrical laws and attaining the most grotesque extremes of sinister bizarrerie."

To communicate the alien nature of the city, Lovecraft busts out one of his favorite adjectives, "cyclopean," and alludes to the same kind of geometric anomalies that he explores in "The Call of Cthulhu."

"It was a terrible, indescribable thing vaster than any subway train—a shapeless congeries of protoplasmic bubbles."

Lovecraft's description of the shoggoth is a superb example of the way he simultaneously describes something while declaring it indescribable. He paints an incomplete picture for us, enticing the reader to fill in the painting with his or her own dreadful imaginings. He gets bonus points for using a word that few people know (congeries), which looks like it's plural, though it is singular. How like a shoggoth! And on top of that, it's a homophone for "conjurees," that is, "those who are conjured"!

"It is absolutely necessary, for the peace and safety of mankind, that some of Earth's dark, dead corners and unplumbed depths be let alone; lest sleeping abnormalities wake to resurgent life, and blasphemously surviving nightmares squirm and splash out of their black lairs to newer and wider conquests."

At the end of the story, Dyer makes his final pitch to dissuade the Starkweather-Moore expedition (and indeed all humankind) from continuing Antarctic exploration for fear of the dreadful things we might discover. As has happened on numerous occasions, his tale turned out to be strangely prescient. Recently, Russian scientists drilled nearly two miles of ice on the polar ice cap to discover a lake with liquid water heated by geothermal vents. In that lake, they have discovered bacteria that have been isolated from the rest of the world for hundreds of thousands of years, if not longer. It is not difficult to imagine that their removal will presage an impending disaster—an idea Lovecraft would have loved.

Pay no charges to messenger

H P LOVECRAFT
10 BARNES STREET
PROVIDENCE R I

For quick service, reply by bearer

URGENT: DELIVER WITHOUT DELAY

RECEIVER'S NUMBER
1631451916321

DATE
22 MAR 1931

TIME FILED
11:13 A.M.

CHECK
88 N=5

TELEGRAM

The World Wide Electrical Printing Telegraph Co. Ltd.

This is a full-rate telegram or electric lettergram unless its deferred character is indicated by a suitable symbol above or preceding the address. The filing time shown in the date line on telegrams and cablegrams is STANDARD TIME at point of origin. FORM HPLHS-001

SENDING STATION:
MCMURDO

SYMBOLS: DL=DAY LETTER NL=NIGHT LETTER LC=DEFERRED CABLE NLT=CABLE NIGHT LETTER SR=SHIP RADIOGRAM

DISCUSSION TOPICS

- Who are the real "monsters" in this story? The Elder Things? The shoggoths? Or the human beings?
- Lovecraft creates his version of an idealized society in the utopian city of the Elder Things. Does their civilization seem idyllic to you? What elements of it do you think Lovecraft yearned for in his own society?
- Lovecraft is vague about the nature of the ultimate horror that lurks within the strange needlelike peaks beyond the Mountains of Madness. Why do you think he introduced this element to the story?

THE SHADOW OVER INNSMOUTH

OVERVIEW

Written at the end of 1931, this 22,000-word story is one of Lovecraft's most popular and enduring tales. It is the only one of his stories to be published in stand-alone book form during his lifetime, issued in a small edition in 1936 by William Crawford, with illustrations by Frank Utpatel. Only two hundred copies were ever bound, making it a prized Lovecraftian collector's item. It was not published in the pulp magazines until 1942, five years after Lovecraft's death.

This is one of the few stories for which initial drafts are still extant. The earlier "discarded" drafts provide an interesting comparison for readers to see the ideas that Lovecraft both developed and abandoned for his final version of the story. As was often the case, even when there were multiple drafts, Lovecraft was not happy with the way the tale turned out, as he expressed in a December 10, 1931, letter to August Derleth:

> [It] has all the defects I deplore—especially in point of style, where hackneyed phrases & rhythms have crept in despite all precautions... I don't intend to offer "The Shadow over Innsmouth" for publication as it would stand no chance of acceptance.

Nevertheless, the story has proven remarkably impactful for fans. The setting of the decrepit seaside town, with its ichthyic residents and sinister cult, seems to provide an endless source of fascination for readers. This story also contains one of Lovecraft's most successful action sequences: the pursuit in the Gilman House Hotel, followed by the narrator's escape from Innsmouth. The sequence is so dramatic that it's been successfully adapted into motion pictures, video games, musical projects, and audio dramas. Late in the story, Lovecraft implies another massive action sequence—the government's raid on Innsmouth—but only through a fleeting offstage reference.

Lovecraft likely took inspiration for this story from a couple of other tales, notably Robert W. Chambers's "The Harbor-Master" and Irwin Cobb's "Fishhead." He was also influenced by a recent trip he had taken to the historical and picturesque Massachusetts town of Newburyport, thirty-five miles north of Boston. He wrote to Clark Ashton Smith on November 20, 1931: "I certainly hope you can get to see Newburyport sooner or later, for its antiquity and desolation make it one of the most spectrally fascinating spots I have ever seen. It has started me off on a new story idea. . . ."

As with "The Call of Cthulhu" and *At the Mountains of Madness*, this story starts with an unnamed first-person narrator saying he's going to reveal the horrible truth, even though he probably shouldn't. It was one of Lovecraft's favorite opening gambits. Although most of the story is told in the first person by the narrator, there are also lengthy sections written as monologues in character voices, including slurred, drunken Yankee dialect.

STORY SUMMARY

Chapter I

The narrator, a young man, embarks on a sightseeing trip along the New England coast to celebrate his coming of age. He stops at the town of Newburyport and visits the local historical society. There he sees on display a strange tiara, oddly wrought of unusual metal and covered with bizarre aquatic motifs. The historian there tells him the piece came from the nearby town of Innsmouth. Innsmouth has a strange history, complete with its own cult. The Newburyport folks try to warn him off, saying Innsmouth folk are unfriendly to outsiders, but this only whets the narrator's curiosity.

Chapter II

The next morning the narrator boards a dilapidated bus and meets the creepy driver, Joe Sargent, who has strange facial deformities that the narrator cannot identify. The narrator describes in rich detail the trip south to the desolate and isolated seaside town of Innsmouth. As they get closer, the narrator sees more strange-looking people lurking in the neglected streets. The bus drops him off at the only hotel in town, the Gilman House. After checking his luggage in the lobby, the narrator interviews the normal-looking clerk at the nearby chain grocery store. The boy shares lots of ominous rumors about the town and its inhabitants, including a very old man named Zadok Allen. He draws a map marked with warnings so the narrator can safely find his way around. The narrator proceeds to explore the city, describing it in detail, until he finally notices an old man whom he assumes must be Zadok Allen.

Chapter III

The narrator plies the half-crazy, half-senile Zadok with bootleg booze, and the increasingly drunken man recounts the secret history of the town. Once a thriving seaport, Innsmouth came under the sway of Obed Marsh, a sea captain who made an unholy alliance with undersea creatures known as the Deep Ones, whom he first encountered on islands in the South Pacific. Marsh traded human victims in exchange for gold and plentiful fishing, and gradually took over the town by means of a cult called The Esoteric Order of Dagon. Those who resisted Marsh and his monstrous allies were systematically eliminated, and things reached a crisis in 1846, when the Deep Ones came up out of the ocean and wiped out all remaining opposition. Zadok says the surviving people of Innsmouth began to interbreed with the Deep Ones, and all of Marsh's children are now half monster. He begins to hint at even more nefarious plans when something terrifies him. He runs away, urging the narrator to get out of Innsmouth as quickly as possible.

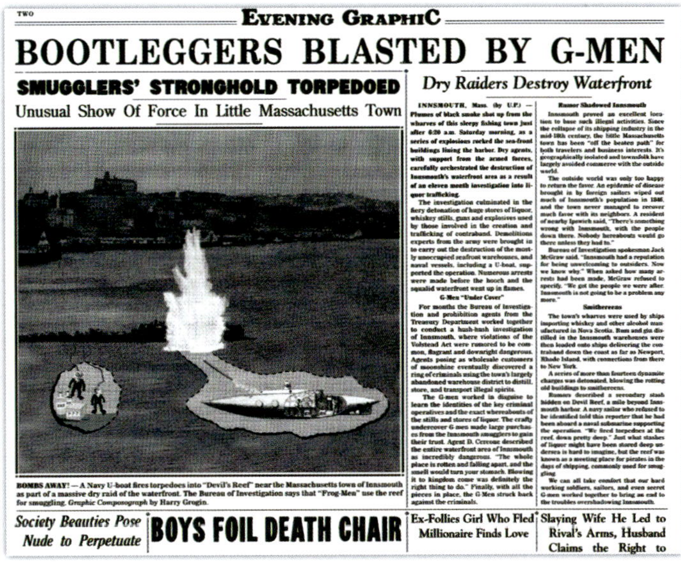

TWO **EVENING GRAPHIC**

BOOTLEGGERS BLASTED BY G-MEN

SMUGGLERS' STRONGHOLD TORPEDOED

Unusual Show Of Force In Little Massachusetts Town

BOMBS AWAY! — A Navy U-boat fires torpedoes into "Devil's Reef" near the Massachusetts town of Innsmouth as part of a massive dry raid of the waterfront. The Bureau of Investigation says that "Frog-Men" use the reef for smuggling. *Graphic Composograph* by Harry Grogin.

Dry Raiders Destroy Waterfront

INNSMOUTH, Mass. (by U.P.) — Plumes of black smoke shot up from the wharves of this sleepy fishing town just after 6:20 a.m. Saturday morning, as a series of explosions rocked the sea-front buildings lining the harbor. Dry agents, with support from the armed forces, carefully orchestrated the destruction of Innsmouth's waterfront area as a result of an eleven month investigation into liquor trafficking.

The investigation culminated in the fiery detonation of huge stores of liquor, whiskey stills, guns and explosives used by those involved in the creation and trafficking of contraband. Demolitions experts from the army were brought in to carry out the destruction of the mostly unoccupied seafront warehouses, and naval vessels, including a U-boat, supported the operation. Numerous arrests were made before the hooch and the squalid waterfront went up in flames.

G-Men "Under Cover"

For months the Bureau of Investigation and prohibition agents from the Treasury Department worked together to conduct a hush-hush investigation of Innsmouth, where violations of the Volstead Act were rumored to be common, flagrant and downright dangerous. Agents posing as wholesale customers of moonshine eventually discovered a ring of criminals using the town's largely abandoned warehouse district to distill, store, and transport illegal spirits.

The G-men worked in disguise to learn the identities of the key criminal operatives and the exact whereabouts of the stills and stores of liquor. The crafty undercover G-men made large purchases from the Innsmouth smugglers to gain their trust. Agent D. Cercone described the entire waterfront area of Innsmouth as incredibly dangerous. "The whole place is rotten and falling apart, and the smell would turn your stomach. Blowing it to kingdom come was definitely the right thing to do." Finally, with all the pieces in place, the G-Men struck back against the criminals.

Rumor Shadowed Innsmouth

Innsmouth proved an excellent location to base such illegal activities. Since the collapse of its shipping industry in the mid-18th century, the little Massachusetts town has been "off the beaten path" for both travelers and business interests. It's geographically isolated and townsfolk have largely avoided commerce with the outside world.

The outside world was only too happy to return the favor. An epidemic of disease brought in by foreign sailors wiped out much of Innsmouth's population in 1846, and the town never managed to recover much favor with its neighbors. A resident of nearby Ipswich said, "There's something wrong with Innsmouth, with the people down there. Nobody hereabouts would go there unless they had to."

Bureau of Investigation spokesman Jack McGraw said, "Innsmouth had a reputation for being unwelcoming to outsiders. Now we know why." When asked how many arrests had been made, McGraw refused to specify. "We got the people we were after. Innsmouth is not going to be a problem any more."

Smithereens

The town's wharves were used by ships importing whiskey and other alcohol manufactured in Nova Scotia. Rum and gin distilled in the Innsmouth warehouses were then loaded onto ships delivering the contraband down the coast as far as Newport, Rhode Island, with connections from there to New York.

A series of more than fourteen dynamite charges was detonated, blowing the rotting old buildings to smithereens.

Rumors described a secondary stash hidden on Devil Reef, a mile beyond Innsmouth harbor. A navy sailor who refused to be identified told this reporter that he had been aboard a naval submarine supporting the operation. "We fired torpedoes at the reef, down pretty deep." Just what stashes of liquor might have been stored deep undersea is hard to imagine, but the reef was known as a meeting place for pirates in the days of shipping, commonly used for smuggling.

We can all take comfort that our hard working soldiers, sailors, and even secret G-men worked together to bring an end to the troubles overshadowing Innsmouth.

Society Beauties Pose Nude to Perpetuate

BOYS FOIL DEATH CHAIR

Ex-Follies Girl Who Fled Millionaire Finds Love

Slaying Wife He Led to Rival's Arms, Husband Claims the Right to

Newspaper coverage of the raid on Innsmouth

PROP FROM *DARK ADVENTURE RADIO THEATRE®: THE SHADOW OVER INNSMOUTH*

Chapter IV

The narrator returns to catch the bus out of town, and he is alarmed to learn the bus has broken down and he will have to spend the night in Innsmouth. He rents a room on the top floor of the Gilman House, where he hears strange, shuffling footsteps in the hall and ominous, croaking noises. As his room suddenly comes under attack, he barricades the door and escapes out a window, fleeing into the night. Roving bands of monstrous fish-frog creatures pursue him, but he manages to get to the outskirts of town, where he sees in the distance the ominous Devil Reef and swarms of Deep Ones. He faints.

Chapter V

The next morning, the narrator walks to the neighboring town without encountering further threats. He goes home and begins to research his own family history. He discovers that he is a descendant of Obed Marsh when his uncle, James Williamson, shows him some old family jewelry that looks very much like the strange Innsmouth tiara he saw in Newburyport. The narrator finally reveals to the reader that years have passed since this trip to Innsmouth, and he intends to return to take his rightful place among the undersea monsters.

CHARACTERS/KEY FIGURES

The Narrator

The protagonist of the story is another Lovecraftian hero who is never identified by name in the text (we learn his intended name was Robert Olmstead through Lovecraft's notes). He is a young man, recently graduated from college, who sets out on a sightseeing trip of antiquarian sites in New England. The narrator shares some characteristics with the author himself, notably frugal travel and dining habits. Olmstead is an atypical character for Lovecraft in a few ways. First, he has a character arc; he ends his story in a very different place emotionally than where he began. While he is of an academic/intellectual bent, he also proves to be a man of action, narrowly escaping an assault on his hotel room and fleeing through the streets of Innsmouth. Through his experience in Innsmouth, he discovers his true ancestry, and in so doing he feels the irresistible compulsion to join his ancestors in the sea.

Zadok Allen

This elderly, alcoholic, and deeply traumatized citizen of Innsmouth disgorges many secrets about the town's past. Zadok gives a spectacularly detailed monologue, providing the historical exposition that makes the story seem plausible. Lovecraft was a teetotaler and didn't have much patience for the intemperate in his personal life. As Lovecraft characters go, Zadok is unusually poignant.

The Ticket Agent

This character is a no-nonsense, no-name railway employee and a fountain of exposition and rumor. He is also a source of unapologetic bigotry, saying "... the real thing behind the way folks feel is simply race prejudice—and I don't say I'm blaming those that hold it. I hate those Innsmouth folks myself, and I wouldn't care to go to their town."

Obed Marsh

Marsh is the Innsmouth sea captain who discovered the South Pacific Islanders who were already engaged in trafficking with the Deep Ones. After trading with them and learning their ways, he eventually brought a Deep One wife back to Innsmouth. Obed created the Esoteric Order of Dagon in Innsmouth and began the practice of interbreeding with the Deep Ones.

The Williamsons

James Williamson is the narrator's uncle and father to Lawrence, the narrator's cousin. Lawrence, a patient in an Ohio insane asylum, has the "Innsmouth look." The narrator plans to break Lawrence out of the asylum so they can fulfill their aquatic destiny together.

THEMES

Ancestral Curse

The notion of being born into a cursed bloodline flourishes here. Olmstead (the narrator) visits Innsmouth without any conscious awareness of his connection to the town, but he discovers from old Zadok Allen he has "the true Marsh eyes." He eventually comes to understand that he has Innsmouth blood and is destined to become a Deep One. Other members of his family are similarly afflicted, one having committed suicide and one being institutionalized. The notion of a familial curse was a compelling concept for Lovecraft, likely having its roots in the fact that both of his parents (for very different reasons) died in Providence's Butler Hospital while receiving care for serious psychiatric maladies. In a fun reversal, Olmstead comes to embrace his fishy destiny.

Miscegenation and Sexual Transgressions

Lovecraft strongly believed that the Nordic races of Northern Europe were superior in nearly every way to all other ethnic groups. He felt it was necessary for races to maintain their "purity," and he was horrified by the concept of miscegenation. He believed the mixing of the races would somehow diminish their vitality. Such opinions about race were much more common a century ago, but this is part of the legacy of racism that makes enjoying Lovecraft so complicated.

Lovecraft's map of Innsmouth

HOWARD P. LOVECRAFT COLLECTION, JOHN HAY LIBRARY, BROWN UNIVERSITY

Lovecraft is generally quite averse to exploring sexuality in his writing (indeed he seems to have been virtually asexual in his personal life) in any overt way. Between his disinterest in human activities and his commitment to presenting himself as a "proper gentleman," he steers clear of primal passions and untoward behaviors in his tales. When he does write about sex, it usually involves humans copulating with monstrous creatures, as in "The Dunwich Horror," "Facts Concerning the Late Arthur Jermyn and His Family," and "The Curse of Yig." This kind of transgression against decency was, for him, potent fuel for storytelling.

Horrors from the Deep

Lovecraft found the ocean to be a source of wonder and fear. Although he lived nearly all his life in Providence, Rhode Island, which sits at the northern end of Narragansett Bay, he was neither a swimmer nor a boater. The smell of fish nauseated him, and he could not abide seafood. The depths of the oceans teeming with unknown and unseen creatures stimulated his imagination. He wrote this in his 1919 story "The White Ship": "Ocean is more ancient than the mountains, and freighted with the memories and the dreams of Time."

Cults and Superstition

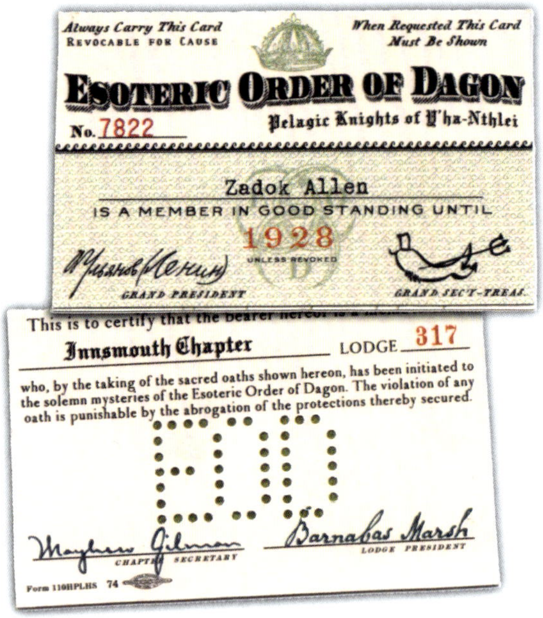

Novelty membership card by The HPLHS

Lovecraft connects the activities of Innsmouth directly to a cult: The Esoteric Order of Dagon. Although he refrains from getting too specific about it, through the cult's rituals and beliefs, the human population of Innsmouth and the Deep One population become hopelessly interconnected. The E.O.D. also serves as an enforcement device, ensuring that citizens of Innsmouth toe the proverbial line and that outsiders are dealt with in a manner that will ensure Innsmouth's secrets are protected. There are many stories in which Lovecraft's antagonists are members of a cult or fringe religious sect. He was an avowed atheist and thought of all human religions as somewhere between a cult and a scam. In his essay "Supernatural Horror in Literature," he wrote: "Much of the power of Western horror-lore was undoubtedly due to the hidden but often suspected presence of a hideous cult of nocturnal worshippers whose strange customs… were rooted in the most revolting fertility-rites of immemorial antiquity."

SETTINGS AND MOTIFS

Innsmouth

The decaying seaside town of Innsmouth, like the town of Arkham, stands out as one of Lovecraft's most vividly realized creations. He invests Innsmouth with tremendous historical and geographical detail, and he even drew a map of it for himself so he could plot out Olmstead's escape. The ominous outcropping known as Devil Reef, which lies just offshore, is equally tantalizing—it is the gateway to unfathomable mysteries. The town has inspired adaptations and sequels in gaming, motion pictures, and music. Subsequent authors have used the federal government's raid on the town, which was only hinted at in the story, as the jumping-off point for additional storytelling.

Y'ha-nthlei

Like the city of the Elder Things in *At the Mountains of Madness*, the cyclopean city of Pnakotus in *The Shadow Out of Time* and the city of Tsath in his collaboration "The Mound," Y'ha-nthlei is a great city built by and for monsters. Rather than being a place of horrors, though, all of these cities are filled with grand, fantastical architecture. Each location presents a sort of idealized urbanization; several of the societies inhabiting his "monster cities" are idealized examples of the kind of benevolent fascistic socialism that Lovecraft admired.

The Collapse of Western Civilization

Lovecraft had a special affinity for the society of mid-eighteenth-century New England. He believed this age, excepting the classical grace of ancient Greece and Rome, captured civilization at its very best. The years after the American Revolution represented, to him, sociological decay and a forfeiture of all that was elegant, graceful, and enduring. He saw the hundred and fifty years of history that preceded his lifetime in Providence as an agonizing collapse, as the city devolved into a pluralistic jumble of immigrants living in a mechanized society bereft of classical architecture.

This perceived collapse of Western civilization is mirrored and amplified in the history of Innsmouth. In the eighteenth century, the town is a prosperous fishing port. But Innsmouth fails to meet the challenges of the nineteenth century, devolving into a hotbed of superstition, miscegenation, and rampant squalor. By the early twentieth century, Innsmouth has become a grotesque shell of its former self and an embodiment of the fate Lovecraft feared was in store for Providence and, ultimately, the rest of Western civilization.

NOTABLE QUOTES

"Thar's whar it all begun—that cursed place of all wickedness whar the deep water starts. Gate o' hell—sheer drop daown to a bottom no saoundin'-line kin tech. Ol' Cap'n Obed done it—him that faound aout more'n was good fer him in the Saouth Sea islands.... Never was nobody like Cap'n Obed—old limb o' Satan!"

This is how the "liquorish nonagenarian" Zadok Allen starts his lengthy monologue revealing the true history of Innsmouth. We are warned he is an unreliable narrator, both drunk and crazy, and Olmstead tries to dismiss everything he says, even though we, as the readers, ironically and instinctively accept his words at face value. When the reader learns that Olmstead may also be an insane and unreliable narrator, the effect is amplified. Lovecraft seldom wrote dialogue, but when he did, he often laid on thick phonetic dialects.

"The sight of such endless avenues of fishy-eyed vacancy and death... start up vestigial fears and aversions that not even the stoutest philosophy can disperse."

Upon viewing the monstrous parade of Deep Ones, Olmstead calls upon philosophy to form a sort of psychological shield against what he is witnessing. Ultimately, though, the horror is so repugnant that no philosophy would be sufficient for the purpose.

"I was not simply the first to succumb to a contagious nightmare hallucination."

As with the quotation above, when philosophy is insufficient to process the horror being witnessed, the next step is to dismiss the horror by categorizing it as a hallucination. It would be even more discomforting if such hallucinations were contagious and caught like a common cold.

"Nothing that I could have imagined... would be in any way comparable to the daemoniac, blasphemous reality that I saw—or believe I saw."

Many Lovecraftian narrators grapple with the reality of the monstrous sights they witness.

"And yet I saw them in a limitless stream—flopping, hopping, croaking, bleating—surging inhumanly through the spectral moonlight in a grotesque, malignant saraband of fantastic nightmare."

Only a Lovecraftian protagonist could witness such horrors and deliver the phrase "malignant saraband of fantastic nightmare" to describe them. Such poetic (with an emphasis on the POE) turns of phrase are what endear his writing to his readers—or scare them away forever.

"... together we shall go to marvel-shadowed Innsmouth. We shall swim out to that brooding reef in the sea and dive down through black abysses to Cyclopean and many-columned Y'ha-nthlei, and in that lair of the Deep Ones we shall dwell amidst wonder and glory for ever."

This quote stands out as a rare instance of a Lovecraftian protagonist having been "won over" to the side of the "bad guys." The final sentence is an echo of the Twenty-Third Psalm, which adds a whiff of blasphemy to the shocking conversion.

Pay no charges to messenger

H P LOVECRAFT
10 BARNES STREET
PROVIDENCE R I

URGENT: DELIVER WITHOUT DELAY

For quick service, reply by bearer

RECEIVER'S NUMBER
329311521

DATE
3 DEC 1931

TIME FILED
2:50 P.M.

CHECK
92 C=10

TELEGRAM

The World Wide Electrical Printing Telegraph Co. Ltd.

This is a full-rate telegram or electric lettergram unless its deferred character is indicated by a suitable symbol above or preceding the address. The filing time shown in the date line on telegrams and cablegrams is STANDARD TIME at point of origin.

FORM HPLHS-001

SENDING STATION:
NEWBURYPORT

SYMBOLS: DL=DAY LETTER NL=NIGHT LETTER LC=DEFERRED CABLE NLT=CABLE NIGHT LETTER SR=SHIP RADIOGRAM

DISCUSSION TOPICS

- Do you think that the interbreeding of the Deep Ones with humans is a manifestation of Lovecraft's fear of people of different races intermingling? Do you think modern audiences are applying contemporary perspectives not intended by the author?
- Does the story have a "happy ending" for Olmstead? Is he headed for immortality and a beautiful family reunion? Or is this guy just bonkers?
- Writing in dialects has greatly fallen out of fashion in modern literature. Do you think it adds to the authenticity of the character or just seems phony?

THE THING ON THE DOORSTEP

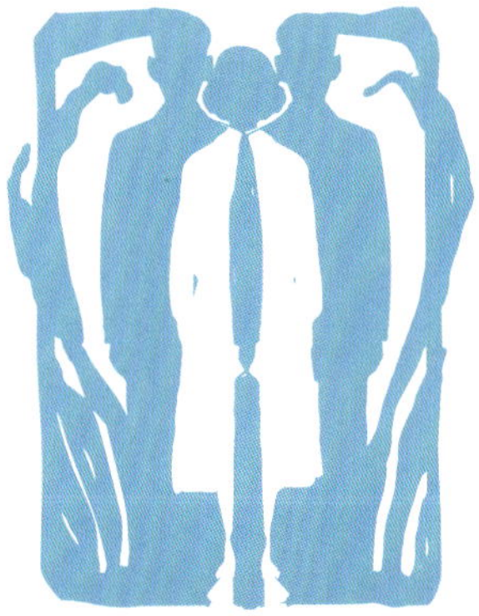

OVERVIEW

This 10,000-word story was written in 1933 between August 21 and 24. Lovecraft was unhappy with the tale and did not originally seek its publication. It remained unpublished until it came out in the January 1937 issue of Weird Tales, just two months before his death.

In his commonplace book, he jotted down a basic plot concept of the story:

> Man has terrible wizard friend who gains influence over him. Kills him in defence of his soul—walls body up in ancient cellar—BUT—the dead wizard (who has said strange things about soul lingering in body) changes bodies with him … leaving him a conscious corpse in cellar.

Lovecraft developed the story into something substantially more interesting. Most noticeably, "The Thing on the Doorstep" features the only significant female character to appear in any of his tales. But Asenath … well, she's not like other female characters. More on this below.

> Glad to hear "Doorstep" did not impress you as being too inadequate—though I still feel a profound dissatisfaction with something about it… I start out trying to find symbols of a certain mood… but when I come to put anything on paper, the chosen symbols seem forced, awkward, childish, exaggerated and essentially inexpressive.
>
> *H. P. Lovecraft to August Derleth, March 4, 1932*

This story was recently adapted into the motion picture *Suitable Flesh*. While the underlying concepts of the story are very much present in the film, it diverges rather drastically from the source material, particularly in its depiction of sex and violence. Like the film adaptation of "The Dunwich Horror," it's hard to imagine that Lovecraft would have enjoyed it.

STORY SUMMARY

Chapter I

The story is narrated after the fact by Daniel Upton. He has shot his best friend, Edward Pickman Derby, and tells the story, attempting to prove that he is not a murderer. Upton recounts his childhood friendship with Derby, a precocious poet, in the days before Upton went on to study architecture and Derby fell in with a group of Bohemian occultists at Miskatonic University.

Chapter II

Derby became involved with Asenath Waite, daughter of Ephraim Waite, an Innsmouth man, now dead, rumored to have possessed occult powers. Derby married the domineering Asenath, and the two took up residence in Arkham's old Crowninshield Mansion.

Chapter III

Upton saw less and less of his old friend, but when they did meet, Derby seemed nervous and frightened, while Asenath seemed increasingly intense. Derby suggested that his wife's occult experiments had "gone too far." Upton wondered if his friend's wife had some kind of remote mesmeric influence upon Derby.

Chapter IV

After receiving a telegram from Maine informing him that Derby had been arrested after stumbling out of the woods like a madman, Upton drove to Maine to rescue his terrified friend. On the return drive, Derby shared his fears that somehow Ephraim had taken over Asenath's mind. Worse still, Derby claimed Asenath was able to take over his mind, even from great distances. Suddenly, in the middle of a panicky rant, Derby's speech and demeanor changed entirely, and he calmly encouraged Upton to forget what he had been saying.

Chapter V

Months later, Derby paid a visit to Upton, and Derby was once again his usual nervous self. He said he and Asenath had had a fight, and that she had left to stay with some horrible friends in New York. He went on to unfold in considerable detail her terrifying practice of swapping her mind with his, taking over his body and leaving his mind trapped in her body. Derby was badly shaken and planned to move out of the mansion back to his old family home now that she was gone.

Chapter VI

Several months later, Derby told Upton he still felt Asenath's will trying to initiate another swap. Derby seemed to be going mad, ranting, "I had to do it… it'll get me… down there in the dark." Upton tried to help by committing Derby to the Arkham Sanitarium. After a few months of treatment, the sanitarium staff notified Upton that his friend had made a sudden recovery. Upton visited and quickly realized Derby was no longer insane, but he was notably not himself.

Chapter VII

The next night, Upton got a phone call from someone with a strange, gelatinous voice, but he couldn't make out who it was. Later, the doorbell rang, and Upton saw a reeking "dwarfed, humped figure" on his doorstep. It tried to speak—sounding like the voice on the phone—and handed him a note in Derby's handwriting. The note begged Upton to "go to the sanitarium and kill it." This confirmed that Asenath was occupying Derby's body, despite Derby having killed her months ago. The thing on the doorstep was Derby in the decomposing body of Asenath Waite.

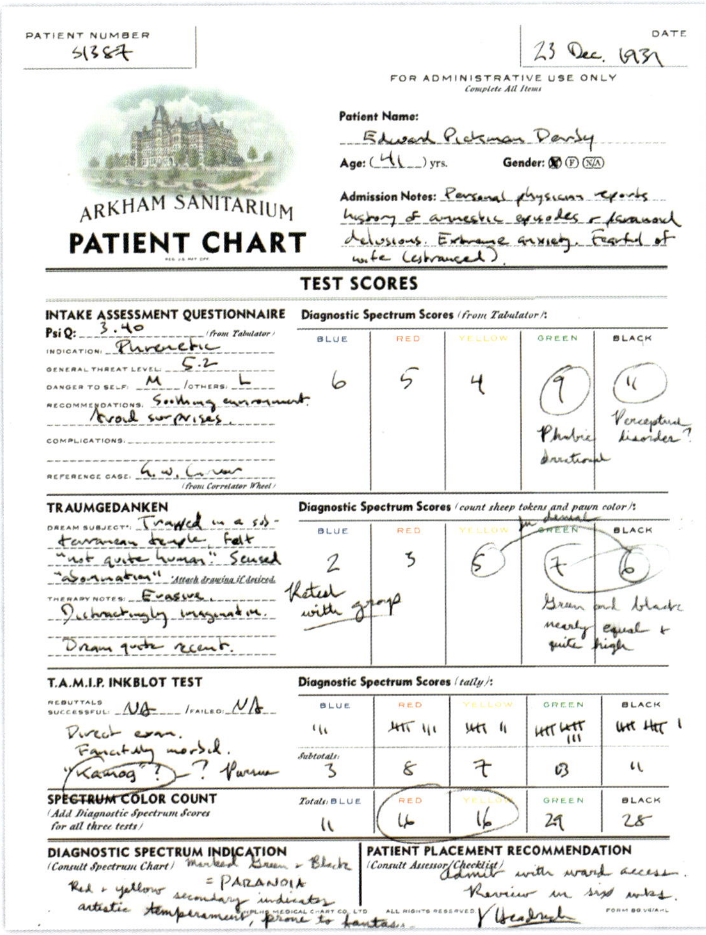

Edward Pickman Derby's Arkham Sanitarium patient chart

PROP FROM *DARK ADVENTURE RADIO THEATRE*®: "THE THING ON THE DOORSTEP"

CHARACTERS/KEY FIGURES

Edward Pickman Derby

There are many parallels between Lovecraft's life and Derby's, represented particularly by the description of Derby as a precocious and "phenomenal child-scholar." Like Lovecraft, Derby marries a woman with a forceful personality soon after the death of his mother. Both are intellectually gifted writers, though Derby is a poet prodigy, rather like Lovecraft's friend Clark Ashton Smith, who published a volume of poetry while still in his teens. Aware of Derby's sensitive nature, Asenath targets him for his "weak will."

Daniel Upton

As the story's narrator, Upton stands out among Lovecraftian characters for having an uncommonly strong emotional bond to a friend. Beyond this though, the author invests his protagonist with little in terms of character development. The only distinct character work seems to have gone into Derby and Asenath.

Asenath Waite

While Asenath is the antagonist in the story, the character we meet is her father, Ephraim, who has killed his daughter and overtaken her body before the story even begins. She's described as attractive "except for overprotuberant eyes; but something in her expression alienated extremely sensitive people." The alienation is likely due to the fact that it's Ephraim looking out through her eyes (and possibly due to the fact she hails from Innsmouth). Many readers find it vexing that Lovecraft's most significant female character is another man who happens to be occupying the physical form of a female. The name "Asenath" is biblical, from Asenath, the daughter of Potiphera in the Book of Genesis.

Ephraim Waite

Ephraim also bears a name from the Book of Genesis. Weirdly, Ephraim is the second son of Joseph ben (son of) Jacob and a woman named Asenath (this would appear to be a coincidence). Ephraim is the same kind of occultist patriarch as Old Whateley in "The Dunwich Horror." Unlike with Old Whateley, Ephraim's motives are not made clear to the reader. Ephraim appears eager to avoid his own death by taking over the bodies of his daughter and others, but the ultimate point of his nefarious plotting is left to the reader's imagination. He was rumored to be able to conjure up storms at sea, for whatever that's worth. He comes from Innsmouth, and there's an implication that his wife (Asenath's mother) was a Deep One.

THEMES

Body Swapping

This story is yet another experiment in which Lovecraft plays with the concept of transferring psyches from one body to another. We see minds removed from their bodies in *The Whisperer in Darkness*. We see Curwen pass himself off as Charles in *The Case of Charles Dexter Ward*. In *The Shadow Out of Time*, Lovecraft uses the "swapping" plot device to replace Peaslee's mind with an alien one. Here, he uses an amalgam of these ideas, allowing Ephraim's mind to move into Asenath's, permitting Ephraim to take over Derby's body to the degree that he could pass as Derby in the world.

Willpower

Ephraim's scheme is wholly reliant on having dominant power over the will of another individual. Presumably, Ephraim targets his daughter due to her inability to fend off his psychic attacks. Once Ephraim has moved into Asenath's body, he sets out to identify a suitable male host with "a fine mind and a weak will." Always one to opine from an egocentric basis, Lovecraft generally held men to be superior to women, but toward the end of his life he relented ever so slightly, saying in an October 1934 letter to Clark Ashton Smith, "The feminine mind … is probably but little if any inferior in total quality."

SETTING AND MOTIFS

Arkham and Miskatonic University

By the time he wrote "The Thing on the Doorstep," Lovecraft seems to have grown so familiar with his own fictional locales that he refers to them and assumes the reader will know what he's talking about. If this was the first Lovecraft story you ever read, some of those references might go right over your head, but that's part of what makes the Cthulhu Mythos so compelling.

While still alive in his own body, Ephraim Waite was known to have consulted the occult books in Miskatonic's library. As a student at the university, Asenath studies medieval metaphysics and joins a group of like-minded "sophisticates." Subsequent authors have embraced this idea, imagining all kinds of specialty courses offered by the legendary university. By the time he wrote this story, Lovecraft was a forty-three-year-old man living at 66 College Street in Providence, right next door to the John Hay Library and near fraternity houses belonging to Brown University. Living so close to the Brown campus might have colored his perceptions, as his descriptions of college students in this story are far from flattering.

Edward Derby winds up confined in Arkham Sanitarium. The sanitarium's name may make readers who are fans of Batman comics think of Arkham Asylum. That is a valid connection. DC Comics writer Denis O'Neil created Arkham Asylum, which first appears in October 1974 in *Batman* #258, as a deliberate nod to Lovecraft's work. Lovecraft, however, never mentions such a place. His works reference the Arkham Sanitarium and Sefton Asylum.

Sexuality

Lovecraft seems to have largely been an asexual person. In a memoir, his wife, Sonia Davis, confirmed that they had sexual relations during their two-year marriage but, for the most part, sexuality is a topic that holds little interest for Lovecraft either in his literary creations or his personal life (as documented in his voluminous correspondence). When sexuality does emerge in his writing, it often manifests in peculiar ways: humans interbreeding with Deep Ones, for example, or Lavinia Whateley coupling with Yog-Sothoth. Some critics have seen sexualized imagery in some of his imagined creatures with their gaping maws and slithering tentacles, but if Lovecraft thought of them that way, it seems to have been only subconsciously.

In "The Thing on the Doorstep," however, Lovecraft creates the bizarre situation of Edward Pickman Derby on his honeymoon having marital relations with his father-in-law, Ephraim Waite, who has taken over his daughter's body. Lovecraft does not (luckily for us, perhaps) explore this strange ménage, but given the circumstances he's set up, Derby's journey is that much stranger. Incidentally, the author and his bride spent their honeymoon frantically retyping a story he had just misplaced. According to Sonia, they finished the job too exhausted to do anything else.

Some have wondered if Lovecraft was homosexual. At times, he exhibited what might be called a "crush" on another man. He gushed rhapsodically about his first meeting with his friend Vrest Orton, and later he also appeared to have a crush on his much younger protege, Robert H. Barlow (who was gay). That said, there's no real evidence to suggest that either relationship was anything more than platonic. Lovecraft had friends and acquaintances who were more or less openly gay, and he seems to have been uncomfortably tolerant of that aspect of their lives, but he was not gay friendly. If he was in the closet, that door was shut tight. The most accurate appellation for him would probably be "asexual."

Yog-Sothothery ~ Nameless Cults

Lovecraft sprinkles many Mythos elements throughout this story without relying upon them as plot devices. He compares Derby to Justin Geoffrey, another fictional poet character created by Lovecraft's friend Robert E. Howard in "The Black Stone." The book of poems Derby writes is entitled *Azathoth and Other Horrors*. Lovecraft mentions the *Necronomicon*, as well as the *Book of Eibon* and *Unuassprechlichen Kulten*, other fictional grimoires invented by his friends. On his terrifying trip to Maine, Derby calls out the name Shub-Niggurath and apparently visits a pit full of shoggoths. But ultimately, the horror here comes from Derby's wife. Or father-in-law. Either way, it's familial horror.

NOTABLE QUOTES

"Witch-cursed, legend-haunted Arkham, whose huddled, sagging gambrel roofs and crumbling Georgian balustrades brood out the centuries beside the darkly muttering Miskatonic."

This is one of the most famous quotes about the fictional town of Arkham. A gambrel roof changes the angle of its slope about halfway up, like a classic barn roof. Lovecraft loved architecture and couldn't say enough about different kinds of roofs.

"It is true that I have sent six bullets through the head of my best friend, and yet I hope to shew by this statement that I am not his murderer."

This an example of one of Lovecraft's terrific opening sentences. It immediately piques the reader's curiosity: How could this be true? Consequently, the reader must read on to resolve this conundrum.

"'I hope you'll forget my attack back there, Upton,' he was saying. 'You know what my nerves are, and I guess you can excuse such things. I'm enormously grateful, of course, for this lift home.'"

Ephraim/Asenath speaks as Edward Derby, attempting to cover up the real Derby's recent panic after his terrifying trip to Maine. It is a masterpiece of understatement. This story has more dialogue than is usual for one of Lovecraft's first-person narrator tales, and none of the characters speaks in phonetic dialect. They do, however, have a kind of hard-boiled 1930s movie vibe.

"glub . . . glub . . . glub. . . ."

This is all that poor Derby can say after he's been trapped in the decomposing body of his "wife." You know things are bad when the infamously verbose author is reduced to repeating monosyllables, clumsily onomatopoetic ones, at that.

"There are black zones of shadow close to our daily paths, and now and then some evil soul breaks a passage through. When that happens, the man who knows must strike before reckoning the consequences."

This is a classic summation that applies to any number of Lovecraft's stories.

Pay no charges to messenger

H P LOVECRAFT
66 COLLEGE STREET
PROVIDENCE R I

For quick service, reply by bearer

URGENT: DELIVER WITHOUT DELAY

RECEIVER'S NUMBER 201521161
DATE 24 AUG 1933
TIME FILED 12:43 P.M.
CHECK 85 P=2
SENDING STATION: ARKHAM

TELEGRAM

The World Wide Electrical Printing Telegraph Co. Ltd.

This is a full-rate telegram or electric lettergram unless its deferred character is indicated by a suitable symbol above or preceding the address. The filing time shown in the date line on telegrams and cablegrams is STANDARD TIME at point of origin. FORM HPLHS-001

SYMBOLS: DL=DAY LETTER NL=NIGHT LETTER LC=DEFERRED CABLE NLT=CABLE NIGHT LETTER SR=SHIP RADIOGRAM

DISCUSSION TOPICS

- Some fans find it infuriating that the only significant female character Lovecraft ever created isn't, in fact, female. Did this bother you? Do you think it's a manifestation of his deeper issues with sex and gender?
- From a dramatic perspective, whose story is this? Is it a tale about Daniel Upton grappling with his weird friend Edward? Or is it about Edward grappling with his weird wife/father-in-law?
- If you were a student at Miskatonic University, what classes would you want to take?

THE SHADOW OUT OF TIME

OVERVIEW

This 25,000-word story, written during the winter of 1934–35, is Lovecraft's final major work. It was published as the cover story of *Astounding Stories* in June 1936.

This story is a fascinating early take on the theme of alien abduction that would become popularized in the 1970s and beyond. The aliens here are not visitors from outer space, but a species of creatures capable of abducting a human through time travel. They're able to swap out the mind of a modern-day person with a mind from one of their own that lives hundreds of millions of years in the past. The swap is eventually reversed, leaving behind a very confused human to grapple with the absence of his own psyche, an unexpected return, and sometimes a very strange recollection of living long ago in an alien body.

Part of Lovecraft's inspiration for the story was probably the novel *Lazarus* by Henri Béraud, which he had read in 1928. It features a man who develops amnesia and an alternate personality. Another influence was the 1933 motion picture *Berkeley Square*. The film involves a man who undergoes a mind swap with an eighteenth-century ancestor, and Lovecraft enjoyed it thoroughly. (The movie starred Leslie Howard, who looked a bit like a more handsome Lovecraft, which might have added to Lovecraft's appreciation.) After a subsequent viewing of the film, he noticed some plot holes. Perhaps he was trying to fix them in his own take on the idea.

As noted by Lovecraft scholars S. T. Joshi and David E. Schultz, Lovecraft's "Notes on Writing Weird Fiction" states, "Conflict with time seems to me the most potent and fruitful theme in all human expression." Despite writing multiple drafts of *The Shadow Out of Time*, Lovecraft was never satisfied with the result and deemed the tale unworthy of the effort it would take for him to type the manuscript. His young friend Robert H. Barlow took on this job, doing his best to decipher Lovecraft's handwriting. The typescript was eventually submitted to F. Orlin Tremaine, the editor of *Astounding Stories*, by another of Lovecraft's young friends, Donald Wandrei. Lovecraft was lucky to have so many admiring friends who had his back. His original handwritten first draft of the story, including illustrations of the Great Race, is in the collection of the John Hay Library at Brown University and can be seen online in the Brown Digital Repository.

STORY SUMMARY

Chapter I

Nathaniel Wingate Peaslee, a professor of economics at Miskatonic University, collapses during a lecture. When he awakens, he is physically awkward and has amnesia, along with a distinct change in personality. He seems like a stranger to his wife and children, who are so freaked out that they eventually leave him. His new personality doesn't appear to care about his family having deserted him. After they leave, he spends his time traveling and studying obscure, old books and remote locations. Five years later, he collapses again. His original personality returns to his body with no recollection of anything that has happened in the preceding five years.

Chapter II

Peaslee valiantly tries to put his life back together. He explores medical histories and finds rare instances of others who have experienced virtually identical symptoms. During these episodes, their "secondary" personality displayed a voracious intellect and an affinity for a wide array of subjects, the same behavior as Peaslee's "other" self. He believes the whole experience was some kind of exchange. He suffers intense and strange dreams, which contain a hint of memories that he can't quite grasp.

Chapter III

As the dreams become more acute, Peaslee embraces the subject of psychology to better understand himself. His youngest son, Wingate, the only member of his family who will have anything to do with him, also studies psychology. Peaslee discovers a myth about creatures from tens of millions of years ago, known as the Great Race. They mastered the secret of time and the ability to swap their consciousnesses with those of beings living in other eras. He decides that his secondary self must have learned of such myths, and the knowledge lingered in his consciousness. Peaslee then rejoins the faculty of Miskatonic University, now as an instructor in the Psychology Department.

Chapter IV

Peaslee's vague dreams give way to more vivid ones in which he sees the horrid cone-shaped bodies of the Great Race. He sees them moving about in a bizarre library-like room, and then looks down and realizes that he *is* one of them. In the dreams, he communicates with other cone-shaped creatures, discovering that their minds come from different epochs of human history. He learns more and more about his dream life amid the Great Race of 150 million years ago. While living among his cone-shaped colleagues, he writes his life story in a volume for the Great Race's library. He also learns of the dreaded creatures they feared.

Chapter V

Peaslee writes what he's learned about himself as a case study for a psychiatric journal. He includes sketches of buildings he dreamed about. A prospector in the Australian outback sends photos to Peaslee of giant stone blocks that look exactly like the dream buildings he sketched. Together with fellow Miskatonic faculty members (including William Dyer, who appeared in *At the Mountains of Madness*), he mounts an expedition to travel to the Great Sandy Desert in Australia to investigate the ruins. The expedition finds an impossibly ancient city that matches Peaslee's dreams.

Chapter VI—VII

Following a massive sandstorm, Peaslee wanders off alone into the subterranean ruins of the city. Driven by a strange compulsion, he makes his way deep into the site—a place he feels he's been before. He plunges ever deeper until he crosses the dusty floors to the ancient library, which he recognizes from his dreams. Marks in the dust suggest something has moved through these long-dead halls in recent times.

Chapter VIII

Driven by his waking memories, Peaslee heads to a specific shelf in the library of the Great Race and removes a volume he somehow knows. He looks at the book and reels at its contents (without revealing what he sees to the reader). He then takes the volume and heads for the surface. His ascent attracts the notice of some monstrous unseen thing. It pursues him and he runs wildly, barely making his way out of the ruins and up into the outside world. Having lost the book during his escape, he confirms that the book was written millions of years ago, by him, in his own handwriting.

CHARACTERS/KEY FIGURES

Nathaniel Wingate Peaslee

Peaslee's psychological complexity makes him remarkable among Lovecraftian characters. Perhaps more than any other protagonist Lovecraft created, Peaslee's rich and complicated motivations, relationships, and emotional life drive the action.

Many characters in Lovecraft's works are afflicted by madness, but Peaslee is the only one to assiduously attempt to study and understand his own psychological ailment. Much of the story's dramatic tension comes from Peaslee grappling with whether

RKHAM

SATURDA

PEASLEE RECOVERING

Miskatonic Professor Fell Unconscious While Teaching Class.

SUFFERING FROM AMNESIA.

May 15.—Nathaniel Wingate Peaslee, a popular professor of Economics in Miskatonic University, is recovering at home to-day after falling unconscious while teaching a class.

Prof. Nathaniel Peaslee
Miskatonic University

Professor Peaslee in the press
PROP FROM *DARK ADVENTURE RADIO THEATRE®: THE SHADOW OUT OF TIME*

what happened to him took place or it is something he has imagined. Lovecraft generally doesn't show much interest in the emotional states of his characters, but here, he explores Peaslee's journey from a place of sympathy and compassion. The story reaches its climax as Peaslee attempts to come to terms with the disturbing truth about his amnesia.

Wingate Peaslee

Of Nathaniel Peaslee's three children, Wingate differentiates himself by being the only one who is confident that his father will recover from his illness. Later, Wingate pursues a degree in psychology, presumably to better understand his father's condition. Wingate shows a level of filial devotion that's uncommon in Lovecraft's stories, traveling all the way into the desert of Western Australia to try to help his father find the truth. This is the only instance of a significant father–son relationship in Lovecraft's works.

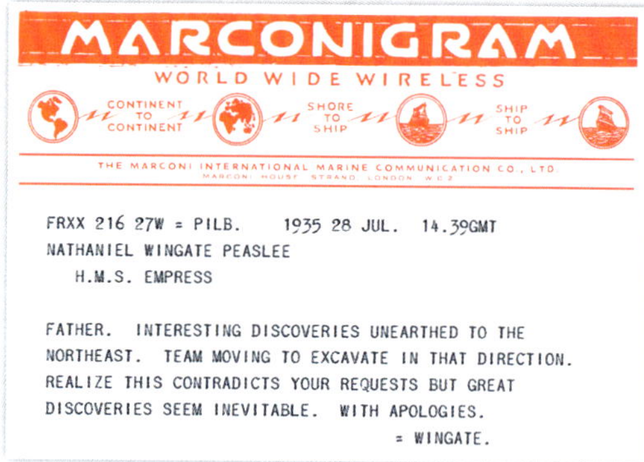
MARCONIGRAM
WORLD WIDE WIRELESS
CONTINENT TO CONTINENT — SHORE TO SHIP — SHIP TO SHIP
THE MARCONI INTERNATIONAL MARINE COMMUNICATION CO., LTD

FRXX 216 27W = PILB. 1935 28 JUL. 14.39GMT
NATHANIEL WINGATE PEASLEE
H.M.S. EMPRESS

FATHER. INTERESTING DISCOVERIES UNEARTHED TO THE NORTHEAST. TEAM MOVING TO EXCAVATE IN THAT DIRECTION. REALIZE THIS CONTRADICTS YOUR REQUESTS BUT GREAT DISCOVERIES SEEM INEVITABLE. WITH APOLOGIES.
= WINGATE.

Devoted son, Wingate Peaslee, helps his father find the truth.
PROP FROM *DARK ADVENTURE RADIO THEATRE®: THE SHADOW OUT OF TIME*

Alice Keezar

As Nathaniel's wife, Alice could potentially take on the challenges of dealing with her husband's new personality, but Lovecraft ignores this possibility; with little fanfare, Alice leaves Nathaniel.

The Great Race of Yith

Another fan favorite, the "monsters" who make up the Great Race of Yith present a fascinating concept. Lovecraft describes them as very large "rugose cones," sprouting several long tubular appendages at the top. But this is only a snapshot of the Great Race at a specific point in time—150 million years ago. Because members of the Great Race have mastered time travel, they know what the past and future of their kind look like. This, combined with their ability to project their minds forward and backward in time, allows them to see the extinction that's coming for their species and to avoid it by migrating en masse into the bodies of beetle-shaped creatures that live in the future. Of course, thwarting their own extinction presumably makes a major change to the time continuum, which could well affect all future species—but Lovecraft wisely avoids this pitfall of time-travel narratives.

The Flying Polyps

These mysterious, horrid entities, feared by the Great Race, are never named. Lovecraft limits himself to describing them as "a horrible elder race of half-polypous, utterly alien entities." They have generally become known by the name "Flying Polyps," a term coined by Sandy Petersen, creator of the tabletop role-playing game Call of Cthulhu® and the game supplement *S. Petersen's Field Guide to Cthulhu Monsters*, published by Chaosium, Inc., in 1988. These somewhat invisible monstrosities are the bane of the Great Race, who have attempted to confine them beneath the city of Pnakotus. Frightful though the Flying Polyps may be, it appears the Great Race was largely able to keep them in line with stout, iron-banded doors and electricity.

THEMES

Cosmic/Temporal Horror

Lovecraft here adds a new angle to his concept of cosmic horror—it's no longer *where* the horrors come from, but rather, *when*. In cosmic horror, he opened the lens of space, embracing its vastness as a source of horrific beings far more consequential than humans. In *The Shadow Out of Time*, Lovecraft plays with notions of things coming from remote eras in the past and/or future that can similarly impinge upon our insignificant lives.

Madness and Pseudo-Memories

Everything we think we know about the universe we hold in the form of memories. Human brains store incoming information and then recall that information as memories—whether it's something that happened moments ago or decades ago. In this story, Lovecraft explores the notion that memory cannot be trusted, depicting a narrator who is painfully aware of that unreliability. Pierre Janet was a French psychologist at the turn of the twentieth century who studied false memory and coined the terms "subconscious" and "dissociation." It's unlikely that Lovecraft knew Janet's work specifically, but the ideas were floating around in the zeitgeist, and were discussed in the kinds of slick magazines Lovecraft read.

As Peaslee grapples with what he perceives as memories too fantastical to be true, he rejects them, labeling them dreams or "pseudo-memories." When the brain manufactures false information in real time, we call it a hallucination and deem the person in need of mental health care. If this happens during sleep, we describe it as a dream and dismiss it as inconsequential. Of course, it turns out that Peaslee is exactly right, and his recollections of life 150 million years ago are perfectly accurate.

The Master Race

Like the Elder Things in *At the Mountains of Madness* or the K'nyanians in "The Mound," Lovecraft takes great delight in building a quasi-utopian society for his monsters. For a story written in 1934, as Nazi Germany was rising to the height of its powers, Lovecraft moves into uncomfortable territory in using the term the "Great Race." The German term "herrenrasse" literally means "master race," and it was used by the Nazis in policies touting their perceived racial superiority.

Lovecraft's politics were extremely conservative early in his life, but as he matured and the world reshaped itself around him, he became far more moderate. Lovecraft tended to discount democracy as a form of government, as he didn't believe the general population had the knowledge or expertise to effectively govern itself. As a result, he was optimistic about authoritarian figures who were rising on the world stage during the 1930s, believing they were individuals who would effectively maintain the common good. He did express concerns about the fascist tendency to effect barbaric solutions when exercising their authority. In most instances, Lovecraft displayed a pointed political cynicism, but when it came to supporting the fascists, he was rather naive, wildly underestimating their willingness to destroy elements of civilization that he cherished, along with millions of human lives, in their quest for domination and power.

Still, Lovecraft imagined the Great Race's society as reflecting his own priorities:

> Industry, highly mechanised, demanded but little time from each citizen; and the abundant leisure was filled with intellectual and aesthetic activities of various sorts. The sciences were carried to an unbelievable height of development, and art was a vital part of life ...

His idealized monster societies never seem to experience issues with economics, cost of living, inflation, unemployment, or other forces that come into play in the real world. The monsters live seemingly idyllic lives of the kind that Lovecraft wished he could have enjoyed.

SETTING AND MOTIFS

Miskatonic University

In Lovecraft's other stories, many of the characters are Miskatonic faculty members. Here, we see Peaslee as both teacher and student, with his son joining him in the study of psychology at Miskatonic. The university's generosity in rehiring Peaslee, not once but twice, after his amnestic episode is remarkable. So, too, is its willingness to fund an international psycho-archeological expedition, not to mention the handsome salary the university must have paid Peaslee, since he could afford to spend five years gallivanting around the world doing obscure private research. Maybe his economics expertise was more practical than theoretical.

Pnakotus

As with his Flying Polyps, Lovecraft never names the city of the Great Race, the remains of which lurk beneath the Great Sandy Desert of Western Australia. Lovecraft fans will hasten to let you know it's called Pnakotus, but such an appellation doesn't come from Lovecraft himself. Among his fictional grimoires, Lovecraft created his first one, the *Pnakotic Manuscripts,* in his 1918 story "Polaris." Lovecraft went on to refer to this prehuman text in numerous other stories. In keeping with the great Lovecraftian tradition, many other authors, including Lin Carter, made use of the *Pnakotic Manuscripts* and, like the fabled *Necronomicon*, the work took on a life of its own in the fan community. Fans have taken the adjectival "Pnakotic" and created the back-formation "Pnakotus" for the desert city. Role-playing and video games have, subsequently, elaborated greatly upon Lovecraft's depiction of the city of the Yithians, which now seems to be inextricably linked to the name Pnakotus.

The territory in Western Australia where Lovecraft located "Pnakotus" is the site of some of the oldest rock formations on Earth, and the world's earliest evidence of life is contained in 3.5-billion-year-old chert in the Pilbara. As with R'lyeh, the author provides the latitude and longitude of the city—22° 3′ 14″ South Latitude, 125° 0′ 39″ East Longitude. As with R'lyeh, this is the middle of nowhere. It is interesting to note that 150 million years ago, Australia and Antarctica made up one contiguous land mass, so the Great Race and the Elder Things would have been practically next-door neighbors.

The Things That the Monsters Fear

As he does with the shoggoths in *The Shadow over Innsmouth* or *At the Mountains of Madness*, Lovecraft tantalizes us by creating beings that are frightening to the Great Race. We don't learn a great deal about the Flying Polyps, but really, we don't need to. The mere fact that the Great Race treats them with abject fear is enough to let us know that we want nothing to do with these invisible, shrieking, nightmarish creatures.

H. P. Lovecraft's "Missing Years"

Peaslee's amnesiac period occurs from 1908 to 1913. It's no coincidence that this five-year window aligns with a key period in Lovecraft's own life. Around the time Lovecraft was beginning work on this story, he wrote in an April 10, 1934, letter to Robert H. Barlow:

> ... when I was 18 I suffered such a breakdown that I had to forego college. In those days I could hardly bear to see or speak to anyone, and liked to shut out the world by pulling down dark shades and using artificial light... my hypersensitive nerves reacted on my bodily functions to such a degree as to give the appearance of many different physical illnesses.

This nervous breakdown affected Lovecraft from 1908 to 1913 and proved to be a painful phase of his life. While not finishing high school seemed of little consequence to Lovecraft, his failure to attend college was a source of lingering regret. It was his involvement with the amateur press movement that gave him a pathway to becoming a writer and enabled him to forge powerful friendships through his correspondence. It is only here, in one of his last stories, that he gives a nod to that strange episode from his teenage years.

NOTABLE QUOTES

"If the thing did happen, then man must be prepared to accept notions of the cosmos, and of his own place in the seething vortex of time, whose merest mention is paralysing."

This quote beautifully encapsulates Lovecraft's notion of cosmic horror. If we understood the true nature of our place in the universe, we would be devastated by the horror of that understanding.

"... [I] was instantly engulfed in a pandaemoniac vortex of loathsome sound and utter, materially tangible blackness."

The author creates for the reader Peaslee's sanity-blasting experience by encouraging us to imagine an impossible soundscape and darkness so intense that it's tactile.

"When a captive mind of alien origin was returned to its own body in the future, it was purged by an intricate mechanical hypnosis of all it had learned in the Great Race's age. ..."

Lovecraft lamented the paradoxes that seem nearly unavoidable in time travel stories and tried to circumvent them by having the memories of abductees routinely wiped.

In some rare cases like Peaslee's, however, the hypnosis doesn't take, and tremendous confusion ensues. If time travel didn't have repercussions, it wouldn't make for very interesting stories.

"There, said the dreams and legends, had reposed the whole history, past and future, of the cosmic space-time continuum—written by captive minds from every orb and every age in the solar system."

Lovecraft's style was heavily influenced by nineteenth-century structure and vocabulary, so it is always striking when a technical twentieth-century term like "space-time continuum" jumps out of one of his sentences. Only Lovecraft could meld Poe and Einstein so effectively. He bridges centuries like a member of his own Great Race. The mathematics fusing three-dimensional space with time was articulated by Hermann Minkowski in 1908, paving the way for the theory of general relativity (Albert Einstein, 1915), great science fiction (Lovecraft, 1935), and plenty of confusion (us, right now).

H P LOVECRAFT
66 COLLEGE STREET
PROVIDENCE R I

Pay no charges to messenger

For quick service, reply by bearer

URGENT: DELIVER WITHOUT DELAY

RECEIVER'S NUMBER 16321415
DATE 22 FEB 1935
TIME FILED 17:27
CHECK 120 S1
SENDING STATION: PERTH

TELEGRAM

The World Wide Electrical Printing Telegraph Co. Ltd.

This is a full-rate telegram or electric lettergram unless its deferred character is indicated by a suitable symbol above or preceding the address. The filing time shown in the date line on telegrams and cablegrams is STANDARD TIME at point of origin. FORM HPLHS-001

SYMBOLS: DL=DAY LETTER NL=NIGHT LETTER LC=DEFERRED CABLE NLT=CABLE NIGHT LETTER SR=SHIP RADIOGRAM

DISCUSSION TOPICS

- Lovecraft liked the notion that, while our species wields power on Earth now, greater species came before and shall come after. How do you feel about this idea?
- Time travel seems to be an irresistible draw for science fiction writers. Are you vexed by some of the issues that arise in time travel stories, or are you content to set physics aside and enjoy a good yarn?
- Have you ever experienced déjà vu, or the uncanny feeling that you're remembering something that hasn't happened yet? What was it like?
- If your mind was abducted by aliens and enabled to meet people from other worlds and other times in history, who would you most like to encounter and why?

Notes

Notes

weldon**owen**

an imprint of Insight Editions

P.O. Box 3088
San Rafael, CA 94912
www.weldonowen.com

CEO *Raoul Goff*
VP Group Publisher *Jeff McLaughlin*
VP Publisher *Roger Shaw*
Publishing Director *Katie Killebrew*
Executive Editor *Jamie Thompson*
Managing Editor *Mary Beth Garhart*
Editorial Assistant *Jon Ellis*
VP Creative *Chrissy Kwasnik*
VP Manufacturing *Alix Nicholaeff*
Production Manager *Tiffani Patterson*
This edition published by Weldon Owen by arrangement with The Book Shop, Ltd.
and the H. P. Lovecraft Historical Society

Designed by Jon Pannier
Edited by Diane Namm

ISBN: 979-8-88674-233-6

This book is part of The H. P. Lovecraft Experience kit and is not to be sold separately.

Manufactured in China by Insight Editions

10 9 8 7 6 5 4 3 2 1

ROOTS of PEACE REPLANTED PAPER

Insight Editions, in association with Roots of Peace, will plant two trees for each tree used in the manufacturing of this book. Roots of Peace is an internationally renowned humanitarian organization dedicated to eradicating land mines worldwide and converting war-torn lands into productive farms and wildlife habitats. Roots of Peace will plant two million fruit and nut trees in Afghanistan and provide farmers there with the skills and support necessary for sustainable land use.